The Dragon Guard Series

By Julia Mills
Books 1 – 7

*There Are No Coincidences.
The Universe Does Not Make Mistakes.
Fate Will Not Be Denied.*

Copyright © 2015 Julia Mills
All Rights Reserved. This book or any portion thereof may not be reproduced or used in any manner whatsoever without the express written permission of the author except for the use of brief quotations in a book review.

DISCLAIMER: This is a work of fiction. Names, characters, businesses, places, events, and incidents are either the product of the author's imagination or used in a fictional manner. Any resemblance to actual persons, living or dead, or actual events is purely coincidental.

NOTICE: This is an adult erotic paranormal romance with love scenes and mature situations. It is only intended for adult readers over the age of 18.
Edited by Lisa Miller, Angel Editing Services
Edited by Maxine Bringenberg
Proofread by Alicia Carmical with AVC Proofreading
Cover Designed by Linda Boulanger with Tell Tale Book Covers
Formatted by Danielle James
Cover Model – Christian Petrovich
Cover Photographer – Golden Czermak with FuriousFotog Portraits and Events

DEDICATION
Dare to Dream! Find the Strength to Act! Never Look Back!

Thank you, God.

To my girls, Liz and Em, I Love You. Every day, every way, always.

Contents

Her Dragon to Slay 7
Her Dragon's Fire 69
Haunted by Her Dragon 171
For the Love of Her Dragon 281
Saved by Her Dragon 366
Only for Her Dragon 454
Fighting for Her Dragon 521

Dragon Guard Series

Index of the Words from the Original Language of the Dragon Kin

Drakes......Male Dragons
Vibrias......Female Dragons
Dragonettes......Young Dragons, either male or female
Mo chroi'......My Heart
Mo ghra'......My Love
Evgren......Sunshine
Ta'mo chroi istigh ionat......My Heart Is Within You
A Thaisce......My Treasure
M'Anamchara......Soul Mate
A Chumann......Sweetheart
M'Fhioghara'......Mate
Fi'orghra'......True Love
Mo' ghra' ru'nda......You Are My Everything
Aonin'......Little One
M'aonin'......My Little One
A Sta'rin'......Little Treasure
A Mhuirnin'......Little Beloved
Mo Mhac......Son
Ma'thair......Mother
Cailin A'lainn......Beautiful Girl
Is breá liom tú anois agus go deo......Love to His Heart
E'adromar a anam......Light to His Soul
Ta' su'il a anseo......Hope to His Future
Leanbh......Baby
Beag amha'in......Little One
Mianach Ini'on......Daughter Mine
Oiche mhaith a mhuirnl'n......Good night, my treasure
Is breá anois agus go deo......Love now and forever
A mhuirnin......My darling
I gcónaí agus go deo. Mine grá......Always and forever. Mine to love.
Teacht anseo, maite......Come here, mate
Chosaint agus a sha'bha'il......Protect and Save
O'n and bean naithe......Amen and Blessings
Is brea' liom tu'......I Love You
Mo maite'......My mate
Tharraingt ar shiúl......Pull away
Briseadh an banna......Break the bond
Tá brón orm......I'm sorry
Go gcasfar le chéile sinn i na Spéartha......Until we meet in the Heavens
Mo a rúnsearc......My secret love
Mo Mhac......Son
A Stor'......My Treasure
Athair......Father
A bheannaigh......Be Blessed
Le creideamh an ancients......With the Faith of the Ancients
Agus beannú na flaithis......And the blessing of the Heavens
A bheith go maith......Be well
Codladh go maith......Sleep well
Deirfiúr......Sister

Her Dragon to Slay
Dragon Guard Series #1

There Are No Coincidences.
The Universe Does Not Make Mistakes.
Fate Will Not Be Denied.

CHAPTER ONE

"Dammit, Grace, pick up the phone," she growled through gritted teeth at the third voicemail she'd had to listen to in the last five minutes.

"Everything okay, Kyndel?' Barney, the *nice* guy in her office, asked.

"Yeah, everything's fine. Just trying to find Grace."

"Oh! Anything I can help with?"

Kyndel thought about telling him her troubles, but Barney had been spending an inordinate amount of time in her office lately. At first, she'd thought he was just being nice, but then he joined her hiking group, and just yesterday he showed up with her favorite no whip, nonfat, iced white chocolate mocha from the *frou frou* coffee shop on the corner. It had been then Kyndel realized she was Barney's newest crush. It had been a long time between boyfriends and Barney was nice, but…um…no. As flattered as she was, there was no way she was having an office romance.

'Don't shit where you eat' was one of the pieces of sage advice Granny had given her just after graduation. Not that it ever truly made sense to Kyndel, but she got the gist of it…keep your personal life *out* of the office.

She saw the puppy dog look on Barney's face and hated to crush his spirit, but Kyndel decided a brisk walk home would be better than leading the poor fellow on, in *any* way.

"No, but thank you so much." Then, to make sure he got the hint and skedaddled, she added, "Have a nice a weekend," before turning her chair and dialing Grace's office for the third time.

Voicemail *again*. Time to pack up and get the heck outta dodge before someone found something else for her to do. Bag on shoulder, scowl on face, and more than a little disgusted, Kyndel headed out of the office.

Never loan Grace the car… Never loan Grace the car… was the mantra playing on a loop in Kyndel's mind. She was madder than a wet hen and getting hotter by the minute. It was *no fun* to walk home after ten hours of work. *No fun* to be abandoned and forgotten by the best friend she'd loaned her car to. *No fun* to make the five-block journey past the park…in the dark.

At twenty-six, she rarely admitted her fear of the dark and held her aunts responsible for the phobia. Had they not made her watch 'The Brain Eaters' when she was only six years old, Kyndel was positive everything would've been just fine. It wasn't that she believed aliens would set loose a horde of parasites to eat every human brain on the planet; she had a *little* more sense than that. It was the feeling of being watched…like someone was hiding in the shadows, just waiting for an opportunity to scare the living daylights out of her. At the mere thought of her 'phantom stalker', the hair stood up at the nape of her neck and she walked a bit faster.

A sudden *thud,* and what sounded like footsteps pounding on the hard ground, had her stopping in her tracks. "What the…?" She gasped, opening her eyes wide, hoping it would help her see through the shadows.

Several tense seconds later—that felt like damn near forever—and Kyndel moved again. This time, her eyes slid side-to-side like the stupid black and white cat clock her granny used to have in the kitchen.

The farther she got from where she'd heard the 'thump', the easier it was to convince herself it had just been kids sneaking into the park after hours. Manlove Park was a well-known make out spot for teenagers. There might've even been a time after moving to the city when Kyndel herself had been convinced to take a walk on the wild side, but that was a story for another day.

Shoot, now I wouldn't know the wild side if I tripped and fell in it.

It had been almost a year since she'd dated the muscle-headed jock from the gym. Three long, tortuous dates and all because he had an incredible body. Of course, dating the douche bag had come at a price. She'd spent the entire time listening to him drone on about his body parts…*and not the good ones*…and *only* when he wasn't checking out every other woman in the joint.

It wasn't that he'd hurt her feelings. Kyndel knew who she was and had never been under the misconception she would be Miss America. She had a few extra pounds and her curves had curves, but she was cute and had a brain, something not everyone could claim. What had pissed her off the most about dating Vinnie was, she'd wasted three whole evenings of her life that she could never get back. The one compliment the jerk had given her had been about her skin; he thought it was beautiful. Her granny always called her complexion peaches and cream and said her freckles added character.

Yeah, cause I need more of that.

She sighed as she thought about how much of her youth she'd wasted hating those tiny brown spots, until the day she realized they weren't going anywhere. It was time to buck up and learn to love them, or stop looking in the mirror. From that day forward, she stopped using makeup to cover them and embraced her 'freckled-self'. She also learned to accept her curves. *If ya don't like em, don't look at em* was her motto. For the most part, she ate right and worked out at least three times a week. But dammit if she didn't love her Ben and Jerry's Cherry Garcia and someone would lose a hand if they tried to take it from her.

A loud *'thud'* echoed between the buildings. Kyndel stumbled to a stop. She looked and listened. The longer she thought about what she'd heard, the easier it was for her to convince herself someone had yelled for help. So, for the second time in about as many minutes, she searched the inky shadows for signs of life. Her anxiety level quadrupled the longer she stood still. She wanted to scream when only the sound of leaves rustling across the sidewalk and the occasional car passing by reached her ears.

Disgusted, she grumbled aloud, "You've gone bonkers, Kyn." The sound of her own voice somehow calmed her rankled nerves and she added, "Get to stepping, girlie."

The clicking of her heels bounced off the brick wall of the library as she hurried past. Resuming her original mantra, she added *Must kill Grace* at the end for good measure.

"I swear when I get my hands on…"

Her words were cut short as the unmistakable sound of a man groaning came from the shadows.

A chill skittered down her spine.

Goose bumps covered her arms.

She counted to three, unable to move…simply listening…praying it was only her imagination. One deep breath later, she slid her right foot forward, prepared to make a beeline for home at a high rate of speed.

The groan came again. Closer than before. More desperate…almost pleading.

The need to help the injured grew within her. Turning towards the darkness, Kyndel searched for the source of the noise.

Shaking so much her teeth chattered, she looked for any sign of the man she *knew* needed her help.

"It's time to make a decision, Kyndel. Fight or flight. What's it gonna be? God knows standing like a bump on a log isn't solving a *damn* thing."

Flight won. She turned, almost running, her satchel clutched tightly to her side like a lifeline.

"Keep your head up and eyes front. Home's only a few blocks away," she reassured herself, with the promise of snatching her best friend bald for the stupid mess she was in.

Feeling guilty and worried for Grace, her heart at war with her brain, Kyndel thought aloud, "Hope everything's okay…"

Grace had always been a little scatter-brained, but she'd never just *forgotten* Kyndel before. It bothered her that there'd been no answer at Grace's office or on her cellphone when Kyndel had tried to track her down before leaving the office. She'd even taken a chance and tried her own home because Grace had a key, but only got voicemail there, too. It was a war between anger and worry that accompanied most of her thoughts about her friend lately.

The running joke was that Grace spent most of her time hooking up with eligible bachelors she met at work. The good Lord *knew* her bestie was gorgeous; five foot nine, long raven hair, blue eyes, and a curvy body without an extra ounce of fat. To top it off, she was a first year lawyer, with a promising career. Grace had it all…brains and beauty, the total package.

Giggling nervously, she gave herself a mental swat to the back of the head. She didn't want anything bad to happen to Grace, just a bump or bruise, even a hangnail would explain being left. If she really had just forgotten, Kyndel was going to be *pissed* and more than a little hurt.

The shadows seemed to be closing in. Fear pushed Kyndel until she was almost jogging in her sensible work heels. Looking over her shoulder, the toe of her shoe caught an uneven piece of concrete, and from one heartbeat to the next, she was falling forward. Arms flailing, mouth stretched wide in a wordless scream, the sidewalk racing toward her face, everything around her seemed to happen in slow motion. All she could think was *that's gonna leave a mark.*

Bracing for impact, she squeezed her eyes tight and prayed…then nothing happened. Opening one eye, then the other, Kyndel found herself hanging above the sidewalk, looking at a pair of the biggest feet she had ever seen—and they were sexy.

Sexy feet? I really am losing it. Wait! Why the hell am I above the concrete?

Warmth radiated from the perfectly muscled arm wrapped around her midsection. Goose bumps emanated from the extra-large hand holding firmly to her blouse, just a little too close to her breast.

She wiggled to change position, the cushion of her well-rounded ass finding the ridges of an incredibly hard set of abs. She trembled. Her heart raced. Just the thought of the man that could hold her upright made up for all her previous mishaps.

Within just a few seconds, Kyndel's world turned on its axis. The scenery blurred as she was effortlessly spun around and immediately found herself sitting atop the body of her rescuer, looking at faded denim covering extremely muscular thighs. Laughing aloud, she asked herself, *wonder what part I'll see next?*

The same muscled arm that had saved her face from certain demise now kept her upright. She did a one-eighty, draped her legs over his thighs, with her knees barely touching the sidewalk, and got her first look at the top half of her rescuer. All she could do was gape. He was absolutely the most handsome man she'd ever seen, with features that looked like they'd been carved by expert hands.

Even with his eyes closed, he gave off the distinctive air of authority. The dim light highlighted his high cheekbones and aristocratic nose, adding to the power she felt radiating from his every pore. His perfectly formed lips made visions of passionate kisses and hot sweaty nights dance through her brain. It didn't help that all he had on was a pair of well-worn blue jeans.

She imagined that denim riding low on his tapered hips when he stood, highlighting the incredibly sexy dimples that sat on the front of his hips. She absolutely knew without looking they were there, and that simple bit of knowledge made her temperature rise another degree, despite the cool breeze.

At the touch of her fingertips against the cool skin of his neck, an electric current arced between them. Flashes of light burst before her eyes. She blinked to clear her vision, then felt for his pulse, strong and steady against her digit. Heat rose from his skin, making her worry he might have a fever. Her eyes wandered down his well-toned body. She scoffed, unsuccessfully trying to convince herself she was only checking for further injury.

Who the hell do you think you're fooling?

She continued her perusal, taking note of his massive shoulders and a chest that could've been sculpted from granite. The light smattering of hair that glistened in the shards of light from the streetlamps emphasized his nipples, which were pebbled from the cool breeze. Her mouth watered and her pulse raced.

What the hell is it about this guy? Is he doused in pheromones? Or am I in heat?

Her eyes landed on the best set of abs she'd ever seen. Unable, or maybe it was unwilling, to stop her hand, she traced the defined lines of his eight-pack, mesmerized by the feel of his skin beneath her fingers. The electricity continued to flow between them. The sound of a horn in the distance pulled her from her musing and brought her current situation into the glaring light of reality. The sexy man that had kept her from breaking her face on the concrete was out cold, and she was paying him back by sitting on his lap and copping a feel.

She scrambled to her feet, surprised her rescuer hadn't moved an inch during her less than graceful attempt to remove her butt from his lap. But there he lay, unmoving, except for the rise and fall of his chest. The longer he remained unconscious, the more panicked she became.

Looking up and down the street and cursing Grace for the hundredth time, Kyndel wished for her car. First Aid class had taught her *never* to move an injured person unless you knew what was wrong. Not that she could pick him up and carry him, anyway. The dude was *HUGE*. At least six foot-three or four, and his muscles had muscles. She prayed he hadn't hit his head on the sidewalk. A concussion could be really bad if not treated.

"You're worried about a concussion now?" She scolded herself. "You've been drooling over the guy while his head is lying on the cold, hard sidewalk. Brilliant, Kyn, just brilliant." Reaching for her satchel, she grabbed her old sorority sweatshirt from inside, wadded it up, and knelt forward to lift his head.

Her fingers tangled in his soft, brown hair. The scattered shards of light made it look like melted chocolate flowing over her skin.

Would it shine in the sun or maybe have highlights? Some lighter brown mixed with red, even a few blond streaks woven throughout?

The silky softness of his tresses turned to something wet and sticky.

Blood!

Kyndel gulped. Panic seized the breath in her lungs as the true severity of the situation smacked her in the face. She fought to keep her calm. Now, there was absolutely no denying he needed medical attention. Reaching into her bag and cursing herself for not thinking of it sooner, she dug around for her cellphone.

Coming up empty-handed, she instantly remembered plugging it into her car charger the night before, not giving it the slightest thought until that moment. Cursing and threatening death to anyone in the immediate vicinity, she sat back on her heels and thought.

All I know to do is run down the street for help.

Looking at the fallen man, then in the direction of the Mini Mart, she reasoned he'd probably be okay. She'd be gone five minutes…*tops*. Run in, use the phone, run back. It all seemed very logical, but fear something would happen to him in her absence kept her in place.

This guy was important to her. That alone had all her red flags flying and bells and whistles screaming in her brain. She tried to push her feelings aside and look at the situation with logic, but that was like holding back a freight train with her pinky finger…*not gonna happen*. Besides, her granny would most definitely haunt her and probably kick her butt if she turned her back on someone who needed help.

"No one's gonna mess with this behemoth, even if he *is* unconscious," she reassured herself. "He probably doesn't have a wallet to steal anyway."

Should she dig in his pockets to try to find one? Some kind of ID?

Nah.

She wasn't keen on trying to explain her hand in his pants if he woke up. Her cheeks warmed at the thought of touching him again.

"What are you doing out at night in just a pair of jeans and bare feet, anyway?" she asked the unconscious man. "Guess it doesn't matter. You need help, whether you're dressed properly or not."

Hooking her satchel over her shoulder, Kyndel stood and took one last look at her 'patient'. Before she had barely moved an inch, a huge, warm hand latched onto her bare ankle.

"What the hell?" she screamed, trying to pull her leg free while looking down to see what new fresh hell had befallen her.

CHAPTER TWO

There was no *bloody* way he could let her get away. No matter how much his body needed to shut down and heal. He had to keep her safe…had to keep her w*ith him*. The mating call and the beast within demanded nothing less.

They'd both suffered a near heart attack when they saw the thug following her. There was no doubt he would've hurt her…*or worse*. Rayne thanked his dragon again for demanding they fly over the city. Heavily populated areas were usually patrolled from the outskirts to avoid detection by the humans. However, on this night, a compulsion that simply would *not* be denied had pulled him to the park…and to the beautiful redhead.

Over the last few weeks, every flight had been a battle. His dragon demanding they fly over the city, the man determined to stay to the fringes as they always had. The beast pushed. The man pushed back. The scent of 'prey' lingering in both their souls.

No matter how vehemently Rayne begged, cajoled, and fought…his dragon persisted. The battle of wills grew in intensity every night. It became tedious. It drained all his strength. It made him restless to want to know what his dragon knew that he did not. When they took to the skies just a few minutes past nightfall on this night, Rayne relented. Finally doing as his dragon demanded.

The closer they came to the city, the stronger Rayne felt his need to find the mystical *something* that eluded him. The Guardsman fought hard, trying to slow his dragon down until he could figure out exactly what they were looking for, but the beast would have none of the man's procrastination. He was single-minded in his determination. The discord between the two entities that shared a soul was something that hadn't happened since Rayne's week of transformation, over a hundred years ago. Since the man's late teens, the two had been in perfect agreement…mighty warriors in sync, sharing the same space, slaying their enemies, no matter how fierce.

Integrating the man and his dragon was one the most important milestones in a dragon shifter's life. Between the ages of eighteen and twenty-one, the conversion began. Man and beast became one and at its conclusion, the dragon would be able to be called forth when needed.

It happened quickly…only a matter of days. The beast became a completely sentient part of the man. Almost immediately, they learned to share the same space, the same thoughts…*the same soul.* The dragon was awake and ready to do what he was created for…protect and defend. The young man was ready to become the warrior *he* was destined to be. The human embraced the awakening of his dragon, the elusive being he'd known was there…just out of reach.

In Rayne's case, his alter ego was an incredibly regal, thousand-pound dragon with red and golden scales. His wingspan stretched far and wide. His roughly ridged brow and spines running down his thick-corded neck were silent reminders of the dragon's prowess in battle, and the scent of fire and ash reminded all that he could breathe fire. Defending his clan with unending loyalty was his prime objective, and one he took seriously. The Universe knew what She was doing. This was their destiny…a Fate that would not be denied.

The human of this duo had been born with a mark, a brand of sorts that resembled a tattoo on his body. Slowly growing, taking shape, and becoming more defined as Rayne grew into manhood, it covered most of his back. This badge of honor laid flat for all to see, unless he experienced extreme emotions or the dragon was being called forth.

Only one other time would these beings experience such a profound change, their true completion—the discovery of their mate. The one person the Universe designed just for them. This woman will become the final and *most integral* part of the union between man and beast. She completes the connection…makes them whole, gives them love, acceptance, and peace. Without her, true balance would be unachievable.

Stories passed down from generation to generation tell of the dragon sensing their fated mate before the man even knew of her existence. The stories tell of a love so strong it fills both to near bursting.

One of Rayne's oldest friends teased him as they left that night. "I bet your woman's out there and your dragon knows. Better get on it, Commander."

It had been all Rayne could do not to punch Lance, the jokester of his Force, especially when he laughed aloud as he walked away.

Once the idea had been planted, it was hard to forget, but Rayne refused to believe *one woman* could be the cause of all the discord he and his dragon were experiencing. It just wasn't possible.

Rayne was incredibly observant. One of the best strategists and trackers in the history of their kin. It was inconceivable something *so monumental* could escape his attention. If the other part of his soul was anywhere nearby, he would *know*.

Division of his focus and concentration, at his age and with his responsibility, was simply unacceptable. He felt like an unsure teenager again. *Not* something any man should experience, especially at a hundred and nineteen years old.

Of course, he felt a little stupid at how wrong he'd truly been and knew his dragon would make him pay for his insolence—one way or another—but...

Now...finally...

His dreams made sense.

He'd repeatedly been visited by a tall, curvy redhead, with the most expressive emerald eyes he had ever seen. The wonderfully erotic fantasies had become so addictive, he'd actually started to count the hours until he could sleep again. In his dreams, she smelled of flowers in the meadow after a spring rain, fresh and clean. The nearly perfect scent called him—completed him. It felt like home.

It had gotten so real, he could *feel* her hands on his chest, discovering his skin. His mouth watered as he remembered how perfectly they fit together. How the taste of her lips lingered long after her kiss. How artfully she teased him until they were both in a frenzy of want and need.

No matter how long he dreamed, Rayne always awoke craving the feel of her skin under his hands. He longed to feel her sweet breath on his neck as he teased her nipple between his thumb and forefinger. He awoke every morning with the taste of her nectar in his mouth and his cock begging for release. The power and reality of his visions made him doubt his sanity.

So when the tantalizing scent from his dreams filled his senses as he flew over the city, he'd almost fallen from the sky. The powerful fragrance overrode all the pollution of the city and grabbed hold of him as he'd glided overhead.

Cautious to remain unseen, Rayne circled closer and closer, zeroing in on his target, using scant bits of his dragon magic to provide cover. At first, he spotted only a man working hard to stay hidden by the shadows. On further inspection, the focus of the thug's attention became evident. The criminal followed *her*...the woman from his dreams.

Anger, violence, and a blind rage he'd never before experienced filled both man and beast. His vision narrowed to a single point...the stalker intending to harm *their* woman. The man's scent was pungent, a horrible mixture of aggression, anger, and filth.

All caution thrown to the wind, neither man nor dragon cared where they were or who saw them. All that mattered was the well-being of the woman that haunted their every thought. The dragon dove from the sky. Rayne shifted back to human form as he descended, hitting the ground on silent feet. In one fluid motion, he launched himself onto the would-be attacker and snapped his neck.

Hiding the body in the shadows, he quickly stepped into the light, looking for his mate. Searing pain tore through his back. The *whoosh* of an arrow sped past his ear, bouncing off the brick wall behind him, alerting him to the presence of hunters— dragon kin's deadliest enemies. Rayne cursed his inattention. So focused on saving the woman, he hadn't scented the area for other dangers, and now he was paying the price. Another arrow grazed his upper arm, the sting of silver burning all the way to his fingertips.

Figures! The bastards have silver-tipped arrows.

It was no surprise that a group of misguided zealots had perfected a hundred ways to kill dragon shifters, and silver topped the list. It was the one true way, *aside from taking the head of the man or the dragon*, to assure a forever death.

Rayne stumbled, momentarily stunned by the influx of poison to his system. Falling into the wall, he cringed as brick scraped his already sensitive skin. Blood flowed down his back. His head bounced against the building so hard he saw stars. Only instinct and strength of will moved him forward. There was no time to worry about his injuries. His woman *needed* his protection, *now* more than ever before. The hunters were so much more of a threat than the petty scumbag he'd already dispatched.

Hunters not only sought out shifters but also exterminated anyone believed to have seen the magical creatures. They didn't need proof, just the belief that someone may have witnessed something supernatural. The sight of them closing in on his redhead pushed the breath from his lungs. His dragon roared in his head.

The bastards were dressed in black from head-to-toe, hiding their faces under masks, like the cowards they were. If not for the monogram of the red scythe lying between their shoulder blades, they would've been completely undetectable to the human eye. Rayne thanked the Universe for his enhanced vision.

Hunching closer to the ground, his pain and weakness forgotten, he prepared for battle. No one would be allowed to hurt his mate. His dragon growled in agreement and lent his considerable strength to the fight to protect her.

She was their future. *No one* would take her from them.

Rayne launched himself onto the closest hunter, delivering a crushing blow to his throat. Although neutralized, the hunter had been able to call out to his compatriots before taking his final breath. The three remaining hunters surrounded Rayne. As they sized each other up, he sent out a silent call to his brethren. Rayne's Force

The begging tone of his voice melted away at Kyndel's resolve, not that it had been ironclad anyway. Sure, he was talking like an escaped mental patient, but it was probably just shock. And the sexy way her name rolled off his tongue definitely helped his cause.

"Okay. I'm giving you three hours, and if you're not better, I'm calling the ambulance and having you forcibly taken to the hospital. You got that, *bub*? Nobody dies on my watch."

He visibly relaxed at her acquiescence. She smiled, unable to help the butterflies his crooked grin created in her tummy.

Why the hell am I agreeing to this crap! Sure, he's the best looking thing I've ever seen, but I swear if he dies at my house, I'll kill him! Sexy voice or not, I'll kick his ass.

She knew she was letting her heart make her decision when she should've been listening to her brain, but he was practically begging. There was just something about this guy that did it for her. She shouldn't be thinking about his hot body, bedroom eyes, or his erotically calloused fingers wrapped around her wrist…but she was. There was no denying what she felt, no denying he was hot as homemade sin, and *absolutely* no denying she wanted to spend more time with him.

"All right, Rayne, you win. I live about five blocks from here. It's the closest place for you to *rest*. We just have to figure out how to get you up and moving. Whatcha say we start with a sitting position and work our way up from there?"

She felt him take a huge breath before tugging on her wrist. In one swift but shaky move, he was sitting, shoulders hunched, trying to hide his pain. He was close enough that she felt his breath on her face, and her eyes closed of their own volition. She leaned closer to his very kissable lips. Imagined what it would feel like to finally make contact. Knew it would blow her mind…and then he groaned.

Moment shattered.

She knew she was blushing and prayed he hadn't realized she'd almost kissed him. As awful as it was and as embarrassed as she was, Kyndel just couldn't help her disappointment.

Snap out of it, girlie! What the hell is wrong with you! When all this is over, I have to get a date, have to get laid! I'm losing my mind!

A small streak of blood slid down his neck, ending her inner dialogue.

"Rayne, your head's still bleeding." She reached around him, grabbed her sweatshirt off the ground with her free hand, and gently pressed it to his head. Once again, she was within kissing distance and this time he was looking right at her. Attraction, hot and fiery, flared to life. She just knew he felt it, too.

They leaned in, their lips meeting. One simple touch unlike anything she'd ever felt. Electricity flashed between them. Kyndel moaned deep in her throat. She felt lightheaded from the contact and braced her hand on his chest to keep from falling into his lap again. His chest vibrated as he groaned. His heart beat against her palm, almost racing the longer they kissed. His chest rumbled again, and this time, she swore he growled.

Rayne jerked away, threw his head back, and sniffed the air around them.

What is he doing? Do I smell bad?

Just as she was about to be offended by the actions of the deranged man she'd just kissed, he looked her square in the eye and demanded, "We have to get out of here…*now*!"

Kyndel huffed her frustration. "That's what I've been saying for the last half hour." She paused, trying to figure out what to do next. "Can you get up? If not, we're gonna need a miracle. There's no way I can lift you."

"I'll get up." He motioned with his hands for her to move back and added, "Take a step back, please."

Please?

Well, at least he had manners, no matter his other oddities. Kyndel stood with a sigh, her knees balking at the movement. Not to mention the extra twenty pounds she carried was slowing her down a little bit. Before she was vertical, Rayne held her hands to help steady her.

How the hell did he get up so fast?

She would've sworn he didn't have the strength to move his big toe by himself, let alone get up before her. Just as she opened her mouth to ask, he once again sniffed the air. His brows furrowed and he grumbled, "We really *have* to get going. Which way to your home?"

This guy really had some odd habits, but she figured it could be worse. He could eat with his hands or burp and fart in public. She snickered at her own joke and looked away when he glanced down at her.

I guess I can deal with sniffing.

The problem was, deep down inside she felt like she was missing something. Like she knew this man was different and that difference was somehow important to her. Being out of the loop irritated her at the best of times, but right now, it pissed her off. Even crazier was the fact that at that moment, he was staring at her like *she* was one brick shy of a load.

What the...?

Pushing all her misconceptions aside, Kyndel pointed over her shoulder and said, "That way. Just shy of five blocks. You sure you can make it?"

Rayne gave a single nod. "I *will* make it. Lead the way."

She turned and he placed his hand on the small of her back. It warmed her to the tip of her toes. Biting the insides of her cheeks to keep from grinning like a loon, she headed towards her apartment.

It's all gonna be okay. He'll sleep. Wake up feeling fresh as a daisy and explain all this madness to me. In the meantime, I'll find Grace and kill her for stranding me. Everything's just great! Really! Just great! Wonder how long I have to say it to make it true? Oy Vey! Thank God it's Friday!

CHAPTER FOUR

It was the longest almost five blocks he'd ever walked. Just when Rayne thought he couldn't take one more step, Kyndel pointed to the next building on the right.

"I'm right there." She looked up at him, concern flashing in her eyes. "Ya gonna make it?"

"Oh yes, I'll make it, rest assured." Pushing the confidence he didn't feel into his words.

The quaint little abode fit what he knew of his mate perfectly. He could see it had been freshly painted a bright white. Frilly blue-checked curtains hung in the windows, giving the perfect backdrop to the flower-filled window boxes.

Four doors indicated four identical abodes, but Kyndel's was by far the prettiest of them all. Flowering bushes lined the walk to the front door and some type of vine gently wrapped around her white picket gate. The house suited the woman that lived there.

"You must have a green thumb," he mused.

"I guess. I've always been able to grow just about anything." She smiled as she answered.

Her horticultural abilities were simply another sign she was indeed his mate. Dragon shifters' mates had special abilities, even if they were human. Most never realized they had them, but the dragon who was the other half of their soul acknowledged it immediately, just as Rayne had with Kyndel, upon seeing her home.

She pushed open the door and crossed the threshold. "No matter how humble, there's no place like home," she said as she let out a breath and quickly added, "come on in. Let's get you laid down. Let the healing begin."

He could hear her irritation and knew she was simply tired and worried and more than a little confused. No matter how selfish it seemed, both the beast and the man were thrilled their mate was concerned. If he'd not been ready to drop to his knees, Rayne would've pursued the sweet scent of arousal that had been coming from Kyndel since he first opened his eyes.

That will have to wait just a few hours.

He stood waiting for her to tell him where to go, even though he could've easily found her room by scent alone. It seemed best to wait for her invitation. So much of what she would learn over the next few days was going to blow her mind. He saw no need in starting something until he could finish it.

It was as if she'd read his mind when she motioned towards the hall. "Second door on the right is the master bedroom. The bathroom's in there, too. Towels are on the shelf if you want to clean up before you 'rest'.

He almost chuckled at the exaggerated inflection she put on the word 'rest' but nodded instead. "Thank you so much for your kindness, Kyndel. I know none of this makes any sense to you, but I *will* explain everything to you once I've slept." He hoped she could feel his honesty, because it would be the basis for their life together.

"Well, like I said before, just don't die on me. You look like a good wind could knock you on your ass right now. Get in there and do whatcha gotta do, since you're so sure it'll heal what ails you. I have my doubts, so all I'm gonna reiterate is...*DO NOT DIE!*"

Rayne chuckled. "If I'm not mistaken, Kyndel, it sounds like you care about my well-being."

"Yeah. Okay. Whatever. I just don't know how I'd explain the big dead man I just met to the police if you kick the bucket. So *don't*, okay?"

"I assure you, beautiful Kyndel, I will not die this night."

He watched her pupils dilate. The tip of her tongue left a tiny wet line across her bottom lip that he longed to follow with his own. He tried to work up the energy to at least take her to bed *with* him. Just holding her in his arms would be magnificent. However, it was useless. Silver coursed through his veins, and he'd lost way too much blood to do *anything* but sleep.

"Get in there and get laid down. I'll use the other bathroom to get changed then I'll bring you something to drink. Do you prefer water or juice? Sorry, I haven't been to the store lately so the pickings are slim."

"Whatever you have will be fine."

He started to head towards the room, which meant walking right towards his gorgeous mate. He stopped just a few inches in front of her. She jerked her head up, and Rayne felt the force of the mating bond pulling them together. He imagined their hot and sweaty bodies entwined, unable to move from hours of enjoying one another.

She cleared her throat, turned on her heel, and headed to the guest bath. He worked hard to keep from grinning. Rayne could tell the mating call was affecting Kyndel just as much as it was him. He once again lamented the fact that he was in such bad shape physically and could not at least explain their connection. He *had* to sink into the healing sleep for a few hours, if only to regain the strength he needed to claim his mate.

Watching her turn into the hall bathroom and just before she closed the door, he called to her. "Kyndel, do not leave or answer the door while I'm asleep. There are people out there that seek to hurt me, and also you by association. Please just give me those few hours you promised."

She answered almost immediately. "Okay, but you have three hours then I want some answers, *Rayne*." The emphasis she put on his name sent shivers running down his spine.

I will never tire of my name on her lips.

He breathed a sigh of relief. He'd used most of what little dragon magic he had left to place concealment wards around her home while they'd stood talking. If by some miracle the hunters were able to break through his enchantments, they would not be able to enter her home without an invitation from the inhabitants…he and Kyndel.

He was sure from her quick response that she would do as he'd asked. She may not understand why, but it was all part of the mating call. One mate would never knowingly endanger the other. It was part of their unbreakable bond. But to be sure, he'd put a magical push in his command. Things were progressing quickly for them. Now to heal so he could claim the one the Universe made for him.

Fate waits for no man, not even the bleeding.

CHAPTER FIVE

"Did that man just order me not to answer my own door?" she asked herself.

"Yeah, he did, and you agreed without a second thought, girlie," she answered herself, doubting her sanity for the umpteenth time since leaving work.

This night just keeps getting weirder and weirder.

At least she felt better in her own home and out of those crappy office clothes. Looking in the mirror, she realized her hair resembled a rat's nest where a family of four had taken up residence for the winter. Dark circles under her eyes made it look as if she'd missed more than a few nights sleep and she looked pale.

As she walked out of the bathroom and headed towards the kitchen, she thought back to the noises she *knew* she'd heard back at the park. Rayne surely hadn't hit himself on the head. A wound that wicked was *not* self-inflicted. There had been so much more going on out there than she knew, and as soon as the sexy man in her bedroom was done with "his rest", she was getting to the bottom of all the weirdness.

With a glass of fruit juice in each hand, she headed to her room. Walking through the door, she gasped. Congealed blood matted his beautiful mane from a nasty head wound, but it was his back that made her want to cry. It looked like a piece of raw meat. Cuts, scrapes, and puncture wounds ran from his shoulders to his waist. Something horrible had happened to him while she stood just a few steps away, unsure what to do.

She'd been worried for her own safety while Rayne was being beaten to a bloody pulp. He'd lain on that sidewalk for what seemed like forever while they *discussed* his need for medical attention, and he hadn't complained at all. The pain must have been agonizing.

Easing his pain was now her number one concern. She thought of the liniment her granny had taught her to make when she was a girl on the farm. A powerful homemade remedy designed to soothe everything from a paper cut to a third degree burn. Granny always said you could take the girl out of the country but you could never get the country out of the girl. That awesome old lady taught Kyndel everything she knew about medicinal herbs. What would cure a headache, indigestion, or help during childbirth, but most importantly, she'd taught her how to make her special ointment. Granny said their kin had always been blessed with the gift of healing, and for the first time, Kyndel was grateful for it.

She remembered the time she'd offered to help a friend at school with an herbal tea for a stomachache. They had laughed at her and said in the *big city,* they had doctors for that type of thing. Kyndel never offered again, but she never gave up on what she'd learned. She kept a small herb garden in the window of her dorm room and told anyone that asked that it was her way to feel close to home. They bought her story and she was happy.

Years later, she now had her own place. Even though it was rented, almost every inch of her backyard was filled with herbs and plants she used for Granny's teas and tonics, but that was only a small part of why she planted everything from acacias to zinnias. More importantly were the beautiful, fresh flowers that brightened her day and the butterflies and birds that flittered about her kitchen window. Having her hands in the dirt grounded her, filled her with happiness, and kept the sadness at bay. Some days it was hard to know she was the only living member of the Masterson family.

Leaving the past where it belonged, she set their juice glasses on the bedside table and walked to the bathroom. While there, she gathered towels, a basin of warm water, and her jar of liniment. All she could think of was Rayne's incredible strength. Yeah, he'd dropped off a couple of times, but she had a sneaky suspicion he'd never been *unconscious*. His reactions while injured were sharper than hers on a good day. Then he walked those four blocks as if nothing was wrong. Not stumbling or slowing, but keeping pace right beside her. It was almost as if he was used to pain. It hurt her heart to think he'd had a hard life. She hoped whatever he'd suffered had been for a good cause and thought maybe it was because of his job.

Oh well, whatever his profession, he definitely has an iron will.

With her arms full of supplies, she returned to his bedside, stopped, and simply stared at the huge man occupying most of her bed. He'd gotten some blood and dirt on her comforter, but nothing that wouldn't wash out. Maybe she'd use that as an excuse to buy the white comforter with pink and lavender hyacinths she'd seen in the Anthology catalog. Something to think about later. Right now, she had to get her pleasantly round ass on the bed and tend to her patient.

She snorted to herself, "Pleasantly round ass…Yep! That's me."

I really am a goofball.

"Okay, big guy, I'm going to wash this dirt and blood off your back, then get some of this liniment on your wounds. I'll get you all fixed up. We need to get that grossness out of your pretty hair, too."

Is it wrong to call a man's hair pretty? Oh, who gives a crap anyway? Not like he can hear me. I really have lost my mind!

It was not enough she had a stranger in her home, who was hurt and spread across her bed, but she was talking to his unconscious ass, too, while he was completely dead to the world. "Oh shit, bad choice of words," she snorted.

He most *definitely* was not dead, and she'd threatened him within an inch of his life to make sure he did not die while in her home. The closer the time came to touch his back, the more her hands shook. It also felt like butterflies were having a party in her tummy. She knew she was being silly, but couldn't control her crazy nerves.

He was injured and needed her help, not to be groped. Not that she would've done that, even with an invitation. She was raised better than that. Kyndel Masterson was a lady.

A little drop of sweat ran down her spine, and it was then she realized what she'd originally thought was nerves was actually anticipation. The little voice in the back of her mind was telling her once she laid her hands on him, things would never be the same. It was like the little voice knew something she didn't.

"He's just a guy," she reasoned.

"Yeah, but he's a mouth-wateringly gorgeous guy," she answered herself, thinking she'd had more conversations with herself in the last few hours than in her whole life, but kept going anyway.

"But he's still just a guy, Kyn. A guy that had a bad experience and needs your help."

Pep talk complete, she placed the basin of warm water next to his shoulder, then scooched herself until she was sitting Indian style with her knees next to his hip. She dipped one of the washcloths into the warm water that she'd added some of her granny's herbal bath oil to. The ingredients in the oil, along with the liniment, would help with some of the soreness. She gently wiped across his shoulders, then rinsed the washcloth in the basin, repeating the process until the water in the basin was yucky. Scooting off the bed, she grabbed the bowl and headed back to the bathroom for clean water and more clean cloths.

When she returned, she was pleased to notice his wounds looked less harsh, almost like they were already closing, but surprised it was happening so quickly. Either her herbs were super charged or he had some kind of kicked up healing power. She refused to believe "resting" was all it took for him to heal like he was.

Once again, she carefully climbed on the bed, resuming her position from before. She worked to wipe all of the gross blood and dirt mixture from his back. When she looked at the basin of water, something seemed to sparkle. It was like there were flecks of glitter mixed with *the muck* coming off his back. *Definitely* not what she expected to see. Question one hundred and fifty two to be answered when Mr. Tall Dark and Handsome Rayne whatever his last name was woke up.

With his back finally clean, Kyndel threw the dirty rags in the laundry basket and dumped the last of the water down the drain. She grabbed a few gauze pads and the butterfly strips from her first aid kit for his deeper wounds before heading back to her patient.

This time, she sat on her knees by his waist, needing the extra height to reach all the way across his wide shoulders. Taking the lid off her liniment, she inhaled the wonderful scent of healing herbs. It was fresh and clean and reminded her of Granny. Just the smell relieved some of her tension and loosened her tired muscles.

Scooping some of the ointment into her hand, she rolled her shoulders to relieve the rest of the tension caused by this man's abrupt arrival into her world and the craziness that had ensued. Looking down at his back, she decided where to start and two things became apparent. First of all, he had many scars from many different times and a wide assortment of weapons. This man was definitely a fighter of some sort. Kyndel only hoped he was one of the good guys. Two, his wounds were most certainly closing up, *on their own*.

There had been quite a few deep lacerations and puncture wounds, which required at least a bandage, if not butterfly strips. Between her last trip to the bathroom and now, they looked like nothing more than scratches. She really wanted to know what made him heal so quickly. But of course, he would have to be conscious for her to get the answers she needed.

Kyndel rubbed her hands together, warming the liniment. Carefully, trying not to wake him, unable to bear the thought of causing him any more pain, she leaned over his back. Her hands had barely touched his right shoulder when the electrical current she'd experienced the first time she touched Rayne happened again. This time, with more force and direction, landing deep in her womb.

She gasped. Her hands flew from his back and she sat staring, looking for anything to explain the shock she'd just received. Kyndel decided she must've shuffled her feet across the carpet on her way out of the bathroom. Of course, that didn't explain the jolt she received in her lady parts, but it pretty much went along with all the other weirdness that had happened.

Taking a deep breath, she gathered her courage and hesitantly placed her hands on his shoulder again. Once again, the current raced through her. Her nipples pebbled against the lace of the camisole she wasn't sure why she'd left on. It was usually one of the first things to go after her blouse, but tonight she felt like she needed an extra layer of protection. Like armor against the draw of the man before her.

I am delusional. I need sleep. My imagination has a mind of its own tonight.

Ignoring the sensations racing through her from touching Rayne, Kyndel began rubbing the ointment into his shoulder and across his bruised ribs. The force of the attack was still evident in the deep purple bruising that decorated his skin. She just knew he'd given better than he'd gotten. This man did *not* lose a fight. It was something she believed with all her heart.

Rubbing the liniment into his wounds, she became mesmerized by the feel of his war-roughened skin against her palms. The warmth created by their contact seemed to soak into every fiber of her being. She could feel him *everywhere*.

A myriad of textures in the beautifully battered skin along his massive shoulders became evident. It tickled the pads of her fingers. Some spots felt softer on the surface but firmer underneath, almost like a scar. The vision of him as a Guardian, a Commander of warriors, someone who'd seen numerous battles, flashed in her mind, explaining the scars and any other old wounds she encountered while she tried to help him heal.

Kyndel didn't even question the image of him leading men into battle as it played out in her mind. It was just a belief planted firmly in her mind, growing into something much larger the longer her hands were on his body. His skin warmed even more. Some of the marks became more predominant. It seemed as though they were taking shape.

As she focused on a particularly intricate set of lines, it took on the appearance of a large wing wrapping up and over his left shoulder. She followed the lines as they swooped down into a large, powerful body with a beautifully massive wing coming out the other side. The picture taking shape before her eyes was mesmerizing.

Glancing to the right, she noticed a fantastically majestic face. The creature's eyes met hers with a flash of recognition and a caress of reassurance. It was a melding of souls, the calling of like to like. All terms that were knew to her but *felt right,* given the situation.

Enthralled with the immerging picture on his back, she almost missed the slight movement of *her* warrior in his sleep. She checked to see if his eyes were still closed. The movement pushed her breasts into the top of his arm. She swore she heard a rumble from deep in his throat. Not really a growl, more like a purr of contentment.

Not willing to break the contact, Kyndel admired his face. It had surely been sculpted by God himself. Inhaling, she drew his scent deep into her lungs. That single, complex aroma reminded her of the breeze right after the rain mixed with something wonderfully spicy. Without thought, she drew more into her being, simply holding it there…savoring it. The image of sweat-soaked bodies wrapped around one another and pushing to their mutual release swamped her consciousness.

She inhaled again as her eyes slid shut. Her breasts grew achy and heavy. Her juices began to flow. She squeezed her legs together to stem the ache growing there. Her eyes snapped open.

There was that sound again.

His back vibrated against her chest. Her nipples grew even harder against the lace of her camisole. The ache inside begged to be quenched. Pushing closer still, she placed her lips on that special spot where his neck met his shoulder. She longed to part her lips and taste his flesh with just the tip of her tongue. She paused, not sure one taste would be enough. It stood to reason he'd taste even better than he smelled.

I shouldn't be thinking things like this about a man I know basically nothing about, but I really gotta find out.

Her only fear was he might wake up and catch her in the act. He seemed totally comatose, and the longer she considered it, the more she was sure she would get away with just one taste. The man was harder to resist than chocolate covered strawberries. The attraction she felt pulling her closer and closer to a man she knew virtually nothing about was irresistible. She knew she should stop, even thought of all the reasons she should. There was just one huge obstacle…HER! Kyndel didn't want to stop. She didn't want to walk away. She wanted, no *needed*, to know what made *this man* special.

Giving in to temptation, she closed the distance between them, tenderly laying her lips to his skin. The spark between them flared to life, spreading from her lips all the way to the tips of her fingers and toes. It was an incredible experience she never wanted to end. A sigh slipped from her lips as the remaining anxiety and tension rolled out of her body.

Forever would never be enough. Cocooned in the delicious warmth of his body was where she was meant to be. She knew it in the depths of her soul. Her body fit perfectly against his, like two pieces of a puzzle made to be together.

She wanted his lips on hers more than she wanted her next breath. Kyndel could almost feel him licking and sucking her aching breasts, sliding into the wetness already gathering in her core, thrusting between her thighs. Her lips moved farther up his neck of their own accord, placing butterfly kisses in the sweet spot behind his ear. The urge to pull his ear lobe between her teeth and bite ever so softly overrode all her sensibilities.

With her next breath, her conscience reared its ugly head. Immediately embarrassed, feeling as if she'd somehow taken advantage of an injured man, Kyndel gently raised herself back to her knees. She scooted a little farther down the bed, stopping when she was once again beside his hip. The feeling she was right where she was supposed to be was unshakable. It made no sense at all and quite frankly, pissed her off just a little bit.

Checking his wounds, her eyes scanned his back. Her jaw dropped open. The picture that had eluded her finally came into view.

OMG! There's a dragon on his back!

It was the most breathtaking image she'd ever seen. What she'd thought were scars formed a magnificent, golden red dragon. The winged warrior completely covered his back, even wrapping around his waist. It hadn't been there twenty minutes before, of that she was sure.

It should've been comforting to know she wasn't losing her mind, to figure out at least one thing about the mysterious Rayne. And it was until she scooted off the bed and took one last look at the tattoo.

Son of a…It's looking right at me.

CHAPTER SIX

Rayne slowly came out of his healing sleep, contentment filling his heart. For the first time in his very long life, all the pieces were in place, Some he hadn't even known were missing. He was whole, complete in a way he could've never imagined. His dragon felt the same way, rolling around on his back, chuffing and blowing little puffs of smoke from his nostrils.

Happy there, buddy? Me, too.

The beautiful scent of flowers in a meadow was all around him. Rayne thought about rolling around to cover himself in the scent, but feared Kyndel might catch him. A warm sensation covered his back and the strong perfume of herbs broke through his mate's scent. It warmed his heart to know the feel of her hands on his skin had not been a dream.

Kyndel had taken care of him with some sort of ointment while he slept. The mating call was riding her hard, pushing her growing feelings for him to the surface. She had no clue what they meant to each other...not yet, but she'd seen him in pain and had done everything in her power to comfort him.

Kyndel...just the thought of her brought what he was sure his brethren would call a goofy grin to his face, not to mention sending blood rushing to his groin. That melodic name described her to a tee. From her fiery mane of red hair to her brilliant emerald eyes that he could literally get lost in, to her spit fire attitude he'd briefly glimpsed when she was angry or frustrated. And he couldn't forget the cute little freckles that dusted across her nose and cheeks. He wanted to spend hours placing butterfly kisses on each one. That led him to wonder if she had those tempting little spots all over her body, which led him to her curves and the hours of absolute splendor he was going to have exploring every decadent inch of her.

She was much shorter than he was and would fit comfortably against him. The vision of evenings spent with her head on his chest as they lay exhausted from hours of lovemaking made his head swim. His mouth watered with thoughts of the hours he would spend between her soft, shapely thighs.

He knew she didn't notice how high her skirt had ridden up as she'd knelt beside him on the sidewalk, and Rayne hadn't minded a bit. The bird's eye view of her beautiful, milky white thighs had kicked his heart into overdrive and driven away his pain. The only thing that kept him from taking her right then and there had been his injuries.

Not that she'd have welcomed his advances. It was as clear as the freckles on her nose that she thought he was an escaped mental patient, even pleaded with him to go to the hospital. Explaining who and what he was to his enticing mate was going to be a treat. She was so animated, so free with her emotions that he looked forward to watching all of them flit across her gorgeous face.

He not only wanted to experience every erotic fantasy he had ever had with her, it was also important he share every aspect of *his life*. Show her his clan, introduce her to the people that were so important to him, make her the center of his world.

The first of his Force to find his mate, Rayne was truly humbled. It was an extraordinary event. There would be days of celebration, feasting for everyone. Their mating brought hope to the entire clan, secured the future of the dragon shifters.

Lying in her bed, drinking in her fragrance, Rayne was content to bask in the warmth of her home. His internal clock told him the three hours she'd promised him had long passed and she hadn't wakened him. He would need to rise and begin a series of difficult conversations with his beautiful Kyndel very soon. Procrastination would only make things harder.

Opening his extraordinary senses, he located her in the other room, sleeping soundly. His poor *mo ghra'* had quite a night. One that could've ended in terror. A shiver ran down his spine at the thought of what her stalker or the hunters might've done to her had he been just a few minutes later. Fate had been with him. He'd made it in time. He'd kept her safe. Her protection was his number one concern from now until the end of time.

Needing to check in, he called out to his brethren. Aidan and Lance answered immediately.

"What's up, Rayne?" Aidan asked.

"Checking in. Bodies in the park disposed of?"

"Nah. We thought we'd leave 'em," Lance teased, then quickly added, *"just playing, dude. Don't get your knickers in a twist."*

Rayne worked hard to remain stern and not laugh at the pain in the ass. All three of them had been friends since they were young. Even though he'd risen to the rank of Commander, they were still his best friends, his brethren. The three of them, along with Devon, Royce, and Aaron made up the most elite fighting Force in the Dragon Guard...in all of dragon kin. They shared a bond of blood and fealty that transcended normal genetics—brethren by choice—by Fate. Their special connection allowed them to communicate over long distances, mind-to-mind, even sense when one of them was in danger.

"My knickers are most definitely not in a twist, asshole."

Both men burst out laughing.

Aidan was the first to recover. *"Ignore him, Commander. He's been an extra kinda butthead this morning, and I drew the short straw, so I'm flying with him."*

"Better you than me." Rayne chuckled.

"Aww, y'all think I'm special," Lance teased in a singsong voice. *"But enough about me...how about that sexy redhead you're thinking about?"*

Rayne was immediately jealous. His dragon chuffed in anger. He knew he was being totally irrational. Logically, he knew his brethren would do nothing to dishonor their bond, but that didn't stop him from wanting to rip Lance's head from his shoulders. Yet another effect of the mating call.

"Chill, Commander. Just messing with ya. Better you than me." Lance was laughing so hard Rayne had a hard time understanding him. The sound of Aidan laughing too pushed back most of Rayne's aggression.

He would have to control the intense feelings of jealousy driving him to kill any other man that glanced in her direction. The little he knew of his mate, he was sure she wouldn't appreciate it. Even after completing the mating ceremony, he would always be overprotective and have the need to be near her whenever possible, but the murderous feelings would dissipate over time. She was the center of his Universe, and he would protect her at all cost.

It took a few deep breaths, but Rayne got his emotions under control before telling his brethren about his mate.

"Her name is Kyndel and she's perfect. And you already know from digging around in my head," he paused and let his irritation at the invasion of his privacy flow through their link, *"that she's gorgeous. She's also fearless. She stood up to me without a second thought."* He laughed. *"She is caring, kind, and more than I'd ever hoped for in a mate."*

Rayne reinforced his mental shields, effectively locking his friends out of his thoughts. There was no way he could take the chance one of them would catch a wayward thought of her creamy thighs or perfect breasts. Since he couldn't stop thinking about her, he'd at least keep from sharing those thoughts.

All of his thoughts centered on how much he wanted to gaze upon her naked body laid out like a feast before him. Images of her rosy nipples, he knew would darken as he worked them with his hands and mouth, taunted him. The beautiful blush, he knew would cover every inch of her fair skin as her excitement grew, teased him.

The sound of Aidan and Lance laughing jerked Rayne from his daydreams. He couldn't help but laugh along. He was truly busted.

"You're a goner, Rayne," Lance cackled. *"Have you explained 'us' to your beautiful mate?"*

"No, but that's the next order of business."

"Good luck with that," Aidan chimed in.

"Yeah, thanks. You two try to stay out of trouble, okay?"

"No promises, lover boy." Lance laughed as he severed their connection.

Shaking his head at the men he called brother and satisfied they had the situation well in hand, Rayne climbed off her bed. It was time to find his mate. Stretching, he was surprised at the lack of soreness in his muscles. Whatever Kyndel had put on his back had reduced the stiffness that usually accompanied accelerated healing.

Looking around her room, he noticed she'd placed a T-shirt and sweat pants on the dresser. Where did his lovely Kyndel get men's clothes in the middle of the night? He picked them up, inhaling only her scent. No one else had worn or touched these clothes since they were washed, and that had been some time ago. Where they from a previous lover? Jealousy raged through his body. He inhaled deeply, scenting her home. All he found was her perfume and that of another female. No other *male* had been there. He and his dragon settled. But the urge to hold her in his arms would not be denied.

Throwing on the T-shirt, he marched out the door, down the hall, and rounded the corner to the family room. What he saw stopped him dead in his tracks. There, curled up on the couch, back facing him with her well-rounded ass pushed outward, was the one the Universe had made for him.

He stood dumbstruck by the gift he'd been given. More than his next breath, he wanted to taste her pouty pink lips, kiss across her jaw, and lavish the little spot right behind her ear that he knew would make her shiver and sigh. His hands itched with the need to cover every single inch of her body with his own. His hunger rose. His cock pushed against the zipper of his blood covered jeans.

He turned and sprinted to the bathroom, ripping the gore-covered clothing from his body. Stepping under the spray of the shower he'd just turned on, not even waiting for the water to warm, he hurriedly washed the evidence of the prior evening's events from his body.

He had to get his hands on her body as soon as possible. That he'd shown the restraint to shower before touching her showed the depth at which the mating call had already taken hold.

She was his *everything*. She deserved the absolute best. Even when they had children, and there would be many of them he was sure, Kyndel would be number one in his heart. There would be adorable little girls with amazing green eyes running around the countryside. A riot of auburn curls swirling around their beautiful faces as they dared *anyone* to get in the way of their fun. Closely followed by little *drakes* with dark hair and violet eyes playing pranks and teasing their sisters.

Less than five minutes later, he was showered and dressed in just the sweatpants she'd laid out for him and running down the hall. He knew he looked a mess…wet hair dripping down his back, wild look in his eyes, and sweat pants tented from his erection.

She was just as he'd left her. An angel fallen to earth especially for him, so peaceful in her sleep. Her long, dark eyelashes curled against her cheeks. He sat next to her delectable bottom, running his fingers through the tangle of red curls streaming down her back. Rubbing along her spine with the back of his hand. Leaning into his touch, she sighed, recognizing him even while sleeping. So receptive to his touch, she accepted his hands on her body.

His light, slow exploration of her body continued. He gently massaged her soft skin through the T-shirt she wore. Needing skin-to-skin contact, he tenderly slid his hand under her clothing. Sparks flew. It was like nothing he'd felt before.

His body leaned toward hers. He was drunk on her scent. She was better than the finest wine and more potent than hundred-year-old scotch. She was exquisite. She was home. She was his heart. He would love this woman for all eternity.

He moved her hair to the side, revealing her neck to rub his nose along the elegant column, marking her with his scent and drawing in more of hers. The tip of his tongue traced an erotic path from behind her ear to the spot where her neck met her shoulder, nipping lightly on the spot that would bear his mark. She shivered, moaning in her sleep and turning to allow him greater access.

His hand gripped her hip as a myriad of emotions flooded his body. The sensory overload from a single touch of his lips to her skin had left him wanting more. His dragon spurred him on. The beast wanted to claim her as their own and would settle for nothing less than Rayne's cock buried deep in their mate.

Slipping the collar of her shirt off her shoulder, he continued his slow, sensual exploration of her body. Her scent, coupled with her responsiveness, was intoxicating. If they lived two thousand years, he would never get enough. Slipping his hand under her shirt, he explored the satiny skin of her stomach, sliding his hand across her ribs until arriving at her voluptuous breasts. His hands shook. His mouth watered. His only thought was of sucking her womanly flesh between his lips.

Letting out the breath he hadn't realized he was holding, he palmed her breast, her already hardened nipple pushing against his hand. She arched into his touch, her lips opening slightly as she sighed in her sleep.

Rayne found her mouthwatering curves irresistible and longed to cover her softness with his hard, needy body. His heart beat out of control as he tasted her shoulder, kissed along her collarbone, and nipped at her jaw, all in an effort to reach her lips. Once there, he savored the sweetness of her mouth. She sighed ever so erotically, whispering his name like a prayer as his lips expertly captured hers.

Kyndel instinctually opened to him. Rayne's tongue slid along hers in a slow, erotic exploration, all coherent thought lost in a haze of desire. It was as if the air had been sucked from the room as he rolled her onto her back and moved over her.

He sighed.

I have found my forever...

CHAPTER SEVEN

Kyndel stretched, slowly coming back to consciousness, not wanting to leave the naughtiest and definitely the most realistic dream she'd ever had. She *felt* his hands on her skin, his mouth on hers, his touch almost burning in its intensity.

She fell asleep thinking of Rayne, so it only stood to reason he had the starring role in the best erotic dream of her life. Squeezing her eyes shut, she willed herself back to sleep, not wanting to face reality when her fantasies were so much better. She never wanted to wake, especially if he continued to kiss her as if she was the air he breathed.

Relaxing back into the couch, she slipped back into her fantasy as if she'd never left. Teeth scraped across her painfully hard nipple. Her back bowed off the couch, pushing more of her sensitive skin into Rayne's incredible mouth.

Her eyes flew open. A mane of silken, wet hair swept across her chest. Before she could question what was happening, a moan tore from her throat. She was on fire. Burning from the inside out. Burying her hands in Rayne's hair, she jerked his mouth to hers. Surprise flashed in his violet eyes a split second before his mouth was on hers.

It was a complete assault on her senses. He took control. His hands grasped both sides of her face, moving her into the position *he* wanted. Their tongues dueled. They fought to breathe, neither willing to end their passion.

Kyndel's hands flew to his back. The marking she'd admired while cleaning his wounds became more pronounced the higher their passion soared. They rippled against her fingertips, almost as if the dragon in the picture was enjoying their desire as much as they were.

Somewhere in the deep recesses of her sex-addled brain, she knew it was too soon to be kissing this stranger, even more so to act upon the demands of her body...but resistance was futile. Nothing wrong could feel this good...*this right*.

CHAPTER EIGHT

Rayne left her mouth, sliding down her body, kissing every inch he could reach. He had to taste her, had to draw as much of *her* into him as possible. The scent of her arousal was driving him crazy. Both man and dragon wanted to taste every inch of her center, enjoy every orgasm Rayne could wring out of her.

He would only stop when she was swollen, tender, and completely spent. Then and only then would he sink into the paradise that was his mate. Fill every inch of her. Feel her pussy contract around him. Be one with her...body and soul.

Holding on by a thread, the need to be deep inside her driving his every action, he slipped his hand under the waistband of her pajama pants. The curly hairs at the top of her mound tickled the tips of his fingers. Moving lower, the heat of her arousal scorched them.

Her pants limited his access. Slowly pulling them over her hips, he kissed and caressed, vowing to keep her naked for all time. Once she was completely bare, ready to devour, he lifted his head and their eyes met.

He was humbled. Her absolute belief that what they were doing was right shone brightly from her eyes. He had her complete trust, even if she had no clue why. His body *and* his dragon begged him to take her before he embarrassed himself like a randy teenager.

"Rayne..." That one word held such feeling, such passion. He was lost, at her mercy for all time. There would be no other.

"Hold on for me, baby. I have to taste you. Okay?"

She bit her bottom lip, looking shy for the first time since they'd met, before giving a single nod.

"Kyndel, do you want me to stop?" Although stopping would probably kill him, he'd do whatever *she* needed.

It took only a second for her to shake her head and mouth the word, *'No'*. He needed no further invitation. Scooting down between her heavenly thighs, tasting the soft sweet skin at her hips, he became lightheaded.

She was full and curvy, everything a woman should be. He placed first one leg, then the other, lovingly over his shoulders, and simply drank in the decadence that was his Kyndel. Immediately intoxicated from the heady scent of her arousal, he licked all around her outer lips, leaving no area untouched.

Her hands tore at his hair. Sweet moans fell from her lips. His resolve to go slow tested to its breaking point. She was by far the biggest temptation he'd ever experienced....and also the sweetest. Slowing to regain his control, he took a deep breath, slowly blowing his exhale against her swollen clit. Kyndel pulled his hair, mewling at the delicate stimulation.

The proof of her arousal glistened in the curly red hair surrounding her pussy. Rayne could no longer resist. Pushing his tongue between her swollen lips as deeply as he could, his heart skipped a beat as her taste exploded on his tongue. Flashes of light and swirls of color burst behind his eyelids from just one taste of her honey.

One finger joined his tongue, tormenting her aroused flesh. Quickly, he added another. Alternating between first tongue and then fingers, pumping in and out, driving her higher and higher, never giving her tender flesh a moment without stimulation, Rayne lapped at the juices that ran from her.

Kyndel was one breath from the point of no return when he pulled back, separated her outer lips with his fingers, and drove his tongue as far into her as he could reach with one steady thrust. Her back bowed off the couch, her thighs tightened around his head, and she screamed his name.

"RAYNE!"

He smiled against her skin, continuing to fuck her with his tongue while teasing her clit with his thumb. Placing his tongue flat on the bottom of her slit, he licked slowly all the way to her clit, sucking the engorged nub between his teeth, nipping lightly. She ground her hips against his face. He ate at her pussy until her head was thrashing side to side. She was speaking in tongues and about to pull his hair out at the roots.

Sucking her clit into his mouth, he bit down with intent, thrusting his fingers into her wanting channel, and curling the tips to reach the sensitive bundle of nerves at the top. Kyndel came with such force he had to work hard to catch all the honey that poured from her pussy. He petted and suckled as she slowly came back to earth. Her sweet sigh of contentment brought a smile to his face.

"Rayne…"

"Yes, *ce'adsearc*."

"That was…that was… *amazing*." Her voice just a breath on the wind as she laid still, completely relaxed, eyes still closed.

Positioning his cock against the swollen lips of her pussy, he rubbed the tip of his swollen head against the clit that still peeked out from her puffy pink lips. Slowly pushing into her, he stopped when just the head of his cock lay inside her. Pushing forward, inch by inch, he teased them both until they were panting, their skin slick with sweat.

Once seated all the way inside her, his cock positioned at the base of her womb, he held still, savoring the way her body contracted around his pulsing cock. He knew without a doubt he could stay locked inside her forever. Unfortunately, he could no longer remain still. Their passion climbed higher, searching for release…a release he could not deny.

Slowly pulling out of her until he was within an inch of slipping from the heaven that was his mate, he pushed back in. Looking to where their bodies were joined in the most intimate of ways, he watched as his cock moved in and out of her, glistening with her juices. Their rhythm increased. She met him stroke for stroke, reaching for her release.

Rayne leaned forward, palmed her breasts, pulling her nipples between his thumbs and forefingers, teasing them to even harder peaks. Kyndel threw her head back, her moans reverberating off the walls of her home. There were no words to describe his mate in the throes of passion. Just the sight of her had him close to losing control. He needed her to come one more time before he emptied into her.

Releasing one of her nipples, he reached between them, rubbing circles over her clit with his thumb. Her pussy squeezed him tighter. He thrust in and out faster and faster until she was screaming her release and milking his cock with such force he thought the top of his head would surely fly off.

Rayne gave Kyndel no respite from his sensual assault. He plunged into her harder and faster, gripping her hips to keep her from bumping her head into the arm of the couch. His balls drew tight against his body, his cock growing even thicker and harder.

"Look at me, *mo ghra'*," Rayne commanded.

Her eyes snapped to his at the same time he pinched her clit between his thumb and forefinger. They exploded together, screaming each other's name. Rayne collapsed forward, holding most of his weight on his forearms, continuing to slide slowly in and out of her. Every touch caused mini contractions in her pussy to tease his slowly softening cock.

When their heart rates began to slow, he rolled them over so that she was pillowed across his chest. He loved the feel of her naked body against his.

"I have never felt anything like that." Her voice was little more than a whisper against his chest.

"Me neither, *ce'adsearc*, me neither."

Kyndel drew patterns in the hair on his chest. Rayne loved the feel of her hands on his body. Even though their lovemaking had been complete and unlike anything he'd ever experienced, he could feel his cock rising again.

She moved, her leg brushing against his growing erection. Her head popped up, her lips in the shape of an 'O'.

"Again?" she questioned with wide eyes.

Rayne pulled her up his body and crushed his mouth to her as his answer. A kiss of raw passion and possession, a branding with his very lips. His tongue swept into her mouth, taking control of her breathing. Rayne's hands moved down her body, gripping her perfectly round ass.

Kyndel moaned into his mouth. It was all the encouragement he needed. He lifted her butt, positioning her so she straddled the tops of his thighs. Sliding his hand between her ass cheeks until he reached her wet, swollen center, his fingers entered her from behind and began to swirl in and out of her as her juices once again flowed.

He kissed his way down her jaw and once again found that little sweet spot behind her ear. Her pussy contracted around his fingers as he sucked and bit down on that sensitive skin. Her legs slid to either side of his hips, dislodging his fingers from her pussy. She moaned at the loss, but immediately began to roll her hips, grinding against his hardened length. With every roll, the head of his cock bumped her clit. He watched the flush spread across her chest and work its way down her body with every touch. Her nails dug into his chest. She threw her head back in ecstasy, speaking in some intelligible language. Kyndel rode him with complete abandon. It was the most magnificent thing he'd ever seen.

Her lovely breasts swaying in his face was a torment he could no longer take. Lifting his head, pulling her chest to his mouth, he sucked as much of her tantalizing flesh into his mouth as would fit. He worried her hardened peak with his tongue and teeth and switched to the other until her hands were once again in his hair and she was moaning his name.

"Oh, God, Rayne. More…please…more," she begged.

He could deny her nothing. Leaning back, he slid his body down just a fraction, lifted his hips, and drove his throbbing cock into her welcoming channel, entering her with such force he touched the bottom of her womb.

Kyndel fell forward, grabbed his shoulders, and sunk her nails into his skin so hard he knew she drew blood. His excitement was driven higher at her total loss of control.

"Rayne…oh God…RAYNE!"

Kyndel screamed her release as Rayne thrust in and out of her, bringing her down from one climax while building the next. With each stroke of his cock, her vagina closed tighter around him. She looked at him with an expression of complete abandon and total satisfaction. His chest puffed with pride.

I put that look on her face.

Feelings he hadn't known he could possess threatened to overtake him. He thought his proudest day had been when he was accepted into the Dragon Guard, but that was a pale memory compared to pleasing his mate.

Kyndel simply stared. A vision…completely naked, haloed by the dawn peeking through the blinds, riding him like a cowgirl. He'd never seen anything more spectacular. She bent forward, laid a gentle kiss to his lips, causing his heart to seize in his chest.

This woman will be the death of me…but what a way to go.

He rocked slowly in and out of her, in absolutely no hurry to leave the warmth of his mate. Their slow dance to the music of their heartbeats and the sounds of their bodies moving in unison continued. He felt the walls of her pussy contracting around him again.

Kyndel closed her eyes. "*This* is heaven."

He swiveled his hips as he moved in and out of her, rubbing all the sensitive spots he now knew made her writhe in pleasure.

"Oh, oh, oh…Rayne."

She rotated her hips in the opposite direction of his as she rode down his length. Their intricate lap dance made it hard for him to think. She leaned forward, her hands landing on his chest and mewled, "Oh God…yes…oh, oh, yes."

"That's it, *ta' mo chroi istigh*, take what you need."

He moved faster, angling himself against her change in position so that every sweep of his cock pushed his swollen head against the bundle of nerves that sent her passion into overload. Their slow burn erupted into a forest fire. Their heavy breathing, the slap of their bodies coupled with their moans of pleasure bounced off the walls of Kyndel's apartment.

She pushed, sitting straight up, just the tips of her fingers still pushing against his chest. The change in position was all they needed. Their eyes locked and from one heartbeat to the next, they were screaming their release.

Kyndel collapsed, boneless and replete across his chest. He listened to her fight to catch her breath, felt her heart beat in sync with his, and didn't even try to stop the smile that crossed his lips.

This is the first of many my love…the first of many.

CHAPTER NINE

She fought hard just to catch her breath. Then realized Mr. Macho Man wasn't having an easy time of it either. His arms came around her, locking her securely in place. Her heart clenched. She felt *cherished*. Kyndel *knew* beyond a shadow of a doubt that nothing bad would ever happen to her as long as Rayne was around. She closed her eyes, reveling in a feeling she hadn't felt since before her parents passed away…the feeling of *truly belonging*.

It was powerful and she'd only known him a few hours. She refused to believe it could be love. But the feeling of coming home, of unconditional acceptance and belonging was undeniable. She also knew as well as she knew her own name, nothing would ever be the same. What had just happened between them had changed the course of her life.

Completely satiated, content to let the worries that usually would have her freaked out to wait, she cuddled farther into his chest. Sex had never been anything like what she'd just experienced with Rayne…*twice*.

Was this the difference between having sex and making love?

Oh, shit! Where did that thought come from? Shoo! Go away!

She'd thought she knew what an orgasm was, but now it was clear she had not. It was utter bliss with Rayne, and Kyndel was determined to enjoy every second of it.

"What are you thinking so hard about, my little *a chumann*?"

"Nothing," she lied. "Just enjoying this moment, right here, right now…*with you*."

Kyndel propped her chin on her hand and looked at the man who had given her more pleasure in the last hour than she'd experienced in all of her twenty-six years. The smug smirk on his lips made her ask, "Pretty satisfied with yourself, huh?" She cocked one eyebrow for effect.

Rayne chuckled. His chest vibrated. Her nipples perked up and her pussy clenched. She worked hard not to let her eyes cross at the scintillating sensations. He rubbed lazy circles up and down her spine, every caress pushing her aching breasts against his taut chest. More delicious friction. Her hips moved against his stomach.

"Does my *mo ghra'* need her *m'fhi'orghra'* again?" he breathed into her ear.

Kyndel pulled back and looked Rayne in the eye. "Did you slip me a mickey or something? I've never been like this in my entire life. I mean, I *like* sex. I'm not a nun or anything." She chuckled. "But I'm in no way promiscuous, either. I usually don't even kiss on the first date. What is it about you? I feel like I've known you my whole life. I'm comfortable with you." She shook her head slightly and sighed. "And I'm not comfortable with *anyone* until I *completely* know them. But you're different, and no matter how I try to deny it, I can't." She stopped and looked away, unsure if she should finish her thought. She decided to go for it. "And what's worse? I don't *want* to deny it."

"Why is that bad, *ce'adsearc*?"

"I'm not saying it is bad…necessarily. I'm saying it's confusing. I got up this morning…" She stopped and thought before continuing, "Or I guess it was yesterday morning, ate my cereal, got dressed, went to work, put up with the bullshit, got off work, and headed home. Was scared half out of my mind, tripped over you, and now here we are. It's a lot to take in, don't you think?"

"Yes." He nodded. "I can see why you would think so."

"And I'm not even going to think about how badly you were hurt and how quickly you healed. I know Granny's ointment is good, but not *that* good." She once again leveled that one raised eyebrow look at him. She wanted to intimidate him, but the grin he was trying to hide said she was failing…*miserably*.

Kyndel felt the muscles under her hands bunch and recognized the gleam in Rayne's eyes. He meant to distract her again, and as good as that sounded, she really needed to get some answers from Mr. Sexy as Sin. After all, he'd promised.

Hopping off Rayne, she deposited herself on the far end of the couch with her back against the arm. Only when the gleam in Rayne's eyes turned to heat did she realize she was sitting there completely naked, her arms crossed under her breasts, displaying them like an offering to the man that could set her pulse to thundering with just a look.

What the hell is the matter with me?

She *never* sat around naked. No one *ever* saw her without at least an oversized T-shirt on, and here she was displaying her ample body for the man that was her kryptonite. He was *definitely* seeing his fill. If his erection, which was growing longer and harder by the second was any indication, he was enjoying the view. She snatched one of Granny's handmade afghans off the back of the couch and tucked it around her, successfully covering her nudity.

Rayne lifted his eyebrow and stared, mimicking her action from just a moment ago. He laughed aloud when she rolled her eyes, then crossed his arms over his chest. She chuckled, letting him know she wasn't intimidated either. They sat staring.

Tired of their staring contest, Kyndel began to blurt out the questions that had been running through her head since she agreed to bring a total stranger into her home.

"Why do I feel so comfortable with you, Rayne? Why do I feel like I've known you my whole life? What is it that pulls me to you? This," she motioned between them, "is not normal. I've *never* felt *this* with anyone before. *Not even my family*. What is it about you that I find so irresistible?"

She spoke faster and faster as she asked all the questions that were plaguing her. All the questions she'd promised herself, just moments ago, not to worry about. Gasping for breath when she finally finished, Kyndel stared at her mystery man, waiting for her answers.

He was just about to answer when his brow furrowed and he looked away. She waited and waited and…

CHAPTER TEN

Rayne took a deep breath and thought for a moment, looking directly into Kyndel's expressive eyes, every emotion displayed for him to see and learn. It was his job to answer her questions, to reassure her everything would be all right. *Better than all right*, it was going to be heaven. All he had to do was make her listen without completely freaking out, or worse, calling the authorities before he could make her see reason. Prepared for the most important conversation of his life, Rayne opened his mouth to speak just as Lance's voice sounded in his head.

"We've got trouble!"

"What's happening?"

"The hunters are closing in on your location. I don't think they know you're there. Your magic seems to be holding, but they're covering three sides of the block and looks like more are swinging around. They're on a fishing expedition, but it's still too close for comfort."

"Thanks for the heads up. I'm handling the situation here. We'll rendezvous in one hour."

"Have fun 'handling that situation' there, buddy boy! I felt a few spikes in your power. Any details you care to share?" Lance coughed to cover the chuckle in his voice, and Rayne imagined strangling him.

"I definitely do NOT care to share," Rayne growled. *"Don't you worry about my 'situation'. You worry about keeping those damn hunters off my ass."*

Rayne cut communications to the sound of Lance laughing and Aidan asking what was going on. Lance better keep his mouth shut or that boy was in for some serious pain.

"Rayne, are you ignoring me? Why aren't you answering my questions?"

He'd completely forgotten Kyndel had no idea he was talking to his brethren or he *could* mindspeak for that matter.

Dammit!

It was getting more complicated by the minute. He wished for the time to court her, to ease her into his life slowly. Give her the time she needed to accept her changing world one step at a time, but that was not what Fate had in store for them. It was going to be a crash course at a hundred miles an hour.

"No, *ce'adsearc*, I'm not ignoring you." He took a deep breath and allowed his instincts to guide him in his explanation. "I need you to listen to me with an open mind. I'm going to ask that you *please* do not interrupt until I'm finished. What I'm about to tell you is going to sound crazy. *I'm* going to sound crazy. But I swear by all I hold sacred, everything I tell you will be the truth, and as soon as I can, I'll *show* you. You'll be able to see with your own eyes that I'm as sane as you. Can you do that for me, *ce'adsearc*?"

She closed her eyes and took a deep breath, then slowly let it out. When she looked at him, he saw resolution and a little trust, even though he was sure she didn't understand where the feelings had come from.

"Yes, I'll listen to what you have to say, but you better be ready to answer my questions when you're finished. God knows *nothing* has been *normal* since I met you. Why should now be any different?"

"Thank you, *mo ghra'*. I promise I'll never betray your trust." He rolled his shoulders. "I'll start with what you just witnessed. I'm the Commander of the Dragon Guard. Through fealty and a bond of blood, I'm able to mindspeak with my Force, a group of men I grew up with, trained with, trust with my life, and by extension now your life. Mindspeak is like what you think of as telepathy or ESP. It's essential to our ability to protect our people. We are the Golden Fire Clan of the Dragon Shifters. My Force and I, along with many others, have been tasked with protecting our people from the hunters, a group of zealots that would drive us into extinction. They were trained by dark wizards, the oldest enemy of the dragon.

"We, the dragon shifters, have been in existence since the days of King Arthur. All the stories are true, just turned into fairy tales for the protection of our kin. As time progressed and the land became more populated, the dragons found it almost impossible to hide their existence. They enlisted the help of a very powerful mage, one of Merlin's line, the original mage. He was able to combine the very essence of their beings with the knight of their choosing. That knight possessed all the characteristics necessary to protect what was theirs, to fight for those that needed a champion and keep their race from extinction.

"The dragons looked for men that were courteous, honest, generous, courageous, loyal, just, discreet, wise, brave, and honorable. All qualities the knights that had fought alongside them for hundreds of years possessed. They made sure these qualities were ingrained in the individual, actually part of their bloodline. The dragons had to ensure that by entrusting their very essence to a group of human men, their power would never be abused.

"My family was one of the few given this honor. My ancestor was chosen in the 6th century, shortly after King Arthur disappeared. Every male in my family has gone through the transformation between the ages of eighteen and twenty-one. From that age forward, we're able to shift from man to dragon and back again…at will. It is a duty and an honor we take *very* seriously. We also retain the magic of our dragon while in our human form.

"One of the most important milestones in a dragon shifter's life, other than his transformation, is finding his mate. The *one* female in all the world created just for him. She *is* the other half of his soul, the completion of the man *and* his beast. She provides them with peace, love, and light. She grounds them...makes them whole. She is the *single* most important person to both entities. Although they have survived and been successful in many endeavors for *many* years, they have never truly lived until they have found her.

"You, my beautiful Kyndel, are *my* mate. You are the light of my soul. You complete me and the dragon that dwells within, in ways I have only dreamed possible. You haunted my thoughts during the day and my dreams at night before I even knew you existed. From the moment I caught your scent as I was soaring over the city last night, I knew you were *the one* for me. When I saw you, it was solidified in my heart that you were the other half of my soul.

"So, *mo ghra'*, you ask why you are drawn to me and feel more comfortable with me than you have felt with any other. It is because we *are destined* to be together. Your soul recognized mine, just as mine recognized yours. Like has called to like. The incredible feelings we are discovering for each other will not be denied. It is Fate. They will only grow stronger over the years. As will our bond. And after our official mating ceremony, you will possess many of the same talents I have. We will be able to mindspeak, and I will teach you to draw on our dragon magic."

Rayne watched and waited as patiently as he could, but finally could take the silence no longer and spoke. "I know it's a lot to take in. I told you I would never betray your trust, always be honest with you, and answer all your questions, and I will. I only ask a little more indulgence on your part. There's a very pressing issue we must address right away.

"The noises I'm sure you heard last evening as you passed the park were caused from a fight between a pack of hunters and myself. They saw me drop from the sky and attacked. I had to 'take care of them' to protect you, my clan, and myself. There are others from their sect that have followed their comrades and are closing in on our location as we speak.

"I have the house warded to keep us from their sight, but they are *very persistent*. Men from my Force assure me they are searching quite diligently to find the one who took out the others from their pack...*me*. We can fight them off and return to our clan, but I cannot... I *will not* leave you alone. They will know you are my mate as soon as they lay eyes on you. They would seek to destroy you to hurt me and to keep us from completing our bond, thus ensuring our offspring never exist.

"I don't want to scare you, my beloved, but I did promise to tell you the truth and I must also ask for you to trust me to keep you safe. We need to get dressed and meet my brethren. We will return to the clan and make plans to take care of the other hunters in the area."

She just sat there staring at him. Her expression one he couldn't read. Her breathing was slow and deep, assuring him she wasn't panicking, but he worried that she wasn't speaking either. He longed to hear her voice. He didn't even care if she yelled at him. He just *needed* her to talk.

Finally, she took a breath and asked, "So the dragon tattoo on your back...is he *your dragon?*"

"Yes and no. The brand across my back is the physical representation of the dragon within." He touched his fist to his chest for emphasis.

Out of all he'd just told her, *that* was the first question she had for him? Kyndel was an incredible riddle he would spend the rest of his life puzzling out. A challenge he happily accepted.

"So I *did* hear noises in the park last night? It wasn't my imagination?" She sounded almost happy, most definitely vindicated.

"No, it was *not* your imagination."

"Those hunters want to kill you and your kind?" He could feel her outrage.

Rayne nodded. "Yes, sweetheart, they do. And you, too. You are mine now, and after our mating ceremony, you will be *our kin* as well. They will use whatever means necessary to take you from me. Something I will NOT let happen."

"And you and your brethren, I think you called them that, y'all can keep us all safe?" She needed reassurance.

"Yes, we can."

"Then I guess we better get dressed and get a move on. But you *will* answer the rest of my questions when we're safe. That's non-negotiable. I'm not sure I believe all this talk of mates and destiny, but those hunters put a hurtin' on you, and I'm damn sure not lookin' forward to runnin' into them."

She stood, wrapping the afghan around her. "Don't think you've gotten off that easy. Our conversation isn't over. I'm going with you, but that does not mean I buy everything you said."

Turning to leave the room, she looked over her shoulder at him. "And no planning any *mating ceremonies* until we've talked."

And with that, she stepped into the hallway…out of his sight.

"Yes, mate, I will answer any and all of your questions as soon as I know you're safe and the hunters are no longer a threat," he called after her.

Rayne, my boy, you hit the jackpot. The Universe does not *make mistakes.*

CHAPTER ELEVEN

She had absolutely no idea why she believed a word out of Rayne's mouth. The little voice in her head that never steered her wrong was saying he was telling the truth, so she decided to run with it. At least he confirmed she *had* heard something in that blasted park last night. She knew with all certainty that he would give his life to protect hers. Not that she would let him do it, but it was a sweet sentiment. He may be some big bad Commander of the Dragon Guard, but she was Kyndel Masterson, and the Mastersons were a tough bunch, even if she was the only one left. Her people knew how to fight and win, especially when someone they cared about was in danger.

Holy shit! Do I care about him? Yeah, I do.

Somehow, in the last twelve hours, he'd wormed his way into her heart.

Well, don't that beat all?

First, she'd just have to help him get rid of those crazy hunter guys. The rest they'd have to figure out later. What would Granny say if she could see her granddaughter now? She'd tell her to get off her butt and get rid of the trouble.

Thanks, Granny, that's the plan!

In retrospect, Kyndel knew she should've asked more questions. Hell, maybe she should've gotten off the crazy train and headed back to her old life.

Endorphins!

It had to be the endorphins created by a whole bunch of the best orgasms she'd ever experienced in her life. That was the only explanation she could come up with for blindly following a man she'd known for less than twenty-four hours.

Kyndel Masterson was not a woman that followed *anyone* on blind faith. That was the kind of shit that got you betrayed, hurt, or worse… *dead*! She'd learned all about that earlier in her life and had promised herself she'd never do it again. With the exception of Grace, *no one* got to be part of her 'inner circle' without the third, fourth, and fifth degree.

It took years for Kyndel to trust, and here she was having sex with and then leaving her home with a man that professed to be a 'dragon shifter'.

Who the hell does that shit?

And if that wasn't enough, he looked her right in the eye and told her they were mates. Mates? Destined to be together and all that happy horseshit.

Destiny? Really? Who believes in that crap anymore?

Was it destiny when she trusted her supposed *friends* at her first ever frat party? They'd slipped her a mickey, she knew it as sure as she knew her name. Kyndel had been drinking beer with Granny and the boys since she was twelve years old and could drink most of them under the table. But that night after half a beer, her world had gotten fuzzy. She remembered using the wall for support as she made her way for the front door and then…*nothing*. Total blackout.

She woke up the next morning in a lawn chair in the front yard of the frat house with a skull-crushing headache and huge holes in her memory. The real blow came when she got back to the dorm. Everyone stopped talking and stood staring as she headed to her room. It was only after a shower and a change of clothes that she found the pictures of her in her underwear on the fraternity/sorority social page.

Handling it like she handled everything in her life, Kyndel picked herself up by her boot straps, held her head high, and acted like nothing had happened. Well…except where Chip Lowery, aka *asshole*, was concerned…

"Nice pics, cupcake," Chip snickered as he walked past her in the cafeteria.

Everyone at her table, as well as the patrons of the four surrounding tables, was instantly silent. Kyndel could feel all eyes on her. She thought of all the witty comebacks she could throw his way, but decided ignoring the jerk was the best course of action and went back to her conversation with Sadie, a girl from Chem 101.

Obviously perturbed with her inattention, Chip the Asshole added at the top of his lungs, "Can I get an up close and personal view of your lingerie collection?"

The cafeteria erupted into laughter. Kyndel wanted to slide under the table or become invisible, but as Fate would have it, she'd left her magic wand at home. So she did the first thing that came to mind...

Standing, she chuckled along with the crowd. Slowly turning in Chip's direction and with a confidence she didn't feel, Kyndel did her best Mae West imitation, complete with swaying hips and bedroom eyes, as she walked to where he was sitting. His eyes were open so wide she thought they might fall out, but knew she had him right where she wanted him.

Stopping in front of his chair, she winked, and in the breathiest voice she could muster, replied, "Anything for you, Chippie," right before she rammed her Doc Marten hiking boot into his crotch.

You could've heard a pin drop as she walked right past him as if nothing had happened. "Oh, and about the private showing, call when you find your dick."

Funny, no one ever messed with her again, and with the help of Corey, a Computer Science major, the pictures disappeared off the web, never to be seen again. Of course, she'd had to endure a month of Corey following her around like a puppy, but eventually she introduced him to Abbey from Art class and they lived happily ever after, at least the last time she talked to them it was wedded bliss.

Shaking her head, she thought about Rayne. She *knew* he would never hurt her. Her little voice was telling her he was being honest. She'd done every test she could think of, had even taken the lid off her little black box...the place in her heart where all her fears were locked away. She'd let the darkness out, trying to drive the out of control emotions from her system, but it didn't work as it had before. Instead of pushing them away, a wave of comfort and security rolled across her, taking all the sad and scary away. It was as if Rayne knew she needed comfort and had given it to her...*unconditionally*.

She watched him closely out of the corner of her eye. He seemed to be in his own little world while he dressed in the clothes they had scrounged from the bag left by the last douche bag she'd let sleep over. The pants were a little short and the shirt stretched to its limit over his awesome chest, but the boots fit...for the most part.

Rayne had questioned her. Well, more like interrogated her at length about this *other male* as he called him.

"Where did these clothes come from, Kyndel?" His tone took on a commanding quality.

"I told you, the last guy I dated for any length of time," she grumbled while looking for a pair of socks that would cover his big feet.

"Was it a long time ago?"

"Was what a long time ago?"

"When you dated this other *male*," he growled at her.

Looking over her shoulder, she found him glaring at her with his jaw clenched so tight she wondered if his teeth were cracking.

"It's been at least a year. Why? What's your problem? Seriously, I don't even remember his name. Was it John? Jack? Jonas?" She shrugged, not willing to deal with whatever he had going on at the moment. "I think it started with a J. Who knows?"

He seemed pacified but still insisted they burn the offending garments. She didn't even try to stop from laughing at his silliness. He rushed towards her, a fierce look on his face and a gleam in his eyes as he lifted her until she had no alternative but to wrap her legs around his waist.

Rayne's lips slammed onto hers. The kiss was raw and primal. He plundered her mouth...demanded her surrender. Left her breathless and more than a little disoriented when he set her back on her feet. Blinking to clear the fog, she could see the unmistakable heat in his eyes. A promise of more mind-numbing orgasms and soul-shattering kisses. Dammit, if all of that didn't sound a whole lot like paradise.

"If you don't stop looking at me like that, we're never gonna get outta here," she teased, grabbing her hiking boots.

"Just keeping you on your toes, *mo chroi'*." He winked and sat next to her while she put on her shoes.

On the way out the door, she looked over her shoulder and realized *everything*, even her little apartment, looked different with Rayne in her life.

Walking down the sidewalk, headed to meet his friends, Kyndel suddenly realized she didn't even know his last name. True to form, she blurted out, "What's your last name?"

Rayne stopped, turned towards her, and smiled. "MacLendon, *evgren*. Why? Wondering how it will sound as your last name?" He winked and her heart skipped a beat before what he'd said registered.

"WHAT? NO!" She stuttered and stammered. "I just wondered. After all, I have trusted you with my welfare and for the time being, have bought into all your tall tales. I thought at least I should know your last name."

She could see him stifle a laugh and thought about kicking him. He spoke before she could decide. "You're absolutely right, *mo ghra'*. I'm sorry I didn't tell you sooner. But you must admit our meeting has been a *bit* unconventional. As soon as we are safe with the clan, we'll have all the time we need to learn about one another. I want to know everything about you and want to share everything I am *with you*.

"I'll also need to meet your parents. It's customary that I present myself and allow your father to question me and make sure my intentions are pure."

Her heart hurt just a little as she answered, "That won't be possible, Rayne. My parents are dead. They were killed in a car accident when I was almost seven years old."

He pulled her close to his body. "Oh, *mo chroi'*, I am so sorry for your loss."

"It was a long time ago, and Granny took good care of me until she passed a few years ago. I'm the only Masterson left, so you'll just have to present yourself to me." She lifted her head from his chest and saw he'd gotten her attempt at humor…not many did.

Might have to keep the big lug around. He gets me.

She slipped out from under his arm and took a step forward. Dwelling in the past was not her thing. Looking forward was the only way she'd made it through the tough times, and she wasn't about to change now. Rayne was immediately at her side. She grinned when he threaded his fingers through hers. The skin-to-skin contact sent warm, tingly feelings straight to her core. She shivered despite herself.

"Are you cold, *mo ghra'*?"

"No, I'm fine." Quickly changing the subject, she asked, "Hey, what are those names you keep calling me?" Kyndel tried to keep the breathy sound from her voice, but with him this close and his hand wrapped around hers, it was an uphill battle.

"It's my family's native language."

"Oh. Okay. But what specifically are you calling me?" Her tone was sharper than she'd intended. Looking up, she smiled, hoping it softened her words.

"*Mo ghra'* means my love. *Evgren* means ray of sunshine. *Mo chroi'* is my heart. I hadn't realized I was using the old language, but it makes sense that I did. Those terms of endearment are truly how I see you."

Trying to keep from blushing at the honesty she heard in his words, she hurried on. "Last night you said something like *tamagotchi astronaut*. I thought maybe you were thinking about video games."

Rayne laughed aloud. He stopped walking, spun her towards him, and placed his hands on her shoulders. He looked deep into her eyes. Kyndel held her breath, sure that whatever he was going to say was going to blow her mind. It was just the way things had been going.

"I said, '*Ta'mo chroi' istigh ionat*'. It means 'my heart is within you'. Because that, my beautiful mate, is how I feel now that I've found you." He paused and she felt the weight of his words in her heart. Not a heavy weight, but a warmth, a promise, something pretty awesome.

"You, Kyndel Masterson, are the keeper of my heart. From the moment I laid eyes on you, you owned me…body, heart, and soul. All my life, I listened to stories of what it would feel like to find my mate. Let me tell you, they paled in comparison to the real thing. There is *no way* I could've prepared for everything I feel from just being in your presence.

"Last night was just a taste of the passion we'll have. I *will* cherish and protect you with all that I am and all I'll ever be. *You* are my sole reason for being. My sun rises and sets with you, *a thaisce*." He had that heated look in his eyes again, but there was also a twinkle, and she soon knew why.

"That means, my treasure." He winked and grinned before pressing his lips to hers.

The world shifted under her feet. She grabbed his forearms to keep from melting into a puddle of goo at his feet. All the tension that had crept up into her as they walked simply disappeared. It had been a long time since she'd felt important, someone to be treasured and loved, someone *truly special* to another person. It was time to relax and see where all of this was leading. God knew she was already addicted to his kisses. Rayne pulled away. She was thrilled to see he was as affected by their kiss as she.

"Kyndel, my love, if we don't stop, I'm going to throw you over my shoulder and head to the nearest bed until neither of us can walk. We'll finish what we have started, of that you can be sure, but now we *must* meet my brethren and get you to safety."

He wrapped his much larger hand around hers and together they made their way to his friends.

CHAPTER TWELVE

One thing was certain, dragon shifters were a hearty stock of men. Kyndel had never seen so much man candy in the same place in all her life. Of course, Rayne was the most handsome of all of them, but she knew more than a few ladies that would give up chocolate for *life* to be with these guys.

The minute they walked into the clearing, a brawny blond with blue eyes she likened to lasers came right over. He bear hugged Rayne, slapping him on the back so hard it sounded like thunder and grinning like the cat that ate the canary. Rayne introduced him as Lance, the one he'd spoken to...*in his head.*

Lance had a cocky grin, a twinkle in his eye, and one little dimple that seemed to wink at her. He was the troublemaker of the crew, no doubt about it. He didn't hide the fact that he was giving her the once over, so she returned the favor, looking at him from head to toe. He stood with his thumbs hung in his front pockets, feet spread about shoulder width apart, and an air that said not to discount his jovial attitude...he was tough as nails when he had to be.

"Well, Kyndel, if you ever get tired of this old man, I'll make sure you know where to find me." He winked, then faster than she could follow swooped in and gave her a hug.

Rayne growled, pulling her from Lance's grasp. "You will keep your suggestions *and* your hands to yourself, *young man.*"

Lance threw his head back and laughed so hard his whole body shook. The other members of Rayne's Force came over, introducing themselves to her, making sure to only shake hands while keeping a watchful eye on their Commander, who was scowling and grumbling.

"There is *absolutely* no reason for any of you to touch her."

"Lighten up, Rayne. I'm just meeting your friends." She chuckled, loving his possessiveness more than she thought she would.

All of the men were extremely polite. Most laughed and carried on while Lance filled Rayne in on the hunters' activity.

It was still daylight. Rayne said they couldn't risk being seen in dragon form, so that meant hiking at least part of the way. Kyndel hated to think about walking through the tall grass of the clearing, but was grateful for a little more time before witnessing the man she'd made love to turn into a dragon.

On their walk to meet the other Guardsmen, Rayne had shared more details about *his dragon.* She had admitted to herself her trepidation at coming face to face with a thousand pound dragon while he talked, but now *there were six of them*!

One thing had bothered her and she asked for clarification. "A thousand pounds?"

"Yes, *mo ghra'*, that is the average weight of our dragons."

"I thought they would be heavier. I mean, from the movies they look *huge.*" Kyndel was immediately embarrassed that she'd just blurted out her thoughts.

Rayne's laughter soothed her when he answered. "Most people think the same thing, but a dragon's bones are hollow. If they were dense like yours or mine when I'm in human form, the beast would be too heavy to get off the ground. We don't have turbine engines like planes to help us fly, just two strong wings and the force of the wind."

"Wow. Learn something new every day," she mused. "Thanks."

"Always my pleasure."

Glancing around their campsite, she thought about what Rayne had explained and tried to imagine them all flying across the sky as dragons. It was then she realized the one with light brown hair and clear amber eyes sitting by himself, surveying their surroundings. He was the one that introduced himself as Aidan. She knew he was keeping watch, but there was something in the way he held himself that told her he was in pain. Not physical pain, but emotional. If his body language hadn't been enough, it was written in his amber eyes as plain as day. She knew these men were warriors, but couldn't stand idly by when someone was in pain. It just didn't set right with her.

"Mind if I have a seat?" She motioned to the rock next to Aidan's.

"Nope, not at all." She felt how forced the calm and friendliness in his voice was.

After a few minutes of silence, Kyndel couldn't stand it any longer. "Enjoying the scenery?" She thought maybe throwing a little humor at the stoic guard might loosen him up.

"Yeah, something like that," Aidan snorted.

"Bet it gets boring."

"Not really. I like the solitude. Gives me time to think and I like the outside."

"Yeah, I bet all of you like the outdoors, seeing as how you guys change into big half ton dragons that can fly and shoot fire from your nostrils." She flinched. "Oh, *shit*! Sorry about that. I shouldn't have blurted that out. I have a bad habit of engaging my mouth before my brain."

She chuckled to ease some of the tension. "I didn't mean anything by that. I was just trying to start a conversation. Standing around and waiting is making me crazy and…"

"It's okay, don't worry about it," Aidan chuckled, and she felt his tension lessen a little bit.

"No, really! I'm sorry. I'm gonna have to get used to this kind of thing if Rayne and I are really going to try to be a couple."

"I'm certain you are going to be more than *just* a couple, from the way the Commander looks at you."

Kyndel couldn't help but feel like she had said something wrong when she watched the smile that had completely transformed his face fall and the grimace from before return. She placed her hand on his forearm and felt him tense. She rubbed one little circle, then removed her hand. "Did I say something wrong?"

"No, *vibria*, you did not. There are just some things that are better left alone."

"Well, Aidan, know that as long as I'm around, you always have someone to talk to if you feel the need."

"I thank you, Kyndel. You make a wonderful addition to our clan and the perfect mate for our Commander. And speaking of our Commander, I think he's done listening to us from behind the tree." He pointed in the direction Rayne was now stalking away from. "It looks like your mate is looking for you, Miss Kyndel."

"You are so busted, buddy!" Kyndel didn't even try to keep from laughing at the way Rayne marched forward like he owned the world. 'The Commander' as most of the men called him, was more than a little embarrassed at being caught spying.

Faster than she could track, Rayne scooped her into his arms and swung her around like her daddy used to when she was a little girl. Their spinning slowed. She slid down his body, stopping when her lips were level with his. His pupils dilated. She felt her cheeks warm with a flush that only came when he was near. Their lips were just about to touch when they were reminded they weren't alone.

"Ahem," Aidan cleared his throat. "I will leave you to it," he chuckled just a bit and turned on his heel.

"I meant what I said, Aidan," Kyndel called to Aidan's back as he walked away.

"Thank you for your kindness, Kyndel. Enjoy your mate," he answered without turning and disappeared before her eyes.

Rayne's breath on her neck as he nibbled her ear made her forget everything but the man who held her tight. The man that made her body burn with the simplest of touches. Her blood boiled. She was immediately wet and needy. The kiss that started as slow and gentle quickly became all about passion and possession.

Rayne ended their kiss as abruptly as it began. Kyndel found herself in his arms, being carried away from the prying eyes of his men. Her feet touched the ground when he stopped on the other side of an outcropping of trees at the farthest point of the park.

Kyndel felt the cold concrete of the wall that separated the maintenance shed they stood beside from the rest of the park at her back. It was a delicious contrast to the hot, hard man pressing against her front. In an instant, she was again lifted and forced to wrap her legs around his waist. She ground her crotch against his denim covered erection. There were just too damn many clothes between them.

She slid her hand under the waistband of his jeans and fisted his hot, throbbing cock, running her thumb through the drop of moisture that had already gathered on the tip. He tore his mouth from hers, threw his head back, and groaned. "Kyndel…*mo ghra'*."

She continued to massage him and grind her hips against the combination of her hand and his hard cock. He thrust against her. Their pace was immediately frantic, her butt bumping against the wall at her back. Rayne tore at the opening of her jeans and thrust two fingers into her weeping flesh.

"Oh my God, Rayne, more…please…more."

He pushed his thumb against her very aroused nub, rubbing circles at the same time he curled his fingers to torment the bundle of nerves at the top of her channel. Kyndel lost all semblances of time and space. She ripped his pants open and his cock sprang free. She fisted him from root to tip, grabbing the moisture from the tip for lubrication, working him faster and faster.

She moaned at the loss as Rayne pulled his fingers from her needy pussy. Faster than she could believe, Kyndel was bent over a fallen log that had been sanded and shellacked for park goers to use as a bench. Her pants were down to her knees and Rayne was massaging the globes of her ass.

"You are the *most spectacular* woman I have *ever* seen."

Kyndel looked over her shoulder to find him looking at her like she was a priceless piece of art. *No one* had ever looked at her like that, but there would be time for that later.

"Less window shopping, more action there, Commander," she teased. Her voice was sexy and throaty, even to her own ears.

He thrust into her with such force that she felt his balls smack against her ass. He felt bigger than before. The fit tighter. She felt the walls of her vagina stretch to accommodate him. The throbbing of his cock magnified by the snug fit. She realized then it was from her jeans holding her knees so close together and thanked God for tight denim.

He held completely still. Seconds ticked by. Her pulse rose. Her vision blurred. It was then she realized from the pulsing of his erection against her contracting pussy that their racing hearts beat as one.

Complete...I feel complete.

CHAPTER THIRTEEN

"Please... Rayne! Please move! Fuck me, *dammit*!" She dropped her head forward in the most beautifully submissive pose he'd ever seen. Her delicate hands were clenched into fists while her forearms supported her weight. She squeezed tight around him, shattering his hard fought control. Leaning forward, he grabbed both her shoulders and began to thrust hard and fast, not missing a beat of his rhythm.

"Oh God, yes! Yes! YES!" Her voice louder and louder as he continued to pound into her waiting flesh. She pushed back, meeting him thrust for thrust. Their movements uncoordinated and frantic. He felt her orgasm building, threatening to take them both over the edge. She was close...so very close, just needed a little extra push.

He took one of his hands from her shoulders, palmed her breast, and squeezing her already hardened nipple between his thumb and forefinger. She went off like a rocket. He followed, roaring his release into the trees.

Rayne couldn't find it in his heart to care that they were being stalked by a crazed band of hunters or that his men were only a few hundred yards away. All that mattered was the woman before him. Leaning down, he rested his chest against her back, inhaling their combined scent and loving every note of it. Moving the collar of her shirt, he lavished her neck, needing to touch as much of her as he could. Her womb grabbed his softening cock, immediately it began to harden again. Heavens, he wished he had time to spend days and weeks inside this woman...and that time *would* come.

As their heartbeats slowed and their breathing returned to normal, he heard her chuckle. "So what was all that about, *Commander*?"

Rayne thought about telling his mate that the sight of her so close to another man, even though it was one of his brethren, had triggered a primal need. The innate desire to be buried inside her...*again*, right that minute, the circumstances they faced be damned, overcame him. More than he needed to breathe, he had needed his scent on her and in her, so that absolutely everyone knew she was his.

When she'd placed her hand on Aidan's arm, Rayne had to hold on to the tree he hid behind to keep from marching over to where she sat, throwing her over his shoulder, and paddling her behind for touching another man. The rational part of his brain knew his very caring mate had seen the sadness inside Aidan and instinctively reached out to ease his pain. The incredibly irrational alpha male and dominant warrior dragon that resided inside of him never wanted those beautiful hands touching anyone but him.

Without thought, he'd marched toward Kyndel and Aidan, not saying a word to any of his men. He gave absolutely no regard to Aaron, another of his lieutenants and Aidan's twin, who had been mid-sentence. Getting to Kyndel had been all that mattered.

Using his enhanced hearing, he listened to their conversation. Just as he had thought, before the mating call had clouded his brain, his mate was trying to comfort his broken friend. Her compassion was one of the hundreds of things he *already* admired about her.

"Well, cat got your tongue?" Kyndel asked while he stood still buried inside her, not sure how to answer her question.

Going with honesty, just as he promised he always would, Rayne simply said, "I was jealous."

She smiled knowingly as he pulled his semi-hard cock from her pussy and helped her to stand. Turning her to face him, he knelt before her, returned the waistband of her jeans to her hips, and kissed the tip of her nose as he snapped and zipped them into place.

As they walked hand in hand back to the other Guardsmen, he thought about their future together. He couldn't wait until they were officially mated and he could hear her thoughts. Being in the dark was not something Rayne was used to.

As they approached, his men had the good sense to give no indication they knew what had taken place between them. Not even Lance smirked in their direction. They'd all heard the stories from the elder couples about the mating call's effect on a dragon shifter. His brethren knew how increasingly possessive Rayne would become until the mating ceremony was completed.

That part of their conversation made her laugh. How crazy was it that those behemoths thought they could do *anything* without attracting attention. Not only were they all HUGE, each was drop-dead gorgeous. The longer she listened in and chuckled, the more predominant the vein in Rayne's head became. When it looked as is if it might pop, she shrugged her shoulders and went back to helping Royce.

She could *feel* Rayne looking at her every five minutes or so. It was the weirdest sensation, like he was *actually* touching her. Goose bumps rose all over her body, making her tingly and causing an almost undeniable ache between her legs. Tamping down on her unruly thoughts, she tried to think of anything but Rayne, not wanting to embarrass herself after just meeting all these men.

Thankfully, Royce distracted her by talking about anything and everything. He was by far the most laid back of the bunch. She asked if his dragon was golden red like Rayne's and was surprised to find out it wasn't. He explained that each man's dragon was colored from their original clan. Royce's was a royal blue with green scales woven throughout. If it was anything like she imagined from his description, he was a *beautiful* dragon. She told him as much and was immediately embarrassed when he laughed and said, "Beautiful? We of the Dragon Guard are not beautiful. We are fierce and unstoppable."

"I'm sorry. I meant no offense."

"Don't fret, Miss Kyndel, I'm only joking. Our dragons are a sight to behold. There was a time when we took to the sky no matter day or night, never fearing anything or anyone. The sun shone off our scales like glitter. It was a truly spectacular sight. As with all good things, people find a way to destroy the beautiful. Overpopulation and enemies have forced us into hiding. We fly at night, unless there is *grave* danger to one of our own."

Kyndel noticed the longer the big man spoke, the more predominant his accent became. His speech became more formal, like from an older time.

"Can I ask how old you are, Royce?"

"Physically, I was one hundred and fifty-six my last birthday. My dragon is over eighteen hundred years old."

She almost swallowed her tongue, then asked the next thing that popped into her mind. "How old is Rayne?" She braced herself for his answer.

"Oh, he is a young one. He just turned one hundred and nineteen his last birthday. His dragon is one of the younger ones as well, only a little over fourteen hundred years."

What the...

Kyndel worked hard not to freak out. She had sex, wild...crazy...*once in a lifetime sex* with a hundred and nineteen year old man *and* she was actually thinking about doing it again, probably more than once.

"How long do y'all expect to live, if you don't mind me asking?"

"We can live to be at least as old as a thousand years, unless our physical body or that of our dragon is mortally wounded. The soul of the man will return to the Universe and the essence of the dragon will pass to the next male in the family bloodline that does not already share his soul with one of the beasts. If the man does not have a successor, the dragon's essence will pass to the next eligible bloodline. That is why from the time we undergo our transformation, we are looking for our mate. She completes the man and the beast in every way possible. This one special woman, created by the Universe for one Guardsman, is essential to the continuation of our way of life...our species as a whole. She holds the seed of life. For you see, a Guardsman can only reproduce with his chosen mate.

"So, Miss Kyndel, you are *absolutely* essential to Rayne's survival. There will be no other for him...*ever*. If he was to lose you or you were to not accept him as a mate, he would live a solitary existence and never know love. It is said that his lifespan would be greatly shortened."

WOW! No pressure. Thanks, Royce.

"But what will he do when I die *years* before him?" Her voice was barely a whisper as she tried to absorb the information Royce had shared with her.

"Once you and he have completed the official mating ceremony, your lifespan will match his. You will live as many years as he does."

"Well, I guess that's a good thing."

"Yes, it's a very good thing," Royce laughed. "Don't look so worried. Rayne is the best man I know. He will protect you with everything in his power and that is *truly* saying something. Now let's get this stuff packed up. It looks like they're ready to head out."

Now, she was marching along with six of the most elite of the Dragon Guard, on her way to only God knew where. Thinking about everything she had learned in the last twenty-four hours. All the ways her world had changed. And most importantly, about the incredibly sexy man the Universe had decided to make her mate.

CHAPTER FIFTEEN

From the way Kyndel's brow furrowed and her teeth worried her bottom lip, Rayne knew she was deep in thought. He'd heard parts of her conversation with Royce and knew it had been shocking. They weren't officially mated, but he was quickly learning her body language and the different tones of her voice. He'd even felt little nudges in his mind. Their souls were reaching out to one another. The ceremonial words of his people may have not been spoken, but they were quickly bonding, regardless.

After two hours of walking, they reached the incline to The Pointe. Rayne called to his men to stop. He needed to get Kyndel some water and see what was troubling her. It was torture to know she was lamenting over things he could help her understand. Bringing her to his side calmed him.

"Come with me, *mo ghra'*. Let's get a drink before we trudge up this hillside."

They sat on a large rock, out of earshot of the others. "Now, what is causing all this stress?"

He held her face between his massive hands, rubbing the tension from her brow. His pride soared as she leaned into his touch.

"Royce told me how old you are and how long you'll live. He told me how important your mate is to you. Rayne, I just met you a little over twenty-four hours ago. How can all this be happening? It's so overwhelming. I told you I'm *not* someone that trusts easily. I mean, I never even *kiss* on the first date, and we did a *whole lot more* than kiss." She paused for a breath and raised that one brow at him again. He would never get tired of her mannerisms.

She rushed on. "I mean, seriously, Rayne, this is *nuts*. I'm traipsing off with you as if I've known you forever. Trusting all that you're telling me, and let's be real here…everything you've told me is something out of a sci-fi/fantasy movie.

"Oh, and don't let me forget…Royce says when we're mated, I'll live as long as you and that could be at least a thousand years." She paused again, but he knew she wasn't finished, so he sat patiently waiting.

"And…and…the thing that makes all of this even harder is if I don't become your mate, you'll spend all those years, almost nine hundred of them, *alone*…without love. But how can this be love? How can this be anything? I just met you!"

She was breathing deeply. He watched her try to get her emotions under control. The look of pleading and utter confusion in her eyes was more than he could stand. He leaned closer, pressing his lips to hers. He slowly kissed from one corner of her mouth to the other. Reassuring, committing, *showing* her love *can* happen in less than a day. The tension left her body. He slowly pulled back, opened his eyes, and marveled at Kyndel's beauty.

Her face in his hands, eyes closed, lips parted ever so slightly, trusting him, whether she realized it or not, to give her answers to all her questions. In that moment, Rayne saw all the reasons why the Universe made *her* for him. Together, they would move heaven and earth.

Slowly, she opened her eyes. The love and complete devotion he saw there was humbling to say the least. She doubted they could already be falling in love, but he could see it there. "*Mo ghra'*, I know everything is happening *so fast*. If I'd had my way, I would have courted you slowly, giving you time to come to terms with each revelation before dumping something else on you, but it didn't happen that way for us.

"I understand you learned things from Royce that I should've told you, and for that I am very sorry. I hope you can find it in your heart to forgive me."

She nodded. He was just about to ask her if she was ready to go when he was interrupted before they'd finished their conversation.

"Rayne, do you feel that?"

Duty called. He stood and helped Kyndel to her feet. They headed towards the others as he answered, *"Feel what, Lance?"*

"Open your senses! There's a fucking horde approaching!"

Rayne kept moving, opening his senses as wide as he could, frustrated with himself that he'd been so focused on Kyndel, he'd once again neglected to sweep the area.

"Give yourself a break, man. You just found your mate. We're here to cover your ass."

"Yes, and thank you, but I'm the Commander. Son of a bitch, you're right. Fifty or sixty, definitely men. One has some serious magic. They all smell of deceit and hate. Fucking hunters!"

Rayne opened his mind to speak to all the Guardsmen. *"We have incoming, less than a mile out. About sixty hunters. They have someone* very *magical with them. Pick up the pace. We have to get as close to The Pointe as possible before we take flight."*

Rayne did the only thing he could think of to get Kyndel as far away from the hunters as fast as he could. He picked her up and threw her over his shoulder. Just as he expected, she was not at all pleased.

"Rayne, put my heavy ass down….*now*. What the hell is going on?"

Trying to be playful while worried out of his mind, Rayne swatted his mate's lovely ass and pretended to growl. "You will *not* call my mate heavy."

He laughed aloud to let her know he was joking before he gave her the bad news. "We are getting away from a pack of hunters that thought to keep us from reaching The Pointe."

"I promise you will pay for hitting my ass, *Commander*," Kyndel promised, and he could tell she meant it. "I appreciate you can move a hundred times faster than I can, but a little warning before bringing out the caveman/superhero routine would be nice. The next time, I'm not gonna hold back. I *will* throw up down your back."

Rayne chuckled despite the situation. "I'll keep that in mind, *mo chroi'*. However, I do hope the next time I throw you over my shoulder, we're naked and you're not protesting."

"Alrighty, children, as much as I'm enjoying the Love Fest, it appears whoever has the magical ability in our group of stalkers can also enhance their speed. They're doing a damn fine job of closing the distance. I'm not afraid to tell you, I just don't like it. How the hell did they know where we were?" Lance questioned.

"Can't you just change or transform or go all dragony *here* and take off?" Kyndel asked.

"Yes, we *could,* and we will if it comes to that, but our dragons' wing span is over thirty feet wide and most of us are at least twenty feet tall. That's a lot of dragon in close quarters. Not to mention, if we all take off at the same time this close to the ground, we could do some real damage to the landscape, which is *never* our intent. That's why we're trying to get to The Pointe."

"They seem to be picking up speed again, Commander," Lance yelled.

Things must really be dangerous. Lance sounds serious for the first time since I met him and he called Rayne, Commander.

"All right men, we're heading for the largest ledge on the right, about half way to the top. Looks like there's a cave and several different outcroppings where we can take a defensive position. Aidan, I want you to call your dragon forth first. You're the quickest to flight and sleekest in the air. We'll need your speed if things go the way they're headed. The magic practitioner is the one we need to identify, followed closely by the asshole leading this merry band of fuck ups. If we're lucky, they're one and the same."

Making it to the ledge with just minutes to spare, Rayne set Kyndel down at the opening of the cave and turned to address his Force. "Aidan, head up to the highest lip and call forth your dragon. I'm hoping when they see you've already transformed, it'll give them reason for pause. Make sure you're ready to bring your dragon fire. Most of all, keep your senses sharp. We have *no idea* what the magician is capable of."

"Yes, Commander," Aidan responded, and up he went.

"Royce, get the swords and shields. We'll fight as men for as long as we can. Aaron and Lance, take the shelf right below us. Transform only if Aidan has taken flight. I want to avoid calling any human attention to us if at all possible.

"Royce and Devon, stay here with Kyndel and me. You'll call your dragons if Aaron and Lance take flight. I'll be the last to transform."

He turned and placed his hands on Kyndel's shoulders, gripping tightly. "*Mo chroi'*, I need you to do whatever I say *without question*. I know that won't be easy for you, but in this case, it is *absolutely necessary*. You have to trust my expertise. It's killing me that you're once again in danger because of me. When we get out of this, and we *will* get out of this, I swear I'm locking you away somewhere safe."

There was a spark in her eyes. He knew it meant she was about to kick his ass. Thankfully, he'd kept her distracted just long enough to get her to safety. He would be in the doghouse, but she would be safe and that's all that mattered.

CHAPTER SIXTEEN

Kyndel was so caught up in what Rayne was saying that she didn't realize he'd used his speedy dragon abilities to take her deep into the cave. When he finished talking, he crushed his mouth to hers. She felt him pouring everything he was into *that one kiss*. He loved her. She felt it. She believed he would give up his own life if it meant she would live. Before she could open her eyes, Rayne was gone and she had a flashlight in her hands.

She could hear him and the other Guardsmen preparing for battle.

"You better not get yourself killed, Rayne MacLendon. I swear I'm gonna kick your ass if you do!" she yelled, knowing damn good and well he could hear every word. Then she added, "And if you live…I'm gonna kick your ass. You really screwed the pooch, big man!"

She imagined his cocky grin and smug chuckle and couldn't stop the smile that spread across her face.

Argh! That man drives me crazy! And I can't come up with one reason why that's a bad thing.

She felt reassuring warmth spread over her, the same feeling she got with Rayne's arms around her. It was like he was right there with her.

No, that's not possible. I can hear him outside the cave, but I know what I feel. I really am losing my freaking mind.

CHAPTER SEVENTEEN

They were all in place. He knew his men could handle whatever the hunters could dish out. They'd done it before. He counted three separate lines of zealots covered in black from head to toe. All appeared to be human, but he'd finally gotten a read on the magical one. The practitioner was leading the group in the middle…the one heading straight to him.

He could feel the tainted magic on his skin. The ones heading in Aidan's direction seemed reluctant to take on a full-grown dragon and had slowed down their approach. The magician was now pushing them, denying them the freedom to retreat.

You should be afraid…be very afraid, idiots.

Aidan was the fiercest Guardsman of their Force, even more so after the loss he'd endured. They could all feel his resolve. The younger of the twins felt he had nothing to live for. It was something that saddened the entire Force, but in this case, it was to their advantage. In dragon form, he would rain destruction down on all comers. The hunters recognized the danger they were rushing headlong into and fought hard against the magic being poured into them. Digging their heels in, they tried to slow their ascent to no avail. The magician was incredibly strong.

Rayne called to Aaron and Lance, *"The leader of the pack is leading the group heading your way. Look at his arrogance. He's marching like he doesn't have a care in the world. Make the son of a bitch cry like a little girl."*

"Hell yeah," Lance gave a war cry.

"It would be my pleasure," Aaron added.

The Commander had put them together for a reason. Lance and Aaron had trained together since right after their transformations. They knew what the other thought before he thought it. What move he would make before he made it.

Rayne tried to feel sorry for the hunters as they marched to their certain demise, but couldn't. They'd chosen their path. It would end at the point of their swords. What a waste of so many lives.

"Take the wizard out first," he called to Royce and Devon. *"He's enhancing their abilities. We have no clue if he'll be able to disrupt our dragon magic, so take no chances. My mate is here. Fight to win."*

"We always do, Commander," his men answered in unison.

Rayne felt Aidan take flight, then the magic from Aaron calling his dragon danced over his skin. Lance was staying in human form for the moment. Apparently, they had a game plan. He wouldn't interfere as long as they took care of the enemy. If anything went wrong, he'd take it out of Lance's hide.

Devon was perched on the edge of the landing with his bow cocked. He was the best archer Rayne had witnessed in all his hundred and nineteen years. He watched the Guardsman take a deep breath, hold it, then let his arrow fly. It rang true, but was repelled by an unseen force. The magician had erected some type of shield.

Rayne studied his opponents. Only the group traveling with the magic practitioner was protected. Proof of his theory came immediately. Lance's sword ran right through the hunter attacking him and Aaron's huge talons had already beheaded two and were ready to take down another. The leader was evading Lance's strikes, but Rayne had faith in his men. He returned his attention to the troop at their feet.

"Call your dragon, Royce. Your magic is older and stronger. We need to take that bastard magician down quickly."

No sooner had he commanded it than a majestic royal blue dragon stood by his side. Royce's dragon definitely mirrored the man. At twenty-five feet tall, five feet over their average, and weighing in at over fifteen hundred pounds, he was a force to be reckoned with. But more impressive than his size were the six-foot spikes running the length of his tail. They pointed in every direction and were positioned on all sides of his twenty-foot appendage. Not to mention, he wielded the oldest and most potent magic of all dragon kin.

The sight of Royce's dragon caused the magician to stumble. Devon used that split second to fire another arrow. The practitioner ducked. The arrow tore straight through the hunter behind him, taking out the next in line as well. The remaining hunters left their fallen, racing forward, with the magician in the lead.

Checking on his men, Rayne saw that Lance held his broadsword at the ready, still facing off against the human pack-leader. Looking for Aaron, he saw he was already in the air helping his twin. Another deviation from the plan. As long as it worked, he would say nothing. If they failed, there would be hell to pay.

Looking back, Rayne saw the leader fighting with a saber. It seemed to be the weapon of choice for the fanatics. They all wore them strapped to their bodies. The pack-leader thrust his blade towards Lance's face. The Guardsman blocked his advance and countered with one of his own. Rayne could see the hunter's arm shake from the impact. The evil grin on Lance's face said it all…he *liked* to play with his prey.

Rayne switched his attention to Aidan. *"How's it going, 'A'?"*

"It's a great day to slay hunters, whatcha say, Commander? You see these bastards fighting against the black magic. They know they are running headlong into death." His laugh was evil but warranted.

"Bet they never expected to see a nineteen-foot tall dragon up close and personal. Feel that fear?"

"Damn straight. My beast can't wait to taste blood."

The hunters had reached the landing below Aidan. Rayne felt his brethren preparing to descend just as Aaron arrived on the scene. His silver dragon so like Aidan's, they both shone like avenging knights in the rising moonlight.

"We'll talk about this after these idiots are dead and fried." The Commander overheard Aidan chastise Aaron through their mindspeak.

"You don't get to have fun all by yourself, little bro," Aaron snickered, and Rayne wondered how long it would be before Aidan smacked him down. He didn't have long to wait.

"Little my ass, you're only two minutes older and you were to cover Lance."

"Lance has it under control. I wanted some flight time, too."

"Rayne's gonna have your head when this is all over. Just stay out of my way, old man." And with that, the brothers engaged the hunters.

Rayne knew Aaron was worried about his twin, but as Commander, he *had* ordered Aaron to stay with Lance. He only hoped the jokester Guardsman wasn't hot-dogging it. This wizard was proving to have a few tricks up his sleeve. He'd obviously studied the dragons and used what he found to hone his skills to mirror some of their own. The practitioner moved almost as fast and had incredible agility.

Royce, in dragon form, and Devon, still in human form, were dispatching hunters as fast as they could. All three of them were protecting the mouth of the cave…*protecting Kyndel*. Chancing once last glance over the ledge as he battled the hunters that had finally reached them, Rayne saw Lance had partially transformed and was burning the bodies of the hunters he'd dispatched. That meant the leader and fifteen or so of his followers would no longer plague their kin.

The wizard shot a bolt of magic directly at Rayne, bringing his attention back to the battle at hand. The Commander dodged just in time. The shot singed the stone beside the entrance to the cave.

Strong magic, just as I thought.

Rayne swung at the wizard's head. The bastard moved to the left, kicking out as he went, connecting with Rayne's ribs and knocking him off balance. Rushing Rayne, the magician struck the Commander in the mouth with the handle of the short sword he drew from the sheath in his belt. Rayne returned with a heavy blow to the wizard's head and several directly to his gut with the handle of his own broadsword.

Rayne quickly changed his mind, he wanted the bastard alive. He needed to question him. The hunters were changing tactics. They needed to get ahead of it, lest they lose any more of their kin.

Raining punches down on the man that would dare to hunt his mate and his people, Rayne could hear the battle all around and above him. It fueled his anger. The wizard fought back with all he had. No matter what Rayne tried, he couldn't break through the magic the practitioner wielded. Getting the upper hand was taking longer than the Commander would've liked.

Swinging with all his might, Rayne stumbled when Kyndel's scent hit him like a shot to the gut. He immediately turned. The magician used Rayne's inattention to get a shot in at his lower back. Lance, who had climbed to their ledge, was right there to hold his sword against the practitioner's neck. Royce, still in dragon form, was at Rayne's side, but the damage was done. One of the hunters had gotten past their defenses. He had Kyndel by the hair, a knife to her neck. The look of determination in her eyes was all he needed to know. She would not be the passive hostage these idiots had planned on.

CHAPTER EIGHTEEN

Kyndel tried to think of anything but the knife at her throat. The boys had been busy while she was stuck in that dark, dank cave. The sounds of their fighting had echoed off the stone walls, driving her crazy with worry. It became impossible for her to take, not knowing what was happening, so she'd crept closer to the cave entrance. Placing her shirt over the flashlight to keep the glow to a minimum, she'd almost run right into the man, completely covered in black, that now held her hostage. If he hadn't had such strange mismatched eyes that glowed in the dark, she would've bumped right into him.

For just an instant, they'd stared at one another. Then he'd moved as quickly as Rayne, getting behind her, grabbing her by the hair, and placing a knife at her throat before she knew what was happening. Kyndel had tried to fight, but he was so much stronger, she hadn't stood a chance. Giving in, she let him lead her to the mouth of the cave.

Rayne's gonna be so pissed. I'm never gonna live down the fact that I didn't stay where he told me to.

But really, was this the middle ages? Put the little woman on a pedestal and come back for her when the trouble is over. She was not the chick that would go along with the macho man routine. Kyndel was *not* some shrinking violet. If their relationship, or whatever was going on between them, was going to work, Rayne was going to have to realize damsel in distress was not her thing. She'd spent the better part of her life fighting for those she loved. She wouldn't stop just because her mate was a hundred and nineteen years old, turned into a dragon, was the Commander of the Dragon Guard, and had antiquated ideas.

Oh crap! I just called him my mate.

Sometime between getting kissed silly and being left in the cave, he had fallen into the group of people she loved. Worse than that, her heart and head had accepted him as her *mate*. That was his word...not *hers*. Being held by some crazy fool that wanted to use her against him immediately took on a whole new level of sucky.

No frikkin' way. I'm not going out like this.

She'd been promised another nine hundred years or so with the man she just realized she loved, and no freak with a knife was going to take that from her. It was the moment of truth. Her captor had trotted her out of the cave, into open air, right behind Rayne.

"You think to hurt my mate, *hunter*?" Rayne sounded lethal.

"No, *Commander*, I mean to kill your mate and watch holy penance rain down on the Dragon Guard, ending them forever."

Oh, damn. This guy had drawn the line in the sand, and her man was about to cross it.

CHAPTER NINETEEN

Rayne forced a calm he didn't feel into his body, and more importantly, his mind. It was not the time for hasty decisions. Hasty decisions led to mistakes. Mistakes led to Kyndel getting hurt.

Unacceptable.

"And exactly how do you plan to do that when your leader is dead and we have your magician at the end of a sword?"

The man holding his mate laughed and jerked Kyndel's head back a little farther, exposing more of her precious neck. The knife went deeper into her skin. A millimeter farther and he would spill her blood. Rayne was quickly losing control. His dragon pushed to get out. Both *needed* to save their mate.

"You have not killed *my* leader. I am not a hunter. And the one you hold is but my apprentice. I am beholden to *no one*, Rayne MacLendon. I *am* your worst nightmare."

With that proclamation, he pushed Kyndel from under the shadow of the cave entrance into the bright moonlight, still holding tight to her hair, knife at her throat.

Leaning forward, the man holding his mate placed his mask covered mouth against Kyndel's ear. "Now, beautiful mate of the *illustrious* Rayne MacLendon, very slowly raise your hands straight up and over your head. Remove my head covering. My hands seem to be a bit full at the moment." He chuckled at the end while Rayne dreamt of breaking his neck.

Kyndel didn't move immediately. Once again, he jerked her hair. She gasped in pain. Rayne jumped forward, but Kyndel met his eyes and shook her head, letting him know not to lose his temper just yet.

He watched as she raised her hands and removed the ski mask as instructed. All the Guardsmen, even those in dragon form, were absolutely still. Shocked by what had just been revealed.

"Andrew," the name slipped from Rayne's lips.

Two silver dragons dropped from the sky, transforming back to men while they descended, landing on either side of Rayne.

"It's just not possible," Aidan was mumbling and walking forward like he was in a trance.

"Oh, yes, *brother*, it *is* possible. The head you saw thrown into the fire that night was not mine. The wizards captured and restrained me with a combination of black magic and blood of the original mage. What you saw was sleight of hand. You were so gullible. You believed it. You gave up on me. Ran like the coward you are. The wizards held me for months with no food. Wouldn't allow me to transform. Tried to take every drop of dragon magic from me.

"When I realized you weren't coming for me, I plotted my revenge against them. When they thought I was weak, they brought me out of the dungeon. I let them believe they had succeeded in my brainwashing. After I learned all their secrets, including how to hide what I am from everyone, even another Guardsman, I killed the whole coven.

"Then I set out to find the hunters and join their ranks. I knew it was the only way to get close enough to kill *you*. The useless zealots were my cover. Even with all I learned from the wizards, I feared if you all focused on me at the same time, you would be able to figure out who I was, especially big guy there." He pointed to Royce, still in dragon form.

"Why don't you join the party as a man, Royce? I'm getting a stiff neck looking all the way up there to make sure you are not plotting anything."

Finally, Aidan spoke. "But why didn't you mindspeak to me? I left that canyon devastated at the loss of my younger brother. I've spent every moment of every day reliving what went wrong. How those wizards were able to get the drop on us. I haven't had one moment's peace since the second I saw what I thought was your head land in that fire. Why would you not come back to the clan when you escaped the wizards? Why would you join with our mortal enemies?"

"Because, *dear brother*," Andrew spat the words like they were poison, "*you* gave up on *me*. You didn't even *try* to find *me*. When we were surrounded by those wizards, you ran and left *me* to be captured. Even before they threw the head of that farmer into the fire, you had already decided I was dead. You gave up on *me*! YOU ARE A COWARD!"

Andrew looked deranged after his outburst. Until that moment, Rayne thought there might be a chance of reasoning with him, but now he was sure nothing was left of the man they knew all those years before. There would be no talking him down.

"But what do you hope to accomplish by killing Rayne's mate?" Aidan sounded like he was talking to a wild animal, trying to calm him, to make him see reason. Rayne just wanted to kill him.

"I was hoping you'd found yours when I saw you sitting on that rock in the park and this bitch had her hand on your arm, but then I saw the great and powerful *Commander* haul her off, and heard the sounds of their pleasure.

I realized she was his and not yours. Unfortunately, plans were already in motion, so I made a revision. I decided then to kill *his* mate, which will drive him mad. He'll unleash his wrath on all in his path and *you'll* have to watch. I'll make sure he saves you for last so that you may feel *every one* of your *brethren* fall, because after all, dear brother, *you* caused all of this.

"We could have waited another day to go hunting. There were enough food stores to last, but you *had* to fly that night. What was so important, *brother dear*? Tell your faithful Guardsmen what couldn't wait. What was more important than your younger brother's life?"

Aidan closed his eyes and shuddered as if in pain. Rayne feared for his brethren's sanity. Finally, he spoke. "I wanted to see the woman from my dreams, the one my dragon and I had scented on our flight over the city the night before. I knew she would be leaving the gym and couldn't resist looking at her raven hair, blue eyes, and curvy figure one more time. I wanted to see if I could glimpse her smile." His words faded as he spoke, so that when he finished, they were barely audible.

"So, for a look at some piece of ass, you allowed *your brother* to be captured and tortured? *You* gave up and walked away? Tell me, *brother*, did you tell your precious Guardsmen what happened? Did you bring them back to the site? DID YOU EVEN TRY TO FIND ME?"

Continuing like he hadn't asked a question, Andrew growled, "Don't bother answering. It doesn't matter. I don't want to hear your excuses or *apologies*. *You* are a *coward* and a *failure*. You will go to your grave knowing you could've saved me. For that, Rayne's mate *must die* and *you* must watch."

Looking at his other brethren, Rayne saw that Aaron looked as mad as he felt. The Commander couldn't tell which brother he wanted to beat the hell out of first. There were definitely some secrets revealed here today that would have to be dealt with, but right now he had to get his mate out of the hands of the madman holding her. He prayed to the Universe that she would forgive him all his mistakes. He was starting to lose count of the number of times she had been in danger in the twenty-four hours since he'd found her. He had to get everyone's head back in the game and bring this stand off to an end.

Just as he was about to move forward, he caught sight of Devon perched on the edge of the opening to the cave, directly above Andrew and Kyndel. Rayne didn't give a damn how his brethren had gotten up there without anyone noticing, just that he had. Now there was hope, and that was all Rayne needed. He couldn't use mindspeak for fear Andrew might still be able to tune in. He would have to rely on the rest of his men to pay attention. The second Devon made a move, they would all have to act to save Kyndel and keep Andrew from getting away.

In the blink of an eye, everything changed. Andrew pulled Kyndel's head back prepared to pull the knife across her neck. Devon looked at Royce and winked. Andrew was so focused on making sure Rayne was watching him, he had no idea what was happening right over his head.

Devon launched himself at Andrew's back. Royce threw his considerable girth at Andrew's side. The knife fell. Devon hit Andrew while he was still reeling from Royce's hit. What no one had planned for was the force of Royce hitting Andrew in the side, coupled with his hand in Kyndel's hair, would throw *her* into the air. She landed with a crunch against the rocks.

Rayne rushed to her side. He ran his hands over her body, feeling for any broken bones or serious injuries. Afraid to pick her up and hold her against his body as he longed to do because of the blow to her head, he placed one hand on her forehead and the other under her head. His fingers found the warm stickiness of blood.

"Royce, get your ass over here. Let the others handle that lunatic. Kyndel is hurt!"

Royce was immediately at his side. "Commander, you have to move back for me to take a look at the wound."

Rayne moved around to the other side of his mate, never losing touch with her. He was staying by her side. He would be there when she opened those beautiful eyes. He would be the first thing she saw.

She has to be okay.

She'd threatened to kick his ass if he died when they first met. Now, he was going to punish her for making him worry. But first, she had to wake up.

"Is she going to be okay, Royce?"

"Yes, I believe she will be fine. I will wrap her wound. The bleeding has slowed, but we need to get her to the lair. The Healer will be able to stitch her up and make sure everything else is okay. The laceration is not that large or deep. It looks worse than it is because head wounds bleed a lot."

Royce had barely finished explaining before Rayne was issuing orders. "Lance, I need you and Devon to construct a makeshift stretcher that I can use to fly Kyndel back to the lair. We have blankets and ties in the med kit. Do what you have to do. I want to take off in less than ten minutes.

"Aidan and Aaron, is the traitor secure?"

He had to make sure they were seeing their brother's crimes and not the young boy they had raised. It may be harsh, but it would benefit them in the end, because Andrew *would* be judged by the Tribunal for his crimes against dragon kin, and more importantly, against his Kyndel.

"Yes, Commander, he is secure. I'll carry him in my talon and Aidan will fly beside," Aaron answered.

Looking over his shoulder, Rayne saw that Aidan was still in shock. Rayne had been the first to see Aidan the night they'd lost Andrew. The younger twin had been inconsolable. Rayne had taken him to the healers who had finally sedated him.

It had taken weeks before Aidan would speak, and even longer before he let his dragon come forth. They *still* took turns checking on him. Aidan had told the absolute truth when he said he lived with the loss of his brother *every* day. Gone was the happy go lucky trickster that played pranks on all of them, alongside Lance. What was left was a hollow shell of the man they had all known for almost a century.

Rayne looked at his Force, the men he was the closest to, closer than any blood relatives could ever be, and was thankful they were with him. They'd been through too many battles to count, had nursed each other's wounds, and buried their dead together for almost a hundred years. These men had been there when his father had fallen and had helped care for his mother until she ultimately followed his father to the Heavens. They were all wounded from tonight's battle, and even though they were already healing physically, they were at the ready to assist him in caring for his injured mate. He would forever be indebted to these men.

Lance jerked him from his thoughts when he yelled, "I have the gurney ready, Commander."

"Good, let's get her in it."

Lance, Royce, and Rayne worked for what seemed like an eternity getting Kyndel strapped in and secured. There could be no mistakes. Royce gave her an injection of some herbs he'd said were safe for her. They would keep her asleep while in flight. It wouldn't be good for her first glimpse of her mate in dragon form to be while she was strapped to a gurney, flying high in the sky.

"I will call my dragon forth. Lance and Royce, secure the straps of the stretcher around my third and fourth toe. That way, once I take flight, I can wrap my talons around her like a cage."

Rayne looked at Kyndel, hurt and bleeding…wrapped like a mummy to a makeshift backboard. He felt a pain in his heart a hundred times worse than any pain from any battle wound he'd ever received.

"She *will* be okay, Rayne. In a day or two, she'll be right back to her sassy self." Lance squeezed his shoulder.

Rayne turned and walked as far from his mate as possible. He called forth his dragon. Lance and Royce were right there with Kyndel. Rayne lifted his paw and his brethren secured his beautiful mate for their trip to the lair.

She would be all right, she *had* to be all right. He would accept nothing less.

With that last thought, he took to the air, leaving his men to dispose of the bodies and bring the traitor home.

CHAPTER TWENTY

Lance and Royce burnt all the dead bodies and readied themselves to return home. Lance worried over the toll he saw this ordeal was taking on Aidan. The man hadn't been the same since he thought Andrew was dead, and now, to know his younger brother had betrayed them all, took away whatever life was left in him. He looked lost and broken, not something that would bode well for the man or his dragon.

Striding towards Aaron and Aidan, Lance could feel the anger rolling off Aaron. It almost overrode the pain coming from Aidan. "You guys all set for the trip back?"

"Yes," Aaron snarled through gritted teeth. Lance tensed at the fury in his brethren's voice, but really couldn't blame the guy.

"Anything I can do to help?" Lance put his hand on Aaron's shoulder and squeezed, showing him he was there if he needed him.

Aaron shrugged off his hand and glared. "This is my mess to clean up. Butt out."

"Look, Aar, I know this sucks." Lance tried to use his nickname from their childhood to lessen the hostility. "We're all here for you. You guys don't have to go through this alone."

"I *said* I'll take care of it," he barked. "They're my brothers. No matter how fucked up they may be, they're my problem, no one else's. Now, for once, do what the Commander told you to do. I don't need or *want* your help."

Lance knew Aaron was just lashing out, but *damn* that stung. He walked towards Royce, who was waiting to transform. "You know he's just pissed because it's easier than all the other things he could be feeling right now," Royce offered, always the most clearheaded of the bunch.

"Yeah, I know," Lance chuckled sarcastically. "Who would've thought I'd be the touchy-feely one this time? Isn't that your job, big guy?"

"Whatever, asshole." Royce slugged him in the arm. At least they could act like things were going to be okay. But Lance knew this was just the beginning of the shit storm.

With everything loaded, Lance and Royce went to the farthest edge, called forth their dragons, and took flight. Lance trusted that Aaron would make sure he and his brothers got back to the lair, but the Universe only knew what would happen after that.

CHAPTER TWENTY-ONE

Andrew knew they were taking him to the lair. He would face charges of treason before the Tribunal, be found guilty, and beheaded. It was a foregone conclusion…one he was *not* going to let happen. He hadn't survived years of torture at the hands of the wizards, then years of hiding with the hunters to be put to death by the people that failed him.

Aaron wouldn't even look at him. The fury rolling off his older brother was enough to suffocate anyone within a mile radius. Andrew saw pure hatred in Aaron's eyes as he secured Andrew's arms and legs with silver chains, the only thing that could contain a dragon shifter.

Then there was Aidan, who resembled a zombie…eyes glazed over, blank stare, no recognition of what was going on around him. Andrew felt no remorse. It was the least of what the coward deserved. For weeks, he'd laid in that dungeon, sure his brothers and brethren would come for him. He was *sure* Aidan would know he was alive. They'd always been the closest, had shared a bond since his birth—but no one came.

He remembered it like it was yesterday,

For months he was starved, beaten and bloody, his dragon clawing to get out. He called out in mindspeak until his head throbbed and his vision blurred. Finally, with no other choice, he gave into the madness. With all hope lost, he planned his survival and plotted his revenge.

First, he convinced the wizards they had broken him. Made them believe he would do whatever they wanted. A master at deception, Andrew fooled them completely. In their quest for power, the wizards were so focused on the spell to combine his power with the blood of the original mage, they paid little attention to him except to keep him clothed in silver chainmail to subdue his magic. The searing pain was a small price to pay to be privy to their plans and learn magic he never knew existed.

Showing no resistance, playing the perfect victim, caused the wizards to lower their guard around him. Eventually, it appeared they had forgotten who he really was. One day, a younger wizard, who'd been sent to bring his food and prepare him for another siphoning ritual, actually sat down and started to talk to him. They each talked about their upbringing and what was going on at the moment. The young wizard relaxed. Andrew felt the magic they all cloaked themselves in as protection against his dragon magic slip away. That one moment of trusting naivety cost the young man and those of his coven their lives.

He shed the chainmail, donned the dead practitioner's robe, and ran. Well versed in their practices, Andrew was able to make his way to the ritual already in progress. He recited the verses from memory while his dragon magic strengthened since shedding the silver chainmail. It flowed through him, fed by his anger and need for revenge.

It came time in their ceremony for the siphoning. The older wizards looked for the protégé. The leader headed for the door to the man's quarters. Andrew threw off the dead wizard's robe, unleashed his dragon magic fueled by hatred and rage, and tainted by the black magic of the wizards' rituals, and prepared to exact his revenge.

Turning their magic against them, he watched as the skin melted from their bodies. Their muscles slid from their bones. They screamed in agony, begging for mercy, and all the while Andrew stood and watched. He relished their screams. They fed the hatred in his soul. Everything noble and chivalrous he'd once been was gone.

His only mission was to destroy the Dragon Guard. Andrew would not let all he'd suffered be in vain. He would destroy them all. Watch their blood stain the ground beneath his feet. But first, he would settle his score with the hunters. The young wizard had shared that the hunters had been instrumental in his capture. Now, they must pay.

Aaron yanked him up by his arms, nearly dislocating his shoulders and shaking him from his memories.

"You'll ride back to the lair with me. I'll carry you in my paw. You try anything stupid and I promise I'll run you through with my talon. No one would hold it against me. You're a pitiful waste of space. Had Rayne not ordered you taken before the Tribunal, I'd end you right here, right now."

"Sorry to be a disappointment to the family, *brother*," Andrew sneered, looking his brother in the eye.

"Don't push your luck, asshole, and do *not ever* refer to me as your brother again. What you suffered was tragic, but what you did after is *unconscionable*. You could've come home. We would've helped you heal. Instead, you chose revenge, and now it will be the death of you."

With no warning except the feel of magic in the air, Aaron called forth his dragon and grabbed Andrew. It took a moment for the traitor to get his bearings. It had been a long time since he'd been near a dragon and that much pure magic. Aaron tipped his head to Aidan and in an instant, there were two silver dragons looking out over the ledge, preparing to return him to their clan to die.

With a single flap of his wings, Aaron was airborne. Andrew watched Aidan rise into the air just seconds after them. Andrew could feel both his brothers flying on autopilot…lost in thought. He sat waiting for the opportune moment to make his move. There was no way he was going without a fight.

As they passed below an especially dense cloud, Andrew pulled out a piece of silver he had hidden in his pocket and jammed it between Aaron's toes. Instinctively, his brother's paw flew open and Andrew found himself falling to the ground.

Aaron and Aidan turned, diving to try to catch him.

Aidan reached him first, swooping underneath his falling body, trying to force Andrew to land safely on his back…but the traitor would have none of it. Andrew straightened and twisted his body any way he could to avoid Aidan's back.

Always the hero, Aaron came to help. Andrew had to work hard to miss both huge beasts. His only hope of escape was to make it to the ground before them. Aidan extended his wing as far as he could. Andrew twisted away, looking up just in time to see Aaron, who was heading straight for the side of a mountain, have to pull up and make a U-turn.

Aidan was still following him, obviously willing to plummet to his death at the bottom of the canyon instead of letting Andrew get away. The only thing he could think of was to magically freeze him in midair. It would wear off before he hit the rocks, but would allow Andrew the time he needed to get away, once they were on the ground.

Andrew landed without incident, another byproduct of his bastardized magic. He watched Aidan hit the ground as a dragon, shake off the residual black magic, and immediately change to human form. The younger of the twins was disoriented and more than a little pissed from the look of it. Aaron landed beside him, having changed to human form on his descent.

The traitor hid behind a large group of rocks not more than two hundred yards from where his *brothers* stood. It had taken a huge amount of his magical stores to freeze Aidan in flight for only those few seconds. He may be sleeker than most in his dragon form, but he still weighed close to a half ton, and that was a lot of dragon to hold still. So there Andrew stood, not far from the idiots, enjoying that he had gotten the best of them.

The great Dragon Guard, what a joke.

He'd tried to get farther away, but just didn't have the magical juice to make it happen. No matter. Aidan and Aaron were too stupid to look farther than their noses. Andrew had learned to mask his scent. He had many newly developed talents, and the black magic to do whatever his dragon magic could not.

Andrew heard them talking about the preparations they would need to make to capture and keep him. How they would need to see the Elders as soon as they returned to the lair to prepare for the Tribunal. They talked at length while Andrew hid and listened.

The dragons were right to prepare for what he had planned. He'd spent a lot of time thinking about his revenge. No matter how long it took or how many attempts, he *would* get those bastards. They should fear him. He was so much more than they could imagine, and he was going to make them pay.

CHAPTER TWENTY-TWO

It'd been almost two full days since Rayne returned to the lair, his bleeding mate in his arms. He'd transformed back to a man *and* kept a hold of Kyndel all while landing, an entirely new experience he never wanted to repeat. Thankfully, his dragon had controlled the process, even brought them down right outside the Healer's home.

All during their flight he prayed for the healing powers Kyndel possessed to do their job. He'd felt them for himself when he was injured, but knew she was unaware of her power. Rayne prayed for instinct and self-preservation to take over and help his mate when she needed it the most.

The Elder Healer, Siobhan, worked diligently to clean and stitch Kyndel's wounds. Rayne cringed as Siobhan shaved a small patch of Kyndel's hair. Not that his mate seemed the least high maintenance, it was just that in his limited experience, females tended to be protective of their hair. He feared she might skin him alive for the little bald spot at the back of her head. Siobhan assured him it was necessary. Kyndel was still one hundred percent human, therefore, the Healer would be staying as close to human medical practices as possible, and that meant doing everything by the book, no short cuts. All anyone cared about was Kyndel's recovery, and for that, he would be eternally grateful.

Siobhan reassured him Kyndel was healing just as expected, maybe even a little ahead of schedule. He felt it too from the hours he sat by her bed, holding her hand, and talking to her. He'd even gotten feelings of warmth and security through their mating bond. It made her continued unconsciousness a tad more bearable, but he *needed* her to wake up. Willed her to open those beautiful emerald eyes, to look at him and give him a dose of her sass. He looked forward to her trying to intimidate him with that one eyebrow cocked and her hands on her hips.

He wanted to pull her to him and kiss those pouty pink lips of hers until they were naked and wrapped around one another. Waiting was killing him. Watching her hour after hour lying there, looking small and helpless, was one of the worst things he had ever endured.

She *would* wake up. She *would* recover. His mate was fearless. She *had* to be okay. He would wither and die without her. Andrew had been right about one thing, if he'd killed her on that rock, Rayne would've lost his mind. He would hunt that son of a bitch down and rip him limb from limb as soon as all was well with his mate.

He looked over his shoulder as Lance entered Kyndel's room and asked, "How's she doing?"

"Still the same. Siobhan was here an hour ago. Said Kyndel is improving, but dammit, I need her to wake up."

"She will." Lance moved to the end of her bed. "You have to give her body time to heal. She's so much more fragile than we are. But she's a fighter, you know that. A little bump on the head isn't going to keep your mate down. She's got fire and spunk. She's your 'Spitfire' after all."

Rayne smiled at the use of the nickname his men had decided on during one of their visits to bring him food and keep him company while he sat vigil. Royce had said her hair looked even more like fire against the white sheets she laid on than when he'd met her. Aidan had squeezed his shoulder and said, "You have quite the little spitfire on your hands there, Commander." It was good to see the old Aidan creeping back into his friend. They would need him at his best to capture his crazy brother.

They'd all laughed and the nickname had stuck. One or all of them came by almost every hour. They would stand by the bed telling her silly stories about his youth, always referring to her as "Spitfire". It was a guarantee she'd be looking to strangle more than a few Guardsmen when she woke up. Not that he cared, he just wanted her back.

Lost in thought, he almost missed what Lance was saying. "Hey bud, why don't you take a walk…get some fresh air. You're going to need to be ready when she's up and about," he chuckled. "Take a few minutes. I'll sit here with her. I promise to call if she wakes."

"I just hate to be away from her. I'm not ashamed to admit that she's my *everything*. If she doesn't recover, I'll cease to exist."

"Rayne, get your head out of your ass. She's gonna be fine," the Guardsman scoffed. "Get outta here for a minute. Get your head straight. You're turning into a whiner." He winked, easing the sting of the truth, but forged ahead, letting Rayne know he needed to get it together. "She needs the *Commander*, not whoever you are right now. Now go."

Rayne stared at Kyndel for just a moment longer. "You're right. I'm beat. I know better than to let the worry get the best of me. A walk will at least keep my butt from growing to the chair."

He stood, laughing off his earlier fear, rubbed Kyndel's leg, and turned to go. "I will only be a minute," he called over his shoulder.

"Take as long as you need. I'll only tell her a *few* of your dirty little secrets." Lance laughed aloud.

Rayne growled at his friend, thanking the Universe Kyndel couldn't hear whatever tales Lance was going to share.

CHAPTER TWENTY-THREE

Kyndel felt like she was floating. Getting the best night's sleep she'd had in years, probably since she was a little girl.

She loved the old two-story house she'd grown up in. It was huge. She had a bedroom and a playroom for all her toys, especially the dollhouse she and her dad built together.

One of her favorite things was working in his shed with him. He would pretend to glue little pieces of wood to his hands, then touch his face, and dance around, yelling for her to pull it off. When she reached to pull his fingers from his face, he would grab her around the waist and swing her in circles. They both laughed until tears ran down their faces. Painting was even better. He smeared paint on her arm, then acted like it was an accident. She got him back when she painted his cheeks and nose red. He looked just like the Raggedy Andy doll her cousin, Lucy, had.

That old house had a big kitchen, too. Her mom loved to cook and bake, especially for the holidays. Kyndel always got to help. She would roll out the dough, ice the cookies, and put sprinkles on the cakes. It was the best, and only got better. Right before her sixth birthday, her mom let her flip the pancakes on the griddle. A few had hit the floor, but her mom had laughed and said, 'accidents happen'. Kyndel could still close her eyes and smell momma's pot roast, just like when they were coming through the door from Sunday school.

Her childhood had been great and she was a pretty good kid, too. Her parents only had to punish her once, and even then, she would swear her dad was biting the inside of his cheeks to keep from laughing. She'd knocked Amy Jo right off the merry-go-round for making fun of her on the playground. The little brat said Kyndel had chipmunk cheeks. The boys had laughed and the girls looked away, like they were embarrassed for her.

Every time Amy Jo passed Kyndel, she made a little "squeak squeak" sound and blew her cheeks up like they were packed with nuts. On the fourth trip, Kyndel lost her cool. She grabbed the handle, dug her feet into the dirt, and stopped the merry-go-round, with Amy Jo right in front of her. The horrible little girl made the stupid face and "squeaked" one more time, so Kyndel hit her right in the shoulder. Amy Jo fell in the dirt and cried like a baby.

Of course, stupid Miss Kidmore saw it and took Kyndel to the principal's office, who called her parents. Dad came to the school. That's how it was in her small town. Everybody knew everybody. Parents came right to the school when there was a problem. You couldn't get away with anything.

She had to write sentences…two hundred of them. Her dad scolded her with a twinkle in his eye. He assured the principal Kyndel would complete her punishment and they headed home. It was horrible to say, but even all these years later, it had been worth it. Amy Jo never teased her again. Then again, she was only at that school for a few more months. Her mom and dad were killed and her whole world changed. She went to live with Granny.

The first day at a new school had been scary. Granny told her to hold her head up, put her shoulders back, and look those new kids right in the eye. Everyone knew Granny and most thought she was a little batty, so Kyndel was left alone. Truth be told, the old lady did have a unique perspective on the world. It didn't matter, she took good care of Kyndel, raising her and loving her the best way she knew how. Granny wasn't as affectionate as her parents. She was rough around the edges and had an opinion about everything, but she taught Kyndel about plants and herbs, making sure her only granddaughter knew how to help people. The old lady had the respect of the people she helped, the ones that couldn't afford a trip to the doctor.

Granny had been front and center when Kyndel graduated with honors from high school, then again from college. The old lady even wore a dress and didn't have her old straw hat on her head. She told Kyndel how proud of her she was and to never forget where she came from.

Kyndel could hear it as if Granny was right there talking, "Kyndel girl, I always knew you were destined for big things. Our little country town can't hold you. Spread your wings, girl. I'm proud of you. Love you, girl."

That was pretty much the same thing her grandmother said to her the last time they spoke. Kyndel was planning to go for a visit. She went home every four months for a long weekend. Granny wouldn't admit it, but she was getting older and needed more help. The silly woman still kept a half-acre garden and another half-acre of flowers and herbs at ninety-two years old. She would tell the boys that came to help they needed to be doing their schoolwork instead, fix them a sandwich, and send them on their way.

When Kyndel got there that weekend, Granny's color was off. Her normally ruddy complex was sallow. She seemed to take just a little bit longer than usual to answer. Weirder still, Granny let Kyndel cook dinner. They sat and reminisced, even talked a little about her parents, which never happened. Her grandmother told her again how proud she was of her and how much she loved her.

The next morning, Kyndel got up and was surprised not to smell coffee brewing. She figured Granny had gotten distracted or someone had come for help, so she started the pot and went to see where her grandma could be. As Kyndel walked past her room, she saw the old woman still in bed at nine 'o'clock. Granny was up with the chickens. She never slept in. Kyndel went in to wake her and just knew she was gone. Granny had died as she had lived…on her own terms.

The matriarch was buried in the family plot at the same little country church, with all of the Mastersons. Kyndel had packed up all the old woman's things she wanted to keep. Then let the ladies of the community come get whatever they could use for people in need, just as Granny had always said she wanted it handled. Kyndel made sure she had all of her grandmother's recipes and formulas packed away. If she had been told once, she had been told a hundred times, "Kyndel, girl, when I leave this earth, you don't let anyone get their hands on my recipes and formulas. They belong to the Mastersons and that's where they will stay. I'll come back to swat your behind if you let them busy bodies get 'em, girlie."

Kyndel kept floating, thinking about everything and nothing at all. She experienced memories of good days and bad days. How she met Grace. How they were still friends all these years later, even though Grace couldn't follow through on anything, *ever*. First dates, bad dates, parties, awards, it was like the highlight reel of her life.

Right on cue, Rayne was with her. Piercing violet eyes that saw everything. Aristocratic nose that crinkled when he was grinning or trying to keep from laughing. His soft, perfectly shaped lips that could bark orders or give the most amazing pleasure imaginable. His square jaw that was always covered with just a hint of stubble that tickled and raised goose bumps when it rubbed her skin. He was every woman's dream lover, but he wanted *her*. God only knew why, but the poor guy believed the Universe had made *her for him*. He had no problems with her extra pounds and more than ample curves. As a matter of fact, he'd threatened her health, or at least her ability to sit down comfortably, if she lost *any* weight.

How he had just happened into her life was nothing short of miraculous. Like it was supposed to happen. She could remember the times before he was part of her world, but those ceased to matter. It seemed as if everything that had ever happened in her life had been working to bring her to *this place* in *this time* to *this man*.

She had none of the self-conscious feelings she usually got from meeting someone new none of the fears that if she trusted too much, he would leave her. Her heart and soul trusted him and *good Lordy* did her body want him every minute of every day.

Weird things just got weirder, but she still didn't freak out, even when he said he could change into a dragon. She'd accepted it as the truth. Granny always said trust your gut, and her gut said he was the real deal. Even her bullshit meter had been completely quiet since meeting Rayne.

Well, except for some guy with glowing mismatched eyes, but as soon as she reached for that memory, it was gone, replaced by thoughts of her mate. It was time to accept that whatever she felt for this man was *real*. But hadn't she already done that? Her heart had. Kyndel knew she loved Rayne.

Now, if she could just wake up and tell him.

CHAPTER TWENTY-FOUR

He walked back in just in time to hear Lance telling Kyndel a story she *really* didn't need to hear...

Rayne was bathing in a stream by their campsite, enjoying the first time in ten days he wasn't covered in dirt, blood, and gore. A bear snuck into camp in search of food. His clothes were hanging from the tree, but when the huge brown bear walked under the limb, said clothing fell onto his big furry back. Rayne ran almost a mile, completely naked, until the bear dropped his clothes before heading back into the forest.

Rayne was putting his clothes back on when he heard female giggles and turned to find three girls, just past the age of consent, sitting on a hay bale, enjoying the view.

Lance was just about to tell Kyndel how Rayne had tried to talk the girls into accompanying him back to their camp until he was run off by their father at the end of a pitch fork.

Rayne cleared his throat and threw his patented scowl at his friend. Lance laughed aloud, tipped his head very slightly, and whispered conspiratorially, "Spitfire, I'll finish this and catch you up on some other good blackmail material later."

Growling low in his throat, a clear warning that Lance would not be talking to his mate alone for a very long time, Rayne added, "You most assuredly will *not*." Lance howled with laughter, patted him on the back, and told the Commander he'd be back later.

Taking his seat at Kyndel's bedside, Rayne grabbed her hand. He rubbed little circles with his thumb while he stared at her face, willing her to wake up. It occurred to him their bond was strengthening, even without the mating ceremony, despite the fact she was unconscious. There was *absolutely* no doubt she was his.

Not that there had ever been.

With that last thought, he drifted to sleep for the first time in three days, slumped in an incredibly uncomfortable chair, holding the hand of the woman he loved.

He awoke cranky as ever, and more than willing to tell anyone that would listen, starting with the Elder Healer.

"Siobhan, this is the *fourth day* and she is *still* laying there. *Do something*." Rayne was tired and frustrated. "I have given you all the time I can. I'm taking her to the human doctors."

Siobhan crossed the room and touched Rayne's shoulder. "You know she's getting better. You can feel it yourself. Her head wound is healing. She's been through a lot in a short amount of time. Her mind and body are working hard to bring her back to you. You *have* to be patient."

"Patient? *Patient* you say? What the hell do you think I've been doing? I sit here day after day, night after night watching her, talking to her, holding her hand, praying to the Universe. It's been long enough, Siobhan. I *need* her to wake up...now." His last words were spoken on a whisper. He crumbled into the same chair he'd inhabited for four days and dropped his head into his hands.

"Commander, this is not a battle you can wage or an opponent you can kill. Your Kyndel is a very strong woman. She suffered not only a physical blow, but she has had a lot to understand and accept. I believe that is what she is doing, and as soon as she has reconciled it all, she will awaken." And with that, she left to check on her other patients.

Hours later Lance found him still at her bedside, telling her stories of what he had planned for their life together. Thankfully, Lance cleared his throat as the story reached an incredibly personal point. "Any change, Commander?"

Rayne jumped to his feet and was in front of Lance in an instant. His temper out of control and his brethren the only one available to take it out on. "Does it look like there's been any change? Would I be sitting here in this damn room like an impotent child if something had changed or if there was anything I could do? What the hell are you doing here?"

He was breathing heavily as he grabbed Lance's shirt and began to shake the other Guardsman. Rayne's control snapped. He'd reached the end of his rope. Needing an outlet for his frustration, he pulled Lance by the shirt until they were nose to nose and snarled, "What have you done to find the traitor that did this to my mate?"

"We can find no trace of him, sir."

Blind with rage, Rayne backed his friend against the far wall, with his hand around his throat. "You will get your ass and that of every Guardsmen back out there and find that piece of shit."

With every word, Rayne squeezed harder and spoke louder until he was roaring.

"Stop yelling, I'm trying to sleep over here."

Rayne didn't even remember moving. He went from strangling one of his best friends to on his knees beside Kyndel's bed. "*Mo chroi'*? What did you say?"

"I asked you to be quiet. I'm sleeping, Rayne." She opened her eyes and just like every other time she turned those beautiful emerald orbs on him, time stood still.

He took her face in his hands and kissed her lightly on the lips, being very careful not to hurt her, but needing the contact to make sure he was not hallucinating. He lifted his head and looked into her eyes again. She was smiling and her eyes were twinkling. Suddenly, his world was right again.

Thank the Universe!

"How do you feel, *mo ghra'*?"

"I was fine until you woke me up by trying to kill Lance. What does a girl have to do around here to get some sleep?" She cocked that one eyebrow at him, and he couldn't help the smile that eclipsed his entire face.

"And…by the way, *why* are you trying to kill Lance?"

Rayne was too embarrassed to answer. And even more so when she looked at Lance and he only shrugged. "I'll leave you two to talk. Glad you are back with us, Spitfire." He made an about face and left before she could get another word out.

"How do you feel, my love?"

"I have a little headache and other than being awakened from the best nap ever, I feel fine. Why?"

"You were hurt and have been *napping* for four days. Don't you remember?"

Rayne watched the thoughts and emotions cross her expressive face. It was as though she was searching her memory for what had happened. Recognition flashed. Her body shivered. *She remembered.*

She closed her eyes. Took a deep breath. Held it for a moment, then exhaled. He knew she was trying to be brave, but could tell from the death grip on his hand she was having a hard time controlling her emotions. When Kyndel looked back at him, she wore a look of fierce determination.

"I remember that jerk had a knife to my neck and was spouting off like a lunatic. He was gonna slit my throat. I felt the knife dig deeper into my skin, then nothing." She stopped and furrowed her brow. "The next thing I know, you're trying to kill Lance and telling me I've been asleep for four days."

Trying to keep the situation light until Siobhan could examine her, Rayne teased, "Well, there's not a damn thing wrong with your memory."

"Nope, not at all.' She chuckled and it was music to his ears.

He knew he should be rushing to get Siobhan, but needed just a few more minutes alone with his mate.

"How do you feel, baby? Is there anything I can get you?"

"I have a little headache. Where's my backpack? There are some herbs in there. I can make a cup of tea that'll take care of it." Kyndel's eyes were suddenly as big as saucers. "Did you say I've been out for *four days*?"

Rayne tucked a little strand of hair that had fallen in her face behind her ear while he answered. "Yes, *a chumann*, you've been unconscious for four days." He dropped the hand that had placed the hair behind her ear to her cheek.

She shook her head and changed the subject. Reaching up, Kyndel rubbed her fingers across his lips, over his jaw line, and into the little curls at the nape of his neck. "You look a little tired there, Commander." She was teasing, but his mate was also incredibly observant. "Did you sleep at all while I was out?"

Rayne leaned into her arm, closed his eyes, and let the scent of her skin reassure him. He spoke without opening his eyes. "I'm fine now that you're awake. I'll sleep when I'm dead." He turned and placed kisses along the inside of her wrist.

After a moment of just enjoying the peace, he felt the need to tell her how truly terrified he was. "You scared the hell out of me, *a thaisce*. Even though Andrew *is* a crazy asshole, he was right. If anything had happened to you, if you were taken from me, I would cease to exist." He rubbed his chin along her arm, marking her, assuring himself she was whole. "I will never let anything happen to you again. I will do *whatever* it takes to keep you safe."

CHAPTER TWENTY-FIVE

Kyndel pulled him to her, tenderly kissed the corner of his luscious lips, working her way to the middle, letting the tip of her tongue sneak out to lick and tease. She made sure she showed attention to every inch of his mouth. It was not until she felt the tension she'd seen in his mouth and jaw completely relax that she deepened the kiss.

She loved this man or dragon or whatever he was. Loved him with every fiber of her being. Her feelings only intensified to know that he stayed with her while she was unconscious. He'd watched over her, made sure she was okay. He said he couldn't live without her and she believed him. *Hell*, she didn't *want* to live without him. He was a good man and he was *hers*.

She moved her tongue along his, teasing and tasting everything that was purely Rayne. It was not a frantic kiss of possession. It was her promise to him of a very long and happy life together. They were alive. They were together. It was all uphill from there.

The kiss grew in intensity. Her hands wrapped in his hair, his hands massaging her ribs. He rubbed the underside of her breasts. She scooted down just a bit, hoping to get his fingers right where she wanted them when the clearing of a throat brought their kiss to an abrupt halt. A growl rumbled from deep in Rayne's throat.

"Do not growl at me, Commander." A tall woman with long gray hair piled on top of her head stood in the doorway, chuckling. "I have to examine your mate, now that she is awake. You do want to take her home, right?" The woman leveled her gaze at him, her grin apparent as she waited for his answer.

"Yes, but you could have waited a few more minutes." Rayne pouted and it was the cutest thing Kyndel had ever seen, although she wondered if he would appreciate the adjective she chose. He winked before continuing, "Kyndel, this is Siobhan, the Healer of our clan."

"Nice to meet you." Kyndel chuckled.

The Healer nodded and smiled, still standing just inside the door, obviously waiting for Rayne to move.

"Oh, Rayne, let her do what she has to." Kyndel smacked his arm. "I really wanna get outta this bed."

Rayne moved to the opposite side of her bed. She saw his determination to stay by her side, but Siobhan had other plans. "Commander, a few of your men are waiting for word of your mate in the outer room. Maybe you could go fill them in while I examine her."

Siobhan peered over the half glasses perched on the end of her nose. A look Kyndel was sure many had seen over the years.

He looked down at Kyndel for her approval. She sighed. "Rayne, I'm a big girl. Go see to those men out there and tell Lance he's sorely mistaken if he thinks I didn't catch that "Spitfire" comment when he left the room earlier."

Rayne threw his head back and laughed. She loved the sound of his laugh and was thrilled the color was coming back to his face. Watching him walk out of the room, she once again marveled at his amazing body.

Kyndel shook her head. "He really is a mess." She hadn't realized she'd spoken aloud until Siobhan laughed.

"I have never seen the Commander act like that. You are good for him. Before you, he was always serious, constantly reviewing the last battle or preparing for the next. I can count on one hand the number of times I have seen him smile since he was initiated into the Guard," Siobhan spoke as she moved around the room.

Kyndel felt her cheeks warm at the older woman's revelations. "Can I ask you a question?" She paused, then continued when Siobhan nodded. "Are you who I have to thank for patching me up?" She reached behind her head to touch the stitches she'd felt the first time she moved, but had waited until Rayne was gone to inspect them. She somehow knew just the recollection of them would upset him.

"Yes, I stitched your wound and gave you herbs comparable to your human antibiotics."

"You know herbs?" Siobhan nodded. "My granny used herbs and plants to heal everything. She was somewhat of a healer herself for the people in her small town. She taught me everything she knew." She looked up at the tall, stately woman with kind eyes beside her bed. She felt the warmth emanating from the Healer. "Thank you very much."

"You are welcome. I was very happy to be able to help. Human physiology is slightly different than ours. I usually only treat those that have already mated with their dragon partners, so I had to guess on a few things." Siobhan talked while she checked Kyndel's pulse. The Healer was very thorough. She felt her arms and legs for any residual pain and finally examined the stitches in her head.

"Your Granny taught you about healing?" Siobhan asked.

"She did. She taught me what herbs and plants cured each ailment. I'm nowhere as good at it as she was, but I can take care of myself without having to pay a doctor."

"You are very gifted, Kyndel. I can feel it and the Commander mentioned it. When you are settled in, I would like to talk to you about helping us from time to time."

"I'd like that," she answered quickly, thrilled to already be finding her way in her 'new world'. "I'd like that a lot since it seems I'm here to stay." She couldn't stop the giggle that escaped.

Needing a few more answers, Kyndel said, "You sound like you've known Rayne for a long time…" She left her thought hanging, hoping Siobhan would get the hint and talk about Rayne without much encouragement.

The Healer was quick to answer. "You could say that. I was there the day he was born. I have administered every test he has ever had and tended to every wound he has received since that day. What is it you would like to know?" Siobhan leveled a knowing glance at her.

Busted! Damn she's good.

Kyndel knew she should've been embarrassed, but she wanted answers to some of her questions more than she cared about a little embarrassment. "Is he really a hundred and nineteen years old?"

"Yes, that sounds about right." She stopped her examination and once again looked Kyndel in the eye. "Is that really what you want to ask, Kyndel?"

Shaking off her nerves, Kyndel answered, "No, that's not what I want to ask. I want to know what happens when we mate. Rayne mentioned something about an official mating ceremony. He mentioned we would be bound together, that I would get some of his abilities. It all sounds so crazy. Is that really what happens?"

Siobhan sat in the chair beside her bed and looked out the window. "Before I answer you, child, let me ask you a question. Do you love Rayne MacLendon?" The Healer folded her hands across her lap and watched Kyndel, waiting for her answer.

"Yes, I do, but I haven't told him yet. I didn't realize I was actually in love with him until that psycho had me at knifepoint and I thought I was going to die. I thought about how terrible it would be to be killed and not have the chance to tell him how I felt." She twisted the blanket covering her lap in her hands, not sure where all the nerves were coming from. She'd never been a timid person and now was not the time to start. "I don't know how it happened this quickly. Somehow, he wormed his way right into my heart. Now, I can't imagine life without him." She shrugged, trying to look nonchalant. "You must think the bump to my head knocked something loose."

Kyndel was surprised when Siobhan touched her hands as she continued to worry with her blanket. "No, child, I do not think anything is loose in your head. That is the way it is with our kin. The Universe is all-knowing and all-powerful. She knows what each dragon shifter needs and She creates the perfect complement in the form of their mate. She has no regard for species or location, only that every dragon shifter, be they Guardsman or not, have that one person that truly completes them.

"It is written in our holy book that 'When the two halves of the same whole meet, there will be instant recognition. Their souls will merge and only then will the dragon shifter know complete peace. They will have found their true home. It will be as if the time before they met does not exist. All that matters is that they become one in mind, body, and soul.'" Siobhan's smile was one of complete serenity. Kyndel knew in that moment, the Healer had known this kind of completion.

"That was beautiful. Is your mate part of the Dragon Guard?"

There was a flash of pain in Siobhan's gray eyes. "He was. He was killed in battle many years ago. I carry him here." She placed her hand over her heart. "And here," she lifted a locket Kyndel hadn't seen until this moment. When she opened the beautifully engraved piece of jewelry, Kyndel saw a spectacular opal dragon scale with a red teardrop in the center.

"My mate was one of the rare white dragons. Not long after we mated, he returned from battle, unable to shift back to human form due to a serious injury. I nursed him in the Healing Caves for almost a week until he was able to shift again. While I was caring for him, he shed this scale. I had placed it with all the others, but my Gareth found it and had this locket made for me to keep it in. He said that only once in every white dragon's life did they produce the rare heart scale, and most shed it without ever knowing. The fact that we had been together when he shed his was our special blessing from the Universe.

"We had many happy years together and even had a son. I believe you have met him…Devon? He is a member of Rayne's Force. Even though Gareth has gone on to the Heavens before me, I hold a piece of his soul in me. We will be reunited one day." She beamed with love and pride while talking of her family.

Kyndel wiped at the tears that threatened to fall. It wasn't until that moment she realized how much older Siobhan appeared than any of the other dragon shifters she'd met. Of course, the Healer was also the first female she'd met.

She was just about to continue her questioning when she heard what sounded like a party approaching her room.

What is going on out there? And why wasn't I invited?

CHAPTER TWENTY-SIX

He'd given Siobhan all the time he could stand. Rayne wanted…no *needed* his mate, and he needed her *now*. It had been entirely *too long* since he'd held her in his arms. The kiss they'd shared before being interrupted had only reminded him of how close he'd come to losing her and how long it had been since he'd tasted her amazing body.

Lance and Aidan were updating him on the search for the traitor. It was as if Andrew had vanished into thin air. They could find no sign of him. The black magic he'd absorbed from the wizards was making it possible for him to elude their search. Rayne told Lance to check with the Elders to see what they knew of the mixture of dragon magic with the taint of black magic. He told Aidan to check in with Royce to see where he was with the weapon preparation and training of the new Guardsmen. Aaron and Devon were still out searching, expected to return any time.

Rayne cuffed Lance on the back of his head and told him to expect as many horrible things as he could think of as punishment for disobeying him during their battle. The surprise that crossed Lance's face said he'd thought his Commander had forgotten and was now worried.

No matter how hard he tried to focus, Rayne could not escape the pull of his mate. Just as he would have dismissed his men, Lance slid past him with Aidan in tow, headed directly for Kyndel's room. He raced after them and collided with Aidan's back just as Lance opened the door.

"Rayne, what's going on out there?" He did nothing to stop the smile that crossed his face as Kyndel called to him.

He pushed past his men and went to her bedside, passing in front of Siobhan. From the looks of things, they were having a bit of girl talk while he was away. Rayne was glad Kyndel had chosen Siobhan to speak to. She was incredibly wise and well versed on the ways of the dragon kin. She was also kind and motherly to all.

"I was coming to see my beautiful mate when these ruffians rushed their way into your room." He directed a scowl at Lance and Aidan while they looked completely unrepentant for their behavior.

Kyndel cocked her eyebrow at the offending Guardsmen, but almost immediately laughed. "You two are incorrigible! You're just in here to mess with Rayne." She pointed her finger. "Don't try to deny it. I can see the guilt in your eyes."

He loved that she felt comfortable enough to tease his brethren. It was even better when she schooled her expression and looked straight at Lance, pointing her finger. "What did I hear you call me when you left before?" Rayne had been on the receiving end of her intimidation and was happy to see it was another's turn.

He almost laughed aloud when Lance lowered his eyes and replied, "Spitfire." Then it was as if the Guardsman had regained his composure when he punched Aidan in the shoulder and gave him up like a bad penny. "Come on, 'A', fess up. Tell her who came up with her new name."

The playful attitude of his brethren had returned. Rayne saw it and knew Kyndel did too by the huge smile on her face. Aidan squared his shoulders, and with a cheeky grin, nodded his head and said, "I did. I came up with that name after I saw how you handled all of us. And you are my hero for keeping your cool when the traitor had a knife to your neck."

Anger and pain flashed in his eyes and as quick as that, it was gone again. Cheeky grin back in place, he chuckled. "Spitfire suits you just like you suit the Commander."

Kyndel reached up and grabbed Rayne's hand, looking at him with a twinkle in her eye before turning back to his brethren. "I guess you're off the hook then, but you better never call me that in public or I'll show you what happens when a spitfire turns into a *wild fire*."

The whole room erupted into laughter as Kyndel asked, "Now, what the heck do I have to do to get to see these dragons y'all keep telling me you can turn into?"

Even though Siobhan had given her a glowing bill of health, Rayne insisted on carrying Kyndel to the clearing a half mile behind the lair. He wasn't letting her go, wasn't taking a chance that she might even stub her toe on his watch. She complained the whole way, which with his enhanced speed, took all of thirty seconds. It made him smile. There would never be a dull moment.

He placed her on the blanket Aidan had spread under a large shade tree on the edge of the clearing. His hand rubbed her perfectly rounded behind that he pinched lightly before jumping out of reach to avoid the swat he knew was coming. She shook her head and he strode away chuckling. He'd made sure she was far enough from them as not to be bumped by one of their dragons, but close enough that she could still see.

Looking over his shoulder, Rayne smiled. He was still trying to wrap his head around how he of all people had been blessed with Kyndel for a mate.

And now she will meet my dragon.

CHAPTER TWENTY-SEVEN

Kyndel watched as Rayne stood twenty yards from her. He was absolutely breathtaking. Looking every bit the Commander she knew he was. He looked her right in the eyes and from one breath to the next, her magnificent warrior became a majestic creature of legend.

She had to tilt her head back as far as it would go just to see to his face, and there staring back at her were the same violet eyes she'd looked into while making love to her fierce warrior. She saw the same love and devotion.

Rayne's dragon was at least two and a half stories tall. A brilliant combination of reds and golds that created a kaleidoscope of colors that sparkled and shined in the late afternoon sun. The dragon unfurled his wings. Kyndel was awestruck at the incredible length. She could only imagine the strength contained in those amazing appendages. The beast had an elegant beauty, making her unable to take her eyes off him.

He laid his long body on the ground, his snout pointing towards her, and chuffed a small puff of smoke. She had no idea how, but she knew he was telling her she was free to touch and explore.

For a moment she could only sit and stare, amazed she felt as safe standing mere feet from a thousand pound dragon as she did a two hundred and twenty pound man. The front of the beast's snout and nostrils were such a dark red hue, they resembled a fine port wine. The peaks and valleys running from his nostrils to his eyes were so numerous she lost count. The variations of colors and textures were spectacular.

The scales around his eyes were lighter and smaller than any other she could see, and there were more of them. They were layered together in an intricate pattern she assumed was to protect his large, crystalline eyes.

Looking up as far as she could see, Kyndel was awestruck at the row of huge spikes starting in the middle of his head and disappearing down his back. She took a few steps backward to take in as much of the incredible creature lying before her as possible. Moving farther down his body, she could see those threatening spikes were not only on his head, but ran all the way down the middle of his neck and stopped at his shoulder blades. They resembled enormous thorns and were accompanied by two lethal-looking curved horns that grew out of his brow ridge, about a yard back from his eye sockets, and extended six feet in front of him.

Kyndel walked closer, placed her hand on the side of his muzzle, and moved towards the wings that were folded into his sides. She touched and rubbed the entire length of his snout until her hand was resting under his violet eyes. He tilted his head to give her a closer look. His scales felt like hand blown glass, but the harder she pressed the more she could feel their incredible strength.

Placing her other hand beside the one already laying on his jawbone, Kyndel let both hands freely roam under his jaw. The scales there were softer and thinner. They felt like the pair of alligator boots Granny wore when she was snake hunting. These softer scales seemed to extend all the way under his massive body.

She finally reached his wings, letting her fingers slide in between the layers of skin folded like an accordion against his massive ribs. It was thick like leather but as soft as silk. The veins she felt running throughout pulsed as she touched them. Her hands found his torso underneath. She felt the raw power coursing through his body. It seemed to flow out of him and into her, a rush unlike anything she'd ever felt.

Still moving down his body, her senses struggling to take it all in, Kyndel came face to face with this colossal back paw. All she could do was gape. She chuckled, realizing she could easily fit between his toes. However, the sharp claws were as long as she was tall. She had no doubt they could tear a man to shreds with one strike.

As she rounded his rear end and came to his tail, she was given glaring clarity that this creature was made to defend. With a ten-foot long tail sporting four-foot tail spikes running its entire length and a triangular shaped spade at the very end, Kyndel knew one swipe and anything in its path would be completely destroyed.

Time stood still as she tried to absorb everything she felt and saw. A wave of what felt like butterfly kisses washed over her. It was then she saw five other dragons standing behind her and Rayne. One was very large with royal blue scales highlighted by a stunning green running throughout. She knew it was Royce from his earlier description. Just as Rayne had said, he was the largest of them all, but even in dragon form, he had a gentler demeanor than the others.

To his right were two silver dragons. One with glittering black scales running down both sides of his body and wings, while the other's underbelly sparkled with the same onyx covering. She knew these were Aidan and Aaron. Twins in human *and* dragon form.

As she continued looking around the circle of dragons, next in line was a spectacular golden dragon. He appeared more compact, as if his muscles were coiled and ready to spring into action. Looking up into this dragon's large face, she immediately knew it was Lance's dragon from the smirk on his face.

She came to the last in the circle and knew without a doubt she was looking at Devon. Although she hadn't spent much time with this Guardsman, she recognized him from Siobhan's description of her mate, his father. He was the most unusual iridescent white, almost like the finest opal. As he shifted from paw to paw, an array of colors appeared and disappeared over his gigantic body. She noticed that in human form, Devon stood an inch or two taller than Rayne, but in dragon form, Rayne was much taller.

Something I'll have to ask about.

She again felt a rush of butterfly kisses, she now knew was dragon magic, at her back. Turning, she found Rayne in human form, walking toward her. "What do you think, *mo ghra'*?"

"It's just *amazing*, Rayne. That word seems inadequate. Spectacular, maybe? I mean, I *believed* every word you told me, but *nothing* compares to seeing y'all with my own eyes." She turned, facing the other members of Rayne's Force still in dragon form. "Y'all have given me a gift I'll never forget. *Thank you very much.*"

Rayne's arms came around her waist as he pressed his front to her back, cuddling her into his warmth. She leaned back, releasing the breath she'd been holding. A tear slipped down her cheek as Rayne gently placed his chin atop of her head. Magic filled the air as the Guardsmen changed back to their human forms. She laughed to herself and mumbled, swiping the tear from her cheek and hoping no one had noticed, "At least they have jeans on when they change back. I'd spontaneously combust if all that muscled man-flesh was naked."

The Universe has a way of taking care of everything.

Rayne spun her around, looking at her like she had something on her face before pulling her in for a hug and asking, "Why are you crying, my love?"

How did he know? Gotta be the bond thingy.

"I'm just *so* happy. I'm home…finally home."

Rayne lifted her off her feet and spun her in circles. "Yes, *mo ghra'*, you most definitely are, and now it's time to make our mating official."

CHAPTER TWENTY-EIGHT

So much had happened. It had only been twenty-four hours since seeing the Guardsmen in dragon form. In that time, Rayne had taken her to meet the Elders, who were nothing like she'd expected. Definitely NOT a bunch of stuffy old men sitting around judging everyone's actions. They were actually cool. All had retired from the Dragon Guard except the oldest of the bunch, Zachary. He was the Elder Healer and the only dragon shifter she'd met that actually looked old…*really old,* in his case. Wisdom surrounded him. Kyndel could only imagine what he'd seen over his many years of life.

The older Elder held her hands, and after several long minutes of just looking into her eyes, told her he was glad she'd finally made it to them. She had no idea what he meant and wondered if dragon shifters got dementia or Alzheimer's, but thought better about asking, chalked his odd behavior up to his age, and smiled. Everyone she met was incredibly happy that she and Rayne had found one another.

After the Elders, Rayne had shown her what she dubbed the Town Square. He kept calling it "the lair", but it reminded her of a little community. There were shops with everything from a bakery to herbs and armor, and even jewelry made from discarded dragon scales. Emma, a very sweet young woman, explained she only used the scales that were broken to make her jewelry. Each trinket she designed had significance. Kyndel was amazed at the beauty and meaning of each piece.

A bracelet with large red bells and smaller multi-color ones caught her eye. The bells tinkled in the breeze and twinkled in the sunlight. It was the most beautiful piece of jewelry she'd ever seen. Granny had always said that every time a bell rings an angel gets his wings. The thought made Kyndel smile. Then Emma told her for the dragons the saying was, 'Every time a dragon kisses his mate, a bell rings'. She laughed aloud, wondering if Rayne had paid Emma to say that. No matter, the young artisan was incredibly talented and Kyndel promised to visit again soon.

Last stop was Siobhan's house. Kyndel would stay there until the next day, the day of their official mating ceremony. On the way there, Rayne explained the Healer would 'prepare' her for the ceremony. It all sounded very secretive.

"What kind of preparations, Rayne?" she asked, not sure she wanted to know.

"Nothing bad. She'll just explain the ceremony and answer your questions." He chuckled.

"But you said 'prepare' like I had to change or…"

Her words were cut short as Rayne captured her lips with his. She immediately opened. His tongue slid alongside hers and all thoughts of ceremonies and 'preparations' were forgotten. Lost to the moment, they pulled apart at the sound of someone clearing their throat. Kyndel looked over her shoulder to find Siobhan grinning from ear to ear.

"It seems I keep finding you two like this." The Healer shook her head in mock outrage. "Commander, if you do not let go of your mate, I will not have time to prepare her for the mating ceremony."

Before Kyndel could move, Rayne plundered her mouth once again, leaving her breathless and blurry-eyed. She watched his swagger as he crossed the path leading back to the center of the lair and laughed aloud.

He is really something else.

A sudden case of nerves caused her hands to shake as she followed Siobhan into the house. The Healer took her down a hallway Kyndel hadn't noticed when she was there before. In her defense, she *had* been unconscious pretty much the whole time, except for when Rayne carried her out, but it did make her wonder how big the house really was.

They entered a beautifully decorated sitting room, with antique furniture and pieces of art displayed on every surface. One thing for certain…Siobhan liked the finer things in life and appreciated her history. The fresh pot of lavender tea sitting on the coffee table gave the room a light, fresh scent. Siobhan motioned for Kyndel to have a seat on the brocade loveseat under a magnificent painting of lilies in a field.

It didn't take long for Kyndel to forget her nerves and for her curiosity to get the best of her. She'd never been one to pussy-foot around an issue. If she was to be mated to Rayne in less than twenty-four hours, she wanted to know every detail.

"So about this mating ceremony. Rayne said you'll answer all my questions. I guess I really have only one, and it's a big one… What's gonna happen?"

The Healer gave her a very motherly smile before explaining everything Kyndel needed to know about the very old and very sacred mating ceremony of the Golden Fire Clan of the Dragon Shifters. They talked into the wee hours of the morning. Siobhan assured Kyndel as they walked to bed that she would always be available for questions…or a cup of tea.

The few hours' sleep she'd gotten did nothing to dispel the unfamiliar nerves that threatened to overtake her as she stood ready to enter the Cave of the Ancients. Kyndel had to admit to herself she was more excited than nervous and ready to get the show on the road.

Standing at the precipice of a future she'd never imagined, Kyndel thought back to the things she and Siobhan had talked about just a few hours ago. The only thing she wondered about was 'the marking'. It all sounded so mystical. When Kyndel asked what the mark would look like, Siobhan got a dreamy look in her eyes and simply said whatever the Universe decided signified their union. Kyndel had decided not to push any more when the Healer looked like she was caught up in a memory too personal to disturb.

Pulled from her thoughts by the two younger Guardsmen that appeared on either side of her, Kyndel placed one arm through each Guardsman's crooked elbow and took a deep breath. One step at a time they led her down the stone passageway to her mate…*to her future.*

She looked at her escorts as they walked. Their uniforms looked like something out of a Knights of the Round Table movie. It seemed apropos since they'd originated in that era. Both young men wore surcoats of the deepest red, trimmed with black and gold rope. An intricate design embroidered on each man's chest depicted a dragon in the throes of battle. The shirt they wore under their surcoats matched the ebony of their pants. Their knee-high, black boots were polished until Kyndel was sure she could see her face in them. As it was, the light from each candle in the sconces lining the corridor to the ceremonial chamber twinkled and shone in the tops as they passed.

They reached the threshold of the Ceremonial Chamber of the Cave of the Ancients. Her escorts bowed and took several steps behind her, standing at attention against the wall. Thankfully, Siobhan had explained only Kyndel, Rayne, and the Elders would be in the chamber during the ceremony. Taking a deep breath to calm the butterflies throwing a party in her stomach, Kyndel crossed the threshold. There was Rayne. Their eyes locked. Her nerves fled. Love filled every fiber of her being. This was the most perfect moment of her life.

CHAPTER TWENTY-NINE

The vision of his mate passing through the archway took Rayne's breath away. There were no words to describe how exquisite she looked standing there ready to begin their life together.

Her wavy auburn hair was piled on her head, curly tendrils framing her expressive face. She'd been self-conscious about the tiny bald spot and stitches at the back of her head. He was glad she'd found a way to camouflage it. The small, white flowers interspersed through the delicate design were baby's breath. She'd told him on one of their walks that it meant 'pure of heart'. Rayne could think of nothing better for her to wear on their mating day.

The off-the-shoulder white gossamer gown she wore gave him a mouthwatering view of the freckles dancing across her peaches and cream shoulders. He thought of all the ways he wanted to touch and tease each of those precious little dots. The corset-like bodice fit perfectly and displayed her ample bosom as an offering he found hard to refuse. It was embroidered with small red flames in honor of his dragon, which was also being united with them today.

A wide, red satin ribbon cinched her waist and the long skirt hugged every one of Kyndel's luscious curves. Her bare feet peeked out the bottom of her dress. He dreamt of sucking each one of those toes between his lips while she moaned in pleasure. Working hard to hold back the growl that was building deep in his chest, he focused on her face.

If anything, his desire for her grew stronger. They needed to get this ceremony started or he was not going to be responsible for what happened. He hadn't been inside his mate's body for five days, and the separation was killing him. Not to mention, she stood just out of reach, looking like an angel fallen from Heaven, and other *men* were looking at her. He knew it was the lack of physical contact over the last few days and the call of the Ancients to complete the mating ritual now that they were in their sacred place that drove his need for her to an all-time high, but he was almost to his breaking point.

Thankfully, the Chief Elder's voice rang through the chamber, "Long ago when knights and dragons fought side by side for King and Country, it became apparent that dragon kin was no longer safe from those that would expose and destroy them. They sought to join with the knights that had so valiantly fought alongside them. Thus, through magic and the will of both dragon and knight, the Golden Fire Clan of the Dragon Shifters was born.

"We are here today in the holiest of places to honor what the Universe put into place all those many years ago. We are here to acknowledge and bless the mating of Rayne Michael MacLendon to the one the Universe made for only him, Kyndel Aislinn Masterson. Will those seeking to witness this union please step forward?"

Out from the shadows stepped the five men Rayne held closer than blood kin, the men that had trained with him, fought with him, bled with him, and now shared the happiest moment of his life. They were all dressed in their finest. Kneeling around the Sacred Circle, they bowed their heads. Royce stood and addressed the Elders, "We, the five of the MacLendon Force, wish to witness and offer our blessing to the union of these two souls, two halves of the same whole. May they live long, fight hard, love harder, and produce many young to flourish when their souls have gone to the Heavens." He knelt again and bowed his head again.

Carrick began again, "Your witness and blessing have been acknowledged and accepted, MacLendon Force. Rayne MacLendon, you may go to your mate and escort her to the center of the Blessed Circle." No sooner had the words been spoken than Rayne was standing in front of Kyndel. He took her hands in his, and because he couldn't muster the will to stop looking at her, he walked backwards until they were in place.

Carrick began again, "The Red Dragons were born of blood and fire. They are notoriously passionate in all areas of their lives. Red Dragons are known for their command and fierceness. The red of their scales symbolizes love and fertility. Red Dragons will lead the charge, conquer the enemy, and defend homeland and family with their very lives. To mate a Red Dragon means to accept all that they are and honor the power shared between mates.

"Now is the time of the marking. May the Universe continue to bless you and yours all the days of your lives." It took only a moment for everyone but Rayne and Kyndel to leave the chamber.

Rayne stood perfectly still, looking into the eyes of the love of his life. He knew there would never come a day he would tire of looking at the gorgeous woman in his arms. Unable to take the anticipation any longer, Rayne lowered his mouth to hers. He stopped right before their lips would have touched and whispered, "*Ta' mo chroi' istigh ionat,*" and with that, he lowered his lips onto hers.

It was the most all-encompassing, devastatingly enraptured kiss they'd ever shared. He felt her in every cell of his body. They were consumed with a heat that threatened to engulf them in the flames of their desire. His body and soul laid open to his mate. He felt it reciprocated. She was just as open to him as he was to her. He was overjoyed they were finally sharing one another's thoughts and feelings.

She flinched in his arms just as he felt a twinge where his neck met his shoulder. They were being marked by the Universe, as mates. Rayne left her lips and trailed kisses across her jaw and down her neck, reaching the tender spot he knew still stung from their brand. He licked and sucked the offending spot until all thoughts of anything but their naked bodies loving one another were banished from both their minds.

Lifting his head from her neck, Rayne looked at his mate. He would spend every day of the rest of his life thanking the Universe for her. He kissed the tip of her nose, looked into her passion-fogged eyes, and whispered, "Now, for the best part. We consummate our mating, *mo ghra'.*"

Lifting her into his arms, he used his enhanced speed to get them home in a matter of minutes. Rayne threw open the door and carried her across the threshold, immediately kicking it closed again with the heel of his boot.

She'd never seen the inside of his home, *their home,* but that had to wait. He needed her naked and in his bed more than he needed to show her the guest bathroom.

Releasing her legs, she slid down his body. Every spot their bodies touched fed the fire that caused his pulse to race and his cock to harden. He steadied her when her feet touched the floor. Together, they let out a long, slow breath. He smiled at how in sync they truly were. She was his. She bore his mark. There was nothing in Heaven or Hell that could tear them apart. Not even death.

Running his hands through her hair, he released the pins holding her curls, careful not to touch her stitches. Baby's breath fell like snowflakes as her auburn mane tumbled down her back. She moaned as he massaged her scalp, pushing her head further into his hands. He rubbed and kneaded down her neck and onto her shoulders, those little freckles teasing him again. This time he did not resist. He kissed and licked each little spot while his hands worked their magic on her still tense muscles.

Kissing across her décolletage, Rayne began to undo the row of tiny pearl buttons holding the bodice of her dress. His breath caught in his throat as her breasts came into view. He untied the ribbon around her waist and her gown floated to the ground. She lifted one foot and then the other as he kicked the garment out of their way with his booted foot. He took a moment just to marvel at the miraculous creature that stood before him in nothing but a white, lace thong.

"Commander, it seems you're a little overdressed for the occasion." She smiled a coy little smile as she lifted his surcoat over his head and reached for the hem of his black undershirt.

Rayne grabbed the same hem and began to tug, but Kyndel placed her hands on top of his. "Let me. It's only fair to return the favor." She looked up at him through her thick dark lashes and winked.

His hands fell to his sides. Who was he to deny his mate anything, even if it was undressing him? She made quick work of his undershirt and ran her hands over his shoulders and across his chest, lightly toying with his nipples. As she rubbed along each ridge of his six-pack and brushed through the thin line of hair leading into the waistband of his pants, Rayne thought he might lose his mind at the sensory overload. Kyndel undid the clasp and zipper of his pants and ran the back of her fingers from one hip to the other. Goose bumps rose on Rayne's skin and he shivered.

She pushed his pants off his hips and followed them to the floor. On her knees in front of him, his erection was right in front of her mouth. She licked her lips and he thought he might die. She captured the small bead of moisture at the tip of his cock with the end of her tongue, and he knew that image would forever be burned into his memory, something he never wanted to forget. Kyndel tasted him again and his eyes slid shut.

When she started to take him in her mouth, his eyes shot open and he grabbed Kyndel's shoulders to bring her back to standing. She resisted his touch, looking up in confusion but assuring him, "No, Rayne, I *want* to taste you."

Their eyes remained locked for just a moment. He had to be sure this was truly what she wanted. Her slight nod confirmed her wishes. Rayne relaxed and laid his hands gently on her upper arms. Kyndel placed her palms on his thighs, rubbing her cheek from the tip to the base of his cock. Her tongue lavished the vein that ran his length, working her way back to the tip, then licking the swollen head like a lollipop. When she dipped her tongue into the slit at the very tip, the muscles in his thighs shook. Rayne was sure his head would blow off his shoulders if he didn't fall flat on his ass first. His breathing sped up and for the first time in his very long life, he wondered if his kin could hyperventilate.

Kyndel sucked as much of his length into her mouth as would fit and hollowed her cheeks. Rayne's fingers squeezed her shoulders of their own volition as he groaned. "*Mo ghra'*, I'm not going to last if you keep doing that."

He felt her smile around his cock at his words. They seemed to spur her on as she worked him in and out of her lips for a few more strokes. He grew larger and thicker, working hard not to explode in her mouth. She moved back to the tip, increasing the suction and pulled him from her mouth with a pop. In a flash, she had sucked one, then the other of his balls into her mouth, licking and massaging with her tongue until he was able to take a long deep breath.

But his little minx was not about to let him rest. She took his length in her mouth once again. Placing both her hands around the base, she worked him in and out of her mouth, sucking and humming until he was helpless but to release into her waiting mouth. She swallowed all he gave, continuing to work her lips up and down until he began to harden again.

It was the most wonderful torture he'd ever endured, but now it was his turn to taste. Putting his hands under her arms, it took less than a second for him to get her on her back in the middle of his bed. One more quick maneuver and he had her legs thrown over his shoulders with his mouth just inches from her center. He rubbed his nose against the wet silk covering his prize. The scent coming from her warm, wet pussy was driving him mad. He had to taste her lest he might die. Slipping two fingers under the lace at her hip, he pulled until the offending material ripped. Throwing it over his head, he inhaled her succulent fragrance. No longer able to stand the torture, the tip of his tongue licked up and down the glistening seam of her pussy.

He groaned deep in his throat as her taste burst upon his tongue. Unable to wait one second longer to have his mouth all over her and his tongue buried deep inside her, he placed his hands under her ass, lifted her pussy closer to his face, and began to feast. He drove his tongue in her weeping channel as far as he could go, licking every inch of her. He curled the end of his tongue and teased the bundle of nerves he knew set her on fire.

Kyndel's hands grabbed his hair, pulling with such force he was sure he'd be bald. He heard her gasping for breath and smiled against her skin. Using the flat of his tongue, he licked her outer lips from bottom to top, teasing circles around her clit on every pass. Her legs tightened around his head. Her heels dug into his back. She moaned and mewled to the Heavens in an unintelligible language as he sucked her swollen nub between his lips, flicking it up and down and in circles with his tongue until she came so hard and long he felt her lose consciousness for just a moment.

Rayne was sure Kyndel had pulled out most of his hair by the roots, but he couldn't care as he continued to drink the honey that flowed from her. He nuzzled and nipped all around her puffy lips until she released his hair and her breathing returned to normal. Carefully lifting her legs off his shoulders, he massaged the muscles in her thighs. There had never been a lovelier sight than Kyndel completely satiated from his attention, looking like a Goddess in his bed.

He kissed her hip and made his way to her belly button where he paid extra attention with his tongue and teeth. When Kyndel started to giggle, he licked his way up her stomach to the sweet spot between her breasts, licking and sucking as he felt her heart beat in sync with his. He palmed both her breasts and gently squeezed as the already raised peaks grew harder against his palms. Kissing up her neck, he paid special attention to the flame-shaped mark. He would never tire of seeing it on her skin. Kissing her neck, he tasted until she sighed and moved her head to the side, allowing him greater access. He spent extra minutes nipping and kissing until her nails dug into his biceps.

She surprised him by grabbing his head and slamming her mouth to his. He opened immediately for her, letting her have her way. His mate was as sassy in bed as she was everywhere else. He loved it. Her hands in his hair and her tongue working his mouth had him ready to explode. He shifted his hips slightly, pushing into her until he could go no farther. He knew he'd done as she wished when she tore her mouth from his, screaming, "Rayne! Yes! Oh God, yes!"

He wanted to go slow this first time in her body as a mated couple, but the feel of her muscles contracting around his painfully hard cock made it impossible for him to hold still. Sliding out of her until only the tip of him rested within her opening, he commanded, "Look at me, Kyndel." And she obeyed.

He thrust into her and pulled right back out, starting a rhythm that she easily met stroke for stroke. They stared into one another's eyes as their passion exploded. He pushed her knees towards her chest, lifting her bottom off the bed, allowing him deeper access to her wet, wanting pussy. He rolled his hips, the head of his cock caressing the sensitive bundle of nerves that made the walls of her vagina close tighter around him and her eyes roll back in her head. He slammed into her, bumping her clit with his pelvis. He watched her struggle to breathe, just as he had trouble drawing his next breath. Only the sound of their bodies slapping together and their heavy breathing could be heard as their frantic pace drove them to completion.

Rayne reached between their bodies, barely touched her clit with his thumb and she was in orbit. Her mouth opened in a silent scream as she reached her climax. Her beautiful emerald eyes that held all the promise of his future locked on his and he was helpless but to follow her over the edge. He would follow her anywhere, even to the end of the earth.

Rayne was flooded with Kyndel's thoughts and emotions. He felt her in his heart and in his soul as he also looked into hers. Both were filled to overflowing with unconditional love and acceptance. They were complete as only true mates could be.

Hours later they lay completely replete, her head on his chest, their legs intertwined, while their bodies cooled from their hours of lovemaking. Rayne reached under his pillow and pulled out a white, silk, drawstring pouch. He placed it in the hand she had on his chest.

Kyndel unwound her legs from his and sat up. "What's this?"

"Open it and see."

She untied the bow and tipped the pouch. Out dropped the stunning bracelet he'd watched her admire in the jewelry store.

"You are such a sneak." She beamed. "I love it, Rayne."

"Emma explained what a bell ringing means to dragons?" Rayne smirked as he asked.

She cocked her eyebrow at him, but the grin on her face took all the bite out of the look. "Yes, she told me."

He took the bracelet from her hands and fastened it around her wrist. "These bells will always be ringing." And with that, he kissed his way up her arm, pulling her body across his as he went.

"Rayne?"

"Yes, mo ghra'?"

"I love you."

"And I love you, a thaisce."

"And this mindspeak thing isn't bad either."

EPILOGUE
6 months later

He knew Andrew was close by, could feel him as if they were standing side-by-side. That was what made not already having him in custody such a kick in the pants. Aidan had spent the last six months following his traitorous brother, hoping to capture him…always a step behind. It was an incredible blow to the Guardsman's ego that his *younger* brother could stay ahead of him. It mattered not that Andrew was tainted with black magic, or that no one, even their Elders, had any idea what the combination of that and his dragon magic could do. It was embarrassing and Aidan was fed up with it. No matter what, *he* should still be able to catch Andrew and bring the traitor back to the clan.

Early in his quest, Aidan found that going back and forth between the lair and the city was wasting an incredible amount of time. Time that could be used for his search. He spoke to Rayne about camping in the wooded part of the City Park where their clan often stayed, but Kyndel had suggested he use her apartment. After all, Rayne had paid her lease for ten years and it was sitting empty. He would forever be grateful to both of them.

The Universe had definitely known what She was doing when She created Kyndel for Rayne. They were perfectly mated and now expecting their first child. Aidan couldn't be happier for them. He had to laugh, though. Rayne was even more protective of Kyndel now that she was expecting and she *refused* to be babied. It was a riot to watch them together.

Unfortunately, his own issues took precedence over the home life of his Commander. Aidan *had* to apprehend the traitor before he hurt anyone else. Andrew was already facing charges of treason from the Tribunal. Not to mention, Rayne wanted him dead for hurting Kyndel, something Aidan couldn't blame his Commander for. If someone ever touched his mate, he could only imagine the rage that would overtake him.

His mate? She was nothing but a dream, a memory he visited every time he dared to close his eyes. The long black waterfall of her hair hung almost to her waist. He knew it would be thick and heavy in his hands. Her eyes were bluer than the sky he soared across on a clear summer day, and her smile lit up his entire world. He leaned back into Kyndel's incredibly comfortable couch and closed his eyes to bring the picture of her back to his mind.

She had a figure that begged to be explored by both his hands and his mouth. He longed to taste every erotic curve and seductive valley. Her full, perky breasts that rode high on her chest would flush across the top when she was aroused, of that he was sure. And, oh heavens, her arousal would be like nothing he'd scented before. She always smelled of honey and vanilla, but when she was aroused, it would be as if her tantalizing aroma had been warmed by the sun. She was sweet and fresh and she would be all his, if he could ever meet her outside of his dreams. He couldn't keep his hands from rubbing against his erection as it pushed against the zipper of his jeans.

Just the thought of the woman he dreamt about every night and had actually scented in this very city repeatedly made his cock stand at attention every time. He tried not to think about her long shapely legs because it brought the image of them wrapped around his waist while he drove into her to the forefront of his mind and made thinking damn near impossible. The longer he sat there daydreaming, the harder it got to deny the need to take his throbbing cock in his hand and handle his arousal on his own.

He unbuttoned his pants and lowered his zipper, his erection springing free. Fisting himself, he began to pump his hand up and down, picturing his beautiful mate. Aidan was completely lost to his own pleasure, imagining his hand was hers, that he totally missed the sound of the key in the lock. A glimpse of very black hair coming through the door was all he saw as cock in hand, he used his dragon speed to run to Kyndel's bedroom.

Hidden behind the door, he scented the air.

Oh shit! It's her…my mate!

~~*~*~*~*~*

Andrew sat across from the little apartment his brother had been staying in for the last six months.

Why didn't Aidan just give up?

If he was trying to show Andrew he was sorry for what Andrew had endured because of his weakness and cowardice, it was too little too late. He was going to have his revenge. He was going to watch the life drain out of every last one of the Guardsmen. He was going to dance on their graves…especially Aidan's.

They left him to suffer at the hands of the wizards, *knowing* he was still alive. The blood oath they'd taken when initiated into the Dragon Guard allowed them to know if their brethren still lived. It was their insurance policy in battle.

Some insurance policy.

Andrew had been alive and trapped, and none of them came to save him. Claimed they didn't know. He *had* blacked out that night, but was sure he hadn't died. He was still here after all, wasn't he?

The wizards bragged about all the ways they had to shield him from dragon magic, but he hadn't heard or read of any that were stronger or could negate the blood bond they shared. His brother, the coward, had left him. The others hadn't even tried to come back for him. They were all cowards. They all had to die.

The looks on their faces had been priceless when Rayne's mate had pulled the mask from his head. He wished he had a picture of their expressions when they realized he was *very much alive.*

Absolutely fucking awesome!

But then that idiot Devon had surprised him. Left him with no option but to flee. Now here he was, barely staying a step ahead of Aidan while making plans to lure those idiot Dragon Guards to their death. They had all underestimated him…in life and in supposed death.

He was so lost in thought he almost missed the little beauty going into the very apartment Aidan was in.

Well, well, well…now isn't this interesting?

Maybe *she* was something he could use to get the jump on his pain in the ass brother.

Her Dragon's Fire
Dragon Guard Series #2

There Are No Coincidences.
The Universe Does Not Make Mistakes.
Fate Will Not Be Denied.

CHAPTER ONE

"Hey, Grace. Busy day?"

"The *busiest*. How about you, Adam?" she asked, not really having time to talk but not wanting to be rude. Adam was, after all, a pretty nice guy…for a lawyer.

"Depositions day four. Thank God, it's Friday. I'm not sure I could take hearing one more dirt bag swear he was with his poor sickly mother when I know damn good and well they were *all* part of the scam."

"I hear ya." She was just about to ask if they had any reliable witnesses when her cell phone rang. Looking at the display, Grace was excited to see her best friend's name. Holding up her phone as if Adam could see who it was, she apologized. "Sorry, I need to take this."

"No worries. Take care."

"You too, Adam," she called to his back as he left the breakroom.

It was the only break she'd been able to squeeze in since her six forty-five arrival that morning, but talking to Kyndel was more important than fresh coffee and a stale bagel.

"Hey you, what's up?"

"Nothing much, girlie. How's tricks?" Kyndel's bubbly voice and southern accent was just what Grace needed to roll away the blues. It had been almost a week since the last time they'd spoken and she missed her best friend.

After seeing each other all the time and talking daily for almost eight years, it was hard for Grace to only have phone conversations with Kyndel. Add to it that she now lived somewhere in God's country with her new husband and his incredibly large extended family, *and* Grace had only laid eyes on her bestie once in the last six months, the young lawyer had to admit she was lonely.

"Same shit, different day, Kyn. Just putting away the bad guys. You calling to tell me you're coming home? …At least for a visit?"

"Soon, doll, I promise. I actually called to give you some good news. You sittin' down?"

"Ummm…" Grabbing a chair, she quickly sat. Kyndel wasn't one to exaggerate so if she said to sit down…Grace sat down. "I am now."

"You're gonna be an auntie!" Kyndel squealed through the phone, her excitement palatable.

"Oh crap! You're…*pregnant?*" Grace was glad her friend told her to sit.

"I am! Isn't it the best news ever?"

Summoning all the love she felt for her best friend, Grace pushed her shock to the side and filled her voice with enthusiasm. "It is, honey. Just the best! How far along are you? When's the due date?"

"About a month." Kyndel laughed. "Don't have a due date yet. We just got confirmation and I wanted you to be the first person we told. Rayne is crazy happy but seriously overprotective."

Grace chuckled. "I bet." She could only imagine how the huge man she'd only met once, but who'd stood beside her friend like an avenging angel, would be protective over his wife and unborn child.

"I talked to Rayne and we're gonna come see you real soon. Maybe you can take some time off for baby shopping…please, Auntie Grace?"

She couldn't help but laugh at Kyndel's little girl voice and lisp as she pretended to beg. "How could I say no to that?"

"Yay!" Kyndel again squealed though the phone. For the hundredth time, Grace marveled at her friend's happiness since getting married. She was happy for her friend… *really*. Maybe a little jealous and most definitely missing the time they spent together, but really pleased Kyndel found her happily ever after.

Lost in thought, she almost missed what Kyndel was saying. "I'm sorry to cut this short. Rayne's brethren are coming to dinner and I have to fry enough chicken to feed an army. I promise to call soon." She paused then added, "I love ya, Grace, you know that, right?"

Brethren? Well, Rayne had spoken with a slight accent. Must be a regional thing.

"Of course I do, you big goofball.' They both laughed. "And I love you, Kyn. Now, take care of yourself and my little niece or nephew. We'll talk soon. "

"I will. You take care of *you*," Kyndel responded and disconnected.

Thinking back to how she and her best friend met, Grace smiled. From the moment they bumped into each other at freshman orientation, she knew they'd be best friends. It didn't matter they were total opposites. It was just a feeling she couldn't deny. Grace was from the city and a powerful, political family, while Kyndel was from the country, raised by her Granny. But none of that mattered. It was an immediate connection that even after all those years, she knew was the only reason she'd made it through college and then law school.

Kyndel may not have wanted to trust Grace at first, but it hadn't taken much time at all for the city girl to charm the country one.

Yeah! Let's go with charm, not pain in the ass stalking.

Grace possessed an innate ability to know when things were as they should be. It was something she'd been born with. She and Kyndel were sisters of the heart and all that sentimental crap from day one.

Yeah, you're not sentimental at all. Keep working on that argument, Counselor.

Kyndel was the one person in the world who didn't treat Grace like a princess, or only wanted to be her friend because one or both of her parents could further their political or social agenda. The girl from the south with fiery red hair never even heard of Ambassador Kensington or his beautiful wife's humanitarian efforts.

Kyndel didn't give a shit. She treated Grace just like everyone else, and after a few short weeks, they were inseparable. Distance couldn't change *that* Grace reminded herself for the tenth time.

It was the weird things about their friendship she missed. Like Kyndel wasn't afraid to call Grace on her crap. She frowned remembering the night Kyndel *met* her new husband. Grace had borrowed Kyndel's car, and then true to form, completely spaced picking her up.

Kyndel assumed Grace was "hooking up" with some random guy, an assumption that bothered Grace more than she let anyone know. Sadly, her best friend wasn't the only one who thought she had a guy hidden around every corner, no matter how many times or how *vehemently* she denied it. Many people over the years teased her about the same thing, so she'd finally given up correcting them, even Kyndel.

In actuality, Grace hadn't been with anyone since her senior year of law school. Walking in and catching Derek screwing Mitzi, the local 'fuck your way to the top' second year law student, had ruined any and all aspirations Grace had for a love life. It was a shock she'd never truly gotten over. She'd been so in love with the asshole she would've forgiven him for cheating. But when she overheard him tell Mitzi he was only with Grace to meet her father and use his connections to further his political career, everything she felt for the jerk died.

As if that hadn't been enough, right before she made her presence known, he told the slut that Grace was a 'spoiled princess' with a fat ass. Walking away and never looking back, Grace decided to focus on school and then her career. Love was for suckers. Anyone who didn't like it could kiss her 'fat ass'. Grace Kensington was going to be an amazing lawyer. She would make sure of it.

And I did!

She never told anyone, not even Kyndel, what she'd heard that night. They all thought she'd walked away because Derek was a cheating piece of crap, which was enough. From that night forward, Grace devoted all her time to studying, and when she graduated in the top ten percent of her class with job offers from five of the most prestigious law firms in the country, it was affirmation all her hard work was worth it.

Month after month of interviewing was tiring. There were great offers from great firms but none felt *right*. She wasn't going to settle. The right firm *for her* was out there, she just had to keep looking.

Finally, Grace's determination paid off. She was called to interview with the State Prosecutor's office. At first, she was sure it was because of her father and thought about not going. Thankfully, she talked herself into it. When the man who later became her boss, the State Prosecutor himself, asked about her family, it was clear he had no idea who she was related to. Grace said they were 'estranged', and then leveled the 'do not fuck with me' look she'd perfected early in her life at him.

The attorney straightened his tie—a move Grace later found out meant he was rethinking his position—and went on with the interview. Out of all the offers from all the prominent law firms she'd received, she decided to work for the State. It held true to her determination to put away the trash preying on those weaker than themselves. Grace Kensington made it her way, and no one could take it from her.

Being a lawyer was the perfect fit for Grace. After all, she'd spent most of her life negotiating with nannies or tutors or whoever she was stuck with while her parents were out *saving the world*. Early on, she'd learned to argue any perspective, of any issue, decisively and effectively, with her eyes closed and a hangover from the party the night before.

At a young age, her favorite nanny, Miss Annabelle, told her she'd make a fine lawyer.

"No one can stand their ground and present the facts like you, Gracie girl." Miss Annabelle's voice echoed in her mind.

She smiled, remembering all the times Miss Annabelle was called to school after Grace defended another student, eloquently eviscerating the bullies with her words.

The debate with Wade Sheffler, the star pitcher, was one of her favorite moments. The topic was the unfair treatment of Mathletes. Grace presented point after point of the outlandish perks the baseball team received, despite the fact they'd yet to have a winning season, as opposed to the lack of perks the Mathletes received. She argued that the incredibly intelligent group held the title of State Champs five years running. It was such a spirited defense she ended up standing on the table in the center of the cafeteria, demanding equal treatment for all academic clubs.

Of course, that was the exact moment Principal Stark made his appearance. Grace was taken to his office and Miss Annabelle was called. Grace remembered the twinkle in her governess's eyes as she assured the principal 'her ward' would be properly reprimanded. The 'proper reprimand' included dinner at Dairy Queen and a night at the movies.

That incident, on top of all the others, solidified Grace's decision to go into law. She would fight for the underdog or put away the ones who preyed upon them. Fate decided she was better suited to put the trash away, and that was exactly what she was doing. Better than *any other* first year associate in *any firm* in the country… and she was doing it her way.

The night she'd forgotten to pick up Kyndel, Grace had been at work… *not hooking up*. The case she was prepping was heinous to say the least. The accused needed to be hanged, shot, and disemboweled before being left out for the vermin, but putting him behind bars would have to do since her other thoughts were illegal.

Kidnapping cases involving young women were happening more frequently, and the police were helpless to find the culprit. These poor victims were simply disappearing… no ransom demands, no bodies found later…*just gone*. The night Kyndel walked home alone the police had finally gotten a lead and asked for a consult with the State Prosecutor's office.

Grace got the assignment and went right to work. So engrossed in her mission, she worked through the night, even showered in the locker room at the gym in their building, changed into the spare clothes she kept in her office closet, and didn't eat. So caught up by the case, it wasn't until lunch the next day she remembered she was supposed to pick Kyndel up from work *the night before.*

When Grace hadn't been able to get a hold of her friend, she was sure Kyndel was ignoring her and knew it was going to take some serious groveling to get back in her good graces. Grace left messages at Kyndel's job, but as usual, didn't hear back from her, then remembered Kyndel's cell phone was in the car Grace borrowed, so that was a dead end too.

Five messages later and countless unanswered calls, it was after six in the evening. Panic had taken over. Racing to Kyndel's apartment, Grace imagined every possible scenario and almost lost her mind when she found the house empty. A week spent not eating, not sleeping, working all day, searching all night and sick with worry, took its toll on Grace.

Finally, on the morning of the eighth day, Kyndel called. Grace was overjoyed. But joy turned to skepticism as her best friend explained she'd *literally* run into a guy while walking home… *and* it was love at first sight.

Kyndel went on and on about Rayne and his family, completely ignoring Grace as she tried to apologize and explain what happened. Over that grueling week, the young lawyer decided to set her best bud straight about the men in her life, or the *lack* thereof. She was even going to tell her the *whole story* about Derek. It had been a long time coming and something that needed to be cleared up between them, but Kyndel was so caught up in talking about the new man in her life Grace couldn't get a word in edgewise.

The woman she'd spent almost every day of the last eight years with, in one way or another, seemed to have undergone a complete transformation. Kyndel was *gushing* over a *man*. The longer Grace listened, the more her instincts screamed there was something her best friend wasn't telling her.

Her suspicions were confirmed when she met Rayne. Grace's *spidey senses* said he was full of secrets but that his intentions were pure. He'd somehow convinced the person who trusted *absolutely no one*, the girl who'd put Grace through every test in the world before calling her a friend, to *marry* him in *less than a week*. It just didn't fit. *Something* didn't feel right.

And I'm not even gonna mention that I wasn't invited to the wedding.

The look in Kyndel's eyes said she was over the moon in love and sickeningly happy. All gagging aside, Grace was *thrilled* for her. No one deserved the love and devotion she saw in Rayne's eyes more than Kyndel. Her life had never been easy, and to see her happy warmed Grace's heart.

Still, no matter how hard she tried to put her suspicions aside and blame them on the envy she felt at watching them together, the fact was, there was more to the story. She just *knew* it. Grace hated herself for being suspicious, but she always followed her gut. It was one of the things that made her good at her job and had saved her too many times to count.

Deciding Kyndel was not in imminent danger and that Grace would get more details when they talked alone, she focused on one of the other changes that rankled her nerves. The fact that one of Rayne's brothers was staying at Kyndel's apartment. It was silly. She knew it was, but it still bothered her.

Not only did her bestie trust the guy she'd married in less than a week, she also trusted *his family*? With her home? *And her plants*? It was a complete turnaround from the Kyndel she knew. Grace had always heard love changed a person, but this was more…she just couldn't put her finger on it.

To add insult to injury, when she stopped to check the plants and pick up the mail, this *brother* was nowhere to be found. Grace knew he'd been there by the intoxicating scent he left in his wake. It was hard work not to get lost in the rich, masculine scent of the woods after a snowfall. She breathed deeply, immersing herself in the intoxicating aroma, wanting to carry it with her. Her obsession had gotten so bad; she was inventing reasons to stop by the apartment more often.

Riiiiigggghhhhttttt. That's why I'm going over there. Just to smell *that man. I don't want to get a look at the man or anything. Oh no…not me. Damn, I'm a crappy liar.*

All she really wanted was to get a look at the guy who made her pulse race and nipples harden from just the way he smelled. He entered her thoughts more and more. She wondered what he looked like and what his hands would feel like against her skin.

Her imagination got the best of her, even when she was sitting in her office, supposedly working. Thoughts of him had her eyes sliding shut. She imagined his lips on her neck and his hands moving under her silk blouse. She shivered as he moved up her ribs, palming her already hard and tender nipples. She scooted farther down in her chair and shivered from the feel of her lace panties rubbing against her aroused flesh.

Oh God, that felt good.

"Grace? Are you still here?" Alice, her assistant, called from the other room.

Jerking herself upright, Grace barely grabbed the desk in time to keep from landing face first in a pile of paperwork.

"Yes! I'm in here," she called through the open door, sounding much more breathy than she should've and praying Alice didn't notice.

Oh, shit! I really need to keep my mind on work. It's definitely safer.

There was enough to worry about with trying to convict a kidnapper and now, Kyndel's pregnancy, without dreaming about a guy she'd never seen… and probably never would.

With my luck, he's the bum of the bunch and bald to boot.

CHAPTER TWO

Three days spent tracking dead end leads. Six months since the brother he'd thought dead pulled 'a Lazarus' with a plot to kill their entire Force. Frustration was threatening to make him pull out his hair. And all Aidan wanted to do was get a good night's sleep before starting the rat race all over again.

"Hey, 'A', what's up?" Lance, one of his brethren, asked through mindspeak.

"Nothing much. What's going on over there?"

"Same. Any luck?"

Aidan thought about ignoring him but answered anyway, trying to keep the frustration out of his voice.

"Not a damn bit. With all the black magic he's got running through his system the little shit can hide almost all his scent. The only signs I could find indicate he's sticking to the populated areas, so tracking him is a real bitch."

"You hear anything from the other clans? Maybe he's taken off across the pond."

"No signs of him anywhere by anybody. Flying blind sucks."

"I know that's right. You need some help?"

"No, I'm good." It would've been nice to have the company, but Lance was the prankster of their Force, and Aidan knew little to no tracking would be done with him around.

"Okay, cool, but ya know I was thinking…"

"That can be dangerous." Aidan chuckled.

Lance laughed aloud. "No shit, but seriously, if he keeps relying on his magical abilities so heavily, the little traitor's gonna screw up and you'll be there to grab him up."

"From your mouth to Fate's ears, bro. This is damn hard on the ego."

"You're good, 'A'. It won't be long now."

"Thanks, man."

"Yep. I gotta run. Royce is bitching about something I may…or may not have done."

"I'm betting on 'may have'." Aidan laughed.

"You know it," was all Aidan heard as his friend severed their connection.

Thinking about the hunt for his brother led Aidan's thoughts down a dark path. He'd spent the better part of six years mourning Andrew's death and dealing with the crushing guilt of having failed his brother. It was Aidan's fault they'd been flying over that exact field at that exact time, the same time and route as the night before. It was his need to catch a glimpse of the one the Universe made for him that cost his little brother his life...or so the Guardsman thought.

Aidan's obsession began months earlier, when the fantasies of a raven-haired beauty with curves begging to be explored began to haunt his dreams. As Fate would have it, the night before he lost his brother, the scent he'd only dreamt of became a reality. It enveloped him and his dragon, making it hard for them to stay in flight. It was a confirmation of every story he'd ever heard about mates. Like called to like. Recognition was instantaneous.

My mate.

So close, he could touch her. It was the best feeling in the world. His heart soared and his dragon pushed to be free to claim her as their own. He felt complete for the first time in all his hundred years. But none of that excused what he'd let happen.

It was his duty as the older brother to protect Andrew. Instead, he'd flown off half-cocked, brother in tow, ignoring all their protocols, intent on getting a glimpse of *his woman*. They were taken by surprise due to his inattention. Overpowered by black magic, Aidan lay unconscious a few yards away while Andrew was taken and hidden.

At least that's how Andrew tells it. Would've been vital information during my six years of torment.

Aidan awakened disoriented, just in time to see what he thought was Andrew's head being thrown into a huge pyre surrounded by wizards, all chanting and swaying.

It had all been subterfuge; Aidan knew that *now*. Not Andrew's head, but the head of a farmer they'd sacrificed for their blood ritual was thrown into the fire. From the information he'd gathered, Aidan learned the wizards spent most of their black magic knocking two full-grown dragons out of the sky then subduing and hiding his brother.

The evil practitioners were forced to perform the additional rite to amass more black magic. It allowed them to virtually disappear, while he struggled to get back to the lair for help. At least Aidan now knew the use of black magic was limited and needed 'recharging'. Very good news for dragon kin.

He'd relived every gory detail of that night every day of his dreary existence, until the moment Andrew was unmasked six months ago. The shock had left Aidan mute and dumbfounded during most of the altercation that injured Kyndel. When he finally got his shit together, Aaron, his twin, had the traitor wrapped in silver chains and Rayne was in dragon form, preparing to carry his injured, unconscious mate to their Healer.

His rage consumed him. To think Andrew, a man Aidan helped raise and trained for admittance into their Force of the Dragon Guard, had sided with not one, but *both* of their mortal enemies. Groups whose sole purpose was to destroy dragon kin. It was unfathomable. Aidan tried to reason it out. Tried to find an excuse for his brother's actions. But the fact remained... Andrew had betrayed *them all*.

He'd escaped the wizards, killed an entire coven, and set out on his own. He *chose* to abandon the clan. He blamed his family, his Force, and dragon kin for his misfortune. Most of all, he blamed Aidan. In his warped and broken mind, Andrew decided revenge was all he had left.

The black magic he'd acquired, mixed with his dragon magic, had somehow enabled Andrew to hide his true nature... his dragon.

Fortunately, after six months of searching and then analyzing what he found, Aidan learned a few things that would give him an advantage in his hunt for the traitor. First of all, by hiding his dragon for so long, it seemed Andrew wasn't able to call him forth *at all*. It made sense that if the traitor still possessed the ability, he would've done so when he was plummeting towards the ground after escaping Aaron's talon. Secondly, Andrew couldn't mindspeak with any of his brethren. In a few of his weaker moments, Aidan had called out to his brother, using their specific link, but felt absolutely nothing, not even a spark. He had no clue how any of these anomalies were possible; no one knew, not *even* the Elders. It was a little scary that the oldest and wisest among them had never heard of a case where a bond as strong as theirs, one of a blood relation, children of the same parents, and the blood bond shared by all Dragon Guard, had been subdued or broken.

The bond Aidan shared with his brothers, Aaron and Andrew, was so strong that even when they shielded their thoughts from one another or were great distances apart, there was still a buzz, almost like a cell phone vibrating in a pocket. But since the night Aidan believed Andrew dead, there had been *nothing at all*. That was the *only reason* Aidan had been so sure his brother was dead. Even when he "reappeared" into their lives, it was as if their bond never existed, something that shouldn't have been possible.

Aidan remembered the day his baby brother was born...

He and Aaron were ten years old. It was a normal day of gathering firewood and playing in the forest. Everything the twins did was an adventure. Aidan was the Commander, Aaron his faithful second. They were scouting the area for scavengers out to pillage and loot their clan. Sticks were their swords and large pieces of bark their shields as they swung at every branch and bush daring to cross their path.

Deep in make-believe battle, parrying with a particularly evil villain, a buzzing began in Aidan's head. He immediately recognized it as another of their blood. The connection was like what he shared with his twin, only a bit different at the same time.

The baby's been born.

His new brother, fresh from the womb and unable to form words, was reaching out to his older sibling. Aidan could feel his happiness, combined with contentment and the feeling of being incredibly loved. The twins raced home, their journey filled with tales of everything they would teach him and the pranks they would play now that there were three of them.

When they arrived, every member of their clan was lined up to pay tribute to the O'Brien family and to get a look at the new baby. After an hour, the twins finally made their way into the family home. As the eldest, having been born two minutes before Aidan, Aaron was first to pay his respects.

When Aidan's turn came, he slowly walked toward the bed where his mother and baby brother lay. Deep in his heart and soul, he knew the new addition to their family would irrevocably change his life. Kneeling beside the bed, he placed a kiss on his mother's cheek and glanced at the bundle lying against her bosom.

Andrew was the tiniest thing Aidan had ever seen. His heart felt like it would burst with pure joy as he reached down to move the blanket for a better look at the baby's face. Baby Andrew grabbed his finger, meeting his gaze with one piercing blue and one amber eye. The amazing gift to their family had the mark of a Special One, and Aidan was the first to experience the wonder and awe of that stare. The connection between the brothers was immediate, growing stronger every day of their lives.

Aidan felt like the most blessed dragon shifter in the Universe. Not only did he have a twin with a connection forged in the womb, but he also now had a bond with his younger brother, established just hours after the young one's birth.

Unfortunately, the latter was blown to hell. No matter the years and the bond, Aidan would do whatever he had to do to catch the traitor and deliver him to the Elders for the Tribunal. The personal cost didn't matter. Andrew must pay for his crimes.

The day Aidan believed his brother died permanently changed him. The scary thing was he knew more changes were on the horizon. Andrew's reappearance sent ripples through the fabric of Aidan's reality. Made him question all he'd ever known. No matter, the little bastard must be caught. Years of training taught Aidan to channel his anger and pain into the hunt. He was a dragon shifter, part of the most elite Force within the Dragon Guard… *this* would not beat him. It would drive him to be stronger, fiercer… have *no* regrets. His only solace was that his parents had long since gone to the Heavens. Thankfully, they weren't witnessing their youngest son's betrayal. Aidan would succeed. He would capture the traitor and restore his family's honor. Failure was not an option.

Shaking himself from his maudlin thoughts, Aidan focused on what needed to be done. He needed a shower, something to eat, and some rest. The hunt for the traitor would continue. Lance and Royce were coming the day after tomorrow for a meeting with the werepanther pack. He hoped they had useful information.

The Big Cats were able get into places he and his kin could not. Max and his pride had been valuable allies over the years and he hoped their natural curiosity paid off as well this time as it had in the past. Aidan was ready to put this whole crappy mess behind him.

Like that will ever happen.

He knew there were answers to be found if he could actually talk to Andrew. Answers that would help them eliminate the greatest threat to dragon kin once and for all. Aidan's biggest fear was that he wouldn't get to the traitor in time and there would be more needless suffering. After witnessing his brother's depravity, Aidan feared for all he held dear. His clan was his first priority, but he couldn't ignore the fact there were others out there needing protection from the lunatic as well.

He thought of his home and everything it meant to him. The last time he'd visited the lair, Rayne and Kyndel announced they were pregnant. If possible, the couple looked *even* happier, and his Commander was more protective of his mate than before. Aidan laughed aloud at the way Kyndel wouldn't stand for Rayne's overbearing attitude. She cocked her eyebrow, smacked his arm, and told him she'd do whatever she wanted. The last he saw them, Kyndel was over Rayne's shoulder, giving him hell, as they headed to their home. They were definitely made for one another.

The Universe does not make mistakes.

A shudder ran down his spine at the thought of protecting a mate *and a child*. He sympathized with Rayne. There was no doubt in Aidan's mind what he would do if someone dared to threaten what was his. They would die.

It was as simple as that. There was *only one* in the world who could complete him and his dragon, and he would do *whatever* it took to protect her and any children they were blessed to conceive. His mate would be *his world.*

His mate?

Yes, he *knew* she was out there. Had known she was close for the last six years but could do nothing about it. His surprise had come when he learned his mate was Kyndel's best friend. Not that it changed anything. He *still* couldn't meet her. There was *family* business to attend to first.

Aidan hated to admit that Andrew had been right when he accused his older brother of going off half-cocked the night they were ambushed. Aidan had been looking for his mate. He knew she was young, barely of legal human age at the time, and studying law at the University. He'd picked up bits and pieces of her conversation with another student while they were walking back to their dorm and could feel her strong sense of justice.

After Andrew's "death", he'd pushed all thoughts of her to the back of his mind. That is, until he walked into Kyndel's apartment and her scent hit him like a ton of bricks. He leaned his head back and closed his eyes, the vision of his mate instantly before him. He knew she'd been in the apartment while he was away. Inhaling deeply, his lungs filled with the lingering scent of vanilla and honey floating on a spring breeze. His vivid fantasies assured him when she was aroused; it was as if her tantalizing aroma had been warmed by the sun.

He dreamed of running his hands through the long waterfall of raven hair that hung almost to her waist. The feel of heavy silk sliding through his fingers made his skin tingle. He wanted to gaze into her eyes, bluer than the sky on a clear summer day, and have her grace him with a smile that lit up his entire world. His hands itched to explore her womanly figure, exploring every curve. As he thought of her amazingly round ass and her long shapely legs wrapped around his waist while he drove into her, his hand rubbed against his erection as it pushed against the zipper of his jeans.

Lost to his daydreams, unable to stop his mouth from watering at the thought of tasting the nipples he knew would be a beautiful shade of deep rose when aroused, Aidan slid a bit farther into the couch. One taste would never be enough. He had plans to spend a lifetime worshipping her… *body and soul.*

She was everything sweet and fresh in the world. He unbuttoned his pants and lowered his zipper. His fully erect cock sprang free and his fist automatically wrapped around his hard length, pumping harder and faster the longer he thought of her…*Grace.*

Even her name is perfect.

CHAPTER THREE

I don't remember ever *being this tired.*

It was ten 'o' clock at night and Grace needed to be back at the office by six thirty the next morning. She was exhausted both mentally and physically. There was no way she'd stay awake for the forty-five minutes to her house. More than that there was *no way* she was sleeping one more night on the torture device pretending to be a couch in her office.

Thankfully, she had clean clothes. She'd hated asking Alice to run her errands, but the wonderful woman said she didn't mind and even had clothes of her own to pick up. Grace paid for *all* the cleaning to ease her guilty conscience and to make sure she didn't show up for work in the same suit two days in a row. Beyond tired, wanting nothing more than some food, a shower, and a bed, she thought about Kyndel's apartment sitting empty, only ten minutes from her office.

She'd stopped by yesterday during a quick lunch break and Rayne's mysterious brother hadn't been in sight, but his unmistakable scent aroused her within minutes of opening the door. Grace wondered if he'd returned. She thought about just going home, not sure she was ready for a face-to-face meeting.

How will I explain stopping by in the middle of the night?

Grace stopped mid-stride. Why the hell did she care what *he* thought? Kyndel was *her* best friend. Had been for a hell of a lot longer than he'd been around. If she wanted to stop by at three in the morning, she would. She wasn't going to drive all the way to her house and risk an accident just to avoid the man who made her hot and bothered as no other ever had.

With her resolve strengthened, Grace closed and locked her office door and headed to the elevator. On the way down, her internal debate continued. When the bell dinged for her stop, her decision was made… she had every right to stay at Kyndel's and *that's* where she was going. Exiting the elevator, she waved good night to Johnny, the night watchman. He smiled, waved, and radioed the watchman in the garage that she was on her way out. Her steps faltered for just a moment with second thoughts, but she saw her reflection in the mirrored glass of the lobby and was reminded of the promise she'd made to herself all those years ago.

I am Grace Kensington, a prosecutor for the State. I handle anything *that comes my way.*

With shoulders squared and spine straightened, she marched on. She *was* going to Kyndel's and if Mr. Smells So Good was there, maybe she could finally get answers to her questions. *After* she had a shower and something that didn't come out of a vending machine to eat.

The drive over was uneventful. She pulled her Volvo into the driveway beside Kyndel's cute little "country in the city" apartment and relaxed. Even though her friend hadn't been back in over six months, all the flowers and plants were still beautiful. Grace always loved plants, but in an effort to keep up appearances, her parents always hired gardeners and landscapers, denying their only child the luxury of tending to her own flowers. They even went as far as having fresh flowers delivered to the house every other day. It was a guilty pleasure of Grace's to be able to take care of Kyndel's gardens.

Stepping out of the car, her *spidey senses* tingled. She looked around and saw nothing unusual, nothing out of place, but couldn't shake the feeling that something wasn't quite right. Walking through the carport towards the back of the house, Grace found nothing but shadows in the dark. Reminding herself for the tenth time to set the timer for the outside lights, she took an extra look just to be sure she was alone.

Would've been easier if I'd remembered the lights. They need to come on at dusk. Anyone could be hiding in all the plants and bushes.

Shaking her head, wondering if her lack of sleep had her *intuition* going wacky, Grace turned around and headed back the way she'd come. As she walked to the front door, her hands instinctively ran over the bushes. Water droplets from the leaves tickled her fingers. She breathed a sigh of relief. Kyndel's place felt like home.

Thank God, her bestie had installed a timer on her irrigation. There was no way Grace had the energy to water plants tonight. She was barely staying vertical, working as hard as she could to get the front door open. As she put the key in the lock, the hairs on the back of her neck stood on end and a shudder ran down her spine. She could feel eyes watching, her *intuition* was screaming to get inside. Whatever was watching her, and she was sure there was something, was *definitely* not friendly.

In a hurry to get in the apartment and lock the door, Grace almost missed the blur rushing towards the hallway. Had it not been for the tantalizing scent she recognized as Rayne's brother, she would've completely freaked out. She was relieved he was there. After the weirdness outside, it felt a lot safer than being alone.

Grace really wished she understood her *spidey senses*. For as long as she could remember she'd had these weird feelings; knew when something was not how it appeared, sensed danger when everything seemed okay. And knew beyond any doubt if someone was lying. Her *intuition* had saved her more than once and for that she was grateful but often wondered where they came from.

Making sure the door was locked, she slid the chain into place and kicked off her shoes. It really felt good to finally have those torture devices off her feet. She was woman enough to admit that she wore them to be as tall as the men at the office. If she was close to their height, they couldn't look down at her. It was bad enough feeling like she should wear a 'These are not my eyes' sign across her more than ample chest, she didn't need to feel 'small' next them also. It was the price she paid for breaking into the boy's club that was the Prosecutor's office, but it didn't mean she had to like it.

Hanging her suit jacket on the coat tree, Grace went to see where the man with the delicious scent went hurrying off to.

I really am a glutton for punishment.

CHAPTER FOUR

Aidan laid his head against the door, completely disgusted with himself. He'd been so caught up in his erotic daydreaming, the woman of his dreams walked right through the front door and almost caught him with his dick in his hand…*literally.*

Really? Big strong Dragon Guardsman, Aidan O'Brien, hiding in the bedroom, too scared to face the woman the Universe made for me. The one I've dreamt of for over six years? Wow, aren't I a catch?

Hiding in the bedroom like a scared little school boy was a *great* first impression. If his senses were right, and they always were, she was heading right for him.

"Hey! Rayne's brother, whatever your name is, I'm Grace, Kyndel's friend. Everything okay in there?"

"Yeah, everything's fine. Name's Aidan, by the way." He tried to sound nonchalant while putting his now limp dick back in his pants. "I was just napping. You caught me by surprise. It's been a long couple of days since I slept." He cleared his throat. "I'll be right out."

"I understand the lack of sleep," she agreed. "It's been a *really* long couple of days for me too. I don't know about you, but I don't see an end in sight." She turned to head back to the living room and called over her shoulder, "I'm starving. You wanna share a pizza?"

A pizza, *really*? She wanted to eat with him? Well, hopefully that meant she hadn't seen what he was doing when she walked in. Lost in his thoughts, he didn't realize he hadn't answered her until she said, "Umm, they do eat pizza wherever you're from, right? Aidan?" He could tell from the decreasing volume of her voice she was walking away.

"Yeah, we do," he chuckled. "Pizza would be great! I'm gonna grab a shower and I'll be right out."

Now, if he could keep his mind, as well as other body parts, focused on eating pizza and not on the irresistible woman on the other side of the door, everything would be great.

CHAPTER FIVE

Grace deserved a gold star *and* brownie points for making it through their pizza dinner without drooling or spilling food down the front of her blouse. Keeping her mind *on* eating and *off* jumping on top of the most beautiful man she'd ever seen was difficult...to say the least.

Beautiful?

Yes. Beautiful was the only word that came to mind, and still paled in comparison to the man himself. He reminded her of the ancient Greek statues she admired on her frequent visits to the Met. His well-chiseled muscles were sleek and without compare. She'd been on the phone ordering pizza when he'd come striding into the living room. Just the sight of him blew her mind. She stood holding the phone, mouth wide open...staring.

It wasn't until the girl from Luigi's said, "Ma'am, are you still there? Does that complete your order?", that Grace spun around, took a deep breath, and finished ordering their dinner.

She took a few extra minutes getting plates and silverware from the kitchen to hide the effect he had on her. It felt like she was back in high school and the quarterback had just smiled at her in the hall. One glimpse of the man she'd had more than one erotic dream about made her palms sweat and her pulse race. His light brown hair, wet and darkened from his shower, was combed back off his forehead with the back hanging past the collar of his well-worn black t-shirt. She was envious of the drop of water traveling down his neck, disappearing into his shirt. It wasn't hard for her to imagine her tongue following its path.

Breathing under control, Grace turned to place the plates on the table at the same time a cell phone rang from the other side of the room. She admired the slight swagger in his walk as his long legs ate up the distance to the weather beaten leather jacket hanging inside the front door. The fit of his faded jeans highlighted the roll and flex of the powerhouse muscles at the top of his legs. He moved with a grace most men his size didn't possess. Aidan was at least six feet four inches of well-toned, completely lickable muscle.

He took the ringing phone from his jacket and answered, keeping his back to her. Grace took full advantage of the view, ogling the almost perfect male physique displayed before her. His neck was corded with well-exercised muscles, leading to a wide expanse of shoulders that made her hands itch with the need to touch and massage. She followed the line of his spine, emphasized by the shirt pulled tight across a back she longed to rub herself against, down to the sexiest ass that had ever been made. *Good God*, it looked tight enough to bounce a quarter off of and damn if her mouth didn't water with wanting to take a bite. He stood with his legs a little less than shoulder width apart. His feet were bare, and although she'd never found feet anything but appendages for beautiful shoes, his were just plain sexy.

I'm in deep shit here.

Grace snapped out of her "hot-man induced" stupor in time to hear him ending his call. Busying herself with wiping off the counters and grabbing napkins out of the cabinet, she once again got her raging hormones under control. What was it about *this man* that reduced her to a mass of want and need? His scent was powerful, there was no doubt about it, but his presence was lethal. Grace had to find some way to stay under the same roof with him *all night* without losing her mind.

I can do it! I've stared down convicted killers. One sexy man isn't gonna do me in.

"So what's on the menu tonight, Grace?"

Lost in her thoughts, she almost missed his question. "What? Oh! I ordered the meat lover's special, a salad, and some garlic knots. Hope that's okay with you."

"I eat anything." He chuckled. "Whatever you ordered is fine."

Her gaze flew to his and before she could comment on his choice of words, his hypnotic, whiskey-colored eyes ensnared her. His stare was a physical touch deep in the middle of her chest that slid down her body, warming every inch. That touch settled in her core, becoming a spark that left her wet and needy. As she stood mesmerized, she saw flecks of brown, green, and gold, flowing like a kaleidoscope through the amber, stealing the breath from her lungs.

The doorbell rang and the spell was broken. She felt a blush heat her cheeks as she reached for her purse. "I've got it, Grace." He shook his head as he opened the door to retrieve the pizza. "Why don't you get the plates and stuff, we'll eat in the living room? Maybe watch some TV?"

She nodded because there was no way she could speak without stammering. Grabbing the stack of plates, Grace headed into the living room. Before she even sat down, Aidan was already placing the delivery boxes on the coffee table and kneeling on the floor across from her.

"Thank you," she said as she opened each box so they could take what they wanted. Grace handed him a plate and proceeded to fill hers with salad.

"Aren't you eating any of this awesome pizza?" Aidan asked with a piece inches from his mouth.

"I prefer to eat my salad first, and then I don't eat as much pizza. I love pizza, but it likes to reside on my backside, so I have to be careful how much I eat." She was chuckling when she looked up and saw Aidan's brow furrowed.

"What's *that* look for?" her voice sharper than she intended.

"Nothing. No particular look."

Grace flashed her patented, fear-inducing stare at him, "Yes, there *was* a particular look. You were scowling at me. Why?"

He sat there staring. This was one of the times she wished her intuition came with the ability to read people's minds. He was definitely thinking hard about something, she just wished she knew what. "Well, are you going to answer me or just sit there staring?" Grace snapped, impatiently.

"I was just wondering why someone as beautiful as you would think they needed to watch what they ate. That's all," he said, like it was something everyone knew. She would've even sworn he smirked had her brain not picked that moment to short circuit.

He thinks I'm beautiful?

Unable to answer, Grace went back to eating her salad and prayed he wouldn't respond. Thankfully, he took the hint and they ate in companionable silence until Aidan grabbed the remote, switched on the television, and flipped through the channels. More than once, she caught herself staring at the near perfect male specimen sitting on the floor, eating pizza, apparently trying to catch a glimpse of every single one of the one hundred and twenty-five channels available. Even breathtakingly handsome men felt the need to work the remote like they were paid by the click. She smiled, thinking it had been forever since she sat and watched TV, and never with someone like Aidan.

Setting her plate on the table, Grace scooted back into the huge overstuffed couch. Pulling her legs under her, she leaned her head to the side, resting it on the arm. Aidan finally landed on a rerun of The Big Bang Theory and stood up. "If you're all done, I'll clear this." He pointed to what was left of their dinner and the dishes. "Sit there and relax. I'll be right back."

Grace raised her head. "I can help."

He leaned over, looking her right in the eye and touched her shoulder. "Just lay there, Grace. You look like you need to rest. I can get the mess."

He stood up and got to work. She couldn't help but rub the spot where he'd touched her shoulder. Even through her clothing, she felt a spark, a current running from the spot he touched straight to her womb, pulling her nipples into taut peaks on its way. She curled farther into the couch, hunching her shoulders, trying to hide her body's reaction. Why did this man have such an effect on her? Her intuition told her she had nothing to fear…he was a good man with good intentions.

It's not his *intentions I'm worried about.*

CHAPTER SIX

Aidan barely kept his composure on the way to the kitchen. Walking with an erection hard enough to pound nails was difficult to say the least, but when he'd scented Grace's arousal, it took all his control not to fall on her luscious body, giving them both the release they wanted...*needed*. Making it to the kitchen, sure Grace couldn't see him, he braced both hands on the counter and took long, deep breaths to regain his balance. *She* made his world tilt on its axis.

He let his head fall forward, exhaling very slowly and counting to ten to get his mind *and* body under control. Aidan thanked the Heavens for the coffee table that sat between them during dinner. It had hidden his obvious erection and saved him from more embarrassment. He'd tried to look away, but Grace was a temptation not even a hundred years of training could help him resist. More than once, he'd wrestled the dragon within to keep the beast from jumping across the table and claiming sweet Grace as their own.

When she insinuated she needed to watch what she ate, Aidan almost lost his cool. He wouldn't have been able to take it if she'd said she needed to lose weight. What was it with women? For some reason they thought curves were bad. Well, he was here to tell her she was perfect, *just the way she was*. Some of her curves were extra curvy and that was definitely all right. The way her skirt hugged the full, round globes of her ass made Aidan want to fall to his knees and worship the ground she walked on. Her ample bosom pushed against the confines of her silk blouse and highlighted the outline of her lace bra. His blood boiled, at least what hadn't already made the trip south. She absolutely captivated him. Hell, even the bright pink polish decorating the tips of her cute little toes made his mouth water.

As if all of that wasn't enough, when she'd blushed, his heart skipped a beat. The light pink flush gave her an ethereal glow. Bless the Universe his mate was spectacular. The way her pouty lips formed a perfect bow made him want to lean across the table for *just* a taste. A comparison of dreams versus reality rushed through his mind. Reality was better, *so much better*. His dragon chuffed in full agreement and growled at the man for holding back. He assured his beast they would be with their mate soon... *very soon*.

In an effort to keep his desire under control, he finished loading the dishwasher and put the leftovers in the refrigerator before heading back to the living room. As he rounded the corner, the sounds of her deep, even breathing reached his ears. She'd fallen asleep. Not surprising. He'd seen how tired she was during dinner. He'd thought about taking her into his arms, massaging her shoulders, and holding her until the bottled up tension left her body. What he wouldn't give to have his hands on her gorgeous, porcelain skin.

When he'd touched her shoulder for just a second, the spark of recognition nearly brought him to his knees. He wanted, *no*, he *needed* to claim her. Needed to look into her beautiful eyes as they both reached the climax their bodies begged for. He smiled, thinking how they were acting like two teenagers. She tried not to look at him while he tried not to get caught looking at her.

Aidan stood, marveling at his good fortune. He and Grace were meant to be together for all time, in this life and the next. She may not know it yet, but he and his dragon knew. The ever-growing scent of her arousal, that drove him mad with desire, let him know her body was already onboard.

Like recognized like, two halves of the same whole, as foretold by the ancestors. He'd listened to so many stories about the incredible feelings finding one's mate evoked, he'd thought he was ready, but nothing compared to the real thing. Aidan *needed* to touch her. His body begged to plunder her mouth and body until neither could think. He wanted to watch her pupils dilate and nipples pebble as he touched every inch of her body.

He smiled, watching her nap. She reminded him of a china doll, perfectly relaxed, not a care in the world. Her dark hair fanned across the arm of the couch, her hands pressed together under her chin as if she'd fallen asleep saying her prayers. The thick fringe of her bangs kissed the arch of her manicured brows and her long lashes curled against her cheeks in little crescents.

A light rose hue highlighted the flawless complexion of her cheeks, reminding him of fairies playing in the garden. Her lips were full and pink and formed a perfect pout, reminding him of a rose bud about to bloom. She was the picture of everything right and wonderful in the world and she was *his*. He wondered if she would think he was crazy if he just stood watching her sleep all night.

She'll probably call the cops. Or worse...Kyndel.

Aidan woke from his Grace-induced stupor when she moved in her sleep. She'd mentioned staying for the night and said something crazy about sleeping on the couch so as not to be a bother.

Not gonna happen.

His mate would sleep in the bed, *period*. She deserved the best, and although the monstrosity of a couch she was sleeping on was one of the most comfortable he'd ever known, there was no way in *hell* he was sleeping in the bed while she was on the couch. If he had it his way, they would *both* be in the bed, wrapped around one another, spent from making love. He reined in his wild thoughts, assuring both himself and his dragon their time would come...*very soon*.

With his mind made up, he carefully moved her hair until it hung over her left shoulder and slid one arm under her head and the other under her knees. Grace curled into his chest and sighed. Her body recognized his even in her sleep. Unconsciously, she trusted him to care for her. He smiled so big his cheeks ached. His chest puffed with pride when her hand landed right over his heart. Walking like a man who owned the world, he took Grace into the master bedroom and tucked her in for the night.

Once again, he found himself standing and staring. He closed his eyes, thanking the Universe for the amazing gift of his mate. When he opened his eyes, she was snuggled under the comforter with a look of absolute peace. His control broke. He leaned forward and gently touched his lips to hers. Together they sighed with complete contentment. He pulled back quickly, knowing if he stayed one second longer they would both be naked.

He used the excuse of checking to make sure she was comfortable to touch her silken skin one last time. Turning off the bedside lamp, Aidan headed to the door. Unable to resist one more look over his shoulder, he paused. His smile grew even bigger. She really was the most beautiful woman he'd ever seen. Wondering how long it would take to get the raging hard on in his jeans under control enough to rest at all, he headed out of the room. She was here and she was his. With that thought and the taste of his mate on his lips, he closed the bedroom door.

Sleep well, my sweet…

CHAPTER SEVEN

Andrew spent the night watching his brother and the woman. It didn't take a rocket scientist to realize she was his mate and they were both trying really hard to avoid the attraction. It made him sick to his stomach. What right did his cowardly brother have to find his mate?

NONE!

Aidan had no right to be happy, no right to find love, no right to live happily ever after. The only thing befitting the man Andrew had spent the first ninety years of his life idolizing was pain and suffering.

At first, Andrew had lain in that dungeon, day after day, month after month, waiting for his brother and the others Guardsmen to rescue him. He'd called out in mindspeak until his head pounded and his ears bled. Then after waiting, hoping and praying, he realized it was for naught…no *one* was coming. On the heels of his feelings of hopelessness came anger and a hate that grew and festered. It was then he began planning his revenge to destroy everyone who had betrayed, tortured, and tormented him.

He'd waited patiently and played the game, gaining the wizards' trust, making them think they'd beaten him. When he saw an opening, he took it. He killed them all. There were other covens out there he planned to annihilate also. It was those first vengeful kills that strengthened his resolve for retribution.

After the wizards, the hunters were easy pickings. They were so filled with hate from the fanatical propaganda they'd been spoon fed their entire lives, that when he showed up with irrefutable information about the weaknesses of the dragons, they'd been putty in his hands. Once he assured them he could help them defeat the strongest Force within the Dragon Guard, they welcomed him into their pack. He'd repaid them by leading them to their deaths, as well. His plan included annihilating the rest of the hunters, but first he was focused on Aidan.

Coward has to pay.

At first, Andrew was going to capture Aidan. Make him feel the same pain and hopelessness he'd endured; trap his older brother in some horrible dungeon to waste away. Then after the debacle on the hillside, Andrew decided killing Aidan outright was the best option, but not before eliminating the other Guardsmen, including his other brother, Aaron.

With them out of the way, Andrew would move on to everyone else responsible for the pain and humiliation he'd suffered. But his plan changed again just a few hours ago. Aidan's mate was in the picture, and Andrew knew who she was. He knew hurting her would be far worse than any physical pain he could inflict on his brother.

Oh yes, the little beauty who'd ultimately been the reason for Andrew's capture would pay. Then Aidan would live the rest of his life knowing he'd failed the woman the Universe made for him. He would live alone and broken, in a prison he could never escape, created by the brother he'd betrayed.

CHAPTER EIGHT

Aidan hadn't gotten a wink of sleep. Every time his eyes slid shut, visions of Grace appeared. Her sky blue eyes, drunk with passion, shining up at him through a fringe of thick black lashes and an amazing expanse of porcelain skin teased him. He imagined kissing every sexy swell, caressing every sensual dip, and tasting every erotic curve. He'd spent the night so excited, he'd finally relented and eased his arousal with his own hand.

The images of her hand and mouth on his hard cock had driven him to come harder than he ever had. Their mating call was working hard and fast, but the timing was all wrong. He needed to catch Andrew before allowing their relationship to progress. Grace was a distraction he hadn't counted on.

Aidan had teased Rayne about his inability to keep his hands off Kyndel, but now he understood Rayne's smile and chuckled answer that someday, he would understand. Paybacks were a bitch, and from his continuously half-erect cock whenever his mate was around, he knew he was being paid back double for the teasing he'd given his Commander.

He'd had lots of time to think about all the ways to woo her, taking his time getting to know her and letting her get to know him. He wanted to share *everything* with her. Wanted to know they had a bond of more than instinct before explaining his existence and the dragon within. But now that he'd met her and spent time with her, there was no way he was walking away, even for a moment. He needed to figure out a way to spend time with her while chasing down his brother.

How he approached Grace was crucial. She was spirited and stubborn. He knew from Kyndel, and now from spending an evening with her, she was intelligent and depended on the facts to make decisions. She was an attorney, after all. He knew from talking to Rayne that Kyndel hadn't explained *anything* to her friend other than their meeting had been love at first sight, they were now married, and he had a large family. Aidan wasn't sure how she would react to the news that they were made for each other by the Universe. He was even more concerned about how she would react to his dragon. But he knew for his sanity, he had to be with her.

Decision made, he headed to the kitchen to make coffee and see if there was anything for breakfast. Some of the other Guardsmen stopped in almost every day to grab a shower, a nap, and something to eat. He had no clue what was left in the refrigerator, if anything. He heard the shower in the master bedroom. Grace was awake and about to be in the shower, naked and wet and… just a few feet from him.

As he was checking the contents of the fridge, he found himself leaning his head against the freezer door, trying to catch his breath. With his eyes closed, all he could imagine was water caressing her generous curves. His hand was turning the knob on the bedroom door before he realized he'd moved. What would she do if he joined her? Let him in to satiate the need he knew was making them both insane, or hit him over the head with a shampoo bottle?

Probably choice number two.

Aidan turned to head back to the kitchen when he heard a moan coming from behind the closed door. With his enhanced hearing, he stood listening as her breathing became labored before she gasped and then moaned. The unmistakable scent of her arousal wrapped around him. It was all he could do to stay standing.

Just a few feet from where he stood, cock pressing against the zipper of his jeans so hard he was sure the design would be pressed into his skin, Grace, his beautiful mate, was pleasuring herself. He grabbed the doorknob again, determined to quench the fire raging through their bodies, when his phone rang in the other room. He was going to kill whoever was on the other end of that call. Spinning around with the scent of his mate's arousal still in the air, he stalked to the other room to answer a phone he really wanted to throw in the nearest river.

It wasn't long before Grace appeared. Dressed in a charcoal grey pinstriped suit and red silk blouse, hair piled up on her head with a little fringe framing her face, she came around the corner and stopped dead in her tracks. Using his enhanced hearing, he knew she was still breathing, so he continued frying the bacon while grinning like the goofball she'd already turned him into.

Her eyes on him were like a caress. He and his dragon reveled in *every* single second of her inspection. He could feel the tattoo, signifying the beast within, rising on his back. The flutters he felt kissing his skin told him the marking he'd had all his life was taking shape, the colors becoming more apparent. The change was always gradual. People who witnessed it often thought they just missed the intricate design at first glance, but his mate would be able to see the beautiful marking in all its glory from beginning to end, for she was as much a part of him as the dragon within and intrinsically more important. He kept his back to Grace, letting her take it all in. It was the first step towards her recognizing him as her mate.

His dragon was breathtaking. Aidan was proud to share his soul with such a regal being. The marking portrayed his beast in flight, accentuating his long lean lines, outstanding musculature, and the incredible expanse of his wings. Those amazing appendages, unfurled in flight, spread from the nape of Aidan's neck and flowed into its silver-scaled body, embellished with thick rows of black scales running the entire length of both sides. A wing came from the other side and wrapped around the man's waist, as if molding itself to him. His majestic head lay over Aidan's left shoulder blade with a determined look on his aristocratic face. His long, spiked tail disappeared into the waistband of his jeans where, unseen by Grace, it continued to wrap around with the large spade at the end lying in the extremely sensitive area next to Aidan's groin.

When he heard her open the door and head down the hall, he realized he was sans T-shirt, but didn't want the bacon to burn or the eggs to get too hard; at least that was the excuse he gave himself. In all honesty, he wanted Grace to see *him*. He wanted her to see his dragon.

Their mutual attraction was a living presence between them. He'd taken care of his never-ending needs last night and knew she'd pleasured herself in the shower just a short while ago. He now wanted to ensure she thought of him while they were apart. He knew he wasn't the most handsome man in the world, but had been told by more than one maiden he was a 'hunk', whatever the hell that meant. He wanted Grace to think of *no one but him*. The Heavens knew he would think of no one but her, *ever again*.

Flashing a little skin to entice his mate wasn't a hardship for Aidan. Now, if he could just get her to reciprocate they'd all be in heaven, but he knew that wasn't happening this morning. She was put together from head to toe, dressed to impress and put away the bad guys. Her hairstyle brought attention to the long, luscious column of her neck. His mouth watered and his lips tingled at the thought of tasting that delectable stretch of skin. His thoughts drifted to the image of his lips at her neck while his fingers pulled the pins holding her stylish coif, causing her beautiful, black tresses to cascade down her back. He forced himself to behave; he needed to feed his mate, get her out the door for work, and follow up on the lead one of the other clans had just called into him.

"I usually only have coffee in the morning," Grace whispered, her voice sounding breathy. He bit the inside of his cheeks to keep from smiling at the sound.

"Well, we can't let all this food go to waste. You *have* to be hungry. You hardly ate anything last night. Grab a plate, it's ready."

Aidan turned back and smiled, very proud of himself. He knew from the way she was breathing and the flush on her cheeks she was affected by what she saw, just as he was, looking at her.

Score one for the dragon man.

"All right, I'll have just a little." She sighed. "And is that coffee I smell?"

"Yep, it sure is. Grab a cup, it's ready too."

After their plates were made, they sat across from one another at the little table in front of the kitchen window. Grace drank her coffee, looked over the rim, and caught him looking back at her. He quickly covered his faux pas by pointing at her plate with his fork. "You better eat while it's hot. Bacon and eggs suck if they get cold and they're rubbery if you reheat them. You're gonna need your strength to put the bad guys behind bars today."

"Did Kyndel tell you I'm an attorney?" she asked with a snarkiness he wondered if she noticed was there. No matter, he loved her fire. It was sexy as hell.

"Yeah, she did. She's really proud of you." He smiled. "She talks about you all the time. Well, when I'm able to get back to the la…home." He barely stopped himself from saying the wrong thing and opening up a can of worms he wasn't yet ready to explain.

She waved her hand in dismissal as she chewed. "She just likes to make it seem like I know what I'm doing."

The stare she leveled at him had probably intimidated more than one person sitting on the wrong side of the law. He figured it was meant to intimidate him as well, but it would take a hell of a lot more than that to make him turn away from her. He admired her strength and intelligence, along with all her other attributes. "What else did she tell you about me?"

If he wasn't mistaken, she was fishing for something. He answered quickly to ease the tension he saw growing in her. "She said you two had been friends since the day you started college."

He watched her relax a fraction. "And that she trusted you with her life."

He watched more of the tension leave her body. "Other than that, she shared stories of the trouble you two caused." He chuckled as he watched the remaining nerves leave her body.

"Yeah, well I'm sure she made it sound worse than it was." Grace smirked, and he got the distinct impression she was remembering all the times they'd raised hell and gotten away with it.

"Did you really throw a red towel in the washing machine with all the Sigma Chi's underwear, forcing them to wear pink skivvies for an entire semester?"

She laughed aloud. It was the most amazing sound he'd ever heard, and the way she looked when all the tension and suspicion left her face was a vision that inspired masterpieces.

"Yes, we did." She chuckled. "And they never had a clue who did it."

Aidan couldn't take his eyes off his mate as she took another bite of her breakfast and lifted her mug toward her lips. He saw her notice him staring. "Do you always watch people eat?" she asked.

"No, but you aren't like anyone I've ever met."

She furrowed her brow. "What exactly am I like?" He was sure that was the voice she used to question clients and witnesses. A tone leaving no room for argument.

"You're beautiful, Grace, just beautiful."

She stared at him, dumbfounded. It warmed his heart. He was sure the very formidable Grace Kensington had *never* been stunned speechless. He bit the inside of his cheeks to keep from smiling for the hundredth time since meeting her, taking the opportunity of her stunned silence to pick up their dishes and turn towards the sink. "Can I get you some more coffee, to go?"

Grace shook her head. "No, and thank you very much for breakfast. I need to get to the office. Witnesses don't interview themselves. Sorry I busted in on you last night." She headed to the door to retrieve her shoes, still sitting where she'd left them the night before.

"No problem, at all. Kyndel's casa es su casa." He chuckled at his own wittiness.

Grace giggled and it sounded like the little bells on the jewelry Emma, from his clan, crafted. "Thanks. I appreciate it. Sometimes I work too late to make it all the way out to my house, but I'll try to pay closer attention to the time and hopefully not have to impose on you again."

She opened the front door and called over her shoulder as she exited, "Have a good day, and thanks again for dinner last night, too."

And with that, she was gone, and Aidan was left smiling ear to ear in her wake.

"Oh, you will be staying here again my beautiful mate, and sleeping is not all we'll be doing."

~~*~*~*~*~*~*

Andrew watched Aidan's mate close the front door and walk to the red Volvo. She got in the car, took a deep breath, buckled her seatbelt, and backed out of the driveway. Andrew waited to the count of twenty before pulling the rented navy blue sedan onto the street. He'd already placed a call to a *guy* he knew with the pretty lady's tag number. He needed her name and address, but this morning he was going to find out where she worked and anything else he could dig up on his own. He had a meeting at noon with a group of rogue wizards who were more than happy to help him with his plans for revenge. Aidan would pay for what Andrew had endured and now, so would his mate.

CHAPTER NINE

Aidan sat on the couch staring at the front door, waiting for Lance and Royce and remembering the last time he'd seen Grace. It had been two days since she'd walked out that door. It seemed like a lifetime and he was climbing the walls. Being in the same house with her and not being able to act on the vast array of fantasies his mind conjured had been torture, but it was nothing compared to being away from her. Not being able to hear her voice or see her amazing smile was going to be the death of him.

He'd prowled the apartment the entire first night before finally throwing himself onto the bed. His head hit the pillow and he was immediately engulfed in her delectable scent. From that point forward, it'd taken supreme effort not to spend every second in bed with his nose buried in her pillow. He thought about carrying it around with him but decided he needed to draw the line somewhere. Getting out of the apartment before he gave up and went running after Grace was the only defense he had. Of course, he'd planned to go straight from his meeting with the werepanthers to her.

He *needed* to see his mate. Showing up at her office would be tricky. She missed nothing. She would be suspicious, but he was counting on the pull of the mating call to make her as needy for him as he was for her. Hell, he'd use whatever means necessary to have her by his side, even her own desire.

Pacing until he was sure he'd worn a path in the carpet, then sitting, then repeating the cycle, unable to keep still for more than a few minutes, Aidan thought about blowing off the meeting.

I can't do that…dammit. But as soon as it's over…

Everything he'd learned about Grace Kensington in the small amount of time they'd spent together kept going around and around in his mind. He smiled, thinking about how she'd admired his body and how the scent of her arousal grew stronger. Even when they were old, surrounded by their great, great, great-grandchildren, he would remember the way she'd looked sleeping on the very spot where he now sat. His angel, fallen from heaven, just for him. So lost in his thoughts, when Lance spoke in the mindspeak of their kind, he jumped.

"Hey, 'A', we're only about a mile out. We had to transform and land on the other side of The Pointe. Be there in a minute."

"What the hell took you so long?"

"Kyndel and Royce were comparing recipes…oomph!" Lance groaned in pain. *"Damn, Royce, that hurt. I think you broke my rib."*

"Shut the hell up then," Royce grumbled.

"All right, you dumb asses. Just get here and don't kill each other." Usually their bickering didn't bother him, but today, all he wanted was Grace.

"I won't kill him, but I'm going to make it almost impossible for him to talk if he keeps up his shit," Royce growled.

"Yeah, yeah, old guy, just keep talking." Lance sighed, but Aidan heard the chuckle in his voice. *"I can see the back of the house. Be there in a minute."*

He loved his brethren, but sometimes Aidan felt like he had a lifetime part in one of the teenage movies the younger Guardsmen were always watching. It never failed, when there was two or more of them together, someone was making wisecracks or playing practical jokes. He remembered the time they were across the country, tracking a pack of hunters who had been attacking smaller clans. The entire Force was holed up for almost twenty-four hours in a cave, awaiting the other clan's Guardsmen to give the signal for them to move in on the enemy. Everyone was antsy and ready to get the hell out of there, but Lance had hidden Aaron's clothes in an alcove outside the cave's entrance. What he didn't know was a nest of rattlesnakes called that particular space their home. Aaron reached in to get his belongings and a full-grown rattler attached itself to his arm.

A rattlesnake bite won't kill a full-grown dragon shifter, but he'll feel like his insides are on fire for about an hour while his enhanced healing works the poison from his body. Aaron launched himself at Lance, snake still attached, and all hell broke loose. It took Aidan, Royce, and Rayne to break up the fight. Then Devon and Andrew held Aaron until he could cool down and the poison left his body. At the thought of his younger brother, his heart hurt, and right on its heels was a rage that threatened to consume him. He would catch Andrew and return him to the Elders… *whatever it took.*

Lance and Royce came through the front door Aidan had been staring at a few minutes earlier. Royce hugged him in the way of their kind while Lance headed straight to the refrigerator.

"What's up with all the rabbit food in here, 'A'? You raid a local farm? I haven't seen a stockpile of fruits and vegetables like this since…" Lance's eyes got big and he inhaled deeply. "Oh, shit! She was here wasn't she? You were both here at the same time and she's coming back, isn't she?"

A shit-eating grin crept across Aidan's face. "Yep, she was here and yes, we were here at the same time." His smile lost a little of its luster. "But that was two days ago and I haven't seen her since."

"Well, go get her, bro."

"I can't just *'go get her'*. I have to go slow, give her time to get to know me."

"Hell with that, 'A', go get your woman."

"Lance, Aidan's right. He needs to handle her carefully. Not all females are as accepting as Rayne's mate," Royce agreed. "From what Kyndel says Grace is very analytical and doesn't believe in what she cannot see." Royce turned back to Aidan. "Have you told the Commander's mate her best friend is *your* mate?"

Aidan shook his head. "No, I haven't told anyone but you two." He shrugged his shoulders. "I let the subject drop with everything that happened the day Kyndel was injured and Andrew got away. Not even Aaron knows." He rubbed his hand down his face. "I know he suspects, but I haven't come out and said the words. I want the traitor stopped before I bring her to the clan." He moved towards the hook holding his leather jacket. "So let's get out there and get this shit over with." Grabbing his coat, he opened the door.

"But I'm hungry, dude," Lance complained as he grabbed two fruit bars and a banana, following Aidan out the door with Royce bringing up the rear. "Guess girl food will have to do for now."

"You're always hungry," Royce answered as he smacked the jokester in the back of the head.

Lance turned, about to throw a punch at Royce's shoulder, when Aidan grabbed his arm. "Can you *please* cut the bullshit? We really need to get the information Max has and I somehow doubt they'll think you two *girls* bickering is helpful to the situation."

Aidan threw his leg over his Harley while his brethren got theirs from the back of the house. He watched as they pushed them to the end of the driveway and got on, ready to drive the fifty-some miles to the meeting place specified by the Big Cats. From the way Lance was favoring his left leg, Aidan was sure he'd mouthed off to Royce again. The pain in the ass would never learn that Royce was older, bigger, and less willing to take his shit than any of the others in their Force.

They may be pains in my ass, but they're my family, and I couldn't ask for better men to have at my back.

CHAPTER TEN

The last two days had been a blur of sifting through files, talking to potential witnesses, filing motions, too much coffee, and not enough sleep. Grace hadn't even left the office. Alice warned Grace that if she didn't leave tonight, the older woman was going to carry her out the front door herself. Not that the tiny slip of a woman could even lift Grace's foot, but it was the thought that counted.

Grace knew one person who could lift her foot and a whole lot more.

Aidan.

No matter how swamped she'd been for the last two days, her mind still wondered about the man who set her body on fire. She thought of his amazing body and images of the two of them quenching their undeniable lust flooded her mind. She shook her head. If she didn't stop the erotic thoughts, she'd never get out of the office and into a shower bigger than a postage stamp.

Grace knew a long, hot shower was all she needed. If she could relax for a moment, her focus would return and the last little piece of the puzzle eluding them in their investigation would become clear. She *had* to find it. *His* identity was somewhere in the mountains of paperwork surrounding her. It was her duty to put 'The Auctioneer' behind bars, along with all his associates. They couldn't be allowed to hurt any more young women.

She thought about Aidan again and smiled. It defied explanation, but she just *knew* he was a good guy, a protector of some kind. There were a few scars on his mouthwatering body. Grace guessed he'd been in a fight or two. One thing she knew for sure was that he gave better than he got. Those scars had been in the defense of another. When she looked into his eyes, there was kindness. She felt at ease, like with him was where she belonged.

Well …after she got past the jolt of electricity that warmed her through and through. No matter how she tried, Grace couldn't help feeling safe around him. A man she'd just officially met and spent less than twelve hours with gave her more comfort than her own parents. It was a feeling she'd only ever felt with Miss Annabelle, and then later in life, with Kyndel.

I miss him.

What the hell was wrong with her? Once again, she shook her head.

I need to snap out of it. Gotta get through this file then I can go home.

She needed a cup of coffee with lots of sugar. Grabbing the money she kept stashed in her top drawer, Grace decided against putting her shoes back on and stood. On the way past her desk, she grabbed a hair tie, throwing her hair on top of her head in a messy bun as she went. Heading down the hall to the break room, she devised a plan to get all the information needed for an indictment.

Turning the corner into the break room, she heard the elevator at the back of the office 'ding'. It was only to be used by the Assistant District Attorneys who had keys. Must be one of them coming back to the office, she reasoned. It was pretty late for an ADA to be coming back in, but it *was* a big case. Everyone in the office wanted to see the douche bag behind bars and his operation shut down. Still, something just didn't feel right.

A chill ran down her spine. Her *spidey senses* screamed for her to get back to her office. She decided against waiting for the coffee to brew, grabbed a Diet Coke and a bag of cookies, and headed for the door. At least in her office there was a phone close by she could lock the door.

Several times on the trip down the hall, she looked over her shoulder. The itch between her shoulder blades said someone was watching, but when she looked, no one was there. The little hairs at the nape of her neck stood on end and she broke out in goose bumps, despite the sweat trickling down her back. Walking into her office, Grace shut and locked the door and sat behind her desk, trying to catch her breath. She thought about calling the police, but what would she say? She imagined how the conversation would go...

"Oh, hello, officer, I'm a first year at the DA's office. I'm here by myself and I have a bad feeling. I think someone's here who shouldn't be. Can you come and check it out?"

"What was that? No, no I didn't see anyone. I only heard the elevator and then the hairs on the back of my neck stood on end. I hurried back to my office, locked the door, and called you."

"What did you say? No, there's no history of mental illness in my family."

Yeah, not going there.

Grace had two choices. She could go see what was going on... *or* get the hell outta Dodge. She'd never been one to run from a fight, and the thought of something bad happening she could've prevented was almost more than she could stand, but red flags were flying everywhere. She looked through her desk drawers for something she could use as a weapon.

Grace wished she'd listened to her father's bodyguard when he suggested she buy a gun. He'd even offered to teach her how to use it. At the time, she'd never imagined having a need for a firearm, even laughed as she told him she would probably shoot herself before anything else.

Definitely rethinking that plan now.

Finally locating the brass letter opener they'd presented to her on her first day, she felt a bit better. It was heavy and sharp. She could make it work. Trying to remember what she'd learned in the self-defense classes she and Kyndel had taken at the Y two summers ago, Grace mentally kicked herself.

I probably should've been paying more attention to what was being taught than the way the instructor's shorts hugged his tight ass.

With the way things had been going, she prayed she was overreacting. How the hell would anyone who wasn't supposed to be in the office have gotten in using the locked elevator? There was no way. But no matter how logically she argued with herself, the feeling of something really wrong going on at the other end of the office wouldn't stop bombarding her senses.

Unable to handle not knowing, Grace took a deep breath and slowly let it out before opening the door. She stuck her head out and looked both ways. Nothing but an empty hall stared back at her. It was eerily quiet except for the hum of the fluorescent lights. Thank God, she'd asked Alice to leave them on when she sent her home.

Listening for any little sound out of the ordinary and hearing nothing, Grace tried to convince herself it was all in her head. Unfortunately, the nagging feeling doubled in strength, screaming, 'SOMETHING IS WRONG'. Pushing her back as close to the wall as she could, she crept down the hall. Reaching the break room, she ducked in and took a minute to gather herself.

Her appreciation of cops grew exponentially. Situations like she was dealing with were part of their everyday jobs. Grace thought her job was stressful, but it was nothing compared to the little adventure she was on. Standing up straight, she prepared herself; it was now or never. Time to go see what the hell was happening. One way or another, she had to know.

She did her imitation of a turtle again... poked her head out, looked both ways, and in the same fashion as before, headed to the back elevator. When she got to the end of the hall, she peeked around the corner and saw nothing. All the doors she could see were closed.

Walking by each one, she reached out and grabbed the knob. All were locked, as they should be. But as she got closer to the lead prosecutor's office, she noticed his door ajar, with a shaft of soft light shining into the hall. She knew Alice always made sure every light was off and every door locked before she left. It had become her unofficial responsibility since they were always the last to leave.

Grace's *spidey senses* buzzed off the charts. It was the strongest warning she'd ever gotten from her internal alarm. Any minute she expected to hear sirens and see flashing lights as she crept towards her boss's door. If there was a way for ears to strain, hers definitely were. When she reached the door, she counted to three then gently pushed it open. Looking around, she found nothing out of place. Walking around the desk to turn the desk light off, she did notice the bottom drawer was open.

Kicking it shut with her foot, Grace turned the light off and headed out the door, locking it as she went. All the way back to her office, she tried to figure out what had happened. Nothing was out of place, but she knew she'd heard the elevator. No matter what she told herself, her crazy *intuition* would *not* stop screaming that something very dangerous was in the office... *with her*.

Packing it in and heading home sounded like the best idea. She was exhausted, and with all that had happened, there was no way she'd be able to concentrate. She blamed her overactive imagination on her lack of sleep and decent food. Even as she tried to dismiss the fear she felt, a shudder ran down her back and the unmistakable feeling of dread filled her.

Throwing the files she wanted to read over the weekend in her briefcase, Grace stuffed her feet into her shoes and headed straight to the elevator. When the elevator on the far end opened, she rushed in, hitting the *door close* and *lobby* buttons at the same time. She breathed a sigh of relief as the elevator began its descent, steadying herself for the hundredth time that evening. A chuckle at her own foolishness slipped out and she ended up laughing aloud to calm her frazzled nerves. Her goofy sense of danger had never been wrong before, but she'd also never been as tired or stressed as she was. It was the only explanation she had, and she was sticking with it.

Exiting the elevator, Grace was surprised to find the security desk empty. Maybe Johnny had gone to the men's room or was on rounds. Hurrying out of the building through the covered crosswalk into the garage, lost in her own thoughts, Grace failed to notice the missing security officer from *his* post at the entrance. It wasn't until she got to the second floor of the parking garage that she realized the overhead lights were off.

The only illumination came from the security lights located on each pillar. Grace knew from an office memo there was a timer to ensure the lights came on at dusk and went off the next daybreak. No sooner had the thought crossed her mind than goose bumps broke out all over her body. She quickened her step, listening more closely for any sounds of danger. Only the thump, thump, thump of her pounding heart and the tap of her heels on concrete were reaching her straining ears.

The trunk of her Volvo came into view. Walking so fast she was almost running, Grace shifted her purse and briefcase from one hand to the other. The keys in her hand reassured her as she prepared to hit the button to unlock the doors. All she wanted was to be safely tucked inside her little car. Movement in her peripheral vision made her whip her head to the right. Grace didn't recognize two men walking straight towards her and didn't want to know them. Her *intuition* said they were *not* selling Girl Scout cookies.

Way to make jokes while the boogiemen are coming to get me.

Moving as quickly as possible, Grace prayed they'd just go away if she ignored them. Only three spaces from her Volvo, she dared to look up and found the first man leaning against the trunk of her car... staring at her. In the glow of the security light, she could see he wore his baseball cap pulled down so far it touched the bridge of his nose. Everything but a very nasty scar running down his cheek and an evil grin were obscured from her sight. The waves of pure hate and aggression pouring from the scary looking man caused her to stumble.

She slowed her pace, but realized too late that the second man had slid behind her. Trapped between the two men, Grace felt like she was drowning in waves of evil and disgust; all directed at her. Her brain was running through every possible way to escape as she squeezed the key fob in her hand, hitting the panic button. The siren-like car alarm screeched, reverberating off the walls of the concrete parking structure. The man in front of her hesitated, looking at his accomplice. She used their second of hesitation to dive between the parked cars on her left... her only thought was survival.

CHAPTER ELEVEN

It had taken all day but it was well worth the time. Aidan had gotten a ton of information from the werepanthers. He now needed time to digest and analyze it all. When they got to the cabin in the middle of nowhere, Aidan scented at least ten Big Cats, but only ever saw four... Max, aka Maximillian Prentice, aka the King, his sister Sophia, and their two personal guards.

He had to laugh at the amount of muscle the King traveled with, but Aidan also knew having different species of cats, all vying for territory, made the Prides do crazy things. It was just one of the many things that made him glad dragon clans all shared the same beliefs and goals. Infighting could tear a group apart and it definitely made daily life a chore for those in power, but Max was a tough SOB. He ran a tight ship and was happy to make alliances that were beneficial for both sides. He'd been a friend to the dragon shifters for a very long time.

This time, just like all the others, Max hadn't disappointed. With all the information his pride gathered about his brother, the hunters, and even the wizards, their Force would finally be able to catch the stupid little bastard. The longer they talked, the more Aidan realized how insane Andrew really was. He was also relentless and driven. A deadly combination that had to be annihilated.

As he sped his Harley around curves and over hills, one detail nagged at him. Max said his panthers caught scent of the traitor downtown, with increasing frequency the last two days. The good news was whatever changes Andrew had experienced with the mixture of his dragon magic and the black magic that allowed him to hide his scent from them seemed to be wearing off. With any luck, they would be able to track and capture him very quickly. They confirmed he'd been staking out Kyndel's apartment, something Aidan already knew from the footprints in the flowerbeds and the broken branches on the bushes close to the windows.

The bad news came from the werepanther spies embedded within the wizard's coven. They'd seen the traitor meeting with the wizard leader. No magic had been used, but the spies reported it was a heated discussion, and the two were to meet again within the week. Aidan needed to find out where that meeting was so he could be there.

Taking just a minute to focus on his surroundings and enjoy the beautiful countryside as it rolled by, Aidan rolled his shoulders, trying to relax. He loved riding in the country. It was the closest thing to flying in the open skies he could find. He thought about Grace, longing for the day she was on the back of his bike, her body wrapped around his while they sped across the open road. He let his imagination run wild with thoughts of his beautiful mate by his side, on his bike *and* in his bed. Before he knew it, the lights of the city came into view.

"I'm heading to Grace's office." He sent to his brethren in mindspeak. *"Where y'all headed?"*

"We'll just follow you into the city and get something to eat before dropping our bikes at Kyndel's and heading back to the lair," Royce answered. *"That cool with you, big mouth?"* he shot at Lance.

"Yeah, I'm cool with that, Grandpa," Lance laughed.

Aidan chuckled with his brothers as they got closer to the address of the State Prosecutor's office. It was late enough in the evening that traffic was basically nonexistent, making the trek from one end of town to the other pretty uneventful.

Stopped at a traffic light a half block from Grace's building, Aidan heard a car alarm ahead on the right. Out of habit, he tuned in with his enhanced hearing to see if anyone needed help. Just as he was about to dismiss it as a false alarm, he heard a scream that sent his heart pounding and had him racing through the still red light.

It was Grace and she was in trouble!

CHAPTER TWELVE

Crawling around in the dark, Grace prayed she was heading *away* from the men trying to get her, rather than toward them. The death grip she had on her keys was the only thing keeping her sane.

If I can get to my car, I'll be safe.

Following the slivers of light glowing under the cars, she reassured herself that if she was getting closer to the security light on the nearest pole, she was also getting closer to her car. One look confirmed her thoughts. The front bumper of her Volvo was just a few feet away.

Grace stayed completely still, head down, holding her breath, trying to hear where her would-be attackers were. When she heard no sound, she raised her head and moved her right leg at the same time. Exhaling, she began scooting her left knee forward. A large, calloused hand grabbed her right ankle. Her hands and knees scraped across the unforgiving concrete. He had her and there was nothing she could do.

Her attacker landed on her back, pushing all the air from her lungs, leaving her unable to breathe. Palming the back of her head, he forced her face into the concrete. She felt him rise to his knees while her mind scrambled for a way to escape. His other hand landed next to her head. She thought of biting him but movement was impossible.

Her mind went completely blank, thoughts driven away by fear of what they planned to do to her. Never one to give up, Grace refused to lie there and be another victim. As she tried to think of a plan, the other man's boots appeared by her head. She felt his fingers in her hair, but couldn't have prepared for the pain that shot through her skull as he used her hair as a handle to jerk her to her feet.

Her scalp was on fire. Tears stung her eyes. Grace prayed. The man's soulless black eyes looked right into hers. "You were definitely in the wrong place at the wrong time, bitch. Pity too. If I had time, I'd show you what it's like to be with a real man," he rasped, his voice gravelly from too many cigarettes. She froze as a sick smile spread across his face, pushing his scar into a crescent shape.

The thought of never seeing Kyndel or her parents ran through mind. Would they know what had happened to her? Then she thought of Aidan and what might've been possible with a man who made her feel things she'd only dreamed about. But the worst were the images of all the crime scene photos she'd viewed throughout her career. The horrible shots depicting victims of violent deaths. It was like a sick slasher film playing on a loop through her mind. She did the only thing she could think of… Grace screamed as if her life depended on it.

Because in that moment…it really did.

CHAPTER THIRTEEN

Aidan raced into the parking garage, following the sound of his mate. Rage and fear fueled his every movement. He'd thought nothing could be as bad as the night he believed Andrew to be dead. Knowing Grace was in trouble made that seem like a walk in the park

Flying around the corner, Aidan sped up when he caught sight of some asshole holding his mate by her hair. Behind her, another man was reaching into the back of his pants for what Aidan could scent was a gun. Thankfully, both men were oblivious to the three Dragon Warriors racing towards them.

Dragon and man lost all control. Rattling the rafters with his roar, Aidan paralyzed Grace's attackers with fear for the few precious seconds he needed. Speeding forward, he launched himself at the man holding his mate. His bike skid to the side, left unnoticed in the dust. Lance and Royce spoke through their link, assuring him they knew what needed to be done.

Getting to Grace is all that matters.

Royce sped past so he could come up behind the thug holding Grace. If Aidan had it his way, the asshole wouldn't be alive that long. Lance jumped from his bike, catapulting himself at the man at Grace's back.

Aidan knocked the man holding Grace into the SUV to his right. The dirt bag dropped Grace as Aidan went in for the kill. The startled thug stood. Aidan charged forward, kicking with such force a wet crack of ribs echoed through the concrete enclosure.

Aidan was on the man instantly, snapping his neck with one quick twist, just as Lance disposed of the second man in the same fashion. Royce grabbed the falling corpse, hauling it between two parked cars to save Grace the shock of seeing a dead body. Kneeling next to Grace, Aidan pulled her into his arms and stood. She curled into his chest, her head in the crook of his neck.

Pulling her closer to his body, he held her tight. She shook so hard he feared she would injure herself. Her fear bled through their growing mating bond, along with her strength. Grace was holding on by a thread. Aidan needed to get her to safety, but first he had to calm his chaotic nerves. Gently laying his lips to her forehead, he breathed in her scent, assuring both he and his dragon she was alive.

I almost lost her after just meeting her.

Even if it meant locking her away, he would never let anything happen to her again. She shuddered in his arms, breaking his train of thought. He had to act fast. Grace was going into shock.

"I need to get her outta here!" he shouted through mindspeak.

"I've got your bike by her car and my coat to wrap her in," Royce answered.

"Thanks." Aidan was glad the largest of their Force was with him. His leather duster would wrap around Grace nicely for the ride home.

"I'm going to take you to Kyndel's on my bike. Can you stand so we can get Royce's jacket on you? It's too cold to ride in just your blouse and skirt." He spoke with a tenderness he hadn't known he possessed.

She held his neck tighter and whimpered. Any tighter and he was sure they would be sharing the same skin.

"Just wrap it around her the best you can," Aidan instructed Royce. *"She's not gonna let go."*

Royce nodded while tucking it around her and in between their bodies, then held Aidan's bike steady while Aidan straddled the seat with Grace clinging to his chest for dear life. Settling her legs across his lap, Aidan noticed she'd lost her shoes in the fight. Reaching down, he wrapped the long flap of his brethren's coat around her feet. Then pried her car keys from her still shaking finger and threw them to Lance. The movement caused her to grip his neck with renewed vigor.

A warmth that could only be love enveloped his heart. Grace had reached for him, and thank the Universe he was there for her. She was clutching his neck, using him like her lifeline, a job he took very seriously. Those criminals had almost taken her from him. Rage once again rolled through him. Only the pressing issue of getting her home as quickly as possible kept him from losing his mind. Starting his bike, Aidan flew out of the garage, leaving the others to clean up the mess.

Arriving at Kyndel's in record time, he slowly turned into the driveway and parked. Using his enhanced speed, Aidan lifted them both off the bike and headed to the front door. Without missing a beat, he unlocked the door and walked through, kicking it shut as he continued towards the master bedroom.

Walking straight to the bathroom, Aidan stopped. He took just a few moments to simply hold Grace. She was alive and safe. He pulled her tighter to his chest. Pushed his nose into her hair, and inhaled, drawing her essence into him. She tensed. He could feel her contemplating getting down from his embrace… breaking their connection.

Grace was a strong, independent woman. He knew she was trying to regain her composure. Stray thoughts continued to flow through their mating bond. She thought she should let go of his neck, but no matter how hard she tried, she couldn't. She had mixed feelings about her dependence upon him. She loved *and* hated it all at once.

It's something you'll get used to mo ghra'. After this, we'll never be apart.

"Grace… *mo chroi'*, can you stand?" He waited. There was no response but he continued anyway. "You need to get a hot shower. We need to get you tucked into bed before the adrenalin wears off. I don't want you going into shock, and from the way you're shaking, I'm afraid you're close."

Aidan loosened his grip on her legs, letting them slide to the floor, while he wrapped both arms around her shoulders to hold her steady. When he was sure she could stand on her own, he loosened his hold and took a step back, but kept his hands on her shoulders for support. Looking into her eyes, still wide with fear, he smiled, giving her the silent reassurance he knew she needed.

The scrapes that decorated her cheek brought his rage roaring to the forefront once again. His dragon puffed smoke, begging to be let out to seek revenge for their mate's suffering. As his eyes traveled down her body, he saw the tears in her clothes. When his eyes landed on her knees, he couldn't believe she was standing. Both knees were raw, with dirt and grime from the floor of the parking garage embedded in the wounds. His need to inflict pain as retribution for his mate rose within him, but Grace's care came first.

And the bastards are dead.

He looked back to her beautiful face and cringed at the fear he saw. "Grace, *mo chroi*, you break my heart with that look." He cupped her unblemished cheek. "I promise on all that I hold sacred, I will *never* let anything happen to you again."

She held her hands up to signal for him to stop talking and he saw her hands had received the same treatment as her knees.

"I know I'm safe with you. I have no idea how I know, but I do. I just can't stop replaying the whole thing over and over in my head."

She tried to turn away from him, but his hold on her shoulders was too strong. One lone tear rolled down her cheek. He pulled her back to his chest. "*Mo chroi*, don't hide from me. I'm here for you, let me help you." His words shook with emotions he thought had died long ago. He knew in that moment he would give his very life if it meant the wonderful creature in his arms never had to suffer another second of pain.

Grace burrowed farther into his chest, rubbing her face against his shirt. She cried out as the cuts and bruises on her cheek made contact with the fabric. Aidan jerked her back. "We have to get those scratches cleaned out."

He lifted her onto the counter, finally unwrapping her from Royce's huge jacket. Throwing the garment into the corner, Aidan asked, "Do you know if there's a first aid kit or something I can use to clean these up?"

"Kyndel has a kit under the sink, with a jar of the ointment her granny taught her to make."

Aidan knelt down and opened the cabinet. He retrieved the box holding the first aid supplies and grabbed the jar of "Granny's Special Recipe", as they'd started calling it around the lair. There was also a bottle of Kyndel's special bath oil, which would come in handy. He smiled up at his mate. "Yes, I'm very familiar with Kyndel's ointment. She's made many jars of it in the months since she married Rayne. We're all wondering how we ever lived without it."

He remembered Kyndel had shown them all how to mix her healing bath oil with warm water to get debris from the wounds and help with the swelling. Filling the basin and sink with warm water and bath oil, Aidan grabbed a handful of the soft cloths and a few towels from the linen closet. Once again, he knelt in front of Grace, preparing to clean her wounds.

She jumped when he touched her foot. His heart broke at the 'deer in the headlights' look she gave him. "Grace, I need you to turn just a little and put your hands in the sink. It'll help get the muck out of those scrapes."

He laid his hand on the outside of her thigh, turning her legs to the side, making it easier for her to reach the warm water mixture. Dunking a soft cloth in the basin on the floor by his leg, Aidan gently washed the wounds on both knees, changing the water several times until all the rocks, dirt, and grime were gone.

Standing, he took her hands out of the water and made sure none of the offending dirt remained on her delicate skin. Tossing the last cloth to the side, Aidan looked at the most beautiful face he'd ever seen. From the first swipe of the cloth on her knees, Grace had closed her eyes. They'd remained closed while he cleaned her abrasions, even when she gasped as he touched an especially deep laceration.

Sitting as still as a statue with her eyes closed, head to the side, Grace leaned just a bit forward. Her adrenalin rush was wearing off. He treated her poor abused face with the same care and attention as he had the rest of her cuts. Aidan needed to hurry and get her in the shower or she was going to fall asleep where she sat.

As much as he wanted to see her luscious body, it was definitely not the time. "Grace, you need to get a shower so I can put the ointment on all those cuts and bruises. I'm going to go into the bedroom to give you some privacy, but I'll be right outside that door." He motioned with his head towards the bedroom. "You holler if you need anything and I'll come running."

He leaned forward and kissed her forehead, inhaling the calming scent of vanilla and honey, reminding him once again she was safe and only a little worse for wear. He leaned back, looked her in the eyes to make sure she wasn't in shock, and gave her shoulders a little squeeze. Her lips curled into a tiny smile that didn't quite reach her eyes and she nodded.

He let his hands fall to his sides and backed out of the bathroom. Aidan kept eye contact to make sure she was okay with him leaving, right up to the second he closed the door. Although she was only a few feet away, he prepared for the longest wait of his life.

With his exceptional hearing, he listened *only* to the woman who held his heart. He cringed at her sharp intakes of breath when her clothing brushed a particularly sensitive abrasion. His fists clenched as the chaos of her emotions when what she'd endured threatened her resolve. He focused to making sure she was still conscious and not in too much pain. Physical pain was such a small part of what his Grace had suffered. When she'd had a good night's sleep and felt a little more like herself, they would start to deal with everything else.

He sat completely still, listening to the water start and the door to the shower slide shut. His dragon pushed him to go to their mate, chuffing and blowing smoke. Aidan pushed back, giving Grace the space she needed. The man and his beast were locked in an internal debate when a tiny sob broke in.

Aidan walked to the door, laid his ear against the wood and listened. What he heard had him ripping open the door and sliding the shower door with such force it bounced off the opposite wall. What he saw stopped him dead in his tracks.

Huddled in the far corner of the shower, with water raining down on her, was his mate. Grace was curled into a ball, sobbing so hard she shook, while biting on a washcloth in an attempt to stay silent. Walking under the spray completely dressed, Aidan picked her up, simply holding her to his chest while she cried. Time ceased to matter. Grace needed comfort… and he would give it to her.

At once, it dawned on him he needed to get her clean before the water turned cold. Grabbing the soap from the holder and the washcloth from her hand, he sat down on the floor of the shower. Washing every inch of her amazing skin, man and dragon reveled in the fact that she was letting him take care of her in such an intimate fashion.

Every so often Grace would glance at him through her lashes, sigh, and close her eyes again. The distant, haunted look in her eyes was something he would move heaven and earth to never see again. When she was as clean as he could get her without moving her off his lap, he washed her lovely mane. Grace closed her eyes and moaned as he massaged first shampoo and then conditioner into her scalp.

Several times he was forced to remind himself, his dragon, and his wayward cock that she was injured. This was about caring for her, *nothing else*. Satisfied that she was clean, Aidan stood, turned off the water, and stepped out of the shower with Grace in his arms. He grabbed the big fluffy towel and jar of ointment from the counter as he carried her to the bed.

Carefully sitting Grace on the bed, he dried her hair then wrapped the towel around her, securing it in the front. "I'm going to find you something warm to wear. You sit right here."

He remembered the big flannel shirt Lance called his "Paul Bunyan Special" hanging in the closet. It would be big enough to cover her three times over, and the best part was he wouldn't have to search for it. Running to the closet, he stripped out of his wet clothes. Grabbing the flannel, he flung the hanger against the wall, threw on a pair of sweats, and made it back to Grace in seconds.

He helped her into his shirt and buttoned it up before helping her stand. Aidan grabbed the bottom of the wet towel and slid it out from under his shirt, letting it fall to the floor. He pulled the covers back and once again sat Grace on the side of the bed.

Kneeling in front of her, he marveled at her strength and beauty, even in her present condition. Neither her mussed hair from the towel drying, nor the bruises, cuts, and scrapes that abraded her tender skin mattered; he couldn't stop staring. She was processing what had happened, but little by little, the spark that was purely Grace was returning to her eyes. His mate was a fighter. She had spirit. She would survive this ordeal and be stronger than before. He just knew it. Grabbing Kyndel's ointment, he unscrewed the lid, scooped out a handful, and rubbed his hands together, warming the ointment for Grace's skin.

Carefully covering both knees and most of her legs with a thin layer of the ointment, he moved to her palms. Lastly, he reached for her face. As gently as possible, with just his fingertips, Aidan spread the ointment across her injured cheek. Grace closed her eyes and leaned into his touch.

When he was sure he'd gotten every mark, he wiped his hands on a clean cloth and threw it to the side. Grace slowly opened her eyes and stared into his. A weight like nothing he'd ever felt hit him square in the chest. Warmth slowly spread throughout his body, burning hotter and faster the longer they held their gaze. Needing to look away lest the wildfire gaining momentum annihilate all his good intentions, he blinked. The spell was broken and he stood to help her into bed.

Grace grabbed both his hands, pulling until he was again looking her in the eyes. "Please stay with me. I don't think I can be alone tonight."

The shadows in her eyes broke his heart, but they were only part of the story. The spark of hope and just a bit of affection froze the breath in his lungs. He would deny his mate nothing… in this life or the next. Smiling, he nodded. Gently lifting Grace, he laid her in the middle of the bed, turned off the bedside lamp, and crawled in next to her.

She turned on her side so he did the same. They lay face to face. Slowly, she moved closer until he could feel her breath against his cheek. "Would you mind holding me, just until I fall to sleep?" she whispered so softly he wouldn't have heard her without his enhanced hearing.

Aidan couldn't speak past the lump in his throat. He opened his arms, welcoming her into his arms and his heart. Grace breathed a sigh of relief against his chest as his arms closed around her.

He stared at the ceiling. Aidan thanked the Universe she was safe in his arms. Closing his eyes, he laid his cheek on the top of her head and enjoyed the feel of his mate in his arms.

CHAPTER FOURTEEN

Aidan spent the first several hours of the night holding his mate as she slept and conversing with his brethren through mindspeak.

"These scum were definitely human," Lance grumbled.

"But the duffle bag they carried is covered in black magic," Royce added. *"And there's a file here concerning an abduction case. There's also..."* He stopped and Aidan could feel his anger through their link.

"What? What is it?"

"They came prepared," the oldest of his Force growled. *"There's rope, duct tape, hunting knives, and another gun."*

"There's a key too. It goes to the elevator at the back of Grace's office. The stench of shit magic was everywhere," Lance rumbled. *"Oh, and I found the security guards locked up in a storage room. Poor guys were embarrassed that someone had gotten the jump on them. But I smoothed it over and said nothing happened here."*

"While we were checking out the key, I found where the file belonged and returned it so no one will be the wiser," Royce detailed. *"We've got your mate's purse and briefcase."*

"Thanks y'all."

"Never a problem," they answered in unison.

Aidan and Royce laughed as Lance bitched about leaving his bike in Grace's parking spot so he could bring her car home.

"Shut up, ya pain in the ass," Aidan chuckled before cutting their connection to the sounds of Royce howling with laughter.

It wasn't long before Aidan heard a car in the driveway, followed by Royce securing his bike in the backyard. Aidan had instructed Lance to leave Grace's keys in the huge terracotta pot next to the back door. The sound of their footsteps faded as they headed back to the lair, while Aidan returned to the puzzle of Grace's attack.

From all the information his brethren had gathered, he was ninety percent sure she hadn't been the target, only a victim of being in the wrong place at the wrong time. Aidan was no less furious, but it *was* a small consolation, and he now had somewhere to point his pent up rage. His next step was to contact Max. Maybe the werepanther spies could connect the dots between the wizards and the prosecutor's office.

Grace hadn't moved a muscle during his conversation with his brethren. Her breathing remained deep and even. Before her attack, she'd been tired from her crazy work schedule. That combined with the adrenalin crash, left her completely exhausted. He was glad she was resting and ecstatic to simply hold her in his arms.

Willing all thoughts of criminals, hunters, and wizards from his head, Aidan relaxed. He thought only of Grace. She was amazing, and she was all his. He never wanted to be apart from her again. Turning more to his side, he wrapped his body around her and stared over her head out the window.

Completely lost in thought, he almost missed Grace's tiny whimper. Rubbing her back, Aidan pushed feelings of calm and love through their link. His mate still squirmed and began mumbling in her sleep. Leaning back, he saw her face drawn in fear and her eyes scrunched tight. She was in the midst of a full-blown nightmare. One Aidan would not let claim her.

Bringing her back against his chest, he cooed comforting words while pouring light and healing through their mating bond. No matter what he tried, her struggles escalated, turning into thrashing, and before he could get them into a sitting position, she was screaming, "No! No! Stop! Please stop..."

Aidan pulled her into his lap, placing his hands on either side of her face, "Grace, baby, open your eyes!" he all but yelled into her face, trying to get her attention over her terror. She continued to scream, tears running down her face while she punched at his chest and shoulders. Grace fought against her nightmare for all she was worth.

Doing the only thing he could think of, Aidan put his nose right against hers, applied light pressure to the sides of her face, and using the same tone of authority he used when instructing new Dragon Guard recruits commanded. "Grace. Wake up. Come back to me."

It was as if he hadn't spoken at all. His panic began to rise. Unable to break the spell of her nightmare and completely frustrated, Aidan he slammed his mouth onto hers. He poured everything he was into that kiss… his fear, anger, and pain flowed into his mate. He gave her the love he already felt combined with the incredible pride swelling within him that she was his.

Grace continued to pound away at his chest and shoulders. Aidan kissed her with a single-minded determination.

She will *wake from this nightmare. It* will not *get the best of us.*

Finally, her thrashing slowed. Her lips relaxed. She kissed him back, still sobbing and shaking. When Aidan would've pulled away, Grace shoved her hands into his hair and with a strength he didn't know she possessed, held him to her, deepening their kiss. He let her guide their passion. She ate at his lips. Thrust her tongue into his mouth. Drew his essence into her being.

He felt her come awake during their kiss, confused but completely lost to their desire as she made love to his mouth, tears still coursing down her cheeks. His conscience said he should stop their kiss, but his heart and soul said it felt too good and too right for it to end. They both needed the closeness to restore some semblance of sanity and security.

He couldn't get enough of her. She made him feel more alive. Her complete trust in him after having suffered such trauma turned him inside out. His blood caught fire. He needed this woman more than his next breath. *Nothing* had ever felt as right as Grace in his arms. She straddled his lap, never losing contact with his lips. Aidan knew *their kiss* was the one thing keeping Grace from shattering into a million pieces. His heart soared as her need flowed to him through their link.

Who am I to deny her what she so desperately needs?

Running his fingers through her hair, he gripped her silky strands lightly and took control of the kiss. He'd let her have her way, let her lead them, but he and his dragon could stand it no longer. He plundered her mouth, thrusting his tongue in and out, mimicking what his extremely hard cock wept to do to her pussy.

Tilting her head more to the side for deeper penetration, Aidan was careful of her wounded cheek. Grace moaned low in her throat. Aidan broke the kiss, holding her head steady as she tried to latch onto his mouth again. He leaned his forehead against hers, trying to slow his breathing and his raging libido.

"M*o chroi,* I've dreamt of kissing you too many times to count, but I have to know that you're okay?" he whispered.

She worried her already swollen lip with her teeth. "Aidan, I *need* this. I need to feel alive, not this fear that's eating away at me." She drew in a shuttering breath. "And I have no clue why, but I know deep in my heart," she placed her hand over her heart, "that I need to feel it with you." She laid her other hand over his heart, raising the spattering of hairs covering his chest on end. Sky blues eyes glowed through a thick fringe of dark lashes and left him punch drunk. All thoughts of anything but his woman fled his mind.

He lightly kissed first one eyelid and then the other. He touched his lips to the apple of one cheek, the tip of her nose, and then the apple of the other cheek, careful of her cuts and scrapes. Each kiss his way of marking her as his, promising he would always care for her. Her needs were his needs. Body and soul, he would always be there for her. He said with his body what his mouth had yet to articulate… she was his *everything*. His world forever revolved around her.

Continuing to lay kisses on either side of her mouth, he caught her sigh of satisfaction while gently nipping at her bottom lip. He moved across her jaw, kissing and tasting until her reached her ear. Sucking her earlobe between his teeth, Aidan bit down lightly. Grace groaned and arched her back, pushing her breasts into his bare chest. She ground her already weeping center against the erection tenting his sweatpants.

Aidan continued his sensual torture, holding his dragon *and* himself at bay. They were primed, ready to take their mate in a way befitting their connection, but this was about Grace and her needs. He was bringing her back and would hold out as long as he could, give her the most pleasure imaginable.

His lips and tongue tormented the side of her neck. His fingers flowed through her silken tresses. He reached between their bodies, slowly unbuttoning his flannel shirt. He liked her in his clothes, it felt right, but the old flannel was keeping them from the skin-to-skin contact he desperately needed.

Patience wearing thin; Aidan could wait no longer. He promised himself to go slow, but he needed to feel every part of his beautiful mate. He needed to imprint every possible inch of her alabaster skin with his body. Every erotic curve and dip of her luscious body called to him. His very being begged to be infused with hers.

When he was finished, there would be no doubt who she belonged to. He pushed the offending article of clothing off her shoulder. With only one button still closed, it slid all the way down her arm, baring not only her shoulder but her perfectly plump breast. Her tightly pebbled nipple the color of a ripe berry made his mouth water. Drawing the delectable tip into his mouth, lavishing it with his tongue, Aidan was sure he'd died and gone to the Heavens.

CHAPTER FIFTEEN

Grace's hands flew to the back of Aidan's head, holding him to her breast. It was an exquisite torture she never wanted to end. Moaning, she panted as he continued to nip and taste her breast. She gasped as he drew as much of her flesh into his mouth as would fit.

Sure she would die from pleasure, Grace was having a hard time catching her breath. Aidan released her breast with a pop, moving to the other, giving it the same fierce attention. She was being consumed by the fire this amazing man stoked within her. Rolling her hips, she tried to ride his very hard cock, but her quest for completion was impeded by his sweats. On every rotation, his cock bumped her excited clit, sending flashes of light through her vision. She needed more. She needed to feel him... *all of him.*

She slid her hand inside his pants, felt the engorged head of his hard cock as she wrapped her hand around the shaft and shivered. Aidan gasped at the contact. In one swift move, Grace found herself on her back, staring into whiskey-colored eyes that caused all thought to flee from her mind. Still holding his erection, looking deep into his eyes, she slowly rubbed her thumb through the moisture at the tip. Aidan shuddered and pumped his hips, running his dick across her palm.

She marveled at the strength contained in his massive body. With his hands planted on either side of her head, holding all of his weight off her, he continued to pump his hips, his cock extending its sensual glide through her hand. His head was thrown back in pleasure and Grace dreamed of tasting every ridge and valley of the spectacularly developed muscles in his neck. He pushed forward and stopped. His head fell forward. Once again, she was snared by those magnetic amber eyes.

I'm under his spell...

CHAPTER SIXTEEN

Sliding down her body, his cock slipped from her hand. Aidan couldn't stop the moan that crossed his lips from the loss. Caught in Grace's gaze he drank in all she felt from their contact. His sensual slide ended with his mouth positioned right above her trimmed ebony curls, glistening with her arousal.

Inhaling deeply, he took her incredible scent deep into his being. His mouth watered in anticipation of the first taste of his mate. He longed to have her juices coat his tongue and flow down his throat. Her scent made him more lightheaded than the strongest ale he'd ever shared with his brethren.

He leaned down, blowing gently on the engorged nub pushing through her curls. Her clit pulsed with excitement. Grace threw back her head and bowed off the bed. Her body pulled tight. Her clit grew harder, pushing farther from under its hood. Aidan placed his tongue at the base of her slit and licked from bottom to top in one slow swipe, forcing her wet, swollen lips to part.

Sucking her firm, sensitive bud into his mouth, he held it gently between his teeth, teasing it fiercely with the tip of his tongue until Grace was grabbing his hair and driving her heels into his back. Juices flowed from her pussy, coating his chin and causing him to lap at her with renewed vigor. He thrust his tongue into her pussy as far as he could reach. Licking and sucking, he captured her nectar, savoring the taste.

Curling the tip of his tongue to reach the very special bundle of nerves he knew would force Grace over the edge, he pushed his finger inside as well, stretching her feminine walls, filling her completely. Grace's thighs tightened around his head as he drove her arousal higher.

He felt her walls contract, gripping his tongue and finger, pulling them farther into her warm, wet pussy. Adding a second finger, he sucked her clit into his mouth. It was the stimulation she needed. Grace went off like a rocket, screaming his name at her release. Continuing to lick and suck her beautiful pussy, he wrung every last tremor of climax from his mate while bringing her slowly back to reality.

Grace sighed, her muscles so relaxed her legs slid off his shoulders. He placed tender kisses on the silken skin above her mound while carefully sliding his arms from under her legs, placing a light kiss on each abraded knee. He continued kissing his way up her body, shedding his pants as he went. Dipping his tongue into her belly button, he smiled against her skin at the giggle that escaped her lips, lax from pleasure.

Reaching the underside of her gorgeous breasts, Aidan left not an inch untouched as he worked his way to her hard, extended nipples, pointing to the heavens, begging to be kissed. He sucked one and then the other into his mouth. Blew a soft puff of air over both peaks still damp from his kiss and watched them pucker and stretch.

Her chest colored with a blush, reminding him of the pink roses his mother had grown all those years ago. He kissed every inch of her sensitized skin he could reach. By the time he arrived at her lips, they were both panting.

I'll die if I'm not buried deep inside her soon.

Braced on his forearms, only a few inches separating their lips, he slid ever so slowly into her hot, contracting pussy. Inch by inch, he joined with his mate. Aidan shook with the effort it took to go slow. Every contraction of her inner muscles pulled him farther into her body, milking his cock, begging him to move faster. Drawing on his great strength, he held back. Sweat ran down his back and his body trembled with anticipation.

Grace was so wet and ready for him, her excitement pooled between them. Completely within his mate, Aidan held still, reveling in the feel of the one meant for him wrapped so tightly around his cock. He watched her face, eyes closed in passion, sweat dotting her upper lip. Her lips parted while she panted. He felt her fighting to gain some semblance of control.

"Look at me, mo *ghra'*. See who is loving you. See everything we are together."

Grace's eyes flew open. The ever-present current jumped between them, sizzling stronger and brighter than before. She wrapped her legs around his waist and held tight as he began a casual slide in and out of her. It was a feeling unlike any other. He promised himself to go slow and he would…even if it killed him. She would know love…*his love*. She would feel safe and treasured…it was his promise to her. Grace owned him…mind, body, and soul.

He could no longer hold back. Their pace accelerated. From one breath to the next, he was pistoning in and out of her wet channel, driving them both to the release they so desperately needed. She met him stroke for stroke.

Grace grabbed his shoulders, crushing her chest to his. Her pebbled nipples rubbed against his chest, the friction causing the most delicious sparks of electricity to arch between them. He shifted his hips, causing his pelvis to bump her clit and his cock to rub her sensitive bundle of nerves with every stroke. Thought was impossible. Aidan could only feel.

He felt her orgasm building, careening towards them like a runaway train, bringing them to the edge of something bigger than either had ever imagined.

Unable to wait a second longer, Aidan commanded, "Come, *mo chroi*. Come with me."

Her muscles contracted so tightly around him he had no idea where she ended and he began.

"Trust me, *mo chroi*. Let go and trust me. I've got you. I'll *always* have you," he groaned his request and thrust into her so hard and fast he felt the bottom of her womb. The exquisite sensation undid the last of their resolve, and in the next breath, they were flying.

He and Grace came with such force their bodies shook. It was hard to stay conscious. The sound of shouting filled the room. His eyes slid shut. Lights flashed and colors burst forth in the darkness.

Aidan felt Grace floating in the ether of their incredible pleasure. As she drifted back to earth, he placed butterfly kisses on her face and neck. Rolling to the side, he placed her across his body, boneless and spent. They shared a peace he hadn't known possible before her. His mate opened her eyes and Aidan was humbled at the overflowing of emotions he witnessed. He watched her fight to keep her eyes open and chuckled as she lost the fight. Her lids slid closed and she was sleeping.

He drew little circles in the drying perspiration on her back and she shivered with a chill. Reaching down, Aidan grabbed the sheet, covering them both. Lying in the darkness of the early morning hours, he grinned like an idiot. He'd made love to his mate. A completeness only possible from joining his body with hers eclipsed his entire being. It was only the beginning.

His thoughts ran wild with the many ways he could keep her in bed for weeks…*maybe months*. The sounds of her sleeping, coupled with the contentment he'd seen in her beautiful blue eyes, were a balm to his soul.

I'm already in love with Grace Kensington.

His smile widened and he drifted off to sleep, happier than he could ever remember.

CHAPTER SEVENTEEN

Andrew headed back to the condominium he was renting across the street from the apartment where his brother and mate were presently sleeping. He didn't have to look in the windows to know they would be completely exhausted from the excitement at Grace's office. He had her name, address, and place of employment, courtesy of his contact. It had been his plan to abduct and torture her this very night, but that was blown to hell by the wizard's hired thugs. Those assholes had shown up and ruined everything. He had no idea what it was all about, but he damned sure planned on finding out during his meeting with the wizard leader the next evening.

After Aidan saved his damsel in distress and sped off, Andrew stayed to watch Lance and Royce dispose of the bodies and cajole the shaken guards into believing nothing really happened. He brushed away the memories threatening his sanity. Memories of the times they were all members of the same Force, working side-by-side…*brethren*. He couldn't stand the weakness those memories evoked. They were his past, a time he could never return to. His brother betrayed him. He'd been forced to make his own way, a way full of revenge and retribution. Lost to his thoughts, he almost missed the werepanther trackers dogging his every step. They were getting closer. Any day they would pinpoint his scent and exact location.

He raced back to his safe house, thinking how relieved he would be after his meeting with the wizard leader. They would perform the ritual. His black magic stores would be replenished. He'd been taught to abhor the use of the hated dark magic, and a part of him was sickened that it was a necessity to stay hidden from the Dragon Guard, but he had to avoid capture and exact his revenge. Andrew would see all responsible for his capture, imprisonment, and torture, pay… along with any who got in his way. He would also uncover the connection between the men in the parking garage and the wizards. It was something that could unravel his plans. He could feel it, and he simply could *not* let that happen.

CHAPTER EIGHTEEN

Grace slowly came awake, dreaming of whiskey-colored eyes and wickedly electrifying kisses. She stretched and winced from the cuts and bruises and a delicious soreness between her legs that had her pulse racing all over again. Aidan had made love to her like no other and driven back the shadows of her attack.

Reaching out, she found the bed still warm from his body. Rolling, Grace breathed in his wonderfully crisp scent and something deep inside fell into place. What was it about *this* man that pushed aside all her usual reservations and insecurities? How could someone she'd known such a short time have slipped past all her defenses? She'd never been the kind of girl to fall into bed with just anyone, but this guy was something all together different.

Her *intuition* assured her he was a good man with good intentions. It would've been easy to think of what they'd shared as a simple fling, but she couldn't. Grace *knew* with scary certainty that Aidan saw her as more than a passing fancy.

And he is so much more than someone to scratch an itch. Although, he's very good at it.

Chuckling at her silliness, Grace stopped short. She'd *never* been silly where a man was concerned...*not ever*. But Aidan completely short-circuited her brain. It was the only excuse she had for lying in bed, giggling like a schoolgirl. Whatever he had, she could bottle it and make a fortune if she was willing to share...

After careful consideration, she found sharing was *absolutely* out of the question. He was hers and that was all there was to it.

Whoa! Mine? Really?

Bolting straight up in bed, eyes wide open, Grace gasped.

Am I sure?

She sat waiting for her *intuition* to kick in; to tell her something was wrong, but... nothing happened.

Well damn! I'm sure.

Not that it made any sense at all, but Grace knew beyond any doubt she was meant to be with Aidan. She was *nowhere near* ready to commit to forever, but knew they were supposed to meet and last night was *most definitely* supposed to happen. He completed something deep within her, something she couldn't explain. Grace was going to enjoy it while it lasted, see where it took them. When he touched her, he made her feel like she was the only woman in the world. She'd even seen flashes of *something more* when she looked into his eyes. Sighing, Grace wondered if she'd ever really felt complete before now.

Swinging her legs over the side of the bed, she stopped. Her scraped knees glared at her. Visions of her attack in the parking garage came rushing back with a vengeance. She shook remembering how scared she'd been. Had it not been for Aidan and his friends, she would be dead. Her body thrown away like yesterday's trash, just another statistic and set of crime scene photos.

I gotta get outta this bed.

Cold chills shot up and down her spine. Flashes of creeping through the office chasing shadows led to those men in the garage, making her *spidey senses* scream. Those two events were connected. Grace just needed to find out how.

With all thoughts of lovemaking and one very edible man locked away for another time, she switched her focus to solving the mystery before her as she headed to the shower.

CHAPTER NINETEEN

Grace is finally awake.

Aidan heard the shower and had to work hard to keep from joining her. He'd been on the phone with Max and a few other contacts, as well as mindspeaking with his brethren, since right before the sun rose. It was torture to leave the warmth of his mate, but he needed to know how Grace's attackers were connected to the wizards. And more importantly, if it had anything to do with the traitor.

His little brother wouldn't live long enough to make it to the Elders and the Tribunal if he had anything to do with Grace's injuries. Aidan would rip him limb from limb with his bare hands...*brother or not*. Taking a deep breath to shake himself out of his rage, Aidan realized Max was talking.

"My cats have seen several *less than honorable* men meeting with the wizard leader. These men smelled of aggression and hate. My boys weren't able to get close enough to know specific details, but they did hear the wizard leader instruct them on the use of an elevator key and where to find 'evidence' when they reached their destination. Definitely sounds like the guys you and your boys took care of last night." Max's voice was low and ominous, obviously upset on Aidan's behalf.

"Damn sure does." Aidan failed at keeping the growl from his voice. "Were your boys able to hear *why* the thugs wanted the evidence or what stake they had in a criminal case being handled by the State Prosecutor's office?"

"No, that's all they picked up, even *with* their enhanced hearing. My cats are still being treated as newbies and not allowed close to the leader, *especially* when he's meeting with outsiders."

"You said there'd been others coming and going. Are they all from the same gang?"

"My spies believe so. They all smell of the same oil and exhaust fumes. One of the guys is an excellent tracker. As soon as he's able, he'll follow them to their hideout." Max sounded pleased with his cats.

"I cannot thank you and your Pride enough, Max. Don't know how I'll ever repay you."

"Don't worry about it. Just invite me to the mating party. I hear you dragons know how to do it right." Max's chuckled.

Aidan laughed. "Our mating parties *are* legendary. I'll make sure y'all are invited. You…"

Looking over his shoulder just as a freshly showered Grace walked into the room, Aidan forgot what he was saying. Dressed in a short blue robe that highlighted her long, alabaster legs, she robbed him of all rational thought.

Max was still speaking in Aidan's ear, but all the Guardsman could do was say goodbye and hang up. He'd call back and apologize later, but with his mate looking better than any dream he'd ever had there was no way Aidan was going to waste time talking on the phone.

Grace's hair was wet and brushed back from her face, making it look even darker than usual. Her cheeks had a blush that reminded him of her arousal. Memories of the night before flashed in his mind. Before he knew it, Aidan was standing in front of her, holding her chin gently, looking deep into her eyes. "How are you feeling this morning, *mo ghra*?" He lightly rubbed under her chin with his forefinger.

Her tongue swiped across her bottom lip and he wanted to follow it with his, but he held fast as she began to speak. "A little sore, but better, thank you." Her voice was little more than a whisper. Her hand touched his forearm and the electricity between them sizzled to life.

Slowly leaning forward, never breaking eye contact, Aidan let his lips lightly touch Grace's. Their eyes slid shut in unison and they both sighed in relief. It was the first real breath he'd taken since last touching her lips.

They opened to one another. Their tongues lightly met and a switch was flipped. His hands slid down her body, gripped the firm full globes of her ass, and lifted his mate until her legs wrapped around his waist. Walking backwards towards the couch, Grace's tiny nails dug into his shoulders. He smiled against her mouth; sure she'd drawn blood.

My mate has claws.

Their kiss was carnal. Breathing for one another, they ate at each other's mouth, unsure where one ended and the other began. Aidan landed hard on the couch, driving his boxer-covered erection against her aroused, silk covered clit. She tore her mouth from his, threw her head back, and rolled her hips. His cock jumped at the contact, the front of his boxers instantly wet from her excitement. If he wasn't buried deep inside his woman before he drew his next breath, Aidan was sure his head would blow off his shoulders.

Aidan distracted himself with Grace's gorgeous neck, bared to him…*for him*. He lavished her succulent skin, savoring his mate. Her taste drove him crazy with desire and filled him with a sense of home and belonging.

His hands slipped under her robe, pushing the material aside until her beautiful breasts were bared to him. Latching onto her already erect nipple, Aidan licked and teased it to a painful peak before scraping his teeth across the very tip. The moan that rose from deep in her throat told him all he needed to know.

We are meant to be…

He slid his hands under the silky fabric of her panties, kneading and massaging her perfect ass while she continued her sensual lap dance, making thought impossible. When he slipped a finger into her weeping pussy, she cried out, grinding for more contact. He curled the tip in a 'come hither' motion, just grazing the magical bundle of nerves seated above with a whisper touch.

Grace bore down, working to increase the pressure, but Aidan used his incredible strength to hold her up, keeping her from getting the contact she so desperately wanted. Her eyes flew open. She speared him with a look he was sure made weaker men shiver and grumbled through gritted teeth, "Aidan, I *need*…"

He slid a second finger into her contracting channel. Her eyes glazed over. Her eyelids slid shut until only a sliver of her arresting blue eyes were visible.

"Yes, *mo chroi*, what do you need?"

"More… Aidan…please…" she panted. "I'm so…" before she could finish, he pressed his thumb against her swollen nub.

She came, screaming his name, her juices further soaking the front of his boxers. Grace in the throes of passion, riding his fingers and shouting his name, was a thing of absolute beauty. His fingers continued their sensual glide, ringing every last tremor of her orgasm from her. She collapsed against his chest, his fingers still deep inside of her.

Tracing patterns in his sweat soaked chest, Grace ran her nails over his extra-sensitive nipples. He loved the feel of her hands on his skin. Aidan sighed while she continued her exploration. She reached the waistband of his boxers. Looked at him through her thick black lashes and batted her eyes.

"You have too many clothes on, sir."

In any other situation he would've laughed. But sitting with his fingers buried deep in his mate's pussy while she looked at him with love in her eyes, all he could think of was thrusting his painfully hard cock into her hot channel.

They stared into one another's eyes. Her hand slipped under his waistband and around his pulsing cock. His eyes all but rolled back in his head. Struggling not to throw her down and have his way with her, Aidan focused on how Grace's hand stretched around his considerable girth. He almost swallowed his tongue when she swiped her thumb over the weeping tip then teased the underside of the head of his penis with the moisture.

"Shit…" he hissed between clenched teeth as she ran her thumb as far down his length she could reach. He was sure she'd studied torture at some point in her life.

Grace lifted her head, nipped at his bottom lip, quickly licking away the sting. She groaned at the loss as Aidan let his fingers slide from her. He quickly grabbed the thin silk straps of her panties and ripped, throwing the ruined undergarment to the floor. Her robe hung open, baring her luscious breasts to him while the belt held fast to her waist.

Unable to resist, he leaned forward, once again sucking her hardened tip into his mouth. Aidan teased and tortured her tender flesh as he untied the belt and tore the robe from her body, leaving her completely bare to him.

The only thing stopping him from being buried deep inside his mate were his own damn boxers. Her nipple came out of his mouth with a pop as he lifted his hips. Bumping his straining cock against the swollen lips of her pussy caused Grace to gasp. He smiled while grabbing his waistband and with one pull tore the offending garment from his body.

The world could've come to an end and it wouldn't have mattered. His single goal was being one with his mate. He lifted her slightly and drove himself into her as far and as deep as he could. His hands flew into her hair. He held her face to his.

"Look at me, *mo ghra'*," he commanded.

Her eyes collided with his. He tilted his hips up and back, making tiny back and forth movements inside Grace's contracting channel, touching every already sensitive part of her, bumping her clit every time he raised his hips. The electricity between them sizzled and snapped like a downed power line on a wet street.

Grace struggled to catch her breath. Aidan's hands were once again on her butt as he kneaded her sensual skin, spreading the juices flowing freely from her arousal as he slipped his finger along the crack of her ass. He teased her rosebud and she pushed her ass farther into his hand. He smiled, knowing one day he would love her there, too.

His hands found purchase on her heavenly thighs. He pumped harder and faster into Grace, lengthening his strokes until he was lifting her completely off his lap and dropping her back onto his dick with every motion. She held his shoulders. Rode him with abandon. Her pussy squeezing him tight on each down stroke. She swiveled her hips when she touched down, grinding her engorged clit against his pelvis. Together, they were approaching the exquisite point of no return.

From the ripple of his dragon against his skin, he knew the beast was enjoying their love making almost as much as he. He drove harder and harder into her as her pussy gripped him tighter and tighter. They both panted as if they were running a marathon. Grace shifted on his lap, changing their position just enough. Their rhythm became frantic, and in the next breath, they came together with such force Aidan was sure the earth had moved.

Their climax went on and on as he emptied everything he had into his mate, slowing his pace when he was sure he would collapse from pure joy. Grace's feminine walls continued to milk his softening cock; he reveled in all they were together. When her contractions ceased, she collapsed against him, fighting to catch her breath.

Brushing the hair from her face, he let himself slide over until he was lying on his side, holding Grace in his arms with her head against his chest and his cock still deep inside of her. He listened as her breathing returned to normal and her body began to cool. Aidan grabbed a blanket off the back of the couch and covered them so she didn't catch a chill.

In the blink of an eye, she's become my world.

He rubbed her back, letting his fingers glide along her spine. Her soft skin felt like rose petals against his calloused fingers. Grace was utter perfection. Her muscles flexed. He knew she was about to sit up. Doing anything to keep contact with her, he rolled onto his back, taking her with him.

When they settled, her chin was propped on her hand, while she lay on his chest, wide-eyed and flushed. He watched emotions war within her and waited while she worked out whatever was bothering her. "What is it about you that makes me trust you?" she blurted out.

He smiled, his fingers resuming their trail up and down her spine, the allure of her silken silk too much to resist. "Maybe we're meant to be together." He shrugged. "Do you believe in Fate?"

She scoffed. A sliver of unease flashed in her eyes. "Is that what you think *this* is…Fate?"

"Hear me out, *mo ghra'*." He watched her internal debate, knowing when she'd reached the decision to listen to him. "I know it's in your nature to base you beliefs on cold hard facts. You believe everything must be logical… have a *definite* explanation. But what if the explanation of why we feel what we feel for each other in record time is Fate? Could you accept that?"

"First of all, what are the names you keep calling me? The language is beautiful but I really need to know what you're saying. It's rather unnerving."

He could feel she was purposely dodging his questions. Could see she wasn't sure how to answer his original question and watched as she realized things in her world had irrevocably changed.

Then he witnessed her rein in her emotions and put on her *lawyer face,* as he was beginning to think of it.

He laughed aloud but quickly commiserated. "I understand it must be incredibly unnerving."

He bit the insides of his mouth and took a deep breath to continue. Her glare looked permanently painted on. Thoughts of kissing the look off her face danced through his mind, but he quickly thought better of it. She would be seriously pissed off if he told her he found that particular look *adorable*. His mate took shit from no one.

And I love it.

Shifting his gaze, Aidan focused on a painting hanging on the opposite wall. "I'm speaking to you in the language of my ancestors. *Mo ghra'* means my love and *mo chroi'* means my heart."

He was happy to see her stern demeanor melting away when he looked back at her and hurried on before she could interrupt. "That's what you mean to me, Grace, and have from the first moment I saw you. You see, I *was* taught to believe in Fate. I *know* in my heart we *are* meant to be together… for all of our days."

Her lips were in the form of an 'o' and her eyes wide as saucers. He'd expected to see some kind of doubt, even anger in her expressive eyes, but what he saw made him want to jump for joy. There was hope, and more than a little of an emotion he was scared to name too soon, reflected back at him.

She collected herself and pulled back the emotions his confession stirred within her. Taking a deep breath, Grace spoke, using what he was sure was her best cross-examination voice. "Let's say for the sake of argument that I buy your theory about Fate… that we belong together. Let me make something very clear…I'm very skeptical, but I *am trying* to keep an open mind."

She paused, squinted, and worried her bottom lip with her teeth before continuing. "How did you know I was in trouble and then make it there in time to save me last night?"

The shakiness he heard in her voice made him draw her closer to his body, lending her his strength while she battled back the emotions threatening to overtake her. When he felt her relax and knew she had herself back under control, he started to explain. "I was on my way to see you. I *missed* you. I wasn't kidding when I said you mean a lot to me. The two days since I'd last seen you seemed like an eternity. I was coming to find you."

He watched as she unconsciously nodded her. His heart soared. She was experiencing the same feelings as he, even if she wasn't ready to *consciously* admit it.

"Lance, Royce, and I were almost to your office when we heard your car alarm go off." He left out the part about being able to hear her scream or that they could communicate directly into each other's minds. It wasn't the time to reveal any of his enhanced abilities.

"We followed the sound. When I saw that asshole holding you by your hair, I damn near lost my mind." He started running his fingers through the ends of her silky mane, rubbing her back at the same time, the touch calming them both.

"My brethren and I have worked together for a long time. It was second nature for us to save you from those dirt bags. I *had* to rescue you, Grace. I didn't have any other choice. I *couldn't* lose you."

He'd taken her hand sometime during his explanation, so moved by the emotions his recollection stirred he had to remind himself not to squeeze her delicate fingers too tightly. Keeping a close eye on her expressions, Aidan tried to gauge where her thoughts were going. He needed to be careful not to spook her or worse yet, make her think he was an escaped mental patient.

"What happened to the men who attacked me?" She met his gaze head on, demanding the truth.

"They were killed in the fight," he answered, gazing right back at her, letting her see he would always be honest.

She nodded her head. He could *feel* her thinking. "Were the police called?" She narrowed her eyes, never breaking eye contact.

"No, they were not." He kept his voice level, waiting to see where she was going with her line of questioning.

"I know this is a long shot but I have to ask. Do you know if they were part of the criminal organization run by a douchebag known as 'The Auctioneer'?"

"I know they were career criminals and part of some bigger scheme, but I don't know what yet," he answered, still wondering what was going on in that brilliant mind of hers. "I want you to know we are *certain* you were *not* the target, but just happened to be there. They wanted to leave no witnesses. Do *you* think they're associated with this 'Auctioneer'?"

She nodded her head. "Before I left the office, I heard the back elevator ding like someone had come up. It's only used by the ADAs and the Prosecutor himself. It was weird. It was so late. It's key-operated and only a very few people have the key. It just didn't *feel* right, ya know?"

Grace paused until he nodded then continued. "I was in the break room getting a snack, so I went back to my office in case whoever it was came looking for me or had a question to ask." She fidgeted with the fringe on the blanket covering them. He could tell she was debating about how much to tell him. He held completely still while she worked it out.

Taking a breath, she held it to the count of five, speared him with a look daring him not to believe what she was about to say, and said, "I know what I'm about to tell you might seem crazy, but I promise it's the absolute truth. It's also something I've never shared with anyone but Kyndel, so if you laugh at me or try to have me committed, I'll kill you." She winked and he gave her a grin to show he was right there with her.

"I'm not even sure what to call it, but I have this *intuition*. Kyndel calls it my *spidey senses*. It's kind of like my own alarm system and lie detector all rolled into one." She hurried on. "Anyway, last night when I heard the elevator ding, I got a really bad feeling, the hairs on my arms even stood on end and cold chills ran down my back." She shivered. "I sneaked down the hall to see what was going on but no one was there, so I went back to my office."

Having a hard time keeping his calm knowing those thugs had been in the same office as his mate, Aidan offered his thanks to the Universe for keeping her safe. He stayed quiet as she moved off his chest, dislodging his cock from its home. His body tensed at the loss of its mate. Wrapping the blanket around herself, Grace sat on the edge of the couch, her hips touching his legs. He missed the contact they'd shared moments ago. Wanted to protect her from her own memories, but respected her need to stay strong. He didn't like it, but he damn sure respected her need to do it, so he sat back and waited.

"I sat there a minute and decided there was no way I was going to get anything done. My nerves were shot. I packed up and headed out, noticing Johnny wasn't at the inside security desk when I got downstairs. It was late, so I figured he had rounds. It wasn't until I was almost to my car that I realized the lights in the garage weren't on… *and* I hadn't seen the security guy at the entrance. Then those awful men appeared."

Her bottom lip quivered. She fisted the edge of the blanket and looked anywhere but at him. He let her battle it out for about fifteen seconds before sitting up, placing his hands on either side of her face, and forcing her to look at him.

"Tell me," was all he said. Then he waited for her to continue, knowing *she* needed to get it out. It was the only way she could start to put the horrific event behind her.

She nodded as much as his hands would allow. "It all happened really fast. One was in front of me, the other behind. All I could think was to dive between two parked cars, but they still caught me and then… you were there."

She collapsed against his chest. He could feel her gulp air while fighting to keep the tears he'd seen filling her eyes from falling. Aidan held her close, whispering words of comfort for a few minutes, but he refused to let her hide from him or her fear. She had to face it to conquer it.

He leaned back and held her away from him. Just this once, he ignored the sparks jumping between them. This was more important than their physical attraction. This was necessary to help *his* Grace get past her trauma.

"You did the right thing, *mo ghra'*. You kept them from hurting you worse than they actually did."

He kissed her scraped cheek to emphasize the damage they'd done and to ease the dragon within, who wanted to hunt down anyone who'd dared even think of hurting their mate. Grace's touch and smell pushed the dragon back.

"Although you didn't know it at the time, you gave me and my brethren the time to get to you…time that made all the difference in the world."

CHAPTER TWENTY

Tears she couldn't stop rolled down each cheek. Aidan leaned forward, kissing one path until his lips touched hers. The chaste kiss he placed upon her lips tore at her heartstrings, but when he laid his forehead against hers, she could only sigh. The tension drained from her body. He'd been with her the whole time, whether in reality or in spirit. Aidan just got her. Grace was filled with so many emotions she thought she might burst.

Grace couldn't stop staring at Aidan. She wholeheartedly believed *every* word he'd spoken. Her *spidey senses* confirmed it. The problem was… she had to decide what to do with this new knowledge. Having already made her mind up to give whatever was growing between them a chance, she felt reassured…almost vindicated.

What she felt for Aidan was amazing… *and scary*, but gave her the first real hope she'd had in years. Knowing her feelings were reciprocated turned her world upside down. She'd prepared herself for a few good months, maybe even a year; sure it would die out like all the others. However, Aidan had said 'for all of our days', not 'just for a little while'. He wanted her *forever*. And God help her, she was floating on air. Not 'happy endorphin' happy, but honest to goodness *happy*.

Pulling out of her euphoria, Grace knew she still needed more answers. Her heart was in dangerous, unfamiliar territory. She did *not* fall in love quickly… or at least never had. Protecting her heart was number one on her list of priorities.

But I'm not sure I need to.

First to break the silence, Grace asked, "So you believe me… about the *feelings* I get?"

"I've learned never to question someone's '*special abilities*.'" He shrugged and smiled. "*Of course* I believe you, and I'm overjoyed you chose to confide in me. More importantly, I'm glad your *spidey senses* helped save your life." He winked and kissed the tip of her nose.

Grace took a deep breath and went on. "Now, I *need* to tell you something else." Aidan nodded for her to continue. "The same *intuition* that warned me about last night's danger is telling me something about *you*."

Aidan's brow furrowed. Grace felt his impatience grow between them. Hurrying on before she lost her nerve, she confessed. "It's telling me I should see what this thing," she motioned with her hand, "between us is."

No sooner were the words out of her mouth than Aidan's lips were on hers. He kissed her hard and fast, then just as quickly, pulled back. Grace opened her eyes, basking in the full glow of his dazzling smile. Her body leaned towards his of its own volition, but his strong hold kept their lips from touching. "We'll be doing a lot more of that later, but right now we need to figure out what those assholes were doing in your office."

She shook her head to clear her thoughts. When her kiss-addled brain cleared, Grace asked, "So you really think those men had something to do with the case we're building against 'The Auctioneer'?"

Aidan slid his arms down her back, picked her up, and shifted his massive body until she was once again sitting on his lap. Grace squirmed to get off but he held her tight. "You might want to stop wiggling around, *mo chroí*. I want to talk about this with you, but I can't be responsible for what happens when your delectable ass rubs against me like that." His breath on her ears raised goose bumps all over her body.

CHAPTER TWENTY-ONE

She gasped then sat still as a statue. Aidan threw back his head and laughed. When Grace chuckled and gave a quick little shimmy to stop his laughing, he loved her all the more. Aidan grabbed her hips and kissed the side of her neck. He'd just decided talking could wait when Lance's voice sounded in his head.

"*'A', you there?*"

He moved Grace down his lap, breaking the contact of her luscious ass with his ready for action cock, but kept hold of her hips. "*Yeah, I'm here. Where else would I be?*" he answered, irritated at the interruption.

"*Well hell, I have no clue. Don't get shitty with me. Max has been trying to get a hold of you for almost an hour. He said he heard from his people in the wizard camp. Something big is happening. You better be sitting down cause you're gonna be pissed.*" Lance paused and Aidan was just about to yell for him to continue when the jokester of their Force added, "*They spotted Andrew in the middle of the shit.*"

"Dammit! How far out are you?"

"*About an hour. We're still in flight.*"

Lance's tone sounded off, almost stressed, and stress was not an emotion his pain in the ass brethren *ever* experienced.

"Who's with you?" Aidan sensed his hesitation so he continued. "*The whole force?*" Aidan paused; praying for any answer other than the one he *knew* was coming. One deep breath later he asked, "*Rayne?*"

"*Yeah, dude, the Commander's here. Sorry. He was right beside me when Max called. There was no way to get away without telling him what was going on?*"

Aidan wondered how much harder this shit was going to get before he got a break. *"Guess Kyndel's pissed too?"*

"She said and I quote, 'Tell 'A' if one hair on Grace's head is harmed, I'll kick his ass.' Then she hugged me and whispered, 'Tell him to keep her safe and bring her to me.'"

Aidan closed his eyes and took a deep breath.

Oh, hell yeah, Spitfire, I'll keep her safe and get her home as soon as I can.

With the cat out of the bag, he didn't have to hold anything back. Not that he planned on it any way, it just felt *right* that the people he called family should know about the woman who held his heart.

"See you when you get here. I have to figure out a way to get Grace ready and back to the lair where she'll be safe. I have a feeling she's gonna wanna see this through to the end."

"Have you told her about us?"

"No, I was trying to take it slow." He chuckled anxiously. *"But that ship sailed."*

Lance chuckled through their link. *"Good luck with that."*

Aidan cut their connection just as Grace jumped off his lap. From the look on her face, he'd missed something important during his chat with Lance.

"What the *hell*, Aidan? You had a death grip on my hips and just ignored me when I asked you to let go."

She narrowed her eyes. He could feel daggers shooting from her stormy baby blues. "What are you *not* telling me?" Grace was using her 'lawyer voice' again and Aidan couldn't blame her.

His mate stood in front of him like a warrior woman from the tales of old. Her hands firmly planted on her hips, her brow furrowed, and her stare so intent her eyes were almost gunmetal grey.

Damn, she's a magnificent creature.

But it was clear her patience was wearing thin. It was now or never… time to tell his Grace all of his secrets.

"Well, what the hell is going on, Aidan?" She tapped her foot, anger filling the space between them.

"You remember just a moment ago when you told me about your *spidey senses*?"

She nodded once, and if possible, narrowed her gaze even more.

"Well, I have some *special abilities* too." He paused, waiting for her to stop him with questions. When she didn't, he continued. "One of them allows my brethren and me to communicate mind to mind. We call it *mindspeak*."

Grace stood there staring at him, as if waiting for more of an explanation to decide if he was bonkers or not, so he rushed on. "There are six of us total. Kyndel's ma…*husband*, who you've met, is our Commander. We've been fighting together for a long time and share a special bond. This connection allows us to protect the people we must, and fight those who seek to eradicate us and our way of life."

Her hands slid off her hips. Her eyes instantly went from little slits of accusation to large saucers of surprise and her mouth dropped open. His dragon pushed him to go to her, to comfort her, but Aidan knew she needed to work this out for herself. His poor mate had gotten one shock after another in the last twelve hours and unfortunately, there were bigger ones to come. Closing and opening her mouth a couple of times, Grace started to pace in front of him.

"So you were talking to one of your 'brethren' just now?" She stepped closer, waiting for his answer.

Aidan nodded, not wanting to disrupt her thought process as she wrestled with this new information. Pacing, Grace spoke as she wore a groove in the carpet.

"And from the way you had a hold of my hips, I'm guessing whatever he told you was *not* good news?"

She looked over her shoulder while passing in front of him. He nodded once, confirming it was most definitely not good news. She stopped in front of him, resumed her warrior stance, and blurted out, "What are you, Aidan?"

Stunned by her direct question, it took almost three heartbeats before he could find his voice. Rising from the couch, still completely naked, Aidan closed the distance between them. He opened his heart and mind wide, hoping she could see all that he was. Placing his hand over her heart, he lifted hers and placed over his heart.

It's now or never.

"I'm going need you trust me, *mo ghra'*. You're going to have to take a lot of what I say on faith… something I know isn't easy for you." He paused while she unconsciously nodded then added, "I'm gonna need you to *trust* me."

He searched her eyes for any signs of doubt or a hint of what she was thinking. All he saw was her want to hear him out and absolute need to believe in him. Aidan knew Grace felt the pull and was looking to him to help her understand what she was feeling.

It's time.

He needed her to *know him*.

"Like I said, there are six of us. Rayne, who you already know. Lance and Royce, who were with me last night, plus Devon and Aaron, who you'll meet as soon as they get here. Just a head's up, Aaron is my twin. And before you ask, *no,* we are *not* identical, but it is painfully obvious that we're brothers."

He winked and continued his explanation. "Now, hold on cause here's where it gets tricky. We're descendants of an ancient race of warriors. Our families were chosen above all others because they epitomized the characteristics of the most revered knights. In the sixth century, shortly after King Arthur's disappearance, our brave ancestors took up the fight against those who would've seen them exterminated. This honor has been passed down generation after generation to the male members of our families."

With his hand covering her heart and his enhanced senses, he monitored changes in her heart beat and breathing. Now, more than ever, he needed her *with* him in every way. He had to know she was truly grasping what he was saying…

Cause I'm afraid I'm about to blow her mind.

He prayed to the Heavens for her *intuition* to help her believe him. Aidan knew the Universe did *not* make mistakes. Grace was his mate, the one above all others destined to be at his side, in this life and the next. She was the other half of his soul, the completion of the man and his beast, but he really wished this part of the mating came with an instruction manual.

"Grace, I need you to keep an open mind. There's more to the story… more that will require your absolute faith in me. I will *never* lie to you, you must know that." He paused, giving his words the impact they needed.

"I want you to open those *spidey senses* of yours wide and let them show you the truth." He smiled to ease their tension. "The men I told you about, my ancestors and those of the men I'm proud to call brethren, were also chosen by the dragons fighting alongside those brave knights.

"You see, the dragons were being driven into extinction by a group of zealots trained to exterminate their kin. That, coupled with the growing human population, made keeping their existence a secret almost impossible. With the help of the original mage, the giant warriors combined their very souls with the knight of their choosing. Once the spell was cast, the *heart* of the dragon resided within the man. Man and dragon learned to coexist and when needed, the dragon would come forth to defend those in need."

He felt her heart pound, heard her breathing escalate, and watched a flood of thoughts whisk through her eyes. "Are you still with me, *mo chroí*?"

Grace nodded. "Yeah, I am." She held his gaze. "No matter how hard I try *not* to believe what you're saying, *everything* in me says you're speaking the absolute truth." She shook her head as if to make it all change, then asked, "How can that be? This is the shit of fantasy novels. How can it be happening right in front of me?"

He pulled her against his chest, thrilled when her arms automatically wrapped around his waist. At the touch of her hands, the tattoo on his lower back began to move. He knew she could feel little shocks through her fingertips and up her arms. Grace pulled back and slowly walked around his body.

Aidan stood still. She had to investigate what she'd felt, it was her nature. Grace had to *see to believe*. This was one of the many ways the dragon *felt* their mate. The beast needed this as much as Grace did. She wasn't only the light to Aidan's soul… she provided it for the dragon also. This was a *very* important introduction.

CHAPTER TWENTY-TWO

Grace stood a step away from Aidan, watching as the beautiful tattoo she'd admired the other day *literally* came alive on his back.

The dragon's silver scales shimmered in the growing morning light. The incredible creature puffed up at her inspection, proud she was taking notice. Moving forward, Grace placed her fingers on the wing tip at the nape of Aidan's neck. The markings rippled, building the electricity flowing between them.

She traced the intricate patterns to the beast's massive body, imagining how beautiful the majestic warrior must look in flight. Caressing its neck, Grace made her way towards its aristocratic head, marveling at the long spikes and curved horns sitting impressively on his brow, head, and neck.

As she reached its eyes, Grace was surprised to see those massive orbs were the same intoxicating whisky color as those of the man who was capturing her heart. Looking into those amazing eyes, she finally understood the statement, 'eyes are the windows to the soul'. She could see the centuries of pride and honor within this fantastic beast. There was understanding and a frighteningly deep recognition that threatened to rattle her resolve. At the same time, it made her feel a part of something important. She'd been irrevocably changed. A sense of belonging warmed her from the inside out.

Love and unconditional acceptance shone out of those huge crystalline eyes. A weight she hadn't realized was present lifted from her shoulders. The connection she shared with the dragon was just as deep and true as the one she felt with the man. The feeling of absolute rightness thrummed through her system. Grace leaned forward, pressing her lips right below the dragon's eye. The emotions flowed freely from the majestic warrior, threatening to overwhelm her.

All she'd been taught about logic and reason did not apply. What she was seeing with her own eyes, was real. She was a part of something so much bigger than herself…so much more than she ever could've imagined before meeting Aidan.

Walking around to stand in front of Aidan, Grace found him with his eyes closed, breathing heavily through opened lips, fists clenched at his sides. She stood on her tiptoes, braced her palms on his chest, and laid her lips to his cheek, just as she'd done with his dragon. His eyes slowly opened. Grace was floored by the sheer force of the emotions that slammed into her.

Aidan's arms came around her. "How are you doing, *mo ghra'*? I know this is a lot to take in and I'm dumping it on you so much faster than I would've liked?"

"Well…I have to admit I *am* surprised that I'm not freaking out. Kinda makes me wonder if I hit my head harder than I thought last night." She chuckled. "I guess it'll take time to completely come to terms with the fact that dragons *are real* and men can change into them.

"You know million dollar movies are made about this shit, right? My *intuition* tells me you're being honest. I can't deny what I just witnessed with my own two eyes, but I *still* need to understand why I feel so drawn to *you*? What is it about *you* that makes me feel like we're meant to be together? That you're somehow what I've been searching for my whole life?" She shook her head. "These are *not* normal feelings to have after only knowing someone such a short time."

"It's easily explained, but once again requires a leap of faith on your part."

She nodded her head for him to continue.

"One of the most important milestones in a dragon shifter's life is finding his mate. She's the one female created by the Universe just for him. She's the other half of his soul, the completion of the man *and* his beast. Their peace, love, and light. She's the one person with the ability to ground them…make them *whole*. Although they've survived and been successful for many years, these two beings only truly begin to live when *she* is part of their life.

"You, Grace, are my mate. The light of my soul. You complete me, and the dragon that dwells within, in ways I'd only ever heard stories about. You've been a part of me from the first moment I knew you existed. The moment I caught your scent over six years ago, I *knew*, but circumstances prevented me from coming to you. When I saw you again all these years later, it was solidified in my heart…*you* are the other half of my soul.

"So, *mo ghra'*, you ask why you're drawn to me? Why the feelings you have for me are stronger and deeper than you've ever experienced with another? It's because we *are* destined to be together. Your soul recognizes mine just as mine recognizes yours. Like has called to like. The incredible feelings we're discovering for each other will *not* be denied. They'll grow *stronger*, my beautiful Grace. Our bond will solidify. After our official mating, you'll possess many of the same talents I have. We'll be able to speak directly into one another's minds. I'll teach you to draw on my dragon magic."

Grace stood still, absorbing all she'd learned since waking a few hours earlier. None of the warning bells or weird feelings that accompanied a deception came to her. If she concentrated *really hard*, she could feel nothing but a need to love and protect her coming from Aidan.

Love?

Yep, that's definitely what it was, and if she was completely honest with herself, she felt it growing within her too.

Well, damn. When did that happen?

Grace knew Aidan was waiting for her to say something. His patience was wearing thin. It was written across his face. She could feel his need to grab her and kiss, to protect and comfort her, but was waiting for her to make the first move…something she truly appreciated.

He gets me.

Finally, she gave in and spoke. "Everything you've said defies logic. I've learned to deal with things from an analytical perspective for the most part. I collect the facts and make my decisions based on what I've collected. All of that being said, I *do know* there are things in this world that defy explanation. They take a leap of faith. My *spidey senses* are one of those things." She winked and chuckled at his cheeky grin before adding, "Are you telling me that you're being completely honest with me no matter how fantastic this all seems?"

He nodded as she covered her heart with her hand. "Good, because it's what I feel in here that makes me say to *hell* with logic.

CHAPTER TWENTY-THREE

Aidan pulled her into his arms…just holding her… never wanting to let her go. *Hell,* he'd felt that from the moment she'd walked through the front door three days ago.

"'A' we're about twenty minutes out, so make sure you're decent." Lance teased through their link.

"We'll be ready." Aidan let his frustration at the situation and the lack of time to spend with his mate flow through their connection.

"You better be. Max, Sophia, and some of their cats are coming, too. He has information you need to hear in person."

"Well hell, the more the merrier, I guess." Aidan's tone was getting sharper by the minute. *"See ya when you get here."* And he cut their connection.

Turning to Grace, he explained. "*Mo ghra'*, Lance and the others are twenty minutes from here, as well as some other associates of ours. They're coming to discuss the men who attacked you and their connection to *our* worst enemy. As much as I hate to admit it, we need to get dressed before they get here."

"Okay, but this discussion is *far* from over. I have lots of questions and I also want to know what the other names you've been calling me mean. Finding out what those guys wanted last night is important, but my questions will have to be answered and…I have a *very good* memory," she agreed with the cheeky little grin he loved on her face.

Turning on her heels, Grace started towards the hall. "You better hurry, *dragon man*, at least I have a blanket on." She chuckled over her shoulder.

Aidan headed after her, smiling from ear to ear. Damn she was fiery, and he loved every feisty inch of her.

CHAPTER TWENTY-FOUR

Grace stood beside Aidan in the garden behind Kyndel's apartment, watching for any sign of his *brethren*. He'd laughed when she asked if they'd be flying in. She hadn't thought it was funny until he started laughing, then she realized what she'd said. It didn't take long before they were both out of breath with tears in their eyes.

Aidan made Grace feel free to be herself. He put her at ease. She didn't have to work for his acceptance; it was freely given…no strings attached.

Best feeling ever…

They hadn't been more than a few feet apart since making love this morning. Grace usually needed her space. She'd never been comfortable with being close to someone for long periods of time, but with Aidan, it just felt right. The need to be close to one another, touching whenever possible, pleasantly surprised her. They were like two puzzle pieces. They fit together perfectly, no gaps, no spaces. Meant to be together. She was learning his unique body language and *knew* he was learning hers.

The tension running through his body as he stood with his arm wrapped around her waist was growing. He continually rubbed his thumb over an especially sensitive patch of skin above the waistband of her jeans. She wondered if he did it to distract her or himself, and decided it was a little of both. Sparks ran through her body from his touch. They kept her grounded and focused. He was infusing her with his strength and determination. She knew he didn't doubt her; Aidan was simply sharing his power and she appreciated it.

While they waited, Grace replayed their discussion over and over, making sure she hadn't missed anything. Looking for some way *not* to believe all she'd been told. No matter how she spun it, she *knew* he was telling the truth. Felt it in her soul. But why hadn't Kyndel told her any of this?

Grace was hurt. Her best friend had kept the biggest secret of their lives from her. Aidan explained secrecy was the only way their kin survived and Kyndel was trying to protect Grace the only way she knew how. He told her no one had known she was his mate until recently. He'd kept it quiet for all those years and she wondered why.

When she questioned him, pain and anger flash through his eyes, along with the ever-present need to protect her. There were *so many* things they still needed to discuss, but there wasn't time with all the chaos. Grace found herself cataloging all her fantastic discoveries like she did with witness testimonies and evidence when she was working a case. It was her way of looking at everything she'd learned and staying sane at the same time. After reviewing it all, Grace figured she understood why Kyndel kept secrets, but didn't make it hurt any less. At least now they could share everything, or at least, Grace hoped so.

Aidan tensed beside her. Following his stare, she saw five huge men approaching. They looked like the front line of the Dallas Cowboys and they were also incredibly easy on the eyes. But none held a candle to the man at her side.

Kyndel's husband, Rayne, or mate as Grace now knew, was in the middle. Most definitely the one in charge, though not the biggest, an air of authority and command surrounded him. When she'd met him a few months ago, something about him set off her *intuition*. It wasn't necessarily bad…it was more of a 'don't f*** with me' vibe. Now, it all made sense.

The guy walking next to Rayne was absolutely the biggest man she'd ever seen. At least a head taller than Aidan's six foot three inches, the giant's chest and shoulders were so wide she now understood the statement 'as broad as a barn'. All of that aside, it was his curly carrot-red hair standing out in every direction on the top of his very large head that made him truly extraordinary. Grace remembered catching a glimpse of him in the parking garage, but he'd been wearing a beanie cap and she'd been busy trying to stay alive, so his hair was a huge surprise in the light of day.

Looking at the line of men quickly approaching, Grace did a double take at the almost identical replica of the man at her side. His twin's light brown hair was wavy and touched the collar of his T-shirt. He walked with purpose; his head held high, shoulders straight, with a swagger just like her mate. Aidan said they weren't identical, but from where she stood, they were as close as two people could be. Watching intently, Grace finally saw it… *his eyes*.

They were a deep, dark blue, reminding her of the Mediterranean Sea she'd seen while on a cruise with her parents when she was ten years old. Grace would never forget the amazing color of the water as it lapped against the side of the ship. A hue that now stared back at her. But instead of being warmed by it, she felt a chill from the emotions raging within their blue depths.

Grace leaned closer to Aidan, seeking shelter the closer 'the brother' got. Her mate's twin must've realized he was scaring her, for in the next instant, his eyes cleared and the corner of his mouth lifted in a sorry attempt at a smile. There was something more going on with him and Grace intended to find out what it was.

Looking down the line, Grace was sure the guy on the end had also been in the garage with them last night. Such a contrast to Aidan's twin, this man reminded her of a surfer with his almost white-blond hair, twinkling light blue eyes, and little dimple that winked at her from the corner of his cocky grin. He was the first to reach them, and before she could raise her hand to shake his, he was scooping her up in a hug.

"Put her down now, you asshole. She's injured and *my mate*," Aidan growled at her side.

The surfer set her feet on the ground and held her at arm's length, giving her the once over. "Well, ya got quite a scratch there on your cheek, Princess. I wondered if you would have a black eye today. Glad to see you don't." He winked and chuckled as Aidan pulled her from his grasp, positioning her on his *other* side.

She looked up and caught all the men trying to keep from cracking up. It was then she realized what the surfer had called her and asked, "What did you call me…?"

"Name's Lance and I called you Princess." He stood waiting for her answer. She could tell he was holding back a laugh.

"Why would you call me Princess? *You* don't even know me," she snapped, unable to stop her temper from rising. She hated that name. Brent, the asshole, had called her that name. It made the little hairs at the back of her neck stand on end to hear it used again after all these years.

"Darlin', in case you haven't noticed, you're a dead ringer for Snow White. You know the princess from the fairy tales? You look exactly like all the pictures I've seen in the books the little *vibrias* read back at the lair." He smiled a smile she was sure had charmed more than one lady out of her panties. "Or I could call you Hellcat after the way you fought those guys last night." He winked and took a step back before Aidan could grab his arm.

"She has a name, *jerk*," Aidan spat.

"I can speak for myself, Aidan." She rubbed the hand he had resting on her waist to ease the sting of her statement, and noticed the wide eyes staring at her from the men he called brethren. She directed her next comment to Lance and decided to be as cheeky as he'd been. "I prefer Hellcat." Then she winked to show she could give as good as she got.

"Hellcat, it is then." Lance laughed aloud with the rest following suit. "We've decided you girls need nicknames, kind of like warning labels."

She lifted her hand to smack his arm. He twisted a little to avoid the slap and chuckled.

"No, no, no…just kidding. Really, we just like to make sure you know how welcome you are to the Force and to the clan." His smile said he had a heart of gold, but the twinkle in his eye said he caused more than his share of trouble.

"One more thing. What does *vibria* mean?" she asked while it was still fresh in her mind.

Lance smiled. "Female dragon."

"Thanks." Grace wondered if she would ever get the hang of this *new* language.

Rayne stepped forward, almost smiling. "Well, since Lance has caused trouble and picked a nickname for you, I guess I can finally ask how you're feeling. Kyndel's worried sick. She can't wait for you to join her at our home. I had to promise to have you there as soon as possible to keep her from coming with us." Grace saw all the love he felt for her friend. She'd never known love like that was possible. Now she had to face the fact she was falling in love with the man standing at her side. Tucking the thought away for another time, she saw the big red-haired man making his way to her.

"I'm so glad to see you're doing better today. I'm Royce by the way. Glad to formally meet you." He smiled the most genuine, pure smile she'd ever seen. This man truly was a gentle giant. His deep brown eyes shone with a kindness rarely seen in *anyone*, let alone someone of his size.

"Royce is our medic, cook, and basically mother to all of us when we are out on a mission," Aidan whispered in her ear. He'd moved and was hugging her from behind, with his chin on her shoulder.

"I am *not* their mother." Royce shook his head. "If I was, I would've kicked all their butts long ago." He smiled his warm, caring smile again. "How are you feeling today, *really*? Anything I should take a look at?"

Grace was blown away by the genuine concern he showed for her. Her cheeks hurt from the huge smile crossing her face. "No, I'm fine, but thank you so much for asking."

It was Royce's turn to smile big and wide. "Sure enough. Anytime. You're one of us now. We'll all have your back." And with that, he stepped back.

Grace watched Royce pick up a huge duffle and move towards the house. Aidan's twin caught her eye, so she asked, "You're Aaron, right?" He nodded at her comment.

"Aidan said you guys weren't identical." Grace held a little tighter to her mate's hand. "But there's no denying you're brothers." She watched for any signs of the storm she'd seen brewing in his eyes earlier, but there was none. Neither did her *spidey senses* give any indication he was anything but ready to get this business settled.

"Yeah, he's my *younger* brother, but I'm the good looking one." He winked and she realized he was trying to make her more comfortable.

Aidan snorted beside her, "Older by two minutes and that's all I've heard for the last hundred years…*shit!*"

Grace spun around in Aidan's arms and grabbed the lapels of his leather jacket, "A hundred years?" She knew her voice was rising, but she'd just received the shock of her life, and that was saying something with all she'd learned in the last few hours.

"Yes, *mo ghra'*. Aaron and I had our one hundredth birthday this year. I told you we're infused with the magic of our dragon. One of the many advantages is a much longer lifespan. We age at a much slower rate than humans."

"Are you two the oldest?" she asked, trying to keep her voice from cracking. The men standing around her laughed.

Oh damn…this is about to get even more complicated.

Aidan loosened the death grip she had on his jacket. He rubbed her palms with his thumbs as he spoke. "No, *mo chroi*, we're the *youngest* of our Force."

"The youngest?" Her voice rose with her panic.

"Yes. The oldest of our Force is Royce. He's a hundred and fifty-six." She tried to process what he was saying, but overload was threatening to take her down.

Before she could respond, Aidan picked her up and moved them to the swing at the corner of the yard. He sat with her on his lap and gently rocked the swing. When he spoke, she could hear his concern. "Grace, I'm sorry I blurted that out. I didn't even think to bring up our longer than normal lifespan or my age when we were talking before. There's so much we have to learn about one another."

He paused. After a few seconds, she slowly nodded for him to continue. "And I never want you to learn anything about me the way you just did. I'm so sorry."

Aidan leaned forward and pressed a kiss to her forehead. The slight tremor in his hands where they held hers told her he was as shaken as she was. Trying hard not to lose it in front of people she'd just met, Grace kept her eyes closed, even when Aidan pulled away.

Deep in thought, she almost missed his whispered, *"Mo ghra'?"*

Grace wasn't ready to open her eyes and face him just yet. The fact that she'd shared the hottest, most intimate sexual experience of her life with a *hundred year old dragon shifter* was blowing her mind. Add to it that he was the *youngest* of the group of men she'd just met and Grace contemplated calling the therapist her mother frequently visited.

Opening her eyes, Grace was met with a look of unconditional love from the man who was quickly stealing her heart. No recrimination for her reaction at the revelation of his age. No rage that she'd confronted him in front of his brethren… just love… *for her*. All of it, right there in his eyes. Aidan hid nothing.

Humbled and overwhelmed, Grace admitted she was experiencing the same emotions within her own heart. Placing her hand on his cheek, she explained, "It's okay, Aidan. I was shocked, but I'm fine now. I know you'd never keep anything from me." Grinning, she continued, "You're pretty sexy for an old man." Then waggled her eyebrows before laughing aloud.

"You think you're funny, do you, *Hellcat*?"

Just a second too late Grace saw the mischief in his eyes. Faster than she could track, Aidan's hands were on her sides and he was tickling her like her grandpa had when she was a little girl. She wiggled and twisted, trying anything to get out of his grasp, but the man was just too *damn fast*.

"Aidan, stop!" She gasped.

"Oh no, *mo chroi*, you made fun of me. This is your punishment."

Grace was laughing so hard it was hard to catch her breath. The more she struggled, the more he tickled. Tears ran down her face. She could tell from his look that he was nowhere near finished.

Doing the first thing that came to mind, Grace slammed her lips to his. Aidan gasped his surprise. She thrust her tongue into his mouth and the switch was flipped. One minute they were laughing and playing, the next electricity exploded between them.

The kiss was off the charts. Like gasoline poured on a fire. They were branding each other for all time. Grace slid her tongue from his mouth and Aidan took control. Palming the back of her head, he positioned her so his tongue could penetrate every part of her mouth, thrusting in and out. Grace loved his dominance. She wished they had time to go back in the house, strip each other bare, and start right where they'd left off.

CHAPTER TWENTY-FIVE

Aidan moved to her jaw. Unable to get enough of Grace, he nibbled and tasted until he reached her ear. Her hands buried in his hair and the moans coming from deep in her throat spurred him on. Kissing down her neck, he savored every delectable inch. Reaching up to move the collar of her blouse, he was so shocked when she pulled his hair that he lifted his head to make sure she was okay.

Eyes hooded with passion, lips swollen from their amazing kiss, Grace was a vision. He leaned in, already missing her taste on his lips, but his mate placed her hand in the middle of his chest and shook her head. They sat looking at one another, breathing like they'd run a marathon, while the seconds ticked by.

Moving first, Grace leaned forward, gently laying her lips on his. She placed soft kisses along his bottom lip, then nibbled his upper lip, begging entrance. Aidan opened slowly, allowing just the very tip of her tongue to breach the entrance. This was different than anything they'd shared so far. His mate wanted control and he could deny her *nothing*.

Aidan wanted to shout his joy to the Heavens. The most beautiful woman in the world, his mate, was sitting on his lap, *kissing him*. He allowed her complete access. She kissed him long and slow, deepening the kiss, touching every inch of his mouth. He was humbled that she wanted to know everything about him.

Grace was building a fire and Aidan was happy to be burned by its flame. The exquisite sensations he experienced at his mate's mouth bathed his mind and body in heat and passion. She kept the kiss slow and deep. He fought not to take charge…not to speed things along. It took all his considerable control to hold both him and his dragon at bay. This was about Grace. She needed to show him what she was feeling.

It was apparent from the time they'd spent together that she needed her independence. Grace had to know she was walking into this with him on *her* terms. His mate was the perfect combination of intelligence, heart, beauty, and breathtaking sensuality. He could feel their mating bond grow stronger with each heartbeat.

His dragon wanted to soar. Grace was falling in love with him. His restraint broke. He lifted his hands to her hair, tilted her head to the side, and deepened their kiss. Aidan was so lost to his amazing mate he missed the scent of the man standing to the side of the swing, until the sound of a cleared throat broke them apart.

Aidan jumped to his feet, placing Grace behind him, ready to face off with the person who had gotten past his defenses. Max stood perfectly still, his hands at his sides while Aidan fought for control. In all of his hundred years, *no one* had *ever* gotten near without him knowing. Now, when he should've been protecting Grace, he'd been caught unaware. His mate played hell with his concentration. It was time to get his head out of his ass until she was safe with his clan.

Max smiled a knowing smile. "Sorry to interrupt, but I'm afraid we don't have much time."

"No problem, sorry to have jumped at you." Aidan tried not to sound as pissed as he was. "I should've been paying attention."

He felt Grace peek around his arm. Stepping to the side, he grasped her hand. "This is Grace Kensington, *my mate*."

Max's eyebrows shot up at the introduction, but Aidan decided to ignore the King's playful attitude. "Grace, this is Maximillian Prentice." He gave Max a pointed look, telling him she was unaware of his 'furry side'.

Holding out his hand, Max grinned. "Pleasure to meet you, Grace. I apologize for the intrusion, but I have some information I'm sure both of you will find *very* interesting."

"Pleasure to meet you as well, Mr. Prentice."

"No need for formality. My friends call me Max." He winked and smiled that same damn smile, making Aidan want to punch him in the mouth.

Aidan knew Max was messing with him. The King of the Big Cats was never anything but a grumpy old alley cat when they talked. *Now,* he was fawning all over Grace just to piss Aidan off. If the mangy tomcat wasn't careful, Aidan was going to follow through with his violent thoughts whether Max was 'royalty' or not.

"Why don't we head over with the others? I'm sure they all need to hear whatever it is you have to say." Aidan pulled Grace closer to his side and headed in the direction of his Force, letting Max follow.

His brethren were all chuckling as he and Grace approached, but it was his twin who just had to say something. "Sorry, bro. Max got to you before we knew what he was doing." Aaron was working so hard to keep from laughing it was difficult for Aidan to make out what he was saying.

"Yeah, bro, we completely missed him until you were already on your feet." Lance chimed in with a wicked glint in his eyes and an evil grin on his face. Aidan knew they were both as full of shit as the pigpens they used to clean as children.

Aidan shook his head. He couldn't be mad at them. *Hell*, he would've done the same if the roles were reversed. "Paybacks are a bitch, assholes," he chuckled, and the whole group erupted into laughter.

"All right, enough screwing around. Max has information we need, so shut up and listen," Rayne growled in a low, controlled tone, his feral smile letting them know he was serious.

CHAPTER TWENTY-SIX

Andrew hadn't been able to think of anything but the wizards' plans for increasing their black magic. The wizard leader had been secretive, giving away no details. The bastard would only say they were working with a powerful man who would be able to deliver exactly what they needed to perform the ritual. The fucking idiot had actually cackled like a loon when he told Andrew how strong they would be once the ritual was complete. He rambled on and on about the wizard army he was building and how they would be unstoppable. His plans included destroying anyone who stood against them, *including* the dragon shifters. Andrew couldn't let that happen. Those worthless, half-witted dragons were *his* to destroy. Only his revenge mattered, not the stupid plans of some crazy wizard.

Immediately after leaving their compound, Andrew began researching how someone as powerful as the wizard leader could increase his powerbase. Hours later, he was still empty-handed. Even the old texts from Merlin's counterparts were a dead end.

Having his power back was all he needed to complete his well-laid plans for revenge. It was imperative he know what the wizards were doing. Andrew was prepared to kill them as soon as he was at full strength. If he didn't, they would turn on him whenever they decided he was no longer valuable. He'd suffered at the hands of their kind before, knew what they were capable of, and had vowed it would *never* happen again. There were other covens filled with stupid wizards he could use in the future, but eventually, they all would die… sins of the brother and all that shit.

If even half the shit the wizard leader spewed was the truth, the power harvested from one ritual would be enough for a lifetime. The maniacal idiot called it the *infinita potestate* or, *Unending Power*.

No sooner had the words left the wizard's mouth than the hair at the nape of Andrew's neck stood on end and he was filled with dread. There was too much he didn't know, and the asshole wasn't willing to share, for Andrew to drop his guard. The traitor had gone off half-cocked once in his life, and look where that had gotten him. There was no way he would be caught unaware again.

Throwing another book onto the growing pile on the floor, Andrew began pacing the creaky floor of his rented lair. There had to be a way to figure out what was going on, how all the pieces fit together. He thought about the men who attacked Aidan's mate. The stink of black magic was undeniable, but when he'd questioned the wizard leader, the jerk shrugged it off… said they were expendable muscle.

On his umpteenth pass across the living room, his cell phone rang. Grabbing it from the table, he barked, "Yeah."

"I need to see you right away. Plans have changed," the wizard leader commanded with his usual air of superiority. It would be a pleasure to watch him die.

Soon...very soon....

"Where?" Andrew asked, his slowly returning dragon senses alerting him to danger.

"Get in the car and drive south. I'll send directions to your cell phone in exactly five minutes," the wizard ordered.

"Look, I'm not into this cloak and dagger shit. Just tell me where I'm going and I'll meet you there," Andrew growled.

"You *will* do as I say. I have to make sure you're not followed. It's up to you. You need me... I definitely do *not need you*."

Oh yeah, this fucker was going to die very slowly and very painfully. Through gritted teeth, Andrew answered, "Fine. I'm leaving now. I better *not* be driving all over hell's half acre for nothing."

"Just drive. You'll have the directions in five minutes. Don't keep me waiting." The call disconnected before Andrew could respond.

Visions of the torture he would bestow upon the wizard leader danced in his head as he started the car. The son of a bitch really thought he was superior.

HA!

He hadn't even figured out what Andrew was; let alone *who* he was. Well, wasn't the self-righteous prick in for a surprise! He smiled, in spite of himself. They would all pay for what he had suffered.

Every last one of them...

CHAPTER TWENTY-SEVEN

Aidan was still fuming. Grace actually talked him into letting her go with them to check out the warehouse Max's people found. She was good...really good, but there was no way he could let her wander into danger. Even if everything had been scouted and scouted again and *should* be safe.

He hated to admit the werepanther trackers were the best. Their sense of smell and ability to move practically unseen was better than any dragon. The panthers followed the scent of the thugs from their most recent meeting with the wizard leader, back to an abandoned auto parts warehouse ten miles outside of town. They'd gotten in and taken pictures.

It was a despicable scene. At least fifty huge cages, big enough to detain a human, lined an entire wall of the middle level. His skin crawled remembering the dirty cots with chains and cuffs attached, lying in wait for their next victim. The assholes were planning something huge, and somehow the traitor was involved. When Grace explained what her office knew about 'The Auctioneer' and the abduction of many young women, it seemed like another piece of the horrific puzzle had fallen into place. They still needed to figure out what fate awaited the girls after they were caught and caged.

Along with the pictures, Max appropriated the blueprints. It was agreed the wizards and their criminal partners were planning to bring the abducted women through the tunnels leading to the lower level of the building. From the diagram, it appeared they could drive right up to the freight elevators, unload their cargo, back out, and be on their way with little or no fuss. Aidan was sure everything would happen in the middle of the night, making it almost impossible for anyone to see. It was the perfect set up.

They needed to see for themselves. Time was of the essence. The werepanthers hadn't seen anyone at the building for hours, and whatever the assholes were planning was happening soon. The wizards were using 'The Auctioneer's' network. Whatever they were doing was guaranteed to be horrific. The Guard had to shut it down.

Any other time, Aidan would be all for charging in and ending their enemies' plans, but having Grace with them changed *everything*. He'd mentioned taking her to the lair to stay with Kyndel. In two-point-two seconds Grace had gone all lawyer on his ass, firing off a list of reasons as long as his arm about why she should go.

If that wasn't bad enough, his brethren sided with her. Especially after she charmed them by producing the file he thought he'd hidden from her. Aidan was pissed. No one seemed to care about Grace's safety. Pride overrode fear for her safety as he watched her explain all she knew about 'The Auctioneer' and the men who worked for him. Grace was intelligent and fearless.

The final nail in the coffin of his fight to take her to Kyndel was the time it would take for him to get her to the lair and then get back to his Force. His brethren were right…he *knew* it. They needed to get to the warehouse and assess the situation so they could prepare for whatever was going down, but he didn't have to like it.

Aidan made Grace promise to stay in the Escalade with the werepanthers, while he, the dragons, and the other werepanthers scouted. She argued vehemently that she needed to see the warehouse. Tried her hardest to convince them she would be able to tell exactly what was going on, but on that point, all the men finally agreed with him.

About time, assholes!

She'd huffed, puffed, and argued with anyone who'd listen as they prepared to leave, until he took her around the corner and kissed her senseless. Aidan would never admit it but he needed that kiss as much, *probably more*, than she did. He would just never get enough of her.

As they raced out of town, Grace on the back of his bike, his brethren riding along side, while the panthers followed in the SUVs, he only wished he could shake the feeling that something just didn't add up.

CHAPTER TWENTY-EIGHT

Grace spent most of the ride trying to come up with an argument Aidan would listen to. She *had* to go into the warehouse. Above everyone else in their convoy, she knew what to look for. She'd been working this case for close to a *year*.

Why couldn't he see that?

Yes, she was scared. There was danger in everything they'd discussed during the intense conversation at Kyndel's, but he had to trust her. If she failed, he would be there. After all, she was not some child to be left in the car while the *big boys* went to face the danger. Sure, Aidan's brethren were all dragon shifters and possessed 'special' abilities, but Grace was no shrinking violet. She had skills…even if they *were* running and screaming.

They're still skills…pfft…

She wanted to ask Aidan about Max, Sophia, and the men who accompanied them. Her *spidey senses* were going crazy, telling her they were *more* than they appeared to be. They weren't dragon shifters, of that she was sure, but they weren't human either.

During their strategy session, she'd watched as Max and Sophia, along with some guy they called Ernesto, exchanged knowing looks. Grace knew Aidan and his brothers did their mindspeak thing. She actually felt a little buzz from her *intuition* when the Guardsmen were talking mind-to-mind. There was none of that with Max and his crew, but something in the way they looked at each other made her think they possessed their own special abilities.

Then there was the way they were 'scenting' the air all the time, putting their noses up and sniffing like they could tell what was coming by the smells in the air. It was all so surreal but had nothing to do with the fact that she needed to convince Aidan to let her go into that warehouse. She had to stop getting sidetracked, but who could really blame her?

I have to get into that building. I have to see with my own eyes.

The pictures would help with her case, but she needed to find evidence of 'The Auctioneer' and his crew's involvement. One little piece of irrefutable evidence would seal the deal and send the lying, kidnapping, asshole away for the rest of his life.

Aidan asked what she was looking for and assured her he would find it. Grace wished it was that easy, but it wasn't something she could explain. She would know *it* when she saw it, and to see it she had to get into that building. It was absolutely the most frustrating situation. Aidan was concerned for her. Hell, she was concerned for herself…, for him …, and for all of the others. Even with all their extraordinary abilities, the wizards they talked about sounded deadly.

But are they deadly enough to take down a dragon? That's the real question…

CHAPTER TWENTY-NINE

Aidan pulled his Harley off the road into a tourist area, a half a mile from the abandoned warehouse, and waited for the others to catch up. It was decided they would approach from the back, through a long forgotten park.

Putting the kickstand down, he helped Grace climb off the back. She immediately started to pace, her frustration a living, breathing entity between them. His mate was upset that he wouldn't let her go into the warehouse. Aidan prayed for the hundredth time that she see he simply could *not* risk her safety. The scene from her attack still played on a loop every time he closed his eyes. There was simply no way she was going to get hurt if he had *anything* to say about it.

He leaned against the seat of his bike, watching her pace and talk to herself. She was preparing her next argument and from the looks of it, he was going to be outmatched. On her third trip past him, Aidan grabbed Grace around the waist. She yelped as he lifted and twisted her until she ended up against him, those amazing blue eyes wide with surprise, staring at him, just as he'd planned.

"What is that beautiful mind of yours cooking up, *mo chroí*?" Aidan waited to see if she would tell him what scheme she was concocting.

Grace worried her bottom lip with her teeth, a sure sign she was going to say something he wasn't going to like. They may have just met, but he was quickly learning her tells, and right now, his brilliant *and* persistent mate was going to suggest something he was sure would shave years off his life.

CHAPTER THIRTY

She took a deep breath. It was now or never. The sound of the other motorcycles was echoing through the trees. She had maybe a minute to convince him. "I want you to hear me out. No kissing me to shut me up or enlisting the help of the others. Just listen to me, *please*."

Aidan nodded and started rubbing circles on either side of her waist with his thumbs. She was sure it was to comfort himself, but it was working for her, too.

"I know you're worried I could get hurt if I go with y'all. I'm worried, too. But I want you to think about one thing." She paused, staring right into the eyes that had become the anchor for her soul.

The brown, blue, and green flecks within those amber depths swirled like a brewing storm. She'd been adrift her whole life, searching for something or *someone* to be hers and hers *alone*. This man with his incredible strength, fantastic heritage, and hypnotic eyes, swept her off her feet and filled the void she hadn't even known was there. Shaken by her revelation, she retained her focus. She *had* to convince him going with him was worth the risk.

"Think of all the girls who've gone missing. Where are they? Why can't we find any leads? What if this is the *one chance* we have to get information that will help us find those girls and the assholes who took them? This could be it. We need to stop this madness. Stop the people taking young woman from those who love them."

Aidan's stare was so intense she didn't dare stop talking. She had his undivided attention and needed to capitalize on the opportunity. "I thought all the way here about how to explain to you what I'm looking for but honestly, I won't know until I see it."

Had it not been for his thumbs still rubbing her sides she would've wondered if he was still awake, Aidan sat *that* still. Hurrying on before he disagreed, she added, "Don't you see? I *have* to do this. I *have* to find out what happened to those girls. I *have* to make sure it doesn't happen to anyone else."

Her voice cracked on the last few words. She wasn't someone who cried easily, but all these missing young women and the prospect of more being abducted broke her heart. She watched his internal debate. He was seriously considering everything she'd said. From the way his brow furrowed and lips pursed, he didn't like where it led. Grace bit her lip to keep from interrupting his contemplation. He had to make this decision himself. The storm she'd seen brewing in his eyes earlier was nothing compared to the powerful glare she was receiving after her well thought out argument. Aidan's eyes were actually glowing. Another extraordinary feature of her mate.

Gripping her waist, he pulled her so close their noses were almost touching, "Okay, *mo ghra'*, you win. You can go with us, but you have to promise to do whatever I say, without hesitation or discussion, no matter what. I need you to understand that you are my world. I know it seems too soon in your culture, but Grace, you are mine. You will be mine for all my days. If anything happens to you, I will cease to exist. You are my everything. I have to know you are safe. I'll give my life to make sure that happens. *Ta' mo chroi istigh ionat*. My heart is within you, *mo ghra'*. Do you understand?"

She could barely breathe. The man she was sure she was meant to spend the rest of her life with was actually going to trust her. No one had *ever* shown her such faith. Grace nodded her head while she swallowed past the lump in her throat.

"No, Grace. I need to hear you say the words," Aidan commanded, still staring directly into her eyes, completely ignoring his brethren and the others arriving all around them.

The brown, green, and blue flecks in his amber orbs were swirling out of control. The storm had broken. He was waiting to hear her agree to *his* terms. She knew without a doubt, he meant *every word* and would take nothing but her complete acquiescence.

"Yes Aidan, I'll do whatever you say, whenever you say it, without question." Grace took a quick breath, her nerves about to shake her apart. "Thank you for trusting me and believing in me. I will *not* let you down."

CHAPTER THIRTY-ONE

Aidan couldn't take it one second longer. He and Grace were bonding so quickly, and even though they were entering a dangerous situation, he and his dragon needed a taste of their luscious mate. Pulling Grace the last inch, he crushed his lips to hers. She sighed into the kiss as he slid his tongue into her mouth. What started as a kiss of possession and domination quickly turned into one of sensual affirmation. They tasted and fed off each other's mouths until they were breathless and in need of a cold shower. Investigating the abandoned warehouse could wait. There was no doubt he could have them a mile into the woods in a matter of seconds with his enhanced abilities.

Lance broke through his muddled brain, laughing as usual. *"Yo, 'A', cool it with the kissy face. The vein in Rayne's forehead is about to burst and I'm sure your mate isn't into PDA. If you don't stop, Max is gonna head over there and embarrass you in front of your pretty lady again."*

"Jealous much, ass?"

Aidan stopped kissing Grace. He held her against his chest until her breathing returned to normal. Lance was right about one thing, she would be embarrassed if she knew the other's had seen them kissing. He would have to explain that dragon shifters were very passionate and help her get over her shyness as soon all the shit was over.

Lance's last words finally penetrated his lust-fogged brain. *"Oh shit, the cat's here too?"*

"Damn straight, so get your head together and get over here." Lance laughed even harder.

Grace lifted her head. He loved to see the lazy look in her eyes and her lips swollen from his kisses, but Lance was right, it wasn't the time. "You were just talking to one of your brethren, weren't you?"

Her question surprised him. "Yeah. How did you know?"

Once again, she worried her bottom lip with her teeth. It took all of his control not to kiss her again. He had to remind himself he was waiting for her to answer his question.

"I noticed a buzzing in my head when everyone was talking back at Kyndel's. Nothing bothersome, just a little noise, like a radio station not tuned in all the way, *staticy,* ya know? Then I realized it only happened when you were looking at one of your brethren. You would shake your head or shrug or grin like someone having a conversation. It happened again just now. I figured it was one of them was telling you they were here and we should stop making out." She chuckled and he was reminded of the tinkling of little bells.

Hugging her even tighter, he sighed. "*Mo ghra'* you're amazing. Yes, Lance was giving me a hard time. I believe the buzzing sound comes from your *spidey senses* combined with our growing mating bond. As I explained before, once we've completed the official mating ceremony, you'll have some of my abilities."

"Well, I'm glad to know it's normal and I'm not losing my mind." Grace laughed as she unwrapped herself from his body.

Effortlessly stopping her struggles, he stood and kissed her forehead. "No, *mo chroi*, you aren't losing your mind, you're sharing mine."

She stood on her toes and kissed his cheek. "Is there anything in there that would embarrass me, Mr. O'Brien?"

"Nothing embarrassing, Miss Kensington, just a preview of things to come." He picked her up and swung her around in a circle before setting her safely back on the ground.

"Aidan, I'm too heavy for you to be picking up all the time." Grace chuckled and squealed at the same time.

He spun her around to face him and bent until they were once again nose-to-nose, "You are *not* heavy. I don't ever want to hear those words come out of your mouth again. I will pick you up any time I like, *mate.*"

His kissed her lips, spun her again, and whisked them over to where the others were waiting. He was going to keep her as close as possible.

She is all that matters...

CHAPTER THIRTY-TWO

From the discussion going on all around her, it sounded to Grace like they were splitting into groups to cover all four sides of the abandoned building, while only a few would actually go into the premises.

Aidan cleared his throat. "There's been a change in plans." He looked from one person to another, catching the eyes of each of his brethren then simply stating, "Grace is going in with us."

"No fucking way, 'A'." Rayne vehemently objected. "Kyndel will kick my ass if anything happens to her! What the hell are you thinking? She's your mate and you're leading her into the danger instead of keeping her out of it?"

Aidan tensed. Grace watched the muscles flex in his arms as he clenched his fists. He took a step towards Rayne and stopped. Tension flared to life between them, "You are right, *Commander*," he growled through gritted teeth. "She is *my* mate and I will protect her with every fiber of my being. This is important to her and therefore important to me. She needs to see the premises and look for the evidence to secure a conviction against the man we all believe is behind the human side of this operation. So, if she says there's no way around her presence on this inspection, then I believe her. You would do well to not concern yourself with the decisions my mate and I make together."

He took another step towards Rayne at the same time Rayne advanced toward him. Tension rose to an uncomfortable level as two of the most formidable men she'd ever seen stood toe-to-toe in an old-fashioned standoff. The pictures she'd seen in old texts of two warriors preparing for battle came to mind, minus the armor and swords. Grace had no idea how long they stood there, but her muscles started to cramp from the stress.

Lance slowly approached the two giants. Placing a hand on each man's shoulder, he joked. "Okay guys, we all know you're both bad asses and that you want what's best for our *Hellcat* here." He winked over his shoulder in Grace's direction.

He squeezed Rayne's shoulder. "Commander, she *is* 'A's' mate. What would you do if someone told you how to act with *Kyndel*?"

Not waiting for an answer, he squeezed Aidan's shoulder. "'A', we all know you'll do whatever it takes to keep your mate safe."

Grace moved closer while Lance was speaking so she could see all three of their faces. She was about to reach out and touch Aidan when she noticed the dimple in Lance's chin begin winking at her and saw the twinkle in his eyes. His next words confirmed her suspicions.

"Now, you boys just kiss and make up so we can go kick bad guy ass, okay?"

She watched the tension drain from both men. They laughed. Rayne reached across, slapped Aidan on the same shoulder Lance had been squeezing a second before, and then apologized. "Sorry, 'A'. You're right. It's between you and your mate." Then the serious look from before returned. "Just keep her close."

"I shouldn't have stepped up to you…" Aidan looked towards Grace. She closed the distance, grabbing his hand in the process. "I know you were only doing what you thought was right. She *is* my world and I'll protect her with my life. Count on it." He squeezed her hand to emphasize his point.

Rayne smiled the first genuine smile Grace had seen since meeting him for the second time. In that moment, she saw how Kyndel could've fallen in love with the big lug so quickly. Then she looked at Aidan. Her heart skipped a beat. She leaned towards him, but before her thoughts could get away from her, Lance chimed in. "See there. You girls *can* play nice."

"Shut the hell up, Lance!" Everyone yelled in unison.

She had no idea how she'd gotten mixed up with this crazy band of extraordinary people, but was damn glad she had.

CHAPTER THIRTY-THREE

Grace started to rethink the whole being thankful thing when Aidan, Rayne, and Max made the executive decision for her to *ride* on Aidan's back as they made their way through the woods. She hadn't believed them when they told her how fast they could run. But…with trees appearing as a blur of brown and green as she was holding on with all her might to keep from being thrown from his back…

Color me a believer…

Her suspicions about Max, his sister, and the others who seemed to go everywhere with them were confirmed…definitely *not* human. They kept pace with Aidan and his brethren effortlessly. The Dragon Guard, which she now understood included Aidan, Rayne, Royce, Aaron, Lance, and Devon, decided to form a kind of circle around she and Aidan, with Lance at her right, Aaron at her left, Royce, the biggest damn man she'd ever seen, behind them and the very quiet one, Devon, in front of Aidan. Rayne led the way, as she was sure he'd done for all the years these men had been a unit. It was still hard to fathom these men were all over a hundred years old *and* changed into dragons at will. Something that old did *not* look sexy.

Max and his crew spread out, and at times, seemed to move faster than Aidan and his brethren. They were doing the 'sniff the air' thing more frequently. Her curiosity was getting the best of her. Grace had to ask Aidan *what* they were.

Laying her head on Aidan's shoulder to eliminate the wind beating against her cheeks, Grace breathed in his scent. It filled her with a calm that shouldn't have been possible when rushing to a place of unspeakable horrors. All the information collected to date indicated human trafficking, but with the addition of the wizards, she had no clue if it was still the case. Settling in for the rest of the ride, Grace tried to come up with a way to keep any other women from being abducted.

Rayne lifted his fist, a signal for all to stop. The same signal she'd seen soldiers use in all those military movies her father used to watch. Everyone gathered behind a maintenance shed on the farthest corner of the property.

"You know the plan. I don't have to remind you it's very important that we get in and get out as quickly as possible. Grab all the evidence you can. Grace can sort out what's what when we get back to the lair."

Rayne looked at Max and his entire crew. Sheer determination was written on every face. Addressing everyone, the Commander barked, "Get me everything I need to end the wizards and catch the *fucking* traitor."

A single nod was all that followed as Rayne looked each person in the eye. The depth of dedication and loyalty on each person's face was incredible. Grace had never witnessed anything like it. These people had immeasurable honor and unflinching dedication to their cause. She was humbled to be part of this group. Lost in thought, she jumped as Aidan placed his lips to her ear, "Are you ready, *mo ghra*? It's not too late to change your mind."

She turned on him, answering through gritted teeth. "I'm *not* changing my mind, Aidan. This is something I *have* to do."

Throwing his hands up in defeat, Aidan grumbled. "You win. But if anything happens to you I'm going to paddle your delectable ass until you can't sit down for a week." To emphasize his point, he slapped her behind as she spun around. Grace stumbled a little at the impact, but refused to acknowledge the effect his touch had on her.

"And if anything happens to you, *mo chroi*," she decided to let him know how much he was coming to mean to her in his own language, "I'll be sure to return the favor." Aidan's chuckle said he'd heard every word.

"She really is a *hellcat*, 'A'." Grace heard Lance remark and knew without a doubt he had a shit-eating grin on his face.

"That she is… that she is," was all she heard before Rayne gave the word for them to take their positions.

CHAPTER THIRTY-FOUR

Andrew felt like such an idiot… a feeling he *truly* despised. Sitting in the middle of nowhere waiting for the wizard leader to show up, he fumed over the wild goose chase he'd been sent on. The need for secrecy was one thing, but driving around aimlessly for hours was useless and *demoralizing*. The arrogant jerk had Andrew go ten miles out of town before sending a series of text messages taking him all over the countryside.

Does he know who I really am?

The traitor knew the black magic he'd absorbed was wearing thin but believed his true identity was still hidden. Early on, he started wearing colored contact lens or dark glasses to keep his mismatched eyes concealed. He wasn't taking any chances they would recognize his one blue and one amber-colored eye as those of *the special one* and determine his true origin. Andrew was sure all the evil he'd perpetrated had blown his special birthright to hell, but it was still a chance he wasn't willing to take. It served those sanctimonious dragons right for leaving him. He would watch every single one of them bleed out at his feet. But first, he had to get this fucking wizard leader to take him to where the ritual was to be held.

The last text message he'd gotten directed him to a beat up old tract home inhabited by the homeless. Andrew refused to get out of his car. He'd sent a message asking why their original plans had changed. The only response he received was, 'The timeline has been accelerated."

Damn cryptic bullshit.

Those idiots acted like they were straight out of a gangster movie from the fifties. Andrew laughed aloud. He'd lived through the fifties and Hollywood's glamorization was far from the truth. The lazy wizards wouldn't have been able to handle any of the real criminals he'd known back in the day. They were the real deal.

As he sat there stewing with his ruffled feathers and bruised ego, he couldn't help but wonder if this would be the final act that completely destroyed his soul. He'd like to believe it didn't matter…that only his revenge was important…but damning your eternal soul was nothing to scoff at. No matter how much he hated all of the people he'd once held most dear, he couldn't shake almost a hundred years of teachings.

Deep down, in the one little spot that remained truly dragon, Andrew knew what he planned to do was wrong. There'd even been times, in the wee hours of the morning, when he could feel his dragon trying to come back to life, but just as the spark of dragon magic was about to take hold, he'd squashed it. No more weakness. He would restore the black magic he'd used and complete his plans…end of story.

Relaxing with thoughts of death and revenge on his mind, Andrew thought he heard several vehicles approaching. One look in the rearview mirror confirmed his suspicions. Five black SUVs, a few feet behind him, parking on both sides of the street.

Could these assholes be anymore clichéd?

The passenger side door of the one directly behind him opened. He recognized the man stepping out as the leader's second. Joe or John or whatever the hell his name was, approached. Andrew rolled down the window, snarling as the warm dry air touched his face. "What the hell is going on?"

"Just tying up loose ends. The timeline has been accelerated. Master Eaton *had* to make sure you weren't followed."

Andrew was sure 'Master Eaton's' lieutenant had just fucked up *royally*. The wizard leader had taken great pains to keep his identity hidden. Several time Andrew asked for his name and the wizard leader had said it was 'of no importance'. Just recently, Andrew found out the power a name could hold over a black magic practitioner. He was sure *Master Eaton* did not want *anyone* to have information that could be used against him. Andrew smiled, filing it away for future use, giving the asshole standing at his car door no indication of his mistake.

"Is this the place or are we here for a picnic?" Andrew let the sarcasm fly.

"You will follow us to the ritual site. Please keep up. Master won't stand for delays." The man did an about face and headed back to his SUV.

"Fucking melodramatic assholes." Andrew shook his head as he raised the window. "This spell better work. If it doesn't…I'll kill 'em all on principle alone."

CHAPTER THIRTY-FIVE

Grace stood with Aidan, Rayne, and Lance, poised and ready to enter the back of the warehouse. It was their job to gather the files from the filing cabinets from the offices on the top level. Her adrenaline was pumping. Sounds of approaching trucks made her *spidey senses* go crazy. She felt Aidan tense at her side, immediately followed by buzzing in her head. Looking to her left, she found Rayne standing still as a statue.

Mindspeak...

As she stared at the Commander, Aidan whispered, "He's talking to Aaron. My brother's at the front of the building with Max and Juan Carlos. They have a clear view of the highway." He paused for just a moment. The buzzing in her brain intensified and he continued. "Four large trucks are turning onto the access road and headed our way."

Thinking about what she'd seen on the blueprints, Grace put two and two together and grabbed Aidan's arm. "There are women in those trucks. I just know it."

He nodded. "Let me see if Royce can see anything."

The closer the trucks got, the louder her intuition yelled that something really awful was about to happen.

"Shit!" Aidan cursed. "Royce confirmed the trucks are moving directly towards the rear of the building and they're heavily armed."

Aidan looked at Rayne. "All humans in the trucks, no sign of wizards, hunters, or *the traitor*," he answered aloud.

Grace noted Aidan's discomfort. She recognized the look. He was second-guessing his decision…apparently a new feeling for him.

It's something I could teach him a lot about.

Grace saw guilt as she studied the man she cared for. Thinking back over all they'd talked about, not one thing came to mind that Aidan, *of all people,* had to feel guilty about. However, she did notice everyone kept referring to a 'traitor', and when they did, both Aaron and Aidan tensed.

So many questions…no time for answers.

"Devon says there are SUVs approaching from the other direction… filled with *wizards*." A murderous look crossed Rayne's face "And…there's a car following the SUVs." He stared directly into Aidan's eyes. "It's the traitor." There it was again, the mention of this 'traitor' He was *definitely* someone Rayne wanted to hurt…*badly*.

No sooner were the words out of his mouth than the buzzing returned. Louder and more irate than before, like a hive of angry bees as opposed to static from a radio. The look on Aidan's face said it all…there was a score to be settled with this 'traitor'. Grabbing his hand, Grace rubbed the back of his hand in an effort to calm him. Between the buzzing in her head, the waves of aggression pouring off Aidan, and her *spidey senses* blaring, she felt lucky to be standing.

"Oh, my…" Grace squealed as Lance's hand touched her shoulder. Turning, she almost fell on her face. Lance laughed. "Sorry about that. Didn't mean to sneak up on you." He paused, still grinning. "How you doing, Hellcat?"

Using the hand he'd placed on her shoulder, Lance pulled her away from Aidan. She looked back as her hand slipped from her mate's. His eyes flashed to Lance and the buzz in her head shut off. Those *men* had been talking about her.

Damn him!

Why talk to Lance and not her? She and Aidan were definitely going to discuss his high-handed tactics. He had no right to keep things from her. She opened her mouth to yell at him. To tell him exactly what she was thinking, but the jerk smiled at her. Not the toe-curling, sensual smile she'd experienced before, but one of pure love and adoration. She knew it was meant to comfort her, but in that moment, she couldn't decide if she should kiss him silly or kick him in the shin.

Holding his eyes for another second, she tried to convey her annoyance. His smile grew and then he mouthed, *I love you.*

Most of the air left her lungs.

He loves me? Oh my God. He just said he loves me.

Lance used her moment of shock and his enhanced abilities to launch them through the woods. "What the hell are you doing, Lance?" She glared at him. "I need to be up there with Aidan. He promised I could gather evidence." She poked him in the chest. "You *all* agreed."

He shrugged. "I'm doing what Aidan asked me to do." She was ready to scream when he added, "Now hear me out before you lose your mind."

Nodding for him to continue while trying to control her temper, Grace counted to ten. How could Aidan do this to her? He *just* said he loved her. Looked at her like she was his whole world. And the whole time he'd been planning to have her moved out of the way.

"'A' wants to make sure you're far away from the human criminals and the wizards. Just until he can make sure it's safe. We didn't know they'd be here when we agreed to you going in. All the Intel said we had time to get in and get out before anyone arrived. *This* changes all the plans. He's trying to do everything possible to keep his word to you, but you have to understand, he's instinct driven to protect you."

Grace got angrier and by the look on Lance's face, he could tell. His next words were rushed. "Come on, Grace, you have to know how he feels about you. I know he explained what it's like for a dragon shifter when they find their mate. It took everything in his power to let me get you out of harm's way. It goes against *every instinct* he has to let you out of his sight, and even though we've been brethren for almost a hundred years, I can assure you he's having a very difficult time with us being together...*alone*. If it wasn't for his hell-bent-on-revenge-little-brother, 'A' would be the one standing here having this conversation with you, not me. He's the only one who can stop Andrew from whatever 'hell on earth' he has planned."

"What do you mean 'hell-bent-on-revenge-little brother'? Aaron's older and he's here with us." She stopped and squinted. "Who the hell is Andrew?" The look on Lance's face said it all...he'd messed up *big time*.

Scrambling to cover up his obvious misstep, Lance chuckled nervously. "Ummm, sounds like you and 'A' still have a lot to talk about." He stammered. "I'm not sure I'm the one to tell you the story."

In any other situation it would've been comical to watch the usually self-assured jokester ready to jump out of his skin. If she had time, Grace would go easy on him, but time was the one thing she was out of. Her *intuition* was telling her this was important. Whoever 'Andrew' was and whatever was going on between him and Aidan was something she needed to understand if she was going to be of any use to her mate.

It was a mission for all the Dragon Guard to eliminate the wizards and the hunters because of their threat to all dragons. But every time they talked about the traitor her *intuition* told her there was *more*, something deeper Aidan was keeping from her.

"Lance, if you don't tell me what the hell is going on right now, I swear I'll yell so loud everyone within a five mile radius will hear." Grace stared directly into the Guardsman's eyes, making sure he knew she meant every word. "I don't think anyone wants their cover blown, do you?" She couldn't help giving him her best shit-eating grin. God only knew she'd already taken enough of his.

He took a deep breath. The buzzing in her head began again.

Aidan... Lance is telling him what just happened...

"You can also tell him I'm *pissed*. He should feel lucky he's up there. It's a lot safer for him. But when we're in the same place again, I'm gonna kick his ass. I don't care if he is some big, bad Dragon Guardsman."

The color drained from Lance's face. The buzzing immediately stopped. At least her asshole mate knew she meant business. Not that it mattered in that moment, but with enough time she'd come up with really creative ways to punish him. Right now she needed answers, and if that meant torturing her mate's brethren, so be it. "Tell me, Lance. Tell me why he would trust you with me if it's so hard to be away from me. Why does he have a brother he didn't tell me about? And I'm guessing that this Andrew is a 'blood-relative-brother', not a brethren like you and the others. What's going on, Lance? Tell me." She put all the emotion and conviction she could in the next word she spoke. *"Please."*

CHAPTER THIRTY-SIX

Aidan owed him big time. This was *way* beyond the call of duty, no matter how many times 'A' had saved his ass. Lance knew things were happening quickly and Grace had been hurt less than twenty-four hours ago, but this shit was important. It was something a mate should handle. What the hell was Aidan thinking bringing her out here and *not* telling her about Andrew?

Now, it was up to him, because Aidan had to be ready to confront Andrew the second he was out in the open. Lance knew it was every dragon shifter's dream to find their mate, but he could make it a few more lifetimes without the hassle. It took everything in him just to keep himself out of trouble. There was no fucking way he could deal with a mate too.

Lance had to explain the nightmare they'd all lived for six years. Explain what her mate had witnessed. What the hell was the Universe playing at? He saw her getting pissed and knew it was now or never.

"All right, Grace, here it is. Before I get started, I want to make sure you understand the *only* reason I'm doing this and not Aidan, is that he *has* to be up there with Rayne and Aaron. He has the deepest connection to their little brother and they need that to capture him and stop whatever he has planned."

She started to interrupt but he put up his hand and shook his head. "I need you to just listen. We don't have much time and I have to make sure you understand. Can you do that for me?"

"You guys are the bossiest bunch of pain in the ass men I've ever seen." She shook her head. "Since I don't have a choice..." She huffed a breath that lifted her bangs off her brow. "Yeah, I can do it. Just hurry the hell up. My intuition is screaming that I need to be with Aidan, even though I want to kick his ass. *He needs me.*"

Lance smiled despite the situation. Aidan said she had a super acute *intuition*. Those extra abilities, plus the mating call, were driving her to be with her mate. He could only imagine what 'A' was going through. Just another reason his best friend had for taking a chunk out of the traitor's hide.

It was up to him. He needed to tell her as much of the story as he could without letting her know Aidan had been looking for *her* the night their lives changed forever. That was something she and her mate could hash out later. No way was he getting any deeper into this mess than he already was.

"All right, here it is in a nutshell. A little over six years ago, Aidan and his younger brother, Andrew, were out on patrol. Aidan got a whiff of something a few days before and couldn't shake the feeling he needed to follow up on it. So they went out to see what it was. The scent Aidan was tracking took all his focus and he was careless, something completely uncharacteristic for *your boy*. He hadn't continually scanned the area like was protocol, and let's just say Andrew always depended on one of us to take care of him, so he wasn't scanning either. He was the youngest of our Force and the younger brother to two of the best Dragon Guardsmen this world has ever known, and to top it off, he was a lazy little shit.

They were flying over a wooded area when they were both *literally* pulled from the sky by what we now know was black magic. The force of the dark spell pushed their dragons back and left the men falling to the ground. Apparently, a coven of wizards saw Aidan earlier when he was out tracking and set a trap for him. However, they hadn't counted on *two* dragons, so from what we now know, they didn't have enough magic to hold them both. In a quick plan B move, the sadistic bastards used their dirty magic to disorient Aidan while they held Andrew and made it look like they killed him. Aidan actually saw what he thought was Andrew's severed head being thrown into their huge ritual fire. They then hit 'A' with another blast of their tainted shit and left him for dead. Hours later, 'A' woke up and made his way back to the lair, but by then there was no sign of the wizards. We searched and searched and found *absolutely* no clues. Now, you have to understand, we have some serious mojo of our own, dragon magic is nothing to scoff at, but those sons of bitches were packing some kind of hyped up, serious power that night." Lance took a deep breath and continued, "We all mourned Andrew's death. I know you know we live a long time, and to lose one of us so early in our lifespan because of the scum of the earth is horrible for all of us, but it hit 'A' the hardest. He felt responsible for Andrew's death and spent every waking minute punishing himself for what had happened. For six years, I watched my best friend in pain and constant turmoil, with no way to help him. No matter what we tried, nothing helped. Then a little over six months ago, everything changed."

"What happened?"

"We were on our way home, trying to get Kyndel, back to the lair." Lance smiled, trying to ease into what was coming next. He was glad for her strength because the rest of the story would send a weaker woman screaming into the woods.

"We were ambushed by a group of hunters led by a magic practitioner able to give them enhanced abilities. Even with all their magically infused powers, we were winning the fight, but somehow, the practitioner got past us and held Kyndel at knifepoint. While Rayne was negotiating her release, the leader revealed himself to be Andrew, obviously not dead, and seriously deranged. After a skirmish leaving Kyndel injured, we captured him, but his infusion of black magic allowed him to escape before 'A' and Aaron could get him back to the Elders for the Tribunal. We've pieced together bits and pieces of what happened, but there are still a lot of holes. The one thing all of our Elders and Leaders believe is that it will take at least one, if not both, of the 'real' brothers to bring him down. For the last six months, 'A' has tracked him. But even with his enhanced senses, Andrew has been able to hide from us. We think it's another effect of the black magic. We also can no longer mindspeak with the traitor and 'A' is positive he's lost touch with his dragon.

Looking directly into her eyes, Lance continued, "In the last week, some of the men who work for Max have been able to catch Andrew's scent a couple of times. We're guessing the black magic is finally wearing off, or he's used all he had stored. Max's men also saw the traitor meeting with the wizard leader and we believe they are associated with 'The Auctioneer' you've been investigating. All of that bullshit is why 'A' is up there and not back here with you, where he truly wants to be. He told me you could tell when he's mindspeaking with one of us, so you know he's been bitching at me the whole time I've been talking to you. Now, I know you have questions, so fire away and I'll do my best to answer them, while we still have time."

CHAPTER THIRTY-SEVEN

Grace stood and stared, not sure what to ask first. She started with one of the last things he'd said. "Kyndel was held at knifepoint? And hurt? But I saw her and she seemed fine. She's *really* okay, right?" Grace was controlling her temper the best she could.

Why does everyone keep things from me?

"Yes, she was held at knifepoint and yes, she was hurt." She felt her cheeks get hot at his admission and knew they were red from her fury.

If this guy had any sense at all, he might want to take a step back. Grace was contemplating punching him since the people she was furious with weren't in front of her and he was. Lance hurried on. "But before you rip my head off, she completely recovered and is healthier than anyone I've ever met."

Grace *just* nodded, thinking the reunion she'd imagined with her best friend was shot to hell.

I'm kicking Kyndel's ass as soon as she delivers her niece or nephew.

"Does Aidan have a plan to catch Andrew? Because if anything happens to him, I *will* cover him in Kyndel's ointment and nurse him back to health just to kill him myself."

Lance grinned. Her hand itched with the need to smack the smirk off his face. Then he spoke, full of himself once again. "We always have a plan, Hellcat."

"On a side note, your nickname for me is *not funny*." She grinned to let him know she wasn't really upset.

Somewhere in the last two seconds, her anger melted away and Grace decided not to be mad at Lance. If she was honest with herself, and she always was, she would've done the same thing if roles were reversed. The buzzing started again and she knew Lance was telling Aidan she hadn't killed him... *yet*.

"I kinda like the nicknames." He shrugged. "And your mate gave Kyndel one, too...not me. We call her Spitfire."

Grace's eyes widened and she smiled. "Well, I have to give him credit for that one." She looked at him with more intent. "I know you're talking to him. Tell him I understand why he has to be up there and why he's worried for me, but *our* discussion, his and mine, is far from over. Make sure he knows it's in no way okay to keep secrets from me."

Grace knew Lance was relaying her exact words from the look on his face. This time, the buzz seemed a little less anxious. She figured being able to feel Aidan's emotions, along with the recognition of his mindspeak, was an added benefit of the mating call thing they all kept talking about. But the fact that her *spidey senses* were screaming at her, telling her first and foremost she needed to be with Aidan, and secondly, Lance hadn't told her the whole story, was about to drive her crazy.

I'll worry about the gory details later.

The pressing issue was getting to Aidan. Something big was about to happen and she needed to be with him. "Tell him we're coming back," she stated, daring Lance to tell her otherwise. "And tell him I'm not taking 'no' for an answer."

Before Lance could respond, Grace spun and started walking back the way they'd come. She knew they were going to try to talk her out of it and she was having none of it. Lance's next words proved her right. "Hey there, Grace, your mate's having a shit fit in my head. Can't we talk about this?"

"Nope. No more talking. I can't explain this crap, but I know I need to be up there with him and that's where I'm going." Grace talked as she walked; knowing Lance caught every word with his enhanced hearing.

"Okay! You got it. I'm just the messenger and I damn sure don't want to get shot." He chuckled from closer behind her than he'd been two seconds ago.

When he caught up to her, Grace saw the familiar twinkle in his eyes. She wondered if he made a joke out of *everything*. Then had a sad thought. What if something had happened to him to make him use humor as a defense mechanism? She'd seen how nervous he was when talking about Aidan and his brothers, but knew he would've busted out a joke or two if he thought he could get away with it.

It was easy to see how Lance and Aidan were so close. Lost in thought, Grace almost fell forward when the ground shook and a sound like the earth caving in on itself made her ears ring. It took a couple seconds for her to realize the sound had come from in front of her. Smoke billowed over the treetops.

With no thought of her safety, Grace sprinted as fast as she could towards the smoke. Her only thoughts of Aidan. Fear that she wouldn't see him again caused her to move faster than she ever imagined her chubby thighs could carry her.

"Grace, I can't let you run in there until we know what's going on. 'A' made me promise to keep you safe," Lance called to her. There was no way she was stopping. He would have to bodily restrain her to keep her from getting to Aidan.

"I really don't give a shit what you promised. He's up there and could be hurt. I *am* going."

I really need to exercise more. I'm gonna need oxygen...

Running had never been Grace's thing. Her words were barely more than a breath as she struggled to keep her pace. "Use your damn mind talk thingy and find out what the hell's going on. Find out if *he's* okay."

A weight lifted as the buzzing in her head started again.

Aidan's okay! At least well enough to communicate.

"What's going on?" she wheezed.

"They have no idea what happened. The trucks entered the tunnels. The wizards were going through one of the loading bay doors with Andrew bringing up the rear when the top of the building just blew off."

She hated the fact that he wasn't even breathing heavily when she was about to pass out. Out of sheer necessity, she slowed her pace while Lance continued explaining. "Rayne, 'A', and the others are trying to get eyes on the traitor. Only a few of the wizards made it out, and since their vehicles were blown up along with part of the warehouse, they've taken cover by one of the outbuildings on the west side. 'A' is screaming his damn head off, telling me to grab you and haul ass the other way."

Lesser men had withered at the look she shot him. It was her best 'I'm gonna take you down' look and had been honed over years of mock trials. Lance answered appropriately. "But I have too much respect for you to do that, even if it means he's gonna kick my ass."

Good man.

They both stopped running and stood behind a small shed, a lot like the one from earlier. "Now all I ask is that you stay close and do what I tell you. I have to make sure nothing happens to you. I've heard enough stories in my lifetime to know you're being driven by forces you just can't fight, so stay close."

She saw the grin and the twinkle in his eye and swore nothing rattled the man.

I'm not going to mindspeak with 'A' until we are closer, but I'm listening to what's going on."

All she could see was an abandoned warehouse with fire and smoke pouring out the top and most of one side.

"*Well hell!* There were girls in the trucks we saw go into the tunnels and now they're trapped. I really need to get down there and help." The fun-loving jokester she'd grown accustomed to was instantly gone. Beside her was a fierce member of the Dragon Guard.

"All right, Grace, we're gonna move closer to the warehouse. Aidan's coming out with the paperwork he was able to save from the flames. He needs to see you just as badly as you need to see him. We'll meet him right over by that group of trees." He pointed to the left. She saw a bench surrounded by trees that must've been a place for the former employees to take a break.

"Stay close." She gasped as he pulled her closer with the arm he laid across her shoulders. "Don't worry, Grace. I got permission from your mate to put my arm around you."

Her eyes shot up and she saw the goofy twinkle she would forever associate with her mate's best friend. At least he had the decency to act like the elbow she shoved into his ribs hurt. "*Oomph*, damn you have some boney elbows."

"Just remember that the next time you think about messing with me."

She knew he was trying to keep her mind off the mayhem just yards from where they were standing, but the longer it took to see Aidan with her own eyes, the louder her *spidey senses* screamed. Something wasn't right about all of this. It just didn't add up. There was more at play than they were seeing.

Nothing she'd learned about the wizards said they would blow up the building after going to all the trouble of procuring it and *definitely* not with their own people in it. It seemed to Grace they were a bunch of cowards who hid behind their power. The story Lance shared earlier only solidified her opinion of the black-magic-yielding-douche bags.

She was having a really hard time staying mad at the incredibly handsome man she'd come to care so deeply for, but it didn't negate the fact that she was still going to give him a rash of shit as soon as she saw for herself that he was all right, *and* kissed him to within an inch of his very long life.

"Okay, here we go. I'm gonna lift you a little off the ground and get us over there as quickly as possible." Lance shifted his arm from her shoulders to her waist. "No wiggling. If I drop you 'A' will chop off my head and throw *me* in a fire."

Unable to speak past the lump in her throat, she nodded. She knew he was kidding, but right now, her focus was the 'tone' her *intuition* had taken in the last few seconds. It was totally different than any time before… sharper, darker… scarier. Her feet left the ground and everything around her was a blur. In less than a minute, she was standing by the bench, watching Aidan emerge from the smoldering rubble. It didn't matter that he was covered with soot and ash from head to toe; he looked amazing to her.

CHAPTER THIRTY-EIGHT

Aidan felt the weight of Grace's gaze. The moment their eyes met, everything that was scrambled and confused just a second before, fell into place. There was his mate, the woman who held his heart. The Universe did *not* make mistakes. She was his. Of course, he would've preferred it if she was about ten thousand miles from the danger, but he couldn't deny the relief soothing his soul at just one look from those beautiful blue eyes.

When all this crap was over, they were going away…*far away*…and *alone*. To a place for just the two of them, no distractions, no wizards or criminals or hunters or deranged little brothers, *just them*. He wanted to spend countless hours showing her exactly what she meant to him.

Our time will come. I promise…

Returning his focus to the present and the paperwork he carried, Aidan hoped it contained the information she needed.

"Rayne, I'm headed out to Grace. Lance is headed in to help." He sent through their link.

"Thanks, 'A'. It's a fucking mess down here."

Just as he was about to answer, a sound he'd hoped never to hear again made him look up. A large military helicopter, a Comanche Stealth like he'd piloted for two tours in Afghanistan, was preparing to touch down in the clearing to the left of the building. It was the only helicopter he knew of that could get as close as it was without being detected, even to their enhanced dragon senses.

What the hell?

Who involved in this unholy mess had the power to commission something so covert? The helicopter was absolutely reserved for military only operations. Who could fly into what appeared to be a secret hideout for a petty criminal and asshole wizards?

There's more at play here than any of us knows, and dammit if Grace isn't right in the fucking middle.

CHAPTER THIRTY-NINE

Andrew knew the wizard leader was an idiot, but now he'd become the *Grand Poo-bah* of all idiots *everywhere*. How in the hell had the idiot with all his supposed power led them straight into a trap? If Andrew didn't have to hide his returning dragon senses from the witless cowards, he could've escaped and left them to die, but as it was, he *had* to save them, too. He simply couldn't risk having them find out who and *what* he was. The cherry on the top of his shit sundae was finding the damn Dragon Guard in attendance.

Without the ritual his dragon would reemerge, he wouldn't be able to stay hidden, and his plans for revenge would be shot to hell.

Unacceptable!

Just as unacceptable was cowering in the bushes with a bunch of spineless wizards trying to figure a way out of a colossal fuck up instead of doing what needed to be done. If not for the smell from the explosives and the cloaking spell the wizards were weaving, the Dragon Guard would've surely found them by now.

Andrew knew the Guard had been lying in wait as he watched them rush to help those trapped after the blast. As soon as he was out of this fucking mess, he would find out exactly what the wizards' real plan was. As well as whom the Dragon Guard was working so hard to save. He would *not* take no for an answer.

Master Eaton needed the power as much as Andrew did if the leader was to keep up appearances. The leader's finely constructed veneer was cracking as he watched his well made plans go up in smoke…*literally*. They continued to search for an escape route, only to find one dead end after another. In desperation, Andrew tried to reach through mindspeak for the first time since his incarceration. Thinking if he could listen in to the Dragon Guard's plans, he could escape without detection.

Hiding in the shadows pissed him off and quite frankly, bruised his ego. There'd been a time, many years ago, when he'd been one of the very few with the ability to listen to *every* conversation within their Force without detection. What he wouldn't give to have that ability again. Reaching out, he felt a slight buzz deep in his subconscious that *refused* to be drawn out. The harder he pushed, the farther from reach his mindspeak moved.

It was just as he suspected; his dragon shifter abilities had been masked by black magic for so long they'd all but ceased to exist. It was the price of his vengeance. No matter. Andrew would pay with his life if it meant each of them felt the pain he'd endured.

Debating the best way to save his own ass, Andrew caught a glimpse of the one sure way out of his debacle and torture his *dear brother* at the same time. Standing just a few yards away, being guarded by Lance, *another useless member of their Force*, was Aidan's mate. Luck was finally on his side. Andrew knew exactly what to do.

Come to me, my pretty…

CHAPTER FORTY

"*Rayne, we have some serious company landing a Comanche out here. Windows are blacked out so I have no idea who or how many are inside.*"

"*What the fuck is going on? Get Grace and get the hell out of here. We'll handle the rest. It shouldn't be long until local fire and rescue arrive.*"

"*Already on the move.*"

Aidan raced across the parking lot, barely slowing as he scooped up his mate and threw her over his shoulder. "*Rayne's waiting for you inside,*" he shot at Lance, continuing towards the woods and the cover he hoped it would provide.

"*On my way. Take care of yours.*" Lance rushed off towards the burning warehouse.

"Aidan, what the hell are you doing? Put me down now!"

Grace was pissed he'd had Lance take her into the woods, and even more pissed there were secrets he and Kyndel had kept from her. He'd seen how relieved she was that he was okay after the explosion, but from the feelings coming off her at this moment, he was going to be lucky if she ever spoke to him again.

"Just hold on, *mo ghra.*" He swatted her ass because he couldn't help it, even though he knew it only pissed her off more. "I have no clue who's in that helicopter, and I have no intention of finding out with you nearby."

"*Dammit* Aidan, you've got to stop the Alpha male bullshit!" She pounded her fists against the back of his thighs.

"*Mo chroi*, I'll do whatever it takes to keep you safe. Helicopters like the one landing back there mean one of two things: either someone very high up in the government is in on whatever's going on, or someone with a lot of money and the need to get away fast has commandeered it. Either way, I'm not taking a chance with your safety."

Aidan stopped and set Grace down in front of him. He stood absolutely still as the waves of anger and frustration poured off his mate. There was no doubt she'd kick his ass right there, on principle alone, if she could. She shook with fury. It was one of the sexiest things he'd ever seen.

Unable to resist, Aidan slammed his mouth to hers. It was raw passion and possession, full of teeth and tongue and aggression. He pulled her so tight to his chest they almost became one. Aidan needed to brand her, to make sure she never doubted *who* she belonged to and more importantly.... *who belonged to her.*

In a flash, his Grace decided to give as good as she got. Her hands slid under his tight black t-shirt, the need to feel her fingers on his skin instantly overwhelming all his senses. The more she tried to possess him, the more he wanted to be possessed. Needing to taste her skin, Aidan nipped and sucked his way across her jaw and down her neck.

Their hunger was so intense he was transported to another time and place. Completely forgotten was the fact they were standing in the middle of the woods, a few hundred yards from where a building had just exploded. Needing his mate more than his next breath, Aidan lifted Grace and backed her against a nearby tree. Papers littered the ground around them, forgotten in lieu of their lust. Using his enhanced abilities, he removed her blouse, sucking her already pebbled lace-covered nipple into his mouth as soon it came into sight.

Grace ground her crotch against his denim-covered erection, seeking the release only he could give her. He let her set the rhythm as he continued to taste every part of her body he could reach. His conscience reminded him it was not the time or the place, but there was no denying the drive of the mating call or his dragon.

Man and beast needed to reconnect with the woman who completed them in every way. With no other thought but feeling her warm, wet pussy wrapped around his painfully hard cock, Aidan slid his hand between their bodies and from one breath to the next, had her naked from the waist down.

Soon, his pants were around his ankles and his straining erection was poised to enter her waiting channel. Looking deep into her mesmerizing blue eyes, he slammed his hips to hers, burying himself to the hilt. Nothing ever felt so right. He held them completely still, her inner walls adjusting to his abrupt intrusion. Her muscles contracted and massaged his hard cock, almost driving him over the edge.

After a few deep breaths to regain control, Aidan began sliding in and out. He wanted to take it slow, but their location and the feel of Grace's juices flowing between them made his thoughts of restraint impossible. Pounding into her faster and harder, keeping one hand under her ass and the other across her back to protect her silken skin, he drove them higher and higher. Grace's nails dug into his shoulders. Her moans louder and louder as she met him stroke for stroke.

Her core contracted harder and faster around his cock. She was close. Tilting his hips, he increased the pressure on her clit and caused the tip of his penis to rub her special bundle of nerves on every slide. Her eyes began to lose focus. Aidan leaned forward and latched onto the sensitive skin where her neck met her shoulder. Her heels dug into his waist until he was sure there would be marks, and he bit down.

Grace came with such force that in the next stroke he was coming with her. As he milked the last waves of her orgasm from her with long steady strokes of his cock, he licked the spot he'd bitten on her neck. He didn't even try to stop the smile spreading across his face as he looked at *his* mark upon her neck. Grace was going to give him hell for it, but he just couldn't care.

He raised his head and looked upon his mate, replete from their lovemaking, his half-erect cock still buried deep inside her. Aidan thanked the Universe for the hundredth time for bringing her into his life. He gave her a quick peck on the lips as he slid from her warm, wet channel. Her baby blues popped open and he was momentarily awestruck.

"What's that look for?" she asked, her voice scratchy and sexy from their lovemaking.

"Just looking at the most beautiful woman in the Universe." He winked, holding her until she was steady on her feet.

She swatted his arm as he bent down to gather her clothing. "You seriously need glasses, Mr. O'Brien."

No sooner were the words out of her mouth than Aidan had her backed against the tree again, her chin between his thumb and forefinger. "Do *not ever* talk bad about yourself, Grace. You *are* the most beautiful woman in the world. The day I met you, all others ceased to exist. My sun, moon, and stars revolve around you. I will not stand for you putting yourself down now or *ever again*."

He hoped he'd gotten his point across. He meant every word. She laid her hand on his cheek. "I don't know what I ever did to deserve you, but I'm glad I did it. Thank you, Aidan."

He leaned his forehead against hers. "I love you, Grace."

He heard her intake of breath. "I love you too, Aidan," her whisper reached his waiting ears. His heart leapt for joy. She loved him. She'd just said she loved him. He grabbed her around the waist and spun her while kissing her until they were both breathless.

They stood looking into one another's eyes. He knew she saw the tears he was fighting to hold back. It just would *not* do to cry in front of his mate.

She cleared her throat and he saw a twinkle in her eye. "I guess I better get dressed, unless you plan on keeping me out here naked for your pleasure all day." Grace wagged her eyebrows, causing him to burst out laughing. "But don't think we aren't going to talk later. It was really unfair of you to have Lance drag me away, and the stuff he told me about you and your younger brother…well, *you* should've told me. " She paused for a moment. "I want a partnership with the man I love, not a dictatorship with a caveman."

"My first thought is and always will be to keep you safe, but I'll work harder to remember to discuss my decisions with you." Grace raised an eyebrow, indicating he'd said something wrong. "I've lived a long time, *mo ghra'*. Give an old dragon some time to change his ways." They both chuckled at his attempt at humor. "And as much as I'd love to keep you naked for months on end, you are right; we don't have time right now."

He handed her the clothes he'd gathered from the ground and teased, "Get dressed before I change my mind." To distract himself, Aidan began picking up the paperwork he'd let fall.

"I'm ready whenever you are," Grace called from behind him as he picked up the last piece of paper. Walking over to where she stood, he kissed her forehead.

"All right, pretty lady, I just have to say, if I had my way we would be heading as far away from here as I could carry you." He saw the fire leap into her eyes and her shoulders square for battle. Holding up his hands in defeat, Aidan chuckled. "But I know better than to try to change your mind once it's made up." Grace relaxed a fraction before his eyes. "So let's creep up to the edge of the woods and see what's going on with the helicopter and its occupants." He pulled her as tight as he could into his side. "Stay right by me, Beautiful. There's no way I'm letting anything happen to you."

As they headed back towards the debris of the devastated warehouse, a shiver ran down his spine. Whatever they were walking towards wasn't going to be pretty, but with his amazing mate by his side, there was nothing he couldn't handle.

CHAPTER FORTY-ONE

And the hits just kept coming. Andrew's incredibly bad luck was worsening. His foolproof plan to get away and run a dagger through his brother's heart was blown to hell when the helicopter landed. Back in the bushes hiding with a bunch of worthless wizards, he wanted to scream just for spite.

What pissed him off the most were the occupants of the biggest freaking helicopter he'd ever seen were just sitting there, doing absolutely nothing but holding up his plans. And of course, there was the part where Aidan had thrown his mate over his shoulder and run in the opposite direction. Talk about failing in epic proportions on all fronts…

Searching for another escape route while focusing on the Comanche, Andrew witnessed no movement. He knew from his time in the Gulf War, similar aircraft were used to move high-ranking officials from site to site. They held up to twelve men, all the gear necessary to guard the assets inside and to launch an offensive assault, if necessary. Whoever was in there was military, had a shitload of money, or *both*.

Andrew bet on the latter since they were in the middle of nowhere, beside a smoldering mess of a building that not even an hour ago was to be the site of a black magic ritual. The people in said helicopter had something to do with either the wizards or the abandoned warehouse.

I would ask what the hell else could happen, but I'm afraid Fate would show me...

CHAPTER FORTY-TWO

They stood at the edge of the woods. Aidan listened to the voices of his brethren through mindspeak and gave Grace the play by play.

"Rayne, Lance, Royce, and Max's men are getting the women out of the rubble. There are six all together. They'd been in the back of the trucks, protected by the thick walls of the trailers during the explosion. The thick, steel walls are all that saved them."

Aidan's grave tone made Grace shiver. "Some of them tried to get out before the guys got there and were caught by falling debris." He stopped and furrowed his brow. "What I can't figure out is what's taking local law enforcement and the fire department so long to get here. I know damn good and well Rayne had someone call."

He looked towards the chopper sitting stationary in the clearing. "And then there's them.' He tilted his head. "What the hell are they doing? Why aren't they making a move?"

"None of this makes any sense," Grace added.

Nodding, he continued. "Aaron, Devon, Max, and Sophia are spread out in the woods looking for the wizards who ran when the building exploded. At least eight of them got away."

Grace let herself be pulled closer to his side. He wrapped his arm around her shoulder and she felt how much he needed the contact. She smiled when he kissed the top of her head, but it was short-lived when she heard, "And I'm sure my little brother is with them."

Still scanning the scene before them, she watched two of Max's men emerge from the warehouse, each carrying a battered young woman. A shiver ran down Grace's spine as she took in their condition. Her determination to see justice rose within her. 'The Auctioneer' and his associates *had* to be stopped. The men she now recognized as Juan Carlos and Ernesto moved with enhanced speed towards her and Aidan.

Grace grabbed the blankets each man had thrown over the shoulders of the young women and spread them out on the grass. The gentle way the men laid the young women down, carefully positioning their unconscious bodies to avoid any further pain, made her heart swell. Juan Carlos handed her a bag of first aid supplies. "Would you clean and bandage their wounds, please?" He kept his eyes on the women as he spoke. "Ernesto and I are going back to help get the others." He finally looked at Grace while he spoke the last few words.

"Sure, I can do that." She opened the bag of supplies. "Be careful." She spoke to his back as he hurried away.

"Here, *mo ghra'*, let me help." Aidan reached for some of the wipes and gauze pads. "If we work together, we can get these two cleaned up before they come back with the others."

Smiling, Grace was once again amazed at the man who stood before her. She glanced towards the warehouse while cleaning the wounds of one of the unconscious women who lay helpless on the ground. Her *spidey senses* kicked up a notch from a movement to her right. Turning her head, she watched men dressed in full combat gear pour out of the helicopter. Ten in all, fanned out in a formation she'd seen in the military movies her father liked to watch.

Reaching across the young woman she cared for, Grace laid her hand on Aidan's. "Aidan, look." She nodded towards the clearing. Before her next breath, her mate was standing fifty feet away using a large patch of foliage for cover. Buzzing in her head began loud and strong.

Hurriedly bandaging the young woman's wounds, she folded the other half of the blanket the girl was laying on over her and moved to Aidan's patient to finish her first aid. Waiting sucked. She didn't want to call out for fear someone would hear her. Keeping the poor, defenseless, women safe was her first priority. Grace worked as fast as she could and tried not to let her nerves get the best of her while she waited for Aidan to tell her what was happening.

CHAPTER FORTY-THREE

The men from the helicopter were obviously military trained and protecting someone important. Covered in tactical military gear, they held automatic rifles like most assault teams. They'd taken a traditional defensive position, five on each side, forming a semi-circle around a tall, bulky man also dressed in combat gear carrying a handgun he kept at his side. The man in the middle didn't have his face covered like the others, but his cap was pulled down as far as it would go, obscuring everything but his mouth and chin. They moved as a unit, obviously well trained and used to working together.

"Rayne, we've got a serious shit storm brewing up here. Eleven men in total, ten protecting one in the middle, just got out of the helicopter, heading towards the warehouse," Aidan sent through their connection.

"What the hell is so important about this fucking warehouse?" Aidan could hear the frustration in Rayne's voice. *"And where the hell is the local law enforcement and fire department?"*

"I don't know, man. But we've got to do something about these assholes right now or they're going to be on your ass."

"You're right," Rayne agreed. *"Aaron. Devon. I need you to get to the rear of the building. The assholes from the helicopter just decided to join the party. 'A' says they're dressed to kill. Bring Max and Sophia with you. I'm sending Royce and all but two of Max's men up to help. Lance is with me. Keep 'em off us until we can get these women out of here. Any luck finding the asshole wizards?"*

"No." Aaron's voice sounded loud, clear, and filled with frustration. *"They have to be using black magic to hide their position. Dev picked up the taint just before you called."*

"Shit! Nothing we can do about it now. See you topside," Rayne growled.

Aidan listened as his brethren answered their Commander while he moved back to Grace and her patients. "*Mo chroi*," he put his hands on either side of her face."I have to go. We have to keep those commandos from getting into that warehouse."

He touched his forehead to hers. "I need you to promise you'll stay *right here*. I hate leaving you but I *have* to go. It's going to take all of us to keep those assholes at bay." Shifting his hands to the back of her neck, Aidan lightly massaged. "You're hidden behind all these bushes and trees. Don't make a sound unless you absolutely have to."

Leaning back, they locked eyes. "If you feel any type of danger or see anyone getting too close, scream like you've never screamed before and I *will* come running." He pressed his lips to hers, pouring all the love and reassurance he could into one brief kiss. She needed to understand exactly what she meant to him and how important it was she stays hidden.

Ending the kiss, but only moving a fraction of an inch, Aidan kept his eyes closed. "I love you, *mo ghra'*… with every beat of my heart."

Grace nodded her head and leaned forward, placing one last kiss upon his lips. Dropping his hands, Aidan stepped back. He saw all the love and devotion he felt for her mirrored in her gaze. With love filling every cell of his being, he turned and sped towards his brethren before he could change his mind. Looking to the Heavens, he prayed.

Please keep her safe….

CHAPTER FORTY-FOUR

She watched, mesmerized as Aidan sped away. Sitting between the unconscious young women, Grace laid the back of her hand on their foreheads, checking for fever. She remembered all the times Miss Annabelle had cared for her during various illnesses and injuries. It made her smile despite her surroundings.

These women looked so young to have suffered such trauma. Grace's *intuition* told her with the right medical and psychological help they'd make it through this ordeal. She'd make sure they got whatever they needed no matter the expense. Completely lost in thought, she jumped when her *spidey senses* screamed something major was happening in the direction of Aidan and the warehouse.

Her mate would lose his mind if he knew she was even thinking of peeking over the edge of the foliage hiding her from view, but she couldn't ignore it. Something catastrophic was about to happen. She had to know Aidan and the others were okay.

Creeping forward, Grace peeped through the vegetation serving as her cover. The Dragon Guard, along with Max and his crew, surrounded the men from the helicopter, who slowly continued toward the loading docks… guns drawn. They didn't appear to have any intention of harming anyone. Their sole focus was to protect the man they surrounded and get him into the still smoldering warehouse. Positioned directly across from Grace and only about fifty yards from the large loading dock doors, she could see Aidan's back. His muscles were flexed, ready to pounce. She jumped when he spoke. "Who are you and what business do you have here?"

The man being protected turned but didn't lift his hat. "This is *my* building. I have every right to be here. It is *you* who are trespassing, whoever you are."

Something about the man's voice seemed familiar. Her *intuition* bounced around in her head. She lifted her hands to her ears to quiet the alarm in her mind.

"If this is your building, then why did you sit in your helicopter and not even attempt to help us rescue those trapped by the explosion?" Aidan asked. She could hear the contained violence in his tone.

"Saving these *people* doesn't concern me. I'm only here to get what's *mine*," he answered. His tone said he knew exactly what was going and didn't give a shit.

"So you knew there were young women being held here and did nothing to stop it?" Aidan asked, anger radiating from every pore, his muscles bunching even tighter.

"I don't have to explain *anything* to you. This is my building and you're trespassing. You and your band of merry men have one minute to get the hell off my property or these highly trained mercenaries will gladly shoot you and throw your cold, dead bodies into the rubble. It's your choice… either way is fine with me."

Aidan took a step forward. His voice shook with rage. "Look, asshole, I don't care who you are, and your goons don't scare me. You're not going into that building until we've gotten all the survivors out. I suggest you take your happy asses back to your fancy helicopter and chill out."

The mystery man took an aggressive step forward, staring at Aidan. Grace counted to six before he spoke. What she heard made the hair all over her body stand on end. It was a voice she'd heard many times before but still couldn't place. Frantically searching her memory while the jerk continued to tell Aidan what was going to happen if they didn't stand down, it came to her with a jolt.

No freaking way. That can't be right.

She shook her head and listened more intently. Disbelief almost drove her to her knees. Her instincts had to be misfiring. There was *no way* it was who she thought it was. As she tried to convince herself she'd made a mistake, the mystery man and Aidan's voices grew louder… *angrier*. The tension in the air threatened to strangle them all.

Just when she was sure she was mistaken, the man in charge reached up and removed his hat. What she saw had her screaming a warning to Aidan without any thought of her own safety. The mystery man, the man being protected by his own small army, was *her boss*, the State Prosecutor, and from the little he'd revealed, also 'The Auctioneer'.

Grace burst from her hiding spot. She thought only of getting to the man who'd lied to her and everyone in law enforcement and keep him from hurting her mate. Running as hard and fast as she could, she screamed for Aidan to get down.

She'd made it barely fifty feet when a burning sensation tore through her left shoulder. Tripping at the pain, Grace just missed the ground as something plowed into her right side, throwing her into the air. Sounds of gunfire and shouting sounded all around her as she landed flat on her back on the concrete. Bones rattled, her head bounced from the impact, and black spots rose before her eyes. Yelling echoed in her head as if she was at the bottom of a barrel.

Trying to clear her vision, she blinked and tried to sit up just as a large calloused hand grabbed her ankle. Grace found herself being unceremoniously pulled across the asphalt, scraping the skin from her lower back and causing her head to bounce a few more times against the unforgiving parking lot. She kicked and fought, trying to get her ankle free from the large paw dragging her away from Aidan. No matter what she tried, the grip around her ankle tightened.

Twisting and turning, Grace grabbed at anything she could to stop her forward motion. Unfortunately, every movement caused pain to shoot from her left shoulder throughout her body and her left arm refused to cooperate, flailing about like a wet dishrag. Kicking with her free foot, she listened to Aidan scream after her as the gunfire and commotion got farther and farther away. Grace prayed her mate would catch up and free her from whoever was dragging her like a ragdoll.

Changing tactics, she tried to get in a semi-upright position, thinking the leverage would her free her ankle. Taking a deep breath, preparing for the torment she knew would come from her useless shoulder, Grace was suddenly jerked from the ground and thrown over a heavily muscled shoulder. All air was pushed from her lungs as her stomach made painful contact with an unforgiving shoulder. Agony radiated throughout her body. Apparently, her ribs had been injured when she was tackled. She almost blacked out as she felt them bend in directions bones weren't meant to bend.

Aidan continued to scream her name, his footsteps pounding on the ground behind her. The man carrying her had a vice-like grip across the back of her thighs she knew would leave bruises to add with all the other injuries she was racking up. Lifting her head, she saw the tortured look on Aidan's face and that of his brethren, as they attempted to catch whoever was carrying her away from them.

"I swear to the Universe if you don't put her down right now, I will flay the skin from your body and watch you bleed, you fucking useless piece of shit!" Grace heard Aidan screaming, the pain in his voice a knife to her heart.

Across the distance, she could see the anguish in his whiskey-colored eyes. The man carrying her began mumbling what sounded like a rhyme under his breath. Her vision blurred. The contents of her stomach planned a speedy getaway. Something warm and wet flowed down her arm and if that wasn't enough, Grace realized that somewhere along the way she'd lost a tennis shoe.

Great! I'm bleeding and I've lost one of my favorite tennis shoes. Could this day get any worse?

Her head weighed a thousand pounds and her vision narrowed to a single pinpoint. She was about to blackout and thought she might've been hallucinating when one second she saw Max and Sophia racing alongside Aidan, and in the next, her mate was sandwiched between two of the largest cats she'd ever seen. Focusing the best she could, Grace realized they were panthers. Really big panthers! Bigger than the ones she'd seen at the zoo.

I knew there was something different about them.

Sadly, she didn't have the luxury of thinking about it as a crazy man, mumbling rhymes, was carrying her deep into the woods. Balling up her fist, she used what little strength she had left to punch her abductor as hard as she could in the back. With only one arm working, it was pretty much a waste of time, but there was no way she would be carried off to God knows where without a fight. The asshole she was draped over squeezed her legs tighter, and that coupled with the constant jarring against her cracked ribs, made her screech in pain. Her abductor's voice grew louder and deeper. Aidan roared in response.

Using the last of her strength, Grace raised her head to look at the man she loved with all her heart. A single tear slid down her cheek. She prayed to God it wouldn't be the last time she saw him. The air around her felt heavy. Little shocks of electricity landed on her skin. The space separating her and Aidan grew larger. They were moving so fast, everything was a blur.

Finding it difficult to breathe and knowing that in a matter of seconds she would black out, Grace yelled. "I love you, Aidan!"

He roared so loud in response she knew the ground shook. The last thing she saw before her world went black was Aidan bathed in bright silver light and the dragon she'd seen on his back materializing before her eyes. It was the most beautiful sight she'd ever seen.

CHAPTER FORTY-FIVE

Luck is finally on my side.

It had all happened in the blink of an eye. Aidan was trying to talk down the heavily guarded man heading into the warehouse, unaware of anything else. It would be his one and only chance to get away from the wizards and the *dragons*. The bonus was Grace Kensington bursting from the woods.

Acting without a second thought, afraid of another opportunity slipping through his fingers, Andrew grabbed her. With an unconscious Grace draped over his shoulder, he flew towards one of the many hideouts he'd secured over the years. It had taken almost all the black magic stored within him to transport them several miles away from the warehouse. He was going to have to move quickly or be caught. The Dragon Guard and those damn werepanthers would be able to locate him very easily with his powers drained, no matter the hundreds of wards he'd placed around the cabin.

Stopping a hundred yards from his destination, Andrew opened the dragon senses he hadn't used in over six years. It was a longshot they'd respond, but one he had to take without his black magic to help him in his quest. Those long unused instincts were raw and dull from inactivity, but slowly reached out into the woods, searching for anything out of place, anything that could stop him from what he had planned.

Finding nothing unusual, he moved from tree to tree, so quickly he was undetectable to the human eye, until he reached the back of his cabin. Andrew breathed a sigh of relief. The wooden doors to the cellar were still secured with his huge chain and lock. Testing the air, he found the black magic wards still in place. They would be enough deterrent to any who came close.

With a few words of Latin, the lock fell away and the doors slowly creaked open. The smell of stale air, mold, and fertile earth assaulted his reawakening dragon senses as he carefully made his way down the rickety wooden steps. Halfway to the bottom, he reached up and pulled a dirty, woven cord hanging from the ceiling. Bright light illuminated the root cellar he'd dug over three years ago after purchasing his secluded hideaway. Every purchase was made with the utmost care, knowing one day he'd use one of them to lure his brother to his doom.

Placing Grace on the rusty old cot in the corner, he secured her uninjured arm to the rail with the handcuffs he'd gotten while readying this place for whomever he may have the pleasure of torturing. Andrew hadn't planned on it being his brother's mate, but would make the most of the opportunities he was given.

While looking at his prisoner, he noticed the wound in her left shoulder was still bleeding. He knew from the scent the bullet was still lodged in the wound. Thankfully, he'd stocked the cabin with clean sheets and medical supplies. After all, it was his brother he wanted dead, not the useless human, whom until recently had no knowledge of what Fate had in store for her.

Of course, she still had to suffer. Had it not been for her, he and Aidan wouldn't have been out on an unplanned patrol all those years ago. His life was irrevocably changed that night. People had to pay. That's all there was to it. So Grace, the mate of his brother wouldn't die, but she would *know* pain, for she would watch her *mate* die by his hand.

CHAPTER FORTY-SIX

Aidan stood completely still. All he could do was stare at the spot where he'd last seen Grace. He was still reeling from the asshole traitor disappearing into thin air with Grace over his shoulder. It had taken Royce, Aaron, and Devon to talk him down from the complete fury consuming him when they disappeared before his eyes. Not once in his hundred years had his dragon come forth without being called. The fear of losing their mate pushed both man and beast to their very limits. Worry and rage surrounded both beings. They would move heaven and earth to get Grace back.

Dragon Guard and werepanther alike were out combing the surrounding area for any sign of Grace. Everyone felt the surge of black magic when she'd disappeared. Max used the extra senses he'd acquired as King of the Pride to tell them Andrew was down to his last drop of tainted magic. The traitor's tricks were finally coming to an end. Without the extra magical help, there was no way he could continue to hide from them. It was sad consolation, but at least it was something.

Rayne and Lance saved the remaining women from the rubble. All six lay on blankets while Siobhan, their clan's Healer, and several of the Dragon Guard trainees, tended to their wounds. Rayne, using mindspeak, called for assistance while Aidan was trying to save Grace. At least they'd saved the young women 'The Auctioneer' kidnapped, and kept them from whatever horrors he had planned. Again, it was little comfort as long as Grace was out there and Aidan had no way of protecting her from whatever the traitor planned to do to her.

As if watching his mate being carried away, helpless to do anything about it *again* wasn't enough, 'The Auctioneer', his bodyguards, and the damned wizards all fled while he chased after his brother. The guilt he'd worked so hard to put away came crashing down on him, but this time it was so much worse…it was *his mate*. After all his promises, he'd failed…*miserably*.

Breathing deeply, Aidan tried to get his raging emotions under control. It was *not* the time to focus on anything but getting her back. His dragon pushed with all his might to come forth again. The beast wanted to tear apart everyone standing between him and the woman he loved. Wrestling the beast from the edge, Aidan assured his dragon they would have Grace back *and* watch the traitor die.

More than anything else, Aidan needed to be out there looking for his mate. She was *supposed* to be at his side. He needed her. All the waiting and uncertainty was overwhelming his rational thought. No matter how many times his brethren reminded him that staying put was the best plan of action, he just knew they were mistaken.

After a heated debate, Rayne convinced Aidan to wait for word from the search parties. He hated to admit that waiting was the best course of action. The only solace was that he'd have a head start when one of the search parties caught Grace's scent. Waiting was killing him, but if it meant getting her back alive and unharmed, he'd do it.

Closing his eyes, he bowed his head and recited the prayer his mother taught him all those years ago, with his own additions. *Dear Universe, creator of all things great and wonderful, Elders of the Dragon Guard and those Great Warriors who have gone before me, I ask you to show favor upon the one who holds my heart. Protect her from those who wish her harm, keep her safe until I again can protect her for myself. Fill her with your loving, reassuring spirit so she knows I will not stop until she is at my side again. It is with all that I hold dear I ask for your blessings and unending power.*

The last words flowed through his mind just as he felt a spark of recognition. A blink of light filled with warmth and reassurance. It started in the center of his heart, quickly spreading throughout his entire being.

Grace!

The trauma of their situation, coupled with the growing mating call, was making it possible for them to mindspeak in its barest form. He didn't care that it was only a spark; it was *something*. He knew she was alive. It was the reassurance he needed. He would find her before the traitor could cause her more pain. Sending a quick thanks to the Universe, he opened his eyes and went in search of his Commander. One step from the makeshift triage area, Rayne spoke in his mind.

"'A', Where are you? Max found something."

"With Siobhan and the girls."

"Head west. Meet you in a minute. Dev's sending us directions as they track the scent."

Aidan opened his mind to all his brethren. He'd shut down their link when he'd lost control and his dragon came forth, not wanting to ravage their minds with his torment. Making a hundred and eighty degree turn, he ran as fast as he could while his brethren continued to feed him directions. They had a lock on Andrew's scent and were following the trail through a completely hidden section of the forest, not five miles from where he'd stood moments ago. He was going to make it in time. He was going to save Grace and he was going to kill his brother for all the heartache he'd caused.

CHAPTER FORTY-SEVEN

Grace floated in and out of consciousness, refusing to open her eyes. It was a game she'd taught herself as a little girl. As long as her eyes were closed, she could be wherever she wanted to be. Reality didn't matter. At the moment, she was warm and safe, snuggled next to the sexiest man alive, *not* laying on something hard and lumpy, and incredibly old from the smell of it. She tried with all her might to return to the dream where she and Aidan were together, not wanting to be in the world where she'd been dragged across the ground, thrown over some crazy man's shoulder, and taken to only God knew where.

Focusing on the memories of Aidan, Grace pictured his beautiful eyes that reduced her to a mass of want and need. She recalled the feel of his calloused hands touching her body, his lips kissing her with such passion she was unable to do anything but give in to their mutual desire. The way his smile shone brighter than any star in the heavens made her sigh. What she wouldn't give to be in his arms again.

That one thought almost broke her resolve, almost caused the tears she held back to flow, but there was no way the asshole who'd stolen her away would win this battle. She knew Aidan was looking for her. He would never let her down. He would search the world to find her. She just had to hold on until he got there.

She tried to relax, but agonizing pain from every single cell of her body kept her from finding any comfort. Figuring out where she was and if there was any chance of escape became the next plan. Listening carefully, she tried to find clues to her location. Unfortunately, her own heartbeat and ragged breathing overrode any sounds that may have been present.

Slowly opening her eyes, Grace found a worn wooden ceiling with sunlight shining through the splintering boards and cobwebs hanging in the corners. Thankfully, the spiders that'd spun those webs were absent. Spiders were the one thing she knew would send her over the edge. Chuckling to herself, she couldn't believe the thought of arachnids could reduce her to a whiney little girl after all she'd been through.

Her body ached so badly she decided to only move her eyes for the time being. To the left she found a wall a few inches from her head that matched the dilapidated ceiling. On her right, there was open space with shadows cast from the sunlight shining through more cracks and crevices.

This is one old joint.

Rolling her eyes up, she found her bangs.

Time for a trim.

Hell, if she got out of this shithole she was taking a week at the spa. No, not if...*when*. *When* she got out of this mess, she was going to the spa and she was making Aidan and Kyndel go with her. She might even let Kyndel's big, grumpy husband come too. She *was* getting out of this mess. Aidan *was* coming to get her. She *was* going to do whatever possible to help with her own escape. It *was* going to happen.

The power of positive thought.

Rolling her eyes down, she found her pink lace bra, pretty much wasted from blood and dirt, but thankfully covering her breasts and right shoulder. To her left she found a huge bandage. Lifting her right hand, Grace felt the metal of a handcuff digging into her wrist. No feeling in her left hand and the pain radiating from that shoulder stopped her from even trying to move it. She let her eyes slid shut and slowly exhaled, trying to relieve some of the tension thrumming through her body.

After a moment of deep breathing, she decided it was time to deal with the problem directly. Preparing for what she knew would hurt like a son of a bitch and doubting her sanity, Grace took as deep a breath as her damaged ribs would allow.

I need to see if there's a way out.

Just as she was about to lift her head, a doorknob rattled to her right. It figured that when she'd decided it was time to move, the psycho was making his appearance. Her luck just deteriorated. Deciding the best course of action was to pretend she was unconscious, Grace stayed absolutely still.

At least when she'd been out, he'd dressed her wounds, and from what she could tell hadn't inflicted any further damage. If he was working with her boss, he knew who she was, and that she had intimate knowledge of the crime boss and his operation. Grace tensed when she thought of the crime scene photos she reviewed, especially the ones where the informants had been beaten to make them talk.

Closing her eyes, she slowed her breathing the best she could. The door swung open. The sound of booted footsteps struck the wooden floor. Playing possum as long as she could was the only move she had in her condition. Hopefully, it would buy Aidan enough time to save her from hell.

Grace wondered what her asshole captor was doing. She knew he was standing there and had been since his footsteps stopped just short of where she lay. His breathing was slow and deep. The asshole definitely had his emotions under control. She only wished she could say the same thing. That he'd not moved since entering the room was unnerving, but she refused to give in. She could lay there as long as he let her. He didn't know it but the jerk was giving her time to figure a way out of this mess or for Aidan would swoop in and save her. She hated the 'damsel in distress' feeling, but *hell*, it was all she had.

Controlling her breathing and trying to keep her muscles loose, Grace imitated sleep, but the longer the standoff lasted, the more impossible her task became. A chair scraped across the floor, making the hairs on her arms stand on end. "You might as well open your eyes. I know you're awake, *Grace Kensington*."

Her eyes flew open, surprised at the familiarity of her abductor's voice. She was positive she'd never heard it before their trip through the woods, and then all she could remember was his whispered mumblings of something that sounded like a demented nursery rhyme. It was the tone and timber of his voice that was so familiar. Staring at the worn, wooden ceiling for a moment, trying to compose herself, she countered. "Well, you know who I am, so why don't you tell me who you are."

"At least turn your head or roll over if you can. Your left arm is useless from where you were shot, so it's not secured. I think we should at least look at one another during our time together, don't you?"

He sounded so laid back, as if they were about to have lunch, nothing like the psychotic maniac who'd tackled her, thrown her over his shoulder, and carried her off. She took a deep breath, preparing to roll over while her mind and body screamed for her to lie still. Rolling to the right, careful not to jiggle her shoulder any more than was absolutely necessary, Grace almost passed out. Pain like nothing she'd ever experienced shot through her body.

She really wasn't a wimp. Having suffered her fair share of scrapes and broken bones as a kid, Grace prided herself on her tolerance to pain, but this shit was intense to say the least. To top it off, as she moved, her lower back stung from contact with the sheet, reminding her the man she was about to look in the eye had dragged her across the pavement. If…no, *when* she got out of here, she was going to kick the dirt bag's ass.

Finally reaching her destination, she opened her eyes to find her abductor. Grace couldn't stop the gasp that sprung from her lips. Sitting no more than five feet from her was an almost exact duplicate of the man who owned her heart. Her *spidey senses* chose that moment to awaken from their shock and begin screaming at her.

Thanks for the heads up there, guys. I already know I'm in deep shit. All my life I wished for you to leave me alone and you chose an incredibly inopportune time to do it, not to mention waking up and stating the obvious when my head's been through the ringer. Give me a break!

Locking eyes with the man she *knew* was her mate's younger brother, several things became evident. If not for the one amber and one blue eye he sported, the man before her could pass for an identical match to her Aidan. Then there were the vibes radiating from him like some malevolent storm. Where Aidan made her feel safe and secure, the man staring back at her made her nervous and agitated. He was filled with so much hate and rage it danced all over her skin and filled the room around them.

Also deep underneath all the dark, hateful feelings, lay what really drove him… hurt, betrayal, and most of all, loneliness. It *almost* made her feel sorry for him. He worked hard to keep his emotions hidden, but her *intuition* told her those feelings were working their way to the surface. He narrowed his eyes while she continued to stare at him. All thoughts of empathy or sympathy for the jackass fled as she looked into his cold, dead eyes. "Well, I'm facing you now. What the hell do you want from me?" She hoped her false vibrato hid at least some of her nerves.

He responded with a smile that chilled her to the bone. "I guess what they say is true. The Universe does not make mistakes," he mused, more to himself than to her. "I won't insult your intelligence. I'll simply confirm what I'm sure you've already figured out. I'm Andrew O'Brien, younger brother to Aaron and more importantly to *you*, Aidan." He paused, never breaking eye contact. "As for what I want from you, it's really very simple. I want to use you to torture my brother. I know you know you're his mate. I'm sure he's told you what that means to a dragon shifter. I want to use you to make him pay for the sins he committed against me some time ago. After I learned of your existence, I knew keeping him from the one person in the world who meant the most to him would drive him crazy."

Her breathing sped up. She could feel perspiration break out all over her skin. She wanted to stay calm, but this guy was bat shit crazy.

CHAPTER FORTY-EIGHT

"I have no intention of killing you. If I wanted you dead, I would've left you in the cellar to drown when the rains came. I simply want to have a little chat with you. I need you to understand what kind of man the Universe has tied you to. I especially want *him* to go crazy with worry, wondering what I'm doing to you, while he relentlessly tracks you down. Then when he thinks he can save you, I want him to die knowing he failed."

He watched as a tear he was sure she was unaware of rolled down her cheek and couldn't stop from adding insult to injury, "By my hand, of course." He purposely left out his intent to inflict at least a little more pain on her, as well.

Taking careful stock of his prey as she processed his intent, Andrew watched the wheels turning. She was an intelligent woman with a great inner strength and fire. He'd meant what he said about the Universe knowing what She was doing when She created this woman for his brother. Grace wouldn't break easily, and as he sat across from her, he wasn't sure breaking her was the ultimate goal anymore. He couldn't deny he wanted her to hurt, at least a bit. After all, she was the root cause of what happened to him.

"So this is all about your need for vengeance? You work with a heinous criminal who kidnaps young women, blows up an abandoned building, hurting those same innocent women, and then drag me to God knows where, all because you need revenge for something that happened almost seven years ago?"

She took a breath, and he again witnessed her incredible strength. "Not to mention you hurt my best friend when she had *absolutely nothing* to do with your sibling rivalry."

Fire danced in her eyes as she yelled at him and he was once again impressed by her conviction. Perfect match for his brother.

Such a shame the bastard would never live to enjoy his beautiful mate.

CHAPTER FORTY-NINE

His next words surprised her. "I am sorry the Commander's mate was injured in our altercation. Collateral damage is something no one can plan for. As for our 'sibling rivalry' as you put it," he lifted an eyebrow to show his disdain for her description, "it appears you haven't been given the whole story and *that* is one of the reasons you're here today. Regarding kidnapping young women, I have no idea what you're talking about, and I definitely did *not* blow up the warehouse. As a matter of fact, that abandoned building was of paramount importance to my future plans. It's neither here nor there now. Plans change. We must adapt."

He tilted his head, making Grace wonder if he was trying to get a different perspective on the situation, her, or both. She also debated whether to believe what he was telling her about not knowing her boss or his criminal activities. Her *spidey senses* said he was being honest, but maybe they'd been knocked out of whack.

"Since our time here is limited, as I'm sure your mate is frantically trying to find you and my diversions will only keep him at bay for so long, I want to make sure you have the correct information about that night all those years ago. I want to make sure you know what a coward Aidan is." He held up his hand to stop her from speaking and she wished she could slug him right then and there, but he continued talking. "Maybe you should tell me what you've been told and then I'll tell you what *really* happened."

They sat sizing one another up. It reminded her of two gunfighters waiting for the clock to strike twelve in the old west. She decided the only way to get this crap over with was to start talking. "Why would I tell you anything? You tackled me, tried to kill me, and kidnapped me, in some misguided attempt to make your brother pay for something he had no control over and has tortured himself for every day since it happened." She took a huge gulp of air and rushed on. "Pardon me for not feeling like I owe you any type of explanation." She glared, letting him know she had no intention of making this easy for him.

"Point taken." He smirked, the look on his face making her palms itch with the need to slap him. This son of a bitch was really looking to have his ass kicked, and if Grace wasn't shot, beaten, and bruised, she would be just the woman to do it.

He began speaking again. "I'll tell you exactly what happened that evening and you can draw your own conclusions. After all, in your business, it is the facts that matter. Right, Grace?"

CHAPTER FIFTY

Her eyebrows lifted in surprise. "Yes, Grace, I did my homework. I know all about you and your insatiable need to see justice prevail. That's why I think you'll find what I have to say very interesting."

He paused again and watched Grace's face. She was working very hard to control any and all reactions, something he knew she used in her profession. "What I need you to understand is that my abduction and subsequent torture was completely my brother's fault."

Again, he raised his hands to stop her protest. "Let's be fair. I gave you an opportunity to tell me what you know but you declined, so in an effort to bring our time together to a successful conclusion, I ask you to let me speak without interruptions. If there's time when I'm finished, you may ask your questions." He watched her struggle to contain her emotions, amazed at how quickly her 'game face' was firmly in place. Apparently, she wanted to know what he had to say even more than she wanted to argue with him. Grace nodded for him to continue.

"Aidan and I weren't supposed to be on patrol that evening. It was supposed to be our first night off in almost two weeks. But the day before, he'd gotten the scent of something that wouldn't let him rest. Do you know what that was, Grace?' He waited several seconds, until she shook her head. "It was *you*. He'd scented *his mate* and nothing would keep him from finding her." The shock on her face confirmed his suspicions… she *hadn't* been told the whole story. He could only guess what other important details had been left out.

"So I agreed to go out with him. He seemed distracted. I didn't think he should be alone. You see, Aidan and I *were* very close. For as long as I could remember, he'd always been there for me. Now that I say it aloud, it occurs to me it probably made his betrayal even worse. But that's neither here nor there. He's a coward and you need to know the truth." He paused, composing himself and shoving away old memories threatening to weaken his resolve. All the old bullshit had no place in his life anymore.

"You see, Aidan was one of the fiercest, most revered of the Dragon Guard. His hunting skills unparalleled by even our Commander. It was as if he had extra abilities none of the rest of us had been given. He seemed to sense danger before any other. But that fateful night, Aidan was in such a hurry to follow *your* scent, to get a glimpse of *his mate*, he ignored all of his training. Knowing his mate was out in there in the world, so very close to him, made him sloppy.

He broke protocol, something we never did, no matter what. He didn't scan the area for danger. It was imperative we always keep an eye out for *any* enemies in the area, especially when we're flying, but he charged headlong after you, acting on pure instinct. He even went so far as to shut down our mind-to-mind communication. But because he *was* my brother and we shared a bond so much stronger than just siblings or brethren, I blindly followed. I *trusted* him." He stared right into Grace's eyes, conveying the depth of betrayal he felt for someone he'd trusted with his very life. "He spent the night watching you study, and then, after he made sure you and your classmate safely returned to your dorm, we finally took to the skies to return to the lair.

About halfway through our journey, the air grew dense and flight became impossible. I tried to contact Aidan through mindspeak but our link was still closed. We were forced from the sky and back into our human forms. I landed, dazed, unable to move, next to a huge fire surrounded by a large group of chanting, hooded figures. Paralyzed, I was unable to move or call out.

I had no idea where Aidan was as I lay floating in and out of consciousness. Finally able to stay awake for more than a few seconds, I realized I was secured to a tree with magically enhanced silver chains. I watched, unable to do more than blink my eyes as the hooded figures danced around their ritual pyre, the air thick with black magic. I heard the moans and pleas for mercy from a human, followed by the wet tearing sounds of flesh and muscle. Then I watched as a severed head was thrown into the fire. The last thing I remember before blacking out again was a flash of bright light and loud chanting.

I awoke some time later, alone and chained in a dungeon. I tried to contact Aidan, but there was no answer. Then I called out to every member our Force. No one answered. It was as though they'd severed all ties with me. I screamed through mindspeak until I thought my head would explode and my ears would bleed, but no one answered. They'd left me for dead at the hands of our enemies.

It wasn't long before the torture began. The wizards tried everything they knew to draw the dragon magic from me. I was starved, beaten, bombarded with spells and rituals, all to no avail. Aware that my magic was constantly regenerating, they kept me blanketed in silver and many different spells and talismans to make sure I couldn't overpower them. They knew the strength and raw power of dragon magic, but no more. The hundreds of thousands of years they'd sought to eradicate the dragon had apparently been done in oblivion, because they had serious misconceptions. Had they been paying attention, they would've known our power is fused within our very soul. There is no way to extract it from us. While the new and creative forms of torture continued, I called out through our link, trying to reach *any* of my brethren.

No one answered. No one came.

I have no idea how long the torture continued, one day bled into the next. It was a large coven so they had shift after shift of wizards constantly battering me, never giving me time to rest or think. It was then I *knew* no one was coming to save me. I was completely and totally on my own and had to figure a way out of the hell I was living." He paused, gauging Grace's reaction to his revelations. "Do you know what that felt like, Grace? Have you ever been totally alone with no one but yourself to depend on? That's the life you're destined to have with Aidan. He will fail. You *will* be left alone."

He watched Grace work diligently to contain her emotions; sure she wouldn't answer his questions but pausing all the same. Her eyes shot fire in his direction. He knew had she been able, she would've killed him on the spot.

"I decided that day to do whatever was necessary to survive. I stopped fighting them, made the wizards think they'd finally won, that I was broken and ready for them to use as they wished. I knew convincing them I was loyal to their cause would be the best way to escape.

"I willingly participated in their black magic rituals, adding my dragon magic when I could and absorbing their black magic along the way. Even though I did my best to convince them of my allegiance, and no matter how many rituals I participated in, they never completely trusted me. The torture stopped but I was only allowed out of my cell for their rituals and never alone or without at least a silver containment talisman." He watched as she absentmindedly nodded her head.

Of course, their doubt was well founded. The whole time I was planning my escape, waiting for the day one of them would let down their guard or I found a weakness in their defenses. When I wasn't planning my escape, I was planning revenge. I dreamt of the day I would come face to face with the *brother* who left me without a backward glance.

When I finally escaped, the first thing I did was kill every single member of the coven, blasting them with the same magic they'd forced upon me." He chuckled to himself. "They definitely were *not* prepared for the 'monster' they'd created. The abilities I'd gained from the infusion of black magic mixed with my dragon magic was nothing anyone could've predicted. That task completed, I set out to payback Aidan and the others of his Force.

I found with all the absorbed black magic, I was able to hide my true identity. Using it to my advantage, I aligned myself with a pack of hunters, another group of fanatics. With all the information they collected, I was able to keep tabs on the clan. They have a very extensive network of spies in every walk of life that I found very useful. It took six years, but finally I perfected the plan to kill them all.

But as I'm sure you were told things didn't go as planned. The hunters were unable to keep up their end of the bargain. They were weak, completely fallible even when filled with magic. The idiots failed to keep the Dragon Guard at bay, the Commander's mate was injured, and I was captured." He paused.

"Of course I was able to escape. And it was beautiful watching both of my witless brothers standing around with their thumbs up their collective asses looking like the fools they truly are. They had always discounted my abilities. I was after all, their *little* brother. Like always, they gave up and headed back to their lair with their tails tucked between their legs. Hapless losers.

One of the downsides of using black magic is that it doesn't regenerate on its own like dragon magic. You can keep it as long as you don't use it, but I was using it daily to hide my true self from the Dragon Guard and the werepanthers, who've always been allies of the dragons."

He watched her eyebrows shoot up for a split second before she schooled her features again. He chuckled. "So you know about the werepanthers." He paused again, thinking aloud. "Interesting. I'm surprised my useless brother introduced you to so much so soon. But I suppose all the action you've experienced did require him to be a little more forthcoming than is usually the 'dragon shifter protocol'.

I spent the next six months aligning myself with another coven of wizards to refuel my store of black magic. It was the only sure way to ensure success the second time around. Unfortunately, the wizards formed another alliance with this criminal you mentioned. I was completely unaware and they weren't smart enough to see they were being double-crossed. I assure you; I had no idea of their plan and definitely knew nothing about any young women."

He stopped speaking as a thought crossed his mind. "Although, now that I think about it, those young women must've been part of the ritual we were to perform. Well, well, well, those bastards *were* keeping serious secrets from me. Not that I should be surprised. It's very hard to find people you can trust when dealing with patrons of the black arts. But I admit I never expected them to get involved with a crime boss. Serves their pompous ass leader right. It's obvious this 'Auctioneer' fellow never intended on letting the wizards have the girls. He used them to provide cover from the authorities. Now the continual use of magic I felt makes sense."

CHAPTER FIFTY-ONE

Andrew came out of his musings. Grace felt his focus on her once again. "You, my pretty little friend," he smiled, his cold dead eyes showing no real emotion, "are an integral part of my plan. Ever since the first night I saw you enter the apartment where Aidan was staying, *I knew*. I knew you were his mate. Finally, all my efforts to make him pay were coming together and in an even bigger, better way than I ever hoped. I followed you and planned to take you from your place of business, but those thugs got there first. I understand now how and why that happened." He continued to smile his dead smile. "Thank you for that bit of information; it will come in handy later.

I thought all was lost, but then you, your mate, and his band of merry men appeared at the warehouse, confirming my suspicions. The wizard leader and his coven aren't nearly as strong as they claim to be. If they were, there's no way the warehouse could've been located by anyone *but* the wizards. For now, I'm sorry to say our time is coming to an end. Your mate is closing in on our location and I must make sure everything is ready for his arrival." He shifted in his seat, crossing his legs, appearing to get more comfortable. "But, as promised, I'm giving you a few minutes to ask any questions you may have."

She stared right into his eyes, saying nothing, amazed at the calm way he spoke to her. Ranting, raving lunatic was more what she'd expected. But then this was his forum; she was a captive audience and he could give his prepared speech the way he'd planned. It was a lot like the criminals she'd watched on the witness stand giving the testimony they'd been coached to give by their attorney. One perfectly orchestrated speech meant to sway the judge and jury to believe in their innocence. And like those same criminals, this lunatic failed in his attempt to convince her of anything but the fact he needed years of therapy.

Grace refused to give him any indication of what she was thinking. He'd been through a horrible ordeal; she'd give him that. But there was no doubt in her mind that Aidan had never given up on his brother. Her mate had mourned the traitor's death and carried the guilt like a noose around his neck. She also knew sharing any of that information with Andrew at this stage of the game would be a complete waste of time. He was just like all the fanatics he'd aligned himself with over the years. Andrew believed in his cause with a single-minded intensity.

As she watched him patiently waiting for her to speak, Grace thought of all the things she wanted to say. Then she thought of all the things her experience told her she should ask him. He was warped, possibly beyond repair, but he was also intelligent. If she could engage him, at least on some level, maybe she could stall him long enough for Aidan to arrive. After all, Andrew said he could feel them getting closer and Grace's *intuition* confirmed his suspicions. It also told her Andrew believed *everything* he was telling her. It was *his* truth and no amount of healthy debate would sway his opinion.

She had to play it exactly right or Andrew would blow a fuse. She just wished she knew what the right play was. The longer she stared at the man who'd killed an entire coven of wizards, injured her best friend, kidnapped her, and planned to kill her mate, all the anger, pain, and fear she felt bubbled over. All thoughts of playing it safe and keeping the lunatic talking fled. She opened her mouth and what came out surprised even her.

"Andrew, I *am* sorry for what you've been through and I *am* devastated for the part you believe I played in that. And whether you want to believe it or not, I know your brother spent every day for over six years letting the guilt eat away at him."

She watched his left eye began to twitch. It was the only indication he heard what she said. Figuring she had nothing to lose, Grace forged ahead. Either Aidan would get there in time or she would be dead. What ever happened, she was sick and tired of having people think they could hurt her and get away with it.

"You know, you just sat there and told me what a coward your brother was and *is*. That *you know* he's going to let me down. You made sure I knew beyond a shadow of a doubt he was completely responsible for what you went through at the hands of those wizards… but let's be honest with each other." She paused, staring into his mismatched eyes, seeing a rising tide of emotion for the first time. "*You* should have scanned the area. You yourself said it was procedure to do so when flying. *You* shouldn't have depended on your big brother to take care of you. After all, *you* were trained as a Dragon Guardsman just like your brother, correct?"

She knew he wasn't going to answer. There was no way he would give her the satisfaction. But what she did notice that renewed her resolve and let her know her strategy, no matter how crazy it was, might actually be working, was the way his fists clenched so tightly his knuckles were white and he was breathing like he'd just run a marathon. His perfectly constructed veneer was cracking. All she needed to do was keep after him and the real bat shit crazy Andrew would appear. She knew having the raving lunatic he truly was out in the open, was the only way she was going to survive long enough for her mate to find her.

"And even more than that, after *you* escaped, why didn't *you* return to your family? Why did *you* think the logical choice was to betray everything *you'd* known for the better part of a hundred years and align yourself with not one, but both of your own kin's worst enemies?"

Grace knew she was poking the bear, placing extra emphasis every time she said 'you', but she needed to drive her point home. It may be the only chance she had. She chuckled in her mind as the most beautiful color of red began creeping up his neck, confirming she was pushing all the right buttons. It could be considered sadistic that she found watching this man come undone a pleasure, but it was all about survival, and Grace would do whatever it took to survive.

"What's the matter, Andrew? Cat got your tongue?" She narrowed her eyes and pretended to think for a moment, a tactic she used more than once to unnerve a witness. "You know what I think? I think you knew *you* were at least partially to blame. I think *you* spent most of the time in that dungeon thinking of ways to blame anyone *but* yourself. I think *you* decided there was no way *you* could live knowing that *you* could've done something to prevent your capture. So you convinced yourself *you* were the victim and took none of the blame."

He leaned forward unconsciously as she continued to pound away at him with her words, just another sign she was getting to him. "I think you knew there was no way your brother would've let that happen to *you* and even more, *Andrew*..." She paused, took a deep breath, and plowed ahead, speaking as quickly as possible, "I think *you* were embarrassed. I think once you started participating in their rituals you were sure there was no way your family would take you back and that was something *you* could *not* accept. I think *you knew* the wizards had done something to keep you from communicating with your brothers. You couldn't accept that you were wrong, that they might've been looking for you. I think you spent your entire life letting your brothers, specifically Aidan, take care of *you* and your own laziness landed you in the middle of your worst nightmare and *you* had to find someone else to blame."

She barely had the last word out of her mouth before the chair Andrew sat in sailed across the room. She flinched when it hit the wall, exploding into a mass of broken pieces and splinters. Next, the small bedside table and lamp flew through the air, along with another chair she hadn't known was there.

All the while, he ranted and raved, face flaming, teeth bared, spittle flying. When there was nothing else to break, he turned on Grace. "You think *I'm* embarrassed?" Andrew roared. "You think Aidan took care of *me*?" He took a step in her direction. Grace worked hard not to shrink back. "You think I *wanted* to go back to the very people who left me for dead?" He took another step forward. "You think..."

He stopped mid-stride and spun towards the door. Standing completely still, his breathing ragged, his shoulders bunched so tight his neck practically disappeared, Andrew seemed to be listening to something Grace couldn't hear.

In the next second, her *intuition* went on high alert. Andrew turned towards her again, but this time she saw a small round pendant hanging from a leather cord in his hand. He was still seething, but in place of the rage she'd seen on his face before, there was now an evil smile that made her gasp.

His voice was low and ominous as he spoke. "I'm so sorry our time together has come to an end, but even through my rusty senses I know your mate is nearby and I have other things to prepare. So this is where we part ways, Miss Kensington."

And with that, he threw the pendant onto her stomach while saying something she could only guess was Latin. Drawing in a breath to tell him to *go to hell*, black spots danced before her eyes, and before the words left her mouth, her world went black...*again*.

CHAPTER FIFTY-TWO

He knew Grace was close, Aidan could feel her in every fiber of his being. He was on the brink of losing his mind. His dragon was straining to get free and find its mate. Both man and beast were frantic to have Grace safe and with them, where she belonged. All the false trails and misdirects Andrew planted made getting to this point infuriating. He silenced everyone around him and stood perfectly still, reaching out with every sense he possessed...*searching*. She was close. Aidan needed to make sure he was heading in the right direction.

Closing his eyes, he thought of the beautiful woman the Universe made just for him. Her eyes rivaled the blue of a summer sky. Her haunting scent drove him wild. His fingertips rubbed together of their own accord, searching for her ebony tresses. He thought of the feel of her porcelain skin as he touched and tasted every inch of her. She was still alive, and he *would* find her.

Aidan knew Grace wasn't Andrew's real target. The stupid son of a bitch was using her to make the situation so much worse. He doubted his end goal was to kill her, but he was afraid of what his younger brother was capable of in his attempts to punish Aidan. He knew from the scent trails they'd followed that Andrew's dragon, no matter how weak, was trying to return. It had to be from the loss of his black magic. As a last ditch effort to plead for his mate's life, Aidan tried to contact him through their mindspeak, but their link was nowhere to be found.

Focusing on Grace, Aidan reached through the growing mating bond trying with all his might to locate her. His brethren and their allies lent their strength to his efforts. Just when he was about to give up, the sound of wood breaking and splintering echoed through the trees. Listening more intently, he heard it again, quickly followed by a spike of pure adrenalin through the link he shared with Grace.

Pushing his enhanced speed to an all-time high, Aidan followed the echo of their mating bond and the noise of breaking wood. The farther he ran, the more he opened his senses, searching for Grace, but also for his brother's traps. Aidan knew he was being lured into something deadly and was more than willing to run headlong into hell, if it meant saving Grace.

As he crested the ridge, Aidan spotted a small cabin.

She's in that cabin!

Sprinting down the hill, still searching for any traps that would slow his descent, he directed their search party to make a loose perimeter around the cabin. Grace was his first priority. He would leave the traitor to the others.

The front door, and what appeared to be a single window in the structure, came into view as he barreled towards his destination. Stopping dead in his tracks, he scanned the area. To his right, trying to remain hidden, was *Andrew*. The brother he'd thought he lost, returning to a complete dragon shifter, as nature intended. But Aidan knew the traitor had learned other, *more dangerous* tricks he had to watch for. Aidan didn't know the man who now inhabited the body of the brother he once considered his closest confidant.

Probing, not sure if Andrew was able to pick up on his intentions, Aidan turned. He knew he was walking into a trap, but nothing would stop him from his goal. The trick would be keeping both Grace and himself alive. The traitor was bringing the fight to him and Aidan would do whatever it took to save his mate and stop his deranged brother.

Seconds felt like hours while Aidan waited for Andrew to make his move. Losing patience, he sent a message to Rayne along their private link. *"Andrew is to my right, hiding behind a tree. Can you sense him?"*

"No, but there's a blind spot where you indicated... must be him. Your connection with him was always stronger than the rest of us. I'll swing around and come up behind him. You wanna hit him head on?" Aidan could hear his old friend holding back his anger, allowing him to take the lead.

"Yeah, let me know when you're in place. Everyone else needs to hold their positions until we get him out in the open."

"I'm on the move."

Aidan felt Rayne disconnect. He took a deep breath and counted to five. When Rayne was in place, Aidan yelled towards the concealed the traitor. "I know you're there, Andrew. You might as well come out and show yourself, *you coward*!"

He waited another count of five, picking up more emotions from Andrew... none of it good. "What are you afraid of, *little* brother? Afraid to stand up to someone your own size? Is hurting women your new game? First Rayne's mate, and now mine?" He continued his taunts until everyone was in place, ready for his signal.

Throwing out the one insult he knew would get a reaction, Aidan yelled, "I know what it is. You're so used to having people cover your ass you don't know what to do on your own. Let's face it; Aaron and I had your back *all your life*. Then you hid behind the hunters, never really getting your hands dirty, just pulling the strings, cavorting with the enemy, always for your own purposes. You don't have the balls to face me. YOU ARE THE COWARD!"

Andrew was losing control, his anger burning hot... his aggression rising, making the air sizzle around them. Aidan heard the crackle of fallen leaves. Andrew was coming in hard and fast, just the way Aidan wanted him. If he could keep the traitor angry, Andrew would make mistakes; mistakes that would help Aidan capture him and more importantly, get to Grace.

Aidan turned just as Andrew launched himself through the air, his short dagger drawn. The Guardsman drew his broadsword, blocking the blade headed for his chest, throwing his brother's momentum off. Andrew landed on his ass. Aidan advanced as Andrew leapt to his feet. The two stood staring.

Aidan could feel the others closing in. Out of the corner his eye he saw a giant cat slinking through the treetops. Immediately recognizing Max, he knew that although they didn't share a mindspeak connection, the King would know what to do when the time came for action.

Aidan again focused on his brother. The last seven years had been rough on Andrew. He looked weathered and beaten. The wildness in his eyes attested to all they'd learned about him since his 'resurrection'. Black magic was deadly shit, and Andrew had been immersed in it for a long time. No matter how he searched, Aidan could find no shred of the brother he'd raised. All that remained was the man who'd held a knife to Kyndel's neck and run off with his mate. A man he would capture and take to the Elders for a Tribunal. A traitor he would kill in the blink of an eye without remorse. No one, brother or not, would hurt his mate and get away with it.

Andrew lunged. Aidan spun to the left, kicking out and connecting with his brother's lower back. Andrew stumbled forward but spun, striking out with his free hand, connecting with Aidan's shoulder. Aidan used the momentum to swing his broadsword at his brother's neck. Andrew ducked, but not before Aidan's sword left its mark on his upper arm. Andrew advanced just as an explosion sounded at his back. Both men stopped, Aidan afraid to take his eyes off his brother but getting a sick feeling in the pit of his stomach as an evil grin appeared on Andrew's face.

"Wonder which one of your precious Guardsmen was caught in my trap?" He paused as if he suddenly had all the time in the world.

Aidan would've given anything to knock the shit-eating grin from his smug face, but he had to keep his cool. Whoever tripped the traitor's trap was sure to be stunned, but would recover. Aidan needed to end this little game and get to Grace. "What the hell do you think you could do that would hurt one of *my* brethren? You're out of black magic and completely out of touch with your own dragon magic. Hell, you even suck at fighting with your short dagger. Been living the high life, have you *little* brother?" Again, he used the taunt he knew Andrew hated the most.

The color rose in the traitor's face as he shook with fury. Aidan could feel Andrew's need to attack but the traitor was holding back. Aidan threw his senses wide open, but could find nothing but his brethren and the werepanthers. Andrew had something planned, but Aidan was running out of time. He needed to force his brother's hand. He needed to get to Grace. Aidan decided the only way to get the bullshit over with was to attack. One way or another, Andrew would be out of the way.

CHAPTER FIFTY-THREE

Andrew watched his brother plot and plan, hoping to come up with a way to get to his mate. Somewhere along the line, Andrew figured the great and honorable Aidan had decided it was perfectly acceptable for Andrew to be collateral damage. As he thought about it, he really couldn't blame him. After all, he'd tried to kill the Commander's mate, and was definitely responsible for the disreputable state Grace was in. But none of that compared to what he'd been through and he just couldn't care. One of his traps had already been tripped. Andrew knew they were surrounded, even though his rusty dragon senses couldn't pick up anyone but the brother who stood in front of him.

He listened for anyone approaching. All Andrew needed was the smallest head start in order for the domino effect of magical traps he'd set to take out at least half the Dragon Guard and allow him to get away. There was no way he was going back to the Elders to be tried as a traitor; he still had work to do, revenge to dole out. He needed to get Aidan in the right spot… at the center of the blast.

It was time for his brother to die. Andrew debated the best way to get Aidan farther into the woods when the Guardsman raised his broadsword and advanced. Andrew threw his dagger up to block a direct hit to his solar plexus, as he pulled the katana strapped to his back from its sheath and moved to the left. Aidan continued his torturous assault. All Andrew could do was defend and work hard to keep his injuries to a minimum. Aidan was a man on a mission…and the mission meant spilling Andrew's blood.

The continued movement further opened the wound on his shoulder. His arm was instantly coated in blood, making it almost impossible to keep hold of his dagger. Aidan wasn't fighting like he wanted to capture him. The sanctimonious Guardsman was fighting like he wanted Andrew dead. He hated to admit it, but Aidan had always been the superior swordsman, and with the fear of losing his mate driving him, he was a force to be reckoned with. Andrew decided to use Aidan's own force against him. He only had to drive him to the spot less than fifty yards away and his getaway plan would be triggered.

As Aidan bombarded him with every move in his repertoire, Andrew attempted to split his concentration between protecting his body and moving backwards. Just a few more steps and they would be there. Andrew raised his katana to block a killing blow, just as all hell broke loose. Explosions sounded all around. Dragon Guardsmen and werepanthers, already shifted into their powerful animals, were running towards him and his brother. Someone had tripped his intricately designed trap, but no one was even near the spot where the key amulet was buried.

Considering the situation completely stacked against him, Andrew turned tail and ran. He threw his dagger at Aidan in the hopes it would slow him down, while heading for a patch of thick brambles he knew hid a stream he could use to hide his scent while escaping.

Andrew ran as fast as he could, pulling on his long forgotten enhanced abilities to fly through the woods. Lifting one of the two remaining amulets from around his neck, he prepared to trigger its magic. He counted on the fact that Aidan wanted to get to his mate and that he could stay at least one step ahead of the others until he activated the amulet. Andrew prayed the Commander was nowhere nearby, because Andrew had less than a fifty/fifty shot at making it out of this cluster fuck.

He saw the hedge of brambles and heard the roar of the stream. Pouring every ounce of energy and rusty dragon magic he could muster into his stride, Andrew pushed himself towards his goal. He could feel someone at his back. Was sure if he turned around, he would see all the men he'd grown up with trying as hard as they could to catch him, but looking over his shoulder would slow him down.

A mere ten feet from the brambles, Andrew's injured shoulder was grabbed from behind. Pulling his shoulder forward, excruciating pain radiated down his arm and across his back. He stumbled and another hand grabbed at the hem of his shirt. Jerking from his would-be captor's hold, Andrew heard his shirt rip as he dove over the hedge of brambles. Sliding down the muddy riverbank, he landed in the stream and was immediately carried downstream by the rapid current.

Lifting his head above the water to speak the incantation that would active his talisman, Andrew saw the Commander standing on the bank, sword drawn, a piece of his shirt in his hand. The traitor should've been ecstatic that he'd gotten away, especially from Rayne, but the look on the Commander's face spoke of vengeance, pain, and suffering. In all the years he'd known Rayne, Andrew had never witnessed such pure hate.

With a healthy dose of fear running through his veins, he uttered the words to activate the amulet to get him to safety. He had no clue how safe he would actually be after all that had happened, but he had a plan, and one way or another, he *would* have his revenge.

CHAPTER FIFTY-FOUR

Aidan was just about to deliver a killing blow. He didn't care if they were blood, he didn't care that Andrew had been his closest confidant, he didn't care that the Elders wanted the traitor brought back to the clan for the Tribunal. Aidan wanted him dead.

Somewhere in the barrage of blows he leveled at Andrew, he'd decided his younger brother was no longer worth saving, no longer worth worrying about. He knew deep inside Andrew would try to get at him. Plain and simple, Aidan was sick and tired of his brother's bullshit. He decided the world would be a better place without the traitor, and Aidan intended to make it so.

Then the world around him exploded. That little son of a bitch had set some kind of magical explosives. As the traitor turned to run, Andrew threw his dagger at Aidan's chest. Aidan ducked, thinking only of Grace lying in that cabin.

"Rayne, get that asshole, I have to get to Grace."

"Go! I'll handle the traitor," Rayne answered. Aidan could feel the pure hatred seething from one of his oldest friends. If anyone besides him could stop Andrew, it would be the Commander.

Aidan all but flew through the destruction his brother had caused. There were fallen trees and eroded earth. Andrew indeed meant to maim or kill as many of them as possible. Aidan had a sneaking suspicion he was the one who was supposed to die, but apparently, things hadn't gone according to the traitor's plan.

Jumping over another especially large crater created by the explosion, Aidan reached the top of a hill. He'd been so caught up in the battle he hadn't realized how far away from the cabin Andrew had pushed him.

Apparently, Grace was unconscious. He'd been trying the entire time he ran to connect with her through their growing mating link, but it was silent. No other reason was acceptable... she was *just unconscious*. As he reached the crest, he looked out over more devastation and finally saw the cabin, off to the left, completely untouched. His relief was a living, breathing entity around him. He ran, his dragon pushing him even faster. Aidan focused on the small structure, as everything around him blurred.

He burst through the door, leaving it hanging by a hinge, and ran to the bed where his mate lay motionless. Wincing, he took in all of her injuries. At least Andrew had bandaged her shoulder, and from the scent, either the bullet had gone straight through or had been removed. Aidan smelled topical antibiotics, so for the moment, infection wasn't a worry.

Pure panic threatened to overtake him that Grace was dressed in nothing but a pink lace bra and jeans. He continued to scent her, and found Andrew had only removed her shirt and cut the strap of her bra to dress her wound. He wanted to grab her up and run as far from the site of her captivity as possible, but first he needed to know that moving her wouldn't harm her any farther.

Sitting on the edge of the bed, Aidan gently laid his hand on her cheek. She was warmer than usual, but he prayed it was because her body was working hard to heal her wounds. Tears filled his eyes as he got an up close and personal look at the damage done to her beautiful face. Make no mistake about it, Grace would always be the most magnificent woman in the world, but his poor mate had so many bruises, cuts, and scrapes, he couldn't find an inch without injury.

Her torso was just as bad. Her ribs were at least cracked, if not broken. He knew if he were able to see her back, there would be more of the same. His heart ached at the pain she'd suffered. Grace was strong. He knew she'd fought hard, but she was no match for his brother. His fingers continued to gently wander over her face and down her neck. "M*o chroi*, I'm here. Please open your eyes. I love you, Grace. Please… *please* be all right."

He cooed and cajoled for what seemed like forever, saying whatever nonsense came to mind. He told her how much he needed her, that he was so glad to have her back, teased her about her new nickname…but she didn't move a muscle. The only sign she still lived was the slow, even, rise and fall of her chest.

When he'd reached the end of his rope, he called out to Devon. *"Dev, bring your mother to the cabin. Grace is alive but I can't wake her. Hurry!"*

"On our way."

Aidan continued to touch Grace as carefully as possible, taking note of her most serious injuries, while talking to her the whole time. He'd heard if someone was in a coma, they could hear everything going on around them. He wanted to make sure his mate knew he was there and would never be apart from her again.

Needing the contact, but also hoping their special connection would somehow bring her back to him, he laid his lips to hers. Just about to give in to his ever-growing grief, Aidan felt the others closing in on the cabin. Devon was the first to call to him. *"We're almost there, less than a minute out, 'A'."*

"Hurry, Dev, I really need her to wake up."

"Keep it together, 'A'. She's gonna need you strong and ready to nurse her back to health when she wakes up," Rayne answered. His Commander was doing whatever it took to keep Aidan's head in the game. They all felt his complete agony at Grace's condition through their long time connection.

"I know. I just need her to wake up." Before he could sink any lower into his despair, Devon rushed in with Siobhan in his arms, followed by his other brethren, along with Max and Sophia.

Devon set his mother gently on her feet next to where Aiden sat on the bed. Looking up at the elder Healer, Aidan searched her eyes for comfort. Siobhan smiled and touched his shoulder. Her warmth and a peace that helped him hold back the anxiety filled him. He had stared down hordes, defended his homeland and his clan against every enemy imaginable, even picked up his fallen comrades and carried their bodies to the lair for burial, but the thought of living without Grace was something he couldn't bear.

"I need you to at least move to the end of the bed, Aidan. I have to examine your mate." Siobhan's soothing voice filtered through his anguished mind. He heard the chuckle in her tone as he moved. He wasn't sure who had put a chair at the end of the bed for him, but he was thankful.

His hands on her legs, the need to touch her an overwhelming force within him, Aidan moved his thumbs up and down, rubbing the inside of her calves lightly as Siobhan ran her fingers through Grace's think ebony hair, feeling for injuries. He watched as the Healer worked her way down Grace's neck, gently prodding and poking to find anything in need of her healing powers.

Aidan cringed as she removed the bandage from Grace's left shoulder and the true extent of the damage became evident. Siobhan examined the wound and got a tub of Granny's recipe. He grinned at the number of times that very ointment had touched Grace's skin in a matter of just a few days.

The Healer covered the laceration and the surrounding area before applying a new bandage. He prayed through the entire examination for Grace to wince in pain or show some sign she was in there, fighting to come back to him. He now knew what Rayne had gone through when Kyndel was hurt. He'd felt bad for both of them at the time, but now he was experiencing the same torment and wondered how Rayne survived those four days.

He was awakened from his musings when Grace's legs moved under his hands. Just about to jump for joy, Aidan realized it was Siobhan moving his mate onto her side to get a look at her back. Siobhan leaned over and immediately stood back up with a perfectly round amulet dangling from the leather strap she held in her hands. The shiny object was deeply inscribed with runes covering the front and back.

"This is what keeps your mate from waking, Aidan. From what I can tell, she's healing very nicely. It seems as though your bond is growing very quickly. Having you near is definitely speeding the process, but this talisman is keeping her unconsciousness. Without having the one who created it here to break the spell, we either need another magic practitioner with greater power, or we need to get her to the Healing Caves of our clan where all the healers can perform the Cleansing Ritual."

Siobhan walked to the end of the battered bed, sat on the edge facing him, and placed her hand on his arm. "It is your choice, son, but you need to make your decision quickly. I have no idea how this was created or what its ultimate intent is, but the sooner the magic leaves her body, the better. I will tell you I find no taint of black magic in or around your mate. I understand your brother has been in collusion with dark wizards and is responsible for Grace's present physical state, so it is definitely a positive I find no sign of it in her." She rubbed slowly up and down his arm. He could feel her healing powers sinking into him, comforting him. "We will all leave you alone to make your decision."

Siobhan went to rise and Aidan grabbed her hand. "There's no need for any of you to leave. I'll take her to the caves. I'll do whatever possible to return this vibrant, amazing woman to her gorgeous self." He bowed his head and felt his dragon chuff in agreement. When he raised he head again, he noticed Devon, Rayne, and Max were no longer in the cabin. *"Where are you?"* he sent directly into Rayne's mind.

"We're making a gurney for you to carry your mate to the caves. It seems to be something we're getting very good at." Aidan could hear the grin in Rayne's voice and appreciated his attempt to lighten the mood.

"Thanks, bro," was all he could choke out for fear the tears he was holding back would fall. His brethren would understand, but there would be hell to pay later.

He looked back to his beautiful Grace, still lying completely still, and realized she was covered with a clean white blanket. Looking farther up her body, he saw Sophia gently lifting her while Siobhan pulled the blanket through to the other side. His mate was covered and ready for her flight. He nodded in thanks to both women.

Rayne called from outside for all to hear. "We're ready out here whenever you are, 'A'."

"You're *sure* it's all right to move her." He leveled his stare at Siobhan, waiting for her confirmation.

"Yes, Aidan, she is well enough to travel. Now pick up your mate and get out of here. I will have Devon call ahead to the other healers. We will be right behind you."

He hugged the Elder Healer, thanking her for all she'd done and would do for his mate. He walked to where Grace lay. Her safety was first and foremost. She'd been through too much in the very short time they'd known one another. He would stand for no more.

Aidan bent and with the utmost care, lifted his mate into his arms. Even though she was still unconscious, he couldn't stop the feeling of completion with Grace in his arms. This was where she was meant to be… always… for all time, cocooned in his arms.

Turning on his heel, he walked out of the cabin. As soon as Grace was healthy again, he would return to this grotesque house of horrors and burn it to the ground. But now he had more important things to handle.

He flew as fast and true as he could while constantly monitoring Grace's condition. It was the longest flight of his life. As he landed, several of the younger healers met him at the mouth of the Healing Cave. They took Grace and the gurney from his paw and headed in. He quickly changed from dragon to man and hurried to his mate.

It had been a very long time since he'd been in the healing caves. Aidan had forgotten how exquisite they were and what an immense power they held. Even with all his worry, he felt the powers of the cave working on him. Relaxing just a fraction, he was able to think more clearly.

Legend stated the Healing Caves knew what each person needed and worked to provide it for them, to restore each to their full self. He sent another of many prayers to the Universe asking for Her help with Grace's healing. He knew she would be okay, he felt in his soul, but nothing stopped his worry. She hadn't moved *at all* during Siobhan's examination or their flight. It was not that the Eder Healer had been anything but gentle, it was just that there was no change in breathing, no slight wincing from the pain she had to be in… *nothing.*

He slowly took in the splendor of one of the most magnificent places in his clan's lair. This holy, healing place was revered and protected. This cavern and its many passages had been formed millions of years ago, when the melting water from thawing glaciers carved the very tunnels he stood in front of as they made their journey to the sea. The many minerals, rocks, and gems still embedded in the walls, floor and ceiling, glittered and glimmered in the light from the many candles hanging in sconces throughout the cave, illustrating its power to all that entered.

There were huge stalactites hanging from the ceiling and stalagmites rising from the floor that seemed to be standing guard. Aidan had heard all the stories from older members of his clan concerning this healing place. When the original dragon shifters found this land and began to carve out their lair, this cavern with all of its magic and wonder called to them. Their leader and his Elders had entered, felt the incredible power of the grotto, and knew in that moment the Universe had shown favor on them. This was indeed the place they would build their clan. That was hundreds and hundreds of years ago and it still served them well.

Trying to hold back the flood of emotions threatening to overwhelm him, he remembered when Siobhan found the amulet that was holding his beautiful mate in stasis and an uncontrollable rage threatened to overtake him.

He'd wanted to kill the traitor before, but knowing Andrew was responsible for Grace's coma now made Aidan want the bastard to not only die, but to suffer while it he did it.

His hands ached to feel his broadsword slice through his brother's body and to watch Andrew's blood soak the earth. Nothing, not even the traitor's hate for Aidan, excused what the little shit had done to Grace. Andrew would know no mercy when they met the next time. The bastard had to die, and die by Aidan's sword was exactly what was going to happen.

So completely lost in his thoughts, he didn't hear Devon and Siobhan come up behind him. Aidan damn near jumped out of his skin when his brethren grabbed his shoulder. "Whoa, bro, what planet were you on? I haven't been able to sneak up on you since we were kids," Devon asked and Aidan saw the look of concern on his friend's face.

"He was thinking of the one responsible for the present condition of his mate, I would suspect," Siobhan stated, confirming what they already knew; she was not only an incredible Healer, but also an unparalleled empath.

"Yeah, I was. Sorry to bring negative energy to the caves. I let my anger get away from me." He bowed his head and breathed deeply, fighting for the control he didn't have.

"I understand. Clear your mind and leave those thoughts for another time. The others are ready to begin the ritual." Siobhan turned and started down the corridor he remembered walking with both his brothers when his father returned, injured from an especially bloody battle.

Devon squeezed his shoulder. "Come on, 'A'. Let's go bring your lady back."

Aidan entered a cavern at the end of a very long passage and found Grace lying on a crystal table covered in a bright white sheet. Her ebony locks flowed over the end like a dark billowing waterfall. Even in this condition, she was absolutely breathtaking. He could see the abrasions on her face and shoulders were healing nicely, confirming what Siobhan said about their deepening connection.

Grace was pulling from his healing powers. He would give them all to her if they would rid her of the magic the traitor had thrust upon her. Aidan continued forward until he stood by her side. Gently placing her hand in his, he took a long look at his mate. He poured all he felt into his gaze, hoping somehow his love and hope for their future would reach her.

He looked up as the healers assembled around the table holding his mate, ready to begin the Cleansing Ritual. He offered one last prayer to the Universe and waited. Grace had to be okay, *she just did.* And if for some reason she wasn't, he would follow her to the heavens, because… Aidan would follow her *anywhere.*

CHAPTER FIFTY-FIVE

Grace was absolutely as frustrated as she'd ever been. That idiot, Andrew, had thrown something at her after trying to be a comic book villain with his ominous speech. Then the lights went out. She couldn't imagine what he'd done. He hadn't given her any drugs or anything that would have made her unable to move, so it had to have been the flashy piece of metal hitting her stomach before bouncing off.

It was only a few heartbeats before she realized she could still hear everything, even feel the breeze on her skin, but just could not move. Grace tried with all her might to yell or open her eyes… do *anything*, but her body simply wouldn't obey. As she listened intently, wondering if the asshole was just standing there staring, she even tried to roll over again, knowing it would hurt like hell but *really* needing to move. She wouldn't put it past Andrew to stand and watch; he definitely was *not* playing with a full deck. But as she lay there motionless, it became apparent she was alone, with no way to get out of the hellish nightmare her life had become.

She must've dozed for a bit because the next thing she knew, the cabin was shaking and she could hear explosions coming from outside. It all made sense. Andrew had gone on and on about the 'things' he had to get ready for Aidan. She prayed with her whole heart that her mate was okay and would somehow find her. She imagined his hypnotic whiskey-colored eyes, the feel of his hands on her skin, and his masculine scent.

She continued praying until her *spidey senses* rang in her head. The longer she waited, the louder they clanged, until she wished for the ability to put her hands over her ears. A loud crash from the vicinity of the door, followed a large gust of wind, and then the most magnificent feeling of warmth and love she'd ever felt.

Aidan!

He'd found her. He was okay and hadn't been injured by the explosions she heard. Andrew hadn't gotten to him. If she could've, she would've breathed a sigh of relief.

The first touch of his hand to her cheek was like a whisper. She could only imagine the mess he saw when he looked at her. Well, her mother always told her she looked good in blues and purples, and she was sporting the whole gamut on her face. Grace wanted to cry out, grab her man, and hug him for all she was worth. Tell him she *knew* he would find her. Make sure he knew she never gave up hope that they would be together again. But no matter what she tried, only her mind screamed… her body remained dormant. Aidan continued to run his finger over her face and down her neck as he spoke to her in hushed, reverent tones. He told her he loved her and her heart almost burst from her chest. She longed to tell him she loved him too. He asked her over and over again to wake up. She wanted to yell as loud as she could that she *was* awake.

The buzzing from Aidan's mindspeaking started in her head. She wondered what they were saying, but just knowing they were near and he wasn't alone, comforted her. His touch was the best feeling in the world. There'd been a time she'd feared never feeling those amazing hands on her body again. She wanted to return his touch, look into his eyes, and tell him everything would be all right, as she listened to the utter heartbreak in his voice.

Grace knew Aidan was a fierce, powerful, warrior, but the thought of sadness coloring the same eyes that had held so much passion and adoration, brought all her anger to the forefront. Anger at what Andrew had done to them. Anger that the man she considered her mentor was actually a criminal mastermind. Anger that they were people trying to hurt Aidan and his kin. Anger at the whole, hellacious situation.

Her inner monologue was abruptly cut short when a calm, soothing voice, exuding serenity, spoke of her condition. She thought hard and finally remembered it was the Healer who was helping the girls back at the warehouse. Grace thanked God the Healer was nearby and prayed she would be able to stop whatever was causing Grace's paralysis. The Healer asked Aidan to move and Grace wanted to burst out laughing at the tone; the older woman was taking care of *everyone*. Grace missed Aidan's touch but was immediately comforted when he put his hands on her shins.

The Healer was gentle as she examined all of Grace's injuries. She knew the older woman didn't mean to, but there were a couple of times she touched places that made Grace want to yelp in pain, although she couldn't, and damn if that didn't piss her off all the more. Grace hoped Aidan or one of the others caught the traitor, or better yet, chopped off his head. She'd spent most of her life believing people needed to be treated fairly and have a chance to at least explain the reason for their crimes; *hell*, she'd made it her career. But that piece of shit needed to die and she couldn't work up any remorse for her feelings.

She felt the Healer's hands at her side and would've winced when she was lifted up and tilted. The pain in her ribs was unbearable, but it ended as quickly as it'd begun. Grace heard the Healer explaining something about the shiny pendant Andrew had thrown at her. Holy crap, he *had* put a spell on her. How the hell was shit like that *even* possible? He really was a twisted little pain in the ass.

She listened while they discussed something about a Cleansing Ritual, and wished she'd had time to learn more about all of this dragon and magical stuff before she it was used on her. As usual, she was late to the party. Then Grace heard the most horrifyingly magnificent news… Aidan was going to fly her back to these 'Healing Caves'. Well, not Aidan as Aidan, but his *dragon*. The beautiful silver and black creature she'd caught a glimpse of as she was being carried away. She *really* wanted to be able to experience the ride with her eyes wide open.

Lifted off the bed and wrapped in what felt like a sheet at first confounded her, but then she figured it would get pretty cold flying through the air. Her effort to push through the spell that continued to hold her hostage was completely exhausting. It was time to lay back and wait to see what happened next. It was really all she could do.

She felt Aidan's arms slide under her and then she was being lifted. Andrew may have thought he could keep them apart, but if anything, they would be closer than ever. It didn't matter that she was basically a paperweight, she felt the sparks of their connection everywhere their skin touched. She knew he felt it too. Cuddled against him the way she was, she could hear his powerful heart beat faster and his breathing speed up. If she could only get any part of her body to move to let him know she was in there. To tell him how much she loved and appreciated him for searching for her and finding her. She only prayed the Cleansing Ritual worked. She prepared the only way a woman trapped inside her own body could for her first trip via flying dragon, Grace laid back and enjoyed the ride.

The 'flight' felt amazing. The wind through her hair and the way it caressed the little bit of skin not covered was nothing short of amazing. She knew they'd strapped her to some kind of gurney because she heard Rayne and Devon explaining it to Aidan. The Guardsmen were some seriously handy guys to have around. She hadn't even thought about how she was going to fly with her mate until she felt them attaching her stretcher to what she could only guess was Aidan's dragon paw. It made her even more pissed at Andrew, realizing what his crazy ass spell was keeping her from experiencing.

Grace had to admit her other senses were heightened, but she was still pissed. She could tell when they flew over a body of water by the change in the smell of the air and the way it was a bit moister on her skin. Gliding over a vegetated piece of land was easy to differentiate by the smell of leaves, grasses, and flowers.

The raw power and energy pouring off her mate in his dragon form was astonishing. She could feel the rush of the breeze and hear the whoosh when he flapped his massive wings. Grace wanted so very much to witness the spectacular sight with her own eyes. There would be other times, of that she was sure, but the first time was extra special and Andrew had stolen that from them. Her *intuition* had been unusually quiet since they'd taken flight. It seemed every part of her enjoyed being in her man's care, no matter what form he was in.

Drifting along, she enjoyed all she could of her first dragon ride, then she felt them descending. It wasn't long before she felt and heard what could only be described as a *thump*. In the next breath, she was being carried, still strapped to the apparatus she'd flown in.

We must've arrived.

She tried one more time, with all her strength that remained, to break the spell holding her hostage, only to once again be denied. She definitely had a new appreciation for the saying "Mad as a wet hen" that Kyndel's granny used to say all the time. She'd seen firsthand how mad a hen could get when she was visiting their family farm. Grace had watched as the poor little animal shook and flipped feathers everywhere, while making the most horrific sounds she'd ever heard. They'd laughed until they were in tears, but she understood the little pullet's anger, and the tears threatening to fall this time were not from *anything* funny.

Grace wondered why she was so sleepy when all she'd been doing was lying about. Then she wished she could've laughed at loud.

Why the hell wouldn't I be tired?

In a little over thirty-six hours she'd been roughed up in a parking lot, made love to the most perfect man in the whole world, been shot, kidnapped, interrogated by a deranged idiot, trapped in a spell, and had her first flight with a dragon. While not all of it was bad (as a matter of fact the making love and flying parts were *seriously* enjoyable, more than enjoyable, they were *freaking fantastic*), the other parts really sucked.

Her brain was getting really foggy as they lifted off the gurney and placed her on a cool, firm surface. She could hear people all around. A familiar electric current she knew only one person could create within her raced up her arm as she started to drift off to sleep. One beautiful word drifted across her mind as she felt him place her hand in his…"*Aidan*", and she let sleep take over.

CHAPTER FIFTY-SIX

Aidan stood as still as possible, waiting for the Cleansing Ritual to begin. He stared into the face of the most wonderful gift he'd ever been given… his Grace. He was completely mesmerized by her beauty, not only on the outside, but even more on the inside. She had a heart of gold, a spirit that could *not* be stopped, and a fierce determination that rivaled his own. He was truly blessed.

The scent of the healing herbs filled the chamber from the incense and candles the healers burned on every surface. They began their chant and Aidan could've sworn he heard Grace's voice in his mind. It sounded like she was calling to him. Closing his eyes, he focused on what he knew he'd heard a few seconds before. In his mind's eye, there was a light shining in the distance.

He increased his focus, knowing deep in his heart Grace was trying to tell him she was there… somewhere, fighting to come back to him. He could feel love, warmth, strength, and a fire to not let evil win. It was his mate. She was doing everything within her power to beat a foe she didn't know or understand. He could feel her confusion and focused all his energy on the light, certain it would bring her back to him.

The chanting of the healers rang in his ears as Siobhan led the Cleansing Prayer along with Eric, another highly skilled Healer. Using everything he'd learned in all his years, Aidan channeled all the energy he could absorb and pushed it into the light, trying whatever possible to make contact with Grace.

His shoulders began to shake; sweat gathered on his upper lip and ran down his back as he continued to push. Almost ready to give up, he gathered all he had left and *shoved* it into his mate. Almost instantaneously, Grace's fingers fluttered against his. He gripped her tighter and began speaking to her, mind to mind. "*Grace, solas mo anam, please, come back to me.*" He pleaded. "*I love you, mo chroi. Follow my voice. Let me lead you back.*" He continued to talk, saying anything and everything that came to mind, not sure he was making sense, just talking to his mate, willing her back.

The healers continued to chant. Aidan continued to coo, cajole, and beg, before ending up telling her all the plans he had for their future together. He worked his way from sublime to sexy. The more heated his description, the brighter the light burned.

He'd reached one of his personal favorite fantasies for their future, when the light just went out. From one heartbeat to the next, it was *gone*. His eyes flew open. He placed his fingers to the side of her neck looking, *praying* for a pulse, but felt nothing. He watched her chest and waited for her next breath... *that never came*. He even laid his lips to hers, hoping against all hope to feel her breath... but there was nothing.

He threw his head back and roared. Long and loud, begging her to come back to him, but nothing changed. He fell to his knees, clinging to Grace's hand like the lifeline she was. The cavern had gone silent. It wasn't until Siobhan laid her hands on his shoulders, kneading in earnest, and whispering everything would be okay, that he realized he was sobbing. Long anguished cries of pain and loss he would never have believed he was capable of. For the first time since he believed Andrew dead, Aidan *cried*, real tears tracking down his face and wetting his chest.

He slumped to the side, resting his head on the edge of the table where she lay, gripping her hand with all his might, still careful not to hurt her in any way. At least he'd stopped screaming, but nothing he tried stopped the tears from flowing. How had he failed her? How had he let this happen? He had one job that truly mattered...to keep her safe.

Fucked that one up. All I've done is lead her into danger.

Plain and simple, Aidan failed. Just like he'd failed in that clearing all those years ago. But this time it was real. There was no subterfuge. She was gone and there was nothing he could do but sit and hold her hand, praying for his true death to come quickly so he might follow her.

With no clue how long he sat there, he listened to the healers leave the chamber. Siobhan gave his shoulders one last squeeze, rose to her feet, and followed the others. He knew he should be doing something, *anything* except sitting on the ground in a heap, but he simply couldn't move. It hurt to breathe... to think. His heart was broken. He'd felt it crack right along with this soul and his will to live when he'd realized Grace no longer lived. His dragon huffed in agreement.

Both souls had a gaping wound, a vast dark hole of nothingness like death itself...the death of their mate. The light of their soul had been extinguished. They would live in darkness until they followed her to the Heavens. He understood what his father meant when he'd told him his life had ceased to be a life after his mother was gone. It was *exactly* how Aidan felt. He couldn't live without her now that he'd experienced life *with* her.

Aidan just sat there, holding Grace's hand, feeling lost and broken. He even stopped praying. He was empty. There was nothing left. The beast inside him felt the same. The once majestic creature lay on its side, curled as tightly in a ball as he could get, grieving the loss of the life they'd lost. He should be searching for the traitor. He should be ripping the very heart from Andrew's chest, but he couldn't leave her, not yet. Grace was gone, but he wasn't ready to let her go.

One by one, the candles in the chamber went out, until he sat in total darkness. The silence almost deafening in its completeness. Only the sounds of the Healing Springs flowing into the deepest cavern from an underground source could be heard. It sounded like little bells tinkling as the water ran down the cave walls and into the lagoon.

The simple sound of the warm, clean water streaming into the cave soothed him. He offered one last prayer to the Universe, imploring the heavenly body who gave them life to bring his Grace back. Aidan prayed like he'd never prayed before. Divine intervention was something he'd been taught from an early age, but when an idea began to form, he was sure it was the Universe answering his plea. He prayed with more earnest, willing the idea to become whole, and just like that, he knew what he had to do. If he worked fast enough, he and his beautiful mate would never be separated again.

Carrying Grace down the long dark corridor, he prayed he was doing the right thing. A calm reassurance filled his soul. He knew he was *absolutely* doing what was required to help Grace. It was sanctioned by the Universe Herself. She was telling him what needed to be done to complete the Cleansing Ritual and rid his mate of the spell holding her hostage. He had to work fast. He had no idea how long it had been since she'd taken her last breath, or even if that mattered. All he felt for sure was the sense of urgency pushing him to act.

When he reached the lagoon, he threw the sheet covering Grace to the side and walked directly into the healing waters, clothing and all. His entire being resonated with the belief his actions would bring his mate back to him, and come hell or high water, he was doing it. He began to whisper what he could remember from the Peace and Healing Chant the healers used when he was injured by a wizard in the 1800's. He surprised himself at how much of the stanza he still remembered, yet another gift from the Universe. Holding Grace close to his chest, repeating the words he *knew* would bring her out of the spell, hope grew in his heart.

He slowly walked the perimeter of the pond continuing to chant, almost singing as he went. The way her ebony locks floated through the water, combined with the little droplets caught in her eyelashes that sparkled like diamonds mesmerized him. It was darker than night in the cavern, but with his enhanced vision, he missed nothing.

He looked at her pouty little mouth and longed for the day she would once again return his kiss. Lost in prayer, Aidan almost missed the slight movement of her eyelids. His laser sharp vision locked on her chest, waiting for the rise and fall indicating she was coming back to him.

Time passed at a snail's pace. Aidan stood waist deep in the healing waters, completely still, waiting for something, *anything* to happen. Then like so many of his prayers, another was answered. Her lips parted and the slightest exhale of air reached his enhanced hearing. Aidan held his breath, afraid to hope, as she took another, deeper breath.

Leaning down until his lips almost touched hers, he felt her breath on his lips. His soul filled with a hope that hours ago he was sure he'd never again feel. Grace was coming back to him! Whatever spell the traitor used had been one of the strongest, to make one mate believe the other dead, but *they* had beaten it.

When he caught Andrew, and he *would* catch him, Aidan was going to get the name of the witch who helped him create such a spell. It wasn't a wizard; the magic wasn't black. The absence of white magic let him know it wasn't a mage or another dragon either. The best way he could describe it was to say it was gray, which meant a witch. A witch who had to be found and neutralized if she was powerful enough to create spells that potent.

Reining in all thoughts except those of his mate, Aidan focused his almost inexhaustible energy on guiding her back to him. Her breathing became deeper and more regulated. With his enhanced hearing, he heard her heart beating steadier and stronger by the minute. He watched as her eyes moved beneath her eyelids, as if she was in a deep sleep, and lifted her hand to his mouth, placing a chaste kiss on her palm.

He moved his head until he could lay his cheek in her hand. Continuing his chant, he walked until he the muscles in his thighs began to shake. Moving to the side of pool, Aidan sat on the ledge while keeping as much of Grace's body immersed in the healing spring waters as possible. He tilted his head back, still reciting the words that were bringing her back to him.

Drifting in an in-between state, not quite awake, not quite dreaming, Aidan heard the barest of whispers. A sound so low and breathy, even with his enhanced hearing he couldn't make out what was said. He only knew it had come from Grace.

He'd opened his senses to his surroundings to make sure the healing caves were abandoned, save him and his mate. Afraid to move, afraid to breathe, he waited for the sound again. Minutes ticked by as he felt what was left of his patience fraying, and then it came. Just a fraction louder, a little less breathy, but amazing nonetheless.

It's my name!

Jerking Grace upright, Aidan stared at her closed eyes. He waited. Her eyes fluttered. Then the most beautiful sight he would ever see in this life or the next, her blue eyes, were looking back at him, a little lost but *so very* awake.

He watched her mouth open and close several times. Holding himself and his beast at bay, he gave her time to get her bearings, when all he wanted to do was crush her to his body and kiss her mouthwatering lips. Her throat worked up and down as a look of pure determination crossed her eyes, then a perfectly melodious sound came from her lips… "Aidan." Her voice was low and gravely from lack of use, but absolutely stunning to his ears.

"Oh *mo ghra'*, you're back." Unable to hold back any longer, Aidan slid his arms around her, pulled her face to his, and kissed her with all that he was. The kiss was long and deep, slow and tender, *complete* in his rediscovery of the woman who owned him body and soul.

Grace slowly responded, quickly becoming a very active participant in their kiss. When her fingers threaded through his hair, he let the tears he'd been holding back fall unchecked down his cheeks. Never had he cried so much, not in all of his hundred years, as he had since finding the woman in his arms. The mighty Dragon Guardsman had been brought to his knees by the one the Universe made for him, and he would happily crawl for the rest of his days to keep her happy and whole.

He moved her until she was straddling his lap and ran his fingers through her wet locks, tilting her head to get a better angle. He held back his passion, not wanting to injure her in any way, but the need to reaffirm Grace was indeed alive and in his arms where she belonged, was all-encompassing. Their tongues touched. Gasoline had been thrown on the fire that was their love. Her hands tightened in his hair as she held him to her.

Aidan smiled, rejoicing in their kiss. He moved his hands down her body, relearning every curve of her succulent skin, as a low moan rose from her throat. Her nipples hardened through the wet, pink lace of her bra, while he continued his exploration. He reached the top of the jeans she still wore and slid his finger just under the waistband, when the sound of a throat clearing echoed through the chamber.

Aidan growled deep in his throat. Moving Grace behind him, he stood, ready to fight, but relaxed immediately when he saw Rayne and Kyndel. The couple was standing on the edge of the lagoon with matching expressions of surprise.

"Well, it looks as if things have changed. We felt your feelings of loss and devastation a few hours ago and feared the worst, but it looks like you have things well in hand." His old friend and Commander smiled as he joked.

"Yes, thank God. Now move your ass and get my best friend out of that water and up here where I can hug her, 'A'." His Commander's very pregnant, very demanding, redheaded mate demanded.

"Yes, ma'am, *Spitfire*." He chuckled.

Turning around, Aidan looked at the mate he thought he'd lost and pure joy filled his being. "I love you, Grace, with all my heart. I'll do everything in my power to *never* let anything happen to you again." He took a deep breath. "I have a very important question to ask you. Grace Kensington, will you be my mate? It's not our custom to ask, but I'm learning quickly that *you* are like no other."

He held his breath as tears filled her eyes. When she opened her pouty pink lips to speak, it was all he could do not to beg her to she say yes. "I love you more than I ever imagined possible, Aidan. I'll be your mate on one condition. You have to stop blaming yourself for what happened right *this minute*." He saw her signature determination envelope her whole face, and decided this was a discussion for another time.

Nodding his head, Aidan doubted he could speak past the lump in his throat. Then burst out laughing when Kyndel yelled from the deck of the lagoon. "All right you two, that's enough of the lovey dovey crap. Congrats and all that shit, but if you don't get up here right now, Grace Elizabeth Kensington, I swear I'm coming in after you!" Aidan could feel Kyndel's happiness at finding her friend alive, while the sadness she'd experienced when she thought Grace lost continued to drift away.

"You will *not* go into that water. Not after I watched you fight to keep your balance under the weight of our child while walking here, *Mate*," Rayne commanded.

Aidan heard the slap he knew was coming and grinned at Grace. "Don't you 'mate' me, Rayne MacLendon," Kyndel growled back. Pregnancy was definitely wearing thin on her already fragile patience.

"I'm bringing her to you now, Kyndel," Aidan called over his shoulder as he reached to pick up his mate. "Rayne, can you light of few of the candles so Grace can see, please?"

He walked out of the healing waters with his mate in his arms. Quickly grabbing a towel, Aidan wrapped it around her shoulders for modesty, and then set her on her feet, facing her best friend. Kyndel was crying and he knew if he turned Grace around he would see the same thing. By his next breath, the women were wound up in the most hilarious hug he'd ever seen. Grace was bent and twisted in an effort to get as close as possible, in spite of the bundle of joy protruding from Kyndel's midsection. He watched as the women embraced, and felt another piece of what his life would be like for all time fall into place. He was reminded of a passage from their holy book describing the exact feeling thrumming through his veins. *"When the two halves of the same whole are truly aligned, every part of their world is in harmony."* Nothing better explained what he was feeling.

The women needed time to reconnect, but Aidan couldn't keep his hands off his mate, the feeling of loss still very fresh in his mind. He moved forward and placed both his hands on her shoulders, lightly massaging, soaking up her essence. He saw that even after almost seven months of mated bliss, his Commander felt the same thing, and smiled at Rayne.

The women finally broke apart. Aidan pulled Grace until her back rested against his front. He kissed the top of her head as Kyndel spoke. "We need to get you out of those wet clothes and have Siobhan check you out. I know you look okay and definitely act okay," Kyndel wiggled her eyebrows and Aidan knew she was referring to the kiss she and Rayne had interrupted, "but I want to make sure you're a hundred percent."

"Yes, *mother*," Grace teased as she turned in his arms. "I guess we better listen to her because she's even bossier now that she's pregnant." The mischief in Grace's eyes made him laugh aloud.

He winked at Kyndel over her head. "Yes, *mo chroi*, we better do as she says." He lifted his mate into his arms and headed toward the mouth of the Healing Caves.

CHAPTER FIFTY-SEVEN

She got a clean bill of health from Siobhan, but like everything else, it was a process. Aidan and Kyndel refused to leave during her examination, which took almost four hours, and that meant Kyndel's very large, very protective mate stayed too. Grace could also hear the other men of their Force outside. Her *spidey senses* were all over the place as they discussed the spell and the talisman Andrew had used on her. She found out not only had she been the recipient of his depravity, but he'd also used several other spells to cause the explosions in the woods.

The son of a bitch basically vanished into thin air just as Rayne was about to catch him. She could tell the men were gearing up to go after him, and wondered if they'd thought about also trying to capture 'The Auctioneer', aka the State Prosecutor, at the same time. Something told her they were connected and the setup at the warehouse hadn't been a coincidence, no matter what Andrew told her in the cabin.

"What are you thinking so hard about, *mo ghra'*?" Aidan asked.

"Something your brother said when he was spouting his crap while holding me captive." She watched as Aidan's brow furrowed, Kyndel frowned, and Rayne began to pace. "He said he had no idea who 'The Auctioneer' was and that he was only there with the wizards to perform some ritual. He did seem very interested in exactly who 'The Auctioneer' was, and even more so once I said he was my former boss." She paused for a minute to think.

"So here's what I've put together after listening to y'all talk about magic and spells and rituals. I'm thinking the wizards needed young women for whatever they were planning to do, which, by the way, I'm *not even* going to think about right now. I think they contacted 'The Auctioneer', and his crew rounded up the girls. But somewhere between kidnapping them and delivering them to that damned warehouse, he got a better offer, or maybe wasn't ever going to let the wizards have them. I'm not sure about that, but I'm sure money's involved somewhere. Whatever he planned, he double-crossed the wizards, thought he could get away with it, but had no clue you big bad Dragon Guardsmen would be there." She winked at Aidan and loved the fact he grinned back.

"I really believe if we find 'The Auctioneer', we'll find Andrew, or the other way around. And if things go really well for us, we'll get the wizards too." She stopped talking and looked around the room at four very stony faces.

Before she could ask what was wrong, Aidan and Kyndel spoke at the same time, "*YOU* aren't going anywhere or catching *anyone*."

She looked at Rayne to back her up, but he was nodding in agreement with the other two. Looking to her side, she saw Siobhan smiling, but before Grace could ask the Elder Healer for her opinion, the woman turned on her heels and left the room.

"*Coward,*" Grace chuckled to herself.

She took a second to look at the best friend she'd ever had and the man she loved more than life itself, reminding herself they were being overprotective because they loved her as much as she loved them. "Okay y'all, I know you're trying to protect me, but I have all the files we'll need to put 'The Auctioneer' away." She grabbed both of Aidan's hands in her own and looked him right in the eyes. "I'm not asking to be in the middle of all the fighting. I'm asking you, Aidan O'Brien, to not keep things from me and use the information I have when you need to, please?"

She watched his internal debate, knowing he'd made his decision before he started to talk. "As long as I can keep you safe, you can be involved. But Grace, my love," she watched him struggle with emotions, "I'll die if anything happens to you again… *my true death*. My heart *cannot* take it." He leaned forward and laid his forehead on their combined hands.

Looking over her amazing mate, Grace saw Kyndel smiling a knowing smile as she held Rayne's hands where they were laid upon her shoulders. Kyndel winked and Grace held back a laugh. Who the hell could've ever predicted all those years ago when she bumped into a sullen redheaded teenager that they would be here, in love, *happy*? Aidan sat up straight, looking her directly in the eyes again. It was her turn to demand a compromise. "And the same goes for you. No getting hurt. Deal?"

He smiled the smile that made her panties wet and her toes curl. "Deal, *mo ghra'*." He leaned forward and kissed her deeply, until the sound of the door bursting open had them jumping apart. She wondered if she was ever going to get to be alone with him again. Grace immediately started laughing when she caught sight of Aidan's brethren, all lined up just inside the door, looking from Aidan to Rayne like children looking to their parents to see who was in the most trouble.

Grace wasn't surprised at all when Lance spoke first. "Hey, Hellcat, glad to see you up and kiss…I mean kicking." He laughed at his own joke, and in the next second, the entire room was filled with the sounds of laughter. She once again caught Aidan's eye, basking in all the love and commitment she felt mirrored in their beautiful amber depths.

It was Kyndel that spoke up and ended the frivolity. "Okay you ruffians, I need to have some girl time with my best friend, so go do whatever it is you need to be doing and we'll see you later."

The entire group grumbled. Aidan and Rayne tried to argue with the redheaded fury, stating they should be able to stay, but in the end, it was obvious Kyndel had all of them wrapped around her little finger. As soon as the door shut, her best friend turned her expressive emerald eyes on her. There was a whole lot of trouble brewing there. The grin that spread across Kyndel's face confirmed her suspicions… this was going to be an interesting bit of girl talk.

They spent the rest of the day and well into the night discussing anything and everything. They laughed, they cried, they even yelled at one another, but in the end, they completely caught up, like the separation they'd experienced never happened. Baby names were discussed. She couldn't stop laughing when Kyndel explained the arguments she and Rayne were having, pretty much daily, about the sex of their child. Grace agreed with Kyndel…it was a boy. Her *intuition* was definitely on board with her thoughts.

One of the sweetest stories Kyndel told her was about the beautiful bracelet on her wrist. It was her wedding present from Rayne, with a special story that made goose bumps rise on Grace's arms. When Kyndel told her dragon shifters believe every time a bell rings, mates are kissing, all Grace could imagine were Aidan's lips on hers. They both laughed until they cried when Kyndel smacked her on the arm to bring her out of her daydream. Grace laughed even harder when Kyndel admitted to having visions of her own mate.

Sometime after their laughing spree and her second or third yawn, there was a knock on the door. Before she could say, "Come in", Rayne was kneeling next to Kyndel, telling her it was time to come home. The look on her friend's face was absolutely priceless. It was a mix between dreamy and adoration. Kyndel told her, and Grace picked up on the buzzing in her head during their conversation, that Rayne and Kyndel were able to mindspeak. She'd even guessed what some of the conversations were about by the looks on her best friend's face. It was a totally different side to her bestie than she'd seen before. It fit Kyndel very well. Since waking up Grace had been able to tell when others beside Aidan were mindspeaking, an interesting new development.

"Go on home, Kyn. Get some rest." She winked. "I'm sure Aidan's not far behind." But as her friend and her mate started to leave, it was Siobhan who came into the room.

"I'm afraid Aidan will not be coming to get you tonight. After you've had a few hours to rest and recuperate, I have the pleasure of answering any questions you may have about our clan and preparing you for your formal mating ceremony." The older woman motioned for her to follow.

Grace spent the next four hours tossing and turning, but sleep eluded her. She got up to see if Siobhan happened to be awake and found her hostess in the kitchen having a cup of tea. "Couldn't sleep?" the Elder Healer asked.

"No, I think I rested enough for a lifetime while I was under that spell." She chuckled.

"Sit down and have some tea. We can have our chat and then if you want to rest before your handsome mate shows up, I am sure there will be time."

"Thank you so much. A cup of tea sounds great." Grace turned toward the counter. It seemed as though Siobhan expected her. There was a delicate tea service awaiting her arrival. Sitting down opposite the Healer, Grace poured a cup of tea and added a spoonful of honey. As they enjoyed their beverage in companionable silence, Grace took in the beautiful décor of Siobhan's home. Antiques were tastefully arranged on just about every surface. A beautiful bouquet of lavenders, pinks, and yellows, could be seen everywhere. She began to fidget, not sure what the proper protocol was in situations like these. Holding out as long as she could, just about to speak, Siobhan started to snicker. Grace looked up and couldn't help laughing along.

"Let me guess, you know I'm about to crawl out of my skin, right?" she asked as the laughter continued.

"My dear, you are no more nervous than most, you just make the cutest faces to go along with your anxiety." Grace watched Siobhan work hard to control her laughing. "Let me put your fears to rest. Nothing crazy is going to happen, I promise. The main purpose of our time together is for you to ask any questions you may have and for me to make sure you are ready for the lifelong commitment you are about to make. So, Grace, are there any questions you have that I may answer for you?"

Grace thought long and hard about what she should ask, and then blurted out the one thing continuing to rattle around in her mind. "Will I be able to turn into a dragon and fly too?"

The Elder Healer laughed again while shaking her head. "No, my darling, you will not be able to transform and fly. It is one of the few things you will not share with your mate, but you will be able to feel what his dragon feels, along with being able to mindspeak with Aidan, and after a time, the others of his Force. You will have enhanced abilities and senses and share a bond with the other half of your soul. Our holy book says it better than I can. It is written, *"When the two halves of the same whole meet, there will be instant recognition. Their souls will merge and only then will the dragon shifter know complete peace. He will have found his true home. It will be as if the time before they met does not exist. All that matters is that they become one in body, mind, and soul.'"*

As they talked, Grace asked question after question, and Siobhan answered them all, putting the young woman's worries to rest. When Grace was all talked out and her brain so full facts she felt like she was going into court, she excused herself, went back to her room, and immediately fell into a deep, restful sleep.

CHAPTER FIFTY-EIGHT

He waited as long as he could. Had been patient while Grace spent time with Kyndel. Aidan knew it was necessary for both of them and was happy with anything that made Grace happy, but he missed her. He'd busied himself while she was with Siobhan making the preparations for their celebration, but he could wait no longer. He was going to see his mate and show her around the lair before their mating ceremony.

He knocked on Siobhan's front door, barely stopping himself from pacing while he waited. When the Healer he'd known all his life answered the door with a knowing smile, she simply said, "Grace is in the last guestroom on the right."

It took all of his waning control not to run down the hall after he thanked Siobhan. He walked as slowly as he could, his heart beating double time and his cock rising to the occasion. Reminding his wayward appendage they were in the home of the woman he considered his second mother, Aidan tamped down his arousal. With thoughts of cutting the tour of their lair short, he entered the room Siobhan had indicated.

There Grace lay, on her side with her hands folded together under her chin, looking every bit the angel she was. He remembered the first night they'd spent together. She'd looked exactly the same after falling asleep on the couch in Kyndel's old apartment. He stood, just staring, offering all his thanks to the Universe.

He moved to the side of the bed, leaned down, and pushed her silken locks behind her ear. She moved her cheek into his touch. Aidan's heart swelled with the perfect love he felt for Grace. He could no longer resist the pull of her delectable lips. Electricity jumped between them. Her quick intake of breath and the movement of her lips against his let him know she was awake and had missed him as much as he'd missed her.

Just as her arms were coming around his neck, he gathered his strength and pulled back. Leaning his forehead against hers, Aidan enjoyed listening to her battle to get her breathing under control. Pride filled his chest at the way he could make her lose control with just a kiss.

"*Mo ghra'*, I want nothing more than to climb into that bed with you and spend the rest of my life making love to every inch of your spectacular body, but Siobhan is in the other room. I also have a limited amount of time to show you around the lair and get you to Kyndel's so you can get ready for our mating ceremony."

She sighed, her breath against his cheek like a spring breeze. "All right, let me get up so we can get this show on the road."

With one last peck on her cheek, he stood and leaned against the wall while she proceeded to get ready. He loved watching her brush her long dark hair, and longed to be the wand of her lip-gloss as it caressed her lips. Aidan laughed aloud when she took her clothes into the bathroom to change, but knew if she hadn't they would've never left the bedroom. Just a few short minutes later, she was ready to go. They yelled their thank you's and goodbye's to Siobhan as they headed out.

He walked with his feet three foot off the ground from the pride he felt having Grace on his arm. Knowing she was his mate and destined to be his for all of their years was amazing. He showed her the Town Square and was completely enthralled as she looked at all their community had to offer with awe and wonder. When they got to Emma's shop, Grace's eyes lit up like a kid in a candy store. Emma made jewelry from the dragon scales that were broken or couldn't be used for any other purpose. He watched as Grace picked up several pieces and listened as Emma explained each one in detail and the significance of their design and color of the scales.

Grace kept going back to one specific necklace. A pendant with three bells in a drop design. There were two on the table, but she continued to touch the one in which the largest bell was made from a shining silver scale like his dragon's. He smiled when Emma explained the significance of a bell ringing to the dragon people, and his mate blushed as she said Kyndel had already shared the story with her. He loved that Grace still blushed and watched as she gave one last long glance back at the necklace then promised Emma she'd be back once she got settled.

Continuing their leisurely walk, Aidan pointed out every building and introduced her to everyone they passed. She was impressed when they reached the Cave of the Elders. Unlike any other cave, the entrance had been carved over time, depicting the journey of the Golden Fire Clan and their quest to preserve their past, grow their community, and enhance the land that was their home.

The intricate design transformed the gateway to the sacred laws and the men that upheld those laws into a thing of majesty. He watched as she absorbed the past, present, and future… a future Grace now shared with all of them. If possible, he was even more impressed with his mate when he introduced her to the Elders.

The four men had lived longer than most, experienced things others could only imagine, and were responsible for the social, political, and economic structure of their civilization. Her eyes lit with an innate understanding from the moment the Head Elder, Carrick, began to speak. They spent over an hour discussing the inner workings of the clan, especially how laws were enacted and enforced.

Of course his Grace would be interested in how they kept order, how had Aidan not thought of that before? They had so much to learn about one another and he looked forward to each discovery. Aidan was incredibly honored when Carrick asked her to be part of the Tribunal when the traitor was captured. She readily agreed and as they left the sacred place, he smiled in response to her overwhelming happiness, once again amazed at how perfect she was.

When they reached Rayne and Kyndel's home, he wanted to make their time together last as long as possible. Walking her around to the backyard, he showed her Kyndel's plants and the swing Rayne had built.

That was where Kyndel found them kissing when she came out to pick flowers for their mating ceremony. Aidan smiled like a loon all the way back to his home. In just three short hours, he would be officially mated to the woman who held his heart. His dragon chuffed in agreement as he entered his home with an extra spring in his step.

CHAPTER FIFTY-NINE

Grace spent the last few hours before her mating ceremony gossiping and primping, getting ready for the *biggest* event of her life. She'd fantasized many times over the years about her wedding and the man she would marry, but never imagined the total calm she now felt and how ready she was to make the biggest commitment of her life. Kyndel asked what her *spidey senses* said when she mentioned how calm and peaceful she was. Grace admitted they had been completely silent, on board with everything she was doing.

Kyndel and Rayne's mating ceremony had been in the Cave of the Ancients. Kyndel gave her as much detail as possible. Both laughed until they cried when Grace commented on the large number of 'special' caves the dragon shifters had, and Kyndel immediately answered, "Well, they *are* dragons. You wouldn't expect them to have 'special' holes in the ground. Thank God!" Their laughing was so loud it brought Kyndel's mate in the room. It took a few minutes to calm down enough to explain their frivolity and Rayne left the room shaking his head.

Dude better lighten up if he's going to live a thousand years with Kyndel.

That was something else she and Kyndel talked about. The sheer number of years they would live. The dreamy look on her best friend's face confirmed all Grace already knew… Kyndel and Rayne were meant to be, just like her and Aidan. Grace told herself once she was back with her best friend she would chew her out for the six months of little to no communication, especially the quick phone call to announce her pregnancy, but seeing how truly happy Kyndel was made all Grace's angst float away. She admitted if the roles were reversed, it would've played out the same way.

Kyndel asked if Grace had seen Aidan's dragon. Grace gave her the details of her abduction. It seemed the two of them talked about the traitor as much as anything else. She really couldn't wait for the day Andrew was locked up, preferably in one of their 'caves' deep in a mountain, *far away*.

She'd originally wanted him dead, but thought he might be able to help them catch 'The Auctioneer' so she revised her thoughts on the subject. Lord knew he'd networked with the elite of the scumbags. When Kyndel explained how she'd seen all the men's dragons, Grace admitted to being a little envious, but knew she'd have lots of years for things like that. She was about to mate or marry or whatever it was called, the man she loved with all her heart.

A knock at the door brought two younger Dragon Guardsmen dressed in their formal uniforms to escort her to the ceremony. Kyndel had explained everyone would be dressed in olde world style, but nothing prepared her for the King Arthur throwbacks.

The young men wore surcoats of the most luxurious silvery gray, almost an exact replica of the color she'd seen when Aidan's dragon came forth. Each was trimmed in black rope with silver thread glittering throughout. On the front was the most intricate stitchery depicting a dragon in flight, so realistic she imagined it taking flight right from each man's chest. They both wore a black long-sleeved undershirt and pants, as well as knee high, black boots polished to a shine. The light from the afternoon sun twinkled and shone in each boot as they walked to an ornately decorated carriage.

Grace felt like Cinderella going to the ball. Each young man placed her hand on their bent elbow, leading her to a carriage that rivaled anything any fairy godmother had ever whipped up with her magic wand. It was deep mahogany with elegant carvings bordering the door and decorating the ledge of the entire vehicle.

As they opened the door, a set of four steps effortlessly rolled to the ground. The young men helped her into her seat and made sure she was comfortable before shutting the door. Grace marveled at the cream, crushed velvet seats and beautiful mural covering all four walls, depicting an entire dragon lair in the midst of a celebration.

As her eyes took in the splendor of something obviously from another time, she saw a bouquet of silver roses tied with a single black ribbon lying on the seat opposite her.

Reaching across, she inhaled their succulent aroma and thought of what was to come. A small card protruding from her bundle of flowers carried a simple message that made her heart beat just a bit faster. *"Today and forever. All my love, Aidan."*

The carriage slowed and Grace knew they were close. Aidan kept the place of their ceremony a secret so she was forced to guess.

He had better be there waiting for me.

She knew Kyndel and Rayne and the other Dragon Guardsmen knew but were sworn to secrecy. They were coming in another larger carriage she'd seen pulling up just as she was entering hers.

They came to a complete stop. A few butterflies flittered and fluttered in her stomach, nothing more than excitement. In a few short moments, she would be mated to the man of her dreams. Grace Kensington had her very own fairy tale with her very own Prince Charming. The only thing missing was her parents, but after almost twenty-seven years of missed recitals and school plays, she wasn't going to let their absence take anything away from her special day.

The carriage door opened and her escorts helped her down. Grace gasped at the sight before her. It was something straight out of an impressionist masterpiece. A meadow filled with every color and variety of flower and fauna imaginable. Four archways pointing to the four corners of the earth, surrounded a raised circle, also decorated with flowers and ribbons. Four chairs that could've been thrones, placed at what she assumed was the head of the circle. It was only Grace and her escorts and she wondered if they were early. She prayed another tragedy hadn't happened in the time it took for her to get to this beautiful place.

The young guardsmen again presented her with their arms. They led her to a clearing two hundred yards from the beautiful meadow. Placing her arms at her sides, the young men took two very large steps back, and stood at attention, as if guarding her from unseen forces.

All her dreams were coming true. As she looked around wondering what was going to happen next, the air around her came to life. Electricity sparkled in the sunlight. The breeze picked up and the delicate ringlets Kyndel had placed all over her head bounced and swayed. Grace looked up, and what she saw was torn straight from the fairy tales Miss Annabelle read to her as a child.

Flying high in the sky were five dragons of various colors, circling around a shining silver dragon with black stripes spanning both sides. As she watched, they made several different formations, but one thing remained constant… the silver dragon was always in the center. She knew it was her Aidan and the others of his Force. They were showing her something very few in this world would ever see…dragons in flight. Her heart swelled to bursting with so many emotions she didn't attempt to identify them. She simply let them wash over her.

The dragons soon disappeared over the tops of the trees and the space around her felt normal again. She guessed the Dragon Guard had placed a magical shield around the area to be able to show her their amazing aerial show. Her escorts arrived at her side and once again led her back to the meadow.

This time, the four Elders she recognized from her trip around the lair were sitting in the chairs at the head of the circle. She knew from her conversations with Kyndel that the Elders had granted her friend special permission to attend her mating ceremony. She smiled when she saw her very pregnant friend sitting on a chair to her right in a gorgeous red gown, holding fresh flowers from her gardens.

Grace looked to her left and there stood the five men Aidan called brethren, dressed in their finest garments, with surcoats depicting what she now knew where the colors of their dragons. Rayne, at the head of the line, stood tall and proud in flaming red, matching both his dragon and his mate's dress, looking every bit the Commander he was. Next was Royce, whose beautiful royal blue surcoat with green accents truly fit the gentle giant who'd come to her aid before she knew dragons existed. Next was Aaron, her mate's twin, dressed in a silvery gray that shimmered and shined in the waning light. He looked so much like her Aidan, yet so different. He winked at her as she looked from man to man.

When she got to the next in line, she had to bite the inside of her cheeks to keep from laughing. Lance was attempting to look regal and noble in his dress uniform of gold and black, but Grace knew the joker who resided underneath the cool exterior wouldn't be caged for long, and just like that, he grinned the cheesiest grin she'd ever seen, making her chuckle despite herself.

He mouthed 'Hellcat' and Grace chuckled. Last in line was Devon, the quiet one of the group. She remembered his dragon almost as vividly as she remembered Aidan's, for its completely unique coloring. He was the most unusual opalescent white and as he'd flown overhead, an array of colors appeared and disappeared over his gigantic body. She looked around for her mate, wondering if he'd gotten cold feet.

A movement to the right of the Elders caught her eye. All rational thought fled her mind. There stood Aidan in all his finery. The most handsome man she'd ever seen. His long, light brown curls pulled back in a queue, highlighting his high cheekbones and gorgeous whiskey colored eyes. His silver surcoat accented the muscular body she knew lay beneath, and his tight black pants tucked into his knee-high black boots, displayed the muscular legs she longed to feel entwined with hers. In that moment, as always, her heart beat only for him.

CHAPTER SIXTY

Aidan was lightheaded from just one look at Grace. She stood across the Ceremonial Circle under one of the archways, an absolute vision of loveliness. Her long ebony hair curled in ringlets, touching her shoulders and he was sure, hanging down her back. Tiny light blue forget-me-not blossoms woven throughout, accentuated her eyes. The same eyes that hypnotized him with the color of the summer sky he'd flown across so many times.

Her porcelain shoulders were bared by her strapless dress of the palest blue, only a slight scar where the bullet had ripped through her shoulder barely visible. Thanks to her body's ability to draw on his healing power, she was almost at a hundred percent. The bodice was cinched tight, emphasizing her ample bosom, causing his mouth to water. He thought about how much he truly wanted to strip her bare and taste every square inch of her amazing body, when he noticed little silver flames embroidered all over her dress in honor of the beast who would also be her mate.

He followed the curves of her body, made even more visible by the corset design of her dress, until he reached the flair of her hips on top of which was wrapped a silver gray ribbon. His eyes continued their exploration down her flowing skirt until he reached her bare feet, peeking from under the hem. The same pink polish graced those precious little toes as the first night he'd spent with this amazing creature. Aidan chuckled as he saw she still had a flower design on both big toes.

Aidan heard Carrick, the Chief Elder, clear his throat just before his voice rang loud and clear across the Garden of Peace. "Long ago, when knights and dragons fought side by side for King and Country, it became apparent dragon kin was no longer safe from those who would expose and destroy them. They sought to join with the knights who had fought so valiantly by their sides. Thus, through magic and the will of both dragon and knight, the Golden Fire Clan of the Dragon Shifters became a reality. It was through the joining of many different clans that we have become the strong and powerful Force we are today.

"We are here today, in the Garden of Peace, a place long blessed by our ancestors who went before us, to honor what the Universe put into place all those many years ago. To acknowledge and bless the mating of Aidan Patrick O'Brien to the one the Universe made for him, Grace Elizabeth Kensington. Will those seeking to witness this union please step forward?"

From the side of the Sacred Circle stepped the five men Aidan held closer than blood, the men who'd trained with him, fought with him, bled with him, and now shared the happiest moment of his life. All dressed in their finest, they knelt around the Ceremonial Circle and bowed their heads. Rayne stood and addressed the Elders. "We, the five of the MacLendon Force, wish to witness and offer our blessing to the union of these two souls, two halves of the same whole. May they live long, fight hard, love harder, and produce many young to flourish when their souls have gone to the heavens." He knelt and bowed his head again.

Aidan watched as Grace struggled to control her emotions and finally gave in, letting a single tear roll down her cheek. He was completely awestruck at the complete majesty of the event. Carrick began again, "Your witness and blessing have been acknowledged and accepted MacLendon Force. Aidan O'Brien, you may go to your mate and escort her to the center of the Blessed Circle." No sooner had the words been spoken than he was standing in front of Grace. Taking her hands in his, and because he couldn't stand not having her in his arms another second, Aidan gently picked Grace up and carried her. When they reached their destination, he carefully placed her on her feet, never taking his hands from her waist.

"The silver dragons were forged from the very fiber of the Universe and because of this, are often referred to as the 'Shield Dragons'. They are protective to a fault and will fight to the death to defend those they hold dear. They have quick and ambitious attitudes and use a combination of their minds and hearts to make all decisions. They love hard, strong, and endlessly. They never lose faith in whom or what they believe in. To mate a silver dragon means to accept all that they are and honor the power shared between mates.

"Now is the time of the marking. May the Universe continue to bless you and yours all the days of your life." Everyone but Aidan and Grace left the meadow.

CHAPTER SIXTY-ONE

Grace stood in awe, staring at the man who held her heart, completely humbled by the abundance of love she felt. She couldn't believe someone like Aidan could love someone like her. It defied all logic, but the belief she felt with every fiber of her being that they were meant to be, rang loud and true. As she fell deeper and deeper into the depths of his hypnotic whiskey eyes, she realized they'd started to glow. The longer she looked, the brighter they glowed. She saw a heat caused by more than passion. Aidan lowered his mouth to hers, stopping right before their lips would've touched, and whispered, "*Ta' mo chroi istigh ionat,*" and with that, lowered his lips to hers.

It was the most all-encompassing, completely devastating, enraptured kiss in the history of kisses. Grace felt the touch of his lips in every cell of her body. She was consumed with a heat that warmed her from the inside out and laid her open… body, heart, and soul, to her mate. She knew there'd never be any part of her, no matter how small, this man would *not* be able to touch. Everything she felt was reciprocated. He was just as open to her as she was to him. It was as though they now shared the same space… inside of her. It was just as Kyndel and Siobhan had described.

There was a slight sting where her neck met her shoulder on her left side. Aidan left her lips, trailing kisses across her jaw and down her neck, until he reached the tender spot. He licked and sucked the offending spot until all thoughts of anything but their naked bodies loving one another were banished from her mind.

She wound her fingers through his hair as he continued to lavish her neck and shoulders with smoldering kisses. She pulled his mouth up to hers and just as she would have kissed the lips of her mate, he pulled back slightly. He looked like a little boy with a secret. She furrowed her brow in mock anger. "What are you up to, Mr. O'Brien?"

His grin widened. "There's nothing in this world I want to do more than make love to my new mate, but there are two things we need to take care of first." He lifted his fingers to her lips before she could object. She chuckled as his eyes widened when the tip of her tongue slid out to taste his finger.

He shook his head. "No fair trying to distract me, *mo ghra'*. The sooner we get this done, the sooner we can *consummate* our union." She laughed aloud as he wiggled his eyebrows for added effect.

She wanted to pout, but knew he was right. "Okay, let's get this show on the road." Before she could utter another word, he picked her up and strode across the meadow to a small gazebo she'd only just noticed.

CHAPTER SIXTY-TWO

Aidan had one last obligation to complete before their union would receive its full blessing from the Universe. He thanked the Heavens for the advancements in technology, for without them he would've had to wait until he could travel over five thousand miles to officially mate his Grace. He knew for certain he would've spontaneously combusted in that time. Sitting her down on the bench in the gazebo, on the far side of the Garden of Peace, Aidan watched as she tried to figure out what was about to happen. "Close your eyes, *m'anamchara*, this is a surprise."

She frowned but complied. He rewarded her with an all too quick peck on the lips. Reaching into the duffle he'd asked his twin to place in the gazebo before the ceremony, Aidan pulled out a small laptop and a silver velvet box. He made quick work of opening the laptop and dialing the people whose blessing would seal their union and allow the Universe to complete the bond that would hold them together for all time. As soon as their faces appeared on the screen, he held his finger to his lips to make sure they didn't ruin the surprise, and pointed to Grace, who still sat with her eyes closed and brows furrowed. "Open your eyes, my love."

Her eyes immediately met his and then lit upon the laptop in his hands and her parents smiling back at her. The surprise and happiness he saw made all his preparations and sneaking around worth it. Had it not been for Kyndel making a few calls and getting him the clearance he needed to speak to the Ambassador, their mating wouldn't have happened.

"Mom! Dad! Oh my God! You're here! Well, not here, but here!" She pointed at the screen as tears of joy rolled down her face.

She looked at him with a look he hoped to see every minute of every day for the rest of his life. "Thank you, Aidan, thank you so much."

He nodded his head, trying to dislodge the lump in his throat. "As I explained to your parents, it's part of the *religious tradition* of my family," he paused and winked with the eye that her parents couldn't see, "that we have a ceremony with only you and I, the holy men who officiate, and our witnesses." She nodded, letting him know she followed the bit of subterfuge he'd had to use to keep her parents from knocking on the front gate of the lair.

"It's also very important that we have your parents blessing on our union, and I knew you would want them here, even if it meant just for a few minutes over the computer."

He turned facing her parents on the screen of the laptop he'd borrowed from one of the much younger *drakes*. "Mr. and Mrs. Kensington, I promise to love and honor your daughter for all the years of my life. Her health and welfare will always be my first thought and she will never want for anything. I ask your blessing on our union."

He waited for three heartbeats that seemed like three years, until her father spoke, "I can see from the sparkle in my little girl's eyes you make her incredibly happy. I'm trusting you with my most prized possession, Mr. O'Brien. You have our blessing."

Aidan felt a weight he hadn't realized was there lift from his shoulders. "Thank you Mr. and Mrs. Kensington. I will do everything in my power to give Grace the life she deserves."

"Mom, Dad, I'm so glad you could be here, even if it is only on a computer screen. I love you both." Grace's voice cracked as she spoke to her parents.

"We love you too, darling. Be happy and we'll be back stateside soon. Please come and visit. We miss you so very much." Her mother was crying by the time she finished speaking.

"We will. Take care of yourselves," Grace answered.

"Thank you again. I look forward to meeting you in person very soon." Aidan was ready to get this over with so he could be alone with his mate, but he would wait as long as Grace wanted. This was her family, a very important part of who she was.

"Bye, Mom and Dad. See you soon."

"Bye, Grace, dear," Her parents both answered, and the screen went blank.

She threw her arms around his neck and hugged him. He felt her body shaking as he rubbed up and down her back, careful to avoid any bumps or scrapes still healing. "Are you okay, *mo chroí*?"

She leaned back. He saw tears of joy and a beautiful smile. "Oh, Aidan, I am *so* happy. Thank you. I know we haven't talked about my family. I'm not very close to them at all, but it just felt like something was missing not having them here, and you took care of it without even knowing it was important to me. If it's possible, I love you even more."

She leaned forward, kissing him long and deep, making his head swim. He thought about abandoning the other plans he had for her and running back to their home, but decided it was his duty to give her everything within his power. Reluctantly, he pulled back from her kiss and watched as the fog cleared from her eyes.

"I have another surprise, *mo ghrá'*. Close your eyes and hold out your hands."

She did as he asked, with a big beautiful smile illuminating her face. He placed the silver velvet box in her hands. "Open your eyes, Grace."

She looked at him and then at the box he'd placed in her hands. "What's this?"

"Open it and find out, *mo chroí*."

Her smile widened. She gasped as she opened the box to find the necklace she'd admired from Emma's shop. Looking up at him, more happy tears slid down her cheeks. "Aidan, you're an amazing man. I don't know what I ever did to deserve you but I'm damn glad I did. I love you with all my heart."

"And I love you, Grace Kensington-O'Brien."

Her eyes widened. "Kensington-O'Brien is it now?"

He raised one eyebrow as he'd seen her best friend do so many times, "Well, I don't care if you keep the Kensington, but you're damn sure taking the O'Brien."

They both erupted into hilarious laughter as he fastened her necklace around her elegant neck. "I know Emma explained what the ringing of a bell means to a dragon and his mate." He left his comment hanging, hoping she'd pick up on his intent. His mate did not disappoint.

"Yes, she did Mr. O'Brien, and this necklace is never going to be quiet."

CHAPTER SIXTY-THREE

The last two months had been mated bliss. Grace absolutely could not imagine life without Aidan. After an all too brief honeymoon, he'd tried to sneak away, but didn't get far before she found him. After a lengthy *discussion,* they *both* returned to the horrible cabin in the woods where she'd been held captive. Aidan called forth his majestic dragon.

Grace marveled at his massive silver and black body and the way the sun shining through the trees made his scales glint and glimmer. She wondered if she'd ever get used to the fact that the man she loved could also become one of the largest and fiercest beasts of legend. His dragon's fire completely consumed the building that had haunted her dreams every day since her rescue. He did it for her, but Grace knew Aidan was glad it was gone as well.

They decided it was best for them to live at her home in the city, since she was working with the new State Prosecutor to catch 'The Auctioneer'. Not to mention, Aidan and his brethren were still tracking Andrew. Together they made an awesome team, both personally and professionally.

She'd been working all day, waiting for him to come home, and was just about to get a glass of wine when she heard the front door open. *"Where is my beautiful mate?"* Aidan spoke directly into her mind.

"She's in the office, missing you terribly."

Before she could draw another breath, she was in his arms. "I do love your enhanced speed, Mr. O'Brien."

"Not as much as I love *you*, Mrs. O'Brien." She adored it when he called her that. She'd decided the morning after their mating ceremony she wanted nothing more than to belong to the handsome hunk of a man now nibbling her neck, *in every way possible*, including her name. She told him she was dropping the Kensington and using only O'Brien as her last name. They made love for the rest of the day, only stopping for sustenance.

CHAPTER SIXTY-FOUR

He continued his exploration of Grace's neck, paying special attention to the double flame brand on her neck…the mark of their mating. Moving to her shoulder, he tasted all he could of his mate. He kissed, licked, and nibbled, removing her top and then her bra for better access. If he had it his way, she would be naked every minute of every day. He worked his way to her waiting breasts, drawing an already swollen, dusty rose nipple into his mouth. He sucked and pulled as much of her flesh into his mouth as he could. Grace arched her back, moaning low in her throat.

They were both panting, pulses racing, when he picked her up and set her on the edge of the desk. Aidan was drowning in the intoxicating scent of warm honey and vanilla. No matter how long they lived, he would never tire of her scent or of the woman in his arms. He *needed* to taste.

Pushing her farther onto the desktop, laying her back as he went, Aidan took a moment to look at his mate. Grace naked from the waist up, lips swollen from his kisses, skin flushed from her excitement, nipples pebbled, and pointing to the ceiling… *absolute perfection.*

He reached for the waistband of her yoga pants, easily sliding them from her body. His cock jumped as he realized she hadn't worn panties and was now completely bare for him. Grace lifted her foot, rubbing his rock hard erection through the denim of his jeans. Aidan rolled his hips, adding to the delicious friction she caused, but had to pull back before he reached the point of no return. He wondered if the day would ever come when she didn't set his blood ablaze and make all reason vacate his brain.

Laying his hand on her stomach, Aidan caressed as he slowly moved towards her pussy. The heat rising from her arousal stung his fingers. She lifted her hips as his fingers slid over the top of her slit. She tried to force him to touch the spot that would send her into orbit.

"Patience, *mo ghra'*, I want to enjoy you," Aidan cooed.

Rewarded with one of her pouts, he almost abandoned the bounty awaiting his mouth to take her puffy bottom lip between his teeth, but the promise of her miraculous taste on his tongue won the battle. He watched as she slowly licked both her index fingers, then her thumbs, and slowly moved her hands to her breasts. When she took her nipples between her saliva soaked digits, it was his turn to pant. His cock pressed against the zipper of his jeans, threatening to rip through the fabric. Aidan bent down, placing tiny kisses along the outer lips of her already wet pussy. As he reached the top of her slit, he watched as she worked her nipples while trying to catch her breath. Aidan blew a puff of air onto her engorged nub. She moaned, looking right into his eyes.

"Aidan…" His name on her lips pushed him to a place only his Grace could take him, a place where only they existed.

He touched her clit with the tip of his tongue, while blowing more little puffs of air on the aroused bundle of nerves until she had her hands in his hair, pulling so hard he saw stars. He pushed his tongue between her swollen lips, her taste exploding on his tongue. The flashes of light and swirls of color he saw from just one taste of her honey were magnificent. Aidan pushed one finger into her aroused flesh and then added another, pumping in and out, driving her higher and higher while tasting her. He separated her outer lips with his fingers and drove his tongue as far into her as he could reach with one smooth thrust. Grace's back bowed off the desk and her legs flew onto his shoulders. She lifted her bottom even higher, pushing his tongue farther into her pulsing channel as she thrashed and screamed his name while he continued to feast.

He smiled to himself at her responsiveness. She never ceased to amaze him with her absolute abandon. Grace was his perfect match in every way. If they lived two thousand years, he'd never tire of her taste.

He continued to fuck her with his tongue while teasing her clit with his thumb. Enjoying his mate too much for it end, he backed off, placing his tongue on the bottom of her slit and licking slowly to her clit. He again sucked her engorged nub between his teeth, nipping lightly. She ground her hips against his face and dug her heels into his back. Aidan alternated between fucking her with his tongue and licking her like the red popsicles she loved so much. By the time he was ready for her to come the first time, she was speaking in tongues and squeezing his head with her lovely, soft thighs.

Aidan once again licked her long and slow from bottom to top. He sucked her clit into his mouth, but this time bit down with more intent on her sensitive little nub. Thrusting his fingers into her wanting channel while curling the tips to reach her very sensitive bundle of nerves at the top, Aidan pushed Grace over the edge. She came with such force he had to focus all his attention to catch the honey flowing from her pussy. He petted and suckled as she slowly came back to earth. The pride filling him was immeasurable, as once again she graced him with his name upon her lips in a sweet sign of contentment, "Aidan…"

"Yes, *a chumann.*"

"I love you." Her voice just a whisper for only his ears as she laid still, completely relaxed, eyes still closed.

"And I love you, mo chroi." He positioned his cock against her swollen, flushed lips, rubbing the head slowly against her clit as it continued to peek out from its hood, coating himself with her essence. He slowly pushed into her weeping channel, stopping just as the head of his cock lay inside.

She contracted, pulling him deeper inside. He pushed forward, inch by inch, teasing them both until they were once again panting, their skin slick with sweat. When he touched the top of her womb, he held completely still, savoring the feel of her body contracting around his pulsing cock. Her inner walls massaged his erection until he was harder than he thought possible. Every time with Grace was like the first, something to be savored. He dreamt of staying inside her forever, held together by the perfect union that can only happen when one is truly made for the other. The only problem was if he didn't move he would come before she was ready again, and there would never be a time her pleasure did not come first.

Slowly pulling out, Aidan hovered at her opening. One slight movement and he would have slipped from the heaven that was his Grace. He pushed forward, watching as his hard pulsing cock disappeared into her. The sight of them joined caused his balls to draw up tight. Their rhythm increased, each stroke of his cock rubbing against her feminine walls. His vision blurred. He would never get enough of her.

Aidan leaned forward, palming her breasts, teasing her nipples with thumbs and forefingers until they grew longer and harder. Grace threw back her head, pushing her breasts farther into his hands. As he felt his release racing to its end, his need for her to come one more time before he filled her with his seed overtook him. He reached between them, using his thumb to rub circles over her clit. She squeezed him tighter and tighter. He ground his teeth together, driving his mate higher until she was screaming her release, milking his cock with such force he thought the top of his head would surely fly off.

Aidan continued his sensual assault, pushing into her harder and faster. He slid his hands down her legs, placed his hands behind her knees, and lifted her legs, changing the angle, driving him even deeper. His cock grew thicker…harder… filling his mate completely.

"Look at me, mo ghra'," Aidan ordered with his limited breath.

Grace's eyes snapped to his. He rolled his hips, bumped the bundle of nerves at the top of her channel, and together they exploded, screaming one another's name. The earth moved as he emptied into his mate.

Aidan let her legs slide down his arms as he leaned over her sweat slicked, orgasm relaxed body and kissed her lips, slowly and tenderly, as her breathing returned to normal.

"I really hate that you can regulate your breathing so quickly. Will I be able to do it someday too?" she asked in the breathy tones of a well-loved woman.

"I'm sure over time, but I must admit, I like you out of breath and completely replete from our lovemaking. It's one of the things I live for."

"If I had the strength I'd punch you in the arm… but I can't feel my arms." She chuckled a throaty chuckle he knew only came after she'd screamed her release to the Heavens.

"Let's have a bath, my love. What do you say?" he asked as he lifted her into her arms and was rewarded with a purr as she curled into his chest.

"Sounds wonderful," she whispered into his chest.

He made it to the third step when Rayne's voice sounded in his head. *"The baby's coming and Kyndel wants you both here."*

There would be no leisurely bath followed by more lovemaking tonight. There was a baby to welcome into the world.

EPILOGUE
Seven months later…

He'd just gotten back from spending the weekend with his clan. Everyone was there, even Aidan and Grace. Rayne's seven-month-old son, James Alexander MacLendon, Jay for short, named after his grandfathers, stole the show. With his long brown curls, emerald green eyes, and toothless smile, he was truly something special. His Commander was the happiest he'd ever seen him and more protective than Lance thought possible. It was the funniest damn thing and well worth the trip.

Lance was staying at Kyndel's old apartment, now that Rayne and Kyndel owned the whole building, while he led the hunt for the traitor. He knew the newlyweds were living in Grace's home about a half an hour from him, but he only saw Aidan when they were following a lead on his crazy ass younger brother. He missed his old friend. For six years, he'd watched 'A' blame himself and mourn the loss of his younger brother. Then after finding out the son of a bitch was alive, Aidan finally claimed his mate. He and Grace were inseparable. Lance guessed that's how it was when you were *in love*. He wished them all the best and couldn't help but feel a *little* jealous.

After all, when all hell was breaking loose, Lance had actually found a ray of sunshine in the form of the one the Universe designed for him. There she was, laying under a pile of rubble, covered in soot, cussing like a sailor… his Samantha, his *mate*. Her long, thick brown braid was all he could see, even as the pile of debris that trapped her quivered and shook while she tried to free herself. The intoxicating scent of lavender, rose petals, and jasmine hit him square in the chest, awakening the feelings he'd recently witnessed in two of his oldest friends. The first meeting of their eyes was magical, sending an electrical current through his body. His pulse raced. Lance had to remind his manhood it wasn't the time or the place to make their connection known, but she'd felt it too. He knew from the way her breath hitched and her pupils dilated.

He tried to deny their connection. Wouldn't go to her, only watched from afar. Even told himself he was there to protect her, since they hadn't caught the traitor or 'The Auctioneer'. Lance knew she suffered not only physical wounds, but also emotional trauma from what she'd been through. It was definitely not the time to drop the "I'm your mate" bomb on her.

Lance also couldn't deny the fact that he just *was not* ready for a mate. Hell, look at what happened to Kyndel and then Grace when they first learned they were the mates of his brethren. One was held at knifepoint and the other trapped in a magical spell; *not* something he wanted his mate to experience. If his Commander, Rayne, and the fiercest of their Force, Aidan, hadn't been able to keep those things from happening, what in all the Heavens would happen to *his* mate? He just wasn't prepared for that kind of responsibility. But no matter what, he still watched.

I really am pathetic.

Tonight was a perfect example. He rushed back from the lair to watch as Samantha left work. He was sure he'd missed her until he spotted her little blue Jetta, still parked in the doctor's parking lot. He looked at his watch, noting it was already six hours past the time she should be leaving the hospital.

I really am becoming a stalker…most definitely a loser.

He knew her schedule by heart, but still called in every day and sweet-talked one of the retired ladies who volunteered in reception to get Samantha's hours.

She must have taken an extra case… again.

From sitting in the waiting area on rainy days or when he simply got tired of sitting on his motorcycle, he knew she took the cases no one else wanted and noted they were almost always children. When he heard she was the most requested resident in the entire hospital, not only because of her skill and knowledge, but because of her incredible bedside manner, he couldn't stop the surge of pride he felt. Thoughts about her bedside manner that had nothing to do with her skill as a doctor, and everything to do with him getting her naked and under him seemed to be on his mind constantly.

Sitting in the shadows for almost four hours, he began to wonder if she was ever coming out. Propping his bike on the kickstand, Lance walked towards the emergency entrance. Just as he crossed the street, the scent of lavender, rose petals, and jasmine caught his attention. His head popped up and there, standing not a hundred yards away, was *Samantha*. From the way she held her head slightly to the side, he knew the muscles in her neck needed a massaging and his hands ached to do just that.

She has to be exhausted. But she's never looked more beautiful.

Using his enhanced speed, he returned to his bike before she spotted him. Being a coward was not something that sat well with him, but Lance had his reasons for staying away and they included eliminating all threats to her life before even considering bringing her into his world.

Sitting on his well-hidden Harley, he watched as she headed for her car. He was completely mesmerized by the sway of her rounded hips as her steps ate up the pavement. Lance lost count of the number of times he dreamt of his hands on those hips. His favorite fantasy played out with her bent over the arm of the huge overstuffed couch in Kyndel's old apartment, his fingers gripping her hips as he drove his hard cock into her hot, wet pussy until they were both screaming their release.

He breathed deeply, trying to dislodge the image of them both naked and spent after hours of hot, sweaty lovemaking from his brain, just in time to see the dark brown braid she always wore cascade down her back as she removed the surgical cap she'd forgotten until now.

Lance held his breath as she undid the tiny pink holder from the end. He'd only seen her hair completely unfettered a few times and it was breathtaking. He longed for it to be *his* fingers running though those curly brown locks instead of hers as she rubbed her scalp and removed a few of the knots he was sure would be present after so many hours bound up.

His cock hardened again as he watched her beautiful curls blow in the wind and prayed for the day he would feel them all over his body. Her hair was soft as silk, he remembered from the brief time she'd spent in his arms as he carried her from the rubble of the abandoned warehouse. Samantha was absolutely breathtaking. Never in his wildest dreams had he imagined scrubs could be sexy, but damn his woman knew how to wear them.

Watching as she got in her car and fastened her seatbelt, Lance wished for the hundredth time that he could go to her, but he knew in his heart the timing was all wrong. The taillights on her car flashed as she backed out of her parking spot and headed towards the road that would take her to the little white cottage with black shutters on the edge of the woods she called home. He adjusted his half-erect cock, threw his leg over the seat of his bike, and waited just a few minutes before following her. His brethren would rag him relentlessly if they knew what he was doing. He'd just have to make sure they never found out.

~~*~*~*~*~*

Seven months! Seven long months of hiding, only leaving the hovel he was holed up in when absolutely necessary. He'd even resorted to paying neighborhood urchins to fetch supplies to avoid going out in public, where those fucking werepanthers, or even worse, the damned Dragon Guard, could scent and find him. He had one amulet left but had to save it until he could locate the illusive witch and have her bespell more of those precious magical discs. If only he and those cowardly fucking wizards had been able to complete the ritual, he would be able to draw on an almost endless reserve of black magic and hide his dragon nature from the assholes who hunted him.

As it was, some criminal they were all calling 'The Auctioneer', who had his sights set on ruling the world, *cue the dramatic music*, had blown up the building and his chances of completing the ritual he so desperately needed. The ritual and the ensuing black magic was essential to his plans for revenge against all the people who'd let him down, tortured him, left him for dead, or just pissed him off in general.

Andrew smiled as he remembered how he'd kidnapped his cowardly brother's mate right in front of Aidan's eyes and kept her from him for quite some time. He heard they'd finally broken through the spell. Andrew wished he could've seen the long hours of suffering his brother endured while he wondered if his mate lived or died.

Of course, it was nothing like *he* had endured at the hands of the wizards, but it was a taste of things to come, things Andrew would make sure his older brothers and all of those worthless Dragon Guardsmen suffered. Added to the memories of the short time he spent with Grace was also the look of pure frustration upon the face of the great and powerful Dragon Guard Commander, Rayne MacLendon, as Andrew activated one of the last of his amulets and disappeared right before the fierce warrior's eyes.

Andrew simply had to find a way to get to that damn witch. It would only take a few of her special amulets for him to be able to leave the horrid place he was calling home and find another coven of witless wizards to help him acquire the black magic he needed to get his plans into motion. Her creative brand of magic allowed him to hide in plain sight from the best trackers in the world *and* hide his dragon nature from all. She was the only witch he knew powerful enough to do what he needed *and* she was proving damn near impossible to draw out of hiding.

He'd never expected the flighty blonde to have enough sense to hide, but apparently, looks were deceiving. She must've run when she learned of the debacle at the warehouse. Scared even though he'd diligently protected her identity. She was a white witch after all, no one would suspect her of being involved in his plan, and for the most part, she wasn't.

The little witch was a means to an end. He'd used her like he used everyone else, but that didn't negate the fact that he needed to find her, *quickly*. His rusty dragon senses didn't work. They only seemed to pick up on members of his old clan. He feared they could use it as a beacon to find him, so he'd shut them down and not used them since the day he sensed his brother and beautiful mate close by. If things continued the way they were, Andrew may have to try again and hope for the best.

He headed to the kitchen for another shot of whiskey. It seemed to be the only thing keeping him from pulling his hair out by the roots as he sat around waiting for news from his spies that something, *anything*, was finally going his way. He watched as the amber liquid flowed into the chipped glass he'd procured from a thrift shop around the corner, on one of the very few trips he made out into civilization.

Awakened from his half drunken musings by a knock on the door, Andrew grabbed the gun he'd taken off a dead body and carefully stalked to the door. No one was due to stop by until tomorrow, but maybe one of the losers he used to do his bidding had found something interesting.

Standing to the side of the door, he sniffed and listened intently. He may not have control over his other dragon senses, but he was definitely using his enhanced sense of smell and hearing whenever he could. He may not like it, but he was a dragon shifter, and if it got him one step closer to executing his plans, he'd use whatever he had at his disposal.

The stench of black magic filled his nostrils. He could hear an accelerated heart beat along with rapid breathing on the other side of the door. It was a wizard, *a frightened wizard*, but a wizard nonetheless, who'd dared to come see him. Maybe his luck was about to take an upward swing. The Heavens knew it was about time.

Andrew didn't stop the evil grin that touched his lips as he reached for the door handle.

Welcome to my parlor said the spider to the fly.

Haunted by Her Dragon
Dragon Guard Series #3

There Are No Coincidences.
The Universe Does Not Make Mistake.
Fate Will Not Be Denied.

CHAPTER ONE

Twenty-four hour shifts were going to be the death of her, especially when they lasted almost thirty. Of course, she had no one to blame but herself. She could've said no when Dr. Monoghan asked her to assist with an appendectomy. "No" had been on the tip of her tongue until she caught sight of the messy blonde curls spilling over the pillow as her mentor pointed towards their patient. She *knew* this was one she couldn't ignore. Monoghan's entire surgical team was male and very good at their chosen professions. Unfortunately, they knew how good they were and their collective bedside manner sucked. There was no way the little tow-headed sprite she'd heard singing would've been able to relax in the presence of the massive amounts of testosterone they spewed.

Grabbing her thirteenth cup of coffee of the day, Sam prayed for no complications and headed in to see her patient. Nothing could've prepared her for the innocent blue eyes surrounded by long thick lashes, topping the cutest little chubby cheeks in the world that looked up at her as she knocked on the half closed door. For a second she thought of another pair of azure eyes that heated her from the inside out, and promised hot sweaty nights spent satiating each other's needs.

Shaking her head to clear her thoughts, she walked to the end of the bed and grabbed the chart. "Hi, Sydney, I'm Dr. Malone. You can call me Dr. Sam."

The sweet girl giggled. "Sam's a boy's name."

"You're right," she smiled. "Unless it's a nickname for Samantha."

Visibly relaxing for the first time since Sam had entered the room, her patient answered, "Oh, that makes sense. There was a Samantha at my old school, but we never called her Sam, she wanted to be called Samantha...Samantha Jane." Sydney thought for a moment. "Sam sure would've been easier."

"It sure would've been," the young doctor agreed, winking at the obviously intelligent child before her. "Did you recently change schools?" She looked towards the woman sitting in the chair, who continued to mess with her cell phone, basically ignoring the child in the hospital bed. It seemed the opportune time for the adult in the room to speak up, but apparently the woman hadn't gotten the memo. When said "adult" didn't even look up, Sam checked the file, not surprised to find that the woman was a social worker, *not* a family member. Sam and Sydney were definitely on their own for this exam.

Probably easier that way....

"It says here you have a tummy ache." She pointed to the chart she still held. "Can you show me exactly where it hurts?"

"Right here." Sydney placed her little chubby hands across her midsection and scrunched up her nose. "But I really just want to go home."

"Now, Sydney, you know the doctor in the emergency room said you need an operation," the woman in the chair stated in a flat, irritating tone, finally entering the conversation, but still not glancing up.

The thought of smacking the woman danced through Sam's coffee-soaked brain. She wondered if *that* would get some kind of reaction from her. Instead of acting on her thoughts, the young doctor turned just in time to see Sydney's eyes fill with tears. Before the first one could fall, Sam asked, "Have you ever been in a hospital before?"

As soon as it was out of her mouth, she wished it back. She knew better. You never asked a ward of the state that question when you didn't know the whole story. What a rookie mistake, one she wouldn't have made had she not been so incredibly frustrated with the woman to her right. The next thing she heard simultaneously broke her heart and filled her with pride.

"Yes, Dr. Sam, I was in the hospital the day the big truck hit our car." Sydney continued in an unwavering tone, simply explaining the facts, all traces of her previous weakness gone. "Mommy and Daddy went to Heaven, and I went to live in the 'big house' with all the other kids. Miss Crutchfield...," Sydney looked over at the woman and rolled her little eyes, "she's my social worker. I have no aunties or uncles, and my nana and pop pop are already in Heaven. It's okay where I live, but I really wish I could go back to my old school to see my friends."

Sam counted to ten in her head, battling her anger, and returned her focus to her patient. Sydney was a tough little girl and one smart cookie. The child went on to tell Sam that the accident had happened about six months ago, and she was waiting to go live with a foster family. She spoke like a miniature adult, using all the correct terms and stating the facts of her situation with detached accuracy while she was examined.

The fact that *the child* was sharing the information and the useless state employee was busy with an inanimate object caused Sam's barely controlled anger to boil again. Why the hell did people with no interest in caring for children become social workers? Shouldn't they at least care about the little people they were responsible for? She'd seen it happen time after time. The people who were supposed to help the "lost children," as her foster mom had called them, didn't give a *damn*. They were there for the salary and the benefits a state job offered, not the welfare of the children.

Sam's constant wish was to somehow improve the system she'd grown up in after the death of her mom and sister. The only way change could happen was to work from the inside…to become a politician or a foster parent. Politics would *never* be something she was good at. Samantha didn't have a politically correct bone in her body. However, she could see herself as a foster parent, being a true advocate for children who grew up as she had. Of course, it would have to wait until she wasn't working thirty hours a day, six days a week.

"I know you do, sweetheart, but today we need to get your sick appendix out so you feel better."

"Can't you just give me some medicine? I really don't want to have an operation."

Before Sam could answer, Miss Crutchfield's monotone voice sounded, causing Sam's fists to clench in an effort to keep from striking the woman. "Sydney, just do what the doctor says. Don't make trouble." And then the woman had the audacity to sigh.

Without a second thought, Sam reached across and grabbed the cell phone from the social worker's hands. When Miss Crutchfield looked up to complain, the woman's face lost all color. Sam could only imagine the expression she wore, but she was just too pissed off to give a shit. The woman was supposed to be *caring* for the sweet child, easing her fear at having surgery, being Sydney's support system, not sitting like a high school girl obsessed with her cell phone.

Samantha leaned down so they were eye to eye and all but growled. "Miss Crutchfield, my name is Dr. Malone. Now, you can either be part of the solution or part of the problem. If you'd like to remain in this room, you'll need to be part of the solution. If you'd like to continue to completely ignore the child who needs your attention, then I suggest you go to the cafeteria and get a cup of coffee while we finish up Sydney's pre-op visit."

Miss Crutchfield's face immediately turned three shades of red. Without a word, she shot from her chair, took her phone from Sam's outstretched hand, and marched out of the room.

The cutest little giggle came from behind the young doctor and immediately calmed her temper. When she looked, Sydney had both of her pudgy little hands covering her mouth while her shoulders bounced with laughter. Just to see the child laughing, no matter how inappropriate, made all the frustration with the useless state employee worthwhile. At least the child wasn't in too much pain at the moment. It wouldn't do to have her suffering. Smiling while holding back her own laughter, Sam teased, "You think that was funny, do you?" Little blonde curls bounced as Sydney nodded. "Well, it was between two adults." Sam leveled her stare just a bit. "Always remember *your* manners."

"Yes, Dr. Sam," the child answered, still giggling.

Letting the subject drop, Sam moved on. "Okay, Miss Sydney, I'm going to show you exactly what will happen during your surgery and answer any questions you have. Then Dr. Schwartz will be in to give you some medicine that'll make you sleepy. Sound good?"

"Yes, ma'am." The child smiled, and all the long hours seemed worth it just to know she could help people who truly needed it.

Once she finished her surgical residency, Sam wanted to be a general practitioner, with children and the elderly as the focus of her practice, no matter where she ended up. Charlie, officially known as Dr. Charlene Gallagher, had teased her from the moment they declared their specialties in med school. Her friend called it Sam's "opposite ends of the spectrum" focus. That wasn't the only ribbing she'd taken, but at least at school Charlie had to bear it, too. Their classmates really had a blast with the fact that Sam and Charlie were roommates and best friends, "the girls with boys' names."

After about fifteen minutes of explaining, complete with a stuffed, cloth appendix, colored Expo markers, and a mini white board, Sydney seemed completely at ease. Sam stayed when the anesthesiologist came in. As her little patient started to yawn, she explained one more time, told the little sweetheart she'd see her in a few minutes, and headed to scrub up.

Hurrying down the hall, Sam remembered the way Sydney had smiled up at her, so trusting and loving. The sweet little girl's smile made all the long hours and millions of cups of coffee worth it. Affirmation that her decision to stay had been the right one came when she entered the Surgical Scrub Room and was confronted by Dr. Monoghan, along with the other three huge, male surgeons from his team. She knew she'd never be considered a "little girl." Sam was a tall, curvy girl and damn proud of it, but she felt almost dainty standing next to the behemoths scrubbing in with her.

Looking through the viewing window, she saw the doors across the large expanse of the operating room open. In came one of her favorite orderlies, Adam, wheeling her young patient into the huge, instrument-filled room. Adam was the best with their pediatric patients, and rightfully so, since he and his wife were working on their own NBA team with three little boys under the age of six, their first baby girl on the way, and them already talking about more. Sam thought they were crazy, but they were good parents and *that* was what was important. Hurriedly, she put on her gown and gloves, then made her way to the operating room to reassure Sydney one last time before they started the countdown.

Sydney smiled up at her. "Hi, Dr. Sam," the little girl half chuckled, half slurred. She was responding well to the anesthesia. Some kids fought it and made the process horrible for all involved, but Little Blondie seemed to be able to adapt to almost anything life threw at her. Smiling down at the sweet child, Sam signaled to the anesthesiologist that he could begin. Time seemed to fly, and thankfully, everything went smoothly. In less than two hours, the young patient was being wheeled to the recovery room.

Samantha stayed with Sydney until the child was in her room and having the first of what the doctor was sure would be many red Jell-O cups. All the nurses loved the little girl on sight, and laughed as she told everyone she only ate *red* Jell-O cups, none of the other "yucky" colors. As Sam was leaving, Sydney called out. "Dr. Sam, I didn't get a hug."

Choking past the lump in her throat, Samantha turned. "You're right. I'm sorry, sweetheart."

Walking the few steps back to the bed, Sam was immediately engulfed in the best hug she'd had in a long time. When she pulled back, Sydney was smiling from ear to ear. The resilience of children always seemed amazing to the doctor. Only a few hours ago this sweet child had been in surgery, and now she was eating red Jell-O and hugging like a bear cub.

"Now, you be good, and I'll be back to check on you in the next day or two." She tweaked the little beauty's button nose.

"Yes, ma'am, Dr. Sam."

Sam was about halfway across the parking lot before she realized her surgical cap was still on her head. As she pulled it off and shoved it in the huge brown messenger bag she'd used since her freshman year in college, her long, thick, braid fell from under the cap and took its place in the center of her back. Laughing to herself, she realized her curly brown mane had been in a braid damn near every day since the first day of her internship almost seven years ago; even weirder was the comfort it gave her hanging against her back. At least her intricate design allowed her to keep the one thing she had in common with her mother *and* follow the rules of the hospital.

Leaving the hospital and the stress of a very long day farther behind with every step, she pulled the end of her braid to the front, removed the ponytail holder, and began unbraiding and finger-combing out the tangles as she went. As each of the strands separated, more of the tension from the last thirty hours also untangled and floated away. Somehow, letting her hair blow in the breeze was just what the doctor ordered. Sam knew by the time she reached her car it would be curling in every direction and she would resemble some wild child, fresh from the woods.

Breathing deeply, she inhaled and blew out all the antiseptic smells of the hospital. She finally had two days off *together,* and doing whatever the hell she wanted for the next forty-eight…no, forty-two…hours was on the top of her list.

There was no regret about losing six hours of her off-time. Sydney was so worth it. It was Sam's job to help a child, and she'd do it again in a heartbeat. Hell, she might even sneak back tomorrow just to check on the child. After all, she *had* told the little darling she'd see her in the next day or two.

Sydney reminded her of all the kids she met when Fate saw fit for her to be in foster care. Sam had been one of the lucky ones. It had taken time, but she'd been placed with a great foster mom, and every day her tragedies from the past were a little easier to deal with. Too tired for a trip down memory lane, she focused on getting to her car.

Reaching into the pocket of her scrubs for her keys, the sensation of being watched raised the tiny hairs at the nape of her neck. Not in a creepy, stalker kind of way, but in a protected, almost special kind of way. As crazy as it seemed, Sam was filled with anticipation and excitement. It was reassuring to know *he* was watching over her.

The feeling of being watched had started after she'd been kidnapped from the very parking lot she now stood in and carried off to the middle of nowhere almost seven months ago. It had definitely been one of the most terrifying experiences of her life…one she would never forget, but not one she would let rule her life either. It was true she'd been fighting for her life that day, but there was no way in hell Sam would be a victim. Nothing, not even bad memories or bullies that preyed on women, could beat her. She still walked to her car by herself, politely avoiding the security guards she knew were told to watch out for her. It reminded her and others that she would *not* live in fear.

Everyone had her best interests at heart, she truly believed that. The hospital mandated psychiatrist recommended she get a roommate to avoid spending time alone after her abduction, but there was no way that was going to happen. Memories of overcrowded rooms at overcrowded group homes, where she could feel the breath of the girl next to her while they slept, reminded Sam she needed her space.

The day she left Momma Maybelle's (the best foster mom in the world) for college, she'd promised herself "things" did not matter, but that she would have the privacy she'd so desperately needed for so many years. So, she'd worked long and hard, saved every penny she could, and two years ago had purchased her own home…a little oasis, away from everyone and everything, where she could sleep crossways on her bed until noon if she wanted.

Sam stopped dead in her tracks.

I sound like a spoiled brat.

Her next thought caused her to chuckle.

Okay, maybe I would share with someone.

The "someone" who came to mind was a big, muscular, hunk of a man with the most hypnotic eyes she'd ever seen, blond spiky hair, and a deep rumbling voice. She'd be willing to share so very many things with him.

Shaking her head in an attempt to restore what little sanity she had left, Sam continued walking, thinking more about how it was like she had a guardian angel…someone who watched over her, kept her safe, protected her. She snorted out loud. "No, not an angel." The man who seemed to consume her thoughts more with every passing day could in no way be associated with the pink-cheeked little cherubs the word "angel" brought to mind. He was a Guardian, big and masculine and….*wow*.

Sam knew with all certainty it was him—the hottest man on the planet, with insurmountable strength, a power that seeped into her very bones the day they met, and a body that awakened dreams of hot, sweaty nights and amazing passion—who watched over her. He'd made her feel safe during one of the most terrifying ordeals of her life, and with the kind of life she'd lived since the fateful day all those years ago, that was really saying something.

Just his presence made her feel…no, made her know…everything was going to be all right—a totally new sensation for Samantha, one she couldn't remember ever feeling. He was different than any other man she'd ever met. It was hard to explain, even to herself. The best description she could come up with was that he was just…more. His touch infused her with warmth and security. It felt…right; not strange or foreign, but meant to be.

Sam knew he'd somehow helped her recover, and was a big part of why she'd gotten back to work so quickly. She was strong and had a determination to accomplish anything she put her mind to, but the trauma of that day had threatened her incredible resolve; and then, there he was. He'd lifted her from the rubble, and the missing pieces of her world had fallen into place. Pieces she hadn't known were missing.

At least two of the other girls who were abducted at the same time were still in therapy. From time to time, Sam checked on them. They'd all been brought to her hospital…therefore, accessing their records and keeping track of them was simple. When her friend Charlie saw her reading their charts, she'd just smiled and walked away. Everyone knew how she felt about bullies, and as far as she was concerned, the scumbags who'd kidnapped them were the worst kind of bullies.

Sam prided herself on her inner strength, something she inherited from her father, or so she'd been told. It had rubbed her the wrong way when the hospital administration decreed she have six sessions with the hospital psychiatrist. She'd adamantly refused until they played hardball and refused to let her go back to work until the evaluation was complete. Doing the six sessions had been tedious and boring. She'd given all the right answers, and once it was complete, she was done.

There was no way in hell Sam was doing any more, even though it was obvious Dr. Simons wanted her to. He often stopped by under the guise of checking on another patient or looking for the head of surgery, but she wasn't an idiot. It was obvious he was checking on her.

Not wanting to draw any more attention to the situation, Sam always smiled and gave the obligatory answers, while inside screaming to be left alone. Dr. Simons even resorted to asking about the cut on her leg when he could tell she was trying to get away. Donning her best smile, she'd tell him it had healed nicely with a minimum of scarring. Why wouldn't he realize there was no reason to rehash the gory details? It was over, she'd survived, and it was time to move on. That was how Dr. Samantha Malone dealt with things. Her continued prayer was that, sooner or later, the good doctor would find another "project" and leave her alone.

Thinking back to that dreadful night, most people would've relived the fear, but Samantha remembered what it had felt like to be lifted out of the rubble by *him*. If she concentrated hard enough, she could actually feel his arms around her. The way he'd moved the huge pile of rubble that had fallen on top of her after the explosion, as if it weighed nothing, would be permanently carved into her memory.

The douche bags who'd grabbed her in the parking lot had obviously cut and run when the bombs went off. If it hadn't been for the two beams crisscrossing over her, Sam would've been crushed when the ceiling collapsed. She remembered struggling and cursing like a sailor on shore leave, trying to get out from under the heap. Suddenly there was daylight, and she was caught in the most unladylike position imaginable. Lying on her back, feet in the air, looking at the sexiest man to walk the earth, Sam was mortified.

Her first glimpse had been of those amazing eyes, the color of the forget-me-nots flowering in the garden behind the house she'd grown up in. So light a blue that in the sunlight they seemed almost colorless, but when they looked at her, they seemed to glow. It felt as if he reached inside and soothed her fears.

Despite his size, he'd been incredibly gentle. She felt a contained aggression emanating from the amazingly muscular arms wrapped around her. His main focus was rescuing her, but he would seek vengeance on her behalf when she was safe. Samantha had been unable to speak, only feel, as he lifted her out of the prison the explosion had created.

When he'd spoken, the little bit of brain function she had left evaporated into thin air. The low rumbling of his voice wove its way under her skin and made her tingle. Since that day, she'd spent many lonely nights letting his whispered words of reassurance fuel her most erotic dreams. She always woke up wondering why he watched her, but never approached.

Samantha couldn't explain, no matter how long she thought about it, how she knew without a doubt he was a good guy. The word "hero" flashed in her mind like a neon sign, and returned every time she thought of him, which happened to be too damned much. Her body and soul knew immediately he was safe…specifically, safe for her.

The adrenaline that had kept her going throughout the entire ordeal bled from her body at the touch of his hand. All of her recognized him as someone she could trust, someone she could lean on, and that wasn't something Samantha Malone ever did. Her eyes slid shut as she remembered how her head lay against his chest of its own volition. She'd taken her first deep breath since the black bag had gone over her head and her back had hit the floor of the dark windowless van she was thrown into.

Her rescuer continually asked if she was okay, if she was hurt, even told her the cut on her leg didn't look too deep. She'd chuckled when he reassured her he was taking her to a "healer." By the time he laid her on a blanket under a tree far from the smoking building, the vibrations of his rich baritone voice had reached deep inside, relaxing her until she felt warm and calm.

At the loss of his warmth, her body ached…just another of the weird things she'd had to work through since that night. How could she feel anything after just a few minutes in his arms? Not to mention the shit she'd been through in those few horrible hours. Sam chalked it up to trauma and shock, but now, seven months later, she still thought about him and heard his strong, steady heartbeat echoing in her mind. She even imagined him walking through the halls of the hospital, and dreamt about him night after night.

Completely on autopilot, Sam unlocked the doors on her old blue Jetta and slid into the driver's seat. She'd thought about getting a new car a few times, but this one fit her like a glove. Besides that, she hated being in debt. Her house was enough for her to keep up with, at least while she was still in her residency. She just had to keep "Bonnie Blue" going for a couple more years. Leaning her head against the headrest, she took a deep breath, letting the stress of the day wash away.

Not surprisingly, as soon as her eyes slid shut crystal blue eyes were gazing back at her. Even in her imagination, she could feel him in the deepest corner of her soul. He was…she searched for the right description…just so much *more* than anyone she'd ever met before. "Larger than life"…that was it! That described him to a tee.

Her mother had said the same thing about her father. Sam always wondered what it meant, but since meeting him, it had all become clear. She could hardly remember her dad…knew he'd been a brave soldier and died in battle, defending the country he loved, from the stories her mom told. He was a hero, medals and all, something she definitely associated with the sexy man who lifted her from her nightmares that day seven months ago.

Lance whispered through her mind. She'd been embarrassed when she'd had to ask the elderly woman who cleaned and bandaged her wounds the name of the man who'd carried her to safety. The healer said his name, and it was as if a breath of fresh air washed over her. It was like nothing she'd ever experienced.

Searching for answers, Sam decided it was a byproduct of all the adrenaline flooding her system. Of course, that didn't explain why she was sitting in her car after working an incredibly long shift thinking about him and smiling.

Damn that man!

What had he done to her? She laughed out loud at her own paranoia.

Like he has any control over you whatsoever.

It was all in her mind. She'd even looked up "Rescuer Syndrome" in her psychology textbooks, and found she didn't have the symptoms or the personality for it. Figuring it might be her completely neglected libido crying out for help, she'd even entertained the thought of dating the cute new pharmacist who continued to ask her out, even though she barely looked his direction and only grunted a few words here or there when he spoke.

The problem was, she didn't feel anything for him, even when he turned his hundred watt smile and what others called incredible charm on her. It was hopeless. She was in lust with a man she'd seen for all of ten minutes, seven damn months ago, haunted by the idea of who she thought he was and unwilling to stop it.

Turning the key in the ignition and hoping the grinding sound she heard wasn't anything serious, Sam blasted Lady Gaga's "Applause," praying it would keep her awake on the thirty minute drive home. Trying to decide whether she was more hungry or tired, she remembered there was nothing in her refrigerator even remotely edible and thought about stopping at the grocery store, but the longer she drove the more exhaustion won out. Even a drive-thru sounded like too much work. Hopefully, the Pop-Tarts she'd gotten a few weeks ago hadn't turned to rocks in the cabinet, and with any luck, she'd be able to locate the single packets of Crystal Light in her junk drawer.

With the dilemma of food settled, she backed out of her parking spot, completely ignoring the extra little shake and shimmy Bonnie Blue made, and headed towards the winding roads that would take her to her little haven in the woods.

CHAPTER TWO

He followed the tail lights of Samantha's car from such a distance they appeared to be little rubies floating in the sky. Constantly scanning the area for anything or anyone that may threaten the beautiful woman who monopolized his thoughts both day and night proved boring, and for the hundredth time that day his mind wandered.

Lance remembered the feel of her in his arms and the gentle slope of her nose leading to her perfectly bowed mouth, begging to be ravished. Her eyes were the deep brown of the mountains behind his childhood home, so deep and dark that when he looked into them, he could feel himself falling into the wonderful, amazing world of his mate. His training taught him to always be prepared, to never let his guard down, but looking into those dark pools of fathomless emotion all those months ago, he'd known he could let go of everything and drift in the splendor of finding the one the Universe had made for him forever.

Watching over her had given him insight into his mate. Samantha was a strong-willed, independent woman, with nerves of steel and a determination rivaling his own warrior spirit. He knew the Universe didn't make mistakes, but he wondered about Her timing. They were still searching for the traitor who'd hurt both Kyndel and Grace. Then there was "The Auctioneer," who seemed to always be on the fringes, not to mention the ever-present threat of hunters and wizards to his kin. Lance had tried, but simply could not justify bringing Samantha into the clan.

Yes, she'd been kidnapped by the human criminal, but he was almost a hundred percent sure she wasn't on the traitor's radar…yet. That would definitely happen if Andrew found out she was his mate. Heavens knew the little fucker liked to mess with the mates of the Guard. Lance also knew the longer he went without at least introducing himself and trying to forge some kind of relationship with the one meant to be his, the harder he made it on himself. They had touched…the mating bond was growing and searching for completion. Soon, he would have no choice but to go to her for both their sakes.

There were days he thought he might die if he didn't touch her, inhale her scent, look into her eyes, but it was something he had to deal with. Drawing on all his years of training helped, as well as dreaming of the day he would claim her and they would never be separated again. What didn't help, however, was the constant prodding of his dragon. His beast simply couldn't or wouldn't understand why the man was choosing to wait. No matter how many times he explained, the centuries old beast thought *he* knew better.

Every day was a new battle between man and dragon, and today had been especially hard. The entire time he'd been with his brethren, his dragon had pushed. It was really distracting, and the conversation he'd had with Royce hadn't helped at all. The older Guardsman was too wise for his own good, and too damn perceptive. Lance had almost slipped up, but smiled as he thought back over their discussion.

"What's up there, loud mouth? Why so quiet today?" Royce teased.

"Nothing, just thinking about the search for the traitor," Lance answered, too quickly.

Royce looked at him with a wisdom that only came from a hundred and fifty-six years of living. "If you say so, but it seems like there's something else."

"Nope, nothing at all." Lance tried not to squirm as he felt the disbelief rolling off his long-time friend and mentor.

"I know shit has been coming at us hard and fast, but if there's something you need help with, don't be a hero…come to one of us. I'd hate to have to kick your ass for hot dogging again." He paused and rubbed his jaw, then smiled. "Well, actually, I'd enjoy kicking your ass." The older Guardsman laughed. "You truly are a burr in my butt, but you're family and I'm here, even if it's to beat you back in line."

Lance knew Royce was trying to ease the tension and get him to open up, but there was no way that shit was going to happen.

"Bring it on, Old Man." Lance winked and smiled, using one of the many nicknames he knew drove Royce crazy.

"That is WISE Old Man to you, 'Pain in the Ass'."

They were both laughing when Rayne had walked over carrying Baby Jay, essentially ending the conversation, something Lance would be eternally grateful to his commander for. It was only a matter of time until Royce figured out what Lance was hiding. He would deal with it when the old man did, but no discussions would take place until Lance was ready.

Bringing himself back to the present, but still lost in thought, he almost missed Sam sitting on the side of the road. As it was, he had to drive ahead almost a half mile to find a place to turn around. He slowed as he came close to where she and her car sat. Since he'd first spotted her, she'd gotten out of the car, opened the hood, and was leaning in to inspect the engine of her little blue car.

The way her pants drew tight against her well-rounded ass caused his blood to race and his cock to harden. He tried to think of anything but what it would feel like to cover her body with his, kiss the sensual column of her neck, hold her generous breasts in his hands, feel her nipples harden against his palms, and finally sink into the woman who haunted him day and night.

Yeah, that's so not working.

The sound of his tires on the gravel pulled her from her inspection of the engine. When she spotted him, her eyes opened wide and her mouth formed a perfect "O," which did absolutely nothing to decrease the growing pressure in his jeans.

"You?" she said in a whisper, still staring in shock.

"Yep, it's me." He hoped quickly changing the subject would stop any further questions, so he rushed on. "What seems to be the problem with your car?" He pointed, hoping she would stop looking at him like he had three heads.

She continued to stare as he approached, but at least closed her oh-so-very delectable mouth. Not that it mattered one damn bit. Samantha was still the sexiest thing on earth *and* was standing right in front of him. As he braced his hands on the frame of her car and leaned in to take a look, she asked, "Do you live around here?"

He loved the sound of her voice. It was a little lower than most women's, and smoky. He longed to hear it whispered in his ear while he tasted and explored her silken skin, with his hands buried deep in her long brown curls, feeling her body moving against his. Taking a deep breath to rein in his wayward thoughts, Lance focused on the gorgeous woman in front of him.

He'd noticed the curiosity with a bit of suspicion in her voice and knew he needed to tread very lightly. His Samantha was a smart cookie, and from what he'd seen, she was also as tenacious as a bulldog. There was no way she would let the subject drop until she was satisfied with the answers he gave her. He decided honesty was the best policy, but that didn't mean he had to tell her everything.

"Not far. I just like to ride out here in the open." He pointed at his Harley. "Riding in the city with all the buildings, people, and stoplights takes all the fun out of it." He glanced over his shoulder and saw she was seriously considering what he'd just said while moving a few steps from him and her car.

Within a few seconds, she'd decided he was being honest. Her shoulders relaxed, and the lines bracketing her intense, dark eyes disappeared. Missing the sound of her voice, he asked, "You live out this way?" Even though he already knew the answer, he needed to protect his secrets.

"Yeah, not too far, just over the next hill at the edge of the woods," she answered as she started back towards him.

His world tilted on its axis. Her long legs, the ones he'd dreamt were wrapped around him, stretched out in front of her displaying all their shapely goodness. The slight sway of her hips and her hair blowing in the wind made him take another deep breath, just too keep from grabbing her and kissing her until neither one remembered where they were.

Lance was about to turn away and the wind changed direction. His entire being was suddenly filled with the scent of jasmine and honeysuckle. Inhaling long and deep, he fought to keep his eyes open. Her scent was absolutely intoxicating. His dragon rolled and purred from just a whiff. He snapped his head back towards the engine and prayed she hadn't noticed his odd behavior. If she had he was screwed. There was absolutely no explanation his lust-fogged brain could conjure.

Deciding he needed to think of anything but the alluring woman at his side, Lance turned and poked around her engine. It didn't take long to find the problem. "How long's it been since you had a tune up? These spark plug wires are beat to hell, and your engine coil looks shot, too."

He heard her feet shuffle in the gravel and couldn't resist looking up. A slight blush covered the apples of her cheeks as she worried her bottom lip with her teeth. For about the hundredth time he was forced to resist the temptation to pull her close. Waiting not so patiently while she worked up the nerve to answer his question, Lance stood mesmerized. When she finally spoke, he had to smile.

"Would it surprise you if I said I just can't remember?" She hurried on, and he listened, loving her voice more with every word. "I know I had the oil changed like eight or nine months ago, and I think I remember them saying something about there being more work I needed to get done, but honestly, I wasn't paying attention. I'd just been called from the hospital. See, I'm a doctor…well almost a doctor…and I'd been called back into work, so I just paid them and left. I know this car is old and I try to keep up with the maintenance, but I work some pretty crazy hours and sometimes I forget to get things done."

She paused to take a breath, and his hands itched with the need to reach out and tip her head back so he could once again look into her eyes while she scrambled to explain the disrepair of her car. The only thing stopping him was the fear that if he touched her without warning she might slap his face. Erring on the side of caution, Lance waited.

"I know I should've gotten a newer car, but I really only go from my house to the hospital and back again. I was hoping to keep this one running for at least another year while I finish my residency. Then when I get a better paying position, I can start paying off my school loans *and* get better transportation." She stopped abruptly, gasped, and speared him with her big brown eyes. "And I have no idea why I just told you all of that. I'm so sorry." She blushed again, and he had to tuck his thumbs in his pockets to keep from touching her.

This woman packed a powerful punch, and he wanted her more than he'd ever wanted anyone or anything in all of his one hundred and twelve years. Just when he was sure he would lose his mind from trying to resist the gorgeous woman standing before him, the most amazing thing happened. She smiled right at him. With that one small act, he knew without a doubt why his commander had acted like a crazy man and Aidan had acted like a lovesick puppy after finding their mates. Lance had no doubt that he would move heaven and earth to see her smile every day of his life, and if all else failed, he would stand on his head or twerk with Miley Cyrus. Whatever it took, he'd do it just to see her smile.

"Is she dead?" Samantha asked, and for the first time he realized she had a slight southern accent. Nothing like Kyndel, his commander's mate, but it was there, nonetheless.

He cleared his throat and chuckled to hide his reaction. "She? Your car's a girl?"

Again her cheeks colored, and he wondered if she blushed all the time. Then he prayed it was only for him, because he knew he would kill any other man who ever made her blush. *WHOA! Where the hell did that come from?*

He quickly shoved all murderous thoughts aside. Samantha was talking again and he didn't want to miss a word coming from those kissable lips.

"Yep! Her name is Bonnie Blue." She said it with pride and he didn't even try to stop the grin spreading across his face.

Damn! She's really something else.

He bit the inside of his cheeks, as he was sure she would not appreciate him laughing at her choice of names for her car. "Bonnie Blue, huh?" She nodded her head and he could tell she was waiting for him to tease her. Instead he moved on. "Nope, she's not dead, but she's not going anywhere tonight. I don't have the parts or the tools to fix her with me right now."

"Well, shit!" She gasped as her hand flew to cover her mouth. "I'm sorry. I shouldn't have said that."

Lance laughed out loud. The longer he laughed the more Samantha relaxed until she was laughing right along with him.

"Darlin', you have absolutely nothing to be sorry about. I've heard worse. Hell, I've said worse," he said, still laughing but using it as a cover to listen to her laughter.

She didn't have the tiny, tinkling, little laugh most women had. His Samantha had a big, full laugh that filled the evening air. The kind of laugh that made other people want in on the joke so they could laugh right along with her.

Keep my Samantha smiling and laughing as much as possible.

And there it was again, *my Samantha*, and thoughts of keeping her happy. What the hell was he doing? He wanted her more every second of every day, even though he knew it wasn't the right time. There was no way he would take chances with her safety. It was time for him to get his head out of his ass and catch the traitor. Then he could be with Sam.

As their laughing died down, she started looking at the ground again and shifting from one foot to the other. He could tell something other than her car was bothering her. "Don't worry about your car...er, I mean Bonnie Blue. I'll get her fixed right up."

"It's not that. It's just that I let my AAA membership lapse, so now I'm going to have to call a tow truck and everyone that I know is working tonight. Guess I'll be walking home." She turned and started back towards her car.

Before he could think about what he was doing, he reached out and touched her arm. Electricity flew between them, making his cock harden. His mind was flooded with images of their bodies intertwined and sweaty while he tasted every inch of her lovely golden skin. It was all he could do to keep from falling at her feet and begging her to be his.

Lance did everything in his power to regain control, to keep himself and his dragon in line as he withdrew his hand and said, "Don't worry about it. I'll have my bre...brothers come and pick her up, and I'll take you home. You aren't scared to ride a Harley, are you?"

He wiggled his eyebrows and was graced with another of her dazzling smiles, while all he could think about was what it would feel like to have her wrapped around him while they rode to her home.

Well hell, I'm totally fucked.

CHAPTER THREE

She'd tried every argument she could think of but nothing seemed to get through Lance's thick skull. He was bound and determined to have his brothers pick up her car and that he be the one to take her home. She even tried calling Charlie, the only person she could really call a friend, but the nurse who answered the phone on the surgical floor said Dr. Gallagher was assisting with another appendectomy. They seemed to be running a special on those lately.

It was either ride on the back of the motorcycle of the guy who'd haunted every damn thought she'd had for seven months, or walk the almost ten miles home. It wasn't that she couldn't walk. It was that she'd been at work for thirty hours, hadn't gotten much sleep the night before, and was only standing because of the sexual tension jumping between her and her now two-time rescuer.

When he'd touched her shoulder, the electric current that ran through her body and landed in her core was potent enough to light the entire metropolitan area. Her panties were immediately wet and her knees weak. She knew he felt it too. His eyes widened and his nostrils flared. He quickly schooled his features and went on to help her with her current situation, acting like nothing had happened. She was sure she'd seen him sniff the air and then smile, but maybe it was her imagination. Otherwise, the man who headlined the best erotic dreams of her life was in need of a psych evaluation.

His brothers arrived a short time later and she damn near lost it. They were the biggest and best looking guys she'd ever seen. Not as good looking as Lance, but she knew loads of women who would let those beefcakes eat crackers in their beds anytime. She kept looking from man to man, searching for physical attributes they might share. He'd said they were brothers, but she saw nothing to indicate they shared any genetic material.

As a matter of fact, the tall red-headed one—well hell, she decided she should call a spade a spade—the carrot-topped giant was in no way genetically related to Lance. She guessed they were just really close friends. His name was Royce, and from the way they bickered and worked together like a well-oiled machine, she could see they'd known each other a very long time. She'd had a few people like that in her life. It was a shame she'd lost touch with them, but they still held a special place in her heart. Without them, she would've never survived foster care before Momma Maybelle came along.

"Look, you pain in the ass, I'm telling you to move the hell out of the way and let me secure the car to the trailer," Royce was growling through gritted teeth.

"Okay, Old Man, I was just trying to help," Lance answered, then looked at her and winked. She'd never noticed it before, but from this angle, she could see a little dimple in his cheek that winked right along with his amazing blue eyes. On anyone else she would've said it was cute, but on his beautifully masculine face, it just made her want to kiss it to see if it tasted as good as it looked.

"You better get your ass outta the way, Lance. You know the old guy has a short fuse these days."

She looked up, surprised the quiet one, who'd barely said "Hi" when they arrived, was actually talking. The longer she looked at him, the more she realized that, just like the giant, there was no way the tall, lean drink of water with light gray eyes, olive skin, and hair so black it shined was related by blood to the muscular, tanned, blond-haired, blue-eyed man who was her infatuation.

"Royce'll be fine, Dev. He just needs to blow off some steam. Since I haven't been around the lai…I mean…home much lately, he hasn't had anyone to argue with. Isn't that right, Grandpa?" She watched as Lance slapped the big man on the back so hard she would've sworn he'd dislocated his shoulder.

"Why don't you two knuckleheads do something besides irritate me? Go over to the other side of the trailer and make sure everything is secure." Royce sounded gruff, but she picked up on the affection he had for the others.

Lance turned and looked right at her, and she felt her heart skip a beat. What the hell was it about this guy that made her body go crazy? He was potent as hell and twice as scary. She had no time in her life for *any* man, let alone one who made her forget all else and dream of endless nights spent wrapped in each other's arms, sweaty and spent. Just staring into his eyes made her want to abandon all else to be with him.

"Devon, you handle that," he said without eye contact. She felt his stare in every cell of her body. Completely mesmerized, Sam stood speechless as he strode in her direction, all sex and wet dreams in ripped jeans and cowboy boots. The muscles in his chest bunched and rolled under his tight gray T-shirt, and she wondered by what miracle his sleeves hadn't burst from the strain of his biceps. He was intense and raw and as tough as nails, but the twinkle in his eyes said he was just as likely to play a practical joke as save a damsel in distress.

Damsel in distress? Where the hell did that thought come from? I really needed to get home and get some sleep.

"You doing okay, Sam?" She heard him speak, saw his lips move, but her brain chose that moment to short circuit. She watched his brows furrow, and before she could answer felt the shock from his touch on her shoulders.

She blinked and shook her head. "Yeah, I'm okay. Sorry, I blanked out there for a minute. Guess I'm more tired than I realized."

"I'm sure you are. Hell, who wouldn't be after a thirty hour shift?"

"Yep, that's the way the job goes." She knew she should move so that his hand would fall from her shoulder, but the heat infusing her exhausted body from that simple touch was absolutely delicious, so she stood there soaking it all in. A second later what he'd said registered in her foggy mind. All the relaxation she'd felt seconds ago disappeared.

"How did you know I just worked thirty hours?"

He looked away for a split second, and when he looked back, he focused on the spot above her eyebrows instead of her eyes. "You told me earlier." As soon as it was out of his mouth he looked her in the eye again.

"No, I didn't. I remember saying I worked long hours, but I know I didn't tell you how long I'd been at work today…I mean yesterday…well, also today. Oh, whatever." She sighed with growing exasperation. "I know I did *not* say anything about thirty hours. How did you know that?" She pushed through gritted teeth, not wanting to alert his brothers to the fact she was about two seconds from losing her cool.

He opened his mouth, about to answer, when Royce yelled for him and her cell phone rang in her pocket. He turned to go and she shivered, her body immediately feeling the loss of his touch. She watched as he walked back to where the others were finishing up with her car. Sam was so entranced by his ass she almost forgot the phone ringing in her hand. Shaking her head, she answered her phone, noting from the caller ID it was the hospital.

Still watching the play of hard muscles under well-worn denim, she couldn't deny he was the best looking thing she'd ever seen, but he was hiding something. She'd picked up on his feelings of unease and tension when she'd called him out. Again, she thought of what a distraction this man was proving to be. Sure, he'd literally saved her ass more than once, but she couldn't shake the feeling he was hiding something, and dammit if she didn't really want to know what it was.

CHAPTER FOUR

Lance knew Samantha was tired. Any other time she wouldn't have accepted his help. He'd had to be persuasive, but it had been worth it. There was nothing like the feel of her arms around his waist and her thighs pressing against his legs as they rode the winding road back to the hospital. He thanked the Universe for his beautiful mate.

However, he wasn't thrilled she was going back to work after having just been there for so many hours, but she had been adamant. He knew if he didn't take her she would just walk, especially since it concerned the patient she'd stayed late to help…a little girl who'd captured Sam's heart. The mating call and his dragon were screaming for him to take her home, but his mate's furrowed brow and unrelenting glare told him she was going back to the hospital come hell or high water. Against his better judgment, they were heading back in the same direction they'd come from just a few hours ago.

He agreed with his dragon …she needed rest, but her determination and commitment to her patients was something he greatly admired. Not to mention her quick mind and immeasurable strength, along with her abundant curves *begging* to be explored. She reminded him of a warrior, defending what she held most dear, something he could totally understand.

That simple realization brought him once again to the fact that he wanted her more than he wanted his next breath. He knew her safety had to come first, but who was he to question Fate if She thought they should spend some time together in the meantime? He'd been fighting his attraction and the mating call for seven months. It was exhausting.

He knew he had to protect her from those who would come back to hurt him again, but he'd also decided sometime in the last twelve hours that he would take full advantage of every excuse to be close to her that presented itself. There was just no way he was claiming her as his mate.

Exposing her to the chaos plaguing his clan was not something he could do. The responsibility of a mate while leading the hunt for the traitor was something he wasn't ready to handle… not to mention the shit he was going to have to deal with from each and every one of his brethren. His mind knew the reality of their situation, but his body, soul, and dragon wanted their mate….*now*. To keep his own sanity he'd protected her from afar, but tonight his best laid plans had been blown all to hell. The last seven months had taught him there were things a person simply couldn't deny, and his attraction to Dr. Samantha Malone was one of those things.

He knew Royce and Devon had paid close attention to his interactions with Sam while they loaded her car onto the trailer. Royce even stopped what he was doing while they discussed whether it was a good idea for her to go back to the hospital or not. There was no way to miss his raised eyebrows and knowing look.

It had taken Devon all of two minutes to recognize her as one of the girls they'd rescued. And in the next minute, Lance heard him telling Royce that Sam had asked Siobhan, Devon's mom and their clan's healer, for his name. His brethren were the closest thing to family that he had and he loved them all, but they were worse than a bunch of women when they all got together.

He pictured how it would happen. Royce would tell everyone who'd listen everything he'd witnessed, ending with a full scale discussion about his future and the woman they were sure was his mate. Before Aidan had found Grace, he would've been in on the fun, but now it would be Royce and Aaron. Then Rayne, his commander, would put his two cents worth into the conversation.

They'd all assume he was going to claim her right away and bring her home. There wouldn't be a moment's peace. He admitted, at least to himself, that he'd given all of them a lot of shit over the years and had enjoyed the hell out of it, but he wasn't ready for what was to come. Paybacks really were a bitch! There was no way he wanted to have a conversation with *any* of them concerning Sam. The only way to avoid it was to be very careful and do his level best to keep his mate away from his nosy ass brethren.

Yeah, that's gonna be easy!

She shifted slightly and laid her head against his shoulder. As she exhaled, her breath stirred the little hairs at the back of his neck. Had they not been traveling fifty miles per hour around curves and over hills, he would've let his eyes slide shut from the sheer pleasure of it. As it was, his cock grew harder, pressing against his zipper until he was sure it would have the design embedded in the skin. He hoped her hand didn't slide any lower than the waistband of his jeans or she would know the effect she had on him. He smiled, knowing he had a similar effect on her. The scent of her arousal had been present ever since he'd taken the first step towards her while on the side of the road.

He felt her relax against his back and her breathing become slow and deep. His tired, overworked mate was falling asleep. Thank the Heavens they were turning into the hospital parking lot, or he would've had to pull over to make sure she didn't fall off his bike. He slowed to little more than idle and coasted into her parking spot. As soon as he cut the motor on his Harley, she stiffened, took a deep breath, and her arms tightened around his waist as she stretched.

"I must've dozed off." She spoke with her head still resting on his shoulder, obviously in no hurry to move.

Lance was definitely in no rush to lose the contact. Nothing had ever felt more perfect than her body against his. Of course, he wanted more, like her *naked* body against the front of his, but he would take what he could get, and what he was getting felt damn good.

"I need to get in there and see what's going on." She sat back and his body immediately missed hers.

He pushed the kickstand down and steadied his bike while she climbed off. Then he followed suit and spun around to find her still standing there. Unable to catch his breath, he stood perfectly still, waiting for her to do or say something. She looked up at him through thick, dark eyelashes, causing his heart to skip a beat.

"Thank you so much for everything. You saved my butt again tonight, not to mention bringing me all the way back to work." She shook her head, and he once again marveled at her magnificent mane. "I have absolutely no idea how I'll ever pay you back, but I *will* find a way."

"Samantha, you have absolutely nothing to pay me back for. Now get in there so you can take care of your special little patient and we can get you home before you fall down."

Her brow furrowed and he watched a myriad of emotions flash through her expressive eyes. He knew the second she'd decided what to say. Her chin popped up, and gone was the demure look he'd received moments ago. Before him stood the warrior woman once again, and she was glaring. "You are *not* staying here and waiting while I take care of Sydney. You've done quite enough. I'll find a ride home with someone. I'm sure Charlie won't mind giving me a lift."

Obviously, she expected him to take her directive without question, because she spun on her heel and was just going to walk away without a backward glance.

Oh, hell no. That shit's not happening!

He gently grabbed her upper arm and spun her around, bending at the same time so that they were eye to eye after her turn. "I understand you're used to taking care of yourself, and that's to be commended, but I brought you here and I'll take you home. *Capisce?*" He winked to ease the sting of his command, but he meant every word. Fire danced in her eyes, and Lance knew they were about to have another discussion.

He would never be sure if it was the close proximity to his mate or the way her scent wrapped around him. Maybe it was the fact that the most fantastic woman in the world had been made especially for him. But whatever it was that caused him to lose his mind, he would forever be grateful.

In a heartbeat, they went from standing toe to toe to him holding her tight against his body, kissing her like she was the very air he breathed. It was pure heaven. Something deep inside his soul shifted. Suddenly, everything wrong with his world was right…complete. He was whole for the first time in his very long life, and the only thing better was the feeling of her lips moving against his. Her tiny nails buried into his back and pulled him even closer to her soft, warm body. Samantha was holding absolutely nothing back. Their bond was almost nonexistent because of its newness, but he could feel her everywhere.

They opened to one another at precisely the same moment, their tongues dueling for supremacy, each trying to take in as much of the other as they could. Lost to their passion, they jumped when the sound of a car door slamming sounded in the darkness of the parking lot.

Sam stiffened and pulled back, looking at him once again through her impossibly thick lashes. He reveled in the half-lidded, sexy look of her eyes and her kiss-swollen lips, knowing he'd done that to her. The blush on her cheeks was an unexpected bonus that had his chest swelling with pride. He refused to give her a chance to remember what he'd been distracting her from. Spinning her on her heels, he walked them towards the hospital. In companionable silence, he enjoyed holding her close for the few minutes it took to reach the entrance.

"Don't think just because you kissed all rational thought from my brain for a few minutes that this conversation is over," she said as they stepped on the curb.

"Whatever you say, *Doc*," he chuckled, hoping to lighten her mood and deciding he liked the nickname.

He looked down to find her still facing forward with her brow once again furrowed. If they didn't reach some kind of compromise in their power struggle, her poor brows would be permanently ruffled. Her body language and the emotions coming from her were filled with confusion more than anything else, something he could most definitely understand. Especially since he was confused even though he had half a clue about what was going on.

They walked through the automatic doors, and the nurse at the desk wore a knowing smile while saying hello to Sam. Continuing down the hall, Lance grinned when Sam squirmed from under his arm at the same time two young women in scrubs came out of a room on their left, turned towards them, and smiled. The one with short blonde hair stopped right in front of Sam. "What're you doing back here, Missy? Didn't I send you home hours ago?"

Sam chuckled. "Yeah, but I had 'technical difficulties,' then got a call that a post-op patient spiked a fever. Of course, Dr. Monoghan and his crew are nowhere to be found, and the floor nurse thinks she needs to be seen, so here I am."

The young woman leveled her gaze at Lance, then slid her eyes back to Sam. "And you just happened to find him in the waiting room?" She tipped her head in his direction.

Sam blushed again. Lance didn't even try to stop the smile that slid across his face.

"No, Lance saved me when Bonnie Blue decided to break down, and then gave me a ride back."

He could tell she was uncomfortable, but had no intentions of letting her off easy. Lance stood still with his signature shit-eating grin planted firmly on his face, waiting to see if she introduced him. To his surprise, Sam didn't miss a beat. "Charlie, this is Lance. Lance, this is Dr. Charlene Gallagher…Charlie." As they were shaking hands, she shifted and started her getaway while beginning to braid her incredible hair.

"If you insist on staying, Lance, you can hang out in the waiting room or the cafeteria," she called over her shoulder.

"I'll be in the cafeteria, Doc," he called to her retreating backside.

"All right, I'll make it as quick as I can."

She picked up the pace…a woman on a mission. He was so entranced by the sway of her gorgeous ass, he completely missed Charlie leaving as well. Shaking his head, he headed towards the elevator to find the cafeteria, his mind a blur of thoughts about his Samantha.

How in the hell was he ever supposed to stay away from her long enough to catch those who threatened not only her, but also the others he held most dear? Royce always told him the day would come when his mouth would write a check his ass couldn't cash. Well, if kissing Sam had been that check, then he would be a pauper selling pencils in the street for just one more taste.

CHAPTER FIVE

The little one was finally resting comfortably in her room. It had taken four long hours to get Sydney's temperature back to 98.6. Sam still had no clue why the child's fever would break and then spike again, only to repeat the cycle about every forty-five minutes. All the tests they ran had come back negative for everything. There was no logical reason for what happened. The bright side was, once they got it all the way back to down to normal, it stayed that way for over an hour with no indication of returning.

The most reassuring sign was that the child's rosy coloring had returned and she'd stopped the constant tossing and turning. All that was left was to chart the final dose of meds, then Sam could find Lance and finally get home to her bed. She hated to admit she was glad he'd stayed. But Charlie had already headed home, and the only remaining option was sleeping in the doctor's lounge…*again*. Sam was ecstatic Lance had hung around.

As she shut down the computer and signed out at the nurse's station, she thought about the man who'd literally kissed her silly. She definitely hadn't seen it coming, but had enjoyed every damn second of it. That was what a kiss was supposed to be…passionate, all-consuming, and….*wow!* As she relived every spectacular second of the best kiss of her life, she moved on autopilot towards the end of the hall.

While she waited for the elevator, a cold creepy feeling slid down her spine. The feeling of being watched made her jumpy, but not the protected, safe way Lance's watching her felt. This was creepy, almost scary.

Nonchalantly, she glanced over one shoulder and then the other, seeing nothing but lab coats, scrubs, and hospitals gowns. There was nothing or no one who looked out of place. But the longer she waited, the more intense and focused the dark, ominous feelings became.

Finally, the elevator indicator flashed red. Sam counted to fifteen, knowing the doors would open any second. She gave one last, quick look over her shoulder, took a step towards the elevator, and ran straight into a wall of hard muscle. Strong, familiar arms instantly wrapped around her, pulling her farther into the elevator. It wasn't until she heard the doors close that the arms gently holding her loosened.

She looked up, immediately snared by the amazing blue eyes she was coming to depend on to be there in her hour of need. The look they held reminded her of the look she'd seen in them the night of their first meeting, complete with brows drawn tight. She realized immediately he wasn't smiling but frowning, almost scowling, and the tension he carried was vibrating through her as he continued to hold her. Even his voice was gruffer than usual when he spoke. He visibly worked to soften both his look and his tone. "I was just coming to find you. What happened?" He was examining her very closely, waiting for her answer. "You seem spooked."

He wasn't happy but was trying to play it cool. She decided to play along and answered, "Oh, nothing…just tired, I guess. Why are you here? I thought we decided to meet in the cafeteria?"

For the second time, he shifted his gaze from her eyes to her eyebrow. He'd done the same thing earlier, and just like then, she was sure now that he was hiding something. Right before he began speaking, he looked back into her eyes. "Just coming to check on you. It's been a little over four hours, Doc. Just wanted to make sure everything was all right." He gave her a little half grin, but the ever present twinkle hadn't returned to his eyes. Still visibly working at relaxing both his body and expression, he asked, "Your little patient doing better?"

"Yeah, her temperature is finally back to normal and she's resting comfortably," Sam answered, still wanting to know what had him on edge but deciding to wait and see if he would tell her on his own.

"Great! Then we can get out of here and you can finally get some rest." He was avoiding any further conversation, but was obviously still on high alert.

The elevator doors began to open. Quicker than she could follow he had her hand in his and was a step in front of her as they exited. She watched him scan the entire area while quickly moving towards the exit, almost as if he was looking for some hidden danger. Gone was the fun-loving guy who'd handled her broken down car without a second thought and had gotten her back to the hospital to take care of Sydney like her knight in shining armor. The man holding her hand now reminded her of some type of soldier or police officer or…bodyguard. Yeah, that was what he was doing. He was guarding her…but from what? She pulled on his hand in an effort to get him to stop, but he only seemed to speed up.

"Come on, Doc, we need to meet Royce in the parking lot. He brought my truck. I figured you'd be too tired to ride back on the Harley."

He smiled his little half smile again but it still didn't reach his eyes. Something was happening that he wasn't sharing with her. Any other time she would've demanded to be told everything, but tonight she was just too exhausted to care. Not one to give up control easily, Sam again thought about calling him out, then decided between fatigue and all the crazy feelings Lance stirred within her, she simply didn't have the strength for a discussion.

The creepy feeling she'd felt a few moments ago had disappeared as soon as she slammed into Lance, once again proving that her mind and body recognized Lance as her safe haven. She was definitely going to need to examine all of this after she'd gotten some sleep.

Lance was a complication she simply didn't need at this stage in her life, no matter what her crazy hormones were screaming. Her intuition was always right. What she'd felt before she bumped into him had been terrifying, but Lance, along with his huge brothers, could pretty much handle anything anyone could dish out. She'd be sure to ask him about it tomorrow when he returned her car. She would be rested and unable to be charmed out of getting the answers she wanted.

CHAPTER SIX

He knew the minute the wizards entered the hospital. The stench of black magic made him nauseous at first scent. His rage had almost gotten the better of him. The only plausible reason they had to be at the hospital was Sam, and there was no way in hell he was letting anything happen to her. Keeping her safe had been all he'd thought about since his first scent of jasmine and honeysuckle in the smoldering warehouse. He'd denied his feelings and the pull of the mating call to protect her, and now those fucking bastards had come after her out in the open, in her place of employment.

WHAT. THE. HELL?

Thank the Heavens he'd been there.

Having no idea how many wizards were in the hospital and not wanting to endanger any innocents, Lance had immediately called for backup, mind speaking with Royce. The big guy decided the guise of exchanging vehicles would explain his and the others' sudden appearance. Lance had to admit he was thankful for the older Guardsman's quick thinking.

"Are you guys here yet?" He called to his brethren in mind speak as he and Sam exited the hospital.

"Already here and waiting, Dude." Devon answered.

"Just you two?" Lance asked as he maneuvered through parked cars with Sam in tow.

"Nope, Aaron and Aidan are inside looking for the dirty fuckers. We figured if their dickhead brother was with the wizards, they had the best chance of catching him. We're going in as soon as you get your girl clear of here." Royce answered, and Lance could hear the chuckle in his voice when he said "your girl." *Dammit*. Lance knew the old man had figured out what was going on.

Sam pulled on his hand and he heard the intake of breath, indicating she was about to speak. He knew the only reason he was getting away with rushing her out of the hospital and weaving through parked cars without a discussion was the fact that she was dead on her feet. Any other time, he was sure she would've put her foot down and demanded he tell her everything.

Just ahead, he saw Royce and Devon standing next to his truck in the parking spot next to hers. Deciding to head off her questioning, he pulled her up the half step she was behind him and pointed to his truck. "Your chariot awaits, milady," he teased, and even threw in a wink, hoping to at least get a grin out of her.

It was all he could do to not laugh out loud when she rolled her eyes and answered, "Thank God."

"Any word from inside?" he asked his brethren while keeping Sam distracted.

"They haven't seen them yet, but the taint of black magic says the wizards are still in there." Royce answered.

"Yeah, these sons of bitches are using all kinds of false trails and misdirects just like Andrew did in the woods." Lance could hear the anger and frustration in Aidan's voice. Lance was thankful Aidan had come along for the hunt.

"Sorry you had to leave your mate, but I'm damn glad you're here." Lance answered quickly.

"No worries, man. She loves hanging with Kyndel and the baby, and I couldn't miss an opportunity to kick these bastards' asses." Lance could hear how desperately Aidan wanted all of this behind them. The Heavens knew it was something they all prayed for.

"And if that asshole little brother of ours is here, then this shit is really gonna be a party." Aaron threw his two cents in. They all laughed to relieve some of the tension.

"Besides, we heard there was a certain beautiful doctor we all needed to meet." Aidan laughed as the badgering Lance was dreading began.

"Yeah, what gives? Trying to keep her all to yourself there? Not cool." Aaron mocked hurt feelings and they all laughed even louder. This was the bullshit Lance had wanted to avoid.

"Now is not the time," was all he said as they reached his truck and the sons of bitches who'd failed to keep their mouths shut. The laughter in his head was almost deafening. Paybacks were a bitch, and the banter they were throwing was only the beginning for all the shit he'd given them during their years together. Oh well, what the hell was family for if not to mess with you every chance they got?

"Hi, Dr. Malone." Royce extended his hand to Samantha, smiling and winking. Lance considered smacking him, no matter how much bigger and older he was.

"Hi…Royce. Just call me Sam." She smiled at his brethren, and he could see her exhaustion was just about to take over.

"Hey, Sam," Devon waved. He was leaning against the tailgate of Lance's Silverado wearing a shit-eating grin. It was completely unusual for the most reserved of Lance's brethren, but confirmed what he already knew…he was in for years of teasing. Something else he'd have to prepare Sam for when the time was right.

"Hey...ah...Devon." She shook her head and once again her fatigue was evident. "Sorry 'bout that. I'm usually good with names, but I've been at work on and off for about thirty-six hours, and I'm runnin' on fumes."

She chuckled and Lance felt jealousy for the first time in his life. He knew it was completely unjustified. His brethren would never do anything but help, protect, and love his mate as a sister, but it was all part of the mating call. It didn't help that his need to care for her exhaustion and the close proximity of the wizards added to his dragon's need to protect. It was time to get the show on the road. Get her home and tucked into bed, and make the nagging dragon within shut the hell up.

"Thanks for bringing the truck. I think *Sam* here is too tired for a bike ride." He accentuated her nickname and was rewarded with another eye roll.

Damn, she's cute when she's sassy.

"I'm not too tired, but I will admit the thought of leaning back against the comfy seats of that big truck sounds like a plan." She leaned slightly towards him, and Lance used the opportunity to pull her against his side. Once again her exhaustion worked in his favor. Samantha didn't even flinch but cuddled into him. He smiled, then realized Royce and Devon were grinning at him like a couple of loons. Dev even winked.

Oh yeah, this just gets better and better....

Lance cleared his throat and glared at both men, but refused to lose the contact with Sam. If they wanted to laugh at him, they could just laugh away...he'd earned it. It felt too good and too right to have her at his side to give a damn. Of course, he would have to come up with a really good reason why he wasn't claiming her right away, but he had time before he saw them again. Right now, he needed to get his mate to her own bed before she fell asleep standing in a damn parking lot.

He moved them to the passenger side of his truck. "Thanks again. I'm gonna get the doc here home. I'll meet up with you later," he said in passing.

His brethren took the hint. "No problem," Devon answered as he and Royce headed towards Sam's parking spot. It was only then Lance realized they'd brought Royce's bike with them. In all the excitement of the wizards' arrival, he'd forgotten that most bikes were too small for the largest of his brethren, and the big guy hated riding bitch.

"Brought your own wheels, huh, Grandpa?" He couldn't resist messing with Royce. It was just too damn fun.

"You better watch your mouth, Pain in the Ass. I might just embarrass you in front of your girl there."

Lance could hear all his brethren chuckling. *"Yeah, yeah, yeah, whatever."*

"Paybacks are a bitch." Royce loved to remind Lance of what he already knew...the big guy *would* get even.

"Whatever, Gramps. You've missed me."

"Right! Like I've missed woolen breeches." With Royce's comeback, all the Guardsmen roared with laughter.

Lance lifted Sam into the truck and made sure she fastened her seatbelt before shutting the door. *"You guys be careful and kick some ass for me."*

"We sure will. Just get your mate outta here. The more I wind around this hospital, the more I'm sure you're right. They were coming for Dr. Malone. Their true trail follows her almost step for step."

Aidan confirmed what Lance feared. They were coming back to collect the women they'd kidnapped earlier in the year. He was glad the other two women who'd stayed in the area were out of state at the moment. It would allow the Guardsmen to keep all the focus on Sam's safety and catch the bastards responsible.

"Thanks again for everything. I'll be in touch."

They all answered as he climbed into his truck, then cut the connection. He needed to think and focus all his attention on scanning for trouble as they made their way to Sam's little cottage in the woods. There was no way he was going to let those assholes follow them. He backed out of the parking spot and headed to the exit.

"You hungry?" he asked, knowing she hadn't eaten anything the entire time he'd been with her, and sure she hadn't eaten much even before that.

The only answer he got was her deep breathing. Glancing over, his suspicions were confirmed...Sam had already fallen asleep. While she slept, he was able to wind around and avoid taking any obvious routes to her home without her questioning his motives. There were no signs of wizards, Andrew, or any humans who didn't belong, but he maintained his vigilance.

Lance would do everything within his considerable power to keep Samantha safe. All of this bullshit proved to him once again how justified he was in not claiming her. His dragon chuffed in agreement about her safety, but was definitely NOT on board with waiting to claim the light of their soul. The two mighty warriors would continue this debate, of that he was sure.

Pulling into her driveway with the headlights off, he once again scanned the area. There was a slight disturbance about five hundred yards behind her house. Pushing more of his considerable power into his mind's eye, Lance focused on the movement and realized it was coming from the treetops. He was then able to locate three more such disturbances and was sure he knew who it was, but needed confirmation. This was, after all, Sam's safety he was dealing with.

"Royce, did you call Max?" He sent directly into the mind of his brethren, not hiding his annoyance.

"Aidan called him when we were unable to locate the wizards. The bastards are gone, and there's no sign of the traitor."

"How the hell did the Big Cats know where Sam lives?" His relief they were patrolling the woods outweighed his annoyance, but he was not thrilled that anyone knew where his mate lived.

"I picked the location out of your mind. Sorry, Bro," Devon answered with sincere regret. His older brethren's talents were growing stronger with age. Lance would have to be careful what he kept out in the open from now on.

"No worries. Just would've been nice to know we had a welcoming committee."

The Guardsmen all chuckled as his last bit of irritation evaporated. He knew they only had his mate's best interests at heart. Lance was going to have to work really hard to keep from making an ass out of himself until all this shit was handled. Between the mating call and his dragon, it was going to be a challenge, one he prayed he was up for.

He knew Maximillian Prentice, King of the Werepanthers, aka Max, was a powerful ally. Hell, he liked the smartass Leo. If not for Max and his pride, they wouldn't have over half the Intel they had on Andrew, the wizards, or the human criminals. Max's werepanthers were able to get into places the dragons simply could not. That rankled some of the Dragon Guard, but Lance really didn't care who found what as long as they eliminated the threat to his mate and caught the asshole traitor. With the Big Cats in the woods, Lance could concentrate on getting Sam settled without having to worry about anyone sneaking up on them.

Stepping out of the truck, he nodded to the giant black cat who'd landed not twenty feet in front of him. The panther blinked its huge green eyes several times, dipped its chin in recognition, and continued his patrol of the woods around Sam's home. Max was a force to be reckoned with as a man, but in animal form, he was downright fierce.

As Lance made his way to the passenger side of his truck, he noticed a few more sets of eyes flashing in the darkness. What had irritated him a few minutes ago was now comforting. Knowing they were out there and had his back, allowing him the time he needed with his mate, damn sure made life easier. Any other time he would've taken the lead, run off after any and all enemies, and not stopped until they were either captured or killed, without regard for his own safety. His brethren all accused him of hot dogging at least once a week for all of their very long lives together, but with Sam in his life, everything had changed.

He stopped dead, hand extended, not quite touching the door handle, realizing for the first time that his world would never be the same. Whether he claimed his mate now or after Andrew and all the others he was colluding with were caught, it was all different, and he wasn't sure how he felt about the changes. Lance knew the Universe didn't make mistakes, but was he really ready for a mate? His dragon pushed hard, letting him know the beast was most definitely ready, but he couldn't stop wondering if *he* was. Deciding it wasn't something he had to think about at the moment, he went back to caring for his mate.

As soon as he opened the door the beauty of his woman hit him square in the chest. Samantha Malone was absolutely gorgeous and amazingly fierce when awake. However, sitting in his truck, body curled to the side with her head leaned against the headrest, sleeping for the first time in a very long time, she completely took his breath away.

Her hair was wound in her signature braid, signifying how exhausted she truly was. He'd never seen her leave it bound any longer than the walk to her car after work. The temptation to taste the succulent skin on her scrumptious neck was hard to resist and caused his body to lean forward of its own volition. Breathing deep in an effort to regain his control, he pulled the scent of jasmine and honeysuckle—her scent—deep into his lungs. His eyes slid shut. He leaned the rest of the way forward until his lips gently touched her forehead. Laying a simple kiss above her eyebrow, he took a moment to enjoy the thought of a normal life with the one destined to be his.

Standing up quickly, he shook his head.

Normal? What the hell is that?

At one hundred and twelve years old, Lance couldn't remember one time his life had been normal. He shook his head one more time and reached across his mate, unhooking the seatbelt. Sliding his arms under her knees and behind her back, he lifted her from the seat. She curled into his chest, laying her head on his shoulder, and he felt another piece of his soul click into place. It just felt right to have her in his arms, depending on him, even in her sleep.

I'm becoming as big a sap as the others. Doesn't that just suck?

Kicking the door shut, the gravel of her driveway crunched under his boots as he headed towards her front door, trying not to think inappropriate thoughts of the amazing woman cuddled against his chest. As he stepped onto her porch, he realized too late her door was locked. Had he had a free hand he would've smacked his forehead for not thinking of it sooner. Then it hit him, she always carried her keys in the front pocket of her scrubs. Carefully balancing his mate with one arm, he retrieved the keys, unlocked the door, and entered her home, not even taking the time to look around. Using his enhanced speed, it took mere seconds to reach the room he knew was hers from all the nights he'd kept watch.

Taking in his surroundings as he gently laid her down, Lance had to smile. The colors were a palette of browns, beiges, and creams, perfectly coinciding with what he already knew of his Sam, but he had to admit the lace and frills surprised him a bit. His mate had a girlie side, and what once would've made him scoff now warmed his heart. This whole mating thing was turning him into a ball of mush. The same shit he'd been ragging on Rayne and Aidan about was happening to him, and Heavens help him, he was starting to not give a shit.

For the first time since laying her down, Sam moved in her sleep. Without a second thought he jumped into action, his only thought for her comfort. He removed her shoes and covered her with the quilt he found neatly folded at the end of the bed. As soon as the blanket touched her, she curled to the side with her back facing him. He marveled at the outline of her perfect form. His palms itched with the need to trace every seductive curve. His mouth watered with the need to taste every erotic dip. The sight of her magnificently rounded behind nearly had him begging at the altar that was his Samantha. His eyes ate up every inch of the amazing creature who was to be his.

He spotted her thick brown braid, and the desire to unleash her miraculous mane overwhelmed him. The need to give her the comfort was alive within him. He knew she needed to rest comfortably and he would do whatever it took to make it so. Sitting lightly on the side of the bed, his hip made contact with her luscious ass and his cock jerked.

Down boy, now's not the time, he told his wayward member, but that didn't stop his imagination from conjuring all sorts of erotic images.

Gently he removed the small pink band, then slowly began to unwind the intricate design her hands had so deftly wound. He was reminded of spun silk as the delicate strands slid through his fingers. He marveled as each tendril naturally curled against her back. As the braid completely fell away, he was unable to stop his fingers from gently massaging her neck. The touch of his fingers on the satin of her skin sent an electric current straight to his erection, causing it to harden even more against the zipper of his jeans. She moaned in her sleep, pushing into his touch, and he knew she felt their connection even as she slept.

Working the tight muscles of her neck, he moved to her shoulders. Letting his hands slide under her scrub top, the need to keep skin to skin contact was thrumming within him. The longer he molded her skin, the faster his heart beat and the more his thoughts of her perfection were confirmed. Even her response to his touch was without flaw.

Her behind rubbed against his hip, and once again his internal debate began. His body, heart, and soul wanted her more than his next breath, but his brain continued to tell him the threats against her needed to be eliminated first. Fortunately, nature had a way of taking care of itself, because as the blood left his brain he acted on pure instinct and leaned forward. He ran his nose along the exposed column of her throat, stopping as he felt her blood pump harder and faster. His tongue slipped past his lips, bathing her pulse in his scent while pulling hers into his soul, marking her, letting all others know to whom she belonged.

Samantha's head fell forward, an invitation for more attention. Who was he to deny his mate? Unable to stop, his hands moved to her waist as he continued to kiss and nip her tender skin. His need built until he was sure he would burst. His hand touched the flesh at her waist and an electrical charge like nothing he'd ever known ran through him, assuring him he'd passed the point of no return.

Using every ounce of strength he possessed, Lance eased back until only his hands at her waist maintained their contact. He watched as she settled back into a deep sleep while his thumbs drew little circles on her skin, unable to give up the last bit of their connection.

A tap on the window woke him from his stupor. He jerked his head around. There looking back at him was a huge pair of green cat eyes and a panther's face with a smirk only the king could give.

Damn cat!

It was truly irritating that the king's beast fit on the small balcony outside Sam's room. Despite his irritation, he smiled at Max's ingenuity for getting his attention. Lance nodded his head, assuming Max needed him outside. The cat turned and the last Lance saw of him was his tail as he leapt from the roof of Sam's cottage.

Sitting a few minutes longer, Lance drank in the beauty of his dark-haired angel. Sighing, he removed his hands from her skin and scribbled a note, letting her know he would return her car as soon as it was repaired. Unable to control himself as he headed towards the hallway, Lance glanced over his shoulder for one last look at her. He wasn't sure who he was trying to fool,—probably himself, most definitely his dragon, and without a doubt the men he called brethren—but in his heart, where there was only the truth, he admitted to himself that he was falling in love with Dr. Samantha Malone. Fate would not be denied. He shook his head.

All right, now I need to get my ass out there and catch those sons of bitches, so I'll never be apart from her again. Wonder if I can stop acting like a love sick idiot for that long?

Turning on his heels, his resolve renewed, he all but flew down the stairs. Locking the door, Lance slid Sam's keys through her mail slot. When he stood again, Max was walking towards him, back in human form and pulling on a T-shirt. The smirk on the Leo's face said it all. "Something you need to tell me there, golden boy?" Max teased, referring to the color of Lance's dragon.

"Don't know what you're talking about, King." Lance answered, braced for what was to come.

"All right, we'll play it your way for now, but I expect an invitation to the mating party," Max chuckled as he stopped a few feet in front of Lance.

"But—" was the only word he got out before Max waved away his response, never one to put up with anyone's bullshit.

"Play it however you want. Not my business." All signs of joking left his face, and he frowned. "What is my business are the signs of trampled foliage, and the lingering scent of black magic. Follow me. Let's see what we can do to catch these bastards."

CHAPTER SEVEN

Sam awoke to the sun shining through the bank of windows in her room and tried hard to work up the energy to move. Her cell phone beeped on the bedside table. She stretched and rolled over to see who had the audacity to bother her on her day off. When she grabbed her phone, she also brought back what appeared to be a business card. The note inscribed made her smile and butterflies flitter in her stomach.

Hope you slept well, Doc. Call you when your car is fixed. Have a good day off. L

She knew she was acting like a lovesick teenager and really couldn't find the will to care. In the privacy of her own home, during the few hours she actually had away from work, Sam was allowed to act like a normal almost twenty-nine year old young woman who was attracted to an incredibly sexy, most definitely sarcastic, sex on a stick "he-man" who'd curled her toes with the most amazing kiss. It added to his appeal that he'd hung around when it wasn't his responsibility to make sure she got home after thirty-six hours of work. Not to mention he relieved her of the stress of dealing with a broken-down car. The icing on the cake, however, were the incredible dreams she'd had that were so real she would've sworn she felt his lips on her neck and hands on her body.

Remembering the phone in her hand, Sam looked at the screen at the same time she shot straight up in bed. *What the...? How did I get into bed? How did I get home?*

She retraced everything that had happened after she finished with Sydney's chart. The last thing she remembered was buckling the seatbelt in Lance's truck. Apparently she'd fallen asleep. It only stood to reason Lance had carried her to bed. She shook her head and read the message on her phone from Charlie.

Your little patient would like to talk to you. Call if you can. Hope you are having a great day off.

Sam had planned on calling Sydney anyway, but needed a shower and a cup of coffee before doing anything. After all, she'd just slept twelve full hours, something she couldn't remember doing...*ever*.

With only one full day off left to get her long list of chores done, Sam jumped in and out of the shower in record time, then brushed her teeth, threw her hair up in a messy bun, dressed in her favorite pair of sweats and "Doctors Do It With Lots of Patience" T-shirt, and headed in search of coffee. While Mr. Coffee did his thing, she called the hospital. The floor nurse gave her the rundown of all the happenings since she'd left the previous evening and then connected her to Sydney's room. The little voice that said "Hello?" warmed her heart.

"Hey, Sydney, it's Dr. Sam. I heard you were asking for me. How're you feeling today?"

"Oh, Dr. Sam, I feel so much better. The medicines you gave me fixed everything. I told them nurses you'd make me better." Her little patient answered with such excitement Sam found herself smiling until her cheeks ached.

"I'm so glad you're better. Nurse Susie said they'll be bringing you some mashed potatoes and chicken strips for dinner to see how your tummy feels with real food in it. Okay?"

"Sure, Dr. Sam, but I really like the red Jell-O and animal crackers."

"I'm sure you do, honey, but we need to make sure your tummy is ready for real food. You don't want to get sick again."

"If you say so," Sydney answered with the enthusiasm only a child could muster. "When will you be back, Dr. Sam?"

"I'll see you first thing in the morning. Be good and listen to what the nurses tell you."

"Yes, ma'am, I will."

"See you tomorrow, sweetheart. Bye, bye."

"Bye, Dr. Sam."

Sam could hear Sydney chattering away about her phone call as she hung up. That little girl was really something special. Sam hoped Sydney was adopted or at least placed with a good foster family very quickly. Thankfully, the beep of the coffeemaker derailed the maudlin thoughts of her horrible experiences in foster care. There was no time to take a trip down memory lane. She had too many things to be happy about and too many things to accomplish for a pity party.

Filling her favorite mug, then adding cream and sugar, Sam looked around for the Pop-Tarts she knew were somewhere. Starvation was setting in and if she didn't want chicken and stars soup for breakfast, it was imperative she locate those yummy toaster pastries. Finally, in the last cabinet she found them…a brand new, unopened box of cinnamon and brown sugar Pop-Tarts, her favorite. With coffee in one hand and breakfast in the other, she headed to the living room to cuddle in her big recliner while she ate.

The day flew by while she did load after load of laundry and cleaned everything that had been untouched for months while she worked day and night. She was mopping floors and listening to Lady Antebellum on her iPod when thoughts of Lance flooded her mind for the umpteenth time. Wondering why he was the one man she couldn't forget, even though their first meeting had been anything but normal and very brief, she sighed.

Her smile grew as she thought about how protected, even special, he made her feel. The kiss they'd shared became like a film clip on a loop, playing over and over in her mind. Her pulse raced and her nipples peaked until they brushed the inside of her T-shirt as she mopped the same spot over and over. That man had the ability to mess with her mind even when he was nowhere around. She knew with a certainty she should be scared. In the next breath, she got the feeling she was missing something. It was the weirdest thing she'd ever felt.

Shaking her head and deciding maybe she needed more sleep, Samantha finished her mopping and headed to her recliner. Her cell phone was sitting on the table, the red light flashing, indicating she'd missed a call. Running her finger across the screen, she laughed out loud. Right there, as sexy as ever, was the object of her infatuation, smiling his signature shit-eating grin. She could only imagine when he'd found the time to take his picture *and* program his number into her phone.

Pressing the key for voicemail, she barely held back the sigh that came from hearing the baritone rumble of his voice. It wove its way inside her heart, warming her throughout, bringing everything she'd been feeling just moments ago roaring to the forefront. Using the focus that had gotten her through medical school, Sam pushed aside her lust-induced fog to hear what he was saying.

"Hey, Doc, it's Lance. Sorry to call so late, but we're still waiting on a part to fix your car. It'll be tomorrow afternoon before it can be driven. I know you have to work early in the morning so give me a call. I'll come get you and make sure you're at the hospital on time. As you can see, I put my number in your phone. Hope you had a good day off. Talk to ya soon."

She all but fell into her chair, stunned and still holding her phone. Her first thought, when she could think again, was that he'd given her a nickname…Doc. Usually, she hated any nickname other than Sam, but with him she liked it. It showed he thought about her in a personal way.

What the hell?

There was no way she had time to be getting hung up on anyone, let alone *that* man. Finishing her residency and getting a permanent position was her focus. It had been all she'd dreamt of since she was a young girl, and a promise she'd made to her dead family. A promise she intended to keep.

Sam liked Lance…a lot. There was no denying she was attracted to him on an almost elemental level…something like the couples in the romance novels Momma Maybelle used to read, in a made for each other kind of way. He was special, and she was sure his easy-going mannerisms were just a small part of who he was. She sensed a deep, intense side to him that he kept hidden from most. He was passion personified. If the kiss they'd shared was any indication, Lance had the ability to turn all her best laid plans into a forgotten mountain of rubble and her into a wanton woman.

She laughed out loud at the thought of her as "wanton" but immediately began to squirm in her seat from the barrage of hot, sexy images that flashed in her mind. A cold shower may just be in her very near future if she couldn't stop thinking of her "hero." Remembering what he'd said in his voicemail, she decided there was no way she was going to ask him to come out of his way to get her so early in the morning after all he'd already done for her. Besides that, maybe a little distance would do her some good. Charlie had to work tomorrow, too. Sam would just give her friend a call. Her house was basically on Charlie's way to the hospital anyway.

Jumping up from her chair with her phone balanced on her shoulder, Sam finished the last of her chores while calling Charlie to make sure she could pick her up in the morning. Of course, Charlie asked about the "hottie" she'd seen with at the hospital. Sam effectively avoided the question by talking about her call with Sydney, and then made an excuse to hang up. She felt bad about not gossiping with her friend like they always did, but for whatever reason, Sam didn't want to share Lance with anyone, even if it was just to talk about how good-looking he was.

Deciding she'd order a pizza since she hadn't made it to the grocery store and the thought of canned soup turned her stomach, Sam dialed up Luigi's and ordered her favorite. In less than thirty minutes, the doorbell rang. Handing the young man all the cash she had, Sam told him to keep the change.

As she looked up to thank him again, two glowing green eyes in the woods across the street caught her eye. Coyotes used to roam the woods and Sam wondered if she should call animal control. It would be a shame if someone's pet was hurt by a wild animal. The longer she thought about it, the more she was sure the eyes looked feline, not canine, and couldn't remember ever seeing any Big Cats in the area. Just as quickly as she'd seen them, they were gone.

Probably imagined it. Need more sleep....

Getting ready for bed, she remembered she hadn't called Lance to let him know Charlie was picking her up for work. Never shying away from anything in her life, Sam surprised herself that just the thought of talking to Lance on the phone made her pulse race. Hoping a shower would calm her nerves, she headed upstairs. Standing under the warm spray, she thought of everything she knew about the man who'd taken up residency in her brain. The instant connection she felt when he rescued her. The way he occupied her every thought. The feeling he'd been watching and protecting her...and then there was the save on the side of the road. If all that wasn't enough, the man was fixing her car. She'd never met anyone like him.

Wrapping herself in her favorite fluffy towel, she made her way into her bedroom and decided texting Lance would be easier than a conversation. She quickly typed, *Thank you so much for fixing Bonnie Blue. Charlie can take me to work in the morning. Talk to you tomorrow. Night, Sam,* and hit send before she could chicken out. When had she turned into such a marshmallow...or worse yet, a girlie girl? She was definitely losing her mind. Momma Maybelle had always said a good night's sleep would cure what ailed her, and that was exactly what she was going to get.

Slipping on her Garfield nightshirt and sliding into bed, Sam pulled up the covers just as the text alert on her phone sounded. Without thinking, she grabbed it and read the words that would fuel the most erotic dreams of her life.

Sweet Dreams, Doc.

CHAPTER EIGHT

Closing his phone after returning her message, Lance stood in the woods behind her house staring at the window to her bedroom. Since he'd been there, he vividly imagined every move she made…everything she touched. When the lights went out, he was certain she was snug in bed, and his body ached to be wrapped around hers. The thought of their bodies intertwined, replete from hours of lovemaking, had been in his mind for so long he thought of little else. He'd been sure she wouldn't accept his offer of a ride to work, but was willing to try anything to spend more time with her away from the chaos and conflict that haunted them at every turn.

Turning his thoughts from his mate and to the asshole he wanted dead, Lance thought about the information they'd gotten from the werepanthers who'd infiltrated the wizard's camp. At the moment he was supposed to be meeting with the other members of his Force to plan their next move, but no matter how hard he tried Lance was unable to stop the images of dark, curly hair and passion-filled, deep brown eyes long enough to focus.

Earlier, he'd made up some lame excuse, cut the mental connection between him and his brethren, and ridden his Harley as fast as he could just to be near her. It seemed like the harder he pushed for the time he needed to eliminate their enemies, the more difficult it became to resist what had been set into motion almost twenty-nine years ago when the Universe created this amazing woman destined to be his mate.

He needed to burn off some of the excess energy pumping through his veins. His dragon and the mating call were relentless. Eighty years ago he would've called forth his dragon and flown for hundreds of miles, but in this day and age that was something used only when absolutely necessary. Running through the woods, Lance used his enhanced speed to mimic flight. The longer he ran, the stronger the need for air became, until he could no longer deny his dragon or himself what they so desperately required.

Deep in the woods, several miles from Sam and civilization, he called forth his dragon. Magic infused his body and filled the air around his beast. He felt a freedom and strength he missed in human form. The golden beast's scales glimmered in the limited moonlight as his wings unfurled and his dragon stretched after his long hibernation. With a burst of energy and good old fashioned dragon magic, he was airborne. Thankfully, the night was foggy with low visibility, providing the cover he needed to enjoy his much needed flight.

Heading out over the ocean, Lance was able to cover many, many miles quicker than even the fastest jet. The deep, dark water provided a mirror of sorts. Once again, he was in awe of the beast the Universe had paired him with those many years ago. Covered with brilliant golden scales from stem to stern and all around, his dragon was fierce in battle, massive in his own right. The huge horns protruding above his eyes curled back over his head and straightened with points that were able to tear the toughest flesh. A line of smaller, but still incredibly imposing, spikes ran all the way down his spine ending just before the featherful, a formation of deadly spikes tipping his tail.

What Lance liked most were the thorn-like talons protruding from the thumbs and tips of his wings and the razor sharp claws extending from every toe. They were smaller than his beast's other weapons and appeared unassuming, but were deadly in their own right. Everything about this incredible creature made him proud to share his being with such a mighty warrior. He looked at the marking, a miniature representation of the beast within that ran across his chest and torso, daily, but nothing compared to witnessing the dragon firsthand.

Time ceased to exist while he was flying, and not until the feel of the air changed against his hide did he realize he had to have been flying for hours. Turning with the expertise of almost a hundred years of flight, he headed back to the woods where he'd flown from. Several times he felt the air thicken, indicating a magic practitioner; not one that practiced the dark arts, but one whose roots were more elemental. He took note of the location and the fact that the magic felt feminine in its origin for later inspection, while hurrying to his destination.

Unable to stop himself, he let the beast fly past Sam's window in the hopes his dragon would catch a glimpse of their magnificent mate. The Heavens smiled upon them. There she lay, her face lax in sleep, more gorgeous than he'd remembered.

Whoa! Who am I kidding?

All the lovesick, sappy shit he'd watched happen to Rayne and Aidan was happening to him even though he'd sworn it wouldn't. What the hell was he going to do?

I'm gonna lose my mind like all the others who've found their mates. Oh, and get my ass busy and catch that stupid son of a bitch traitor.

The dragon landed in the woods with a stealth and grace unexpected from a being so large. Within seconds, the beast was replaced by the man, dressed in the clothes he was wearing before the transformation. Just one of the many wonders of dragon magic he'd learned to accept without question from the moment the heart of his beast settled into his soul.

Making his way to his Harley, Lance heard the sound of large paws hitting the fallen leaves on the forest floor. Using his enhanced sense of smell, he located the two werepanthers quickly approaching from the rear.

Continuing his trek, he was joined by Max in human form, wearing only a pair of jeans, and a huge golden brown cat with deep hazel eyes aiming a throaty "tsk tsk tsk" in his direction.

Lance looked to Max and pointed at the cat on his other side. "I'm not sure, but I believe I'm being scolded by the fur ball."

The cat in question hissed as Max answered while laughing. "Yes, it appears Juan Carlos does not agree with your evening flight."

"Well, not all of us can change into something small enough to slink around in the dark and drink milk from a saucer." He laughed at his own joke and was rewarded with a growl emanating from deep in the werepanther's throat.

Max, still chuckling at his side, spoke up. "All right children, let us play nice."

"Yeah, I'll play nice. You gotta rubber mouse I can throw for Sylvester over there?"

Juan Carlos's growl grew until Lance could see his body vibrating. "Chill out JC. I'm just messing with ya."

"Juan Carlos does not 'chill out' very well," Max answered for the still growling and hissing cat. "Finish patrolling this area and I'll be right with you," the king instructed his lieutenant.

Lance figured he was about to get a lecture he really wasn't in the mood for, so he decided to head it off at the pass. "Anything out of the ordinary?"

"Nothing since we found those latent traces of black magic. After thinking about it, I believe they were from the first time she was kidnapped. I'm sure they had originally planned to take her from here but were unable to find the chance and opted for the hospital parking lot."

"You're probably right," Lance answered. Still considering what the Leo had said, he almost missed the next revelation.

"I believe your mate may have seen me earlier this evening when—"

"Samantha…. Her name is Samantha, and how the hell did she see you?" Lance rounded on him, unable to control his emotions when it came to his mate.

The amusement in Max's eyes was evident.

He knows…busted!

Standing still, Lance waited for the Leo to answer. "Had you not been so quick to correct my use of the word 'mate,' you would've known I'm sure she only saw my eyes shining in the darkness as she retrieved her pizza from the delivery man." Max shook his head and chuckled at Lance's expense. "She only looked for a split second. I'm positive she explained it away as her imagination. I simply wanted you to be aware in case the subject presented itself."

Instead of apologizing, Lance opted to ignore the whole damn mess and moved on. "I'm sure you're right. Thanks for keeping watch while I try to track down Andrew and his merry band of losers."

Lance knew Max wanted to say more, but in true regal fashion took the high road. "You are most welcome. It'll benefit all of us when this mess is brought to an end."

"Damn straight. Well, I'm sure I'm due for an ass chewing from Rayne. I'll be back in the morning. Thanks again."

"No need for thanks. Just make sure I'm invited to the mating party." Max laughed and winked, making Lance's hand itch with the need to punch the king in the jaw.

Before the Guardsman could draw a breath to correct his friend and major pain in the ass, Max changed back into a large black panther and sauntered off through the woods.

"Damn cats just can't mind their own business," he mumbled to himself as he walked towards his bike.

Lance knew damn good and well Max had been talking to Rayne, who was getting all his information from Royce and Devon. They were the elite Dragon Guard and the powerful Werepanther Pride, but at this moment, they were acting like a bunch of gossipy girls. Usually Lance enjoyed talking shit and causing trouble, but this was the first time he'd been on the receiving end, and that sucked.

CHAPTER NINE

The sound of her alarm blaring across the room roused Sam from the hottest dream she'd ever had. It started so innocently, all smiles and crystal blue eyes, but quickly evolved into hot, sweaty passion that left her with the urge to run naked through the woods. Well…maybe walking quickly, because running was so *not* happening. God knew Sam only ran when there was an emergency at the hospital, and before that, when Miss Sizemore, her high school PE teacher, had demanded it. Tired of listening to the alarm, she decided it was time to get the day started. Charlie would be picking her up in a little over an hour, and Sam definitely needed a shower followed by a very strong cup of coffee to clear the erotic cobwebs.

Walking past the windows covering almost one entire wall of her bedroom, she stopped to admire the sun as it started its ascent. The oranges, reds, and yellows against the deep blue of the early morning sky reminded her of all the beauty in the world she was often too busy to appreciate. As the golden glow grew, Sam had a flash of déjà vu. She felt herself looking through the windows, in the not so distant past, watching a huge glistening figure fly through the sky.

The creature's impressive wings exuded power as they propelled him gracefully across the skyline. She was captivated by the picture unfurling in her mind. The beast performed an intricate ballet with tricky body rolls and fanciful dips just for her. She caught sight of a large crystal blue orb gazing directly at her as what she now knew to be a dragon came within a breath of her window. The emotions reflected within seemed to settle within her very soul, filling the little dark places previously forged by loss and loneliness. There was a familiarity, a sense of like recognizing like on a core level begging to be explored.

Her phone vibrated against the wood of her bedside table, shaking her from her daydream. As she made her way across the room, the reflection in the mirror over her dresser caught her attention, forcing her to take a closer look. Looking back was the same face she remembered from every day for almost twenty-nine years, but with a major difference…Sam looked happy.

The corners of her mouth were upturned, her eyes sparkled, and the warmth she felt inside emanated in a beautiful glow haloing her head. Sam chuckled, thinking she may have actually gotten *too* much sleep. Her phone sounded again and she resumed her trek across the room. A quick look at the clock told her she'd spent may too much time inside her own head, something that was happening more and more since meeting Lance. If she didn't hurry, Charlie was going to be in her driveway honking the horn before Sam even had her scrubs on.

Flipping open the phone as she headed to the bathroom, she almost tripped over her own feet when the nine little words displayed on the screen made her pulse jump.

Have a great day, Doc. See you soon.

She smiled and continued to the shower. While drying off, she couldn't shake the feeling of strong, muscular arms wrapped around her body while soft, full lips kissed and tasted her neck and shoulders. Laughing at her own silliness, she finished getting ready and headed down the stairs, following the mouth-watering aroma of fresh brewed coffee. Thank God for coffee makers with timers.

Supersize travel mug in hand and messenger bag over her shoulder, she was stepping out the door when she heard the telltale sounds of gravel crunching in her driveway, signaling Charlie's arrival. Locking the door with the key she'd found on the floor inside her door, Sam hurried to the car, getting ready for what she hoped was an uneventful day.

Almost ten hours later, the true meaning of "dumb luck" was alive and well in Sam's world. To say her day had been a disaster was an understatement. Patients who should've been easy required extra meds or procedures. Two surgeries were cancelled because patients' vitals were unstable. Even technology was against them…the computers crashed not once but twice. And to top it off, the cafeteria was out of Diet Coke.

She'd just been paged for what seemed like the hundredth time when her phone vibrated in her pocket. Running for the elevator, she heard "Dr. Malone to Orthopedics" over the PA and wondered how she was going to be on two different floors at the same time.

"Rough day, Dr. Malone?" asked a tall, scruffy looking man with sunglasses covering not only his eyes but most of his face.

She hadn't realized he was there until he'd spoken. He was perched against the railing at the very back of the elevator, hidden in the shadows. Her phone shook the coins in her pockets just as she was about to answer the stranger's question. The message that appeared relieved some of the pressure tightening the muscles in her neck.

Hey, Doc. Bonnie Blue is good as new. Where can I bring the keys?

She didn't stop the smile that crossed her lips and chuckled as she returned the message. *Come to the fourth floor nurses' station. See you there.*

The elevator doors opened and a cold chill swept down her spine. She shivered as the jacket of the man who'd spoken to her brushed her elbow as he made his way into the hall. Something about him was off. The air around him seemed heavier than anywhere else. The words "dark and creepy" floated through her mind.

Shaking off the negative feelings the stranger had stirred, Sam made her way towards the patient they continued to page her about. It dawned on her the strange man had called her by name, but her badge was well hidden under her lab coat.

Once again chills skated down her back. Before Sam could dwell on her encounter, Charlie yelled from down the hall and the young doctor was on her way to the next emergency. All thoughts of weird men in elevators and sexy blue-eyed rescuers were forgotten for the moment.

Almost an hour later, Mrs. Robinson's stitches were replaced and her arm immobilized to avoid a repeat performance. Sam was throwing away her gloves when a low rumbling voice drifted from the hallway. Her skin tingled and her nipples hardened. She'd never been so glad to have a lab coat on in her life.

A jolt of pure adrenaline shot through her at the sight of the man. With his back to her, leaning against the wall with a cell phone to his ear and his right ankle thrown haphazardly over the left, he was lethal. Her eyes hungrily traced the line his faded jeans made from his cocked hip to his incredibly well-proportioned behind, and ate up the powerful muscles that simply refused to be contained by the well-worn denim. Working her way back up the other leg, helpless to doing anything but admire his incredible ass once again, her mouth went dry.

Lance moved his shoulder and his faded baby blue T-shirt pulled even tighter across the impressive expanse of his back, begging to be explored. Hundreds of hours spent studying musculature didn't come close to the education her eyes received looking at this one man. He was a study in dichotomy, all hard muscles and lines of a well-honed body against the tenderness and willingness to help others she'd already witnessed.

A throat clearing behind her caused her to stumble as she spun around, only to be confronted by a man who looked like he'd walked right off the pages of GQ. He was incredibly attractive, nothing like the man behind her but a damn fine specimen of manliness in his own right. Where Lance was rough and raw, this man was suave and refined. He was at least six foot two, with striking green eyes set in light olive skin surrounded by thick, dark lashes. His super dark, wavy hair parted on the side in a devil may care way of the male stars in old movies, and Sam knew it was done by a "stylist," not a barber. His thick full lips, presently curled into a one-sided grin, had without a doubt made more than one woman swoon.

The suit he wore was obviously tailored for him because nothing off the rack fit that well. Her years surrounded by male doctors had taught her a thing or two about the designer things in life, and this man definitely wore it well. She knew if she looked down at his feet there would be a pair of designer loafers. Unlike others she associated with who wore this type of attire, this man seemed friendly, almost approachable.

Almost?

Yes, she would definitely say almost. There was a contained aggression just under the surface she hoped to never witness.

His grin morphed into a full blown smile when he spoke. She wasn't surprised to hear a slight South American accent. "Dr. Malone, I presume?" he asked with an outstretched hand.

"I am; and you would be?" she countered while shaking his hand, surprised to feel calluses across his palm and the tips of each finger.

"Max Prentice, a friend of Lance's." He motioned behind her as he spoke.

"Oh, I see." Not sure what to say next, Sam was thankfully saved when a very large warm hand engulfed her shoulder. Electric shocks flooded her system, making rational thought damn near impossible. Immediate recognition allowed her to relax into his touch while trying to hide her reaction from the man facing her.

"Are you bothering the good doctor, Max, my man?" Lance's voice was even deeper and more powerful when spoken so close to her ear.

Max's smile became mischievous. "Not at all. I was merely keeping her company while you were otherwise engaged."

She worked hard not to sigh as Lance massaged her shoulder while he spoke to Max around her. "I'll take it from here. Why don't you grab a cup of coffee? I'll meet ya in the cafeteria in a few. Cool?"

With a wink she figured was for Lance's benefit, Max turned on his heels and headed towards the bank of elevators at the end of the hall. The heat at her back increased as she felt Lance so close their bodies should've been touching. "So Doc, how's your day been so far?"

It was barely a whisper right against her ear. The low rumble of every syllable stirred her need and want. She felt the slightest touch of his lips on the curve of her ear as he inhaled deeply. The next thing she knew she was spun around, and what she saw was a look the exact opposite of what she'd expected from his actions mere seconds before.

Lance's brows were furrowed, his lips in a firm thin line, and his eyes darkened to a stormy gray. The grip he had on her upper arms tightened. He looked side-to-side and began moving them just a few doors down the hall towards a room she knew was empty. He kicked the door shut and sat them both on the edge of the bed housekeeping had yet to make.

"What the hell are you doing, Lance?" Sam jumped up and faced him, hands on hips, eyes narrowed, waiting for his answer.

The staring contest lasted all of ten seconds before he exhaled and his head slumped forward. Sam waited while he composed himself, not moving a muscle…just watching. Slowly, his head came up and she was speared with a stern, dark look, rimmed with worry and a touch of fear.

Fear? What does this big hulk have to be afraid of?

Still waiting for him to answer her question, Sam began to let out the breath she'd just realized she was holding. Just as she was about to give up and break the silence, Lance spoke.

"Dammit, Doc, I'm sorry. I shouldn't have done that. And my explanation is probably going to make you think I need a one way ticket to the psych ward, but here goes. I have to ask…have you seen or talked to anyone other than a patient or colleague today?"

She could tell he thought what he was asking her was important, so instead of fighting, Sam decided to go with it and see where they ended up. "Yeah, I did. But how did you know?"

"I promise I'll answer. But first, what did he look like?"

"I don't really know. He was in the back of the elevator I ran into after being paged. I remember thinking it was weird he had sunglasses on indoors, but then I got distracted by your text, and then the elevator doors were opening. He rushed past and was gone before I got out."

Lance leaned forward from his perch on the bed, absorbing all she'd said. His hands were gripping the sheets so tightly his knuckles were white and the muscles in his forearms bulged. Sam replayed the incident in the elevator in her mind. Lance stared at her with such intensity she had to concentrate not to fidget.

"I didn't know he was there until he spoke. Then I realized after he was already gone that he knew my name, but my badge was under my lab coat so there was no way he could've seen it. For a second I thought maybe he was a former patient, but I would've remembered someone so creepy." Sam shuddered, remembering how eerie he'd made her feel.

If possible, Lance's look became more intense. His grip on the mattress increased until she waited to hear the tearing of fabric. Backing down was not an option. Sam had to know how he knew what happened earlier and what the hell it had to do with him literally dragging her into an empty room. Rushing on before he could distract her, she demanded, "Now it's your turn. What the hell happened back there?"

"When we were standing together in the hall—and here's where you're gonna think I've lost my mind—I smelled him on you."

"You mean you smelled his cologne on me, or something like that? And wait…you know him? Well enough to know what cologne he wears?" She narrowed her gaze. "Who is this guy, Lance?"

"He used to be one of my bre…brothers, and he's very dangerous."

Lance stood up and closed the distance between them. She could now see that damn dimple in his cheek, winking at her up close and personally. As her eyes took in every detail of his almost perfectly chiseled face, he spoke more softly, making his low, gravelly voice roll through her, raising goosebumps on her arms. "So I guess that means I'm gonna have to stay real close, Doc, and make sure nothing bad happens."

He wound his arm around her waist, bringing her tight against his warm, hard body, and her immediately hard nipples rubbed against the lace of her bra. Unconsciously, she arched into his touch. The look in his eyes stole her breath and made her body weep. Thoughts of what his naked body would feel like against hers were all she could see in her lust-soaked mind.

Lance wiggled his eyebrows and just that quick, he'd gone from the big, bad protector to the grinning jokester. Lost to the powerful man who held her close, her eyes closed, effectively cutting off his hypnotic gaze while she tried to regain at least some of her equilibrium. When she reopened her eyes, he was studying her.

Too many emotions to identify drifted across his expressive face. There was something he wasn't telling her. She could see it…even feel it in his touch. His smile was brilliant, but the lines of tension bracketing his eyes told her the revelation that his prodigal brother was in the hospital bothered him more than he was willing to admit. None of this was what she'd expected when she'd first seen his text. More things to contemplate was not what she needed. But Sam knew with all certainty, no matter what else was happening, there was no way to deny the pull of the man who held her tight.

Just as their lips were about to touch, the PA overhead broke them apart. "Dr. Malone, Code Amber, Room 212. Dr. Malone, Code Amber, Room 212." Without another thought, she spun from Lance's arms and raced out of the room.

"What the hell's happening, Doc?" Lance called after her.

There was no way she could answer past the fear like a weight on her chest. The loud speaker had just announced that Sydney was missing!

CHAPTER TEN

Lance caught up with Sam as she entered the stairwell. The waves of fear radiating from his mate would've crippled a lesser woman, but not his Sam. He wanted to make her stop and tell him what was happening, but from the look on her face and the way her muscles were drawn tight, he knew he'd end up with her knee in a very personal part of his body. Instead of speaking, he kept pace and pushed as much of his strength as he thought she could handle through their very new, very weak mating bond.

As Sam threw open the door marked with a large number two, she worked hard to school her expression and put on an air of professionalism. The woman he recognized as Charlie came rushing towards them, talking in hushed tones, stopping Sam in the middle of the hall.

"The nurse had checked on her not more than ten minutes before. Sydney asked for more red Jell-O. When the nurse returned, the child was gone. No one saw her and nothing in the room has been disturbed. It looks like she simply got up and walked away."

"She *has* to be somewhere. Sydney couldn't have gotten out of here without someone seeing her. She told me she was going to the children's room after lunch. Did someone check there?" Sam inquired. Lance could tell she was holding on by the skin of her teeth. The need to touch her was alive within him, but he also recognized *her* need to remain independent and professional.

"They've looked everywhere. You were paged when it was determined she was not in the hospital," Charlie answered, taking on a completely professional tone he was sure she used in an attempt to keep Sam calm.

"We have to look again. There's no way she would've gone anywhere on her own. She knew I was coming back before heading home. There was something she needed to show me."

Sam walked around her friend and headed towards what he now knew was the child's room. Lance followed closely behind, sending a mental message to Royce and Devon, who were presently camped out at Kyndel's old apartment. He explained the situation and asked them to meet him at the hospital ASAP. Grabbing the cell phone from his back pocket, Lance sent a text to Max to meet him where he stood.

The hair on the back of his neck stood on end as they entered Sydney's room. Rage caused his vision to blur. Andrew, that traitorous little fucker, had been in the room. From the power of his scent, the traitor had been there within the last fifteen or twenty minutes. In an effort to hide his anger, he called out to his brethren again.

"Royce, Dev, you close?"

"Less than five minutes out. What's up?" Royce answered immediately.

"Andrew's involved in this somehow. I'm in the child's room and his stench is everywhere."

"What the fuck?" Devon's anger flared through their link.

"How long ago did this happen?" Royce was just as angry but much better at keeping his composure, always looking for a solution to the problem.

"Less than thirty minutes from the scent." Lance scanned the room and listened to the conversations all around, looking for any clue to help locate the missing girl. Glancing at her chart, he sent the image of her angelic face to both men.

"We'll start with the emergency entrance and work our way around. Devon's calling Aaron. He was already on his way to the apartment. We'll find her, bro."

"Yeah, I know but it needs to be sooner rather than later. Doc is about to lose it and then what the hell am I gonna do?"

"You're gonna man up and take care of your mate, you giant pain in the ass."

Lance was grateful to his elder brethren for trying to ease his tension, even if it did mean he got his own shit thrown back at him.

Fucking paybacks!

Not to be outdone, he answered as only he could. *"Yeah, Old Man, I'll man up. You just try to keep up."*

"Keep up hell! I'm always at least three steps ahead of your pansy ass."

"Okay, ladies, you're both pretty. Now, let's find this little girl," Aaron chimed in, apparently getting close the hospital, *"and kick my little brother's ass while we're at it."*

"Hell yeah," they all answered in unison.

"Everybody keep in touch. We're outside the hospital now." Royce stated.

"Be there in a minute." Aaron responded.

"Thanks," was all Lance could say as Sam turned. For the first time, he saw true fear in the eyes of the woman claiming his heart faster than he could've ever imagined.

Putting the conversation his brethren were having at the back of his mind, Lance opened his arms. Without hesitation, Sam walked into them. He held her close, realizing he'd been a fool to ever think he could stay away from his amazing mate. Even facing the horrible situation unfolding around them, it just felt right to have her in his arms.

Inhaling, he took her scent deep into his lungs, calming not only himself but the dragon within, who was threatening to burst forth from the pain, fear, and torment radiating from their Sam. Max appeared in the doorway just as Lance was about to tell Sam his brethren were outside looking for Sydney.

Lance watched as the incredibly observant King of the Cats scanned the room and took a single, deliberate breath. Max's green eyes glowed and met Lance's with instant recognition. One nod of his head and Max disappeared. It was one of a handful of times Lance wished he could communicate mind to mind with the werepanther as he did his own kin.

Sending a quick mental message to his brethren that Max was on the way, Lance began quietly questioning Sam, deciding now was not the time to disclose he knew who was responsible for the child's disappearance. "What was security able to tell you?"

"Only that they've checked everywhere and she's not in the hospital. They've even looked in the basement and all the 'employee only' areas. The police have been called and should be here any second. Hospital Security waited to call them because they were sure she'd just wandered down the hall."

Lance could hear the anger and frustration in her voice as she spoke into his chest. He wanted nothing more than to rush out and help with the search for the child, but could feel deep in his soul how much Sam needed him. Instead of rushing into battle as was his way, he told her what he hoped would ease some of her pain. "I called my brothers while you were talking to Security. They're out scouring the grounds and surrounding area for Sydney right now."

She slowly lifted her head, raising her hands at the same time and pushing against his chest, trying to look anywhere but at him. He'd wondered how long it would take until she realized she was depending on him and tried to get away. Refusing to be shut out, he tightened his grip on her waist with one arm, while using the thumb and forefinger of his opposite hand on her chin to bring them eye to eye. He saw himself reflected in her deep, dark eyes, along with all the fire he expected from his strong, determined mate. Before he could say what he intended, Sam was already off and running.

"Dammit, Lance, let me go! I'm going out there to find her myself. There's no way that little girl left this hospital by herself, and there is absolutely no way you're stopping me from looking for her." She ended her declaration on a low, ominous tone, with her teeth gritted and her fists drawn tight against his chest.

Waiting for her to take a few breaths, Lance tried to decide how to keep his mate from running straight into danger. Sam was smart…way too smart for *his* own good. There were things he wasn't ready to reveal, but decided the only way she was going to listen was for him to be logical.

"I understand you're scared, Doc. I know Sydney means a lot to you, but you can't go running off half-cocked. We have to have a plan. My brothers are searching and they're *very* good at what they do." He watched as she considered his words, but didn't give her time to raise the objection he saw brewing. "Let me call them and see if they have any leads. Then you and I can decide what our best move is…okay?"

She worried her bottom lip with her teeth until it was red and swollen. Under different circumstances, he would've loved to kiss all her worries away, but now was not the time, no matter what his mind and other much more persistent parts of his body were telling him. He'd heard stories of the potency of the mating call, but had never imagined what it would be like. He was having a hard time thinking of anything but Sam's lush body spread naked before him. With a hard-fought restraint he didn't know he possessed, he pulled his errant thoughts back to the problem of finding the missing child, and more importantly, keeping his mate safe.

Releasing his hold on her and moving towards the window, he took his cell phone from his back pocket. He hated deceiving Sam in any way, but how could he explain he spoke directly into the minds of his brethren and they into his? Pretending to dial, Lance lifted the cell phone to his ear and called out to the other members of his Force, all the while speaking into the phone. "Any news? I have one very antsy doctor up here who's ready to run out and start looking on her own."

"We're getting close. Andrew's gotten refueled with black magic since the shit storm in the woods. There were a few false trails, but they were weak and evaporated quickly. Luckily, he wasn't able to hide the little one's fresh clean scent. We finally located his path and are closing in," Royce growled, more than a little pissed off.

"I swear to the Heavens when we catch this son of a bitch I'm taking him down where he stands. Fuck the Elders and fuck the Tribunal. This bastard needs to die!" Usually the most quiet and serene of all his brethren, Devon was practically screaming through their mind speak…proof that this shit with Andrew was wearing on all of them. The stupid douche bag had just gone farther than any of them would've thought possible by taking a child.

"No can do, Dev. The little fucker is mine," Aidan countered. Lance hadn't even known he was there.

"Not if I find the piece of shit first," Aaron seethed. Well damn, almost the whole crew was there.

"How the hell did you two get here so quickly?" Lance asked the twins. All the shit they'd all endured for almost a year hit them the hardest of all. Andrew was their younger brother, blood of their blood. How the hell they'd kept their sanity was beyond Lance's understanding.

"Aar was at the house looking over some of the information Grace dug up on 'The Auctioneer' when we heard you call Royce. We headed over to see if we could help find the little girl and kick our brother's ass," Aidan answered. Having a brother he'd devoted so much of his life to, caring for and training, only to have Andrew betray all of them and their way of life, had to feel like a dagger to Aidan's heart.

"The son of a bitch has gone too far this time. Whoever finds him needs to kill him. END OF STORY! No one hurts a child. NO ONE!" Devon was literally screaming fury.

"Okay Dev, you're right, but don't pop a vessel before we find him. Woosah, bro, woosah." Lance chuckled even though he didn't feel it, in an effort to calm his brethren. The Guardsmen going off half-cocked was what Andrew was hoping for. The dirty little traitor wanted them to make mistakes so he could keep spreading his special brand of crazy.

"I know, dude, but a child? Really? What the fuck? This shit is making me crazy!" Devon answered. Lance could hear him trying to calm down and regain his focus.

"I know, man, I know. Now we have to find her before his crazy ass loses it all together. Let me see if I can get Doc to chill, and then I'll come help you search." Lance wondered how in the hell he was going to keep Sam from going with him.

"Do what you can, but from experience, I can tell you that you might as well just give in. Your girl's gonna win the argument every time." Aidan chuckled and all the others followed suit.

Before Lance could think of a witty comeback, Royce chimed in. *"Ya know, Pain in the Ass, I can't wait to watch your mate kick your ass. She doesn't seem like someone who's gonna take your shit lying down."*

The roar of the laughter was almost more than Lance could stand. He knew he deserved everything they were throwing at him, but *damn*, it stung!

"Yeah, yeah, yeah, Old Man, yuck it up. Your time's coming."

"I'm sure it is, but I'm not the one going through it now, and I'm not the one who said he'd never have a mate. Sucks to be you, Pain in the Ass, sucks to be you." If possible, the laughter from his brethren grew.

"All right, you assholes, let me see what I can do up here. I'll be down when I can. Find. Sydney." He shook his head as their laughter died down. *"And thanks."*

He kept the conversation between his brethren in the back of his mind as he closed his cell phone and turned to locate Sam, not looking forward to the discussion he knew was to come. The room had cleared some while he'd been talking to his Force. The atmosphere was sad and desolate. Looking from person to person, he tried to locate the only face that mattered to him. Not seeing Sam, he approached her friend, Charlie. "Hey, where's Sam?"

"Oh hey, Lance. She went to the ladies' room. She's really worried about Sydney." Her brows furrowed and she tilted her head to the side like she was thinking. Then she looked at her watch. "You know, she's been gone longer than I'd realized."

Charlie turned towards the door, still wearing a befuddled expression. Deciding he needed to check on his absent mate, Lance reached out and stopped the young doctor's progress to the door. She glared over her shoulder and he could see why she and Sam were such good friends. They definitely shared strength of will.

"Let me go check on her and see if there's anything I can do to help. Why don't you check with the police to see if they have any new information?" he suggested.

Watching her inner debate, Lance saw when she resigned to letting him handle the situation. "Okay." She hesitantly relented before reaching out and grabbing his arm. "But you better take care of her or you'll have to deal with me." She looked directly into his eyes and he saw with all certainty that she meant every word she said.

"Yes, ma'am, you have my word." Before he could say anymore, Charlie released his arm and spun on her heels, obviously satisfied with his response.

Without another thought, Lance headed into the hall following the scent of his wayward mate. As he passed the nurse's station, he asked if there was a doctor's lounge nearby, and was directed to the restrooms next to the elevators. Looking towards the end of the hall, Lance realized Sam's scent was heading in the exact opposite direction…towards the stairs. Dread slithered down his spine as he headed towards the door, Sam's scent increasing in intensity with every step. He was immediately pissed with himself.

I never should've taken my eyes off her.

Racing down the two flights of stairs using some of his enhanced speed, but not wanting to draw any attention from the people searching for Sydney, he called to the men of his Force. *"Doc snuck out while we were talking. I'm following her scent but keep an eye out."*

"Told you she would get what she wanted one way or another," Aidan chuckled. *"Which exit did she take?"*

"Side exit next to Emergency. I just came through the door," Lance growled, ignoring the dig from Aidan.

"I'm closest. I'll circle around the backside. She already knows me, so if I see her, she won't freak out," Royce responded.

Lance could hear the smile in his oldest friend's voice and thanked the Heavens Royce didn't comment any farther on the whole "mate" thing. True to form, Lance couldn't resist messing with the elder Guardsman, even though getting Sam back was his priority. *"And the Heavens know she'll be able to see your pretty hair from a mile away."*

"Afraid she'll like my pretty hair more than yours, smartass?" Royce laughed.

Lance felt instant jealousy coming from the mating bond once again. He knew he had nothing to fear from his long-time friend, but the need to have Sam in his arms and mark her as his own damn near brought him to his knees. As soon he found her, he was going to kiss her silly, then swat her ass until she couldn't sit for a week. Just the thought of her luscious rear end caused his cock to jump in his jeans.

Damn! This mating shit just doesn't let up!

To make matters worse, his dragon was right on board, feeding the erotic images racing through his mind and riding him hard to take action.

Finally answering Royce to take his mind off his issues, Lance teased, *"Whatever, Grandpa. I doubt she's into carrot tops."*

Lance missed everything Royce said as he rounded the corner of the hospital and looked across the parking lot. Standing across the street, holding the little blonde-haired beauty while she licked an ice cream cone, was Andrew.

With no other thought but to rescue the little girl and kill the bastard holding her, he tore across the lot, yelling through mind speak to all that could hear. *"Andrew's across the street holding Sydney! Get your asses around here!"*

Reaching the last grassy area before the street, a city bus passed in front of Lance, momentarily blocking his view. His next look showed Sydney standing alone on the sidewalk still eating her ice cream cone. Racing across the street, he stopped as soon as he stepped onto the curb, not wanting to scare the child.

His brethren were shouting directions to one another through their link as they searched for the traitor. Aaron and Aidan took off to the right, Royce and Devon to the left, working like the well-oiled machine they had always been.

Lance walked slowly towards the little girl, who seemed to not have a care in the world except for enjoying her ice cream. Sydney stopped and smiled. "Are you Lance?"

Shocked that she was so calm, and even more so that she knew his name, Lance stopped a few feet from her and squatted so they were closer to the same height. He'd been around enough of the young *vibrias* at the lair to know his size could be intimidating, not that Sydney seemed scared in the slightest.

Examining her with all of his enhanced senses, he was relieved to see no harm had come to her. It was small consolation, but at least Andrew hadn't slipped so far into insanity that he would harm a child. The traitor had obviously used the child to send some kind of twisted message. Lance would figure it out later. Right now, he needed to make sure he wasn't missing anything and that Sydney was really all right before deciphering the actions of a mad man.

Continuing to check the child for injuries both physically and emotionally, he could see why Sam was so fond of the child. Sydney was a mini version of the vibrant woman herself. The intelligence in her eyes shone bright, and she had a strength not often associated with someone so young. He found no fear at all after having been kidnapped and then left on the side of the road. "Yes, I am. Are you Sydney?"

Blonde curls bounced in every direction as she nodded. "Yes, sir." She took another lick of her ice cream just before it dripped on her hand. "Do you know Dr. Sam?"

"Yes, I do."

"Do you know Andrew?"

Her question concerning the traitor caused his muscles to tense. Lance worked hard to keep the tension from his face and voice. Sydney was definitely perceptive enough to pick up any change in his demeanor, and he needed her to tell him everything she knew. "Yes, I do. Do you?"

She thought for a second while she took another lick of her cone. When she answered, he could feel her confusion, but still no fear. "Well, not really. He said he was a friend of Dr. Sam and that she said it was okay for me to go with him to get a treat. Then he brought me out here and we walked around for a few minutes." She looked around and then frowned. "He's kind of weird." No sooner had the words left her mouth than her eyes grew big and round, she gasped, and smacked her hand over her mouth. The child let her head fall forward and then looked up at him through her thick dark lashes. "Sorry. It's not nice to say bad things about people. Please don't tell Miss Crutchfield."

He bit the insides of his cheeks to keep from smiling. "Your secret's safe with me." He winked to secure their pact. She once again held her head high and smiled a sweet smile that only came from one so young.

"Thanks! You're pretty cool."

"Thank you, Miss Sydney. You're pretty cool yourself."

The child blushed and for the first time in his very long life, Lance wondered what it would feel like to have a child of his own. Shaking his head in the hopes of restoring his sanity, he decided it was time to get the child back into the hospital and see what she could tell him about her abductor.

"It's a little chilly to be standing out here in just a robe and slippers, Miss Sydney. Whatcha say I pick you up and we head back over to the hospital and see if we can find Dr. Sam?"

"Okay, Lance." She took the few steps that separated them, and without any hesitation wrapped her one free hand around his neck as he lifted her. Once again, he pictured himself with children of his own, little girls with big blue eyes and long, dark, curly hair, creating as much trouble as possible.

He carried Sydney across the street as she slurped the last of the ice cream from her cone and frowned. "What's the matter? Don't like the cone?"

She scrunched up her button nose and shook her head. "Nope. I only like the ice cream."

He chuckled and headed to the large trash can sitting next to a bench on one of the grassy sections in the parking lot. As he leaned over to let Sydney drop her empty squishy cone into the receptacle, the unmistakable scent of jasmine and honeysuckle wafted under his nose. He turned just in time to see Sam barreling towards them. Stray strands of her unruly mane had escaped from her braid and were blowing in every direction. Her dark brown eyes were wide and cheeks bright red with exertion. She jumped the few inches onto the grass and launched in their direction, grabbing both of them in a huge bear hug.

He put his arm around Sam in an attempt to keep her from hitting the ground, then stepped backward until he felt the bench against his calves before collapsing with both ladies in his lap. Sam held onto both of them for all she was worth. Lance rubbed long, smooth strokes up and down her back, hoping to help calm her frazzled nerves.

As her breathing returned to normal, he felt the fear, frustration, and tension bleed from her body. With her body leaning heavily against his chest, he could feel her trying to get control of her emotions. His heart swelled as Sydney's little hand landed on Sam's shoulder and the little girl began to rub little circles of comfort. The child looked up at him, shrugged, and whispered, "Is Dr. Sam okay, Lance?"

Before he could answer, Sam lifted her head and looked first at him and then at the little one still rubbing her shoulder. "Yes, Sydney, I'm okay. I was just very worried about you." She reached up, gently taking the child's hand from her shoulder, and simply held it between hers. "Are you all right? Did he hurt you or scare you at all?"

Sydney smiled and shook her head. "Nope, not at all. He bought me an ice cream cone from the cafeteria, and then we walked around over there where the flowers are." She pointed her little chubby fingers to the left of the hospital. "Then we went over there." She pointed behind where they were seated. "Andrew said there were real pretty flowers there, but we didn't get to see them because he said Lance was coming to take me back to the hospital. He promised to show them to me another time."

Sam looked up into his eyes. He could see she was looking to him to validate the child's story and to somehow make her feel better about all that had happened. He only wished he could. She looked back to Sydney, and asked, "Why did you leave the hospital with a stranger?"

For the first time since meeting the little beauty, Lance felt her tense and saw confusion cross her face. "He wasn't a stranger." She paused and looked from Sam to him and back to his mate again, fear just beginning to leak into her gaze. "Andrew said he was your friend, Dr. Sam."

Sam's back went stiff, and she immediately took a deep breath. He watched as she fought to control her emotions. She relaxed a little bit as she began to speak. "Andrew is not a friend of mine, sweetheart. I don't even know him."

Tears filled the little ones eyes. Never one to deal well with tears, Lance hurriedly tried to diffuse the situation. "Andrew's actually a friend of mine, Sydney. He probably just misspoke when he said he knew Dr. Sam." Both women exhaled. "Did Andrew tell you anything else?" he asked.

Sydney smiled a watery grin in his direction and giggled. "He said to tell you…." She paused, and he held his breath as she thought hard about the information the traitor had shared with her. Lance felt his anger rising. What the hell was wrong with that fucking loser that he would use a child to relay a message?

Her eyes brightened, but what she said sent chills down his spine and made Sam sit up straight. "Now that he had your attention, he'd be seeing you soon. He's a silly man, Lance, isn't he?" She giggled again, completely unaware that she'd landed smack in the middle of danger.

Not wanting to scare the child, he chuckled with her. "He sure is a silly man, Sydney. Did he say anything else?"

She shook her head. "Nope, he just showed me his eyes. Did you know he had one blue eye and one brown eye? No wait…that's not right, he said the other one was amber…whatever that means." She shrugged and smiled her sweet innocent smile, letting him know she really was unharmed.

"I did know that." Not wanting to discuss the man responsible for so much pain and suffering with the little cutie or his mate any longer, Lance quickly changed the subject. "Why don't you give Dr. Sam a hug? I think she needs it. Then let's get you back into the hospital. There are lots of people that want to see you."

Sydney climbed across his lap and grabbed hold of Sam's neck with such vigor she reminded him of a little bear cub. His mate's arms immediately wrapped around the child, and both sighed as if all was right in their world once again. Sam was amazing, absolutely stunning, and incredibly intelligent. She had a capacity for compassion he'd been sure no longer existed in a world where people like 'The Auctioneer' and Andrew were allowed to exist. In a nutshell, she was perfect.

For what seemed like the millionth time, he wondered how the hell he was ever going to keep from claiming her until he and his brethren could dispose of the traitor. If Lance had it his way, he would grab her up and head to the farthest end of the earth, where he could keep her safe from everyone and everything. There he could spend endless days and nights kissing, touching, tasting, and simply adoring every inch of her luscious body. He'd spent so very many hours imagining what it would be like to sink into her incredible body, to feel her warm, wet pussy grip his incredibly hard cock, that the visions were damn near real enough to touch.

He felt his cock rise and immediately shut down his thoughts. What the hell was wrong with him? There was no time for daydreams, especially ones involving sex with the most perfect woman in the world, and definitely not when there was a child present. Lance was becoming the same pussy-whipped wimp as Rayne and Aidan.

Sam was his mate, the Universe made her especially for him. He knew beyond a shadow of a doubt they were meant to be together in this life and the next, but there was no way he was going to give up his spine to have it all. Maybe that was the way his brethren wanted to play it, but not him. He still had free will. He was a Dragon Guardsman with the most elite force in the world. He refused to walk around like a lovesick puppy, mooning over his magnificent mate, bitching like a whiney little girl because he couldn't claim her as quickly as he wanted.

Sure, he'd been watching her from the shadows for over seven months. Sure, she monopolized damn near every thought he had both waking and sleeping. But he was stronger than the rest, better at controlling his emotions than the others. All he had to do was catch Andrew, make him give up the wizards he was working with, and use that information to eliminate 'The Auctioneer'. All the while keeping his distance from Sam, but still making sure she was safe and out of the line of fire.

Piece of cake.

Lance could almost hear Royce's voice; "Yeah, right, shove that oversized head of yours just a little farther up your ass."

Fuck that! He could do it.

First order of business, get the ladies occupying his lap back into the hospital and reconnect with his brethren for an update on the search for Andrew. Then he needed to come up with a plan of action to accomplish his goals in the least possible time. Decision made, he was just about to tell Sam and Sydney it was time to go when his mate lifted her head and speared him with her gorgeous dark brown eyes. Helpless to do anything but stare back at her as a myriad of emotions crossed her beautiful face, he felt his recently fortified resolve start to crumble. Not willing to give up without a fight, he patted her on the back and put his plan into motion.

Grinning, he said, "Okay ladies, enough of this goofin' around. Let's get you two inside."

Sam smiled, pulled Sydney the rest of the way into her arms, and slid her delectable ass across his thigh. The unintentional sensual contact caused his already semi-erect cock to stand at attention further, testing his resolve to resist the lure of his mate. Only the threats against her safety and that of the child she held in her arms kept him from kissing her until neither one could draw a breath without the other.

He grabbed Sam's waist and helped her stand while holding Sydney to keep her from feeling his body's reaction to her. It also removed the greatest temptation he'd ever dealt with from touching his traitorous body. While gaining her footing on the grassy surface, Sam stumbled, Lance reached out to steady her, and his hand made contact with the silky skin just above the waistband of her scrub pants. The resulting electric shock caused them both to gasp.

In unison, their eyes met. Her pupils dilated, and her breathing sped up right along with his. She licked her lips, and the want to follow her tongue with his made him see double. Breathing deeply, he realized that staying away from Dr. Samantha Malone was going to be the single hardest thing he'd ever done.

He groaned to himself, realizing exactly how much shit he was going to have to put up with from his brethren. He really was turning into a cream puff, and he feared there wasn't shit he could do about it.

CHAPTER ELEVEN

Andrew watched as the Dragon Guard ran around like chickens with their heads cut off. They were looking for him with the hopes of taking him back to the Elders and the dreaded Tribunal. That shit was absolutely *not* happening if he had anything to say about it. Thankfully, John, a lackey of the wizard leader Andrew had been aligned with during the horrible debacle at the abandoned warehouse, had turned up at his door after going rogue.

Together Andrew, John, and the others they'd "collected" along the way performed several small rituals, partially rebuilding their store of black magic. It was nowhere near what it had been before the fight with his brother, but it was better than nothing. Had Andrew been able to find Kyra, the white witch who created the most powerful amulets he'd ever seen, he would've had no problem evading those he'd once called brethren. But as Fate would have it, the witch was hiding in the mountains surrounding Dark Lake, and with her powers she might never be found.

It was incredibly frustrating; after three months, he'd finally tracked her using his Dragon Guard training. His rusty skills and less-than-par sense of smell got him to within a mile of the little witch before she just disappeared as he was closing in. It was as if she'd just evaporated into thin air, leaving no trace at all.

His only consolation was the realization that a Guardsman's mate lived close by. He'd originally believed it was the witch herself, and still wondered if maybe she was too, but that was a problem for another day. He would know the one he sensed when he found her, and if he was lucky enough, he'd know the Guardsman she was destined to be with also. This was information he could use to his advantage.

No one could hide their fate from him. He was The Special One, and that afforded him abilities no other possessed…endowments that had been buried under black magic but now were reemerging, never to be put to sleep again. There was a time in the not-so-distant past when he'd been sure those abilities were gone forever, but dragons were resilient and so was everything that made them special. The longer he went without high levels of black magic, the more predominant his old talents became. Of course, that also meant it was easier for the Dragon Guard and those damn werepanthers to track him. He had to be extremely careful while he continued his hunt for the witch. It would really suck to be caught and not finish his plans for revenge. Kyra was the key. She had to be found. He would settle for nothing less.

Then there was 'The Auctioneer', who John assured him could get them what they needed to perform the Grand Ritual. The ancient magic would provide them with enough dark power to last for years. However, it also presented a problem he hadn't foreseen or prepared for…human sacrifice. No matter how hard he tried, Andrew couldn't justify the taking of innocent lives.

What a time to grow a conscience.

He'd done some really shitty things in his quest for vengeance, but it had always been to people who deserved it, never anyone innocent or not somehow involved in his world. He'd started with the worthless wizards who'd held him hostage and tortured him, then moved on to some useless fucking hunters. Those who'd died while he tried to ambush the Dragon Guard were simply fanatics who hated for the sake of hating and believed their lives were worth more than others. Andrew had taken pleasure in proving them wrong.

Then there were the Dragon Guardsmen, the ones he'd once called brethren, which ironically included his *real* brothers. They'd done nothing to help him in his greatest hour of need; left him for dead after his dragon had literally been forced from the sky and his human form thrust upon him. Where had they been? Lazy fucking cowards had been caring for the yellow-bellied loser with whom he shared blood. The one he'd once held in the highest regard; his brother, who'd run off into the night and left him at the hands of those magic-hungry wizards.

Andrew did feel bad that the commander's mate and his brother's mate had been injured in his bid for revenge, but if Rayne and Aidan were half the men they claimed to be, their women should've been safe. No permanent damage had been caused. He'd heard through his extensive network of spies that both women had recovered, and Rayne's mate had given birth to their first child.

Aidan and Grace had also been officially mated. Apparently, he hadn't ruined their lives at all, but added to them, and that meant they had more to lose when he sent the Guardsmen to their forever deaths. Andrew would watch as the realization came over them when they were about to lose it all…just as the light left their eyes. There would be no regret, no second thoughts, just the complete joy of finally avenging all he'd endured because the Elite Dragon Guard were pussies and couldn't save him.

Shaken from his thoughts by the sound of the little blonde-haired beauty's sweet voice, he watched as the biggest idiot of them all acted the part of the hero. Lance was so sure he was saving Sydney from certain death.

As if!

Andrew's heart may have been hardened by all he'd suffered, but there was absolutely no way he would ever hurt a child, especially one as special as little Sydney. The Special One's intuition was always correct. Had the fucking smartass taken a moment to pull his big head out of his ass and use the dragon senses he'd been given by the Universe, Lance would've realized how incredibly unique the little girl was. The jerk would also know that no matter how much life had hardened Andrew, there would never come a time when he would intentionally hurt a child.

Kick the ass of one of those self-important, egotistical, full of themselves Dragon Guardsmen? Hell yeah, but never a child. Sydney had a means to an end…the only way Andrew could be sure to get the Guard's attention and remind them he could and *would* take what he wanted simply to make a point.

Once again, he was roused from his musings, this time from the approaching Guardsmen. He'd been watching from behind some foliage since he'd placed the child on the lawn for the idiot Guardsman to get to safety, but it was time to go. Just as he rounded the corner of an old brownstone he knew had a basement perfect for eluding capture, he caught the scent of jasmine and honeysuckle. That was the scent he remembered from his trek through the wilderness while in pursuit of his elusive witch, and again earlier in the elevator.

Andrew turned just in time to see Dr. Malone make contact with Lance and the precious little *vibria*. In a split second everything became clear. The doctor was the big dope's mate. He knew Lance had been standing guard over her since the day all hell had broken loose, but Andrew had missed the mating signs.

His strategy to use Sydney to get the asshole's attention had been only because he knew Lance was never far from the good doctor, but now his plans could be taken to a whole new level. Again, he lamented that a female might be injured in his bid to make the bastards pay, but what else could he do? If they were incapable of keeping the most important people in their lives safe, how was it really his fault? After all, he was The Special One, meant to make a mark in this world and the next. No one ever said it had to be a positive mark.

CHAPTER TWELVE

If she had to explain one more time what had transpired from the time she ran from the hospital until she walked back in carrying Sydney, Sam was going to run screaming through the halls. At least they believed neither she nor Lance had anything to do with the child's disappearance, and were responsible for dispatching what seemed like an entire squadron armed with a detailed description of Andrew the Asshole.

The first person she saw when she exited the elevator had been Miss Crutchfield. It had taken all of Sam's very limited control not to punch the useless bitch right in the mouth when the social worker accused Sam of somehow being complicit in the girl's disappearance. Miss Crutchfield reached for Sydney, acting as if she cared about the child's well-being, and the child had burrowed further into Sam's body, refusing to be separated from the doctor. Detective Smithers had eventually relented and let Sydney stay with Sam until she calmed down. Charlie was then able to take the little girl back to her room.

Lance had been less than thrilled when they were separated. She knew he had growled, which she should consider strange, but for some reason thought it fit him. He wore an expression almost identical to the one she remembered from the day he'd saved her from the blast…fierce, unrelenting, and definitely dangerous, but when he looked at her, his expression softened. The slight dip of his chin let her know he would make sure everything turned out all right for *all* of them.

She tried to doubt him, tried to dislodge the belief she had in him. Experience hadn't always been kind to Samantha. It had taught her that believing in someone else usually ended with her being lonely and her heart broken. But no matter how hard she tried to dispel the feeling of confidence in the insanely sexy, completely overbearing man, just the opposite happened. It grew. It was like he was easing his way into her heart and she was helpless to do anything about it…unsettling to say the least.

They were done questioning Lance, and Sam watched him pace just outside the door of the room she remained sequestered in. She'd seen Max and heard them talking about someone coming to "represent" them, but didn't catch the attorney's name. Apparently, Lance was very well-connected to have a lawyer he could just call and have appear whenever he needed. Charlie poked her head in to let her know Sydney was resting comfortably. That had been almost fifteen minutes earlier, just after the detective's partner had left Sam sitting and staring at a blank wall with the promise that her questioning was almost complete.

Her muscles were cramping and her patience frazzled as she heard raised voices outside the door of her makeshift interrogation room. Lance was making his frustration with her continued containment known for all to hear. Just as quickly as the commotion had broken out, it ended. All that remained were whispered voices.

Not wanting to be left out, Sam stood and quietly moved closer to the door the young detective had thankfully left ajar. She recognized Detective Smithers's voice as he tried to exert his authority, and then Lance's as he insisted he be able to see Samantha. The discussion was just about to dissolve into more yelling when a woman's voice came from farther down the hall.

"Lance, please do not strike the detective." It was a command, not a request.

Had Sam not been sure Lance really was about to punch the detective, she would've laughed at the sound of authority the mystery woman possessed. As it was, she smiled her first real smile since handing Sydney over to Charlie when Lance answered, "Yes, Grace," like a little boy who'd been caught with his hand in the cookie jar, and not the huge, muscular man threatening to hit an officer of the law.

Sam was immediately impressed as the female lawyer wasted no time stating her purpose. "Detective Smithers, my name is Grace O'Brien. I represent Mr. Kavanaugh and Dr. Malone. I understand you've questioned both my clients and have been given the information regarding the alleged kidnapper, but are still holding Dr. Malone. May I ask why?"

The detective stuttered, and when he answered he sounded frightened. "I just have a few follow up questions, Ms. O'Brien, and at no time did they ask for an attorney."

"Did you read them their rights?" Grace immediately countered. "And it's Mrs. O'Brien."

"No, no ma'am. They aren't under arrest, only being questioned regarding the child's abduction." The detective's voice shook.

"But you repeatedly denied Mr. Kavanaugh access to Dr. Malone, and have not allowed Dr. Malone contact with anyone since she returned with the child, correct?"

"Yes, but—" The detective tried to answer but the attorney had obviously heard enough.

"There is no 'but,' detective. You have violated my clients' rights. The questioning is over. Should you have any further questions…here is my card. Please contact me and I will make the necessary arrangements."

Sam heard a mumbled "Okay" before the door she was standing beside swung open and Lance was sweeping her into his arms. Unable to mutter a word before his mouth slammed against hers, she was robbed of all rational thought. He kissed her like a man possessed. His tongue demanded entrance, accepting nothing but her complete surrender. His tongue slid along hers as their teeth crashed and he became the very air she breathed.

There was nothing to do but kiss him back. Sam's need to taste every part of this extraordinary man grew within her. In the next instant, she heard the door slam shut and felt his hands grip her ample backside. She was lifted until her hips met his, and she felt the wall at her back. Helpless to do anything but what her body demanded, Samantha completely let go for the first time in her life.

Lance tore his mouth from hers, gasping as he kissed and nipped along her jaw line. Goosebumps rose all over her body. Her nipples pebbled against her the lace of her bra, and her panties were immediately wet with her arousal. This was what she'd dreamt of. *He* was touching her body, bringing her pleasure like it was something he'd done hundreds of times, not like it was their first time together.

He bit the tender dip between her shoulder and neck and all coherent thought flew from her mind. Their hips met over and over, the feel of his massive erection continually bumping her engorged clit, setting off fireworks behind her eyelids and pushing her closer to the point of no return.

He groaned, grabbed both her hips, and held them against the wall as he placed his thigh against her hot, wet crotch. His mouth returned to her neck as she rode his leg, seeking her release. Sam felt his hand at the waistband of her scrubs, her body moving on its own to allow him access. His large calloused hand grazed her hip before stirring the short curls of her mound. He rubbed and teased her outer lips, staying just a breath from her clit as it pulsed in anticipation of his touch. His lips against her ear caused her to shiver as he whispered while sliding his middle finger into her, "Gods, Doc, you feel so *damn* good. So hot and wet…and ready for me."

He worked his finger slowly in and out of her, keeping her right on the edge, teasing to the distraction. Time stood still as he drove her higher and higher. His next words came as a command. "Open your eyes, Doc. Look at me."

Her eyes snapped open just as his thumb and forefinger pinched her clit and she exploded, riding his hand with abandon. Filled with a feeling she didn't understand, but didn't ever want to end, she stared into his amazing blue eyes, held captive by their intensity. In that moment their souls touched, and the resulting explosion felt like she was being massaged from the inside out. Sam wanted to scream to the Heavens, but only whimpered to keep the people just outside the door from hearing. He continued to kiss, touch, and pet until her breathing returned to normal and she collapsed against his chest, replete from the best orgasm of her life.

He pulled his finger from her and straightened her clothing as she continued to rely on his strength to keep her upright. While thinking of all the ways she would like to repay him and wishing for the time to act upon her thoughts, there was a knock on the door. She struggled to climb off his knee while pushing against his chest, suddenly embarrassed by what had just transpired.

He pushed his hips against hers, holding her hostage against the wall and grabbed her hands. She felt the wetness on his hand from her release and his still hard cock against her stomach. Her eyes snapped to his as the unmistakable heat of her blush rose in her cheeks. He grinned and shook his head. "No way, Doc. You aren't hiding from me or from what's happening between us."

She continued to stare, not sure what to say next. Thankfully another, louder knock on the door, followed by a deep voice she remembered from the other night, saved her from commenting.

"All right, jackass, we're all packed up out here and ready to go. You wanna save the kissy face for later so we can get going?"

Lance's smile grew. Sam wanted to hide under the bed, completely mortified that his brother knew at least some of what happened between them. Her face grew hotter and she knew her cheeks were flaming red, but he continued to hold her as he answered Royce. "We're coming, Old Man. Don't get your panties in a twist. Just making sure Doc's okay after her questioning."

"Well, hurry the hell up. Everyone out here is ready to go."

"Be right out, Grandpa."

"I'll Grandpa you, you giant pain in the ass," Royce grumbled.

Through gritted teeth, she whispered, "Let me go, Lance. There are people out there waiting for us."

"They'll wait, Doc. I need to make sure we have an understanding. What happened here was not a one-time thing. There's something between us that needs to be explored. When time permits, we're gonna 'explore' until we can't explore anymore. And when we catch our breath, we're gonna start all over again; understood?"

He tried to look intimidating and she was sure he'd scared many people in his life, but the twinkle in his eyes and the dimple in his cheek made it impossible for her to do anything but roll her eyes at him. He squeezed her hands just a little tighter and she nodded.

"Not good enough, Doc. I need to hear the words."

She saw his steel resolve reflected back at her and had no doubt he would keep her in that very position for as long as it took her to voice her agreement.

"Yes, Lance. I agree."

"Good." He winked and moved a half a step back, releasing her body but still holding her hands.

As the cool antiseptic air of the hospital moved between them, Sam missed the warmth of his body, craved what she'd never felt with another. He let one of her hands fall to her side but wound his fingers through the other as they headed for the door. At any other time in her life, she would've fought to get away, to be by herself, to regain her composure.

Samantha was a loner. She'd never even spent the entire night with any of her lovers, always finding an excuse to escape and return to her solitary life. But there was just something about Lance that made her throw all her old habits, along with her common sense, out the window. If she wasn't careful, he was going to find his way into her heart, and that was something she in no way was ready for or had the time for.

They exited the room to find Royce and Devon, along with a stunning, dark-haired woman Sam knew immediately was the attorney she'd heard speaking to the detective. There was a man at the woman's back with the most unusual amber eyes. From the possessive way he cupped her shoulder, Sam knew he had to be the attorney's husband. An almost identical copy of him, but with deep blue eyes, stood to his right. They were huge, and it appeared their muscles had muscles. She knew immediately they were more of Lance's brothers.

"Hey, Samantha…I mean Sam," Devon waved.

"Hi, Devon," she answered, and looked to the gentle giant. "Hi, Royce. How are you?"

"I'm fine, Samantha. How are you holding up?"

"Good, thank you."

He and Lance gave each other a hard time, but she could tell they truly cared for one another as only brothers could.

Sam looked at the woman smiling sweetly in her direction just as Lance began to speak.

"Doc, this is Grace." He pointed to the woman, who returned her smile as she waved. "And the mad man behind her is her ma…ah…husband, Aidan."

"Nice to meet you, Dr. Malone," the couple answered in unison.

"Just call me Sam. Thank you so much for coming to my rescue. It seems y'all have had to do that a lot lately." She chuckled and was about to move forward to shake hands with the couple when the one with deep blue, almost haunting eyes spoke up. "I'm Aaron, by the way, since the wiseass isn't gonna introduce me."

And just like that, all residual tension from Sydney's abduction, their questioning by the police, and all that happened between them was gone. The entire group was laughing like they didn't have a care in the world. She felt Lance's arm go around her and her body, which he'd apparently taken command of without her knowledge, cuddled into him.

When she got home and had a few minutes to herself away from the intoxicating allure of this man, Sam was definitely going to examine her own mental stability. There was absolutely no way she could be falling for the big, overbearing, overgrown child at her side. She didn't have time for a relationship. She had plans and goals, things she needed to accomplish. Even as she thought of all the reasons she shouldn't fall for Lance, his hand found a little patch of bare skin at her waist. The electric shock from just that small caress caused her heart to race.

I'm up shit's creek without a paddle, here.

CHAPTER THIRTEEN

Lance stood in the hall, laughing with his brethren, his arm around Sam, and a sense of pride beyond anything he'd ever imagined filled his being.

She's really mine.

There was no way he could stay away from her. He'd been a fool to think he ever could. One taste of her passion sent him past the point of no return and he wanted more, as quickly as possible and for as long as possible. He and his dragon were working overtime with visions of all the ways they could enjoy their perfect mate. But there was still the problem of the traitor. Not to mention that for the first time in Lance's very long life, he was going to have to be careful and think of the consequences of his actions before acting.

Not going to be easy….

Sam's safety and that of the little girl she held dear was all that mattered. No way was he letting anything happen to her. It was even more inconceivable after what they had shared. He'd seen first-hand what Andrew was capable of where the mates of the Dragon Guard were concerned. He also had personal knowledge of what it felt to lose someone special. It was a feeling he'd sworn many years before to never feel again. He would do whatever possible to make sure he never did.

Sam tensed next to him. He was surprised she didn't move from his side when her friend Charlie approached, pushing Sydney in a small wheelchair. The child was all smiles and only had eyes for his mate.

"Hi, Dr. Sam," the sweet girl giggled. Lance watched each of his brethren fall under her spell. "Dr. Charlie said I get to leave the hospital and go stay with Ms. Grace and Mr. Aidan. Isn't that cool?"

His body immediately felt the loss as Sam jumped from his side and stood in front of Grace. He could feel her confusion and more than a little suspicion. Taking his cues from Aidan, since he was mated to Grace and seemed to be doing okay, he hung back and waited.

Firing her question at Grace, Sam's voice was sterner than he'd thought possible. "What is the meaning of this, Mrs. O'Brien? Are you also a doctor? How can you remove this child from the hospital?" Sam's shoulders rose and fell as she took a long deep breath. She was just about to lose her composure, but it was her fight, no matter how much he wanted to jump in.

Grace's face showed complete patience and understanding as she answered his mate. "I understand your confusion, Dr. Malone, but I'm sure you'll agree that the hospital has proven they are *not* able to keep Sydney safe." Sam nodded and Grace continued. "Lance explained the situation when he called for my help. I took it upon myself to get an order of temporary custody for Sydney, while also preparing any paperwork I may need to ensure you two were released from the less than legal questioning you were forced to endure. Since I didn't know your complete legal name and address and was unable to get back in touch with Lance," Grace shot him a look that he knew had caused many criminals to cringe, "I used Aidan and myself as temporary guardians and our address as her place of residence until other arrangements can be made. You are more than welcome to stay with us until everything is sorted. We have a big house just outside the city, and have made provisions for her safety."

He could tell from the tension in Sam's shoulders she still wasn't happy with what was going on. Lance had so much to learn about his mate, but he did know she needed time to think things through and having this sprung on her didn't sit well. As Sam's unease rose, his need to comfort her became almost overwhelming, something so foreign he wasn't sure how to react. Just about to move to her side, he stopped short when Aidan's voice sounded through their link. *"Chill out, Bro. Grace has it under control. Your doc is just protecting what's hers. You need to stay put and let her work it out. No hot-dogging. You hear me?"*

"Yeah, I hear ya, asshole, but that doesn't mean I have to like it," Lance grumbled.

"Damn, how the mighty have fallen," Aidan chuckled through his mind. *"I'm loving this shit."*

"Isn't it great to see the little pain in the ass all tied up in his underwear?" Royce threw his two cents into the conversation.

Before Lance could answer, Aaron decided to get in on the fun. *"I cannot wait until they are formally mated. She's gonna give him a run for his money. Couldn't happen to a nicer guy."*

Feeling ganged up on and truly despising each and every one of his brethren, Lance was plotting his reply when he heard Sam speak, more in control of her emotions than before. "I'd definitely like to go with you and make sure you have everything Sydney needs. She's still recovering from her surgery and a fever we have yet to diagnose. I apologize for losing my temper. Thank you very much for taking care of all the paperwork. My dealings with her social worker could be described as hostile at best." Sam halfway chuckled, and he could feel her acceptance of the situation through their growing bond.

Grace smiled and took a few steps forward until she stood in front of his mate. She reached out and grabbed Sam's hand, holding it for a just a second before speaking again. "You'll get used to us taking care of one another the more you get to know us. The guys tend to take things too far and act like Neanderthals. If you have any problem with that one, you just let me know." She dropped Sam's hand, pointed right at him, and winked. "Together, I'm sure we can take him down a peg or two." And with that, the two women laughed like lifelong friends. He could only imagine what hell was coming his way.

Not wanting to think about it any longer, Lance walked over and slid his arm around Sam's waist, turning them to face Sydney. "You ready to go, kiddo?" he asked.

"I sure am, Lance, but I don't want to ride in this wheelchair. Can you carry me?"

He looked down at Sam for confirmation. When she nodded, he knelt down to let Sydney crawl into his arms. She latched onto his neck as he stood, turning to face the others. "Have you met everyone, Sydney?"

"Yes, I did, while you and Dr. Sam were talking in the other room. Mr. Royce said I should ask you what you were talking about."

The whole group erupted into laughter as he frowned and Sam blushed. Lance knew it was one of about a million things they were going to use to get back at him for all he'd done to them. Looking down at Sydney, who was patiently waiting for his answer, unaware she was being used to get back at him, he thought quickly. "We were deciding what to have for dinner tonight. I heard a rumor that you like cheese pizza."

The child's eyes lit up as she nodded her head and looked to Sam. "Can we have cheese pizza, Dr. Sam? Please, please, oh please?"

Forgetting her embarrassment, Sam smiled. "Yes, we can have cheese pizza, but we also need to make sure they have red Jell-O and animal crackers in case your tummy starts to hurt again."

"Oh, I already told Miss Grace, and she said Mr. Royce and Mr. Devon would stop at the store for us. Isn't that cool?"

Again, the entire group was laughing. For the first time in many years, Lance was truly happy. Not cracking jokes and acting like an idiot to keep everyone going, but truly happy, and it was all because of the woman standing by his side. He really was an idiot to have thought he could stay away from her. The Universe may not make mistakes, but She damn sure knew how to screw with a guy's sanity.

Four hours and countless bouts of laughing later, the fridge was packed with red Jell-O and the cabinet with animal crackers, along with anything else Royce decided Sydney might need. The big guy was going to make a kick-ass dad. He'd literally thought of *everything*. Eight large pizzas had been devoured while they watched *How to Train Your Dragon*, a DVD Grace had gotten Aidan as a joke. Sydney loved it and he and his brethren watched while barely keeping a straight face. Where in the hell did cartoonists get their crazy ass ideas?

He'd decided to walk the perimeter of Grace and Aidan's land to make sure all the young Guardsmen and werepanthers were in place. He knew what happened at the hospital had just been a prelude to Andrew's true plan. The little bastard was really good at creating chaos.

Lance nodded to Jace, one of the youngest of the group but by far the most promising. "Anything suspicious?"

"No, sir, nothing at all." Lance cringed at the use of "sir." He knew it was the way Rayne and the others were training them, but he hated how old it made him feel.

"Good. Just make sure you stay alert."

"Yes, sir. Absolutely, sir."

"Good job, but you can drop the 'sir' crap with me. Lance is fine." Lance chuckled, not wanting to break the young man's spirit but really hating that he'd been called sir three times in the span of thirty seconds.

"Yes, si…ummm….yes, Lance."

"Better." He nodded his approval and the younger man smiled. "Now stay alert and let us know if you hear *anything*."

"Yes…Lance."

The young man was going to make an excellent Guardsman, but he really needed to lighten up. Chuckling, Lance turned on his heels and resumed his perusal of the grounds. As usual, Royce had done a great job with the tactical positions of all the men, and he could sense the werepanthers moving through the trees.

For the first time since leaving the hospital, he realized Max had been missing in action. Pulling the cell phone from his back pocket, Lance dialed the king while finishing his inspection. Four rings later, he left a short message asking the Leo to give him a call. Something seemed off. It wasn't like Max not to be right in the middle of things.

Lance had seen Sophia, Max's sister and second-in-command, when all the Big Cats arrived. She'd briefly spoken with Royce to confirm the plans before disappearing with her pride members to shift and begin their security sweep. He was glad the panthers were on their side. Their ability to blend in and get information far surpassed that of the dragons. It pricked his ego just a bit, but as long as they were allies he didn't see the harm in them all sharing talents. Lance remembered more than one time Max had called for backup, needing the muscle and raw power of the dragons, so he figured in the grand scheme of things, they were all equal.

He stopped and spoke to a few more of the young Guardsmen as he made his way back to the house. Lance could see why Aidan had agreed to stay with Grace after their mating instead of all the way back at their lair. The couple stated they needed to be closer to Grace's job with the State Prosecutor's office, at least until 'The Auctioneer' and his band of thugs were safely behind bars, but Lance could also see how the huge estate fit the couple. With the high stone walls enclosing the massive expanse of land, it gave them the privacy they needed and kept his long-time friend from feeling the claustrophobia that sometimes plagued their kin when they stayed in the city too long.

Thinking of Sam, Lance imagined she would want to stay at her home after they were mated, then quickly shut down that train of thought. There was no way he could move forward with the official mating. He was resigned to the fact that he couldn't stay away from her, but officially mating was out of the question with the traitor on the loose.

He hadn't even started preparing her for the mind blowing revelations he was going to have to drop at her feet. What would happen when he told her he had the soul of a dragon living within him, and when needed, could call him forward? Lance stopped dead in his tracks.

What the hell am I going to do?

Rayne and Aidan had dealt with the same issues and their mates had responded favorably. Would Sam? Something told him he wasn't going to have it as easy as his brethren had.

Looking through the patio doors, he watched Sam and Sydney laugh while playing what he assumed was "Slap Jack." If not, they were beating the hell out of a defenseless tray table. Lance couldn't tear his eyes away from his spectacular mate. She was mesmerizing. Her dark brown eyes danced with joy and she had the most adorable dimples when she just let herself go and enjoyed the moment.

His thoughts returned to a few hours prior when he'd held her close and watched her every emotion as she came completely undone in his arms. What he wouldn't give to sink into her warm, welcoming body, stare into her deep, dark eyes, and lose complete control with her.

Studying her more closely, he imagined all the ways he wanted to explore her magnificent body. His cock made its presence known, his mind awash with images of him and Sam loving one another. Samantha Malone was his in this life. He just couldn't wait to begin their life together. Lance had spent so many years running from Fate, telling himself after the loss of his mother and sisters all those years ago that he would never let another woman close.

His failure to protect his family had been his driving force for close to a hundred years. If he'd only stayed with his family while undergoing his transformation he would've been there to protect them, but his mother demanded he go to the lair of the most elite Dragon Guard and train with the best.

The loss of his father in battle had been devastating. It was something that had torn away at his mother's soul bit by bit with debilitating loneliness. Lance never knew how, but she'd carried on for her family...for her children. She'd wanted the best for them, and swore to uphold the promise she and his father had made on the day of his birth. Lance would be trained by the most elite Dragon Guard Force, and there would be no discussion about it.

Lance had traveled for the better part of six days on foot to reach the lair of the Golden Fire Clan. Alexander MacLendon, Rayne's father, had been the commander of their Force and one of his father's most trusted friends. Lance had grown up listening to the stories of the battles fought and foes defeated by these mighty warriors and their brethren.

For three long months he trained night and day, learning everything he could from the best Dragon Guard Commander their kin had ever known, while becoming fast friends with his son, not having any clue what Fate had in store for them. On the day his mentor deemed him ready to return home, there was a huge feast in his honor. They partied the night away, not knowing his own clan was under attack. The next morning Alexander sent him on his way, but not before decreeing Royce would accompany him back and assist with further training of any younger, newly transformed kin.

The older Guardsman was a silent traveling companion, only speaking when asked questions, and most answers were no more than a few words. Lance had to admit he'd been glad to have Royce close by when his first long range flight almost ended with him hitting the side of a mountain as Lance tried to somersault in the air. Royce yelled loud and long through the mind speak of their kin, reaming him for his foolishness, but Lance had still done it again just to prove he could. Afterward, they had walked for almost an entire day before Royce would allow him to call forth his dragon and soar again. Lance smiled as he thought of all the years he'd been a thorn in the old man's side and how it had all started.

His levity was short lived as he remembered what they found as they crested the ridge just above his clan's lair. The Golden Dragon Clan had been completely decimated, the stench of black magic permeating their lungs with every breath. Feelings of loss and despair threatened to overtake him as he ran from pile to pile of smoldering debris, envisioning the vibrant clan members who'd been reduced to nothing more than ash at his feet by the treacherous wizards.

Lance slowed as he came upon the broken remains of the wheelbarrow he'd repaired the day before leaving for training. Following a trail of blood, he found what was left of his mother and younger sisters, huddled together with hunters' arrows protruding from their chests. They hadn't stood a chance.

He and Royce had immediately buried his fallen clan members, performing the Rite of Passage to ensure each soul's safe journey into the Heavens. The longer they worked to honor the dead, the clearer what had happened became. The only remains present were those of women, children, and elderly members of the clan...no Guardsmen. The atrocity had obviously been planned to deliver the most devastation to the clan and to all dragon kin. Lance called out through the mind speak unique to his clan, alerting the warriors of his findings. Only two of his clan answered. They detailed the bloody battle they'd been in and the loss of the other Guardsmen of their Force. After much discussion, it was determined those who'd killed the women and children were part of the same wizard coven who'd also killed their Guardsmen.

Lost in the memories of how he and Royce, along with the two surviving Guardsmen of his clan, had tracked down the hunters and wizards, exacting a justice befitting the crimes they'd committed against his people, he missed Sam walking towards the window. Not until she tapped on the window was he thrust back into the present and face to face with his future. He could see the concern in her eyes and could only imagine what expression he wore after reliving the most devastating loss of his very long life. Trying to reassure his mate and throw off the haunting memories, he plastered on his infamous shit-eating grin and threw in a wink for good measure. He knew he'd succeeded when she smiled back at him.

Sliding the door open, he almost hit the ground as Sydney catapulted across the room and latched onto his leg. They all erupted into laughter as he pulled the child up his body and into his arms while making his way to the couch. Collapsing in a heap with the child in his lap and Sam at his side, Lance chuckled, "You ladies really think you're funny, don't ya?"

"We...are," Sydney laughed.

"We'll just see about that," he said as he tickled her sides, careful to avoid the spots where he sensed her weakness, until she was begging him to stop.

"Not fair," she giggled after finally regaining her breath.

"Hey kiddo, you sneak attacked first. I was just defending myself." He winked at Sam, adoring the fact that she was relaxed and having fun. Leaning his head forward, he whispered into Sydney's ear and smiled as she covered her mouth with both her little hands, trying to keep her giggles contained.

He counted to three in her ear and half tossed, half sat the little one on the other side of Sam, while he moved closer to her hip. They both attacked at once, tickling Sam's sides until she was squirming with tears running down her cheeks. Somehow amidst their fun, Sam wiggled free, and before he could catch her was across the room with arms thrown out in front, trying to protect herself from more tickles. He knew he could get past her defenses if he really wanted to, but decided he would let her think she had the upper hand, at least for the moment. Besides, watching her ample breasts move up and down as she struggled to regain her breath was a hell of a show. Once again, his imagination ran away with him and he felt his cock growing hard. He quickly reminded himself there was a child in the room.

In an effort to distract his wayward thoughts, he decided to mess with Sam instead. "You really think you're safe over there, Doc?" he teased.

"A whole lot safer than between you two."

"But Dr. Sam, we were just playing around," Sydney grinned. Lance almost laughed out loud as she winked at him, so sure she was suckering the young doctor.

He looked up just in time to catch the look of adoration for the child on Sam's face. A warmth that would never go away as long as he had her enveloped his heart. There was no other like his mate. Thank the Heavens his brethren couldn't see his sappy display of emotions or hear his thoughts. There was no denying the growing love he had for Sam, or his need to be near her as much as possible, but if he could avoid the inevitable shit storm from his brethren a few times, he wouldn't miss it. The mating call was working overtime to make sure he did everything he'd sworn to never do, especially with Andrew and 'The Auctioneer' still out there threatening what was most important to him. He would protect these two special ladies and any other like he had been unable to do for his mother and sisters.

In an effort to keep the dark thoughts at bay, he decided to play along with Sydney. "Don't ya think Dr. Sam cheated by sneaking away, Sydney?"

Blonde curls bounced all over as she nodded her agreement. "I do. Maybe we should go get her." She shook with excitement, waiting to see if he agreed.

"No. No. No," Sam commanded from across the room, trying her best to sound tough but failing miserably with her barely contained giggles.

"Aw, come on, Dr. Sam," Sydney begged.

"I think you've had quite enough excitement for today, Miss Sydney. How about we go up to that pretty room Miss Grace got ready for you and get you tucked in for the night?"

"Do I have to?" the little girl whined, shocking Lance by looking at him for confirmation.

Never one to get between two women, no matter how small one might be, he smiled and looked into the sweet child's pleading blue eyes. "Whatever Dr. Sam says goes. She's the boss and knows what will make you all better." Sydney's bottom lip curled and she batted her long dark lashes at him in what he recognized was a last ditch effort to get her way.

Finding it hard to resist, but knowing Sam would kick his ass, he decided on a compromise. "How about a piggy-back ride upstairs instead? How does that sound, Dr. Sam?"

They both looked to Sam. She nodded her agreement, and Sydney's pout disappeared, turning immediately into a smile. She crawled across the couch towards him with a twinkle in her eyes and a mischief he knew all too well. "Can you two both read me a bedtime story?" She climbed into his lap and hugged his neck.

"Sure," they agreed in unison.

As he stood and swung Sydney onto his shoulders, his eyes caught Sam's and the connection between them sizzled to life. Her eyes widened and she gasped, letting him know she felt it too. He quickly turned towards the stairs, knowing the sooner he got the little sweetie to bed, the quicker he got to be alone with Sam, and nothing was going to keep him from being alone with his mate. Nothing at all.

CHAPTER FOURTEEN

Sam tried to look anywhere but at Lance's ass as he ascended the stairs in front of her, but it was useless. The way his well-worn jeans fit perfectly against the most amazing butt she'd ever seen made it impossible. The man was like a drug. No one had ever affected her like he did. When he'd kissed her earlier, there was nothing she could do but obey her body's demands to let him have his way with her…and what he'd done had been nothing short of delicious.

His touch ignited the most amazing sensations. Just the thought of the way he made her feel had her squeezing her legs together in an attempt to stem her arousal. The longer she followed him the more errant her thoughts became, and all attempts to stop her excitement failed as she felt the tell-tale wetness in her panties. What the hell was she going to do? There was no way she could be around this man and not crave his touch, not want to run her hands over his incredibly muscled body. But Samantha had goals, things she wanted to accomplish, and she feared he could derail all her well laid plans if she let this thing between them go any farther.

Then there was Sydney and the man who'd kidnapped her. Sam believed with all her heart that Lance and his brothers were the only way to keep the little girl safe. After all, they'd rescued Sam more times than she wanted to think about; but that left her with a dilemma. How could she stay close to the child but away from the man who haunted her every thought and made her body burn?

Figuring there was no way to answer the question without lots more thought, Sam decided she needed to get her raging libido under control before they got to the end of the hall. Instead of Lance's behind, she wondered what bedtime story Sydney would like. She really hoped it was one she knew, since the huge house they were in did not look "kid friendly."

"You still back there, Dr. Sam?" Sydney asked from her perch atop the amazingly tall man before her.

"I'm here, Sydney," Sam answered as they entered the room Grace had graciously gotten ready for her little patient.

She watched as Lance bent at the waist and Sydney jumped from his shoulders, bouncing on the bed. Her hands itched with the need to reach out and touch all of him.

Shaking her head, hoping to clear some of the lust-induced fog from her brain, Sam switched her focus to Sydney. The child was absolutely amazing. After all she'd been through, she was jumping, laughing, and singing "Three Little Monkeys Jumping on the Bed."

There was no way to stop the smile that spread across Sam's face as she watched the two people who'd become so important to her in such a short amount of time having so much fun. They laughed and played as she got out one of the pink, frilly nighties Royce had picked up and a soft, fluffy towel for her to use after her bath.

Sam filled the tub with warm water and bubbles before heading out to grab Sydney, just then realizing it was quiet in the other room. What she saw stopped her in her tracks. Sitting with his back against the headboard, legs stretched out and ankles crossed, Lance held the child against his chest with his cheek resting on her cute blonde curls. Apparently, she'd been more tired than Sam realized.

Walking to the bed, the young doctor sat on the edge. Her hip rested against his, causing the same electrical current that always accompanied his touch to ripple through her body. He showed no sign that he felt it. Sam wondered if maybe it was all in her imagination, but then he turned his eyes to her and she saw what she felt reflected in their mesmerizing cornflower hue. His slow, sexy smile fed the fire their proximity started, and her thighs involuntarily clenched together in her body's attempt to stem her excitement. For a moment she thought she might actually have her hormones under control, then he spoke. His low rumbling voice made her pulse race and her palms sweaty.

"I think your little patient here is down for the count, Doc."

Rubbing her hands on her thighs, she nodded and tried to speak past the lump in her throat. Her already smoky voice came out softer than she'd intended. "Sure looks like you wore her out."

Sam knew he'd recognized the change in her tone for what it was when his eyes slightly closed and his tongue trailed across his bottom lip. Her mouth watered. All she could think of was what it would feel like to draw those puffy pink lips between her teeth. Looking at the floor, drawing on every single shred of self-control she had, Sam noticed his boots. He must've taken them off when he and Sydney were playing.

Instead of cooling the fires raging through her body, the picture of him shedding every thread of clothing and standing before her completely naked embedded itself in her mind. Lost in thought, she almost fell on her ass when he laid his hand on hers and spoke. "Whoa there, Doc. Don't fall."

He slid his hand to the inside of her thigh and held her in place. The heat from his touch made her pussy gush, and before she knew what was happening she'd laid her lips on his. Lance immediately took control, nibbling and tasting across her bottom lip, along her jaw, running his tongue along the outside of her ear. When he whispered, goose bumps rose all over her body. "You're killing me here, Doc. Let me lay this little bundle down, then I can show you what you do to me."

She nodded and stood, not thinking of anything but finally comparing her imagination to reality where the mouth-watering man was concerned. When all her plans for the future and her fear that Lance could somehow keep her from achieving her goals threatened to stop her from exploring what was between them, she pushed them to the back of her mind.

She'd spent every day since she was six years old being responsible, never doing anything that could remotely get in the way of becoming a successful doctor. Even the few men she'd dated had been "safe," with absolutely no possibility of becoming more than a passing fling, but Lance was different. There was something about him, something she couldn't put her finger on. That *something* had taken root deep inside and refused to be ignored. He possessed the ability to turn her inside out. Sam was going to find out what made him so special and pray she made it out alive.

Her next thought was cut short as he crushed his mouth to hers. Lifting her until she was forced to wrap her legs around his waist, Lance moved them out of Sydney's room, gently closing the door as they went. His sensual assault continued and somewhere in the back of her mind she realized they'd entered another room and he'd closed the door. However, it wasn't until she felt the mattress under her back and he'd stopped kissing her that she opened her eyes. Looking up at him made her feel giddy, not unlike the expensive champagne Charlene's parents had gotten for them when they'd received their undergraduate degrees.

She could feel his gaze, just as she could feel his hands slowly moving across her ribs and his erection rubbing against her swollen clit through their clothing as he rolled his hips. Never in her life had she wanted to be naked in front of a man, but in that moment, it was all she could think of. He smiled his sexy smile that turned her insides to jelly, then spoke, and absolutely any thought of anything but getting as close to him as possible evaporated from her brain.

"You're driving me nuts, Doc. I can't think when I have you in my arms like this," he whispered as he lowered his head. When his lips touched her neck, the spark of recognition was stronger than ever before, pushing a low moan from her throat and causing her hips to move in unison with his.

When his hand closed over her breast her nipple hardened to an almost painful point, her back arched, and she could no longer keep her eyes open. His mouth moved her scrub top off her shoulder as he tasted every inch of her collarbone, setting her skin on fire. He groaned as she felt the material pull tight, unable to be stretched any farther. The material ripped, and he responded, "No worries. I'll buy you a new one. I can't wait another second to taste every delectable inch of you."

Before she drew another breath, her bra joined her ruined scrub top and his mouth latched onto her breast. Her hands were in his hair as she pushed more and more of her aching mound into his mouth. He ate at her like she was the best thing he'd ever tasted. His teeth ran across the tip of her nipple while his tongue licked the same spot to ease the sting. When she was sure she would lose her mind, he released her breast with a pop and immediately dove onto the other, giving it just as much attention.

She writhed against him as her juices flowed and her clit pulsed. Sam was quickly losing control when she felt his hand slide past the waist band of her pants, shoving them down along with her panties. Lance lifted slightly to continue removing her pants, losing contact with her body, and she groaned at the loss.

"Just a little patience, Doc. I'm working as fast as I can," he chuckled. "Heavens be damned, aren't you just the sexiest thing?"

Before she could reply he had her completely disrobed and was pulling his shirt over his head.
Damn, that man moves fast.

In the next second, her brain short-circuited as she took in the absolute masterpiece of a male specimen hovering above her. He was chiseled perfection, with wide shoulders begging to be touched and a chest rivaling any gracing the pages of any magazine, anywhere. Sparingly sprinkled light, coarse hair highlighted his spectacularly drawn dragon tattoo.

It was incredibly intricate in its design, and the gold scales covering the massive beast's body seemed to shimmer. A faint memory came to mind, but was pushed away when his lips touched her sensitive skin once again. She ran her nails across his already raised berry-tipped nipples, teasing the little hairs around them. A shock that caused her womb to quiver shot through her body when she touched the base of the dragon's neck. He shivered in response and growled, "Enough, woman. I won't wait any longer to taste you."

He slid down her body, kissing and tasting, until his face was just above her mound. When all movement stopped, she looked down her body and found him staring. Every other time in her life, she'd been embarrassed to be seen naked. Sam had curves and hips, and God had given her perky double D's that some men just didn't appreciate. But this time was different. The look in Lance's eyes said he liked what he saw, maybe even loved it. He found her desirable and sexy.

Another time, she would've questioned how someone who looked like him could think someone who looked like her was sexy, but his hungry gaze answered any questions she had. The shit-eating grin Sam was quickly coming to know as his go-to look appeared and he kissed the skin right above the curls covering her outer lips. Nipping lightly, his voice vibrated her aroused clit when he whispered, "Hold on, Doc, I'm gonna feast. You smell like Heaven, and I intend to have my fill."

With that, he pushed his tongue through her sensitive lips and lifted her legs onto his shoulders. Her eyes slid shut as he licked her from bottom to top with the flat of his tongue. All the air was sucked from the room and flashes of light exploded behind her eyelids as he speared her with his tongue. Sam lost her breath when he bent the tip, tickling the bundle of nerves at the top of her channel. He was taking her to outer space as she grabbed his hair to keep from blasting off.

CHAPTER FIFTEEN

Her taste exploded on his tongue. Swirls of color burst into his vision from the first taste of the honey dripping from his beautiful mate. Lance pushed one finger into her aroused flesh, quickly adding another as he pumped in and out, driving her higher and higher. He separated her outer lips, driving his tongue as far as he could go with one smooth thrust. Sam's back bowed off the mattress, and her thighs tightened around his head as she thrashed and spoke unintelligible syllables, finally putting her fist in her mouth to keep from screaming out.

He smiled against her hot, wet pussy, pleased as could be at her responsiveness to his touch. He fucked her with his tongue and fingers while he drew circles on her clit with his thumb. Not wanting to waste one drop of her nectar, he placed his tongue flat on the bottom of her slit and slowly licked from the bottom to the top. On his second swipe, he sucked her engorged nub between his teeth and nipped lightly. She ground her hips against his face while he ate as if it was his last meal, sure he could live on the honey flowing from her for the rest of his life. He alternated between fucking her with his tongue and licking her like the best ice cream cone he'd ever eaten until she was tossing her head from side to side and biting on the fist she still had in her mouth. He feared she would draw blood.

Lance lifted up on his forearms. At the loss of contact, her eyes snapped open. "*Mo chroi'*, you can take your fist out of your mouth. Aidan had all the bedrooms soundproofed for just this reason."

Not giving her time to question, he returned to the banquet of his mate, licking her long and slow, determined to make her scream his name, never wanting to hear anything more in his life. He sucked her clit into his mouth and bit down on her swollen nub with more intent, thrusting three fingers into her wanting channel while curling the tips to reach her sensitive bundle of nerves. Sam came with such force the juices poured from her pussy. He worked hard to get every drop. Petting and suckling her swollen lips, he felt her slowly return to earth. He smiled the largest smile possible, filled with pride and completion. His grin damn near made his cheeks hurt as it grew when she sighed his name, "Lance…."

"Yes, *a chumann.*"

"That was…. You were…. Oh my God," she whispered as her limp hand flopped across her eyes, and he saw the bite marks on her hand.

He overflowed with love, contentment, completion, gratitude, and faith that things would work out. The most beautiful woman in the world lay before him, completely relaxed from the way he had loved her. Lance let her legs slide carefully off his shoulders until they rested in the crook of his arms. Spotting the scar on her leg from her injury at the hands of 'The Auctioneer's' men, he bent and kissed the entire length, acknowledging what she'd suffered, but more importantly, that she'd survived.

He positioned his cock against her swollen, flushed lips and rubbed the head slowly against her clit where it peeked out of its hood. Coating himself with her juices, he slowly pushed into Sam, stopping when the head of his cock lay just inside her contracting channel. Each clutch pulled him deeper inside, making breathing almost impossible. He gritted his teeth as he pushed forward, inch by inch, teasing them both until all he heard was their panting and the sweat running down his back. When he touched the top of her womb he held still, savoring the feel of her hot, throbbing channel massaging his pulsing cock.

His erection grew harder. He was sure the top of his head would blow right off, but Lance would not hurry. This was something to be savored. The first time with his mate, the one the Universe made just for him, was exponentially better than any story he'd ever been told. He almost regretted teasing his brethren about how they'd acted after finding their mates now that he was experiencing it, but he couldn't be bothered thinking of them when the gorgeous creature who was meant to be his was looking at him with pure desire in her eyes.

Lance dreamt of staying buried deep inside Samantha forever, held together by the perfect union that only happened when mates came together. Unfortunately, if he didn't move soon, he was going to explode like a randy teenager and embarrass himself with the only woman who would ever matter to him.

Slowly, he pulled out of the heaven of his mate and hovered at her opening. The slightest movement would have caused him to slip from the only place he wanted to be. Pushing forward, he watched his pulsing cock disappear into her warm, wet pussy. The sight of them joined caused his balls to draw up and his eyes to cross. Their rhythm increased, each stroke of his cock rubbing against her feminine walls. His gaze wandered from where they were joined up the long erotic curves of his Samantha. She was all woman and all his. He marveled as her large, full breasts bounced with each bump of his hips against hers. His mouth watered as he remembered the taste of those deep, rose-colored nipples.

Leaning forward, he palmed her breasts, bringing her knees that were still draped over his arms up to just under his hands. He rolled her nipples between his thumbs and forefingers, and was rewarded with his name tumbling from her lips in a low, slow mantra. With her legs bent higher, he could sink deeper into Sam, feeling an unparalleled closeness. His cock buried to the hilt in his delectable mate drove all sanity from him. Swiveling his hips, he bumped her clit with every movement.

Samantha was held captive, unable to move as he used all of his body to tease her to a frenzied peak. She thrashed her head from side to side, throwing her long curly mane in every direction as she chanted his name, the last coming out as a scream to the Heavens. "Lance…Lance…Lance…LANCE!"

"Hold on, *solas mo anam*," he grunted through gritted teeth, barely holding back his own climax. Lifting her legs just a fraction, Lance wanted her to see where he entered her. "Look at us, *mo ghra'*. Look where we're joined together. See where we are loving one another."

Her eyes snapped open and watched as he took long deep strokes in and out of her. Unable to hold back any longer, he ground his pelvis against her clit. Sam screamed her release as her pussy poured so much of her precious juices that they dripped between their bodies. Her contracting channel squeezed his cock until he shouted, emptying his seed into her. Their climax went on and on until he was sure he would collapse. When her pussy's hold on his cock began to relax, he moved in and out of her quaking body with slow short strokes, bringing her back to earth and allowing both their racing hearts to return to normal.

His legs shook from exertion, something he couldn't remember ever happening. If he died in that moment, he knew it would be for all the right reasons. Sure Sam was too far gone to notice, he used his enhanced speed to pull her to his chest. Twisting, he landed with his back on the bed and the amazing doctor draped across his sweat soaked chest. His fingers trailed up and down her spine, enjoying the silkiness of her gorgeous skin. She half-heartedly shivered in response to the electricity bouncing between them, unable to react, too replete from their lovemaking.

"Are you cold, Doc?" he asked, not wanting her to need for anything with him in her life.

"Mmmmm…," she mumbled, not moving.

He chuckled and grabbed the blanket folded at the end of the bed, throwing it over both of them. His fingers ran through her hair and he marveled at the softness. He found it captivating that each strand fought to curl in its own direction, then he almost groaned out loud.

When in the hell have I ever taken the time to think about a woman's hair, let alone watch how it curls?

He was so gone where his woman was concerned there was no going back. While he was buried deep inside her, a calm like he'd never known filled him…body, heart and soul. The pieces of his soul he hadn't known were missing snapped into place. He was whole for the first time in his life. Waiting for the fear to set in or to feel the need to run that never came, Lance had an epiphany…contentment was his new best friend, and he enjoyed the hell out of it.

Sam cuddled farther into his body, laying her arm across his chest. Her breathing slowed and it wasn't long until she had fallen into a deep sleep, exhausted from all the excitement of the day. While one hand continued its exploration of her many, many curls, he threaded the fingers of the other through hers. For several long moments Lance stared at their intertwined hands, amazed at how perfect they were together.

Each part fit together in perfect harmony, one made for the other, to be together forever. He knew his brethren would have a field day with all he was feeling and thinking, but for the first time, he really didn't give a shit. He could take as good as he gave, and the Heavens knew he'd given really damn well over the years. But Sam was worth every single thing his brethren were going to throw at him….

He rubbed tiny circles on the back of her hand with his thumb, dumbfounded again by the softness of her skin. There would never come a day when he would tire of touching every single part of her. Her long, thin fingers were tipped with short cut, well-manicured, unpolished nails, which he knew was due to her profession. It wouldn't do for a surgeon to have long talons while operating.

He snorted at his own *faux pas*, thinking of the times he himself sported a rather impressive set of talons, and immediately wondered what his mate would think of his dragon. The beast chuffed in his mind, assuring him she would be impressed. Again he snorted. Damn if his dragon's ego didn't rival his own. Just another example of how the Universe does not make mistakes.

It took his feet falling asleep for him to realize they were still lying across the bed. He'd been so absorbed in Sam that the rest of the world, even his feet and legs hanging over the side of the bed, had ceased to exist. Using his enhanced speed and hoping not to disturb her slumber, he quickly righted their position and covered them with the fluffy down comforter that matched the room's décor.

"Damn, bring a sexy woman into my life and I become a fucking interior decorator," he chuckled to himself.

It wasn't long until he felt his eyelids growing heavy. Not remembering the last time he'd spent the whole night with a woman, let alone wanted to, he pulled Sam closer. Not only did he want to spend the night with his mate, he wanted as much of her bare skin touching his as possible. Smiling, he turned to his side, bringing the fronts of their bodies as close as possible. Spending the last precious seconds before falling asleep looking at the face of his Samantha, absolutely mesmerized by her beauty, Lance drifted off to sleep happier than he'd ever been.

An annoying buzz woke him from the best sleep of his life. After deciding to ignore it and finding that impossible, he followed the noise to the pocket of his jeans, where his cell phone refused to shut up. Noting it was still dark outside, he figured he'd at least been asleep three hours. Breathing a sigh of relief when the obnoxious sound ended, he'd just closed his eyes when the noise began again.

Apparently, someone *really* needed to talk to him. Careful not to awaken his sleeping mate, Lance slid from the bed, grabbed his jeans, and headed to the bathroom. Once the door was shut, he answered the call. "This better be fucking important," he growled.

"Well, hello to you, too." Max's smooth voice floated from the receiver and Lance could tell he was smiling.

"Like I said, this better be important. It's the middle of the night, and I was…." He stopped short, not wanting to share even the slightest detail of what he'd shared with his mate with anyone. Lance had never been one to keep anything to himself. He shook his head at the protective feelings growing within him.

"Did you hear what I said?" Max's tone had changed to irritation and Lance knew he'd missed something.

"Nope, sorry. Still waking up."

"Yeah, I'm sure it has nothing to do with one very charming doctor." The smile was back in Max's voice, and Lance wanted more than anything to knock the cocky grin he imagined the king to be sporting right off the big cat's face. Taking several deep breaths to get himself back in control, Lance listened while Max continued. "Like I was saying, Juan Carlos and I are at your doctor's home, patrolling the woods, and have found something I think you need to see for yourself."

"Is it Andrew?" Lance was immediately on guard.

"Yes, but that's not all. You need to get out here. Your traitor is not the only one who has been watching Dr. Malone. There's an interesting new development you need to see."

"All right, Max. I'll be there in thirty minutes," Lance snapped.

"See you then," Max replied and disconnected the call.

Lance shoved his legs into his jeans, grabbed his dirty T-shirt from the floor and headed for the door. Just as he grabbed the doorknob, he thought of Sam. He definitely didn't want her to wake up after all they'd shared to find an empty bed without an explanation.

Digging in the drawer of the bedside table, he found a pad of paper and pen. He scribbled, *Doc, got a call about Andrew. Had to check it out. See you for breakfast. Hope you slept well. Ta' mo chroi istigh ionat, Lance.*

He knew she didn't know the language of his kin and had truly never thought he would speak the words to anyone, but in this case they fit, and he was ready to say them to her. His heart *was* within her, and would be for the rest of their life. Looking at her, once again amazed she was actually his, he smiled for about the hundredth time. Laying the pad next to her phone so she was sure to see it, he slipped out of the room, down the stairs, and out to his Harley, dressing on the way.

As he sped down the long driveway, he spoke directly into Royce's mind. *"You up, Old Man?"*

"I am now, you pain in the ass," the older guardsman grumbled.

"Yeah, yeah, yeah, get over it. Max called. They found something, and I have to run out to Sam's house."

Lance could feel his old friend become instantly alert. *"You need backup?"*

"No. Thanks. Can you keep an eye on Sam and Sydney til I get back?"

Royce chuckled and Lance prepared for what was to come. *"No way! How the mighty have fallen."* He laughed. *"Seriously though, I'm happy for ya, man but that doesn't mean I'm cutting you any slack. I'll take care of the girls. Call if you need us."*

"You know I will and…thanks."

Just thinking of Sam in the house with most of his brethren damn near turned him green with jealousy, but it was the best place for them. They would be safe. He had to get this shit handled and get Andrew out of their hair so he could move on with his very long, very happy life with his amazing mate.

"No problem. See ya when I see ya."

Knowing the old man had everything covered, he sped towards Sam's house wishing he could call forth his dragon and take to the skies…the suspense was killing him. What the hell had Andrew done now?

CHAPTER SIXTEEN

Perched high in the mountains, he paused in his search, trying to determine which trail was the real one. All the misdirects were really pissing him off, but it was also what he'd expected. After all, Kyra was the best magic practitioner he'd ever seen. Because of all her false trails, Andrew had almost been spotted by the werepanthers stationed in the woods between Dr. Malone's cottage and the Black Lake.

As if that wasn't enough, it was the king who padded in his direction. Did they actually think he was stupid enough to believe Sam would be there after all the chaos he'd caused not more than twelve hours ago? His returning dragon senses told him she and Sydney were still in the city. He was sure they were at his brother's home, the brother who'd left him for dead. Good thing the son of a bitch had married well complete with a fortress…stone walls and all. There would come a day when Andrew would march in and take Aidan's head, but at this point he wasn't prepared to penetrate the grounds. Not until he was full to overflowing with black magic and armed with a shitload of Kyra's amazing amulets.

When he'd returned to his hideout after his fun at the hospital, John and the others were waiting with several new recruits, one of which was able to perform rituals that raised his level of black magic. The young wizard was also able to scry for the witch. That led Andrew to the same mountains he'd followed her to before. She had to have a hideout somewhere in the rock formation, and he damn well intended to find it.

He wasn't going to hurt her. Andrew just needed more of her amulets. Of course, if Kyra required a little extra persuasion, he would do it. Her amulets were the key to the success of his plan and time was running out. All the dragons, including both of his brothers, were within his reach and he was not about to let them get away. Then he remembered the commander had yet to make an appearance.

Wondering what it would take to get Rayne to leave his mate and child, Andrew almost missed the sound of a motorcycle stopping in front of Sam's home. It could only be one person, the mate of the lovely doctor. An idea began to form in his demented mind, one that made his heart race and an evil smile grace his lips. All it would take would be one text message to John, and Andrew could kill two birds with one stone. Not exactly kill, but definitely use as bait. All he needed to do was get close to see what was going on with the idiots on the ground, and his best idea so far would be a go.

CHAPTER SEVENTEEN

During the entire ride he thought of Sam. Images of her in the throes of passion would not stop their continual loop through his mind. All he thought about was containing whatever catastrophe Andrew had caused and getting back to Sam as quickly as possible. Preferably, before she left the comfort of the king size bed he'd left her naked and sleeping in.

Catching sight of a large black panther slinking through the darkness, Lance turned into the woods at the rear of Sam's house. Magic touched his skin. From one breath to the next, the deadly predator transformed into the King of the Big Cats. Max closed the distance between them in a pair of faded jeans. For the first time the Leo didn't possess his trademark smug grin.

"What's up, Max?" Lance asked, now sure that all hell was about to break loose from the look on the other man's face.

"Follow me. I want to show you what we found." Max turned without waiting for a response, heading towards the scent of fresh water.

In just a few strides Lance was side by side with the king. The silence was almost deafening. None of the usual sounds associated with the woods were present. It was as if everything living had vacated the premises. Then the stench of black magic smacked his senses. It was pungent, and if he wasn't mistaken had the tinge of death about it.

His enhanced vision confirmed what his nose already told him…something had died not far from where he stood, and huge quantities of black magic had been involved. There were scorch marks and dead vegetation everywhere he looked. The sound of a stream, full from the recent rains, was loud enough that he knew it was just over the ridge.

Max stopped and pointed. Not a hundred feet from where they stood sat a pile of burned animal carcasses in the center of a pentagram, large rocks sitting on each of the five points. Melted black wax stained four of the stones with white covering the stone sitting atop the demonic symbol.

Lance walked closer and his dragon roared in his mind. The senseless loss of life was something they both found absolutely unforgivable. For his beast it was something infinitely more personal. The massive warrior whose heart and soul resided within him was of the earth, an elemental, and the senseless death of those precious creatures touched something deep inside.

"You okay, man?" Max asked, sounding like he was miles away instead of a few feet.

Time slowed as Lance's dragon pushed, continuing to roar, demanding justice. The Guardsman breathed deeply, consoling his beast the only way he knew how. He told the dragon the day would come when they would catch the one responsible and make him pay for his crimes. Slowly both beings calmed.

Lance answered the king through gritted teeth. "Yeah, I'm good. The big guy," he patted his chest to indicate the dragon within, "had a moment over that." He pointed to the pile of dead animals.

"Yes, our cats were not pleased, to say the least."

"I don't smell Andrew near this abomination," Lance growled, looking for any piece of ground not bearing the mark of the dark ritual that had been performed.

"You're right. His scent isn't here. I'll show you where he has been in a moment. I found another scent you should remember."

Lance centered himself and sifted through all the scents assaulting his enhanced senses. One he'd hoped to never smell again became clear. Mixed in with the various wizards and a few hunters, he could make out the unmistakable scent of at least two of the men who'd protected 'The Auctioneer' at the abandoned warehouse.

"What the fuck are wizards, hunters, and henchmen for the human criminal doing in the same place, performing death magic?" Lance spoke more to himself than Max.

Walking the perimeter of the ceremonial space, Lance was close enough to see ten animals of various sizes and species had been murdered. From the look of it, the ritual had taken place while he and the others were occupied with Andrew's bullshit. It only stood to reason the traitor had somehow been involved. It was right up the little fucker's alley, but something still didn't make sense.

"You know what I can't figure out, Max? Why was Andrew not here? He's a selfish little asshole. There's no way in hell he would miss the opportunity to be part of a ritual of this magnitude. It was obvious at the hospital he was running low on dirty magic. So what gives?"

"What Juan Carlos and I have been able to piece together tells me Andrew isn't with this group, at least not at the moment. Follow me. I'll show what we found of your traitor."

Used to having everyone follow his every command, Max had already turned and was heading towards whatever they'd found of Andrew. Lance chuckled as he jogged to catch up. "You know, you could wait for a guy to at least answer before taking off there, King."

"I'm not accustomed to waiting, dragon. Keep up or get left behind," Max teased with his patented "cat that ate the canary" grin firmly in place.

"Oh, I'll keep up. Don't you worry—" His next words were cut off by the hiss of a large cat from overhead. The panther landed firmly on the foliage covered ground, only a few feet from Lance, teeth bared, head lowered in what the Guardsman could only assume meant he was pissed.

Max laughed at his side. "Juan Carlos takes your comments as a form of disrespect." Then to his lieutenant, still in cat form, he said, "Stand down, old friend; our Guardsman here thinks he's funny. He means no disrespect."

"You know, Max, your boy there really needs to lighten up." Lance chuckled but kept one eye on the panther. It wouldn't do to have Sam see him all torn from a fight with a big cat. Especially since she didn't know they existed.

"As I've told you before, Juan Carlos does not chill out, but I can assure you he's only trying to intimidate you." The golden panther growled low in his throat but let them pass, following as they headed towards the base of the mountains.

"This way." Max pointed to a trail that had been carved out from repetitive use.

The king's tone became hushed and more intense. Before Lance could ask what was up, Max stopped. "Here's where the traitor's trail becomes very distinct. I believe he's searching for 'something' or 'someone.' As we moved farther up the mountain there were definite signs of residual white magic, and if I am not mistaken—which I rarely am—" The Leo looked back at Lance and winked, always the consummate asshole, but apparently trying to ease some of the growing tension. "It's the same white magic, yet unbastardized by black magic, that we felt in the woods when we chased Andrew and rescued Aidan's mate. The magic practitioner who was here is at least a close relative, but more likely the same witch who created those blasted amulets. And it is *she* the traitor is looking for."

"That explains a lot. When I flew over this area the other night...." Before he could finish, Juan Carlos, still in cat form, growled. "Yeah, yeah, yeah, I know you didn't approve." Lance shook his head at the panther. "Anyway, there were a few times I felt the presence of white magic. That must have been her, too." He smiled. "Well, it looks like the stupid fuck-up is having a bad run with his motley crew," Lance joked. "The wizards are performing rituals without him, and his little witch is hiding from him. Andrew never did play well with others."

"It would seem you are right, and he appears to be part cat," Max curled his lip in disgust, "since I'm sure dragons do not have nine lives." Lance laughed out loud and the Leo continued. "I'm really looking forward to ending any he may have left." The king growled. It was the closest Lance had ever seen the leader of the Big Cats come to a show of real anger. Max was always calm, cool, and collected, even when they were in the middle of battle. It truly was time to catch Andrew's ass and make him pay for all he'd done.

"How far up did his scent go?" Lance asked as he used his enhanced sight to catch any signs of Andrew's trail.

"It stopped at the second rise and restarted towards the back. It's spotty and the stench of black magic is all around. He's recharged since the hospital and is using it to lay false trails as much as possible." Max stopped. Lance could see the wheels turning in his mind.

When the king spoke again, his tone was low and ominous. "He will not give up. The white witch is important to him, but she's in her element here and able, at least for the time being, to stay ahead of him. Follow me."

Both men turned and walked back through woods. Neither spoke until they reached Sam's backyard. "I will have members of my pride come clear away the ritual site and show proper respect to the animals that gave their lives." His tone became little more than a whisper. "Round up your Force and meet us back here tonight. If we find the witch, I'm confident she can help us find the traitor."

Unable to help himself, Lance saluted, and the low growl that came from behind them let him know he'd once again offended Juan Carlos. Max chuckled. At least the king had a sense of humor, even though he spoke with a Latin accent that sounded like he belonged in one of the mafia movies the younger Guardsmen were so fond of. "You got it, Max. I'll round up the troops and we'll see you back here tonight."

Lance turned to wave goodbye and all he saw was the tail end of a very large black panther making his way into the woods. If the sun hadn't almost been up, Lance wasn't sure he would've seen the cat without his enhanced vision.

Max really needs a course in etiquette.

In no time at all he was back on his Harley, speeding towards Sam and hoping she was still naked in bed. Lance had plans for an amazing wake up call.

CHAPTER EIGHTEEN

Well, at least he had confirmation Kyra was hiding in the mountains he was searching, but Andrew was pissed that Master Eaton and some of his remaining followers had hooked up with hunters and were performing rituals so close to his hideout. Worst of all, they hadn't reached out to him.

He was sure no one was aware of the little coven he was acquiring with all the rogues. He and the Master had left things on good terms as they'd both run for cover when the shit hit the fan at the abandoned warehouse, so why had the wizard leader not reached out to him? Luckily, Andrew had learned that a ritual could be performed using animals, but he still had to wonder if the presence of the humans working for 'The Auctioneer' meant they were still trying to grab human women for a Grand Power Ritual.

Andrew hadn't been able to hear what the idiot and the king talked about as they left the edge of the mountain and returned to Dr. Malone's house. There was at least one other werepanther in the woods, and Andrew couldn't waste what black magic he had left to conceal himself when his witch was close. Once he had her and she'd made his amulets, then he could once again come and go as he pleased. Those fucking dragons needed to watch their backs. Andrew was going to strike hard and fast. The others of his group of rogues had gotten his message. If they knew what was good for them, they were making the preparations he'd ordered. There would be no time to waste once he found Kyra.

Sure that it was okay to move without detection, Andrew scooted out of the foliage he'd used for cover. He ascended the mountain using another, less traveled trail. It wouldn't do for the werepanthers to locate his scent again. Andrew needed to be careful now that the sun had almost completely risen.

His little witch could use the daylight to her advantage, and his patience with her continued avoidance of him and his needs was at an end. It was way past time to take down the mighty Dragon Guard. Those "wastes of space and air" needed to pay for leaving him in the hands of the wizards to be tortured. And then there was Aidan, the brother who'd left him for dead. Andrew had a very special kind of vengeance planned for him, one that would send shockwaves through all of dragon kin.

Focusing on the task at hand and putting all thoughts of retribution from his mind, Andrew climbed the mountain using long forgotten hunting and tracking skills. Kyra was here. He would find her. He *had* to find her.

CHAPTER NINETEEN

Lance spoke with his brethren the entire ride back to Aidan's. Royce was going to handle calling Rayne, and would also speak with Max later in the afternoon. The oldest of their Force was still nagging in Lance's ear when he drove through the gates.

"I know you're not listening to a damn thing I'm saying, but your mate is gonna be asking questions. She's no dummy. You better get your shit together and have the talk before it gets out of hand. We were lucky only the little one has made an appearance this morning. By the way, I've spoken to Grace and we need a background on Sydney. There's just something about her. I can't put my finger on it, but she's way more perceptive than anyone is giving her credit for. I'd swear she can tell when we're mind speaking."

"Whatever, Old Man. I swear you just find things to worry about. I'll handle Doc, and if Grace is cool with tracking down Syd's background, then go for it. You just need to chill the hell out. Think about it. If all goes well, we'll have the traitor back at the lair before sunrise tomorrow." Lance threw the kickstand down on his Harley and was striding towards the door in one smooth movement. *"I'm on my way in the back door and heading up the back stairs to see Sam. Let me know what Rayne's got to say…later."*

Royce laughed. *"Just take care of her, you pain in the ass. The Heavens know the Universe was way too good to you when they made Samantha."*

"Don't I know it, Old Man, don't I know it."

Lance smiled from ear to ear as he took the steps three at a time, his erection tenting the front of his jeans by the time he grabbed the doorknob and quietly opened the door. The sight of her long curly mane spread across the pillow and the golden glow of her bare back where the sheet was draped at her waist almost brought him to his knees. Remembering there was a very inquisitive six-year old in the house, he reached back and locked the door. There would be no interruptions for the next hour or so. He needed to wake his mate, and he took his job very seriously.

CHAPTER TWENTY

She came awake slowly to the amazing feeling of Lance's lips kissing and tasting the sweet spot behind her ear. He whispered all the scrumptious things he wanted to do to her body. The feel of a warm muscled chest at her back and large calloused hands kneading both of her incredibly sensitive breasts, coupled with his low rumbling voice, made her nipples hard and her pussy dripping wet.

Their bodies were so completely fused together that the short, coarse hairs covering his legs tickled the back of hers as they moved. Her hips began to roll back and forth of their own accord. Every motion brought her ample backside in contact with his very aroused cock. One of his amazingly talented hands continued to torment her breasts, alternating between the needy globes, as the other worked its way downward.

His light, sensual touch left a path of sparks, each landing directly in her womb, and amping up her arousal until she panted and moaned. When his fingers tickled the short curly hairs covering her mound, her hips jerked forward, trying to drive his fingers to her already pulsing clit.

"What's the matter, Doc? Have an itch you'd like me to scratch?" he chuckled in her ear. The vibration against her body robbed her lungs of the air needed to answer, so she nodded, and continued to move in any way possible with the hopes he would ease the ache he'd started before she lost her mind.

Always the tease, Lance lightly slid his finger all around her outer lips, coming close to her throbbing nub on every turn, but never touching where Samantha so desperately needed relief. Unable to control herself any longer, sure she would lose her mind if she didn't have release in the next few seconds, she started to turn over.

The movement caused his rock hard penis to slip into the crack of her ass, making contact with the very bottom of her slit. Both she and Lance gasped as his strong arms closed around her, holding her completely still. He exhaled long and slow. She felt him *everywhere*. Then he spoke, and she was sure she could come just from the sound of his voice against her ear.

"Hold still, *m'anamchara*. You're driving me crazy. I need to feel you come apart in my arms before I completely embarrass myself," he panted. Sam felt better knowing that he was just as affected as she was.

If Sam could've, she would've laughed. How in the hell could he ever embarrass himself when the very thought of him made her wet and needy? She'd dreamt of having this man naked and wrapped around her for so long, she'd almost thought last night was just another of her erotic dreams. But here he was again and she was greedy for more. Her next thought was stolen from her mind as he simultaneously leaned her forward at the waist and slid his cock into her waiting channel.

"Lance…oh my God, Lance…," she moaned, her voice sounding low and breathy.

Her contracting womb pulled all of his long, hard length into her. She could feel him pulsing against her feminine walls as he held them completely still. He slid his leg between hers, opening her legs and changing their position just enough that when he began to slide out of her, he bumped the sensitive bundle of nerves at the height of her channel. She saw stars behind her tightly closed eyes. When his fingers touched her engorged clit, she came with such force she fought to remain conscious. He continued to move in and out as she floated back to earth, building another orgasm before the shocks of the first had stopped.

Sam needed to look into his crystal blue eyes to make sure he was really there, loving her. She had to know she wasn't dreaming, so she attempted to roll over once again. This time his grip on her body loosened. Sam felt immediate loss as his still hard cock slid from her overly sensitive pussy.

Her peaked nipples rubbed against the short hairs on his chest when they were finally face-to-face. Shivering at the delicious tremors rushing all over her body, Sam tried to gain a modicum of control. The longer her chest was in contact with his, the more tingles she felt. It was as if the brilliant dragon tattoo on his chest was moving right along with them.

Lance smiled a cock-sure smile, as if he had a secret he was deciding if he should share. Then he chuckled, "You cold, Doc? Why not let me warm you up a bit?"

Before she could process what he'd said, his lips were on hers. Her brain and body went into overload. It was a kiss of epic proportions that short circuited her brain. Samantha could only feel. His kiss of complete dominance robbed the room of all air. They were breathing for one another. A kiss so deep and completely sensual Sam knew she'd been marked for all time… there would never be another. No matter what happened in the next minute, hour, day, or lifetime, at least a part of her would always belong to him. In the next breath it was all teeth and tongue, so hot she felt as if he'd set a fire and was stoking it. His hands gripped her butt, melding her body to his as he moved onto his back.

Her legs slid to either side of his hips and his cock bumped her clit. She immediately sat up, leaning forward on her knees with her hands braced on his pecs, his erection poised at her opening. Looking deep into his eyes she saw a wealth of emotion, making the butterflies in her stomach flit and flutter. It was totally humbling to have a man like Lance look at her like she was his everything.

Excitement coursed through her veins at the heat he did nothing to hide. He wanted her, really wanted her. He looked like he could and would eat her alive. The thought of what his talented lips could make her feel had her lower body shifting until just the head of his penis sat inside her pussy. Shocked that she could be excited again after having just returned from Heaven, she slid farther down his shaft as his hands gripped her waist. Sweat dotted his upper lip and lines bracketed his eyes, letting her see the effort it took for him to allow her to take control and go slow.

When he was seated completely inside her, they both sighed. It was as if their joining was what they'd both been waiting for their whole lives. No matter how many times they made love, it would always be just like the first. She continued to look deep into his eyes, an invisible tether tying their souls together, binding them as no other.

Unable to deal with all the emotions welling up inside her, Sam began to move slowly up his cock. When he would have slipped from her, she began her downward stroke. He moved his hips in unison with hers, and on every down stroke of his length she rotated her hips. Their intricate dance pushed out all thoughts of anything but the incredible man she was astride. Their motions sped up, pushing her right to the brink of release. Sam could tell from the throbbing of his cock buried deep inside her he was too, but she needed something more, something she articulated with her sex-addled brain. He pushed her farther onto his erection just as she shifted forward.

Sam mewled at the contact. "Oh, oh, oh, yes…," she chanted, riding him harder and faster.

"Yes, *ta' mo chroi istigh*, yes! Take whatever you need. Come for me." The tone of his voice, breathless from their lovemaking, shot through her, pushing her.

Lance reached between their bodies and laid his thumb on her pulsing clit. Sam was sure he'd read her mind when he gently pushed, and she was screaming her release right along with him. Their orgasm went on and on as he worked himself in and out of her body, prolonging their ecstasy.

Sam collapsed against his chest, gasping to get a breath, and grinned against his sweat soaked chest as he wheezed right along with her. Never in her life had she thought she could bring a man as strong and vibrant as Lance to his knees, but from the sound of his breathing, she'd done just that. Her eyes closed as her breathing returned to normal, and with a smile on her face, she drifted to sleep.

CHAPTER TWENTY-ONE

Lance felt Sam completely relax. It wasn't long until he realized she'd fallen asleep with his half-erect cock still buried within her warm, wet pussy. Not wanting to sever their connection, he was content to lie with her draped across his body while he thought about the miraculous gift he'd been given by the Universe.

Dr. Samantha Malone was perfection. She was smart and intuitive. A more superb woman had never been born. The way she took command of every situation, so sure of herself, and unwilling to back down until every option had been exhausted, made him respect her as no other. But it was her heart and compassion that drew him in like a moth to a flame. The light of her pure, unselfish, giving soul shone like a beacon. He truly was the most blessed man to walk the earth. His dragon chuffed in agreement, basking in the afterglow of the incredible connection they were building with their mate.

Sam moved in her sleep, curling slightly to the side. His cock slipped from her and she moaned. Even in her sleep she missed the connection of their bodies as much as he did. Slowly sliding off his chest, his mate settled in against his side, breathing a sigh of relief that caused the dragon marking on his chest to ripple. The beast within loved the attention, and was definitely pushing Lance harder than ever to mark Samantha. The battle of wills that had been a constant since the day they laid eyes on Sam continued, until Royce spoke directly into his mind. *"Okay, lover boy. Time's up. Rayne's on his way and Jace and I have played as much Candyland as we can stand."*

"What's the matter? Did the little girl kick your ass, Grandpa?" Lance chuckled.

"I think the child cheats," the elder guardsman grumbled, and Lance was sure he heard an agreement from the younger Guardsman.

"You guys are such wimps." Lance laughed outright and was rewarded with two disgusted scoffs in return.

"Just wait until she plays with you, and then tell me that she isn't a shark", Royce retaliated. *"Now get your ass outta bed and get down here before the commander gets here, or I'll send the little one up to roust you."*

"We'll be down in a bit, Old Man. Just keep your shirt on," Lance said, appreciating all that his long-time friend was doing for him by keeping Sydney busy so he could spend time alone with Sam. *"Oh, and Royce?"*

"What now, pain in my ass?" Royce almost growled through their connection.

"Thanks for everything." Lance said with all sincerity, and then rushed on before Royce could recover from his unfamiliar show of affection. *"See ya in a few."*

He promptly cut their connection to concentrate on waking the beautiful woman who was to be his for all time.

After thirty minutes of kissing and cajoling, he finally had her out of bed and in the shower, but was sporting another impressive erection. He wanted to follow her into the bath and quench their desire. However, he was sure that would take hours, because once he started making love to his Samantha again, he had no plans of stopping until they were unable to walk. Unfortunately, their time was short. Making sure to not get sidetracked, he'd showered prior to waking her, giving him no excuse.

Damn, I still want her with every fiber of my being.

Dressed and sitting on the edge of the bed, he thought about the months since he'd rescued Sam and recognized her as his mate. Lance wondered if she had any idea how much she'd come to mean to him, or how hard he would work to give her the life she deserved. It was going to be a battle keeping her out of harm's way until Andrew and 'The Auctioneer' were caught, but if he had the last few days to do over again, there wasn't one damn thing he'd change. It had been foolish to think he could resist her. Every time he looked into her eyes he saw their future. For the first time in a very long time, Lance looked forward to living a thousand years. There was no doubt he could do anything with Sam at his side. It was time he laid all his cards on the table.

Royce had been right when he said she was no dummy. His mate was going to have a lot of questions, and the more of his Force she met, the more questions there would be. With Rayne on the way and a fight sure to happen, Lance knew there wouldn't be time to explain until he returned. He hoped for everyone's discretion.

One thing was for sure, Grace had already filled Kyndel in on everything. Devon and the old man's inability to keep their mouths shut made sure everyone knew Sam was his mate and didn't know anything about dragons…or the men who turned into them. She was sure to be pissed that he'd kept secrets. Of course, that was if she didn't call the men in the white jackets to lock him in a padded room before he could get it all out.

The bathroom door opened. As the steam cleared, his brain turned to mush. Standing in the doorway was his mate, dripping wet from the shower and relaxed from their lovemaking. Her long curly mane was wet, making it appear darker and causing the curls to hang long and loose. Samantha had a towel wrapped around her curves, but thankfully she was tall, so it just barely covered her breasts and fell right at the top of her thighs. He knew if she raised her arms he would see the short curly hairs covering her mound. His mouth watered, remembering her taste, and his cock jumped in his jeans, wanting to sink into the heaven that was his mate and forget about everyone and everything.

"Damn, Doc, you look…wow…you're just…you're everything good and right and wonderful. I changed my mind. I'm not sharing you with anybody."

He loved the way she blushed and gripped the towel a little tighter. Her pupils dilated and her lips opened just a bit. The alluring scent of jasmine and honeysuckle signaling her arousal assured him he affected her the same way she did him.

"Whatcha say we just stay up here for a while? I can have one of the guys bring us some food, you can lose the towel, and…."

She took two steps towards him and stopped. The way she smiled tied him up in knots. There was nothing he wouldn't do for this woman, all she had to do was ask. Then she spoke, and the smoky, low tone of her voice rolled over him. Lance wondered how he'd survived as long as he had without her.

"I thought you said we had to discuss a way to find Andrew? As much as I want to stay here with you—and trust me, I *really* want to stay here with you—" She winked, and for just a flash the dreamy look filling her dark eyes told him she was being completely honest. "I have to make sure Sydney is safe. But I'll make a deal with you. We get this Andrew guy taken care of and we can spend as much time together as you like."

The little wiggle of her eyebrows at the end of her proposed compromise made him laugh out loud. He stood and closed the distance between them, unable to stay away from her any longer. His arm automatically went around her waist, while the thumb and forefinger of his other hand gently lifted her perfect chin. Looking deep into her dark brown eyes, he was lost.

"Do you know how great you are? That just seeing you, even when you don't see me, makes all the worries of the day just float away? I have come awake every morning since I met you, wanting to see you, making sure I could at least catch a glimpse so that my day would be complete. To have you here in my arms is a dream come true." She tried to lower her eyes but he held her chin firm. "Please don't look away. I know I'm not the most romantic guy and I tend to joke instead of talk about anything close to my feelings. But know this Doc…I think you're amazing, and I pray you give this thing between us a chance."

He hoped he was being direct enough to let her know he had no intention of ever letting her go, while being vague enough to keep her from running away from him. Never had he imagined he would feel like he did about

Sam. Every time the subject of love or mates had come up in the past, Lance was always the first to say there was no such thing as love or that it would never happen to him.

Sure, he'd heard all the stories about "the one the Universe made" for each dragon shifter, but decided at a very young age to make sure that shit did *not* happen to him. He had been so wrong. Every sappy little thing all the Elders had told him was true. The sun, moon, and stars rose and set in Samantha, and he would do everything in his considerable power to keep her right where she was…in his arms.

"Lance—"

That's all Sam got out before Rayne's voice sounded in his head. *"We're here, you crazy pain in the ass. I hear there's someone we need to meet and a fucking traitor to catch once and for all. So haul your ass down here."*

"Be right there, your highness," Lance laughed, realizing he'd missed his commander and friend. This being in love shit really was making him a sentimental bastard.

"Yeah, you better be or I'm sending Kyndel and Grace up to get you." He could hear the smile in his friend's voice.

"See ya in a minute."

Lance's focus returned to Sam, but now her brows were furrowed, a frown gracing her lip, and her body stiff. When she spoke he could hear her anger, but also that she was hurt by his inattention. "Were you just ignoring me?"

He dropped his hand from her chin as she used both hands to push away from him. Doing the only thing he could think of, he pulled her close, locking her hands between them, and slammed his mouth to hers. He slid the tip of his tongue along the seam of her lips, begging for entrance. She did her damnedest to keep them closed.

Never one to give up, Lance decided to try nipping and tasting in an effort to soften her up. There was absolutely no time to explain that he was in no way ignoring her, but actually talking to his commander in his mind. Yeah, that would go over like a fart in church and have her ordering a straight-jacket in XXL. So he distracted her until the time was right to share all his secrets.

Lance left no part of her scrumptious lips untouched. There was no way he would ever get enough of the woman he held in his arms. Helpless to do anything but continue kissing her, he moved along her jaw, only stopping to whisper, "Damn, Doc, you taste amazing," before working his way down her neck.

It was only when her head fell backward, allowing him greater access, that he knew the tension was over, at least for the moment. When she grabbed the front of his shirt and her well-manicured nails bit into his chest, he thought about throwing caution to the wind and taking her back to bed. But he didn't want his mate to meet a pissed off Rayne MacLendon, so he summoned his incredible restraint and pulled his lips from her neck.

Taking her hands from his shirt and putting them back on the knot that kept her towel from hitting the floor, Lance placed his hands on her shoulders and took one step back. He knew the only way they were going to make it out of the room in the next twenty-four to forty-eight hours was if he limited his contact to her fabulous curves.

Sam finally opened her eyes and the sleepy, lustful look she gave him threatened his resolve. His woman packed a powerful punch. She was the ultimate temptation in a very sexy package. There was just no other way to think of her.

Clearing his throat, Lance hoped he sounded like he had his shit together when he spoke. "Doc, there's another of my brothers downstairs, and he's ready to get the plan for tonight underway. There's nothing I want more than to strip that towel off your body and kiss every damn inch, but I like my ass where it is, so that'll have to wait." He would've laughed out loud at the look of disappointment in her eyes if his cock wasn't so hard he was sure he could pound nails with it. "Now, get your pretty little ass dressed and I'll be sitting over by the door." He wiggled his eyebrows for effect. "Enjoying the view."

She grabbed his hand as he turned to head to his seat. "On one condition."

"And that is?"

"We talk as soon as we're done with whatever planning y'all are doing to catch this guy. I have more questions than answers, and you have to promise not to kiss me to shut me up."

He barked out a laugh that he was sure they heard even through the soundproofing. "Yes, *mo chroi'*, I'll answer all your questions, but I make no promises about the kissing."

"Yeah, we'll see about that, tough guy," she said in a sassy voice that made the tiny bit of blood powering his brain make a beeline for his cock.

Lance watched the hypnotic sway of her curvy hips as she headed for the bathroom, grabbing the clothes Grace had left outside the door while they had been otherwise occupied. All he could think was that Samantha Malone was the best thing in the world, and she was all his

CHAPTER TWENTY-TWO

After four hours spent listening to six of the biggest, most alpha men she'd seen in her entire life bicker about the best strategy for almost everything, Sam needed a break. Sydney had offered a bit of a distraction, but these men were a force unto themselves. There was no way the child could compete.

Sam met the dark-haired man with striking violet eyes, his gorgeous red-headed wife, and their absolutely adorable son before she even stepped off the last step on her way to find coffee. It was obvious Rayne was the leader of group. She recognized military training in the way they discussed their plans. Not for the first time, she wondered why they were handling this Andrew asshole and not bringing in the cops. Lance told her the kidnapper had been one of his brothers before he'd done something awful and was basically disowned. She just added the Andrew situation to the list of questions she already had for Lance.

Right before she was sure she would go insane from testosterone overload, Grace and Kyndel returned from their trip to the grocery store. Simply having other females who were taller than four feet made things easier. It wasn't that she'd truly suffered. Lance had been incredibly attentive the entire time, making sure she was comfortable, asking if there was anything he could get her. He even stole kisses when he thought his brothers weren't looking.

There was never a time when she didn't feel him either looking at her or thinking about her. Sam wasn't sure how she knew what he was thinking, but there it was, just another weird occurrence since Lance had appeared in her world. She laughed at the looks the other guys gave him. Apparently he didn't bring many women around. That simple fact made her way happier than it should've.

When she wasn't listening to the men, she and Sydney were playing Candyland and Chutes and Ladders. The little girl was such a doll and so incredibly intelligent…a real joy to be around, and quite the game player.

The ladies walked in carrying bags and the conversation at the kitchen table ceased. Everyone headed out to bring in the supplies. Sam could only imagine how much food it took to keep the huge men fed. They were like the front line of a football team, and that was without Royce. He was a mountain all by himself.

Sighing at the looks of complete adoration Rayne and Aidan gave their wives, she smiled at the welcome kisses they received from their men. It curled her toes from across the room, reminding her of the kisses she and Lance had shared not so very long ago. Stepping up to the door leading to the garage, Sam came face to face with the object of her fantasies. The twinkle in his eye and shit-eating grin on his face told her he had a least some idea of what she was thinking.

Before she could move out of the way, he shifted the groceries he held to the side and grabbed her around the waist, and his lips landed on hers. Sam was helpless to do anything but kiss him back. Their kiss was hot, entirely too quick, and completely scrambled her brain. When he set her back on her feet, she counted to three before she could catch her breath and get out of the way of the others.

Devon smiled as he passed by with a knowing look in his light grey eyes. Sam blushed as she walked towards the SUV, still loaded with food. Kyndel met her, chuckling. "Guess I should've told you that our guys are seriously into PDA."

Feeling the embarrassment fade away, Sam laughed right along with her. "Yes, I really need to talk to Lance. He picks the most inopportune times to manhandle me."

No sooner were the words out of her mouth than she heard laughter from every direction. Within seconds, everyone in the house joined them in the garage and loved her joke. It was so cool, she laughed right along with them. Royce touched her shoulder. Sam was once again amazed at the warmth she saw in the huge man's eyes.

"If you can figure out how to make that pain in the ass behave, we'll all be forever in your debt."

She searched out the face of the man who'd started the whole damn thing, only to find him looking at her like she was the only person in the room, maybe even the world. Caught by his gaze, Sam didn't even realize he was moving until he stood right in front of her. His hands closed on her shoulders, and even through her shirt, the electricity of his touch shot through her body, making her ache to feel him everywhere.

Lance's smile was so sweet and the little dimple in his cheek that seemed to appear just to torment her made Sam wish they were alone. When he pulled her so close only a breath would fit between their bodies, she was helpless to do anything but follow his lead. Her body leaned forward of its own volition. She had no doubt she would've kissed him no matter who was looking, but at just that moment, Aaron did his best impression of Freddy Mercury.

"And another one's gone, and another one's gone, another one bites the dust."

The entire room erupted in laughter so loud she was glad the nearest neighbor was almost a mile away. The tender moment was thankfully gone before she'd completely humiliated herself.

Several hours later, after all the groceries were put away and the biggest dinner she'd ever seen had been devoured, the men resumed their talks in the kitchen while Sam, along with Grace, Kyndel, and the kids, were in the living room watching *Cars*. Sydney was sitting between Samantha and the little boy, explaining the movie to anyone who would listen like she was the newest edition to Siskel and Ebert. Lost in her thoughts, Sam jumped when the child's hand landed on her leg.

"Dr. Sam, Miss Grace is talking to you."

Sam smiled at the elegant brunette, trying not to laugh. "Sorry about that, I was at least a million miles away."

"No problem, I was just letting you know I filed the paperwork to change Sydney's guardianship to you. The police reports and hospital employee accounts definitely support that she's not safe there. Even Dr. Monoghan agreed Sydney needs to be monitored by a healthcare professional for at least a few more days to make sure her mysterious fever doesn't return."

Grace spoke with such a professional air there was no doubting she was an attorney, but with a wealth of feelings in her words. It was obvious she'd fallen under Sydney's spell, just like everyone who'd met the little girl.

"Do you think the judge will go along with your request?" Sam asked, not really caring what the paperwork said as long as Sydney was safe and Sam could see her. It was hard for Sam to admit, after spending so much of her life alone, that both Sydney and Lance had come to mean so much to her so quickly. Sam simply could not imagine her life without them.

All her plans and goals for the future were still running through her mind, but now they were evolving, going places she'd never imagined. It was like Samantha had no control over the path she would take. A power so much bigger than anything she'd ever known was directing every decision and action, and Sam was just along for the ride.

One thing was certain…this unseen force was doing its level best to tell her that the two very persistent, blue-eyed people who'd burst through every one of her defenses were going to be very present in her future, and there wasn't a damn thing she could do about it. Never one to take anything lying down, she tried to get pissed about all these changes to her well laid plan, but the anger never came.

She realized Grace was talking while she had taken another little trip to la-la land, and refocused to hear what the attorney had to say.

"Yes, I believe he will. He's very concerned with child welfare and has been on the bench forever. Not to mention, he's a personal friend of my father. He knows me well enough to know the request is justified. I expect to have the signed paperwork back in just a few days."

"Your father's an attorney, too?"

"He was when I was very young, but gave it up for politics. He's been with the Embassy for years now, and my mother's involved in so many humanitarian efforts it's hard to keep track. They travel at least three hundred and sixty days of every year. They haven't even met my husband except through Skype."

Sam watched as Grace closed her eyes and took a deep breath before continuing. "Sorry about that. Guess old wounds run deep." Grace gave a half smile and looked to the charming red-head who'd been looking on with concern.

When Grace spoke again it was with affection in her voice. "Had it not been for Kyndel and her granny, I would've ended up just another spoiled socialite wasting her life."

Before any of them could respond, Aidan's voice came booming from the kitchen. "Thank the Heavens for Kyndel and her granny!"

The men all laughed, and the look that came to Grace's face could only be described as true love. In the next instant, Rayne was kneeling beside Kyndel, whispering and making his wife smile as well. Sam wondered how she'd missed him coming into the room, but before she could think about it any further, she was being lifted over the back of the couch and into the arms of the man who had turned her world upside down. Sydney giggled and Lance ruffled the little girl's curls.

He turned back to her and with that one look, it was as if she was falling into him. She was floating towards a future that would be filled with love, warmth, and incredible happiness. He'd snuck in, and was now as much a part of her as the blood flowing through her veins. The depth of emotion in his eyes said all that and more was reciprocated. For the first time since she'd lost her family, Sam actually felt love coming from another person. Any other time, she would've done everything possible to throw up all her defenses and keep him at arms' length, but none of the old fears came. Quite the opposite…she felt comforted. It was a completely new sensation, one she could really get used to.

"We have a couple of hours before heading out, Doc. Got any ideas what we can do while we wait?" He wiggled his eyebrows. She couldn't stop the laugh that bubbled out.

"Well, there's a certain little girl who needs a bath and her pj's."

His smiled turned more sweet than salacious as they both laughed when Sydney moaned. "Oh man, Dr. Sam. Can't I play with Baby Jay just a little while longer?"

Kyndel saved the day, already one of the best moms Sam had ever seen. "Jay has to have his bath and jammies too, Sydney. But maybe, if you're a good girl and do what Dr. Sam said without a fuss, you can come and have a bedtime story with us. Sound good, kiddo?"

"Can I? Can I, Dr. Sam?" Sydney flew off the couch and danced around.

Lance let Sam slide down his body. She had to work really hard to keep her focus on the child and not on his amazing body, or his obvious happiness at having her in his arms. Sam turned towards the still bouncing and twirling little girl and extended her hand. "Of course, sweetheart."

Sydney grabbed her hand, pulling Samantha towards the stairs and yelling over her shoulder. "See ya when we're done, Lance. Hurry, Baby Jay, so we can have a story. Night, everyone else." And then she blew kisses as they ascended the stairs.

Everyone downstairs laughed and said their goodnights. They may not all be blood, but they were definitely a family. Sam was happy to have them for however long they were a part of her life. She'd learned early in life that nothing was forever, but in the deep recesses of her mind, she really wished this could be.

CHAPTER TWENTY-THREE

Lance watched as the door to their bathroom opened and Sydney ran towards him, a cloud of steam in her wake. She jumped on the bed and pounced on his chest, hugging him around the neck for all she was worth.

"Can you come too, Lance? I want you to come to Baby Jay's room with us. Please?"

There was no way he could say no to that sweet little face. Then he looked up. Sam was walking towards the bed, and his mind went blank. The steam from Sydney's bath had made her hair even curlier, and her cheeks were flushed from the heat. She looked even younger, and definitely more desirable. Lance was a goner.

If Syd hadn't been in the room, he would've already had Sam against the wall, naked and panting. He might've already been alive one hundred and twelve years, but real living hadn't started until the day Samantha Malone entered his life. He was the idiot Royce had called him for all those years to have ever imagined being anywhere but with her.

With Samantha by his side, Lance was a better person. She was his strength. Hell, she was his everything. There was no way Andrew, 'The Auctioneer', or any other idiot who sought to hurt them would get anywhere near his mate. She was his. He would fight to his dying breath to keep her happy and healthy. Oh yeah…and naked as much as possible, but that came later.

"So are you coming with us, Lance?" Sydney impatiently asked again.

"Absolutely, Syd." He set her on the floor and stood beside her. "Let's hit it, kiddo."

She giggled and grabbed his hand. "You called me Syd. I like it."

"Well, then I'll call you Syd all the time."

She laughed, grabbing Sam's hand too. "Let's go, you guys. Baby Jay's waiting for me. I just know it."

They all chuckled and headed into the hallway.

Wanting to make sure Rayne and Kyndel were ready for the intrusion, Lance called directly into Rayne's mind, knowing Kyndel could hear him, too. Her mind speaking skills were becoming damn near as good as any of theirs, and it hadn't even been two years since she and Rayne had mated.

"Hey, bro, we're on the way. Is the coast clear?"

"Get your ass over here. I love my son, but I really want some alone time with his mom before we head out."

"I hear ya, man." Lance chuckled. *"Be there in a sec."*

Sydney pulled on his hand. When he looked down, she crooked her finger in a "come here" move. With his face close to hers, she put her chubby little hands on his face and her mouth to his ear. What she whispered had him almost falling on his ass. "You were talking to Mr. Rayne in your head just now, weren't you?"

He pulled back and looked into her angelic face. For the first time since meeting her, Lance saw a knowledge in her bright blue eyes so much older than her years. He placed his lips to her ear and answered. "Yes, darlin'. Can we talk more about this when it's just you and me?"

She whispered back and he held back his laughter at the seriousness of her tone. "Yep. I don't think Dr. Sam knows. She might freak out, huh?"

"Yeah, she might."

"Okay," she nodded her head and turned, running the last few steps to Jay's room.

Sam came up to his side and he grabbed her hand. Just as he raised his other hand to knock on the door, she spoke. "What was that back there about?"

Schooling his expression, he answered as he knocked. "Now Dr. Malone, would you want me to betray Syd's confidence?" Lance winked, hoping his humor would distract her. Thankfully, Kyndel opened the door. Any other conversation was drowned out as Sydney yelled "Hello" to everyone and began asking Jay what story he wanted to hear.

One hour and four stories later Jay was crashed, and Sydney could barely keep her eyes open. Lance had spent a large portion of story time wondering exactly how the little girl he'd only known for little more than a day was able to tap into their mind speak. Somehow, he didn't think she knew what they were saying, just that they were talking directly into each other's minds.

Grace could do the same thing as a side effect of her Spidey senses, and he wondered if that was the case with Syd…but she hadn't mentioned any special talents. He would definitely have to talk to the old man after their excursion and see what he might know about it, but for now it was bedtime. Scooping Sydney off the loveseat, he said "Night" to all as he, Sam, and the sweet bundle in his arms headed to the child's room.

The little sweetheart barely got through her prayers without yawning, and was asleep as soon as her head hit the pillow. The complete adoration he saw in Sam's eyes was just one of the hundreds of things he'd come to love about her. Lance paused, waiting for the internal groan at his continued sappiness, but it didn't come…instead, the feeling that all the pieces of his life were finally in order filled him. He wondered how many years of teasing he would have to take from his brethren. Then he smiled, because for the first time, it really didn't matter. Sam was worth all the shit he would take from them.

Looking back at the one the Universe had made for him, he found Samantha grinning like a little girl with a secret. She turned and headed for the door, and he was helpless to do anything but follow. As soon as the door closed, she started to laugh. He pulled her to him, giving her the most intimidating look he could muster, which made her laugh even harder. Lifting her feet off the ground, Lance walked towards their room.

She squealed and he asked, "What exactly is so funny, Doc?"

"Put me down and I'll tell you."

"Tell me and I'll put you down," he countered, and laughed out loud as she glared at him.

"All right, you win." She pretended to be upset.

He set her feet on the floor, sure to keep her close. "Now, tell me what's so funny?"

Sam bit her bottom lip and Lance almost forgot what he'd asked. All he wanted to do was nibble on her luscious mouth himself. Sam spoke, restoring a bit of his focus. "You were looking at Sydney with such tenderness, then in the blink of an eye, your look changed to one of almost confusion, and then relief. It just tickled me to watch all the thoughts and emotions cross your face."

"Tickled you, huh?" And with that, he opened the door and walked her backwards, thinking of all the ways he would like to tickle her.

"Don't get too cozy in there, Romeo," Royce yelled on his way by. "You've got less than thirty minutes before Rayne wants us downstairs and ready to go."

"Whatever, Old Man. You worry about your shit…I got this covered."

"Yeah, right, whatever you say, Pain in the Ass." Lance heard Royce chuckle and knew there was more to come. "Feel free to kick his ass, Sam. Holler if you need any help."

"Get lost, Gramps," Lance yelled into the hall, only to hear his long time friend's cackle in return. Had Sam not been in his arms, he would've kept their banter going, but with only thirty minutes to enjoy his mate, there was no way in hell he was going to waste it on Royce.

Lance had originally planned to tickle Sam into submission. That had all changed. His every thought now revolved around kissing as much of her body as he could in the time he had remaining.

It a rough job…but one I take seriously.

CHAPTER TWENTY-FOUR

Finally luck had been on his side, and when it counted the most. As soon as the idiot, Lance, had driven away and the werepanthers were busy cleaning up the mess from the ritual, Andrew had been able to truly search for Kyra. Thankfully, the little witch made a fatal mistake and ventured out in the light of day, thinking she was safe.

She'd led him right to the front door of her hiding place. Andrew stood staring for the longest time, not believing something really had worked in his favor. Then the sound of crashing and rather creative cursing came from inside the tiny, dilapidated structure. He guessed it could have been called a cabin several hundred years ago, but all he saw was rotten wood held together by the vines that had grown in and around every available hole and crevice.

It reminded Andrew of the stories his mother and brothers used to read to him about fairies when he was a very young *drake*. As soon as the thought crossed his mind, he shut it down. Memories like that were for losers. His parents were dead and his brothers were assholes. He hated the fact that since his dragon senses had returned, so had the memories he'd worked diligently for years to lock away. If there was time, he decided he would ask Kyra for a spell or potion to make his past permanently disappear.

The look on her face when she opened the door to find him standing there had been priceless. Andrew had to give her credit for her moxie. She hadn't tried to run. Didn't even scream. She only hung her head and muttered, "Oh, shit!"

He pushed her back into her hidey hole, secured the door, and proceeded to tell her what he needed. Of course, she'd been resistant. Kyra could cuss like a drunk and had a right hook like a prize fighter. It took several hours for the mark on his forehead, where a particularly large piece of quartz had nicked him, to heal. In any other circumstance, he would have laughed until he cried at some of the names she called him, but he couldn't take the chance she would think he had gone soft. "Son of a fuckin' fairy's fat-assed cousin" had a particularly memorable ring.

After his constant reassurances that he wasn't going to harm her didn't work, he tied her to a chair to lower her resistance, and through gritted teeth (hers), they reached a compromise. She would make the amulets he needed and allow herself to be detained until after he had the Dragon Guard subdued. After that, he would let her go on her merry way with the promise never to contact her again. There was no way in hell the last part was going to happen, but she didn't need to know that. Andrew did whatever it took to get her to wield her special brand of magic.

Kyra bitched and moaned the entire time they worked, reminding him she was a white witch and her magic was not to be used to hurt others. Andrew did what he did best…he lied. Knowing she doubted every word he uttered, Andrew poured on his long forgotten charm along with the persuasive manner he'd mastered over the years until she finally given in. Although he was sure she did whatever it took to get rid of him, that didn't matter, he'd get what he wanted.

Helping with the ingredients gave him a look into the construction of her talismans, even though their true power came from the witch herself. Kyra worked with complete confidence and a true love of her craft. Andrew opened his long unused senses, still clouded with black magic, and focused on the tiny violet-eyed sorceress.

It only took a few moments and he had confirmation of what he'd suspected since meeting Kyra. She was an intended mate of a Dragon Guardsman. Had he not muddied his senses with tainted magic for so many years, he would be able to pinpoint which one, but as it was, just the knowledge she'd been created for one of the men who'd left him for dead was enough.

Trying to think of all the ways he could use the newfound knowledge to his benefit, and coming up with nothing, Andrew moved on to what was important…his vengeance. They would all be dead by his hand. Kyra would be his to use as he saw fit, without their interference.

As he sat perched in a particularly large crevice with a spectacular vantage point, Andrew waited for the Force he'd once belonged to and their allies to arrive. He kept trying to feel bad for leaving Kyra chained in her hideout while he, John, and the others tainted her magic by setting traps throughout the woods, but he couldn't allow her to see. He was certain she would do everything in her considerable power to warn the useless Dragon Guard, and there was absolutely no way he would let that happen.

Thinking of all the ways he was finally going to have all he'd worked for since his escape, Andrew planned the next steps in his grand scheme. It monopolized his every thought…making everyone responsible for the hardships he'd endured pay. When he was done, John may be allowed to live, at least for a little while. The rogue wizard was instrumental in building their group to over forty members in a very short time, and he was always available. His attention to detail had been invaluable when planning the impromptu attack. The rogue wizard had absolutely no conscience, which proved essential. The important feather in John's cap was that he had intimate knowledge of Master Eaton's methods, and was willing to act as spy and go-between. All things to be considered after the Guardsmen were sent to the Heavens.

Andrew thought back over his plan one more time, and pictured where all the traps were placed, along with the "special surprises" he had left. Waiting sucked, but it would all be worth it. John sat down beside him, looking around as if he was also running through their plans. When the rogue wizard spoke, it was in hushed tones.

"Everything is set and ready to go. Everyone is in position. I can't think of anything we missed. How are you feeling, sir?"

He hated when John spoke like they were spies in some stupid James Bond movie, but Andrew knew it was left over from the many years he'd spent serving Master Eaton. The wizard leader had an over exaggerated sense of importance, and liked to play the part of leader more than actually doing any of the work.

Andrew answered, still looking out over the woods behind Dr. Malone's home. "I'll let you know when the Dragon Guardsmen are bleeding out at our feet."

The rogue wizard hummed his agreement. "You're going to accomplish what no one else could do…to destroy the Force of the Golden Fire Clan. The stories of their Guardsmen are legendary. The wizards and hunters have sought to exterminate them for centuries. You'll be the most feared and sought after wizard in the country."

Hearing the awe in John's voice reinforced his decision to let the man live while he was still useful. Sooner or later, the rogue would have to be eliminated, because no one could ever know Andrew was one of the mighty dragon kin. Not until all had been made to pay, and he was ready to return to the clan that had betrayed him and destroy them as well.

Forgetting the rogue wizard was waiting for his reply until he cleared his throat, Andrew merely grunted in John's direction. Andrew wanted to be feared. It would make recruiting other wizards, and those with less than respectable personalities, much easier. When all was said and done, it was going to take an army to spread his vengeance, and an army was what he would have.

Smiling at the sounds of approaching vehicles, anticipating the chaos he was about to cause, Andrew's heart raced. Those assholes had absolutely no idea what was waiting for them. All the better.

John tensed next to him. Just a few more minutes and Andrew would finally feel the relief that came from exacting revenge on those who deserved it. His brothers would die by his hand. How could this night get any better?

CHAPTER TWENTY-FIVE

Sam wondered how many more times she could pace the same circle before she lost her mind or wore a path in Grace's expensive carpet. Sydney and Jay were playing their hundredth game of stack the blocks and knock them down. Watching how well the little girl played with the baby made her both happy and sad. Sydney was an incredible child. Sam had no doubt she would grow up to do amazing things, but wondered if everything she'd already suffered was too much.

Sydney would've made a wonderful big sister. Hopefully that could still happen for her. When Sam thought of the little darling not being a part of her life, it made the young doctor even sadder. Not wanting to spend the entire week they'd given her off from the hospital brooding and worrying, she tried to think of other, happier subjects. Of course, her sexy obsession popped into her mind, creating a delicious distraction from her worries.

Remembering the way he'd kissed her until she thought she might lose her sanity, and his promise to come back safely after kicking Andrew's ass, made Sam sigh. Lance had almost lost his mind when she'd suggested her going along with them. He'd even enlisted the help of his brothers to convince her otherwise.

Each of them gave her countless reasons why she and the other women needed to stay put. They were right, and she knew it, but Sam had never been someone who let others fight her battles. Lance and Royce had explained that the fight with their lost brother was a battle that had been going on long before she'd entered the picture. All of it pissed her off and added to her need to pace and fret.

Looking at her watch, she realized they'd been gone almost eight hours. It was still early in the morning. The smell of Sydney's waffles cooking brought Grace, Kyndel, and Jay to the kitchen. Together, they had all eaten and talked until just a few moments ago.

Heading down the hall opposite the living room, Sam found a workout room. Deciding a few minutes on the stationary bike might just work off some of her excess energy while the kids played, she walked through the door. Exercise had never been something she liked. Actually, she avoided it at all costs, but there had to be something to do while the minutes dragged on. Pedaling to the tunes of Florida Georgia Line blaring from her earbuds, Sam was so lost in her pretend journey she almost fell off the bike when Grace touched her shoulder.

"Oh shit. I'm so sorry, Sam. I thought you saw us come in. You okay?" The pretty brunette smiled.

Sam could tell it was taking all of Grace's control not to laugh, so the young doctor laughed to ease the tension. Everyone, even the kids, followed suit.

"No problem. I was lost in thought."

"I guess so. You looked right at us when we came in," Kyndel commented as she sat Jay in the corner surrounded by huge rectangular cushions. Sydney climbed over one of the hedge-like furnishings and started building with the Legos while the baby watched with rapt attention.

The ladies removed their jackets to show tank tops and yoga pants just like the ones Grace had loaned Sam. They sat facing each other and began stretching. "We're gonna do some yoga if you'd like to join." Grace exhaled as she leaned forward for the third time.

"Yeah, we're not really into exercise, but decided if we did it together it might not be so bad," Kyndel added, rolling her eyes.

"Sure," Sam shrugged. "It's got to be better than this stupid bike. My fat butt is aching from the seat." She climbed down and sat between the girls, starting to stretch with them.

When she raised her head again both Grace and Kyndel were smiling knowing smiles in her direction. "All right you two, what's going on?"

"Nothing," they said in unison, chuckling.

It was Grace who spoke first. "Really, it's nothing. We're just glad Lance has someone, and that you fit in with all our craziness."

"Oh," was the only thing Sam could think to say. The two women continued to stare at her, so she figured she might as well be honest. It had worked for all her years so far.

"Well, whatever it is between us is pretty new. Who knows how long it'll last? I'll admit, he *is* something else, but I have no idea if he's looking for a relationship or just a fling. Not to mention, I have about a year of my residency left. After that I might be offered a position where I am…if not, I'll have to find something permanent."

Where in the hell did all that come from? Over share, much?

Kyndel and Grace nodded as she spoke, then gave each other a quick, conspiring look. They knew something she didn't. Sam didn't know them well enough to be blunt, but she really wanted to know what was going on. Bending at the waist, Sam wondered if she should pursue the conversation. After all, Kyndel did say they were all very open about almost everything.

The fact remained they were such an incredibly close-knit group that they knew things she didn't about Lance. If the roles were reversed, Sam knew she would be pissed if he talked about her and whatever relationship they may or may not have without her present. So she kept her mouth shut and stretched until Kyndel got up and started the DVD.

While they were bending, stretching, and breathing, she noticed that every so often one or both of the ladies would get a faraway look in their eyes. Sometimes they would nod or shake their heads. It seemed weird, but before Sam could think about it any longer their exercise got much more intense. Her focus switched to keeping her balance and breathing instead of looking around.

I really am out of shape. Oxygen, anyone?

Then she thought about Lance and how he'd kissed and touched her everywhere. Image after image of his face in all of its masculine glory played in her mind. His crystal blue eyes twinkling when he was joking, and almost glowing when the look turned more heated. Each expression was more intense than the other. Every image reinforced what he'd told her…he wanted to be with her.

"Earth to Sam," Kyndel called. Both women chuckled as Sam jumped for the second time since they'd entered the room.

"Were you on Planet Lance just then?" Grace laughed.

Sam felt her cheeks heat and laughed. "I sure was."

"Don't be embarrassed on our account." Kyndel motioned from herself to Grace. "We both understand completely. Been there, done that. Rayne monopolizes every spare minute I have, even if he isn't in the same room." The dreamy look returned to Kyndel's eyes as she raised her arms overhead and stretched.

When Kyndel turned her head to the right, Sam saw a flame shaped mark at the slope between her neck and shoulder. It reminded her of a tattoo, but not really as dark or defined as any she'd seen. It didn't look like a birthmark either. Sam tried to get a better look, but didn't want her new friends to think she was a stalker, or worse yet, a nut job, so she continued to stretch.

Unable to keep her curiosity at bay any longer, she asked, "When do you think the guys'll be back?"

Again Grace and Kyndel looked at one another, and she was sure some unspoken communication passed between them. Their look held too much weight to be just a look. It was Grace who spoke first.

"No clue, but Aidan promised to call as soon as he could."

For the first time since meeting her, Grace's eyes didn't quite meet hers, a sure sign they weren't telling her something. Before Sam could think of a way to ask without being rude, Sydney called her name and Jay yelled.

All three women turned in unison to see Sydney trying to protect the structure she'd built with outstretched arms while she carefully hunched over it. The Legos stood just slightly taller than the baby. He looked like a miniature Godzilla, hell bent on destroying Tokyo, as he tried to maneuver around Sydney while holding onto the corner of his walker. Sam couldn't keep from laughing, and was glad to hear the others found it as funny as she did.

Grace reached the children first, grabbed Jay before he could destroy Sydney's creation, and swung him in the air before securing him to her hip. She kissed the top of his head and lovingly scolded, "Jay, my dear, you can't tear down Sydney's building. She worked really hard on it. It's fantastic."

She was rewarded with an "Uh huh" from the beaming Sydney and a long string of baby talk from Jay. Grace passed by Sam as she carried Jay to his mother. It was then that Sam noticed a mark similar to Kyndel's on the attorney's neck. Hers was a little larger and looked like a flame with wings, but was located in exactly the same spot as her friend's. It was also the same "not quite tattoo definitely not a birthmark" brand.

Her brows furrowed as she wondered why both women would have comparable marks in the same spots on their necks. Earlier, they'd talked about being in college together, making Sam wonder if maybe it was a sorority thing. If Lance kept her around long enough, she would have to work up the courage to ask, because it would drive her nuts until she knew their origin.

Finally, feeling like she might actually be able to sit still and read or watch TV, Sam called to Sydney, "Hey girlie, get your toys picked up. Let's go have a rest before lunch."

"Awww, man, do we have to?" Sydney complained.

Before she could answer, Kyndel spoke up. "Jay has to go down for a nap, pretty girl. So you go rest with Dr. Sam, and we'll all meet you in the kitchen when he wakes up; cool?"

Sydney smiled. "Sure, Miss Kyndel. See ya later, Baby Jay." Sydney waved as she made her way towards Sam, but stopped right in front of Grace first. "You gonna have lunch with us too, Miss Grace?"

"I sure am, Sydney, but first I have to take a shower." She pinched her nose between her thumb and forefinger, indicating she really needed one after their workout. Everyone laughed, and Sam realized how much happier she'd been since meeting Lance's extended family.

Sydney skipped over, grabbed Sam's hand, and started to pull her towards the door. "See you guys later," she hollered over her shoulder, obviously intent to get the resting part of their day out of the way. The little girl had just started running towards her room when what sounded like an explosion came from the first floor, followed by the shouting of male voices so loud Sam could barely hear her own thoughts.

Calling to the child, the doctor turned to see what the hell was happening. All she could make out were very loud, very angry male voices, all vying to be heard. Her foot touched the bottom step and it was as if a switch had been flipped. What had been deafening shouts and angry voices was all at once complete and utter silence, with all eyes trained on her. The look they gave her was one she'd seen at another time in her life, one she'd done everything in her power to never see again. She started shaking her head as Royce walked towards her, refusing to believe it was happening again.

CHAPTER TWENTY-SIX

It felt like they'd been combing the woods behind Sam's house for days when in all actuality, it'd been just a few hours. It was ironic how now that he had someone to get home to, the things he once thought were fun just seemed tedious.

There were signs Andrew had been there and that he'd acquired more people than the last time they met him. Déjà vu struck as Royce sent out a call that black SUVs were coming down the single-lane gravel road leading to their location. Devon gave them even more bad news, *"Guess what boys? I believe 'The Auctioneer' and his thugs are here."*

Rayne immediately barked new orders while Lance stayed hunkered down in the same spot he'd started in. It seemed like forever while they waited to see who was actually running the shit show for the evening. They all had first-hand knowledge of what happened when they went in clueless, so Rayne ordered them to wait. It was absolute torture. Lance saw the werepanthers prowling the treetops and envied the Big Cats; at least they got to move around.

He tried to keep his thoughts on what was happening all around him, but no matter how hard he tried, the beautiful woman that was to be his was all he could see. Sam was one of a kind, a true original that he had no doubt would make his life exponentially better just by being in it. Lance wanted to start that life right away. He had held back, worried, and tried to stay away, but when push came to shove, everything he had ever been taught was true…Fate would not be denied. They were meant to be together, and no crazy ass traitor or human criminal trying to ruin the world was going to keep them apart. He'd come to terms with that, and would do whatever it took to help her see she was his mate forever and always.

The images of Sam's smile, her dazzling, dark brown eyes, and the way she responded to his touch flooded his mind as he waited, making him wonder if this shit would ever be over. The longer he thought of her, the more he could feel her through their growing mating bond. Lance grinned like a loon as he felt how happy and content she was. He didn't give a shit if any of his emotions were leaking through to his brethren. They could tease him all they wanted; he had Sam, and that was all that mattered.

Impatient to catch the little rat bastard and get back to his mate, he called out in the way of his kin to any who was listening. *"What the hell? Are we waiting for an engraved invitation?"*

"No, Pain in the Ass, we're trying to find Andrew, and whoever's with him," Royce growled.

"And we'll move when I say to move." Rayne stated in full commander mode.

"Yeah, yeah, yeah, I know, but this is fucking frustrating." "No, shit, Sherlock. You think you're the only one bored shitless and ready to catch the little asshole, and be done with all of this fucking waste of our time?" Aidan asked. Lance could feel his anger through their link.

"All right ladies, while y'all are having your bitch session, something's happening about halfway up the mountain. How 'bout we all pay attention, then we can handle our shit and get the hell outta Dodge?" Aaron said, trying to sound calm.

"I guess I'm not surprised he'd hide on higher ground after all the silver we found hidden everywhere on the ground. I can still feel magic in the air, but I'll be damned if I can find where it's coming from." Devon grumbled.

"I'm trying to get a bead on the humans, but they have the stench of black magic all over them. I can't be sure what I'm seeing is all there is." Royce mumbled, obviously thinking out loud. *"I'm almost positive at least five or six of the men with 'The Auctioneer' are actual wizards. The black magic is just too strong for them to be anything else."*

"And there are seriously dense spots of the noxious shit at the base of the mountain. None of the human criminals or those who came with them have made it that far. I have to think Andrew has some wizards with his nasty ass too." Devon confirmed what they were all thinking… Andrew and 'The Auctioneer' were not playing together in this sandbox.

Lance hoped Rayne and Royce had some kind of strategy planned to make this all work. If they left it up to him, Lance would run screaming, broadsword drawn, slicing any and all in his path to pieces. He was fucking sick and tired of all of it. It was time for it to be over. Andrew needed to be caught and taken to the Elders for the Tribunal, or killed dead on the spot. Both worked for him. 'The Auctioneer' needed to be caught, also, and made to rot in jail for the atrocities he'd inflicted on all those poor women. Secretly, Lance hoped for about five minutes alone with the stupid son of a bitch for the crap Sam had gone through because of his filth and greed.

Lance remembered the pockets of white magic he'd felt the night he'd flown over this very area. Figuring it was something he was going to have to share, he took a deep breath, and went for it. *"I was out here a few nights ago and felt pockets of really strong white magic. I was gonna come back and investigate, but shit came up. I'm thinking we need to find that witch; maybe she can help."*

"She?" Royce asked.

"Yeah, definitely a she. The magic was very feminine."

"Is it like what we can feel on the forest floor?" Aidan asked.

"Kind of, but don't you guys feel like there's something more added to what we can detect out here?" Lance knew he wasn't making much sense, but they'd all known him long enough to decipher his gibberish.

Thank the Heavens Aaron had his back, and jumped in before there were any questions Lance would rather not answer. *"Now that I focus on it, I see what you mean. I pretty much didn't bother with it before because it's white, but now I can tell there's something else mixed with it. Royce, you need to get your old senses over here and see what it is."*

"Okay dickhead, me and my old senses will get right over there," the oldest of their Force grumbled. *"Y'all losers would be lost without me."*

"All right, let's find out what's going on. Max and the other cats are going to work their way up the mountain, so we have a few minutes," Rayne stated, taking charge once again.

A few minutes seemed like several hours, but Aaron finally spoke. *"The old man hates to admit it, but Lance is right. The magic is female in origin, and hold onto to your hats, sports fans, it seems it's been contaminated with black magic that has a tinge of dragon in it. Sound like anyone we know?"*

"That fucking son of a bitch!" Aidan snarled. *"And why the hell are you so perky about this shit, Aar?"*

"Because, 'A', he's here, and we have a scent, one he can't fuck with. Lighten up a bit and think about it. We're gonna get his pansy ass tonight." Aaron answered. Lance could feel his confidence. It seemed to reenergize all of them.

"Glad to see you guys finally decided to show up." Rayne barked. *"Now let's spread out and find the stupid bastard, and any person stupid enough to follow him."*

In the slow, methodical formation they'd been using for over a hundred years, the MacLendon Force began creeping toward the base of the mountain with senses wide open to detect any movement or traps. Devon was watching 'The Auctioneer' and his men, who seemed to be content with lying in wait. The problem was none of the Guard knew what the criminals were waiting for. Lance guessed they wanted Andrew, but how would that fucking loser be of any use to a thug who kidnapped and sold young women? Deciding he really didn't give a shit as long as they rounded them all up, Lance continued his trek through the woods, listening to the information his brethren were sharing.

Reaching the opposite side of the mountain from Royce and Aaron's location, Lance started for the first path he saw. *"I'm heading up the middle path,"* he called to anyone who was listening.

"Get the fuck down...," was all Devon got out before all hell broke loose.

From the sheer pandemonium coming from where 'The Auctioneer' and his thugs were hiding, it appeared someone had prematurely fired a grenade launcher, causing a chain reaction of epic proportions. Clods of dirt and pieces of trees flew everywhere. Continued explosions were deafening, especially with his enhanced senses wide open.

Lance immediately shut down his heightened hearing, praying the ringing in his ears would stop sometime this millennium. Rayne directed them to continue their search for Andrew. The traitor had been there. They were all sure he still was, so until Andrew was tucked away in a cave somewhere in Outer Mongolia, or better yet minus his head, he would continue to be their main focus.

Andrew was dragon, and therefore knew too much to be allowed to continue his insane plan of vengeance. Lance watched as some of the werepanthers jumped from the trees, landing as men, and stalked the human criminals, preparing to stop the chaos. Sure their allies could handle the idiots, Lance focused on his side of the mountain while listening to the others report in.

Just a few hundred feet up, he began to sense rather than see movement on his left. Signaling to the others of his Force, Lance got as low to the ground as possible, looking for anywhere his six foot two inch frame could take cover. He had to get an estimate of how many combatants they needed to neutralize.

One bush in particular shook more and more as the blasts from below continued. He truly thought 'The Auctioneer' had a little better control of his minions than what they were witnessing. It would help get his ass put away for his crimes, and give them something to joke about later, but was completely uncharacteristic of what they already knew of the criminal.

Moving towards the shaking bush, Lance felt an especially dense pocket of white magic farther up the mountain. In a snap decision, he followed the trail, hoping to find the witch. He pictured the spot he was sure held many of Andrew's followers and sent it out to his brethren. The trail of white magic grew stronger with each step, reaffirming his decision to investigate.

If Andrew had found the magic practitioner, which Lance was sure he had, then it only stood to reason the traitor wouldn't leave her unguarded. And being the paranoid asshole he was, Andrew himself would be guarding her…or at least be close by. She was a powerful practitioner. Lance could tell from the way her magic leaked all over the mountainside from her anger. Power that the traitor would want.

If there was one thing Andrew wanted more than revenge, it was power. He'd always been jealous of anyone he couldn't beat, no matter if they were older or stronger or had more experience. The stupid son of a bitch had to be the center of attention, and would do whatever it took to get there. His recent resurrection and bid to the rule the world by any means necessary was no surprise. Stopping him was pretty much all that mattered to any of them.

Just above him, Lance could see the outline of what looked like an old tin roof covered in vines being held up with more of the same vegetation. He directed his senses and opened them wide. The witch was definitely inside. His original assumption had been right. She was pissed and powerful.

Moving with all the stealth of years of battle training, Lance made his way towards the structure, keeping watch for anyone or anything who may be lying in wait. He slid around the back of the cabin and waited to the count of ten for any sign of movement. He "felt" the interior to make sure there were no surprises. All he could sense was one seriously feisty witch.

I hope she doesn't turn me into a frog.

His dragon seconded that thought, and decided neither one of them would look good as a green, slimy amphibian. Creeping towards the front, staying out of the moonlight as much as possible, the Guardsman finally reached the only way in or out of the cabin. Slowly opening the door, he caught a glimpse of the smallest woman he'd ever seen, trussed to a chair with duct tape, and with a red bandana hanging out of her mouth.

Her vivid violet eyes spat fire and the chair she was in began rocking side to side as she tugged at her restraints with surprising strength. Lance held his hands up, hoping she understood he meant her no harm. The closer he got, the broader he smiled. Finally, she stopped struggling. He removed her gag and put his index finger to his lips to make sure she knew to keep as quiet as possible.

Nodding in agreement, she opened her mouth wide, moving her jaw side to side to loosen her muscles before speaking. Her voice was high and clear even when she whispered, reminding him of the fairies he'd met in the hills of Ireland. That was where the likeness ended. Her attitude was all witch and all sarcasm.

"Okay, dragon man, let's get me out of this damn chair and find that asshole."

He was shocked. "You can tell what I am even though I'm shielding?"

"You betcha. I'm a helluva lot older than I look." She winked at him, ending any misconception he had about the tiny white-blonde sorceress needing his help for anything, except to escape from the duct tape.

He carefully pulled the duct tape from her right hand, trying not to harm her in any way. About halfway through, she leaned close and whispered, "Rip that shit off. I'll heal. You're wasting time. I can hear all the chaos that idiot's causing."

"What you hear isn't Andrew's doing. It's a friend of his. Maybe you've heard of him, 'The Auctioneer'?" Lance questioned as he finishing releasing her hand.

"Nope, can't say as I have." She took a long deep breath, and in the next second ripped the duct tape off her other arm, managing to stifle the scream he could see straining her throat.

Two deep breaths later, she spoke. "Name's Kyra, by the way. I figure you already smelled I'm one of the good guys for yourself, but just so we don't have any misunderstandings, *no black magic is welcome here*."

She started taking the tape off her ankles one at a time. At least it was over her pants so there was no more pain…just tons of tape to get through.

"That little fucker came to me about six or seven months ago with some sob story about needing to hide from y'all. So, I made him some amulets, then he came back for more. I've never been one to get caught up in disputes between clans or any other sects. I work for whoever I can barter with or can pay me. The first time, he paid. This time, we were to barter specialty ingredients. But as soon as I was finishing the talismans, the shithead tied me up and one of the idiots with him mentioned blowing things up. I knew the stupid shit had messed with my magic." She squinted her eyes and Lance had to wonder what she was thinking, then continued. "And that just *pisses me off*," she finished, whispering through gritted teeth. Lance knew she would've been screaming had the situation allowed it.

"So you didn't design them to blow up?" he asked, curious to see exactly what she was capable of.

"Nope, sure didn't. I designed some to hide scent and some to stun a person if they get close enough. Nothing that would blow up. I've taken a vow to do no harm unless necessary for survival, so you can see where making amulets that blow up just might go against that. Now, I don't know how much you know about witches…." She looked at him, waiting for an answer, and only continued after he shook his head to indicate little to nothing. "Well, if I violate my vows, I get a visit from the Council, and that never ends well for someone who goes against any of the rules…especially if that witch is not part of a coven."

She stood up and shook out her arms and legs. He was once again amazed at how short she really was. No taller than five foot one or two with petite features, but a power rolling off of her small frame that rivaled his own. The saying, "dynamite comes in small packages" came to mind.

"Something funny there, dragon man?" she said with a look he feared meant he might end up a frog after all.

"Not at all and the name's Lance. I was just thinking how appearances can be deceiving."

"You got that shit right there, Lance. Now, what are we gonna do to catch the asshole and make him pay for pissing me off?" She shook her head and frowned, not waiting for him to answer before she started talking again. "I should've known better. I thought I sensed dark magic on him one of the times we met, but I couldn't get a good read so I let it go. Douchebag had a good sob story. I even hid up here in this shithole that used to belong to my nanny to avoid him after word came through the grapevine that he was in some shit a few months back. Bastard found me anyway. Then earlier tonight, I got nothing from him with black magic in it, just read long unused dragon magic. The loser that came to help him though, that asshole stank with the nasty shit. Which sucks, but also means I won't get nicked for the changes in the amulets."

He held back his laughter as she then cussed a blue streak. Just something else that didn't fit the visual. One thing was for sure, she was right that it was past time to get the hell out of Dodge. Smacking himself in the head, he remembered t he'd forgotten to tell any of his brethren what he was up to.

"Hey, Rayne, I found the witch, and she's as pissed as we are. Fucker double crossed her, too."

"You sure we can trust her?" Rayne asked, ever the commander.

"Yeah, I'm sure," Lance answered, looking back at her and waving for her to hurry up.

"I'm close. I got your back," Aaron added.

"All right, Max and I have a clusterfuck to clear up down here. Find that sniveling coward." Rayne sounded as pissed as Lance had ever heard him, and from the sounds of continued gunfire, he had a reason to be.

Lance watched through his commander's eyes for a few seconds. Thankfully, his longtime friend and leader trusted him to do so, and he saw the problem they were dealing with right away. 'The Auctioneer's' goons had spread out too far, and were so poorly trained that they were actually shooting at one another. Any other time Rayne probably would've just let them kill each other, but they were on the hunt for Andrew and forced to stop the gunfire in order to get the coward to show his face.

Opening the door just wide enough for the top of him to fit through, Lance used every enhanced sense he had to make sure it was safe to take Kyra out and found nothing dangerous. The little witch slipped out in front of him, putting a silver disc hanging from a leather strap over her head as she passed. He tapped her shoulder and motioned to her necklace.

"Amulet for cover and protection," she whispered in answer. "I'd give you one but your dragon magic would just null any spell I could put on it. You must be pretty old there, blue eyes." Again she winked and he chuckled under his breath, thinking about the sexy woman waiting for him. Damn, he missed Sam.

Signaling with a cock of his head that they were going down the back way, he calmly grabbed her shoulder when she tried to lead. As she looked over her shoulder about to object, Lance gave her a "yeah, right" look and started walking. She shrugged and let him pass. He damn sure had to admire her confidence…which made him think of Sam…*again*.

At the edge of the cabin, he stopped and waited as Kyra came up to his side. Leaning down, he whispered, "One of my brethren is just over that ridge."

She nodded and he was sure she could see Aaron, which made him wonder what else she might be able to see or sense, so he asked. "Can you see or hear anything?"

Kyra squinted her eyes, tilted her head to the side, and focused on something beyond his comprehension. A few seconds later, she shook her head. "Nope. That son of a bitch has altered my amulets so much that I can't track them."

"Well, then we're doing this the old fashioned way." Lance felt the grin on his face and figured Kyra thought he was nuts. But when she grinned back, he knew they were going get along just fine.

"All right kiddies, let's get moving," Aaron sent straight into Lance's mind.

"What took ya so long there, bro?" Lance chuckled.

"Had to tie up a young wizard who thought he could sneak up on us. When he wakes, hanging over that cliff over there, he may rethink his plan." Aaron laughed in his head, but Lance could feel the tension thrumming through him. They could all feel how close they were to catching Andrew, but for his actual brothers, it had to be bittersweet.

"Damn, wish I could've been there."

"From the look of things, there are enough of them spread over this mountainside for you to have as much fun as you want. All we have to do is get the little one there to safety."

"Little one?" Lance scoffed. "Scan her for a sec. She's no one to be fucked with."

Two seconds later Aaron answered. "Holy shit! No, I guess she's not, but she's still a tiny little thing. Let's get her to Sam's house and then kick some ass." He could tell his brethren was more than ready to have a go at the traitor, and nothing was getting in his way.

"I'm heading down," Lance answered Aaron, then whispered to Kyra, "You ready?"

"Damn straight," she answered. "And I can tell you're talking to one of your clan. I'm sure you big strong dragon guys have decided I need to get out of your way, but let me tell you one thing…." She narrowed her eyes. "If we run into that little fucker on the way down, I'm gonna kick him in the balls."

He mock saluted. "Yes, ma'am." She was a real piece of work and funny as hell. His dragon was trying to tell him something about the little witch, but Lance didn't have time to figure it out. Later, after he got home and held Sam in his arms for about a week, he'd look at what about Kyra made his dragon pause. At this point, Lance would take all the help he could get to catch Andrew and end this bullshit once and for all. He knew Rayne would probably kill him if he let the little witch so much as raise a finger. The commander was definitely old school when it came to females, but Lance would let her get a few kicks in if the chance presented itself.

Leading the way, he headed them towards a crevice covered by a huge bush. The blasts from below had lessened, but the sound of gunfire still broke through the night air as he listened to Rayne directing Aidan and Devon. The wizards 'The Auctioneer' had brought with him were providing cover for the humans. Sick and tired of waiting for something to happen, he decided on a new plan. *"Aaron, come get Kyra. I think I know how to draw Andrew out."*

"Dude, that's not what Rayne wants." Aaron half-heartedly warned.

"Yeah, well this shit is taking too long. The bastard came for my mate, so this is my fight. Get Kyra to safety and hurry back."

"Whatever you say. You're gonna do what you want any way. It's your ass." Aaron laughed. *"Be right there."*

In less than three heartbeats, Aaron came up behind them. Kyra turned and whispered, "Hey, you the cavalry?"

"Yeah, you might say that. I'm your way down the mountain," Aaron smiled, but Lance could tell he wasn't thrilled.

She turned back to Lance. "You gonna raise hell, dragon man?"

"That's the plan," he grinned. "But I'll bring him to ya so you can get a couple kicks in before he's off to solitary, deal?"

"Deal!" Kyra's grin said she was going to do a whole lot more to the traitor than a few kicks if she ever got her hands on him. Made Lance damn glad that look wasn't meant for him.

He nodded to both of Aaron and Kyra. "See you at the bottom."

They nodded back and Aaron added through their link, *"Watch your ass."*

"Sure thing," Lance answered, and took off back to the cabin. He knew for certain the little coward would come back for the witch, and he planned to be waiting when he did.

CHAPTER TWENTY-SEVEN

Waiting sucked! With the fucking Dragon Guard scouring the mountain, and 'The Auctioneer's' buffoons making enough noise to wake the dead, Andrew's followers were getting nervous. He was getting text after text asking what they needed do or if they should retreat.

Retreat? No fucking way!

They'd come too far and waited too long. This would be the day he finally got to begin his revenge against the Dragon Guard. Andrew could feel it in his bones. All they had to do was be patient; those idiots would screw up, and he would capitalize on it.

It had been heartbreaking to watch the Guardsmen take apart most of the booby traps he'd set on the ground below. Thankfully, they missed a few of the amulets he and John added their special touch to. All they had to do was trip over them and the stupid Guardsmen would be out of commission for quite a while.

From his perch he could see Rayne and the werepanthers were effectively handling 'The Auctioneer's' crew and even some of his wizards. He knew they were some of the weaker members of Master Eaton's coven.

Funny how the lead wizard and his stronger followers hadn't come to the fight; but then again, they might just not be where Andrew could see them…*yet*. When this was all over and at least one of the useless Dragon Guard was neutralized, he was going to approach 'The Auctioneer' and Master Eaton to form an alliance.

John had assured him repeatedly that neither had any idea what Andrew had been up to for all these months. Together the three of them could make all his plans for revenge a reality; and then, of course, he would kill them, too.

Then there was Kyra. She would remain useful until the end *if* he could keep her from setting him on fire or banishing him to some unknown world. She was powerful. He had to do everything in his power to keep her from finding out what he was really doing with the amulets she'd made. Andrew had almost ripped John's head off when he'd entered the cabin without hiding who and what he was. Andrew was sure the little witch sensed what John was by the look of pure hatred in her eyes.

Andrew hoped he could convince her he was only using John to keep the big bad dragons from finding him. Kyra was smart, but he was smarter. It may take some seriously fast talking, but Andrew knew he could outsmart the white witch. It also helped that he was not in any way associated with the idiots who were blowing the woods to bits. It would go a long way to convincing her to keep working with him.

The men are restless. We need to move, appeared as a text message on his phone. He wondered if it was the men or John that were restless.

Not yet, was his response.

They would wait until he told them to move or they would die. It was as simple as that. He wanted as many Guardsmen as possible on the mountainside. It would give him the best possible chance of capturing, wounding, or killing at least one of them, with capturing being at the top of the list. He wanted them all to feel just a taste of the pain and humiliation he'd felt before giving them their forever death.

Andrew thought again about Kyra and wondered whose mate she was. Did the Guardsman know? Since she was left completely alone and not even watched by a Guard-in-training, he had to think they had no clue she existed, and that gave him an idea to draw them out. With a quick text to John to keep all their cohorts in place, Andrew headed back to the cabin to fetch the little witch. All the waiting was getting them nowhere. It was time to light the fuse.

CHAPTER TWENTY-EIGHT

Aaron was right. After taking a little more scenic route back to the cabin, Lance was able to pinpoint several heavy pockets of black magic, indicating the locations of hiding wizards. Even though he wanted to eliminate their natural enemies, Andrew was the target du jour. Lance had to think the little shit was calling the shots, and wondered exactly how stupid the wizards were to follow such a loser.

Coming up on the shack from the rear again but the opposite side from last time, Lance opened his senses completely. He searched for Andrew or anything out of place that might tell him if the shithead was nearby. Finding nothing, he walked to the front, opened the door slightly, and had to grin.

Standing over Kyra's work table was the stupid fucking bastard who'd turned all of their lives inside out. In less than a second Lance's broadsword was drawn and he was charging towards the unprotected back of the traitor, all the while screaming through the link to his brethren, *"The stupid son of a bitch is up here!"*

Not surprisingly, Aidan was the first to respond. *"Fuck me! Be there in two!"*

Lance was sure the rest all said variations of the same thing, but the sounds were drowned out by the sounds of his broadsword slamming into Andrew's katana. The lazy mother fucker wanted to fight, and that made Lance's day. He lived for the fight. The heat of the battle fueled his actions. He was doing what he'd trained his entire life to do…slay the enemy who threatened the dragon kin way of life, no matter who that enemy was.

Apparently the asshole had been training since the last time Lance watched him swing a blade. The traitor's advances were measured and compact. From the look in his eye, Andrew was trying to find an opening. The stupid asshole was obviously delusional. The traitor thought he could take down one of the best swordsmen ever born?

Not only had Lance been alive longer, but he'd had some kind of blade in his hand since he could walk. To add to his natural ability, he'd trained with Rayne's father until the day of Alexander's forever death. Those countless hours of instruction at the hands of a true master had given him the confidence to believe there wasn't a fight he could not win.

"So you've been practicing, you piece of shit. Scared you're gonna get your ass kicked?" Lance taunted.

"Scared? Of you? Hardly! I don't have to practice to beat the likes of you. You're the joke you've always been," Andrew countered, but Lance could see the fear growing in his eyes. The coward would have to fight on his own without the help of his magic or his friends.

"Yeah, we'll see how tough you are when you're covered in silver standing before the Tribunal."

"Not gonna happen…." The traitor tried to continue their banter but was definitely out of shape from the way he panted, not to mention the sweat dotting his upper lip.

Continuing to drive Andrew farther back with one swipe of his blade after another, Lance was eating up the dread growing in the mismatched eyes of his one-time friend. The traitor was mere feet from the back wall when a sound like cracking wood began just to the left of where they fought. Unable to look, Lance continued to tear away at the meager defenses Andrew had left.

Aidan and Aaron yelled in unison, "Get the fuck away from there, you pieces of shit!"
Without warning, the entire wall that had been cracking fell away. A quick glance revealed the twins fighting five or six sword-wielding wizards. Andrew took advantage of the split second distraction to swipe at Lance's arm. His blade missed the target, but Lance felt a ribbon of fire break out over his ribs. Trusting his enhanced healing, he refocused, and in a series of intricate thrusts and parries, had Andrew flat against the back wall, essentially taking away the traitor's ability to swing his blade. Just as Lance was about to land a debilitating blow, he felt three stabs across his back and the immediate burn of silver entering his system.

Son of a bitch! Someone has silver tipped arrows?

Immediately after, Devon spoke directly into his mind. *"Hunter down. You cool?"*

"I'm cool. Hunters, too? What. The. Fuck?"

"I got this! Kick the little shit's ass for all of us." Lance felt Devon's concentration go to his own fight. Lance prayed to the Heavens for strength.

His pain caused him to stumble, giving Andrew the space he needed to renew their fight. The bastard actually got an almost satisfied look in his eyes as he watched Lance struggle to compensate for the arrows in his back.

Ignoring the pain and weakness quickly spreading through his body, Lance fought to regain the upper hand. He pulled from the strength of his dragon. The beast responded by pouring all he could into the warrior. The man he'd once called brother slowly moved towards the opening left from the missing wall while trying to fend off the barrage of strikes from Lance's broadsword.

Unable to keep Andrew from reaching the outside, Lance looked for the best place to continue their fight while keeping the coward as far from his misguided followers as possible. Lance spotted a small ledge not more than a hundred yards from where they fought. If he got the traitor out on the ledge the fight would be over. There was no way Andrew would take a chance on falling. He was just too much of a coward.

Lance's dragon continued to pump a steady stream of power into him, enhancing it with his ancient dragon magic. The beast was attempting to keep the silver from spreading until the Guardsman could defeat Andrew and go into his healing sleep. He quickly checked, and the Dragon Guard, along with their allies, were winning the battle, but he could hear them talking about the ones who were getting away.

Through the eyes of his brothers he could see Max was sending the werepanthers out to try and round them up. Any other time he would've laughed at the thought of those idiots coming face to face with the Big Cats, but at that moment he was just a bit busy.

Nearing the ledge where he planned to end their confrontation, Lance began to take more controlled strikes, concentrating much of his strength into each downward swipe. The resulting clang of metal on metal was music to his ears. He watched the vibrations reverberate up the traitor's arms, causing him to put both hands on the grip of his blade just to keep it from falling from his hands. Lance loved that Andrew was completely on the defensive as the Guardsman continued to attack with everything he had left. The terror now emanating from Andrew was icing on the cake.

"Looks like you might be a little outmatched, *asshole*." Lance couldn't help but taunt the little fucker.

It took several seconds before Andrew responded, and when he did his voice was winded. "I'll watch you beg for your life this night, you worthless piece of shit."

Lance had to give the little shit credit…he talked a good game. But Lance was well aware that every strike Andrew threw was weaker than the last. There was no way the traitor could outlast him. Measuring the distance to the ledge, Lance changed tactics. Instead of a full frontal attack, he began going for Andrew's left side, essentially herding him in the direction he wanted him to go.

When the traitor finally stepped back onto the ledge, Lance went in for the kill. "You ready to give-in?"

"I'd rather die," was Andrew's response.

Lance smiled. "Suits me just fine."

The Guardsman struck over and over, giving the asshole exactly what he'd just asked for. When Andrew stumbled back, Lance knew there would never be a better opportunity. With all that he was he pulled his broadsword over his head, preparing for the kill.

Just as he started his downswing, Royce's voice sounded in his head. *"Behind you!"*

Lance couldn't respond to the big guy and was unable to do anything but continue on the course he'd begun. He had to trust that Aidan or Aaron, who he knew were close, would do whatever they could to help out.

The Guardsman's blade clashed with Andrew's as the traitor held it overhead, trying whatever he could to protect himself. Lance felt the sting of countless arrows pierce his skin. Victory was in sight. One final blow and the traitor crumbled under the force of Lance's blow.

Unfortunately, the Guardsman couldn't stop his forward motion. He catapulted over the fallen Andrew, sliding towards the lip of the ledge. The hunter's arrows, still sticking from his back, pushed farther into his flesh. He felt the burn of the silver heads spread in every possible direction. His weakened dragon fought against the debilitating poison, but was unable to thwart its effects.

Lance's brethren were all shouting directions in his head; however, his arms and legs grew heavier by the second, and a fog invaded his brain. In a last ditch effort, he reached back and grabbed Andrew's outstretched leg to use as an anchor. Although he would always think of the traitor as the "little asshole," Lance prayed Andrew's six foot, two hundred pound frame would be just enough to keep him from going over the ledge. The Guardsman's forward motion slowed right before he felt his legs go over the edge.

The next thing he saw was the ground racing towards him. Rayne screamed into his head, *"Call your dragon!"*

But the beast had given all that he could, and although the giant warrior tried, there wasn't enough of his ancient magic remaining for him to materialize. Lance was sure he wouldn't die, but knew it was going to hurt like a son of a bitch. He counted the seconds in his head and knew when he was close to hitting the ground. He brought up all the images of Sam he'd tucked away to take his mind off his inevitable destination. He wondered how pissed she'd be when she saw him all messed up, then thought how much fun it would be to play doctor with *his doctor.*

Sure the ground was close, Lance took the deepest breath possible and braced for impact. It was then he actually understood what the men of his Force were all screaming.

"SILVER!"

In his next breath, something hard and cold pierced the skin of his back, sliding completely through his body. Squinting, he saw the blade of a broadsword protruding from his chest.

"Fuck!" was all he could wheeze out before he saw feet, so big they could only belong to Royce, stop right beside him.

The older Guardsman was on his knees, talking faster than Lance could track. "Stay still, you pain in the ass. Let me see what I'm working with."

For the first time in all the years he'd known the old guy, Royce sounded panicked. Lance could feel his dragon pushing with what little power he had left, but both man and beast knew it wasn't enough. There was no way the Guardsman would be able to stay conscious much longer.

Grabbing Royce's hand, he waited until the gentle brown eyes of his oldest friend looked at him, and then said all he could. "Protect Sam and Syd." With a sigh, he and his dragon lost the fight and their world went black.

CHAPTER TWENTY-NINE

Those fucking Guardsmen had done it again. They'd found a way to ruin all his plans *and* they had Kyra. *What. The. Fuck?*

True to form, the cowardly wizards with him had scattered when the fight got to be more than they could handle. Only John came forward when the assholes raced to help the dope. Thank the Heavens for the hunters, although Andrew was pretty sure they'd come with Master Eaton's men. He'd had absolutely no contact with any hunter packs since the incident on the hillside almost a year ago.

At least one good thing came out of the evening; Lance was either dead or dying. Served the idiot right for thinking he could defeat The Special One. It had been close, but what those losers needed to remember was that Andrew always had a backup plan…even his backup plans had backup plans.

The rogue wizards thought he was stupid when he'd told them to place piles of silver around the base of the mountain. Guess he'd shown them. Fate had showered favor upon him for a moment and Lance, the dope, was sporting a broadsword through the chest. Andrew would gloat when he and the rogue wizards were back together.

There would be fewer of them. He should feel bad about that, but it was all about getting his revenge and not about how many followers he could amass. Like the old saying went, "You gotta break a few eggs…." Andrew was sure many had been killed, either by 'The Auctioneer's' incompetence or the useless Guardsmen, not to mention the werepanthers he'd seen chasing them through the woods.

Getting Kyra back was definitely on his to-do list, but would have to wait until he was able to regroup and see where he stood with personnel and supplies. Andrew was alive and able to fight another day. Although running through the woods was less than dignified, he'd avoided capture.

Put a big ol' mark in the win column.

Andrew was no more than a half a mile from his hidden vehicle when the sounds of human feet being followed by much larger, much heavier paws, reached his ears. Turning his head, he caught sight of one of the rogue wizards John had introduced him to running for his life. One minute the rogue was up, and the next he was taken down by a large caramel-colored panther.

The Big Cat was trying to detain the man, but teeth and claws combined with a scared shitless wizard was heading towards disaster for the practitioner. Andrew sped towards the SUV expertly hidden by branches and vines, thankful he hadn't been the werepanther's prey.

When he was safely behind the wheel and careening down the unused, single-lane gravel road, he texted his second, *Returning to base.* After several long minutes of wondering if the rogue wizard had survived, Andrew's phone vibrated on the seat next to him, *Assessing the damage. See you tonight.*

He would've liked to have been there to see how many of their flock survived, but with the sun rising and the only amulets left hidden, there was no way he could risk being caught. John was competent. Andrew would simply have to trust the man to do his job. If not, Andrew would return to the original plan and kill him as soon as he had Kyra back in his possession.

CHAPTER THIRTY

It had been an hour since Royce had told her that Lance was hurt. Sam knew he was alive. She could *feel* him, something she was going to have to examine later. When Royce explained there was a state-of-the-art medical facility in the basement and that a "healer" from their family was on the way, she'd damn near punched the big man in the gut. She knew their brief conversation would've been comical in any other situation, but at that moment she was out of her mind.

"I'm a doctor, Royce. Let me help."

"I know you're a doctor, Samantha, and a very good one, but Lance has a few unique…medical conditions that require a 'specialist.'"

She'd seen him look over her head with concern, and Sydney had squeezed her hand. Sam had glared over her shoulder to find Aidan looking back at the big man. It was obvious some type of silent communication was taking place, but she had no clue how.

Letting her anger take over, Sam took a step forward, standing toe-to-toe with a six foot ten inch giant, and threw as much attitude into her voice as possible. "Dammit, Royce, take me to him! I can help!"

The resignation she saw in his eyes swamped her with fear. Her knees trembled, but she refused to show weakness. Lance needed her to be strong.

"Please…," was all she could get past the lump in her throat.

"I promise you can go down just as soon as Siobhan has gotten here and had a chance to look at him."

Without another word, Royce turned and headed towards a door she hadn't seen before. Grace was immediately at her side, directing her back into the family room where Kyndel sat with Jay.

Sydney crawled up in her lap, and that's where they'd been ever since.

Devon returned and she heard the voice of an older woman. The timber of the woman's voice seemed to lower the tension level in the house exponentially. When Sam asked Grace and Kyndel about her, both ladies smiled and assured her their family healer was the best in the world. While all of that was well and good, Samantha was a trained surgeon, top in her class, and working to be one of the best in the country. She needed to be down there. Sydney sat on the floor next to Jay. Sam paced, trying to think of a way to get past the young man guarding the door. Seeing Lance was her number one goal. She'd lost everyone she'd ever loved without being able to help. There had been no goodbye or prayers for a happy ending, only caskets and flowers and weeping mourners. That shit was *so* not happening this time. She was *not* losing him, not as long as Sam drew breath.

Her pacing halted and she stared out the window. Was it true? Did she love him? Despite all her misgivings and thoughts of her future, since Lance had burst into her world Sam hadn't been able to imagine her life without him. He'd haunted her every thought. Even when he'd been watching her, she'd longed for more. Now that she had it, imagining a future with him was almost too easy. There were things he wasn't telling her, and that would have to be dealt with, but what mattered was that he was hurt, needed her help, and they were being kept apart.

She paced the other direction and ran right into Grace. Both women grabbed the others' arms for support.

"Oh Grace! I'm sorry. I didn't see you there."

Grace shook her head. "No! No! It's my fault. I was following too close. I thought you were headed into the kitchen and maybe we could talk over a cup of coffee."

Little red flags went up. She grabbed Grace's arm again. "What is it? What has happened?" Sam whispered, fearing the worst.

"Oh, Sam, I'm sorry. I didn't mean to freak you out. It's nothing like that. There are just a few things you should know about our family. Things Lance should've told you but wasn't able to with all that's happened." Grace smiled sweetly, and Sam wondered if these things were answers to the questions piling up in her mind.

"Sure, coffee sounds great, and if this conversation will get me down there with him, all the better."

Sam turned and headed for the kitchen, not waiting for an answer. Lance needed her. She knew it like she knew her own name, like she'd known every time he was near. It sounded weird even to her, but she could feel his need for her. He was reaching for her with his mind instead of his body. Maybe all the stress and lack of sleep over the last couple of days was making her loopy. Hopefully, Grace and Kyndel would have the answers she needed.

Sitting at the table, Sam watched the other women approach. Kyndel moved the kids and their toys into the breakfast nook with them. When she met the red-headed woman's eyes, Kyndel smiled and chuckled, "You surely didn't think I was getting left out of all the fun, did you?"

Grace took the seat across from Sam and Kyndel pulled another next to her best friend. Whatever they had to say was important, that much was obvious. The butterflies in Sam's stomach fluttered like when she'd had a big exam at school. The others seemed completely relaxed, leading her to believe it was nothing ominous. Her mind ran wild, wondering what it could be, and decided maybe it was something as simple as making sure she understood they were family by choice, not blood related. Surely they knew that didn't matter to her.

After popping up and hurrying to grab the refreshments, Grace returned with cookies, a full coffee pot, mugs, sugar, cream, and milk for the kids. The attorney went about making sure everyone was well taken care of before taking her seat. It was like she was stalling. Sam's tension amped up, and her suspicions were confirmed when the raven-haired beauty sat down, took a deep breath, and said, "So how are you *really*?"

Deciding to answer instead of be an ass, Sam said, "I'm scared and frustrated and heading towards pissed. I don't understand any of this. Why in the hell would you have medical facilities in your home? Why does your family have its own healer? What can this healer do that I can't? For Christ's sake, I am a doctor. Why can't I go down there and help? Is he really okay, or are you just preparing me for the worst? I know you don't know much about me, but everyone I ever cared for has passed away. If he's already dead, just tell me."

Sam fired questions one right after another. The lump that had been growing in her throat since she sat down caused her last words to be barely more than a whisper.

Both women were frantically shaking their heads. Kyndel was the first to speak, "Dammit, I'm so sorry we've freaked you out. Lance isn't dead, honey. It takes a hell of a lot more than what he's been through to take out one of our guys," the redhead said as she made a circle indicating the three of them and continued.

"What we need to talk to you about is the reason why Rayne and the others haven't let you see him yet. I've had to argue with my lovely husband for the better part of an hour to get him to let us talk to you. He still thinks we need to wait for Lance to get better, but I know if it was my man laying down there on a gurney and I had no idea what was happening, I'd be tearing the doors off the hinges to get to him. Am I right?" Her southern accent only accentuated the meaning and feeling behind her words.

Sam nodded her head. Of course she wanted to get down there. She had no idea what kind of future they had together, if any, but she was falling in love with the big lug. She knew she could help him, if they would just let her. Motioning for Kyndel to continue, she took a sip of her coffee.

It was Grace who picked up the conversation. "Okay, what we're about to tell you is going to sound insane, especially because you haven't known us for long. When Lance wakes up, I'm going to kick him in the shins for not talking to you before he went running off, but then again, I remember what the first few weeks are like." She got a dreamy look in her eyes.

Sam smiled, knowing exactly what the other woman was talking about. Lance was a force to be reckoned with. All she wanted was to have him safe and sound and in her arms.

Kyndel swatted Grace's arm and both ladies giggled like schoolgirls. They had the kind of friendship Sam had always wished for…like sisters. Maybe if things worked out with her blue-eyed hero they would all end up friends? Stranger things had happened.

Interrupting Sam's wayward thoughts, Grace spoke again. "I can only think of one way to tell you all of it, and that's to start at the beginning. When Aidan told me all of this, he asked that I not ask any questions until he was done, but I'm not like that. If at any time you need to stop me or ask a question, just jump right in, okay?"

Sam nodded, growing more leery by the minute. Grace took a deep breath and started. "You know all the stories you've heard of knights and dragons?" Sam nodded. "Well, they're absolutely true. But there's a huge twist they left out of the story books we were read as children and the history books we studied in school. They were as real as the ones in *Dragonheart* about 1500 years ago, but they aren't like that now. As time progressed and the world became more populated, the dragons weren't able to hide their existence any longer. They enlisted the help of a very powerful mage."

Sam felt her brow furrow and both women sitting across the table from her grinned.

"I know what you're thinking, but I assure you, we are completely sane. There really are mages and magic and a whole lot of other shit, but that's for another time. Back to my point; the mage was able to combine what made the dragon special, its soul and its magic, with the knight of its choosing. The knight had to possess all the characteristics necessary to protect their clans, to fight for those that needed a champion, and keep their race from falling into extinction."

"King Arthur?" Sam felt her eyebrows shoot up almost to her hairline and her eyes get big.

Grace laughed but continued. "Yeah, that guy was real too. But I have no idea about Guinevere. I do, however, know that your mate was named for a great warrior from that time, but you'll have to ask him about that.

"Anyhow," Grace drew a breath and shot a look at Kyndel, who was sitting on the very edge of her chair. "King Arthur had a code of conduct for his knights, a list of sorts, of characteristics that a man had to have to even be considered to be one of his knights. The dragons looked for men who had the same qualities as the knights they'd fought beside for thousands of years. These warriors had to be courteous, honest, generous, courageous, loyal, just, discreet, wise, brave, and honorable. They made sure these qualities were so ingrained in the individual that they were an integral part of his bloodline. It was imperative the dragons ensured that their power was never abused. You see, dragons are fire made flesh, and fire is power.

"The men you've met here are descendants of the men who were given this honor. It all started in the sixth century, shortly after King Arthur disappeared. From that point forward, every male from the chosen families has gone through a transformation between the ages of eighteen and twenty-one." Grace stopped and looked Sam right in the eye. "You okay so far?"

She thought for a moment, considered yelling "PSYCH" to see if the other women followed along, and then answered. "Yeah, I'm good."

Grace and Kyndel exchanged a knowing look. Sam braced herself for what was to come next. Kyndel spoke. "I can see from the way you're looking at us you think we've lost our minds, or maybe we're just messing with you to keep you from thinking about your man. That could *not* be further from the truth. We're telling you all this so that you can get down there with him. Once you're there, you'll see and hear things that defy all rational explanation. It's going to be real, I promise, but you're still gonna freak, even though we're telling you all of this.

"So Grace told you all about the dragons, but now let's talk about the guys and what it all means right here, right now. Okay?"

Sam nodded her head, wondering exactly what the fiery red-head with the emerald eyes and southern accent could possibly say that would be any crazier than what she'd already heard.

"Well, now she," Kyndel motioned towards Grace, "said something about a transformation. Before I go down that path, I wanna ask you a question. You know that tattoo on Lance's chest, the big dragon that looks like he's flying off to battle?"

"Yes…." Jealousy ran through Sam at the thought of Kyndel looking at Lance's chest. She shoved it down but still felt antsy. First of all, she'd never been jealous in her entire life and had no clue what the hell had caused it to happen now. Then there was the fact that it was obvious Kyndel was head over heels in love with her husband. Other men had ceased to exist to the redhead.

Shaking her head, Sam said, "Go on…."

"All right then, keep that tattoo in mind while I'm telling you the next part of our family's history. See, after the boys go through what's called their transformation, the men they have become can then call forth the dragon that lives within." Kyndel paused and Sam could feel how much she wanted her to believe what she was saying, but there was no way any of this could be true…was there?

Kyndel continued. "By calling forth, I mean they can actually shift from man to dragon and back again. Now, I see you think I've been smoking something really good, or maybe I drank the Kool-aid, but I'm telling you the absolute truth. If you'll bear with us just a bit longer, I'm going to prove everything we're saying. Can you do that? Will you do that for Lance?"

Kyndel wasn't playing fair if she was going to throw Lance in Sam's face. She wished she could say it didn't matter, but that would be a lie and she really tried to never be dishonest. Two deep breaths later, Samantha nodded.

"Now, the men we love and their brothers, they consider it an honor that their families were selected. They take the duty associated with it very seriously. They protect the dragon way of life and help those in need whenever possible. They are kind of like superheroes without the capes."

The ladies both burst out laughing. It didn't take long before Sam was laughing right along with them. It felt good to let go of some of the tension thrumming through her body, but it didn't negate the fact that they were both certifiable.

When the laughter died down and they all had a fresh cup of coffee, Kyndel went on. "I have a question for you, Miss Sam. Has there ever been a time when you were talking to Lance and he seemed to be about a million miles away, and when you asked him about it he made some excuse?"

"Yes, it's happened. Why?" Sam asked suspiciously, preparing for what was to come.

"When the man and the dragon were merged, they began to share the magic that is inherent to the beast. One of the many benefits of that sharing is that the warrior can speak directly into the minds of other dragon shifters, or vice versa."

Kyndel reached across the table and touched Sam's arm. "Think about it before you call the men in the white suits. Haven't you always felt like there's something different about Lance? Something special? And when you met his brothers, didn't the weirdness kind of get hiked up a notch or two?"

Samantha had to admit that everything Kyndel was saying about Lance being different and the interaction between him and his brothers being anything but normal was true. But really?

Dragons? Telepathy?

Could any of this be true? The longer she thought about it, the more Sam decided she really needed to know the truth, for her own sanity and for the growing love she felt for the goofy man with the hypnotic blue eyes.

"I know what you're saying about the guys is right. They do act 'differently' when they're together, and there have been times when I could've sworn Lance was carrying on a conversation I couldn't hear…but all of this is just too crazy. I mean, really? Psych ward, shock treatment, institutionalized for life, *crazy*."

Sam looked out the window, then back to the two women who'd been nothing but gracious to both her and Sydney. Resigned she was going to listen to all they had to say, if for no other reason than to get to Lance, Sam relented. "I'm listening…go on."

Both women smiled, and Grace started again. "One of the most important milestones in a dragon shifter's life, other than his transformation, is finding his mate. The one female in the entire world created just for him. She's the other half of his soul, the completion of the man and his beast. They say their mate is the peace, love, and light that both man and beast need to survive the many years they have left in this life and the next.

"This woman grounds them, makes them whole, and is the single most important person to both entities, *ever*. They've existed longer than we can imagine before meeting their mate, but only truly begin to live when they're able to share their life and love with the one the Universe designed for them.

"We believe," she motioned between herself and Kyndel, "and so do the men, that you are Lance's mate. The one meant for him."

Sam started to shake her head and Grace held up her hands. "Just seeing you two together solidifies that belief, and if I had any doubts, they all went up in smoke when I saw how hard you fought to get down there with him. The fire in your eyes says it's a need inside of you to protect what's yours."

"Yes, I care about him and I owe him my life, but I seriously doubt that I'm his…*mate*. He's a nice guy. We're getting to know each other, but I have plans for my life and my career. Those things *have* to come first. I've been trying to get down to him because I know I can help him. I'm a trained doctor, after all."

Grace looked at Sam like she was sure the woman had looked at many defendants across the courtroom in her life. When the attorney spoke, there was steel in her voice. "You can lie to yourself, that's fine, but I'll tell you one thing. Lance believes you're his mate, and that may just be the one thing that saves his life." She paused, and Sam could tell she was deciding what to tell her.

"What is it? Just tell me."

Grace shrugged. "The bond between mates is almost immediate, but very weak in the beginning. The more time you spend together and the more…intimate that time is, the quicker and stronger the bond grows. Because he believes you're his mate, even though he's in his 'healing sleep,' which is kind of like a coma, he'll seek you out. That's the main reason Kyndel and I decided we needed to tell you everything we could, so that you can go down there and be with him…help him heal."

There were several seconds of silence stretching on like an eternity. Sam refused to be the first one to speak. They could give in first. She wasn't the one telling fairy tales while the man they all cared for was hurt and needed their help.

Positive their standoff would go on forever, Sam jumped when Sydney's little hand touched hers. She looked down and the little girl was smiling. The child made a "come here" sign with her finger, then whispered, "They're telling the truth, Dr. Sam…promise."

Sam jerked back and stared into the little girl's eyes. There'd always been a maturity to the child that exceeded her years, but at that moment there was a look of resignation and belief. Sydney was attempting to relay that all Sam had heard had been the complete truth. Unsure what to do, the doctor asked, "How do you know that, Sydney?"

"I can hear them when they talk to each other, up here." She placed her chubby, little finger on her temple, and grinned.

"You can...*hear* them?" Sam asked, not sure what was happening, but afraid she might miss something if she blinked.

"Not what they're saying, but I know when they're talking to each other." Sydney nodded and continued. "I told Lance and he said we would talk about it when you weren't around, but then he got hurt. Hope he doesn't get mad that I'm telling you now." She stopped and squinted, like she was thinking really hard about something, and then said, "Nah, he won't get mad. He loves us, right, Dr. Sam?"

Samantha felt her eyebrows shoot up. Breathing deeply, she tried to think of some way to answer the child who was looking at her like she had all the answers. In the blink of an eye, it all made sense…he *did* love them.

What other man would rescue a woman from certain death and ask for nothing in return? Or watch after the same woman for months on end without ever making contact? Even more than that, what normal man would willingly take on the responsibility of a little girl who needed protection, then go after the man who'd tried to kidnap her?

The list of things Lance had done for Sam was unimaginable. No other person she'd ever known, aside from her parents, had given her so much. There was no denying there was something between them.

He looked at her like no other ever had. He touched her and it was as though there'd never been any other man and there never would be…ever. He made her feel like she could be Sam, the Sam she was meant to be, and nothing or no one would stand in the way of her dreams. He wanted her for her, nothing more. She didn't even care that he called her "Doc." If Sam was honest, she liked it. It was *his* name for her.

"Yes, baby, he loves us," she answered.

Her thoughts went on and on, leading her to the dream she'd almost forgotten. At least she had thought it was a dream. It seemed like a dream. What else could seeing a golden dragon flying over the woods behind her house be? With her new "information," she figured it could be almost anything. Sam was almost yelling but couldn't stop…she had to know. "Is Lance's dragon golden?"

Both women smiled so brightly she could feel their relief. Kyndel spoke first. "Yes, sweetpea, his dragon is a brilliant, glittering gold."

Not able to sit any longer, Sam stood and paced, soon realizing Sydney was pacing alongside. The little girl said she could hear when Lance and his brothers were talking in each other's minds. Could that be true too? Could all of what they'd just told her be true? It was completely mind boggling and more than a bit disturbing, but she was beginning to believe at least some of it.

Sam thought about the amazing man who'd haunted so many of her thoughts for so long. If what they were saying was the truth, he needed her more than she'd originally thought, and she was wasting time questioning everything. There would be time later.
Lance was all that mattered.

"All right, let's say I believe at least some of what you're saying. Can I *please* go down and see him now?" Sam asked, unable to keep the pleading tone from her voice.

"Absolutely, honey, just one more thing," Kyndel responded. Sam worked hard to not roll her eyes.

"The only thing that can kill one of our boys is silver poisoning or beheading. Right now, Lance has part of a silver blade sticking out of his chest. From what I've heard it was coated in liquid silver as well. The dragon within him is able to dispel the silver, but only after the blade has been removed."

"Then why the hell haven't they removed it?" Sam interrupted.

"Because the blade is in the bottom part of his heart and Siobhan, our healer, is afraid he won't be able to heal fast enough to keep from bleeding to death. His dragon was weakened during the fight. His beast is unable to help with healing as much as he usually would, and that's where you come in.

"We're all praying your strength, plus your medical knowledge, will help get that blade out of him and get our pain in the ass back to his lovable, irritating self."
Sam worried her lip with her teeth and slid into doctor mode. It was way safer for her emotions and her heart than girlfriend or mate, or whatever the hell she was to him, mode. Thinking of her rotation in Cardiac Care, Sam remembered a case study she'd read about an army surgeon who'd been able to remove large pieces of shrapnel from a man's heart on the battlefield and the soldier had survived. All she had to do was get down there and see if the same procedure would work for a silver blade.

"What the hell are we waiting for?" Done wasting time, Sam turned on her heels and headed towards the door still being guarded by the young man whose name she couldn't remember.

When he stepped in front of her, she looked him dead in the eye and in a low ominous voice said, "You're probably a hundred times stronger than I am, but I promise, if you try to stop me from going through that door I will fight as dirty as I know how to get past you. I was a foster kid. We know how to fight dirty and we know how to win."

His eyes widened. She knew he'd been told not to let her pass, but could see he wouldn't fight with her either. Sam was about to muscle her way through when the door opened and a pair of very tired violet eyes looked down at her. His attempt at a smile was weak at best. She couldn't blame him…it had to be hard to see one of his own hurt.

Rayne placed his hand on the younger man's shoulder. "It's fine, Jace, let Dr. Malone pass. Hopefully, she'll be able to help."

Without another word, he turned and headed back down the stairs. Jace moved and she took that as her cue to follow. The stairs turned at a right angle, and as she rounded the corner, a blindingly bright light caused her to stumble. When the spots cleared from her eyes, Sam saw antiseptically white walls and a painted gray floor, not unlike the operating rooms at the hospital.

Quickly scanning the area as her feet took her down the last few steps, Sam saw the state-of-the-art triage and surgical area. It had to have cost a fortune, but she guessed when you lived hundreds of years, you had time to save some serious coin. What she wasn't thrilled to see was a tiny little woman with platinum blonde hair praying or chanting or whatever the hell she was doing over Lance. Rationally, Sam knew she had no claim to him even though Grace and Kyndel said they were mates, but just the thought of the curvy little woman touching Lance made Sam see red.

She made her way over to where they had Lance. Her first instinct was to throw herself over him and cry, but she was a doctor and doctors didn't act that way, no matter who was on their table. Sam took her millionth deep breath and put her professional persona firmly in place. She was going to save his life…and then she was gonna kick his ass.

CHAPTER THIRTY-ONE

The one big difference between this setup and the hospital was no heart monitors or IV's, none of the usual equipment doctors used to track the patient's vitals. Maybe it had something to do with the whole "being a dragon" thing. The smooth, calm, feminine voice she'd heard earlier sounded beside her. Sam turned to find a very tall, stately woman with striking gray hair smiling at her.

"You must be Dr. Malone. I'm Siobhan, the clan's Elder Healer. It's a pleasure to meet the one the Universe has made for our Lance."

The older woman held out her hand and as Sam shook it, the young doctor tucked away the words "clan" and "Elder Healer" for another time, figuring that was going to be happening a lot while she was with Lance's family.

"Just call me Sam," she answered, trying to smile but really eager to get to look more closely at Lance's injuries.

"Sam it is then. I'm sure you want to look at our patient." Siobhan motioned towards Lance. Sam could see they had covered the blade protruding from his chest with a sheet.

Do dragons have to worry about infection?

A real quick glance around the room showed her that no one was wearing masks or gloves. Infection must not be a worry.

Making her way to his bedside, Sam looked at the little blonde who was propped on a stool, chanting something that sounded like Latin. Siobhan spoke quickly, pointing to the other woman who was so enthralled in her own verse she had yet to look up. "That is Kyra. She is a white witch. We are hoping her magic can keep the silver from spreading."

Sam felt her eyebrows rise for the tenth time in the last hour, and wondered if they might just get stuck up there.

A witch? Really? Dragons weren't enough, there had to be witches too?

What the hell else were these people going to tell her was real? Next, they were going to say people could turn into cats or dogs…*what the hell*? Slowly shaking her head to clear the craziness, and reminding herself that there were all kinds of beliefs out there, Sam decided if they wanted to believe in a witch they could. It was their right. For her, she was going to believe in her education and training and find a way to help the man before her. Mate or not, she *would* save him. She *had* to.

It was worse than she'd imagined. He was pale and lifeless…still the most handsome man she'd ever seen, but everything that made him Lance was sleeping right along with the man. Sam longed to see the twinkle in his crystal blue eyes and his shit-eating grin that made her smile even when she wanted to kick his ass. But most of all, Sam wanted to feel the low rumble of his voice tumble through her as he said her name.

Pushing all thoughts of anything but saving him aside, Sam removed the sheet and barely held back a gasp. They hadn't been kidding when they said there was a blade sticking out of his chest, and from the way he was propped up on a bunch of pillows, it went all the way through.

Taking a deep breath, Sam examined the area around the wound. She wondered how they knew it pierced his heart without an x-ray. "How do you know the blade has touched his heart without an x-ray or an ultrasound?" Sam looked around again and saw none of the huge equipment she relied on at the hospital.

"As a healer I am able to feel what the injured are feeling, and I can see what is going on inside their wounds," Siobhan calmly answered.

Sam worked hard to school her features. She really didn't want to alienate the very people trying to save Lance's life, and oh yeah…they were his family, too. No pressure there at all; she imagined rolling her eyes. The closer she looked at his wounds, the more she was sure they could get the blade out *and* keep him from bleeding to death if they all worked together. However, she was going to need at least an ultrasound picture to be sure they were working in the right place.

Siobhan—at least she thought that was her name—may be able to see what was going on in there, but Sam couldn't. There was no way she was letting anyone, even herself, perform any kind of surgery until she saw exactly where the blade was inside his body. Being completely professional, she calmly asked, "Can someone run up and get my cell phone, please? I think I left it in the family room by the couch." She heard someone run up the stairs before she had the whole question out of her mouth. "And do we have rubber gloves? I know you guys probably don't get infections, but I would feel better if we used them."

A box of gloves appeared at her side. She met the healer's eyes as she grabbed a pair. Maybe the woman really could see inside people, because it damn sure felt like she was looking inside of her.

"Thank you. I want to call the hospital and see if we can borrow an ultrasound machine. I appreciate that you've been taking care of your people with your special abilities, but for me to cut into his chest," Sam motioned towards the man who was quickly becoming a habit she didn't know how to quit, "I have to be able to actually see what's going on in there."

"I understand, dear, and I want you to know that I will work with you, not take over or impose our way of thinking on you. I am going to ask one thing though, and I hope you can help me with it." Siobhan spoke in her smooth, calm way, and when she touched Sam's arm, the doctor swore she felt warmth spread throughout her body. Sam instantly felt more in control of her emotions. Maybe there was something to the whole dragon magic thing.

She nodded for the healer to continue. "I want you to open your mind to all you have been told, and anything else that may seem unusual to you as we try to bring your mate back to us."

Sam stood listening, unsure what to expect. Siobhan simply smiled, giving her a look the doctor remembered from her childhood. It was a motherly look that said "You might be able to fool yourself, but I can see right through you."

The healer went on. "Whatever you think you know, I can see how much you care for Lance. I know he cares for you, and *that* will be the key to his survival. Because he is dragon and the Universe has made you just for him, you two share a special bond. I can feel he is resisting the pull, trying to protect you from his pain and suffering. But he is going to need your strength."

Sam listened to every word Siobhan was saying, waiting for the other shoe to drop, and then it did. "You are going to need to make him open up to you. It will be difficult because you are not officially mated and do not wear his mark, but I know that you can do this, Samantha. I know you can save his life."

Wow! No pressure.

Unable to speak, Sam turned back to Lance, watching the incredibly slow rise and fall of his chest. The sword had pierced the wing of the majestic dragon adorning his chest. She touched the magnificent beast that appeared to be racing into battle and felt the shot of the electricity that always accompanied touching Lance…much weaker, but still present. As she skimmed over his special marking, it rippled and writhed under her touch.

The colors became slightly more vivid and she could feel the ridges pushing against her fingertips. The tattoo was responding to her touch. Looking into the vivid blue orb that held barely a shadow of the twinkle she remembered from her dream, it all became clear. No matter what she believed about men who could shift into dragons, healers who could look inside the human body, or even witches who chanted to keep people alive, one fact remained…Sam was falling in love with the blue-eyed smart ass who could set her body on fire with a wink and a smile.

Continuing to touch the dragon on his chest, she noted his breathing had slowed. Taking his pulse, hers began to race…his was slow and thready. Out of habit, she reached for the stethoscope that usually hung around her neck. Frustrated, she lashed out before she could stop herself, "I NEED MY PHONE!"

Everyone around her stood still. The room was engulfed in silence except for the damn chanting. Immediately embarrassed for her outburst, she hung her head. "I'm sorry," she whispered.

A large, warm hand touched her shoulder. Sam looked up to find the biggest guy…wait, dragon…she'd ever met. "Don't worry about it, Samantha, we're all freaking out. I keep thinking any minute he's going to jump off that table and call me Grandpa."

Royce looked at his brethren lying lifelessly on the table and smiled a sad smile that didn't reach his eyes. "Here's your phone. Let me know where to go and I'll get everything you need."

She nodded, took the phone, and moved towards the corner of the room. By the time Charlie answered her call, Sam was somewhat under control and able to ask for the supplies and equipment she needed. The fact that her long-time friend didn't ask any questions, other than if Sam was okay, spoke to the depth of their friendship.

Returning to Lance's bedside, Sam spoke to the gentle giant who stood watch over his brother. "Charlie will be waiting for you outside the hospital by the fire exit nearest the Emergency Room." She met his eyes. "Thank you," was all she could get out before he just disappeared.

Dragon men can really move....

Doing everything possible to think of the man before her as just another patient, Sam remembered what Siobhan had said about opening herself up to everything she'd learned and to Lance.

Deciding to try a mental exercise the psychiatrist had taught her after her kidnapping, Sam closed her eyes, took several deep breaths, and thought about the amazing man who'd invaded her very soul from the first moment he looked down at her soot covered face. His dimple winked at her. His eyes twinkled with the mischief of at least five teenage boys.

She remembered what it felt like to have his arms wrapped around her and the feel of his skin against hers. The longer she thought of him, the quicker the images came, ranging from the gentle way he dealt with Sydney to the passionate way he played her body like it had been designed for his hands alone. He was like no other man she'd ever known, a force unto himself who wreaked havoc and made her look forward to the craziness. Opening her eyes, she stared at his handsome face that even the blood loss and silver blade sticking out of his chest couldn't diminish, and felt the spark deep in her heart reach out to him.

Totally out of her element, not sure what to make of what she was feeling, Sam took a leap of faith and followed her heart. Focusing all her thoughts on that spark, she fed her affection and new feelings of love into it. The more the spark grew, the more she could actually feel Lance. He was around her, and within her, giving her his strength and making her feel like there was nothing she couldn't do. He was also pissing her off, because as she tried to lend her strength to him, he was trying to block her somehow.

Not truly understanding what was happening, Sam followed her instincts. She grabbed his face and leaned forward. When their noses almost touched she spoke to him in her best "I am the doctor, you are the patient voice."

"Listen here, dragon man, you *are* going to let me help you any way I can. You *are* going to stop trying to keep me out. You *are* going to stop protecting me. You *are* going to get better, because then I *am* going to kick your ass for keeping secrets from me."

She heard some snickering from behind her and was positive she felt more than that coming from the man lying on the table. "Now that we have that all worked out, just lay there and behave."

Sam truly had no idea if he'd heard her or if it was her wishful thinking that made her believe she'd felt him react to her words. But as she and Siobhan went to work making sure they were ready when Royce returned, she felt the light within her grow brighter. Sam was sure some of her energy was flowing to him.

First order of business, Sam moved the chanting witch (Kyra, or whatever her name was) across the room, far away from Lance, and far away from *her*. The healer assured her the tiny woman could do whatever it was she was doing from anywhere. Buying into the fact that men could change into dragons was as far as Sam was willing to stretch for the day, but Lance's family believed "the witch" was doing something to help their cause, so Sam wouldn't completely banish her…just remove her from sight.

Royce returned in record time. Once the equipment was all set up, she and Siobhan worked tirelessly for hours. It was a true collaboration. As the healer worked to remove the sword, Sam followed its path, stitched his heart muscle, and ensured the blade didn't pass through anything that would cause more damage. She was amazed he only bled a small amount, and remembered that Siobhan had told her that Lance would be able to regulate most of his body's functions as long as they worked quickly and she continued to keep the bond between them open.

As they worked, more people from what they called their clan entered the room, forming groups in the four corners of the room. So engrossed in saving Lance, it wasn't until she turned to grab more sutures that Sam realized they were actually chanting. It was nothing like the sounds of the tiny witch. Theirs had more of a sacred feel. It was the Latin she'd learned in medical school, and the longer she tuned in, the more she understood they were actually praying not only for Lance, but that she and Siobhan would be given all they needed and all would be better for the experience.

Sam was completely humbled at the solidarity and commitment to one another these people shared. It was something she'd never known, even when her mother and sister were alive. These people had no real extended family…it had always been just them. To see and feel the bond that ran between them energized her and made her believe there might actually be a chance for her and the man they all swore was her mate.

When the blade was removed and Samantha had tied off the last stitch, the healer slathered the wound with a thick layer of ointment that smelled of herbs and flowers. Any other time she would've had a fit, but after all she'd witnessed in the last ten or so hours, Sam had to believe Siobhan knew what she was doing. The people who'd been chanting were now placing candles on every available surface. In groups of four, they surrounded Lance's bed and offered what she could only imagine were more prayers of healing and support.

Unable to stand any longer, Sam dropped in the chair someone had placed at the foot of his bed and leaned forward. Her head fell onto her folded arms. Trying to get comfortable, she bumped his bare foot. Just the touch sent a familiar electric current streaking through her body, more intense than anything she'd experienced before. It was a good sign.

Completely exhausted, both physically and mentally, her body still reacted to his touch, and it was so much stronger than when she'd been touching the dragon on his chest prior to the surgery. Never a religious person, Sam took a moment and offered a really quick prayer to whatever higher power was listening. Then she drifted, not quite sleeping, but not quite awake.

Days passed. Sam was beginning to think Lance might never wake up. The only time she left his bedside was to shower and change clothes, afraid that if she stayed away too long, the bond she could feel tying them together would somehow cease to exist.

Sam hated to admit she was starting to depend on the feelings of warmth and acceptance coming from Lance. They *had* to be coming from him. She'd never felt them before the day she'd completely opened herself to him. Sam never wanted it to end. When the thought of returning to work invaded the routine she'd set up while caring for Lance, she pushed it away, not wanting to think what would happen if they spent long hours and miles apart.

Somehow Siobhan knew what she was feeling, and without preamble, explained that once the bond between mates was formed, not even their "forever death" could sever what they had together. The older woman told her the story of how her own mate had gone to the Heavens many years ago, and how their connection was still just as strong as the day it had formed.

Sam saw the momentary flash of pain in the other woman's eyes, which was immediately replaced with a smile so sweet it brought a tear to the doctor's eyes.

"My Gareth was a Dragon Guardsman, just like your Lance. I lost him during an especially brutal battle with the wizards and hunters many years ago. I carry him here." The healer placed her hand over her heart. "And here," she said as she lifted the locket Sam had admired often over the last few days. Siobhan opened the beautifully engraved piece of jewelry to show Sam a spectacular opal dragon scale, with what looked like a red tear drop in the center.

"My mate was one of the rare white dragons. Not long after we were mated, he returned from battle, unable to shift back to human form due to a serious injury. I nursed him in the healing caves for almost a week until he was able to shift again. While I cared for him, he shed this scale."

She gently stroked the scales within the locket. "I'd placed it with all the other broken scales, but my Gareth found it and had this locket made for me. On the day he gave it me, he explained that only once in every white dragon's life did they produce the rare heart scale. Most shed it without ever knowing. The fact we'd been together when he'd shed it was our special blessing from the Universe.

"We had many happy years together and were blessed with a son. I believe you've met him…Devon?" Sam nodded. "Even though Gareth has gone on before me, I hold a piece of his soul in mine. We will be reunited in the Heavens again one day." Siobhan beamed with love and pride while talking of her family.

For the first time since this entire thing started, Sam let her tears flow freely, surprised that not one was in sadness. All were happy tears of hope and love. Siobhan held the doctor's hand. Once again, warmth that defied explanation made its way up Sam's arm, filling her with a calm sense of well-being.

"There is one more thing I need to talk to you about, love," the elder woman began. Sam wiped her eyes on her sleeve while she listened. "I know the girls explained a lot to you about our kin. I can tell you have not completely come to terms with what the future holds for you and our Lance, but I feel it is my responsibility to make sure you know that our lifespan is considerably longer than that of humans. If you decide to officially mate with Lance, yours will be also."

Sam sat for a minute, contemplating what she'd just learned, and wondered if her life would ever be normal again. She snorted in the most unladylike fashion when she realized her life had never been normal, so why start at this point? Siobhan grinned like she knew what Sam was thinking, and actually chuckled when Sam snorted.

"So are we talking a hundred years longer or something?"

"Actually, we are talking about a thousand years, and that is just in this life. None of us knows what the next life holds," the healer said so calmly Sam had to do a quick rewind of the conversation to make sure she'd heard correctly. She was sure her eyes were going to bug out of her head.

"One thousand years? Really?"

Siobhan grabbed both her hands, but Sam was pretty sure the warmth trick wasn't going to work this time. "Yes, dear, but there is nothing to fear. You will have your mate and all his brethren by your side. Days filled with love and family."

"It all sounds really cool, but don't you guys get arthritis or diabetes or high blood pressure?"

Siobhan laughed. "No, Samantha, we do not. We are designed to live long, bountiful lives protecting our kin and any other who may need our help."

"If you say so, but I was thinking eighty was going be a lot of years. I definitely need to think about the whole thousand year thing." Sam tried to make light while inside she was freaking out.

"I promise I did not tell you to scare you or make you doubt what I can tell you feel for him." Siobhan motioned to Lance, still lying motionless. "But to make sure you know everything about us."

"Well, thank you for sharing. I truly appreciate it. It's just gonna take a little time to fully absorb it all."

On the third day, Sam could no longer keep Sydney from visiting Lance. The negotiations and promises were over. As soon as they got downstairs, she was once again completely amazed by the little girl's maturity and loving nature. Syd sat beside Lance's bed with her books and dolls, reading and acting out story after story. There were times when the little girl was talking or singing that Sam could actually feel love flowing through their connection. The doctor had to believe it meant he was making his way back to them.

Sydney visited at least once a day from then on. There were times it appeared as though she was actually carrying on a conversation with him, but Sam chalked it up to the little girl's imagination. Grace had spoken with the judge handling Sydney's case, and now the four of them, Aidan, Grace, Sam, and Lance, were listed as her guardians. The order would remain in place until Sydney's safety was no longer an issue. If Sam had it her way, the child would remain with them forever.

Them? Forever?

Was she really considering making a go of it with her Dragon Man? She shoved it into the "Things to Think About Later" part of her brain and moved on.

The huge incision across his chest visibly healed more each day, until on the sixth day. That day the stitches dissolved, leaving a jagged puffy pink scar…further proof that all she was being told, no matter how unbelievable, was the truth.

His heartbeat was strong and steady, although still slower than she liked. Siobhan assured her it was normal for all dragon shifters. All of his brethren, as Sam had been told they were called, were in and out every day, all day, and Kyndel came down a few extra times to administer the ointment that was her granny's recipe. Sam had never believed in herbal remedies, but then she'd never believed men could turn into dragons, either.

Max, whom she'd met at the hospital, his sister, and two men came to visit during Lance's convalescence. Their mannerisms were anything but normal. The large, darker skinned one with onyx eyes actually sniffed Lance's arm, then looked to Max. Sam was sure the silent communication thing was happening between them, but it was different than when the dragons did it…completely inexplicable, but different nonetheless. Max and his group were big and muscular, but leaner, more compact, more graceful than Lance and the others. The dragon shifters were graceful, but these others were just…more so. They were very polite and seemed genuinely concerned for Lance's welfare, but Sam couldn't help feeling they had secrets of their own.

Her hand to forehead moment came when Devon came down just as Max and crew were leaving. She must have been looking at them with a questioning look, because the usually quiet Guardsman asked, "You can tell, can't you?"

"What?" she asked, trying to school her features.

"You can tell they aren't human. You've been around us long enough you're starting to notice the difference," he stated so matter-of-factly that it took her a minute to respond.

"Busted," she shrugged, waiting for him to go on.

"They're werepanthers."

Sam knew she was looking at Devon like he had three heads, but she couldn't stop. Then he said, "Like we change into dragons, they change into panthers." Devon smiled, like it was every day a person found out there really were people who could turn into something more, before asking, "You okay, Sam?"

"Okay is a relative term. I will be as soon as you tell me what else is out there and why the darker one smelled Lance's arm."

Devon thought for a moment and then agreed. "But if he," Devon motioned towards Lance, "gets pissed, I'm blaming it on you."

"Deal," she agreed.

"Juan Carlos was 'scenting' to see if there was silver left in Lance's body. He told Max it's almost gone."

"I think I need some of those supercharged senses," Sam laughed, trying to relieve the tension.

"You will," he responded, but she decided to let that go for another time.

She listened as he told her about more spectacular things than she'd ever even imagined. They talked into the wee hours of the morning. If Devon hadn't looked her straight in the eye or stalled for even a second before answering one of her million questions, Sam would've sworn he was messing with her…kind of like her initiation into the family. But he didn't, and she knew he was being blatantly honest. When she finally rested that evening, her dreams were full of all they'd discussed. She added it to the list of things she was going to wring Lance's neck over when he woke up.

The last night before she had to return to work, Royce came down to visit. As he was getting up to leave he asked her to come outside for a minute. Scared Lance might wake up while she was gone, Sam stood, but didn't move until one of the younger healers who'd been making the rounds told her he would keep watch and come get her if there was any change.

As they made their way through the house, Sam noticed it was completely abandoned. "Where is everyone?"

The big guy didn't answer, just kept moving. When they reached the french doors leading into the backyard, Sam saw lights and heard voices. Royce threw them open, and everyone she'd met over the last week screamed, "SURPRISE!"

In the course of all the craziness, Sam had forgotten her own birthday. Not that she ever really celebrated it, but at least she usually remembered the day. It was incredibly touching that these amazing people had thought of her. They were accepting her into their fold, making her one of their own, even though she still held out that she would be returning to her life as soon as she knew Lance was healthy and the threats against her and Sydney had been eliminated.

For a brief second, Sam wondered how they'd known, and then got so caught up in the festivities it was several hours before it dawned on her that she'd forgotten to ask. Figuring it would have to wait until later, Sam made her way back down to Lance.

The young healer had been replaced by Jace, a newly "transformed" member of what they called the Dragon Guard. He seemed like a good kid, but looked no older than the high school kids she'd taught CPR over the summer. Sam knew sooner or later her brain was going to explode from all the new things she was learning, and she hadn't even touched on the "special language" she'd heard them speaking. It reminded her of the Gaelic she'd heard Charlie's parents speak the few times they'd visited.

Sam gave Lance his nightly sponge bath and realized she was actually holding her breath, waiting for him to open his eyes. She longed to hear, "Doc," in his low baritone rumble that worked its way under her skin and made her pulse race, and to feel his lips on hers.

Taking a deep breath, she wiped across his chest with a clean cloth to remove the bath oil infused water, marveling again as Lancelot—as she'd started calling the dragon on his chest—responded to her touch. Sam thought back to her dream featuring the amazing beast and recalled every detail of his massive body. Something about that dream seemed real.

At the time, she'd dismissed it as her lack of sleep, but after all she'd learned in the last week, Sam had to wonder if it was real. Had Lance actually flown past her window, watching and protecting her even in his dragon form? Kyndel and Grace said she was the mate of not only the man, but the beast. Could it really be true? Why would she doubt that if she was willing to believe the rest?

Her hands moved along Lance's amazing body, touching every muscle, caressing the definition of his eight-pack, making her mouth water with the need to taste. She knew she should feel bad about getting excited while he lay there unmoving, recovering from an almost fatal injury, but her body had a mind of its own. It also didn't help that the longer her hands massaged his tanned skin, the stronger the feelings of lust coming through their connection grew and the stronger the electric current between them sparked. Somewhere in his healing sleep, as they all called it, Lance was aware of what was going on and knew she was caring for him. It was just something she knew…without explanation.

Siobhan explained it was the combination of massive amounts of silver and the way his dragon had drained his strength to keep Lance up and fighting that was prolonging his healing time. Sam would've thought it might've had something to do with the huge blade they'd removed from his chest and said as much to the elder woman.

The healer just laughed and told the doctor he'd healed from much worse almost overnight. It was completely inconceivable, yet she was watching it happen, living every moment of it, and not able to dispute one thing she'd learned.

Deciding it was truly masochistic to continue torturing herself any longer, Sam rushed to finish. Her resolve almost evaporated as his cock jumped when her hands came near. She reminded herself she'd taken an oath to care for the sick and injured, not molest them where they lay.

Laughing at her own silliness and the way she was hiding behind her profession, Sam just shook her head. The three women she was quickly coming to call friends warned her that as the mating bond grew, so would her need to be with her mate. They had not been lying. There were times just looking at him made her nipples pebble and juices flow.

More than once she'd had to excuse herself to the ladies room to splash cold water on her face and take a few deep breaths. Even then, she could still smell his masculine scent on her hands and clothing where they'd come in contact with his sensual skin. It was a tantalizing aroma that reminded her of the air right after a lightning strike, cool and fresh, but electrically charged with an undertone of musk that sent her pulse racing and her temperature rising. The man was a damn drug. No matter how hard she tried to deny it, she feared she was addicted.

Settling into the huge recliner Royce had brought down for her the first night, Sam dreaded the morning. It meant leaving Lance and Sydney and the place she was quickly becoming to think of as a second home. If anyone had told her a couple of weeks ago that she would ever enjoy sharing her space with anyone, Sam would've called them a liar, but now she was finding it hard to think of her life without these people.

She had no clue what that meant to her plans for the future. Siobhan had expressed how desperately their clan needed healers, especially ones who could treat human mates *and* dragon kin. Could she do it? Could she leave behind all she knew and go to only God knew where and live with people who could do things she'd once thought only existed in books and movies?

The longer she thought, the more Sam realized the real question was…could she live without Lance.

CHAPTER THIRTY-TWO

Three weeks? Three fucking weeks? And Samantha wasn't even in the house after all that time. Rayne had decided it was okay for her to return to work, and Lance hadn't been awake to go with her. Thankfully, the commander had her under constant protection, either by those of their clan or Max's men. He and his dragon were having a difficult time rationalizing that they were not the ones protecting her. It was maddening.

Every few minutes Lance had to convince both man and beast that no one would dare touch her. It was one of the most difficult things he'd ever done. It pissed him off more than he wanted to admit. All of him, body and soul, needed to be near her. Needed to hold her. Needed to connect with her.

He didn't even care that all of his brethren were going to razz him relentlessly. Lance just wanted Sam as soon as possible. Being without her for those long weeks had left a huge dark hole in his soul that only her light could fill. He needed her to feel complete. He needed her more than he needed his next breath. For what seemed like the hundredth time while Siobhan poked and prodded, he talked himself down from certain madness. His dragon pushed and chuffed, but there was nothing Lance could do.

His brethren, especially Royce, would just kick his ass if he tried to move before the Elder Healer gave her permission. He'd been warned, and from the look in their eyes, they meant what they said. Lance sat as still as possible and endured the exam. Whatever it took to get the hell out bed and to his mate was what he was going to do.

He'd never been out that long, even when he'd damn near had his arm and leg blown off in the Gulf War. What was even weirder was he had no recollection of what had gone on outside of his healing sleep. He hadn't felt like he was floating, hadn't had any dreams. He hadn't even fantasized about Sam. It was just one big, black blob of nothingness. Siobhan explained it was because both he and his dragon had been completely drained. The silver had simply taken over. The Elder Healer explained in detail how Kyra, and as many healers as could make the trip, had chanted to keep him from crossing over into the Heavens. But it was when she spoke of his mate that he was filled with a pride he'd never known.

"She is truly a gifted doctor and an amazing woman, Lance," Siobhan stated.
He could see his Doc had made quite the impression on the Elder Healer.

"But she is struggling to come to terms with all she has learned and the impending changes in her life." She looked at him and he braced for the lecture he knew that look prefaced.

"Grace and Kyndel did a good job of explaining how our kin came about, dragon shifters, and mates, but it would've been better coming from you. Having a mate means her needs come before yours, even if your needs are just your fears rearing their ugly little heads."

He attempted to interrupt to defend himself, but she stopped him cold with a pointed stare. Nodding for her to continue, Lance settled back and took his verbal punishment, because he knew she was right.

"I was there when Alexander brought you to the lair. I know the responsibility you felt…still feel to this day for the death of your family, but you have to put that behind you. The Universe has given you a mate, a woman made especially for you, your perfect complement in every way. It is the dream of every dragon, be he Guard or not, to find his mate. You, my boy, cannot let your past get in the way. Andrew is still out there, and this human criminal that is apparently somehow in league with him, but that does not change the simple fact that your future has come to you. You have to grab it with both hands and live it. It is time. It is what your mother and sisters would want for you." She paused, and he knew she was giving him a chance to respond, but his surrogate mother had literally stolen the words from his mouth.

"She does not know the story of Andrew and his betrayal, so that is up to you to explain or not. I also have not shared with her my beliefs about Sydney. Samantha loves that child, and I can tell that you are falling for her charms as well." Siobhan winked. He knew it was for his benefit. "Our beliefs about her origin need to come from you."

He knew she was right, but wondered what his amazing mate would think of their theory. No matter, he wasn't a coward. Sam had to know the truth. She had to see they were meant to be together. He damn sure wasn't letting her over-think their destiny. She was his, just as much as he was hers. Lance would do everything in his considerable power to make her choose him and their future. If that didn't work, he'd ask his brethren for help. At this point he had no dignity and no shame. All he had was the love that filled every fiber of his being for the woman who was meant to be his in this life and the next.

Hours later, he was finally allowed to get out of bed with a clean bill of health. The first stop was the longest, hottest shower he ever remembered taking. As the water flowed over him and the steam filled the bathroom, he thought of all he'd learned since his return to the living. It was obvious Sam felt the pull of the mating call and had opened herself to their bond in order to save his life.

Being able to feel her had been one of things allowing him to not run off like a crazy man looking for her as soon as his eyes had opened. The bond that would allow her to share his dragon magic and all its benefits was still new, and weak, but now that he was awake, Lance planned to do everything to make it as strong as possible and to get the gorgeous Dr. Malone to be his mate for all time.

He couldn't wait to have their official mating ceremony, and knew exactly where it would be held. Thankfully, Aidan had paved the way for them to have their own unique location for the sacred ritual that would bind them together for all time.

Finally feeling almost like himself, Lance dressed in a pair of jeans and grabbed his favorite boots. He had to laugh at the story Jace told him about the very boots he was shoving his feet into. Apparently, the twins decided the newly initiated Guardsman should be responsible for cleaning the mud, blood, and gore from Lance's boots and do his best to restore them to their original, comfortable condition. Lance remembered all the things he'd been subjected to during his first years in the Guard, and figured Jace had gotten off pretty easy.

Pulling an old gray T-shirt over his head, he felt the pull of his still healing scar, proving that fucking bastard traitor had slathered the sword Lance had been impaled on with some sort of bespelled liquid silver. He knew the fucking shit was almost out of his system, but couldn't wait for it all to be gone. Scars might be cool for some guys and prove they were tough, but Lance knew he was tough.

He'd only gotten one foot in the kitchen when he was damn near tackled by a four-foot ball of energy topped with a mass of curly blonde hair and a squeal that could break glass.

"You're up! You're up! You're up!" Sydney screamed as she climbed his leg like it was the old oak outside his home at their lair.

Lifting Sydney into his arms, she turned towards the crowd gathering and continued to scream, "He's up! He's up! He's up!"

Rayne walked in carrying Jay, who looked as though he'd grown a foot since the last time Lance saw him, and smiled. "Yes, Miss Sydney, I told you he was awake and would come up as soon as he was dressed."

His commander turned his attention towards him, speaking as he advanced. "She's been pacing and stalking the door ever since word that you'd awakened reached us up here." Clapping Lance on the back, Rayne continued. "Glad to have you back."

Lance nodded. "Glad to be back." And the floodgates were opened.

All the Guardsmen, Grace, Kyndel, and the werepanthers who'd stopped by, took their turn welcoming him back. The last to approach was his oldest friend, Royce. The look the big guy gave him said it all. They may antagonize each other beyond all reason, but when push came to shove, they were brothers through blood and loyalty, and nothing could change that.

"Glad to see you up and around. You damn sure milked it for all it was worth, you pain in the ass."

He could've heard a pin drop as they all waited for his rebuttal. Never one to disappoint, Lance grinned and winked. "Aww shucks, Gramps. Ya missed me, didn't you?"

Royce's mouth moved with what Lance was sure was a damn good comeback, but there was no way to hear it over the laughter that had erupted. After that, it was hours of storytelling and planning, all centered on the fucking loser and 'The Auctioneer'.

Lance listened and added what he could, but Sam monopolized his thoughts. He checked the clock on the stove at least thirty times, and at one point, swore it wasn't working. The goofy looks he got from all in attendance told him it was, and worst yet, they knew exactly what was going on. The night dragged on, with the best part being tucking Sydney into bed and reading her a bedtime story.

When he left her room after about fifty goodnight kisses, Lance went straight to the room he'd shared with Sam before the battle, but only traces of her amazing scent were to be found. It was then he remembered Siobhan telling him she'd spent every night in the recliner next to the bed where he'd convalesced.

Making a beeline for the basement, Lance lifted her pillow and inhaled jasmine and honeysuckle. His cock jumped as images of Sam flooded his mind. It was all he could do to not jump on his Harley and ride to the hospital, but he knew he had to wait for her to come to him.

Grace had texted Sam to give her the good news even before he'd emerged from the basement, so he'd refrained from bothering her again. The attorney told him Sam was doing everything possible to get someone to cover the second part of her double shift. His prayers had been answered when his phone vibrated on the counter after finally being located in Sydney's doll bag, and the message said, *Getting off at midnight.*

Lance spent the next hours alternating between pacing and sitting on the stairs tapping his foot. His only distraction came when he ventured to the back yard to pick flowers for Sam from one of the many gardens.

The grandfather clock at the top of the stairs chimed when midnight arrived, and his dragon chuffed. Both man and beast were ready to reconnect with their alluring mate. It felt like an eternity before he heard the younger Guardsman stationed near the gate mind speak to one of the others right outside the house, alerting them to the fact that Dr. Malone was on her way up the drive. Lance was pleased to see they extended her the proper respect, and knew he had Royce to thank. The big guy was the only one of them who still adhered to the old ways.

Trying to look calm, cool, and collected, he damn near jumped out of his skin when the door opened and he got his first glimpse of the most wonderful woman ever created after three very long weeks. Sam paused for just a second, threw her brown leather messenger bag to the side, and started towards him. He saw that she was nervous and knew no matter how hard it was, he had to let her come to him. It had to be her decision. So he waited, holding the flowers he'd picked and looking into her dark brown eyes.

Sam stopped five feet in front of him, and for the first time since coming through the door, looked like she truly wanted to be there. When she spoke, her smoky voice wrapped around him. The pieces of his world that had seemed askew since opening his eyes fell into place. All was right with his world. "How are you feeling?" she asked.

His mouth was so dry, he barely forced out his answer. "Fine, now that you're here, Doc."

She graced him with a spectacular smile. He could see stars in her eyes, and the hairs on his arms stood on end. No longer able to stand not having her in his arms, Lance stood and closed the distance between them. The moment their skin touched, the resulting electric current made him weak in the knees.

If he'd been anyone else, he would've written her a sonnet or spoken beautiful words expressing everything he was feeling, but he was who he was, so he did the only thing he could, he kissed her with his entire being. Lance poured all the love and devotion he felt for Samantha into his kiss. She sighed, opening to him completely, filling him with pride that she trusted him.

Dropping the flowers and pulling her as close as he could, their kiss caught fire. He knew it would only be minutes before the need to have her naked beneath him took over. She climbed his body, as blown away by their passion as he. He grabbed her ass, lifting her until he could feel her hardened nipples against his chest. Only their clothes kept him from her luscious body. Unable to wait any longer, he slid his hands down the back of her thighs and pushed her legs until she wrapped them around his waist.

Taking the stairs three at a time and never losing contact with her incredible mouth, Lance raced to their room. The feel of her hands in his hair, her nails scratching his scalp, and the way she continued to lose control spurred him on. Balancing her on his raised thigh, he barely got the door open before she started to grind against his leg.

He could feel the heat of her excitement through their clothes. His mouth watered to taste the honey he knew was flowing from her pussy. The door bounced off the wall. Lance stepped across the threshold and kicked it closed with his booted foot, not missing a beat in his quest to bury his throbbing cock into his wet and ready mate.

Lance's knees hit the bed at the same time Sam unwound her legs from his waist and slid down his body. The friction was enough he thought he might explode in his jeans. Pulling back from their kiss, he grinned as Sam moaned at the loss. The lustful half-lidded look she gave him had him pulling her scrub top over her head and tearing the bra from her body. Just the sight of her breasts short-circuited his brain. His mouth latched onto one hard nipple while his thumb and forefinger worked the other, and then he switched. All the while Sam mewled and writhed, holding him fast to her breast.

He released her nipple and threw his head back, trying to catch his breath. The feel of her hands on his zipper had him snapping to attention. Before he could grab her, she knelt before him and was working his jeans downward. He placed his hands under her arms.

Sam looked him right in the eyes, shaking her head. "Please, Lance, I want to do this. I *need* to do this," she panted, and whatever blood was left in his brain headed south. There was no way in this life or the next he could deny her anything. Just the thought of her lips on his cock made him gasp for air.

With the first lick of her tongue across the tip Lance saw stars. "Damn, Doc! You're gonna kill me," he hissed, and was rewarded when he felt her smile against his rock hard cock.

Sam sucked him into her mouth so slowly he thought his head would surely fly off his shoulders. Resisting pumping his hips, Lance glimpsed heaven when the tip of his erection touched the back of her throat as she hollowed out her cheeks and swallowed. She slowly let him all but fall from her mouth, then ran her tongue up and down the slit he knew wept with precum.

He fell from her mouth and groaned, never wanting it to end. As if reading his mind, she ran her tongue along the vein running the length of his cock. He became so hard, he was sure he would explode or die from anticipation. Her tongue lavished the ridge under his mushroom head, causing him to moan so loudly he knew everyone in the house could hear despite the soundproofing.

Holding on by a thread, Lance panted like a dog, but there was no way he would take this from his mate. She wanted control, and he would give it to her even if it killed him. He moved his hands to her shoulders and kneaded. Breathing faster than when he'd been forced to run twenty miles without using his enhanced abilities, Lance wondered if any of his kin had ever died of cardiac arrest. Didn't matter. He would be happy to be the first if it meant feeling her mouth on him for just a moment longer.

Sam surprised him by sucking all of his considerable length into her mouth in one quick motion, but she damn near threw him over the edge when she massaged him with her tongue and swallowed around his swollen head. The muscles in her mouth and throat milked him until his eyes crossed beneath his closed lids.

He squeezed her shoulders, careful not to hurt her, and spoke through gritted teeth. "Doc, *mo ghra'*, I'm not going to last if you keep doing that." The sound of his pained voice would've made him laugh if there had been any air left in his lungs.

Sam mumbled, "Mmhmm," and the vibrations against his aroused cock caused his body to break out in a cold sweat. Never before had he experienced anything like it. He grabbed her hair and realized she still wore her signature braid.

All thought flew from his mind as she pulled him from her mouth, and quicker than he knew she could move sucked one, and then the other of his balls in to her mouth. Sam licked and massaged with her tongue while working up and down his penis with her fist. Just as he was sure he was going to embarrass himself, she took his length in her mouth, placed both her hands around the base, and worked him in and out of her mouth, sucking and humming until he could do nothing but release. He floated back to earth, realizing she was still working her lips up and down his semi-erect cock.

Lance had suffered the sweetest torture possible from his mate's luscious lips, and it was his turn. Within seconds Sam was flat on her back with a stunned expression, lips rosy and swollen from the way she'd just loved him. Using his enhanced speed, he stripped the rest of her clothing from her body and threw her legs over his shoulders.

Chuckling as she gasped, he blew on her weeping center, rubbing his nose against the warm, wet silk covering what he wanted most, her aroused scent driving him mad. His only option was to taste her or die from want. Tormenting both of them just a bit more, he ran the very tip of his tongue from the bottom to the very top of the glistening seam of her pussy, bypassing her engorged nub, and smiled when she grabbed his hair, trying to direct him to where she wanted him most.

At the first taste of his mate on his lips, Lance groaned deep in his throat. With no restraint left and his dragon pushing harder than he'd ever felt, he buried his tongue deep inside. Needing more of her, he placed his hands under her ass and lifted her as close as possible to his face to feast on what would be his for all time. He licked every inch he could touch, drinking in all that she was.

Sam gasped and mewled, struggling to breathe as he continued his assault, happy to go on until she collapsed from exhaustion. He placed the flat of his tongue at the bottom of her outer lips, applied just a little pressure, and licked all the way to her clit. Her bright red nub slid neatly between his lips, and he used the tip of his tongue to tease it until she came so hard he struggled to swallow all her juices. He nuzzled and nipped all around her inflamed lips until she released his hair and her breathing began to slow.

Lifting her legs gently off his shoulders and massaging from her ankles to her thighs, Lance marveled at the sight before him. Never had there been a lovelier sight than his mate completely satiated, barely able to keep her eyes open.

He kissed her hip and made his way to just below her belly button. Sam's throaty chuckle was music to his ears. Kissing his way up her stomach to the sweet spot between her breasts, Lance nipped, enjoying the gasp from her luscious lips. Palming both her breasts, he squeezed the already raised peaks and sighed as they pushed against his hands. He kissed her neck, paying special attention to one of his favorite spots right behind her ear. She rolled her head to the side, allowing him greater access. He spent a few extra minutes tasting and kissing until her nails dug into his biceps.

Enjoying the taste and feel of his mate, knowing there would never be any place better than in her arms, love exploded in his heart and soul. He shifted his hips the tiniest bit and pushed into her until he could go no farther. Sam gasped, "Lance! Yes! Oh God, yes!"

He wanted to go slow the first time in her after so long, but the feel of her muscles contracting around him, driving him higher, made it impossible for him to hold still any longer. He slid out of her until only the very tip of his cock rested inside her opening. "Look at me, Samantha," he commanded, using her given name. Her eyes locked with his.

Pushing back into her as fast and hard as he could, Lance pulled right back out, starting a rhythm that she met stroke for stroke. They continued to stare into each other's eyes as their passion rose. Pushing her knees towards her chest, he lifted her bottom off the bed. Their new position allowed him the deeper access to her weeping channel he sought. He rolled his hips, touching every inch of his mate that he could. The walls of her vagina closed tighter around him. They lost eye contact when her eyes rolled back in her head. It was just as well because he felt a grin of pride spread across his face as he fought for air.

He slammed into her, bumping her clit with his pelvis as her breathing accelerated and the pulse in her neck pumped ferociously. The sound of their bodies slapping together, coupled with their heavy breathing, was all he could hear as he watched Sam racing towards her release.

His balls drew up tight. Reaching between their bodies, he barely touched her clit with his thumb and watched as she flew apart. Her bottomless brown eyes snapped to his, and there within was the promise of their future. That one look from the most important person in his world pushed him over the edge. His orgasm triggered another in her. Lance finally understood the true meaning of bliss. They collapsed, spent, fulfilled, and incredibly happy.

He awoke to the sun shining through the blinds and a tiny little knock at the door. Carefully, he moved Sam from her place draped across his chest and watched as she curled onto her side, sweetly falling back into a deep sleep. He slipped out of bed and into his jeans.

Opening the door just enough to slide into the hall, it was just barely closed before Sydney jumped into his arms, talking a hundred miles a minute, and smiling from ear to ear. "Grace and Kyndel said to wait until you came out. Royce said he would play another game of Candyland with me, but I really wanted to see you and Dr. Sam. I don't wait very well. Can we go in and see her?"

"Dr. Sam is still sleeping, Syd, but we can go down and make some breakfast, maybe play until she gets up. Cool?"

She clapped her hands and bounced in his arms. "Yay! Let's do it! But you better put a shirt on, you silly dragon."

He damn near dropped her and could feel his eyes go round when she called him a silly dragon, but then he remembered all Siobhan had told him about the little sweetie and couldn't help but laugh along with her.

"If I'm a silly dragon, then you are most definitely a silly girl," Lance teased as he sat her on her feet and mussed the curls on her head. "You head on down. I'll grab a shirt and be right there."

"Okay," she sing-songed and skipped towards the stairs. No sooner had he put his hand on the doorknob then she called to him. "Lance?"

"Yes, darlin'?" he answered, looking over his shoulder.

"Love you," she said before continuing her trip to the stairs.

He stood motionless as he watched her disappear down the stairs, smiling as he entered the bedroom. The sight that caught his eyes, coupled with what had just happened in the hall, made him believe he was the most blessed of all dragon kin.

Sam was still curled on her side, facing him with a look of absolute peace on her face. Her long curly hair spread out behind her made his fingers itch to run through the silky tendrils as he had all through the night. It was truly one of his guilty pleasures, to unwind her hair from the intricate french braid she frequently wore and watch as it resumed its true wild form. He would never tire of simply looking at her.

A few weeks ago he'd feared turning into a sappy shell of himself, but now he welcomed all the love and devotion he felt thrumming through his veins. He'd mistaken love for weakness, when in essence it was the strength that brought him back to life, and the unyielding force that made absolutely anything seem possible.

Knowing if he didn't leave right away he would end up back in bed making love to Sam, Lance grabbed a clean T-shirt from the drawer and pulled it over his head as he made his way down the stairs. He could hear the sounds of Syd explaining the finer points of block stacking to Jay, along with his brethren laughing and joking in the kitchen.

Deciding caffeine was a necessity after the night he'd spent loving his mate, he headed straight for the kitchen. As soon as his bare feet hit tile, the jokes started. Of all the taunts he listened to as he poured a cup of coffee, Aidan's damn near caused him to spit coffee across the counter. "Hey there, macho man, what's with the moony eyes? Did cupid shove an arrow up your ass?"

When he could speak again, Lance smiled the grin he knew pissed them all off and said, "He damn sure did."

Chuckling at their stunned silence, he joined Syd on the floor, helping build block castles while the child told stories of princesses trapped in towers and the knights who saved them. Jay crawled from structure to structure, wreaking havoc while putting everything possible in his mouth. Kyndel passed by a few times to make sure they were all getting along, while picking up toys that had spread all over the house. Aidan told him Grace was locked in her office with some new information concerning the whereabouts of 'The Auctioneer' as he passed by on his way to join his mate.

It wasn't until his stomach growled that Lance remembered he hadn't eaten this morning. "Hey, Syd, you hungry?"

He could tell she was thinking about it before she nodded. "I am. Can we have chicken nuggets and french fries?"

"We sure can," he answered, standing and scooping Jay up at the same time. Syd grabbed his hand as they made their way to the kitchen. He imagined what it would be like to take care of Sam and his kids. Little girls with long dark curls and his blue eyes, charming everyone they came in contact with, and blond-haired boys with big brown eyes who were always causing trouble. Kyndel met him at the refrigerator and took Jay for his bottle and nap while Syd climbed up to the breakfast bar.

Lance was bent down placing the nuggets and fries in the oven when he felt his mate's arms wrap around his waist. Standing and turning to face her at the same time, he was once again amazed that someone as brilliant and beautiful as she was had been designed just for him.

"How did you sleep, Doc?"

She got a dreamy look in her eyes, barely speaking above a whisper. "Great. And you?"

"Best night I've ever had." He kissed the tip of her nose and pulled her closer.

Out of the corner of his eye, he saw Syd struggling to climb off her barstool. Putting his mouth to her ear, he whispered, "There's a little girl back there dying to see you."

She blushed the most spectacular color of pink and twisted in his arms. "Hey, pretty girl, get over here and let's have a huggy party."

Syd hit the floor running and squeezed between their legs. Sam stepped back as Lance picked the child up and held her on his hip. The little sweetheart kissed both of their cheeks while looking from one to the other. He saw something brewing her eyes and winked at Sam before speaking. "So tell me, little bit, what's on your mind?"

He and Sam waited as Sydney looked down, took a deep breath, and then began, "I was thinking...." She looked between the two of them. "Will I have to go back to the 'big house'? 'Cause I really like it here with you and all the other dragons, and Miss Kyndel and Baby Jay and Miss Grace."

When she finished, her head dropped forward, avoiding their gaze. Sam and he looked at each for a few long moments. He could see the conflict in his mate's eyes and feel her love for the child through their bond. Making the first real decision of what he thought of as his new life, he answered. "Syd, we're going to do everything possible to keep you with us. That is, if you're sure you want to stay."

The last word was barely out of his mouth before both of his girls threw their arms around his neck and Lance understood the true meaning of "huggy party." The term *"My girls"* continued to roll around in his brain, but it only took a few seconds for him to realize that's exactly who they were...His. His to love. His to protect. His to have in his life for all time. It just felt right.

"All right you two, we need plates and silverware, ketchup, and something to drink. The chicken nuggets and fries should be just about done."

The girls released his neck. Sydney practically jumped out of his arms and headed to the fridge, while Sam collected plates, utensils, and cups. As they ate, they discussed plans for the day. Samantha let them know she had two days off. He grinned to himself, thinking she was going to need a hell of a lot longer than two days off if things went as he had planned.

They spent the rest of the day walking the grounds, picking flowers since the ones he'd picked the night before were now gone, and playing hide and seek. Later, they watched *The Little Mermaid* and *Cars*, two of Syd's favorite movies. At about eight-thirty, Sam announced it was bath time and that he could meet them in Sydney's room in about a half an hour for bedtime stories.

Left to his own devices, Lance wandered towards Grace's office. What sounded like a serious conversation could be heard as he walked up. Not wanting to eavesdrop, he resisted the urge to use his enhanced hearing and instead stepped over the threshold.

"Glad you could join us," Aidan said as he looked up from the pile of papers neatly stacked in front of him.

"Hey, dude, how you feelin'?" Aaron asked.

"I'm good. Thanks, man," Lance answered as they slapped each other on the back.

Rayne took charge as he had for as many years as Lance could remember. "Glad to have you back. We were just discussing what Grace has learned about 'The Auctioneer' and the traitor. Max's men are trying to find a way back in with the head wizard. The little information they did get proved he and the human criminal are working together. It also appears that Andrew has formed his own group with the wizards who severed ties to the Master."

The volume of grumbling increased and Rayne shot a look at each member of their Force, indicating he was not finished speaking. As the noise died down, he continued, "So what we put together from the shit storm in the woods was correct. Andrew is running his own show and still has a connection to black magic; however, we believe it isn't as powerful or as plentiful as before."

Kyra spoke from her spot next to Grace. "Now that I know the son of a bitch uses black magic, and I have the 'taste' of it, I can scry for a location. He has one hell of a shielding spell, so unless I'm close I have no clue how reliable it'll be." She narrowed her eyes and spit through gritted teeth, almost growling. "But I can promise once we catch him, I'm gonna have a party torturing the shit out of the little fucker."

Lance looked around the room as each of his brothers either bit the inside of his cheeks or coughed into their hands to avoid laughing at the tiny, platinum-haired witch who vibrated with anger. Kyra was definitely not over the fact the little fucker had duped her into making amulets for him, then twisted her white magic with his filthy black magic. Siobhan shared with Lance that her Council was not holding any of Andrew's actions against Kyra, and it seemed as though she'd been accepted into their motley crew, at least by most of his brethren.

They continued to discuss strategy for capturing the asshole and stopping 'The Auctioneer'. There was no way any of them were going to let harm come to those they loved.

He looked at the clock on the wall and realized it was story time, so he said his goodbyes and headed out to see his girls. In the hallway, he damn near ran right into Royce. The big guy looked frustrated and tired. "What's up, Grandpa?"

"I'm really not in the mood for your shit tonight, Pain in the Ass."

He cut off the big guy's attempt to slide past him and put his hand on the older man's chest. "Seriously, what's going on?"

Royce took a deep breath and stared over Lance's head for almost an entire minute. When the big man responded, Lance could hear the sheer exhaustion in his friend's voice. "Nothing. Just the same shit, different day, and I'm late to the party." He nodded towards the door Lance had just come through.

Seeing his oldest friend was in no way ready to talk about whatever was bothering him, Lance decided to let it go for the moment. "All right, I'm heading up to tuck Sydney in. Talk to you tomorrow."

Royce grinned, and even though it didn't reach his eyes, Lance knew something good was coming. "Go get 'em, lover boy. I'm sure Sydney's not the only young lady you're 'tucking in'." He wiggled his eyebrows and scooted past Lance, chuckling all the way. He let the old guy have that one since it seemed to lighten his spirits.

Heading towards the stairs and going over his plans for the evening, Lance stopped dead in his tracks and listened to the wonderful sounds of Sam and Sydney's laughter. He had to be the luckiest son of a bitch. Walking into Syd's room, he saw both ladies sitting cross-legged on the bed, dressing the child's dolls for bed.

"What's all the ruckus in here?" he asked as he ran to the bed and picked Sydney up. Tossing her into the air, he sat down as she landed in his lap.

It took a moment for her giggling to die down enough to speak, and when she did, she sounded like a cartoon character. "That was fun, dragon man. We're getting the babies ready for bed. Can you read my story tonight, please?"

"Sure can, short stuff. Let's get these babies to bed and get you tucked in."

Sydney jumped off the bed, placed her dolls tenderly in the beds she'd fashioned out of small towels, and covered them with one of Jay's blankets Kyndel had given her. When she was finished, she came right back to bed, jumped in, and pulled up the covers.

"Can we read *Sleeping Beauty*?"

"Yes, we can," Sam answered, appearing at his side a minute later, carrying the book and a pink plastic cup filled with water.

Thirty minutes and a bunch of yawns later, Lance and Sam kissed Sydney goodnight, turned on her nightlight, and headed back to their room. After excruciatingly long months watching and protecting this amazing woman, it was the best feeling ever to have her hand in his and her scent filling his lungs. He fell more in love with Samantha Malone every second he spent in her presence. With this woman by his side, there was no doubt he could defeat every foe and conquer every challenge set before him. She was a beacon in his darkest hour. She captivated him completely…body and soul. She was all things right in the world. She was everything, and she was his.

As soon as the door closed, he had her in his arms, needing to reconnect with her even though he'd spent the day by her side. There would never be a time he felt like he'd had enough of his magnificent mate. He'd made fun of Rayne when he met Kyndel and couldn't stop touching her even when they were marching through a field. He'd made jokes when Grace came into Aidan's life and his brethren could not keep his lips off her even when they were facing down a parking lot full of combatants, but now Lance understood.

There was no feeling in the world like being with this woman, his woman. Lance slowly lowered his lips, gently touching hers, kissing her like they had all the time in the world, tasting every square inch of her succulent mouth, absorbing all of her that he could. And when she opened for him, he leisurely slid his tongue into her mouth…exploring, stoking the flame that constantly burned between until he was sure he would spontaneously combust.

Lance moved along her jaw, tasting and teasing, marking her as his. Her hips began to move against his erection, the friction making him light-headed. He painstakingly pulled away from her, and together they groaned at the loss.

The passion he saw in her dreamy eyes almost made him rethink his plan, but he knew there were things they needed to discuss…one very specific question he needed her to answer. Walking them to the couch that overlooked the terrace, he got them each a beer from the fridge Aidan made sure was in each room and sat down facing her.

He took a moment to just look at his mate, soaking in the goodness radiating from her. "Damn Doc, you're gorgeous," he said, and was rewarded with a soft blush on her cheeks. She took a long draw of her beer, and all he could think of was what she would taste like in that moment.

Reminding himself that there were things they needed to talk about, Lance took her hand in his, looked her in the eye, and said, "I know everyone explained a lot of stuff to you about who we are while I was out. I'm so damn sorry I didn't do it before the shit hit the fan. I have no excuse. I just thought there would be time when I got home, and then…well…you know." He shrugged and was glad to see her smile. "To be honest, I was surprised you didn't punch me when you got home last night. I mean, I'm glad you didn't, but I wouldn't have blamed you," he went on as she chuckled, and he was happy she wasn't telling him what a jerk he was. "So what questions do you have? I can see the wheels turning up there." He tapped the side of her head. "I'm an open book…ask away."

Sam paused and worried her bottom lip with her teeth, a sign he knew meant she was deciding what to say. He could feel that she had a ton of questions, but waited for her to work it out for herself. After several long minutes, his mate straightened her back and looked him square in the eye. She backed down from nothing.

"At first, I was pissed and couldn't believe you'd hidden things from me. But the longer I thought about it, and the more time I spent with your family, I realized I probably would've done the same thing. There are things about me I don't share with anyone." She paused, and his curiosity was peaked, but he let her continue. "Then, I realized I wouldn't have believed you anyway. My mom always said things happen for a reason. Guess this was definitely one of those times."

"Yeah, I suppose you're right, Doc, but I'm really sorry I left you hanging like that. And…." He had to pause, because for the first time since finding his family dead, Lance was almost overcome with emotion. "I want to thank you for saving my life, for opening yourself up and lending me your strength, and for taking care of me while I recovered. Siobhan was sure to tell me what an amazing doctor you are, which I already knew, but it was cool to hear how much respect she has for you. It takes a lot to impress her, and you definitely did." He took her beer bottle, placed it next to his on the side table, and took both her hands in his. "Now, ask me whatever you want."

Almost before he had finished speaking, she blurted out, "Am I really your mate or whatever it's called? Are we really meant to be together?"

Somehow he wasn't surprised she'd asked. Siobhan had told him how uncomfortable she was with their fated future. "Yes, Doc, you are. I don't know exactly how it was explained to you, but I can tell you I've heard A LOT of stories in all my years, and not a damn one prepared me for that day in the abandoned warehouse when our eyes met. I guess the best way I can explain it is with a passage from our holy book. 'When the two halves of the same whole meet, there will be instant recognition. Their souls will merge, and only then will the man and dragon know complete peace; they will have found their true home. It will be as if the time before they met their mate does not exist. All that will matter will be that they become one in body, mind, and soul with the One the Universe made for them.'" He waited and watched while she came to terms with what he'd just said.

"I know that I feel things for you I never imagined possible. I also know that ever since I did what Siobhan asked and 'opened' myself up to you, there are times I can actually feel what you feel." It was an incredible feeling of belonging and love that Sam acknowledged, at least partially, what was happening between them. "I've seen firsthand that you guys are way more than what you appear, but you have to understand, I've been on my own since I was six years old."

She stopped and closed her eyes. He could see what it cost her to think about the past. Lance rubbed circles on the back of her hands, giving her the time she needed. They sat in silence for some time.

When she finally spoke, he was thankful for his enhanced hearing, because she barely whispered. "My dad was killed while deployed during the Gulf War. I was barely walking and my sister was just a few months old. He was an army medic. I never really knew him, but I imagine he was like you…strong, fearless, and bound by some inner calling to help those who needed it. He protected those he loved. My dad is why I became a doctor. It was the least I could do to honor the man who gave so much and loved us so completely."

She looked at him with tear-filled eyes. He wanted nothing more than to wrap her in his arms and take away all the pain she'd ever felt, but he knew his mate would have none of it. She spoke of his strength and fearlessness without recognizing those very traits in herself. Sam was a true warrior, his perfect match in every way.

"Mom, Sarah, and I lived a really simple life. Mom was a school teacher. She always told stories about Dad and showed us pictures to make sure we never forgot him. It was like I got to know him through her memories.

"She never wanted me to ride the school bus. Said it was dirty and stinky, and since she taught just two blocks away at the junior high, she dropped me off and picked me up. One day during a particularly bad thunderstorm, she was late. I waited until all the other kids were gone, then one of the teachers took me to the office and called Mom's phone. There was no answer. Then they called her school. The secretary said she'd seen her leave ten minutes earlier, so we figured she was caught in traffic from the rain. It was then that we heard the sirens. I *knew* something was wrong.

"We waited for another hour before the police arrived. They wanted to speak to my teacher alone…she was also a close friend of my mom's. But there was no way I was going to be left out. They finally told us a drunk driver had run a stop sign and T-boned my mom's mini-van. He was going so fast that he pushed them onto the curb and the vehicle flipped. Both my mom and sister were pronounced dead at the scene.

"I wasn't really sure at the time what everything they were saying meant, but I knew one thing…I was alone. Both my parents were only children, and all four of my grandparents had passed before I was born."

Lance's pain at the story his love was telling made him wish to go back in time and endure all her pain and suffering for her. She'd lived through her trials and learned from them. Samantha was stronger because of them and helped people every day.

"My teacher took me home with her. I stayed there until a social worker showed up. Then I was taken to a group home. There were lots of foster homes after that, and I finally landed at Momma Maybelle's." A feeling of contentment flowed through their bond. Lance knew his mate truly loved this woman.

"She was the first person besides my mom's friend who acted like I mattered, acted like she cared. I stayed with her until I graduated from high school. She was so proud the day we got the letter that I'd been accepted into one of the most prestigious colleges in the country with a full scholarship. We had a huge graduation party, and all the kids she could find who'd been in foster care with me came.

"Maybelle and I stayed in touch until she died during my junior year. It was a true testament to the wonderful woman she was that every foster kid still in the area came to her memorial service. There's not a day that goes by that I don't thank God for my mom, dad, and Momma Maybelle. Without them, I would've been just a statistic, one of those kids we patch up in the emergency room and send back out it in the world to fend for themselves.

"Now I tell you this because for some crazy reason, I want you to really know who I am and to let you know that all of this," she motioned between them, "scares the shit out of me. Everyone I have ever loved, leaves."

He watched a lone tear travel down her cheek and gave up. Letting her hands drop, Lance grabbed Sam around the waist and lifted her onto his lap. She struggled for a minute, but he held her as still as possible until she gave in and cuddled against his chest. His kissed the top of her head and inhaled the beautiful scent of jasmine and honeysuckle that would forever remind him of the gift he'd been given.

As long as he had breath in his lungs, no one would ever cause this woman another moment of pain. She'd suffered enough. It was his job to make all her days as wonderful as they could possibly be.

"I'll never leave you, Doc and even if one of us goes to the Heavens before the other, we will still be connected…heart and soul. I know you were told about how long we live. I want to make sure you understand that once we're officially mated, if that's what you want, you'll have the same increased lifespan."

She jerked back from him with a surprised look on her face. The way her pouty lips formed a perfect circle made him want to ditch all the talking and have a taste of his lady love. However, it was time all of it was worked out between them. She needed to feel comfortable with everything she'd learned before he could ask her the question he and his dragon longed to hear the answer to.

He chuckled and nodded. "Yes, *mo chroi'* we'll live almost a thousand years together in this life, and for eternity in the next."

Her brow furrowed as she asked, "What did you just call me? And what is the language I hear all your brethren and Siobhan speak occasionally?'

"It's the language of our kin. Not many use it anymore. Most of us mind speak because it's a helluva lot quicker, but the older members of our clan still use it all the time. As for what I called you, I said, 'my heart,' because Samantha Malone, that is exactly what you are." He watched while she digested what he'd just said, and added, "*Ta' mo chroi istigh ionat, mo ghra'* which means 'my heart is within you, my love.'"

Placing his hands on either side of her face, Lance looked into the depth of her dark brown eyes and spoke with more sincerity than he thought he could ever possess. "I love you. With everything that I am. I know that you are the one person in the Universe who completes not only me, but the beast within. I cannot and will not live a moment of my life without you."

CHAPTER THIRTY-THREE

Love? He loved her? Really? Could it be true? She damn sure had learned to not discount what she doubted. Hell, men who shifted into dragons was real; it was probably not out of the realm of possibilities that he at least thought he loved her. Sam looked deep inside herself, even the parts she kept locked away, while he continued to gaze at her with his hypnotic, crystal blue eyes.

She took his hands from her face and held them in her lap. "I have some incredible feelings for you that I can't explain, and I'm pretty sure I don't want to. But I have to be as honest with you as I want you to be with me…." She paused and watched as he held his breath, but never once lost eye contact. Unable to speak above a whisper, she said, "I am terrified. I don't think I'd survive another loss."

It was the single hardest thing she'd ever admitted to anyone in her life. Sam was prepared for him to tell her she was weak or silly, or any wide variety of insults that were swimming around in her mind, but he didn't. He completely surprised her by smiling and massaging up and down her arms. When he spoke, she could feel strength pouring from him, filling her, and calming her fears. "I completely understand, *mo ghra'*. We have a lot more in common than either of us knew. It's time to share my past with you."

Lance told her about his father who was killed in battle when he was a child, and about his mother and sisters, who sounded like wonderful, beautiful, strong-willed women. He talked about how he'd traveled for days to reach the clan with the Dragon Guard that Rayne's father commanded, and how he'd trained for three long months.

She felt like her heart would shatter into a million pieces as he told her how they'd come to find all the people of his clan dead from an attack by black magic wizards. She felt her tears fall as she pictured him finding his mother and sisters, killed by the people that he'd been training to protect them from. The only thing she could think to do as he relived the most traumatic event of his life was to wrap her arms around him and lend him her quiet support.

Sam cried for all he had lost. The longer he spoke, the more it became undeniable they *were* meant to be together. It was destiny that they share the good times and the bad times, but most of all, they were meant to heal each other and be exactly what the other needed.

She had no idea how long they sat in silence and didn't care. Wrapped in his arms was the safest, most peaceful place in the world. Reveling in the strong, steady beat of his heart in her ear and the deep, even rise and fall of his chest, reaffirmed her belief in the sanctity of life. It gave her hope that she really could love and be loved without drastic consequences. He woke her from her musings when she heard the sensual rumbling of his low-voice.

"You okay down there, Doc?"

"Yeah, I'm good." She sat up and looked at the man who'd stolen her heart. "I'm so sorry you lost your family. I know it was a long time ago, but I can tell how much they meant to you and how much you loved them."

Feeling tears come to her eyes again, Sam took a deep breath, but it was Lance who spoke. "You are right, *evgren*. I did love them very much. I still carry that love to this day, but it is *you* who makes my heart beat. It is you I love more than life itself." He placed his hand over her heart, and she knew he could feel how hard and fast it was beating, but she didn't care. It was time to be honest with him.

Sam looked down at his hand on her chest and marveled that she found even his hands sexy. Knowing how those incredibly talented fingers could make her body sing made it difficult for her to think. It was now or never. She had to tell him how she felt.

Raising her head, she found him looking at her. She felt him deep inside, burning brighter and filling her with so much love and acceptance she thought she might burst. Instead, she blurted out all she was feeling. "I love you, too. I didn't think it was possible for me to love anyone ever again. In fact, I've worked really hard for all these years to keep people at arm's length, but there's no way I can deny what I feel or what you've come to mean to me. I love you. There's no other way to say it. I do. But I swear, if you ever put me through what I went through the last three weeks, I *will* kick your ass."

The last word was still on her lips when he slammed his mouth to hers, kissing her with a fiery passion. He stole the breath from her lungs and all thought from her mind. When they came up for air, she could think only of getting her amazing man naked. By the look in his eyes, he thought the same thing. But…there were still a few questions she needed answered.

She laughed out loud as he groaned when her hands touched his chest to keep him from continuing their kiss. "What gives, Doc? I'm dying here." As he spoke he raised his hips, letting her feel exactly how happy he was to be kissing her. It was then her turn to groan.

He laughed and tried to close the distance between them, but Sam kept her arms firm. "I have just a few more questions."

He groaned even louder, flopped back against the couch, and let his head fall to the side. "You really are trying to kill me. I just know it."

She play punched him in the stomach. He grunted, picking up his head and winking at her, but it was the shit-eating grin and damn dimple that made her giggle like a schoolgirl. Breathing deeply to regain control, she asked, "Did you fly past my window in dragon form the first night we officially met?"

His grin grew wider as he nodded. "Sure did." He placed his index finger on his lips, making the "shhhh" sound. "But keep that between us; I'm not really supposed to be flying that close to town unless it's an emergency."

Another giggle bubbled out of her and she chalked it up to a side effect of being in love. "I promise, and I want to see him again for real when I know for sure I'm awake." When he tipped his head in agreement, she went on. "Is everyone's dragon the same color as yours?"

"No, our dragons are all originally from different clans, and therefore, we're all different colors, except for Aidan and Aaron. They're the same because they're blood relatives and twins. Integration happened as time passed. We don't adhere to the color sects any longer. We live with the Force with whom we trained or pledged our fealty."

He stopped talking and she thought about what he'd said, wondering if, or when, she would get to see the color of the other dragons. Then she remembered something she really needed to ask, so she powered on.

"Now, Sydney said she told you that she can tell when you and your brothers were talking into each other's minds, and she said you told her to keep that little tidbit from me. Is that true?" She gave him her most intimidating look, the one she reserved for children and seniors who refused to take their meds.

"Yes, I did," he said and didn't even have the decency to look ashamed. "But in my defense, I didn't know how the hell she could tell, and I didn't want you freaking out and leaving me."

He pretend pouted, and when that didn't work he tickled her until she surrendered. When she was able to speak again, Sam said, "No more secrets. Got it, dragon man? And since we're on that subject, why is it she can do that?"

He furrowed his brow and pursed his lips. "No one is sure, but Siobhan has a theory—" She tried to butt in but he shook his head and gave her a look before continuing. "But we need to talk to the Elders of our clan and have Sydney talk to them to be sure."

She frowned at him. He quickly grinned, and said, "There's nothing to worry about, *at all*. I promise. Whatever it may be is a blessing, something really cool. We just need to be sure."

Knowing he was telling the truth from their bond, Sam let it go but gave him one last look to let him know she wanted answers as soon as possible. He had to be the most patient man in the world as he sat waiting for her next question like he had all the time in the world.

Well, he kinda does.

Smiling at her own funny, she asked, "Who the hell is Andrew? What all has he done? Every time his name or one of the names you guys call him came up while you were healing, everyone spoke in your language. I'm guessing they were waiting for you to give me the scoop."

"Well, Doc, there's a long answer to that, but I'm gonna Reader's Digest it for you the best I can. Over seven years ago, Aidan and his younger brother, Andrew, were out on patrol. Aidan had gotten a whiff of something a few days prior and couldn't shake the feeling he needed to follow up. So they went out to see what it was. The scent Aidan was tracking took all his focus and he was careless, something completely uncharacteristic for any of us, but especially 'A'. He's one of the best trackers any clan has ever seen. Anyway, he hadn't continually scanned the area like we're all trained to do, and his pansy-assed little brother, who always depended on one of us to take care of him, wasn't scanning either. Andrew was the youngest in our Force and the younger brother to two of the best Dragon Guardsmen this world has ever known. And to top it off, he was, and I imagine still is, a lazy little shit."

He paused to take a breath and she quickly asked, "'A' is Aidan, right?"

"Yep, sorry about that, force of habit. Anyway, the guys were flying over a wooded area when they were both literally pulled from the sky by what we now know was black magic. The force from the dark spell pushed their dragons back and left the men falling to the ground. Apparently, a coven of wizards had seen 'A' earlier in the week and set a trap for him. However, they hadn't counted on two dragons. From what we now know, they didn't have enough magic to hold them both. In a quick plan B move, the sadistic bastards used their dirty magic to disorient 'A' while they held Andrew and made it look like they sacrificed him. 'A' was sure he'd seen Andrew's severed head thrown into their huge ritual fire, and before he could do anything about it, the assholes hit him with another blast of their tainted shit, leaving him for dead.

"Later, 'A' woke up and made his way back to the clan for help. By the time we got back there, the cowards had run and hidden their tracks. The search went on hours with no clues to be found. Now, you have to understand. We have some serious mojo of our own. Dragon magic is ancient and nothing to be scoffed at, but those sons of bitches were packing some kind of hyped up, seriously nasty power that night.

"We all mourned Andrew's death. You know we live a long time, and to lose one of us so early in our lifespan because of the scum of the earth is a horrible loss for all of us, but it hit 'A' the hardest. He felt responsible for Andrew's death and spent every waking minute punishing himself for what had happened. For six years, we all watched our friend and brethren in pain and constant turmoil, with no way to help him. No matter what we tried, nothing helped. Not even Aaron, his twin, could reach him. Then almost two years ago, everything changed.

"We were on our way back to the lair. Trying to get Spitfire…I mean Kyndel…back to the lair," he smiled, and she took the opportunity to butt in.

"Kyndel lets you call her 'Spitfire'?"

"She damn sure does, and Grace lets me call her 'Hellcat'. It was our way of letting them both know they were accepted into the clan. I can't believe you didn't hear it while I was out."

"I did, but I was so focused on you and…." She paused. Was she really going to admit this to him? Yeah, she sure was. "I was so worried about you that I remember little else besides taking care of you and Sydney and sleeping." Sam tried to bow her head to avoid his knowing eyes, but Lance had other plans as he used his thumb and forefinger to lift her head until they were eye to eye.

"Thank you," he said so softly she had to strain to hear him, before kissing her on the very tip of her nose. "You brought me back. I'll forever be grateful. I love you, Doc."

Trying to regain her composure, she asked, "And I'm guessing that 'Doc' is my nickname?"

"You got it. Now, let me finish this story, because I have something I need to ask you. That day in the clearing, we were ambushed by a group of hunters led by a magic practitioner pumping them with enhanced abilities. Even with the black magic, we were winning the fight, but somehow, the magical guy got past us and held Kyndel at knife point. While Rayne was negotiating for her release, the SOB pulled off his mask and there stood Andrew…not dead, and seriously fucked in the head from his time with the wizards. Kyndel was hurt when we caught the asshole. Then he used the black magic he'd gotten from the wizards, mixed with his dragon magic, and escaped before 'A' and Aaron could get him back to the Elders for the Tribunal.

"It took us a while, but we've pieced together bits and pieces of what happened. There are still holes, but we're some tenacious sons of bitches. The one thing all of our Elders and Leaders believe is that it will take at least one, if not both, of his 'real' brothers to bring him down. 'A' and Aaron take turns leading hunting parties tracking him, but even with our enhanced senses, the traitor has been able to hide from us. We think it's another effect of the black magic. We also can no longer mind speak with him. 'A' is positive the traitor's lost touch with his dragon. But I think his beast is coming back to him, especially after that shit at the hospital. There was a touch of dragon magic mixed in there, too.

"Andrew was also there the day you were kidnapped, and used the explosion to capture Grace in an effort to lure 'A' into a trap. Thankfully, Grace is one tough cookie and held on until Aidan was able to rescue her, but we almost lost her to a fucking spell.

"Taking Sydney to get to you was the last fucking straw. Andrew's a spineless, useless coward who attacks women and children instead of coming right at us. I met Kyra out there on the mountainside and learned how he'd used and exploited her as well. So as far as I'm concerned, if I have a chance to take him down, I'm doing it…to hell with the Tribunal."

Lance breathed deeply. Sam could see and feel the incredible amount of anger he kept at bay. She rubbed his chest, trying to soothe him and the beast she knew dwelled within her miraculous mate. She wondered what the Tribunal was, but decided to ask another time.

After several minutes, he started talking again, but she could still hear the rage in his voice. "Then there's 'The Auctioneer' and his band of idiots, who are responsible for your kidnapping. Killing that shit for brains will be too good for him. He needs to suffer." She smiled at his righteous indignation for what she'd suffered, loving him all the more for it.

"I know somehow, someway, Andrew, the leader of the wizard coven, and this asshole crime boss are all connected. You should talk to Grace to learn all about the 'The Auctioneer'. He was actually the State Prosecutor, her boss, until that day at the warehouse when she recognized him and later exposed him to the world for the dick he really is. She's been researching and collecting information to put him in jail as soon as we catch him. She can tell you anything you want to know. Please, tell me that's all the questions for now, because I *really* have something I want to talk to you about." He almost whined the last sentence, so even though Sam had other things she wanted to know, she let him off the hook for the time being.

"I'm done for now. What's your question?"

He lifted his hips slightly and faster than she could track, retrieved something from his back pocket and hid it in his front pocket. Amazed by how fast he could move, she looked for what he'd gotten. She could see the outline of a small cylinder under the denim, but had no idea what it was, and as soon as he started speaking, she was captivated once again.

"Doc, I love you and you said you love me. I know you're the woman I'm meant to spend all my days with, in this life and the next, and I'm praying you feel the same way."

He stood with her in his arms, gently set her on the couch, and knelt before her. For the first time since meeting him, she saw tears glistening in his eyes. Sam worked as hard as she could to keep her emotions under control, but knew he could see the moisture in hers as well. "Samantha Anne Malone, *mo ghra' ru'nda*, my mate, *solas mo anam,* you complete both the dragon within and the humble man before you. Will you be my mate now and forever, on this earth and in the Heavens, with the blessing of the Universe that made you for me and me for you?"

She didn't know whether to jump for joy or cry from happiness, but she was sure sitting there dumbfounded was all she could do while she caught her breath. As if all he'd said was not enough, he pulled out a golden velvet box. Her jaw dropped as he opened the hinged top and presented her with an absolutely gorgeous aquamarine ring. The brilliant emerald cut stone was such a light blue she was sure when the sun hit it just right it would look colorless and shimmer like no other. The band had an intricate design that resembled the scales she'd seen on the tail of the amazing golden dragon that glided past her window all those weeks ago. She continued to stare as he spoke.

"This ring was given to my mother by my father at their official mating ceremony two hundred and eleven years ago today. It was fashioned from his scales, and the stone was one he found while tracking a specifically heinous pack of hunters in Brazil even before he knew she existed. He'd carried it with him for years, and knew the moment he scented my mother, his mate, she would wear it as a token of his undying love for her. She, like you, was human by birth, and he wanted to adhere to as many of her customs as he could out of respect for his mate. Something I also plan to do.

"Mom gave it to me the day we received word Dad had succumbed to his forever death, and made me promise I would give it to my mate, just as he had given it to her." He paused and she watched him battle his emotions before he spoke again. "I would be the happiest dragon who ever took to the sky if you would wear my ring and be my mate." He watched her for a minute, and then spoke again. "And happy birthday, *mo chroi'*. Sorry I was out for the party." He winked, and she wondered if she would ever get tired of his silliness. "So what do you say, Doc?"

All thoughts of residencies and careers, plans and goals, flew from her mind. The only thing she knew without a doubt was that no matter how she'd fought it, no matter how much she denied it, this man was a part of her, a part she could not and would not live without. They could figure out the rest. As long as they were together, everything else would fall into place. Sam tried to speak, but only squeaked, so she nodded her head. He smiled that beautiful smile she knew was just for her. It lit up her entire being just as he'd said she did to him.

Within the span of two heartbeats he had the ring on her finger and she was in his arms, spinning around and around. They were kissing and spinning, and moving across the floor, happy to have found one another. Her only regret was that her mom and dad would never know the man who'd stolen her heart, but even that thought was driven from her head when her back touched down on their bed and he gently landed on top of her. Their eyes met. The love and adoration she saw shining down on her made all the years before fade away.

Lance spoke and his chest vibrated against hers, causing her already peaked nipples to rub against the lace of her bra. His lips were almost to hers. They shared the same air, and then she heard and felt him whisper, "I love you, Doc."

Their lips touched and together they celebrated all that they were…and would be together.

CHAPTER THIRTY-FOUR

Andrew waited outside the huge iron gate that resembled something out of a gothic novel. It surrounded the biggest, most ostentatious estate he'd ever seen. Sitting in the nondescript sedan he'd rented early that morning, Andrew waited impatiently to be allowed entry into the lair of 'The Auctioneer'. It was the best case of hiding in plain sight he'd ever seen.

He'd looked up the property after receiving the address via email. County records indicated it was owned by some drug lord's ex-wife. The loser was rotting away in Federal prison, not to mention Andrew's research had turned up that she had restraining orders against him in twelve states and eleven countries. He figured the boys in blue were not wasting much time monitoring the goings on at this address, and 'The Auctioneer' would've known about it from his previous job as State Prosecutor.

The meeting he was waiting to attend had taken so much posturing and pandering and playing nice by all parties, that there had been a time last week when Andrew thought about killing everyone associated with any of the alliance bullshit and doling out his brand of justice.
Fortunately, John talked him off the proverbial ledge. After all, Andrew's right hand man had been the one who was approached by a minion of Master Eaton's after the fuck up on the mountainside. When the rogue explained how important it was to build the relationships, even if it was just to get to the next step before disposing of every idiot in the place and taking over himself, Andrew had to agree.

Neither had any idea what the other parties were after. Maybe it was just a way to draw them out, but 'The Auctioneer' and Master Eaton could be valuable. They had connections it would take Andrew years to forge that he didn't want to waste. Everything had led to him sitting outside, waiting like a peasant to be admitted to a stolen residence.

Andrew came alone, something John wasn't thrilled about in the slightest, but he really didn't give a shit. The rogue wizard tried to convince Andrew he needed to be there to sense any magical traps that might be set. Andrew laughed to himself, thinking if the bastard knew who he really was, John would shit where he stood.

During the time Andrew had spent in the company of Master Eaton and then the rogue wizards, he'd learned the fanatics had collected tons of information about the dragon shifters. Surprisingly, a majority of it was spot on, but the part that was complete bullshit was fucking hilarious.

The shock of his hundred years came when he'd found an ancient text, written in the language of the mage, all about The Special One. The information was frighteningly correct and enlightening. There had been things even *he* didn't know detailed in the volume.
Andrew had damn near had a heart attack, if dragons were able to have heart attacks, because it appeared the wizard had actually begun to translate the old language. The book mysteriously disappeared the next day. When John had asked him if he'd seen it, Andrew simply shook his head.

It would never be found. There was no way he was leaving that shit laying around. Andrew was having a difficult enough time hiding his returning dragon senses and enhanced abilities. What the fuck would he do if the contacts he painfully stuck in his eyes daily to hide one amber eye and one blue eye fell out? The paranoid sons of bitches were already questioning him at every turn about his magical training and teachers. One or two might've left without a word when they'd questioned him closer than he was comfortable with, and those bodies had been a pain in the ass to dispose of without getting caught. He really didn't look forward to doing it again.

He'd already had a meeting with Master Eaton a few days earlier, and figured from the questions he was asked they were coming to him because of his use of white magic. Of course, he'd assured the Master he could deliver whatever they needed. Andrew thanked the Heavens he'd done so much reading on the subject when searching for Kyra. He'd been incredibly convincing, and that had gotten him to the next step.

Andrew made it clear to John he would walk away if the assholes asked for things he couldn't or wouldn't deliver. If they knew the tiny, white witch's location then he would definitely play ball, but other than that, he would set the terms, and they would deliver or they could kiss his ass.

Thinking of Kyra, he was somehow sure she was with the dragons or they were protecting her. He knew she was a mate to one of them, and had narrowed it down to either Royce or Devon, but really had no clue and didn't give a shit.

His cell phone vibrated on the seat next to him. A message from John appeared. *Everything okay?*

Pissed that he was being bothered when he'd left very specific instructions he would make first contact after the meeting, Andrew turned off his phone. Little bastard could sit and wait until Andrew was good and ready to answer.

Still fuming, he glared at the screen/touchpad gate control when it sounded. "Mr. O'Brien, I am opening the gate. Proceed to the fountain and park to your left. One of my associates will be waiting at the door to make sure you've followed my instructions, and escort you in if all is as it should be."

Andrew wanted to rage. He wanted to tell them they could take their self-entitled bullshit and shove it up their asses. They were nothing but dirty black magic wizards and fucking thugs, not fit to lick the bottom of his riding boots, but that wouldn't get him what he wanted and needed.

Speaking in his most politically correct voice, he answered, "As you wish."

No sooner were the words out of his mouth than he heard the whine of the hydraulics opening the gate. The huge gates were only about three-quarters open when he hit the accelerator and sailed through. All he could think was that this shit had better be worth it, or John would find his head separated from his shoulders, no matter how useful he'd proven to be.

Getting into the house was easy. Of course, The Auctioneer's henchmen frisked him at the door. He'd almost laughed out loud. What the hell did he need a gun for? Even if they didn't know what he was, which he was sure they didn't, they were assuming he wielded some seriously strong white magic. If he had been, he could've conjured whatever he wanted with a single word spell, not even an amulet needed. It was confirmation they had no idea what white magic could or could not do. How incredibly short-sighted of Master Eaton. First rule of combat…know your enemy.

It seemed impossible, but the stupid fucking leader of the largest coven of wizards in the country had no clue what devastation his oldest and deadliest enemy could wreak on the world. Yes, they fought to destroy dragon kin, but all other magical covens sought to eliminate anyone that held the power of black magic. The Master *had* to know that. How could he not know what each was capable of?

An evil grin slid across Andrew's lips as he wondered if maybe he wasn't the only imposter in the bunch. Suddenly very interested in the meeting that was about to happen, he even felt a spring in his step.

Whistling as he waited in the chair he was assigned on the far side of a replica of a fifteenth century dining table, Andrew took in his surroundings. Thankfully, Master Eaton and his ass kissing followers came in first, taking up the entire side opposite him. There were ten of them in all. It was the Master's show of strength.

"Good to see you again, Andrew. I trust all is well since we last spoke?" The pretentious asshole gave a single nod in his direction, then waited for Andrew's answer while he picked imaginary lint from his custom made suit. Bastard had come into some money recently, probably from his new partner. What a change from the tattered ceremonial robes the wizard usually wore.

"I am wonderful," Andrew responded. "You look well," he said, hoping the Master would just sit there and shut up, but of course that didn't happen.

"Yes, things are *very* good, as I told you when we met. I hope you thought about what we discussed and will be ready to give Mr. A what he wants when he asks." The wizard raised his eyebrows in an attempt to intimidate. Deciding to ignore him, Andrew rolled his eyes as he waited to see what the human criminal had planned for his grand entrance.

Thankfully, he didn't have to wait long, and wanted to laugh at the pomp and circumstance 'The Auctioneer', aka Mr. A, provided. Eight men in black suits and ties with white shirts, wearing sunglasses, and smelling of gunpowder, filed into the room, taking their places around the perimeter. The big boss continued to deal with military men, making Andrew wonder if Mr. A was ex-military himself. He then decided he didn't give a shit.

Mr. A entered the room and took the seat at the head of the table, not sparing either Master Eaton or himself a look. The glorified thug opened the large file he carried and began sorting papers. On his heels came two more men who took up their posts on either side of his king-like throne. They were dressed as the others, but much larger.

Finally, the self-important bastard looked up and spoke. "Thank you for coming, Andrew." He nodded in his direction. "And you for making time in your schedule, Master Eaton." Another nod at the other man followed.

"I have asked you here to see if we might combine our forces in an effort to more effectively and efficiently reach our personal and common goals. The fiasco in the woods was unfortunate, and quite frankly, embarrassing. I have dealt with the ones in my employ responsible, as I hope each of you have, as well."

Andrew wanted to laugh out loud. No one from his camp had done anything wrong. In fact, they'd been the ones who'd actually accomplished something. He was still waiting to hear, but he was almost certain Lance had received his forever death when he fell onto the pile of silver. His spies had reported the unmoving Guardsman was carried from the field with a sword through his chest.

The dragon within stirred every time he thought of what happened, grieving for one of his own. Fucking dragon traits! If he hadn't gotten so painfully low on black magic and used white magic on top of it, Andrew guessed the damn things would've stayed at bay. But as it stood his dragon was awake, and not looking to nap any time soon.

Andrew nodded his agreement as Master Eaton prattled on about the changes within his ranks. Obviously bored, Mr. A spoke over him. "Here is my proposal." He slid a stack of papers towards both men. "Take a few minutes to look over the sections that apply to you personally while I have lunch brought in."

As if he had telepathic powers, the door at the rear of the room opened and in came three young women pushing carts piled high with food. He could smell everything from fresh fruit to many different kinds of cooked meat, and wondered exactly what the ploy was. Heavens knew this glorified thug did nothing, even lunch, without an angle.

Andrew declined food, but did accept a glass of Bushmills single malt whiskey. It had been years since he'd had a taste of his homelands. As the warm amber liquid slid down his throat, Andrew reviewed the document before him. It was just as he had suspected…they thought it was he who'd learned to wield white magic, or someone in his group, which was true up until the mountainside incident. Time to lie like the snake he'd become. Based on the terms he was reading, the alliance would definitely provide the things he needed to move forward.

Mr. A cleared his throat. The waitresses cleaned up the empty dishes, refilled their glasses, and exited through the same door they had entered. "Now that you gentleman have had time to review my proposal, can I assume since you're still here that the terms meet your approval?"

Master Eaton spoke first. "Yes, it is quite satisfactory."

Mr. A nodded and looked to Andrew. "Yes," he answered.

Their host clapped his hands together. "Wonderful! Andrew, one of my associates will show you to your room. Please get your things moved in as soon as possible so that we may get to work. Also, I will need a list of those who will be joining you here. As I am sure you saw in my proposal, I'm limiting it to ten, including yourself. I trust that will be satisfactory."

Andrew nodded, thinking there was no way he was having any of his compatriots stay in this compound with him. As long as they remained on the outside, they were free to work independently of Mr. A's operations. Free to stay on the path he'd set for them. Andrew agreed to join with these two, but he would never tell them everything he knew…that was just bad business. His ultimate goal was and would always be to destroy the Dragon Guard. Everything he did was towards that end, and he would succeed. Working with Master Eaton and Mr. A was only be a means to an end.

Andrew had an idea. If he could simply bide his time and learn all he could about the inner workings of both operations, then when the time was right, he would be able swoop in and take over everything. The wizards who followed Master Eaton and the hired thugs who followed Mr. A would follow whoever they believed had the most power, and in the end it would be Andrew.

He could see in their eyes that they discounted him, just as those fucking Guardsmen had always done. The idiots thought they could treat him like the "little brother" for his entire life. The ones he dealt with at this moment thought he was expendable, and he was going to use that in his favor.

First order of business was to get Kyra back. Her magic was one of the most important parts of his plan, as well as this alliance. He would sacrifice girls if that was what it took, and he would fill himself with an unending fount of black magic. All to see the fear in those he'd once thought of as brethren as he removed their heads from their bodies. Hell, he might even have a few werepanther pelts to decorate his walls before it was over. Those douche bag cats would suffer just for their association with the Dragon Guard.

Mr. A stood. "Gentlemen, please excuse me, I have other appointments. We will talk in the next few days."

He stepped towards Andrew with his hand outstretched and they shook. The cold dead look in his eyes confirmed what Andrew's heightened sense of smell had already told him. The man was dipping into the black magic. It seemed the boys had gotten started without him.

Andrew exited the room as the other two men were shaking hands. There was too much to get ready for the next phase of his plan to stand around playing nice. As he exited the mansion, he pulled his cell phone from his pocket, turned it on, and called John. "Change of plans," was all he said before disconnecting the call and exiting the property. Things were about to get interesting, and those fucking Guardsmen had better enjoy every minute of every day, because theirs were numbered.

CHAPTER THIRTY-FIVE

When she returned to the hospital the day after accepting Lance's marriage, or mating, proposal, wearing the absolutely gorgeous ring he'd given her, her coworkers had freaked out. If she had a nickel for every time someone said, "We thought you'd be the last one of us to ever get married," she would be a rich chick.

Dr. Monoghan approved her request for six weeks off on the spot. He even congratulated her, assuring her spot would be waiting when she returned. Charlie pulled her to the side, surprised she was returning at all. When Sam had told her it was Lance who insisted she only take a leave and come back to finish her residency, her friend swooned a little, telling her how lucky she was. Wholeheartedly agreeing, Sam spent the rest of the day missing her mate, counting the hours until she could head back to him.

It had taken them a week to get everything ready to go to the lair, as everyone kept calling it. She was kind of freaked out, not knowing what to expect. Lance, Grace, Kyndel, and even Siobhan spent tons of time answering all her questions, with the most coming when all the girls got together and discussed the mating ceremony. Every woman had their own unique story to tell, each just as magical as the other, demonstrating how important and special this rite was to their culture. She chuckled when she realized it was the men who did all the planning. Sam's imagination ran away with her as she thought of the things her extraordinary mate might come up with.

It was also incredibly interesting to learn that when the dragons had entrusted their souls to the knights, almost all the female dragons had been destroyed by the wizards and the hunters. The dragons had been searching for answers, with extinction knocking at their door. Their Elders met in the most ancient and holy of places, praying continually to the Universe for almost twenty years for an answer. It was the night before the Joining Ceremony, while the mage and the dragons were making preparations, that their prayers were answered.

Two lovebirds entered the cave where the Elders prayed deep in the earth, surrounded my miles and miles of rock. They landed on their altar at the center of their Prayer Circle and began to sing a beautiful song. These words appeared in the air above them as their melody rang out. "From the human race, women with great power will be born. Not the power to maim or destroy, but the power to love, to heal, to uplift, and to rebuild. The beautiful ones will be created as the perfect complement for the men who take up our spirits. One woman destined for one man, to live on Earth and in the *Heavens joined* for all times. When the time is right, they shall discover one another. The two will become one, and the woman will provide the man and the beast with love, light, and hope. Together they shall provide heirs that will allow our great race to continue for all eternity."

She'd asked if there were any female dragons left, but no one answered. Sam got the idea they had avoided the question. She let it drop but tucked it away for another time.

The best surprise of all came when Grace called her into her office the night before they were to leave. She had been trying to find her iPod for Sydney when she heard, "Hey, Sam, is that you?"

"Yep, sure is," she said as she headed towards the door. "Whatcha need?" She flopped on the couch just inside the other woman's office.

"I just got a call." Grace paused, and Sam braced for whatever was to come. "It was from the judge handling Sydney's case." Grace smiled, and Sam let go of the breath she hadn't realized she was holding.

"Tell me, Grace! You're killing me here." Sam knew she'd raised her voice, but there was no way to stop it. She was freaking out.

"We got the approval to take her out of the county. Sydney gets to go the lair with us, and will be there for your mating ceremony."

Sam jumped up and ran around the desk, hugging Grace for all she was worth. "Thank you, thank you, thank you!"

"It was you who made the best impression on the home visit. And I quote, 'In all my years in child services, I have never seen a foster parent care so deeply for her ward.' That was just one of the positive comments the new social worker had to say. It was all you, love."

Sam's vision wavered as she let the tears fall. She really did love that little girl.

Kissing Grace on the cheek, she ran out of the office, hollering over her shoulder, "Thank you Grace! You're the best! Gotta go tell Syd and Lance!" The sound of laughter was all she heard as she raced down the hall.

They hardly slept the rest of the night. When morning came and it was time to head to the lair, the girls had all of their luggage at the bottom of the stairs. She and Sydney made breakfast and then lunch for everybody. The waiting was killing them.

They were down in the basement looking for a doll when Lance took them back upstairs with the guise of forgetting something, but as soon as they stepped onto the patio at the back of the house, both she and Sydney stopped short. There, standing not a hundred feet from them, were five fully mature, absolutely breathtaking dragons. She looked at Sydney, who smiled ear to ear while squealing her delight, and then at her mate, who wore his patented shit-eating grin, complete with dimple and twinkling eyes.

As Sam turned back to take in the splendor of the moment, Lance moved behind her and whispered, "You asked if we were all the same color. I figured showing was better than telling." She nodded, still unable to speak.

When her brain finally started to work again, she asked, "Aren't you guys afraid of being seen?"

"Yes, but we took care of it. Close your eyes and try to clear your mind."

It took a few seconds and a few deep breaths, but finally her mind was empty. In the next heartbeat, she could see an array of translucent colors, reminding her of the "rainbow" from an oil-covered puddle when the noonday sun shined upon it. She gasped and her eyes flew open. "What was that?"

"That, *mo chori'*, is a shield created from our combined dragon magic. I shared what I could of my enhanced vision so you could see it." He sounded so proud.

"This is what it'll be like once we're officially mated?"

"It'll be so much better, Doc…so much better," he said as he kissed her cheek.

They stepped off the wooden deck and walked toward the men in their dragon forms. The beast closest to them was biggest by far. It was the most vibrant royal blue, with deep green scales running throughout, and resembled the pictures of the water in the Caribbean she'd seen in the travel magazines Momma Maybelle had strewn all over her house.

From his sheer size, she was sure it was Royce, but when he lowered his head and looked at her, it was the gentleness deep in the brown orbs that confirmed it. Something told her he'd suckered more than one opponent into thinking his gentle nature meant he wouldn't tear them apart, and they'd been sorely surprised.

Behind Royce and to the right were two silver dragons with glittering black scales running down both sides of one and covering the underbelly of the other. They were nowhere near as massive as Royce, but formidable in their own right. The dragons bent their front legs until their knees touched the grass, and bowed their massive heads. She saw whiskey eyes in one and blue in the other, confirming it was Aidan and Aaron, twins as men, twins as dragons.

Kyndel was standing to her left. Even if Sam hadn't already known from the flaming red of the scales on the next beast that it was Rayne, the loving smile of his mate and the constant "da da da da" of Jay were dead giveaways. To top it off, there was the commanding way he held himself and the laser stare from his violet eyes.

Standing at the back had to be Devon, who although the others said was coming out of his shell, still talked way less than everyone else. Sam recognized him from his mother's description of his father's dragon and the heart scale she'd seen in Siobhan's locket. His beast had to be the most unique of them all, with opalescent white scales covering his entire body. As he took a few steps towards them, an array of colors appeared and disappeared, making his gigantic body seem even more magical than she knew it to be.

He stood just a bit taller than Rayne's dragon, but not nearly as tall as Royce's. His body was sleek, with a longer, thinner tail like the twins. The one thing that remained constant as she looked from dragon to dragon was the array of deadly spikes and thorns adorning their bodies, reminding her how lethal they would be in battle.

Filled with gratitude for what these men had done for her, Sam said, "Thank you so very much; so very, very much."

Each dragon returned to standing and dipped their heads in acknowledgement. Lance spoke from behind her ear, causing goose bumps to rise on her arms. "Do you want me to ride with you? Royce volunteered to take us. Or do you want me to call forth my dragon for you and Syd to ride?"

She spun in his arms and looked him square in the eye. "I want you to fly, please?"

"You got it, Doc." He swooped down, laid a really quick, really amazing kiss on her lips, and before she had her eyes open, called forth his beast.

Standing before her was the golden dragon from her dream, even more magnificent than she remembered. He truly reminded her of everything she'd ever read about the knight, Lancelot. She would have to remember to tell him the nickname she'd given his dragon when they reached their destination.

At this angle, she could see that on his proud chest the gold looked more like silk. Moving forward, completely unafraid of the huge beast before her, Sam stood on tiptoes to feel the underbelly of the dragon that was also her mate. He shivered in response to her touch, and she felt the earth quake a bit with him. It was a giddy feeling to know she had that effect on something so large and powerful. Stepping back so she could see his face, she wasn't surprised to find that even in his magical form, Lance appeared to have a smirk on his face.

In unison, the dragons of Aidan, Rayne, and Lance held out their front right paw, palm up, and placed them on the ground. She glanced over to find Grace crawling into Aidan's colossal paw. She and Sydney followed suit by climbing into Lance's front paw. The child vibrated with excitement and giggled. "This is the coolest thing ever, huh, Dr. Sam?"

"It sure is, Syd."

Once they were seated, he closed his long massive toes around them and she heard the click of his imposing claws. Lance had always made her feel safe…protected. Witnessing his dragon and feeling the raw power thrumming through him only solidified all she knew. This man…this dragon…would protect her and all she held dear with everything he was, and *that* was truly saying something.

Settled in with Sydney by her side, the wind from his long, powerful wings ruffled their hair. They felt his body lower slightly, and with no more movement than getting off the couch he launched them into the air. Magical was the only word that came to mind as they soared through the sky.

The flight to the lair was absolutely awe-inspiring. Had Sam not been actually sitting in the palm of a thousand pound, prehistoric beast gliding across the sky, she would've sworn she'd fallen through the looking glass. But it was real, completely and totally real, and simply the best thing aside from meeting Lance that had ever happened to her. Surreal didn't even begin to describe the experience. Sam had the most wonderful man in the world to thank for it.

Sydney constantly asked questions or commented on the things they saw. The child's enthusiasm was infectious, and before long, they were playing I Spy, but on a whole new level.

Sam could only imagine what they looked like from the ground. Rayne's red dragon led the way with them right behind, Aidan and Aaron on either side, and Royce and Devon following. She knew the dragon magic hid them from sight, but was sure that back when a dragon soaring in the sky was a commonplace event, it had been spectacular to watch.

Looking at her watch, Sam was shocked to see they'd been in the air almost three hours.

Time just flew by. I crack me up.

She could feel them descending and the butterflies in her stomach began to flutter with loads of excitement and a healthy dose of nerves. Lance had explained so much, but talking about it was way different than actually seeing it.

They touched down, and after a dozen steps Lancelot stopped completely. He lowered his paw to the ground and opened his palm. Climbing to the ground, Sam noticed they were high atop a ridge overlooking a lush green valley with a thriving community right in the center. It had to be her mate's home. Across from where she stood was another larger mountain with hundreds of caves and outcroppings. The whole place looked like it had come right off a movie screen.

Sydney yelled, "Hey Dr. Sam, let's go!"

Sam turned to see men where a few minutes ago there had been dragons. They were all dressed in the same clothes she remembered them wearing back at Aidan and Grace's. She once again stood in awe of the power of their magic.

"Yeah, Doc, let's go!" her mate yelled as he lifted Sydney onto his shoulders. She caught up to them, and together their entire party walked down the path to meet the people who would become her extended family.

CHAPTER THIRTY-SIX

Sam and Sydney were welcomed by everyone they came in contact with, just as he knew they would be. However, it didn't stop his chest from puffing out with the pride he felt from presenting the one the Universe had made for only him to his clan.

The girls wanted to see the village right away and there was no way he could deny either of them anything, even if he did want some alone time with his spectacular mate. When they reached the Town Square (as Kyndel had renamed the center of their lair), Sam and Sydney's eyes flitted from one thing to another, taking it all in. This was the commerce center of the lair, holding all the merchants and craftsmen, as well as the school for the children. They stopped at shop after shop and bought little trinkets along the way, but it was Emma, the jewelry artisan's studio, that had them both staring in awe.

Emma made jewelry from dragon scales that were broken or misshapen and not useful in any other way. She was by far the most gifted craftsman in their clan, and according to Siobhan, just recently her powers as a mystic had manifested. It appeared she was adjusting well, at least until she touched Sydney's hand while explaining a specific piece of jewelry.

It happened in a split second. He was sure that neither of his girls noticed Emma's eyes glass over or the way she slightly swayed. She looked at him over the child's head, then quickly averted her eyes. He called to Rayne and Royce through their link. *"Emma, the jeweler, has mystic powers. I completely forgot Siobhan telling me about it after I woke up. I just witnessed them for myself when she touched Sydney. Can one of you talk to her and see what that was all about? I don't want to upset Sam until I know what it is."*

"No problem. Kyndel, Jay, and I are headed that way," Rayne answered.

"Maybe she can help locate the traitor," Royce added. *"I need to head that way, too. See you there."* And they all cut their connection.

Royce had been acting weirder than usual since Lance had awoken from his coma. The few times he'd tried to talk to him, the big guy had completely blown him off. The older Guardsman had also been spending a lot of time alone, which was seriously unusual for him. He was usually the caregiver and mother hen of their Force.

Lance had been so wrapped up with Sam and making sure she and Sydney were safe until he could finally get them to their clan's lair that he'd let Royce off the hook too easily, but that shit was going to change. As soon as he and Sam's formal mating ceremony was complete and they'd had a proper honeymoon, he was going to nag and badger his old friend, as only he could, until he got answers.

Bringing his attention back to the girls, he was happy to see them enjoying themselves. Wanting to show them his home and spend some quality time with his mate, he called to them. "Come on, you two. There's a lot more to see."

They picked up several more pieces of jewelry, and he listened as Emma explained each piece in detail and the importance of the design and color of scales. He smiled when Emma explained the significance of a bell ringing to the dragon people. As they walked towards him, they were chattering on and on about all the pretty pieces they'd seen.

"Did Emma make the bracelet Kyndel wears and the necklace Grace wears?" Sam asked.

"Yes, she did," he answered. "Why do you ask?"

"Interesting they have bells on them...."

He didn't let her finish before he kissed her quickly, but with all the love he felt.

He heard bells ringing and the sound of Sydney laughing. Looking over Sam's shoulder, he could see Emma and the child holding bells the artist had crafted from larger dragons scales and grinning from ear to ear.

"Very funny, you two." He winked as Sydney ran to him and Sam.

"Well, Emma did say that every time a dragon kisses his mate a bell rings." Sam laughed and he was once again reminded how truly lucky he was.

They continued their leisurely walk as he pointed out other buildings and continued introducing his family to everyone they passed. Sam was obviously impressed when they reached the Cave of the Elders. Unlike any other cave, the entrance had been carved over time, depicting the journey of the Golden Fire Clan and their quest to preserve their past, grow their community, and enhance the land that was their home. The intricate design transformed the gateway to the sacred laws and rules of their society into a thing of beauty.

If possible, he was even more proud of his mate when he introduced her to the Clan Elders. These four men had lived longer than most, experienced things most of them could only imagine, and were responsible for the social, political, and economic structure of their civilization. Her eyes lit with an excitement he'd only seen when they were alone. She practically glowed from the moment the Head Healer, Zachary, began to speak. The oldest known living member of all dragon kin had seen more battle and performed more healing than any other. He had a wisdom that literally flowed from him into anyone willing to accept it, and Lance's Sam was more than willing.

Lance watched as Zachary took Sam's hands in his. The amazing energy of the aged dragon flowed all around them. He spoke in a voice weakened from age, but still clear and direct. "You have incredible healing powers, with an empathy that surpasses even mine. I can imagine you have healed many. I know you will be very important to both humans and dragon kin." His mismatched eyes met Sam's, and Lance saw her slowly nod. The Elder and his mate talked until Sydney yawned loudly from where she played at his side.

Carrick, the Chief Elder, knelt down beside her, and Lance almost gasped out loud. Never before had he seen the leader of their clan on the floor. Carrick's deep voice bounced from wall to wall even though he spoke barely above a whisper. "Are you having fun, little one?"

"Yes, sir, I am," Sydney answered, completely unimpressed by the person speaking to her, but incredibly respectful.

"I hope you enjoy your time here. Maybe you will come see me again someday."

"That would be cool. I can bring more toys next time," the child responded.

Carrick's booming laughter was all they could hear for several seconds as it echoed all throughout the cave. "Yes, my dear, that would be perfect."

As they said their goodbyes, Lance couldn't help but wonder what is was about Sydney that drew the Chief Elder's attention. He was beginning to get a list longer than his arms of questions needing to be answered, but the first order of business was to officially mate the miraculous Samantha Malone.

CHAPTER THIRTY-SEVEN

Forty-eight hours after her first dragon flight, she was preparing to be mated to the man who'd stolen her heart. His home sat at the edge of the lair of his clan, with a lush wooded area behind it. It was freaky, but also reassuring, that his home so closely resembled hers. Painted white with black shutters and windows everywhere, the main difference was that his was over twice as big as hers.

Her wild mane would not be tamed and she refused to wear it bound in her usual french braid. Frustrated and staring at herself in the mirror, Sam was just about to give up when Siobhan appeared with four stunning golden hair combs. When the doctor held them in her hands, she realized they were carved from the scales of a golden dragon. As she raised her eyes, the older woman simply nodded and returned to securing Sam's hair in a complex design of braids and curls. As the healer worked, she added tiny, light blue forget-me-not blooms throughout the design. Sam never wore very much makeup and thankfully was blessed with her father's skin tone, so she got away with a dusting of powder, a little mascara, and burnt honey lip gloss.

Earlier in the day, a large box had been delivered, containing dresses for both she and Sydney, along with a note from Lance. "For my beautiful ladies. Elder Carrick and the others have given permission for Sydney to attend the ceremony with us. See you there. All my love, Lance."

Their gowns were absolutely beautiful. Sam's was made of golden gossamer, and draped over one shoulder while leaving the other bare. As she shook it out, getting ready to try it on, she marveled at the way the light made it sparkle, almost like there were little diamonds woven into the fabric.

Slipping the dress over her head, Sam was amazed at the perfect fit. It had obviously been handmade. She wondered when Lance had found the time to order it. The bodice was fitted, and a dark gold satin ribbon tied around the waist, making her hips look rounder and fuller.

She frowned at her reflection, having always hated her hips, and the words Lance had spoken when she mentioned losing weight whispered through her mind. "I love you, *mo chroi'*, just as you are. Your body was fashioned by the Universe to be everything I ever wanted or needed. You are perfect, inside and out. I love every curl of your gorgeous hair that wraps so lovingly around my fingers. I love the sweet way the tip of your nose turns up ever so slightly. I love the way your pouty lips open so readily at the touch of mine. Most of all, you , *mo ghra'*, must know that I will die a happy man if it is in your arms, pillowed by the fullness and curves that signify you are all woman and all mine." Just at thought of her mate she was once again calm. It was amazing…absolutely amazing.

Looking in the full length mirror, she noticed small, dark amber flames embroidered all over the skirt from the waist to the hem. They made her think of the marks both Grace and Kyndel wore on their necks. Marks like the one she knew she would wear for all to see as soon as she was officially mated to Lance. He'd explained that each varied slightly, but always had some kind of flame involved in the design, a design that was never known until the time of marking.

She pulled Sydney's dress from the box just as the little one ran into the room. Her curls, which had a few minutes earlier been neatly bound with gold ribbons, were bouncing all over, daring anyone to tame them. Sam shrugged and figured there were other things to worry about. "Here's your dress, Syd."

"Ohh, that is so pretty!" She hopped up and down, clapping.

In the blink of an eye, she had her pink robe thrown on the bed and was standing in front of Sam wearing the cutest little lace slip. "Arms up, cutey pie. Let's get you ready to roll," Sam said as she slid the dress over the child's head.

Sydney looked like a doll. "Why are you crying, Dr. Sam?"

"I'm so happy, Syd. Just really, really happy." Sam dabbed at her eyes with a tissue, thankful for waterproof mascara. "Grab the ballet slippers out of the box and put them on. We don't want to keep whoever is picking us up waiting."

"They're golden, Dr. Sam. I love them," Sydney said as she placed her foot in first one shoe and then the other. "Here's yours, too," she said as she placed them in front of Sam's feet.

They spent the next few moments primping in the mirror, and were just heading out of the room when the doorbell rang. Sydney ran to the door and yelled, "Who's there?"

"Jace and Tomas, Miss Sydney, here to escort you and Dr. Malone to the ceremony." Sam recognized his voice through the door and nodded for the child to let them enter.

Both of the younger Guardsmen resembled characters from a movie featuring King Arthur dressed in their best uniforms, which made sense since they'd actually come from that era in one way or another. Both wore surcoats of a rich golden color trimmed with braided black and gold rope. On each, the expertly stitched dragon in the throes of battle was so realistically done Sam half expected it to jump off their chests. The long sleeved undershirt and pants they wore were coal black, and their knee high, black boots were polished to a high shine that shone in the late afternoon sunlight.

Jace and Tomas moved to either side of the door, facing one another as Sam and Sydney exited. When the ladies reached the edge of the porch, the Guardsmen joined them with arms bent. Tomas was so tall that only Sydney's hand reached his forearm, but the look on her face told Sam all she needed to know…Syd loved every minute of it. Sam slid her arm through Jace's, and together the four of them followed the round patio stones to the gate at the corner of Lance's yard, leading to a small wooded area. She had to laugh when they reached the gate and found a narrow golden carpet covering the path Sydney had spotted from the bedroom window.

She and Jace followed the other pair. They'd walked about twenty paces when Tomas stopped beside a large stump covered with lace, holding the largest bouquet of baby blue roses accented with golden baby's breath Sam believed had ever been created. There had to be at least four dozen roses, and they smelled like heaven. The card attached was simple but poignant. *Always and forever. Lance.*

She took one from the bunch when Jace thankfully offered to carry them. As she would have turned away, she spied a small nosegay with the same blue and golden flowers. When Tomas handed it to Sydney, the little sweetie looked like she might melt on the spot. Flowers turned even little girls to mush. Sam would have to remember to thank Lance for thinking of absolutely everything, and making the day as special for Sydney as he had for her.

They continued down the path, talking and taking in the wondrous scenery. The butterflies in her stomach grew, but more from excitement than nerves. By the time they went to bed tonight she would be mated to the man of her dreams.

Sam heard the sound of water and wondered what her wise-cracking mate had planned for the start of their amazing life together. Just a few more steps and they cleared the trees to find themselves standing beside a small lake.

A grotto in the corner had water flowing over large polished rocks and into the body of water before them. The natural landscaping was flawless, but the decorations surrounding the lake were breathtaking. Maypoles decorated with hundreds of ribbons hanging from the top and flower garlands winding around the length dotted the perimeter in ten foot intervals.

The lake itself had large lily pads with multicolored flowers covering most of its rippling surface. Tied to the whitewashed dock with gold cord was a small, swan shaped craft. The young Guardsmen led them down the dock and made sure both were secure in their seats before one climbed in the front and the other the back. Each grabbed an oar and began rowing the boat to the grotto.

As they slowed, she saw a gazebo decorated to match the maypoles, with four incredibly ornate chairs resembling small thrones positioned in a semi-circle inside. The chairs were empty one moment, and in the blink of the eye the four Elders she'd met when she first arrived at the lair appeared. Lance had shown her just how fast their enhanced speed made them, but damn, even old guys moved fast.

Tomas jumped out and pulled the boat onto the grass, and Jace helped both of them onto the shore. The young Guardsmen bowed while motioning with a flourish for Sam and Sydney to follow yet another piece of the golden carpet to the spectacular structure Lance had prepared. The Elders all nodded their greeting. Sam placed Sydney in the small chair to the right of the steps leading into the gazebo.

Her mate was nowhere in sight, and for just a moment, she wondered if he'd gotten cold feet. A rustling to her left alerted her to the arrival of Lance's brethren. The five men of his Force were dressed in their finest, similar to the garb worn by their escorts, but in colors matching their specific dragon.

Rayne was at the head of the line, standing tall and proud in the reddest of reds, looking every bit the commander he was. Then came Royce, whose beautiful royal blue surcoat with green accents truly fit the gentle giant who seemed to care for everyone. Next, Aaron and Aidan, standing tall and dignified, were dressed in a silvery gray that shone in the waning light. Devon was at the end of the line in a stunning white iridescent surcoat that barely did justice to the dragon he'd shown her. All the men smiled, filling her with true acceptance of a family she'd never expected to have. It was overwhelming and beautiful, but she still hadn't seen the man she loved.

No sooner had the thought crossed her mind than he came striding around the gazebo,-looking better than any man had a right to look.

But damn, he does that in a pair of ripped jeans and faded T-shirt…dress clothes just up the ante.

His shimmering golden surcoat with black cord and embroidery accentuated the amazing body she knew lay beneath. His smile lit up the twilight. He looked nowhere but into her eyes. The electrical current that was always present when they were together snapped to life. Sam recognized it in him, too, as his pupils dilated and nostrils flared. Her body reacted to everything when they were together, and she hoped she would make it through the mating ceremony without dragging him behind the gazebo and making love to him until neither could think. She would've sworn he could read her mind when his smile widened and he winked, suggesting they shared the same thoughts.

Lance stopped ten feet from her, almost at attention. Sam held her breath, waiting for what would come next. Carrick, the Chief Elder, cleared his throat, then his voice rang out loud and clear. "Long ago, when knights and dragons fought side by side for King and Country, it became apparent that dragon kin was no longer safe from those that would expose and destroy them. They sought to join with the knights that had fought so valiantly by their sides for centuries. Thus, through magic, and the will of both dragon and knight, the Golden Fire Clan of the Dragon Shifters became a reality. It was through the joining of many different clans that we have become the strong and powerful Force we are today.

"We are here, at the Lake of Life, a place long blessed by our ancestors that went before us, to honor what the Universe put into place all those many years ago. To acknowledge and bless the mating of Lancelot Michael Kavanaugh to the one the Universe made for him, Samantha Anne Malone. Will those seeking to witness this union please step forward?"

From their place next to the gazebo stepped the five men Lance had called brethren since the moment she met him. The men she knew had trained with him, fought with him, bled with him, and now shared the happiest moment of both their lives with them. They knelt as one and bowed their heads.

Rayne then stood, addressing the Elders. "We, the five of the MacLendon Force, wish to witness and offer our blessing to the union of these two souls, two halves of the same whole. May they live long, fight hard, love harder, and produce many young to flourish in this world when their souls have gone to the Heavens." He knelt next to his men and bowed his head once again.

Carrick began again. "Your witness and blessing have been acknowledged and accepted, MacLendon Force. Lancelot Kavanaugh, you may go to your mate."

She didn't even see him move before he was standing in front of her with a look in his glowing blue eyes that made her feel loved, adored, and incredibly humble to have found real love. He took her hands in his, and she felt all the emotion and power he held within just from his touch.

Carrick spoke. "The Golden Dragons are warriors born of the sun and the harvest. The Heavens shine favorably on all of Her winged warriors, but the ones born with golden scales are near and dear to Her heart. They have great intuition and reason. Their exteriors are strong and sturdy. They use those characteristics to protect all they hold dear. Although they appear to never take anything seriously, their emotions run deep, and once they have pledged their fealty, they never turn their backs. Their love never tires, but instead seems to grow stronger with each passing year. To mate a golden dragon means to accept all that they are and honor the power shared between mates.

"Now is the time of the marking. May the Universe continue to bless you and yours all of your days." She knew the Elders were leaving by the boot strikes on the wood of the gazebo, and she saw Lance's brethren exit after Royce had collected Sydney.

She had no idea how long they stood there ensnared in each other's gaze before Lance pulled her the last few inches to him. He lowered his head and stopped right before their lips touched. She felt his breath on her lips as he whispered, "*Ta' mo chroi istigh ionat,*" and then he kissed her. A more all-encompassing, completely and devastatingly enraptured kiss had never been shared between two. The first brush of his lips reached every cell of her body. A heat unlike any she'd ever known consumed her from the inside out and laid her open, heart and soul, to her mate. The moment was perfect. And then as if a switch had been flipped, she could feel what Lance felt, confusing her for an instant, but then the piece of her soul she hadn't known was missing slid into place and she was soaring. It was one thing to be told someone loved you, but to feel what they felt was beyond belief. It was even better than Grace and Kyndel had explained. The love they shared defied all explanation. It simply was.

A twinge on the left side of her neck made her flinch. Lance left her lips, taking a moment to look into her eyes before trailing kisses across her sensitive skin until he reached the tender spot. He licked and sucked until all thoughts of anything but their bodies loving one another were banished from her mind. She wound her fingers through his hair as he continued to lavish her neck and shoulders until Sam was sure she would catch fire.

She pulled his mouth up to hers, and just as she would've kissed the lips of her mate, he pulled back slightly and winked. Sam furrowed her brow in mock anger. "Are you trying to kill me, Lancelot?"

Unable to stop herself, she laughed out loud. Her mate looked puzzled at her outburst as she hurried to explain. "While you were recovering, every night when I gave you your bath and I spoke to the dragon on your chest. I nicknamed him Lancelot. Today when Carrick said your given name was Lancelot it was hard not to laugh. Just now when I said it out loud, it reminded me." She shrugged, and hoped he understood.

Lance threw back his head and she saw the mark on his neck as he laughed his marvelous booming laugh that made her tingle all over. "That's priceless, *mo ghra'*, absolutely priceless."

She reached up, touching the brand that looked like a flame with an arrow through it. As she touched it, Lance moaned low in his throat, almost a growl, and touched the spot on her neck where she'd felt a twinge during their mating ceremony.

Sam was sure her eyes would roll back into her head at the intense feelings and heightened arousal she felt as he tenderly rubbed it with just his fingertips. As she looked into his eyes, he nodded. "Yes, Doc, they match, and if we don't stop touching them soon, there will be no stopping us." He wiggled his eyebrows and the dimple in his cheek winked at her as she removed her hand from his neck.

Lance guided her to a blanket laid on the grass she hadn't seen earlier. Once they were seated, he produced a small golden box and a set of papers rolled with a golden ribbon tied around it. "What's this? You've done enough," she smiled while looking at the beautiful decorations and thinking of the magnificent ceremony he'd just given her.

"Aww, Doc, I'd give you the world just to see that smile," he said with love and honesty she could feel. He leaned forward and kissed the tip of her nose. "You are all that matters," he whispered, and the depth of his emotions brought tears to her eyes.

Unable to speak, she nodded and then gasped as she opened the box. There, lying against the gold velvet, were the beautiful earrings she'd admired at Emma's jewelry shop…two delicate golden bells, fashioned from golden dragon scales, hanging on petite golden chains from emerald cut aquamarine jewels, nearly identical to the one she wore on her finger. "They are so beautiful." She laid her hand on his cheek and sweetly kissed his lips. When she would've deepened the kiss he pulled back, grinning from ear to ear. "Put them on, *mo chroí*. I want to see them hanging from your pretty little ears."

As quickly as she could, she removed the tiny gold hoops she'd worn for her mating ceremony and put them on. Shaking her head slightly, Sam smiled slyly as the bells from her ears rang. "You know what happens when a bell rings," she giggled.

He pulled her onto his lap and kissed her with an assurance of their love filled tomorrows. The kiss was slow and passionate and so complete she simply melted, but then she was mated to Lancelot Kavanaugh. What else was she to do? Their kiss continued until both were panting and fighting to keep their clothes on.

Using his enhanced speed, he set her back on the blanket and pointed to the papers she still held. "Have a look at those, please Doc. I might explode if I'm not making love to you as soon as possible."

Dispensing with formalities, she ripped the ribbon off the papers and sat speechless as she saw the bold type at the top of the first page. FINAL DISPOSITION OF LEGAL GUARDIANSHIP. She read on to see that she and Lance had been named as Sydney's permanent and legal guardians…her parents. She launched herself at Lance, crushing her mouth to his. She had to be the luckiest woman in the world to have him, and now the little beauty, in her life.

"I love you with all my heart," she thought to herself while still kissing her miraculous mate.

"But I love you more, Doc," she heard in her mind, and pulled back, shocked.

"What did you say," she asked out loud.

"I said, I love you more," he repeated directly into her mind. *"And now we share everything."*

She sighed as he kissed her again, giving him all that she was and all she hoped they would be. For the first night of their very long lives, she loved her mate…her husband…as it was always meant to be…two souls joined forever, blessed by the Universe.

Sam had a family, she had love…they had it all.

EPILOGUE
FOUR MONTHS LATER

The Universe had given them all a beautiful day for the first birthday of their commander's son. Birthdays had never been anything they celebrated. They were warriors who lived hundreds of years. What use did they have for such things? But now that three of Royce's brethren had found their human mates, birthday parties seemed to be on the horizon. He truly hoped they didn't want to celebrate his. He'd never told anyone the date, but he was sure the other Guardsmen knew how and where to find it. He just prayed they didn't go looking.

When Lance and Sam arrived with Sydney, he'd made sure to give his closest friend as much shit as possible. For almost a hundred years, Royce had put up with everything from snakes in his bedroll to Vaseline on the doorknobs to being called Grandpa at every turn. Now that the jokester was mated, Royce took every opportunity to remind Lance of all the things he'd said about mates and his reluctance to have one of his own prior to meeting Samantha Malone. In all truth, Royce was so incredibly proud of Lance for not only claiming his mate, but also officially adopting Sydney. Their little family was a true miracle, and he was sure it would grow one day as well.

Walking into the kitchen, Royce ran right into the bane of his existence, Kyra St. Croix. She had been staying with Rayne and Kyndel since they found her on that mountainside all those months ago. The moment he'd scented patchouli and rose petals, he knew she was to be his mate. From the moment of his birth he was taught that the Universe does not make mistakes, and he'd waited for the day he would find the one made especially for him.

But a witch? Was it a sick joke? Did the Universe have a sense of humor? Yes, she was a white witch, but he'd learned the hard way that any magic but dragon magic was unreliable, and could be bastardized and twisted to the practitioner's whims.

It was a fact she'd been helping them with their search for Andrew. He'd heard her praying to her goddess on several occasions, begging forgiveness for the part she'd played in what happened to Grace, Sydney, and Lance. Royce felt the pain in her voice when she knelt before each of them, asking for their forgiveness. It was one of four times in his one hundred and fifty-six years he'd actually cried. Thank the Heavens none of his brethren had seen. The moment had been heart wrenching and the pride he'd felt immeasurable. But the fact remained…she was a witch.

He'd sought out the Elders, specifically Malachi, for answers about what Royce considered a travesty. The older dragon had been on this earth almost as long as Zachary, and even though no one knew how long that actually was, everyone knew it was longer than they could imagine. The Elders were picked by the Universe Herself to guide and counsel their clan, each given a specific area of their community to oversee. Malachi's area of expertise was anything spiritual, and mates definitely fell under spiritual.

The Elder answered with a knowing look on his face. "You know, my son, the Universe does not make mistakes. She creates the one who will complete you and your dragon. Your mate will bring the light to your souls. You two will meet when the time is right."

"Yes, I understand all that, but a witch…a magic practitioner? How can that be?"

"Every time a dragon shifter finds his mate, a transformation not unlike the one you experienced when you accepted your dragon occurs. It is unique for each coupling. Yours will be no different." Malachi smiled. "And I am sure it will be enlightening for both of you."

"But she's a witch. I always understood that our mates were to be human."

"Yes, you are correct, but I am sure you have been told that each mate has a special quality, one that has been in their heritage for generations. It is that trait that the Universe makes our 'beautiful ones' unique enough to be the mate of a dragon. Yours is no different. She is half-human. Her mother was a witch and her father a police officer."

"She is only half witch? That is remarkable with all the power I feel inside her."

"Yes, she is indeed powerful, and has lived many years on the fringe of her kind, sought after by many who would taint her magic. She has resisted all forms of temptation to remain in the light. She is a gift, Royce. Find a way to accept her."

Royce exited the Cave of the Elders with more questions than when he'd entered, more frustrated than he could ever remember. He walked for hours, thinking and looking for answers to the questions plaguing him. His walk took him to the Garden of Peace. One of the most blessed and spiritual places in the lair, it had always given him comfort. But on that day, there was none to be found. No matter how long he prayed or how many ways he tried to reason out his fate, he got no answers, and even now had no clue how to proceed.

"Excuse me," the little witch whispered.

He shifted to the side-and went to the refrigerator as she all but ran from the room. He stood with the door open, staring at nothing, until Devon's voice broke the silence. "She's a really cool lady. Nothing like any other witch we've encountered. You really need to give her a chance and stop scaring the hell out of her, Old Man."

He spun around. "Scaring her? I scare her?"

"Hell yeah, you scare her. You're a foot and a half taller than her and weigh about a hundred and seventy pounds more than she does, but I figure it's the perma-scowl you've been sporting since we brought Lance back from that fucking mountain that makes her afraid you'll run her through with your blade," Devon reprimanded. Royce knew he must be acting badly for the most laid back, quiet member of their Force to call him out.

"I'm not trying to scare her. I'm just…I…I'm…."

Devon laughed. "I hear ya, man, but you better get your shit together. You know Andrew is coming for her. If all that Max's men found out is true, he has more help than ever before. We have to take the little fucker down, and to do that you have to have your head in the game."

They stood staring at one another until Sydney ran in the room asking for juice boxes. Royce knew his friend was right. The battle brewing was one they had to win. They'd been pussy-footing around long enough. The traitor had to be brought to justice for the good of all dragon kin. All he had to do was get his head out of his ass long enough to put a hundred and twenty years of hate and bias aside, and keep his mate safe until he could claim her. Oh yeah, and talk to her without gritting his teeth. Easy…riiiight….

~~*~*~*~*~*~*

Better accommodations and unlimited resources were definitely a plus. It had taken some serious dancing to get Master Eaton and Mr. A to believe that all the wizards in his employ had either been killed or abandoned him, but Andrew had done it. His plan had also cut off the information John was able to collect from all his sources.

After all, the rogue was supposed to be dead or in hiding, so they had let them dry up. John came up with another plan, which so far, was working spectacularly. He'd "purchased" microscopic spy cams for Andrew to place all over the mansion. These little black dots transmitted back to John, where he recorded, watched, and reported everything he saw.

The newest of Mr. A's endeavors was an oldie but goodie, with a few changes. His hired thugs were rounding up homeless bums to use for the blood ritual planned for the end of the month. It was sooner than Andrew would have liked, but he planned to work day and night to be ready. He was absorbing all the black magic he could from the little rituals Master Eaton performed damn near daily, using whatever animals they could procure. Then there were the ones he and John and their band of merry wizards performed weekly that provided a boost. Getting to them without being followed was always a little bit of a hat trick, but so far so good.

He was also trying to recreate Kyra's amulets and playing around with white magic, which naturally adhered to his returning dragon magic. There were times he felt as if he had a one stop occult shop running through his veins. All he had to do was recreate the blast from the night he'd escaped the wizards and he would have everything he needed to kill those who'd wronged him, and those in his way. He'd been taught that blood magic would kill his soul and had shied away from it as much as possible. But then it occurred to him…who needed a soul when he was about to have everything he wanted and more than he'd imagined?

His phone vibrated on the desk. The text from John that appeared was just what he'd been waiting for. *The ancient text has been located.* Andrew walked to the bar, poured two fingers of Bushmills, and looked at the full moon hanging low in the sky.

Twenty-nine days…just twenty-nine days.

For the Love of Her Dragon
Dragon Guard Series #4

There Are No Coincidences.
The Universe Does Not Make Mistakes.
Fate Will Not Be Denied.

CHAPTER ONE

The sound of boots hitting the wet ground drew Royce to the mouth of the cave he had called home for the last thirteen days. In the distance, he could see his brother Rian, Head Elder of the Blue Thunder Clan of the Dragon Shifters and winner of Most Arrogant Brother of the Year one hundred and fifty years running, making his way towards him. His daily visits had grown old on day one and did little more than exponentially add to Royce's nasty attitude. Deciding to prepare for the inevitable lecture, he moved back to his camp chair by the fire and stirred the logs in an effort to calm his turbulent mood. All was wasted when Rian called to him before he had even crossed the threshold, "So tell me, *little* brother, how long are you going to hide in these caves?"

"Hide? What the hell are you talking about, Rian? I am *not* hiding," Royce answered through gritted teeth, ignoring the 'little brother' dig. So what if the asshole was an inch taller and a year older? He had grown soft over the years and Royce had no doubt he could take him in a fight. The thought of using his pompous ass of an older brother's face to work out some of his frustration *almost* brought a smile to his face.

"Aye, brother, you are. You're hiding from the wee lass with platinum curls and violet eyes," Rian answered with a cocky grin that made Royce grit his teeth and the brogue of their ancestors.

"Damn you! Stay the hell outta my head!" Royce barely contained the roar he felt building.

"Tsk, Tsk, Tsk…did I hit a nerve?" Rian held up his hand to keep Royce from lashing out again. "If you don't want the entire clan to see what you're truly feeling towards the little witch, I suggest you learn to shield your thoughts while you sleep. It's obvious that no matter how hard you fight it, the mating call has its hooks in you." His brother raised one eyebrow and smirked, "At least I have the decency to block you out before your 'hormones' take over. I'm not sure the younger of the clan will be so courteous…should your thoughts reach them."

Rian chuckled and Royce worked hard to control his temper. He was well aware of where his thoughts regarding Kyra went when he let his guard down. How could he not think of her in all the ways a dragon shifter was supposed to think of his mate? She was, after all, the One promised to him by the Universe. She was absolutely gorgeous. Yes, she was short, only five foot two, but she was a force unto herself. Her long platinum hair reached to her waist and was both straight and curly and seemed to just be shy of being tamed all the time. Her violet eyes were vibrant and expressive and held a wisdom that went beyond her age or her experience. She seemed to glow with energy and exuberance, and her heart seemed to lead her no matter the magical power she wielded. But that did not negate the fact that she was a witch, and no matter what he felt for the beautiful woman, he would *not* mate with her. She was witch! A *fucking* witch!

At first, he tried to justify it with the fact that Kyra's father was human, which worked for about five seconds - just long enough for him to remember the other half of her lineage. The half that came from one of the most powerful and highly regarded white witches in all the world, *mommy dearest*, the Grand Priestess Calysta St. Croix. That alone gave her immense power. Power that crackled and sparked all around her. Power that he knew could twist and corrupt even the purest of hearts. Although he had to admit, that he felt nothing but goodness and light in Kyra, and for a few brief hours every day when he was so tired he just dropped onto his pallet, his treacherous mind and heart imagined a life with her, but he knew there was *no way* he could trust it. Everything could change in the blink of an eye and he was not going to be caught unaware, not again. He would fight Fate with his last breath. A lonely, loveless life was better than living every day waiting for his mate to turn in to a power-hungry piece of trash that would slay all he held dear to gain the power she thought she deserved.

He shook himself from his thoughts. One glance at his brother and he knew Rian was just gearing up to spout more BS, and true to form, big brother did not disappoint. "Even if I hadn't been able to see the turmoil in your head, I've had visits from Stefan. Not only is he the clan's Spiritual Elder…you *do* remember that he's also our uncle and the man who helped raise us after Mother's death, do you not?"

"You know I really hate when you get the high and mighty 'I'm the Head Elder' tone in your voice, Ri. And you know *damn* good and well that I remember who he is and all that he's done for us. That's *precisely* the reason I wanted to talk to him. Stefan was there when mother and Rhianna were killed. He tried everything in his considerable power to keep our mother and sister with us. It was he that identified the spell Ilsa had been trying to work and sanctioned her execution when father was unable to do little more than breathe and grieve. Who better to know how I feel about witches than he?"

"That was a long time ago, Roy, and the Universe does not make mistakes…"

"SHUT THE HELL UP!" Royce roared, letting all the frustration, anger, and helplessness he felt at the cards Fate had dealt him, freely flow.

For the first time that he could ever remember Rian just stood, staring…not speaking, not spouting pious recriminations, just waiting to see what would come next. It was something Royce had never experienced in his very long life; his brother was actually listening. Royce took a deep breath and began again, "I understand what a wondrous gift a mate is, but Kyra is a witch and I *cannot and will not* live my life with a witch…white or not."

He let his head fall forward into his hands and sighed, the weight of all that had happened in the last six weeks bearing down on him like a boulder. How could the Universe, in Her infinite wisdom, pair him with a magic practitioner? Yes, Kyra was beautiful and intelligent and had a heart ten times bigger than her tiny five feet two inch frame should be capable of containing, but she was a witch!

He spoke his thoughts out loud, "I have seen her capacity for goodness. *Hell*, I could actually *feel* her agony and regret as she apologized to Grace and Lance for unknowingly helping Andrew." He turned and watched as Rian took the seat across the fire, still not speaking.

"I damn near cried *myself* when she knelt before Sydney and apologized, promising with complete sincerity that she would do everything in her power to stop the man that had almost taken her new daddy from her. I can feel that her intentions are pure, but what scares me is the power I feel within her; it is immense.

"I know Rory and I were much closer to Ilsa than you. Father always took you with him, making sure you learned everything you needed to know to become the next leader of our clan, but you have to remember how much we trusted her. She was like a second mother to us all. She took care of us, kept us out of trouble, made us all believe she was *family* and then…"

Tears filled his eyes and the lump in his throat grew so large that he could barely breathe. A memory so strong it felt as though he had been transported back in time began to unfurl in his mind and he was helpless to do anything but let it play out.

There in front of him was the home where he and his brothers had spent their youth, looking the same as it had all those years ago. He could see the beautiful stained glass windows that decorated every turret, each depicting a famous dragon in the throes of battle. His fingers itched with the need to touch the ivy that lovingly grew in every nook and cranny of the brick structure, and he almost laughed out loud remembering all the toys that he and his brothers had hidden from one another in those tangled vines, only to be found and used for ransom in one of their many games of war.

He watched as a much younger version of himself made his way around the house, a large buck slung over his shoulder and a huge smile on his face. His father had dispatched him that very morning to rid the lair of the deer that continued to raid almost every garden. It was with great satisfaction that he remembered hanging the carcass from the tree while others of their clan began to gather and congratulate him on his hunt.

The hair at the nape of his neck stood on end, just as it had so many years ago, when his mother's blood-curdling screams cut through that beautiful fall day. The earth shook from the responding roar of his father's dragon, miles away. Unable to stop the flood of memories that had irreparably changed his life, his heart raced and sweat rolled down his back as he watched a younger version of himself race through the house and up the steep wooden staircase that led to the bedrooms. Just as he reached the door of his parent's room, his point of view changed. No longer was he an innocent bystander, but an active participant. He had slipped into his much younger body, doomed to relive one of the most horrific events of his life. The actions that had rushed by and fought for his attention only seconds before, now moved in slow motion.

Fury and disbelief caused bile to rise in his throat in reality just as it was in his memories. His mother, Riona, hands extended over her head, tied to the bedposts, legs stretched wide and knees bent with her feet secured, just as was their custom during a pure dragon birth. The coppery scent of fresh blood flooded his senses as it dripped from the dagger that was clenched in Ilsa's hand, their long time nursemaid. The chant that escaped her lips was guttural and ominous, nothing like the sweet melodious voice that had sung him to sleep more times than he could count. He watched, helpless to stop what pure evil had already set into action, as the blade descended and cut a wide path through his mother's already ravaged abdomen. Riona fought with all her might against her restraints while begging for her most trusted companion to stop the madness that had obviously befallen her.

Royce raced forward and grabbed Ilsa by the waist, turning as he went in an effort to get her and her deadly stiletto as far from his mother and unborn sister as possible. The one time confidant struggled to stay upright while still slashing her blade in Riona's direction. In her bid to escape Royce's grasp, Ilsa tripped, her blade missing her mark and plunging into Royce's shoulder, ripping his skin, tearing tendons and muscles, stopping only when it grated against his collarbone. Unable to pull her blade free, the nursemaid began tearing at his face and chest with her nails that had somehow become talons since he saw her that morning at breakfast.

As he battled to control the rampaging woman that had attacked his mother, the room filled with members of their clan, all attempting to save his family from what looked to be certain death, even for a dragon of her breeding and power. Out of the blue, wave after wave of pain, anguish, anger, and fury threatened to drive him to his knees. His father had finally reached his mother and with no thought except of his ravaged mate, his usually well-secured shielding blew away. All the outrage and pain from what his beloved was suffering rolled unchecked through the unique bond the Head Elder shared with all that had pledged their allegiance to him. From clan member to clan member, their turbulent emotions added to their leaders, making the room thick with a mixture of anger, sorrow, and a growing need for retribution at what had been done to their queen.

With one last burst of energy, Royce subdued Ilsa and handed her off to several clan members, who proceeded to bind her hands and feet and gag her. He immediately made his way back to his mother's bedside and stood opposite his father and brothers. His father gently held his mother to his chest, unfazed or unaware of the blood that ran from her body or the tears that stained his cheeks. Never had his father been a man that let his emotions show, but there was no denying the depth of anguish and fear the older dragon felt when faced with the loss of his mate. As he watched, his father attempted to infuse his mother with the strength and incredible healing powers of all his years and stature. Royce could see the majestic blue-green dragon that lived within his father attempting to push to the forefront, the need to save his mate just as powerful as that of the man's. The sheer strength of the beast caused its image to be transposed over and around his mother and father.

Movement at the door alerted him to the arrival of his Uncle Stefan, the clan's Spiritual Leader, and Niall, one of the oldest and most powerful healers of all dragon kin. The crowd parted as the Elders rushed to aid Riona. His brothers backed away, allowing the men to kneel at the bedside. They laid their hands upon his mother's still bleeding stomach and began the Healing Chant. Within seconds, the entire room was enveloped in the revenant verse of healing and prayer meant to call upon the Universe and add strength to the couple as they fought with all that they were to heal the damage done to the once peaceful, vibrant woman, now clinging to life in her mate's arms.

The scent of incense and candles filled the room as, one after the other, the healers his uncle had summoned began to appear. He could feel the massive power of his clan pouring into his parents as they melded into one entity with the common goal of saving his mother and unborn sister. They prayed with one voice and all the power they could muster to save the first purebred dragon female to be born in over a thousand years. Rhianna was to lead the way to the resurgence of their race and give strength to the human mates each dragon shifter was promised by the Universe.

They chanted through the night, while Niall used everything in his abundant arsenal to heal Riona and Rhianna. The tiny, premature baby girl was born sometime in the wee hours of the morning, and although she was barely breathing and pale as the snow on the mountain tops, she was beautiful to all that saw her. She shared Royce's head of bright red curly hair and the one time she graced them by opening her eyes, the brilliant blue that shined behind those tiny lids were an exact replica of his mother's. The tiny babe had looked right into his eyes and an unbreakable bond was instantly formed. Royce willingly funneled all the energy he had left into her tiny body, praying with all that he was that she would live, that he would have the chance to watch her grow and flourish and live the life the Heavens intended.

But at daybreak, just as the warm golden rays of the first light of day crested the mountainside, the two most important people in Royce's life simultaneously took their last breaths. The complete and utter silence of the moment rang in his ears. Everyone in attendance watched as Ronan, their Head Elder, gently laid his wife upon her pillow, placed their tiny daughter into her arms and covered them both lovingly with the blood soaked sheet. He stood watching them, as if by sheer will alone he could wish life back into them. The vast darkness felt endless, but no one moved. He wondered if they even breathed. Then, in the blink of an eye, his father threw back his head and roared. Raw power and emotion blasted through the entire lair. Windows shattered and the very timbers of their home trembled from the sheer weight of his anguish. One by one, each clan member added their voice to their leaders until the ground shook and trees toppled.

As quickly as it had begun it stopped, like a switch had been flipped, and the powerful ruler of the Blue Thunder Clan of the Dragon Shifters was gone…one second there, the next not. Royce looked out the window over his mother's head as the growing light of a new day shone through the shards of glass still stuck in the window pane, and there, flying towards the sun, was his father's dragon. He watched the beast get smaller and smaller as a crippling loss filled him. Turning his head he saw what he was feeling reflected on the faces of his brothers.

Unwilling to relive any more anguish he called upon the strength his dragon, and together they pushed him from his dark revelry back to reality. The residual effects of the overpowering emotions left him spent and panting. While attempting to regain his control, he looked up to find Rian leaning against the wall of the cave, head bowed, with sweat dripping from his brow. "You ok, Ri? What happened?"

"You happened, little brother. You and your blasted memories of the past. You and your ability to relive events as if they are happening all over again. I had no idea we were taking a stroll down memory lane until it was too late. A heads up next time would be nice." He turned and faced Royce. The sweat that dotted his upper lip and the slight tremor in his hand gave away the power the memory had over him.

"Now you see why I cannot mate with her, no matter how impressive her lineage or how sterling her reputation. Ilsa had never done anything remotely dark. *Hell*, her parents were two white witches from highly honored covens that hadn't practiced or even spoken of the dark arts for centuries. She was of the great mage's lineage for Heaven's sake! She lived with our family, our clan, for hundreds of years and was mother's closest friend. That piece of shit, waste of skin and bones helped *raise* us, and in the time between breakfast and lunch was overtaken by a dark spirit seeking the power only the sacrifice of a female dragon and child can yield."

He paused, trying to regain some semblance of control. With none to be found, he continued, his voice a low snarl. "She *slaughtered* our family."

The look that crossed Rian's face let Royce know his older brother was uncharacteristically thinking before speaking. His older brother turned, stopping with his feet shoulder width apart, his hands clasped behind his back, reminding Royce of all the speeches Rian had given before the Guard had flown off into battle, but was sure this oration was not to be uplifting. He braced himself for the recrimination he was sure would follow. The voice that reached his ears was one he hadn't heard since childhood. "Royce, I know this isn't what you wished for or could've ever seen happening, but *it is* your reality and you need to find a way to accept it. You've been given a gift, one that every dragon shifter hears tales of from their first bedtime story and wishes for from the second of their transformation.

"As much as you don't want to hear it, you *will* listen…The Universe does *not* make mistakes. She and She alone knows what you *need* even if you don't. Most times She acts in spite of what you believe is right for you. You have to find your faith. It is not your destiny to die alone and loveless. You more than any of us deserve to be happy, to have an entire clan of your own running around and to have a woman at your side that reminds you to *lighten the hell up*!"

Both brothers burst out laughing, the tension breaker needed before they ground their teeth to nubs. Royce knew his brother was right, in theory, and he was instantly filled with regret for burdening Rian with his personal problems after the horrible hand Fate had dealt *him*. "Ri, I'm…"

"Shut the hell up, Roy. Do you really think I'd be working so hard to pull your stubborn ass out of the past if I was still stuck there? What's done is done. But you, my *little brother*," Rian stopped, eyebrow raised and took a step forward, "have a bright future just waiting for you. All you have to do is grab it."

"Ya know I really hate that you know what I'm going to say before I get it out of my mouth, and I know you're right, at least for the most part, but there are no guarantees she won't fall to the dark arts."

"*Dammit*, Roy, pull your head out of your ass! Guarantees? You want *fucking guarantees*? Life has no *guarantees*! We get what we get and it's up to us to make the most out of it!"

Rian turned and stood staring towards the mouth of the cave. Royce could see his brother's shoulders rising and falling as he took deep breaths to regain his composure. It was an uncommon occurrence for his older, and although he hated to admit it, wiser brother to lose his temper. There had to be something else going on besides Royce's inability to accept his mate. He listened as Rian's breathing and heart rate returned to normal, but decided not to resume the conversation. If Rian wanted to he could, but Royce was fine with letting the subject die the death it deserved. Of course, his brother liked the sound of his own voice just about as much as he liked anything, so Royce was not surprised when Rian began again.

"I've seen your little witch in your mind, just as you see her with your own two eyes, and more importantly, with your heart. You're drawn to her, just as it's meant to be. Your dragon pushes for you to go to her, but you hold the past in front of you, shielding, protecting you from real happiness, from life as it was intended. You have to stop holding on to the past as some sort of tribute to mother and Rhianna. They are gone, Royce, have been for over a hundred years. Father's gone on to join them in the heavens and they're looking down on all of us, wishing they could bitch slap some sense into *you*. You're not honoring their deaths by refusing the one person you are meant to spend all of your days with both here and in the next life…"

Rian paused, and for the first time since Royce had arrived at the clan of his birth, he realized how tired his brother looked. Something was weighing on him, something he wasn't sharing with him. Just as he was about to speak, Rian held up his hand and looked him right in the eye. "No justifications, you are dishonoring them."

Before Royce could respond, the space that Rian had occupied was empty. Royce was left feeling even angrier and more confused than before. He paced beside the fire, looking to the mouth of the cave every few minutes, not sure who or what he was waiting for, but sure things were about to go to hell.

~~*~*~*~*~*~*

*Drip…drip…drip…*Kyra watched the raindrops slide off the leaves and fall into the huge puddle that had formed outside the makeshift shelter Lance and Devon had built for her. Each *splat* seemed to accentuate the incredible amount of time that was passing and the utter failure of her quest to catch the little shithead that had tricked her into helping him hurt the nicest bunch of people…and dragons, she had ever met. They actually *cared* for one another and saw each other as more than a means to an end. It was something she had never experienced before.

Smiling, she remembered how her 'escorts' had reacted when the first raindrop had fallen about an hour ago. It had been absolutely comical as the two big bad Guardsmen bickered like little boys as they constructed the lean-to that kept her and her supplies somewhat dry. She had laughed so hard tears had run down her face. Lance and Devon were worse than a coven full of teenage witches and *that* was saying something. About an hour into her wait, she'd wondered if it had occurred to them how the bright blue tarp secured to the ground behind her and attached to two large pieces of wood in the front stuck out like a sore thumb on the side of the mountain they were perched upon.

"You do know I won't melt, right?" She yelled. "That was the Wicked Witch of the West. I'm the Short Sarcastic Witch of the South," she snorted at her own joke and heard them laugh along.

"Yeah, I'm pretty sure you won't melt. I've heard only sugar melts. However, all your witchy goodies may and after thirteen days of absolutely no sign of the traitor, I'm not taking a chance that we'll miss him the first time you get a jingle or whatever happens on your magic mirror," Devon answered, and she could tell that he and Lance were moving closer.

She shifted her bags to the side to make room for their larger than usual bodies when the toe of a soggy, worn-out cowboy boot entered her view. "Hey, Snarky Witch," Lance chuckled at his own joke and the thought of kicking him in the shin made her grin, "Looks like the weather is clearing up. Since we've established you won't melt, how about you get packed up and let's see if we can find the little asshole?"

"Thank the Goddess," she mumbled as she grabbed the handles of her bags. "I'm *so* ready to find that shithead and give him a swift kick in the ass." She stood and walked out into the reappearing sunlight.

When she saw them, she laughed out loud. "You guys look like a couple of drowned rats. You sure you don't want to head back and get some dry clothes before we continue."

The last word was barely out of her mouth before they answered in unison, "*Hell, no!*"

She raised her palms in a sign of surrender. "No problem. I just don't want your mate," she looked at Lance, "and your momma," she looked at Devon, "to get pissed at me when you both get the sniffles."

"We don't get sick," they answered in unison.

"You two really need to talk one at a time or take your ventriloquism act on the road," she laughed as she placed her bags on a rock and turned to start taking down the shelter.

"We can get it. You just cop a squat and we'll be on our way in a minute," Lance winked and she wondered if his new mate, Samantha, ever got tired of his constant joking.

Then she remembered the dreamy way they looked at one another, as if no one else existed, and she *knew* the answer. Unfortunately, the image of the largest man she'd ever seen with brooding brown eyes and absolutely luscious lips burst into her mind. It didn't matter that she'd barely ever seen them in anything but a frown or heard little more than a grumble come from them, his lips were still completely kissable and occupied her thoughts way more than they should. She hadn't seen the man she knew Fate had picked out for her for almost two weeks. Apparently, he had left before sunrise the morning after Baby Jay's first birthday party. *Jerk!* He'd been completely unbearable and basically anti-social, even to his brethren, during one of the most joyous occasions his clan had known. It was a huge deal that the Commander of the Elite Dragon Force and his beautiful mate had been blessed with a son, and an even bigger deal that in the middle of the search for the traitor that had damned near killed the child's mother, the entire Force had taken a day off to celebrate the little would-be warrior's first birthday.

She'd tried everything she could think of to get him to speak to her but had failed…totally…miserably, and then completely lost her nerve when she crashed right into his chest. To make matters worse…he had *growled*…really growled at her when her hand had landed just above his waist. *What the hell!* He was six-foot ten and she was five-foot two; her hands only reached so far and she was about to fall on her ass. It had been one of the most embarrassing moments of her life*, and* she knew Devon had witnessed it all. Thankfully, he'd had the decency to never mention it.

Dammit, she was no wimp! Kyra St. Croix had never cowered from anything in her life. She was the daughter and heiress of Grand Priestess Calysta St. Croix, the leader of the oldest and most powerful coven of Earth witches in the world. She'd made it through every test that could have been thrown at her when her right of succession had been questioned, completely based on her 'mixed race'. Was it her fault her father was a human? That her mom had a thing for mortals? She had only laid eyes on the man three times in her entire life. That was the way of their coven. Not one she really agreed with, but who was she to buck thousands of years of a tradition she really didn't care about? He seemed nice enough, but three times in seventy-five years did not a daddy-daughter relationship make. He was a sperm donor in her eyes, plain and simple. She had endured forty days and forty nights in the Forest of Darkness, with only what she could scavenge to survive and infused with a magic-dampening spell to prove she had what it took to lead the prestigious coven.

Not that any of that really mattered. There was no way her mother would ever forgive her for leaving, skulking off in the night, to avoid being paraded from dragon clan to dragon clan to identify her mate. She was not a show pony, or worse yet, a beauty queen on tour. Her mother had refused to listen, insisting that they needed to locate her mate as soon as possible with no explanation why. Only after a few months of arguing had Kyra overheard the conversation that changed everything.

She had been heading back to her room after one of the absolutely worst training sessions in the history of training sessions. One that made her want to rip out every last strand of her hair and scream to the heavens. Training had never been something she enjoyed, whether she was doing it or receiving it, and it had definitely never been her lifelong dream to instruct orphaned teen witches with raging hormones. All the talk of boys, hair, and *New Kids on the Block* triggered her gag reflex, ranking right up there with talking about her feelings and painting her toenails…shit that made her *ass twitch*. Lost in thought, she almost ran into the wall when she heard her mother say, "Kyra will do as she is told," from behind the half-closed door of her mother's office. She slowed and leaned against the wall, pretending to review the training schedule stuck to the clipboard in her hands.

Calysta was talking to one of Kyra's many aunts, detailing her contact with the leaders of the dragon clans in the area concerning the 'new development'. Not surprisingly, they had all agreed that Kyra needed to be 'united' with her mate as soon as possible. *WOW! Romance much?* Even though her mate had been predetermined by Fate hundreds of years before she was even a twinkle in her daddy's eye, it pissed her off that her mother was trying to control it. Kyra wasn't looking for a fairy tale love story or anything mushy, but the chance for them to meet on their own terms would have been nice.

It was not the first time since her fiftieth birthday that she had cursed the dragon tattoo on her right hip. Like most things her mother was involved in, one of the coolest things to happen to Kyra had taken a swift slide down a slippery slope. At first she had been excited, kind of giddy, even though that was not an emotion she'd really ever experienced. The prospect of being a part of something bigger than herself, something that had absolutely nothing to do with her mother or her aunts or her coven, was exciting.

The marking that spelled out a huge part of her future was beautiful and majestic, and it fit Kyra. She just knew it was meant for her and that she belonged to the beast it represented and the man with whom he shared his soul. The blue dragon with ever so faint touches of green was in flight and appeared to be simply enjoying the air through his wings and on his scales. He was slightly tipped to the side, so that one wing appeared higher than the other and in just the right light, she could make out the depth of emotion glowing in his deep brown eyes. He had opposing horns and a tail that was long and barbed and she knew would be treacherous in battle but was elegant in flight. More than anything, the tattoo was hers and what came with it was her destiny, and hers alone. The other witches gushed over it and wished for their own. She listened to the giggles and whispers until she thought she might scream.

Kyra was a *NOT* a girly-girl, never had been. She didn't gush or giggle or even gossip like the other girls had when she was younger, and as the years passed, she'd pretty much avoided every female-centered conversation she could. It just wasn't her thing. But when the beautiful blue-green dragon that looked like it was flying through a perfect sky had appeared, she'd immediately felt a sense of purpose…*of belonging*. In that moment, she had realized that's what she'd been missing and it was within her reach. Then in came momma! Leave it to Calysta to insert herself smack ass in the middle of a situation that had absolutely nothing to do with her. What the hell was it about Kyra that made her mother incapable of letting her have any kind of life that was her own? Goddess knew that the Grand Priestess had done *nothing* but groom her to take over the coven from her first steps. She had never been a *real* mom. There had been no tea parties, no Barbie dolls, and no make-up tips…absolutely nothing but hour after hour of training in one form or another.

She had been so lost in her anger that she had almost missed her aunt's comment about 'The Prophecy'. If it was possible, she got even madder with each word she heard. So mad that power began to build in her veins, making her hair lift around her face. Her anger was spiraling out of control until a crack began to form above her head. It had been years since she'd lost control, but just the prospect of her mom ruining the one thing she wanted for herself was the last straw. She had quickly ducked into the storage room beside her mom's office. Leaning against the wall, attempting to regain her control, a plan came to mind. A way to show her mother and all those other bitches that she was through with their crazy ass plans for *her life*.

Several hours later she had come up with a plan that would help her get her hands on the actual Prophecy and get the hell out of dodge. She knew that it would take a few days, but then she would be rid of all the bullshit that came with her mother, her aunts, and their full-of-shit coven. Her prayers for a less complicated life were going to be a reality, she would see to that.

That had been twenty-five years ago. From the moment she had stowed away in the back of that eighteen-wheeler, after hiking almost fifteen miles to the nearest highway in the dead of night, she'd never looked back. There had been times she knew her mother and the coven were looking for her and had even talked to Calysta a few times over the years when she knew it was safe and absolutely necessary. Thankfully, she was truly gifted in the Cloaking Spell department, thanks to her mother's bloodline.

Her magic had manifested at an early age, more powerful than anyone had imagined. It had quickly become second nature to her. She had gotten good at hiding who and what she was or at least making it damn near impossible for anyone to find her, from the moment she decided to disappear. The purity of the dragon magic of her newfound friends called to her white Earth magic, and it had been second nature to drop her guard and let them know exactly who she was. Had the scumbag, Andrew's, dragon magic not been buried so far within him the first time she met him, she would have recognized him for what he was and things would have gone very differently and people she now cared about would not have been hurt. That was just one of the many reasons she wanted to kick his ass until he begged for mercy and then turn him into the snake he was.

Somewhere along the way she had decided she should find out more about her father, but all she had was a faded Polaroid and a rusty old pocket knife. Her mother had claimed she'd lost touch with him after finding out she was pregnant and running back to her coven. Every time they had 'the discussion', the little hairs on the back of Kyra's neck stood on end and she got a ringing in her ears telling her Calysta was lying. They always fought. Kyra always begged. Calysta always avoided until Kyra wore her down and then it ended the same way, with the same lie. She finally had given up ever getting the information she so desperately wanted from her mother. Eventually, she had figured since he was human, and she was over seventy-five, that he had passed away, just another thing in a long list of things that her mother had taken from her.

"Shit!" She yelled as cold drops of water splashed her face and chest, ending her trip down memory lane.

"Wake up, Witchy Poo," Lance chuckled while Devon laughed and shook his head.

"You had to throw water on the last dry shirt I have?"

"Sure did. We're ready to go. I called your name. You didn't answer. So I threw water at you." The biggest hundred-year old kid she had ever known shrugged. She saw the glint in his eye and knew the best was yet to come.

"Besides, you said you wouldn't melt," he winked and she was once again reminded of a bad little boy just waiting to be scolded. Goddess bless Sam for signing up to deal with him for all time.

"No, but I may call in the flying monkeys if you two don't behave yourselves."

"Hey! I didn't do anything," Devon pretended to pout while Lance laughed so hard Kyra was almost afraid he might fall off the side of the mountain.

"No worries, Dev. I'll direct them to the pain in the ass over there…" No sooner were the words out of her mouth than a familiar pain hit her square in the chest. Devon's eyes widened and Lance stopped laughing. 'Pain in the ass' was what Royce called Lance and *everyone* knew that. Everyone also knew that the six-foot ten-inch wall of muscle with red curly hair and deep brown eyes had snuck out before dawn the night after Jay MacLendon's first birthday party and had basically been incommunicado ever since. That had been thirteen days ago.

Thirteen long, miserable days and nights of her lamenting over the last time she'd seen Royce and the conversation between him and Devon that she'd overheard. Unintentional eavesdropping had been a part of her life from a very young age. She had always been short and then stopped growing at twelve. So at five foot two, she went unnoticed…*A LOT*…and that allowed her to hear things that she otherwise wouldn't have. She had replayed the Guardsmen's conversation over and over and always came to the same conclusion. Royce was surprised that he could intimidate her. It was almost as if he was scared of *her* and that shit just didn't make sense. What the hell could she do to a hundred-plus-year-old dragon shifter who was chock-full of his own special brand of magic, chivalry, and goodness, with the ability to change into a thousand pound beast of war and knock down skyscrapers like they were Legos, not to mention the whole fire breathing thing?

At first she thought it was because he recognized her just as she had recognized him and just wasn't ready for the whole 'be together forever in this lifetime and the next' gig that Destiny had decided for both of them. Then she thought it was the fact that she had unknowingly helped that little shithead, Andrew, hurt some of the sweetest people in the world that just happened to be part of Royce's clan. But she knew he was there the day she had apologized and been forgiven by each and every person, even little Sydney. Hurting people was not something Kyra ever wanted to do in any way, shape, or form, and especially not with her magic. Not only because she had taken the Pledge to *'do no harm'*, but also because she just wasn't a villain. *Hell*, she didn't even have an evil laugh.

At the age of thirty, she had pledged her magic and her life to the Goddess of the Earth, assuring both her coven and the Universe, as well as the blessed Goddess that she would only ever use her gifts in a positive manner. It was kind of like the Hippocratic Oath that doctors took before they became licensed, but much more comprehensive and punitive. In its simplest form, the Pledge meant DO NO HARM, and since she was supernatural, if she did intentionally do harm to any living thing she would be low-jacked and the 'powers-that-be' could zap her ass. It was incredibly painful but with no long lasting effects. If, Goddess forbid, she got a couple of zaps, the Council showed up and that was something she *never* wanted to have happen.

The Council was made of up of the oldest, most powerful witches in existence, who had absolutely no sense of humor or patience for rule breakers. She had only ever seen them once, and it had been another time where she was somewhere she wasn't supposed to be but had gone undetected. A man she'd known her entire life had gone completely off the rails, killed people, irreparably damaged the Earth, and had completely turned to dark magic. It had taken ten of the most skilled from her mother's coven to capture him and the Council's punishment had been swift. One minute the accused was screaming and spitting venom and the next he was on fire. Poof! Gone! Pile of Ash on the ground! Definitely not something Kyra ever wanted to experience firsthand.

She was shaken from her memories when Devon's hand touched her shoulder. "Come on, let's get this over with. I'm ready to go home and relax. Kyndel invited me to dinner and Jay and I have plans for a rousing game of roll-the-ball." He winked and she knew he was trying to get her mind off the one track it had seemed to be stuck on ever since meeting the dragon they all called 'the gentle giant'. Devon's beautiful smile and twinkling grey eyes didn't hurt anything either. He didn't make her feel anything but friendship, but he was sweet and really nice to look at, as were all the Dragon Guardsmen.

"Alright you two knuckleheads, lead the way." Lance pointed towards the direction they had been heading before the downpour.

Laughing, they began their trek, joking and teasing, but the fun was long forgotten after several hours of endless walking. Kyra was hot, tired, and seriously pissed, convinced they were just wasting time, aimlessly marching around the hillside. She was just about to suggest a break when a chill ran down her spine and her hands began to shake. Without saying a word, she dropped into the lotus position with her backpack on her lap and began pulling out her supplies, completely ignoring Lance's bitching and Devon's inquiries about her wellbeing. It took only a few seconds and she had the silver-framed mirror that had been her great-great-grandmother's, a vial of blessed water from the Black Lake, and her special herbs, and was working her Scrying Spell. She could hear the two Guardsmen discussing what she was doing but concentrated on the task at hand. They had been around her long enough to know she wasn't wasting time. Any other explanations would have to wait.

The spell took less than five minutes and had a side effect she had only experienced one other time in her life. Not only did she get a location on Andrew, but she also had a vision of what he was planning. The scene that played out in her mind was like watching a horror movie, only she could feel what each character felt. Her heart raced and a cold sweat broke out all over her body, but she was stuck watching the complete annihilation of a quaint little community tucked in a once beautifully lush valley. Everything she saw was from Andrew's point of view so although she hadn't seen him, she knew he was there, but that was the only thing that felt familiar.

She searched the faces of the dead and injured for any indication of the target of the asshole's destruction, but nothing looked familiar and there wasn't any sound to help. All she knew was that he was somewhere off a rocky coast with turbulent waters and he was having a great time hurting anyone and everyone in his path. The silent movie of destruction went on and on. When she was sure she couldn't take any more pain and suffering and had decided to see what the guys thought about what she had seen, her heart ceased to beat and her lungs refused to hold air. There, standing in the middle of the war zone, was Royce. His brow was furrowed, his brown eyes scanning the area for those that most needed his help. Her heart broke when she saw the cuts and bruises covering most of his beautiful face and his torn, bloody, and soot-covered clothes.

The horror show unfolding in Andrew's mind switched to slow motion as Royce moved from person to person, helping the living from the rubble and getting them to safety. He wasn't the only one working rescue, but he was the only one that mattered to her. He shouted something and she cursed the lack of sound. In the next instant, a taller version of Royce (was that even possible?) appeared to his right. The resemblance was uncanny. The new guy's hair was short and curly, auburn instead of bright red, and he was not all muscular and hunky, more long and lean, which only added to how absolutely tall he was. The two worked furiously to clear away the debris, looking for someone or something specific. Even though only a vision, she could tell they were engaged in a constant stream of mind speak, another wonderful perk of being magical.

An ominous sense of danger filled her and once again her breath stilled in her lungs. She watched as both men turned in unison and began running almost faster than her eyes could track. They were obviously screaming orders to anyone that could hear from the expressions they wore and the way their mouths moved. The feeling of impending doom engulfed every cell of Kyra's body as she felt Andrew's enjoyment grow. The sick son of a bitch was enjoying what he was seeing and delighted that more was coming.

Horror movies had never been her thing and to have the man that was her mate in a starring role in one that would be a reality was seriously freaking her out. Sifting through everything she had ever learned that was stored in her goofy brain, she looked for a way to pull out of the vision. Finally, she found what she thought might work, but true to form, a bright light burst before her eyes. Vibrations of an explosion she knew was taking place in her mind gave her the sensation of falling, right before her world went black.

Two sets of very large hands shook her and babbled frantically. If she had been able to, she would have screamed out loud when Lance said he was going to throw her over his shoulder and run like hell, but it was Devon's response that almost stopped her heart.

"*Dammit*, Lance, settle the hell down. She's magical...*really magical* and super powerful. Give her a minute to pull herself out of whatever happened before you go all caveman. We have no idea what she was doing besides scrying, and she told us that was just for location, so apparently her witchy senses found a lead and she took it. Besides, if anything happens to her, Royce will lose his shit. You and I both know it. She is his mate. He knows she's his mate. He's just being pigheaded. There is no way in hell he could handle her getting seriously hurt."

She could hear the rocks crunch under Lance's worn-out cowboy boots and knew he was pacing, his second favorite pastime.

"I know, *dammit*, but you know I suck at waiting. When she hit the ground, all I could think was snake bite, but there's no way one would come anywhere near us. Then she started digging in her goodie bag and I thought it was no big thing, but now...what the *hell*? Her eyes were like...gone, rolled back in her head, and she was shaking so hard I thought she would fall to pieces." He paced the whole time he spoke.

When he stopped, she knew he had knelt down as the denim of his blue jeans brushed her arm. She imagined him staring at her face, not sure what to do and then he spoke. "Did you hear how fast her heart was beating? I wish Sam was here, she would know what to do."

"Dude, you gotta chill. I've seen stuff like this before with some of mom's patients. Give her a little time and she'll bring herself out of it. Kyra is a fighter. You just have to be patient."

"Yeah, yeah, yeah...patience. You're all Zen and I'm about to lose my shit. I really hate you sometimes, Dev."

Devon's chuckle relieved even more of the tension that had invaded her body during her vision. "I'm not Zen, I'm just not crazy like you. Now, sit down and wait for her to find her way back."

She heard the rustle of someone digging in her duffle bag. "You want a protein bar?" Devon asked.

"Yeah, throw me a couple and a bottle of water, please," Lance replied, and she could still hear the concern in his voice.

She was once again amazed at how these people, these dragons, cared so much for one another and *for her*. They'd only known her a short time and had definitely met her under less than desirable circumstances, but nonetheless, they had accepted her as one of their own. It was an amazing feeling and one she would always cherish.

She felt as if she was slowing floating upward, despite the hard ground beneath her back. The feeling returned to her fingers and toes slowly, with pins and needles working their way up her arms and legs. As soon as her mouth worked again, she whispered, "That bottle of water better not be to throw in my face."

Though her vision was blurry, she could make out the smiles that spread across the men's faces. Of course Lance was the first to speak, "What the hell, Witchy Poo? You decide you needed a nap?"

"Yeah, that was it," she chuckled, as Devon helped her sit up.

As soon as the warmth of his hand hit her shoulder a flood of images from her vision came rushing back. The water she was drinking flew out of her mouth and she shouted details as fast as she could. "It was so pretty and calm, but I could feel the darkness coming. I could see and feel everything but couldn't hear a damn thing. I know the little asshole was there. I could see everything through his eyes and he was so excited about the awfulness that was coming."

She used Devon's knee to help her up while still shouting about all she had just seen. "Everything was fine one minute and then...BOOM..."

"What the hell are you talking about, Little Bit?" Lance shouted and grabbed her by the shoulders, bending enough to look her right in the eyes.

Kyra blinked a few times and took a deep breath, trying to get her bearing in order to make sense of what she'd seen.

Lance spoke again, softer and more worried than she could have ever imagined, "Come on, Kyra, snap out of it. Tell us what you saw. What made you collapse?"

"I...he...it was..." She closed her eyes and took another deep breath. When she opened them again, both Devon and Lance were staring at her, expectantly. She took two steps back and snapped, "Stop looking at me like I have two heads."

They both laughed, helping all the tension associated with the horrific vision she'd just experienced drain out of body, finally straightening out the thoughts in her head. The ending of her vision flashed before her eyes and for the first time in her life she thought she might just faint. Without further thought, she screamed, "We have to find Royce! He's in danger. There's gonna be an explosion!" She reached out and grabbed a hand from both men and started to pull.

"Come on! What the hell's wrong with you?!" she shouted.

Neither man moved, just stood and stared, looking at her like she had two heads. She pulled so hard she could feel sweat dotting her upper lip. Completely frustrated and more than a little pissed, she dropped both their hands and spun around, only to find herself lifted in midair by Lance and deposited on the same big rock she had been propped against just moments earlier.

Just about to scream…again…she realized they were both using mind speak. Her heart raced as she felt the seconds tick by. She had no idea how long they had until whatever it was that Andrew was planning happened, she only prayed that they could get a warning to Royce in time.

Lance and Devon were deep in conversation with the others of their Force, not paying any attention to her, when she decided that waiting sucked and she was going to do whatever it took to stop the devastation she had witnessed. Her escape plan would have worked if the damn dragons didn't move so fast. Devon grabbed her by the arm before she could get both feet on the ground and held fast. When she turned to give him her best 'Go To Hell' look, he was giving her his, and since he was about twenty years older and a foot taller, his was better. She started to hunch her shoulders and then realized she had absolutely nothing to be ashamed of. The man she was supposed to spend the rest of her life with was in serious danger. It didn't matter that he couldn't stand the sight of her, or that she already had feelings for him, she had to save him along with the others she'd seen lying dead or broken around him.

"What do you think you are doing, Kyra? We're talking to Rayne and trying to get a hold of Royce. Wait just a fucking minute," he scolded.

She glanced over his shoulder to see Lance's devil-may-care attitude gone, replaced by a warrior, out for blood, ready to protect one of his own. It was intimidating to say the least, but she refused to back down. Royce needed their help. The threat was real and growing every second.

"Hurry," was all she could get out before she was deposited back on the same damn rock and told to stay put.

Thank the Goddess she didn't have to wait long. Lance grabbed the large duffel she'd dropped on the ground and reached for her hand, "We can't get Royce to answer. Rayne is on his way to the Elders. Come on, we're taking you back to the lair. You can stay with Kyndel and Grace while we go see what the hell is going on."

"No fucking way!" she screamed. "There is absolutely no way you are leaving me to sit at home like the *'little woman'*. Whatever is threatening him is magical. I could feel it and the last time I checked, *dragon man*, I'm the magical expert around here."

"There is no way in hell we're taking you anywhere near that kind of danger or that piece-of-shit traitor," Lance yelled back as he grabbed for the arm she had pulled from his grasp.

As soon as his fingers touched her skin, a powerful shock caused him to cry out, "WHAT THE FUCK?" He pulled back his hand, looked at his fingers, and then at her with suspicion.

Any other time she would have been embarrassed that her anxiety and fear had caused her to use her powers without conscious thought, but not this time. The man that she was supposed to spend her life with was in trouble and she knew with all certainty that she could save him. Remembering what she'd told the last group of teenage witches that she had ever trained, 'Suck it up Buttercup, you're a real witch now', all those years ago, she squared her shoulders and looked a man she would otherwise call friend straight in the eyes.

"I'm sorry I hurt you, but I'm not sorry it happened. I *am* a witch, in case you forgot," she poked him in the shoulder for added effect. "And whatever or whoever is trying to hurt Royce is also trying to hurt all the people around him," she poked him again and this time he had the decency to at least take a step back.

"They are using magic. Strong,"…poke…"powerful,"…poke…"old magic. I have a duty to protect them. So we can play this your way and I'll just sneak out and do what I can by myself…" she placed both hands on her hips. "Or we can work together. Either way *I. am. going.*" Not waiting for an answer, she turned on her heel, threw her back pack over her shoulder, and stomped in the direction of their SUV. At this point she didn't give a shit if they followed or not, she was going to save Royce. She was going to save them all and then she just might kick her supposed mate's ass for getting into trouble in the first place.

On the ride back to the lair, she explained in vivid detail everything she had seen in her vision while Devon relayed the information to Rayne and the other Guardsmen, making sure they were ready to head out as soon as she and the guys returned. She found out along the way that the big dude she'd seen standing next to Royce was his older brother, the leader of his own clan. *Well, hell*, she thought to herself, *more family to deal with*. Lance went on to tell her that Royce had gone back to the clan of his birth and for the first time in thirteen days she knew where he was. She almost laughed out loud as she thought, *Damn, little ole me sent the big ole dragon man running home.*

Her levity immediately turned to sadness when she realized he really was running from her. All those silly little dreams about someone that would love her unconditionally and want nothing more than for her to love him back were *bullshit*. Sure, she'd seen firsthand that it could happen. She thought about Lance and Sam and all the other mated couples she'd met while staying with their clan and knew in her heart it was possible, but for some reason it wasn't in the cards for her and Royce.

A sadness weighed her down as they rounded the corner and turned onto the barely visible dirt road that led to the dragon shifter's lair, but Kyra was a fighter. She had been through worse things and figured worse was still to come, so she shoved her sadness aside. It was time to show these cavemen what a girl with some magic could do. Yeah, sure they were bigger, but hadn't they heard about dynamite in small packages?

~~*~*~*~*~*

Andrew had spent the last two weeks plotting and planning, amassing magic from every source he could find. It was apparent that Master Eaton and his followers were still doing blood sacrifices from the amount of magic buzzing through them. He could see their dark glowing auras and was sure they could light up a small city.

Thankfully, John had located a Siphoning Spell that allowed him to pull a little from each wizard within close proximity without detection. For the first time, he had more black magic flowing through his body than he could ever remember, and unlike before, his newly acquired power did not snuff out his dragon senses. On the contrary, the beautifully pure dragon magic seemed to simply avoid the taint of the dark, almost like the two polar opposite powers had decided to coexist within him.

He'd always been told he would possess extraordinary abilities because he had been born a "*Special One*". The ancient text John had acquired for him confirmed it and had only strengthened his resolve to do whatever it took to exact his revenge. The text was written in the old language, but thankfully, he and John had found another book that helped with the translation. The more he learned, the more fascinated he became. Just yesterday he had translated the beginnings of the Prophecy. He was intrigued when he recognized the word 'sorceress' and couldn't wait to learn more.

He finished packing his supplies just as a knock at the door sounded outside his wing of the mansion he shared with Master Eaton, Mr. A, and a handful of their followers. When he had first decided to move in with the leader of the most powerful wizards in the country and the State's Attorney-turned-crime boss that specialized in human trafficking, he'd had his doubts, but with the help of his right-hand man and some very handy surveillance equipment, they were making great headway towards achieving his plans for revenge.

"Come in," he called out, knowing it was Andy, one of Master Eaton's favorite wizards, from the beat of his heart and the smell of bacon on his clothes. Andy had been appointed the unofficial cook of the mansion and it seemed bacon was always on the menu.

The door opened and the small round face with puffy pink cheeks he was expecting came into view. "Good morning, Mr. O'Brien. Master Eaton wanted you to know that everyone is loaded and the jet is scheduled to take off in two hours," the small chubby wizard spoke without ever once meeting Andrew's eyes. Poor little man was scared shitless and Andrew loved every damn minute of it. Wielding the power he possessed was intoxicating, and knowing that by tomorrow, at this same time, one of the men he held responsible for all he had endured would be removed from the earth and sent to the Heavens where he belonged. It was a shame that the others wouldn't be there to see it happen but that couldn't be helped. He needed to strike while the iron was hot and prove to himself, along with everyone else, that he could take down a dragon shifter. *Hell*, they all doubted their existence and thought he was insane. Wouldn't they shit their pants if he revealed they already knew one…*him*? He laughed to himself as he followed Andy down the corridor and out the front door to one of the fifty or so black SUVs the crime boss owned.

He rode to the private airfield in silence, thankful the others had agreed to let him ride alone, save the driver. Thinking over his plan, he made sure every 'I' was dotted and every 'T' crossed. There would be no second chance. They had to get in, destroy the Blue Thunder Clan, and get out without a trace. It would be the one time he would be able to strike without any warning.

Ever since Kyra had been captured by the Guard all those months ago, he had been keeping the last Cloaking amulet powered up with an infusion of dragon magic and black magic. Several times he'd had John scry for him to be sure it was working. He had to believe it was the purity of his returning dragon magic that kept it going. The little witch had mentioned that he had bastardized her Earth magic, creating something altogether different and unknown. He knew he should feel bad for deceiving her after all she had done to help him, even if he had lied through his teeth to get what he wanted. But knowing that she had taken up with the Dragon Guard against him eliminated any guilt he felt.

Pulled from his thoughts when the SUV stopped, he gathered his things and climbed out onto the abandoned airstrip. There, sitting before him, was the luxury jet Mr. A had 'acquired' on a recent 'business trip'. Andrew had absolutely no idea where the known crime boss and basic blight upon the earth went for his business, or what exactly occurred there, but as long as it got Andrew what he wanted he would continue to turn a blind eye and reap the benefits.

"Welcome, Mr. O'Brien," Adrienne, a cute young brunette with deep blue eyes that served as Mr. A's executive assistant chirped as he stepped onto the charcoal gray carpet leading the way to the stairs into the plane.

"Hello, Adrienne, and thank you," he absently responded, while another of the hundreds of lackeys the mobster seemed to always have available relieved him of his bag.

Unsure whether he should let something so important out of his sight, he held onto the handle for just a beat and then decided he didn't want to call too much attention to his supplies, so he said, "Please make sure that is stowed over my seat." The young man nodded his understanding and preceded Andrew up the steps.

"Have a safe trip, Mr. O'Brien. See you when you return," Adrienne called out as he entered the plane. Not for the first time, he wondered how Adrienne, a sweet girl, had gotten mixed up with such a horrible man, but quickly decided he was no one to judge and didn't care. She was a grown adult and not his to worry about. The little human was of no consequence to his plans and therefore expendable. However, that did not mean he wouldn't mess with her mind for fun. And just to show himself he could, he looked over his shoulder and smiled, pleased to see her blush at his attention. He shrugged. Maybe he could find a way for her to be useful somewhere down the line, if for nothing more than to look at.

All thoughts of silly young girls flew from his mind at the first glimpse of the empty plane before him. His face must have mirrored the questions in his mind because the young man that had carried his bag onto the plane answered his unspoken inquiry, "Mr. A and Master Eaton were delayed and will be here momentarily. Can I get you a drink and some hors d'oeuvres?"

"No, thank you. I'll just grab a seat and read while I wait," Andrew responded, less than thrilled at the delay.

Not only was it terribly inconvenient, not to mention rude, to be left sitting and waiting, but he detested the fact that they were out doing something he knew absolutely nothing about. He trusted no one, least of all his 'partners'. It was obvious none of them told the other two the whole story or the whole truth about anything they did or their ultimate goal. Each man had his own agenda and would do whatever it took to grab the prize at the end of their respective journeys.

Andrew settled into a seat at the very rear of the plane with the ancient text opened in his lap. It had been covered and made to look like any ordinary book to avoid any unnecessary questions. No one could know that he had possession of one of the most ancient and dangerous volumes of spells, prophecies, and supernatural knowledge ever written. It was only by luck that John had overheard a few young witches talking about it and had been able to befriend them long enough to get into their leader's home and steal the book. His protégé had assured him that he had not been seen, but further warned that the Grand Priestess he had liberated the book from was one of the most powerful he had ever encountered and would definitely try to get it back. Just another reason he was thrilled his amulet was keeping him hidden from everyone.

It was almost forty-five minutes later when he finally heard the sound of people approaching the plane. Before he could return the book to his bag, Mr. A entered the plane with Master Eaton, several wizards, and a few of his thugs in tow. Master Eaton was the first to speak and actually had the decency to apologize, "Sorry we are late. We were unavoidably detained, but the cargo is being loaded and we will be in the air in the next twenty minutes."

"No need to explain, Eaton. Andrew knows there are many moving parts to all our plans and delays are to be expected. Get buckled in so we can have a drink and enjoy our flight."

The asshole actually had the nerve to wink in Andrew's direction like they were friends. If the scumbag had not been essential to all his plans, Andrew would have killed him where he stood, but as it was, he needed him for at least two more weeks. If all went well, as soon as the next full moon was high in the sky, there would be nothing any of them could do to stop him. Until then, he would bide his time, put up with all their bullshit, and revel in the moment he watched the life drain out of their useless bodies.

Deciding to play along, he smiled, knowing it did not reach his eyes and said, "Absolutely. No harm done. I was able to catch up on some much needed reading."

Master Eaton looked from one man to the other, his fear from the building tension and innuendos that were being freely tossed around was palpable. In an effort to end the pissing contest that Mr. A seemed to perpetually be ready for, Andrew chuckled and motioned towards the flight attendants. "Besides, I have been tortured with the tantalizing aroma coming from the galley and would love to have a bite to eat and a drink while we wait to get our voyage underway."

Seemingly pacified, and the tension level decreasing by the second, everyone took a seat while the attendants served the drinks and passed around an extravagant assortment of hors d'oeuvres. Eating and drinking with a plane full of idiots ranked right up there with having all his teeth pulled without anesthetic, but it was a means to an end and he would do whatever it took to destroy everyone that betrayed him. He took comfort in the fact that in just sixteen days the moon would be full, and as long as things went according to plan, he would have all the power he needed to deliver the vengeance those fucking dragon assholes deserved. All he had to do was play the part, and the Universe knew he was *good* at playing his part.

~~*~*~*~*~*~*

There was absolutely no way she could have prepared herself for a flight to the coast of an entirely different country on the back of a dragon. When they had reached the lair, all the Guardsmen had been in the clearing behind Rayne's home, ready to transform and head out to stop whatever plan Andrew was cooking up. She had tried repeatedly, using every spell and magical charm she could think of, to get another read on Andrew, but the bastard had either charged his Cloaking amulet or found another way to avoid her detection. The only other thing she could think of was that he was surrounded by other magical beings and their magic was essentially spilling onto him, keeping him hidden. She decided that as soon as they landed, she would do a Detection spell to see if she could locate any high concentrations of black magic. That way she would be able to track the people he was with and the guys could catch him before he could hurt Royce or any of the innocent people the fucking traitor cared nothing about.

Rayne had told them that no one, not even Carrick, the Head Elder, had been able to get a response from Royce or his brothers, making them believe that something or someone was blocking their communication. Thankfully, there was a special connection between all the dragons that shared a blood bond, fueled by their dragon magic, that let them know Royce was still alive, not in what condition, just that he was alive.

She had watched as the mated Guardsmen kissed their loved ones goodbye, unable to stop the heaviness that settled in and around her heart. That was how she had always imagined a mate would be…loving and caring and totally devoted. Deciding her pity party should wait until everyone was safe and she was off somewhere by herself, preferably at least a hundred miles from all things dragon, she had bent down to give the waiting Sydney a kiss on the head. There was just something about the little blonde-haired beauty that brightened even the darkest moments. After everyone had been hugged, kissed, and wished a safe trip, Lance asked if she was hitching a ride with him or taking her own broom. Everyone laughed and some of the sadness fell away from the group. Lance had a way of making everyone laugh, even when faced with eminent danger.

The men had walked about a hundred yards farther into the clearing, and from one moment to the next, the men she knew became the dragons she had imagined. Two shimmering silver and black, one striking red, one glimmering gold, and a brilliant white – all majestic, all fierce, all exuding more power and magic than she had ever experienced, and all ready to do whatever it took to protect one of their own.

The strange feeling that only came when the Guard were using their mind speak slid through her mind. A hand on her shoulder made her jump just before Sam said, "Lance is ready." And then the beautiful doctor did something completely surprising. She hugged Kyra. A real hug that without words let her know that she was truly accepted into their family…that she mattered. It took all her control not to let the tears she felt welling up fall. As soon as Sam let go, Kyra turned away and all but ran towards the dragons. Nothing had ever touched her like that one simple gesture.

Their flight had been amazing and her enhanced night vision had definitely come in handy. Flying over the open water in the middle of night had been amazing. She'd seen whales, dolphins, and all kinds of sea creatures she'd only ever seen in books and movies. She felt like a little kid on her first grade field trip, not that she had ever been on a field trip or even to a school, but she had heard about them. There was no way she could have stopped the giggles that bubbled over even though she knew the Guardsmen could hear. It might have been the only chance she would ever get to ride a dragon and she was damn sure going to make the most of it.

On the ground and making their way through an incredibly dense forest towards the lair of the Blue Thunder Clan, she wondered how she was going to avoid the giant of a man that had flown halfway around the world to avoid her. No matter what Devon had said, she knew she was the reason he'd left. Just to confirm that fact, there were times she would get a glimpse of what he was feeling or thinking. She quickly learned that the difference between what he felt towards her when he was awake and what he felt when was sleeping or had let his guard down was as different as night and day. Not that she had a clue what to do about it.

When he was awake, he pushed all thoughts of her as far from his consciousness as possible, and when that wasn't possible, she felt how angry and frustrated he became. It was like he was being forced to listen to techno music after an all-night bender…*shitty*. But when he was asleep, she felt affection, attraction, the desire to get to know her better, and the need to protect her at all costs. She had spent hour after hour wondering what it all meant and had even contemplated talking to Siobhan, Devon's mom and their clan's Elder Healer, about it. No matter how many times Kyra came into contact with the older woman, she was impressed with her compassion and the acceptance she felt from her, however, Kyra had never gotten around to it and she was out of time. In the next hour or so she would be face to face with the man. If he had not been in danger, there was no way she would be anywhere around him. He had made his feelings known and there was no way she was forcing herself on him. It was a 'take care of business and get the hell out' situation.

Before she could sink any farther into her self-examination, a strange feeling fell over her. She felt covered with a sick slimy feeling that literally tried to invade her pores. It was as if she walked through motor oil flowing from a waterfall. Each step she took made it harder to breathe. Her feet felt like they were tied to bricks. Kyra stumbled and reached forward, using Aaron's back for support. The Guardsman spun around with a half-smile, obviously ready to tease, but his expression immediately changed when he saw her struggle to stand.

"Kyra," he reached out to keep her from falling forward. "What the…"

She couldn't make out what came next and she fell to the ground, tearing the backpack from her shoulder. Aaron knelt down in front of her, still obviously shouting, trying to get an answer to what was happening, but she was unable to make out any of his words. In her peripheral vision, she could see the others, spread out in a circle, protecting her from whatever seemed to be coming just for her. She searched her bag for the protection against the onslaught of the black magic that she was coming to recognize. It had a signature all its own, one of betrayal, hate, and retribution.

Finally, at the bottom of her bag, her fingers touched the cool silver disc she sought. Snatching it out, she let her bag fall to the side and shoved her head through the leather strap attached to the powerful Protection amulet she always made sure was charged and close at hand.

The instant the weight of the ancient pendant touched the center of her chest the oppressive weight began to lift. She counted to ten and was finally able to draw her first full, clean breath. When her vision cleared, Aaron was kneeling in front of her, hands on her shoulders, gripping just shy of the point of pain and repeating her name over and over.

She put one hand on his and tried to smile, "I'm okay." Her voice sounded scratchy even to her ears, confirming that she had been sucking air like a fish out of water during her battle with the dark magic.

She swallowed and continued to reassure her protector and the others she knew were still standing guard, "Seriously, I'm okay, but Andrew is close and he's not alone. He's attempting to work a serious Barrier spell. I must have walked right through the perimeter he set. One second I was breathing the beautiful fresh scent of the sea and the next I felt like I was drowning in motor oil."

The Guardsmen turned to face her and listened intently to the information she had about the traitor. Aaron stood and the spot he vacated was filled with the Dragon Guard Commander, Rayne. He looked at her intently with a look of concern mixed with anger in his deep violet eyes. When he spoke it was the voice of a commander, not the voice of Kyndel's caring mate or Jay's loving father that she was used to. "Are you sure you're alright?"

"Yeah, I'm sure." She smiled her best 'it'll be okay' smile and made sure it reached her eyes. "But I'm getting damn tired of this son of a bitch sneaking up on me and knocking me on my ass. I have my pride ya' know?"

The Commander smiled and the tension level all around her dropped a notch. Before anyone could interrupt, she continued, "He's not far, no more than twenty miles away, and he's not alone." She closed her eyes and imagined the face of the traitor, the man she had believed needed her help all those months ago but only gave her what he seemed to give everyone…*betrayal*.

"There are at least eight of them using magic, maybe others. I can't read anyone non-magical while they're working the spell. They're using blood magic, but it doesn't feel like they performed the sacrifice here."

She grew silent as she realized they were merely warming up. Her eyes opened of their own volition and she saw five fierce warriors hanging on her every word. *Damn! No pressure*, she thought to herself.

"He's only working a Barrier spell. It'll take most of the night to complete and it's meant to seal anything that draws breath within its confines. We need to find Royce and get everyone out from behind the barrier that little piece of shit is building."

As she stood up, she was struck with a thought, "Hey! Don't any of you big lugs feel the effects of the spell…*at all*?" She felt her eyes grow wide but couldn't help her surprise as they all shook their heads.

"Well, *damn* I knew you guys were strong and dragon magic was nothing to mess with but…well…" She rubbed her hands down her face, still in awe of the vast amount of power surrounding her. "Just *damn*…that's all I got."

Laughter rang through the forest as she gathered up her backpack and secured it on her shoulder. Devon handed her a bottle of water, a concerned look still haunting his grey eyes. "You sure you're okay? That's the second time in just a few hours you've taken a fall."

Kyra swatted his shoulder and teased, "Way to make a girl feel special, Dev."

At least he had the decency to look embarrassed, because Aaron and Lance chose that moment to pick on her like the big brothers she had always wished for. "Yeah, *little witch*," Lance joked, using the nickname he knew irritated her the most. "Your ass has been hitting the ground a lot lately."

"I hear you've taken to fainting, 'Sarcastic Little Witch of the South'. All this raw power makes you swoon, huh?" Aaron teased and she wondered when Lance had found the time to tell them all about her new 'title'.

"Swoon my ass, dragon man," she laughed.

Before they could continue their banter, Rayne spoke, "Alright, there'll be time for this shit later. Right now we need to get to Royce and Rian and see what we can do about evacuating the area." He pointed to Aidan, who had been suspiciously silent during the whole incident, "'A', you take the lead." He looked from man to man, "Lance to Kyra's right, Devon to her left, Aaron and I will take the rear. Let's get moving."

She felt the weight of the Commander's stare right before he spoke, "Kyra, let me know if you feel *anything* unusual. I want no more sneak attacks and I want Andrew's head on a pike," he finished on a growl with a look of utter contempt and untold anger in his eyes.

"Absolutely," was all she could get out before he disappeared behind her and they started to move forward.

That is one pissed off dragon, was all she thought as they marched towards Royce, hoping they could stop whatever the traitor had panned.

Exactly one hour later, she felt the familiar sensation associated with the mind speak of the Dragon Guard. Curious by nature, it always bothered her when she knew they were talking but couldn't hear it. She smiled when she remembered that her Auntie Della had told her how dragon mates shared special abilities and that one day she would share everything with hers. Her smile fell as she realized that was not what the future held for her. If she was not mistaken, and she was sure she wasn't, her mate would rather eat nails than share anything with her. *Stop your fucking whining, Kyra. Now is not the time*, she thought to herself.

Rayne's voice sounded from behind. "I finally got a hold of Rian. He said Royce is on the outer edge of the lair, holed up in a cave."

She felt a whoosh of air as he sped past her, "I'll lead the way and Rian will meet us on the other side. Let's go."

Their hike continued and the buzzing from their mind speak rose higher and higher until she was sure she could reach out and grab the words. She concentrated on the flow of energy and found one strand more intense than the others. Following it, she found Aidan, his blue eyes turbulent with worry and anger. Not wanting to disturb him, but desperate to know who he was trying to connect with, she followed the trail as far as it went. There at the end was not a face, but a huge inky stain filled with pure malevolence and contempt. The emotions coming from the horrible mass of evil made Kyra feel dirty from the inside out. Just as she was about to retreat, she sensed a familiar signature, one she despised more with every passing second. It was Andrew. Aidan was trying to track his treacherous brother through the special link between brothers, searching for the one that had caused so much pain to so many he loved. It was then that she knew why he had been so quiet and withdrawn. Aidan was seeking out the little bastard, and if the powerfully hostile feelings were any indication, Aidan intended to end his brother's life if given the chance.

Feeling like a Peeping Tom and sure that she had time to keep Aidan from making a mistake he couldn't take back, Kyra pulled back, but kept a small foothold in the brothers' connection. If Aidan found Andrew before they did and tried to act without his brethren, she would know and would do whatever it took to ensure the traitor's capture without harm to the living. Andrew had to pay for what he had done, but not at the cost of any of the souls of the people she had come to think of as family.

It only took about fifteen minutes longer before Rayne gave the sign to stop. Kyra looked around in the dark for signs of someone other than the Force she traveled alongside. As she looked towards the skies, she realized the sun would rise in less than an hour and sent a prayer to the Goddess for everyone's safety. She'd never been an incredibly spiritual person, other than her magical connection to the Goddess and the Universe, but standing alongside the fiercest warriors she'd ever known, ready to battle one of their own turned traitor, made her realize how much she had truly come to care for each and every one of them and all they held dear. More than that was the understanding that even though all of them, including her, were incredibly hard to kill, they were not immortal. She knew there was no way she would allow one of her new friends to fall to the traitor that spread death and disaster like it was pixie dust. Andrew thought he could best them with magic. The arrogant prick thought he could best *her*. He was over-confident and cocky and she *would* bring him down.

No matter what she thought about her mother, she had to give Calysta credit for one thing. She had taught Kyra to fight and fight was what she would do. Fight for her friends. Fight for the magic that Andrew abused. And even fight for the hard-headed giant that refused to accept their fate. Andrew was in for a surprise in the form of a five-foot two pissed as shit white witch. *Watch out shithead. I'm coming for you,* she thought as hard as she could toward the thread that lead to the traitor. She wanted him to know she was coming and she wanted him scared.

"Well, you lot look like you're about to do something stupid. Mind if I tag along?" The sound of an unfamiliar voice with a slight accent pulled her from her mental assault on the traitor.

Her anxiety lessened when she saw Rayne embrace the stranger and when he called him 'Rian', she knew she was looking at the back of Royce's older brother. The man was the tallest person she had ever seen. He stood more than a head taller than the leader of the Dragon Guard Force and Rayne was over a foot taller than she was; just another reminder that she was the shortest person *in the world*. Rian turned towards the group and Kyra gasped at the incredible family resemblance. It was absolutely uncanny, but the longer she looked, the more obvious the differences became. His hair was an auburn, not bright red, and his eyes were a glowing blue instead of the warm brown she liked to sneak glances at when Royce wasn't paying attention. She knew from her vision that Rian was a good inch taller than his younger brother, and now that she had a closer look, she verified that he was long and lean, where Royce was bulk and muscle and possessed a raw power that made her tingle all over, even when she tried with all her might to ignore it.

When he spoke, she felt none of electricity that even a grunt from Royce caused. "Thank you so much for coming. I have no clue what threatens us this evening, but I am grateful that you have come to help protect those I hold dear."

"We are going to stay hidden in the caves and give Kyra a chance to work her magic for any clues about our enemies while we prepare our defense," Rayne explained.

In the blink of eye, Rian was standing next to Kyra and had her hand in his. He greeted her like the gentleman of old with a chaste kiss to the back of her hand, but the wink was all cocky dragon shifter. She could tell he was messing with her, but she was unsure how not to offend the Head Elder and brother of the man who occupied too many of her thoughts. When he spoke, she was sure he was just trying to get a rise out of her, "You are even lovelier in person." He stepped back and looked from her toes to her head and back down again, "And just the tiniest little thing I have ever seen."

Rian stepped towards her again, gripping her hands a tad tighter. "And you are a strong little witch, aren't you?"

Before she could respond, Devon stepped towards them and clapped Rian on the back. "Stop teasing her, Ri. She's had a rough couple of hours and she's here to help. We wouldn't have even known about the threat without her."

Devon turned towards Kyra as he skillfully removed her hand from Rian's and moved her back a step. "Ignore Rian, he's trying to get a rise out of his little brother. Isn't that right, Royce?"

She spun around like a child's top and found the man that had done everything possible to avoid her standing not twenty feet away, with the same look of disdain she remembered from their last encounter. Before she could think of a smart ass comment to save face, Rian chuckled, "I knew the little platinum-haired beauty would bring you down from your perch, *little brother*."

Fuck! Now why did he have to go and do that? was all she could think as the woods rang with men's laughter.

CHAPTER TWO

Royce zeroed in on the face that had haunted his every thought for the last two weeks. Kyra was absolutely the most beautiful woman he had ever seen. Her lightly tanned skin begged to be touched and at the moment, the full pink lips that he had dreamed of tasting more times than he cared to admit, were drawn in a tight line, but still so very tempting. He tried to look away, but the curvy figure that made his fingers itch with the need to explore and experience every erotic inch drew his eyes. Her strength, independence, and power literally filled the air around her and were the complete opposite of her petite height. He thought about throwing her over his shoulder and taking her far away from all problems that loomed in front of them, but that wasn't reasonable or logical and damn sure wouldn't change the past.

He watched as she looked everywhere but at him and his heart hurt at the discomfort he caused her. If only she wasn't a witch. He would welcome her with open arms and enjoy every minute of eternity with her. But the fact remained that she was a witch, and there was no way in hell he was going to be bound to anyone with the capacity to turn on the people they love at a moment's notice and the power to take their life without thought. He shoved the thoughts of his mate to the back of his mind and focused on the men he called brethren and the brother he wanted to punch. Rayne swatted his arm, "How have you been, my friend? I have missed you."

"I've been fine, just trying to keep this loser in line." He looked towards his brother and noticed Kyra had moved farther to the back of the group.

"Oh yeah, he's been a lot of help. Hiding out in the caves, staying in dragon form for days at a time and brooding over his beloved." Rian cackled as the words Royce had prayed his brother would keep to himself, spewed from his mouth.

Of course, his brethren joined in the fun and Royce was left to play along when all he wanted to do was punch Rian in the mouth and get back to his nice, isolated cave. With the hopes of changing the subject from his recent brooding, he asked, "So what brings all of you here. Need a field trip?"

"No, Kyra was finally able to track Andrew. She had a vision that literally knocked her on her ass and it led us here…to you." The same shit-eating grin that Royce had seen on Lance's face for the better part of ninety years threatened his hard fought patience on this occasion more than it ever had. Just as he was about to tell his brethren to go to hell, what Lance *actually said* reached his muddled brain and his natural instincts along with his dragon took over.

In the span of two seconds, his need to protect his mate overrode his doubts *and* his common sense. Using his enhanced speed, Royce moved to Kyra, snatched her up and landed on the ridge over the cave he was calling home in less than a minute. He held her close, drew her unique scent into his being and reveled in the peace he felt for the first time since he had laid eyes on the witch. *How could something so wrong, feel so absolutely perfect?* he wondered to himself.

Slowly, the longer they stood together, the more he felt her relax. His hand caressed her back, enjoying the feel of her body under his fingertips, memorizing every dip and curve. His mate was tiny, but she was powerful, and not just because of her magic. Her inner strength shone like a beacon to a ship trying to find the shore. She stirred under his touch and sighed as his fingertips skimmed the side of her breast. Kyra was intoxicating. No matter his disgust for her kind, being this close caused his dragon to push him to claim her as their own. He tried to recall the memory of the day he found his mother, bloody and dying by a witch's hand, in a last ditch effort to stop the incredible desire he felt for the woman meant to be his, but his want and need would not be denied.

The feel of her breath on his chest through the fabric of his shirt, assured him that she was just as affected by their embrace as he. The rays of the dawn began to peek over the horizon, painting an unforgettable backdrop for their encounter. Warm yellows and deep reds blended together creating a masterpiece against the dark blue and purple of the retreating night. It was the second most beautiful thing he had laid his eyes on in the last few minutes. He carefully turned Kyra in his arms, wanting to share one perfect moment in time with the one he could never truly have. She moved without question or hesitation. He felt even their heart beats coming into sync as the mating call and their combustible chemistry did as Fate had intended. Unable to resist, Royce let himself enjoy what he could never keep.

Kyra relaxed into him and her much smaller, soft hands lay atop his which had closed around her curvy waist. He smiled as her fingers lazily caressed the back of his hands. From the motion he knew she was unaware of her actions, and it meant all the more. To know that she was not swept away in the mating call alone was a comfort. She was soft where he was hard. His mate was short where he was tall. He imagined the picture of them together looked strange to others, but somehow they fit together perfectly. Like two pieces of a puzzle, cut to perfection, one to complete the other.

Royce tensed as his mate shifted from one foot to the other, the motion causing her body to brush against his erection. The temptation to take what was rightfully his grew within him and he found himself wanting the woman in his arms more with each passing second. He remembered that she was a witch and knew full well that he couldn't live his life with the very species that robbed his family of so much, but none of that seemed to matter to his body or his dragon.

The sun had reached the midway point in its rise to christen a new day when Royce gave in to his desires. He spun Kyra around in his arms and lifted her until she had no option but to wrap her shapely legs around his waist. She gasped at the contact and he took the opportunity to latch his lips to hers, sliding his tongue along hers. An electric current radiated throughout his body, driving his desire higher.

His hands roamed her body as she writhed and moaned against him. Needing to taste more of his mate, he tore his mouth from hers, nipping and kissing his way along her delicate jaw line. A taste like no other burst upon his tongue. His cock strained against the zipper of his jeans until he was sure he would find its impression there. Kyra pulled his hair and her well-manicured nails bit at his scalp as she mewled and rode his erection through their clothing. He ate at her neck like a starving man using the last drop of his hard-fought determination to keep from throwing her down on the rocks and taking her as his body and dragon both demanded.

She cried out and the increasing scent of her arousal told him she was close. The heated aroma of patchouli and rose petals wrapped around them like a blanket, fueling his passion, creating their own private oasis from reality. Knowing this was the first and last time he would ever have the opportunity to witness the one made for him in the throes of passion, he sucked her earlobe into his mouth, running the tip of his tongue along the edge and meeting her hips thrust for thrust. He drove her higher and higher until her movements became frenzied. At just the right moment, he bit down on her earlobe. Quickly drawing his head back, he watched as Kyra screamed her pleasure to the Heavens. It was the most exquisite sight he had ever seen. With her head thrown back, her long tresses blowing in the sea breeze, her cheeks flushed, and her lips rounded in pleasure, she took his breath away. The image burned itself into his brain, there for all time, to pull up when he needed to remember what perfection it was to hold his mate in his arms.

As her orgasm subsided, she raised her head and her eyes slowly opened. He was mesmerized by the brilliant violet of her eyes and wealth of emotion he saw in their half-lidded satisfaction. The side of her kiss-swollen mouth tipped in a tentative smile and his world shifted on its axis. He was midway down a slippery slope and the beautiful creature in his arms had just pushed his descent into overdrive. Royce knew one thing for certain, if he stayed in her presence one second longer, he would be lost forever and there was no way he could allow that to happen.

He spun to his right, placed her on a flattened boulder and sped away, thanking the Universe for his enhanced abilities. It was a dick move, he knew it was, but there was no way he would ever trust her…she was a *witch* and capable of untold evil, not to be trusted. As he entered the cave he was inhabiting, he heard the words that simultaneously made him laugh and cringe… Kyra's voice filled with anger and regret that tore at his soul. Her words were completely accurate and cut to the quick leaving his soul hemorrhaging. *That fucking dick!* And then came a sob that broke his heart.

He moved as far back in the cave as he could go to keep from hearing anymore, but it was useless. Kyra was magical and they had been around one another far too long. Even if they hadn't just shared the most passionate moment of his very long life, he would still be connected to her, still be able to feel her above all others. He had been delusional to think thousands of miles and an ocean could change fate. Only he could change his fate. Only he could walk away from what the Universe had planned for him.

He spoke to Devon through their unique link, asking him to come and fetch Kyra. Devon was the only one of his brethren besides Rayne with enough discretion to simply get the little witch off the mountain and back to the safety of his Force without commenting or sharing with the others. As his brethren made his way to Royce's mate, Devon filled Royce in on Kyra's visions and what was being planned to stop Andrew from hurting anyone. Guilt came at him from every direction: guilt that he had not been there to protect her, guilt that he could not help her through her visions, and guilt that he had been so lost in his own worries that he had completely cut communication with everyone. It was the most self-centered thing he had ever done and all because he couldn't accept the fact that he was fated to share his life with a witch.

His dragon continued to roar in his head, angry with the man for his inability to put the past behind him. Royce could tell that Devon had reached Kyra and was unable to stop himself from walking towards the mouth of the cave to see if he could hear any of their conversation. What he heard made him respect Kyra more than he already did.

"What are *you* doing here, Devon?" she asked and he could hear the hurt and resentment in her voice that she tried to hide.

Before his brethren could answer, Kyra spoke again, "Oh, let me guess…the coward sent you to bring me down? What a piece of… *Whatever!* I can get down by myself. I made it seventy-five years before him and I'll make it a hell of a lot more after him."

"Kyra, don't…" Devon pleaded.

"Don't what, Devon? Get the hell out of the way."

From the sound and direction of her footsteps, she had already figured out there was a rock formation at the rear of the ridge that worked like steps. The heels of her boots hit the rock with such force he could only imagine the fury that was rolling off of her. To confirm his thoughts, Devon sounded across their unique link, *"What the hell did you do to her? She is pissed, my friend! Pissed on an extreme level. I'm waiting for the steam to come rolling out of her ears. If I get turned into a toad for something you did, I'm not going to be happy."*

Royce paused, not sure how to answer, and his silence must have been enough for Devon to figure out what happened, at least in theory. *"OH! What the fuck man? I can only imagine what happened. You can't do that shit to her. You need to get your head out of your ass."*

Royce could feel his long-time friend's anger and knew that he was right. In all the years they had been brethren, he'd never heard Devon as upset and disappointed as he was in that moment. He was right. Royce had to get his shit together and he told him so. *"You're right. I'd like to blame the mating call, and that is part of it, and the fact that she is really a great lady and when I heard she'd had a hard time of it and…. I just…It was…She is…"*

"Yeah, I know she's great, asshole. Who do you think has been watching after her day after day while she puts her ass on the line to help find the fucking traitor? Not you. Not the one that is supposed to be protecting her…me! And she's also loving and giving and caring, but more than all of that, she is hurting because she has no clue why you are rejecting her. Now, I can only assume that something happened between the two of you and once again you've rejected her, and that is wrong on a level I never thought I would see from you. Dude, you are an idiot, and so very, very stupid. I hope she makes you pay dearly, because she does not deserve anything you are putting her through."

Royce was disgusted with himself. Disgusted at what he had done to a woman that from all accounts did not deserve his messed up shit. But more than that, disgusted at the jealousy he felt…jealousy that he had absolutely no right feeling. He should be thanking the Universe that one of the best men he'd ever known was looking after Kyra, but instead, he and his dragon wanted to run out of the cave they were hiding in, claim what was theirs, and do everything in their considerable power to keep her away from any other men. Instead he thought about all he had lost at the hands of one of her kind and how there was no way he would ever be able to fully trust that she would not turn on him or those he loved. With thoughts of death and betrayal swirling around his mind, he turned around and walked deeper into the dark dankness of his dwelling.

"Tell Rayne and Rian I'll meet them at the ridge. I'll take first watch and lead the men in from the other side."

He knew ignoring everything his good friend had just said was low, but it was also his own form of self-preservation and he was taking the only way out he had.

"I never thought I would say this, but Royce O'Reilly, you are a fucking coward. I'll tell them, but you better have your head on straight…forever is a long time to be alone." And with that his friend severed their connection.

~~*~*~*~*~*~*

"Kyra, be careful. You're gonna fall if you don't stop stomping around," Devon sounded as pissed as she felt.

"Whatever, Devon, I'm *not* stomping. I'm *trying* to get my big ass off this damn mountain and back to the others. I just want to find that little asshole and go home." She stumbled onto the final step and would've fallen if it hadn't been for Devon's quick reflexes.

"Thanks," was all she could get past the lump in her throat. Embarrassed, but not willing to show it, she pulled her arm from Devon's grasp and started to take the last step again, but her escort decided it was time to talk.

"Are you sure you're okay?" Devon asked, and the sincerity in his voice was almost her undoing, but then she remembered what a fool Royce had made of her just moments ago and let her anger be her shield.

She squared her shoulders and since Royce wasn't there, turned on her friend, "Yes, Devon, I'm sure I'm fine."

The Guardsman looked frustrated, worried, and more than a little pissed off, but for some reason she could tell none of those emotions were pointed at her. She watched as he quickly regained his composure. "Just remember, I *am* your friend and I'm here if you need to talk."

Once again a lump formed in her throat. *What the hell is wrong with me?* she thought. She never cried, never got choked up. Kyra St Croix did not let people get to her. She thought back to many years earlier and remembered the exact moment she had closed the doors on the part of her that allowed others to hurt her, the part of her that trusted in someone other than herself. Then she pictured the exact moment that she knew there was something more for her in her future. The truth that she would have one person to whom she meant the world, to whom she was connected…body and soul. That would think of her wants and needs instead of just what she could do for them…the day her dragon marking appeared. But today, those days seemed like eons ago and proved to be the dreams of a much younger, much more naïve young woman. It was time to kick ass, take names, and put the mushy shit to rest.

She looked Devon in the eyes, showing her strength and her resolve and said, "Really, I'm good. No worries, okay?"

Devon's eyes said he wasn't buying it, but at least he had the decency to put on a good show, "Okay, Killer. You ready to kick some traitor ass?" He smiled his crooked smile.

"*Hell*, yeah. I'm ready. Let's get this show on the road!" She chuckled as they took the last few steps to the bottom of the mountain and headed back to where the others were planning their defense.

It was obvious Rian had rallied the troops by the sheer number of people milling around the makeshift headquarters he and Rayne had ordered set up. It was positioned at the south side of the lair under the cover of a huge rock formation and hidden by a dense grouping of trees. Devon had explained on their way back that the Blue Thunder Clan was much smaller than theirs and had not had a man find his mate for almost a hundred years. Once again fate had stuck up her middle finger and dared the world to say anything about it. Here was a clan of some of the hottest, most loyal, fierce men she'd ever met and they were without mates. And here she was, tied to the one person in the world that couldn't stand the sight of her. *Yeah, it's a wonderful life alright*, said the little witch in her head.

Before she could sink any lower, Rian was at her side, "Hey there, little witch, long time no see. Have fun while you were gone?"

She could tell from the shit eating grin on his face he had his own ideas about exactly what had occurred between her and his brother, but there was no way she saying a damn thing. Instead she decided to play along. "Yep, sure did. I was out sightseeing. Beautiful country you have here and by the way…I have a name."

Rian chuckled and pointed towards a small tent nestled in a quiet little corner. "Rayne ordered that set up for you so that you may work your magic in peace. Your bags are ready and waiting." He began to walk, so she followed, wondering why he thought she needed an escort.

When they reached their destination he simply stood, looking out at the landscape, his eyes seeing much more than the nature before them. Kyra watched a million thoughts fly across his face…a face that looked so much like the one she wanted to punch that she wondered if that was where the similarities ended. Not wanting to disturb him, she stood waiting since he had chosen the entrance to her makeshift workspace as his place to perch. He slowly looked down and she was once again reminded how amazingly tall both he and his brother were, especially when compared to her stature.

His blue eyes were no longer sparkling, but held questions that she feared he was going to ask. Not one to wait for the inevitable she spoke first, "Was there something else you needed before I get to work?"

Rian grinned but it didn't reach his eyes. "As a matter of fact, there is. I know my brother is being a first rate asshat and I've been debating whether I should explain his behavior or not. Since you are here I think it's my duty as his older brother and the bane of his very existence to explain the source of the burr up his butt."

She scoffed, "I hate to inform you but I've taken the title of 'Royce's bane of existence' from you, Your Highness, or Elder, or whatever I'm supposed to call you."

He laughed out loud and she was reminded of the one time she'd heard Royce laugh. It was bold and full and made you want to laugh right along with him. "You're supposed to call me Rian, and someday, Brother. That's why I'm going to tell you what it is that keeps my brother from falling at your feet and worshipping the ground you walk on, like his heart and dragon are begging him to do."

She tried to interrupt, but he held up his hand for her to wait and continued, "I know you don't believe he wants you, but let me assure you, little wi…*Kyra*, that he most definitely finds you the most beautiful and alluring creature on the planet, and rightfully so. You were made especially for him, just as he was made for you, and had he and our whole family not suffered a terrible loss in our younger years, I have no doubts that the two of you would already be mated and off making babies, or at least practicing. But as Fate would have it, we *did* suffer a tragedy and of all of us, Royce has been the one that refuses to let the past rest."

He looked over her head and kept talking, "When we were much younger and still living with our parents, my mother was pregnant with our sister. The baby was thought to be the one our prophecies spoke of, the child that would bring female dragons back to our kin. From the day my mother knew she carried a girl, dragon shifters from all over the world sent their blessings and some even came to visit our humble clan.

"As the time of the birth came closer, my mother and her most trusted friend, the woman that had been part of our family for my entire life and had helped raise all of us boys, Ilsa, were engrossed in making sure everything was perfect for our little Rhianna to enter the world.

"One day very close to the birth, we were all out and about doing whatever, when my mother's scream ripped through the beautiful fall day." His last words were barely a whisper and she looked up to see tears filling his eyes. Completely unprepared for any show of emotion from the man she had thought incapable of anything but cracking jokes and issuing orders, Kyra just stood and watched as Rian struggled for control.

When he began again his voice cracked, "Royce was the first to arrive and what he saw, I am afraid, scarred him for life."

Rian continued and the story he told was like a dagger to her heart. She simply couldn't imagine the loss they had suffered and that it came at the hands of someone they loved and trusted made it all the worse. The pain and anguish rolling off the man before her was overwhelming, even though she was about the most untouchy-feely person in the world. She was helpless to do anything but close the distance between them and hug him for all she was worth. His hands landed on her shoulders and gripped just shy of the point of pain. Untold minutes later, he urged her back a step and they locked eyes, "I have yet to tell you the most important part. Ilsa was a white witch and she was sacrificing our mother and sister to a demon to gain power. So you see, Kyra, its Royce's prejudice that keeps him from your side, *not you*. Fate has given you the task to drag him out of the past and into the future that awaits both of you."

Kyra felt as if she had been punched in the gut. She wanted to simultaneously laugh and cry. Fate had not only flipped her off, but now She was laughing about it. When Kyra was alone, she was definitely going to ask the Goddess what it was she had done to deserve this steaming pile of shit that was her life. Never one to mince words, she said what she was thinking, "What the hell am *I* supposed to do? I can't change the fact that I'm a witch. I'm sure it doesn't help that I'm also one of the strongest around *and* I helped Andrew hurt the people he loves, even though I didn't know what the piece of shit was up to."

She stepped around him and started to pace while she spoke, "I mean seriously, what do *you* want me to do? He hated me before he even knew me. He hates what I am at a cellular level and is unwilling to see past that to find out *who* I am. You think I can change that?"

She threw her hands in the air as she continued to pace, not caring that every dragon shifter in the vicinity could hear what she was saying. "And…*and* if all that wasn't enough, Fate in Her infinite wisdom, decided to tie us together. Did you know that now that we have…?" She stuttered to a stop and took a breath as she felt the telltale heat of a blush on her cheeks.

There was no way she was going to tell Rian that she had made out with Royce like a cheerleader on Homecoming with the quarterback, and had for the first time in her life climaxed. She had no idea how much these dragon guys actually knew about witches, but was sure they didn't know that only a witch's one true mate could bring her to completion and as soon as that happened, there would *never* be another. Not even a little kissing under the bleachers with someone that wasn't him. Since their 'trip to the mountain top' had led to just that, the rest of Kyra's very long life, at least where love was concerned, had been decided. She figured she should've been upset, but it was just confirmation of what she had known from the first moment she had laid eyes on the gentle giant with caring eyes and curly red hair…she was truly and rightly screwed.

Realizing she and Rian were just standing there, staring at one another, she hurried on. "There's no changing his mind. *Hell*, he ran across an ocean and is sleeping in a cave to be rid of me! He's had longer than I've been alive to feed and nurture his hate of witches. There's nothing I can do. I'm going to help catch Andrew and then I'm going to disappear. Let your brother live his life cause I'm damn sure gonna live mine. I won't give him the opportunity to shame me again!"

The second the words left her mouth, she knew she had said too much. Damn her temper and damn her inability to keep her mouth shut. Not wanting to deal with Rian any longer, she tried to step around him in the hopes of hiding in her tent, but he was having none of her avoidance. He stuck his arm in front of her and refused to move it until she acknowledged him. Holding her position, she turned her head and glared, waiting for him to speak.

Her heart beat in her chest while she waited, and she wondered if witches could have heart attacks. When he spoke, it was the voice of the Elder of the clan, not the voice of a brother, he used, "You are right, he will not shame you again. I won't allow it. But neither will I allow you to run and hide like he has done. I tried to be patient, but you two are your own worst enemies."

"I do not know what occurred between you two earlier and it's none of my business. I can however, assume, and whether you know it or not, your actions have doomed you both to a life of utter loneliness."

She felt her eyes widen…he knew. *Well, hell, he's definitely more than just a pretty face*, she mused in her head.

"Just like witches, dragon shifters also will have no other after they have found their mate. The details are a little different." He winked and then immediately resumed his command of the situation, "But the results are the same and that is something I could never allow for my brother, or for you now that I've met you."

"While I appreciate your stance on the subject, I'm not sure what you or I, for that fact, can do about it. Royce has made up his mind and now I agree. There's no way in *the world* he and I belong together."

Rian was just about to speak when a tall, younger version of the man standing before her appeared over his shoulder. "What's up, Brother. Holding Royce's mate hostage? You know, you're gonna get your ass kicked for it, right?"

Rian closed his eyes for a split second and took a deep breath. She watched as he put a patient smile on his face, lowered his arm, and turned to look at his doppelganger. He looked back to her and she saw affection shining through the myriad of other emotions in his eyes. "Kyra, let me introduce Rory, the youngest of the O'Reilly family and biggest pain in the ass you will ever meet. Rory…this is Kyra."

"Now that was not nice, Bro," Rory chuckled as he slapped Rian on the back and then turned his hundred watt smile on Kyra. "Hey, there."

He reached around his brother and threw out his hand for her to shake. She laid hers in his and he squeezed slightly before letting go. "You really are a little bit of a thing aren't you? And have more power than witches twice your size." He looked at his hand and flexed his fingers, as if he could still feel her power. "Really glad to meet you. Have you dragged Roy outta that cave and given him a good whack to the head yet?"

"Rory, now's not the time," Rian interrupted. "Kyra needs to work her magic so we can see exactly where Andrew and the other miscreants are located before it's too late. Go see Rayne or Aidan. I'm sure they have something useful you could be doing. I'll be right behind you."

"Aye, aye, Captain," Rory saluted and smirked. He looked at Kyra again, "Great to meet you. Look forward to getting to know you better, *Sis*." He winked and headed over to where the warriors were preparing for battle.

"Sorry about that," Rian apologized. "Rory takes the title of 'little brother' to a whole new level."

"But you love him," Kyra added.

"Yes, I do. I love both my brothers and will do whatever it takes, including beating the shit out of them, to see them happy." She tried to interrupt, but again he put his hand up to stop her. One day she was going to smack that hand down, but not today. She was tired and hungry and needed to scry for the asshole before it got any later.

Aidan called from the other side of the camp for Rian, so whatever conversation they were about to continue was thankfully cut short. He did, however, leave her with a parting promise she could've lived without, "We'll talk later. Do what you need to do and grab a little rest. I think dinner will be ready soon and if all goes well, we'll have the traitor captured before he's able to hurt anyone else." Not waiting for her answer, he turned and headed towards the men, walking like the leader she was now sure he was.

Kyra climbed into her tent and found all her belongings, along with an air mattress, sleeping bag, table and two chairs, and a little vanity. They had obviously taken great pains to make up a tent that was feminine while still useful, and she appreciated their efforts. At the thought of all that needed to be done, a weariness soaked into her bones. It was then that she realized it had been almost thirty-two hours since she'd last slept and she opted for a little siesta before getting to work.

Finally settled and ready to sleep, her eyes refused to close. *Figures*, she thought. Staring at the roof of her tent, she ran through the conversation she'd had with Rian. First of all, she thought of Rory. How freaky was it that there was *another* brother she knew nothing about and what on the earth did they feed them that made them so damn big? The youngest of the brothers was a carbon copy of Rian. If they hadn't told her any differently, she would have sworn they were twins: both muscular and strong, but long and lean, where Royce was quite the opposite. The differences didn't end with their body types but she really wasn't into thinking about anything that could lead her to obsess over Royce…not tonight, not ever again, if she could help it.

She planned what to do to locate and stop Andrew from the shit storm he was planning while trying to bring to the forefront whatever had been trying to stay buried since Rian told her what their family suffered at the hands of a witch gone mad. Sleep came over her while she was thinking about all she had learned. With her defenses down, she began to remember the story that was passed from the Elders of her coven to each witch, right before she was taught the Siphoning spell.

Kyra dreamt of the Circle of Witches with her mother at the head, the ceremonial fire burning in the center and all the faces of those that had trained with her waiting eagerly to hear what Grand Priestess Calysta had to say. Her mother explained exactly what the Siphoning spell was *supposed* to be used for and that it was a grave offense, punishable by a sanction from the Council, if ever used maliciously or to harm another.

The room became deathly quiet as Calysta told of a witch many years before that had been of their coven, but accepted a calling and had gone to live among another race. She told of the witch's many years of dedicated service to her adopted family and their kin and how very respected she was to all that knew her. Abruptly, the story turned dark and the Grand Priestess' voice lowered to an ominous whisper. She reminded each who listened about the allure of the dark evil and how very important it was to be ever vigilant against any force that would threaten to turn them from the light. Kyra hadn't noticed that day, nor had she thought about it since, but in her memory she could see a fear and sadness in her mother's eyes that ran deep.

After a few minutes of silence, Calysta finally spoke again, "You see, my little ones, a true sister of my heart, one of the best witches I had ever known, was taken from us by dark forces. She was tempted in a very short time to turn her allegiance from all she held dear in exchange for a power so malevolent that it caused her to not only take the life of the one she loved, but also that of the woman's unborn child."

There was utter silence. No one moved, no one spoke, and she tried to remember if anyone even breathed. All she remembered was every heart beat in the room beating as one, in a slow pounding of dread. Then her mother spoke, "So beloved ones, as your power grows so does your responsibility. You must always do everything in your power to remain in the light, and if you should ever feel yourself growing weak, you *must* call on your sister witches. But even that may not be enough.

"So to make sure we never forget, we share the name of our fallen sister with all of our coven. When times are hard and you feel you need a reminder of all you stand to lose, you only need speak her name and you will be filled with a strength born of our collective love and devotion to the Earth, the Goddess that blesses us all. Della will hand each of you a pink candle, together we will light them and invoke the protection of the Power of All. I will speak her name and the invocation will be complete."

For the span of two heartbeats the room was in complete darkness, then slowly filled with candlelight. Calysta, Della, and all the other elders were spread around the perimeter of the circle holding large red candles wrapped in sage. Calysta looked into each girl's face and then said…

"Dammit, Kyra wake up. You've been asleep for almost two hours, dinner's ready, and Rayne is anxious for you to get started. He wants us in place before nightfall but needs you to tell us where to go." She was immediately awake and staring into Devon's face.

"Shit, Devon, seriously? I was just about to remember something very important. You waited two fucking hours and couldn't wait ten more seconds?" She knew she was yelling and being unreasonable, but *dammit,* she really wanted to remember that name.

Devon's look of total confusion would have been comical any other time, but not in that moment. "I heard you talking and thought you were awake, so I peeked in and you were tossing and turning and calling out."

She jumped up and flew at him, "What was I saying? What did you hear?"

The look of concern told her Devon was worried, but instead of lecturing like she expected, he told her what he'd heard. "You were talking about the Earth and the Goddess and then you said something in Latin that sounded like *illuminati.* That was all I could make out."

"*SHIT!* Two seconds longer, that was all I needed…just two more seconds." Her head fell forward and her eyes closed of their own volition as she ran her fingers through her hair. The thought of pulling out a handful or two crossed her mind, but she decided it served no purpose. A few deep breaths to get her disappointment and anger under control and she was able to think straight again. Why couldn't she remember who her mother had been talking about and why would that memory, out of all the others, rear its ugly little head now?

Not willing to spend any longer worrying about what she couldn't change, she raised her head and squared her shoulders. "You said something about food?"

Devon chuckled, but she could see the tension thrumming through him. He was worried about her and not doing a very good job of hiding it. "Yes, I did. I figured that would get your attention."

"What are you saying, Dev? That I eat a lot?" She faked annoyance at his comment in an effort to ease the tension.

"No, no, no, I would never say that to a lady. I…"

"Pfft…a lady?" Kyra scoffed, unable to stop the laugh that bubbled out. "There's no lady here."

Devon burst out laughing with her and she knew order had been restored, at least for the moment. She walked over to the tiny camp-style vanity, grabbed her hairbrush, and attacked her long tresses in an effort to excise a few of the tangles and at least look like a civilized human when she faced the Guardsmen outside her tent.

Feat accomplished and her massive mane tamed with a hair tie, she and Devon exited the tent and headed towards a long table packed with the largest, fiercest men she had ever seen. Their sheer size never ceased to amaze her. Shoulder to shoulder, they sat eating and talking about the battle to come and the common enemy they would all put their lives on the line to eliminate. They were a wall of muscle and might and unwavering determination…Andrew didn't stand a chance.

~~*~*~*~*~*~*

He watched from a distance as Kyra and Devon exited her tent and walked towards the others. It was obvious they were becoming good friends. Logically, he was happy she had someone to watch after her, someone to confide in, and was glad it was Devon. He was a good guy who would protect her, as well as counsel her as needed. At least that was what he kept telling himself as his jealousy grew and his dragon growled his fury when Devon's hand touched her elbow as they walked across the uneven ground.

Stop looking at her. Stop thinking about her. This is the way it has to be, had become a constant mantra in his mind from the moment he grabbed her just a few short hours ago. He had relived holding her in his arms, the feel of his lips on hers and the amazing sight of her eyes half-lidded with passion. It had gotten so bad that he had cursed the Universe, cursed Fate, and punched the rock wall of the cave until his hands were bloodied and beaten. When that didn't work, he had contacted Stefan through their unique link, but of course the Spiritual Elder gave him the same advice he'd been giving him for the better part of two weeks…*put the past in the past and move on.* If only it was that easy.

When he held her in his arms he could feel that they belonged together. A sense of completion encompassed him and he felt true peace for the first time in his very long life, but then his doubt and prejudice snuck in. He remembered how much he loved and trusted Ilsa. How in the blink of an eye she was twisted into some evil shade of herself and had killed the heart of his family without remorse. Andrew also came to mind. Royce had helped raise him, watched him grow into a fine Dragon Guardsman following in the footsteps of his father and brothers, and now they were all fighting to protect those they held dear from his treachery. How could he trust? How could he believe?

"Hiding in the bushes, little brother?" Rian startled him, just another side effect of his jumbled emotions. No one, including his older brother, had been able to get the jump on him since he was a young Guardsman still in training.

"No, I'm waiting for instructions. Did Devon not relay my message?" he bit out.

"Yes, he did, but I had to wonder why you didn't just tell me yourself? I tried to contact you and it was as if you had shut out the whole world…*again.*" Rian raised a single eyebrow. A sign that he was irritated with Royce.

"I was preparing. We've been fighting the fucking traitor since his reappearance and he escapes at every turn. I want him finished!" He poured all the rage and resentment of his situation into his words hoping to deter any further 'mating' conversation, but true to form, Rian had more to say.

"Oh, little brother, if you can't be honest with me, at least be honest with yourself. I see it in your eyes, hear it in your voice; you want your little witch with every fiber of your being. The mating call is upon you and soon there will be little you can do to stop it. I'm sure your 'liaison' on the ridge only strengthened the bond growing between you and Kyra."

Royce started to speak, but in true regal fashion, Rian held up his hand for him to remain quiet and continued, "You can try to deny it, but remember, we *are* brothers, both real and believed, and there is no way you can hide this from me. Even when you try to block the world, your emotions still flow through our familial bond. I know you are torturing yourself and for what? To avenge mother? To avenge Rhianna?" Rian grabbed his shoulders and pulled Royce a few feet forward until their chests almost touched.

His older brother looked him in the eyes and spoke with all the authority of a Head Elder, patriarch of their line, and older brother. "They are dead, Roy, and no amount of penance on your part can ever change that. There is no way to bring them back. Let it go. Move on, and for all that is holy, *stop torturing that little witch.* She does *not* deserve it."

Royce pulled from his brother's embrace and turned away. "It is just that easy for you, isn't it? To put it all away in a nice neat little box and move on?"

There was silence from where he knew his brother still stood. When he dared look, Rian's head was thrown back, eyes closed, and if he wasn't mistaken, his older brother was praying. Royce stood in awe at the complete reverence he felt encompassing his brother. It was several moments before Rian's head came forward and Royce could see a sense of peace. When his brother spoke, it was his brother, not the leader of a clan. "No, Royce, I don't put it away in a box. I keep it here," Rian's fist struck his chest with a loud *thump,* right over his heart. "And I use it to remind me to enjoy every minute of every day, to take my joy where I find it. We've been given the opportunity to live very long lives, but not *one second* of it is guaranteed. It is *our* responsibility to *use* what we have been given, not squander it. I know mother and Rhianna are at peace because I believe prayers are answered."

His brother paused and Royce could see him carefully choosing his words.

"Roy, you are wasting your life. Your mate is here. She is everything anyone could ever want and she was created for you, just as you were for her." Royce felt his brow furrow, Rian knew something Royce didn't, and he only prayed the jerk was going to share.

"After our last conversation I thought about why the Universe, in Her infinite wisdom, chose a witch for your mate. Stefan and I even prayed with the Elders for an answer, and not until this moment did it all become clear. It is because you insist on letting the past cripple you instead of taking your lessons and moving on. Fate has forced your hand and you, dear brother, have fallen right into Her trap." Rian paused. Royce could see the wheels turning and wished he would just get on with it. His patience was wearing thin.

When the winds changed and the scent of patchouli and rose petals reached his senses, it was all he could do not to repeat his actions from earlier. Kyra's scent was intoxicating, no matter her origins…her very being called to him. He felt like a drowning man with no desire of rescue. He searched the crowd of people moving about for just a glimpse of his mate and like magic, the object of all his angst was before him, walking towards her tent. Thankfully, she was alone. There was no way he could be responsible for his actions if even Devon had been near her at that moment. All his and Rian's discussions of her and their situation had heightened his mating instincts and pushed his dragon to damned near distraction over the need to feel her in his arms again. Only one hundred and fifty-six years of training and determination kept him from going to her.

The grin on Rian's face said he had smelled Kyra's scent also, and it may not have called to him as it did Royce, but it did confirm that Royce suffered and his brother really didn't care. "What trap, brother? What the *fuck* are you talking about?" Royce snapped, unable to keep his ire in check.

"Tsk, tsk, temper, temper, little brother."

"Temper, my ass, Rian. I'm tired of being screwed with. Now just tell me what you figured out and let's be done with this miserable discussion. You're accomplishing nothing but pissing me off."

"Wake the hell up, Roy. Do you really not know that when you grabbed your mate and spirited away with her, tasting of what you consider 'forbidden fruit', you sealed not only your fate, but hers? Are you *really* that stupid?"

"Stop the damn riddles, Ri, just tell me," Royce spit.

"Fate has blessed you with Kyra and made sure she is half-human to abide by the wishes of the original Elders, but She also made her half-witch, to make you finally move on. To be whole and have the love you so richly deserve. To do that you will have to put your bullshit aside and grab onto your future with both hands and a clean heart and conscience or…you will be forced to live a lonely, loveless life. But you, little brother, have added your own little twist, you have now doomed Kyra to the same fate if you cannot love her for who she is, not *what* she is."

"*Dammit*, Rian, I swear I'm going to knock you on your ass if you don't explain yourself without the damn riddles. How did *I* doom Kyra to anything?"

"I would've thought in your hatred of witches you would've learned all there was to know about them, but I guess you have blindly hated for so long that even *you* missed something vital to *your* particular situation. The moment you took Kyra in your arms and 'consummated', so to speak, your relationship," Rian winked and Royce wanted to punch the condescending smirk right off his face, but held back if only to find out what Rian had to say. "You made it impossible for Kyra to ever even find solace in another's arms."

Royce stood dumbfounded, not really understanding but drawing his own conclusions, and not liking any of them. Unable to speak, he motioned for Rian to continue. What he heard would have driven a lesser man to his knees. As it was, he had trouble drawing breath. "What you failed to realize before your rash actions was that only a witch's one true mate can bring her to completion. She can have other lovers but never climax. Still, a few witches I know find immense pleasure with others and refuse to even look for their mates, not that you care about those instances. What is important to you is that once an Earth witch has found her mate and he has brought her to her peak, there can *never* be another…in *any way*."

The world seemed to darken to a single point over Rian's shoulder. How could this be? How could he be responsible for Kyra's future in such a way? He knew what Fate had in store for him and had been slowly learning to accept that he would be loveless, that there would be no mate, no children, nothing like he had seen the others of his Force experience. Although he was not thrilled with the prospect, he couldn't think of another way around it, but to know that someone else's life was being irrevocably damaged because of his decisions was like a weight around his neck.

He did the only thing he could think of…he struck out at Rian with all his might, hoping to knock the all knowing smile right from his lips, and with any luck break his nose in the process. The sound of breaking bone was just what he needed to help with his guilt and pain. But Rian knew him too well and was prepared. He moved to the right causing Royce to catch only air. The force of the swing knocked him off balance and before he could stop, he was lying flat on his back staring up at Rian and, unfortunately, also Rory.

"You really need to work on your delivery, big brother," his younger brother scoffed as he extended his hand.

Royce took Rory's hand and stood, embarrassed by his action but still pissed about what he had just learned. "Thanks," he offered and then grumbled, "What the hell are you doing here? This is *not* a family meeting."

"I wasn't looking for your grumpy ass. I was actually looking for Ri. Seems *your* little witch needs to speak to him and was unable to locate him. She asked if I would tell him she was looking for him and that she would be with Rayne and the others, so here I am." Rory was grinning the same shit-eating grin he had seen on Rian's face entirely too much lately.

Not willing to deal with anymore of their bullshit and feeling the undeniable need to lick his proverbial wounds, he turned and stomped farther into the forest, but not before he heard Rian in his mind, *"Don't cut connections, Roy. We'll be preparing for Andrew and I'll need to be able to get a hold of you."*

"I have no intentions of cutting anything. You do what you need to do and I'll do the same. Leave the connection open while you plan. I'll add what I can. I'm headed to high ground to scout," Royce replied. He hoped Rian was too focused on whatever Kyra had to tell him to realize that his only intention in asking him to keep the line open was to hear her voice. Yes, the looming battle mattered. Catching Andrew mattered, but he had to hear *her* voice. She was an obsession. An obsession he knew he couldn't have, but craved with all he was.

"Will do. Let me know what you see and Roy..."

"Yes?"

"Get your head out of your ass before it's too late."

He didn't respond, just nodded as he made his way to the hidden trail he had found earlier during his stay at the base of the mountain. If only it was as easy as simply 'pulling his head out of his ass'. Didn't Rian, or any of them for that matter, think he would have already done it? He wanted love. He wanted to know what it felt like to have Kyra in his arms, his life, and his bed, every minute of every day until the end of time, but how could he lay over a hundred years of pain and bigotry to the side? When it was only his destiny in question, he had strengthened his resolve, made his decision, and was making peace with it. But now, both of their fates rested squarely on his shoulders, and he had no clue how to save either one of them.

The trip to the concealed lookout point, where he had spent countless hours since returning to his homeland, was spent listening to all that Kyra had gleaned from scrying and several other Location spells. He damned near jumped off the mountain and flew back to camp when it was decided that she, Devon, and Aidan would head out to make sure the black magic perimeter she had gone through on the hike to the lair was not closing in around them. Only Rian's voice warning him that he needed to stay put kept him in place. Luckily, Rory decided to tag along and opened their unique link, allowing him to listen in as they hiked.

The second the evil magic touched his mate, not only did he hear the concern in his brethren's voice at her discomfort, but he could feel its inky darkness trying to invade her soul.

He was nauseous and knew it came from Kyra through their strengthening bond. His heart ached at the discomfort he knew she felt and he wondered if maybe there was a way for them to make a life together, but his musings about the future were cut short when a familiar voice sounded through Rory's open link. "Well, what do we have here, fucking Dragon Guardsmen and their pet witch? Tell me boys, is today a good day to die?"

Royce moved faster than he'd ever thought possible as he yelled to Rian, *"Andrew's there! He's with them! That little fucker just threatened her life!"*

He could hear Rian and Rayne shouting orders and knew there was help on the way but he was not leaving Kyra's safety to anyone else. It was his responsibility. The farther he traveled, the more intently he listened to the ranting of the lunatic they had once called friend and brethren. "So Kyra, I see you have chosen the losing side."

"Win or lose, at least they tell the truth, Andrew," Kyra responded. He was amazed he heard no fear in her voice, only anger and the residual effects of the black magic.

"When did I ever lie to you, my sweet?" Andrew responded.

"You told me they were after *you* and that you only needed to hide from them. You never mentioned that you were going to take my pure, white, Earth magic and destroy it with your piece of shit black magic. You never mentioned that you were out to hurt, even kill, innocent women and children. You're a dick and a liar...a *fucking* liar." By the time she finished, she was screaming and Royce could feel her fury.

"She really is sexy when she's pissed off isn't she? The flush on her cheeks just brings out her beauty." He had no clue who the traitor was talking to, but he wanted to rip his head from his neck. Just the fact that the little bastard was daring to talk to Kyra made him and his dragon roar in anger.

It was Aidan that responded, his voice vibrating with animosity and outrage. "Andrew, stop this shit! You've done enough. It's me you're pissed at, me you want to hurt, so let's settle this between us. Leave everyone else out of it." It was amazing how calm his brethren sounded considering that stupid little asshole had tried to kill Grace, Aidan's mate.

Royce arrived on the scene just in time to hear Andrew laugh, "But, Brother, you're not the only one that left me to die. How would it be fair for you to pay for everyone's sins?"

Andrew continued, obviously enjoying the sound of his own voice, "I wonder if the Blue Thunder Guardsmen know what you did. Do they know that the mighty MacLendon Force is actually made of cowards? That they are willing to leave a member behind to be tortured because they are too scared to mount a rescue? Oh, well, since it is obvious you are allies, they'll find out soon enough. You will betray them just as you betrayed me."

Just behind Andrew, Royce could see Rayne, Rian, and the others surrounding the traitor. He caught his Commander's eye with a questioning look. Rayne answered through their link, *"He has himself protected with some kind of spell or something. It seems to be specific to dragon shifters. We can't get in. I think he closed it when the others reached a certain point. My best guess is he is trying to grab Kyra."*

Royce immediately saw red, *"There is no way in hell that son of a bitch is touching a hair on her head."*

"Glad to have you back, Brother. No, let's get her out of there and catch that little shit."

Aidan was still trying to reason with whatever was left of the younger brother he loved while Royce was trying to find a way through the shield Andrew had constructed. As he crept around the perimeter, he noticed footsteps heading off in the other direction. It looked to be about fifteen or twenty men and some were dragging something very heavy if the indentations in the ground were any indication. As he worked his way around he listened to the conversation taking place to his right, but tuned into the forest. He found a small break in the shield at the same time he heard a voice off in the distance. "Make sure the amulets are exactly where the map indicates. We don't want those big guys to break free."

It all clicked into place and he yelled through mind speak to Rayne and Aidan, *"It's a trap! That little shit is keeping us busy while the others with him set a trap."*

He saw Aidan shift Kyra even farther behind him and was both irritated and proud that she fought to stay in the forefront. Aidan told Rory and Devon what Royce had figured out and together they slowly pushed Kyra farther and farther from the traitor. Andrew continued his posturing, so caught up that he didn't notice their slight movements.

Rory had taken up the rear position. As soon as he reached the boundary, he slid his foot through. Everyone listening breathed a sigh of relief that at least they could get out. It sounded like Andrew's monologue was coming to an end, so Royce urged the Guardsmen with Kyra to simply grab her ass and haul her out of there. Rory reached for her just when Andrew spoke up, "I'm sure by now you cowards have called reinforcements and I'm surrounded. How thrilling! I am absolutely quaking in my boots. I knew when I saw you were all here that it wasn't a family reunion, but I decided to stop by and say hi anyway."

He turned to leave and then swung right back around. "Oh, I almost forgot…Kyra, have you ever heard the Prophecy about the Earth witch destined to mate dragon shifter royalty?"

Andrew stared right at Kyra and Royce felt the hair stand up on the back of his neck. "Well, after the little show I watched of you and Royce on the ridge, I guess you have found your mate. Does he know you are destined for bigger and better things, or that the very witch that killed his mother came from *your* coven? Might make for some interesting pillow talk, ya think? Catch ya later, little witch."

Royce was stunned, unable to think, let alone move. Everything was happening around him and he just stood there like a stump. Andrew disappeared into thin air. Rory had Kyra thrown over his shoulder and was speeding to safety while she screamed obscenities he had never imagined. Rayne was ordering every available man to find the traitor and follow the tracks Royce had found in the forest to gather up the followers.

Rian yelled along their unique connection for him to get his ass back to camp, but all he could do was focus on the last thing the traitor had said. Could it be true? Did she know? What the hell was he going to do now?

CHAPTER THREE

Andrew looked on from his hiding place high over the Dragon Guard's encampment. Things had not gone according to Plan A, but that was the beauty of having a Plan B and C, along with his returning dragon senses. The moment he sensed the Dragon Guard's proximity to his own, he had revised his plan. His partners were not thrilled, but after using his considerable charm, Mr. A and Master Eaton had relented and headed back home, leaving all the underlings with him to delay the dragons with a wild goose chase.

He did feel bad that his dark magic bothered Kyra as much as it did. Even though she was with his sworn enemies, he still admired her. They could have been great partners if not for her destiny. When he had read the part of the Prophecy pertaining to the witch and the dragon, he had immediately known it was her. It was an added bonus that the Grand Priestess, who he now knew was her mother, had kept personal notes stashed in the volume. It truly helped put the pieces together. The look he had seen on her face when he mentioned Ilsa had been priceless, and he was sure Royce was waiting in the sidelines somewhere, but Andrew could not figure out why he left Rory and the others to protect her. Surely, he would not trust his beloved mate to any but himself.

He thought back to the scene he had witnessed on the ridge. The lovers definitely looked to be hitting it off until Royce was called away. The longer he replayed the memory, the more Andrew realized his original assumption had been incorrect. Royce's speedy departure, the look of devastation on Kyra's face, and the way her shoulders had fallen forward as if in defeat spelled out something totally different than his first thought. Royce had *not* been called away. He had simply left his mate without a backward glance. *That* explained why Devon had shown up. Royce had called his longtime friend to get her safely back to the others. *What an interesting development*, he pondered. The wedge he was hoping to drive between them was already firmly in place. It was up to him to make sure it was permanent.

What an added bonus that Aidan had been present. It had been the first time since that fateful day at the cabin that he had laid eyes on his brother. It always amazed him that no matter what he did to his older brother, Aidan still tried to reason with him. Like, as the older brother, he *had* to try to save Andrew. He laughed out loud at the mere thought that he needed saving. Royce would be the first to fall, he decided, if for no other reason than the fact that he had hurt Kyra. She held a special place in Andrew's heart, no matter her loyalties. Only thirteen more days until the full moon and he would take the life of the oldest of the MacLendon Force. If others fell, all the better. But it was Royce that had to fall first. Before it was all over they would all die, and Aidan would be left to watch the devastation of his kin, the most worthless race to ever take breath.

The vibration of the cell phone in his pocket stirred him from his musings. The message read: *Heading to airfield. Take off in ninety minutes.* Everything was coming together nicely. He needed to touch base with John to make sure preparations were underway for what would be the beginning of the end of the dragons. Swiftly reaching the forest floor, he dialed his second. His partners believed John dead and that was just the way Andrew wanted it. He would use their resources and make them believe they all shared a common goal, but the truth was, there could only be one victor and he meant to be that man.

John answered just as Andrew was about to hang up. "Yes, sir?"

"Things are on schedule?" he asked as he made his way to the hidden motorcycle the others had left him.

"Yes. I was able to locate another Earth witch. She is much younger and not near as powerful as the previous one, but she is competent and very easy to deceive. With our infusion of dark energy, the amulets will be just what you wanted." John sounded as excited as Andrew had ever heard him, which increased his confidence that they would deal the first crushing blow to the Dragon Guard in his bid for revenge.

"Perfect. I appreciate your efforts."

"Thank you, sir," John replied, and Andrew smiled at his second's readiness to please.

"Have you located the other pieces of the Prophecy?"

"No, sir, I have not, but I am very close to decoding the symbol you sent me from the witch's book. At first I believed the four intertwined circles with the star at the center was simply the witches' way of marking the spell with their elemental symbols, but under a magnifying glass, I have found that where each circle touches what originally appeared to be a solid line is actually script written in an ancient runic language. I have several scholars working on the translation that I believe will lead us to the other texts and the rest of the Prophecy." John's optimism was contagious. Andrew felt better about their plans just being around him. "Good work, John."

"Thank you, sir, but it was your studious observation that concluded that the text we have is incomplete."

Andrew smiled, letting John's praise pass. There would be time for congratulations when he was the only dragon shifter left in existence. When his betrayers were exterminated and forgotten, then he would rejoice.

"I'm heading to the plane. I will contact you when we have arrived back at the mansion." He disconnected before John could respond. It was important that his second remember his place. A little praise was fine to keep the young wizard working towards Andrew's goal, but there was no way he could let him get overconfident, especially when he had yet to decide if John was to live or die when his mission was complete. Actions were all that mattered to Andrew. As long as John did what he was told to the best of his abilities and continued to be useful, he would live…it was as simple as that.

He uncovered the small motorcycle hidden under a pile of brush and headed down the dirt path he knew lead to the airfield, plans churning in his mind. It had been a productive trip to the old country. At least with his new plan he did not have to keep Royce contained and weakened for the remaining days until the full moon. No, the entire Force would think they had run him off. He laughed at their stupidity and reveled in the things to come. Vengeance was within his grasp.

~~*~*~*~*~*

If she wasn't convinced that she was destined to die alone with twenty cats, she damned sure knew it after Andrew's declaration. That was what had been hiding in her memory. The name her mother had spoken that night all those years ago…*Ilsa*.

What a picture! A witch with twenty cats, alone in the forest in a little cottage. All she needed was a broom and a pointy hat and she would personify every stereotype ever concerning witches in the history of the world.

At the mention of the long forgotten witch and her connection with what she had been told, it had felt as if all the blood drained from her body. It was not the rush she had imagined, but more like a smooth flow towards the forest floor. It seemed like it took a long time when in actuality, it was almost instantaneous and she had seen spots before her eyes. The action happening all around her had seemed really far away, like she was at the end of a very long hallway watching a movie on a small screen TV.

When Rory had thrown her over his shoulder and ran, reality had come rushing at her like the waves during a storm. Her heart raced, cold sweat covered her body, and there was simply not enough air to keep her lungs inflated. A branch had smacked her ass as they flew away from the chaos, snapping her back to reality. It was then that she realized she needed to be following Andrew instead of running away. She should have been embarrassed at the things she had called Rory for manhandling her, but in reality, she didn't give a shit. He really was the 'bastard son of a one-eyed troll-faced griffin' and she stood by her opinion. It had been even worse that he had laughed at her as she spewed insults meant to piss him off. Who in all the Heavens did he think he was to mock her. They all constantly teased her about turning them into toads, and she was about two seconds from making their taunts come true.

But none of that really mattered. She was just using it to keep from thinking about what had really happened. Royce had heard everything Andrew had said. Things that she had forgotten but was sure he would think she was keeping from him. Not that he had *ever* taken the time to talk to her or given her a chance to say anything. He had condemned her from the beginning just because of her heritage. He had his reasons and the Goddess knew they were justified, but wasn't a person supposed to be innocent until proven guilty? Wasn't that what the humans believed, and wasn't she half-human? She had spent the last twenty-five years waiting for the day she would meet her mate, building it up in her mind to be something grandiose, like a fairy tale. Well, one thing was for sure, the book was better than the movie and worlds better than reality.

She listened to the men packing up and figured she should be doing the same, but her pity party was still in full swing and who was she to cut it short? It was her party and she would cry if she wanted to. It was the first ever true 'girlie-moment' she had allowed herself and she was going to soak it all up.

Devon had tried to talk to her, but she'd kept her back to him and the sleeping bag pulled over her head until he had given up. When she was ready to talk, which should be in about thirty years or so, then she would seek him out. Until then, Kyra wanted to be left alone. As soon as they got home, she was going to move away from the Dragon Guard's lair. She would still help them, but there was no way she could be around them day in and day out knowing there was no future for her there. She had made amazing friends and prayed that they could stay close. It was the first time she'd had real friends that weren't witches and she really liked them, *dammit*. Maybe if she left, Royce would return. He was an integral part of their Force and had been missed. With her gone, there would be nothing to keep him away.

The tears she had held back when around the others dampened her tiny travel pillow. She could count on one hand the number of times she had allowed herself to cry in all her years. Kyra had been taught to be strong, to resist anything that could be seen as weakness, and if by chance she was ever hurt, she was taught to suck it up and hold her head high. Yeah, well, that was not happening this time. She was wounded and there was nothing but a good old fashioned cry that would make it any better. Deep in her heart she knew she had fallen a little in love the first moment she had laid eyes on Royce and that it had grown over time. It was silly, really, but something she had no control over. The Universe, the Goddess, and Fate had all conspired and she had been all too happy to oblige.

There had been a split second of blessed recognition and the fire of need that can only occur when encountering one's mate for the first time when she met Royce, but it was quickly followed by suspicion and regret:

two things she saw every time she looked at him. Kyra would have given anything, even her magic, to see love reflected in his deep brown eyes, but that was not to be. She was a witch, and like her ancestors, she had been condemned without a trial. At least there was no fiery stake or noose hanging on a tree.

What would her mother, the great Calysta St. Croix, think of her now? Would she condemn Kyra a failure? Brand her unworthy and think of her as the daughter that was to mate a dragon shifter and bring honor to her coven but instead could not convince her intended that she was worthy of a conversation, let alone someone with whom to conceive heirs? Had her mother known that the people slaughtered by Ilsa were members of her would-be mate's family? *Probably, knowing dear old mom*, she thought. If so, why had she not prepared Kyra for what was to come? So what if they hadn't spoken in years? Calysta knew how to contact her if she had really wanted to. Kyra carried on like she was hidden from her mother, but she knew deep down inside that if the Grand Priestess wanted to find her, she would.

Deciding pity parties were not all they were cracked up to be and that crying only gave her a headache and made her nose run, she threw back the covers. When she looked in the tiny mirror she kept in her pack she added a few more reasons for not crying to her list…red, puffy eyes and blotchy skin. She really was not cut out for any of this prissy shit. Damn Royce! Damn him to hell for making her act like a girl.

She packed up her belongings while making a mental list of all she needed to accomplish both personally and to help fight Andrew. It was then that she had remembered while the stupid putz, Andrew, had been ranting she had worked a Spell of Recognition, essentially trapping a piece of his aura in the Goldstone pendant she wore around her neck. The Goldstone contained copper to bind the malevolent parts of the traitor's aura and allow Kyra to use what was left to locate and track him. All she had to do was activate it.

Lighting the candles she had yet to pack and sitting cross-legged in the middle of her tent, she pictured Andrew as she had first seen him, a man in need of her help, and then as she had come to know him, a traitor and poster boy of all that was wrong in the world. Methodically, a picture began to form in her mind. Having never worked this spell other than when she originally learned it years ago, she was amazed at the clarity of the image and the accompanying thoughts.

Of course Andrew was scheming, but he was also relaxing, enjoying his flight. He was headed back to whatever hole in the ground he was calling home. She couldn't get a location or picture of the house because he was not thinking of the actual structure, only what had to be done when he returned. His thoughts were jumbled, but he kept returning to that damn Prophecy. If she ever ran into the dumbass that had found it absolutely necessary to write that crap out, she promised herself she would kick his ass. *Had to be a man, a woman would NOT be that stupid,* she thought as she continued to sift through what she could of Andrew's thoughts. Now that she had made initial contact, doing it again would be simple. She had a leg up on the jerk, at least *something* positive had come out of their little meeting in the woods.

Not wanting to face the Dragon Guard any more than was absolutely necessary, she fiddled around in her tent listening to what was going on outside. Rayne was obviously pissed. More than once he had roared, actually *roared*, that he would see Andrew skinned alive for all he had done. It had been a huge weight off her shoulders when the Commander had ordered Devon, Lance, and Aidan, along with several of Rian's clan, to return home. He was sure whatever evil Andrew was concocting would take place on their home turf, and he wanted his mate and child along with all the other innocents protected.

The men had raced off to catch a plane bound for the west. At first she thought it was funny that they weren't transforming and flying themselves and then realized it was daylight. The expenditure of magic to conceal their beasts in the light of day would have been too much, at least that was what she guessed. She was at the flap of her tent about to offer her help when she heard Devon ask Rory to watch after her and make sure she got back safely. Tears threatened to fall again, the big old softy was a true friend, one she was sure would be with her throughout her lifetime.

Time seemed to fly and before she knew it, the sun had set. Rory appeared at the flap of her tent, "Hey, Kyra, okay if I come in?"

"Yeah, come in," she answered, ready to get the hell out of there. Hiding was not something she was good at or enjoyed.

"We're gonna be heading out in a few minutes. As your appointed bodyguard, I wanted to make sure you were ready." He grinned and she wondered how old he was. It had to be older than her but he acted like a frat guy looking for a party most of time.

"I've been ready for a while, but I really need to talk to Rayne before we leave. I was just trying to stay out of the way while you guys were getting ready to head out."

"Sure you were," he said with more than a little suspicion in his voice. "I'm sure spending all day in a dark, dank tent is exactly what an Earth witch enjoys above all else. Just as I am sure your self-imposed exile had nothing to do with my pig-headed loser of a brother."

Busted! she thought, but was unwilling to let Rory know he had hit the nail on the head. "No, I took a nap after being carried like a sack of rotten potatoes through the woods and basically dismissed like an errant child. Then I worked a spell or two to make sure that schmuck was not anywhere near Kyndel, Sam, or the others we left at home, and finally, I packed up so I was ready to go when it was time to leave."

He smiled a knowing smile and she imagined smacking it off his face, but before she could act upon her thoughts, he shrugged, "Have it your way, but I do want you to understand something." It was as if a switch had been flipped. Gone was the playful youngest brother that everyone thought was clueless, only to be replaced by an intense, bold Guardsman. Even his voice sounded different; deeper and more commanding, "It does not matter to Rian or I where you came from or what you are or even that Ilsa was of your coven. As far as we are concerned you are to be our sister, and it will happen sooner rather than later.

"For as long as I can remember I always knew Royce would be the first of us to find his mate. *Hell*, Rian and I've had a bet going for over fifty years about when it would happen. I'm happy to say that I won." A small twinkle in his eye told her the clown was still in there, but it didn't stop him from resuming with a stern tone, "Royce is and always will be the heart of our family. Many over the years have mistaken that as weakness. Of course, my big brother has corrected their misguided assumptions with extreme prejudice, but that does not negate the truth of it.

"When we were young, before Ilsa lost her mind, she explained the importance of our trio to us and made us promise to always be there for one another. It has not been easy, most of all for Roy, but we have done our best. As I am sure you can imagine, Rian is the head, not only figuratively, but also in reality. A strong leader, willing to make the hard decisions, highly respected not only by our clan, but all of dragon kin, and also a gifted strategist.

"As I said, Royce is the heart. His compassion allows him to see the whole picture and keep balance in the fight we face against those that would destroy all we hold dear. He has a depth that keeps us all from indiscriminately killing those who oppose us. He is the life force that pumps through both clans." He stopped and she once again saw the levity in his gaze and a slight grin on his face.

Several minutes passed as he looked everywhere but at her, and it was then that she realized for all of his bravado, Rory was embarrassed to say what part he played in their family dynamics. Never one to hold back (Well, until recently anyway) Kyra asked, "And you, what part are you?"

Rory laughed, "You truly are a bold little witch. You're going to need that fearless abandon to deal with my brother on a daily basis for all of eternity."

She felt her smile fall and a sadness she had forgotten, at least for a few minutes, descend back upon her. Trying to turn away, she found Rory standing in her way, "I know it's hard right now, but I promise the big dumbass *will* come around. You two are destined to be together. Haven't you heard…the Universe knows what She's doing?"

Thankfully, he was so tall and she was so short and they were so close together, that when she looked straight ahead she only had to stare at the logo on his t-shirt. Rory continued, "To answer your question, I am the hands. I make things happen. Now, do not misunderstand; we are all men of action, but I am more willing to leap without looking than my brothers. I take the risks they have to think about. The older I get, the more I realize how true the old witch's descriptions were."

He walked away and looked out the open flap of her tent. Kyra was immediately aware of the fact that he was mind speaking with someone and wondered who, but was unwilling to interrupt or ask. She began gathering up her bags just as Rory turned around and smiled. "I know you can tell when we're talking to one another in the way of our kin and I have nothing to hide. It was Devon, checking on you. He takes his role of protector very seriously."

It was nice to know someone cared. She felt her spirits lift. "He's a good friend," she smiled and then added, "and a hell of a poker player."

"I have been known to play a hand or two if the stakes are right," he winked at her, all traces of the warrior gone.

"We usually play for shots. Can you handle your liquor, dragon man?" she joked, feeling more and more like her old self.

"You just wait, little witch, just wait and see."

He grabbed her duffle bag and exited the tent ahead of her, being sure to stop and hold the flap to keep it from falling on her head. She thought a lot about all they had discussed as she rode back across the ocean on the back of his noble royal blue beast. Only her night vision allowed her to see the ribbons of green strewn throughout that added depth and reminded her why his family's clan was called Blue Thunder.

Leaning forward to rest against the base of his neck, she let her eyes slide shut. No matter how hard she tried, she could not banish the hope that Rory was right, that she would still be his and Rian's sister. That Royce would accept their fate. One thought followed her into her slumber. *Hope was a scary bitch.*

CHAPTER FOUR

He and Rian stayed another day after Rayne and the others had headed back to make sure the younger Guardsmen were prepared to defend their lands until the conflict with the traitor was over. The Elders came to see them off, his Uncle Stefan among them, and looking none too pleased. After all the pleasantries were dispensed, he and Stefan moved to the side to speak privately.

Royce was the first to break the awkward silence, "I'm sure you heard about the newest development in Fate's plan to ruin my life?" Royce asked.

"Ruin your life? Royce, my boy, you need to stop focusing on everything that is wrong and instead look at what is good. You have never been one to back down from a fight, nor have you ever been the bringer of doom and gloom…quite the opposite. You are the one that searches for the truth. You make others see reason, find the goodness, see the quest to the end. Now, because you are faced with a real challenge, one that hits at *your* heart for the first time, you are giving up, accepting an unfulfilled life without a fight. What a pity." His uncle shook his head just as he had done when he was a boy and failed at learning some valuable lesson.

The shame Royce felt caused him to lash out, "I have not given up! I have accepted what is. You taught me that the Universe does not make mistakes, that Fate will not be denied. Did you ever think that might be a load of bullshit? That sometimes, something somewhere, just gets fucked up? That it is up to us to set it right? We were given free will to choose our path. I cannot find a way around the fact that she is a witch, a witch from the same coven as Ilsa. Remember her? The witch that murdered my mother? Then shoved a dagger into a baby before she even had a chance to draw her first breath? Do you remember, Uncle?" He spat the last words out with enough venom that Stefan actually flinched.

Several moments later, as Royce felt his temper begin to subside and the guilt of what he had just said began to rush in, his uncle spoke, "Yes Royce, I remember. But I remember so much more of your mother and of Ilsa than that one day. Don't you? Don't you have any happy memories to draw from, or are you so focused on your own guilt over what happened that you can't remember anything else?"

Stefan could not have inflicted more pain if he had run Royce through with a sword. The truth of the Elder's words rang throughout his entire body, and pointed out a fact he'd never realized. When he thought of his mother, he did *only* think of that day, of what he found when he entered that room, and he *did* feel guilt. Not just your garden variety, 'oh shit, I better never do that again' guilt, but real, bone-deep, almost debilitating guilt. Sure he had family memories and his mother was always in them laughing, smiling, loving them all, but sometime between entering that room, finding his mother, and returning to the outside world, he had tucked every other thought of Riona away and replaced them with remorse that he could not save her and his sister and a need for vengeance against a woman already slain.

His head dropped forward and for the first time in his life he felt one hundred and fifty-six years old. Stefan laid his hand on his bicep and Royce could feel the Elder pouring healing energy into him. It was his Uncle's gift, to be able to help heal the soul, and one of the many reasons he was so incredibly valuable to their kin. Royce finally raised his head and met the eyes of the man that was like a second father to him and the recrimination he expected to find was surprisingly absent, all he could see in the Elder's light green eyes was forgiveness and hope.

His words only reinforced what his eyes already said, "You will get through this, my boy. I have to believe you will learn to accept that sassy little witch for exactly who she is and have a chance at a life filled with joy and love, but she is not going to wait around forever. Kyra is strong and independent, Royce, and you have hurt her. The choice is yours, it always has been, just don't take too long to make it. I have a feeling your mate has even more determination than you to live a loveless life, in place of forgiving *you*."

Stefan's last words rang in his ears the entire flight back home. As if that wasn't enough, he and Rian entered Rayne and Kyndel's home to find all the women crowded around Kyra, engaged in a heated debate. The sound of the door closing against the frame stopped the debate, but the glares and looks of complete disgust he got from Kyndel, Grace, and Samantha would have leveled a lesser man. They lasted for several tense moments, in which Royce prayed for one of his brethren to save his ass, but those losers simply left him to his fate.

Kyndel was the first to move, essentially ending the standoff, but he knew bigger trouble was on the way when her eyebrow lifted and her hands landed on her hips. Grace followed with the same stare he had seen her level at Aidan to win many an argument, and Samantha simply folded her arms. But the look on Kyra's face and the way she quickly looked out the window to avoid even the sight of him was what made his heart ache. Was Stefan right? Would she leave before he could truly get his shit together? Was that what he wanted or did he want her and the promise of a future?

The glares continued and no one, not even his brothers offered any assistance. *Hell*, Rory even plopped his ass on a barstool and chuckled like he was watching football on a big screen. It seemed only the children were glad to see him. Jay, Rayne's son, toddled over and grabbed his leg while Sydney, Lance and Samantha's daughter, flew at him demanding to be hugged.

He picked up Jay and headed to the family room, a child on each hip. The conversation began again as soon as he had exited the room, and he fought the urge to use his enhanced hearing to eavesdrop. *If they wanted to say something to him, they could damn well talk directly to him.* At least that was what his bruised ego thought.

He knew he was messed up and knew the situation had to be fixed, but had no clue how to do it. To be honest, he needed five minutes where he wasn't thinking about the steaming pile of shit his life had become. The kids were a great distraction. He pushed his wallowing away, and instead gave pony rides and played airplane until both children were yawning and cuddling in his lap. The thought of what it would be like to have his own children in his lap crossed his mind, but he quickly squashed the errant idea. How could he imagine children when he couldn't imagine a life with their mother? *I am truly screwed and have no one to blame but myself*, was all he thought as he stood to take the children to their parents.

Samantha took Sydney and said good night while Kyndel hoisted Jay onto her hip, also saying her farewells and headed upstairs. Royce made his way to the fridge and grabbed a beer. As he leaned his butt against the counter, he realized only the men of his Force and his brothers were present. From the looks on their faces, he was sure he was not going to like what they had to say. He was shocked when Lance was the first to speak, "Alright, old man, what's up? This is your intervention. It's obvious you feel the mating bond, *hell*, we can all feel it through you. You are repressing so hard, you are pushing out at us."

Everyone in the room nodded in agreement as Devon spoke, "I know you want to rip my head off every time I'm near her, even though you told me to watch after her. I can feel it. Your emotions are bleeding through to all of us."

Royce looked from man to man as each nodded in agreement. Was what they were saying the truth? Had he repressed and avoided what he was trying *not* to feel for Kyra so much that he was projecting it to all around him? The truth of the situation was written on every face looking back at him. Not only was he screwing with his world, he was screwing with theirs.

"*Shit!*" He squeezed the bottle in his hand so tight that it cracked before setting it on the counter behind him. "I'm sorry. I had no idea. As soon as Andrew is neutralized I'll head back to the caves."

"Fuck that!" was growled from every Guardsman in attendance, but it was Rayne that stepped forward and spoke, "No, you will not. You will face this like you have faced every other challenge in your life…head on. I have fought by your side for more years than I care to remember and I've never seen you doubt yourself like you are now. I gave you time and space to come to the right conclusion, but obviously you aren't going to. Either you are too hard-headed or too blind to see what is right in front of you. As your friend and your Commander, I'm ordering to you to remove your head from your ass and do what needs to be done to rectify the situation you have caused."

He and Rayne had been friends since the Commander had been barely old enough to hold a broadsword, and Royce could not think of a time that his friend had ever spoken to him with such disappointment and anger. Rayne was not the only one pissed. The hits just kept coming.

From the corner of the kitchen Aaron spoke, "Look old man, I know your issues. *Hell*, we've all got 'em, but this is *your mate* we are talking about, your future…forever, you get it? You get one shot at this shit. That's it, no do-overs, no regrouping, one shot, and you are fucking up *royally!*"

Never one to keep quiet, Lance chimed in again, "Practice what you preach, Gramps. We've all had to listen to you be right about every damn thing under the sun for so many years that your monumental screw up now took us all by surprise. Trust me, I should be happy to see you be wrong, just this once, but I'm not *and* I'm not letting you screw up your entire life *or Kyra's*. It was you that pushed me to claim Sam, even with all that was going on around us. Yeah, I cursed the very air you breathed, but in the end, as much as it hurts to admit, you were right. That woman is the best damn thing that ever happened to me, just like Kyra is the best part of you."

Frustrated and feeling more than a little ganged up on, he spoke before he thought, "The best part of me? How the hell do you figure? She's a witch with more power in her petite frame than any of us can imagine. What the hell am I supposed to do if she gets seduced by the dark like Ilsa did?"

He looked at Rian and Rory for help, but they only sat looking at him like he was a lunatic, so he continued letting all his feelings of bitterness and defeat fuel his words, "What will you do, you sanctimonious asshole, if she loses her shit and comes after your family? Sacrifices Samantha and Sydney right before your eyes."

Royce spun around and nailed Rayne with a look of pure contempt, "Or you, my dear Commander hear your beautiful wife call for help, so pained and helpless, and you arrive just in time to see the dagger plunge into her heart! Tell me, *fucking* tell me, what you wouldn't do to keep that from happening?" He was shouting so loud he could feel the windows rattle in their panes. He looked from man to man, but they were looking over his shoulder with complete pity and untold compassion, not the anger he thought would come from his outburst. It was then that he heard a tiny sob, almost inaudible. That one little sound reached directly into his chest and squeezed his heart until he thought it would stop beating.

His rage forgotten, he spun around so fast that he almost knocked the table over. There, standing at the entrance to the kitchen, was Kyra, looking as if it was he that wielded the dagger. Her violet eyes were as big as saucers. Her tiny hands were covering her mouth but not stopping the heart-wrenching sobs that crossed her lips, or tears streaming down her cheeks wetting the collar of her lavender blouse.

Unable to stop the need to comfort his mate a living being within him, he took a step in her direction. In response, she threw her hands up in front of her and shook her head until he thought she would fall from the force of her actions. Royce stopped where he was and his hand reached for Kyra of its own volition, while his dragon roared with the need to hold the one who was to be theirs.

His heart beat with such vehemence he was sure it would jump from his chest. He counted twenty beats while he stood gawking at the most beautiful woman ever created. Even grief stricken, she was absolutely perfect and in those seconds it didn't matter what she was, it only mattered that she was his. He tried to take another step towards her and this time she took a step back, her eyes widening even more. *She's afraid of me*, he thought, and a sadness unlike any he had never known filled him. When she spoke he felt his heart break. Her words cut deep and true and the worst part was…he deserved them. Her voice was barely above a whisper and clogged with tears, "That is really what you think of me? That I could hurt a child? That I could hurt any of the people that I have come to love as much as my own blood…maybe more? You really think I'm a monster, don't you?"

Before his eyes, she went from a wounded pup to fierce warrior. She threw back her shoulders, scrubbed the remaining tears from her face, and bunched her fists at her sides, ready to take on whatever foe came at her. Damn shame he was the enemy. Her next words rang clear and true, "I am not the monster, Royce O'Reilly, you are. You have a black heart, incapable of compassion or reprieve. A few moments ago I would have given anything, absolutely anything to have you forgive me, to have you accept me as your mate. I was willing to forfeit the very magic that runs through my veins for a chance at forever with you."

Her breath came fast and heavy and he knew it was the fury he felt all around him. Before he could come up with anything to say, she took a step forward and shook her fist at him, "But no more. That fucking ship has sailed. I refuse to waste one more second of my life on *you*! I may never know the love of a mate, but I have the love of friends and family and that will sustain me for all of my years."

She leaned forward slightly and he saw fire dance in her eyes. When she spoke it was deliberate and each word was another dagger to his heart. "I don't want *you*, Royce. Your shit can remain your shit. Keep it *forever*. Let it fester and rot for all I care."

He stood completely confounded, unsure what to do or say or *even think*. Then her last words reached his ears as she turned to leave, and what was left of his world crumbled, "We could have had it all, but you blew it."

The minutes ticked by as he stood watching his future walk away from him and he was unable to stop it. Kyra had hit the nail on the head: *he blew it.* Fucked up…*royally,* and it took losing it all to make him realize what a grade A asshole he truly was. Devon appeared at his side and the pity on his face was more than he could take. He knew there would be more of the same and they would all have some sort of advice that he really didn't want to hear, so he did the only thing he could…he left.

The walk home was filled with a running loop of all that Kyra had said. The look of complete betrayal on her face and the pain that seemed to radiate from her every pore was something he would never forget, and he had caused it all, every last drop was his burden to bear. It wasn't until he heard his boots hit the wooden planks of his porch that he realized he was there. He opened the door and none of the joy he had imagined at returning met him. For the first time since building his home almost eighty years ago, he realized how empty it was, that it was a monument to all he had thrown away in his own stupidity.

Sleep eluded him. He grabbed his hundredth beer of the evening and prayed that it would at least numb some of the anguish he felt, but the anguish remained. The wooden floors of his home had a whole new groove from his constant pacing. The sun came up over the horizon and the memories of having Kyra in his arms came rushing back. He relived the short time he had been with her, the only time he would ever be with the one meant to be his. He wished for his cave by the sea, if only to have the sound of the waves to calm his grief.

He had just stepped out of the shower when he heard the front door open and close. Rian called out, "You alive back there, Bro?"

"Yeah, let me get dressed and I'll be right out."

"Hurry the hell up, your breakfast is gonna get cold," Rory added.

Great, it's family bonding time, he thought. "Be right out," was his only response.

He walked out to find a feast covering his kitchen table. "What's all this?" he asked.

"Kyndel and Grace were up early this morning, cooking up a storm. I guess Sam had been at it too before she headed to the hospital with Devon in tow. We were in the guest room and the smell of these damned addictive blueberry muffins woke us up." Rory popped a whole muffin in his mouth and groaned like it was manna from heaven.

"Ya'll could've stayed here. Heavens knows there's tons of room."

Both brothers stopped mid chew and shook their heads. It was Rian that responded, "No way, Bro. You needed some alone time after the ass kicking you took."

Rory spit orange juice halfway across the kitchen and then continued laughing until he could barely stand. Apparently, his loss and humiliation was funny to his younger brother. Just the thought of last night had him standing and throwing his half-eaten breakfast into the sink. Regaining his composure, Rory apologized, "Dude, lighten up. I wasn't laughing at you. Grow the hell up. I just couldn't believe that our diplomatic big brother, who reminded me to not mention what happened last night all the way here, just let it fly like that. I'm sorry I laughed, but you gotta admit that shit is funny."

Rian jumped to his own defense, "I said don't talk about it, all I did was explain why we stayed at Rayne's."

"Po-TAY-to...Po-TAH-to, Bro. You fucked up. Admit it."

"I will not."

Unable to keep the grin from his face even with the pain of the events of the previous night still raw within him, he slapped both his brothers on the back. They may be complete and total jerks, but they were his family and he loved them more than his own life. He was sure they had shown up to provide a distraction. With their goal accomplished, he grabbed a biscuit and another cup of coffee and sat down.

"What's the plan for today?" Royce asked as he finished loading the dishwasher and made another pot of coffee.

Rian looked at his watch before answering, "We are to meet at the clearing in about forty minutes."

"Alright, let me run and get my boots and we can take off."

Just as he was about to turn the corner into his kitchen he caught the tail end of his brothers' conversation. "You think he's gonna be okay, Ri?" Rory asked as concerned as Royce had ever heard him.

"I don't know Ror, I just don't know. Forever is a long time to be alone." Rian sounded sad and defeated, something he had never heard from his older brother and leader of the Blue Thunder Dragon Shifters.

Royce felt hollow and empty. Rian was right...forever is a *really long time* to be alone.

~~*~*~*~*~*

The full moon was quickly approaching...quicker than Kyra wanted. She had finally been able to figure out that whatever Andrew was scheming needed the power of a full moon, and of course the little shithead was in luck, because the one coming was a Blue Moon. Its power was twice that of any other..... *not good news*. She had been keeping tabs on the traitor through her Goldstone, but it was getting harder and harder as he was exposed to copious amounts of black magic that nullified her white magic's reach.

With only six days left, Kyra felt no closer to answers than she had when the whole mess started. She was completely engrossed in a new grimoire that Rian had found for her when the doorbell rang. Grumbling about not enough hours in the day, she was stunned when she opened the door to find the King of the Big Cats and his lieutenant standing on her little porch. His cheeky grin said he had caught at least a little of her grumblings and she couldn't stop the blush that heated her cheeks.

Maximillian Prentise was a force to reckoned with in the shifter world. He was the undisputed King of all the Big Cats, older than anyone dared ask and the most powerful creature she had ever encountered, although his power differed from that of dragons or witches. His felt as old as time and was a mixture of many cultures. As Max had amassed his pride, which contained many species, he had been blessed with a part of each of their origins and thus some of their unique magic. Not all of it was as white and untainted as what she possessed, but it was of the Earth and nowhere near anything dark.

Max chuckled and she realized she was just staring. "Well, *hell*, Max, you surprised me. Come on in."

"Sorry we didn't call first. We were talking to Rayne and he said you might need some assistance, so we popped right over." She was sure the timber of the King's voice, combined with his slight Latin accent, had made more than one woman shiver, but all she heard was his much appreciated offer to help.

Kyra moved out of the way as both gentlemen entered the cottage she was calling home. She was always amazed how cat-like their movements were, even in human form. To the clueless observer she could only imagine how refined they appeared, but no one that had ever seen them in action would describe them that way. They were intense and savage, definitely someone she was glad to have on her side.

Her brow furrowed as she asked, "You practice magic?"

"But of course, *bruja pequena*. Not as well as you, but we've picked up a few tricks along the way." He winked and reached for a duffle that Juan Carlos, his lieutenant, had been carrying.

She cleared a space on the dining table and watched as Max unpacked bottles of herbs and liquids, along with a huge box containing roots. Next came an intricately carved mahogany box detailed with what she could only assume were pieces of gold. Lastly, he pulled out a large piece of lavender velvet and spread it over the area she had cleared.

"Now, tell me what you know so far. The dragons are warriors. Their explanation of what you know was…spotty at best." Max smiled and she could see the respect he had for his allies.

"Well, to be honest, I don't know much. I spelled a Goldstone to peek in on Andrew, but he and his band of merry idiots have been using so much black magic that it is basically useless."

She dropped the pendant on the table and continued, "I did get a clear enough picture of the full moon to know that whatever he's planning needs that kind of lunar power." She knew it wasn't enough, but she was just about at the end of her rope. If Max couldn't help, she would need to contact her mother, and Kyra would rather chop off both her arms and try to swim than ask for Calysta's help.

The perceptive Leo picked up the Goldstone and whispered a phrase she couldn't quite make out, but was sure was ancient Incan. When he looked back up, his deep green eyes were glowing and more feline than human in appearance. She had heard that he could channel any and all of the cats he ruled at any time, but witnessing his power was kind of freaky. A movement behind Max drew her attention and she only then realized that the space occupied by the strong silent bodyguard now housed a large golden brown panther with deep hazel eyes. The spark of recognition in the animal's eyes was amazing.

Max followed her gaze and chuckled, "Juan Carlos has been with me a long time and our bond runs deep. The use of magic from his homeland brings out his beast. Never fear, the man is still in there and very much in control. Now, your Goldstone should work a little better. I cleared away some of the taint. It won't last forever, but it may give you a look or two that could help."

"Thanks! And I'm not worried about Juan Carlos," she barely contained the giggle that threatened to escape. She felt like a kid at the zoo, but was embarrassed to admit her thoughts.

"Let me guess, you want to feel his fur?" Max asked with a twinkle in his eyes that showed even a King could have fun.

She nodded her head. "It just looks so soft the way it shines in the sunlight."

The werepanther in question padded towards her. It was not until he rubbed against her leg that she realized if he stood on his hind legs he would be taller than her and probably would outweigh her by a good fifty pounds. Power surrounded the animal. She could feel it pulsing against its containment, ready to spring forward when needed. Her hand touched the top of the feline's head as he circled her. One swipe from top of head to tip of tail and she was convinced he was actually covered in the finest silk on earth.

The spell was broken when Juan Carlos' cat purred and the vibration against her leg caused her to stumble. Before she could fall forward, Max was there to keep her on her feet. He laughed out loud and her embarrassment faded away.

Juan Carlos in human form and dressed as before appeared beside her, quick to apologize, "So sorry, I forget how petite you really are. Are you okay?"

"Absolutely. No harm done. Thanks for letting me feel you up." She winked to show she really was okay and the room erupted in laughter once again.

"Now, let's do what we came here to do," Max said, ever the King. "I was told you have a grimoire that contains very old magic."

"Yeah, Rian brought it over a little while ago. I haven't gotten through much of it, and since it is all pretty much new to me, it is slow going."

She lifted the heavy book right before Juan Carlos took it from her hands. "Let me get that for you." He handed the book to Max like it weighed nothing and she was once again amazed by their strength.

The King opened the volume and began reading with his lieutenant looking over his shoulder. "Would you like some tea or something?" Kyra offered.

Neither looking up from their reading, they answered in unison, "Yes, please."

Heading to the kitchen she filled the kettle and placed it on the stove. After the cups and tea were on the counter, she stood gazing at the beauty of the garden behind the little cottage she inhabited. Kyndel had said she had a knack for nature, but nothing could have prepared Kyra for the amazing picture she saw as she waited for the water to boil. Her gaze landed on every blossom and vine, marveling at the infinite wisdom of the Earth and Her ability to provide everything anyone ever needed. She continued her perusal when she saw movement under the huge oak tree at the far corner. Concentrating her power on the spot that had drawn her attention, she gasped as the image came into view. There, leaned against the tree, looking like he had lost his last friend was Royce. Long muscular legs stretched out before him, crossed at the ankle, with his hands loosely folded in his lap. His chest rising and falling against the faded gray t-shirt that stretched tight across his bunched muscles reminded her that he was completely at rest in that moment. His head was thrown back against the bark of the tree, the contrast only accentuating the fiery color of his hair. His perfect lips were barely moving in what she could only assume was a prayer and his deep brown eyes that always held so much emotion were closed in reverence.

Her body and soul longed to go to him, but her head reminded her of the horrible things he had said and that he truly believed she was evil incarnate. The pain of his words kept her from throwing open the door and running to him, but the damned hope that still dwelled in her heart made her watch and wish. The sound of the whistle on the kettle made her look away, but nothing could stop the pain she felt knowing what the future held.

Luckily when she returned to the dining room, Max and Juan Carlos had found something they believed to be useful. Together, they spent the rest of the day and well into the night preparing amulets, keeping her from obsessing over what would never be.

When the werepanthers finally left, Kyra fell into bed completely exhausted, but happily satisfied with what they had accomplished and the plan they had come up with for stopping whatever Andrew had planned. She was excited to tell Rayne what they had come up with and too see if she could get any more information from her Goldstone now that Max had cleansed it.

For the first time since learning of Andrew's deception and the part she unwittingly played in it, she fell into a peaceful sleep. She seemed to float on clouds, looking over some of the happiest times in her life. First was her sixteenth birthday when she was literally Queen for a day. Another, later in life spent learning spells and practicing with her aunties, and then she landed on the day of her fiftieth birthday celebration. For the last twenty-five years it had been one of her most cherished memories. Now it held a pinch of bittersweet melancholy, but as it played out, her recent pain was forgotten and she was transported back in time to the exact moment the dragon marking appeared on her right hip, along with the recognition of all that it meant for her future.

She had dreamed of a faceless man that night who was all she imagined the ancient warriors blessed by the Universe to be. Now she had firsthand knowledge of the Dragon Guard and as her dream continued, that knowledge, along with twenty-five years of life experience out from behind the walls of her coven, blended into the past and evolved into a whole new picture.

She was dancing with an incredibly tall, well-muscled man that held her loosely against his body as they moved to the music and filled the younger woman she imagined she used to be with such nervous excitement she almost vibrated with it. The man leading her through the dance was confident and had a strength she could feel where their hands and bodies touched. He had a low baritone voice that calmed her nerves and a laugh that made her happy just to hear it. Every so often his large hand would graze up her spine and slowly slide back down to the small of her back, leaving a trail of sparkling energy in its wake.

He leaned down and whispered in her ear, raising goosebumps all over the real life sleeping Kyra and making her wish she knew what was said. In her dream she giggled and a slight blush touched her cheeks. The dance continued even when a much slower, sensual song was played. Her escort pulled her even closer and as she laid her head against his chest, he placed a chaste kiss upon her crown. The scene continued for several moments and ended with Kyra telling her Aunt Della how much fun she'd had and how much she liked *him*.

Kyra continued to dream and relive moments from her life, some exactly as they had occurred and others changed as only can happen in fantasies. When she happened upon the memory of her vision in which Royce was standing in the aftermath of an explosion, she thanked the Goddess that they had been able to stop that from happening.

In her dream, she felt the caress of the sea air on her skin and saw the waves crashing against the rocks just as they had the day Royce had taken her to the ridge. Not wanting to live through that ordeal again, she tried to change the direction of her thoughts, but they would not be deterred. She was destined to watch her most humiliating experience unfold before her eyes.

The feel of his hands at her waist warmed her throughout, sending an electric current directly to her womb. As he spun her around and their lips met, she was lost to the image running though her mind, waiting for the moment her fate was sealed and the one man that was to love her forever would run away like the coward he was; but it never came.

Instead, as soon as she had reached the first climax of her already long life, she watched as Royce pulled the Kyra of her dream towards him until they looked into one another's eyes. Slower than she thought possible, his lips touched the corner of her mouth and gently nipped and tasted from one side to other, taking special care in the middle to let the tip of his tongue just barely slide across her lips and ever so lightly touch the tip of hers, igniting her senses and causing a series of tiny contractions in her womb. With her legs still locked around his waist, she moved against his erection seeking to give him pleasure like he had shown her, but he would have none of it. He exerted his considerable control by placing his hands on her hips, essentially trapping her right where he wanted her.

She sighed her resignation as he worked his way across her jaw and down the column of her neck, the rough stubble of his beard tickling and exciting. He lavished special attention to the spot where her neck and shoulder met, causing her to strain against his hold. She felt him smile against her skin just before he bit down on the tendon lying just below the skin. The slight pinch made her jump and he took the opportunity to position his cock right against her opening. All that separated them was their clothing, and if she could've had one coherent thought, she would've worked a spell to remove the offending material from both their bodies, but as it was, Royce was relentless. He kissed and sucked the spot he had bitten until she was a mass of want and need.

As if that was not enough, he wrapped one arm under her bottom further trapping her body against his. He then used his other to take one of her straining nipples between his thumb and forefinger and torment the hardened peak until she was certain she would lose her mind. He definitely knew how to use the difference in their sizes to his advantage, and as the real life Kyra experienced the dream as if it was really happening, she panted for more.

The sound of his excitement roughened voice in her ear drew her farther into her dream, "I want you, Kyra, and with all that I am I swear I have to have you."

His words became actions as she watched him use his enhanced speed to move them from the ridge overlooking the ocean to the cave he had been living in. Although she had never seen it in the real world, her imagination took over and it was a mere matter of seconds before her mate had her lying on a pallet of sleeping bags and blankets beside a roaring fire. She closed her eyes just as his fingers touched the buttons on her blouse, but Royce was having none of it. His fingers stilled and he spoke with an authority she'd heard on several occasions. Her eyes snapped to his as he spoke, "Look at me, Kyra. This is about us, together, always as one. From this day forward you hold my heart, you are my home, and you are my reason for living. Never shut me out, I want us to share every second of our very long lives together."

Minutes ticked by as they simply stared into one another's eyes. She watched as the firelight magnified the plethora of emotion Royce felt and she sighed in relief that she was not alone in the depth of her feelings. Slowly, he began working to open her buttons once again, kissing the spot right above each new opening and then returning to gaze into her eyes.

Her hands moved of their own volition, exploring every inch she could reach of his massive body. When they slid under the material of his shirt, the electric shock resulting from their skin to skin contact caused her to gasp. Royce's lips found hers and the fire that had been smoldering was set ablaze.

His tongue slid alongside hers as his hands covered her breasts and his calloused roughed palms rubbed against her raised nipples. She arched into his touch and he groaned into her mouth as her nails dug into his back. He rolled until she was seated atop his lap and ripped her open blouse from her shoulders. A moment of embarrassment was quickly erased by the look of complete adoration and undeniable lust in his deep brown eyes. His hands slid up her sides, and as he spread his fingers wide, she was engulfed in his touch. Fingers from each hand made their way under her bra and the sensation they ignited had her fighting to keep her eyes open; it was like nothing she had ever experienced. In the next breath, cool air caressed her breasts. She shivered at the sensation, "Are you cold, *a sta'rin*"?

Speech escaped her, so she shook her head right before he leaned forward and licked the very tip of her breast. Lost to the sensation, her head fell back and her fingers tangled in his hair, pulling him as close as possible. Royce seemed to know what she needed even when she didn't as he sucked as much of her breast into his mouth as would fit and continued torturing her nipple with his teeth and tongue. Her hips moved against his considerable length, the friction of her clothing pushing her towards another release.

Royce moved to her other breast, showing it the same attention, while his hands landed on her waist. He ripped open the button and unzipped her jeans, sliding his hand inside her panties and teasing the curls seated at the top of her mound. Once again their eyes met and the undeniable want and need he showed her was humbling. Never had anyone looked at her with such reverence and *heat*. Lost in his gaze, the slight movement of his hand did not register until the tip of his finger grazed her clit. Her world tilted both figuratively and literally as he rolled them until she was once again on her back and he was lying beside her, his finger tracing the outer lips of her pussy.

She lifted her hips in an attempt to drive his attentions back to the tiny nub of nerves that she knew would bring on her release, but her mate would not have it. The look in his eyes and the grin on his lips said he was enjoying torturing her.

He leaned forward, kissed between her breasts, and nuzzled both of the tender globes, placing kisses on the underside before moving down her stomach. His kisses became deeper and he nipped her skin under her belly button as he worked her jeans farther down her body. Her hips lifted and in the next instant she was completely bare. Any other time in her life she would have been mortified. No one had ever seen her completely naked, not even the very few lovers she had taken over the years. She knew her breasts were smaller than most, her hips too wide, and her belly too rounded, but none of those insecurities came to life. Both dream Kyra and the one living out her fantasy through her dreams were amazed. Royce looked at her like she was a goddess, and for the first time in her life, she felt like one.

Very gently he lifted first one leg and then the other over his shoulders, lowering his body, keeping eye contact, and running his hands up and down her legs the entire time. When he spoke, she could hear what the effort to go slow cost him and she adored him all the more for it. "I have to taste you, *m'a mhuirnin'*. The scent of your arousal is driving me mad."

As he lowered his head, Kyra knew she should feel self-conscious. She had never shared anything this intimate with anyone, but with Royce and in her dream, it seemed perfectly natural to give all that she was to her mate. The first swipe of his tongue against her aroused flesh had her clawing at the blankets and screaming to the Heavens in an unknown language. Her pussy contracted around his fingers as his tongue continued to lick at her like she was the best thing he had ever tasted.

She felt her arousal building as he inserted another finger, stretching her walls at the same time his thumb found her clit. He bent the fingers moving inside her upward and touched the bundle of nerves she had previously thought a myth. Her orgasm hit her like a storm, her pussy clamped tight around his fingers, her legs tightened around his head, and she rode the waves of the most powerful force she had ever felt. He continued to pet and taste until she was lying boneless beneath him, her fingers lazily running through his hair.

He removed first one leg and then the other, kneading the muscles of her thighs and setting off a whole new series of tremors in her womb. The smile that brightened his face was full of satisfaction, and if she was not mistaken, pride. Always the smartass, she teased, "Proud of yourself there, stud?"

Royce chuckled and the vibrations, coupled with the way his chest hair tickled her skin, made her gasp and raise her hips. He winked and his grin turned playful. "Oh yeah, I'm proud," he said as he slid two fingers back into her still weeping channel. Kyra pushed against his fingers and mewled at her renewed arousal, shocked that she could feel anything after what they had just done. But her mate was not to be denied and it felt so good to be joined with him that she rode his hand until they were both panting.

She whined as Royce removed his fingers, but was relieved when she felt the head of his erection at her opening. He pushed forward and stopped just inside. Her hips lifted and her pussy contracted harder and faster, trying to pull him in, but he held completely still. "Look at me, Kyra," once again a command, and once again, she obeyed without question.

"I need to go slow, *m'aonin'*. You are tiny and I will not hurt you." His hands held her hips still and his gaze darkened. "I want you more than my next breath" He breathed deeply and she saw sweat dotting his upper lips as he moved a few inches further inside. She focused on his eyes and could feel their combined strength. In that moment she knew with absolute certainty there was nothing they could not achieve as long as they were together.

He groaned as she felt the head of his cock touch the mouth of her womb. He was buried so deep inside of her, she had no idea where she ended and he began, and she didn't care. The lines between dream and reality blurred. All that mattered was that they were together. Together as they were meant to be, together forever.

"You are driving me absolutely crazy," he said through gritted teeth as he gently pulled out of her only to slowly return. His cock stretched her inner walls, filling her completely. He was a big man on all accounts and every inch of him was hers. Unable to stay still any longer, she fought against his hands on her hips and pulled herself up, nipping at his neck to quicken his pace. When he refused to speed up, she drove her hands into his hair, scratching his scalp as she pulled his mouth to hers. He immediately opened to her and she kissed him with all that she was. She worked her tongue along his, tasting all that he was, then slid it in and out of his mouth showing him what she wanted him to do with the cock he now had buried deep inside her.

His pace quickened but it was nowhere near what she wanted from him. She wanted him to lose control. She wanted him as crazy for her as she was for him. He had said he was, but she needed him to show her. She continued her assault almost to the point of no return when she wrapped her legs around him and lifted her ass completely from the pallet. The change in position pushed him farther inside. Her pussy massaged and gripped his throbbing cock. The light in his eyes turned ravenous as he thrust in and out of her with such force she was sure they were moving across the dirt floor. Nothing mattered but the man loving her as no other ever had. Everything was as the Goddess and the Universe had intended.

They screamed their mutual release to the Heavens and she saw love in the depths of her mate's eyes. A love so pure and true it brought tears to her eyes. She saw his lips move but couldn't make out what he was saying and then her world went black. In the distance she heard an annoying buzz and promised death to whoever dared to interrupt them.

Reaching towards the noise, her hand hit a flat, hard surface. Her eyes flew open and immediately shut again as they were assaulted by the bright light of the morning sun. Slowly, she opened one eye and then the other, looked at the ceiling and then the wall in front of her. She grabbed her cell phone and shut off the alarm, thanking the Heavens for the blessed silence. It was then that reality kicked her square in the ass. She was in her bed in the little cottage Rayne and Kyndel had let her use. It was morning and she was alone. Not in the cave on the side of the mountain by the sea with the man of her dreams. Not making love and letting the world spin on. Nope! The whole damn thing had been a dream. *Well, ain't that fucking grand?* she thought. *Even my dreams are out to get me.*

Unwilling to face the day for at least another thirty minutes, Kyra rolled over and pulled the covers over her head. *Hope is not only a scary bitch, but she really fucking sucks*, was her last thought before her cell phone rang and she was forced to face the day.

CHAPTER FIVE

Royce was sleep-deprived, frustrated and wanted to be anywhere but where he was headed. For the fourth night in a row he had dreamt of Kyra. Crazy, erotic, wake up and relieve yourself in the shower dreams that taunted him throughout the day, reminding him what an epic failure he was. When his phone rang about fifteen minutes ago and Lance had told him they were all being summoned to go over a plan that Max and Kyra had devised, he wanted to scream and throw his phone against the wall, but then decided that would help absolutely no one and he hated putting contacts in a new phone. So he had climbed out of bed, taken his obligatory shower and headed out the door, praying that someone had made a pot of seriously strong coffee. One good thing had come out of his wake up call…he now had confirmation that Max's visit to Kyra's home the day before had been completely 'professional'.

Royce had ended up at her front door after enough discussions with his brothers to last three lifetimes, two trips to see Malachi, daily trips to the Garden of Peace, and just plain missing the friendship he had shared with the mates of his brethren. Left with no options, he had decided to go over and see if Kyra would at least talk to him. He hoped she would let him explain that he was sorry for the things he had said. Pleading insanity had occurred to him if that was what it took to get her to talk to him.

But then he had gotten there and the King of The Big Cats had been with her. Royce had tried to reason that it was all about catching the traitor and the alliance the dragons shared with the werepanthers, and he had turned to go with the intention of coming back later. Then he had heard Kyra's magical laughter and he had walked away, hat in hand, overcome with jealousy. The next few hours had been spent in the gardens behind the little cottage, propped against a tree praying to the Universe for guidance in his journey to seek his mate's forgiveness and attempt to live the life they were meant to have.

Somewhere along the way he had heard a voice he thought gone forever…his mother. Riona O'Reilly had made her presence known in death the same way she had in life, with elegance, grace, and a smack to the back of his big head. At first he had dismissed what he'd heard as a figment of his imagination, but when the voice practically yelled, "Royce Alan O'Reilly, *mo mhac*, do *NOT* ignore me!" he had literally ducked to miss the hit he knew from experience followed those words.

He had looked as far as he could see for all the blooms and found himself alone. He shook his head and thought what a shame it was that somewhere along the line he had lost his mind. After another look around for an explanation of what he'd heard, he settled back to continue his conversation with the Universe and heard the voice again. "I *swear* to all that is holy, you have gotten even *more* hard-headed over the years. I am *still your mother* and you WILL acknowledge me!"

He jumped up, looking for one of the young *vibrias*, sure that Lance had put her up to messing with him. That damn *pain in the ass* was always up to something and it was usually at Royce's expense. After walking the entire garden, he found no one, or even footsteps that indicated anyone but him had been there in the last few days. Sitting on the bench on the other side of the garden, his thoughts quickly returned to his mate and the mess he'd made of things. *"You're a fucking idiot,"* he thought, and knew it was the truth. He was a bone deep, no hope for redemption idiot, with absolutely no legitimate reason for acting like he had. It was like all the crap of the past had been blown away the night he arrived home. Yeah, it had sucked on a level he hadn't experienced in all his years, but it had also opened his eyes to the fact that he was holding onto something that should have been reconciled years ago. All he was left with was the truth that he needed to fix what he had broken and the knowledge that he had no clue how to do that.

The first few days had sucked. He had replayed the look on Kyra's face and all she had said after the heart-wrenching sob that had shredded his heart over and over, every time more painful and exponentially more shameful than the first. He could feel the pain and anguish he had caused the one person in the world that he was supposed to protect above all others, and he found it hard to face his reflection in the mirror. The look of utter betrayal in her vibrant violet eyes haunted him day and night. He felt the vehemence in her words, her complete and total belief that she would never be seduced by the dark, a belief that came from deep inside her soul and resonated in his.

All his other attempts to speak with her had failed. He knew she was avoiding any place he might be. If he showed up and she was already there, she seemed to vanish into thin air. He was sure his brethren were helping her stay away from him, but there was no way he was going to ask. They had just started speaking to him again and he was not going to bring up the subject of his mate to anyone. Best not to poke the dragons. So he had shown up at her door, only to walk away empty-handed and lost.

Lost in thought, he almost fell off the bench when a honey bee had stung his ear. "Ow…Shit…Ow," he howled as he grabbed his ear and then swatted the offending insect. Insects never messed with his kind, recognizing a larger, more lethal predator on instinct, but that little guy hadn't cared. Not willing to leave the solitude of the garden, he sat back down but watched for anymore of the obviously insane bugs. It was then that he heard laughter in the breeze and was sure he felt a kiss right on the spot the bee had stung. It wasn't until he heard the lullaby his mother always sang when he and his brothers were hurt or afraid or just needed a reminder that she loved them more than life itself, that he was sure he had lost his mind, but actually welcomed the insanity.

"Alright *ma'thair*, I give up. You must be here. Either that or we will find out if they make straight-jackets in XXXL."

Once again he heard his mother's laughter and this time it warmed his heart. "Yes, *mo mahc*, I'm here. Just as I promised to be all those years ago, never far from the treasures of my heart."

He felt the tears well up and refused to let them fall. He was dragon, he was a Guardsman, and he was strong. As if his mother could read his mind, she responded, "Yes, you are strong and honest and loyal and everything your father and I ever hoped you would be, just as your brothers are. We could not be prouder of you than we are, but tears do not make you weak, *mo mahc*, on the contrary, they make you strong. They show you have compassion and you of all people, know that."

Not surprised that whatever had allowed his mother to speak to him from the Heavens had also allowed her the ability to read his heart and mind, he answered, "You are right, *ma'thair*. I'm sorry."

"You have no reason to apologize to me. I'm your mother and it's my job in this life and the next to be there for you through the good and the bad. It's your little mate that you should be apologizing to. You have hurt her, Royce, hurt her in a way the sweetling should never have had to endure."

His head fell forward in shame and all he could choke out was, "I know. But how am I to accept a witch as a mate?"

"Did you think that holding on to all that hate and forsaking the one you are supposed to love above all others would honor my memory? Make me proud? Bring me back?"

His mother's words were like arrows being shot one at a time at his heart, each hitting their target with increased accuracy. When he spoke it was through gritted teeth to hold back the need to roar his failure for all to witness, "I don't know what I thought. I have no excuse. It happened and now I wish I could take it back, but that's just not possible. I want to make amends. Tell her I'm sorry and ask for another chance, but she won't even look at me. She even avoids me."

"Like you avoided her and went all the way back to our clan to hide in a cave and lick the wounds you yourself caused?" his mother countered, and he imagined her just the way she had looked every time he and his brothers had gotten caught doing something they shouldn't. Only this time, it was his entire future on the line and his mother's disappointment in him was debilitating in its intensity. Unable to speak, he merely nodded.

"Royce, my love, you have to make this right. You cannot live your life alone and loveless, nor can you condemn that beautiful, vibrant woman to the same fate. She is your match in every way. Kyra was sent to you because the Universe knows you better than you know yourself. She is the answer to all the questions you haven't even thought to ask and she will heal you in ways you can only imagine. My dear, sweet boy, she is the answer to every prayer you will ever pray. So crawl across broken glass if that is what it takes, but make this right for both your souls." He felt the caress of the wind on his cheek, like the kisses he remembered from so long ago, and the tears he had held back wet his cheeks.

"I know you are right and I can feel that Kyra is all I could ever want or need…right here," he laid his hand on his heart. "And I can almost imagine our future together. Then all the memories of that day come flooding back and it is just too much to imagine a life with a witch."

"Royce, you wound me. Your father and I raised you better than that. Is a witch really all you see? You really do not see a beautiful woman, with a heart full of love and the strength to stand by your side no matter what comes your way?"

He could imagine the look of disappointment in his mother's eyes and the way she used to shake her head in disgust. He was just about to speak when she started again, and if possible he felt even worse.

"When have you ever let your head completely rule *any decision*? Why in all of the Heavens would you simply walk away from the source of all your future happiness? Royce, this is simply unacceptable."

The longer he listened to his mother, the more he realized what a complete idiot he had been and *knew* it was something he had to rectify as soon as possible. Riona was right. He had literally turned his back on the greatest gift a dragon shifter could ever receive all because of his own stupid prejudice. Royce only hoped Kyra would accept him after all he had done.

When his mother spoke again, her tone was filled with love and pride. She had heard his thoughts and she approved. "I love you, my son. Now fix this before it is too late," and with those last barely audible words, he felt the spirit of his mother return to the heavens.

He looked to the sky and whispered, "I will, *ma'thair*, I promise I will."

It was a promise he meant to keep, if only he knew how. He knew Lance had made it clear that Kyra would be at the meeting for his benefit, and he was well aware that they would be surrounded by every Guardsmen from both clans and the werepanthers along with the mates if the girls had it their way, so the meeting was not the place to have a personal conversation. He walked along thinking of all the ways he could get her attention and make her talk to him and coming up with absolutely nothing, when he was flanked on either side by his brothers, both sporting shit-eating grins. "You two left the house early this morning. What's up?"

"Nothing," they answered in unison, and he knew they were both lying, but with all he had to think about he let it go.

Rian was the first to break the silence, "So what's up with the meeting? I was talking with Carrick when Rayne called."

"Carrick? What were you talking to him about?" Royce asked, not hiding his concern.

"Can't one Head Elder just talk to another? After all, he has been at this since before we were born and he was one of father's closet friends," Rian replied. Royce could tell there was more to it.

Before he could probe any farther, Rory spoke up, "I see your little witch is in good company today." He nodded towards the entrance to the Grande Hall and there was Max holding the door for a smiling Kyra.

Royce immediately saw red, or maybe it was green, and his dragon pushed for the man to stake his claim and run the mangy cat away from their mate. After several deep breaths, he was able to speak, "She is free to speak to whomever she likes."

"Yeah, you keep telling yourself that, Bro," Rory chuckled and smacked him on the back just as they reached a group of his brethren waiting to enter the hall.

Lance was the first to speak, "Hey, Gramps. How's it going? You coming to training after the meeting?"

"I am," was all he said as the lingering scent of patchouli and rose petals assaulted his senses.

"We have a few that are ready for their Swordsman test. Thank the Heavens you'll be there to administer it," Devon added, smiling like all had been forgiven. Royce knew he had put him in a terrible position when he asked him to look after Kyra and he would be forever grateful for all his brethren had done.

"Oh, yeah? Do we have anyone good?" he asked, trying to think of anything but Kyra, just a few feet away and still ignoring his very existence.

It was Aaron that answered, "There are a few. The others just need more practice. They could really benefit from your sparring."

"Then they shall have it, and I'll bring this useless lug with me," he pointed towards Rory. "He's been known to be handy with a blade. After all, he had the best teacher around."

Royce smiled, just about to give himself credit, but Rian was quicker, "Damn sure did…ME!"

The group erupted into laughter and then Rayne appeared with Kyndel on his arm. "Would you all care to join us inside?"

"Sure," they all answered and followed the Commander.

As soon as Royce spotted Kyra at the front of the room his heart skipped a beat. He was once again amazed at how absolutely gorgeous she was and for the first time noticed the beauty of the aura that surrounded her. It was a spectacular mix of red and orange that reminded him of the sunrise they had shared all those days ago and indicated the depth of her strength, passion, and courage. The longer he admired her, the brighter the white light mixed with the red and orange became, telling him that his mate was in perfect balance with everything within and around her. It was just as his mother had said. She was everything he could have ever hoped for.

His mind reeled with thoughts of how to make her at least talk to him when Max appeared at her side. Royce took a step forward before he was able to get his emotions under control. Of course, it didn't go unnoticed by his brethren. Devon moved to his side and spoke under his breath, "You okay?"

"Yeah, I'm good," he answered, not sure who he was trying to convince.

Thankfully, Rayne appeared at the front of the room and called the meeting to order before anyone else could speak. After explaining all they knew so far, Max spoke and Royce had to continually remind himself to listen and not think of all the ways to skin a cat. When the King yielded the floor to Kyra, Royce held his breath. It had been over a week since he had heard her voice above a mumble from across the room, and he realized in that moment how much he had missed it.

Her voice shook with nerves and her fingers fiddled with the strands of her hair that had fallen over her shoulder. His heart and dragon begged him to do whatever possible to ease her stress. Doing the only thing he could think of, he focused all his energy on Kyra and pushed reassurance, confidence, and the tiniest bit of love through the bond he had only found existed a few days ago. It was weak and fading due to his negligence, but it was the only tie he had to her and the only way he knew to help.

He watched as her shoulders lifted and she stood a little taller. Her voice became clearer and the shakiness disappeared. He could see her searching the crowd for who had helped her. It saddened him that because of his own prejudice and ignorance, she didn't recognize her own mate's energy, but he had no one to blame but himself. He gave no indication it was him and soon she was so engrossed in her presentation that she gave up the hunt. As she spoke, he was filled with pride at how intelligent and intuitive she was, but his pride damn near overflowed during the question and answer session. A younger Guardsman, Jase, asked, "How can you be certain he will perform his ritual on the mountain by Black Lake?"

"I am sure because I lived on that mountain and I know the power the mountain holds, as well as the power of the Black Lake. When the conditions are optimal, as they will be in five short days, the combination of those two places will quite literally glow with power. Now, as I stated, I have no idea what he has planned, but I know he will have to harvest a ton of power to even attempt to take out you behemoths." The room roared with laughter and appreciation at her assessment of the Dragon Guard.

When they settled down, she began again, "I also know he'll want everyone working for him holding as much power as possible, so they will all be in attendance. It's my belief that we will be able to stop him *and* capture him before he can gain the power he seeks, let alone work whatever spell he believes will harm all of you."

The men all clapped at her words and Kyra beamed. He had thought she was beautiful before, but the woman standing before him now was simply magnificent. His need to be near her overrode his common sense and he started towards her. Devon's hand on his shoulder stopped him and he spun around to tell his brethren to 'Fuck off' but Devon's words halted his rage, "You can't go to her here, not now, not in front of everyone. Save it for later."

He sighed and nodded, knowing what his friend was saying was true. Not that it stopped the ache in his heart and soul to go to her, only her forgiveness would soothe that.

The questions continued until Rayne stepped to the front and called their meeting to an end. Royce followed the others towards the door but not before one long last look at Kyra. She was caught up in packing her supplies and unaware of his attention, but he still took in all that he could before he left the building and headed to the training pit. The others' chatter was a buzzing in the background as he thought about his situation and looked for any glimmer of hope or for a way that he could make amends. Luckily, they reached the training area before he had to admit that he had once again come up empty-handed.

He, Rory, and Devon watched all the young Guardsmen for the better part of an hour before pairing off with ones that needed the most help. Their sparring went on until the first glimpses of dusk touched the sky. Tired and in desperate need of a shower, Royce and his brothers headed for home. They had steaks marinating and cold beer in the fridge, and for the first evening since he had gotten home, Royce was going to relax. The Heavens knew that all the problems of the last few days would still be there in the fresh light of a new day. Who knew, maybe a little reprieve was just what he needed to find a solution.

Their steaks had been amazing and they had laughed until the wee hours of the morning. The fresh new light of day shone through the window, and aside from the headache that only came from the three O'Reilly brothers, two fifths of Bushmills, and a case of Budweiser combined, Royce was no closer to an answer than when he had fallen into bed still clothed. He should have been happy that he hadn't had another erotic dream starring Kyra, but in all honesty, he missed it and he knew that made him more pathetic than he was willing to admit.

Standing in the shower and praying for aspirin, he heard his brothers in the kitchen and prayed they were making coffee. Once the water was off, he listened to their conversation.

"Do you think Kyra will come around and forgive Roy?" Rory asked.

"Yeah, she'll come around. No one, even a witch as powerful as her, can resist the pull of the mating call, and I guarantee you the mating call is working on both of them," Rian answered and Royce could tell he was smiling.

"I know, but she is still really pissed," Rory said. Royce could hear the uncertainty in his younger brother's voice that mirrored his own.

"She is and she has every right to be, but did you see her sneaking looks at Roy when he wasn't looking yesterday?" Royce immediately felt lighter than he had two seconds before. Could Rian be right, was she looking at him with something other than a scowl?

"I saw, and I also know he was trying to help her when she was all nervous and fidgety. Do you think she knew it was him?" Royce could tell Rory was smiling now too, and that made him feel better about the mess he had created.

"Nah, she had no clue. For all she does know about our kin, thankfully, there are a few things she is still clueless about." They both laughed.

"I think we need to help this situation along, Ri. I'm tired of waiting and *damn* tired of watching both of them mope around." Rory sounded determined and Royce wondered if it was time to walk out there and shut the gossip session down.

But Rian's response stopped him dead in his tracks, "Already taken care of little Bro, already taken care of."

~~*~*~*~*~*~*

Watching butterflies flit around the garden out the window over the sink while waiting for the coffee to brew was the most restful thing she had done in the last twelve hours. After the meeting with all the Dragon Guard, she had been in a planning session with Max and Rayne until just before sundown. By the time she had gotten home all she had wanted was a huge glass of wine and a hot bath. Over an hour later, well pruned and buzzed, she had fallen into a dreamless sleep. When her alarm had gone off at eight a.m. she'd hit the snooze until it had finally shut off on its own.

She wondered what it would feel like to have nothing more pressing for an entire day than to float on the breeze, land on flower petals, and enjoy the sun on her wings. Butterflies might have the most perfect life ever; or maybe it was cats. Either way, they damn sure had it better than she did. It was becoming harder and harder to stay mad at Royce. She was still hurt and still cringed every time she thought about what had happened, but then she would catch him looking at her and it all kind of faded to the back. Every time their eyes met she could feel how much he wanted to talk to her, see in his eyes that he was sorry, but then he would take a step towards her and she would find an excuse to leave. No matter how pitiful he looked, she was not ready to listen…not yet.

So instead she tried to stay busy every waking minute, even if it meant wondering what it would be like to be anything but what she was or to be anywhere but where she was. The last few drops of coffee dripped into the pot and she grabbed her favorite mug to pour her first cup of the nectar of the Goddess.

Heading to the dining room, she almost spilt her coffee when the ringing of the doorbell startled her. She grumbled to herself as she grabbed the knob. When she saw who had seen fit to make an appearance, her first thought was to slam and lock the door and run and hide under the bed, but she knew it would only prolong the inevitable. Instead, she smiled her sweetest 'eat-shit' smile and used the nicest tone of voice she could muster, "Hi, Mom. How's it going? Long time no see."

Calysta swept past Kyra and sat primly on the very edge of the couch. It had been a long time since she had laid eyes on her mother but not much had changed. She was still tall, thin, and elegant. Her hair might have had a few more silver strands, but for the most part it was still a perfect strawberry blonde and hung past her butt in cascading waves. Her aquamarine eyes shone bright and moved across the room, taking in everything and disapproving of it all with a slight downturn of her mouth and a crinkle across the bridge of her nose. *Some things never change*, Kyra thought as she sat in the chair directly across from her mother.

"So what brings you to my door?" Kyra asked.

In the tone that had always made Kyra want to run screaming from the room, Calysta responded, "Well, darling, if Mohammed will not come to the mountain, the mountain must come to Mohammed."

"So I'm Mohammed in your scenario?"

"Would you not say I have been patient? Twenty-five years seems sufficient enough for you to sow your wild oats or whatever it is you took off to do." Condescension dripped off the Grand Priestess' every word.

Kyra counted to ten in her mind and took a few deep breaths before speaking, and even then she knew she sounded pissed, "Sowing my wild oats? That's why you think I left. At fifty years old, you thought I needed to drink and have sex with strangers to make my life complete?"

"Do not be crude, Kyra. I simply mean that you needed to be free from what you saw as an oppressive situation." Calysta sniffed and Kyra wanted to laugh, but instead waited for her mother to continue. "For the first few years I expected you to show back up, but as time went on I realized you felt the need to punish me."

Kyra really wanted to laugh at the theatrics but it was almost too pitiful to be funny. She did, however, look around to see if maybe some of her aunties were peeking in the windows or had snuck in when she wasn't looking, a performance like she was witnessing was usually not wasted on just one person. But she saw no one and her mother was apparently waiting for her response.

"Mother, we had this conversation the day before I left. I did not leave for any other reason than to live my life the way I saw fit. If you could have seen reason I would have stayed, but as always, things had to be your way."

"I blame this on your human side. If your father had been a wizard none of this would have happened."

Kyra had heard enough, and if her years on her own had taught her one thing, it was that she did not have to listen to anything she didn't want to hear. She calmly stood, walked across to her mother and spoke in the calmest voice she could muster, "Mother, my human side is all that has stopped me from smacking you across the face more times than I'd like to admit." Calysta gasped and feigned fear.

"And that human side you like to criticize is the only reason I was chosen by the Universe to have a dragon shifter as a mate, or did that little fact slip your mind?" She paused to see if her mother would at least try to deny what Kyra was saying, but true to form, Calysta just sat looking regal.

"No, I'm sure it didn't since that was all that really mattered. Admit it, Mother, you had always suspected that I would be the one. I would even go so far as to say that the chance at having a dragon shifter as a son-in-law was the only reason you were ever with my father. Goddess knows you couldn't have what you wanted without a little human in the mix."

Finally Calysta started to speak but Kyra was too angry and still had things she needed to say. "Don't, Mother, just don't. I'm talking and for once you're going to listen. You came to my home uninvited, and did not even have the decency to ask me how I was. Twenty-five years, Mother…twenty-five years and not even a fucking hug or 'how are you' or a 'you look well'? Just some shit about bringing the mountain to Mohammed?" Kyra knew she was screaming and could not have cared less.

"It was always about that damn Prophecy. It was never about me." She paused in an effort to control her temper, but nothing short of throwing her mother out on her ear was going to help.

"Tell me, Mother, why are you here? *Really*. Not some bullshit reason you think I'll buy but the Goddess honest truth. You know I never found the Prophecy. You also have always known where I was or at least the general vicinity. You are, after all, Calysta St Croix. So what is it Mother, what do you want after all these years?"

"I only wanted to see if you were alright. No matter what you think of me, Kyra, I am your mother and I do worry about you. I admit I kept tabs on you but I gave you your space. I let you do whatever it was that you thought you needed to do, but now I think it is time that we come together as a family again."

Kyra knew she was lying, knew it like she knew the back of her own hand, and she knew that she should keep her close just to keep an eye on her, but in that moment it was either make her mother leave or run the risk of snatching every last strand of hair from her head. So she did the only thing she could think of, she marched over to the door, threw it open, looked her mother right in the eyes and said the words she had longed to say for more years than she could remember, "Leave Mother, just go. I do not want to see you or talk to you and as for coming together as a family…I have a new family so there is really no reason for us to see one another again,"

"Now, Kyra, you listen to me," Calysta's voice rose with every syllable, but Kyra was not moved.

"No, Mother, you listen to me…get out." The last two words were whispered with all the venom Kyra could stir up.

Calysta stood in front of Kyra for just a second before storming out and getting into the backseat of her Mercedes, complete with driver. Kyra slammed the door but not before she caught sight of Royce standing at the end of her walk with a bunch of flowers in his hand. *Great! Just fucking great!* she thought as the slam of the door shook the frame. And if all of that wasn't enough, she still had not had her coffee.

~~*~*~*~*~*

After a serious internal debate, Royce had decided that confronting his brothers about their conversation, especially Rian's ominous comment, would only lead to a discussion he was neither ready for nor wanted to have. He appeared in the kitchen like nothing was wrong, had breakfast with his brothers, and finally escaped by telling them he needed to talk to the other men…which wasn't a complete lie.

Royce showed up at Devon's with the full intention of feeling him out for information about Kyra. He knew his friend had taken his request to watch over his mate very seriously and that they had formed a quick friendship that Royce envied more than he was willing to admit.

Devon answered the door with a smile and a knowing look that had Royce laughing out loud. He realized it had been a while since he had truly laughed without the aid of alcohol and felt like a tiny piece of the boulder he was carrying on his shoulders had been lifted. "I guess you know why I'm here?" Was all he had to say before Devon clapped him on the shoulder and invited him in.

"Yeah. Honestly, I'm surprised it took you this long." Devon chuckled. "You want some coffee?"

"Yeah, thanks." Standing in Devon's kitchen, he was suddenly struck with an incredible sense of unease, and realized for the first time in a really long time that he was *nervous*.

His incredibly perceptive friend noticed, too. Handing him his coffee, Devon got right to it, "So what are you gonna do, Bro?"

"Well," Royce chuckled. "I have no idea." Unable to stand still, he began to pace the length of the long galley kitchen, his long legs eating up the distance in only five steps before he had to turn and retrace his steps. "I *fucked up*, Dev. I mean *fucked up* on a royal level, and I have no clue what to do to make her see that I'm sorry and that I've changed. I mean, don't get me wrong, I'm still a work in progress, but I now know that she has an iron will and the inner strength of a Titan. *Hell,* she makes me look like a lightweight and we all know I have some seriously strong convictions. But her determination to do what is right and keep her magic as white as possible is a living force within her."

Devon nodded his head while Royce continued to pace and ramble, everything he had been thinking for the last week and a half pouring from him. "Our bond is growing. I know I kick started it on the ridge that morning, but I'm shocked at how strong it's getting in such a short amount of time. I thought with the lack of contact it would fade, but it's the opposite. There are times I can feel her thinking about me and *damn man*, it makes my freaking day, and then I remember that she hates the very air I breathe and well…you know…"

He felt like he was a young man again, trying to ask a girl out for the first time, only this time it wasn't a trip to a barn raising…it was for *all eternity*. Devon stood looking thoughtful as Royce continued on, "I know I have to talk to her, but how? She avoids me like the plague and looks at me like I'm wanted for mass murder."

Devon barked a laugh, which surprisingly made Royce feel better. He stopped pacing and stood across from his longtime friend. "Dude, she does *not* think you have the plague and as for how she looks at you…well, I think you might be projecting your fears about her anger just a bit." He held up his hand indicating with his thumb and forefinger just a little bit, and then threw his arms wide open. Both men laughed long and hard, a much needed respite from the worry Royce had been spreading while he spoke.

As their levity wound down, Royce grabbed the mug of coffee Devon had poured and headed out the back door to the patio. He sat on one of the large wooden chairs he remembered watching Devon construct, sand, and stain years ago, and thought about all he had experienced and all that was still to come. Deciding to share something he hadn't told anyone, he sighed, "My mother spoke to me the other day."

"I'm not surprised," Devon answered, only confirming what Royce had always known, his friend was the most accepting and spiritual of all his brethren.

"Yeah, she told me to get my ass in gear and do whatever it took to win Kyra back." He looked out over Devon's well-manicured lawn, not really seeing anything, but looking for answers in the landscape.

"She's right, ya' know? Kyra has already started falling in love with you. I can see it as plain as day. Don't get me wrong, she's fighting it. She's still hurt and really not sure she can ever trust you, but she can't help what she feels. Kyra is magical, Bro, *seriously magical,* and Earth witches have their crap to deal with regarding mates and forever and everything. Did you know that she has a tattoo on her right hip that is a damn near exact match for yours?"

Before the last word was all the way out of Devon's mouth, Royce was standing toe-to-toe with his friend, barely containing his rage and snarling, "*How the fuck* do you know she has a tattoo *anywhere* on her body?"

Devon grinned and that only caused Royce to push his chest against his brethren's, an act of aggression among dragons. "Touch a nerve there, *old man*?"

His friend took a step back and it was all Royce could do not to step right back up to him. Grinning, Devon said, "She told me about it. Explained how she's known since her fiftieth birthday that she was to be mated to a dragon shifter. That the mark appears like once every thousand years or so to a white witch the Goddess deems worthy of the honor, and that her mom, the leader of their coven, went *ape shit* when she showed her and tried to run her life, hence the reason she's on her own.

"She also said that a couple days after the mark appeared she had a crazy dream, and when she woke up she thought she was losing her mind, because she knew all these new words she'd never heard before. It wasn't until Lance said one of them to Sam that she realized, she knew what it was. She understands the language of our ancestors."

If possible, Royce felt even worse. Kyra had been deemed worthy by the Goddess herself and fashioned by the Universe just for him and he had pissed all over it by being a dick. To top it off, he had just acted like a total asshole to one of his best friends…*way to go, loser*, ran through his head. "Shit, I really am the lowest form of life. I'm sorry, man. What the *hell* am I gonna do, Dev?"

"You're gonna do what men have been doing since the dawn of time…you're going to grovel, my friend. Beg like your life depends on it because, let's face it….*it does*."

Royce knew Devon was right but he had no clue how to go about it. He was the one that had been doling out advice for most of his life. He'd never had to think about what he would do if the shoe was on the other foot, and now faced with a mess bigger than anything he had ever counseled anyone on, he was lost. His next thought spurred him to action, *but I'll be damned if I give up*.

"Thank you, Dev. I'm going over there right now. I'll camp out on her front porch if I have to."

He headed out the door and Devon's parting words of advice made him smile, "Take flowers, women love flowers."

He ran into the Town Square, as Rayne's mate had named the commerce center of their lair, and grabbed the biggest, most beautiful bunch of fresh cut flowers he could find. Wasting no time, he walked as fast as his long legs would carry him. It was time he and Kyra talked, time to resolve their issues and get on with their lives. If she would only listen to him, he knew he could show her that he had changed and that all he wanted was to share his life with her. The slamming of her front door and the look on the woman's face that exited stopped him dead in his tracks. *Maybe now is not the best time*, he thought.

Royce stared at the door that had just been slammed and then looked at the tail lights of the car making its way out of the lair and wondered what the hell had just happened. Unsure what to do, he walked towards the door, hoping a brilliant idea would just come to him. By the time he stepped onto her porch no such idea had occurred, and he had reached the point of no return, so he did the only thing he could do…he knocked. Waiting to the count of twenty and deciding Kyra was not going to answer, he stepped back and looked around her tiny porch. Not wanting to show up at the training pit with a bundle of flowers, he was just about to lay them on the porch swing when the door creaked open and Kyra looked around the corner.

Her face was flushed with anger and her eyes looked everywhere but at him, but he could still see the fire burning in them. He knew he should have apologized for the intrusion and walked away, but his feet refused to move and his heart was screaming to stay. Not to mention the thousand pound beast with whom he shared his very soul that was doing everything but blowing smoke to let him know that they *needed* their mate.

She spoke, and he let her voice just roll over him, "Did you need something?"

"I wanted you to have these," he said and handed her the flowers.

Kyra hesitated and he was afraid that she would decline his gift but after a few seconds of an inner debate he watched in her eyes, she tentatively reached out and took them from him. "Thank you. They're beautiful," she said, still looking at the bouquet.

As her head tipped forward and she smelled the huge pink blossom at the apex of the arrangement, he wished for the day her lips would be that close to his again. Just the thought brought memories of the brief time he had actually held her in his arms and the many erotic dreams he'd had recently.

He cleared his throat, "Everything okay?"

She looked up at him under her lashes, only accentuating how much smaller than him she was and shrugged, "Doesn't everyone have family drama?"

"Family?" he asked.

"Yeah, that was dear old mom," she answered with so much emotion, he immediately remembered what Devon had told him about their strained relationship.

At a loss for words, he let his heart speak for him, "I'm sorry you had to deal with that."

"Whatever, it's not like I expected anything different. I'm actually surprised she showed up. I was sure I had been officially written off, or maybe that was just wishful thinking." His heart clenched at the sight of her sad smile, and all he wanted to do was hold her until her hurt was long forgotten.

She quickly composed herself. It was like for just a few moments she had forgotten to be upset with him, and he'd had hope, but then a wall had been instantly constructed between them and her eyes became shuttered. Kyra was closing him out and that was something he could not let happen. Throwing caution to the wind, he took a step forward, pleasantly surprised that she didn't move away. "I wanted to talk to you…please?"

He watched her struggle with her decision and prayed to every deity he had ever heard of for her to just give him a chance. When she speared him with her violet eyes his heart skipped a beat and he thought he might pass out, but then she slowly nodded and it beat like he had just run a mile. "Come on in. I need to put these babies in some water," she nodded towards the flowers and reached back to push the door open farther. "Besides, we seem to be drawing a crowd."

He followed her gaze and saw that both of his brothers and more than a few of the Guardsmen were nonchalantly trying to hear their conversation. He shook his head and followed Kyra through the door, vowing to kick Devon's ass for spreading the word of his whereabouts.

Once inside, all thoughts of anything but his mate fled. Her scent was everywhere, making his dragon roll on his back and damn near purr in ecstasy. He looked around the small cottage he had visited more times than he could remember when Rayne had been building the big house. He had even slept on the very couch that still occupied center stage in the living room, but this visit, everything seemed different, brighter, better, just because of the home's inhabitant. Little things that screamed her presence were lying here and there, making it feel warm, inviting, and lived-in.

Kyra headed straight to the kitchen and he heard the water running while she filled a vase for her flowers. He stood in the dining room just taking it all in and picked up a pendant from the table. A large golden stone beautifully bound in copper with a heavy chain attached. The stone seemed to flair to life in his hand. He could feel Kyra's energy and a distinctly feline energy that he could only assume was Max's, but then fading into the background was another. It seemed heavier than the others and dark, but also familiar somehow.

Lost to what he was experiencing, he was surprised when Kyra spoke and he realized she was right beside him, "What do you feel?"

She stared at the stone in his hand and he knew that's what she was talking about but wished it was something much more personal that had spurred her inquiry. "I feel your energy and a Big Cat, Max, I'm guessing?" he slyly asked, trying to keep his jealousy from showing through, but promising himself to talk to the King whenever the chance presented itself.

She nodded and waited for him to continue. "And something in the distance that is dark but familiar." As soon as he heard the words he had only thought moments ago, his old suspicions tried to rise up, but there was no way he was going to blow the only chance Kyra may ever give him to try to make things right. With renewed focus, he looked at her beautiful face, listened to the sound of her breathing, and watched her pulse flutter just beneath the skin at the base of her neck, a spot he wanted to taste almost as much as he wanted his next breath.

She spoke and it was barely above a whisper, but filled with excitement, "You can feel him? Really?"

"Him who?" Royce asked, keeping his jealousy on a tight leash but needing an answer as quickly as possible.

"Andrew. I spelled that Goldstone to work as kind of a tracking device. A way to give me a look at what was going on around him, maybe even show me where he is, but he is using and surrounded by so much black magic that it only takes a little while before I can't read it anymore. I even had Max cleanse it for me using his brand of magic, but that lasted less than a day and then *nada*. But until you said you could feel him, I never thought about the connection of your dragon magic to his." She was excited. It made his heart beat faster to see her eyes light up and he wanted to shout that he had done that, but it was just a tiny step towards his ultimate goal.

"Do you mind if we hold on to it together and see what comes to light?" she tentatively asked, and he could only guess that she was scared of his response because of his earlier recrimination of all things magic.

Wanting to reassure her that he was a changed man and needing to help her, he readily agreed, "Absolutely. What do you need me to do?"

Kyra looked surprised at his eager acceptance, further confirming that he was on the right path. It may not have been going how he had planned, but he was spending time with his mate and she was no longer looking at him like he kicked her puppy, so he was putting it in the win column.

"Take a seat," she pointed to the chair at the head of the table and took a seat next to him. "You're so damn tall, I'm getting a crick in my neck from looking up at you," she chuckled and he laughed along, happier than he had been for a long time.

She lit a candle and set it between them. When she reached for his hand, he braced for the touch he had thought lost to him forever while trying to hide any reaction that would make Kyra turn from him. "Hold the stone in your fist and then wrap your other hand around it," she instructed.

He complied, sad when their connection was broken, but almost immediately, she put one hand on top of his and the other underneath. Her hands were so small they barely covered just the back of his, but the warmth he felt from her touch was unlike any other. His body began to react and he thanked the heavens that his shirt tails covered his growing erection. He had no clue how he would explain that and was sure that she wouldn't find it complimentary.

"Now, focus on the flame and think of Andrew, not the traitor that you want to catch, but the man he was before all of this happened. That is the part I have no knowledge of, the part I can't connect with. I have a feeling he has more dragon magic than he realizes, and if we can use that to tap in, then we can get a better sense of what the little shithead is planning."

He wanted to laugh at what she had said, but her demeanor told him she was dead serious, so he focused and remembered Andrew as he had been when Royce had trained him. How proud Andrew had been to be accepted in the Guard and the incredible bond he and his brothers shared. The bond between the brothers had been as strong as he shared with his own and he wondered if maybe Aidan or Aaron might be able to connect with Andrew better than he, but he didn't mention it out of the sheer need to spend time with Kyra. If he couldn't help her, he would most definitely suggest it, but that was *after* he had done everything he could.

The flame danced and swayed hypnotically as the stone grew warmer in his hands. The longer he watched the more he could make out images in the golden glow, and in the next second, he was able to feel what the traitor was feeling and the bastard was excited. The picture developing in the flame showed a ritual fire surrounded by at least fifty people, some hooded, some wearing amulets that resembled the ones Kyra made, but dirtied by black magic. The group chanted the words Andrew and another man, obviously also in charge, fed them.

Royce caught glances of the area surrounding the fire that only confirmed what Kyra had said. He was planning a ritual on the mountain beside Black Lake. The picture faded from view and Kyra slumped back in her chair, severing their connection before she spoke, "He must have come in contact with more shit magic," she huffed, and it was then that he realized how discouraged she was.

"You should be proud of yourself. That was amazing," he praised.

Kyra's eyes raised, wide and full of skepticism, making Royce chuckle, "No, seriously," he laid his hand on her knee. "You should be proud. You just confirmed what you thought all along…he is going to perform a ritual at Black Lake on the mountain and we can be there to stop him."

He tried to convey the pride and acceptance he felt, and for a moment he thought it might be working, but then Kyra suddenly stood up and walked to the far end of the table. "Thank you for helping me with that, but given your dislike of all things magic, I'm sure that's not why you're here."

His reprieve was over and she had all her defenses at the ready once again, waiting for him to make a mess of things again, but there was no way he was going to let that happen. He took a deep breath and let his hands fall into his lap, waiting for a just a few seconds and listening to her heartbeat. The rapid beat told him that she was just as nervous as he. Everything in him screamed to do whatever he could to make her feel better. Using the voice he reserved for the mates of his brethren, he began, "I came here to apologize. I know it'll never be enough, and if given the chance, I'll spend every day for the rest of my life making it up to you. I am so incredibly sorry for everything that I did to push you away. I'm a complete and total idiot. It's the only excuse I have and I know it's like a raindrop hoping to fill the ocean…it will *never* be enough." He stopped and watched his mate, looking for any sign that his words were having the desired effect, but he just couldn't tell.

Desperate to know what she was feeling, he reached through their growing mating bond, only to be smacked in the face with so many emotions and feelings that it took him a minute just to recognize them all. Kyra was swamped with confusion, frustration, anger, disbelief, and a pain that forced the air from his lungs. Just as he was about to pull back, he felt a little touch of hope. It was like a light in the darkness, and right behind that beautiful, warm, glowing light, was the tiniest spark of love. Just enough to let him know there was a chance. A chance that she would forgive him, a chance that she could truly love him, and a chance that the tiny little spark he saw burning deep inside her heart could be stoked and fed until it was a blaze that could not be contained. That was his deepest desire for them and he hoped with all he was that he could make her believe in the possibility of their future as much as he did.

"I know you've been told what happened in my past." She nodded and he saw pity in her eyes, pity that he did not deserve.

"Don't feel sorry for me. It was a long time ago and absolutely no excuse for what I said or how I ran away from you that beautiful morning on the ridge. It happened and I refused to deal with it until now. When faced with the prospect of letting go of my hate and anger, I somehow thought that would also make me give up the memories of my mother. I was wrong…dead wrong. I now have it on good authority that all the great things about her will be with me forever. But that does nothing to change the fact that I hurt you."

He cleared his throat and looked away, needing to find a little balance. In the split second it took him to glance out the window and back to his mate, something became crystal clear…she *was* his balance. She was the one person in existence that could make him feel right, whole…complete. She was all he would ever need. All he had to do was make her believe that he could be the same thing for her.

CHAPTER SIX

Hours later, after Royce left, Kyra grabbed a bottle of wine and a glass and made a beeline for the patio. The sunset, cool breeze, and quiet were just what she needed after that afternoon. It hadn't been bad, really, just filled with so much inner turmoil that she needed to get away from herself. She knew she hadn't given him the answers he was looking for and part of her really, really wanted to. The thought of running into his arms, forgetting all the bad shit and riding off into the sunset had been her go-to thought the entire time they talked. But Kyra lived in the real world and knew that they had issues that had to be resolved before she could ever trust that he wouldn't simply change his mind again and leave her a crazy mess of heartbroken witch. There was *no way* she would survive that again, especially if she let her old friend, Hope, have a foothold in her heart.

She chuckled at her own dramatic flair and took a long sip of her wine. The sigh that followed came from somewhere deep in her soul and personified everything she was feeling. Her head fell back, her eyes closed, and for a few minutes all the worries of the world washed away. A cool breeze blew and the crickets chirped. It was paradise, and then her cell phone rang, shattering her momentary serenity. An unfamiliar number flashed across the screen and she hesitated to answer. The phone ceased its clatter, the silence in the absence of the song "Everything She Does Is Magic" almost deafening. She had made that tune her ring tone so many years ago she no longer remembered the reason for it, but nonetheless, had never changed it.

Maybe it was because I had a mad crush on Sting, she giggled to herself, and then almost dropped her glass of wine when it rang again, same number flashing across the screen. This time she answered right away, "Hello?"

"Kyra, honey, is that you?" The voice, a blast from the past, asked.

"Yes, Auntie Della, it's me," was all she could get out, so shocked that the oldest of her mother's true sisters was reaching out to her.

"It is so good to finally hear your voice, *Little One*." She smiled, remembering the thousands of times she had asked her auntie to stop calling her that and was surprised at the comfort it gave her now.

"Yours too, Auntie," she said as she pictured the round-faced, cherub of a woman that had been her only confidant during her horrible teenage years. Kyra remembered how her watery, light blue eyes would shine with understanding when Calysta had done one thing or another to piss off her only daughter. As the years came and went, it was always Auntie Della that was there with a kind word, sage advice, and a hug. She could have very well been the Grand Priestess, her powers were stronger and better practiced than Calysta's, but that had not been her dream. Della took pride in training and nurturing the young. So early in life, the sisters had made a pact to stand together and carry out their individual duties to the best of their abilities for the good of the coven. And that stood all these many years later. But it did not stop the elder witch from having her niece's back whenever necessary. Kyra knew her well enough, even after all the years they had been separated, to know something was wrong from the tone of her voice.

"What's wrong?" Kyra asked, dispensing with pleasantries.

Her aunt paused and tension poured through the line, "Have you seen your mother?"

"Yes, she was here earlier today," Kyra answered, her suspicions rising. "Why do you ask?"

"Oh dear, *Little One*, I'm sorry. I was hoping to at least give you warning. I only just learned that she had gotten word from the dragons that you were with them."

Unable to contain her shock, Kyra practically yelled, "She WHAT?! What the hell?! From WHO?!" If Royce had anything to do with the impromptu visit from her mother, she would be a widow before she was even a wife.

"Calm yourself, how many times have I told you I do not like that language?" Ever the model of decorum, a throwback to her true generation, her aunt scolded.

Two deep breaths later, Kyra still saw red, but apologized all the same, "Sorry, Auntie Della. It's just that her visit was…well…"

"I can only imagine, sweetheart and I *am* so sorry. If only I could have warned you."

"It doesn't matter now, what's done is done," Kyra said, still trying to calm down. "But I really need to know who contacted Mother, please, Auntie."

"Let me find the letter." Kyra heard the sound of papers being shuffled as her aunt mumbled about messes.

Several tense seconds later, Della came back on the line, "The letter is signed Elder Rian A. O'Reilly, Blue Thunder Clan. But are you not mated to a Golden Fire shifter, dear heart?"

Her blood boiled with the need to kick a certain pompous, arrogant, dragon man's ass, but she vowed to contain her fury until she could get her aunt off the phone. "Long story, Auntie. I'm not mated to anyone yet, and as it stands, I may never be."

"That will not do, *Little One*. You need your mate, just like the flowers need the rain."

She could feel one of Della's philosophical rants coming on, and as much as she had missed her aunt and wanted to reconnect, the only thing that mattered in that second was finding Rian and putting her size five boot squarely up his ass. Using the voice that had gotten her out of more trouble than she could even remember, she said the one thing she knew her aunt longed to hear, "I know you're right, Auntie. I'll do *whatever* it takes to be the dutiful mate and you *must* come to the mating ceremony as soon as the details are set."

Thankfully, her aunt bought her act as she had so many times during Kyra's life. "Oh, Sweetling, you have made this old witch very happy. Know that I am always here for you, *Little One*, you only need call. I love you, my dear."

Her aunt's unconditional love had seen Kyra through many dark times and would get her through more, she had no doubt. "Thank you, Auntie Della, I love you, too."

"Blessed be, *Little One*."

"Blessed be, Auntie."

She barely had the call disconnected before she was in the house, boots on, and heading for the front door, all thoughts of relaxation a distant memory. Rian was about to see what happened when you fucked with Kyra St. Croix. On her way to Royce's home, she regretted not having her aunt read her the entire letter, but then decided torturing it out of Rian would be so much more rewarding.

The door opened before her fist could hit it the third time, a very surprised and smiling Royce stood just over the threshold. The smile slid from his face and his brow furrowed as she nearly spit her words at him, "Where the hell is your asshole brother?"

"You will have to narrow it down a bit. They're both assholes." Any other time she would have laughed at his response, but in that moment it was all she could do to keep from screaming.

"Rian," she growled through gritted teeth.

"He's at the training pit." Kyra spun around and flew across the yard, Royce's yelled "Why?" a whisper in the distance.

She reached her destination in record time and marched right up to the asshole that was the focus of her anger. He smiled a smile she was sure had made many women swoon, but instead of swooning, Kyra punched him right in the stomach as hard as she could. His resulting grunt let her know she had hit her mark. She pulled back to strike again when her fist was engulfed in a much larger hand, that even in her fury she recognized as her mate. The feel of his breath on her ear as he whispered, "I know he deserves to have his ass kicked, but here is not the place," threatened her resolve to kick his brother's ass, but even Royce could not stop her from getting the answers.

Sounding winded, with his hand rubbing where her fist had landed, Rian spoke, "What the hell, little witch? Isn't Royce the one you are supposed to be beating on?"

She started for him again, fighting as hard as she could against Royce's hold, "You stupid, arrogant prick, I'm going to kick your ass all the way back across the ocean."

A crowd was starting to form around them, not that Kyra cared as she prepared her next insult, but before the words could leave her mouth, she was lifted in the air. She heard Royce bark, "Follow me...*now*," at his brother as everything around her became a blur. No matter how many times she had seen the dragon shifters use their enhanced speed, nothing was as cool as riding along, even if she was mad enough to chew nails.

A moment later, her feet touched the ground again and she recognized that they were at least two miles from the training pit, in the middle of the woods. She quickly blinked to gain her equilibrium, and wasn't surprised to see not only Rian, but also Rory standing in front of her. The warmth at her back and the hand on her shoulder said that Royce was at her back, whether just a coincidence or by design. Had she not been so angry, she could have kissed him for standing with her, even though he had no clue why she wanted to kill his brother. Tucking all thoughts of the sexy man behind her away for later consideration, she narrowed her eyes as Rian spoke, "Exactly what has you so hostile this evening?"

Not only was he smirking at her, but his tone was dripping with an arrogance that set her teeth on edge. She got almost a half a step towards him before she was pulled back against Royce's chest and his mouth was once again at her ear, "He's baiting you. Trust me, he can keep this up all day."

Feeling the truth in Royce's words, she cut off Rian's next words and asked, "Why did you contact my mother? In what part of your inflated ego did you think that reuniting my mother and me would do anything but make me want to rip your head off and spit down the hole?"

Before Rian could respond, she felt Royce tense behind her and his chest vibrated against her back as he spoke, "Is it true, Ri? Did you contact her mother?"

"I did," he responded with no remorse.

"What *exactly* were you thinking?" Royce asked, before she had a chance.

"Well, dear brother, I was hoping that bringing her mother here would help with both the magic needed to take the traitor down and your…" he cleared his throat and motioned with his index finger between she and Royce, "*relationship issues*."

Faster than she could track, Royce was out from behind her, had punched Rian in the face, and was standing over him roaring, "What the *fuck* is wrong with you?" Royce reached down and picked up his brother by the front of his shirt, still screaming. "What the *hell* gives you the right to put your arrogant ass in the middle of everyone else's business? Get a damned life of your own and stay the hell out of mine and…" he pulled Rian until their noses touched and snarled, "Leave. Kyra. *Alone.*"

Rian hit the ground with a thud and Royce stood looking down at his brother as if seeing him for the first time. Rory slowing approached and looked from one brother to the other. "Okay, so now that family counseling session has concluded for today, can we all put our fists away and kiss and make up?"

"Fuck you, Rory," Royce ground out, still breathing like at any moment he might spontaneously combust.

Kyra stood silent, unable to move, taking in the sight before her. No one had ever stood up for her before. Even her Auntie Della had only provided moral support. But there was Royce, the man she was sure she would never forgive or be able to trust, the man that had hurt her more in just a few months than her mother had in fifty years, punching his own brother in the face in her defense. All the anger she had felt moments ago seemed to float away, only to be replaced by a bone-deep fatigue. Royce seemed to sense she was suddenly working really hard just to stay on her feet as he once again took his place at her back and this time, pulled her to him.

Rian climbed to his feet and wiped the blood from his already healing nose and lip while Rory looked like he was watching a tennis match, looking from one brother to the other. The silence was broken when Royce spoke over her head. "Rian, apologize to Kyra," he demanded.

Time stood still. All three brothers looked at one another and she knew that had she not been there, looks would have been replaced by words and punches. As it was, she could feel the violent conversation they were having in mind speak. It almost made her smile to think they were being civilized for her benefit. Several tense moments later, Rian spoke, "I am very sorry, Kyra. I thought I was doing the right thing. As my brother has pointed out, I may have overstepped. I hope you will accept my apology and we can let bygones be bygones."

She had absolutely no idea how to respond. On the one hand, she thought he really was sorry, or at least afraid Royce might just kick his ass. Maybe being the Head Elder had made him soft. But on the other hand, he had brought her mother back into her life and she knew that was not something that was going to just go away. Twenty-five years was all the reprieve she was going to get.

"I accept your apology, Rian." There was so much more she wanted to say, but simply did not have the energy.

Rian and Rory walked away, talking about training and plans for their return home, while she was perfectly content to stay right where she was, cocooned in Royce's warmth, surrounded by his incredible strength. His stubble tickled the outside of her ear and his breath caused goosebumps to rise on her arms as he whispered, "I better get you home, *a chumann*. It'll be dark soon and I still have to meet with my Force."

"And I'm so tired I might fall asleep standing here," she chuckled.

"Well, let me make it easier for you," and with that, he lifted her up and they exited the woods the same way they had entered.

When they got to within a hundred yards of her home, Royce set her on her feet and took her hand. She was surprised at how natural it felt to walk hand in hand with the man that occupied her every dream, and the constant electrical current that flowed between them had her wet and needy by the time they got to her front door. "Here you are, safe and sound," he said, his voice sounding lower and rougher. It made her smile to know that she affected him just like he did her.

"Yep. Thanks for everything. Sorry if I embarrassed you earlier…"

"Stop right there," Royce interrupted. "You had every right to come after Rian. He was wrong and deserved a hell of a lot more than he got. I'm sorry I hit him before you had the chance. Years of history between brothers got the best of me." He dropped her hand and slowly moved his hands up and down her arms, leaving little electric shocks along the way.

"The only reason I moved the conversation away from the clan was because my brother is used to being in charge and loves an audience. If you had confronted him in front of the other Guardsmen, he would've played it up and you never would've gotten the apology he owed you."

No matter how hard she tried to hold it in, she yawned, and was immediately embarrassed. Royce laughed low in his throat, and as she tried to turn away, he captured her chin between his thumb and forefinger. He leaned down until they were looking into one another's eyes. "Please don't hide from me," he whispered and looked at her like she was the only thing that mattered in the world.

Time stood still and he leaned forward until their foreheads touched. "You need your sleep and I have to get to Rayne's." He kissed her on the forehead, his lips lingering and making her wish for more.

He straightened up and smiled the most beautiful smile she had ever seen, and somewhere deep inside, Kyra knew it was just for her. "Go on, get some sleep and I'll see you tomorrow." He turned her towards the door and stood waiting as she opened the door and walked inside.

"Night, Royce."

"Night, *mo chroi*, sweet dreams, Kyra."

She shut the door while he stood watching, and waited as she listened to his footsteps move farther and farther away from the door. *He really is trying to show you that he wants to be forgiven*, she thought to herself. She got her shoes off before she fell into bed and had the best dream of her life.

~~*~*~*~*~*~*

Royce walked home as the first light of the morning sun shone through the trees, more pissed than he could ever remember being. When Rayne and Rian had decreed…not suggested, not discussed…just decreed, that Aidan and Aaron would accompany Kyra to place the amulets around the mountain the night before the full moon, he had lost his mind. He knew she had been working extremely hard to come up with a way to capture Andrew with minimum harm, further proving to Royce that she would never hurt a living a soul without extreme provocation, because if there was anyone that needed to be 'harmed' to within an inch of his worthless life, it was that lowlife traitor.

At first, he had tried the politically correct approach and had said that Kyra and his brethren would need back up. Both leaders had agreed and then promptly assigned the task to Kellan, Brannoc, Lennox and Pearce – the Commander and the three oldest and best Guardsmen from Rian's clan. Royce knew all of the men, had fought beside them, and had it been any other situation, he would have felt they were more than capable. But this was Kyra's safety they were talking about, and he was not willing to leave her wellbeing to anyone but himself. Even the promise from Kellan that they would leave their connection open, allowing him to monitor every moment that Kyra was out in the open, did little to calm his ire.

The debate had waged on until Rayne announced the conversation over. It was the first time in over a hundred years that he had wanted to inflict pain upon his friend and Commander. As he had tried to make his escape, Rayne had stopped him to explain, "I know you're pissed, old friend, and no one understands more than I, but with all that has happened between you and Kyra, I need for you to stay behind. I can tell you from personal experience that you will forsake all others to protect her, now more than ever, and you will not be able to focus on anything else. If I had it to do all over again, I would have had someone else protect Kyndel."

Rayne's explanation had only served to add insult to injury, so when Aidan joined him on his walk home, Royce was less than cordial. "I'm not in the mood, 'A'."

"Yeah, I know, you're just letting that shit fly all over. Which with your ability to put your emotions on lockdown is really saying something. Grace just told me she can feel your anger. That's why I came this way. I can only imagine the others can too and trust me, I understand. I know you don't want to hear this, but I agree with Rayne. If I had it to do all over again, I would have let someone else protect Grace. *Hell*, I did! And when the shit hit the fan, I thought I could do better and took over and we all know how that turned out." Royce could feel the remorse his brethren still felt from all his mate had suffered, but Royce was still pissed.

They walked along in silence for a few moments, only to be joined by Aaron. "What's up?"

"Not a fucking thing, Aar," Royce snarled.

Aaron threw his hands up in mock surrender and chuckled, "Alright big guy, I get that you're pissed, but you know that 'A' and I aren't gonna let anything happen to your girl. And the cast of Highlander has our backs, so we got this shit covered." Aaron laughed at his own joke and Royce recognized it for what it was…his brethren's attempt to lessen his worry, if only that was possible.

He continued to walk, and before too long the twins thankfully said their goodbyes. As he made his way through the trees that provided his home with extra privacy, he saw Devon sitting on the steps leading to his front door, with his elbows propped on his knees and his head in his hands. Royce knew his friend sensed his presence long before he had been able to see him, so he spoke as he crossed the front lawn, "I'm not in the mood for company, Dev."

"Yeah, everyone within a fifty mile radius knows you're not in the mood, but I need to talk to you," Devon responded and rose.

Royce entered his home, assuming his friend would follow, so he wasn't surprised when his voice sounded right behind him. "I just came to apologize." Royce turned to face his friend, completely confused by his Devon's declaration.

"What the hell do you have to be sorry for?"

"You asked me to take care of Kyra and I tried, but now I'm gonna be stuck here with you while she leaves the lair," Devon answered, and Royce could feel his friend's remorse, which went a long way to cooling his temper.

"Don't worry about it, dude. Not your fault," Royce consoled.

Devon shook his head, "I should've seen it coming. She mentioned she had come up with a magical answer that she was sure we could use to capture the douchebag. Now that they have the amulets crafted, Kyra and Max are sure that the familial bond the twins share with the traitor will help her activate the spelled charms without Andrew being able to detect them."

Royce scoffed as he handed Devon one of the beers he'd gotten from the fridge, "Yeah, that Cat and I are gonna have a serious conversation just as soon as he shows his mangy face, and I don't give shit if he's the King or not."

"I hear ya, just be carefu. They *are* allies and all that happy horseshit."

The two men drank their beers and stood on Royce's front porch watching the sun rise, both lost in thought. It was Devon that broke the silence, "All you have to do is make it twenty-four hours, Bro, and then you'll at least be in the same vicinity as your mate. I think you lost your mind before Rayne explained that 'A', Aaron, and Kyra will set the amulets while Rian's Guard watches their backs. Then Kyra will be tucked away in Sam's old house that has been warded against everything anyone knows a ward for, until we all get there right at dusk. As soon as the useless waste of space crosses the perimeter that Kyra's bespelled amulets have created, he will be contained on the mountain. Then we kick ass and take names, something I have waited far too long for, what about you?"

"Yeah, but that is a helluva a long time for Kyra to be almost seventy miles away from me.... seventy miles that I will have to race across if anyone dares try to hurt her."

Devon slapped Royce on the back and headed down the stairs, "I am liking the change in you. Have faith, old man. She lived on that damn mountain, knows it like the back of her hand, and is small enough to hide in places no one else will even think to look. It's all gonna be okay. You two are working through your issues. Not even that demented piece of shit is gonna stop what you and Kyra are building."

Royce sighed and hoped that everything Devon had said was true. There was *no way* he was going to let anything happen to his mate, not after he had finally found his way to her. He reached through their link and calmed the moment he felt her resting peacefully on the other end.

"I need a couple hours of sleep and you should get some, too. Kyra will be here until late afternoon, so you'll have time to see her before they go," his friend said as he disappeared in the trees.

Sleep? Was he serious? Royce thought as he headed back into his home and started the coffee maker, wondering how he was not going to lose his mind while Kyra was out of his sight.

He knew the second Kyra awakened and fought the urge to race to her. To keep his mind busy, he entertained the thought of using whatever means necessary to make her see that she would be safer staying right where she was, but knew that she would never do that. She had a score to settle with the traitor, the same as everyone else he had hurt, and Royce could not deny her the chance to bring him down.

Royce spent the better part of the morning and most of the early afternoon training and sparring. It didn't keep his mind as busy as he would have liked, but it kept him busy enough that when Sydney yelled from the side of the training pit that lunch was ready, he was surprised at how long he had been at it. "Royce, come on. Mom says lunch is ready and you better hurry," her little giggle made him smile. The blonde-haired blue-eyed beauty was one of the only people that could make him smile, even in the darkest of times.

If someone would have told him six months ago that Lance, the biggest pain in the ass of his Force, the man that swore he would be a bachelor until the day he died, would have a wife, an almost six year old daughter, and be the picture of domestication, he would have called them a liar. But it had all happened and Royce could not be happier for him. "I'm coming, Syd. Let me put the swords away and wash up, and I'll be right there."

"Okay, but Mom says if you don't get in here, I get your cookies."

"I did not say that, little missy," added Sam, her adopted mother and beautiful mate of his friend.

'Mom," Sydney giggled. "I was trying to get him to hurry. I'm hungry and those cookies are calling my name."

"Take your time, Royce," Sam called to him and then lifted her daughter onto her hip. "And as for you little girl, veggies before cookies."

He listened to them laugh as they went back into the house, and he wiped down the blades that had been left and put them away before washing his hands and face and heading to lunch.

Royce had barely gotten one foot in the door before Sydney flew at him from her seat at the table. He picked her up and swung her around, mesmerized by her laughter, and thought what a miracle it would be to play with his own children one day very soon. Sydney's hand on his face brought him back to reality. "Whatcha smilin' about, Royce?"

"Just thinking what a cutie you are and how lucky I am that you're my girlfriend."

Sydney giggled, "I'm not your girlfriend, silly old dragon. Kyra is. And she's gonna be your wife soon, but first you gotta help her."

"Oh, you think so, do you?" Royce said while he put Sydney in her seat next to the window and spoke to Sam through the mind speak of their clan, *"How does she know anything about Kyra and me, and what is she talking about 'me helping her'?"*

"We might as well talk out loud. She can tell when we are talking like this and is almost to the point that she can listen in," Sam answered while bringing hamburgers, fries, and fresh cut vegetables to the table.

"Sydney, honey. Royce wants to know how you know about him and Kyra."

Royce sat down next to the sweet girl and helped her get her food while she explained, "Sometimes when I'm just playing or reading or goofing around, I get pictures in my head. Mom and Dad said it's cause I'm special," she crinkled her nose and Royce could not resist the urge to give her a little peck right over that crinkle, and was rewarded with another of her sweet giggles.

"Well, they're right, Sydney girl. You are about the most special girl I've ever known."

Sydney rolled her eyes, "You really are a silly old dragon." She got up on her knees and held his face between her hands, "But I love you any way." And she kissed him on the tip of his nose.

His eyes watered and he noticed Sydney's show of affection was having the same effect on her mom. He choked back his emotions, helped the little darling sit back down and asked, "So tell me what you saw about Kyra and me?"

"Well…you guys were walking and talking and holding hands. Then," Sydney scrunched her face and put her napkin over her face before whispering, "You guys were kissing…yuck."

Sam and Royce laughed and that was when Lance walked in, "Now, that's not fair. Y'all are having a party without me."

Sydney jumped off her chair and ran towards him screaming, "Hey, Daddy!"

Lance grabbed his daughter and kissed her on both cheeks while she giggled on and on. When the laughter died down and everyone was once again seated at the table, Lance asked, "So, what was so funny?"

Sydney was the first to answer, "I was telling Royce about Kyra and him and I told him I saw them kissing." She shook her head and added, "Ewwwww…just like you and Mommy kiss sometimes."

Everyone laughed and finished filling their plates. Lunch conversation was kept light, but as soon as the dishes had been cleared away, Sydney headed out to play on the swings and Royce asked, "I guess her abilities are getting stronger, huh?"

"They damn sure are, but at least for the moment they are limited to people she knows or people she has met. Siobhan found an old Prophecy that talks about *the vibria born of human parents and the last female born of two dragons lost in plain sight.* She's sure Syd is the first and has an idea that Emma, the girl who owns the jewelry shop, is the other, but the old book she found it in was damaged and that's all she knows. She has talked to as many Elders from as many clans as she could and is still contacting more. What she knows so far is that they all thought it was just a myth, a story told by the campfire, and that it has anywhere from three to five different parts involving at least three different species of magical beings. Who knew when you told me Sydney was special when we first rescued her from Andrew, how special she really was?"

"Well, *shit*! I'm not sure if I should say congratulations or run for the hills," Royce laughed, mostly because he had no clue what else to do.

It was Sam that answered and her face showed the truth in her words, "Sydney is our miracle, and whether she is part of some grand plan or just the most beautiful little girl that ever walked…we love her with all our hearts." The couple grasped hands and smiled. Royce really was happily surprised at what a difference six months and two wonderful ladies had made in his friend.

But the smart ass he had known forever was still lurking right below the surface and always ready to give him a hard time. Looking at his watch, Lance remarked, "Don't you need to be seeing about a witch, my brother?"

Royce looked at the clock on the stove and swore, *"Dammit,* I sure as hell do." He stood, clapped Lance on the shoulder and kissed Sam on the top of the head before thanking them both for a great meal. He yelled his goodbye to Sydney, hopped the fence, and ran across the pasture to the little house Kyra was staying in, looking forward to seeing his beautiful mate before she left the safety of the lair.

He had never been happier to find someone home alone as he was when he reached out with his senses right before he opened the gate leading to Kyra's front door. He was just about to knock on the door when it opened and a pink-cheeked Kyra was standing, glaring at him with her hands on her hips. "I wondered if you were going to at least come and say goodbye. Cut it kind of close, didn't you?" To further drive her point home, her little bare foot tapped against the floor.

Unable to resist his beautiful mate one second longer, he lifted her until he could look into her violet eyes and slammed his mouth to hers. She opened immediately, and as their tongues met, he felt the sensations ripple throughout his entire body. Her petite hands gripped his shoulders and her muscular legs wound around his waist.

There had been a time he had worried about their height difference, but all those fears floated away when he felt the perfection of Kyra in his arms.

The longer they kissed, the faster his heart beat and the harder his cock pushed against the zipper of his jeans. He lifted his foot to slam the door shut, with plans to relieve her of every stitch of her clothing, until a wolf whistle sounded behind them. As quick as his enhanced abilities would allow him, he placed Kyra's feet on the floor and spun around to face his brethren. "Sorry, Bro, did I interrupt?" Aaron grinned as Royce groaned. He had been so wrapped up in Kyra, he hadn't even sensed his brethren's approach.

"Not at all," he grumbled and Kyra appeared at his side, smirking. *Damn*, if he didn't love her spunk.

"Come on in, Aaron," his mate called over her shoulder as she turned, grabbed his hand, and headed into the house. "Just made some iced tea for the road. It's in the fridge. Gotta finish packing and then I'll be ready to go."

Royce's good mood evaporated as he thought about the long hours they would be separated. *"You better keep her safe or I promise I will kick your ass,"* he sent directly into Aaron's mind.

"No worries, lover boy, I won't let anyone or anything harm a hair on her pretty little head," Aaron answered and Royce could hear the grin in his voice.

"You just worry about keeping her safe, I'll worry about her pretty little head...and everything under that, too.

Aaron laughed long and loud through their link as Royce grumbled, *"Too many damn brothers...and they all think they're funny."*

CHAPTER SEVEN

Everything that could be done was done, everyone that was going with them knew their orders forwards and backwards. All he had to do was wait twenty-four more hours and he would be on his way to the mountain. In theory, the ritual they were working was simple, but if after all he had been through in the last seven years had taught him anything, it was that nothing ever went off without a hitch, especially where those fucking dragons were involved. And with Kyra working with them, he had to be even more vigilant.

Master Eaton's insistence on going along also bothered him. Andrew was pleased with the addition of power but leery of the Head Wizard's motives. Andrew had seen the sidelong glances and heard the whispering that stopped the minute he entered a room. Andrew smiled, happy for the return of his enhanced hearing and the great fortune that none of the idiots he was working with had any clue who or what he really was. *Hell*, they still hadn't figured out that the warriors they had encountered on their mission across the sea had truly been the elusive Dragon Guard, and he was happy to let them live in their ignorance. He had tried to explain but the ignorance of those around him knew no bounds.

He hated putting all his eggs in one basket, but when this plan had come to him in a dream, he knew it was the only way he was going to have the revenge he so richly deserved. He would amass an almost limitless amount of power, as would the chosen of his followers. Of course, it might leave them little more than mindless zombies afterwards, since they were only wizards and did not have dragon magic to counteract the damage of the powerful dark magic combined with the evil ritual required to extract Earth magic and twist to his will, but that was a chance he was willing to take. He had taken steps to protect John, his assistant, the only one that mattered at all to him. The dark magic practitioners would hold the power for just shy of a day, from the time the Blue Moon was high in the sky until the next night when they would flood the entire lair of the dragon shifters that had betrayed him with a spell that would leave them helpless, ripe for the killing. It was then that he would go from house to house relieving each member of the MacLendon Force of their heads, saving his dear brother Aidan, the worst offender of them all, for last.

Andrew chuckled to himself as the words of the spell repeated over and over in his mind. He meticulously went over his plan…he would work the ritual that allowed them to absorb the magic of the moon, mountain, and lake, combined with the 'Blood of the Unknowing' as the grimoire had called it. It was one of the oldest incantations he had ever seen and had taken him weeks to translate. The Spell of Soul Destruction was one he had planned to use over and over, for it could be placed on its intended victims with little to no power if the magic practitioner wanted the person to slowly fade away and die a gut-wrenchingly painful death. In some ways, Andrew wished that was what he could do to his brother. However, he had suffered a few setbacks and things up to this point were taking way longer than he wanted. He was opting for the full power version that would stun all in its path, leaving them mindless and ready for death. He had added his own special touch ensuring that the men would be hit the hardest of the clan.

The mighty Golden Fire clan would be left without their precious Dragon Guard to fade into obscurity. He would then come in and build his own clan. One that was not afraid to take what the greatest predators of the world deserved….*everything*. His thoughts churned of all he would do when the untraceable phone in his pocket vibrated, drawing him from his visions of grandeur. John's message was simple, *Confirming tomorrow night. Four total. Supplies located.* Andrew's smile grew. His second in command continued to exceed his expectations and as soon as Master Eaton and Mr. A were eliminated, he would bring John out of the shadows. The young wizard had more than earned Andrew's trust and a place at his right hand.

The phone he used for everything else rang in the next minute. The name on the caller ID made his skin crawl. Mr. A, the human crime boss, was calling. One of the worst human beings he had ever had the displeasure of meeting, and definitely only a means to an end. Andrew looked forward to the day he slit the mobster's throat. He calmed his thoughts and cleared his throat as he answered, "Good Morning. I trust you slept well, Mr. A?"

"Yes, thank you, I did," the crook's smoke-roughened voice slid through the phone like a snake, slippery and sneaky, and made Andrew's skin crawl. "I was just speaking with Master Eaton and he assured me everything is set for tomorrow night. I'll be in Vegas awaiting your call when all has been accomplished."

Andrew took a deep breath, holding back what he truly wanted to say and replied, "As you wish."

"I understand it will be another twenty-nine days before we can execute the next step?" the mob boss asked. Andrew knew he was only checking to make sure both he and the wizard master were telling the same story. What neither of them knew was that they would be dead long before the next full moon…by Andrew's own hand, but that was a surprise for another time.

"You are correct," the traitor answered.

"Excellent. I will leave you to it then and look forward to speaking to you tomorrow evening." Not waiting for a reply, the thug hung up. Andrew knew it was just one of the little power plays he used to keep up the illusion that he was in charge, an illusion Andrew was going to enjoy smashing almost as much as he was going to enjoy destroying the dragons.

~~*~*~*~*~*~*

Royce watched as Kyra, Aidan, and Aaron drove away, a feeling of complete and utter dread settling in his gut. The Blue Thunder Guardsmen, following in a second SUV, gave him a little more reassurance that things would be okay until he could get there. He had grilled his brethren while Kyra packed, until they both had threatened to gag him, tie him up, and dump him in the stables until they were long gone. He had stopped, but still worried that they would not be able to keep her from getting hurt. Grace touched his arm before speaking, "Now you know what we go through every time you guys head out without us. Sucks, huh?"

He knew she was trying to take his mind off being away from Kyra and it had worked. "It sure does," he chuckled.

"Wanna come to the house for something to eat? Kyndel, Jay, Sam, and Sydney are coming to keep me company, and I'm sure their husbands will not be able to stay away for long." She laughed and Royce was reminded how well she and Aidan worked as a couple. Just another reminder that the Universe knew what She was doing, something he had doubted before, but now knew was a hard and fast truth.

"Thank you so much, Grace, but I'm gonna head back to the house," he touched her hand that was still on his arm.

"Well, you know where we are if you change your mind." The beautiful attorney turned and walked in the direction of the home she and Aidan used when they were at the lair.

Royce stood staring in the direction his mate had traveled, sending a prayer to the Heavens that she would be okay until they were reunited. He knew they were a long way from reconciliation, and that he was the only one to blame for their issues, but if the kiss she had given him before Aidan had interrupted was any indication, then there was hope.

Heading towards his home, he reached through their fragile mating bond. It was already becoming second nature to constantly check on her and he was sure she was feeling it too. He had entertained the idea of explaining the bond to her, but then decided it was still too early. Because of his ignorance and hate she didn't trust him yet, and knowing that they could feel what the other was feeling, and in some cases get glimpses of what the other was seeing, might be more than she was ready for. It made him smile to remember how much more at ease she had been around him earlier in the day. They had even joked about all her magical supplies and her significant lack of anything but blue jeans and boots when she was packing.

He had caught her sneaking looks under her long, full lashes, and more than once had stopped himself from finishing what they had started before Aaron had so rudely interrupted. Nothing could have prepared him for the way she kissed him right before she left. He had been leaning down to pick up her bags when she snuck under his arm, grabbed his face and laid her full, perfect lips to his. As she poured more passion and affection than he could have ever imagined her small frame was able to hold, he had been completely lost to her. That one kiss made him believe that no matter how long it took, she would find her way to forgiving him and they would be together.

Royce puttered around his house until he was ready to scream. There were only so many things he could do to distract himself from constant thoughts of Kyra in harm's way and him too far away to be of any use. He wandered out to his patio and watched the last sliver of the sun disappear behind the mountains in the distance. His thoughts returned to Kyra for the millionth time. He knew they would have arrived at Sam's cottage within the last thirty minutes or so, and that his mate and brethren would be heading towards the mountain to place the amulets. Before he knew he had moved, he was about a mile into the woods behind his home heading in Kyra's direction.

He had no clue how long he paced along the tree line before reaching through the mating bond once again. Kyra was concentrating and he could hear the words of the Perimeter Binding Spell repeating over and over in her mind. The touch of Aidan and Aaron's dragon magic caused his beast to growl with teeth bared and paw the ground in his mind, ready to stake his claim. Royce pushed back with all his strength, persuading his dragon that the magic he felt was no threat, but friendly. When his beast was finally pacified, Royce focused on his mate again and was immediately worried. She was tired and beginning to doubt that she could do what needed to be done. Without a second thought, he poured strength and confidence through their link, just as he had when she had spoken before the Guard days earlier. His heart soared when she accepted what he gave her without reservation, and he knew that somewhere in her heart, she knew it was him.

He stayed connected until he could feel that she was almost finished and only moved away from their connection when Devon spoke directly into his mind, *"How ya holding up, old man?"*

"I'm okay. Just trying to keep busy."

"I hear ya'. Want some company?" Devon asked.

"Nah. I'm good. I think I'm gonna watch an old western and turn in early. Thanks though." Royce absently responded.

"Alright, holler if you need anything. Catch ya in the morning."

"Thanks, Bro. See ya then," Royce said, and ended the conversation.

Iced tea in hand, he settled into his recliner, grabbed the remote, and started his favorite John Wayne movie. The movie picked up right where he had left off the last time he'd watched. He looked on as The Duke slid off his horse, sauntered towards his leading lady, and kissed her passionately. It was the last straw, Rayne had told him to stay away while Kyra was working her magic, but Royce was sure she was finished and tucked away in the safety of Sam's house. The night was cloudless and darker than usual, dark enough to hide a thousand pound dragon in flight. Before he could talk himself out of it, he was out the back door and in the clearing beyond the trees. He called forth his dragon and took to the skies, using a small amount of his magic as added precaution against detection. Rayne would forgive his need to be with his mate, but not even his longtime friend would keep the Elders from punishing him if he were seen.

Seventy miles by dragon flight was over in less than forty-five minutes. He landed deep in the woods between the house and Black Lake, quickly transforming from dragon to man. Almost halfway to his mate, the sounds of paws on the forest floor sounded behind him and the scent of panther filled his senses. Standing still, he waited until he felt the telltale magic of transformation and then turned to find Juan Carlos, Max's lieutenant, looking less than thrilled to see him.

His patience already pushed to its limits, Royce spoke, "When did you guys get here? Max around?"

Juan Carlos' rough Latin accent reached his ears, full of judgment and criticism, "The King will be along tomorrow morning. We've been here about fifteen minutes. The dragons are guarding the right side and front, we took the back and left. I was told you would be coming tomorrow with the others."

"Plans change."

For one of the only times since Royce had met the werepanther, he grinned. It was just for a few seconds before resuming his serious demeanor but it was progress. "Well, you better get to your mate before your clan knows you're here. You did a good job hiding your entrance but you know everyone is on high alert waiting for the traitor and they are gonna sense your presence sooner rather than later."

"Thanks."

Without an answer, the man turned back into the panther and disappeared into the woods. Royce shrugged and ran as fast as he could until he reached the sliding glass doors that led to Kyra. Using his enhanced strength he popped the lock on the door, and using a broom and a landscape brick he picked up off the deck, secured them once again as soon as he was inside. He followed the sound of the shower to the second floor and found Kyra in the bathroom.

Steam and the scent of patchouli and rose petals poured from the entrance, called to not only the man, but the beast. Her voice drifted to him and he chuckled as he realized she was singing 'That Old Black Magic'. Even when he was running from her he had loved to hear her speak or laugh, the sound like a tinkling of bells ever present. Her singing voice was no different; it was beautiful, just like the woman.

He slowly walked towards his mate, not sure she would be glad to see him, just knowing he had to see her. The steam enveloped him and it was as if he was transported to another place and time where only he and Kyra existed. He drew back the curtain and marveled at the sheer beauty of the one the Universe had made for him as the water and suds flowed down her back and over her perfectly rounded ass.

Unable to stop himself, he reached out, letting his fingers trace her spine. He followed a single drop of water, suddenly parched with a thirst only his mate could quench. Kyra spun around and gasped, her hands automatically covering her breasts and the curls of her mound. "Royce..." his name a whisper on her lips as she stood staring.

"Kyra..." was all he could squeeze past the lump in his throat.

Seconds ticked by as they stood staring at one another. As if unable to resist the attraction any longer, they flew at one another. Their lips met with the fire and passion Royce had always imagined would happen when mates came together. Water soaked through his clothes, wetting his skin as Kyra climbed his body, as lost to the intensity of their attraction as he was.

She ripped at his clothes, seeking the contact they both craved. The moment his shirt hit the shower floor and their chests touched, he was lost. The sensation of her satiny skin, slicked by the water against him, broke his resolve to go slow. He could never remember wanting anything as much as he wanted to sink into the warm welcoming heaven that was his Kyra.

Sitting her on the bench at the back of the shower, he ripped the remaining clothes from his body and threw them out of the way. He fell to his knees and looked into the eyes he wanted to look into every day for the rest of his life and all through the next. As hard as it was to wait, he searched her eyes for confirmation that she wanted what was about to happen between them as much as he did. A slight nod was all the encouragement Royce needed. The need to taste her pushed his every movement as he leaned forward and drew as much of her breast into his mouth as he could, teasing her already taut nipple with his tongue until Kyra mewled and drove her hands into his hair, holding him in place as the warm water poured down his back.

 He released her breast with a pop and moved to the other. His hands traced her sides, reveling in every erotic curve and sensual dip. The suds still falling from her long tresses, sliding over her silken skin served as the paint, while his hand worshipped the masterpiece that was his mate, embedding her beautiful form to memory for all time. He kissed down her body, paying extra attention to a cluster of freckles to the right of her belly button. Kyra giggled at the sensation and then moaned as he lightly nipped and relieved the sting with his tongue.

 As his hands made their way down her body, he felt a slight fluttering under his left hand. Pressing every so lightly, he felt it again, and when he lifted his hand he saw a small replica of the dragon he had carried on his left shoulder and arm since his transformation. He ran just his fingertips across the amazing marking and felt it move once again just as Kyra threw back her head and moaned, drawing his attention back to the woman in his arms.

 He pulled her to the edge of the seat and slid first one and then two fingers into her weeping pussy, moving them in and out, curling the tips every so often to just graze the bundle of nerves at the top of her channel that made her tiny nails dig into his shoulders and her legs to close tighter to keep him from ever leaving her warmth. Kyra's breathing became rapid and her moans louder as he moved faster and used his thumb to brush across the tip of her swollen clit. The contractions of her womb drew his fingers farther into her warmth, her juices flowing so freely that he felt them run down his arm. Knowing she was close to completion, he bent his fingers, rubbing her special bundle of nerves on every pass and used his thumb and forefinger to gently pinch her clit.

 Kyra all but jumped into his lap as she screamed her release. He watched in awe at the sheer elegance of his mate, her head thrown back in passion, her neck bared to him, and a flush that only came from complete satisfaction working its way all over her body. His lips found the sensual column of her neck and tasted every inch he could reach while his fingers continued to slide slowly in and out of her still quaking pussy as her orgasm subsided.

 Slowly, she lifted her head and Royce followed the motion by kissing up her neck. He whispered, "You are absolutely breathtaking, Kyra St. Croix," as he kissed the outside of her ear. Before she could answer, he lightly bit her ear lobe causing her to gasp and her pussy to spasm against his fingers still deep within her.

 In one fluid motion Royce removed his fingers from Kyra, stood, and carefully leaned her against the tile, tilting his hips against hers to hold her in place while his hands found her breasts and began kneading her excited flesh. He hissed as the tip of his erection brushed against the curls covering her mound, the sensation threatening to drive him back to his knees. As coherent thought left his mind, he slammed his mouth to Kyra's. He kissed her like she was the very air he breathed, pouring his remorse over his actions of the past, his belief that they were meant to be together, his faith in her as a person and a witch, and the growing love he felt for her and her alone, into that one kiss. It seemed to go on forever and the need to be buried deep inside his mate grew, like a wildfire fueled by the love and passion of the ages. Their love had already overcome so much and he had faith that it was one of the strongest forces in the Universe. The lure of the little witch that had captured his heart was unlike any other and would sustain him, nourish him, and let him be the man Kyra needed him to be.

 Pulling back just slightly, he held Kyra in place with his hands as he rolled his hips and let just the head of his cock slide into her wet warmth. The sensation was like nothing he had ever imagined. Kyra's eyes snapped open and he was caught by the intensity of the feelings he saw reflected there. His heart leapt for joy at the heat, passion, and affection he saw, but felt the sadness at her continued pain of his stupidity. He saw the tiniest bit of trust, like a seed trying to take root, and vowed to nurture it until it was vibrant and in full bloom.

 Kyra's legs came around his waist and the familiarity of the action was comforting, but the resulting contraction of her pussy around his cock drove his desire higher and pulled his cock farther into her channel. He slowly pushed forward, feeling her muscles stretch against his size and letting the overwhelming flow of her juices provide lubrication for their passion. When he felt the mouth of her womb with the tip of his erection, they both sighed in unison. He knew deep in his soul that the feeling of complete connection with their soul mate was what they both had unknowingly been searching for all their adult lives. A sense of belonging and completion flooded their mating bond and Kyra's eyes widened.

 The need to move and feel her move against him took over. Holding Kyra steady, he pulled almost completely from her warmth before pushing all the way back in. His slow, steady pace accelerated until he could hear the sound of their passion-soaked skin slapping together and the feel of his mate meeting him stroke for stroke. Their motions became frantic and the second before he lost control, he barked, "Kyra!" Her eyes flew open and their mutual release echoed against the tiles of the shower.

The feeling of being with his mate was like nothing Royce had ever experienced. A feeling of euphoria came over him as he continued to slowly move in and out of Kyra and marveled as he watched her return to earth. When she had calmed, she graced him with a lazy smile, and he let his half-erect penis slide from the haven of his mate.

Afraid he would fall to the ground, Royce stepped back until the shower bench touched the back of his legs and sat down, pulling Kyra to his chest. She curled into him and he could've sworn she purred. He kissed the top of her head and thanked the Universe for second chances. Kyra was a gift, one he would spend his life proving he deserved. He only prayed that she would bestow her grace upon him. He promised with his every breath to unconditionally love her for every second of every minute of every day of this life and the next. His only wish was for all her tomorrows to be filled with nothing but bliss.

The water still poured from the shower and it was then that he realized the steam had diminished. He quickly rinsed the remaining shampoo from her hair and body, feeling truly fulfilled that she let him care for her. He grabbed a fluffy pink towel from the counter beside the shower and wrapped Kyra in it before heading to the bedroom.

Her eyes drooped as she tried to conceal her continual yawns. All the while, he reveled that the lazy smile he had put on her beautiful lips remained. He enjoyed running the soft towel over her enticing curves, making sure every inch of her body was dry. She watched while he quickly dried his own body and then giggled when he lifted her with one arm while throwing back the covers with the other. He positioned himself sitting up with his back touching the headboard, his legs stretched out in front of him and Kyra curled in his lap, keeping as much of their skin to skin contact as possible. As he pulled the covers over them, he felt her tense and then begin to speak, "Royce..."

He laid his index finger to her lips and whispered, "Shhhh, there will be plenty of time to talk later. Get your rest. Tomorrow's a big day. Let's just enjoy being right here, right now...*together*."

Kyra sighed and her breath tickled the hair on his chest. As she snuggled closer against him, for the first time in his very long life he understood what it meant to be truly at peace.

~~*~*~*~*~*

The sound of voices and the smell of coffee had Kyra opening her eyes, even though all she wanted was to curl up against Royce and stay in bed for maybe another a week or two. She stretched and smiled as she felt little aches that only came from being well-loved. Debating whether she should move or not, she let her eyes slide closed, only to pop open when a low, smooth voice that made her body tingle sounded from the vicinity of the door. "Good morning, *cailin 'alainn*. Did you sleep well?" Royce sat down next to her as he spoke.

She rolled to her side facing him, and nearly purred, "Yes, very well." As she inhaled, the scent of fresh air and sunshine filled her senses. The thought of running her nose up and down his exposed thigh, just to have that scent embedded in her very soul, crossed her mind. Her cheeks flushed with embarrassment.

Royce chuckled and asked, "What were you just thinking?"

Instead of answering, she asked, "Why?"

"The look on your face was pure delight and the way your cheeks blushed told me that it was definitely a thought I would like to make a reality."

A nervous giggle flew from her lips as she rolled to her back and pulled the comforter over her head to hide from Royce's incredibly perceptive gaze. The mattress moved as his leg brushed the blanket, and in the next second, she was looking into the same deep brown eyes that had held so much passion the night before. "I thought we agreed you wouldn't hide from me," Royce chuckled.

"Yeah, yeah, yeah," she answered. "We agreed but I was..." She bit her lip to stop from embarrassing herself.

"You were what, *a chumann*?"

"Nothing," she answered and tried to roll away, but the huge muscular arm lying across her waist kept her in place.

"Tell me...please," he asked and grinned. Not the way he grinned at her before, but this time, like a little boy just before he is about to do something that he knows will get him in trouble but was going to do it anyway. There was a twinkle in his eyes that hadn't been there before, and little lines bracketed his eyes that she knew only came when someone was truly happy. When he spoke she could hear that happiness in his voice, "or I might have to resort to tickling the answer out of you."

"You wouldn't do that to me," was her answer, but she saw the truth in his eyes...he most definitely would and he would enjoy every minute of it.

"Have it your way," he said and his hands grabbed her sides.

She laughed wildly and when he paused for her to take a breath, she wheezed out, "I was just...well, I was thinking...*oh, hell*. I thought you smelled good, alright? That's the truth."

Kyra turned her head to the side to avoid looking at Royce and showing how embarrassed she was at what she had just admitted.

A sweet lingering kiss on her neck, just below her ear, and then he whispered, "I think you smell delicious, *mo chroi*, absolutely delicious." To show the honesty of his words, he ran his nose the entire length of her neck, inhaling.

A slight kiss on her cheek and then she felt his breath on her lips, one brush of his lips on hers and then… "Royce, Kyra, breakfast is ready!" Aidan yelled from downstairs. They groaned in unison and then burst out laughing.

With a kiss to her forehead, the man that she wanted to trust more than anything in the world stood and walked towards the door. His last words left her smiling all the way to the breakfast table, "There will be a hell of a lot more of *that* later."

After breakfast was cleared and Royce had been properly teased for showing up in the middle of the night, the guys headed out to relieve the others and Kyra headed upstairs to unpack the rest of her supplies and avoid the other Guardsmen that were coming to eat and rest. She had laughed out loud when she heard Royce just outside the kitchen window warning them against even looking at her. The afternoon flew by as she alternated between thinking about all they needed to accomplish before the sun came up the next morning, and if she was ever going to truly be able to forgive and forget and completely trust where Royce was concerned. Just his name running through her mind caused her pulse to race. If she knew for sure things could always be like they had been during the night, then she would run headlong towards Royce and never look back.

Unfortunately, Kyra had learned too many times, and always the hard way, that just because she wanted things to be a certain way, didn't always make them happen that way. She was a survivor and part of that came from learning from her mistakes. For one of the first times that she could remember since leaving the coven, Kyra prayed, and not just a "please help me get outta the mess I have created" prayer. She prayed a real, honest to goodness, talking to the Goddess, looking for guidance prayer, and when she was finished, felt as if the weight of the world had been lifted from her shoulders. Her future with Royce was still one big question mark, but at least she knew somehow they would both be alright.

Hours later, every supply she thought she could ever need was out and ready to go. Kyra took a shower, braided her hair to keep it out of her way, and dressed in her favorite jeans and boots, along with her lucky black t-shirt with a fluorescent green outline of a witch on a broom and the words…'O'Cedar Makes Your Life Easier'. Slowly, she walked down the stairs, listening carefully to make sure she was alone, and was in the kitchen making a tuna sandwich when Aidan came through the back door. "Hey, whatcha makin'?" he asked and grabbed a glass of tea.

"Tuna sandwich. Want one?"

"Sure, that would be great. I'm starving," he answered and took a long drink of iced tea.

"Anybody else coming in? I'll make a few if they are," she asked as casually as possible, but Aidan's laugh told her that he knew what she was really wanted to know.

"Royce is with Rayne and Rian. They got here about an hour ago and they're all going over the plans again. I've heard them so many times, I can recite them forwards and backwards and I needed to talk to Grace…*alone*. Even mind speak can be crowded when you have brethren like mine." He smiled, and the amazing love he felt for his wife was like a light shining straight from his heart. He and Grace gave her hope that everything would turn out for her and Royce.

"I completely understand. Try growing up with at least a hundred other witches…crowded does not begin to describe it. And try getting a hot shower after seven a.m. without using your magic…*pfft*…not happening."

They laughed together as she brought their sandwiches to the table and refilled their drinks. She and Aidan ate and talked about their childhoods and families and even football before she felt the sensation that accompanied the mind speak of the Dragon Guard. Aidan nodded once or twice and then said, "The sun is going down and Royce wants you to make sure the wards are as strong as they can be, so that you are protected until you have to come outside right before midnight."

Any other time she would have gotten pissed and told him to mind his own business, but after spending time with the dragons and feeling at least some of what Royce was feeling, she knew he was being the macho caveman to protect her, and it warmed her heart. She nodded and then began walking from window to window, repeating the Warding Spell. Then she repeated it on the doors. She finished, returned to the table, and mock saluted. "Tell 'dragon man' that the wards have been reinforced." She almost got the words out before she collapsed in her chair, laughing. Aidan joined in and let her know that her message had been received and Royce was chuckling, as well.

Aidan stood and said, "I've gotta get out there. Duty calls. Lock the door behind me and one of us will be back to get you in just a little while."

She rolled her eyes but followed his instructions, settling in to watch cartoons and wait to finally catch the scumbag that had caused so much misery to so many people.

A knock at the door startled her from her half sleeping, half watching TV position on the couch. One look through the peephole showed Aidan and Aaron. She opened the door and they both said, "He's with Rayne," in unison before she could even ask the question. Either they were mind readers or she wasn't very good at hiding her emotions. *I'm going with B*, she thought to herself.

"We have people watching every route into this place and there have been no signs of our demented little brother or anyone that works for him. Royce wants you out by the mountain and hidden long before Andrew gets here. For once, everyone agrees, so we are here to make that happen. You ready to go?" Aaron spoke with his usual cockiness, but this time it filled her with confidence instead of pissing her off.

"Thanks, guys," she said as she headed up the stairs. "Let me grab my bag and I'll be ready to go."

Within two minutes she was back, backpack over her shoulder, ready to head out. Aidan opened the door. "After you, milady," he said and winked. She grinned, and together they all walked into the darkness to meet the others and put the traitor in the deepest hole they could find.

The trip through the woods had been a whole lot more fun than hiding between a fallen log and a rock at the base of the mountain. For the first twenty minutes she had run through what was going to happen, making mental check marks as she went. Amulets spelled with the Perimeter Spell that would allow the idiots in but not out, placed and activated with magic from the traitor's brothers…check. Containment Spell memorized and ready to work as soon as Andrew closed his circle…check. Nerves of steel firmly in place…check (well, maybe a half a check). It was going to be scary as shit to walk out and face Andrew and all his followers, even with the knowledge that their magic was 'stuck', for lack of a better term, within them by the special Containment Spell her Auntie Della had given her. After that she would use a very safe, very literal Siphoning Spell that would remove Andrew's black magic and put it into a vessel. She had made sure the specific spell she was using was one hundred percent white and would only take the power from the host and store it in an inanimate object. There was no way she would risk her immortal soul or her tenuous relationship with her mate to extract the traitor's magic. The urn she had chosen was the final step to ensure that no one, not even her, would ever get ahold of the darkness it would contain.

The sweet young jewelry artisan, Emma, had crafted a wide bottomed, slim necked vase out of silver and iron; silver to prevent any shifter of any kind from touching it, and iron to prevent any witch, light or dark, from accessing it. The stopper was also a combination of the powerful metals and would immediately be covered with wax from a candle used in a ritual to avoid detection and escape. Kyra had taken every precaution she could think of and had even spoken to Auntie Della to be sure.

She wished the Goldstone she had been using to track the dirt bag still worked, but he was apparently so immersed in black magic, even the thought of him obliterated everything good and pure. It was still hanging around her neck, but only as a beautiful accessory, nothing more.

As she sat there waiting, the moisture from the ground soaking into her jeans, every minute or two she would get the feeling that Royce was thinking about her or that he was trying to tell her something. It was a special, comforting feeling that reminded her of what she sensed when the dragons were mind speaking. If she concentrated on the point where the feelings originated, she could almost hear his voice. Kyra closed her eyes and concentrated until the sound of footsteps demanded her attention.

Holding her breath, she listened for any sign of the identity of the group heading towards her. Andrew's voice, one she would never forget no matter how long she lived, was clear and pompous, "Is everyone in position and ready to ascend?"

"Yes, sir," was the prompt reply that squelched across the radio.

Had it been any other time, she would have laughed at the haughty air in his voice. It was as if he was the general commanding his troops. *What a dick*, she thought as a hand on her shoulder caused her to jump. Thankfully, she had already put her hand over her mouth to avoid making any noise. Turning her head as far as it would go, she saw Aaron, a look of fierce determination on his face. When he smiled, it was almost scary and didn't reach his eyes. She knew it was his game face and was damn glad she would never have it pointed at her.

"You good?" he mouthed.

Kyra nodded in response and turned back to see if she could at least count feet through the brush that helped provide her cover. Aaron tapped her shoulder, evidently he knew what she was doing because he held up both hands, fingers extended, indicating ten, and then held up a single hand with all five fingers extended and mouthed the word, "Groups."

Great! Super! Fifty dark wizards, led by a madman, trying to extract powerful pure white Earth magic and twist it to something dark and evil to destroy only the *Goddess knew* how many people…*no problemo. Yeah…riiiigghhhtt.* Her mother and auntie had always said she was powerful and this was one time she really hoped they knew what the *hell* they were talking about.

Andrew's voice cut through her thoughts, "Let us begin."

She knew the moment each wizard stepped over the perimeter she and the Guardsmen had set. It was not an uncomfortable feeling, just an awareness of every foot that touched the ground inside. She could see that Aaron felt it too by the slight widening of his eyes. In an instant, he was again ready for this battle. Kyra could see how personal it was for him and wished for a quick end to the pain Andrew continued to cause the people she called family.

The awareness that Royce was thinking of her was ever present and she longed for it to be him beside her. She knew it had to be a blood relative of the douchebag, but that did not stop her wanting her man with her before she had to go face fifty pissed off wizards. Her thoughts halted, *my man*? Where the hell had that thought come from? She was not sure she had forgiven him for all that had happened, and damn sure knew she wasn't ready to hand him her heart. She didn't trust that he wouldn't turn on her again. But nonetheless, her crazy ass mind was being led around by her heart and they were *both* already thinking of him as *her man*.

She immediately knew when the last person had crossed her magical border and slid her hands into the gloves she needed to handle the vessel. With the vase in her hands, she turned to Aaron and nodded. She followed in his footsteps to the back of the mountain, remaining completely concealed. They climbed a path she herself had made and spelled when the mountain had been her home. From an especially dense patch of shrubbery and weeds, they waited for Andrew to begin to close the circle.

Two wizards, dressed in hooded cloaks, outlined the circle in white chalk, so completely infused with black magic it made her eyes water. Andrew was joined at the head of the circle by a tall, thin man with a long pointed nose, whose silky black robe was adorned with a variety of symbols, indicating he had reached Master status in the wizard community. The others around the circle were dressed in plain woolen, indicating they were new or had not achieved any recognition. Kyra's mother had believed that it was important to know all they could about their enemies. As a young witch, Kyra had hated learning all the crap about anything other than magic, but now was grateful to at least understand a bit about what she was facing.

The traitor wore no robes and had a sword strapped to his back and a dagger shoved in the side of his belt. She was sure it was a show of strength and wanted to laugh at his arrogance. A spell traveled a damn sight faster than a sword could cut, but she was grateful that he believed he was protected. False vibrado would help bring the little shithead to his knees.

When the chalk circle was finished and the two had returned to their places, Andrew began to speak, but not the words that would close the circle. Instead he droned on and on about all they would achieve with their ritual and their goals for the future. Kyra could feel the hate and rage pouring off Aaron and wondered if he could feel hers. Finally, after what seemed like hours, Andrew asked the wizards to join hands.

Before the traitor spoke the third word of his ritual, Kyra had begun her Containment Spell. When she was finished, she felt the sweat dot her upper lip and roll down her spine. Aaron leaned in and whispered next to ear, "Everyone is ready when you are. You say when and we all walk out together."

Kyra nodded, absently listening to the words of the ancient ritual Andrew and the Master Wizard standing next to him were attempting to work. The constant chanting of the other wizards lent reverence to the proceeding, and would have been spiritual had they not been tainting purity with evil and then planning to use it to kill. Kyra's heart sank when she recognized the old Latin word for blood…*sanguis.* To add insult to injury, she was sure the full translation of what the bastard traitor had said was Blood of the Unknowing. These filthy assholes had killed an untold number of innocent people just for their blood. It turned Kyra's stomach and strengthened her resolve to kick the ass of every single piece of shit standing in that circle, beginning with the biggest dick of them all…Andrew.

She felt the rite coming to an end and prepared herself for what was to come. As soon as Andrew spoke the closing words, he and his followers would be expecting a flow of magic from the moon and mountain directly into their souls. When that did not happen, Kyra had to be right there with her vessel and her spell. One final prayer to the Goddess and a happy thought to the spot in the center of her heart where she felt Royce the most, and she nodded to Aaron. She felt him speak to the Dragon Guard and thought, *It's now or never, Kyra girl. Time to kick traitor ass, Earth witch-style.*

~~*~*~*~*~*

Aaron's voice rang loud and clear in Royce's head, "Thirty seconds." He spent every one of those seconds pouring confidence, strength, and love through their bond, and would have yelled his joy to the Heavens when he felt her thinking of him. It was obvious she had purposely focused on their connection even though he was sure that she still had no clue what it was.

Aaron's command of "Now," pushed all other thoughts to the back of his mind. The traitor was less than fifty yards away and it was time to put the little fucker away.

Using their enhanced speed, the Dragon Guard surrounded the circle where Andrew was standing as leader. Royce would have laughed out loud at the assorted looks of surprise and fear on the wizards' faces had it not been that he and all his brethren wanted to rip their heads off and feed the bodies to the scavengers.

He located Kyra where Aaron had placed her between him and his twin, with Rian at her back. It was comforting that she was so well protected, but he would have felt so much better if he had been there himself. Kyra immediately began her spell while the guard stood at the ready, swords drawn. Andrew turned to face her, along with the gaunt man standing next to him, and began speaking so quickly he could barely make out the words. From the bit of Latin he remembered, they were trying to stop the words she was speaking. Their followers, however, seemed to be stuck in the original spell. They all stood, holding hands, swaying and repeating the chant Andrew had instructed them to say, completely unaware of the turmoil brewing all around them.

Royce watched closely as Kyra held her ground. His heart and his dragon pushed him to go to her as her hands shook and her voice quivered, so when Andrew drew the katana from his scabbard and the master drew a pistol, it was all he could do not to call forth his fire. The traitor advanced on Aidan, shouting how he would finally take his head, while the wizard walked to the center of the ritual circle, and shouted, "EXSOMNIS!"

The wizards in the circle snapped to attention and as one unit, did a one eighty, pulled swords and daggers from under their robes, and moved towards the Guardsmen. Always ready for a battle, the dragon warriors ran headlong towards the sorcerers, unfazed by the four to one odds. Royce watched Aaron and Rian continue to protect Kyra while Aidan locked blades with the little brother he had thought lost so many years ago, but truly wanted dead and buried for good this time.

With his enhanced vision, Royce could see what looked like thick gray smoke coming from a blackened spot on the ground, close to what would have been the center of the dark wizards' circle, and flow into the vessel that Kyra was holding. The longer it flowed, the more her arms quaked and the vase shook. He remembered she had told him it was made of silver and iron and that iron was harmful to witches, explaining why she was wearing heavy black leather gloves, making holding onto the vessel even more difficult.

Royce struck down every wizard in his path in his race to get to Kyra. His dragon pushed with all his force against the confines of Royce's mind and body with the need to protect their mate. So involved in fighting a particularly skilled sorcerer while watching Kyra, he was hit at the base of his skull by what he recognized as the handle of a sword. His knees immediately hit the ground at the same time he heard Kyra scream his name. Thankfully, Rory was quicker than any of their enemies and was there in the blink of an eye to decapitate two wizards with one strike.

Nodding to Kyra that he was okay, Royce and his younger brother continued to massacre the opposition. Only Kyra's voice raised in pain stilled his blade. When his eyes found her, she was leaning with her back against Rian, tears streaming down her face. Aaron was off to the side fighting a group of magicians, while the Master Wizard was descending upon his mate, chanting ugly Latin words in a low guttural tone. It was then that he saw magical sigils forged from silver hanging off the hood of his robe. Two of the symbols he recognized from his youth, and knew they were used to nullify a personal attack. Ilsa had always made sure that he and his brothers knew basic symbols of protection in case they were ever attacked, and thank the Heavens he knew those. Unfortunately, the most experienced practitioner was blocking whatever spell Kyra had worked that was supposed to keep him from using magic against her. The rite he was throwing at her, combined with the energy used to work the Siphoning Spell, was causing his mate serious pain while she tried to finish what she had started.

"What the fuck, Ri? Make her stop! It's hurting her!" Royce shouted directly into his brother's mind.

"I tried! But your mate is tougher than nails, she won't stop!" Royce could never remember a time he had ever heard his brother so panicked and that only served to make him crazy with worry.

"Pick her up! Get her the hell outta here!"

"Don't you think I tried? But she just dug her heels in and threatened to hurt my...manhood." Rian answered and Royce could hear his embarrassment at being bested by, as Rian called her, 'the little witch'.

The battle raged on around him, while he took out every opponent that dared challenge him, all in the effort to get to Kyra and get her to safety. Their eyes met and he shouted for her to leave, but she simply shook her head and looked away. The need to protect his mate was beginning to overtake all common sense. He was ready to call forth his beast and burn them to the ground when a beam, resembling starlight, began to shine on Kyra.

He followed the ribbon of light to the outstretched palms of a tall, full-figured woman with long gray hair flowing around her face, accentuating her glowing blue eyes. The light seemed to fortify Kyra as the woman slowly walked towards her. His mate mouthed the word, 'Auntie' and new hope surged throughout every Guardsman, but none so much as Royce. They all fought with renewed vigor, striking down the remaining wizards that had not run in fear.

Royce was within a few steps of Kyra when the clash of blades and the sounds of bitter insults reached his ears. Looking to his left, he saw Aidan and Andrew still engaged in a battle to the death with Andrew, who was hurling insults and yelling every vile thing imaginable. Aidan, ever the honorable man, was fighting with the utmost skill and enduring all his brother's taunts in an effort to capture the traitor instead of killing him.

Andrew aimed a violent thrust at Aidan's heart, but the seasoned warrior stepped to the side just in time. The momentum propelled Andrew over the side of the mountain. Every Guardsman that was not fighting ran to the edge of the mountain, only to see the traitor being carried off by several of his followers. A cry of sheer horror sounded behind the men watching their greatest enemy get away. They all turned, swords at the ready, to witness the older witch driving a bright green light into the Master Wizard. He was on his knees, attempting to fight the assault the older, obviously more experienced sorceress was piling upon him.

The elder witch took a half step back and the failing Master got in an exceptionally strong burst of magic, but Kyra was right there to help out and within minutes the dark wizard was laying on the ground, unconscious. Both witches stepped back as Kellan and Brannoc stepped in, grabbed the wizard by the arms, and began dragging him away. The Master Wizard sprung to life and pointed his dagger at Kellan's heart. Always quick to react, Brannoc ran the assailant through with his broadsword. The dead wizard dropped to the ground, just another casualty in Andrew's bid for vengeance.

Kyra completed the siphoning of dark magic, spoke the spell that would seal it while applying the wax of the ceremonial candle. She finished just as Royce ran to her side, grabbing her and lifting her until their lips met. One hard and fast kiss, with a promise of so much more, and he was being introduced to his mate's Auntie Della. The woman, he found out on the hike back to Sam's cottage, was responsible for the strong vibrant woman that he looked forward to spending the rest of his life loving. The longer the older woman spoke, the more Royce could see the resemblance between Kyra and her aunt. Mannerisms, facial expressions, and an inner belief in everything that was right and good with the world, were just the most obvious of the similarities.

Aaron and Rian carried the vessel containing the dark magic back to the house. Once there, it was loaded into a silver lined lead box with a spelled lock, awaiting transport to the werepanthers. Apparently, Max knew of a witch doctor in the rain forest that could dispose of the tainted magic without harm to anyone.

The battle had been a victory even if Andrew had gotten away. They had kept him from getting the dark magic, thinned his ranks by at least forty dark arts practitioners, and only suffered minor wounds themselves that were already healing. Kyra, Della, Royce, and all the Dragon Guard crowded into the small house and partied until the wee hours of the night. When Kyra tugged on his arm and yawned, he picked her up and yelled good night to all that were listening as he took his mate upstairs.

He felt her head fall against his shoulder, heard her breathing slow, and knew she had already fallen asleep. As they entered the bedroom, he used his foot to softly kick the door closed behind them. After pulling back the covers, he gently laid Kyra on her side, thankful she had already showered and changed, because nothing would make him wake her, especially when she looked like his very own angel peacefully dreaming. He stood staring just a moment longer, and then stripped down to his boxers and climbed into bed beside his amazing mate. When Kyra snuggled against him and breathed a sigh of relief against his chest, he looked to the ceiling and whispered, "You were so right, Mom, she is worth *everything*."

CHAPTER EIGHT

It had been the best night's sleep he'd ever had and all he could think about was getting Kyra back into his arms. Royce had felt his reluctant mate kiss him on the cheek and then get out of bed a few hours earlier, whispering for him to rest as long as he liked, that she was going to see her aunt. The ringing of his cell phone woke him with a start, and when he looked at the screen he frowned. "What the *hell*, Rory? You couldn't just mind speak? I hate waking up to a ringing phone," he grumbled while his younger brother just laughed.

"First of all, I tried to mind speak to you for about an hour, and then Rian tried, and even Devon, but all we got back was static, also known as snoring." Rory howled with laughter and Royce contemplated hanging up, but before he could decide, his brother began again, "Anyway, I finally gave up and called. And secondly, it is damn near ten o'clock. And you are late! Rayne and Rian want to have a debriefing since the traitor got away. So make yourself beautiful and get your ass out to the lake."

Rory hung up before Royce could tell him to *stick it*. Jumping out of bed, he threw on his jeans and a clean t-shirt, grabbed his boots and socks, and headed downstairs as quickly as he could. Hearing Kyra's voice coming from the kitchen made him smile. She was all he would ever need. All he had to do was convince her that he would *never, ever* do anything to hurt her again. His mate's Aunt Della was the first to speak, "You look well rested and in a hurry this morning, my boy."

He chuckled at her use of 'my boy'. It had been years since anyone had called him anything but 'old man' or 'gramps'. He knew witches aged as slowly as they did and wondered how old Kyra's aunt actually was, but would never ask a lady her age. "I did sleep well." He looked towards Kyra, and just the glimpse of her violet eyes from under her full dark lashes made his pulse race and the tiny grin on her very kissable lips made his heart soar. His mate was a tough witch that took shit from no one and he loved that about her, but he also adored that she had a sweet, sensitive side, reserved just for him.

Remembering they were not alone, he turned again to Della and asked, "And did you sleep well?"

She nodded before speaking, "I did, thank you. And I have enjoyed spending time with my favorite niece."

"Auntie, I'm your only niece." Kyra shook her head and laughed.

"That makes no difference, you are *still* my favorite and don't you give me any back talk. I can still whoop your butt."

The kitchen erupted in laughter just as Kellan walked in the back door. "Hey, nobody invited me to the party," he joked, causing them all to laugh even harder.

As the fun died down, Kellan cleared his throat and began to speak, "I'm sorry to take you away from the fun, but the vein in Rayne's head is about to pop and Rory sent me to get you."

Not wanting to spend one second away from Kyra, but knowing it was unavoidable, Royce nodded. He turned to Kyra and pulled her to him. "I won't be gone long and then we can head back to the lair and show your aunt around… sound good?"

"Sounds awesome," she replied, but he could see that something else was on her mind.

He leaned down until they were eye-to-eye and asked, "Everything okay, *mo ghra'*?"

She nodded and said, "Perfect." But he could see that something was still bothering her. He debated skipping the meeting and staying to find out what was on her mind until Rayne's voice sounded in his head, *"You have ninety seconds…"* His Commander's voice left no room for argument. He gave Kyra a quick kiss and ran out the door with Kellan in tow, promising himself he would find out what had put that faraway look in his mate's beautiful violet eyes.

Four hours! Four fucking hours later, and if he had to listen to one more person detail the part they played in the battle the night before, he was going to pull every last red hair from his head. The gathering had begun just as he had expected. Rayne spoke as the Commander in charge of the mission and let them know that werepanthers with magical abilities were already being dispatched to gather Intel. They all knew that Andrew had survived his fall but were holding out hope that maybe he had succumbed to his injuries, or was injured badly enough that they would be able to swoop in and capture him. They knew they had delivered a serious blow to his followers, killing approximately forty and hopefully leaving him vulnerable. But the best part had been the destruction of the Master Wizard.

Royce felt pride that Kyra and her aunt had been able to defeat the dark practitioner. When they had first gotten back to the cottage after the fight, he could sense Kyra's worry that he would turn on her again. After all, he had all but called her a murderer-in-waiting and swore he would never have anything to do with her less than two weeks ago. But everything had changed, and that situation had definitely been really screwed up. On the mountain, she had defended herself and all the Dragon Guard against a powerfully evil wizard, and she had defeated him. He could not have been prouder and he had told her so in front of his brethren.

Rian's voice brought him back to reality, acting as the Head Elder of the allied clan and adding his congratulations along with the promise that his and Kellan's Forces would always be allies of the Golden Fire Clan and the MacLendon Force. From there, everyone had to put their two-cents-worth in, while all Royce wanted to do was get back to Kyra. Finally, it felt like it was wrapping up and he tapped into his and Kyra's mating bond. The anxiety and frustration he felt had him standing up and waving his goodbye to the leaders of the group.

He made it to the back door of the cottage in record time, even for a dragon shifter, using his enhanced speed. The conversation between Kyra and her aunt stopped as soon as he opened the door and the look on his mate's face said it all…she was worried and it had something to do with him. Unsure what to do as both women looked first at him and then each other, he opted for the wait-and-see approach. Trying to play it cool when he felt anything but, he asked, "So are you ladies ready to head back to the lair?"

"Auntie Della is gonna head back home. She has lots to do and feels like she has been gone long enough." He could feel the tension in her words and knew there was more to it than she was saying. A quick sidelong glance from Kyra to her aunt told him he was right, but again he decided to wait and see if she would tell him what was happening. He longed for her to trust him, to confide in him, and knew he would do whatever it took and wait as long as she needed to have that.

"I'm sorry you can't join us. Can I have one of the guys give you a ride?"

"No, dear, I have my own way." Della stood and hugged Kyra, placing a kiss on the top of her head, before turning towards Royce. "Take care of my niece. She is everything to me."

He nodded, "And to me. I won't let anything happen to her. I promise."

Della stood still, staring into his eyes for a few heartbeats longer than normal. When it was obvious she'd seen what she was looking for, she smiled, nodded, and said goodbye. Royce stood, watching Kyra try to look everywhere but at him, and he had no clue what to do. He wanted her to tell him what was going on, wanted to be able to help her with whatever was bothering her, but knew that if he pushed her she would completely shut him out, and that was something he could not let happen. Thinking that talking was better than just standing like a stump he asked, "You hungry?"

Royce watched as Kyra visibly relaxed and he immediately felt better. When she answered, her voice sounded a little less strained than it had when she had spoken a few minutes earlier. "Yeah, actually I am. I hadn't realized how hungry until you just mentioned it."

"Great, whatcha hungry for?"

"A burger and fries sounds awesome." She stopped, her eyes got wide, and she stammered, "I mean is that…ummm…do you want…or do you like…oh hell! Do burgers and fries sound good to you?"

Unable to keep a straight face, he chuckled his answer, "Absolutely one of my favorite foods." He had seen that Kyra was nervous, but then was overjoyed when she regained her spunk and attitude. They were as much a part of who and what Kyra was as her violet eyes and Earth magic, and that was the woman he was growing to love more every minute of every day. "There is a diner not far from here that makes homemade ice cream and the best milkshakes I've ever had. Burgers are pretty great too," he said and was delighted when her eyes lit up.

Kyra jumped up and ran for the stairs, hollering over her shoulder, "Let me change my jeans and grab my boots and I'll be ready to go."

A couple of hours with Kyra, watching her expression when she was thinking or happy, or trying to come up with a snappy comeback, would go down in history as one of the best times of Royce's life. She made fun of him when he curled up his nose as she dipped her fries in mayonnaise, and called him a chicken when he said there was no way he was putting a mayo soaked fry in his mouth. But the look that would go into the special place he had already built in his mind, the one where he kept every beautiful image of Kyra that he never wanted to forget, was the look she had when she had taken a drink of her fresh peach milkshake. Her eyes had gotten almost as big as saucers and twinkled like they had stars in them, while the straw had slipped from her lips as they vibrated ever so slightly when she hummed, "mmmmmmm." It was a look of pure bliss, and one he wanted to see over and over…. preferably when she was naked.

The drive back to Sam's home was filled with silly stories of her childhood and her Auntie Della. A couple of times Royce almost asked about Kyra's mother, but knew from his glimpse of their relationship and her obvious avoidance of the subject, that for the time being, it was better left alone. As they turned down the gravel road leading back to Sam's old house, she said, "Enough about me, what about your childhood? I mean besides what I already know."

She gasped and he knew it was because she had inadvertently alluded to his loss. He reached across the seat and grabbed her hand, "Hey, look at me."

He waited as she slowly turned his way. If he hadn't been driving he would have pulled her into his lap so that she could feel the beat of his heart and truth of his words, but as it was, he used the connection of their hands and the growing strength of their bond to let her know that everything he was saying was the absolute truth. "It's okay. That's all in the past and I'll tell you anything you want to know. Unfortunately, we have company."

He nodded out the windshield and watched as her gaze followed his. She groaned at the sight of all the Guardsmen, not a hundred feet in front of them, loading up in preparation to head home, causing him to grin. He jumped out of the car and ran around to help her out just before Aaron yelled, "I smell burgers and fries from Millie's and I bet you didn't even bring me a doggie bag."

"Isn't that a dragon bag?" she giggled under her breath, and Royce could tell that it was intended for his ears only. As all the Guardsmen laughed, he made a mental note to remind her how sensitive dragon shifter hearing really was, but guessed by the surprised look on her face that she had just figured it out.

"Good one, little witch, good one," Aaron yelled across the distance, and Royce felt Kyra relax. Just the fact that she cared whether her silly comment had bothered another showed him exactly what a great heart his mate had, and that one of his best friends had eased her discomfort strengthened his belief that everything between them was going to be okay.

"Thanks, Bro. I owe ya one," Royce sent through their unique link.

"No worries. She's definitely a keeper," Aaron sent back, and Royce could hear the sincerity in his brethren's words.

"That she is," Royce answered.

He placed his hand on the small of Kyra's back and guided her to the house, loving the electrical current that flowed between them even through her clothing. It was something he had been told about by the older clansmen, and had even heard from his brethren that had found their mates, but he'd never imagined how wonderful it would feel. He knew that she felt it too by her harsh intake of breath and quickening of her heartbeat. As soon as they were inside, his control snapped. He lifted Kyra onto the kitchen counter, pushed his lips to hers, and kissed her with the fire and passion of a dragon shifter being ridden hard by the mating call. His hands slid under her blouse, the feel of her skin driving his desire higher and higher the longer he touched her. Just as he was about to pick her up and speed upstairs, the sound of a throat clearing pulled him from his mate.

"I guess I really am gonna have to start calling ahead," Aaron chuckled.

Royce leaned his head to Kyra's and sighed. Then he turned to face his friend while she sat behind him. "I really wish you would."

"Sorry, but the crew is about ready and I wanted to make sure you guys were all packed up."

"Thanks, man. We'll be out in just a few minutes." Royce said as he turned and helped Kyra down.

Once her feet hit the floor, she scooted around him and was hurrying up the stairs, shouting that she wouldn't be but a few minutes. Both men shook their heads and chuckled.

With only three SUVs to accommodate twelve huge Dragon Guardsmen and one tiny witch, the ride back to the lair was crowded but fun. Aaron, Aidan, and Rory rode in the same vehicle as Royce and Kyra, ensuring that they laughed the entire time. Royce watched as Kyra laughed until tears rolled down her face at the stories his 'supposed' friends and family told about his mishaps throughout the years. He knew he should have been upset, but just couldn't be as he watched how much fun his mate was having.

Their arrival home was met with a big party at Rayne and Kyndel's. His brethren all found their mates and children happy to see them in a way he only now understood that he had Kyra in his life. Every available surface was covered with food and drink and many from the clan stopped by to share in the celebration, wishing them all luck in their continued efforts to capture the one that had betrayed their entire race. Kyra was never far from his side, something he took as a very good sign, even though he saw the same worried look in her eyes that he had witnessed earlier, when she thought he wasn't looking.

After watching Kyra fight to keep her eyes open for about thirty minutes, he grabbed her hand and together they made the rounds, thanking everyone and saying good night. The walk to Kyra's was nice, but with every step they took Royce could feel his mate's tension growing. Finally, when they reached her front door and she practically ran in, he asked the question that had been driving him crazy since that morning, "What's wrong Kyra? What has you so worried?"

"Nothing," she answered too quickly, as she busied herself with unpacking her supplies onto the table.

Not willing to let the subject drop, Royce walked over to her and stilled her hands with his. When she finally looked up, he could see frustration and worry, just as he had expected, but also pain, and that was not something he could just ignore. He laid his hand on her cheek and looked into her eyes, trying to show her how much he cared and that he would do anything to help her before he spoke. "What is it Kyra? What have you been keeping from me all day?"

She shook her head but it was without conviction, so he stood, touching her face and waiting for her to tell him. When she spoke her voice shook, "My mother is missing."

Royce sat down in the nearest chair and pulled Kyra onto his lap. She laid her head on his chest as he rubbed little circles on her back and hummed the same tune his mother had when he and his brothers needed comfort. He waited until her breathing returned to normal before he asked his next question.

"What can I do to help?"

"That's just it, there's nothing *anyone* can do to help," her voice cracked and she burrowed farther into his embrace.

"There is always something that can be done. Just tell me what you know and we'll figure out how to get her back."

Kyra jumped off his lap and started to pace. One her third trip past him, Royce spoke, "Talk to me, Kyra. Tell me what's going on."

"I don't know what's going on. I have no idea what happened. Mom showed up, yelled and left…just like always. Auntie Della shows up, helps save my ass only to tell me that my mother never made it home after our fight and…"

She stopped dead in her tracks and stared out the picture window into the night. Royce used all his considerable strength, but it wasn't enough. He could see the tension in her body, feel it flowing through their bond and had to go to her. Placing his hands on her shoulders, he leaned down and asked, "And what, Kyra?"

Her shoulders slumped and she looked at the floor. He heard her swallow several times before she finally spoke in a voice that sounded far away and lost, "And that as the only heir to the Grand Priestess and of a ruling age, I have to go back and run things until my mother is found or the Council decides who is to rule in her place."

It was definitely NOT what he was expecting her to say and for a split second thought he might have misheard but then he replayed her words again and knew he had definitely heard everything Kyra had said correctly. Trying to keep his dragon from making an appearance and his brain from exploding, he said the only thing he could think of, "If you have to go, I'll go too. Who knows, I might be able to help."

Kyra shook her head and moved out of his grasp. When she spoke, the sadness in her voice nearly broke his heart, "You can't. Until the decision is made by the Council as to who will be the next Grand Priestess, no one that has not been initiated into our coven can enter…no one."

"There has to be something we can do. You are my mate and I am yours, they cannot keep us apart," he said through gritted teeth, trying to keep his temper in check but failing miserably.

Her sadness was like a dagger to his heart and her next words drove it deep, "You really mean that? You really *believe* we are mates?"

The shock of her words made him stutter and he saw uncertainty flash in her eyes. That uncertainty renewed his resolve to make her see that he more than believed they were mates, he *knew* with all that he was that she was to be his. When he spoke he was sure to pour his whole heart and soul into his words, "Knowing that you are my mate, that you were created just for me, is my reason for living, the one thing in all the world that tells me the future is full of hope and promise. It is what I am staking forever on. I have no doubt we will live long happy lives filled with more love than any couple has ever known."

She threw herself into his arms, hugging his neck and sobbing so hard that within minutes, the collar of his shirt was wet. As he felt her begin to calm, he once again sat down and pulled her into his lap. She looked up, not quite meeting his eyes, and he could see she was embarrassed for her outburst. Needing to comfort her, he quickly spoke, "Never be embarrassed about anything you feel or think or say or…just *anything* with me. We are in this together. Always remember that…*always together*."

They spent the next several hours discussing everything from where her mother could be to how long she thought it would be before she could come back to him, or that he might be allowed into her coven. He saw how upset she was by all that was happening and how she hated that it was out of her control. Royce wished there was something he could do to make things easier for his mate, but could come up with absolutely nothing.

He handled the whole thing pretty well until she told him she would be leaving first thing in the morning. He almost lost control. For a moment, it was hard for him to breathe, as if all the air had been sucked from the room. He felt as if he had just gotten her and now had to let her go. Had he been younger and more prone to tantrums he would have yelled and screamed about how life wasn't fair. Instead, he repeated that old saying about absence making the heart grow fonder and assured them both that there was no way in the world he was giving Kyra up. It may have taken him a while to realize she was all he could ever want, but now that he had, there was nothing that could take her from him, not even a missing mother and a Council of witches.

In the wee hours of the morning, they made their way to bed. They held one another, kissing and touching, drinking each other in. It was never rushed, just a slow exploration of what they truly were to one another. Royce used his hands to memorize every inch of Kyra's body, tucking it away in his heart to pull out and relive when missing her got to be unbearable, like he knew it would. He reveled in the feel of her hands on his skin and when they made love they were one…mind, body, and soul. The missing pieces each had been searching for their entire lives, were found that night in each other.

Morning came, no matter how hard they tried to hold it off, but as they looked into one another's eyes, there was no sadness…only hope. Royce walked Kyra to the car her Aunt Della had sent for her and kissed her one last time, laying his heart at her feet, letting her have all of him, showing her that he was a better man for just having her in his life, assuring her that very soon they would be together again. He repeated the words that would forever be engraved on his heart…*always together*. When she smiled he knew she felt the depth of his commitment, but more than that, she believed it, she *believed* him.

The car pulled away and Royce stood staring down the road it had traveled long after the taillights had disappeared. Unsure what to do with himself and wanting to be as close to Kyra as possible, he walked back into her house. He inhaled her scent, touched her charms that lay on the table, and finally ended up back in her bedroom. Sitting on the end of the bed, he let himself fall back and his eyes slide shut. Not even the constant messages from his brothers disturbed him as he begged, "Just bring her back to me. I can hold out as long as it takes as long as I know she'll come back." He had no clue who he was asking, if it was the Universe, the Goddess, or Fate, but when he felt a whisper of a breeze, like a kiss on his forehead, he knew everything would work out. He smiled as he thought, *Thanks Mom.*

~~*~*~*~*~*

It had been ten days since she had gotten to the coven that she had grown up in, the coven her mother had governed, the coven she had never wanted to return to. Kyra knew it was her duty and that she was doing the right thing, but that did not make being away from Royce any easier. Every moment of every day, whether she was asleep or awake, she was thinking of him. She missed him more with each passing day and looked forward to their daily phone calls.

He told her everything that was happening at the lair and with everyone she had grown to love over her time spent there. Sometimes, he would be with some of them when he called and she would get to talk to them too. Her favorite was Sydney. The child was just a doll and always said exactly what was on her mind, something Kyra could definitely relate to. The conversation she'd had with the almost six-year old just the night before had been running through her mind all day. "Hey Syd. How ya doing?"

"I'm okay."

"Just okay? You sound kinda down," Kyra asked, genuinely worried that the ever bubbly child seemed sad.

"Yeah…well…it's just…can you keep a secret Kyra?" Sydney asked.

Curiosity peaked, Kyra answered, "Sure can. Remember I told you witches are the best secret keepers."

Sydney giggled and Kyra knew she was starting to feel better already. "Okay, I'll tell you, but I gotta go in the other room." Kyra heard Sydney tell Royce she'd be right back and then waited.

Just a minute later Sydney said, "Okay. I'm back. Now you have to pinkie swear even though we can't touch pinkies, that you won't be a blabber."

Kyra wanted to laugh, but knew from experience that Sydney was being serious and would be pissed if she laughed, so all she said was, "I pinkie swear."

She imagined Sydney's sweet little face considering her swear while listening to the silence and then finally the little girl spoke, "Okay, I know you won't blab 'cause you're my best friend."

Kyra's heart swelled. Sydney was one of a kind and the best little girl she knew. It made her happy that the child trusted her. "Thanks Syd, I'm honored to be your best friend."

"Cool!" she exclaimed and then grew very serious, "Kyra, are you ever coming home?"

Kyra could barely speak past the lump that immediately formed at the child's question. Clearing her throat she answered, "Of course I'm coming back, Sweetheart. Why would you ask that? Is that your secret? You think I'm not coming back?"

"No…yes…well…not me but…" Kyra waited and listened as Sydney took a deep breath. Finally she began again, "Not me, Royce. Royce is scared you're not coming back. I heard him tell Daddy when they were outside and I was supposed to be playing with Jay. He told my daddy not to tell anyone, but that it was killing him. Do you think it really is? Is Royce gonna die if you don't come back? Please tell me you're coming back."

Sydney was almost crying by the time she stopped speaking and Kyra's heart hurt that she was not there to reassure her, to make her feel better. She felt even worse that she was putting Royce through so much so early in their relationship. "Yes, Baby Girl, I am most definitely coming back to you *and* to Royce. I have things to take care of but I *will be back*. Royce was just being silly when he said it was killing him, like when you think you're gonna die when your mommy makes you eat your veggies before dessert. It's something people say when they really want something to happen. The next time you hear him say that, give him a big hug, kiss his cheek, and tell him you love him. Can you do that for me?"

"I can! I can!" Sydney squealed. "I'm so glad you're coming back and that Royce isn't gonna die."

"Me too, Baby Girl, me too."

"I'm gonna take the phone back now. Love you, Kyra."

"Love you too, Syd." Kyra heard the child running and then she heard Royce's low, smooth voice asking, "What was that all about?"

"Just girl talk," she answered, her heart pounding from what Sydney had just told her.

"Oh, I see. Keeping secrets from me already, huh?" He chuckled, and for the first time that day she truly believed everything was going to be alright. They talked for about an hour and it took another ten minutes of goodbyes before they hung up.

It was those phone calls that kept her going and made her believe that when she did get to leave the coven *he* would be waiting for her. Maybe Hope was turning out to be Kyra's friend after all.

~~*~*~*~*~*

"Tomorrow will be three weeks and as of yesterday, Kyra still had no idea when the Council would make their decision and let her come back here, or at the very least, let me go to her. What the *fuck* am I supposed to do, Dev?"

"You're going to keep your head up, believe in the wisdom of the Universe, and keep the faith. Kyra will be back here before you know it and then you can plan your mating ceremony. Make things official. Live happily ever after. *Hell*, have babies while you're at it." Devon laughed out loud and took a long draw off the beer he had been nursing since they started their conversation.

"Yeah, I know you're right, but this is making me crazy. Did I tell you that I'm so out of my mind I thought I saw Kyra in the Town Square yesterday and started running after her until the girl turned and I realized it was Tanya, the baker's daughter?" Royce scrubbed his hands down his face as Devon chuckled and headed into the kitchen for another beer.

"Well, at least you stopped before you accosted her. She's to be mated to Winston, one of the younger Guardsmen, and I'm sure her father would've been less than thrilled with you, mistake or not," his friend said as he walked back into his living room.

"Yeah, real funny, asshole. But none of this solves my problem. I miss her, Dev. I mean *really* miss her. I can't eat. I can't think. I don't sleep. I just walk around thinking of her. I spend part of every day at her house, touching her things, inhaling her scent, just being where the memory of her is the strongest. I'm acting like a lovesick teenager and at my age, that is *nuts*. I literally count the minutes until I can call her, at least hearing her voice makes me feel almost like myself again."

"Well, how long til you can call her today?" Devon asked.

Royce looked at his watch and sighed. "About three hours."

"Then let's get some of the guys over here, watch some football, eat junk food, and forget about women for a while. You in?"

"Sure, anything to get my mind off this mess."

For three whole hours, he and his brethren yelled at the TV, drank beer, and had a blast, but the second the alarm sounded that is was time to call Kyra, Royce disappeared out the back door and moved far enough away that he could talk to his mate in private. He dialed her number and listened as the phone rang and rang and then her voicemail picked up. It was the first time since they had been apart that she hadn't answered when he called. Worried something was wrong, he dialed again and again, and every time only got her voicemail. Walking back to the house like he had lost his last friend, he tried to get ahold of her one more time, and when her voicemail picked up again, he said what had been on his mind every second of every day for three weeks. He said the only thing that mattered, "I love you, Kyra."

When he was sure he could face his brethren without acting like a love sick puppy, he walked through the back door, grabbed a beer and sat down to finish watching the game. Devon looked at him and all he could do was shrug, not ready to share the news that for the first time since she'd left, he was *truly* worried that she wasn't coming back. The game ended with Kellan and Aaron trash talking and Lennox and Lance getting everyone to agree to play poker.

When the grandfather clock that had been his parents' chimed that it was three am, he used his brother's favorite saying, "You don't have to go home but you have to get the hell out here," to clear out the crowd.

Slowly but surely all Guardsmen left, and as he shut the door, the silence and emptiness almost overwhelmed him. He paced from one end of his home to the other while his dragon roared in his head. Both man and beast had reached the end of their rope and there was only one thing that would make it better…they had to go to Kyra.

Royce raced to his room, threw some clothes in a bag, and grabbed the keys to his Harley. He told himself to remember to call Devon in the morning and let him know what he had done so they wouldn't send every member of both Forces to look for him. Looking around to make sure he had everything he needed, he shut off the lights and walked out the door. Jumping off the porch and heading to the side of the house where he parked his Harley, he stopped dead in his tracks as the scent of patchouli and rose petals smacked him in the face. He spun so fast the landscape around him was just a blur and there, standing at the end of his walk, was Kyra. They looked at each other for three long heartbeats and then she held up her phone and said, "I love you, too."

CHAPTER NINE

Royce ran to her and all Kyra could do was stand and stare. It was the most surreal moment of her life, one she had hoped would happen but had truly doubted she would ever experience. After everything that had gone on between them, she'd had no clue if they would ever truly find their way to one another. While she was at the coven she had done a lot of thinking about the future. She had talked to her Auntie Della as well the others, and they all said the same thing, "You have the Goddess *and* the Universe on your side, you just have to be patient and things will work out." But patience had never been her thing, and the longer they were apart, the more the gaping wound that had once been her heart bled.

Early that day, or maybe it was the day before, she had no idea what time it even was, let alone what day it was, the Council had shown up unannounced and called Kyra and all the Elders Witches into the library. With little pomp and no introduction, they began speaking of the welfare of the coven, the immense responsibilities of the interim Grand Priestess, and the lifelong commitment that position required in case that Calysta was not found. They had droned on and on until Kyra was sure her head might explode.

When the ancient witch leading the proceedings finally took a breath, Kyra had requested to speak. She had explained in the most eloquent and politically correct way that she could muster that she was not the right person for the job regardless of her bloodline. Eyebrows had risen all around the table, but she had pressed on, stating that she had been on Sabbatical (her Auntie's words, not hers) for more than twenty-five years and therefore not familiar with the inner workings that such a prestigious position required. By the look of disdain on the faces of the Council members, she was sure she was losing the battle and then Priestess Agatha Montage had spoken and Kyra's heart sank, "We understand your hesitation at accepting such a time-honored position. However, you are a direct descendant of one of the most powerful bloodlines in our history. From all reports you, Kyra St. Croix, are the most powerful witch of your line and that is something we simply cannot overlook."

The silence was deafening. Only the sound of her heart breaking could be heard and then she blurted out the thought that had been running through her mind since the assembly had begun, "But I am mated to a dragon-shifter of royal birth. I bear his mark on my right hip and he is my one true mate ordained by the Goddess." She spoke so fast that she wondered if anyone had understood what she had said, but the stunned looks told her they had indeed heard and it meant something way more important than even she knew.

Her claim was verified by her aunts, along with a show and tell of the dragon tattoo on her hip. The Council then looked to the Coven Elders who unanimously nominated Della to be their Grand Priestess. A date for her induction had been set and after more talks, the Council had finally adjourned their assembly. When Kyra returned to her room, her cell phone was blinking that she had a message. She pressed the button and as Royce's voice filled the room, her heart filled to almost bursting …He said he loved her!

It seemed to take forever for her to get her bags packed, arrange for a ride, and say her goodbyes. But when she had finally been in the car, headed back to the man that held her heart, everything felt right for the first time she could *ever* remember. She had thought *that* was the best feeling in the world, but she had been wrong. The best feeling in the world was the exact second Royce's arms closed around her. It was like coming in from the cold after a long hard winter. He was all she would ever need.

He pulled back and knelt in front of her, more love than she had ever fathomed existed shining from his warm brown eyes. The words that followed she would carry in her heart for all time. "Kyra, *mo ghra'*, every second that we were apart the hole in my heart grew larger, until I was sure I would cease to exist without you. Having you here, *really here*, is a blessing and one I will not squander. I know our life together won't be perfect, nothing worth having really is, but it will be ours and anything we have together is better than the pain of being apart. You are the best part of me, the light of my soul and the completion of all that I am, man and dragon. I love you with every beat of my heart, every breath that I take, and every thought that I have. All I want is to be by your side, to be your mate, to love you every day that I draw breath and even the ones that come after. So I ask you, Kyra St Croix, will you be my mate, now and forever…*Always together!*"

Words escaped her and all she could do was nod her head. Royce smiled a smile that would forever be branded on her heart, an expression that personified all his hopes and dreams for their future, right before lifting her high into the air and swinging her around, shouting his joy for all to hear. Thankfully his closest neighbor was far enough away that no one was awakened.

Their first night back together and most of the next day was spent in bed. They made love, talked about the future, and only after he plied her with coffee and her favorite maple iced donuts did they begin talking about their mating ceremony. The longer he explained all the dragon shifter customs, the more questions she had, until he suggested that she speak with Siobhan, the Elder Healer and Devon's mother. Kyra had met her when they had worked together to save Lance's life and had spoken many times since, if only in passing, so she was more than willing to speak with her. A phone call to see if the healer was available and a long shower in which Royce gave new meaning to 'washing her back' and they set off to Siobhan's house.

His brethren seemed to have been lying in wait, because at every turn, one of them popped out to presumably say hello and welcome her back, but it was when they ran into Lance, Sam, and Sydney that she knew her dragon man had been busy telling their news to his family and friends through their mind speak. He had kept her so preoccupied that she had missed the telltale signs of their special communication, *something I never should have told him about*, she chuckled to herself.

Sydney had squealed from across the clearing and run towards she and Royce, "Kyra! Kyra! You're back!"

Royce had grabbed the child mid-run and hoisted her to his hip. Sydney kissed his cheek and hugged his neck, all the while telling Kyra how happy she was that she was home. "And Royce is happy, too. See? See his happy eyes? And his heart is singing, I can hear it."

Her parents had caught up by then and everyone laughed at the child's sweet way of describing his happiness, but Sydney was not to be deterred. She grabbed Kyra's hand and placed it over Royce's heart with her smaller one on top. "See? You can feel it," the child almost demanded. Not wanting to hurt Sydney's feelings, Kyra concentrated on the spot where their joined hands touched her mate's chest, and she felt it. It was the feeling you get when you hear a song that makes you want to sing along or a laugh that makes you want to laugh too. It was happiness, there was no other way to describe it. Her eyes met Royce's and she could see that he had felt it too.

"You're right, Syd. I can feel it."

Looking vindicated as only an almost six-year old could, she remarked, "Told you so."

The entire group burst out laughing, and after congratulatory hugs and promises of dinner together were exchanged, Kyra and Royce continued their walk to Siobhan's. They discussed Sydney's developing abilities, coming to the same conclusions they had already heard; she was special, but no one really knew how or why.

Royce had told Kyra that she would speak with the Elder Healer alone, but her nerves still threatened to get the best of her as Siobhan led her into a beautifully decorated sitting room adorned with hand crafted furniture from some of the most elegant eras. Calysta had insisted that Kyra learn about the finer things in life, something that had bored her to tears when she was younger, but in this setting, she was glad she had some clue what she was looking at. Not only was the furniture of museum quality, but every available surface was adorned with figurines, sculptures, or crystal pieces that would make any curator of any museum in the world jealous. The older woman even served tea from an antique tea service decorated with small lavender flowers that Kyra was sure dated back to the seventeenth century.

They chatted about a little of everything while they enjoyed their tea, and as soon as they were finished, Siobhan began, "Let me formally congratulate you on your mating. I knew our gentle giant would come around, and from the look of things, all is going very well." The Elder Healer smiled a knowing smile and Kyra was suddenly uncomfortable. She had never been a prude, but her relationship with Royce was new and discussing it with Siobhan felt like talking about sex with her aunties…*awkward*.

"Yeah…well, we had a rocky start that's for sure. I think maybe I should pinch myself to make sure I'm not dreaming, but then if this is all a dream, I'd rather not wake up." She chuckled to hide her nerves, but somehow knew the older woman was wise to her ploy.

The healer laughed out loud and all the tension Kyra had been feeling fled. Then Siobhan said, "I never had a doubt you two would find your way. I have lived many years with the belief that the Universe is all knowing and all powerful. She knows what each dragon needs and She creates their perfect complement in the form of their mate. She has no regard for species or location, only that you carry the special traits of the human race and that every dragon shifter, be they Guard or not, have that *one person* that truly completes them. She makes no mistakes."

Siobhan's voice had taken on an almost reverent tone. "Mating with a dragon shifter is not only romantic, but also spiritual. Our holy book says, *'when the two halves of the same whole meet, there will be instant recognition. Their souls will merge and only then will the dragon shifter know complete peace. They will have found their true home. It will be as if the time before the two met does not exist. All that matters is that they become one in body, mind, and soul.'*

"I know that Earth witches also have predestined mates chosen by the Goddess. What a tremendous blessing that your world and Royce's aligned. Dare I say the life you two will share will indeed be epic?" Siobhan seemed to get a faraway look in her eyes and when she next spoke, her words were filled with such love and devotion, Kyra felt honored the healer chose to share them with her.

"The bond of a dragon shifter and his mate is sacred and something that will exist even when you have both gone to the Heavens. My Gareth, Devon's father, was a member of the Dragon Guard and also one of the rare white dragons. Our love was and is timeless. Although he was killed in battle many years ago, I hold a piece of his soul in me." Siobhan laid her hand over her heart. "And I live every day with the belief that we will be reunited in the Heavens again one day."

The rest of their visit was spent with Kyra asking every question she could think of and some that seemed to come out of nowhere. Siobhan answered everything the best she could and together they lit candles and spoke the Mating Blessing, "Mother of All Universe, we thank you for our very life. Please be with these two souls, Royce and Kyra, as they dedicate their love and devotion to not only each other, but also to You. As you blessed our Elders with the wisdom to further our race, also bless Royce and Kyra with long life, much love, and a happiness that knows no bounds. May they have many children and when they ascend to the Heavens, may You find favor with those that have honored You with their lives and their love."

Kyra hugged Siobhan just before a heavy knock at the door let her know that Royce's patience had come to an end, and she had to admit to herself that she had missed him even though they had only been apart a few hours. The older woman called for him to come in, and without even a glance in any other direction, he came straight to her, kissing her until she forgot her name, let alone where she was. Only Siobhan's chuckle brought her hurtling back to Earth and had her burying her face in Royce's chest to avoid eye contact.

His laugh rumbled beneath her ear and soon they were all laughing together. Siobhan assured Kyra that it was not the first, nor would their kiss be the last she had witnessed. She further added that she was looking forward to the day it was her own son and his mate kissing in her living room. Royce and Kyra thanked the healer and promised to visit again soon.

Instead of heading home, Royce steered her towards the Town Square. Although she had been there at least a hundred times, this time was different, better somehow. She and her mate were walking hand in hand, browsing from shop to shop, and everyone they passed smiled and said hello, and some even offered their congratulations. All she could figure was that being in love, truly in love with your soul mate, really did make the world a better place.

They were discussing the mating ceremony and she had just commented that she was glad he had to plan it instead of her, when the woman that ran the flower shop yelled across the thoroughfare and asked to speak to Royce alone. Excusing himself with a quick kiss and a promise to hurry back, he jogged across the street as she continued to window shop. Every merchant in the lair was incredibly talented, but none so much as Emma, the jewelry artisan. She created gorgeous pieces out of otherwise unusable dragon scales, that rivaled anything Tiffany's had ever displayed.

Kyra looked over, saw that Royce was still talking to the florist and decided she had time to pop in, say hi, and see what new pieces the jeweler had created. The little shop always felt so warm and inviting, and smelled of apples and cinnamon, even though Emma swore that she rarely ate in the store, let alone cooked in it.

Kyra was greeted with a big smile and hug from the sweet young woman. No matter how many times she saw Emma, she was always so surprised at the magic she felt in her presence. She had asked the jeweler about it on an earlier visit, only to learn that she was an orphan, found in a basket in the woods many years before by Mary, the sister of Malachi – the Spiritual Elder of the clan, and raised by the woman and her mate, Samuel, until their passing. The love for her adoptive parents was evident when Emma spoke of them, and the fact that she had taken up the trade of her father was a true testament to the power of that affection.

The ladies talked as Kyra browsed. There were so many beautiful pieces, but she kept coming back to what she thought was a bracelet. It was almost completely made up of tiny bells that had been fashioned from royal blue dragon shells, with a few green ones that only served to accent the brilliance of the blue, all hanging from a thin golden chain. When she picked up the jewelry, the tinkle of the bells reminded her of the laughter of the fairies her Auntie Della had taken her to visit when she was a child.

Kyra laid the piece across her wrist and Emma giggled. When Kyra looked up at her, her brow furrowed in question, Emma replied, "It's an anklet."

Together the women laughed and Emma helped Kyra try it on. It was as if it had been made especially for her and as she took a few steps one way and then the other, the sound of the bells filled the tiny shop. Royce chose that moment to appear. He walked straight to Kyra and kissed her long and deep. Only when she was sure she was going pass out did he pull back, but kept her tight to his side. As her wits returned, she looked up, and in the cheekiest tone possible, complete with her pretend English accent said, "Did ya miss me, love?"

Her mate answered in kind, "Aye, I did." Then placed a kiss on the very tip of her nose before adding, "Besides, I heard the bells ringing and had to kiss ya'."

"Huh?" was the only reply she could think of, and thankfully, Royce was quick to explain.

"Every time a bell rings, a dragon is kissing his mate. Ya' didn't want me to mess with Fate did ya'?"

"Absolutely not!" she giggled and then showed him her ankle. "I was just trying this on. Isn't it beautiful?"

"It definitely is. Our Emma here is very talented," Royce commented.

The fact that Royce had taken the time to compliment Emma and the resulting blush on the jeweler's cheeks, just made Kyra love her mate all the more, if that was even possible. Reluctantly, she knelt down, removed the anklet and handed it back to Emma, promising to return and purchase it when things settled down a bit. Emma once again congratulated them and asked Kyra to come have coffee with her any time she could. Kyra left smiling, and wondering how she had ever lived so long without all the awesome people of the clan in her life.

~~*~*~*~*~*

It was finally his mating day and Royce was more nervous than he had ever imagined possible. He owed a huge debt of gratitude to the men of his Force, their mates, and his brothers, because without them he never would have gotten everything ready in just three days. Now, standing in the garden behind the house Kyra had been staying in, he was sweating bullets, praying she liked everything he had prepared. He'd had to get special permission for the first of many surprises he had planned for her.

The Elders had agreed to let him fly Kyra to Serenity Landing, the summit of the mountain that housed the Cave of the Ancients, where the ceremony was to take place. It was both special and symbolic of their relationship. His mate, no matter her stature, lifted him higher than he ever thought possible, and it was only fitting that he mark her as his own at the highest spot in the entire lair.

He watched as the two younger Guardsmen dressed in surcoats that almost exactly matched the royal blue of his beast, dismounted their horses and walked towards Kyra's front door. Using his enhanced vision, he saw a dragon that matched the one he had worn on his arm, chest, and shoulder since his transformation embroidered in golden thread across the front, and the black and golden rope trimming the top and sides. His mind wandered for just a moment as he remembered Kyra's tiny dragon tattoo, an exact match for his, and his mouth watered with the need to kiss that very spot and feel it react to his touch.

The sound of Lance's whistle brought him back to the present and alerted him that it was time to transform. He called forth the dragon that had been with him for as long as he could remember. Magic filled the air, and from one moment to the next, Royce's human form was replaced with his majestic royal blue beast. The massive warrior was as excited as the man to lay eyes upon their mate for the first time on their mating day. Neither was disappointed as Kyra exited the rear of the cottage, a Guardsman on both sides and a smile that shone so bright, even the sun paled in comparison. Her look of surprise was priceless, and the look of adoration that followed, absolutely breathtaking.

The dress he'd had made for her was perfect. It was the lightest color of lavender the seamstress could find to highlight the mesmerizing color of her eyes. Through the eyes of his dragon, he saw the tiny flames, just a few shades darker than the gossamer of her gown, that seemed to have no pattern but only served to accentuate the beauty of the woman wearing the garment. The royal blue satin sash around her waist showed off her beautifully full figure that would be his source of endless pleasure. As she walked towards him, the sun highlighted the slight tan of her shoulders, bare and tempting.

As they approached, the dragon laid on the ground, getting as low as possible for the Guardsmen to help his mate onto his back. Once she was in place, the dragon stood and prepared for flight. A quick thought to Lance had his brethren telling Kyra to hold the soft scales at the base of his neck. Just the feel of her hands on his scales caused the dragon to shiver. It was a unique experience for mates, and one both man and beast would not have traded for anything in the world.

The flight was less than ten minutes even with the detour around the mountain, but the feelings that flowed from Kyra through their mating bond let Royce know how much she enjoyed herself and the joy she felt that they were to be one for all time. Landing on the far side of the plateau, two more of the younger Guardsmen were standing at the ready to help Kyra down and escort her to her place next to the raised platform where the Elders would be seated. He noticed five chairs, but was more concerned with keeping his eyes on Kyra so the thought of the extra chair was completely dismissed.

He was delighted at her oooohs and ahhhhs as she took in all the flowers, ribbons, and bows they had placed on the archways leading to the dais where he would mark her as his for all time. The tears of happiness that filled Kyra's eyes when she saw her Auntie Della sitting to the side were worth every second of arguing with both the Elders and the Elder Witch he'd had to endure to have her present.

Once she was in place, Royce's dragon moved behind a huge outcropping on the backside of the summit. Calling forth his dragon magic, he transformed back into the man that wanted to be done with the ceremony and alone with his mate more than he wanted his next breath. He watched through the foliage as the Elders ascended to their places and had to smile when Rian was among them…fifth chair explained. Just about to thank his mother for her presence even from the Heavens, he spotted his Force as they took their places to the left of the platform. Not only the five he was proud to call brethren appeared in surcoats matching the color of their dragons, but also the four Guardsmen from the Blue Thunder Clan and his younger brother Rory. The visiting Guardsmen in their royal blue dress uniforms, so like his, took their places behind the others. The two lines of men served as a reminder of his past and present. Each played a monumental part in molding him into all that he was… a man, a dragon, a warrior. and on this, the most special day of all…a mate.

He looked to Kyra, the one created for him by a Universe he had thought had failed him and a Fate he was sure was out to destroy him, and was completely humbled. She was the embodiment of everything Royce needed to be complete, whole, and…*happy*. She was his future and all he would ever need. Unable to wait a second longer, he walked to his place, dead center of the Sacred Circle Kyndel, Grace, and Sam had created with small flower-filled ceramic vases. After a few seconds of silence, it was Rian that spoke, not Carrick as he had expected. Royce stood a bit taller, it was an incredible honor to have his own brother speak the words that would bind him and Kyra together.

"Long ago when knights and dragons fought side by side for King and country, it became apparent that dragon kin was no longer safe from those that would expose and destroy them. They sought to join with the knights that had so valiantly fought by their sides. Thus through magic and the will of both dragon and knight, the Dragon Shifters were born.

"In the infinite wisdom of our Founding Elders, clans were set up, one for each color of dragon, each assigned a region in which to make their home and to protect. Over time, some have flourished, some have ceased to exist, and others have been born from the joining of many. As the Head Elder of The Blue Thunder Clan and brother to Royce, it is an incredible honor to stand among those of the Golden Fire Clan. We are brothers in blood, brothers in battle, and brothers in loyalty.

"We are here today, in this most holy place of tradition, to honor what the Universe put into place all those many years ago. We are here to acknowledge and bless the mating of Royce Alan O'Reilly to the one the Universe made for him and him alone, Kyra Renee St. Croix. Will those seeking to witness this union please step forward?"

The ten men he was proud to call brethren stepped forward as one unit, and together, Rayne and Rory walked a few paces ahead. All the Guardsmen knelt and bowed their heads. After a few moments of silence, Rayne stood and faced the Elders "We, the five of the MacLendon Force, wish to witness and offer our blessing to the union of these two souls, two halves of the same whole. May they live long, fight hard, love harder, and produce many young to flourish when their souls have gone to the heavens." He knelt and bowed his head again.

Rory then stood and addressed the Elders, "We, the five of the Aherne Force of the Blue Thunder Clan, wish to witness and offer our blessing to one born of our blood and the mate of his heart. May their lives now and forever be a testament to all we hold dear…love, honor, and loyalty. As you are one, let your strength see you many years and the children of your children smile upon you." He also knelt and bowed when he was finished. Royce was in awe and would always remember that Kellan, although the Commander of the Force, had let Rory bestow the blessing. It was an honor that would not go without thanks.

It was Carrick that spoke after the moment of silence following Rory's blessing, "Your witness and blessings have been acknowledged and accepted MacLendon and Aherne Forces. It is truly a blessed event to have two such honorable clans together. Royce O'Reilly you may go to your mate. Please escort her to the Sacred Circle and before the Elders assembled here."

Royce walked towards Kyra, never once breaking eye contact, took her hands into his, and placed kisses upon both, before slowly walking her back to the Elders. It took all his considerable restraint to not grab her up and rush, but the sheer reverence of the moment made him go slow and savor every second.

Once they were in place, Rian spoke again, "The blue dragons were born of sea and sky. They are symbolic of the vastness of life and infinity, and they possess the ability to experience life from all aspects. They are highly protective and incredibly magical. Blue dragons are known for their patience and loyalty. The blue of their scales symbolizes the boundless sky and the deep calmness of the waters. Blue dragons will see every advantage, protect home and family with their very lives, and welcome the rising tide of change with calm acceptance. To mate a blue dragon is to accept all that they are and honor the power shared between mates."

It was Carrick's voice that rang with clarity and power, "Now is the time of the marking. May the Universe continue to bless you and yours all the days of your life," and with that everyone but Royce and Kyra followed the path that led off the mountain.

~~*~*~*~*~*~*

Time stood still as Kyra stared into Royce's eyes. She watched as a fire blazed in their deep brown depths, helpless to do anything but gaze upon her mate. Royce lowered his mouth to hers, stopping right before their lips would have touched and whispered, "*Ta' mo chroi istigh ionat,*" and then touched his lips to hers.

Just the tender touch of his lips to hers started an ache deep in her soul that spread like wildfire through her entire body, igniting a passion that would burn bright and hot for eternity. They opened completely to one another, baring all that they were to the other half of their soul. Kyra could feel Royce in every fiber of her being, and felt a part of herself binding to him. He was becoming as much a part of her as she was of him.

A small light, barely a glow, started in her heart and then flashed to encompass her entire being. In that flash, Kyra experienced everything that Royce was feeling, and knew with all certainty that he shared her emotions as well. She felt a twinge on the left side of her neck, and Royce immediately left her lips, trailing kisses across her jaw and down her neck until he reached the tender spot. He licked and sucked until all thoughts of anything but their naked bodies loving one another vanished from her mind.

When they finally stopped kissing, Royce led her to the same path the others had used to exit the plateau, but when she would have continued down the path, Royce steered her to the right and through the opening of a cave that had been decorated with the same flowers as their mating ceremony. As her eyes adjusted, she saw candles burning on every available surface and a pallet of thick fluffy blankets stacked high in the center. It was her dream from all those weeks ago coming to life. They walked in silence until they stood at the edge of the blankets. When Royce spoke, his voice echoed all the love and passion she was feeling. "Our first kiss was on a mountain top and I spent more nights than I care to admit lying on a cave floor dreaming that you would be mine. I thought it only fitting that we spend our first night as a mated couple here. I hope you agree."

Unable to form a single coherent thought, she threw herself into his arms and kissed him as if her very life depended upon it. Her hands slid under his surcoat and soon it hit the ground, along with the black t-shirt he had worn under it. His bare skin under her fingertips set off a series of electrical currents that caused an ache only Royce could cure. She slid down his body, randomly placing kisses and tasting special spots she planned to revisit. She appreciated every inch that was her mate and enjoyed the hiss from his mouth as her body rubbed against his straining cock.

She removed his belt, unbuttoned his pants, and let her hand follow the trail of deep auburn hair that disappeared into his pants. Her fingers stretched to cover the girth of his erection and she smiled as it pulsed against her palm. Working her fist to the tip, she let her thumb caress the weeping tip, spreading the warm proof of his excitement all around. Royce threw back his head and in her mind, she heard his strained voice, "*Kyra, mo ghra', I love you with all that I am.*"

Her surprise momentarily stilled her hand and she answered just as he had spoken, "*And I love you, my very own dragon man.*" Royce began to move his hips, dragging his cock through her palm. She listened as his breathing became ragged and watched the pulse in his neck beat a staccato rhythm as she marveled at the mark shaped like a flame riding a wave that she knew had not been there before. A piece of the conversation she'd had with Siobhan came to mind and she instantly knew it was their mating mark, and that she had a matching brand on her neck.

Passion shut off all further thought of anything but the man before her when more evidence of his ecstasy puddled in her hand. She worked her fist up and down his generous length, feeling him grow even harder. Using her free hand and with his help, she shoved his pants to the ground. As he kicked them out of the way, she placed her free hand on his thigh and leaned forward, taking as much of his cock into her mouth as she could. His essence on her tongue was like nothing she had ever tasted. He tasted of sea and air and purely Royce. She let her tongue massage the bulging vein that ran the length of the underside of his erection and felt him throb in reaction. Slowly, she let him slide from her mouth, only to tease the slit at the tip with her tongue. Royce's hands held her head and she could feel the building tension as his fingers gently flexed in her hair. With her hand on his thigh, she felt his muscles quiver and knew he wanted to move his hips but was using his considerable strength to hold back. Longing to see her mate completely lost to their passion, she sucked his cock back into her mouth until it touched the back of her throat, sucked until her cheeks hollowed, and swallowed. The resulting groan from Royce and the shift of his hands to her shoulders in an attempt to push her back and dislodge his cock from her mouth let Kyra know he was close to where she wanted him. Her need to give him the same pleasure he had shown her and the feelings that were flowing between them spurred her on.

She slid her lips over him and once again hollowed her cheeks, but this time, she moved her fist up and down the base of his cock, and with her free hand, she massaged his balls. He shouted, "Kyra…Kyra…*mo chroi…*

Unable to answer, she merely hummed, "mmmmmhhmmmmmm?' the vibrations a happy accident that caused him to groan loud and long.

He tried to pull from her mouth as hard as she tried to keep him there, and the result was a give and take in which they met one another stroke for stroke until she felt his balls in her hand tighten. He changed his tactics by sliding his hands under her arms and tried to lift her from the ground, but Kyra doubled her efforts, quickening their pace until he roared her name to the heavens and she felt the warm wet flow of his essence down her throat. Kyra swallowed every drop and worked him in and out of her mouth until his breathing slowed. Only then did she let him fall from her lips.

Royce knelt before her, placed his hands on her waist, and looked at her like she was the most beautiful thing he had ever seen. "You are absolutely amazing, my *a sta'rin'*. You and your love saved me from myself."

Ever so slowly, he leaned forward and placed a kiss on first one temple and then the other, above one eyebrow and then the other. He continue to show tender adoration with his lips, touching as many places as he could, until he had worked his way all the way down her throat. His journey continued to the very top of the lavender gown she was still wearing. Every inch of her décolletage knew his attention, while his hands slowly worked the zipper of her dress downward and then her gown hit the ground, leaving her in nothing but the lavender lace thong the girls had given her at her 'bachelorette' party. Royce leaned back and ran his eyes slowly from her baby pink toenails that Grace had demanded be painted to her shoulders and back again. She felt her nipples harden to just shy the point of pain, and the wetness that until now had gathered in her pussy wet the inside of her thigh.

"You are the most beautiful creature ever created, Kyra O'Reilly, and you are all mine," he whispered right before his mouth slammed to hers and he laid her back on the soft pillow of the pallet he had prepared. They kissed and tasted until she was sure she would never be able to live without his touch. She felt Royce *everywhere*, in her heart, in her soul, and in her thoughts. The sensual overload was indescribable, and combined with his hands on her body, made her insane with need. She felt his fingers slide under the lace on her hip and a slight tug later, she was completely naked and utterly at his mercy.

Kyra lifted her hips in an effort to get his wandering hands where she needed them most, but Royce only placed one hand flat on the skin above the curls that covered her mound and held her still. His hands were so large that as he moved his thumb back and forth, he brushed the tip of her very excited clit, raising goosebumps all over her body. She screamed her frustration and ever growing arousal at the ceiling, using only his name, "Royce...oh my Goddess...Royce..."

She could hear the smile in his voice as he answered, "Yes, *ce'adsearc*. Yes. I am here."

His body moved against her and she opened her eyes to see him kneeling between her legs. Their eyes met and Kyra was snared, unable to do anything but look into the eyes of the man that was hers forever. He placed his hands under her ass and gently pulled her closer to him. She felt the head of his cock touch the outer lips of her pussy and her hips lifted in response, causing him to slide between her outer lips and bump her clit. She tried to move her hips forward, tried to push him farther inside, and the movement caused both of them gasp. She watched his eyes become half-lidded and finally, his hips began to move.

She rolled her hips to meet his thrust and his thick, hard cock slid all the way into her wet warm pussy, only stopping when he reached the very bottom. They both sighed and the feeling of utter bliss rolled over and around them...they were truly one in all ways. Savoring the feeling of her womb contracting around his hard, throbbing cock, they paused, savoring the moment. The emotions freely flowing between them only heightened Kyra's excitement.

Royce's looked at where they were joined and spoke with incredible reverence, "Look at us*, mo ghra'*, look at where we are joined...*always together.*"

The sight of their bodies joined amped up her need to move, to feel release from the orgasm that was barreling towards her. She moved with renewed vigor against her mate, watching him glide in and out of her pussy. Royce needed no more motivation, he drove in and out of her, rolling his hips every time their hips touched. The change in motion made the head of his cock rub against the bundle of nerves at the top of her channel and her clit to make contact with the base of his cock on every stroke. Unable to do anything but feel, she let go of everything but the love and devotion she felt for her mate and reached for his hands. His fingers slid between hers just as she screamed her release to the heavens and heard Royce roar his.

She slowly returned to earth as Royce continued to slowly move in and out of her with their hands still clasped. "Hey there, *a sta'rin'*, how you doin'?"

She knew she wore a goofy grin and really didn't care as she purred her answer, "Perfect, my love, just perfect."

Royce let their hands fall apart, pulled completely out of her, picked her up, and moved her to the top of their pallet, laying her gently on her side with her head on a feather pillow. He laid facing her and smiled. Kyra had no idea how long they laid there, just gazing into each other's eyes, before he pulled a royal blue velvet box with a beautiful white ribbon tied around it from under her pillow and handed it to her.

"What's this?" she asked.

"Open it and find out," was his answer.

"But I didn't get you anything."

"I have everything I want, right here...*you*. Now, open it or I'll tickle you until you do." He grinned and she wondered if a day would ever come when she would grow tired of just looking at him.

She carefully pulled the ribbon, untying the perfectly crafted bow and laid the ribbon across Royce's chest. He laughed out loud and asked, "Am I gonna get unwrapped soon, too?"

"If you're lucky," she answered and winked.

Nothing could have prepared her for what she saw when she lifted the lid on the box. Her words came out jumbled, but thankfully Royce understood, "Oh my…when did you…I was gonna…"

Sparing her anymore verbal diarrhea, Royce leaned forward and kissed her while taking the anklet she had admired in Emma's shop from the velvet box. Only when she was breathless, did he leave her lips, kissing her chin, then the base of her neck, and the spot between her breasts. He worked his way down her body, randomly placing kisses that drove her wild. Kyra was shocked that she could feel herself getting wet again so soon after having the best orgasm of her life. When Royce kissed the sensitive skin right above her mound, her hips lifted of their own accord and he chuckled, but sadly, moved on.

He kissed the inside of first one thigh and then the other, the back of one knee and then the other. His stubble tickled and she giggled in response. Finally, he lifted her leg so that he could kiss all around her ankle. She had never imagined her ankle as an erogenous zone, but with Royce, *everything* was an erogenous zone. He placed the anklet around her ankle and made the bells tinkle with their special song. Kissing his way back up her body made her feel the flush of arousal and the joy of love. When he reached her lips, he kissed her long and deep, speaking directly into her mind, *"Every time a bell rings…"*

"A dragon kisses his mate," she finished for him, feeling the depth of his commitment.

"I adore you, a thaisce, and I promise you a life of endless happiness and incomparable love."

"Oh Royce, I love you."

"And I you, Kyra, and I you."

As she drifted off to sleep in the arms of the man she was meant to love, she knew everything that had happened had been worth the love they shared, and that there was nothing she wouldn't do, for the love of her dragon.

EPILOGUE
SIX MONTHS LATER

Devon had overslept for the fourth straight morning, making him almost late to escort Sam to the hospital...*again*. It was the last day of her residency and his last day to keep her safe in case the traitor or the human criminal came after her again. Lance had tried to guard her but since he freaked out every time any man even spoke to his mate, Rayne had asked for volunteers. Devon had had nothing better to do, so he had jumped at the chance and that was over six months ago.

He actually enjoyed his time in the hospital. Sam was a really great doctor and he loved watching the way she dealt with her patients. She had a real gift. Devon had always loved healing, and the fact that his mother was the Elder Healer of their clan, said it was in his blood. He might have chosen to follow in his father's footsteps and join the Guard, but healing called to his heart.

"About time, Bro," Lance said as he answered the door.

Devon grunted in his direction, not really in the mood for any of his smart-assed brethren's shit after another night filled with dreams of a faceless woman begging for him to save her.

Lance's hand on his shoulder stopped his forward progress. *"Don't forget to bring her straight to Rayne and Kyndel's. We'll all be there waiting to surprise her and congratulate her on finally, officially being Dr. Samantha Malone, MD."* He used their unique link to keep Sam from hearing their plans.

Devon nodded and tried to smile. He was so happy for Sam, and it was cool to see Lance happy for his mate, but today was *not* a good day. Saved from more conversation by Sam's entrance, he breathed a sigh of relief and thanked the Heavens for the travel mug of coffee she shoved into his hand. "You ready to go, Mr. Bodyguard?" she asked.

"I'll meet you in the car," was his answer, and he exited so the couple could have some privacy to say goodbye.

Sam ran out the side door, jumped in the SUV, and they rode together in companionable silence. As he drove, Devon thought more about the dreams he continued to have. At first, he thought it was just that...a dream. Probably caused by too many hero/action movies or too many conversations with his mother about mating, but by the end of the second one, he had changed his mind. They were too real. He could feel her terror, and on a few occasions, had caught the scent of sand and the sea. Scenting a dream was strange, even for a dragon shifter. They had to be some sort of premonition. It was the only explanation, but of what? As they reached the hospital parking lot, he shoved all thoughts of dreams and damsels in distress to the back of his mind and escorted Sam to work.

Several hours before the end of the day, Sam was called to the Emergency Room. There had been a multi-car pile-up on the freeway and all the injured were being brought to her hospital. On the way down in the elevator, Devon noticed Ernesto, one of the werepanthers from Max's Pride, and nodded. Luckily, Max had agreed that Ernesto, who was a male nurse already employed at the same hospital as Sam, could work her schedule, allowing her to be protected even in the restricted areas of the hospital. Devon had no idea where the werepanther was any other time or how he mysteriously appeared just when Samantha was heading to such an area, but he knew the Big Cats were good at getting in to places no one else could, and making impossible things happen, so he didn't question. He was thankful for the help.

Once Devon had watched the huge doors marked STAFF ONLY close, he headed to the waiting area to watch TV until Sam emerged and he was back on guard duty. It wasn't long until the Emergency entrance was flooded with EMTs and Paramedics pushing gurneys and caring for the injured. Every seat in the waiting area was filled within minutes and the family and friends of those involved in the accident still continued to pour in. Devon offered his seat to an elderly woman that was crying into a tissue and excused himself.

Not wanting to be far from Sam in case Ernesto was called away, he positioned himself at the reception desk right outside of the Emergency Room. He had seen others shooed away, but for some reason, the nurses always let him hang out and even got him coffee from *their* coffee maker, saving him from the horrible vending machine coffee. The clock ticked by another hour and there were still gurneys lining the halls with patients that needed to be seen. Every available doctor had been called from other departments and Charlene, Sam's best friend and fellow doctor, was called in on her day off to deal with the never-ending flow of patients.

Needing to stretch his legs and get some fresh air, Devon stepped outside, sure to keep the large doors at the end of the hall in sight. Watching a cluster of dragonflies flitting around the blossoms of an azalea bush, his mind wandered, and for the first time he heard the voice of the woman from his dreams during his waking hours. She sounded even more desperate than when he was deep in slumber. *"Help me, please."*

He closed his eyes, focused on the echo of the voice, and spoke to her the same way he communicated with his brethren, *"Who are you? Where are you?"*

There was a slight intake of breath and then she answered, *"Can you really hear me? Please tell me I'm not dreaming."*

He looked around to make sure one of his brethren wasn't pranking him and saw nothing or no one that even looked familiar. "Yes, I can hear you." He paused, realizing she hadn't answered his questions and decided to try a different approach to get the answers he needed. *"My name's Devon. What is yours?"*

There was no answer and the silence droned on until he was sure either he had imagined her or she had decided to screw with someone else. As he reentered the hospital, the voice came again, and this time it was louder and clearer, and if possible, more panicked. *"Help me, please?"*

His lack of sleep and frustration got the better of him and he snapped, *"How the hell am I supposed to help you when won't tell me where you are or who you are?"*

Again his question was met with silence, but this time it made him want to yell or hit something, or act in ways completely uncharacteristic for him. There was something about her voice, something that he felt every time he heard it, something that called to him. He wanted to chalk it up to the fact that he was a sworn protector and she needed help, but he knew it went deeper than that. Shaking his head to clear the cobwebs, he decided she was gone for real this time and took his seat next to reception.

It wasn't long before Sam came out looking like she needed a weeks' worth of sleep. Trying to lighten the mood, he teased, "How's tricks, Doc?"

She smiled and leaned against the desk, "Busy and beat, my friend. How about…"

He missed the rest of what Sam said because at that moment, his senses were assaulted with the scent of sand and the sea. It wasn't a dream this time. It was real…and *nearby*! Without a word, he followed the tantalizing aroma, immediately locating its origin. A gurney quickly moving away from him with long dark tresses hanging off the side and an elegant olive-toned hand lying precariously on top of the white blanket covering the patient it transported was the source.

Devon raced to catch up but just missed the elevator as the doors closed. Using his enhanced senses, he listened as the orderly pushing the gurney asked his companion to press the button for x-ray. He raced back to reception, grabbed Sam by the arm and quickly walked back to the elevators.

"What's going on, Dev?" Sam asked, and it was the concern in her voice that made him stop and explain.

"You're going to think I'm nuts, but the woman that was just wheeled to x-ray has been talking to me, through mind speak…*in my dreams*." He waited for Sam to tell him he was crazy, but all she did was push the down arrow and smile at him.

"You aren't taking me to the Psych ward are you?"

"No, silly man, we're going to x-ray."

"You believe me?" He was as surprised as he had ever been.

"Of course I do. Of all the things I've seen hanging out with you guys, this is tame," she laughed as the elevator doors opened and they stepped inside.

When they arrived at their destination, Sam used her access to look up the patient, but came back knowing no more than they did before. "She is listed as a Jane Doe and they have no idea what's wrong with her. She has no outward injuries, but has been unresponsive for almost six weeks and shows no signs of improvement."

His heart sank and it apparently showed on his face, because Sam touched his forearm before saying, "I'm so sorry, Dev. Is there anything else I can do?"

"I don't know, Sam, I just don't know," he answered, and it was then that everything clicked into place. The mind speak, her scent, his undeniable need to help her no matter the cost, it was all there, but he had been too frustrated and too tired to see it. Devon blurted out what he was thinking, "Holy shit, she's my mate."

~~*~*~*~*~*

It had been six months since the failure on the mountain top and the death of Master Eaton. Six months since his own brother had tried to kill him, not that Andrew wasn't also trying to kill Aidan, but his was a bid for vengeance and Aidan was doing it out of a sense of honor; *what a fucking waste*. As if that was not enough, he had seen Lance…alive and well, just another failure in a long list of crap that hadn't gone his way.

The death of Master Eaton had been devastating and proven that Kyra was definitely one hundred percent with the Dragon Guard. He had tried to find out who the older witch that had helped her was, but was still no closer to an answer. One good thing had come out of it. All the wizards had looked to him as their new leader and Andrew had embraced the role. He had even gotten John into the mansion, hidden behind a full beard and horn-rimmed glasses, but at least they were under the same roof, eliminating almost all the 007 spy bullshit. With John readily accessible day and night, they were making real progress deciphering the Prophecy.

Just that morning, John had come to him with a complete translation of the portion pertaining to the Earth element. He reread the script, confirming what he already knew. *A powerful white witch, sworn to the Earth, of long regal lineage made whole by human love, must mate a dragon of royal descent marked by devastating loss and the heart of not one clan, but two.* It was obvious to him after seeing the connection between Kyra and Royce that they were the two referred to in the ancient text.

  He had told John to use every available wizard to locate the other texts and knew his second in command would do whatever it took. For some reason he could not explain, he knew that the Prophecy was the key to his future and there was no way he was giving up until he knew every word. Of course, that did not mean that he wouldn't try everything in his power to bring down the ones that had betrayed him and left him for dead if the chance presented itself.

  Mr. A had made it clear that as long as they continued to provide magical cover for his operations, he would provide muscle for Andrew's. So in the last six months, while he and the wizards had searched for a way to take down the dragons and amass as much dark magic as possible, Mr. A had kidnapped young men and women and shipped them to buyers overseas with little to no detection from the authorities. Amazing how much easier it was to transport victims that had been subdued with a Stunning Spell as opposed to tied up and threatened.

  There had been accidents….. victims had been accidently killed or scarred and unable to be sold, in which case Andrew tried to save them by giving them the chance to learn magic. For some it worked and for others…well, they became collateral damage. A few times someone that actually showed promise was hit by a stray spell and maimed or killed. One such young woman had been struck down, and no matter what they tried, she had remained comatose.

  Andrew felt so bad for the beautiful young woman with long brown hair and delicate features, that he'd had John and another he trusted drop her at the hospital. He knew it was stupid and made him look soft, but she was sweet and he could tell that she had never hurt anyone in her life. She had also displayed a high degree of magical talent and her accident had been a loss to his cause. There had been something familiar about her, not familiar as in he had met her or her people before, but that something inside her was something he had encountered before.

  The parchment pages of the archaic grimoire crinkled as he turned them. He recognized the smell of old blood and stale magic on every page, making him pay closer attention to the spells, sure something contained within could help him in his bid to destroy the dragon shifters once and for all. He was just about to call it a day when the Latin words for *forever death* and *shapeshifter* caught his eye…*mortem in aeternum and versipellis… mortem in aeternum and versipellis…*

  The words echoed in his mind as he made his way through the mansion in search of John. If his instincts were right, this was the break they had been waiting six *fucking* months for, and he was not wasting one more *damn* day sitting on his ass.

~~*~*~*~*~*

  The concrete beneath her back was hard, damp, and cold. The iron shackles that were locked around her wrists and ankles burned along with the chain that weighed heavily across her chest, stomach, and thighs. As long as she didn't move too much, the chain stayed on what was left of her clothing and she avoided further injury. It had been at least a day since her captors had made an appearance, and she was so dehydrated that her lips cracked with the slightest movement. Even when they did appear, they only fed her two or three crackers and a piece of cheese, followed by warm water that tasted like a plastic bottle. Hunger and thirst had become her constant companions.

  Opening her eyes and seeing nothing more than she did with them closed because of the complete darkness, she let them slide shut and prayed for the millionth time to the Goddess. She had tried to count days and it was difficult with the light depravation, but she was pretty sure she had been locked away for about six months, give or take a week or two. All thoughts of rescue had left her a long time ago, her prayers had turned dark, and all she wished for was a quick death.

  As she finished her plea to her Maker, the sound of the key in the lock of the large iron door signaled the arrival of her captors. She knew there were always two by the sound of their heartbeats and that one was a woman by the smell of her perfume, but only one ever spoke, and it was always the man. The creak of the heavy door and six footsteps on the concrete floor and then the voice that she would never forget sounded. "Good evening Calysta, how are you this fine evening?"

Saved by Her Dragon
Dragon Guard Series #5

There Are No Coincidences.
The Universe Does Not Make Mistakes.
Fate Will Not Be Denied.

CHAPTER ONE

"I hope you can hear what I'm saying. If not, I've been sitting here for the last ten days talking to myself. It would be a real shame if they carted me off to a padded room before I even knew your name." Devon chuckled as he brushed his mate's long, dark hair, wishing with all his heart that she would open her eyes, move, talk...*anything*.

The nurses were letting him handle more of her daily care. It made him feel useful and like he was helping her. The connection they already shared was deeper than any he had ever heard of, defying the history of his kin. That they could actually mindspeak before the official mating ceremony and marking was unfathomable among his kin, and it made him long to know *all* the ways their union would be unique.

His mate was special. He felt it in the depths of his soul. Devon smiled as he remembered all the times over the years he had heard the exact same words from his brethren. It was just their way. Every dragon shifter thought *his* mate was the most extraordinary creature ever created, how could he not? The Universe made one astonishing woman for each dragon shifter...and *only* him. She completed him and the dragon within in every way possible. A dragon's mate brought light to their soul and love to their life. But *she* was so much more. It was reflected in every person...dragon, mate, or human...that came into contact with her. They were drawn to her, as though she was the light that would fill their darkness.

At first he thought it was because of her condition, combined with a desire to help. But the longer he cared for her, the more it became clear that *she* was the reason. They wanted to be near *her*, almost like being in her orbit would somehow make them better people. At least that's how he thought of it, because if he didn't, his jealousy and that of his beast would become unbearable.

Even the physicians that were very clinical in their dealings with his mate had a difficult time giving up hope. Each gave him a daily report that was logical, clinical, and detached, but he could *feel* there was more they wanted to say. Their comments consisted of things like, "the longer the coma lasts, the less likely she is to wake, but nothing is impossible" or "she shows no sign of deteriorating or improving, she is just existing, but she is strong, so there is hope". Then they would give her another long look and he could see them wishing her well. It only further proved she was exceptional.

Devon marveled at the way her long, dark lashes curled lightly atop the curve of her high cheekbones. Her soft, olive skin glowed, and even under the harsh fluorescent hospital lighting, they still held a slight blush. His fingers slid from her hair to the slope of her neck and tingled at the connection. His mate, soft and warm to the touch, was absolutely captivating. His mouth watered to taste the very spot his fingers caressed. He willed the strong emotions he already felt for her through their growing mating bond, and he prayed she could feel how important she was to him. For just a moment, he closed his eyes and let dreams of their future follow the feelings he shared. He grew impatient for some change in her condition and was willing to try damn near anything to get her out of that bed and into his arms.

He quickly squashed his maudlin thoughts, instead letting them drift to her daily sponge baths. He had been pleasantly surprised when the nurses had asked him to help but turned away when they uncovered her breasts or pubic area, no matter how much he wanted to look. Not that looking away did anything to stop his imagination. Those brief moments had fueled some of his best erotic dreams. The nurses chuckled at his modesty, but he'd explained that it was a matter of respect and trust to the one that already held his heart. The women had *ooh'd* and *aww'd* and told him what a great guy he was, making him regret his decision to share. What her caregivers didn't understand, and he couldn't explain, was that although she was to be his for all time, they hadn't *really* met yet, and when she did wake, he wanted her to know that her needs *always* came first...*in every way*.

He knew in his heart that everything would work out. There was no way the Universe, in Her infinite wisdom, would bring them together only to rip *her* from his grasp before he had the chance to do anything other than watch her motionless form in a hospital bed. She *would* wake up. She *had* to wake up.

Unwilling to think of any other alternative, he thought of her voice and the way it caressed him from the inside out when she spoke directly into his mind. It completed him in a way he had only imagined, and miraculously, his dragon was content for the first time in years. Unfortunately, it was also exasperating and confusing, because no matter how hard he tried, it was always the same...beautiful but *incomplete.* She would call out and he would answer, there would be a pause and then she would call out again. He was sure she heard his voice by the way she would ask if he was still there, but for some reason she never answered his questions or responded to anything he said. It made him wonder if she heard the *sound* of his voice but not the words, making true communication with his mate just out of reach. Devon's most earnest prayer was to have her in his arms. However, the longer her condition remained unchanged, the harder he searched for 'unconventional' ways to bring her back to the land of the living.

Stopping the dark thoughts that threatened his optimism, he instead continued his one-sided conversation with his mate. "You've been quiet the last few days. I even took a nap to see if maybe you would talk to me then.

Sam says you're probably saving up your strength for when you wake. I'm sure that's the case, but…I miss you." The last three words were whispered for her ears only.

Devon sank into the recliner he kept beside her bed, wrapped his hand around hers, and brought it to his lips. He gently kissed the back of her hand and continued to stare at her face, imagining the first glimpse of her smile or the utter joy of witnessing passion reflected in her eyes. He knew from the hundreds of times the doctors and nurses had checked her pupils that they were the palest green, with just a touch of blue, reminding him of the sea as it met the coastline where he played as a child. His heart ached to see them sparkle as she giggled or light with fire when she gave him hell for one of the many things he was sure she would get after him about, *anything* but the dullness that came from her coma.

He brushed an errant hair from her forehead and almost fell from his chair when a voice from across the room said, "No change?"

Devon had been so wrapped up in his mate he completely missed Aaron's approach, something that hadn't happened to the experienced Guardsmen since right after his transformation. Praying it would go unnoticed, he had to smile when Aaron laughed. "Sorry, bro, didn't mean to sneak up on ya."

Devon let go of his mate's hand and scratched the scruff covering his jaw, realizing he couldn't remember the last time he'd shaved. "No change at all," he sighed his answer, his eyes never leaving his mate.

"What's Sam say?" Aaron asked, his usually joking tone replaced by concern.

"She said there is *another* specialist coming today." He shook his head and added, "I finally gave in and called Mom. It'd be an understatement to say she was pissed. After she finished yelling at me, she had me call Lance to bring her down here."

Feeling incomplete without contact, Devon reached out and once again wrapped his much larger hand around his mate's. He and his dragon needed the connection more with every day she stayed just out of their reach. His thumb rubbed circles on the back of her hand and wrist. Her long, elegant fingers naturally wrapped around his hands and he thanked the Heavens that she was not as petite as Royce's mate, Kyra. At five-feet-two inches, Devon always feared one of them would somehow hurt the little witch, even with her immense magical power.

Devon had breathed a sigh of relief that his mate was at least five-feet-eight inches tall. He was even more pleased that after what the doctors were saying had to be almost four weeks in a coma and with her only nourishment from bags and tubes, she still had ample breasts and curves that made his palms itch to explore. She was everything a woman should be. She was *perfect*. But he would still be careful. She was considerably smaller than his six-feet-three inch frame and delicate in comparison to his muscular physique.

"Your mom yelled?" Aaron asked, jarring Devon from his daydreams.

He nodded. It had been one of only three times he could remember his mother raising her voice in all of his one hundred and twenty years. Siobhan Walsh was the epitome of patience and tranquility. As one of the most talented healers in all of dragon kin and an Elder of their clan, she embodied calm, cool, and collected. However, that had all gone to hell in a hand basket when her only son had called from the hospital, and it had gotten worse when he told her that he hadn't been avoiding her for the last ten days but had been at his mate's bedside. But the cherry on the sundae was when he told her that said mate was unconscious and unresponsive. Her bellow (that's the only way he could think to describe it) had been just as loud as when she'd caught him and some of the other young *drakes* peeking under the tent of the older, more 'physically developed' *vibrias* when he was not yet a teen.

"Yeah, she yelled. Then told me she loved me before slamming the phone in my ear." Devon tried to laugh, but it came out more like a cough.

Aaron walked the rest of the way into the room, grabbing a chair on his way. "Don't worry, Dev, you know she's just shocked and even more worried. Hell, you never keep anything from her." He straddled the chair backwards, laying his arms across the back, looking equal parts comfortable and bored.

"Yeah, I know, and I know I should've called her earlier, but I really thought the coma was from a bump on the head or something simple and might last a day or two. I was so sure my mate would wake up and everything would be fine, I just didn't want to bother Mom. Well, as you can see," he paused, letting his head fall forward, "I was wrong, *really wrong*. It's just that Mom has enough on her plate with Grace having twins. Heaven knows the entire clan is celebrating the first set of twins in almost a hundred years and the happy couple, or at least your brother, is losing their minds. I was sure we could handle this without bothering her. Again…I was mistaken."

"Isn't that some *shit*? My brother's gonna have twins! Well, Grace is going to have them, but you get what I mean." Aaron chuckled. "A's in hog heaven when he's not worrying about Grace, and I think she's going to banish him from the house if he doesn't stop trying to coddle her." He quickly added, "I'm telling you right now, he's *not* staying with me."

Aaron stopped, looked around the room, and then said, "Did I tell you, they've completely moved back to the lair? Siobhan wants them close and Kyndel, enlisting Rayne for backup, demanded they move back to the lair.

I'm just thankful Aidan is carrying on the family tradition. I can't imagine a mate, much less a baby…and two? No *fucking* way!"

His brethren was laughing, but Devon could hear the longing in his voice. It was hard enough that the twin Guardsmen had lost their parents, but then their younger brother had betrayed dragon kin and was lost to his own hatred and insanity. Insult to injury was that Devon had found his mate, leaving Aaron the only bachelor on their Force, a situation that just had to *suck*.

Deciding they both needed a break, Devon let go of his mate's hand and stood, gripping Aaron's shoulder. "Let's get a cup of coffee before Mom gets here. Ya know there won't be time later."

Aaron nodded as he stood, returning the chair to its place against the wall as he headed towards the door. He glanced towards Devon's mate then back to his friend. "You sure you want to leave her?"

"Yeah, even *I* have to get away every once in a while to keep my sanity, just not for long. I'll stop by the nurse's station, someone will come and stay with her while I'm gone. Sam put 'round the clock care in her official orders so my girl is never alone." He stood staring, unable to stop his fingertips from caressing her cheek.

Devon leaned as close as he could get to her ear and whispered, "I'm going with Aaron to grab a cup of coffee, *a chumann*. Be right back." He pressed a kiss to her forehead, lingering an extra heartbeat to inhale the scent of sand and sea. One simple whiff calmed his soul and the dragon within, who was *not* dealing well with their mate's condition.

When he stood, he saw that Aaron had silently moved to just outside the door, protecting their tender moment from prying eyes in his own way. His quick-to-temper and always-a-smart-ass brother was not usually so considerate, and Devon had to wonder if there was more to his friend's newfound manners than just courtesy.

Turning as he approached, Aaron spoke before Devon could thank him, "You ready to go?"

Taking the hint, Devon nodded. "Lead the way."

After a quick stop at the nurse's station, the Guardsmen headed towards the elevators. One more glance down the hall reassured Devon all would be well in his absence. Melanie, one of his favorite nurses, was heading into his mate's room. Once inside the lift he asked about another of their brethren. "Has anyone heard from Kyra and Royce?"

Aaron nodded. "I talked to the old man this morning. They're no closer to finding Calysta than when they left." Aaron chuckled. "Royce is definitely ready to put some distance between him and his brothers. He grumbled about them always 'being under foot' before Kyra wrestled the phone from him and said everything was good. She sounded more tired than I thought possible, but said she has some strong leads and gave me a long list of her witchy stuff that she needs sent. I asked if she was worried about her mom and she said 'not really', but it was just a cover. There's definitely something up." He shrugged. "I gave the list to Jace and told him how important it was that it go out today. All in all, *grumpy grandpa* and his mate sounded good…just beat." Aaron finished just as the doors opened and the scent of fresh coffee and food invaded Devon's senses, making his stomach growl.

Aaron laughed out loud, clapping him on the back. "Hungry, dude?"

"I guess I am," Devon chuckled. "I think Sam's surprise party was the last time I ate anything other than sandwiches and chips from the vending machine in the waiting room."

"I know I'm going to sound like the old man, but you really have to take better care of yourself. Your mom's gonna give you another dose of hell when she sees you. I didn't want to mention it, but you're kinda looking like Grizzly Adams there. It'd be a damn shame if you scared your lovely mate as soon as she opened her eyes." Aaron laughed at his own joke, and for the first time in ten days, Devon laughed, too.

"You're right. I look like a bum. I've been spending every waking minute here or on the road. I leave long enough to run home, shower, and change clothes, then haul ass back here. I'm trying to at least be presentable to speak to the doctors and nurses that come in every day, but it's just so *damn* hard to leave her. I'm always afraid she's going to wake up and I'm not gonna be there."

Devon turned away from his brethren, hiding the emotions that speaking of his mate stirred within him, and grabbed a tray, heading towards the food. He decided eating before his mother arrived and the sermons began was a good idea. It was going to be bad enough when she saw his shaggy hair and almost full beard without a lecture on how important it was for him to take care of himself.

They ate in companionable silence for a few moments until Devon asked, "Did Kyra mention if she thought Andrew had anything to do with her mother's disappearance?"

Aaron took a drink of his iced tea, then shook his head as he answered, "I asked and she said there were no signs of the traitor or any witches or wizards, for that matter. She said every spell she used registered the same thing…really old, really dark magic that was definitely from the earth, but had no human or magical practitioner's signature attached at all. When I asked what the hell that meant, she sounded really frustrated, cursed a little bit, and admitted she didn't have a clue. Her next step is to call her Aunt Della, something she didn't sound thrilled about. Freaky, huh?"

Devon furrowed his brow and nodded. "Damn sure is." Before he could contemplate what fresh hell was coming for them this time, his mate's voice sounded in his head, *"Are you there? Please, help me…"*

"I'm here, sweetheart. Can you hear me?" He waited less than two heartbeats before jumping to his feet, tray in hand, and headed for the trashcans, his brother and their conversation completely forgotten. Aaron's voice from behind brought him back to reality.

"Dude, what's up?"

Devon pointed to his temple and answered, "She's talking again."

Aaron grabbed the tray. "You go on, let me throw this shit away and I'll be right up."

Unable to speak, waiting for a reply from his mate, Devon nodded and jogged towards the elevators. Once the doors closed, Devon called to her again, *"Baby, are you there? Can you hear me?"*

As he stepped out of the lift, she spoke again, *"Please help me. I can't find my way."*

"I'm here. You're not alone. I'll do whatever I can to help, but you have to talk to me. You have to tell me what you see or feel or smell…anything."

He spoke quickly as he raced down the hall. Crossing the threshold into her room, he had to swerve not to run right into the back of one of the young healers from his clan. Quickly taking in the scene, Devon saw his mother, Lance, and Sydney standing at his mate's bedside. Then he saw two more of his younger clansmen, who were training with Siobhan, unpacking candles and incense, placing them on every available surface. It was obvious his mother wasn't wasting any time. He knew she was aware of his presence but had yet to acknowledge him, and if truth be told, he wasn't looking forward to their first interaction since her abrupt goodbye earlier.

He made his way to her bedside and Lance was the first to speak, obviously trying to relieve the tension filling the room. "Hey, Dev. How's it going?"

Devon continued to call to his mate while greeting their visitors. Before he could answer, Sydney, Lance's daughter, came running towards him, arms outstretched, a huge smile on her sweet face. He grabbed her just as she jumped and swung her into the air before settling her on his hip. Her arms came around his neck and she kissed his cheek as she whispered, "Miss you, Dev."

"I miss you too, Syd. How have you been?"

"I'm good. Been going to classes." The room erupted into laughter at the matter of fact way the child spoke. She was most definitely six going on twenty-one. "When are you and your mate coming home?"

They reached her bedside just as Devon answered, "I don't know, Syd. The doctors say we need her to wake up first." He hated that he didn't at least know her name. It sounded so impersonal to say 'her' or 'my mate' all the time.

The perceptive child in his arms hugged him tighter and said, "It's okay. She knows you're here and she's *really* happy 'bout it."

He snapped his head to the side and looked right into Sydney's big blue eyes. "What did you say?"

Sydney rolled her eyes in mock irritation, placed her hands on his cheeks, and stared deeply into his eyes. When she spoke, it was slower than her normal cadence and with a great deal of deliberation, "I said…she knows you're here…and she's really happy 'bout it."

In any other situation, he would have laughed at Sydney's actions, but the sheer gravity of the situation stole the air from his lungs. It took a few seconds for him to find his voice and when he did, it came out as barely more than a whisper, "You can hear her? Can she hear you?"

"Of course I can hear her." Sydney shook her head like his questions were ludicrous, and he was reminded once again that the child had wisdom well beyond her years. When she spoke again, it was on a giggle. "And why wouldn't she be able to hear me, silly dragon?"

It was then that Devon realized the room was as quiet as a tomb and all eyes were on him and the little beauty. Slowly her hands slid from his cheeks and once again wrapped around his neck as she hugged him tight. She spoke and his heart skipped a beat, "She's trying her best to wake up, but the black fog won't let her."

Thankfully, Siobhan chose that moment to speak, because there was no way he could. "Sydney, why don't you jump down and come over here and tell me what you and Devon's mate talked about."

The child gave Devon one more hug and a kiss on the cheek before sliding to the floor and skipping over to his mother. He watched as she went, impatient to hear what she had to say, not sure what to make of the fact that his mate could hear the girl but not him. He knew Sydney was extraordinary and that her parents and Siobhan were doing everything possible to understand all her exceptional abilities, but he was almost afraid to hope that the little girl could actually help wake the woman that was meant to be his.

"Sam's heading this way," Lance spoke directly into his mind.

"Is she alone?" Devon asked.

There was a pause and then his brother answered, *"Charlie is with her and the specialist will be here within the hour. There's also a nurse on the way to draw blood."*

The words had barely been spoken when Sam stepped into the room with her friend and colleague in tow. Sam was quick to speak in an effort to distract her friend from the young healers gathering up the candles and incense they had just placed. "Hey, why wasn't I invited to the party?"

"Mommy! Mommy!" Sydney yelled. All thoughts of anything but her mother forgotten as she ran to Sam.

Devon watched the scene unfold before him with a new perspective and a happy heart, knowing someday that would be his mate and child. Lance joined his family as the healers finished hiding their magical paraphernalia. Dr. Gallagher, aka Charlie, Sam's oldest friend and colleague, was more interested in getting to her patient than paying attention to the people around her, so everything out of the ordinary went unnoticed. He watched as she checked his mate's vitals, recording them on the chart.

Sam soon joined her friend at his mate's bedside, and although it was crowded, he stood his ground. As he listened, the two doctors discussed what would happen when the specialist came in and the treatment options still open to them, making sure they had all their bases covered. Lance once again spoke through mindspeak. *"I told Sam what Syd said about the black fog and she's ordering another MRI and CAT scan, whatever the hell they are. She also said something about checking medical journals."*

"Thanks, bud. Hope she can figure it out."

"Me, too. Trust me, if there's a way, Doc will bring her back to you."

Devon smiled at the way Lance used his wife's nickname, another testament to the incredible bond between mates, one he could not wait to share with his. The sound of Sam's voice pulled his attention. "I need you to sign this paperwork so I can have some additional tests done." She smiled and barely winked, letting him know that she was aware of the conversation between him and her mate.

Devon nodded as he signed and asked, "Will these take place before or after the newest specialist examines her?"

Sam smiled and touched his arm. He could feel the reassurance she was pushing towards him and appreciated her efforts. When she spoke, he was once again reminded what an amazing doctor Samantha Malone truly was. "I'm going to wait and see if she orders any others so we can do them all together. I just wanted to get this paperwork out of the way before I forgot." She moved to the side, letting the phlebotomist closer to take the blood that had been ordered.

The young man carefully extracted the samples and Devon worked hard to keep his jealousy and that of his dragon in check. Logically, he knew the man's interest in his mate was purely professional, but his heart and beast saw the man as a threat, one they wanted very badly to exterminate. The longer he watched, the more the need to remove the young professional's hand from the end of his arm became a living force within him. His feet took a step towards the younger man of their own volition. Only Sam's hand on his arm and the sound of Lance's voice in his head kept him from continuing his forward motion. *"Whoa there, brother. Chill out."*

Devon jerked from the jealous fog and shook his head before answering his friend, *"Damn, what the hell was that?"*

His brother's answering laughter further calmed Devon and his dragon, *"That my friend...is the mating call. Ain't it grand?"*

"No, not really, smartass," he chuckled and moved behind his mother until the lab tech left the room, just to be safe.

"Yeah, well, it gets easier, but trust me, it never goes away."

Before he could respond, Siobhan spoke, "How long do we have before the specialist gets here?"

Sam answered, "About thirty, maybe forty-five minutes. Charlie and I are going to my office to wait for her. Sorry y'all, but everyone except Devon will need to move to the waiting room while Dr. Lawrence does her examination." She winked in their general direction and then followed her friend out the door.

"Can we go get some ice cream, Dad?" Sydney asked as soon as her mother was out of ear shot.

"Sure we can, *leanbh*," Lance answered as he lifted Sydney from Siobhan's lap. "Anybody else want some ice cream? I'm buying," he added as he turned to head out of the room.

"Yes!" Everyone answered, almost in unison. Devon watched as they filed into the hall.

His mother was the last to stand. Turning, she reached for his hands. They stood looking at one another for a few seconds before she spoke. "You know I love you with all my heart, but if you ever pull a stunt like this again, I *will* beat you black and blue."

Devon felt his eyes grow large and had to work hard not to laugh at the vision her words inspired. He knew his mother was being serious, but just the thought of her beating anyone, especially him, was truly funny. Eager to put an end to their feud, he apologized. "Mom, I'm so sorry. I know I should've called right away, but I truly thought it was nothing serious and I could handle it without bothering you."

He barely had the words out of his mouth before she dropped one of his hands and swatted his arm. "There will never be a time when you are *bothering* me. I am your mother and the healer of your clan. Don't you EVER forget that." She emphasized her point with another swat to his arm.

Knowing better than to belabor the point, he quickly answered. "I really am sorry, Mom. Won't happen again."

Siobhan smiled her 'approving mother' smile, then hugged him and kissed his cheek before leaning down to grab her oversized leather bag. As she turned to leave the room, he heard her say, "See that it doesn't." He barked out a laugh and saw her shoulders shake as she tried to hold in her own glee. Calmness settled over him to know that he and his mother were once again in good standing. She was an important part of his life and he hated when they disagreed.

Devon settled into his recliner laid his hand over his mate's, and spoke, "Well, *a chumann,* here we are again…just you and me. And now you've met my mom."

He raised her hand to his cheek. At the skin to skin contact, an electric current shot through his body, making a beeline to his cock. His eyes slid shut and his breathing became labored. The longer they touched, the more intense the feelings became, until his erection pushed against the zipper of his jeans and he was forced to let her hand fall from his face.

The sound of voices in the hall alerted him to the arrival of Samantha and the specialist. Devon took a deep breath and used his considerable self-control to rein in his raging libido just as the doctors entered the room. He stood while Sam introduced her companion. "Devon Walsh, this is Dr. Jane Lawrence. Dr. Lawrence is the top neurosurgeon in the country with a specialty in trauma."

He sensed her nervousness and knew she hurried with the introductions to avoid the personal questions that would inevitably come. Without answers, both Devon and Sam worried that Dr. Lawrence would become suspicious of their relationship with the patient. It was something they were getting good at avoiding as the days ticked past and more unfamiliar doctors came to examine her. The hospital had been incredibly lenient due to Sam's sterling reputation, but he doubted it would work with the woman before him.

With a smile and nod, Dr. Lawrence reviewed the chart Samantha handed her quickly, making small notes in the margins. Without looking up, she commented, "I see you ordered another MRI and CAT scan, was there a change that prompted this new testing?"

He saw Sam's eyebrows rise at the other doctor's question, but was impressed with her quick thinking. "There was eye movement and increased dilation during her last exam. You will see that in Dr. Gallagher's notes."

"Oh, yes, here it is," Dr. Lawrence answered in a somewhat underwhelmed tone and Devon recognized her question for exactly what it was…a way to double check her colleague's work. He would have laughed out loud at the outrage he saw on Sam's face had he not feared one or both women might kick him in the balls. Besides, there was something just a little *different* about Dr. Lawrence that he couldn't get a read on.

After a few more moments of strained silence, the specialist returned the chart to the hook at the end of the bed and without a word, moved closer to his mate. She stood staring, making him wonder if she was trying to divine a diagnosis. Dr. Lawrence's intense stare and lack of movement was odd to say the least. The longer it lasted, the more uncomfortable Devon grew. He looked to Samantha for direction, only to find her looking like she was about to pounce. Her brow was furrowed, her mouth turned down in a frown, and her fists were clenched to the point of making her knuckles white. He spoke through the link shared amongst all his brethren and their mates, *"Sam…"*

Her eyes snapped to his and she gave a quick shake of her head. *"Hang on just a sec,"* was her only reply before she returned her stare to the doctor.

Devon counted to thirty before Dr. Lawrence's stance relaxed, glancing first at Sam and then Devon. Looking back to the patient before speaking, she began, "From what I can see, this woman has been through a substantial trauma, but that is not what keeps her from waking. I cannot pinpoint *what* is keeping her in the coma and I am not sure further testing will reveal anything new, but it can't hurt either."

Sam was the first to speak. "Excuse me, Dr. Lawrence, I mean no disrespect, but you didn't even *touch* the patient. How can you make any assumptions about her condition?"

Instead of answering, the specialist spun on her heel and walked towards the door. Devon was sure she was about to leave without further discussion and was surprised when she shut the door and leaned against it. Smiling slightly, she crossed her arms over her chest and spoke, "Maximillian Prentise sent me." With that declaration, her eyes flashed from totally human to very feline and back again in a split second.

"Well, shit," Devon said under his breath, forcing a chuckle from the doctor.

"I'm sorry I didn't tell you right away, but Max's message was very brief and he neglected to let me know that her attending physician was also dragon." She smiled the first real smile since entering the room.

"I'm not a dragon shifter but my husband is, and I had no idea Max was even aware of the situation," Sam remarked.

He could have kicked himself for not recognizing the good doctor as a shifter. For the second time in the same day, Devon had let his concern for his mate override his senses. It was a mistake he wouldn't make again. All at once everything fell into place and Devon filled in the blanks. "Ernesto has been checking in on her. It didn't even occur to me that he would tell Max. I'll have to call the King and thank him."

"Ernesto just happens to be my brother. Our parents were both Pride Healers. I am part of the pride but travel so much that I rarely see any of them in person. However, that does not stop our Leo from calling me when the need arises and I believe this is such an occasion," Jane said, and Devon could feel the affection she had for her brother and her King.

Dr. Lawrence was so much more relaxed and approachable that Devon began asking questions. "Have you seen anything like this before, Doctor?"

Dr. Lawrence moved away from the door and came to his mate's bedside, picking up her hand as she answered, "Please call me Jane." She looked at him and grinned. "I have. I understand you have a very skilled healer in your clan and a powerful white witch, as well. Is that right?"

Both Devon and Sam nodded as she continued, "I have very little magical knowledge or ability to sense its use, that is one of the reasons I became a doctor instead of a healer, but I would say that your girl here is a casualty of a powerful sorcerous accident."

She paused, looking at both of them for emphasis. When she spoke again, it was with a bit more conviction, "It is really the only explanation. She has no wounds, bruises, or contusions. All her tests, scans, and x-rays are normal, and she continues to thrive, although unresponsive. Lastly, her overall health is not declining, like we typically see in coma patients."

Silence filled the room as Devon and Sam absorbed Jane's words. Dr. Lawrence finally broke the silence, speaking directly to Devon. "I would get your healer to assess your mate as soon as possible."

He grinned and hurried to explain as Jane frowned. "The healer is my mom and she's here in the hospital with others from our clan eating ice cream as we speak."

All three laughed as Jane moved towards the door. "Then I'll leave you to it. I have to be south of the border for another consultation early tomorrow morning."

She reached in her pocket and handed him her card. "Please don't hesitate to call if you have any questions or need me for anything."

"Thank you very much, Dr. Lawrence," he and Sam answered in unison.

"Jane, please, and it was my pleasure." She waved goodbye and disappeared into the hall, right before a bouncing Sydney entered with balloons tied to each wrist.

"Look, Mommy! Look, Devon! They had balloons in the gift shop," Sydney squealed.

Before either could answer, Lance appeared with a pink stuffed cat under one arm and a purple unicorn under the other. Devon burst out laughing as Sam commented, "And it looks like they had stuffed animals, too."

Sydney nodded, making her blonde curls bounce. "They sure did. Aren't they cute?"

"They really are," Devon laughed and shook his head at his friend, who proceeded to elbow him as he walked by.

"Just wait until you have kids of your own, dude. Paybacks are a bitch and I have a long memory," Lance smirked and raised his eyebrows, letting Devon know his brethren was looking forward to the day he could return the favor.

"Enough, you two," Siobhan interjected. "I want to know what the doctor said."

A quick glance at Sam and Devon knew it was up to him to explain. "Well, Dr. Lawrence is a werepanther, as well as being the leading neurosurgeon in the country. Max sent her to help us out. She believes we are dealing with something magical, not physical, which goes along with the black fog Syd told us about."

He continued as his mother nodded, "She knew of you and Kyra by reputation and felt your expertise was just what we needed."

For the first time in what seemed like hours he looked at his mate. It was the longest he had been in the same room without touching her since recognizing her as his own. He moved to her side, immediately threading his fingers through hers. His mother spoke, breaking the spell that just being near her created. "Then close that door and let's see what we can find out. If what Max's doctor said is correct, then we are going to need Kyra as soon as possible."

Turning to her trainees she instructed, "Please set up the candles and incense again. We will perform the Discovery Ritual as soon as you are ready. Lance, since you are the closest, can you please close the door?"

The Guardsman obliged, quietly closing the door. It was then that Devon realized somewhere along the way Aaron had disappeared. "Hey, has anyone seen Aaron?"

"Oh *shit*, yeah. He went back to the lair. Something about making sure Jace sent a package to Kyra. But dude, he was acting really weird and when I asked what was up, he just ignored me and left." Lance shrugged, heading back to his wife and daughter.

"Well, okay then. I guess I'll catch up with him later," Devon said right before his mother announced they were ready to begin.

"Are you able to stay for the ritual, Samantha?" Siobhan asked.

"Yes, ma'am. I'm officially off duty, so I'm all yours," Sam responded as she cuddled closer into her mate's chest and Sydney hugged her leg. "We'll all be right here."

"Good. Now, if everyone will please form a circle around Devon's mate and hold hands," the Elder Healer instructed. "And Sydney, if you will stand next to me?"

"Yes, ma'am, Ms. Siobhan," the child answered, pulling her mom along.

As soon as all the candles were lit and the circle complete, Siobhan began to pray, *"Dear Universe, Heavens and Elders of Olde, we come to you, humbly seeking answers that only your infinite wisdom can provide. Your child, mate of Devon, is suffering. We ask for your guidance in putting an end to her torment. Please direct our actions and fill our hearts and minds with the knowledge essential to bring this child back into the light of your grace. We thank you for all you have given us and strive to honor you in all that we do. Your humble servants."*

When the prayer concluded, Siobhan, along with the other healers, began the healing chant Devon had learned as a child. Their low, reverent tones filled the room with hope, love, and healing. He felt the energy of each person in their circle flow through him, and if he concentrated hard enough, he could actually identify each person. Sydney's was as bright as the sun and filled with such an unbridled joy that he took a few extra seconds just to enjoy the feeling. Sam and Lance's combined and burst at the seams with so much love he felt honored they chose to lend it to his mate. His mother's was bold and confident and led the way for all the other healers, but the underlying tone of a mother's love was evident and made him smile.

He had no idea how much time passed as the chant of the healers grew in intensity and volume. The feelings he had been admiring became an entity in and of themselves. It was then that he realized Siobhan, Sam, and Lance had opened the link to all their kin and each dragon shifter was lending strength to their cause. In a rush, he felt the strong immovable force of his old friend, Royce, and the fire and determination of Kyra, Royce's mate. Right behind that was the support of the Blue Thunder clan, Royce's clan of birth. The sheer rush of power threatened to drive Devon to his knees. He would be forever indebted to each and every person for their unwavering support.

The chant swelled to an unprecedented crescendo in their hearts and minds. Then, as if a switch had been flipped, all was quiet, only the sound of hundreds of heartbeats beating as one broke the silence. Siobhan thanked the Universe, the Heavens, and the Elders of Olde, as well as every dragon shifter for their help. Devon was just about to speak when the phone in his pocket vibrated. Letting go of his mother's hand and that of a younger healer, he retrieved it, recognized the number as Royce's and answered, "Hey, old man, thank you for your help. What's up?"

"Kyra needs to talk to you…hang on a sec."

He heard the phone change hands and then the unmistakable southern accent of Royce's mate rang loud and clear. Kyra was practically screaming, almost out of breath and definitely upset. "It's magic, Dev! Fucking magic is keeping your girl asleep! I can feel it like I feel the wind on my face. I can't tell the origin without being right there, but I can tell that it's a mixture of at least two different types and more than one practitioner."

She paused to breathe and Devon asked, "What can we do to find out who and what it is?"

"You can't do anything, but I damn sure can! We're packing to head back right this minute. It's almost dark here, so Roy can go all dragony and we'll be there in no time."

Devon interrupted, "But what about the search for your mom? I can't ask you to leave that to come back and help us."

"Well see, that's the beauty of family…you don't have to ask, I'm coming and that's all there is to it."

"Seriously, Kyra, she's your mom."

"Yeah, and you're Royce's brother, which makes you my brother, and you need my help more than Calysta does. She's old and powerful, so whatever shit she's gotten herself into will have to wait until you and your mate are all happy and shit…*Capisce*?"

Devon laughed out loud. "*Capisce.* I don't know how I'll ever thank you. Know that I appreciate it from the bottom of my heart."

"Just have a jumbo bottle of wine ready to celebrate when we get her awake and we'll call it square," the little witch chuckled before continuing, "Roy wants to talk to you. See ya soon, Dev."

"Thank you again, Kyra."

Once again he listened as the phone passed from one to the other, then Royce's low, rumbly voice came on the line. "We'll be there by first light. You still at the hospital?"

"Yep, I am," he answered and then quickly added, "Royce…thanks, man."

"Not a problem, Dev. Just returning the favor for all the times you watched over Kyra. See ya soon."

"Fly safe."

"You know it," was the older dragon's response before the line went dead.

Smiling from ear to ear at the prospect of finally knowing the cause of his mate's condition, Devon turned, only to be greeted by eight pairs of eyes full of questions. "That was Royce and Kyra. When we were praying, Kyra felt the magic that's keeping her from waking."

He reached out and touched his mate as he spoke. "They are headed back as we speak. Kyra couldn't get a lock on what kind of magic or who had worked the original spell, but she could feel its power. Royce said they'll be here before daybreak."

Everyone smiled and congratulated him, but it was Sam's expression that gave him pause. Her brow was furrowed as she worried her bottom lip with her teeth. Unease slithered down his spine, forcing him to ask, "What is it, Sam? What's wrong? Do you think Kyra's mistaken?"

Samantha jumped as if he had scared her and hurriedly answered, "Oh! Crap! No! I'm sorry, Devon. I was just thinking…there's no way we can do what needs to be done to help your mate here in this room, or even in the hospital, without causing suspicion and running the risk of people asking questions we can't answer. Physically, I'm sure she can be moved, but I'm not sure how to get around the legal mumbo jumbo to get her out of here. Having you on the chart as a 'relative' was fairly easy, but faking discharge paperwork could cost me my license, not to mention it is *really* illegal."

"So what do we do now?" Lance asked, pulling his mate to his side.

Devon thought for a moment before asking, "What exactly does the hospital need to make her discharge legal and keep you out of trouble?"

"You'd need to be made her health care surrogate and that requires a legal document," Sam answered, worry still evident in her voice.

Devon grinned and chuckled. "Well, I happen to know an awesome attorney that I bet can help out."

"Oh shit, I didn't think of Grace," Lance said as he continued to comfort his mate and then quickly added, "don't you dare tell her…she'll kick my ass."

The room erupted in laughter as Devon dialed Aidan's number, with all the different conversations taking place, he excused himself to complete his call. He leaned down, kissed his mate on the forehead, and headed into the hall. After a few rings, Aidan answered, "Hey, dude, we were just talking about you. Powerful ceremony. Did it help? How's she doing?"

"Pretty much the same, thanks, but we did learn something that might help and I need Grace's help. But I wanted to make sure she was feeling okay before I bothered her."

His friend sighed heavily into the phone and when he finally answered, Devon had to work hard not to laugh. "Yeah, she's fine. *Hell*, she's better than I am and she's the one that's pregnant. I keep telling her to take it easy and she keeps telling me to shut the hell up. So yeah, she's good. Whatcha need?"

"During the ritual Kyra felt the magic that's keeping my mate in a coma, but without being in close contact, she can't identify the type or the user. She and Royce are headed back so she can work her magic. Until now, hanging at the hospital was okay, but with this new information, there's no way we can do what has to be done without drawing attention to the fact that we're *different*. We need to move her to the lair and that's where Grace comes in. Sam says we need a legal document giving me permission to make decisions to keep everything on the up and up and most importantly, to make sure our fine doctor stays out of trouble."

"Okay, hang on, let me take Grace the phone," Aidan answered.

A second later Devon heard his brethren curse. "Shit, Babe. Where the hell did you come from? I thought you were resting."

"And I thought you were going to leave the mothering to me?" Grace responded, making Devon laugh.

"Grace, honey…"

"Don't you 'Grace honey' me, Aidan O'Brien. Give me the phone." Grace's tone was priceless and one Devon recognized as her 'lawyer voice'. His poor friend was completely outmatched and obviously loved every damn minute of it, even though Devon was sure Aidan would never admit it.

"Hey, Devon, how are you?" Grace's sweet, concerned voice was such a contrast to how she had just spoken to her mate. Devon hoped she didn't hear the laughter in his voice.

"I'm good. How are you and those babies?"

"Oh, we're fine. Thanks for asking. I'm only a little over six weeks and not even showing yet. Mostly I'm tired of your *brethren* and his constant hovering."

Devon chuckled. "I'm sure it's a pain in the ass, but it's only because he loves you. Remember how Rayne was with Kyndel?"

"Oh, crap, don't remind me. I'll go stark raving mad if Aidan gets that bad."

"I hate to tell ya, but you better get ready. Your boy's got an extra dose of protectiveness when it comes to you."

"Thanks, Dev…thanks a lot," Grace giggled. "Now, I caught most of what you said. I'm guessing you need a health care surrogate form, which will be a little tricky since we don't know her name, but I'm sure Judge Walton will give us a hand, considering Aidan and I helped him find the thief in his office. Give me a few hours and I'll get back to you. I'm assuming we need this like yesterday?"

He grinned at the way Grace asked her rhetorical question. "Yep, sure do. Sorry for the rush," Devon answered, truly sorry for asking for such a huge favor and in a hurry to boot.

"Not to worry. Now take care of your girl and I'll get back to you as soon as I can."

He could tell that his friend's mate was already deep in thought, but he wanted to convey his appreciation for her help. "Thanks, Grace. I don't know what I'd do without you."

"Remember that when I need a babysitter," she laughed. "Talk to you soon."

"Talk to ya later," and with that he hung up and headed back to his mate and family.

Lance immediately asked, "What next, Bro?"

"Well, it looks like we wait to hear back from Grace. You guys can head out if you want. Thanks for everything. I'll let you know as soon as I hear anything at all." He knew he was giving them the bum's rush, but it felt like forever since he'd been alone with his mate. Although she still slept, he felt the unwavering need to tell her what was going on and to just *be* with her…*alone*.

The knowing smile on his mother's face told him she knew exactly what he was feeling, but it was Sydney's yawn that sealed the deal. Sam picked her daughter up and motioned to her mate as she spoke, "Miss Priss here needs to get home, have a hot meal and a bath, and then a good night's sleep. Whatcha say there, Syd?"

The sweet child nodded, laid her head on her mom's shoulder, and then answered, "Can I have chicken tenders and watermelon?"

Lance laughed as he joined his family. "Yes, sweetpea, you sure can. Now, let's get outta here and let Devon get some rest. Sounds like tomorrow's gonna be a helluva day."

Sydney squirmed in her mother's arms until Sam set her on the floor. She ran over and hugged Devon's leg until he lifted her to eye level. She kissed his cheek and whispered, "Sweet dreams, Devon. Tomorrow you get to meet your mate."

He answered, "Sweet dreams to you, too, punkin. From your mouth to Heaven's ears."

As Sydney climbed down and returned to her parents, Devon looked into the faces of his family and friends and saw the same hope he felt reflected back at him. He felt compelled to speak. "Thank you all again for all your help. I couldn't have done *any* of this without you. I owe you a debt I'm not sure I'll ever be able to repay, but I'll damn sure try."

Lance stepped forward with his signature shit-eating grin plastered across his face and Devon prepared for whatever his pain-in-the ass brethren was about to say. As usual, Lance did not disappoint. "Now, don't go getting all teary eyed on us, Dev. I'd hate for your mate to wake up and think she was stuck with a crybaby."

Quicker than Devon could answer, Sam was beside her mate, smacking him on the arm and chuckling. "Leave Dev alone or I might just have to tell him about your less than manly response to 'Finding Nemo' the other night."

Everyone roared with laughter as Lance's face turned an exceptionally brilliant color of red. Never one to be outdone, his brethren did the only thing he could…he smacked his mate on the butt, grabbed his daughter, and jogged across the room to avoid Sam's swinging hand. Their antics once again reminded Devon how lucky he was to be a part of such an amazing family and clan.

As the laughter died down, Lance and his family exited, saying one last goodbye. The younger healers followed with their bags of candles and supplies, leaving only his mother behind. She stood looking from him to his mate and back again. It was several long moments before she spoke, and her words were overflowing with love. "You need to get some rest, Son. We made great strides today, but there is still a long row to hoe, and you are going to need your strength."

She paused and smiled before continuing, "And you might want to think about a shave and haircut before you officially meet your mate." She let the laugh she had obviously been holding at bay out and the sound of it comforted Devon in a way nothing else could. He stood on the precipice of one of the most important events in his very long life, and was so incredibly grateful for all the woman standing before him had done to make him the man he was. He closed the gap that separated them, nodded while placing his hands on her shoulders, and said, "As soon as she is safely at the lair, I promise I'll shave and get a haircut. And...Mom?"

"Yes, Son?" Siobhan answered, looking at him as only a mother can look at her child.

"Thank you for everything." As soon as the words crossed his lips, he pulled her into a hug that lasted until a nurse coming to take his mate's vitals knocked on the door.

Devon recognized her as Melanie, his favorite of all of the nurses, and one that didn't usually work in the evenings. "What are you still doing here?" he asked.

"One of the night shift girls is home with the flu, so I offered to stay and help out until her replacement gets here. Sorry to interrupt," Melanie said as she headed to his mate's bedside.

"You're not interrupting, Melanie, I'd like to introduce my mom, Siobhan. Mom, this is Melanie, one of the best nurses in the world. Mom was just heading home."

Melanie blushed and giggled. "Thank you, Mr. Walsh." Then she looked to his mother and stretched out her hand, "Nice to meet you, ma'am."

The ladies shook and Siobhan replied, "No need for formalities, just call me Siobhan and I am very happy to meet you. Thank you for taking such good care of our girl here."

"It's my pleasure." It was obvious Melanie was about to say something else, but the cordless phone in her hand interrupted.

As she moved away to answer it, Devon walked Siobhan to the door and watched as she met up with the young healers waiting by the elevators. He watched until they were out of sight before turning on his heel and returning to his mate's bedside. Melanie was just finishing her exam and as soon as the young nurse was gone, he took a deep breath, reached for his beloved's hand, and sank into the recliner, thankfully still positioned next her bed. It was the first time in ten days that he actually relaxed, simply wanting to spend the next few hours talking to his mate.

Devon brought her hand to his lips, taking her scent into his lungs. His eyes slid shut and his dragon all but purred as her scent infused every fiber of their being. The need to rest overrode his need to talk.

"I have so much to tell you, Sweetheart, but I can barely keep my eyes open. I'm gonna put my head down for just a few minutes and then we'll talk, okay?" He chuckled at himself as he actually waited for her to answer.

He laid his head on the pillow of their joined hands and spoke directly into her mind, *"Rest well, mo chroi', big things are just over the horizon."*

Devon waited as long as he could, but when his mate didn't answer, he gave up his battle and drifted off into a deep, dreamless sleep.

Stuck somewhere between completely asleep and barely awake, Devon could hear a very persistent, extremely annoying buzzing sound that he swore he would destroy if only he could locate its origin. The offending noise stopped, only to immediately begin again. When the cycle of buzz...stop...buzz started for the third time, he forced his eyes open. The flood of light from the huge window across the room let him know he had slept through the night.

As he lifted his head, it became apparent that his six-foot-three inch frame was not meant to spend the night doubled over in a recliner, and he would pay for his decision to spend the night as a pretzel. He stretched, feeling every one of his one hundred and twenty years right before the horrendous buzzing sounded again. Finally conscious, he realized it was his cellphone and fished it out of his back pocket, answering just before it went to voicemail.

"Hello?"

"Good morning to you, too," Grace chuckled on the other end of the phone. "Long night?"

Devon grinned at the lawyer's sunny disposition so early in the morning, remembering how much his brethren, her mate, hated mornings. He cleared his throat before answering, "Actually, I slept pretty well...just waking up. How are you?"

"I'm good, always was an early riser and seems as though pregnancy has amplified that condition," she answered. "Aidan is less than thrilled," she added with a chuckle. "But what I really called for is to let you know that the judge is signing your paperwork as we speak and I just got off the phone with the hospital administrator who is waiting for the fax. As soon as Sam gets there and signs the release orders, you'll be free to bring your mate home."

"*Hot damn*, Grace, that's great news! Thank you so much!"

"Sure thing, Dev. Gotta run. Got some bad guys to put away. Talk to you soon." Devon smiled at the attorney's response.

"Be safe out there," he said at the same time Royce and Kyra walked into the room.

Devon disconnected the call and stood to welcome his friends. "Morning, guys. How's it goin'?"

Kyra hugged him hello before answering, "We're good. Talked to Lance and he said you were working to get her back to the lair, but we wanted to stop by anyway and see if there was anything we could do to help."

Devon shook his head. "Just hung up with Grace and the paperwork is on the way. As soon as Sam signs her part, we'll be good to go. Thanks for coming."

"No problem. Great news, Bro," Royce finally spoke.

"Damn straight. If you guys want to head home to grab food and sleep, I can holler when we get there and are all settled in."

The look of relief on Royce's face said it all, his oldest friend and the oldest of his Force needed some shut eye. Kyra picked up on her mate's exhaustion and said, "If you're sure you're okay, I'm gonna take the big guy here home so he can rest his old bones."

Her giggles were cut short when Royce grabbed her up and threw her over his shoulder. "You better put me down, old man, or I swear I *will* make good on my threat to turn you into a toad."

Royce barked out a laugh while placing the feisty witch on the ground. Kyra winked and pointed at her little finger before teasing, "Got him right where I want him."

The older Guardsman returned his hands to her waist and growled, "Be careful, little witch, or I *will* carry you out of here with your pretty little ass in the air."

Kyra blushed and elbowed Royce in the gut. The resulting 'oomph' assured Devon that the couple before him was more in love than ever, only serving to reinforce his belief that *the Universe does not make mistakes*. Kyra's quick response reminded him why he liked her so much. "Yeah, yeah, yeah, says the guy that still can't find his boots."

"Kyra..." Royce growled.

"Royce..." Kyra growled back. She might have been convincing if she hadn't started giggling.

Deciding he needed to grab some coffee and make arrangements to get his mate back to the lair before Sam arrived, Devon said, "I don't even want to know."

"No, you don't," Royce was quick to respond. "If you're sure you don't need us, I'm gonna take you up on the offer to get some rest. I'm beat."

"No problem. Get outta here and I'll talk to you soon." Devon hugged Kyra and shook hands with Royce in the way of their kind.

As soon as the couple was out of sight, Devon spoke to Aaron through their unique link, *"Aar, you up?"*

"Yeah. What's up?" was the groggy response he received a few seconds later.

"Looks like I'm gonna get to bring her home today, so I need a favor."

"Good news, man. Whatcha need?"

"Thanks. I need to see if you can bring my SUV to the hospital and then take my Harley back to the house?"

"Not a problem. I just need to grab a shower and mainline some caffeine and I'll be right there."

"Thanks."

"No problem, buddy."

Devon felt Aaron sever their connection and decided mainlining caffeine was the best idea he'd heard all morning. He kissed his mate and headed to the cafeteria in search of coffee and food.

Twenty minutes later, filled with eggs, bacon, toast, a couple of blueberry muffins, and three cups of coffee, Devon stood waiting for the elevator, thinking about all that needed to be done between the time he got her home and when she would finally open her eyes. Just as the doors to the lift opened, he heard the unmistakable squeal of Sydney and the tap of her little shoes on the tile. He turned just in time to pick up the running child before she made contact with his leg.

"Good morning, Dev. Ready to take our girl home?" Sydney asked, her eyes shining bright with excitement.

"Our girl, huh?" Devon asked, winking to assure the child he was playing.

"Well, duh. She's one of us, ya know?"

"Yes, darlin', I know."

Sydney giggled and kissed him on the cheek right before her parents appeared behind them. Having let the elevator go, Devon leaned forward and pressed the call button again while asking, "Going my way?"

Lance and Sam smiled, answering in unison, "Sure are."

"To what do I owe the honor of the entire Kavanaugh clan's presence this fine morning?"

"Sydney has a checkup scheduled," Lance answered.

Samantha added with a wink, "I have some paperwork to get done so we can get your mate home and awake. By the way, just a head's up, Kyndel is cooking up a feast. Rayne is rearranging search schedules to keep as many of you guys at the lair as he can until Kyra knows what we are dealing with and well…you've talked to everyone else."

Once again Devon was filled with an incredible sense of gratitude. "Thank you all so much," he said as the doors of the elevator opened and they all stepped in.

Their group exited the elevator as soon as it stopped on their floor and headed down the hall. Sam stopped at the nurse's station, while Devon, Lance, and Sydney continued on their course. Once inside his mate's room, he took up his usual spot at her bedside, but this time with Sydney on his lap. When he reached for her hand, Sydney mimicked his movements and laid her smaller hand atop their joined ones.

"She's sleeping," Sydney said in a tiny voice, staring at his mate's face.

Devon leaned forward until his head was next to the child's and looked between the beautiful woman and the sweet little girl. "How can you tell, Syd?" Devon asked.

"I can feel it…here," she answered and placed her hand over Devon's heart.

His curiosity got the best of him and he had to ask, "What does it feel like?"

Sydney tilted her head to the side and squinted her eyes while she was thinking. A moment later she said, "When she's sleeping, I feel floaty, like when I jump on the trampoline at Jay's house."

He had so many more questions but didn't want to make Sydney uncomfortable, even though he doubted that was possible. The child was remarkable and until her parents knew the extent of her special abilities, they had all agreed not to draw any more attention than was absolutely necessary. Devon answered the only way he could think of. "That's really cool, Syd. Thanks for the help."

The little girl nodded and returned her hand to his and his mate's, apparently content to just sit with him. Her father, however, was another story. Lance was pacing back and forth and sighing at least once every pass. Devon turned his head and watched a few trips before asking, "What's up, bud?"

Lance stopped and looked out the window, arms crossed, legs shoulder width apart, and blew out a long, slow breath. He answered without turning around, "Nothing…everything…oh screw it. Nothing I can't handle." He spun around and speared Devon with a look that said he was done, but then added, "And let it go until you have your world straight and then we'll go grab a beer or twelve and solve all the problems of the world. Deal?"

His brethren obviously needed to talk, but not in front of Sydney and Devon respected that. He also knew Sydney was getting better at listening in to their mindspeak unless it was the link between mates, so he understood why their normal form of communication wouldn't work. With no other options, he nodded his agreement but added out loud, "Ya know I'll hold you to that beer *and* the talk."

Lance half-heartedly chuckled and nodded. "Yeah, yeah, yeah, I know…you're a dog with a bone."

"Daddy, you're so silly." Sydney laughed and jumped down, running to her dad.

Devon smiled as he watched Lance ruffle his daughter's hair and listened to Sydney's resulting laughter, thinking how much his brother had grown since meeting the two women in his life. The alarm on Lance's phone rang, reminding him of Sydney's appointment. The two said their goodbyes and once again, Devon found himself alone with his mate.

Needing to make sure Aaron had not gotten sidetracked, he called to him, *"Hey bud, how long til you get here?"*

"Pulling into the parking lot. Impatient much?" Aaron answered, and Devon could hear the grin through their link.

"Actually, I am." Devon laughed. *"See ya in a minute."*

He shut down their connection and grabbed the overnight bag he had been keeping in the closet. Ten minutes later he was shaved, had on a fresh shirt, and was ready to get the show on the road. He'd just decided to go check on Sam's progress when she and her friend, Charlie, entered the room, greeting him in unison. Sam continued, "We have the paperwork you need and also…" She pulled a bag from the hospital gift shop out from under her arm and handed it to him. "A pair of scrubs for her to wear home. Is Aaron here, yet?"

"You called, doctor dear?" came from the hall, and within seconds Aaron was standing in the doorway, a fresh cup of coffee in hand. A look of surprise flashed across his face before he schooled his features and walked to the far side of the room, speaking as he went. "Are we ready to get the hell outta dodge, Bro?"

Aaron had made kind of a wide berth around the doctors and Devon wondered about his strange behavior, but could only focus on getting his girl home. Devon grinned. "Yep. Sam and Charlie just got here with her paperwork. How about you and I go out in the hall and sign it while the ladies change my girl's clothes?"

"Deal."

Ten excruciating minutes later, Sam called to them that they were ready to go. He and Aaron worked perfectly together, just as they had hundreds of times, to get his mate transferred to a gurney and into the elevator. Charlie had insisted they get an orderly, but the men had it done before she could complete the call.

As soon as his mate was loaded into the back of his SUV and he was buckled into the driver's seat, Devon breathed a sigh of relief and headed out of the parking lot. A few pieces of the puzzle that were his chaotic life fell into place as he turned onto the road leading to their lair with Aaron following closely behind.

He called his mother and let her know they were on their way and then called to Royce through the connection of their Force. *"Hey Royce, we're headed your way."*

"Congrats, Bro. I'll let Kyra know and we'll meet you at your mom's."

"Thanks, man."

"Anytime, Brother." And they both cut their connection.

The rest of the trip was without incident and he spent the time telling his mate anything and everything he could think of concerning his clan, his brethren, and their lair. He knew he was repeating things he had already shared and wondered for about the hundredth time if she really could hear what he was saying, or if she would remember.

He entered the lair and maneuvered the narrow streets that led to Siobhan's house. His mother was waiting on her front porch as he pulled his SUV into the driveway while Aaron parked Devon's Harley on the street. Before he was out of the truck, Royce and Kyra appeared from behind the house, carrying two large duffle bags, with what he guessed were the witch's supplies. Rayne, Kyndel, and their son, Jay, could be seen making their way down the sidewalk. Aidan and Grace were missing from the 'family reunion', but he knew Grace was at work and was sure her mate was at her side, which only left Lance, Sam, and Sydney, who he had just left at the hospital.

Not wanting to waste any more time, Devon motioned for Aaron to help get his mate out of the SUV and into his mother's home. They were joined by his Commander and Royce, and together the four well-trained warriors made quick work of her transfer. Siobhan directed them to the room that had been his when he was younger, but had been remodeled several times over with the passing years. He wasn't at all surprised to see she had it completely ready for his mate and any situation that may arise with her recovery. No sooner had the guys wheeled the gurney into the room than Kyra and Kyndel appeared at Siobhan's side.

"You guys get out of here for a minute and let us girls get her settled into bed," Kyndel said as she handed her son to his father and made a shooing motion with her hands.

The men looked at one another, shrugged, and then turned and left. Down in the kitchen, they raided his mother's fridge while Devon got the play-by-play of the latest soccer game he'd missed. He continued to keep one eye on the clock and one ear on the bedroom until Kyndel appeared in the doorway, giving the all clear. Devon practically ran out of the room, wasting no time maneuvering the long halls lined with his mother's menagerie of antiques and knickknacks to get to his mate. He burst through the half-closed door and right into the middle of Siobhan and Kyra's conversation.

Both women looked at him and almost in unison said, "Good! You're here. We need to talk."

Devon nodded, heading towards his mate's bedside, needing to be near her. "Okay. Whatcha need?"

The ladies looked at one another, Siobhan nodded once before they turned back, and Kyra spoke, "I want...well, *we* want," she motioned towards his mother, "to start the spell to find out what's going on with your girl right away...like...*now*." She rushed on and Devon wondered why. He was just as anxious, probably more, to have her awake. Then Kyra said the one thing he hadn't thought of and his blood ran cold.

"She's been out a long time, Dev, and I'm afraid the longer we wait the harder it's going to be to identify the magic and/or the magic user and rid her of whatever it is that isn't letting her wake up."

The little witch turned and paced. "I could just kick myself for not thinking that it could be magical when you first told me about her, but I was so wrapped up in Calysta's shit that I figured she was human and it was a human problem, but Dev...she isn't human. Well, not completely human any way. I'm not sure what she is, but I do know it's good and pure, nothing dark or evil about your girl."

She walked towards him and he saw the love and concern in her eyes. When she grabbed his free hand, she squeezed for a second and looked him right in the eye. "I'm no doctor and I understand that moving her probably took a lot, but I truly think we need to get started right away. Call Sam and make sure it's cool physically and all that. I'll head down and see what havoc my hubs and the rest of the crew are causing. You holler when you decide."

Kyra dropped his hand and hugged his neck then looked at his mate, touching her arm just above where his hand held hers. Devon could feel the little push of love and magic that Kyra gave her. It made his heart swell to know that his 'family' was already growing to care for her as much as he was. He watched Kyra go and sent a real quick thought to Royce, *"Kyra's the best. You're damn lucky, Bro."*

His answer made Devon smile. *"Don't I know it, Brother. Don't I know it."*

He had almost forgotten his mother was in the room until she appeared at his side. Concern flowed from her fingertips where they rested on his shoulder, prompting Devon to ask, "What do you think we should do?"

Siobhan took a moment to answer and when she did, he was glad he had asked. "I will tell you what I told Kyra. When I focus on your mate, I feel strength, courage, and a desire to emerge from the cocoon she has been forced into. I have yet to feel any real consciousness that I can use to try to communicate with her, but she *is* in there and her spirit longs to be free. I think we should proceed. You and I will stay linked to your mate in every way we can to make sure she is okay, and Kyra will do what she does best...locate the magic and the sorcerer."

Devon nodded as his mother spoke, internally agreeing with every word she said. He took the cellphone from his pocket and called Sam, glad she answered right away. "Hey, Dev. I was just thinking about you guys. How's everything?"

He quickly explained what he, Kyra, and his mother had talked about. Samantha readily agreed and said she, Lance, and Sydney would be there within the hour. After thanking her and disconnecting the call, Devon told his mother it was a go and called to his brethren, *"Royce, tell Kyra we're ready."*

The older Guardsman answered immediately, *"She heard. She's on her way."*

Before he could respond, the tap of the little witch's boots against the hardwood of his mother's floors could be heard heading his way. Kyra rushed through the door, she and Siobhan immediately becoming engrossed in clearing the large dressing table across the room for all their supplies. Devon stayed with his mate, telling her what was about to happen and assuring her that he would be right by her side every step of the way.

In less than an hour, all the members of his Force that were in attendance, along with their mates and children, were assembled, and the time had come to begin the ritual. Devon, Siobhan, Royce, Rayne, Kyndel, Lance, Sam, and Sydney formed a circle around his mate. Kyra moved around the room, chanting in Latin and magically lighting the hundred or so candles that adorned every available surface. She then walked the entire circle, sprinkling what he recognized as thyme, which she explained was a feminine herb used for healing, while she spoke an incantation in English that closed the circle.

He watched as she pulled a deep indigo candle and the heirloom mirror he knew she used for scrying from the brown leather messenger bag that was slung across her body. Kyra handed the mirror to Royce, lit the candle, and asked everyone to focus their attention and energy on the flame. She then asked the Goddess to reveal the spell that was holding his mate captive and to show her the face of the one that had cast it. Time slowed and minutes felt like hours, but finally he saw recognition in the witch's eyes and watched as she mouthed, *"Fuck!"*

From there things moved very quickly. Kyra seemed to fly around the circle, handing each person an antique silver pill box filled with what she explained was rosemary, thyme, and cinnamon, herbs that promoted strength of memory, healing and well-being. She went on to say that the Uncrossing Spell would break the hold of the offending magic. True to her words, it was mere minutes from the time that she returned to her spot next to Royce and spoke the words of the spell that Devon could actually feel a weight being lifted from the room. The flames of all the candles dimmed and then shot up before returning to normal.

Kyra threw salt on the scrying mirror and gently placed a large silver disc with what he recognized as black tourmaline, often used for its protective qualities, embedded in three intertwined circles on its surface on his mate's chest. She spoke words from a language he could only guess was as old as time and every candle in the room was extinguished, leaving them standing in total darkness.

Devon stood completely still, praying to the Universe that all had gone as planned. Kyra's hand on his shoulder caused him to jump as she took the pill box from his hand and placed it in a ratty old burlap bag. With his enhanced eyesight, he watched as she did the same with every person in the circle, then gathered the amulet from his mate's chest and shoved it into the bag as well. After uttering a phrase in Latin, she used the toe of her boot to break the circle of thyme and turned back towards the group.

"We're almost done. You guys have been great. We just need to go to Siobhan's Blackthorn tree, burn all of the talismans, and bury them under its roots. Follow me, please."

Kyra headed out the door, holding the burlap sack in front of her like trash as they all followed. Devon called to Aaron, who had opted to hang out in the kitchen during the ritual, *"Can you go up and stay with her while we finish this?"*

"Gotcha covered," was his quick response.

"Thanks."

Devon was sure his mate would be fine and Kyra had said before they began that it would take some time after the spell was removed for his mate to wake, but he still didn't want to take the chance that her first glimpse of her new life would be while she was alone and frightened in a strange place. He knew Aaron would call to him if anything changed and take care of her until he could get back.

Kyra had them form a circle around the tree, said a quick incantation, poured kerosene on the bag, and lit it ablaze. It took less than two minutes for the bag to be reduced to nothing more than a pile of ash. Devon was sure it was because of her intense magical power, not to mention the healthy dose of kerosene she had used. Royce dug a small hole, brushed the pile of ash into the hole, and covered it again.

Devon had to hold back his laughter as Kyra jumped up and down on the overturned soil and spoke in Latin. He was glad to see the smirks on Lance and Royce's face that mirrored his own. When the time was right, he planned to ask her if jumping helped with the magic or if it was just because she was so petite. It wasn't that he didn't respect her ability. It was just a crazy sight to see a five-feet-two, platinum-blonde witch jumping up and down, chanting in the moonlight. When she stopped and walked towards Royce, Devon saw her grin and knew she thought it was funny, too.

"Can you all please join hands?" Kyra asked right before she prayed. *"Thank you to the Goddess of All, whom without your goodness and light we would be lost and alone. Thank you to the Universe for your great wisdom and the life that flows through us. Thank you to the Heavens above, below, and all around for providing us with the proof of yesterday, the reality of today, and the hope of tomorrow. Blessed be."*

Everyone repeated, "Blessed be."

"Okay, you crazy kids. Let's go get something to eat and we can discuss…"

Kyra's next words were drowned out as a scream tore through the air. Devon's heart felt as though it was in a vice as *"Please help me! He's gonna kill me this time!"* rang through his head.

CHAPTER TWO

She floated towards consciousness and *knew* it was different this time. Her mind was clear, more focused, and thankfully…*without the damn black fog*. It was as if the sun had decided to shine after being hidden for so long. She knew the surface was quickly approaching and with it came the first deep breath she had taken in what seemed like an eternity. Her entire being was filled with the fresh, crisp scent of a summer storm combined with sea and sun. It was *his* scent, and although she had no idea who *he* was, her heart recognized him as important. Her mystery man had talked to her, held her hand, and kissed her forehead when she was lost, alone, and terrified in those sparse moments when the fog had receded. Every other moment was nonexistent. There was just…*nothing*, and she was left feeling empty, except for…*him*.

When her eyes opened, she was pleased to confirm that she no longer inhabited the cramped dormitory style room at the mansion of the wizard that kidnapped her, as well as many others. Even better, she was nowhere near the empty field where they had trained them to work terrible magic. It was the training that had landed her in the horrible black nothingness…hopeless and helpless for days, weeks, months. *How long have I been out?*

Not ready to think of anything but the fact that her eyes were actually open, that she could see *something*, she focused on the pale yellow walls and beautiful floral paintings that adorned much of the available space. Everything was bright and happy. Hope infused the very air she breathed, it was even in the light of the small crystal lamp and white candle burning at her bedside.

She shook her head slightly, causing her nose to make contact with the pillow. Once again the wonderful scent of her rescuer filled her senses with hope and her heart with longing. It was unclear how she knew he was responsible for her return to the land of the living, but deep inside, she just *knew*. Testing her mobility, she rolled her head to the other side and felt only the slightest twinge of sore muscles in her neck. Spying the half-opened door, she listened to the happy conversation coming from the other side. No more grumbling, anger, and fear, it was a blessed change from the recent past. Resuming her inspection of her surroundings, she saw more candles - pink, silver, and black - lit throughout the room and smelled what she thought were spices. The candles and scents were familiar, but for some reason her brain failed to latch on to the memory.

The harder she tried to remember, the farther away the recollection floated. She closed her eyes and focused, but still nothing came. The sound of approaching footsteps jarred her from her thoughts as anticipation built. She was finally going to see the man who had given her faith that she would wake up and the strength to survive the black fog. She took a deep breath as the breeze from the opening door touched her arm, loving the feel of freedom. One more deep breath and her eyes opened of their own volition, no longer willing to wait. It seemed they were even more ready than her to see their hero. Instead, the sight before her tore the breath from her lungs and caused her heart to beat with such force that she was sure it would burst from her chest. Unwilling to be held captive again, she searched for a way to escape or anything to use as a weapon.

When she came up empty handed, she did the only thing she could…she screamed as loud and as long as she could. Then she prayed that someone would save her from the repeat of her past torment. Curling into a ball and shoving herself against the headboard in the farthest corner of the bed, she continued to scream, both aloud and in her head. The startled man before her threw out his hands and slowly backed away, shaking his head and saying something she couldn't make out over her own shrieks.

Feeling lightheaded from lack of oxygen, her screaming died out, but only long enough to draw another breath. The sound of thundering footsteps heading in her direction caused her to pause. Fear piled on top of fear and threatened hysteria, leaving her paralyzed. One glance at the stranger told her that he was in the exact same spot and just as confused as she, which made no sense, but nothing had in so long she had stopped expecting it. The sound of splintering wood drew her attention as the door bounced off the wall. All she saw was a blur before she was enveloped in pair of extremely warm, extremely strong arms. One breath and the unmistakable scent of a summer storm filled her lungs, easing her panic.

Unable to grip her rescuer with her arms held tight to her sides, she simply burrowed into his body with the hopes of somehow fusing their bodies together. He was the perfect barrier between her and her abductor. His chest vibrated under her cheek as he whispered words of comfort and she knew at once he would never let anything or *anyone* hurt her. As her pulse and breathing slowed, she felt his head turn. He addressed the man behind him. "What the *fuck*, Aaron? What did you do?" His words sounded angry, but his tone was questioning.

"Me? What the *hell*, Dev?" The man across the room answered. The sound of others entering the room and whispers could be heard as he continued, "I walked in, looked out the window, and she started screaming. I didn't know she was awake and damn sure didn't have a chance to speak."

Warm hands rubbed up and down her spine, and for the first time in her life she understood why cats purred. Just his touch made her want to live in the safety of his embrace for all time, but she could tell from the tension in his body that it was not the time for *friendly* hellos. When he spoke again, it was in little more than a breath beside her ear and made goose bumps rise all over her body. "What happened, Sweetheart? Can you lean back just a bit and talk to me…*please*?"

The tone he used was gentle and caring and left her no choice but to do as he asked. At her movement, he loosened his arms just enough for her to lean back against the headboard but kept his hands at her waist. His continued touch gave her the encouragement she needed to look into his eyes. She was left breathless, not from fear but from the sheer depth of emotion reflected in her rescuer's eyes. She knew it was wrong to think of a man as beautiful, but all other words escaped her. His nearly black hair was tousled with a few strands haphazardly slung across his furrowed brow. The look in his fathomless grey eyes was intoxicating, and the thick, dark lashes that lined his gorgeous eyes would make any woman jealous. The patrician line of his nose, his high cheekbones, and his strong jaw reminded her of the gladiators she had seen in the old movies Pops used to watch. She wondered if his stubble would tickle against her skin, but it was his mouth that drew and held her attention. The light pink color against the deep tan of his complexion and the perfect bow of his full lips made her mouth water. It was only through sheer strength of will that she was able to resist the urge to lean forward for just a taste.

She watched those perfect lips move and realized he was speaking. Not wanting him to think she was ignoring him, or worse yet, daft, she shook herself out of her stupor and focused on his words. "Tell me what happened. What frightened you?"

The weight of his words settled in and around her. Taking a deep breath, she nodded slightly and answered, tentatively pointing at the man now pacing in a tight circle by the window. "It's him. He's going to try to take me again."

It was as though her words sucked all the air from the room. Both the man in the corner and the man in front of her said, *"What the…?"* at exactly the same time, and gasps could be heard from the vicinity of the door.

"Dev, I swear I've never seen this woman before that day in the hospital with you!" the man she *knew* as her abductor shouted from across the room.

The one holding her answered him while maintaining eye contact with her. "I know, Aaron, I know. Something's not right. We just need to chill out for a second and figure this *shit* out."

Then he spoke to her, "It's gonna be okay, but there's *got* to be a mistake. That's Aaron," he motioned over his shoulder. "He's my bre…friend, and I *know* he didn't abduct you. *Hell*, he didn't even know you until I told him about you. He helped me watch after you in the hospital."

Hospital? Had she been in a hospital? She remembered him saying something about doctors during one of her too sparse, too brief moments of cognizance. Then there were the pokes to her arms and the humming sound she now knew must've been medical equipment. *How long was I out? What day is it?* A million thoughts ran through her mind and then she heard him like she had all those times before. *"I promise to answer all your questions, as soon as possible, but right now we need to figure out why you think Aaron had anything to do with what happened to you."*

Her eyes snapped to his, only to find him waiting patiently for her response. It should've seemed weird that he could hear her thoughts and even weirder that he could answer directly into her mind, but it didn't. Instead, it seemed *right* and made her feel closer to him…safer somehow. His voice was all she had to cling to while fighting the black fog and it was his voice that would help her again. Nodding her agreement, she looked over his shoulder and was surprised at all the people watching. *When did they all get here?*

There was a tiny woman with platinum hair and bright violet eyes that glowed when she smiled. The light around her was bright and friendly and when combined with the aura belonging to the biggest man she'd ever seen in her entire life standing protectively behind the petite woman, it was obvious they meant her no harm. She smiled as she watched the couple look back and forth between the man holding her and the man in the corner, like they were at a tennis match.

The mismatched couple was joined by a very pretty, tall, dark haired woman and a handsome blond man that reminded her of a surfer. They were partially hidden by what was left of the door. It was also apparent there were others just outside the door, all extremely interested in what was going on in her room.

Unable to bear all the attention, she bowed her head and lowered her arm. A finger under her chin lifted her face until once again she met her rescuer's expressive gaze. "You have nothing to hide from and nothing to fear. Everyone here is your friend, I promise. I'm Devon. What's your name?"

She opened her mouth to answer then shut it again. *What is my name? Surely I know my own name?* She opened her mouth again but nothing came out. Her mind was a complete blank. Not her name, where she was from…*nothing*. She could see pictures in her mind of an older couple that she knew to be Mom and Pops. Not her birth parents, but a wonderful couple that had raised her and loved her more than anything. She knew they were long dead and missed them terribly. The image of the farmhouse just outside the city where she had grown up and lived, even after her parents' death, floated through her consciousness. So did the one stupid night she had decided to go see a movie and never made it back.

The harder she tried to remember, the more pictures that flashed through her mind. It was like a highlight reel of her life…just glimpses of people and places she had known throughout the years. The longer it lasted without her name, the more worried she became. The rapid rhythm of her pulse beating in her ears, combined with the single drop of sweat rolling down her back, were clear indicators that she was heading into a full blown panic attack. A few deep breaths did nothing to calm her nerves as sweat broke out across her upper lip. The man holding her looked on cautiously, obviously sensing her fear and confusion. In one swift motion he pulled her onto his lap, where her legs fell on either side of his thighs, leaving them positioned chest to chest. His fingers wound into the hair at the sides of her head. He looked deep into her eyes and crooned, "Breathe with me, *mo chroí'*. Nice and slow."

She took one breath and then the next, never breaking eye contact, following his lead. The panic began to recede, her shoulders began to relax. He smiled and she was rewarded with his low rumble of approval. "That's it, *a chumann*, just breathe. You're fine. Nothing and no one will ever harm you again."

Then he spoke directly into her mind, offering further reassurance. *"Don't worry, your name will come back to you. You've been unconscious for quite a while. I'm sure you just need time to adjust."*

"Thank you," she answered aloud and took another long, deep breath. This man with the compassionate eyes and soothing voice was like a drug. A very potent, very addictive drug she already knew she never wanted to be without.

Devon, that's what he'd said his name was, spoke again, and his words brought the reality of the situation into complete, unfiltered focus. "You said you were abducted, right? And that you think it was my friend," he pointed to the man in the corner, "that did it?"

Her voice failing, she nodded, and the man from her nightmares all but yelled, "It was *not* me. I think you better have Sam look at her again, Dev. She must've hit her head or something when she was freaking out." His voice sounded different than she remembered. It was deeper and held a bit more of an accent.

Devon turned and looked over his shoulder. "Aaron, relax, I'm trying to figure this out. But maybe you're right, she was really freaked." He winked at her as he swung his head around to look over the opposite shoulder. "Sam, you wanna take a look? Make sure everything's okay?"

The pretty dark haired woman slowly walked towards them. Devon smiled and motioned as she stood at her bedside. "This is Sam. Actually, Dr. Samantha Malone and she's awesome. Is it okay if she just takes a look real quick to check everything?"

At the prospect of being separated from him, her hands gripped his forearms even tighter, making him chuckle. "It's all right, Sweetheart. I'm not going anywhere. Although I do think you'll need to get off my lap for Sam to have a good look at you."

The heat from her blush warmed her cheeks and her eyes closed in embarrassment. It was the doctor who spoke, easing her tension as she lightly touched her shoulder. "Don't worry. He's just messing with you. Get used to it. They're all a bunch of overgrown teenagers."

Giggling more to herself than the others, she loosened her grip on his arms and started to crawl off his lap. In the next second, she found herself back on the bed, sitting next to Devon. Her eyes grew big as she looked up to find him smiling. "*Damn*, you're strong," flew from her lips before she could stop them, and again she blushed as her hand slapped over her mouth.

Laughter filled the room as Devon joked, "Why thank ya, ma'am," in what she was sure was his best southern accent.

Shaking her head, Samantha reached for a weathered brown messenger bag and pulled out a stethoscope, blood pressure cuff, and penlight. The doctor knelt before her, motioning to Devon, "He's just happy you're awake. You'll have to excuse his goofiness, it's a welcome change from the worry. Now, let's see what we've got going on here."

The doctor's words warmed her heart. *I'm gonna need to get used to the teasing? He's happy I'm awake? He cares that I'm okay?* It was a lot to wish for and she couldn't help but hope it was the truth. Devon made her feel almost normal again. She loved the feel of his arms around her and the look in his eyes when... Her thoughts were cut short as Sam stood up and the voices in the room grew louder. One look revealed a newcomer - a tall, elderly woman whose long, grey braid swung as she spoke. She was engaged in a serious conversation with the tiny blonde.

"Everything seems to be fine." Sam's words drew her attention and she watched as the doctor returned her instruments to her bag. "No signs of trauma, nothing unusual. I would say something light to eat and then a good night's sleep will make all the difference in the world. You're making a miraculous recovery for someone that's been in a coma for at least a month."

"A month!" She gasped, unconsciously grabbing for Devon's hand. He automatically threaded his fingers through hers and pulled at their connection to get her attention. "Yes, Sweetheart, the doctors are sure you were unconscious for at least four weeks. I only found you twelve days ago and just got to bring you here to my mother's home earlier today." He motioned to the older lady.

A commotion at the door cut off her next question. What she saw next had her doubting her sanity. Standing not two steps inside the door was an exact replica of the man that stood next to the window. Her eyes flew to the first man to make sure he really was there, and then at the second, and back to the first again. The longer she looked from one to the other, the more certain she was that Samantha had been wrong about her condition. She *had* to be losing her mind.

Devon words sounded far away and muffled. "What is it? What's wrong? Talk to me, *mo chroi'*."

She could hear his distress and worked hard to focus. "It's them." She pointed behind him at the two identical men, her voice shaky with fear. "How are there *two* of them?"

Squeezing Devon's hand as tight as she could, trying everything she could to anchor herself to him. He had promised to protect her and she knew he meant it. Just about to beg for that help, her words were cut off when the tiny blonde shrieked, "Oh shit! It all makes sense now."

She moved around the older woman, stopping between the two men. Her eyes were brighter than before, and she smiled a knowing smile. "You," she pointed to the man by the window. Then swung around and pointed at the other and said, "And you...are twins."

The one she was facing said, "Yeah, *no shit*. And...?"

"And when we finished the ritual, I was just about to tell y'all that I had sensed a crazy mixture of black magic, Earth magic, and what I thought was dragon magic during the Cleansing. But she screamed, we ran, and well...now...here we all are." She took a breath and continued her explanation, "I'm now *positive* it was that stupid dickhead." The tiny woman put her hands on her hips and continued, her brow furrowed like she was deep in thought, "It kinda felt like him, but it's been a while since I've had a good sense of his special brand of crazy and *never* when it was mixed with any Earth magic but my own." She spun around and spoke to the older woman. "His dragon magic is seriously stronger than before."

The mention of the guy the tiny woman had called 'dickhead' caused Devon to tense and every other male to growl in anger. Apparently, there was a nasty history between her true abductor and the nice people that were trying to help her. She wondered what he had done to make them so mad and was just about to ask when the petite blonde woman took a few more steps in her direction. Stopping at the end of the bed, she grinned nervously. "I'm *so sorry* for blurting all that out. You must think I'm a *fucking* loon."

A picture of her mom in the greenhouse behind the barn, the entire back wall covered with bookshelves that overflowed with old books and notebooks came to mind. Mom had called them her 'Recipe and Spell books'. She giggled and surprised even herself with her response, "That's okay, my mom was a witch. Well, not my birth mom, but the woman who raised me. She did spells and made teas and ointments for people who needed her help. It's all good. I know you're not crazy. Besides, you have a beautiful light. You're a really good person."

"Well, thanks." The petite witch's smile lit up her whole face. "I'm Kyra, and that's my mate, Royce," she pointed to the huge man with extremely red hair.

Kyra's next words came out rushed. "So here's the deal. These two are twins." She motioned to the two guys that had freaked her out just moments ago. "And they have a little brother that's bat shit crazy, Andrew. He's the one that I believe abducted you. Now, I know all of this is hard to believe, but I want you to do two things for me and I promise you'll see that what I'm saying is the truth. Cool?"

She looked at Devon and he nodded his approval. She could feel him lending her his strength and reassurance through their joined hands. Figuring she had nothing to lose, she answered the only way she could, "Sure, what do you need me to do?"

Kyra motioned for Aaron to come towards her while she spoke, "I want you to focus on Aaron and get a good read on his spirit. Can you do that for me?"

She nodded her head, looking right at him. His aura was brilliant. It shone blue and red with bright white all around. There was absolutely nothing malevolent about him. Looking at his twin, she saw exactly the same colors, but with bits of green and yellow added to the mix. The additional colors had to be from the gorgeous brunette at his side. The love between them was evident and something she longed for.

Looking back to Kyra, she smiled and said, "Their auras are clean and bright. You're right, they're nothing like him. But the resemblance is scary…*literally*."

Kyra laughed. "Wow! You're quick. Two at once, I'm impressed. I can see where you'd think they look like their younger, *demented* brother, but the more time you spend around these two, the less they'll look like the little shithead, I promise." The petite witch winked before speaking again. "Now, one more thing to make *really* sure and put all your fears to rest."

The tiny woman motioned for the twins to join her at the end of the bed before she continued, "Do you remember the color of Andrew's eyes?"

She thought for just a second and took a deep breath to brace herself, calling up the memory of her abductor. In a split second, it all came rushing back…*the day she woke up in the strange locked room with two young men and an older woman. She pictured the man with little round glasses who brought them food and clean clothes. He'd been somewhat kind when he instructed them to get ready to meet their Master. The wait was awful. The sudden sound of a key in the lock made her hands shake. She, along with the other three, had collectively held their breath as the one they all called Master O'Brien walked into the room. His smile had been chilling and his eyes cold.* The scary recollection vanished and blessed reality returned. *His eyes! That's it!* She screamed, "His eyes! One is blue and one is the color of whisky!" She pointed to the men standing on either side of Kyra, "Yours are blue and yours are whisky!"

The remaining tension in the room evaporated. Aaron visibly relaxed for the first time since she had laid eyes on him, and she immediately felt bad for having freaked out. He turned to leave and she called to him, "Aaron…?"

He stopped, turned, and half-grinned. After a moment's hesitation, he took a step back. "Yes?"

She tried to stand but her legs buckled, causing her to land in a heap on Devon's lap. "Take it easy, Sweetheart," Devon said as his arms steadied her.

When she looked back to Aaron, his hands were out, ready to catch her should she fall. It just further confirmed that he was absolutely *nothing* like the man that had her kidnapped and held her against her will. She smiled up at him. "Thank you so much. I guess a month in bed makes for weak legs," she chuckled and then met his eyes. "I wanted to tell you how *very sorry* I am that I accused you of having anything to do with what happened to me. It was *completely* my mistake." She looked away for just a second and when she looked back, he was grinning. "I hope you won't hold it against me."

He shook his head and scoffed. "*Hell, no.* Don't think about it again. My little brother's an asshole. He seems to hurt everything he touches. I'm just glad you're gonna be okay and I promise you…he *will* pay for what he's done." He looked over her shoulder and gave a quick nod before he touched her shoulder and said, "Now, take care of yourself. Cause Dev's been a *real* pain in the ass while you were out."

The room erupted in laughter as Aaron left, assuring her he would see her later. From there it was a parade of faces and names as she met everyone. Devon said they were all members of his *Force*. She had been so busy trying to put names with faces that she had forgotten to ask what that meant.

Nerves almost got the best of her when she met Siobhan, Devon's mother, but the elderly woman was so gracious and welcoming, all her insecurities simply melted away. "It is nice to meet you and I am so glad you are feeling better. I heard the good doctor say you should eat and get some rest. Kyndel has cooked up enough food for an army and her cooking always makes me feel better. Would you like me to have them bring you a plate?"

Her stomach growled before she could answer. Siobhan chuckled and Devon barked a laugh as her cheeks warmed for about the hundredth time. *At the rate I keep embarrassing myself, I'm never gonna need makeup again.* His voice brought her out of her thoughts. "Would you like to sit at the table or eat here in bed?"

She really wanted to get out of bed but knew she would hit the floor if she tried to stand on her own. "I…" Her words were cut short as Devon picked her up and carried her to the small table in the corner of the room. He delicately placed her on the cushioned chair then knelt before her. She sighed as just the tips of his fingers touched her cheek. "Never hesitate to tell me what you want or need, *a chumann,* your happiness means everything to me."

Thankfully, Siobhan spared her from trying to speak past the lump in her throat when the older woman returned with a tray containing two heaping plates of food and two huge glasses of iced tea. As she placed the tray on the table, she said, "I know I gave you a lot, but I wasn't sure what you liked, so there is a bit of everything. Just eat what you can. Don't worry if you can't eat much, it has been a while since you had solid food. Whatever you get down will help your strength return."

"Thanks, Mom, I'll make sure she eats." She looked up to find a lopsided grin on his lips and a twinkle in his eye.

Everything looked and tasted delicious, but Siobhan had been right, she was only able to eat small bites, and even those seemed to take much longer than usual to swallow. Every time she paused, Devon would give her a look that said 'you *need to eat',* which made her giggle nervously. The tea absolutely hit the spot. It was a blend of black and green tea and she could taste herbs just like her mom used to blend. It became increasingly obvious that she was more thirsty than hungry. When her glass was empty, Devon handed her his, saying, "Drink as much as you like. I'll go get us some more."

Kyra and Siobhan entered the room with Devon close behind, just as she was finishing his drink. He placed two fresh glasses of tea on their table and grabbed two chairs from the corner for the ladies. Once seated, Kyra spoke first. "I know you must be tired but I wanted…I mean, *we* wanted," she looked to Siobhan and then continued, "to talk to you about your memory."

When she nodded for them to continue, it was Siobhan who spoke. "You said your mother was a witch, correct?"

"Yes, ma'am, she was."

"And from what you said, it sounds like she was an Earth witch, one that specialized in healing. Does any of that sound familiar?" Devon's mom asked.

She felt all eyes on her as she answered. "That's what she always said. Her talents came from the Goddess and were passed down from generation to generation. Everything she ever taught me she said had to be used for good or we would get in trouble with the Council."

"Did your mom belong to a coven?" Kyra asked, leaning forward like her answer was very important.

"She did. They were a small group. There were only five left, at least that was what they said the last time I talked to them about a year ago. They're all healers in the small communities around our farm."

Siobhan spoke and the waves of acceptance and reassurance flowed over Anya. "Our Kyndel is a lot like your mom was, only not magical, just an extremely strong healer. I am also a healer and Kyra is a white witch, as you already know. She performed a rite to find what was keeping you unconscious and removed the offending magic. We were hoping that it cleared up all the effects of the tainted magic, but apparently some residual effects remain. We think we have a way to help you with that."

She almost jumped off the chair, so excited to hear what they had to say. They were going to help her remember who she was! "Absolutely, what do we need to do first?" she asked.

Both of the women and Devon smiled, but it was Siobhan that spoke. "First of all, *you* need to get a good night's sleep."

When she would have argued, Kyra spoke up. "She's right, you really do. The magic we got rid of earlier was some nasty stuff and you did just return to the land of the living. Rest up while Siobhan and I get all the goodies ready. Tomorrow at twilight we'll all be calling you by your name," the little witch added, looking just as excited as she felt.

Kyra and Siobhan explained everything that would happen during the ritual, and she was surprised how much it sounded like the spells that her mom and her friends had worked. All through the evening, the people she had met earlier stopped back in her room to tell her how happy they were she was feeling better and to say goodnight. Devon was lucky to have such a tight-knit group of family and friends. She was confused about who was actually related and which ones were just friends, but none of that seemed to matter. They all seemed great.

Kyra's husband came in to get his wife and Siobhan also said goodnight, leaving her and Devon alone for the first time since she had awakened. She listened intently as he answered all her questions about his life. It was so cool to hear how he and the men she had met had been friends since they were teenagers. Devon didn't seem all that old, but when he talked about his friends and family, she felt a kind of timelessness that made her think he was older than he appeared. She blamed it on his slight accent but couldn't shake the feeling that she was missing something she would easily identify any other time. It wasn't that they had ever met before, it was something deeper. He was unique…*special* in some way.

She ducked her head, trying to hide a yawn, but he was way too perceptive, commenting as he stood, "You really do need to rest."

Without another word, she was in his arms again and he was walking towards the bed. Although she had spent the evening with Devon, the air from the open window had kept his scent just out of her reach. She inhaled deeply, her eyes closing on their own and she wondered if anything had ever smelled as good as the man holding her.

He gently laid her down, kissing her on the forehead before he stood and headed towards the door. *Is he going to leave without saying goodbye?*

A chuckle whispered through her mind right before she heard his voice. *"No, Sweetheart, I'm gonna try to get this broken door closed and then I'm going to get some sleep in that big comfy chair over there."*

"But…"

"But, nothing," he cut her off. *"I have slept by your bedside for almost two weeks and I'm not about to stop now."*

He turned and with just a look made it clear that she should agree…so she did. "Okay, if you're sure."

"I am. I've spent many nights in that chair and a few more won't hurt." She watched as he made his way around the room, blowing out the candles that hadn't already burnt down.

When he was finished, he sat down and began taking off his boots. The play of muscles underneath his faded black T-shirt made her hands itch to feel them for herself. Committing each movement to memory, knowing the day would come when she would need to recall just being in the same room with a man like Devon, she closed her eyes and took a deep breath. *That man is lethal!*

Fighting sleep, she pried her eyes open just as he turned off the light. She gasped, surprised by the feel of Devon's lips on her forehead and his whisper falling gently on her ears, '*Oiche mhaith a mhuirnl'n.*" In her mind she heard, *"Goodnight, my treasure."*

"Night, Devon," she said several seconds later, finally finding her voice and giddy that he thought of her as his treasure.

The springs on the chair creaked and she imagined Devon getting his very large, very muscled frame into some kind of comfortable position. She debated telling him that he could go sleep in his own bed, but the words wouldn't come. Being honest with herself, she knew it was because she was scared to be alone. Promising herself that tomorrow night, after she knew her name, she would make sure he got a good night's sleep in his own bed, she snuggled in. Feeling satisfied with her decision and growing more tired by the second, she drifted into blissful sleep.

Consciousness came all at once. She went from a delicious dream of Devon to eyes wide open, the sun from a new day shining bright. Choosing to return to her dream, she rolled over, only to be met by a pair of the bluest eyes she had ever seen topped with a head of curly blonde hair.

"Morning, I'm Sydney!" The beautiful child announced, whispering loudly.

"Well, good morning to you, Sydney. How are you?"

"I'm good. We gots to whisper, cause Mom said not to come in here until you were awake. I was gonna sit and wait, but you were talking and I thought maybe you were awake with your eyes closed, big people do that sometimes, but you weren't but now you are so…"

She giggled at the child's precociousness and then wiggled herself into a sitting position. "So we can talk?"

Sydney nodded and her blonde curls bounced all around. The little girl was absolutely beautiful, inside and out. When she looked into the child's eyes, she could see what most called an 'old soul'. Like most children, Sydney had very few boundaries, and within the next minute was all the way up on the bed, spreading out paper dolls and telling a story about how the prince saved the doctor and the lost little girl.

The child stopped and looked up, cocking her head and furrowing her brow. "You are kinda like me and Mommy. You got saved by Devon just like we got saved by Daddy."

It wasn't a question. It was a statement made without reservation. "What makes you say that?" she asked, extremely interested in Sydney's answer.

"You were 'napped by Andrew, just like me and Mommy. Well, Mommy was 'napped by the other bad guy, but he lives with Andrew so it's kinda the same thing." Sydney made a sweeping motion with her hands before continuing, "And just like Daddy came and got me and Mommy, Devon came and got you. He's a real cool guy. You should like him."

She laughed out loud. "You think I should, huh? What if he doesn't like me?"

Sydney handed her the paper doll princess and a change of clothes. "Sure he likes you, silly, he likes you lots."

It was absolutely preposterous that she was having such a personal conversation with a child, but there was something special about Sydney, obvious in the way she spoke with such conviction. It was then that she realized she had absolutely no idea how old the child was. "May I ask how old you are?"

"Sure you can," Sydney beamed. "I'm six! How old are you?"

"Well, that's kinda tricky, because right now I don't remember."

"Like you don't remember your name?" Sydney asked, with a look of concentration on her face.

"Yes, that's right."

"That's easy, you're Anya! Why didn't you just ask? I heard it last night, in here." The child pointed at her temple while continuing to play.

Anya? Yes! That's it! That's my name! Anya Sloane! Speechless, she sat looking at Sydney, unsure what to do. The little girl continued to talk as Anya sat completely stunned, focused only on the fact that she finally remembered who she was. The fact that a little girl she had just met knew who she was when she herself did not would have to be examined later, because at that moment she was just ecstatic to feel whole again. The next few minutes became a blur as chaos ensued. Sydney climbed into her lap, Sam and Devon entered the room, and her brain reengaged causing her to shout out, "OMG! I KNOW WHO I AM!"

The adults raced to her bedside, Sam took Sydney off her lap, and Devon sat down beside her. When he grabbed her hands there was an instant recognition, a spark that emanated from their clasped hands ran throughout her body and landed deep in her soul. When he spoke, his voice amplified the electricity between them. "You remembered? *Tell me.*"

"Anya…my name is Anya Sloane, but it was Sydney. Not me. *Sydney knew.* She just said it like she'd always known." Her words came out so fast that she had no idea if they even made sense. She just knew for the first time since the black fog had tried to destroy all she was that she had a name! In response, Devon pulled her onto his lap, covers and all, placing a kiss just under her ear that raised goose bumps all over her body.

His voice next to her ear made her want to curl into him and return the kiss, but they had an audience, so she settled for leaning against his chest. "You knew her name, Syd?"

"Well, course I did, Dev," Sydney answered with an unspoken 'DUH' punctuating her sentence.

It was Sam that asked, "How did you know, honey?"

The child shrugged and repeated her earlier action by touching her temple. "Just did, Mom."

Before any more questions could be asked, Lance, Aaron, and Aidan rushed into the room, closely followed by Rayne, the Commander she had briefly met the night before. Lance came directly to his family. "What's up? We *heard* her scream."

He looked from Sam to Devon with a knowing look that made Anya wonder what was up, but before she could ask, Devon answered, "Sort of. Actually it was Sydney. Our resident Super Girl who knew her name."

Sydney giggled as Devon said, "May I introduce, Anya Sloane."

"Nice to meet you, Anya," she heard in one form or another from everyone in attendance. She smiled around the room, instantly embarrassed at her appearance. *What the hell? I haven't even brushed my teeth!*

"No one here cares about that, Anya. We're all just happy you finally have a name," Devon whispered.

His comment warmed her heart, but the fact remained that she was still in her pajamas with bed head and morning breath and her room was quickly filling up with people she had just met. It was then that she remembered Kyra and Siobhan were preparing for a ritual to help her remember. Not wanting them to waste any time, she turned to Devon. "You need to call your mom and Kyra. I don't want them to waste time getting ready for a spell we don't need."

Before he could answer, Royce and Kyra appeared. Wasting no time, Kyra hopefully asked, "Is it true? Did you remember?"

Anya nodded. "Actually, it was Sydney that remembered…or knew…" She trailed off, not exactly sure how to explain. Thankfully, the little girl was quick to pick up the conversation.

Sliding from her dad's arms, she rushed to Kyra. "I knew her name, Kyra. It was just right here." Sydney pointed to her head again as Kyra laughed out loud.

Royce picked up the child, who quickly kissed his cheek and hugged his neck. It was obvious Sydney was loved by everyone, and Anya could see why. Her spirit was pure white with yellow, blue, green, violet, and pink – everything good and right – swirling throughout. When the big man spoke, Anya could hear nothing but love, "You're something special, Little Bit."

"So are you, silly ole dragon." She hugged him tighter, bringing tears to Anya's eyes.

A collective gasp went up and Anya felt all eyes on her. She turned, looking at Devon, unsure what had happened. "Everyone out," he barked, obviously misinterpreting her tears for something other than happiness.

She struggled to explain, but in the blink of an eye the room was cleared and they were left staring at one another. Never one to deal with commands or confusion well, she jumped off his lap and sat on her knees across from him. "What was that for? Everyone looked at me like I had three heads. Then you issued an *order* and they left…just gone…*poof*. Did I do something wrong?"

Anya knew her voice was getting louder and sharper with every syllable, but she was feeling more herself and more frustrated by the minute. When Devon spoke, she could hear, as well as see, his struggle to remain calm. "Absolutely not. You did nothing wrong. It was just that…well…did you hear what Sydney said?"

"Of course, I heard what she said. I thought it was precious. She's so sweet and so loved by all of you, it was just amazing to watch. Made me all teary-eyed"

Relief colored his expression. "They were happy tears?"

"Yes, Devon." She swatted at his leg for emphasis. "They were happy tears. Couldn't you tell? Now what's bothering you?"

He smiled but she could see the unease in his eyes. The deep breath he took before speaking only confirmed it. "Did you hear *everything* she said?"

"Yes, *dammit*!" frustration coloring her words. She knew she'd been in a coma and had holes in her memory, but she wasn't brain dead after all. "What's wrong? What did I miss?" She narrowed her eyes and tried for an intimidating look. "What are you *not* saying, Devon?"

He reached out to touch her hand, but she moved before they touched. The hurt on his face stung, but she was confused and well on her way to pissed. His touch would be a serious distraction, so she stuck to her guns, no matter how much her heart told her to close the distance between them. He hung his head, speaking without looking up. "I guess it's now or never. I'd hoped to wait and talk to you about this after you had time to get to know me better, but as they say, 'Out of the mouths of babes'."

As if in slow motion, he lifted his head, his pained expression shattering her resolve to avoid his touch. She reached out, laying her hand on his knee and was more pleased than she should have been when he covered it with his. "Anya, Sydney called Royce a 'silly ole dragon'. Did you catch that?"

"Yeah…and…?"

The deep breath and slow exhale Devon took made Anya tense, preparing for some devastating revelation, but what he said made her want to hug and strangle him simultaneously. "I am…we are…well, the men are…" *Huge sigh.* "Dragon shifters…"

Anya laughed right out loud, all the fear and tension fading away until she literally fell back on the bed, laughing uncontrollably. Tears poured down her face and still, she laughed. It was just what she needed to rid herself of all the bullshit that had bottled up since her kidnapping. She laughed so long that Devon picked her up and plopped in the chair beside the bed with her in his lap.

Trying to get her laughter under control, she took a deep breath and looked up. Devon was half grinning, half scowling, with one eyebrow cocked higher than the other. His expression caused her to bust out in a renewed set of giggles that she worked as quickly as possible to get under control when his expression turned more scowl than grin.

A staring contest immediately began, one that Anya had no time for. Patience had never been a virtue she possessed nor had any aspirations to acquire. She was and always had been more of an instant gratification girl. *Damn! It's good to remember at least part of who I am!* The situation at hand was no different than any other and she handled it exactly the same way she always had…leap first, look later. "What's all the freaking out about? Think about it, Devon. I can read auras…*see people's spirits*." She stopped and thought for a moment and then asked, "You do know what that means, right?"

"I thought I did…now I'm not so sure."

"Okay, here it is: Reader's Digest version and all. When I look at people, I see *ALL* of them. I can see *you* and *your dragon*." She shrugged and waited for his response.

"Oh…" was all she got, so she kept explaining.

"And even if I couldn't see everyone's parts and pieces, Mom and Pops were pretty powerful witches and very active in the 'community', so I've met a lot of people with special abilities. Shifters are pretty easy to spot once you've hung out with a couple dozen. The auras are different. Although I *will* tell you that I always wanted to meet a dragon." She waggled her eyebrows to ease the tension coming from Devon. When he chuckled, she gave herself a mental high five and then asked, "Was that why you were so worried?"

For a split second she thought he was going to have another 'moment', but he quickly schooled his features and answered, "Yeah. It's not every day someone just *knows* about us. I was afraid with all you've been through it might somehow screw with your recovery."

Devon suddenly became very intense, gripped her upper arm, and leaned forward until they were almost nose to nose. When he spoke, she could feel the weight of his words to the bottom of her soul. "There is absolutely nothing I would *not* do to keep you safe and happy, Anya. *Nothing.*" He slammed his mouth to hers, kissing her as if life itself depended on that one kiss. She responded immediately and felt something inside her click into place…something she hadn't even known was askew. All rational thought ceased when his tongue slid alongside hers, igniting a wildfire that left her breathless and holding onto the man before her for dear life.

Anya was sure she would melt from the heat of their passion but was unwilling to move away from Devon. From one heartbeat to the next, he released her arms, leaned back, and smiled a lazy smile, all the worry of just moments before gone. She gave herself a mental shake to make sure she hadn't imagined the last few moments. But one touch to her sensitive lips, still tingling from his kiss, coupled with the feeling of pure excitement coursing through her veins, assured her it had really happened. They stared at one another until a knock at the door caused her to jump.

"Come in, I know y'all have been pacing the hall the entire time," Devon called out, keeping her captive with his heated gaze.

The words were barely spoken when the door flew open and *everyone* piled into the room. Sydney was the first to speak. "See…I *told you* Anya knew. Sheesh, you guys freak out about *everything.*"

Everyone laughed until Kyra asked, "Do you remember everything, Anya? Any holes in your memory?"

Anya turned and looked at the tiny witch while searching her own mind. She was disappointed to find gaps of blackness remained, all surrounding her abduction and the man the others referred to as Andrew. She wasn't sure if it was lingering effects of the strange mixture of magic she had been bombarded with, or her subconscious protecting her from the trauma. Either way, she *had* to remember and was certain Kyra could help her do it.

"There *are* gaps. Mostly about what happened at the mansion and that guy…Andrew."

She cringed just a little when she said his name, feeling how much just the mention of it upset Devon and everyone else in the room. Although she really wanted to avoid upsetting the people that had been so kind to her, the truth was the truth and it had to be handled.

There was no missing the look Devon threw over her shoulder and Anya turned to see the exact same expression on the face of every man in the room. It was one that promised retribution and violence. In her heart, she knew that whatever had caused such hatred had to have been horrific and the curious side of her really wanted to know, but she had learned long ago that everything had a time and place and later…much later would be better.

Siobhan spoke and Anya acknowledged the calming vibes she was projecting with the serene tone of her voice. The power of the healer was immense and explained why Devon had so many of the same qualities despite his warrior exterior. "Anya, if it is okay with you, we can proceed with the memory ritual. Kyra and I have combined an Earthen spell with a ritual of ancient dragon origin that will bring your hidden memories to the surface. This extraordinary combination has an added benefit of allowing you to put your recovered memories in a metaphysical 'box' inside your mind, where you can then draw them out and deal with them when you are ready."

"I remember Mom doing that a time or two with some of those she helped. It's definitely worth a try. Thank you."

Devon tensed and Anya met his eyes. He spoke in her mind before she could speak. *"Are you sure you feel up to this? There's no rush, Sweetheart. If you need time to rest and gain your strength, take it. Mom and Kyra will understand."*

She knew he had her best interests at heart, but she felt like a part of her life had been stolen and was ready to take back what was hers. "No, I want to do this and the sooner the better," she answered out loud.

He reluctantly nodded but his words reassured her. "If you're sure, then I'm sure."

Anya placed her hand on his cheek, trying to show him as much as tell him how thankful she was for his support. "Thank you very much."

Devon opened his mouth to speak, but his words were cut off when Aaron teased, "Enough of the mushy shit, you two. I'm hungry and Sam says we have to wait for Anya before we can eat. So chop chop." He snapped his finger for effect.

"Oomph," was all she heard before the laughing began again. One glance and she laughed, too. Aaron was rubbing his stomach and Kyndel was grinning from ear to ear, even winked when their eyes met. *She and I are gonna get along just fine.*

"You guys get the hell outta here and let Anya get dressed. We'll be right out," Devon joked, but everyone took the hint and filed out.

Aaron was the last through the door, throwing a wink over his shoulder and mouthing, "I'm starving."

Anya giggled as the door closed and immediately gasped. In one fluid motion, she found herself standing with Devon positioned behind her, his arms around her waist. Her legs shook and her knees threatened to buckle, but she refused to fall. His words at her back strengthened her resolve. "Just relax and lean on me. Let your legs get used to holding you again."

Anya concentrated on first one leg and then the other, pouring as much energy as she could to her weakened limbs. The tremors slowed and then stopped completely as she felt her strength returning. She lifted her right foot, testing her balance, and then placed it just inches in front of the other. Repeating the process, she was completely thrilled when she was still upright. Devon's praise only added to her exhilaration. "You got this, *mo chroi'*. Let's see if you can make it to the end of the bed."

Feeling like she could climb Mt. Everest, Anya nodded and took first one step and then another until she reached her destination. She was panting like she had run a mile and sweat was rolling down her back, but she was as happy as she could ever remember. Devon helped her take a seat on the trunk at the end of the bed and knelt in front of her. His hands on her thighs caused her pulse to race and her already hardened nipples to rub against the soft cotton of her nightgown. The corner of his mouth raised and she wondered if he had any idea what *that* look did to her heart rate.

She shivered at the sound of his voice. "You sit right here, and I'll go run you a bath. It'll help your sore muscles and get you prepared for a busy day."

Unable to speak past the lump in her throat, she nodded and watched as Devon headed to the bathroom. Her eyes zeroed in on the incredible display of male anatomy before her. The muscles in his well-toned backside rippled and tugged at the denim of his jeans, and for the first time Anya could remember, she was jealous of the worn fabric. Her fingers tingled as she imagined them caressing and kneading those toned, hard muscles. Her thighs clenched together as moisture wet her panties.

Closing her eyes, she counted to ten and gave herself a quick reality check. *He's helping you, that's all. It doesn't matter that he kissed you. It was just a heat of the moment kind of thing. Stop thinking about him naked, it'll only get you in trouble.*

His voice stopped her inner monologue, but what he said made no sense to her lust soaked brain. "Lavender or citrus scent?"

"Huh?"

He looked around the door frame and repeated, "Lavender or citrus scent?"

When she didn't answer right away, he explained, "Kyndel makes bath oils infused with healing herbs and…well, I guess you'd call it her special brand of love." He chuckled. "And I wondered if you preferred lavender or citrus scent. She makes a lot of different ones but those two suit you."

She held back a girlie giggle at his continued attentiveness to her needs and answered, "You pick. Whichever's fine with me." *This man is gonna be the death of me…but what a sweet way to go.*

She grinned and looked towards the window. A grandfather clock somewhere beyond the door chimed twelve times and she gasped. Devon was in front of her in a flash. "What's wrong? What happened?"

His hands moved up and down her arms, across her back, and across the tops of her legs feeling for injuries and leaving tiny little tingles in their wake that fueled the libido she was trying so hard to control. "I'm fine. Sorry. I just *heard* what time it was and realized everyone's waiting for me so we can eat. We need to hurry."

Devon laughed. "I assure you Aaron has already conned them out of food. There's no way he waited longer than thirty seconds after leaving this room, and I'm sure the others followed suit. *We* don't miss meals around here."

"Are you sure?" she asked, still worried.

He leaned forward, letting his forehead touch hers and looked her in the eye. "I'm positive. Now let's get you into the bath. It's *you* that needs to eat. You need your strength to get back on your feet."

With no further warning, she was in his arms again and being carried to the bathroom. He sat her on the corner of a gorgeous roman style tub, citrus scented steam rising from the wonderfully aromatic bubbles. "Here are some towels," Devon pointed to a wicker stool stacked high with white fluffy towels.

"And here," he pointed to a matching stool on the other side, "is a robe. I'll be right outside the door, just holler when you're done and I'll come escort you out."

He turned to leave, and although she knew it was totally inappropriate, she was a little disappointed that he didn't even try to sneak a peek of her naked. *Get over it, Anya. Why would he want to see you naked?*

The thought had barely made it through her mind when Devon stopped in the doorway, looked over his shoulder with a fire burning in his eyes that hadn't been there before, and said, *"OH, I* will *see all of you,* m'fhiorghra' *but only when you have the strength for what comes next."* He winked and exited the room, leaving Anya more breathless and aroused than before.

She soaked in the miraculous tub, enjoying the heat of the water and the feel of the herbs working the soreness from her muscles, invigorating her tired body. Wanting to get her hair washed before the water cooled, she turned on the water and attempted to situate herself under the faucet. As she shifted onto her knees, Anya realized a second too late that the bottom of the tub was more slippery than she thought. Her butt went one way, her knees the other, and without warning she slid under the water with an audible *yelp*!

Before Anya could resurface, two large hands were pulling her from the water as she spit and sputtered warm soapy water in a most unladylike fashion. Embarrassment damn near overwhelmed her as she refused to open her eyes, simply feeling around for the hand towel she knew was on the side of the tub. Devon's hand met hers as he handed her the cloth and the same electric charge as before ran through her system, landing squarely in her womb. The sound of water pouring into the tub stopped.

After she had wiped her face, Anya sat perfectly still, eyes squeezed shut. She prayed Devon would just leave her in peace to die of embarrassment. Instead, he spoke. "Are you okay, *a chumann*?"

She heard the smile in his voice and the thought of simply sinking under the water again bounced around her brain, but she figured he would just fish her out, so she answered. "Yes, I'm fine." Anya knew she sounded like a petulant child and Devon's bark of laughter only served to confirm her thoughts.

"What were you trying to do?"

She pouted a moment longer before answering. "I wanted to wash my hair, but the tub was slippery. My top half zigged when my bottom half zagged and well…you know the rest."

"Are you gonna open your eyes?"

"Nope."

"Why?"

"Because…"

"Please?" She could hear him trying to hold back a laugh and bit the inside of her cheeks to keep from smiling. She was embarrassed…*not* flirting with the irresistible man that had once again saved her silly ass.

"Nope." She worked hard to say that one word without laughing at the sheer ridiculousness of the situation.

"Okay, if you're not gonna open your eyes, how about I help you wash your hair?"

He didn't wait for her answer, which was good, because she had no clue what she would've said. The softness of a towel touched her shoulder, causing her eyes to fly open. The cocky grin and twinkle in his eyes told her that Devon knew *exactly* what he was doing, but in the end, she really didn't care. Just having him close made her feel better, whole, complete, and quite frankly, it was worlds better than anything she could remember, so she decided to enjoy it. The towel he had secured to her shoulders covered her breasts, protecting her modesty and showing her what a gentleman Devon really was.

With his hands on her shoulders, he carefully moved her in a semi-circle until her back was to the faucet. Only after he checked the water temperature no less than four times did he speak. "Lean back against my hand and let's see what we can do."

Anya let herself relax into his touch. The warmth of the water against her scalp was heavenly, but when his fingers followed, she sighed despite herself. *What is it about his touch that makes it hard to breath?* She had no clue but never wanted it to end.

His voice beside her ear sounded like how silk sheets felt against bare skin as he whispered, "Is the water warm enough?"

She almost forgot to answer, so caught in the web of desire he weaved. When she did, it sounded breathy and "Fine," was the only response she could muster.

Far too soon, Devon was shutting off the water and helping her return to a sitting position. He began gently massaging her scalp with a towel, drying the excess water from her locks. If she wasn't careful, she could get used to all this attention and would damn sure miss it when it was gone.

He wrapped the towel around her hair, folding it on top of her head. "Can you get up on the ledge and get dried off? If not, I can call one of the girls to help."

"I'll be fine." She grabbed his wrist and pulled him just a bit closer so he could see the sincerity in her eyes as she spoke. "Thank you very much, Devon. I don't know wh…"

He cut off her words with just the touch of his lips to hers, lingering slightly before pulling back. It was just long enough to make Anya's heart race. When he looked into her eyes, she saw a passion and excitement that matched her own. His voice was rough and his breathing ragged as he said, "the pleasure was all mine, *mo ghra'*."

He stood, and from her vantage point, the effect their kiss had on him was blatantly evident. Her eyes took a leisurely stroll up his body. She grew breathless the longer she looked, but she looked all the same. Every part she could see, and some she imagined, were perfect. She made it all the way to his amazing jawline, completely mesmerized. *Even the man's stubble is sexy. I wonder...* her thoughts stopped dead in their tracks as she spotted the corner of his oh-so-kissable lips raised in a cocky little grin that said she was right and truly busted.

Winking, he turned to leave and reminded her, "I'll be right outside the door. Yell if you need me."

Anya lifted herself onto the edge of the tub as soon as the door clicked shut, mentally berating herself for getting caught looking, *no*, make that drooling over that damn sexy man. It only took a few moments for her to dry off and get bundled into the plush pink robe he left for her. She had just wrangled her libido under control and wanted to walk when Devon returned, but he insisted she'd had enough exercise until she had something to eat and proceeded to pick her up and carry her to the bed, making her temperature rise yet again.

Almost immediately he left, allowing Anya to get dressed and brush through her thick, wavy hair before facing the whole crew. When he carried her into the dining room, they all stopped what they were doing and seemed genuinely happy to see her. Kyndel set a plate of food in front of her while Grace filled her glass with tea. Sydney climbed onto her lap and kissed her cheek before telling her to try the cookies.

The rest of the day passed in a happy blur. Most importantly, she, Kyra, and Siobhan prepared for the ritual that would return her memories. The two very talented women taught her to make the 'box' in her mind that Siobhan had earlier mentioned. It was cool to think she would be able to store her recollections instead of being overwhelmed by them returning all at once.

About an hour before nightfall, they all gathered under the Blackthorn tree in Siobhan's backyard. Anya watched from her place on a blanket Devon had prepared for her as Kyra lit the ceremonial fire and instructed everyone to form a circle around the blaze, enclosing both women inside. Just as they had planned, Kyra sprinkled rosemary, sage, periwinkle, and dried blueberry–herbs that stimulate memory–into the blaze while Siobhan recited the Ritual of Remembrance that had been used by the ancient Elders of her clan. The words became a part of Anya as she listened to the Healer's tranquil tones.

"It is the will of Anya, your child of light, to greet her past for what it is. Together, all in attendance, we call the spirits of the past to meet the breath of the present that the future may bring forth life. She brings her heart and mind from the dark of the past to the light of the future. She welcomes all that has come to pass with open arms. We ask for your guidance from the Heavens, the Universe, and the Goddess of All."

The flames grew higher and burned brighter, almost touching the leaves overhead, then they suddenly extinguished. The darkness of the night descended and left the group in the light of the third quarter moon with the serenade of the frogs from the nearby pond as background music. Anya sensed Devon just before his hand touched her shoulder, the heat from his touch calming her rattled nerves. Siobhan appeared before them and spoke as she knelt. "It will take time for the memories to resurface, and when they do, the 'box' in your mind will feel full, heavy even. I suggest you not attempt to open that box on your own or alone."

Devon spoke first. "She won't be alone. I have no intention of leaving her side."

Even in the limited light, Anya saw Siobhan smile, beaming with pride at her son's declaration. She was a little confused by the healer's reaction but felt such relief she didn't ask questions. Siobhan touched Anya's arm right before she stood, still smiling from ear to ear. "It looks like you are in good hands, my dear."

Later, everyone gathered in the kitchen, eating cookies and cake until Sydney announced it was bedtime. After all the goodbyes and goodnights, happily snuggled into bed, Anya fell asleep before Devon returned from his home. She had almost suggested he just stay there in his own bed, but like the night before, she chickened out and kept her mouth shut. Sleep came easily, knowing he would be there if she needed him.

Logically, Anya knew she was dreaming but still felt herself being sucked deeper into the dream world of her memories. The scene came into view and a voice she had hoped to never hear again asked, *"And who are you?"*

Scared and still hurting from the bumpy ride in the back of a windowless panel van, Anya simply stared at the tall, unshaven man with mismatched eyes. Undeterred by her lack of communication and with a look of concern that surprised her, he questioned, "Can you at least tell me if you're okay?"

She nodded and looked at her feet, unable to bear his intense stare. He spoke to another, the one she remembered as John. His long face and little, round glasses perched on the end of his crooked nose would have made her smile any other time. "Was she injured on the ride over?"

"Not that I am aware of, sir, but I can have her examined."

"See that you do. Can you not see that she is special...important?"

"As you wish, Master Andrew."

Her memories continued, one right after another, until she felt as if they were tearing her apart. One moment she was watching them as if they were a movie, the next she was an active participant in scenes she'd already been forced to endure in real life. Anya summoned her strength, convincing herself that she could make it to the end, that she could get the answers they needed to capture Andrew and make him pay for all he had done.

However, her memories refused to be tamed and the film of her life continued. *The sound of thunder and the smell of ozone from a nearby lightning strike filled her senses, making the hair at the nape of her neck stand on end. She looked to her left and saw Bill, a man in his early twenties whose only mistake had been walking his dog, lying dead, a look of utter fear and pain forever etched on his face. Tears streamed down her face for the man that had been grabbed off the street and forced to learn a twisted breed of magic.*

Unable to look away, she was left unprotected when the sick little son of a bitch they had paired her with fired off a spell. Anya felt the sting above her heart several seconds before she lost all feeling in her extremities. As she tumbled to the ground, her last sight was of Master O'Brien running toward her, yelling. Her only solace was that the black fog wasn't there this time.

"Anya, wake up! Anya, honey, *dammit*, wake up!" She could hear Devon's voice just out of reach.

Fear rising in his voice, all but screaming, she could hear him trying to coax her awake. "Anya, *mo ghra'*, please, *please* wake up. You're freaking me the *fuck* out."

She felt Devon's arms slide under her body and once again found herself on his lap, still unable to respond to his pleas. She fought hard, his fear for her well-being giving her the strength she needed to finally break free from the net of her memories. Her eyes flew open and she gasped. Devon straightened his arms just enough to see her face and immediately pulled her back to his chest, holding her tight. His chest rose and fell under her cheek with a sigh of relief.

She listened to the strong, steady beat of his heart. The continual *th-thump, th-thump, th-thump* allowing her to shove her memories back into the 'box' in her mind and close the lid. Devon spoke words of comfort in what she remembered from her mom's teachings to be the language of his ancestors, his strong hands rubbing a swirling pattern up and down her spine. She recognized a few of the words and smiled despite herself when he called her *his heart*.

The grandfather clock chimed four times and Devon kissed her on the head then pulled back enough that she could finally see his face. Worry filled his eyes, and when he spoke, she could feel it in his words. "You scared the hell out of me, *mo ghra'*.'"

He took a long, deep breath before continuing. "When you called out to me, I felt *real* fear for the first time in my very long life. I've faced off hordes, monsters, and crazy wizards hell bent on ruling the world, but none of them scared me like the sound of you terrified and out of my reach. I tried everything I could think of to wake you and still you fought the nightmares. The prospect of losing you made my blood run cold."

Devon looked at her, the weight of his stare reaching the far recesses of her soul. "Now may not be the appropriate time, but I won't waste another minute without making sure you understand that *you are mine*, Anya Sloane–mine to love, mine to shield, and mine to cherish for all time. I will fight *whatever* threatens your happiness and health, even if that means jumping in your dreams and battling the devil himself."

Time ceased to exist as the true meaning of the words became clear. *He's claiming me as his mate!*

"*Yes,* m'anamchara*. I am. Just as the Universe intended,*" he answered directly into her mind.

Their discussion was cut short by the doorbell. "That'll be Aaron and Aidan. Your mind was opened to mine while you dreamt and I saw it all. As Andrew's only living blood relatives, I asked the twins to come over. I think with their help, I can piece together where he is, or at least get close." He stood and placed her back on the bed, kissing her forehead and then her lips before standing. "Try to get some sleep while I talk to my brethren. When the sun is up and you are rested, we can all fill in whatever blanks are left...*together*, okay?"

Anya wanted to disagree with Devon's decision to talk to his brethren without her and she definitely wanted to talk to him about the way he made his intentions towards her known. But at the thought of arguing, fatigue overtook her and she yawned long and deep. They both chuckled. Then he leaned forward to pull the covers up, giving her one last kiss before heading out the door.

The muscle in his jaw clenched and he stood just a little taller and straighter as he walked out, telling her that he was furious but trying to keep it from her, just another thing they would be discussing sooner rather than later. Anya fell into a dreamless sleep with the thought of brilliant grey eyes and the tingle of Devon's kiss on her lips.

CHAPTER THREE

"Is there anything that little fucker can't twist into complete and total shit?" Devon growled through gritted teeth, his anger and that of his dragon burning hot and bright. He ground his teeth, clenched his fists, and paced until he was sure there was smoke coming out of his ears.

Aaron and Aidan listened as he recounted every horrible second of Anya's nightmares, and together they came to the same conclusion…Andrew *had* plans for her. The traitor saw something in her, something more than *his mate*. Devon remembered hearing the little bastard say that she was *special* and he had seen the glint in Andrew's eyes when he looked at her. It made Devon's beast roar! There was no way in hell that fucking traitor was going to lay a finger on Anya *ever again*.

Lost in thought, he had to ask Aidan to repeat what he was saying. His brethren replied, "I just wondered if our *dear* little brother was the one that had Anya dropped off at the hospital. Grace said her file stated they found her propped in an empty wheelchair just inside the Emergency entrance. From what you've told us, seems like he's running a pretty tight ship, so it only stands to reason that he had enough heart to save her life. It had to have something to do with what he saw as 'special' about her, right?"

"Yeah, gotta be. I know that when she was in the hospital and I watched how everyone responded to her, they all seemed to go above and beyond. She's definitely something amazing," Devon answered and his brethren chuckled as he hurried. "I know. I know. We all say the same damn thing, but can't you feel it, too?"

Aaron smirked then surprised Devon with his words. "There's something different about her, for sure. I've been trying to put my finger on it since that first day in the hospital. And before you get all territorial and crazy, it's a familiar feeling, like a sister kinda thing, ya know?"

Devon wished he could say that he and his dragon hadn't thought of punching Aaron in the mouth, but he'd be lying. The mating call was riding him hard, especially since Anya's experience in dreamland. His brethren's words had almost pushed him over the edge, but when he thought about what had been said, he realized Aaron hit the nail on the head. There *was* something familiar about her, besides being his mate.

Aidan spoke up. "Grace and I talked about the same thing. She even asked if there was a chance we'd met Anya before, but I *know* we haven't."

A knock at the backdoor momentarily halted the conversation, as Lance, Royce, and Kyra walked in. Before Devon could ask what was happening, Lance spoke. "Heard there was a party. Anyone make coffee?" the jokester of their Force asked as he proceeded to start a pot when he found it empty.

"I hollered at the pain-in-the-ass when Aidan told me what was up, and Kyra came to make sure Anya was okay," Royce answered Devon's questioning look.

Kyra looked around before asking, "She get back to sleep?"

"Yeah, I checked on her a few minutes ago," Devon responded. If truth be told, he had stayed linked to her the whole time. There was no way she would ever go through anything alone again, if he had anything to say about it.

The little witch nodded then turned and began taking the ingredients for breakfast from the refrigerator. *Looks like they're here for the long haul.* Devon smiled. Never one to waste time, Royce asked, "What exactly happened? 'A' said she remembered and the shithead was definitely involved."

"Yeah, Andrew's at the center of it, and it looks like he thought he could use Anya for something he was planning."

Devon was again interrupted when Rayne appeared with a box full of food. "Front door was open and my hands were full. Kyndel will be over when Jay gets up."

The Commander sat the box on the table and turned to Aidan. "Your mate said to tell you she's working from home today. She and Kyndel were on the phone when I left." He turned back to Devon. "Now, bring us all up to speed. You take the lead."

Rayne's resolve to do whatever it took to catch the traitor, even letting another Guardsman lead, matched the determination of every Guardsman in the room. Andrew had been responsible for more pain and suffering than any single being Devon could ever remember. He quickly retold everything he had witnessed in his mate's dream, careful to give every detail.

Each member nodded when he explained the way the traitor had said Anya was special and the extra attention he paid her. Aidan explained their theory about Andrew ordering her dropped off at the hospital and Lance asked, "Did you ever scent him or any other black magic when you were with her?"

"No, nothing," Devon answered. "But then she'd been in the hospital for a while at that point, and I was sure she'd just bumped her head. The thing that pisses me off is the little fucker saw something in her he wanted to exploit. We've all noticed there's something extraordinary about her, but he wanted to *use* her. If he had any idea she was okay, I'm sure we would've seen him or his flunkies."

Just the thought of Andrew even looking in Anya's direction made Devon itch to get his hands around the traitor's neck. His dragon chuffed his approval of the Guardsman's thoughts. Thankfully, Kyra's voice brought him back to reality and made him focus on something other than homicide.

"I told you I sensed something inside your girl that was 'more than human' when we were trying to get her awake. If I could sense it, then I'm sure the asshole could to. His dragon magic is way stronger than before, add to that the filthy shit he's messed up in and the addition of Earth magic, I'm sure he sensed she's more than she appears. The longer I think about it, the more convinced I am that a Concealment Spell was used on Anya early in her life."

Devon tensed and Kyra rushed on. "Now before you go gettin' all Alpha male, chill and listen. It's all white magic, nothing harmful and nothing I can't get through with just a little time. My guess is that her adoptive parents used it to protect her, which if the way you describe Andrew's interest is any indication, then thank the Goddess. When Anya gets up, we need to talk to her and see if she remembers anything."

Kyra turned back to the stove and Aidan picked up the conversation. "I get the feeling from what you've told us, Dev, that Andrew's gearing up for something but isn't ready yet. If he's grabbing people off the streets and giving them magical training, then he's still a ways from putting whatever bullshit plan he has cooked up into action, right? What do you think, Kyra? You're the resident magical expert." He asked as Royce's mate brought a huge skillet of scrambled eggs and a plate full of bacon to the table.

"Roy, hun, grab the plates please," Kyra said before answering Aidan. "Yeah, I'd imagine he's at least a week or two from even a small number of his "recruits' being anywhere near ready to cast spells with any accuracy, and that's only if he's been enhancing their abilities with his own. Kidnapping Anya was random and lucky for the asshole. He had no idea that she was anything other than a mundane, someone without magical abilities."

"In our language it's called a *gandraíocht,* without magic," Siobhan said as she entered the kitchen.

"Sorry we woke you, Mom," Devon said as he stood, giving his mother his chair and grinned when he saw every Guardsman on their feet as well.

"I've been awake since Anya's nightmare. Once I knew you had it under control and heard that Andrew was involved, I began researching. The smell of coffee and breakfast is the only reason I am here. Thank you Kyra for feeding the army." Siobhan smiled and began filling her plate.

The others followed suit and silence filled the room as they devoured almost everything in sight. Devon thought about all he had learned from Anya's memories and all he knew of Andrew's propensity for violence, coming to the conclusion that they would have to strike first, eliminating the traitor and his continual threats once and for all. It was also glaringly obvious that they needed more manpower to find where the shithead was hiding out.

As soon as breakfast was over, Kyra and Siobhan excused themselves to further research ways to identify and remove Anya's Concealment Spell while Devon began to lay out the beginnings of his plan to catch the traitor.

"From what I saw, Andrew is held up in a mansion with a huge open field either on the property or very close by. During all of her memories, Anya was either in the house, in that field, or walking from one to the other. The only time a vehicle was even mentioned was when she was first abducted."

Heads nodded around the table as Devon and Aidan both opened laptops and Royce and Rayne began spreading out maps of the area. While his computer was booting up, Devon said, "Royce, I hate to ask this. I know you've had about as much family as you can stand for a while, but do you think Rian, Rory, and their Force would be able to come help out? I have a feeling…"

"Already spoke to my brothers and Kellan. They'll be on their way as soon as the sun sets. Bro, you're *thinking* loud enough for every dragon within a thousand miles to hear." The older Guardsman chuckled.

"Thanks, man," was all Devon could say.

"Why don't y'all just hug it out and then we can get back to work," Aaron joked from the corner and was rewarded with a smack to the back of the head from Royce.

Always the Commander, Rayne stepped in before things got any further out of hand. "Time to get to work."

Devon took over. "'A', can you look through tax records in about a hundred mile radius from the hospital for expensive homes or estates? Focus on anything that's in the name of a trust or a company. I'll take empty, abandoned, or bank owned properties."

"Can you guys mark them on the maps?" he asked Rayne, Royce, and Aaron without looking up.

"Why a hundred miles from the hospital?" Aaron inquired. "I'd think he'd be farther away. Especially if what Kyra said about his dragon coming back is true. Wouldn't he be afraid we could sense him?"

"Andrew had Anya taken to Sam's hospital, but I don't think it had anything to do with our lovely doctor. I believe it was because it's the closest one with specialists on staff. If he'd wanted Sam's attention, the traitor would've made sure she knew Anya was there. Andrew's also lazy and paranoid. He would never let anyone travel farther than a hundred miles one way, they would be too far out of his control," Devon commented while clicking away at the keyboard.

A few uh huhs and grunts of agreement were all he heard as Aidan began calling out addresses meeting his specifications while he searched through thousands of records. Hours passed as they mapped location after location. Devon was shocked at the sheer number that met their requirements. When Rayne announced they had over thirty properties, the Guardsmen took a break to regroup and think of ways to narrow their hunt for the traitor.

Even though he had been linked to Anya the entire time, he missed her touch, her scent, *hell*, he just missed *her*. Entering the room, he propped the broken door back against the frame and spoke through mindspeak to Jace. *"Hey, bud, I have a huge favor to ask. Can you head to Home Depot and get a replacement door for one of the bedrooms in my mom's house?"*

"What the hell? You guys partying without me?"

"Don't I wish. No, I got a little over zealous." Devon chuckled.

"You got it, Bro. I have to go pick up Kyra's magical supplies that I sent the other day. Thank the Heavens Rory just sent them right back." The younger man laughed.

"Thanks, man. I owe ya one."

"Naw, just remember me when it's your turn to run training. Aaron's been kicking my ass."

"And I'll keep right on kicking, my man," Aaron interjected, making Devon laugh out loud and Jace moan.

"Well, shit," Jace groaned. *"When I am gonna learn* everyone *can hear me?"*

The older Guardsmen roared with laughter and Jace went on. *"Oh well, I'm headed into town. See ya in a couple hours."*

"See ya, kid. Thanks!"

"Stay outta trouble or you'll be cleaning the stalls for training, young'un" Aaron jokingly added. His brethren really did enjoy giving the younger guys hell.

Not to be outdone, Jace added, *"I hear ya, old man,"* and quickly severed their link.

"That kid's a smartass," Aaron chuckled.

"And you like him all the more for it."

"Damn straight. Now hurry up and visit with your girl while we raid your mom's fridge. We got lots more to do," Aaron joked and Devon could tell he already had his mouth full of leftovers.

"Yeah, yeah, yeah." Devon snickered as they both cut the connection and he turned to find Anya watching his every move.

"How long have you been awake, Sweetheart?" he asked as he made his way to her side.

"I woke up a few moments before I heard your footsteps." She pushed up into a sitting position, turning towards him with a serious look on her face.

Devon sat down on the side of the bed, grabbing her hand in the process. She may have something serious she wanted to discuss, but he and his dragon had been without her touch for long enough. The spark that accompanied their clasped hands made him smile and when he looked up, he found the same look on Anya's face. She glanced at their combined hands, back to him, and exhaled a breath he hadn't realized she'd been holding.

"You were just talking to Aaron and another dragon when you walked in, right?"

Surprised, Devon nodded and said, "Yeah. How did you know?"

"I could hear it." Anya pointed to her temple with her free hand. "It was kinda like when I hear you, but it felt like it was on a different channel or something, sort of out of tune with static in the background." She shook her head, trying to make sense of it.

Devon's smile grew as he explained. "Well, that's pretty much what it is. One of the perks of being a dragon shifter is that we're able to *mindspeak* with those of our clan, our Force, other dragons, and most importantly, our mate. That's what allowed me to hear you while you were in a coma and how I can hear your thoughts when you have your guard down or you're projecting. I wanted to ask if you have any psychic abilities or ESP, or maybe even shared some of your adopted parents' magic."

Anya shook her head and Devon continued. "The only reason I ask is because, although we are destined to be together, it's pretty unusual that we would have a mind-to-mind connection so early on, especially before actually meeting. It's also extraordinary that you could hear my conversation with Aaron. I know abilities grow the longer mates are together, but apparently you've had them right from the get-go."

Anya still shook her head but was deep in thought. Devon paused while she digested what he had just said, but she was quick and immediately asked, "Why could I only hear your voice and not what you were saying when I was in a coma?"

"I'm not really sure, that's something I want to ask Kyra and Mom. Hopefully they'll have an answer. My best guess is that it had something to do with the magical fog both you and Sydney described. It blocked part of our connection."

"And about this mate stuff…way to drop a bomb on a girl and then walk away," Anya smacked his knee. "I need a little more explanation than 'you are mine, Anya Sloane'." Devon burst out laughing at the way Anya attempted to imitate his much lower voice when she spoke the last few words.

She looked up at him and bit her bottom lip, effectively shredding a hundred years of hard fought self-control. In one sweeping motion, Devon tugged on their combined hands, pulling Anya into his lap, and slammed his mouth to hers. The electrifying sensation when their lips met sent a current throughout his body that landed squarely in his dick and made him crave every inch of his mate. Their tongues met as she opened completely to him. Her nails dug into his shoulders, spurring him on and pushing their passion higher.

His hands massaged and caressed her generous curves, bunching the material of her cotton gown until he touched the bare skin of her lower back. Anya's scent filled the room as her arousal grew, making the man and his beast crazy with desire. His dragon purred at the glory of having their mate excited and wanting in his arms. Their kiss went on and on, and visions of their spent, naked bodies flashed in his lust-addled brain.

She arched her back and moaned into his mouth as just the tips of his fingers slid inside her panties. Goose bumps raised on her heated skin as he sought to memorize every inch of his delectable mate. His fingers grazed the curls at the top of her mound and Anya rolled her hips, grinding against his erection as it tented the material of the sweatpants he had yet to change.

Devon fought for control, telling himself and his dragon it was not the right time to claim her. His brethren and mother were within earshot and Anya was still weak from all she had been through. The longer they kissed, the harder it became to see reason. Summoning all his resolve, he pulled his mouth from hers. Anya moaned at the loss, and with a strength he didn't know she possessed, pulled him closer.

Unable to stand one more second of sexual torment, Devon laid Anya back on the bed, following her down, never losing contact with her luscious mouth until he lay cradled between her thighs. Her legs wrapped around his waist and their hips met stroke for stroke, the only thing keeping him from burying his throbbing cock deep inside and claiming her for all time was their clothing.

He reached for the hem of her gown just as her hands slipped under the waistband of his sweats and her nails bit into his ass as she held him close. His mouth tore from hers as he moaned long and low. Their pace increased as the thread holding the last of Devon's restraint broke. Rising to his knees, he smiled as Anya groaned at the loss of contact and immediately gasped when he grabbed her wrists, lifted them over her head, and secured them with his much larger hand.

Her eyes burned with passion and her kiss swollen lips begged for more attention, but it was her hardened nipples pressing invitingly against the thin cotton of her gown that caught his attention and caused his mouth to water. He held her gaze as he lowered his lips to her breast. Her sharp intake of breath was music to his ears as he sucked as much as he could of her ample breast into his mouth, gown and all. With tongue and teeth, he licked and sucked first one breast then the other until she was writhing beneath him. The entire room smelled of sand and sea and…*Anya*.

Leaving the heaven of her voluptuous chest, hating that she was still clothed, he kissed and nipped down her body, her hands still held captive. With his teeth, he worked her gown up over her hips, baring the silky skin of her stomach, demanding to be tasted. Taking a deep breath and pushing his needs as well as those of his dragon back, he kissed from one hip to the other, right along the top of her panties, dipping his tongue just under the elastic, enjoying the lift of Anya's hips and her pleading moans. "Devon…Devon…oh, oh…please, Devon…*please.*"

"Please what, *mo ghra*? Tell me what you need." He crooned as he continued to taste and torment them both.

"I…I…you…" was the only response he received. Anya took a deep breath and pulled against the grip he had on her wrists. "Please…Devon. Let me…touch you." Her passion-filled voice proved she was as lost to their lust as he. Devon loosened his grip, allowing her to pull free. Her fingers dove into his hair as she attempted to direct his movements. He chuckled against her skin and stuck to his slow, torturous seduction.

Sliding farther down her body, he buried his nose against the moisture that soaked the crotch of her panties and inhaled. Her scent filled his entire being, making his head spin. Completely lost to his mate and with both hands free, he slowed her movements with a hand on her hip as the fingers of his other hand slid inside the leg of her undergarment. His index finger touched her curls wet with her arousal, and Anya's hips shot off the bed, despite the hold he had on her. He traced her outer lips up one side and down the other as slowly as possible, marveling in her perfection. Anya pulled at his hair, her hips thrusting as she tried to force his hand to where she needed him most.

Her mind was open to his, allowing him to share everything she felt, and enhancing the incredible experience of being with his mate for the first time a hundred fold. She threw back her head, baring her throat to him. Her complete trust in him flooded his heart and mind. He watched her cheeks grow more flushed with excitement and her lips draw into a perfect 'O'. She panted his name as he let his finger slide into her warm, wet pussy, and he couldn't help his grin as *Oh My God* floated through her mind. The air was pushed from his lungs and his heart nearly burst with the love he already felt for his amazing mate. She was *absolutely perfect*.

Unable to take one more moment without her taste upon his tongue, Devon fisted the side of her panties and pulled. The sound of the ripping material made his dragon roar in triumph. The offending material flew through the air as he removed his finger, and before Anya could react from the loss, he thrust his tongue deep inside her. He curled the tip of his tongue, teasing the bundle of nerves at the top of her channel and loved the muffled yell of his name against her fist. Anya's legs came up over his shoulders and closed around his head, her heels digging into his back as he licked, sucked, and tasted.

Anya's taste exploded on his tongue, making him see stars and thirst for more. It was like nothing he'd ever experienced. The more he tasted, the more he wanted. There would never be a time in their very long lives together that he would not crave his mate.

Feeling her orgasm building to its crescendo, Devon placed the flat of his tongue at the base of her slit and licked from bottom to top in one fluid motion, sucking her clit between his lips when he reached the top. He held her throbbing nub lightly between his teeth, teasing with the tip of his tongue causing Anya to thrash and mewl. She pulled his hair until he was sure he would be bald. Through their bond, he felt the moment that she could take no more and bit down. Anya screamed her release against her fist. He thrust his tongue into her as far as he could reach, drinking her nectar until the spasms of her orgasm began to subside. Devon continued to lick and suck grinning as she sighed with complete satisfaction and her legs slid from his shoulders.

He lifted his head to see her lazy smile and half-lidded eyes, in that instant, his world became complete. It wasn't that he hadn't known she was his, of that he had no doubts, but to have her in his bed with the look of a well-loved woman, and to know he had put that look on her face, was worth every second of every day for the past one hundred and twenty years. There was no doubt she was his…*forever*.

Devon rose to his knees and slowly crawled up Anya's body, placing his hands on either side of her head when he had reached his destination. He gazed into her eyes, pouring all that he felt into that one poignant look and spoke the words he had waited his whole life to say. "*Ta' mo chroi istigh ionat*, Anya Sloane. *Is breá anois agus go deo.* My heart is within you. Love now and forever."

Tears came to her eyes and for a second he thought he had gone too far, but the smile that came to her lips was a thing of beauty, and when she uttered, "Now and forever," back to him, he was helpless to do anything but lower his lips to hers.

Their tender moment was cut short by the sound of Aaron's voice in his head. *"Dude, I'm sorry to do this to ya but Max, Sophia, and Juan Carlos just pulled up. Rayne called them to help. You better…ah…well, you better get your ass out here before the vein in his head starts throbbing."*

Although he was pissed at the intrusion and so hard he thought his dick might burst, Devon still snickered at just how uncomfortable his brethren sounded at having to disturb them. He was sure the others knew what had just happened, even though they had tried to be quiet, but he couldn't work up the energy to care.

Mentally chastising himself for putting his needs before those of his mate's, he moved to sit back, but Anya held him tight, forcing him to look back down at her. He was surprised to see her smile from before replaced with a scowl. She shocked him further by speaking directly into his mind, *"I'm still getting the hang of talking to you this way and us sharing thoughts, but I know what I just heard. Let me tell you one thing, Mate, what we just shared was amazing, and I won't let you or your worries ruin it. We have to take our joy where we can find it. So cut the shit, all right? I'm healing faster than ever, and as for the rest, you'll get it all handled. I have faith in you."*

Devon was humbled by the complete belief and conviction he felt in Anya's words. Without another thought, he leaned down and kissed her breathless, showing her with his actions where words failed that he appreciated her trust.

When their kiss ended she spoke, somewhat breathless, "Since I can't return the favor, how about I promise to make it up to you?" She winked and reached between them, the back of her fingers grazing his still partially erect cock.

Devon shuddered slightly and chuckled at the sly half-grin on Anya's face as she continued. "You better go wash up, change clothes, and get out there. Sounds like you have important company."

"I'll help you get ready first."

"No, I'm fine. I feel much stronger today, and if something happens that I can't handle or I get weak, I'll call you."

Devon hesitated, but when she put the palms of her hands on his chest and pushed, he felt her strength and relented, making her promise again to call him if she needed anything. Despite her griping, he still helped her up and into the bathroom before he washed up and shaved. She was sitting on the edge of the tub when he walked back in after dressing.

He gave her his best glare and reiterated, "Call me if you need *anything*."

"I will. Now get outta here so I can get ready."

He swooped in for a kiss and smiled from ear to ear when she muttered, "Best kisser ever," under her breath as he walked out the door.

Still smiling and unable to work up any guilt at all for taking the time to properly say good morning to his mate, Devon turned the corner into his mother's dining room and found a horde, not only his entire force and their families but also a few of the younger Guardsmen, along with Maximillian Prentise, King of the Big Cats. Max's sister, Sophia, and their two most trusted lieutenants, Juan Carlos and Ernesto were also in attendance. All eyes snapped to him when he entered the room and not one to let a moment pass, Lance, aka The Pain-In-The-Ass, was the first to speak. "Glad you could join us, Dev."

His comment broke the silence and the room erupted into roars of laughter. Devon crossed the room to where the King and the other werepanthers were seated. Max stood as Devon extended his hand and as the men shook, Devon said, "I want to thank you for sending Dr. Lawrence to help us, and you," he turned towards Ernesto, "thank you for involving your Leo. I will forever be in your debt."

Max was the first to reply. "There is no debt. We're in this together. The traitor has taken from us all. Besides, I'm hoping we might finally get an invitation to a dragon mating celebration."

"You're at the top of the guest list. All of you are." Devon looked at each werepanther and then around the room at all the others, smiling at his good fortune.

Never one to be left out, Aaron snorted. "Well, aren't we just one big happy family..."

Rayne cut off whatever was to come next in his commanding fashion. "I asked Max to help with the search. While you were otherwise occupied," the Commander raised an eyebrow before continuing, "we have narrowed it down to five properties from our original thirty with two at the top of the list."

Kyndel quickly interrupted. "We came," she motioned to Grace and Sam, "to see if there was anything Anya needed and maybe get her out for some fresh air."

Devon nodded. "I left her getting into the tub."

It allowed him to completely focus on finding Andrew, knowing Anya would not be alone. He had felt her strength and conviction to take care of herself but couldn't stop worrying or checking in to be certain she was okay.

The girls and children headed out of the room, but not before Sydney ran over, stopped right in front of him, and crooked her finger in a *'come here'* motion. When Devon leaned down, she kissed his cheek, then turned and ran to catch up with the others. He stood grinning and headed to the table that was completely covered with maps.

Aidan began explaining. "These two, although as far away on either side of the hospital as possible, are our best bets. The county records show that their lots are enormous and remote with damn near a forest for cover. The houses themselves are located in the back corner of each property, and they have huge open spaces just as you described from Anya's memories. These are definitely where we should start. Kyra had no feeling one way or another, so we'll have to do it the old fashioned way."

"I recommend we split up into two groups, comprised of both dragons and panthers, and go tonight," Max suggested as he turned towards his sister. The look they shared let Devon know they were speaking through the feline version of mindspeak. A swift nod from Sophia and she and Ernesto headed towards the door.

Max looked back to the group and explained. "Sophia is going to call Raphael, Fausto, and Benedicto. They're the best trackers in the Pride."

"Your help is truly appreciated," Rayne acknowledged and turned to Devon. "This is your show. Lead away, my friend."

It was almost an hour later when Jace knocked on the door and hollered, "Hurry, this son of a bitch is heavy!" Royce laughed as he opened the door and the two younger Guardsmen hauled a brand new, solid oak door across the threshold.

"Did ya get the biggest and heaviest they had, young'un?" Royce asked.

Jace grinned a wide, shit-eating grin. "I got solid oak. Thought y'all might need the extra reinforcement."

Devon shook his head. "You've been spending way too much time with Aaron and Lance."

"Hey! Not cool!" was heard from the vicinity of the kitchen, but it was the smell of sand and sea that drew his attention. He spun around and there, standing in the doorway between the hallway and the living room, was

Anya. His feet moved of their own volition, and within seconds he had his arms around her and was lost to her loving gaze. Sydney squeezed between them and tugged on his belt loop.

"Doesn't Anya look pretty, Dev? I picked out her top. Purple's my favorite color," Sydney chattered on until Devon relented and picked her up.

She placed one arm around his neck, the other around Anya's, and kissed them both on the cheek. "Love you guys. Now let me down, I need a cookie."

Devon watched as Sydney ran into the kitchen to get her cookie before he looked back to Anya. She had her head bowed and he could feel her embarrassment at the child's words. Placing his forefinger under her chin, he gently lifted her head until he was looking into her eyes and smiled. "You are absolutely gorgeous and it has nothing to do with the shirt, although it's nice, too," he chuckled. "You could be wearing a burlap bag and would still be the most beautiful woman in the world."

He kissed the tip of her nose and pulled her tight against his chest. "You are perfect and you are mine," he whispered just before their lips met.

"Ahem, there'll be time for that later, you two." Rayne's voice sounded behind them.

Anya jumped and tried to pull away, but Devon held her tight, speaking against her lips, "He can wait another minute."

He kissed her until she once again relaxed in his arms. Pulling back, he winked and helped her to the kitchen table, thrilled to see how much better she was walking. Kyndel appeared with a plate of food and a big glass of her special tea. Kissing Anya on top of the head, he said, "Eat up, *evgren*. I need to make sure Jace and Liam aren't tearing down more than they're fixing."

One quick trip down the hall assured him the young men had everything taken care of. When Devon returned to the kitchen, Anya was laughing and talking with the mates of his brethren, Sydney, and his mother, but all conversation halted when he approached the table. Devon snorted. "What the hell? Is this a ladies only conversation?"

"Sure is," was Sydney's quick response, causing everyone in both rooms to burst out laughing.

"I see how it is." Devon feigned annoyance but winked towards his mate. It was then that he noticed her rubbing the inside of her left wrist.

He knelt at her side, taking her hand in his. "Is your wrist bothering you?" he asked, examining the area she had rubbed to a bright red circle.

"It started itching while I was in the tub, so I put some of 'Granny's Special Recipe' that Kyndel gave me on it. The irritation stopped for a while but now it's back with a vengeance." Anya looked from her wrist to him while she spoke.

Devon could feel small raised bumps that seemed to almost vibrate when his thumb rubbed over them. Worried his mate was having an adverse reaction to something in his mother's home, he pulled her wrist closer and used his enhanced vision to examine the affected area.

"I'm just gonna take a quick look," he said offhandedly, concern for Anya's well-being outweighing his manners. What he had originally thought to be a rash began to take shape before his eyes. It took just a moment for him to identify the small marking as it continued to materialize on her wrist.

"I'll be a son of a…" he mumbled under his breath and looked up at Anya.

Concern evident in her eyes, he quickly explained. "I'm not sure how it's happening but you're being marked."

Her eyes grew wide with fear, making Devon hurriedly explain. "It's nothing bad at all. I promise." He touched her knee with his other hand and pushed love and reassurance through their mating bond.

"It's the mark of a heart scale. It's said that only once in every white dragon's life do they produce the rare heart scale and most shed it without ever knowing. I know we haven't had time to talk about it, but…my dragon is white."

"I have only ever personally known one other white dragon, my dad. He actually found his when he and my mother were together." He looked up at Siobhan to find her looking at the locket his father had given her. "He had a locket made for her to hold his heart scale and told her that it was their special blessing from the Universe. I think you developing this particular tattoo is pretty awesome, but I have no clue what it means."

Siobhan spoke from across the table. "There has to be something in one of the many volumes of history I have or are housed in the Elder's library. Let me do some research and I am sure we can find the origin of this miracle."

"Miracle?" He and Anya asked in unison.

"Yes, whatever is happening here is most *definitely* a miracle. Can you not feel it all around us? *Your* mating is special, we just need to see exactly how special." Siobhan assured everyone listening and then turned to

Kyra. "Would you mind joining me? It is now more important than ever to find out if Anya is under a Concealment Spell and remove it if necessary."

"Absolutely," the little witch answered, kissing her mate as she stood to leave. Kyra stopped beside Anya and touched her shoulder. "It's just like I explained, honey, nothing to worry about. We always have shit of some kind or another stirring around here. We'll get this all figured out. You got a good guy there." She kissed Anya's cheek and patted Devon's shoulder before jogging after his mother.

Devon watched a million emotions flash across Anya's face and was driven to comfort her. Doing the only thing he could think of, and with the help of his enhanced abilities, he scooped his mate up as he stood and then sat in her chair with her cuddled against his chest. Anya fought his hold and mumbled something he missed. Putting his ear right in front of her lips, he asked, "Pardon?"

"Put me down. Everyone's looking at us," she whispered, her breath ruffled his hair and stroked his ear, causing his eyes to slide shut.

Clearing his throat and attempting to push back his dragon he answered, "Yeah, and…?"

"And it's embarrassing."

"I'm sorry you're embarrassed, *mo chroi'*, but we are an affectionate bunch."

"But…"

Her comment was cut short when Grace spoke from across the table. "Seriously, Anya, you're gonna have to get used to it. They're all a mess and it only gets worse the longer you're with them. Heavens help you if you ever get…ohhhhhhhhhh…"

In a flash, Grace was picked up out of her seat and was being carried towards the door by her obviously adoring husband who shouted, "Max and Rayne will catch you up, Dev. We'll be back later. It seems my mate needs to *rest*."

Devon chuckled. "See, told ya."

"Okay, I guess." Anya giggled, but he could see it was going to take time for her to get used to their ways.

"Max needs to get back to his Pride to prepare for tonight, so if you're done causing trouble, could you get in here?" Rayne called from the dining room.

"Oooooo….oomph," came from Aaron in the corner. Devon turned to flip him off just in time to see Kyndel rubbing the back of her hand and his friend rubbing his stomach for the second time in two days.

"Kyndel's getting good with the backhand, Bro. You better watch out or move quicker," Devon joked through their link.

"Damn, she's fast." Aaron chuckled.

"She's murder with a wooden spoon, too," Rayne added to the conversation. *"Now, get your asses in here,"* he added quickly, switching from friend to Commander mid comment.

Both Guardsmen chuckled as Aaron headed towards the dining room and Devon stood, not wanting to let his mate go. He sat her back in her chair, kissed her forehead, and said, *"I gotta go. Have fun with the girls and Jay,"* right into her mind.

Anya grabbed his arm and pulled until they were eye level. She laid her lips to his and answered back in the same fashion. *"Thank you."*

The sound of her voice in his head got better every time. Wanting to grab her and run as fast as he could to his home but knowing he had to prepare for their nighttime surveillance, he sighed, pulled back from her lips, and headed towards the dining room. He had one foot over the threshold when Max's laugh reached his ears. "It's good to see that some things never change. I thought werecats were bad, but dragons fall hard."

"And it's the best plummet in the world, King," was Devon's quick comeback. When he looked around, he smirked to see Rayne, Lance, and Royce nodding in agreement.

Aaron cleared his throat. "I don't give a shit how great it is, I'm not giving up the single life. What about you, Max?"

The King's answer was cut off when Rayne began explaining their plans for finding Andrew, apparently tired of waiting. "Since you were otherwise engaged," Rayne raised an eyebrow at Devon and shook his head before continuing, "Max and I have set the teams. You lead the team with Aaron, Royce, Max, Ernesto, and Raphael. Everyone else will be with me."

"Except Sophia," Max interjected. "She will be with the Pride handling another matter."

Devon wondered about the sudden change in the Leo's demeanor but knew it was none of his business. It was more important that he catch up on all that had been discussed in his absence. Royce spoke up, spinning the largest map on the table so that everyone could see. Pointing at the most eastern point of the circle they had drawn to indicate the hundred mile radius around the hospital, he explained, "I believe this property's our best bet. The house is almost completely hidden by trees. There's an iron fence across the front and halfway down both sides, then it turns into a five foot rock wall. *Hell*, the large clearing even has cover."

Aaron handed Devon a picture that had been printed from the county records showing nothing but a huge expanse of trees, bushes, and foliage of all varieties. And then an aerial view in which he could see the large open area and the roof of an absolutely enormous home, along with everything else Royce had described. He had to agree that if he were hiding out and training a group of black magic wizards, it would be the property he would use. The only problem he could see was the huge iron gates and the security cameras he saw everywhere. More to himself than anyone else, he asked, "What the *hell* are we gonna do about all those cameras?"

He was surprised when Max answered. "Raphael is an electrical wizard. Once we've arrived at the property, he'll find the main switch and disable them. I'd imagine there are people watching the feed, therefore, we'll need to move quickly, but I'm sure even you dragons can keep up."

Laughing, Lance answered. "I hope your people don't have a problem watching dragon ass as we take the lead."

For the next several hours he and the men debated every possible scenario until Devon was sure they had everything covered at least ten times over. Plans changed halfway through and it was decided everyone would go to the first property. After looking at both, it was the best possible choice. If it proved not to be the one, then they would be doing the same thing the next night. His gut said this was the one and if Devon had learned anything, it was to follow his gut.

~~*~*~*~*~*~*

Anya spent the afternoon trying to ignore the weird sensations in her wrist and listening to the conversations all around her. It had been so weird to actually meet the King of the Big Cats, as Devon had called him, Maximillian Prentise. Her parents had known a few jaguar shifters over the years, so Anya thought she knew what to expect, but the Pride members had been *nothing* compared to their Leader. The power seemed to roll off of him in waves and his feline characteristics were almost completely masked, making him appear human. His sister, Sophia, was drop dead gorgeous and also had no distinguishable panther characteristics.

Ernesto's voice seemed familiar and Devon's voice in her head confirmed her thoughts. *"Ernesto is a nurse at the hospital and took care of you during some of your stay."*

She acknowledged Devon's words with a nod and thanked Ernesto for all he had done to help her. The last man, Juan Carlos, was taller, more muscled, and had a much darker complexion than the others. When he shook her hand, she felt a raw, almost untamed power that wasn't present in the others. Anya wondered about his differences and decided it was something she would ask Devon about later. Royce called from the dining room and again she was left in the kitchen with instructions to take it easy, something that was really beginning to get on her nerves.

She knew she was supposed to be getting to know the girls and it was something she really wanted to do, but the plans Devon was making held her attention. "Did you hear me, Anya?" Sydney asked, interrupting her wayward thoughts.

"No, Sweetheart, I'm sorry. My mind keeps wandering."

The child rolled her eyes but smiled before whispering, "You were leaves dropping on Devon and Daddy weren't you?"

Anya giggled. "Yes, Syd, I was *eaves dropping* and I shouldn't have been. It's not a nice thing to do."

"That's okay, I do it all the time," the little beauty said in a matter of fact manner, making Anya laugh out loud.

"Well, it's not polite, little miss," Sam answered from across the table.

Both Sydney and Anya giggled before whispering, "*Busted!*"

"We better behave," Sydney said amongst her chuckles.

"Yeah, we better." Anya looked up to find Kyra almost jogging towards her. "What's up?" Anya questioned.

"Can you come with me? Siobhan and I found something and I want to see if it works."

"Sure," Anya replied as Sydney jumped off her lap. Before she could stand on her own, Devon was at her side, practically lifting her from the chair. "What the…"

"I'm going, too," Devon replied before she even had the chance to ask the question.

Grabbing his forearm, Anya turned to chastise Devon when the mark on her wrist made contact with the tattoo on his arm, and the resulting electrical charge caused her to stumble against his hard body. His chest was heaving and the sound of his heart pounding under her ear made it sound as if he had run miles instead of just a few steps. Looking up with wide eyes, she could see that his surprise mirrored her own. When he spoke, his voice was little more than a growl. "What the hell was that?"

"I have no clue." She narrowed her eyes, about to speak when the tattoo on his arm wiggled under her fingertips. Dropping his arm like he had the plague, her eyes shot to his.

"What's wrong, *mo chroí*?" Devon asked with concern.

Eyes wide, shaking her head, she looked from Devon to his arm and back again, I...your arm...I..." She stopped and took a deep breath. "Your tattoo...*moved*. I felt it kinda...*wiggle*." Anya wiggled her fingers to help explain.

She watched as Devon turned his arm over, inspecting every inch before looking at her. "I didn't feel it, but I was a little preoccupied with the shock you gave me," he said, eyes narrowed, thinking so hard she could almost hear his thoughts.

His words surprised her and she blurted out, "*I...shocked...you?*"

"Well, yes. I know you felt it, too." His eyebrows rose and then his brow quickly furrowed.

"You know I did, but I thought it came from you."

"I think it came from both of you," Siobhan called from the doorway. "A similar occurrence was documented in one of the journals I just read. In very special cases when the mating marks touch, a 'shock' of sorts happens. I know that your dragon brand and the marking on your wrist," she motioned from one to the other of them before continuing, "are not mating marks, but they are enough like them that I believe we can ascertain it is the same phenomena. The author of the journal entry believed it was due to the combination of the magical abilities of both people."

Kyra jumped in, so excited her small frame vibrated as she spoke. "And that's why I'm positive you've been under some type of Concealment or Protection spell for most of your life. I felt the magic in you before. And now that you and Devon are together, it seems to be growing, even without the official mating ceremony."

The tiny witch took a step forward. "We just need to perform a little spell and then we'll know for sure."

There was no way Anya could have said no, even if she wanted to, with Kyra standing there bouncing from one foot to the other, her eyes wide, nodding her head in reassurance. The waves of pure belief rolling off her were strong enough to power a city.

Devon started to speak but Anya cut him off. It was time he learned that she could speak for herself. "Sure! Let's do it!"

That was all it took. Kyra jumped up and down, clapped her hands, then ran over and did her best to get her tiny arms around both of them for a hug. Anya caught Devon's scowl right before he schooled his features, and spoke through their link, *"It's going to be fine. And...I can speak for myself."*

"I know that you can. I just worry that you're not giving yourself time to heal. And..."

"And what?"

"Nothing."

She knew he wasn't telling her everything, but Kyra had their hands in a death grip and was attempting to pull them towards the door while talking a mile a minute, explaining the ritual they were about to perform. Only Royce slowed her down. "Kyra, honey, let them walk," Royce commented, barely able to keep the laughter out of his voice.

"Oh shit! I'm sorry." Kyra snorted, dropping their hands and stepping back. "I just love solving puzzles and helping the people I love."

Royce leaned down and kissed the top of her head. "We know you do, *mo ghrá'.*" The chuckle he had been holding in bubbled out.

The love Anya saw between the couple was absolutely adorable and adorable was *not* a word she had ever thought she would use where Royce was concerned. He was *huge*. "It's okay. I'm glad you're here to help," Anya assured. "I'm ready if you are."

She pulled from Devon's arms, but he wound his fingers through hers, not letting her get away and walked beside her. Figuring it wasn't worth the argument, she nodded and followed Kyra. As they made their way down the hall, she remembered Siobhan's words and asked, "What did your mom mean when she said 'dragon brand'?"

"When we reach the age of transformation, between seventeen and twenty, the dragon within that has lain dormant becomes a *true* part of us. When that happens, the barely discernible marking we've had since birth grows bolder and brighter. It takes its place as it was meant to be...the physical representation of our dragon. Each dragon shifter carries the brand of *his* dragon somewhere on his body."

He paused as he motioned for her to enter Siobhan's study ahead of him, and then went on. "With my shirt on, you are only able to see his tail." He traced what she had originally thought to be a beautifully artistic tattoo while he spoke. "He actually covers most of my upper arm, shoulder, and even a small part of my shoulder blade."

Devon leaned his head forward and pulled the hem of his shirt down, revealing the head of a majestic opalescent dragon perched at the base of his neck. It seemed impossible, but there it was right before her eyes, unlike any tattoo or marking she had ever seen. A square shaped snout with a rather imposing short, thick, curved horn right between the nostrils, an imposing brow that protected two silver-grey eyes so like those of the man her heart already recognized as hers. There was no denying he and this creature were one. The recognition in those soulful eyes drew her closer and beckoned her to touch.

Her fingertips smoothed over the glistening scales of the bridge of its nose and Anya felt them move. Instead of being scared like before, she was intrigued and continued her slow exploration until her fingers were just under its eyes. It was miraculous how close to reality her imagination was. As a child she had been obsessed with dragons and knights and read every book she could find, always sure the writer had the story wrong and that dragons were actually the good guys.

"We are," floated through her mind and she chuckled.

"Yeah, Mom and Pops explained that to me after I read an especially horrible story where the dragon was slaying women and children. It had me swearing to never read again." She laughed. *"I think I was eight at the time."*

Devon cleared his throat and stood. Her hand that had been on his neck slowly drifted downward, stopping right over his heart. The steady beat reverberated through her and it was then that she realized their hearts were in sync.

"As they always will be." Devon's words, low and seductive in her mind, conjured images better left for a less crowded venue.

Having caught her thought he snickered, but coughed into his hand when she pretended to scowl at him. With his hand on her lower back, he directed her to the loveseat directly across from Siobhan and Kyra, but Anya needed to be sure of one more little detail. *"I will be seeing the rest of that dragon sometime soon, right?"*

"Of that you can be sure, mo chroi'. *Of that you can be sure."* The look in Devon's eyes matched the tone of his voice and Anya shivered in anticipation.

Thank goodness his mother spoke and broke the spell, even though the look on her face said she knew *exactly* what she had interrupted. "The Detection Ritual is very simple. Kyra will light a red candle, sprinkle some thyme, and say the incantation. Then you will sleep with a Revealing Amulet under your pillow. Sometime in the near future, the amulet will tell us if you have been magically protected. We can go from there and decide how or *if* to remove it."

"Sounds easy enough. Can you do it right now?" Anya inquired as Devon tensed beside her.

"Absolutely," Kyra responded while placing the large red candle and the herb bowl in the center of the table. She completed the spell in a matter of minutes and only after she had blown out the candle did Devon relax. He watched with squinted eyes when Kyra handed her the silver engraved amulet she was to put under her pillow.

Anya squeezed his hand and joked, "Did you think I was gonna vanish into thin air or something?"

His laugh was forced and his smile fake when he answered. "No, not at all. I trust these ladies completely."

"Yeah, that was convincing," she switched to their silent form of communication as everyone else left the room.

"Dammit, Anya, I'm worried and that's not something I'm good at. I'm a warrior. I look at the obstacles, formulate a plan, and use that plan to eliminate anything keeping me from the goal. I do not lament over a decision...I act. The only goal in my life is keeping you safe." He finally looked at her and there she saw a whirlwind of emotion.

Since they were alone, Anya spoke out loud. Her tone was sharper than she originally intended, but the longer she spoke the more her passion on the subject became evident. "Talk to me, Devon. You're not in this alone. If I truly am *your mate* and we're going to spend the next *forever* together, then you have to learn to include me. I'm not some damsel in distress, and I will *not* have you making decisions for me. I want a partnership, not a dictatorship."

Devon sighed long and deep, and Anya felt his emotions deep in her heart. She wanted to push him, to make him talk, because waiting was killing her; but she knew he needed the time so she bit her tongue and waited. The tick of the clock on the mantel echoed throughout the huge narrow room, seeming louder every second that passed. Time seemed to be going in reverse. Finally, he spoke and what he said rocked Anya's world. "You, Anya, *mo chroi'*, are the realization of every dream I've ever dreamt, every wish I've ever made, and every hope I've ever had. You are my today, my future...my forever. The moment I scented sand and sea, I felt complete for the first time in my very long life. I cannot, and most definitely *will not,* let anything happen to you. It's my nature to act first and ask questions later, and that instinct is the strongest it's ever been since finding you." He paused and she held her breath, waiting for him to continue.

"For you, I will try as hard as I can to include you in my decisions. Just give me a little leeway. It's gonna take some time, but I'd do anything to make you happy…*anything*. *Tá túgrá mo chroí go síoraí*…you are my heart forever."

Anya sat staring into his incredibly expressive grey eyes, dumbfounded. Like every woman, she had dreamt of finding the perfect man, falling in love, and living happily ever after, but even her wildest dreams paled in comparison to the man sitting next to her. When she finally found her voice, all she could say was, "Good answer."

Devon barked out a laugh and stood. Anya thought he was going to help her stand as well, but instead, he dropped to one knee, took her hands in his, and looked into her eyes. While she struggled to breathe he said, "Anya Sloane, although we met just a few days ago, I cannot imagine my life without you. You are the *solas mo anam* and the *bualadh mo chroí*. Without you, my life will be dark and lonely. It is with the blessing of the Universe, the Heavens, and the Goddess of All that I humbly ask you to be my mate, now and forever…joined as one."

Anya had no clue what to say. She definitely had feelings for the man, feelings she'd never felt for *anyone*. Love was there, mixed with a big dose of lust and passion, but her heart was definitely controlling everything where Devon was concerned. It was obvious that their futures were woven together by Fate or Destiny or whatever mystical being controlled these kinds of things. There were just too many things that fit together for their relationship to be mere coincidence.

Looking into his eyes, Anya could see love and fire, devotion and strength, and…*her* happily ever after. The one she had dreamt of almost every day of her life. She said a real quick prayer to the Goddess that she was doing the right thing and was immediately filled with the '*warm fuzzies*', confirming that her parents were sending her love and hugs.

She slowly nodded her head and said the words that would change her life for all of eternity. "Yes, Devon Walsh, I would be honored to be your mate."

Quicker than her eyes could track, Devon was standing with her in his arms, kissing her, branding her as his. The kiss was so raw and intense that Anya was sure they would burst into flames. With his mind open to hers, she felt the depth of his commitment, his undying loyalty, and more love than she ever imagined. She could feel all that he was and all he ever hoped to be. His thoughts of her made her feel more cherished, more adored, and so completely consumed that she was humbled to have someone so perfect in her life.

Anya was so swept away in the magic of the moment that it took a second for her to realize he had lifted his lips from hers. As her eyes slowly opened and she looked at the man she *knew* she was supposed to spend the rest of her life, something deep inside her soul slid into place.

When he spoke, his low, rumbly voice made her shiver. "Well, Darlin', as much as I want to throw you over my shoulder, sneak over to my house and hide out for a month or two, my brethren are just about to drive me mad. They've been calling the entire time we've been in here. Rayne wants to go over our plans for tonight one more time, seems like something has changed."

He held her head between his hands, laid his forehead on hers, and grinned. "I love you, *mo ghra'*."

"I love you, too."

~~*~*~*~*~*

It had been over a month since the young girl he had heard the others call Anya had been injured. He knew John had dropped her off at the hospital and hoped she was okay. Andrew toyed with the idea of going to check on her many times, but with his returning dragon powers and only a small supply of amulets to hide his identity, it wasn't a risk he was willing to take. The thought of sending someone else also occurred to him, but then he would have to admit she mattered and that shit was just not happening. Partly because it showed weakness and partly because he still had no idea what the hell it was about her that seemed special, familiar…*important*.

He thought of her every time he was researching the Prophecy and wondered if there was a connection he had yet to uncover. The Heavens knew he was wandering around in the dark with all the mystical bullshit and had already made mistakes that had cost them valuable time, a commodity they really didn't have. It was as if he would take one step forward and two steps back. John had even tried to accept the blame, but Andrew knew *he* had fucked up by assuming that the section referring to the white witch and the dragon with royal blood was the representation of the Earth element. Nothing written by the Ancients was ever straight forward. He had no clue where that piece of the puzzle went but was happy he finally had it, because the second text was proving to be a real thorn in his side.

When they had finally located the dusty old book in the bottom of a crate of useless shit at an estate sale, he had been sure they were making real headway, but the damn thing wasn't even written in the same language as the first. This one had roots in the ancient dragon language and there were indicators that it had been written in more than one place by more than one person. It had been too many years to even think about since Andrew had read the ancient words, but as he poured over them, the translation slowly returned. Just that afternoon, he had deciphered the first few lines of another element's representation in what he prayed would be the piece of the Prophecy that would bring those fucking dragons to their knees. *Born to an extinct race, thought to be one but actually two. Both with destinies blessed by Fate, neither knowing the other exists...*

He had no fucking clue what it all meant, but he would figure it out if it was the last thing he did. Just about to begin translating again, he heard a knock at the door. The scent was John's, but he was not alone. Not wanting anyone but his trusted second to know of the book's existence, Andrew quickly shoved it into his bottom desk drawer, along with his notes before commanding, "Enter."

"Please excuse the interruption, Master, but Samuel," he motioned to the man at his side, "has information I believe you will find valuable."

Andrew narrowed his eyes and opened his senses, inspecting the small, round man before him to determine if he was worth the bother. He remembered Samuel to be a new 'recruit' that had been picked up only a few nights ago. He smelled of sweat, fear, and a sweetness that made Andrew wonder if the man was sick or hiding candy in his pockets. When he was sure the man was too scared to tell him anything but the truth, he steepled his hands under his chin and growled, "Tell me."

All the color drained from Samuel's face as sweat broke out on his upper lip. His hand visibly trembled when he raised it to wipe away the moisture, and his voice shook as he answered, "Master, thank you. The others were talking about a girl that was injured some time ago that they believed dead." He paused, audibly swallowed, and took a deep breath that did nothing to calm his nerves.

Andrew sat perfectly still, waiting for the man to get to the point and enjoying the fact that he scared him shitless. "Before I was...well, that is to say...before I came here, I was a CNA at a hospital about hundred miles from here and there was a girl fitting her description in an unexplained coma."

Leaning forward, he waited for the man to continue, but short on patience and needing an answer, Andrew stood, rounded the desk, and advanced until his six foot three inch frame towered over the quivering mass of humanity. He waited three seconds and then asked, "Has her family come?"

"No...no..." Samuel stopped, closed his eyes, took a deep breath, let it out, opened his eyes and began again. This time, although his voice shook, his words were at least coherent. "The only person I ever saw with her, besides the doctors and nurses, was a huge dark-haired man that looked like he might have been a professional wrestler."

Andrew's scowl deepened and he growled low in his throat, something that had been happening with more frequency as of late. When he spoke it was low and ominous sounding, making Samuel take a step back. "Was there anything else you noticed about this man?"

The smaller man looked constipated, but Andrew could practically hear the wheels turning as Samuel sought to give him the information he requested. Almost a full minute later, the man's eyes widened and he spoke so fast Andrew thought he might hyperventilate. "He had a huge tattoo that came out from under the sleeve of his T-shirt and ran down his arm past the bend of his elbow."

Andrew nodded, keeping a tight rein on his temper. "Thank you, Samuel."

Turning to John, he ordered, "Please take our new friend here back to training and see that he is given extra rations and placed with Jason, our most promising instructor. Thank you, John."

John eyed Andrew, obviously seeing the rage building at the information he had just received. "As you wish, Master," was all he said. Grabbing Samuel's arm, John all but dragged the man towards the door, quietly exiting.

As soon as he was alone, Andrew exploded in a fit of rage. He swept everything from his desk, reveling in the sound of breaking glass and cracking plaster as anything not nailed down smashed against the wall. The splintering of wood as he threw one chair after another across the room helped to cool his temper and when there was nothing left to demolish, he stood in the middle of the room, threw back his head, and roared. It was the first time he had heard his dragon in over seven years and the sound only fueled his hatred. "I *knew* she was special! I *fucking* knew it! And now those Heavens be damned, good for nothing, piece of shit dragons have her!"

Looking for something else to break and coming up empty handed, Andrew sunk onto the couch, the only thing he hadn't destroyed, threw back his head, and stared at the ceiling fan as it turned around and around. He thought of all those fucking idiots had taken from him, all the pain and misery they had caused him, and decided he had no choice but to go to the hospital and take the girl back. She was important. He didn't know how, but that didn't matter. What mattered was that he could *not* let the dragons have her, especially that shithead, Devon Walsh.

A plan started to form in Andrew's mind and the first step meant making a call. All he had to do was locate the phone under all the debris that littered his office.

CHAPTER FOUR

Devon was about to pull his hair out. They had been over and over their plans and still Rayne droned on. He watched as all his brethren sighed and rolled their eyes, but none were willing to stop their Commander. He, like all of them, had suffered at the hands of the traitor and felt the need to put the bastard's reign of terror to an end, but for Rayne, he not only felt what had happened to him, he also felt what each of his men had endured as well. It was one of the things that made him the most respected Force Leader in all of Dragon kin. However, sometimes he went overboard and no one, not even the King of the Big Cats, could find it in their hearts to stop him.

Thankfully, Kyndel's call from the other room telling him that she and Jay needed to go home caused him to stop for a minute. Max used the interruption to announce that he and his people also needed to head back to their Pride. The rest followed suit, and soon the house was empty except for Siobhan, Anya, and himself.

Devon shut off all the lights except the one his mother always left burning and headed to where he knew his mate lay sleeping. He was glad to see that Jace and Liam had finished hanging the door and took pleasure in shutting out the world with a barely audible click of the latch. Turning on his heels he stopped short. There, lying on her side with her hands clasped under her chin, blissfully asleep, was his very own angel.

The crickets' song blew through the window on the cool night breeze as Devon stood staring, thanking the Heavens for bringing her safely to him. His dragon pushed to be near their mate and the man was happy to oblige. Quickly he made his way to her and carefully lay on top of the blanket she was under, careful not to disturb her. Unable to be so close and not touch, he wrapped his much larger body around his mate. Anya cuddled back into him. It was the best thing he'd ever felt and when his name crossed her lips on a sigh, he knew he would do whatever it took to hear that every day for the rest of his very long life.

For almost an hour he just lay with Anya in his arms and enjoyed how perfectly they fit together. Then his mind wandered to what they would find later in the evening. It wasn't until Rory, Royce's younger brother, spoke through their shared link that he realized he had fallen asleep. *"Hey sleepyhead. Time to rise and shine. We'll be landing behind the Great Hall in five. Where do you want us?"*

Looking at the clock on the bedside table, he noted the time and then answered, *"You can head over here. I'm at Mom's. There's enough food, beds, and showers that you guys can relax a bit before the fun begins."*

It was Rian, the older of the O'Reilly brothers and Head Elder of their clan that answered. *"Thanks, Devon. We'll be there in ten minutes."*

"Back door is open. Make yourself at home. See ya when you get here."

Quicker than he wanted, he heard the Guardsmen from the Blue Thunder Clan approach the back of the house and knew it was time to leave the warmth of his mate. Holding her close for just a moment longer, memorizing the feel of her body against his, drawing as much of her tantalizing scent in as he could, Devon felt as if they were in a world all their own, one that was completely his mate...*his Anya*.

Of course, reality kicked in the door as Aaron's voice sounded in his head. *"Yo, lover boy, get your ass out here. Everyone's here raiding the fridge and talking shit."*

With a sigh, he answered, *"I'm on my way...asshole."*

"Hurry it up or I'm letting Rory come in and get you."

"You bet your ass, Bro," Rory chimed in.

"I'm coming. I'm coming..." Devon groaned.

They all laughed and simultaneously cut their connection. Devon snuggled with Anya for just a bit longer then grudgingly crawled from her warmth. Without looking back, for fear that he wouldn't have the strength to leave her, he headed out the door and followed the sounds of his brethren to the kitchen.

He wasn't surprised to see Rayne, Rian, and Kellan, the Commander of the Blue Thunder Force, in the dining room discussing their plans and pouring over the maps and pictures they had collected earlier in the day. Even less of a shock was the party that was happening in the kitchen. There was not a square inch of the table that wasn't covered with food and drink. The men were all kicked back, eating, talking, and getting ready for their mission.

"What the hell is this? A briefing or a party?" Devon growled, trying to keep the smile from his voice and off his face.

"A little bit of both. Can't miss an opportunity to fight the bad guy, have a drink, and eat some of Kyndel's amazing cooking," Rory answered with a mouth full of food and a huge glass of tea in his hand.

"I hear congrats are in order, my man." Lennox from Rian's clan stood and shook his hand, the others quickly following his lead.

"Thanks, guys. I appreciate it."

"So when do we getta look at yer bonnie lass?" Pearce asked, wiggling his eyebrows and grinning ear to ear, his usually hidden Irish brogue alive and well, reminding Devon of Gareth, his father.

"Never, if I can help it," Devon joked and the room erupted in laughter.

Before the situation could get any farther out of hand, Rian called from the other room, "Get in here. We have work to do."

All the men groaned but did as the Elder commanded, filing into the dining room and circling the table. Rayne began just as his cellphone rang. Devon took over the briefing until his Commander returned just a few moments later.

All eyes turned as Rayne said, "After talking it over with Juan Carlos and Raphael and taking a closer look at the property specs, Max would like to send a group of his scouts in to check out the property tonight. As much as I hate to admit it, the werepanthers are better at getting in and out without detection in their animal form than we are in human form. I told him to keep us posted."

Devon paced, frustrated at the delay. His need to do something…*anything*, to make Andrew pay for all he had done to those he held most dear had his dragon chuffing in his head. Both man and beast were ready to put the traitor in a box and let him rot for all eternity. Rayne's hand on his shoulder pulled him from his thoughts of vengeance. "I know it sucks to wait, but I really think it is best. One more night is not going to give Andrew any more of an advantage, and this way we will have the best intel possible."

"I know you're right. It's just…"

"It's just that you want his head on a spike for daring to hurt your mate," Rayne interrupted.

"And Kyndel, Grace, Sam, Sydney, Kyra, and everyone else that little fucker's demented revenge has harmed." Devon growled.

Rayne nodded. "We'll get him. Go spend some time with Anya. I think everyone is heading home and it sounds like Rian and his crew is commandeering your house."

Turning and addressing the group before Devon could respond, the Commander spoke, "We'll meet back here at noon tomorrow. That should give Max and his men time to get here. Get a good night's sleep. By tomorrow at this time, the traitor will be eliminated…*one way or another."*

Rayne's words hung in the air as each man nodded, a solemn promise of retribution burning in their eyes. In complete silence, the men cleaned the kitchen and left his mother's home with only a nod in Devon's direction.

Checking the house one last time, Devon headed back to his mate. He was glad to see that she was still sleeping peacefully, no matter how much his heart ached to see her gorgeous eyes and beautiful smile. Filled with nervous energy and the need for action, he knew there was no way he could lay still beside her, but the allure of his mate was too much to resist.

Kneeling beside her bed, he laid his head on her pillow, getting as close as possible without disturbing her. He watched her lashes flutter against her cheek as her eyes moved behind her closed lids. Because he feared she was heading towards another nightmare, Devon opened his mind completely to hers and entered her dreams. The image of an older couple working in a garden, laughing with a young dark-haired girl came into view. When the child looked up, he smiled at the younger version of his mate and when she called the gentleman 'Pops' he relaxed knowing he was watching one of Anya's happy memories.

He stayed linked to his mate and watched more of her childhood memories until the constant growling and chuffing of his dragon drove him from her bed. Several laps around the house and more than a few strong words to the beast he had shared his soul with for over a hundred years proved useless. It was not long before Devon found himself walking the path that led to what Kyndel had named the Town Square.

As he looked at the darkened store fronts and empty wooden carts the artisans used to display their goods, the enormous stone fountain at the center of the square caught his eye. Devon had no idea how many times he had passed the beautiful sculpture in the fifty or so years since it had been placed in the Square, but for the first time the giant stone dragon with his wings wrapped lovingly around a beautiful woman and two children gave him pause. The speech the Head Elder, Carrick, had given on the day it was dedicated had brought to light the symbiotic relationship between the dragons and their mates.

It was then that he read the beautiful words written in the old language, embossed on the brass plague, secured at the dragon's feet, *E'adrom ar a anam. Is brea' ar a chroi. Ta' su'il anseo.* All those years ago he had simply thought of the words as a nice sentiment, but now he truly understood their meaning. Anya was the light to his soul, the love to his heart, and the hope to his future. She was *everything* and he wondered how he had ever lived without her.

The sound of a door closing came from the alley between the jewelry store and one of the bakeries. Using his enhanced speed, Devon moved towards the sound, sure to stay under the cover of darkness. The sounds of footsteps echoed against brick walls and the shadow of a person lengthened onto the sidewalk. He opened his senses to make sure it was someone from his lair but only heard static. Shaking his head he pushed harder, but still only scratchy sounds that reminded him of a poorly tuned radio came back. He was poised to attack when he heard the mumblings of a familiar voice and a scent he recognized as one of his favorite people.

Not wanting to scare the young woman, he cleared his throat and called out, "Emma? Everything okay back there?"

"Oh, shoot!" She squeaked, obviously startled, then she quickly recovered. "Devon? Is that you?"

Thankful for his enhanced vision, Devon saw her face right before he answered. "It is. What are you doing out so late?"

"You wouldn't believe me if I told you," she muttered under her breath.

"Try me," he chuckled.

"*Damn*, I always forget you can hear everything."

He could tell she was stalling and decided to wait her out. She kept walking in his direction but refused to meet his eyes until she was right in front of him. As Emma looked up, she stretched out her hand. A long gold chain flowed over her palm and Devon caught sight of one of the young artisan's beautiful creations, a pendant glowing in the moonlight made out of one of *his own* dragon scales. Obviously damaged, but exquisitely refashioned into a smaller version of its original shape with just a slight lopsidedness that gave it character. The scale had been polished to a high sheen and on its own was eye-catching. However, it was the tiny bell hanging from a delicate golden chain of only two or three links directly in the center that drew his eye. It had been made from one of the reddest scales he had ever seen and appeared as more of a heart shape than a traditional bell.

Emma spoke, her voice taking on a faraway quality. "Two days ago I awoke with an undeniable urge to create *that* pendant. Now don't get me wrong, I've been inspired before, but this was almost like a compulsion. I *had* to make this exact pendant. When I realized I didn't have any white scales available, I tried to work with others and none of them worked. Several hours later, I gave up and headed out for a walk."

She pointed over her shoulder at a wooded area that had been built into a large park with walking trails and playground equipment for the young *drakes* and *vibrias*. "I was walking over there, completely focused on the design that would *not* leave me alone, when I found *this* scale lying atop of pile of leaves. I have no idea how it got there, but since you are the only white dragon in existence, I *know* it's yours, and I'm pretty damn sure I was supposed to find it."

Emma shook her head and continued. "If I have learned anything, it's that when things happen around here that are completely and totally crazy, it's best to follow them through to the end." She looked down at her hand, still holding the necklace between them, then back up at him. "I have worked pretty much every minute since then and was actually headed to your mom's to leave this for you."

She held up her other hand to stop the comment that he was just about to make. "I know what you're thinking…how did I know it was for you and your mate? Well, let me ask you a question first,"

Devon nodded his head for her continue.

"Does your mate have light green eyes?"

"Yes," was all he could say.

"Does her name start with the letter A?"

He nodded, unable to speak at the woman's accuracy.

"Then this is for her," Emma nervously giggled, turning the pendant over in her hand.

Devon smiled at the tiny tinkle the bell made as it rolled in her hand. His eyes widened as he saw the perfectly painted 'A' in the exact color of his mate's eyes on the underside of the charm. "How?"

After a moment's pause, he looked up to see Emma's intense stare taking in his every expression. Her smile was slow but sweet, followed by a shrug. "I have no freakin' clue, but I know that for the first time since I awoke with this design in my brain, I feel like I can go home and finally get some rest."

She grabbed his wrist with her empty hand, turned it over, and gently laid the necklace against his palm. Her smile grew as she winked and said, "Give it to your girl. Hope she likes it."

Devon was just about to thank her when Lance's voice sounded in his head. *"Dev, you up?"*

Signaling with the index finger of his empty hand for Emma to wait a minute, he answered his brethren. *"Yeah. Everything okay?"*

"Not really. Sam just got a call from Charlie at the hospital. Seems like a man just showed up there asking about Anya. He didn't know her name but gave an almost perfect description. Of course, Charlie gave him the SOP about giving out information being against the rules and told him nothing. The guy seemed to accept that but did ask repeatedly if she was okay. He left without causing any trouble, but she was freaked and wanted us to know. Sam was just about to hang up when Charlie laughed and said the guy had one blue eye and one brown eye."

"*Fuck!*" Devon spat.

"*My sentiments exactly. The little son of a bitch must be desperate to be out in the open without his lackeys.*"

Devon looked to Emma, thankful her house was on the way to his mother's because getting back to his mate was all he could think about. "Thank you. Anya will love it, and I apologize for cutting our visit short, but something's come up I *have* to take care of. Let me walk you home on my way." He placed his hand on her shoulder, turning her around, and directing her towards their homes.

"Oh, that's okay…"she started to argue.

Shaking his head, Devon cut in, "My mother will kick my ass if I let you walk home alone in the dark, not to mention, I'd feel like shit."

They both chuckled as he hurried them along. Although it only took a few moments, it seemed like forever before they reached Emma's quaint red brick cottage. He had been talking to Lance, Aaron, and Royce through mindspeak the whole time and knew his brethren were all just a few seconds from Siobhan's home. With his link to his mate wide open, he watched as the young woman disappeared into her home, then using his enhanced speed, ran towards his mate.

He saw Royce standing just inside the backdoor and called ahead. *"Everything okay?"*

"Yep. We knew there was no way the shithead could be inside the lair, but Kyra wanted to check on Anya and we all agreed. Better safe than sorry."

"Thanks, old man," he answered as he made his way to the front of the house.

"Everything cool up here, Bro?" Devon asked Lance as he rounded the corner.

"Yeah. Aaron's out in the woods on the north side just to be sure nothing and no one is there that shouldn't be. We're not as confidant as you and Grandpa that the little fucker can't get close to us."

"I heard that, you pain in the ass." Royce growled through their combined link.

Heading through the front door, Devon chuckled at his friends' constant bickering and called to Aaron. *"See anything out of the ordinary out there?"*

"Nothing," was the only response.

Expecting more, Devon waited until he reached the door to his mate's room before speaking to them all. *"Thanks, you guys. I'll be out as soon as I check on Anya."*

"Take your time, I'm heading in to make coffee and find something to eat," Lance replied.

"Damn, do you ever get enough to eat? Royce asked. *"And Kyra already has the coffee on."*

"No and thank the Heavens." Lance laughed.

Tuning out his brethren's banter, he entered Anya's room, gently closing the door behind him to find the woman of his dreams still asleep, blissfully unaware of the commotion going on all around her. He had been linked to her all evening, even more so after Lance's call, and knew that she was sweetly dreaming the night away, but his dragon would take nothing less than actual touch and scent before he would stop his growling and chuffing.

Devon moved to her bedside, carefully sat on the edge of the bed, and lifted her hand to his lips. The incredible spark of recognition flared between them as he touched her soft skin. The calming scent of sand and sea washed over him and his beast, making his dragon back down from the constant pushing to be free. The beast was pacified for the time being but sat ready to attack at a second's notice. Movement under the fingertips that gently held Anya's wrist sent a flood of electric shocks down his arm and the mark that signified his dragon pulsed in response.

Turning her hand in his, he saw the marking was fully formed and darker than before. He remembered the necklace in his pocket, shifted slightly, and pulled it out into the open, the tiny bell sending its clear tone into the air. Devon had been so lost to his own thoughts and then surprised by Emma's appearance, not to mention her amazing story of how the pendant had come to be, that he hadn't even realized it *also* resembled a heart scale. Gently returning the necklace to his pocket for safe keeping, he then kissed the mark on her wrist. Pulses of recognition filled his entire being and caused his cock to jump. He smiled to himself, thinking of all the ways he planned to love her for the rest of their very long lives together.

Satisfied that his mate was fine and in no imminent danger, Devon placed a chaste kiss on her temple, reluctantly stood, and headed back towards the kitchen before he gave into temptation and joined her in bed.

He entered the kitchen to find every member of his Force and that of the Blue Thunder Clan crowded around the kitchen table discussing what to do next. Rian commented on his arrival first. "Hey, Dev. Guess it's a good thing we let Max and his crew take the first pass tonight, huh?"

"Definitely was. I just wish one of us would've been at the hospital to catch that fucking asshole." He looked around the room and watched everyone in attendance nod in agreement.

He turned to Lance. "And I'm damn glad Sam wasn't working tonight."

"You and me both, Brother, you and me both."

It was then that Devon realized Aaron was absent. "Where's Aar?"

Aidan answered from across the room. "He said he had one more thing to check on and then he would be back. Sounded kinda weird but wouldn't tell me where he was going." The Guardsman shrugged as he added sugar to his coffee.

"Well, he'll have to catch up when he gets back," Rayne commented as he walked in from the dining room. "I just got off the phone with Max and it seems you were right. Andrew and about fifty others are holed up in the mansion we researched. From the magic surrounding the place, it seems they are mostly novice and for the most part just humans that are being magically trained, which goes along with what Anya has been able to tell us and what you have seen in her memories." The Commander nodded to Devon before continuing. "The Leo has no doubt we will be able to get in and out before any of them, including that piece of shit, knows what hit them. We'll go with our original plan. Everyone good with that?"

Devon watched as everyone nodded in agreement and was just about to speak when Rian stood and addressed the group. "Since the sun will be up in a few hours, I'm gonna head back over to Dev's, grab a shower, and get some training in before tonight's raid." He crossed the room and clapped Devon on the shoulder as he passed. "You better get some sleep, lover boy."

Devon thanked the group as everyone stood and headed out. Less than a minute later only he, Royce, and Kyra were left with a table top of half-filled coffee cups and the remnants of a tray of cinnamon rolls. They cleared the table in silence, all obviously deep in thought when Kyra spoke. "I think I should go with you tonight."

The words were barely out of her mouth when Royce growled through gritted teeth. "No fucking way, *mo chroí'*. You're not getting anywhere near that little piece of shit."

Spinning on her heels and advancing towards her mate, Devon saw fire in Kyra's eyes. With the hopes of preventing a fight between two of his dearest friends, Devon quickly interjected. "Kyra, I need you here to protect Anya. With all of us gone, there's no one I trust more to keep her safe."

His words hung in the air as he felt the brewing tensions fade away. Kyra laughed. "Damn, you know how to take the wind out of a girl's sails, Dev." She continued forward, walking directly into her mate's outstretched arms.

Royce mouthed, *"Thank you,"* over Kyra's head and Devon grinned in response.

"Now, you two chuckleheads get the hell outta here and get some rest and..." He paused until they were both looking at him, then said, "Thank you so very much. I couldn't do this without either of you."

"Oh yeah, you could. It just wouldn't be as much fun." Kyra giggled.

Royce turned her in his arms and gently pushed his mate towards the back door, speaking over his shoulder, "I'm gonna take you up on the offer to get a few more hours sleep."

"Me, too," Devon called to his friends as he shut the door and turned out the kitchen light. Heading back to Anya, he let all thoughts of the traitor drift away so that when he slid into bed next to her, his only thoughts were of her and the perfect way their bodies fit together.

~~*~*~*~*~*

Andrew barely made it back to the mansion before his temper got the best of him. He left his car running in the driveway, driver's side door wide open, and the front door of the mansion barely on the hinges as he shoved his way through the throng of wizard wannabes blocking the path to his office. Slamming the door, he was greeted by an empty office with nothing but his nineteenth century solid oak Ambassador's desk and leather high back office chair to toss around. Unwilling to destroy the only two pieces of furniture left, he pushed open the hidden panel beside the floor to ceiling bookcases and disappeared down the long hidden passageway to his hidden workout facility.

Throwing his trench coat, suit jacket, and dress shirt into a pile in the corner of the well-appointed room and kicking his shoes in the opposite corner, he strode towards the long punching bag that hung from the ceiling in the center of the room. He poured every bit of frustration and anger he felt at the loss of the young woman he *knew* was not only special but somehow imperative to his vengeance against the dragons. Sweat poured down his face and back. His fists, as well as the tops of his feet, bled from the sheer voracity of his attack while his temper raged on. Visions of the sanctimonious Devon Walsh sweeping in and saving the damsel in distress fueled his ire as his punches and kicks landed one right after another. Only the sound of the concrete cracking under the huge steel bracket that held the bag to the ceiling stilled his fists.

Making his way to the small refrigerator across the room, he pulled out a cold bottle of water, took off the cap and drank it down, reaching for a second bottle while pitching the other towards the trashcan. Only when the second bottle had been emptied and thrown away did Andrew lean against the wall and take a long, deep breath. He looked around the room, not really seeing any of the equipment, only remembering what the young doctor said when he inquired about the girl's condition. Dr. Gallagher, as her nametag had identified her, had spouted hospital policy and deflected his questions quite effectively, but it had been what she didn't say that let him know the young woman was awake and well and for that he was grateful. What he absolutely hated, and was not sure how to rectify, was the fact that she was with those fucking dragons.

Andrew slid down the wall until his ass made contact with the floor, thankful he had at least one place in the world to let pretenses go and think. He thought about the vibes he had gotten from the young woman his men had taken from outside the movie theatre all those weeks ago. It was obvious she was magical. Not like Kyra or any of the other witches or wizards he had ever known, but magical all the same. She was filled with goodness and light, and something very old with an almost reverent feeling to it. That magic is what had compelled him to have her taken to the hospital where he knew she would sooner or later recover.

Sure that word of his arrival and disappearance had reached Mr. A and not wanting the glorified thug to accidently stumble upon his private lair while searching for him, Andrew jumped in the shower he had installed and quickly redressed. Taking a different route that lead to the gardens behind the mansion, the traitor reentered through the French doors into the dining room. All conversation ceased and the handful of his followers that surrounded one end of the long, antique dining table refused to meet his eyes. Apparently, word of his less than joyful return had spread. Silently reveling in the fact that they feared him, Andrew strode out of the room with his head held high.

Just as he rounded the corner to the hallway that led to his office, he spotted John carrying several large books, a look of genuine accomplishment on his face. At the sound of Andrew's boots on the hardwood floor, his assistant smiled and said six words that truly lifted Andrew's spirits. "I translated more of the prophecy."

~~*~*~*~*~*

Anya awoke cocooned in the warmth of Devon's body, his scent filling her senses. The feel of his breath on the nape of her neck as he spooned her felt as natural to her as breathing. She very slowly and carefully rolled until she was face to face with the man that had wormed his way into her heart. Up close, she could see how incredibly long and thick his dark eyelashes were as they curled against the tops of his cheeks. She thought of the expressive grey eyes they outlined and her heart beat a little faster.

Her fingers seemed to have a mind of their own as they lightly stroked the tiny laugh lines that emanated from those expressive eyes, making her smile to herself. Butterflies chose that moment to take up residence in her tummy as a collage of everything from Devon's silly smirk to a full blown laugh paraded through her mind. *How is it possible he has come to mean so much to me in such a short time?*

"*Because I am as much yours as you are mine.*" She squeaked in surprise and then giggled as the arm he had draped across her waist tightened, pulling her tighter against his hard body.

Anya swatted his shoulder. "How long have you been lying there playing opossum?"

With his eyes holding her captive, he leaned forward until their lips all but touched and whispered, "I'll sleep when I'm dead. I don't want to miss a second of having you in my arms."

His lips touched hers and the fire she had seen burning in his eyes poured into her. She opened completely to the man she was sure she was meant to spend the rest of her life with and felt the incredible depth of his love and commitment. Their kiss went on and on until she was sure she would spontaneously combust until a knock at the door surprised them both.

"This better be good," Devon growled against her lips.

"Wake up on the wrong side of the bed, *lover boy*?" He could hear the contained laughter in Rory's voice.

"What do you want, Rory?" Devon's growl was very pronounced, his chest rumbling under her fingertips.

"Don't kill the messenger, dude. Rayne and Rian are waiting in the Great Hall with the others. They've been calling you for over an hour, but apparently you've been *incommunicado*."

"I swear privacy is a dirty word around here," Devon grumbled under his breath, still holding her tight.

Anya buried her head in his chest to keep from laughing out loud at the conversation going on over her head, but her efforts were for naught when Rory answered, "We live in each other's heads ninety percent of the time and you want privacy? What? Are you new here?"

"Rory!" Devon all but roared. Instead of frightening her as it would've before she'd met this wonderful group of dragons, it caused Anya to giggle uncontrollably, which made Devon's chest jump against her cheek with his own barely contained laughter.

"I'm going…I'm going. But they're just gonna send someone else or Heavens forbid…*me* again until you get your ass outta bed and get over there," Rory complained.

"Go away, Rory. Tell them I'll be there in a few minutes." Devon commanded as he rolled his eyes.

"Yeah, yeah, yeah. I'll tell them," Rory muttered as she heard his retreating footsteps.

Anya almost felt bad for the other Guardsman but knew he was a smartass and loved picking at anyone he could. Devon disturbed her thoughts and giggles with a kiss to the tip of her nose before pulling farther back from her. He paused for a moment and just stared. Unable to bear his look, she looked down for a second, and when she looked up again, he was still gazing at her, wearing a knowing a smile. When he spoke, she could feel the emotion of his words to the depths of her soul. "I am absolutely the luckiest man in the world."

She felt her cheeks warm from the emotion his words stirred within her. When she would've looked away again, Devon's fingers held her chin captive and spoke with a reverence she had only heard uttered in a prayer. "Believe my words, *mo ghra'*. From the moment I found you, you became my reason for living. The Universe may have made you, but you are *mine,* and I am the happiest dragon alive for it."

Tears gathered in her eyes and her heart beat faster than she ever imagined it could at his words of love and commitment, but it was his last statement that made her heart fill to near bursting. "All of my love…now…always…forever." He sealed his pledge with just the touch of his lips to hers and in the next instant, much to her disappointment, was climbing out of bed.

Anya couldn't stop grinning as she watched him pull jeans over his boxers and covered the chest her fingers itched to touch just one more time with a worn grey T-shirt. It was obvious Devon noticed when he raised one eyebrow and the side of his mouth rose in an adorable smirk, but he confirmed it when he winked and asked, "Enjoying the show?"

She scooted up in the bed and crossed her arms behind her head, trying to portray a calm she didn't feel. Furrowing her brow and pursing her lips like she was making a tough decision, Anya tried to keep the laughter from her voice when she answered. "Well, yes, I believe I am."

Less than a heartbeat later, she found herself wrapped in his arms, breathless from the amazing kiss of her mate. Moaning deep in her throat and grabbing his shoulders to pull him closer, she poured all she felt for the amazing man she was fated to love forever into that one kiss. All too soon, Devon pulled back and Anya was happy to see he was as breathless as she. His voice was lower and more raspy than usual when he said, "I cannot wait for the rest of our lives together."

He stopped and sighed. "Unfortunately, my brethren are giving me a headache with their continual bitching in my head."

A quick kiss on her forehead as he returned her to bed and he was at the door. "I'll be back as soon as I can, *mo chroi'*."

She sighed as the door gently closed and smiled. *Forever will never be long enough...*

CHAPTER FIVE

Using his enhanced speed and cutting through all the wooded areas, Devon arrived at the Great Hall in just a few minutes. It wasn't because every few seconds one or the other of his brethren were bellowing in his brain, although he was going to kick some ass when he saw them, it was completely and totally because he hated every minute that he was not with Anya. Every second in her presence made him love her more. It was as if he had known her forever, not just a few days.

Ready to kick ass and take names for being disturbed, Devon pushed open the huge double doors to the Great Hall and stomped in, only to be stopped in his tracks by the presence of not only the King of the Big Cats, but Carrick, the Head Elder of his clan. Deciding to play off his abrupt entrance, he called out, "I'm here, let the party begin."

Unfortunately, both Aaron and Lance were in attendance, so his efforts were thrown by the wayside when they both cracked up, causing everyone else to follow suit. Aaron was the first to recover and spoke as Devon made his way to the huge round table in the center of the enormous room. "Nice try, Slick."

A slap on the back from Lance as he passed by was accompanied by, "She's got you all tied up in your underwear."

Before he could respond Rayne added, "Another one bites the dust."

The Commander's out of character comment triggered another round of laughter that only calmed when Carrick cleared his throat. The men gathered around as the Elder spoke. "I wanted to tell each and every one of you, especially Aaron and Aidan, that I understand how hard it is to hunt down one of your own. It is not what we as men or dragons ever want to do, but all too often it is a task we must undertake. May the Universe bless you with success."

Devon watched as their regal Leader exited the building and wondered if he was talking about the rogue Carrick and his father had hunted down all those years ago. Max's voice shoved thoughts of the past behind and Devon focused on the information the King and his guards were able to obtain.

"The pictures you gave us were incredibly accurate. Gotta love technology and all that shit. The only notable difference is the overgrowth of the foliage, but that is to our advantage as it provides excellent coverage. Raphael was also able to get a closer look at the security system and disabling it will be no problem. The only thing that might give us pause is access into the mansion itself. Every entrance is locked and magically warded except for a hidden entrance that I am sure leads to the basement. It's completely covered with overgrown plants and vines. Something tells me *nobody* knows it even exists. All of my men agree that one small explosive would blow the door and clear the tunnel."

"Hell, yeah," Lennox cheered from across the table.

"You'll have to excuse Lenn, he has a flair for explosions." Rory chuckled while Rian and Kellan shook their heads.

Devon looked at the large Guardsman with spiky black hair and a wild look in his eyes and nodded. "It's all you, Lennox. Just don't blow us all to the Heavens."

"Aye, just let me at 'em."

"Sounds like we have a plan. So, if there's nothing else, I suggest everyone do what needs to be done and we'll meet back here at nine tonight," Rayne said and then turned to Max. "And we'll see you and your crew at the abandoned Quicky Mart about ten miles from the property at ten thirty?"

"That you will," Max answered. Devon was once again amazed at the nonchalance with which the King did damn near everything, including planning to invade a fortress filled with crazy, half-trained wizards and a clearly deranged traitor.

Everyone went their separate directions and Devon headed out to the training pit. He had been keeping tabs on Anya through their mating link and knew she was happy and relaxed. So instead of heading back and spoiling her good mood with his nervous energy, he decided to train for an hour or two.

Striding into the barn and grabbing a broad sword, it dawned on Devon that for the first time he truly was nervous about a mission. He had no clue how many times he had flown, ridden, or run headlong into battle without a thought but to vanquish the enemy. His brethren teased that he was the 'Zen Guardsman', and until a few days ago that had been true. He had always been the voice of reason and the go-to guy for reassurance, but all of that changed the moment Anya had entered the picture.

He shook his head, psychoanalyzing himself, and it was then that he realized he still had his confidence, his inner peace, and his resolve that what he and his brethren were doing was absolutely honorable. The only thing that had changed was his undeniable need to return home after battle, to spend hundreds of years learning everything there was to know about the one the Universe had made for him.

Thankfully, Rian called out from across the pit, jerking Devon from his self-analysis. "Aye, Dev. Fancy a bit of sparring?"

Devon chuckled at the clan leader's brogue. It seemed it only made an appearance when Rian was distracted or fighting. "You're on," he answered, swinging his sword to test the balance.

Rian advanced and within seconds they were engaged in a mock battle for their lives. The clash of the blades drew the other Guardsmen and trainees until a crowd formed around them, and Devon could see the other men making bets on who would bow out first. Never one to go down easily, he poured everything into each thrust of his sword.

The taunts started about an hour into their duel, but when Devon noticed Rian's arm shaking, he used it to his advantage, and within minutes had the bigger and older Elder disarmed and standing at the end of his blade.

"Will you look at that shit, Roy? Dev just spanked Ri but good. Guess I owe you fifty bucks." Rory chuckled to Royce.

Rian put his fist over his heart, acting incredibly disheartened and in his best British accent, he crooned, "Et tu, Royce? Et tu?"

The entire pit erupted in laughter as Devon and Rian made their way back to the barn to clean their swords and grab something to drink. "You've gotten better with a sword than I remember, Devon."

"Thanks Rian, but I think the last time we trained together was about fifty years ago. I'm sorry to say I've had more occasions than I care to admit to hone my skills, especially in the last few years."

"Yeah, Andrew has definitely caused more than his fair share of trouble." Rian paused and Devon could tell he was deciding whether to share something or not.

When the Elder spoke again, his tone no longer held the levity from just moments before. "Carrick has asked Kellan and our Force to stay and assist with Andrew's containment…and he requested I serve on the Tribunal."

The tension in Rian's body and the almost haunted tone of his voice said neither of those requests were welcomed but had been agreed to out of a sense of duty. Devon was just about to respond when Anya spoke directly into his mind. He smiled at the tentative tone to her voice, *"Devon?"*

"Yes, mo chroi'*,"* he answered while saying goodbye to Rian.

Her giggle made him smile as he almost jogged towards his mother's home. *"I just wondered what you were up to. Your mom is researching and the other girls went home…"*

"And you're bored?"

"Well…"

He received more than one questioning look when he laughed out loud for no apparent reason but really didn't care, his mate was reaching out to him and he couldn't be happier. *"I'll be right there, love."*

"Thanks."

Taking the same shortcuts he used just a few hours earlier, he was at his mother's home in less than a minute and had Anya in his arms in the next two seconds. After a lengthy hello kiss that had all thoughts of anything but her naked body wrapped around his and his name on her lips, he reluctantly set his mate a few inches away and took a deep breath. He grinned as he took in the dreamy look in her eyes and the way she struggled to catch her breath.

Noticing him looking at her, Anya raised one eyebrow and put her hands on her hips before teasing, "Pretty happy with yourself, huh?"

Acting like he had to think about his answer, Devon pursed his lips and looked to the side before answering. "As a matter of fact, I am," he snickered.

Anya swung to swat his shoulder but Devon was quicker and grabbed her hand, pulling her close to him once again. Holding her against his chest, he looked into her beautiful, light green eyes and saw his forever. He kissed her forehead and asked, "Wanna take a walk? See the sights?"

The excitement he saw in her eyes answered his question before she exclaimed, "Oh, yes! Please?"

Before he could answer, she was wiggling out of his arms and calling over her shoulder, "Just let me grab my shoes."

When she returned, Anya had not only put on the sandals Grace had loaned her, but had also pulled her hair up in a cute ponytail that sat high on her head. Grabbing his hand, she pulled him towards the door, chatting away about all Kyndel and Grace had told her about the lair and more specifically, the Town Square.

They walked along, arm-in-arm and Devon introduced her to everyone they passed, prouder than he had ever been. He had to admit, at least to himself, that he had been happy when his brethren had found their mates, but there was absolutely nothing that compared to having Anya in his life. The stories he had heard his entire life did not come close to the feeling of finding the one the Universe had made for him.

Caught up in his thoughts, he almost missed Anya's question. "Is there a florist here?"

"Yes, there is. Did you want some flowers?" Her question surprised him and then made him worry that he was not providing her with everything she wanted or needed.

She immediately shook her head. "Not for me, but I would like to get your mom some to thank her for her hospitality." A pained look crossed her face and her head fell forward, causing him to stop and spin her around until they were face to face.

Lifting her head in surprise, he cut off the words she was about to speak when he asked, "What's the matter, *mo ghra'*?"

"Nothing…it's just that…oh *hell*!" Her voice gained confidence and she squared her shoulders. "I forgot I don't have any money. I don't even know where my purse *is*!"

Devon schooled his features and bit the inside of his cheeks to keep from smiling at her obvious distress. His mate was strong, independent, and absolutely adorable, and he would do whatever he could, even holding in his laugher, to make sure she stayed just as she was. He was irritated with himself for not realizing she needed her own things. Having a mate was uncharted territory but one he was going to enjoy every second discovering.

"Not to worry. I'll take care of it. And in the very near future, we'll take a trip out to your farm to grab your things, okay?"

The look that crossed her face was reminiscent of the way Sydney and Jay looked on Christmas morning and her squeal of delight warmed him through and through. "Oh my gosh, thank you so much, Dev. Everyone has been so great to me and I am so thankful, but I really do miss my stuff."

She threw herself into his arms and hugged him with a strength he hadn't realized she possessed. The clearing of a throat sounded behind him and they broke apart right before Sydney slammed into his leg. "Boo!" the little girl screamed. "Did I scare you? Huh? Did I?"

Feigning fear, he shuddered and clasped his chest. "You did! I think you might've given me a heart attack."

"You're so silly, Dev," the child giggled while turning to his mate. "Did I scare you too much, Anya?"

His mate knelt down and shook her head. "No way! Come on, Syd, you know girls are tougher than boys."

Sydney's giggle turned into full blown laughter as she agreed, "We sure are!" Throwing herself into Anya's arms, the child gave her a big hug before stepping back and asking, "Where y'all going? Dad is taking me to get some ice cream. You wanna come, too?"

As fun as spending time with one of his favorite people in the whole world sounded, Devon truly wanted to show his mate around the lair and then spend some alone time before he had to embark on the hunt for the traitor. "Not today, Syd. How about a rain check?"

The sweet girl took his refusal in stride. "You got it. Just don't forget, 'kay?"

"It's a date! No way I'm gonna forget that." He helped Anya up as Sydney ran the few steps back to her dad. It was then that Devon realized Lance hadn't spoken at all.

"What's wrong, man? It's not like you to be so quiet."

"Nothing," was the only response he got from his brethren, but Sydney was more than willing to spill the beans.

"Daddy's upset cause Andrew was at the hospital last night, but Mommy went to work anyway and wouldn't let Daddy come, too. But Jace and Liam went to keep her safe and Ern…Ernes…the panther man is there, too."

"Ernesto?" Devon helped, seeing the frustration on the child's face.

"Yep! Him!" Sydney bounced from one foot to the other.

Seeing the obvious frustration on his brethren's face, Devon used their link and said, *"Ya know Jace and Liam are not gonna let anything happen to Sam, and if for some reason Andrew or one of his minions get past them, Ernesto is damn good. It's the cat in him."*

"Yeah, I know. It's just…oh hell. It's just if anything happens to her…" Lance's voice trailed off and for the first time Devon could truly relate.

"I know, Bro, but you can't think that way. Sam's smart and there's no way she'll go anywhere without an escort. Just keep the faith. She'll be back here where you can watch over her before you know it."

"I know you're right. She's just so damned stubborn."

"And dedicated, and an amazing doctor, and tough as nails…"

"You are so right." Lance finally chuckled. *"Thanks, man."*

"You got it."

Tired of waiting for her ice cream, Sydney pulled on her dad's arm and all but yelled, "Are you guys done talking in your heads? I need my ice cream!"

All three adults barked with laughter as Lance swung his daughter into his arms and kissed her cheek. "Yes, Syd, we're done." Turning to Devon and Anya he winked. "Catch you two later."

"Bye guys," they called in unison as father carried daughter towards the ice cream shop.

Not one to miss anything, Anya asked, "Is Sydney a dragon shifter, too?"

Devon shrugged. "No one knows what Sydney is except a very loveable, happy, super intelligent little girl with more special powers than anyone ever thought possible."

"Not even Kyra or your mom?"

Shaking his head, Devon answered, "Not even Kyra or my mom. Sydney was hurt in a car accident that killed her parents and Sam was her doctor. Sam had been in the foster care system and couldn't bear to see the sweet child go through what she did. Long story short, Lance finally claimed her as his mate and they adopted Sydney and they are living the dream."

Accepting the abbreviated explanation he had given her, Anya nodded as they once again began walking towards the Town Square. Her eyes lit up as they turned the corner and the epicenter of his clan came into view. It didn't take long until she was completely engrossed in their little community, marveling about all the different shops and stopping to look at *everything*. Devon once again noticed how everyone they came in contact with seemed drawn to her. Each person told her how happy they were to meet her and asked how she was, truly interested in hearing her answer. The baker gave her a loaf of bread and some bagels, the florist refused to take payment for the flowers she picked out for Siobhan, even the grouchy old dragon that ran the stationery store smiled and offered to create special invitations for their mating ceremony. Devon was amazed at the incredible reception Anya received from his kin.

He was disappointed, but not surprised, when Anya stopped and looked in the window of Emma's shop and it was closed. There was a note on the door apologizing, explaining that the jeweler had been working overtime on a special piece and would reopen the next day. He watched his mate's eyes light up at all the beautiful jewelry in the window and imagined how excited she would be when he presented her with the beautiful pendant Emma had created.

Several hours later, laden down with more packages than he could ever remember carrying, even during the holidays, he and Anya made their way back to Siobhan's home. Walking up the front steps, Anya asked, "Am I ever gonna see your house?"

Stopping at the door and turning to look into her eyes, he answered through their ever-growing mating bond. *"You will most definitely see OUR home...very soon, mo chroi'."*

He watched her eyes grow wide, heard her sharp intake of breath at his innuendo, and cursed every single package in his hands for standing between his body and hers. Apparently reading his thoughts, she grinned and chuckled directly into his mind, *"I'll hold you to it."*

Anya opened the door since his hands were full, but Devon still insisted she go in ahead of him. He heard her mutter something about macho men and laughed to himself. If she only knew that not only was he minding his manners, but there was no way *in hell* he was giving up the chance to watch the gentle sway of her beautifully rounded behind as she made her way into the house.

After all of their bags were emptied and Anya was satisfied with the floral arrangement she had created for his mother, who was still researching in her study, Devon steered her down the hall and into the room they were now sharing. Giving into temptation, he sealed his lips to hers as soon as the door was closed behind them and kissed her like he had longed to all afternoon. Lifting her and making his way to the bed, he carefully sat on the edge with Anya straddling his lap, their lips never leaving one another.

Their kiss went on forever and would've led to them both spent and sleeping in each other's arms had Royce's voice not sounded in Devon's mind. *"Rayne just called for us to meet at the Great Hall. He said he didn't get a response from you so I thought I'd holler before he sent Rory after you again."* The older Guardsman chuckled through their shared link as Devon groaned. *"Be fair warned, the girls are all on their way to Siobhan's to keep Anya company while we are out tonight, since it's her first time and all."*

A giggle from Anya let him know that she had overheard at least part of his conversation with Royce. He wondered about the increased powers she had already received from their yet to be official mating, but another voice in his head made him lose his train of thought. *"Yo, lover boy. You get the message that we need to be at the Great Hall as soon as possible?"*

"Yeah. Your older brother just told me," he growled at Rory.

From the laugh in Rory's voice, Devon could tell Rory was enjoying interrupting him again way too much. *"Well, ya better hurry or ya know Rayne will just send me to get you."*

"Yeah, yeah, yeah, smartass. I know." And then more to himself than anyone else he added, *"I am seriously rethinking my choice of giving Rayne back the command of this mission."*

"I'm sure you are, lover boy." Rory laughed through their link right before cutting their connection.

As Anya went to move off his lap, her knee brushed across his rock hard cock as it pushed against the zipper of his jeans. She gasped as he pulled her hard against his body and slammed his mouth to hers, making promises with his kiss that he had yet to speak. Her hips met his as she rode his cock until stars burst behind his closed eyelids, and all he could think of was his mate naked and writhing beneath him.

Devon stood and turned to lay them both on the bed when Anya tore her mouth away and laid her forehead against his. Trying to catch her breath, she whispered, "There is nothing I want more than to make love to you, but I'm afraid I would have to kill Rory or *anyone* that interrupted us. So you, Mr. Walsh, better get your sexy ass out of here and do what you have to do." She stopped and kissed the tip of his nose, then continued, "And I will be waiting right here when you get back."

Loving that she was already comfortable enough with him to tease, he returned the gesture by gently tossing her on the bed and spinning around. Looking over his shoulder, he smirked and barked, "So you think my ass is sexy, huh?"

Anya threw back her head, her laughter filling the room and Devon with incredible happiness. He walked towards the bathroom to grab a quick shower, serenaded by the music of her laughter and thoughts of what his life would be like with her by his side. Only after he was clean, dried, and dressed, and sure he would be able to hold back his desire, did he return to the bedroom.

Finding Anya dressed and ready to greet the girls, he kissed her thoughtless one more time and together they followed the sounds of women talking and Sydney laughing. Satisfied that she was okay and would be kept busy while he was gone, Devon headed out into the night to meet his brethren. Almost an hour later, thirteen proud Guardsmen piled into three black SUVs and headed to meet their allies and finally bring down the fucking traitor that had caused so much pain and turmoil among their kin.

They met the werepanthers at the designated spot, and within ten minutes all the vehicles had been hidden and the dragons, along with the King and his men, were running in three different directions towards the mansion the traitor called home. It had been decided early on that they would split into three groups, converging on Andrew's hideout from both sides and the back. They had all agreed that not even that idiot would try using the front door for his escape, if he attempted one at all.

Devon listened to the Guardsmen calling out everything they could see through mindspeak. Each group contained at least two werepanthers that did not have access to the dragons' special form of communication, but that had been taken care of. Max was in Devon's group and every few minutes he would relay the information to the Leo as discreetly as possible so that he might pass it along to his men.

As they drew close to the mansion, Devon could feel the men's excitement as they got closer to the perimeter of the property. The prospect of finally putting the asshole traitor in a cage and ending his bullshit revenge was all they thought about.

Max held up his fist, signaling their group to stop. Raphael moved forward and Devon watched as the panther removed several small tools from the pockets of his cargo pants and set to shutting down the security system. Less than five minutes later, Devon was sending word to his brethren that they were free to breach the walls of the compound.

He listened intently as Rian's group made their way to the back of the house. It was there that Lennox would set the charges that would allow them access into Andrew's fortress. Thankfully, they had not been noticed, and according to Max's play-by-play from Raphael, the security system was still offline but sending a signal to the wizards, mimicking it was in working order.

"Lennox and I just got to the tunnel entrance. The 'mad bomber' says to give him five minutes and then we'll be good to go," Rian sent through mindspeak to all the dragons.

Devon told Max what Rian had said and watched as he passed the information onto his Pride. Within seconds, Max gave a nod, whispering, "Raphael's good. His patch into their security is holding strong."

The tension was palpable as the seconds ticked by, everyone waiting for Rian's signal. Devon grinned, listening to Lennox's excitement as he prepared the explosive. *"He truly is our very own 'psycho',"* Rory joked.

"You gotta love a man that gets such pleasure out of his job. Just make sure he doesn't blow all of us up, too, Ri," Lance laughed.

"Ha Ha, you guys are freaking hilarious!" Lennox grumbled.

"So, if you ladies are finished with the coffee club, maybe we can get this fucking show on the road." Rayne growled, his frustration evident.

"Sounds like the Commander is wound a bit tight." Aaron sent through their unique link.

"No shit. I haven't heard Rayne so keyed up since the day the traitor returned," Devon answered, still keeping an ear open to Lennox's progress.

"Ernesto senses movement heading towards the basement from within the house," Max whispered from behind.

Devon immediately sent the message to all the Guardsmen and began moving through the overgrown foliage. Rayne issued the command that all teams form a loose perimeter close to the house, and Devon listened as all teams confirmed they were moving in. The main objective in those few moments was to run interference if any wizards should wander outside and keep Lennox hidden until the device could be detonated.

Devon felt as if he could hear the seconds ticking by in his head. Everyone had gone completely silent. The anticipation that ran through both dragon and panther alike was thick enough to cut with a knife. Only Lennox seemed to be unfazed as he continued to mutter to himself.

Rian broke through the Guardsmen's mindless chatter and whispered ominously, *"I can feel the traitor just inside those fucking walls. His dragon is weaker than most and shrouded in a cloudy mess of magic, but it's there intermittently. Thankfully, the beast cannot sense us…yet."*

The warriors' anticipation turned to anger and the need for vengeance with confirmation that the traitor was just a few feet away. Always more empathetic than most, Aidan spoke cautiously and flooded their common link with a calmness Devon admired. *"Take a breath, Brothers. Stick to the plan. We'll have…"*

His words were cut short as Lennox roared, "OH FUCK!" And a matching shout of "OH SHIT!" came from the other side of the small door they were trying to access.

"WHAT THE HELL?" Rian and Aaron bellowed as the ground shook and a sharp, quick heaviness tore through the air in waves, building pressure within Devon's head until he thought his eardrums might pop. The sound that followed was one he had heard many times when deployed overseas but had hoped to never hear again, especially with his brethren in such close quarters.

Devon ran as hard and fast as he could towards the back of the mansion that was now unrecognizable as flames from an explosion ate away at the structure. Amidst the chaos, Rian yelled, Lennox cussed, and every dragon and panther scrambled to regroup while still trying to stick to some semblance of the plan they had worked so hard to perfect to achieve their ultimate goal…*capturing the fucking traitor.*

~~*~*~*~*~*

Andrew felt the floor beneath his feet tremble only seconds before a sound unlike any he had heard before tore through the structure. His heightened senses picked up the sweet smell of almonds, closely followed by the bitter smell of burning rubber, triggering memories of a past he had hoped long forgotten. Realizing almost too late what was happening, he shouted to John and shoved aside the access panel to the hidden tunnels. Running ahead, yelling directions over his shoulder so that his second would make it to the safety of his hidden room through the dense darkness, Andrew caught a fleeting sense of dragons. Sure they had been the cause of the explosion he ran to escape. No matter how fleeting and unwelcomed, it was the first time in nearly eight years that he had been able to 'feel' the men he had once called brethren. One in particular he had hoped never to have to deal with again rang loud and clear for a few seconds. Rian O'Reilly was the eldest of the mighty O'Reilly brothers and a real pain in the ass.

Andrew was pissed that the dragon assholes had been able to get so close and inflict such damage right under his nose, but he also took comfort in the fact that more of his inherent dragon power was returning. Even as he fled for his life, his devious mind was concocting a way out of his present dilemma and how to use all he was regaining to his advantage.

Rounding the corner, he felt the tremble of an aftershock right before the breeze from falling stone and debris reached his back. Turning to be sure John was still following, Andrew saw his second taken down by a large misshapen piece of the tunnel ceiling. Indecision stilled his feet for only a few seconds before he spun around and ran to save the only person he had been able to trust since his brothers' betrayal.

Lifting the enormous piece of rubble like it was little more than cardboard and throwing it aside, he saw John unconscious, blood running from the huge gash on the side of his head. Carefully tossing the injured man over his shoulder, Andrew ran full speed through an avalanche of stone and dirt, barely reaching his inner sanctum before hearing the passage they had just run through completely collapse.

The chamber was awash with toppled and demolished exercise equipment. The long punching bag once hanging perfectly in the center of the room was askew with the heavy metal brace hanging from only one of its thick metal bolts. Andrew made his way to the far corner where several practice mats were strewn about. Kicking them into place, he laid John down, grabbed the towels that had once been stacked neatly in the corner, and rolled them into a pillow to elevate his head.

Ripping one of the remaining towels into strips, Andrew applied pressure to the man's head wound, trying to remember if he had any first aid supplies stowed in the cabinets. John remained unconscious and unmoving for hours, even when Andrew returned with antiseptic and bandages from his search and did the best he could to stop the bleeding and prevent infection.

Waiting for his assistant to regain consciousness and thinking of the ruin he was sure his lair had become fueled his ever-growing hatred for the dragons, the same pieces of shit that had abandoned and betrayed him all those years ago. He took a small bit of comfort in the fact that it was almost certain Mr. A and his useless band of simple thugs had been killed in the blast. It then occurred to him that the humans they had been magically training may have suffered the same fate, and for just a second, he was filled with remorse.

Trying to use some of his newly returned dragon senses, Andrew opened his mind and reached out but only heard the roar of an open connection. Waiting was not something he had ever done well, especially after his years bound and held captive by the dark wizards, so after checking John's dressing and making sure the man still lived, Andrew ventured through what was left of the doorway to assess the damage and search for a way out. He had traveled less than a hundred yards when he came upon a wall of rock and rubble. After almost an hour of digging, it became clear that it was deeper than he could plow through on his own and he headed back to check on his second.

Clearing away the debris from his makeshift kitchen, Andrew found the prepackaged food and bottled water he had always been sure to replenish, just in case of an emergency. Laughing to himself that he was indeed in the middle of an emergency, he ate and paced, trying to formulate a plan of escape until he grew tired and made a pallet for himself on the cold stone floor.

John's breathing was slow and labored, making Andrew wonder if he had also sustained internal injuries. Many years ago he would have been able to sense the true extent of his assistant's condition, but those long hidden abilities had not returned. Staring at the ceiling, he remembered the ancient volume John had carefully stowed under the oversized coat he seemed to always wear.

Andrew retrieved the book and settled back on his mat, deciding if he was going to be stuck in a hole in the ground, he could at least translate more of the Heavens damned Prophecy that he knew held weight for his own future. He was thankful for the return of his enhanced vision, because he had yet to unearth the flashlight he knew was in the large steel chest still buried by the rubble. The more he read, the more frustrated he became as he realized the piece they had translated just a few days ago was incomplete and what he was looking at in that moment was yet another passage.

Hours later he had translated the first two sentences. *A calling to heal, a hidden nature, a history long forgotten…all protected in the heart of a woman destined to complete a warrior and his beast. The revelation of all she is brought forth from the joining with her mate.*

Andrew had at first been sure the text referred to Samantha, but she and the asshole had been together for quite some time and Andrew knew from all his well-placed spies that she was a brilliant doctor, but still simply human. His eyes burned and his vision blurred as he tried to complete the last sentence, but when he nodded off and the book landed on his chest, he knew it was time to grab a few hours rest.

Changing John's bandage and looking for any improvement in the man's condition, Andrew drew solace from the fact that at least his second's heart beat and he still drew breath. Once again settling onto his makeshift bed, staring at the cracked ceiling of his decimated abode, he added the loss of his home and the souls he had been training for his cause, John's injury, and the death of the man that provided him financial support to the list of atrocities the useless, good for nothing, piece of shit dragons had committed against him. The rage he held at bay from the first rumble of the explosion filled him with a new level of hate that only the blood of his enemies would cool. Andrew renewed his vow that he would not rest until he watched the life drain from each and every one of them…especially the brother that had left him for dead and the other brother that protected the coward.

CHAPTER SIX

Anya paced the floor for countless hours trying desperately to reach Devon through their mating bond after a flash that resembled an explosion had torn through her mind. Awakened from where she had fallen asleep on the couch, her heart beat hard and fast and her cheeks were wet with tears. In that instant, she felt a fear and anger she knew was not her own, but belonged to Devon. When she had called directly into his mind to make sure he was okay, everything had gone blank. It was almost as if the black fog had returned, but this time she could feel the tether between she and her mate holding strong. It was all that kept her from falling victim to the despair that stood on the outskirts of her thoughts, ready to pounce should she lose hope…at least she knew he was alive.

Siobhan also assured her that Devon was well and attributed his 'radio silence' to the explosion she had witnessed. At first, Anya hadn't contacted Kyra or the other girls, but as time went on, worry got the best of her and she called the tiny witch. Kyra answered her cellphone on the first ring and answered the question Anya had yet to ask. "I can't reach Royce either, but I can tell he's okay. Any ideas what the hell is going on with the big lugs?"

Loving the fact that Kyra never lost her sense of humor, Anya answered. "I had a horrible dream complete with an explosion, then woke up scared and pissed. It took a second, but I realized I was seeing and feeling what Dev was seeing and feeling, then everything on his end went dark. Like you said, I can still *feel* him."

"Well shit! That explains a lot. I was up reading, got a creepy feeling, and then Royce's thoughts just disappeared. Wonder if Kyndel, Grace, and Sam felt the same thing?" Kyra asked.

"No clue. I didn't want to call and wake the kids, and Grace looked so tired when you guys were over here earlier, I decided to try you first," Anya answered.

"Good call, but if it goes on much longer, I think we should at least check in, ya know?"

"Yeah, you're probably right. I just wish I knew what was going on before making that call." Anya grumbled.

"You and me both. Wanna wait together?" The little witch sounded like she needed the company as much as Anya, who readily agreed.

It wasn't long before Anya heard a knock at the door and was surprised when she found not only Kyra but also Grace at the front door.

"Look who I found on the way over." Kyra chuckled as she walked in carrying a basket that Anya could tell from the delicious aroma contained oatmeal cookies. At this rate, if she didn't start working out, her butt was going to be the size of Texas. These ladies knew how to cook and it seemed like the guys were *always* hungry.

"Oh Grace, I'm so glad you're here. I wanted to call but didn't want to disturb your rest."

"That's what Kyra said. I appreciate the thought, but I couldn't sleep. I was up working when I heard a blast in my head and then nothing. I can feel Aidan but no communication…*at all*." Worry was written all over the attorney's face, driving Anya to hug her before she was through the door. "Kyndel felt the same thing," Grace said against Anya's shoulder and then pulled back. "Hope you don't mind, but I called her when I ran into Kyra. She and Jay are on their way. Apparently, the little guy is up and cranky. Guess he can tell something is wrong, too."

Grace made her way into the kitchen, filled the tea kettle, and took the tin of Kyndel's special tea from the cabinet while turning on the stove. "Anyone talk to Sam?"

A knock at the door stopped all conversation. Before Anya could get there, the door opened and Sydney came running in, Sam close behind. "Anya, Daddy and the other guys were in a 'splosion, but they're okay, just can't talk in their heads." A quick hug to Anya's leg and the little girl was on her way to the kitchen, still talking over her shoulder. "Mom's kinda freaked out, but I told her everybody's okay. I can still hear them, especially Rian. He's really loud and sounds really mad."

Anya couldn't help but laugh. Sydney was absolutely one of the coolest kids she'd ever met and so intelligent it bordered on scary, but the best thing was that she accepted her gifts without question. Catching up and kissing the child on the top of the head, Anya looked to Sam who was shaking her head and smiling, before asking, "Wanna glass of milk or juice, sweetheart?"

"Milk, please," Sydney answered absently while inspecting the contents of Kyra's basket.

When Anya returned, Samantha was sitting next to her daughter, trying to convince her to have one cookie and a banana. Anya didn't have the heart to tell Sam that her money was on Sydney winning that *discussion*. Her thoughts were interrupted when Siobhan appeared, a welcoming smile and words of welcome for all. The healer stopped next to the little girl. "Those cookies look really good, Sydney."

"They are, Miss Siobhan," she said around a mouthful. "You should try one."

"I think I just might. Thank you, dear." And then turning to Anya, Siobhan asked, "Any change?"

"Not at all. I never thought I would miss someone else being in my head, but I have to admit it's kinda lonely without him."

"Don't ever let him hear you say that. You'll never live it down," Siobhan joked and everyone laughed along.

Soon, cups of tea had been made for all, Sydney was coloring, and Jay had fallen back to sleep on his mother's shoulder. The tension in the room seemed to have calmed a bit, but the wait still dragged on. Anya looked around the table, amazed at how comfortable she felt with people who only a few days prior she hadn't known existed. It wasn't like she'd never had friends. Goddess knew people always talked to her, no matter where she was. All of her life perfect strangers had gone out of their way to say hello or ask how she was. Over time she had gotten used to it, but with these people it just seemed natural, like she was where she was supposed to be for the first time in her life.

It wasn't that she hadn't loved her adoptive parents. She had been thankful every day for all they had given her. It was just that she had always felt different, like she didn't quite fit. But since waking up and meeting these incredible people, all of that had changed. Kyra's voice drew her from her thoughts. "Hey, do you mind if I grab the amulet from the Detection Ritual? Might as well make myself useful while we wait. Maybe it'll tell us something."

"Sure. It's under my pillow." The words were barely out of her mouth before the witch was heading out of the room, nervous energy filling the air in her wake.

"I don't know about y'all but my ass is falling asleep in these wooden chairs. Since it looks like we're gonna be here a while, how about we go in the living room where the furniture is cushioned." Kyndel stood, not waiting for an answer and left the room, Jay peacefully sleeping in her arms.

Sydney jumped down and followed, with the rest not far behind. Kyra returned, amulet in hand, smiling from ear to ear. "Look at this." She pointed to the markings across the top that were glowing a soft red color. "We got something."

Turning to Siobhan, she asked, "Do you mind if I use your study to see what it is?"

"Not at all, dear. I'll come along to help."

Anya watched as the two women walked out, Kyra explaining how she was going to extract the information from the glowing talisman. Sydney had gone from coloring to playing with Jay's blocks, singing while she built. Anya recognized the tune as one her mom used to sing when she was a child and began to sing along. The sweet child smiled up at her and then, without warning, stood and ran the few steps and jumped into her lap.

"*Oomph*...hey, Syd," Anya wheezed.

"Sydney!" Sam scolded from across the room.

"Don't worry about it," Anya said over the child's head.

Sydney snuggled into Anya's lap, still humming the song. They cuddled for a few minutes before the little girl turned her head and spoke to her mom. "I can hear Daddy. He's saying a bunch of bad words and talking about Andrew. He said he's gonna kick his...butt."

Sam laughed. "Thank you for not repeating your father's bad language."

Sydney continued, "Aidan and Aaron are there, and so are Royce and Dev. Sounds like they're throwing rocks around. Everybody's mad and Rian is *still* yelling." She turned completely around and looked at Kyndel. "Rayne's growling, but not like when he plays with us, more like the mean bears we saw in that movie the other night." The ladies all laughed, a layer of the tension lifting from the group.

Anya hugged the girl. "Thank you, Sweetheart. I'm so glad you can hear them. We are all really worried."

Sydney nodded. "I could feel it." She touched her chest over her heart and then stretched until her mouth was next to Anya's ear and whispered, "Devon's talking to you in his head, even though he knows you can't hear him. I didn't listen on purpose, promise, but he said he loves you."

Anya hugged her tight and whispered back, "It's okay, Baby. Thank you for telling me."

Sometime during her conversation with the little girl, Sam had come to stand beside them. "Hey, Syd, how about we go grab a nap in one of Miss Siobhan's extra rooms? I have a feeling tomorrow…well, later today, is going to be crazy."

"But Mom…" Sydney whined and Anya bit the inside of her lips to keep from smiling.

"No 'but mom' kiddo," Sam scolded as she lifted Sydney from Anya's lap. "I know you're tired and I can barely keep my eyes open. I'm sure Daddy will be here before you know it with all the other guys, and you're going to want to see everybody."

"Okay, fine," Sydney grumbled.

"Tell everyone goodnight."

"Goodnight," she parroted over her mother's shoulder, still not happy with her situation.

"Night y'all," Sam said as she disappeared down the hall.

"Has Dev told you anything about his plans for your mating ceremony?" Kyndel asked almost immediately.

"No. I just figured we would plan it when this mess with Andrew was over."

It was Grace that answered. "*You* won't be planning anything. In dragon culture, it's the male that plans the mating ceremony. He takes care of every detail, even picking out your gown."

The dreamy look on the faces of her friends told Anya all she needed to know…these men knew what they were doing when it came to making their mating official. It was then that she realized that even though her parents had told her much about other species and cultures, there were still so many things she didn't know. She opened her mouth to ask about the mating ceremony when Kyra burst into the room. Barely able to contain her excitement, the tiny witch spoke so quickly it took Anya's brain a second to catch up.

"Oh my Goddess! You've been under a helluva Concealment Spell. One like I've only ever read about. Your parents had some serious mojo! I hope you don't mind, but I called my Aunt Della and she's looking through the library at the coven for a way to remove it."

Kyra paused for a breath and Siobhan came up behind her, looking at Anya and asking in a very motherly tone, "Are you all right, my dear?"

She thought for a moment before answering. "Yeah, I'm good. I know Mom and Pops only ever did what they thought was best. If they placed the spell, there had to be a good reason. I just hope you can remove it. I'd kinda like to know what I don't know, ya know?" She giggled at her own goofy speech and the others laughed along.

"I have every faith in our Kyra. If there's a…"

No one heard the rest of what Siobhan was saying as a collective gasp filled the room. Anya could only guess that like her, the other girls heard the voices of their mates.

"*Dev?*"

"*It's me,* mo ghra'. *Were you expecting someone else?*"

"*No, goofball. I was…well…I mean it's been…*"

"*I know,* evgren. *It sucked. I thought I was gonna go crazy when I was unable to reach out or hear your thoughts. Then I found out no one could speak to their mates. Hell, there were a few minutes that we couldn't even talk to each other. We think it was the sound waves from the blast that interfered with our mindspeak.*"

"*I'm just so glad you're all right. I mean I could feel you the whole time, but it was really hard not being able to talk to you, especially after I saw the explosion in my dream.*"

"*Sorry about that. I had no idea what was about to happen or I would've shielded you.*" She heard true regret in his voice but needed him to understand they were in this whole crazy thing together, no matter how rough it got.

"*You better never shield me from anything, Devon. We talked about this. What happens to you, happens to me. I never want you to go through anything alone. We're partners, no matter what. Good, bad, or ugly.*"

"Yes, ma'am." Anya wasn't sure if she should kiss him or kick him when she heard the chuckle in his voice. Getting her big bad dragon to stop treating her like the little woman she most definitely was *not* wasn't going to be an easy task. He continued, *"I've got to get back to the search, but I'm coming home with the first group right before dawn. I'll tell you all about it then."*

"Okay. Be safe."

"I will. I love you, mo ghra'.*"*

"Love you, too, Dev." And she truly meant it.

Lost in thought with what she was sure was a goofy grin on her face, Anya was unprepared for the six-year-old ball of energy that once again landed right on her lap, singing a very happy tune. "Mommy talked to Daddy. Mommy talked to Daddy."

She smiled at Sydney's delight, unable to stop from singing along for just a minute. When the darling girl took a breath, Anya jumped in. "And I talked to Devon and Grace to Aidan and Kyndel to Rayne…"

"I know, silly. I heard them all, even Aaron when he was talking to Rian. He's not very happy 'cause they still can't find Andrew."

"I can only imagine."

Her next comment was interrupted when Sam took Sydney from her lap, saying, "Now that we are sure everything is okay, I think we should get home, little miss. You need to get at least a little catnap before Daddy gets home. I'm somehow sure you'll be up the moment he touches down."

"Touches down?" Anya asked.

Sam nodded as she explained. "Lance and Rory are flying back while it's still dark to see if they can spot any of Andrew or Mr. A's followers that may have gotten away. Rian's sure Andrew is still inside and he has confirmed Mr. A died in the blast. They just want to make sure any that may have escaped can be rounded up and held accountable for their crimes."

"I see," Anya responded and immediately felt bad for all the others that had been abducted like her. They hadn't been responsible for their situation, and now they were either dead or being hunted down.

Grace must've sensed her thoughts when she said, "Anya, if there are any that were forced into Andrew's plot, like you, I'll personally make sure they are given the rehabilitation they need to return to their old lives."

While Anya thanked Grace, she saw Sam cross the room out of the corner of her eye. The women exchanged a look and Grace rose to follow Sam and Sydney into the kitchen. Anya looked at Kyndel, who was watching her best friend and shaking her head. When the Commander's mate turned around, she explained. "You remember we told you about what Mr. A and his thugs had done to Sam?"

Anya nodded while the other woman continued her explanation. "Well, we didn't get to the part where Mr. A was actually Grace's boss, the State's Attorney, at the same time he was a human trafficker and building the city's largest crime syndicate. A couple of his thugs broke into the State Building to steal some incriminating paperwork while Grace was working late one night and she was caught in the crossfire. Thank the Heavens, Aidan got there in time, but she was still injured. Then when the warehouse where they had taken Samantha after she was kidnapped blew up, my poor bestie was captured by Andrew and we thought we'd lost her. Grace was hoping to get a chance to put her old boss in jail for the rest of his life. I know she's glad he's been stopped, but I think it's kind of a letdown that she didn't get to be the one that clicked the lock and threw away the key."

Kyndel's chuckle sounded hollow and her smile didn't reach her eyes. "Both girls suffered at that asshole's hands, and I think they just need a few minutes to let reality sink in." She sounded almost haunted when she spoke of the others' trauma, making Anya feel bad for the Commander's wife, who was so incredibly empathic that she suffered also.

It was then that Anya realized she could hear their whispered voices from the other room and if she focused, she could actually make out what they were saying. She chalked it up to another benefit of the mating call the other girls had been telling her about.

Having a difficult time blocking out Grace and Sam's conversation, Anya told Kyndel she needed to see what Kyra was up to with the amulet and hurried towards Siobhan's study. As she approached, she caught part of Kyra and Siobhan's discussion about the best way to remove the Concealment Spell. She lightly knocked on the door to let them know she was there before walking in.

"Come on in, Anya," called Kyra.

"Thanks," she answered, stopping just inside the door when she found them both sitting cross-legged on the Oriental rug in front of the fireplace. Every available inch between and around them was covered with open books, notebooks, and loose pages. Judging by the discoloration of the paper, they were very old.

Siobhan began to explain. "From the strength of the Concealment Spell and the traces of 'other' magic Kyra sensed from the amulet, we are once again combining her Earth magic with dragon rituals."

Kyra picked up the explanation when Siobhan paused. "I spoke with my Aunt Della. Who, by the way, cannot wait to meet you." The smile on the tiny witch's face said she loved her aunt very much. "Anyway, I told you I had called her. Well, she called back and gave me all the information she could find about Concealment Spells, which was *loads*, thank the Goddess. She also said you must be *superhuman* to have endured all the magic thrust upon you and not be crazy. Most people can't take it without some really crazy side effects."

They all chuckled as Siobhan sifted through the stacks of books and papers before coming up with what resembled a large recipe card. "Here it is!"

She handed it to Kyra, who quickly scanned the writing and then said, "Okay, chica, this is gonna work pretty much the same as the Detection Spell, only there's no amulet. *Hell*, we don't even have to light a candle, just form a circle, recite the ritual, and wait. I know the waiting part will suck, but I'm adding an indicator that will tell me when the concealment is lifted so we'll know right away, cool?"

"Absolutely," Anya responded and quickly added, "I don't think I'll ever be able to thank you both enough for all your help."

Siobhan stood and stepped over the clutter on the floor, stopping right in front of her. "Having you here and seeing the look of utter bliss you put on my son's face is thanks enough."

Before she could respond, the older woman pulled her into a fierce hug. It was only a few seconds before she felt a much smaller set of arms come around her from behind and heard Kyra's melodic voice. "And I think it's freaking cool to get another sis."

These beautiful, magical people never ceased to amaze Anya with their kindness, generosity, and love. She had loved her mom and pops very much, but always felt like something was missing. The longer she spent with Devon and his clan, the more she understood what family *really felt like.*

~~*~*~*~*~*~*

It had been a hell of a night and all he wanted to do was crawl into bed with Anya and hold her while he slept for a few days, but his mother and Kyra apparently had other plans. Devon wasn't surprised when he walked into Siobhan's house to find Sam, Grace, and Kyndel huddled in deep conversation around the kitchen table. He had left Aidan and Rayne digging through the rubble with Aaron, Rian, Royce, and Kellan, and had watched Lance and Rory fly overhead from the SUV window while he drove the rest of the Blue Thunder Clan back to the lair. Rian had told them to rest because they would have the shift tomorrow night, and Rayne had told him to drive them, informing Devon that his constant worry over being away from Anya was driving them all crazy. Max had concurred as he and his panthers piled into vehicles to return to their Pride. Devon shrugged, not apologetic in the slightest for the strong feelings his mate evoked. He did note that he was going to have to work harder to keep them to himself, something he had not had to do since he was very young.

Ain't love grand?

Devon knew he should've felt bad for leaving the others behind in favor of seeing Anya, but he just couldn't work up the guilt. The mating call was relentless and his dragon felt it just as strongly, making the beast damn near intolerable. The long hours of silence between them after the blast had only exacerbated the situation. He had spoken to her and knew she was doing fine, but that did not negate the fact that he *needed* to *see* her, *hold* her, *take* her scent into his body, and *feel* her skin against his.

He was just about to ask where his mate was when he heard the words of a ritual and felt Kyra's magic pulse through the air. Rushing down the hall to his mother's study, he threw open the door just as Kyra said the words, *"We ask for the blessing of the Universe, the Heavens, and the Goddess in our quest to rid this woman of the Spell of Concealment."*

Marching to Anya, he stood behind her, waiting until the ladies raised their heads and let go of one another's hands before spinning her around. He slammed his mouth to hers and reveled in her immediate response to his kiss. She opened for him and he tasted deep of all that she was until they were both panting and more than a little excited. He saw the blush on her cheeks and loved that he had put it there. Devon didn't care who saw, he wanted to fly her to the top of the highest peak and scream for all to hear that Anya was his mate and he loved her with every fiber of his being.

The sound of Siobhan clearing her throat and Kyra giggling brought his thoughts back to the study and what he had just walked in on. Never one to mince words, he looked first at his mother and then Kyra before asking, "So, anything anyone wants to tell me?"

Anya's eyes grew wide and he realized his tone may have been a bit stronger than he intended, but he was just a little pissed that no one had bothered to either give him a heads up or wait until he got back. Devon knew Anya thought she could take care of herself, but she was *his mate,* and he would be damned if even his mother would perform magic on her without his permission. He was just about to say what he thought when Anya pulled from his arms and planted her fists firmly on her hips. The look she gave him said she had heard at least part of his thoughts and did *not* agree.

Devon held up his hands and opened his mouth to explain, but she would hear none of it. "Dammit, Devon, I *can* take care of myself and if I want your mother, or anyone else for that matter, to perform a spell, a ritual, or an appendectomy, *I'll be damned* if I'll wait for *your* permission."

She leaned forward on her tippy toes until their noses almost touched, in what he assumed was an effort to intimidate him. He used his considerable control to keep from laughing at how cute she looked, guessing it would only infuriate her more. When she spoke again it was through gritted teeth, "You are my mate, but that does *not* mean that you get to dictate everything I do. Siobhan and Kyra found a way to remove the Concealment Spell and I wanted it gone as soon as possible, so we did the ritual." She shrugged. "It's done, so I suggest you deal with it, but the choice is yours."

He sensed she was about to turn away in order to make a dramatic exit and solidify her position on the matter, but there was no way he was letting her get away, they had been apart for way too long. Taking one step to the right and stopping her movement, he scooped her up, tossed her over his shoulder, and headed towards the door. When he turned down the hall, he looked back at Kyra and his mother and winked as they laughed at his exit.

Anya laid silently over his shoulder as he made his way to the other end of the house, but he could feel her frustration and was sure he was going to get an earful when they were safely ensconced in the privacy of her room. He could not have been more wrong. After shutting and locking the door to make sure they weren't interrupted, he carefully placed Anya on the bed and stood back…waiting for what he thought was sure was to come.

Instead of yelling or even chastising him for his high-handed behavior, she smiled sweetly, scooted to the edge of the bed, and proceeded to remove first one sandal and then the other. Never saying a word, only smiling sweetly, she stood, kissed the tip of his nose, and turned to the right. As she walked away from him, she removed first her blouse and then her bra, letting them fall to the floor while giving him a mouthwatering view of her beautiful back and the curves that had his hands begging to touch.

He watched as her jeans slid to the floor and his breath caught in his throat as her panties slid down her legs. She expertly stepped out of them, striding the last few steps to the door of the bathroom, gloriously naked. He all but panted as he took in the seductive sway of her ass and knew he would find every way possible to keep her unclothed as much as possible in the future.

His dick hardened to the point of pain when she stopped in the doorway, slowly turned to the side, giving him a view of her absolutely perfect profile, and then looked longingly over her shoulder. He had taken one involuntary step in her direction when her words stopped him in his tracks. "I was going to invite you to shower with me, but now I find myself needing time alone." She slowly licked her lips, the trail of her tongue making his cock jump as he imagined her beautiful lips on his body.

The spell she had woven fell away with the click of the lock on the bathroom door. Standing in shock at the way his mate had just played him like a fiddle, he groaned when her next statement reached his ears. "Act like a Neanderthal and throw me over your shoulder again and see what other tricks I have up my sleeve. Paybacks are a bitch, Dragon Man."

Devon had no clue how long he laid on the bed while the scent of sea and sand mixed with Kyndel's special bath oil filled the room, driving him crazy with desire. He imagined the water glistening on her olive skin and the bubbles sliding over her generous curves. The beautiful aroma and his musings, combined with her striptease, made him want nothing more than to break down the door that stood between them and show her what a Neanderthal he could truly be. Of course, that would only further prove her point and probably land him on the couch, or worse yet, back at his house with Rian's men. He shuddered at the thought.

He realized after the fact that his actions could have been misconstrued as high-handed. But he had been sure that once they were alone he would be able to explain his actions and make her see that sometimes his desire to keep her safe overrode his ability to let her do things for herself. It was obvious she valued her independence and had told him how important having a true partnership was to her. He would move heaven and earth to have her happy, but letting her put herself in danger without even consulting him was not acceptable and something she would have to understand. Devon somehow figured it was not the last *discussion* they would have on the matter.

Trying to decide how to approach Anya while wondering if she would ever emerge from the bath, he welcomed the distraction of Rory's voice in his mind. *"Hey, Dev. Thought I'd catch ya up while lover boy here is talking to his pretty doctor. We saw nothing. If anyone did get away, they're good and hidden now."*

"Thanks for trying. Did you let Rayne and Rian know?"

"Sure did and Rayne said to holler at you." For the first time Devon could ever remember, Rory wasn't being a smartass or joking around. He just sounded tired.

"Cool. Thanks."

"You got it. We're about to land in the clearing behind your house. I'm gonna grab a shower and some shut eye."

"Enjoy, Ror. Catch ya later."

"See ya, Dev."

Deciding he better start groveling before Anya spent all the down time he had hiding in the bathroom, he tapped on the door and asked, "Everything okay in there, *mo chroí'*?"

"Just great," was her quick response.

Leaning against the door, he whispered, "M*o ghra'*, would you please come out and talk to me?"

No answer, only silence, had him closing his eyes, leaning his head against the door, and praying to the Heavens for the right words to explain his actions. It was then he remembered something he had read just a few days before. Taking a deep breath, he started, "Anya, *a mhuirnin*, do you remember the fountain we saw in the Town Square?"

"Yes."

He breathed a quick sigh of relief at her response and continued. "When the Elders had the sculpture built, they placed a very special saying at the base. The words are beautiful in both languages, but I truly never understood their meaning until you came into my life. It says 'Light to his soul. Love to his heart. Hope to his future.'" He paused and swallowed past the lump that was growing in his throat. "You are all of that and more. There are times that I think I only learned how to breathe after I met you."

He heard movement on the other side of the door and felt the emotions his words stirred within his mate flowing through their bond. When she didn't speak, he went on. "I know you think I try to control you or keep you from things, and I guess you're right to a certain extent, but it's only because I love you more than I ever thought possible. I *literally* cannot imagine my life without you in it, and for a guy that's been alive for a hundred and twenty years…that's saying something."

He heard her move closer to the door and pressed on. "I want to make you *happy*. I want you to have everything you ever wanted and things you never knew possible. I'll spend *every day* of our lives together doing *everything* in my considerable power to see you smile, and when you do…so will I, because I'll know that I put that look on your face."

He felt her hand against the door and put his opposite hers. "So when I freak out because you're involved in a ritual when I'm not around, or I throw you over my shoulder because I want to be alone with you, it's not because I want to control you. It's because I simply adore you and the very thought of you doing anything that could result in you getting hurt stops my heart in my chest. All I can think of is getting you away from anyone or anything that may even remotely cause you harm. And if you think I'm being an overbearing Neanderthal, you should know that my dragon is a hundred times worse and about a thousand pounds bigger."

The lock clicked and the door opened just enough for him to see Anya's beautiful face. Her first words should've surprised him, but made sense the more he got to know her. "Even when your mom is involved?"

"Yes, *mo ghra'*, even when Siobhan is involved."

"But…I mean…" She stopped and shook her head.

He pushed the door and was overjoyed when she stepped back to let it open all the way, but disappointed that she was wearing a robe. Pushing his errant thoughts and those of his beast to the side, he said the only thing that came to mind. "Without you, there is no me. It's as simple as that. Devon Walsh as a single being ceased to exist the moment my soul recognized yours as its mate."

The need to hold his mate was a physical ache in his chest, but he wasn't sure she was ready for his touch. Always full of surprises, his mate reached out and entwined her fingers with his. Devon welcomed the electric shock that always accompanied her touch. His soul literally singing as she closed the space between them and snuggled into his chest. Their hands still clasped between them, he wound his free arm around her waist and let his hand rest on her hip.

Lost to the feeling of Anya in his arms, she surprised him when she said, "It's weird how much you mean to me in such a short period of time, but I was taught not to question such things. We all have a path and I know in my heart that you are mine but…" She lifted her head and looked as fierce as she could while cuddled against him. Her raised voice let him know she meant business. "You cannot go all caveman on me just to get your way."

Not waiting for his response, she laid her head back on his chest and once again snuggled close. He decided to enjoy holding her in his arms and to let her think she had won…*this time*. He loved her fire and spunk, but it was the way she turned him inside out with just a look that made him feel like he could fly without his wings. Even his dragon chuffed in agreement.

"So are you gonna tell me what happened out there? What blew up?" Her muffled words reached his ears.

"I am," he said as he pulled back. "Stand right there. I need a shower. The smell of smoke and ash is horrible. I'm sorry if I got any on you, but I just couldn't keep my hands to myself." He winked and then said, "Don't move. Two minutes, tops."

He didn't wait for her reply. He simply used his enhanced speed to race to the tub, strip, shower, and pull on the pair of clean boxers he always kept in the drawer in case he couldn't get to his house.

Returning to his mate, who still stood where he had asked, he gently lifted her into his arms, carrying her to his favorite chair in the corner. Devon answered her question once he was comfortable and she was settled on his lap. "The werepanthers found a forgotten entrance into the mansion. It was covered with dirt and overgrown with weeds. After looking at the blueprints in the county records, Rian found that it led to a tunnel under the mansion, so it was decided that Lennox would use a small amount of explosives to clear the way. All was going as planned until he was discovered by an overzealous wizard. Just as Lenn set the charge to blow, the wizard fired off a spell. The two combined, causing a chain reaction that blew the back of the mansion and most of its inhabitants all to hell."

"Thank goodness none of *you* were hurt," she murmured.

"Nothing serious. Lennox was knocked on his ass and Rian got a nick on the arm from flying debris, but the worst part was having our mental communication knocked out."

"Are you sure Andrew was even there?"

"Yeah, Rian sensed him when we breached the perimeter and then once after the blast, but that was really faint. He's sure the traitor is trapped somewhere beneath the structure but when I left, they still had no clue where, and that place is *huge*. Not to mention that now about seventy percent of it's just a big pile of rock and ash."

The longer they talked, the more the exhaustion he had felt before their disagreement returned, instead of the words he planned to say coming from his mouth, he yawned long and loud. Anya giggled as she pushed off his lap and held out her hand to him. "Come on, big guy, let's get you tucked in. You need to rest before the craziness resumes."

Having a hard time keeping his eyes open, he took her hand and followed her into bed. *How did I ever sleep without her in my arms* was Devon's last thought as he kissed the top of Anya's head and drifted off to sleep.

CHAPTER SEVEN

Sometime in the wee hours of their second or third night in captivity, John drew his last breath. Time was irrelevant when only his intermittent dragon senses let him know if it was day or night. Andrew had gone from his first deep sleep since the explosion to completely awake the second his assistant's heart beat for the last time. The traitor had knelt beside the only person he had dared to trust in over seven years and let the pain of loss wash over him. He had known the man was in bad shape and tried everything he could to keep him alive while attempting to dig through the debris that kept them trapped. Getting his second the proper medical attention had been his first concern, but he had failed.

He shed no tears, nor did he beg the Heavens to return John to life. Andrew only vowed retribution in a reverent whisper. An oath made to his fallen comrade assuring John's spirit that he would make every fucking piece of shit dragon pay for the man's suffering and death.

Several hours later, Andrew walked out into what was left of the tunnel he had been attempting to clear since the blast, but instead of turning towards the exit, he turned back towards the mansion and walked the hundred feet of partially cleared concrete to the wall of fallen rock. He bent over and began digging into the mountain of debris, not stopping until he had cleared a six feet by four feet section almost two feet deep and then collected the smoothest rocks he could find, setting them aside.

After making sure everything was like he wanted, he returned to his makeshift abode and rifled through the cabinets that had fallen off the walls until he found a clean sheet. Kneeling next to the body of his assistant, Andrew wrapped John in the white cloth, picked up his lifeless body, and carried him to the crypt he had just built. Carefully he placed the body inside and then covered it with the stones he had set aside.

Standing in silence for several long minutes, Andrew then did something he had thought long forgotten. He prayed to the Heavens and spoke the words of the Dragon Burial Rite. *Elders of Olde, Heavens above, and the Universe that controls it all, receive this soul into your keeping. Protect him on his journey to the other side. Prepare him for what is to come in the afterlife. He is 'kin fole eile' and is deserving of my gratitude.*

It was the only way he knew to assure John's soul was not stuck in the ether, roaming the Earth as a specter. They had never spoken of religion or faith and Andrew had no knowledge other than the little he had been exposed to of the coven in which John had practiced his wizardry, or their beliefs regarding death, so he had drawn upon the only thing he knew. He had recited the words from his mother and father's *sochraide*.

Returning to the hidden room, unable to settle his tumultuous thoughts of revenge, Andrew tested the integrity of the brace that secured the large punching bag to the ceiling. Finding it lacking, he dug the boxing dummy he rarely used out of the closet and proceeded to punch and kick until sweat wet his hair and ran down his back. With every strike he imagined the face of a different Dragon Guardsman. The one that came most often was the one that had betrayed him and left him for dead and was now responsible for the death of his comrade. They would all pay, but it would be Aidan, the ultimate coward, that would suffer the most.

Andrew had gotten a fleeting impression that his brother was near a few nights ago. It stood to reason that the assholes would be searching for him in the debris of the mansion, but they had no knowledge of his hidden tunnels, and because the mansion had belonged to a former drug lord, the passages were not on any blueprint or map of the property. As he continued to rain blows down on the mannequin, a plan formed in his mind. If he could dig out, he might be able to surprise them while they worked, and with any luck at all, at least one of his loser brothers would be in attendance.

Deciding to put his plan into action after a bottle of water and one of the few protein bars he had left, Andrew delivered one last blow that had the dummy slamming against the opposite wall and falling in pieces on the floor. The sinister grin he felt cross his lips was nothing compared to the dark thoughts invading his mind. He promised John that every last one of the Dragon Guard would lose their life by his hand, leaving their mates as nothing more than grieving widows and their children fatherless. If the rumors were true, he was to be an uncle, and what a pity those babies would never know their father. *What a pity indeed…*

~~*~*~*~*~*~*

Three crazy days went by with no sign of Andrew. Devon stayed at the lair all day, even though Anya barely saw him, between him planning their mating ceremony and meeting with the other men. Every time he came back she would try to get details about their wedding, but he would smile his panty-dropping smile and tell her to be patient. Patience was not something Anya had ever been good at, and it seemed that nothing had changed.

They had talked about returning to her farm to pick up some of her stuff, especially the heirloom hair combs that had been worn by every woman in her mom's family on their wedding day for the last two hundred years. Anya knew Devon would do everything possible to get her there, but he was so busy she felt bad about asking. She had even suggested pushing the date of the ceremony back a few days until things settled down, but Devon shook his head so hard she thought it might fly off. Then he told her in no uncertain terms they would be officially mated by the end of the week. After that she decided never to broach the subject again.

The search for Andrew seemed to be taking its toll on everyone. All the girls talked about their mates being worn out and grumpy. Earlier, she watched Devon walk in just as the sun was making its daily appearance after a long night of searching for the traitor, covered in soot and the smell of smoke, and looking so tired her heart ached for him. He tried to hide his exhaustion as he made his way to the bathroom, jumped in and out of the shower, then came to lie down beside her. Bone-deep exhaustion poured off of him in waves as he fit his hard, warm body behind hers and held her tight. Anya prayed she was giving him as much comfort as he gave her and vowed she would make her own way out to her farm. There was no way she was going to ask Devon for one more thing. –He had enough on his plate. She could handle one little day trip to her own old home.

The soft sounds of Devon's snoring reached her ears and she smiled, glad her man would at least get a few hours rest. Resigned that she would ask one of the girls to accompany her to the farm, she settled into Devon's arms and followed him to sleep.

The few hours they slept seemed to recharge Devon's battery. He left whistling after a huge breakfast and several cups of coffee. When he kissed her goodbye, she could feel how happy he was and giggled at the silly images of him dancing down the street that he placed in her mind.

Convincing Kyra to go with her to the farm had been easier than she'd expected. The Earth witch was extremely interested in going through her mom's notebooks and seeing the other witch's greenhouse. When Anya told her she could keep anything she liked, Kyra's eyes lit up like a Christmas tree and they were out the door in five minutes flat.

"I'm figuring we'll be back before Dev and Roy, so I just left a note on the kitchen table at our house and Siobhan knows where we are if anyone is looking for us," Kyra assured her as they buckled into her little blue Mini convertible the witch called her 'broom'.

"I left one in our room, too," Anya added.

"Kyndel and Grace know where we are and Sam is at the hospital…" Kyra chuckled, "Damn, it's almost more trouble than it's worth just to take a little ride, huh?"

"I was just thinking the same thing," Anya agreed.

The rest of the trip was filled with chatter of her mating ceremony and Kyra talked about her mom, Calysta. Anya listened intently to the description of the magic the younger witch had felt while looking for the Grand Priestess. The more Kyra told her, the more she was certain her mom had talked about something similar.

"That sounds an awful lot like something Mom and her coven dealt with when I was younger. I don't remember the specifics, but I'm sure it's in one of her notebooks." She stopped and thought for a second before adding, "All I really remember is Mom and Pops talking about making sure 'nothing followed them home'. I was young, so I kept looking out the window for a puppy or something, but now I have to wonder what they were really talking about."

"Yeah, there's some scary shit out there, and the stuff I felt when we were traipsing over the countryside and through the caves on the coast of Royce's homeland made me shiver. It was dark and evil. Mom's a tough old bitch and I'm sure she can handle it, but… " Anya watched her shudder at the memory and figured whatever it was had to be more than scary if the incredibly powerful white witch and her huge mate were worried.

Changing the subject, Anya asked about Kyra's mating ceremony and listened intently as her friend painted a romantic picture of one of the happiest days of her life. It wasn't long before they were turning onto the long, two-lane dirt road that led to the only home she ever remembered. Pulling into the gravel driveway, Kyra went on and on about the fields of wild flowers on either side of the lane and the herbs whose fragrance decorated the cool breeze.

No sooner had they parked the car than Jedidiah, Pop's oldest friend and the caretaker of the farm came strolling out of the barn. Smiling and waving, Anya called to him, "Just here to pick up some clothes and stuff. Everything okay?"

"Sure is, Little One. Everything okay with you?"

She had called earlier in the week to let Jed and his wife, Dot, know where she was and had explained about her 'accident'. Jed and Dot were witches in her mom's coven and still practiced the craft, something Anya was thankful for, given the changes in her life since they had last seen each other.

"Yes, sir. Couldn't be better. Dot around?"

"No. She's over at the house. Grandkids are coming in later today and she's cookin' up a storm."

"Jed, this is Kyra. She's…"

Her introduction was cut short when Jed cut in, "One powerful little witch." He extended his hand to shake and went on, "Nice to meet ya. Who's your kin?"

Anya and Kyra both laughed out loud before Kyra responded while shaking Jed's hand. "Nice to meet you, too, sir. My mom is Grand Priestess Calysta St. Croix and my auntie is Della St. Croix."

"Well, hell. It really is a small world. My Dottie was friends with a Della St. Croix when I met her about a hundred years ago. Wonder if it's the same one?"

"I would imagine so. To the best of my knowledge, they broke the mold when they made her." Kyra and Jed both laughed at her joke.

"Tell her we asked about her and let her know to come on out any time." Jed walked over and gave Anya a one-armed hug then said, "I'll let you girls get to it. I still have chores to get done and I'm sure Dot's got a list a mile long for me when I get home."

"Thanks, Jed. Give Dottie my love," Anya called after the tall, thin man as he ambled back towards the barn.

"I sure will. Take care of yourself, Little One."

"Little One?" Kyra asked, and Anya saw the glint in her eye, assuring her Devon was going to hear about her nickname.

"Yeah, that's pretty much what everyone has called me for as long as I can remember. The story goes that when I came to live with Mom and Pops I was wrapped in so many blankets that it took forever to find the baby in the bundle, and Pops said he didn't know they made 'em that little. Somehow that became 'little one' and it stuck."

She shrugged and quickly changed the subject. "The greenhouse is out back if you wanna check it out while I gather up my stuff. There should be bags and boxes out there in case you find anything you want to keep. Jed and Dottie already took what they wanted, so anything still there is fair game."

"You sure you don't need any help?" Kyra asked, staring longingly at the greenhouse.

Anya swatted at her friend's arm. "Like you would be any help at all." They both laughed and Anya added, "Get over there and have fun. I'll holler at you when I'm done."

Kyra gave her a quick hug then turned. "You're the best," she yelled over her shoulder as she practically ran in the opposite direction.

As Anya turned towards the house, she caught sight of the pasture where her pops had taught her to ride. And then, like he knew she was thinking about him, her favorite horse, Romeo, trotted into view. Unable to stop herself, she ran to the gate and threw it open just as the horse met her halfway, nuzzling her cheek. The look in his large charcoal eyes told her he had missed her as much as she had missed him.

Pulling him to the fence, she climbed up a rung and then slung her leg over Romeo's bare back. It was as if they had never been apart. He galloped for several laps around the pasture and she could feel that he was as happy as she with the wind blowing against their faces. It was almost as good as old times. All too soon, her ride came to an end as Jed walked out of the barn with Romeo's feed. She thanked the man for his help with her dismount and for taking such great care of her 'friend'. Making her way back to the house she decided to ask Devon about bringing her horse to the lair.

Anya walked in the kitchen door of the only house she had ever remembered living in and welcomed the smells of home. She was happy to see that Dot had been watering the herbs that sat in the window above the sink and loved the fact that no matter how long her parents had been gone she could still feel their presence. Making her way to the back of the house and up the steep wooden staircase, she thought about Devon and sent him a wave of love through their mating link.

Over the past few days she had been able to talk with Siobhan and had learned so much more about dragon culture, specifically what it really meant to be mated to a Guardsman. Anya had been amazed at the depth and richness of the centuries old race. There were things the Elder Healer told her that seemed familiar, but most of it was new and incredibly interesting. Anya considered herself extremely blessed to have been literally made to be part of a race of ancient warriors.

As she walked into her room an eerie feeling of déjà vu came over her and the marking on her wrist tingled. She stopped and felt her surroundings like her mom had taught her, nothing more than memories of her childhood and the happiness that had been shared filled her senses. Shaking off the weird feelings, Anya retrieved two suitcases and a duffle bag from the closet and stuffed them full of clothes, accessories, and old pictures. When her room was all but bare, she headed downstairs and into her pop's office.

Leaving her bags in the hallway, Anya headed directly to the huge painting depicting the landscape outside the very window she stood beside. Carefully sliding the framed canvas to the side, she quickly entered the combination to the safe and took out the heirloom hair combs accented with teardrop opals. Tears filled her eyes as she thought of all the women that had worn the very combs she held in her hands on the most special day of their lives. She reached to shut the safe and once again the marking on her wrist tingled. Trying to ignore it, she spun the dial on the lock and pulled the painting back into place. Instead of fading, the tingling spread up her arm and when she looked at the marking, it appeared to be raised.

Several things happened at once. Devon's voice sounded in her mind, a dark shadow blocked the sun from the window, and Kyra burst into the room yelling her name. Before she could ask what was going on, the little witch had her by the arm pulling her down the hall and out the kitchen door. With all the commotion she couldn't make out what Devon was shouting in her head or what Kyra was babbling on about. Grabbing the wooden railing before she fell down the stairs, Anya looked up to see four full grown dragons landing in the pasture beside the barn. She had read tons of books when she was growing up, most of them containing dragons, and not one of the descriptions did what she was looking at justice.

The largest of the group, which by size alone she figured had to be Royce, was a brilliant royal blue with green highlights. There were two silver dragons, each with unique black markings. They had to be brothers and therefore, Aaron and Aidan. But it was the white dragon whose scales seemed opalescent in the sunlight that drew and held her eye. She felt the connection she had with the beautiful beast and knew it was her mate. He was absolutely gorgeous, and as he touched down, she got a look at the curved horns protruding from his head, the imposing row of spikes that started at the nape of his neck and ran to the tip of his tail, where a huge three-sided spade looked as if it could take out a forest with one swipe.

Her inspection of the majestic creatures was short lived as the air around her filled with magic and in the next second Devon was striding towards her in just a pair of jeans, closely followed by Royce, Aaron, and Aidan. She smiled at her mate, still awestruck from what she had witnessed, but the look that he gave made her take a step back. The brick of the house dug into her back as she took in his furrowed brow, downturned lips, and the way he marched up the four steps and placed his hands on either side of her head.

Anya started to speak but Devon's lips were on hers before she could think of what to say. He kissed her long and deep, holding her captive with just his mouth. Lost to his kiss, she was shocked when she found herself once again thrown over his shoulder and hauled back into the house. Acting like he knew his way around, Devon walked them straight into the family room and placed her not so gently on the couch, kneeling in front of her. He placed his hands on her thighs and leaned so close she could see blue and green flecks swirling in his turbulent grey eyes.

Their staring contest lasted about five seconds, but felt like a lifetime. She had just started to smile when Devon opened his mouth, "What *in the hell* are you doing in the middle of fucking nowhere *by yourself?*"

She felt the smile fall from her face, but not before the thought of kicking him in the balls crossed her mind.

~*~*~*~*~*~*~*

Devon knew he was acting like a raving lunatic, but the harder he tried to keep his mouth shut and hear what Anya had to say, the harder his dragon pushed to take action and the madder he got. How many times had he told her not to go anywhere without him until Andrew was caught? What *the fuck* had she been thinking? He knew he would never get answers as long as he kept talking, but there was a disconnect between his brain and his mouth, and apparently his mouth still had loads to say.

"*Dammit*, Anya, were you trying to get yourself captured or killed?"

The look on her face said he should've found a way to shut up approximately ten seconds earlier. Her eyes widened, her lips flattened, she took a deep breath, and he heard her counting in her head. When she spoke, it had a low and ominous ring to it and a part of him thought he actually heard her growl. "Yes, Devon, that's exactly what I was trying to do. I wanted to get captured again because it was just a freakin' party to be scared out of my mind twenty-four hours a day and made to practice screwed up magic. Oh, and let us not forget being in a coma and thinking I was gonna get eaten by some damned black fog. Best time I ever had."

She pushed against his chest hard enough that he had to stand to keep from falling on his ass. Anya stood and stepped around him, her voice getting louder every few words. "It couldn't have been because I knew how tired and busy you were, or how much you wanted us to be able to be mated this week. It couldn't have been because I wanted to keep a promise to my mom and not have you bring me out here to get these." She thrust her hand out and in it he saw a pair of absolutely gorgeous combs. The exact combs she had told him about. He immediately felt like a dick for losing his temper.

"Of course it had to be because I'm some ditzy broad that you have to watch over all the time." She stood in the doorway and he watched the rise and fall of her shoulders as she took several deep breaths. When she turned, the tears in her eyes nearly brought him to his knees. But it was her words that cut him to the quick. "You're never gonna change and that is why this," she motioned over her shoulder towards him, "is never gonna work."

Unable to move, he watched her walk out of the room and heard the kitchen door slam as she left the house. He sank to his knees, and that is where Aaron found him almost thirty minutes later.

"Are you praying or did she kick you?" Aaron joked, but Devon could see the concern on his face.

Not sure how to answer, he spoke the truth. "I fucked up. She ripped out my heart and I'm praying for a way to make it right."

Aaron sat in the chair beside where Devon still knelt and gripped his shoulder. "You know I got nothing, but I will admit seeing you lose your shit and not act all Zen makes me feel like you might actually be human."

Devon snorted and Aaron continued, "But I seem to remember some advice you gave the old guy and it seems like it might work for you, too." His friend squeezed his shoulder before letting go and standing. "You better grovel, my man, and make it good."

He sat in the same spot for a little while longer and then ventured out to the backyard where Kyra and his brethren were sitting around talking.

The little witch was the first to look up and nodded towards the greenhouse as she said, "Your girl's in there. Said she wanted to be alone."

Without a word he walked towards his mate. He wondered if pirates doomed to walk the plank felt like he did in that moment. The sound of singing stopped him dead in his tracks just beyond the corner of the little structure. It didn't surprise him that Anya had a beautiful voice and it made him feel a little better that the song was a happy one. He listened for a moment longer and realized he was only avoiding the inevitable. He had royally screwed up and it was time to face the music and beg for forgiveness.

Thinking back, he could never remember a time when he was scared of anything before Anya. He and his brethren had battled damn near everything there was to fight, and there had been times the outcome was not a foregone conclusion. But never once had he felt the true, blood curdling fear that was coursing through his body at that moment.

Taking a deep breath, he walked the last few steps and pulled open the door. He knew she heard him from the slight stutter in her melody, but she picked right up and kept her back to him, paying particular attention to a large, flat, clay pot of herbs she was weeding. Her hands deftly pulled the unwanted greenery while leaving the fragrant herbs untouched. It was obviously a task she had performed many times and one that brought her comfort.

Devon had to admit to himself that he had avoided listening to her thoughts or reaching through their link for fear of what he would hear, but listening to her sing and watching her do something she enjoyed made him drop his guard and slowly travel into his mate's mind. It wasn't surprising to him that she was reasoning through what had happened. For the most part, she was giving him the benefit of the doubt, which made him feel just a little more like shit than he had before. Saying a real quick prayer, he closed the distance between them and touched her shoulder.

Anya spun around and speared him with a look that made him second guess his decision to mend fences, but Devon knew it was now or never. "I'm so sorry for what I said and how I acted. If you'll give me a chance, I really want to explain my actions."

Seconds ticked by as his mate simply stood and stared. He had stopped listening to her thoughts right before he began speaking and refused to invade her privacy any more than he already had, leaving him to read the emotions as they flashed through her eyes. Most of them were nothing he ever wanted to see again and he chastised himself for putting them there. At least she was still standing there and hadn't smacked him in the face, something he counted as a blessing. He pressed on. "You know we've been digging through the wreckage of that damned mansion for almost four days with no sign of Andrew. I'm not sure I explained how strong Rian's ability to connect with other dragons is, but he's super powerful, and if anyone can sense that fucking traitor, then it'll be him. Well, today he felt him. It was subtle, almost like a whisper, but it gave us a starting point instead of just digging around aimlessly like we have been.

"Aaron, Aidan, and I grabbed every piece of equipment we could and got about ten feet down when Rian got a serious ping on his radar. I'm sure having the traitor's brothers around helped, but anyway, this time Rian heard a specific thought, one that has us all a bit jumpy. The stupid son of a bitch is about to dig his way out and we have no idea which way he is heading, but he is planning something big as revenge."

He had Anya's attention. She was listening to his explanation and in that moment, it was as much as he could hope for. She had taken off her gardening gloves and had her hands folded in front of her body, acting as a barrier between them. She had yet to smile, but she also hadn't told him to go to hell. *Put one in the win column.*

"I tried to reach you through mindspeak but when you didn't answer, I figured you were resting, but Royce said he couldn't reach Kyra either. Then Aidan said Grace had said you two left together earlier in the day and still weren't back. I have to admit I kinda lost my mind."

"Kinda? Yeah. Kinda." Was all she said and each word was punctuated with a roll of her eyes.

"Roy and I raced back to the lair, saw the notes you and Kyra had left, and took to the skies. It wasn't until we were already in the air that I realized Aaron and Aidan were with us."

He stopped and thought about his next words very carefully. "I'm sorry, really sorry, Anya. I know that doesn't fix what I did. I know it's happened before and I can't promise it won't happen again. Heaven knows we've been together less than a week and I've already had to apologize three times for the same damn thing, but I swear on my life, I'm trying to give you the space and independence that you need. And I'd like to tell you that it will get better after Andrew is caught, but I won't lie to you. All I can promise is to try to respect your wishes and most definitely not make an ass out of myself again.

"Hell, ask any of my brethren. I bet none of them can remember the last time they even heard me raise my voice. They all call me the 'Zen One', but since you came into my life, the calm flew out the window. I'm restless when you are not by my side, I spend every minute we're apart wondering what you're doing and praying that you're safe. The guys even made me come home the other night because my thoughts were bleeding through my link with them. Know how long it's been since that happened?" She shook her head right away and he had to hold back his smile when her hands fell to her sides.

"At least a hundred years ago, and it's all because of you, *mo ghra'.*" He took a step forward and was rewarded with a tiny grin, but then she raised her hand and placed her palm flat against his chest.

"I know you're trying, Devon. Believe it or not, I can feel it right here." She laid her free hand over her heart. "But that does not change the fact that you barged into *my home* and yelled at *me* for being there. Not only is that about the dumbest thing I've ever heard of, it's humiliating. It's like you don't trust me to take care of myself or think I'm incapable. Well, I've got news for you, mister, I've been doing it for a long time and I have no plans of stopping any time soon. I may not be a witch or a dragon or anything but a simple human, but my parents taught me a thing or two, and aside from your crazy ass traitor and his stupid wizards, I've done a damn fine job of staying out of trouble."

To emphasize her point, Anya propped her hands on her hips and raised one eyebrow, and he could tell from her stare she was daring him to say otherwise.

A knock on the door had them both calling, "Yes?" and then chuckling as Kyra walked in.

"Sorry to interrupt, but Jed and Dot are out here and we have stalled them as long as we can. Dot felt the magic in the air and saw the shadows, so they came over to meet your 'beau'." She made air quotes with her fingers and winked when she said beau, which caused Anya to giggle.

He looked at her and before he could ask she explained, "Jed and Dot were my parents' oldest friends and part of their coven, not to mention they take care of the house and farm since Mom and Dad died. They've always been like another set of parents. We better get out there and meet them before they end up in here with us."

Anya reached down and grabbed his hand as they headed for the door. She hung back when Kyra exited and turned on her heel, looked him square in the eye, and whispered, "This discussion is far from over."

Devon groaned a little inside but realized she was still holding his hand as they made their way into the waning sunlight. He was further encouraged when she introduced him to the older couple as her fiancé. Everything seemed to be going fine until he heard Royce's voice in his head. *"This mating shit ain't easy, is it Bro?"*

"There's the understatement of the year."

His older brethren's laugh echoed in his head just as Jed said, "You better take good care of our little one, I know a spell that…"

"None of that, Jedidiah," his wife scolded and swatted his arm as everyone else howled with laughter.

CHAPTER EIGHT

It had been two days since her fateful trip to the farm, and two days since what Anya was calling the 'defining moment' in their relationship had occurred. Fighting with Devon sucked and Anya knew she had overreacted, but dammit, she was not going to be ordered around by anyone. No matter how sexy he was or that he made her wet and needy by just being near.

Kyndel, Grace, Sam, and Kyra had commiserated while they celebrated her last night of freedom. They all had tales about the pigheadedness of dragons as mates, especially Kyra, whose story made Anya's look like a schoolyard spat. Luckily, each had attested to the fact that it had all been worth it. Their words were sweet, but it was the love she heard in their voices and the genuine affection she saw when the couples were together that gave her hope.

She admitted that she'd never really had a serious boyfriend, swearing the girls to secrecy and then almost fell out of her chair when they all admitted to the same thing. There had been guys she'd dated and guys that were friends, but none she ever wanted to spend any real time with and none that made her feel the way Devon made her feel or made her think of forever. She had felt so reassured when every single one of the others nodded in agreement.

She remembered how her mom had always said she was too stubborn and too headstrong for any ordinary man. *If only you knew how right you were Mom.* But then again, maybe her mom did. It wouldn't surprise Anya at all if Sadie Sloane had been wise to Destiny's plan for her adopted daughter all along. It would be just like her mom to keep someone as special as Devon a secret from her until she was ready.

To his credit, since his fit of temper, Devon had been trying really hard to see her side of things. He didn't even freak out when she, Grace, and the others went into town to pick up something special for her to wear on her mating night. They all laughed when they spotted Jace and Liam following them, but it did not diminish the fact that Devon was trying.

Siobhan had been the greatest help of all. Not only had she explained the mating ceremony and more of the dragon culture, but she had given valuable insight into the inner workings of her son. Anya laughed when the healer told the story of her mate, Gareth, on the day Devon was born. She chuckled as she remembered Siobhan's words. "Because I am a healer, I thought we could forego all the craziness that usually went along with the birth of a dragon shifter. History dictated I would have a male, which has been the way of our people for almost a thousand years, hence the reason a perfect match from the human race is created for every dragon. The birth of any dragon shifter was and still is highly celebrated, but the pomp and ceremony surrounding the birth of a Guardsman's child goes far beyond outrageous. I had let my mate know I wanted no part of it, only me, Gareth, and our child were to be present for the birth. It was decided after much debate and many arguments that we would go to the Healing Caves when I was ready to deliver, along with *one* of the other healers, and return to the lair after the birth.

"I did not take my mate's inability to keep *anything* from his brethren into account. Nor did I realize the lengths he would go to make sure I was safe. Sometime between when my labor started and the birth of our son, Gareth had called four more healers and several of their mates to assist with the birth. From one contraction to the next I was surrounded by a team of people and a beaming father-to-be. He had also shared the blessed event with *one* of the men on his Force, who then shared it with his mate and her with another. By the time my beautiful baby boy made his screaming presence into the world, a full-fledged party was underway just outside the entrance to the cave.

"As I came back to me senses, the sounds of the celebration reached the back of the cave. I was much too happy to be upset. I had an amazing mate, a healthy baby, and a family that wanted nothing more than to celebrate a new member of our clan.

"I tell you all of this, my dear Anya, not to say that you should not make your wishes known or stand up for yourself, especially where my son is concerned, but to illustrate an important ingredient for your future sanity. Dragon shifters are warriors…leaders…an entire breed that was created with the sole purpose of fighting evil in the world, protecting those in need, and ensuring the survival of their race. The weight of their existence can cloud their judgment, making them act irrationally, especially where the One that holds their heart is concerned.

"I can promise that his overbearing tendencies will lessen the longer you are together, but they will never completely go away, and if you or your children are in danger, the beast within our Devon will roar and defend you all to his dying breath. His dragon simply will not allow him to hang back and think of your feelings or wishes, it will demand he act and do so quickly."

Anya's musings were cut short by a knock at the door. There, standing just outside her bedroom door were Sam and Sydney, holding a large, light grey gift box bound with shimmering pearlescent ribbon and a beautiful matching bow. Syd danced on tippy toes and squealed, "Happy Mating Day! We brought a present for you, Anya, and you're gonna love it!"

"Come on in. Let's see what it is."

She moved to the side while they entered, Sydney dancing all the way to the bed, singing, "Anya's getting mated" at the top of her lungs to the tune of Ring Around the Rosie. Sam laid the box on her bed and Sydney climbed up beside it, bouncing on her knees and switching to an "Open it. Open it" chant. The child continued as Anya carefully untied the bow, lifted the lid, and stood speechless, completely overwhelmed by the gorgeous gossamer gown delicately folded within. With shaking hands, she lifted the gift card with her name perfectly scripted across the front. The world around her slipped away as she read the words inside…*Today we begin our lives together. Now…always…forever, Devon.*

Lifting the garment from the box, Anya marveled at the attention to detail and the absolute beauty she held in her hands. The fabric shimmered in the sunlight. The same sunlight that highlighted the opalescent flames exquisitely embroidered in a sporadic pattern the full length of the skirt. She spun towards the full length mirror, holding the dress in front of her, stunned at her reflection. It had thin, white satin straps delicately sewn into a sweetheart neckline with a corset type bodice she was sure would show off her full bust to perfection. *Damn man truly thinks of everything.*

The vision before her seemed unreal. There had never been a time she could remember thinking of herself as pretty. Cute, maybe…cleans up nice, probably…never pretty. But standing there holding what would be her wedding dress, her makeup expertly done, and her hair in a loose twist secured with the combs that had been her mom's, wavy tendrils hanging loosely around her face and cascading down her back, she felt truly beautiful.

"Anya, you look like a princess," Sydney squealed behind her.

"You are gorgeous, girl. Now, let's get you into that pretty frock and on your way to the ceremony. I know a very nervous dragon that can't wait to see you," Sam agreed, grinning.

Reality set in as Sam zipped her into her dress and wrapped the thick pearlescent satin ribbon around her waist. It was as if her life had been pulled from one of the books she'd read as a child. She was the princess that had been saved by her knight in shining armor. He had battled the forces of evil to bring her back to life and they were going to live happily ever after. The only difference was her knight was also the dragon, and that plot twist was just fine with her.

One quick look in the mirror and a swipe of lip gloss was all she had time for before Sydney announced, "Jace and Liam are here."

Walking down the hall, she accepted hugs and wishes from all the girls. Siobhan had told her no one but the Elders, Devon's Force, Devon, and she were allowed at the mating ceremony, but she knew her friends were getting ready for the party following their nuptials.

Just as Sydney had said, the younger Guardsmen stood right outside the front door in full dress uniform. They looked like they had stepped right out of a Knights of the Round Table movie, which she guessed made sense based on their heritage. Black pants tucked into the top of their polished knee-high black boots and a long-sleeved black undershirt gave the perfect backdrop for the shining white of their surcoats. She was amazed by the almost exact match to the color of Devon's dragon's scales. The fabric even had an opalescent glow in the waning light of the sun. Black and gold braiding trimmed the top and sides, but it was the dragon in the throes of battle embroidered on the front that made their uniforms complete.

Both turned toward the walk when they saw her, putting their arms out for her to grasp. Once she was settled between them, they escorted her down the steps and toward three majestic Palominos, not unlike the ones she had helped her pops train for most of her life. Tears filled her eyes at the continued thoughtfulness of her mate, and the stunning way flowers had been woven into each horse's mane and around the reins. Even the blankets under their saddles matched the men's surcoats.

The young men helped Anya onto the most decorated of the horses and stood by while she got situated to ride side saddle before climbing upon their own mounts. Their ride to the ceremony took them through the woods behind Siobhan's home and past the home she would share with Devon. Each tree along their path was wrapped with a twinkling white ribbon and a huge white bow holding a spray of three large white Calla Lilies. It was one of the most striking things she had ever seen.

As they exited the trees, another young man, also in dress uniform, stood holding the largest bouquet of white roses she had ever seen. Her horse slowed, as if the animal knew something she didn't, and then she heard the young Guardsman communicating with her mount mind-to-mind. He approached with a huge smile, handed her the flowers and bowed before returning to his post. The card attached read…*Only a few minutes and you will be mine…now…always…forever, Devon.* She sat still for only a moment and then she, Jace, and Liam continued on their way.

They circled a small lake and stopped at the base of the mountain on the other side. Jace turned, and for the first time during their journey spoke. "Devon said you were an expert rider, I just want to make sure you can maneuver the trail to the first ledge."

Anya's eyes followed his gesture to a narrow path carved into the side of the rock and she nodded. "Not a problem. Lead the way."

Grinning, Jace turned forward in his saddle, made a clicking noise with his mouth to signal the horses, and led the way up the side of the mountain. The trip was slow but extraordinarily beautiful. Not only was the natural scenery breathtaking, but large white bows with white Calla Lilies that matched those from the path were attached to vines and outcroppings that sporadically grew along their trek. It felt like a dream.

They stopped on a landing that led to the mouth of a huge cave. Moving faster than her eyes could follow, Jace dismounted and was at her side to help her down while Liam took the reins and kept the horse still. Once her bare feet touched the white patterned carpet strewn with red and white rose petals, the young Guardsmen escorted her to the mouth of the cavern. Her hands slid from their arms and Jace presented her with her bouquet. Once the flowers were secure in her arm, he and Liam took their positions on either side of the entrance.

She took a few steps and stopped, overcome by the splendor of one of the most magnificent places she had ever seen. The raw power of the cave spoke to Anya. She listened with her heightened senses to the story it had to tell. It was remarkable that the longer she spent with Devon and his clan, the more acute normal everyday things like hearing became.

The minerals, rocks, and gems embedded in the walls and ceiling glittered and glimmered in the light of the many candles hanging in sconces throughout the cave. There were huge stalactites hanging from the ceiling and stalagmites rising from the floor that seemed to be standing guard, protecting the sanctity of a place she could feel held great significance to the dragons, and therefore to her. Following the white carpet, she made her way deeper into the cavern and soon heard the sound of water flowing and gently splashing into what she imagined to be a pool.

Only a few feet ahead, Anya saw an entrance brightened by several candelabras and knew it was where she was to go. Stepping over the threshold, she saw the stream she had heard flowing down the wall, the water tinkling like little bells as it made its way into the lagoon covered with white water lilies. She looked around the grotto at the huge white Grecian planters filled with bunches of the enormous white roses and flowers from lily of the valley plants. A raised platform stood to the side of the pool with four chairs loosely resembling thrones upon it and a circle with an archway strewn with white ribbons and flowers in the center.

She spotted a small white chair to the side of the platform, remembered what Siobhan had told her, and walked to it. As soon as she was seated, the Elders Devon had introduced her to a few days ago appeared on the platform, reminding her how quickly dragon shifters could move, even the older ones. The Head Elder, Carrick, gave her a nod while the others smiled serenely in her direction. A rustling to the right drew her attention as the men of Devon's Force filed out, dressed to the nines in surcoats that she knew matched the color of each man's dragon.

Rayne was at the head of the line, standing tall and proud in the reddest of reds, looking every bit the Commander he was. Then came Royce, whose beautiful royal blue surcoat with green accents truly fit the man and the beast. Next, Aaron and Aidan, dressed in a silvery gray that shined in the waning light, stood tall and dignified. Aaron winked and grinned, making her giggle just a bit. Lance was at the end of the line in a stunning golden surcoat that she had to imagine depicted his beast perfectly.

The butterflies in her stomach were throwing a serious party as silence filled the chamber and just when she was sure she would faint, Devon appeared from the same direction the others had come. He smiled from ear to ear, looked better than a man had a right to, and winked when he took his place in front of the other Guardsmen. Anya stood, placed her flowers on her chair, and waited. Only the sound of Devon's voice in her head kept her from hyperventilating…*You look absolutely gorgeous…*

~~*~*~*~*~*

Devon watched Anya across the chamber, both man and beast ready to have her as theirs for all time. She looked like a goddess in the gown he had commissioned. It fit her like a glove, accentuating all her attributes and making his mouth water with the need to taste every inch of her luscious body. He saw on her face and heard in her thoughts how much she enjoyed all his preparations on her most special of days. When he looked into her eyes, he felt the last piece of the puzzle that was his life click into place. The electricity that was always present when they were together snapped to life and he watched her eyes widen in recognition of their magical connection.

He held her eyes as he strode towards her, falling more in love with every step. Stopping in front of her, the scent of sea and sand filled his senses and wrapped around him, making his dragon chuff loud and long in his head. Taking her hands in his, he led Anya to the center of the Sacred Circle and watched as she held her breath. *"Breathe* mo ghra'*, just breathe,"* he whispered into her mind and was rewarded a stunning smile.

Carrick cleared his throat and his voice rang out loud and clear through the chamber. "Long ago, when knights and dragons fought side by side for King and Country, it became apparent that dragon kin was no longer safe from those that would expose and destroy them. They sought to join with the knights that had fought so valiantly by their sides for centuries. Thus, through magic and the will of both dragon and knight, the Golden Fire Clan of the Dragon Shifters became a reality. It was through the joining of many different clans that we have become the strong and powerful Clan we are today.

"We are here at the Healing Caves, a place long blessed by our ancestors that went before us, to honor what the Universe put into place all those many years ago. To acknowledge and bless the mating of Devon Reid Walsh to the one the Universe made for him, Anya Brynne Sloane. Will those seeking to witness this union please step forward?"

From their place next to the Elders, the men his heart knew as brothers stepped forward. These men had trained with him, fought with him, bled with him, and now shared the happiest moment of his life. They knelt as one and bowed their heads. Rayne then stood and addressed the Elders. "We, the five of the MacLendon Force, wish to witness and offer our blessing to the union of these two souls, two halves of the same whole. May they live long, fight hard, love harder, and produce many young to flourish in this world when their souls have gone to the Heavens." He knelt next to his men and bowed his head once again.

Carrick began again, "Your witness and blessing have been acknowledged and accepted MacLendon Force." The Guardsmen stood and stepped back to their original position.

Only the sound of the water flowing into the grotto could be heard as he stood staring into the eyes of his very own angel. Thoughts of her body against his flooded his mind until he was sure no amount of self-control would keep him from taking Anya in his arms and running to their home.

Carrick began again, "The white dragons are warriors born of the sun *and* the moon. The Universe shines favorably on all of Her winged warriors, but the ones born with white scales hold both the favor of the day and of the night. They are a powerful sign of purity and wisdom combined with tremendous spiritual energy. Their calm exterior hides the heart of the beast and allows them to take those that oppose them by surprise. Loyalty and strength of will are their two greatest attributes and they use those to protect all they hold dear. Love and devotion run deep within those with white scales and grows deeper as the years pass. To mate a white dragon means to accept all that they are, and honor the power shared between mates.

"Now is the time of the marking. May the Universe continue to bless you and yours all of your days." The sounds of the others exiting the chamber only served as background noise to the beating of their two hearts as one. Devon had no idea how long he stood looking at his magnificent mate, but he knew with every fiber of his being there would never be a day he would not welcome the sight.

He felt his eyes begin to glow and saw a heat that was more than passion reflected in Anya's gorgeous green eyes. Devon lowered his mouth to hers, and as their lips touched whispered, "*Ta' mo chroi istigh ionat*," into her mind. The experience was unlike any other, a flame ignited in his heart and spread throughout his body, filling every cell with the bond only true mates share.

Anya broke their kiss with a hiss, a twinge to his neck telling him that they were being marked by the Universe. "No worries, *mo chroi'*, it's only the mating mark."

He lowered his mouth to her neck, running the tip of his tongue along the lines of the double flames signifying their bond, to ease the sting. Anya's hands grabbed his head, holding him in place, moaning his name. Her body arched into his, causing his already hard cock to rub against the cradle of her stomach.

With a reluctant groan, Devon pulled back from his mate, sure to keep her body against his. He watched as her eyes flew open, full of fire, passion and questions, "What…"

"I know, *a mhuirnin,* there's nothing more I want to do than disappear with you for a year or two, all alone…somewhere secluded…." He kissed her forehead and sighed, "But we have a party full of people waiting just below."

She pretended to pout, the sight more than he could stand. His lips once again found hers and he poured all they were together into that small joining, making promises of what was to come. Their bond was complete. They were connected soul to soul, heart to heart, destiny to destiny for all their days on the Earth and all those after.

Pulling back once again, Devon set Anya an arm's length away to help him resist the temptation she would always be and grinned as she struggled to open her eyes. Even heavy-lidded, he was humbled by all he saw shining back at him, knowing there was *absolutely nothing* he would not do for this one woman…*his woman.*

The mark on her wrist rippled under his fingertips. His dragon tattoo and the beast within responded in kind and his mating mark pulsed with the power of their bond. Anya gasped and her pupils dilated. "What was that?"

"That was us, *mo ghra'*. Just us," he chuckled and turned, pulling his mate to his side.

Walking out of the cave, a voice Devon thought lost to him forever floated through his mind, *"She's a keeper, son. Blessings o' thuas."*

"Thanks, Dad." was all that came out as emotion gripped his heart.

~~*~*~*~*~*

The trip down the mountain in Devon's lap atop his handsome filly felt like a dream. She kept touching the mating mark as it pulsed on her neck and looking at the one on her mate. It was a truly surreal experience. She had been able to hear his thoughts and he hers from the very beginning, even when she was in a coma. There had even been times when they could feel each other's emotions, but after the kiss that damn near fried every brain cell in her mind, it was as if they shared *everything…they were one*. Then she remembered Siobhan's words. "It is written in our holy book that *'When the two halves of the same whole meet, there will be instant recognition. Their souls will merge and only then will the dragon shifter know complete peace, they will have found their true home. It will be as if the time before they met does not exist. All that matters is that they become one in body, mind, and soul.'*

She most definitely felt the 'one in body, mind, and soul' thing, but it was *her* that had found her true home, been saved from a life of loneliness by her very own dragon. Devon pulled her close, causing goose bumps to rise when he whispered, "We saved each other, *mo chroí'*."

She was sure her heart would burst from the emotion she felt pouring from the amazing man holding her in his arms. The horse slowed and she followed Devon's gaze to find all of their friends, and some she was beginning to think of as family, gathered around the lake ready for a serious party. Tents, chairs, decorations, and a band she recognized as werepanthers began to play as soon as Devon dismounted, still holding her close.

The party-goers formed two lines facing one another in a boy-girl fashion and when Devon set her at the entrance to their receiving line. The Guardsmen, all of them, even the Blue Thunder Clan, lifted their swords making an archway for them to walk under. It was exactly backwards from every wedding she had ever attended and made all the more special for it. At the end of the line stood Siobhan and Carrick, and as the couple neared, the two Elders bowed their heads. Anya could hear the older couple blessing their union. Tears filled her eyes at the outpouring of affection she felt from everyone in attendance. She was no longer an orphan, she had truly found her family.

Her happy tears turned to giggles when Max stepped right in front of them, bowed, and asked for a dance. Devon growled low in his throat, quickly informing the King that *he* had the first dance. *"And every one after that,"* she heard him add in his mind. Max smiled his 'cat that ate the canary' grin, winked, and told her he would catch up with her later.

Kyndel and Grace quickly redirected them to the huge four tier cake at the center of the festivities. Anya wasn't surprised to find Sydney standing close by eyeing the gorgeous confection, and laughed when the child asked, "Are you gonna cut it now? My tummy is dying to taste it."

"You got it, Syd. We'll cut it right now," Devon quickly answered.

Sam appeared with a pearl handled knife and cake server engraved with DW and AW enclosed in an elegant heart. Leaning close, the young doctor whispered, "We made it as much like a regular wedding reception as we could. Now that there are more of us, it was easy to convince the guys."

"Yeah, right, like we had a choice," Lance scoffed from behind his mate, love evident in his every word.

Anya looked up to see Grace, and Kyra approaching. She was immediately drawn into a group hug as all the girls descended, squealing, "Welcome to the family," in unison.

Kyra whispered close to her ear, "The spell lifted while you were in the cave. Let me know when you feel any changes."

The next few hours were a blur of well wishes and partying until she thought she might collapse. She was glad to see Dr. Gallagher, Charlie as she was instructed to call her, and to finally be able to thank her for her excellent care during her time in the hospital.

Max did finally commandeer her for a spin around the dance floor, much to her mate's chagrin and to the laughs of the werepanthers in attendance. Before she could make it back to Devon's side, Aaron swooped in, asking to dance with the 'bride'. She smiled at his use of a very human word and agreed.

The dance had barely begun when he asked, "Are you happy, Anya?"

"Happier than I've ever been. Why do you ask?"

"It's important to Devon and that makes it important to me." She felt the honesty and conviction in every word he spoke.

"You know him really well, huh?"

"Yeah," he chuckled. "You could say that. Why?"

She looked away, wondering if she should ask what she really wanted to know and then deciding *What the hell?* and went for it. "Do you think *I* make *him* happy?"

Aaron threw back his head and laughed so loud some of the guest turned and stared before answering. "Honey, if he were any happier, he'd have to be two people. He *absolutely adores* you. I have never seen him happier...*ever*...and I've known his ugly mug for a helluva lotta years."

She couldn't help the giggle that bubbled over and hugged his neck. "Thank you so much," she whispered before pulling back.

"Hey, hey, hey, what the hell's going on over here," Devon asked, pretending to be angry.

"I'm trying to steal your mate and there's not a damn thing you can do about it," Aaron joked as he danced Anya a few steps from Devon, winking for her to play along.

Following Aaron's footwork, Anya stepped a tiny bit closer, right before an arm slid around her back and slipped between she and her dance partner. The grin on Aaron's face said he had achieved exactly what he intended...*to drive Devon crazy*.

Anya gasped as she was lifted into the air and twirled down Devon's arm until she fell flush against his body. Breathless, she looked into his glowing grey eyes and recognized both the man and beast whose souls completed her own. He spun her with the finesse of Fred Astaire, weaving a spell as the tune the band played provided the perfect score. Devon's hands moved expertly over her body, leaving a trail of heat and desire until Anya was sure she would be but a pile of ash in his hands.

Their erotic dance of love and seduction continued, her desire building higher as the music's sensual beat kept time. Devon kissed along the bare skin of her shoulder, paying special attention to his mark, the one that told the world she was his. With lips and tongue he tasted his way to her ear, nipping at her lobe before kissing away the sting.

His chest rumbled under her hands as the rolling timbre of his deep baritone voice sang one of her favorite songs in the language of his ancestors, the words stoking the fire burning in her lust-addled mind in English, *"I want you forever, forever and always. Through the good and the bad and the ugly..."* It was one of the songs she had always hoped would be played at her wedding.

She felt his arousal stiffen against her stomach, taking comfort in the fact that he was as lost to their hunger as she. Anya rolled her hips in time with his, teasing him with her body, promising all her love. One song ended and another began just as they reached the very edge of the party.

There, hidden in the shadows, he lifted his head and stared deep into her eyes. The corner of his mouth lifted in a grin and when he spoke, his voice was deep with desire. "You need to be careful, *mo chroi'*, a newly mated dragon can be a dangerous creature."

She batted her eyes and crooned, "Oh, yeah?"

"Oh yeah," he growled, lifting her into his arms and speeding away from their guests. The trees were a blur in her peripheral vision as they sped down the path she had earlier ridden to their mating ceremony. The freedom of traveling at the enhanced speed of a dragon shifter was exhilarating. What should have taken almost a half hour was over in mere minutes. She felt Devon slow and then stop completely. Anya turned her head and saw the beautiful home she knew to be his. "Ours...*m'fhiorghra'*, always ours," he breathed, closing the distance between them. When he kissed her deeply and completely, the bond they already shared strengthened and the pieces of her heart she once thought lost forever came together.

She shifted in his arms trying to deepen the kiss, but instead of responding, Devon pulled back, grinning as she moaned at the loss. "I hear there is a human custom where the man carries his mate over the threshold."

"Yes...there is."

Slowly and deliberately, Devon once again lowered his lips towards hers. Excitement coursed through her veins, but he stopped right before they touched and growled low in his throat. "Then we are going to do this right."

He kissed her like a man possessed, flooding her with an undying love that both excited and humbled Anya. In the background, she heard the door slam, followed by the pounding of his footsteps as he tore through the house. All thought flew from her mind. The antique lace that lined the bodice of her gown teased her hardened, sensitive nipples and she felt her panties dampen as her arousal soared.

She felt the softness of down at her back and the hardness of her mate at her front as Devon settled on top of her. She felt him holding back most of his weight, always thinking of her comfort first. Thankfully, her gown was strategically slit to the thigh on both sides, accommodating her legs as they wound around his waist. They pulled apart, panting as if they'd run for miles.

Devon rolled his hips, effectively holding her body captive while his heated gaze enthralled and mesmerized. His hands worked their way from her hips, across her ribs, resting lightly at the sides of her breasts, his thumbs landing so closely to her nipples that she arched her back to force his touch. Smirking at her response, he continued torturing her, branding her until he reached the straps of her gown. Slowly inching them down, his smile grew, and the look of mischief joined the fire in his eyes.

Anya lifted her head, trying to once again capture his lips, but Devon moved quicker than she could track. Looming over her, he growled. "I have never wanted anything as much as I want you now."

"Then have me, Mr. Walsh. Have me and never let me go."

~~*~*~*~*~*

He had been digging continuously since burying John. If his inner clock was correct, it had been almost three days. The only time he stopped was to grab a bottle of water and a protein bar, of which he had none left. There would be no sleep until he reached daylight.

Andrew had forgotten the sheer power that came from the dragon within and although his beast had only partially returned, he was using every ounce of its incomparable force to claw his way to freedom. The stones jagged edges tore at his skin and dug into his knees through the denim of his jeans. His lungs filled with dust and soot the deeper he dug into the wall of rubble, the need for vengeance fueling his every movement. When he thought he couldn't pick up one more rock, the image of John's lifeless body, bloody and broken by the actions of those fucking Guardsmen, spurred him to continue.

When that wasn't enough, he only had to think of the years of torture at the hands of evil wizards he had endured all because his brother, the one he trusted more than any other, had left him for dead. He even thought of the years with the hunters and vowed to include them in his scheme. Visions of what he had planned for the dragons had evolved until he was finally prepared to exact his revenge. Andrew had cursed the Universe and Fate for what they had put him through, but understood it had all been part of his Destiny. Had he not suffered all that he had, he might never have been strong enough to do what had to be done.

There were times he would get a flicker of recognition, one where his dragon felt the call of another. But as quickly as those came, they disappeared, only serving to let him know the bastards were close and obviously still searching for him. Several hours earlier he had felt one such tremor and had halted his excavation to avoid detection. When his senses calmed and he felt nothing else but the isolation of his captivity, he began again.

Mindlessly throwing one rock after another over his shoulder, he had no idea how long the sounds of crickets had been filtering into the tunnel before he recognized them for what they were…the sounds of freedom. Opening his senses, he felt the movement of the trees and even heard the faint sound of a deer's heartbeat in the distance. His mind and body filled with a renewed vigor at the prospect of escape and his hands dug deeper while his body struggled to work harder than he ever imagined possible.

Summoning every ounce of his remaining strength, Andrew pushed his fingers between an unusually large boulder and the fallen beams and rock wall of the tunnel where it had become wedged. He felt the skin peel away from the flesh of his fingers, his knuckles leaving a lasting imprint in the stone, but still he pressed on, sure that freedom was just a few feet away.

Andrew's feet, shoulder width apart, dug into the concrete floor as the slab remained stuck tight where it had fallen during the blast. Bending his knees, he took a huge breath, counted to three, and pulled with all he was. The boulder trembled under his grasp, the edges began to crack, and in one swift move the rock dislodged. The cool night air rushed in as he was forced to throw it over his shoulder or be crushed under its weight.

Stumbling to freedom, he all but crawled to the edge of a field, the stalks of wheat long past harvest serving as cover. Leaning against one of the few remaining fence posts, he clutched the ancient volume John had protected with his life, filled his lungs with fresh air, and began plotting his next move.

He looked back to all that remained of what he had called home, taking in the total devastation. "Those fucking dragons aren't gonna know what hit them," he growled to anyone or anything within the sound of his voice.

CHAPTER NINE

Anya's words were music to his ears and the only invitation he or his dragon needed. Their mate wanted to be loved and they were both of a mind to give her anything her heart...*and body,* desired. Wanting their first time as an officially mated couple to last as long as he could stand, Devon kissed the column of her neck, nipped across the apex of her shoulder, and dragged the tiny satin strap of her gown down her arm with his teeth. Kissing his way back to her mouth, marking every inch of her as his and his alone, he kissed her breathless and then repeated his efforts on her other shoulder.

The more he tasted the more Anya panted, making her breasts a temptation he could no longer resist. Kissing across the neckline of her dress, letting his tongue dip under the satin ribbing to taste the decadent flesh made his mate moan with pleasure and push into his touch. He pulled the zipper at her side down, kissing every inch of naked flesh as it became visible. Anya writhed under his ministrations, grabbing his head and trying to force it where she most wanted his touch. "Patience, *a chumann*. I have a lot of time to make up for."

She groaned her disapproval as he continued his slow perusal. His mouth watered as he peeled away the cloth of her bodice revealing the voluptuous breasts and berry-colored nipples begging for his mouth. Licking across first one and then the other, he was rewarded with an, "Oh Heavens, Devon...*please...*"

Loving her responsiveness, he took the nipple between his lips, sucking and nipping until Anya bowed her back, holding him to her chest and mewling his name. His hand kneaded the other breast, working her nipple to an even harder point between his thumb and forefinger.

The scent of her arousal filled the room with the tantalizing aroma of the beach on a summer day. His dragon pushed and roared in his head, demanding he continue undressing their beautiful mate, both man and beast driven to taste her nectar. Releasing her breast with a loud pop, Devon latched onto the other, working her dress farther down her body and over her beautifully rounded hips. His fingers stilled as he felt the lace of her underwear.

His mouth moved from her nipple, kissing the valley between her breasts, leaving a trail of heat and seduction down her body, tasting and marking every inch he could reach. He reached the silk of her panties and inhaled long and deep, immersing himself in Anya's wonderfully unique scent. Unable to resist any longer, he knelt between her thighs, all but tearing the gown from her body and throwing the offending material over his shoulder as soon as her feet slipped free. Her panties were the next to go, leaving her gloriously naked and open to do with as he pleased.

Anya was a feast for the eyes when clothed, but naked she was absolutely stunning. As slowly as his growing need would allow, his eyes worked their way from the deep red of the polish that covered her toes, up her shapely legs that very soon would be wrapped around as many parts of his body as he could get them, to her soft thighs he could not wait to have pillowing his head. Her rounded stomach told him she was a real woman, not some little girl without curves, curves that fueled his wild imagination and begged to be kissed over and over again.

"Devon?" His name on her lips drew his gaze.

"Yes, *mo chroí'*?" he crooned, massaging up and down her thighs, sure to brush the outer lips of her pussy on every pass and enjoying that her hips jumped at every touch.

"Devon...I need..." She gasped, unable to complete her thought as his index finger ran up and down her slit, already wet with the proof of her arousal.

"What is it you need, my love?" He teased, enjoying the sight as her breathing grew even more ragged and she found it hard to hold still. Devon took in the vision of Anya in the throes of passion, her head thrown back, eyes closed tight, mouth open as she called his name like a mantra and knew he had glimpsed heaven.

"I...oh God, yes..." She wailed as he pushed his finger through her folds and teased the opening, her juices wetting his hand. Her pussy contracted around the tip of his finger, attempting to pull his digit into her warm wet passage. Adding another finger, he began gliding them in and out, her honey providing the perfect lubrication. His thumb drew lazy circles around her swollen clit while his fingers continued to work her arousal higher. Every few swipes he would bend the tips of his fingers to gently brush the very special bundle of nerves that made his mate moan in pleasure.

Needing to taste her more than he needed his next breath, he quickly removed his fingers, and before she could whine at the loss, drove his tongue into her pussy as far as he could reach. Her taste exploded on his tongue, flashes of light bursting before his eyes. He devoured Anya like a man possessed, grabbing every drop of the nectar that flowed from her. She tasted of sunshine and honey and everything good and right in the world. The more his tongue moved within her, the more of her heavenly juices he took in until he felt drunk. Her hands pulled at his hair and he was sure he would be bald, but he simply couldn't care. Her legs came over his shoulders and closed around his head, making breathing almost impossible, and still he consumed all she had to give.

He felt her tense just a second before her orgasm overtook her. Screaming his name, she came on his tongue, filling his mouth until her juices ran down his chin. He continued to lick and tease as she came back to earth.

Looking up, he found her smiling a lazy smile and gazing at him through passion-filled eyes. His only thought was to keep that exact look on her face for the rest of their lives together.

His cock pulsed against the zipper of his black pants and it was then that he realized he was still completely dressed. Not wanting to leave his place between her thighs but needing to feel her skin against his, Devon stood in one fluid motion, threw off his surcoat and tore the black long-sleeved T-shirt over his head. His hands reached for the buckle of his belt, only to be knocked away by Anya's much smaller ones.

His eyes flew to hers. "What…?"

"It's my turn, Mr. Walsh," she winked. He had no idea how she had moved so quickly, but when she looked at him with such mischief in her eyes and a grin that was perfect parts sweetness and seduction on her lips, all thoughts of anything but being buried deep inside her fled from his mind.

Anya undid his belt and button and then slowly slid his zipper down, never once losing eye contact. She pressed her body to his, the heat of her skin against his better than anything he could have ever imagined. Her hardened nipples pushed against the muscles of his chest and he longed to taste them once again. With her thighs pressing against his, she turned their bodies until the bed bumped the back of his knees. His pants slid down his legs, held up by his knee-length boots. Devon started to bend to remove the offending footwear but Anya's hands on his shoulders stopped his progress

Shaking her head, she gently pushed until he sat on the side of the bed and then drove the breath from his lungs as she kneeled before him. The look she gave him as she glanced up through the fringe of her long dark lashes would have killed a lesser man. Needing to be inside her more than he needed his next breath, Devon grabbed her shoulders, trying to pull her onto his lap, boots be damned. But once again she shook her head, denying him the pleasure he so desperately needed. His mate had a plan, one she would not abandon, no matter how close to death she pushed him. *But you'll die with a smile on your face, old boy*, he chuckled to himself.

Lifting first one foot and then the other, Anya removed his boots and then his pants. She ran her nails, painted the same deep red as her toes, up his shins and across his thighs, stopping inches from his straining cock, eager to have her touch. Anya painted figure eights up and down his thigh, the friction of her touch against the smattering of short dark hair raised goose bumps all over his body while she wove her web of seduction.

Her thoughts were completely open to him, letting him feel as well as hear that *his* pleasure was her only focus. She wanted to please him in every way possible and mark him just as he did her. Anya wanted the world to know he was hers, every bit as much as she was his.

All thought fled from his mind when her lips closed around his cock and she sucked as much of his considerable length into her mouth as she could fit. He had been so lost to their combined thoughts, he had once again missed her movement. With slow precision that threatened all his years of hard fought patience, Anya worked him in and out of her mouth, her tongue massaging the pulsing vein that ran from base to tip.

His head fell back, his eyes slid shut, and his body shook with the sheer power it took to restrain himself from lifting her off the floor, throwing her on the bed, and burying himself deep inside her. The pleasure she gave him threatened his very sanity.

"*I can't hold on much longer,* mo ghra'. *You are killing me,*" he sent directly in her mind.

Her answering chuckle was maddening and incredibly sexy. "*I have faith you'll hold on, Dragon Man.*"

Any response he might have had was driven from his mind when she pulled her head back until only his mushroom head lay in the confines of her miraculous mouth. The tip of her tongue dipped into the slit at the very tip, causing his cock to jump and the muscles in his thighs to shake. She continued her exploration, licking all around the ridge while her hands closed around his balls and massaged. Her nails scratched against his ass, adding a whole new dimension to the web of love and seduction she wove.

In one swift motion Anya sucked him deep into her mouth, the tip of his cock touching the back of her throat. She hollowed her cheeks and swallowed while her hands worked the base of his shaft. He fell back, his arms keeping him semi-upright as his balls drew up tight and he released into her mouth, his shout echoing throughout the entire dwelling.

As he floated down from the best orgasm of his life, Anya's thoughts of undying love and complete adoration filled his heart and mind while she continued to work him across her sweet lips. Needing to feel her skin against his more than anything he reached forward, pulling his already hardening cock from her mouth and slid his hands under her arms.

Anya resisted, and almost quicker than his eyes could track, and with a strength he could only attribute to their incredible love, pushed him onto his back. Devon watched, totally captivated as she climbed over his body with the grace of a jungle cat. Her heavy breasts swung side to side, hypnotizing him with their movement, her hips following in the same seductive dance. As she came closer, he saw the evidence of her desire wetting her thighs and moved to roll them over so that he could ravish his mate to his heart's content.

Her hands on his chest and the look in her eyes stilled his movements. Anya licked her lips, her tongue wetting a trail across the top and then the bottom. Unable to look anywhere but her mouth that had just given him untold pleasure, he moaned in total bliss when she straddled his waist, his straining cock fitting perfectly between the cheeks of her beautiful bottom. With her eyes locked on his, she rocked her hips back and forth slowly, lifting ever so slightly, dragging his erection through her juices.

Devon growled low in his throat, fisted the comforter under his body and pulled. The sound of fabric tearing reached his ears at the same time Anya lifted up on her knees and gripped his cock, positioning it at her opening. As she slowly sank down, her walls quickly adjusted to his girth, fitting around him like a glove, and they sighed in unison, the sound of complete bliss. Their first joining as dragon shifter and mate was a thing of ultimate joy and untold beauty. Never had two people fit more perfectly together.

He resisted the urge to move, feeling through their connection how important it was to her to control their first coupling as what she called, man and wife. Her feminine walls contracted around him, making rational thought damn near impossible.

"You're going to kill me, *mo ghra'*," he rumbled, wheezing with the effort to find enough air.

"Can you think of a better way to go?" she chuckled and he was glad to hear she was as breathless as he.

Finally, just as Devon was sure he would lose his mind, Anya lifted, tightening around him as she raised high enough he feared falling from her tight, warm sex. But just before that happened, she descended, rolling her hips when she touched down. She started a rhythm, rising and falling, tightening and rolling, driving Devon and his dragon nearly insane.

His hands cupped her breasts, feeling the pebble of her hardened nipple against his palm as he squeezed her silky skin. The sight of his mate riding him with such wild abandon brought the beast to the forefront, the dragon would no longer be denied. Grabbing her waist, he rolled them until Anya's gorgeous green eyes were looking up at him. Her legs automatically tightened around him, her hands grabbing his shoulders for purchase as he began thrusting into her.

His control completely shattered as she met him thrust for thrust, the sounds of their flesh slapping against one another mixed with their harsh breaths filling the room. They worked each other roughly. Had he not been able to hear her thoughts, Devon would have feared hurting her, but Anya was just as lost to their passion as he, enjoying all they were together. The faster they moved, the louder she moaned. Her hands slipped from his shoulders and he felt the bite of her nails as they slid down his back. His dragon roared and the man arched his back, thrilled he had driven her to such heights.

Her pussy contracted tighter and tighter around him as his cock swelled and his balls again grew tight. They were both so very close that he would do whatever possible to see them release together. Reaching between their bodies, he rubbed his thumb against her clit. Anya's nails bit deeper into his back, she bowed up until only the weight of his body kept her from coming off the bed and shouted in an unknown language. She was frantic beneath him as he slammed into her, bumping her cervix on every thrust.

"Look at me, Anya," Devon sent directly into her mind as he lightly pinched her swollen nub between his thumb and forefinger. Anya's eyes snapped to his and together they bellowed their release to the Heavens. Her pussy contracted around him, holding him tight, milking him of his last drop. When she began to relax, he moved slowly in and out of her, wringing the last of her orgasm from deep within. He smiled as she shivered from his semi-erect cock rubbing against her sensitive walls.

Her eyes began to clear, a satisfied sparkle replacing the clouds of euphoria. His heart clenched in his chest and his dragon purred when she stretched beneath him, the lazy grin of contentment once again gracing her lips. Unwilling to leave the haven of his mate, he rolled to his side taking her with him until their heads rested comfortably on the pillows at the head of the bed.

Bits of torn fabric and down floated about as he positioned their bodies, causing Anya to giggle. "You ripped the comforter."

"And I'd do it again and again," he answered, taking her mouth with his while he reached under her pillow to retrieve the light grey, velvet drawstring bag he had placed there before the ceremony.

He pulled up and chuckled as her mouth followed his, trying to prolong their kiss. "Just one second, my love. I have a present for you."

Anya looked between them at the velvet bag and then back to his eyes before furrowing her brow and pouting. "But I don't have anything for you."

Devon pulled her close until he could feel her breath on his cheek and whispered, "I have everything I'll ever want or need, right here…*in you*."

Tears filled her eyes, but he knew from her thoughts they were what the other women had called happy tears. Scooting into a sitting position, he lifted Anya and set her across his thighs before handing her his gift.

She gently tipped the bag and Devon watched as the exquisite necklace Emma had created slipped into her hand. Her lips formed a perfect 'O' as she gasped in surprise and pleasure. "Oh my…Devon… This is beautiful. Is it made of *your* scale?"

"Yes, *mo ghra'*, it is. Emma designed it for our mating day. It is a one of a kind work of art…just like you." The same happy tears he had seen fill her eyes just a moment ago wet her cheeks as she threw her arms around him.

When she sat back, Devon took the necklace from her grasp and secured the gold chain around her neck. The tiny bell tinkled as she moved. "I love that sound," she crooned.

"Do you know what it means when a bell rings?"

She tipped her head and thought for a moment before answering, "No."

The bared column of her neck caught and held his attention as he spoke. "Every time," he kissed below her ear, "a dragon," he kissed her mating mark, "kisses his mate," he kissed her jaw, "a bell rings." He kissed the apple of her cheek. With the tip of his index finger under her chin, he turned her head until their noses all but touched and breathed, "And this little bell is gonna earn his keep," just before capturing her lips.

"*I love you, Devon,*" whispered across his mind.

"*And I love you, Anya Walsh, with all that I am and all I will ever be.*"

~*~*~*~*~*~*~*

Anya awoke suddenly, an excruciating pain radiating from deep within her core, shooting throughout her body and robbing her lungs of air. It felt like she was burning from the inside out. The mark on her wrist throbbed, and with every pulse new pain radiated up her arm. Every movement forced a whimper from her lips, even the sheet on her body seemed heavy. Not wanting to disturb Devon, she slowly sat up, letting her legs that felt too heavy to lift fall over the side of the bed before she tried to stand. Her legs shook violently with every step, forcing her to grab the bedpost to keep from falling.

Panting like she had just run a marathon, Anya pushed off and stumbled to the chair as black spots filled her vision. A cold sweat broke out all over her body, her teeth chattered as she shook uncontrollably, caught between the chill of her skin and the fire burning just under the surface. Bending forward, she let her head fall between her knees and gulped air like a fish out of water, sure she was about to faint.

Attempting a deep breath, she sat back as an especially horrible wave of pain slightly receded and waited for her vision to clear. Flashes of light burst between the black spots whether her eyes were open or shut, and visions of things she had never before seen appeared as memories in her mind. Gathering her strength, Anya stood once again, painstakingly making her way to the bathroom.

She leaned heavily on the basin, letting the water run until she was sure it was cold. Some of the water she aimed for her face hit its mark, but much of it covered her chest and arms and wet the floor beneath her feet. Another wave of pain began building in the pit of her stomach, promising to be far worse than the last. Leaning on the sink she pushed to stand, a glow reflected in the mirror shown in her peripheral vision, snapping her attention to the reflection.

Her hair hung in dripping, matted strands around her face, her normally light olive skin so pale it appeared translucent, and her lips an almost blood red. She looked alien, but it was her eyes that scared her the most. They glowed so bright, they lit the darkness where she had forgotten to turn on a light and when she moved closer to the mirror, she could see flashes of something deep within, changing the shape of her pupil. The longer she looked the faster it flashed, making it impossible for her to give the form she saw a name.

Fearing she was possessed or suffering some horrible side effect of the magic Andrew had subjected her to, even entertaining the comment made by Kyra's aunt about her sanity, Anya turned as quickly as she could and attempted to call for Devon. No sound came from her throat, only the strangled whisper of a wounded animal. As she took a breath to try again, the ball of fire she had felt building burst forth, blanketing her inside with molten lava and driving her to her knees.

She screamed within her mind, praying Devon would hear her distress and come to the rescue, but her calls only echoed within her own mind and mixed with the roar of a static she had never before experienced. The pain seemed to be never ending, wave upon wave building until she actually prayed for death. Then as if a switch had been flipped, it disappeared. She lay on the floor between the bathroom and the bedroom, curled in a fetal position, panting like a dog, quaking uncontrollably.

It took several moments, but finally she rose to her knees, used the door for support, and stood once again on shaky legs. Taking a few deep breaths, praying that whatever had decided to attack her had moved on, she took first one step and then another until she made it out of the room and stood at the top of the steps. She gripped the wooden railing, and taking one step at a time, made her way to the bottom of stairs, her butt making contact with the bottom step as the waning strength in her legs gave out. If her mouth were not so dry that her tongue stuck to the roof of her mouth, and had her throat not burned from thirst, she would've crawled to the couch and tried to sleep off the effects of whatever had just occurred. But thirst won out and she found herself once again summoning her strength and struggling to stand.

Slowly, and with incredible focus, she made it to the kitchen sink, filled a glass from the closest cabinet with water, and drank it down in one gulp. She repeated the process several times until her throat no longer burned. Exhausted and barely able to put one foot in front of the other, she shuffled to the couch. Falling onto the soft, overstuffed cushions, she pulled the throw from the back, letting it cover her body wherever it fell.

Anya was shocked when the clock on the mantel chimed four times. What had felt like an eternity of pain had taken less than ten minutes. Hovering between consciousness and delirium, she reached for Devon with her mind and was glad to find him blessedly dreaming of children that resembled the perfect combination of them both. Lulled to sleep by the tick of the clock, she was immediately jerked awake when the fire that had threatened to overtake her just moments before returned with a vengeance.

The ball of fire not only surged within her body but also all around. It felt as if the blood in her veins boiled and her heart would burst from her chest. A compulsion so powerful it broke through the pain forced her to her feet and drove her out the front door to the clearing just past the row of trees that surrounded Devon's home. Anya fell to her knees, the sticks and pebbles digging into her hands and legs.

Struggling to breath, unable to see more than shadowy shapes, she screamed for her mate with her mouth and mind. His answering roar assured that he had received her distress call and was racing to her side. Her vision darkened to a single fuzzy dot in the distance just as her lungs seized in her chest. She pitched forward, her cheek hit the ground, and darkness overtook her just as she felt Devon's hands on her body.

~~*~*~*~*~*

Devon awoke to an empty bed and complete silence blanketing the house. He called to Anya through their bond, received no reply, and then yelled her name. He had made it two steps from the bed when her cry of pain and fear rang loud and clear in his head and his ears. Following their mating bond, he flew down the stairs, burst through the front door, and ran as fast as his enhanced speed would carry him until he found Anya in the clearing, naked and unconscious.

Pulling her into his lap, holding her to his chest, he bellowed, *"SHE'S FADING! I can feel it! Please help me, I think she's dying!"*

The answering calls from all his brethren filled his head. Lance yelled, *"I'm bringing Sam and we're grabbing Siobhan."*

Time stood still as he rocked back and forth, Anya limp and cold in his arms, barely breathing. He whispered words of love and comfort, pouring all his strength and healing powers through their bond while he prayed to the Heavens for her safety. The sounds of footsteps approaching from all directions reached his ears as Anya gasped and bowing up pushed off his lap.

Devon scrambled after her as blood-curdling screams poured from her lips. Magic stronger than he had ever felt filled the air, stinging his naked skin and making it difficult to breathe. His brethren called their arrival through the haze surrounding them, but his eyes were glued to his mate as she lifted just slightly off the ground, as if hanging from invisible wires. He reached to pull her from her magical bonds when a bright light exploded, temporarily leaving him blind and deaf.

Rough hands pulled at his arms and shoulders, dragging him away from the last place he had seen his mate. Everything went deadly silent but still he struggled against his brethren while he and his dragon roared their insistence to be with Anya.

Aaron's voice cut through the chaos. "Open your fucking eyes, Devon! You are *not* gonna believe this shit!"

His eyes flew open. At first blurry, his sight immediately cleared, but what he saw had him not only doubting his vision but also his sanity. There, standing not fifty feet from where his bare ass sat on the cold hard ground stood a full grown, *female*, green dragon.

She was absolutely gorgeous. Smaller than his dragon in height and weight, more compact, but imposing nonetheless. The creature before him was absent horns on her snout or head, possessing only a row of short but deadly spikes running the length of her spine and tail, ending in a three-sided Caudal spade, not unlike his own. He had no doubt of the power lurking within her and could feel it begging to be unleashed. His dragon pushed hard at his confines, growling within Devon's head to be allowed an up close and personal meeting with their mate's new form. Her light green scales with just a touch of blue were an exact match for the woman's eyes and glittered in the moonlight. One look into the glowing crystalline eyes trying hard to focus told him the gorgeous beast before him was his mate, even as his mind struggled to make sense of what had just happened.

"Devon? I'm scared. What's happening? Where am I?" Anya asked, her fear a living being between them. Hearing her fears and knowing that she thought she was once again trapped in magic, Devon stood and took a step towards her.

The well-being of his mate took precedence over all else. Not caring who saw his nudity, Devon strode towards the beautiful creature that was his mate, speaking as he went. *"I'm here, mo chroi'. I'm here. I know you're scared, but you're gonna have to trust me and not freak out. Can you do that?"*

"Yes...but Devon..."

"Stay with me, sweetheart." He interrupted, stopping a few feet from her paw and then adding, *"Now, look down at your foot."*

She resisted for just a second before following his instruction. He watched and listened as the beast before him lowered her head. The bond between them was deeper than before, allowing him to see what she saw. The picture of a dragon's paw shone large and bright in her mind while she worked hard to make sense of it. *"Devon? But I...? What is...? Am I...?"* she whimpered.

He moved under her massive head, making eye contact and letting her see that he loved her just as much in that moment as he ever had and he would take her any way he could get her. *"Yes, mo ghra'. You are dragon."*

~~*~*~*~*~*~*

Anya was shocked as every Guardsman and all their mates came forward, touched her paw, and offered their love and support. She could feel their confusion that matched hers, but she also felt their unconditional acceptance. She wasn't sure if dragons could cry but knew her eyes filled with tears. Siobhan was the best, offering as much explanation as she could. "It would seem the mark on your wrist was a clue we all missed," the healer chuckled. "We know you were adopted, now we just have to find out where your birth parents came from, other than the obvious Green Dragon Clan. I was a young girl, just barely mated to Gareth, when they were savagely attacked and all of dragon kin believed them lost to us forever. There are several books that detail dragon heritage, in which I am sure I can find out more of your special lineage, *mianach ini'on*. I trust you two have things to deal with, so I will go research and return as quickly as I know more."

It was Kyra's words that gave the most comfort and pretty much put her situation into perspective. "Well, we know what all that magic was hiding."

Nerves almost overtook her when Carrick and the other Elders appeared and offered congratulations. Malachi, the Spiritual Elder gave thanks to the Heavens for not only the first female dragon in nearly a thousand years, but also the return of the Green Dragons, long since taken from the Earth by their enemies.

Carrick told of a story he had heard on several occasions, but until that moment had dismissed as fiction. He said, "An older dragon I was called to give last rites to told of a female dragon, one of the last and mate to the Commander of the Green Dragon Guard Force, which escaped the fighting when her clan was attacked. She took refuge in the caves high above her homelands where most never dared to venture.

"Soon after her exile, she realized she was pregnant and in due course gave birth. Unfortunately, without proper nourishment, the added strain of caring for her young, and a harsh winter, she fell ill. Using what little magic she had left, she concealed herself and her child from detection and left the caves. Her condition worsened as she traveled and she began to count her remaining days. Fearing for her child's safety, she came upon a couple overflowing with white magic and kindness. With her last bit of life, she placed the child on their doorstep and hid in the bushes until she was sure they had retrieved the baby.

"Knowing her child was safe and would be cared for, she made her way into the woods and perished, returning to the Earth as is our way. I believe you may be that child, Anya. We, the Elders, will do whatever we can to assist you. Know that we are here for you always, *mianach ini'on*."

Carrick stepped back and Zachary came close, also assuring her they would be assisting Siobhan in the search for her lineage. The oldest of the Elders confirmed Carrick's story, letting her know he had heard it on several occasions and would contact anyone he knew that might remember. He also called her *mianach ini'on*, which Devon told her meant 'daughter mine'.

It was Riordan standing guard, looking every bit the General he was that shocked her the most. He knelt before her paw and looked up right into her eyes. His eyes took on the vertical slit of his dragon and he growled low in his throat, speaking directly into her mind and Devon's, *"You carry a heavy weight, beag amha'in, you bring hope where it was thought long gone. I will be your sword, should you ever need it. Your mate is formidable and one I admire above all others, but know that I protect you both and any that come from your union with my very life."*

He unsheathed his sword, drew it across the palm of his hand, and placed it on her paw, *"This is my blood, willingly shed as will always be the case."*

Without another word, he stood, shook Devon's hand as she had seen the other Guardsmen do, and then walked to the far edge of their circle, holding his sword at the ready as he had promised.

Devon's voice in her mind calmed the chaos. *"They are all going to be here to help you with whatever you need. Whatever* we *need."*

"What did Riordan call me?"

"He called you beag amha'in. *It means Little One."*

They both chuckled at the way things had come full circle right before Sydney came running towards her. In all the confusion, Anya hadn't realized that she hadn't seen the little girl.

"Anya! Anya! Look at you!! I knew you were something cool, just couldn't see the picture," Sydney screamed as her little blonde curls bounced all around.

Without any fear, the child climbed up on her paw and motioned for her to bend her neck. When Anya paused, afraid she would hurt the child, Devon instructed, *"It's just like bending your neck any other time, only now you have more of it to bend. Go slow and don't let your head fall forward."*

Following his directions to the letter, Anya lowered her head until it was almost on the ground, and her eyes were just shy of Sydney's. The girl reached out and stroked the soft scales under her eyes, cooing as she spoke. "You make a pretty dragon, Anya. I can't wait to watch you fly."

"Me too, Syd. Thank you," she thought towards the child and was rewarded with a huge smile letting her know Sydney had heard her words.

As the sweet girl climbed down she said, "I love you, Anya."

"Love you, too, Syd."

It was only a few minutes before Devon began shooing everyone away, telling them he needed to be alone with his mate. After another round of goodbyes, she and her mate were finally alone in the clearing.

It took several hours, coupled with her mate's impenetrable patience and unyielding strength, but Anya finally came to terms with her new state of being. Along the way she learned to walk without leveling everything in her path, to lie down without falling over, and to spread her wings. She had asked to fly but Devon had chuckled and said, *"Maybe you should learn to turn back into the beautiful woman I mated first."*

And that was the hard part, returning to her human form. Devon told her to picture what she looked like as a woman and pour her dragon magic into that thought, which proved to be way harder than it sounded. She watched as he changed back and forth over and over, making it look effortless, but still she remained a dragon. Dropping to her haunches and huffing smoke, she complained, *"I'm gonna be a dragon forever."*

Devon laughed, which sounded really weird coming from a thousand pound dragon and said, *"Then we'll be dragons together."*

"That's not the point," she whined, embarrassed at her weakness, but seriously scared she wasn't going to able to change back.

"Anya, open your mind completely to me. Just like it was when you first transformed," Devon commanded, and without thought she obeyed.

"See the image of me in human form?" He asked with his tone less stern.

"Yes."

"See you standing next to me?"

"Yes."

"Now, feel the path my magic takes."

She felt, as well as saw his dragon magic travel along an invisible thread and fill the picture with life. Her magic followed the same path, and from one breath to the next, she turned from dragon to woman and found herself in the arms of her mate.

After showering, eating, and making love on every available surface, they fell asleep on the couch, only to be roused by a knock at the door. Grumbling about people showing up uninvited and unannounced, Devon opened the door to Aaron, Lance, and Rory with only a towel around his hips. Thankfully, Anya had kept the robe she'd worn after their shower close by and had thrown it on while her mate searched for his towel.

Not waiting to be invited in, Aaron slipped past Devon and plopped down on the couch right next to her. "So how's life, *vibria*?" He asked in a chuckle.

"*Vibria*?"

"Female dragon. You know.... your newest soul mate?"

She hadn't thought about it that way but she guessed he was right. There was a feeling of another consciousness residing in her soul and she stored that information along with several questions away for the next time she and her mate were alone. Not sure she should share the fact that Devon had found a small tattoo, the exact likeness of her dragon on the back of her left shoulder, she decided to wait. But she still smiled when she remembered how the marking had raised and moved against her skin as he had kissed it.

Remembering Aaron was waiting for an answer, she hurriedly said, "It's cool...weird...but cool."

"Yeah, I bet."

Devon's shout interrupted their conversation. "What the fuck? When were you gonna tell me? The shithead is loose?"

Lance backed away, raising his hands in surrender as Rory answered, "Don't kill the messengers. Rian heard the traitor's thoughts for just a second, right after you put out the call that Anya was in trouble. He ran off to follow the trail as soon as he saw your mate's dragon. Rayne and Aidan followed when you sent us all away."

Lance picked up the explanation. "The three of us have been hanging out, pretty much driving Sam and the girls crazy, waiting for information. Aidan finally sent word that they have a scent, so we headed this way to see if you two had come up for air." He paused and turned to Anya. "The girls said to pack a bag and head over whenever you're ready. And I should warn you that Sydney is about to go nuts waiting to ask you what it feels like to be a dragon, so be prepared."

"No worries." Anya laughed and looked to Devon. "You better get ready and go catch yourself a traitor."

He shook his head as he walked towards her, sitting next to her before he responded, "Nope. I'm staying with you. We were just mated yesterday. You found out you were a dragon shifter and went through your first transformation. There is no way I'm going anywhere. My place is at your side."

Turning towards him until she was almost in his lap, Anya looked right into his eyes and said, "Devon Walsh, you *will* go with your Force and hunt down the stupid son of a bitch that has caused so much pain and hurt so many people." He started to interrupt, but her index finger on his lips stopped his retort and she continued, "I know exactly what we've been through in the last twenty-four hours, but that does *not* negate the fact that the little shithead needs to be stopped and you guys are stronger when you work together. I'll be fine. You can even drop me off at Lance and Sam's on your way out and I *promise* to stay put until you get back, deal?"

"Deal," he reluctantly agreed, his eyes promising they would continue the conversation when they were alone.

"Great!" Aaron clapped his hands as he stood and walked towards the door. "We'll meet you lovebirds at Casa de Kavanaugh," he called over his shoulder. "Head 'em up and move 'em out," he said as he pushed Rory and Lance out the door, shutting it as he went.

She and Devon looked at each other and in unison said, "Something's up with Aaron?"

Devon barked out a laugh as he pulled her onto his lap, kissing her neck before she could react. Still giggling, Anya pushed against his chest. "Hey, we're supposed to be getting ready to go."

"Yeah, yeah, yeah…in a minute," he mumbled against her neck in between kisses. When his lips touched her mating mark, heat shot directly to her pussy and all thoughts of anything but the delicious man she was destined to spend her life with evaporated. She sighed, letting her head roll to the side to grant him greater access. The bell on the beautiful necklace he placed around her neck jingled at the movement.

She felt Devon smile against her neck right before, *"See, told ya…"* floated through her mind. Followed by, *"Is breá liom tú anois agus go deo."*

Life just did *not* get any better…

EPILOGUE

It had been two weeks since Devon had bellowed his distress call across their mindspeak, fearing his mate was dying. Two weeks since Aaron had made a lame excuse to the woman he knew was to be his and had sped away into the night to help a brethren, only to see the first female dragon in nearly a thousand years. Two weeks since he had shared an incredible kiss with his mate. And…more importantly…two weeks since the one the Universe had made for him had run away, traumatized from what she had just witnessed and knowing the most guarded secret of his entire clan.

Aaron had been happier than he thought possible when Dr. Charlene Gallagher had agreed to dance with him during the reception following Devon and Anya's mating ceremony. The party was still going strong, even though the couple had fled hours earlier. Dragons liked to party and especially if it was in celebration of something as monumental as one of their own finding his mate and making it official.

Aaron had spent the majority of the evening watching the good doctor, Charlie as she like to be called, while trying to work up his nerve to speak to her. He had repeatedly yelled at himself for being a coward and his dragon had all but roared in his head, demanding the man at least get close so he could scent the one meant to be theirs. Finally, when he was afraid the party would end and so would his chances of even talking to her, he had made his way through the party-goers and asked for a dance. His heart had almost left his chest when she readily agreed.

The feel of her in his arms was something Aaron would never forget. Then she had truly blown his mind and said yes when he asked if she would like to take a walk away from the noise.

Charlie was smart and witty and had a voice like fine whisky that rolled all over and through him. He knew he would hear that voice in his dreams as she screamed his name while he gave her more pleasure than she had ever known. He hadn't planned on kissing her. *Hell*, he'd been having a hard enough time keeping up his end of the conversation. But there was just something about the way her dark blonde hair and deep blue eyes shone in the moonlight that had made him lower his lips to hers. She must have felt it too because she met him halfway and when they touched, sparks flew. An electrical current ran through his body, making him wonder if he glowed with the feelings this one woman brought out in him. And then Devon had called and Aaron had taken Charlie back to the party, making some stupid excuse for having to leave. Never in his wildest dreams had he imagined she would follow him.

He knew Charlie was hiding out in the cottage Sam still owned and had lived in prior to meeting Lance. The brief kiss they had shared had started the mating call, which allowed him to keep track of her…to make sure she was okay. About twenty times every day he walked towards his Harley, prepared to go to her and explain *everything*, and every time he lost his nerve. Part of him thought maybe this stupid shit would wear off, but then the part of him that remembered their kiss, remembered what it felt like to have her in his arms kicked in, and he knew sooner or later he was going to *have* to make things right.

Aaron had never really wanted a mate. He knew every other Guardsman did, but it was just not something he really ever thought about, when he did, it gave him the willies. It was not until he had glimpsed Dr. Charlene Gallagher that he actually considered a life with another person. As it was, just the very thought of her drove him crazy and his dragon had gotten damn near impossible to deal with.

After the first week, he had gone to Sam for advice. She had laughed, explaining that her best friend was hardheaded and had a terrible temper to boot. Her suggestion was to give Charlie time to cool off, time to come to terms with what she had seen, and then Samantha was sure her friend would come to him for answers. He saw the sadness in his brethren's mate's eyes as she explained that Dr. Charlene Gallagher had also cut communication with her, only calling to tell her she had taken vacation from the hospital and to ask if she could use the cottage. The tears he saw in the young doctor's eyes and heard in her voice when she said Charlie had asked not to be disturbed tore at his heart. Never one to be overly emotional, Aaron chalked it up to the mating call, thanked Sam, and left to go lick his proverbial wounds.

Any other time he would have talked to Devon and Royce, they were the brethren with the most level heads and best advice. However, Royce was off with Kyra searching for her mother and Devon had his hands full with a mate that just transformed into the first female dragon in nearly a thousand years, AND was a dragon from a long lost clan. So...there was no way Aaron was bothering either of them.

He had considered talking to his twin but once again, Aidan had his own issues. Aaron's brother and his mate were pregnant with twins, the first in almost a hundred years, and Aidan had gone into hyper-protective mate and dad mode. Although it was absolutely hilarious to watch, it didn't help with Aaron's problems. He was close with all his brethren, but he wasn't ready to relive the whole story again, so that left just one thing…*training*. Andrew was out there on the loose, planning only the Heavens knew what. It was the perfect opportunity to focus all of Aaron's anger and frustration on the little brother he had grown to hate.

Since it was still early and the younger Guardsmen were busy with the tasks Rayne and Rian had given them, he shoved his earbuds into his ears, blasted Metallica, and started off on his run. Running had always been something he hated, especially after his years in the service, but the longer he went without Charlie, the more the solitude of tearing across the countryside fit his mood. He emptied his mind of everything but the music blasting in his ears, the sights and scents around him, and the rhythmic pounding of his feet against the ground.

Passing the ten mile mark and still going strong, lost to his thoughts, he damn near ran straight into the huge lake in front of him when the scent of roses punched him right in the gut. Shaking his head, Aaron looked around, only to realize he had run straight to Black Lake, which coincidentally was less than a mile behind the cottage his mate now occupied. *Dammit, this Fate will not be denied shit really sucks!*

~~*~*~*~*~*~*

Hiding out in the same cave, on the same mountainside, where his resurrection had occurred almost two years ago should have seemed poetic. But he was starving, injured, and without any resources whatsoever, making misery all Andrew knew. The hunting trap he had stepped in on his hurried escape across the wheat field had torn the muscles and tendons in the calf of his right leg, and without proper nutrition, even his returning dragon abilities were struggling to heal the wound. Thankfully, the cave had a small stream running through it, so he could stay hydrated and keep his cut clean. The few small animals that used the creek as their water source had become his only source of food, but the supply was dwindling as the word spread about the predator hiding in their midst.

His only solace was the ancient text he had taken with him when he had escaped from the ruins of the mansion. With little else to do, he divided his time between translating the old dragon language and plotting his revenge against everyone that had been a part of all he had suffered, including John's death. John was the only person in nearly eight years Andrew had dared let close, and the fucking dragons had taken that from him, too. Sadness filled him as he pulled page after page of his assistant's notes from the book. His spirits lifted slightly when he found one page in particular that detailed all they knew about the prophecy. It was only bits and pieces, but he would do whatever had to be done to find the whole prophecy and use it to destroy anyone that got in his way.

A powerful white witch sworn to the Earth, of long regal lineage made whole by human love, must mate a dragon of royal descent marked by devastating loss and the heart of not one clan but two.

The vibria born of human parents and the last female born of two dragons lost in plain sight.

Born to an extinct race, thought to be one but actually two. Both with destinies blessed by Fate, neither knowing the other exists…

A calling to heal, a hidden nature, a history long forgotten…all protected in the heart of a woman destined to complete a warrior and his beast. The revelation of all she is brought forth from the joining with her mate.

Another page, one much older and most certainly written in blood, fell from between the last page and the back cover as he shifted his position. The moment he saw it, he remembered John showing it to him before and wanted to scream for not following up on it from the beginning. Thankfully, his assistant had possessed the wherewithal to remove the page from the ancient grimoire and hide it away for safe keeping. This one, very old piece of parchment held the spell to deliver the forever death to any shifter ever known.

Smiling his first real smile in days, Andrew lay back on the stone floor and closed his eyes. *Those fuckers are not going to know what hit them.*

~~*~*~*~*~*

In the last week her captors had resorted to torture in an effort to get her to reveal the location of the grimoire that contained the most powerful and most deadly spell known to magical practitioners worldwide. This new development, although painful, gave Calysta a little more insight into her captors…they were working for someone magical. Only the most experienced witches or the oldest families with long lineages knew of the existence of the spell. To all others it was only a myth, passed from person to person as a warning to the evil of meddling with things one didn't understand.

On the surface it looked like a simple summoning spell, but the ritual was written so that as each step was completed another would appear, erasing the previous, each step becoming more complex, more dark, and more deadly. It was written so that a single, experienced witch with incredible power may work the spell without deadly repercussions that would span her entire line. And only on Samhain, when the veil between worlds was the thinnest. Legend stated it was created by a dark Priestess trying to find the soul of her long dead lover in order to place said soul in a waiting body, thus allowing them to once again wreak havoc on an unsuspecting world. Simply known as Thanatos, the name of the witch's lover and also meaning death, the spell drops the veil between Earth and Hell, allowing only the witch working the spell to bring over any*thing* her heart desired, and only that witch can restore the curtain between worlds.

The spell was only ever recorded in one grimoire and had always been entrusted to the most powerful Priestess to keep hidden. Since taking her place as the leader of her coven, Calysta had protected the book and its contents with every resource she possessed. It was hidden in plain sight, spelled to look like an ordinary instruction manual in the library of her coven, warded more heavily than any single artifact in their vault. Only she and Della knew of its location, and both were willing to die to keep it safe and out of the hands of evil.

The most recent indignities she had suffered had come at the hands of her female captor with the male standing watch. They always came in together and, until yesterday, only *he* had spoken. His voice was low and gravely with a bit of an accent that she knew she had heard before but simply could not place. The female was younger and Calysta could tell from the reluctance pouring off of her, far less certain about what they were doing. The Grand Priestess had caught the last bit of an argument between the two as they entered her cell the day before. The man had growled her name, Mara, right before a loud slap had echoed throughout the chamber, followed by a very female whimper. Calysta gave her credit for not crying out and thought if only Mara were to visit her alone, she might have an opportunity to convince the younger woman to help her. But it was obvious they still feared her power, even though she was kept chained in iron to a cement slab in an iron-lined room, malnourished, and close to dehydration.

Face down on the slab, arms shackled over her head, iron chains thrown across her abused back, Calysta rolled her shoulders, trying to find a position that would let blood flow return to her fingers. She hissed as pain from the burn marks she had received yesterday shot through her body. The bitch had shoved acid soaked iron daggers into her back and then rinsed her wounds in a mixture of salt and deadly nightshade to keep them from healing and increase her suffering.

It was apparent to Calysta that the Goddess, the Universe, Fate…whoever…was not going to let her die. The almighty powers had a plan for her and she was going to have to carry it out, whether she wanted to or not. Pulling on the strength of her ancestors and the power that would always be a part of who she was, Calysta began to chant… *"Heal me now and make me whole. Take my pain, refill my soul. Let the scars remain, no one can know. Bring peace and comfort, let your light brightly show."*

She prayed with all she was. It was her last chance. Finishing her tenth or maybe it was her eleventh time through the chant, the sound of iron scraping concrete reached her ears. But it was the unmistakable scent of sulfur that had her pulling against her restraints. *"What hath hell wrought?"* was her last thought as pain pushed her into the oblivion of unconsciousness.

Only for Her Dragon
Dragon Guard Series #6

There Are No Coincidences.
The Universe Does Not Make Mistakes.
Fate Will Not Be Denied.

CHAPTER ONE

"We haven't had this much to drink since college," Charlie slurred as her head fell to the side. "And I still have the incriminating photos to prove it." She giggled. "I wonder what your hubby would think of that."

"Oh, you know Lance, he'd just ask for a repeat performance." Her best friend, Samantha, chuckled.

That was the problem...

Charlie didn't know Lance, at least not like she thought she did. And what hurt the most was that she felt like she didn't know Sam anymore either. There'd been a time when they'd shared *everything*, a time when the longest they could go without talking was twenty-four hours. When Sam married Lance Kavanaugh a little over a year ago, that all changed.

As if that wasn't bad enough, things got exponentially more complicated a couple of weeks ago.

The guy who said 'Life changes in the blink of an eye' definitely knew what he was talking about. One minute Charlie had been kissing the sexiest man she'd ever met, and the next she had been looking at a dragon...*a freakin' dragon.*

Of course, Aaron had told her to go back to the party before he'd sped away, but Dr. Charlene Gallagher did *not* take orders. She followed the man that continued to haunt her dreams at what she thought was a safe distance. Running in heels across the forest floor, barely able to see his back, Charlie seriously doubted her judgment. That was before she heard the sounds of someone in distress. As the daughter of a policeman, and a trained doctor, she rushed headlong into the clearing.

It had taken her brain a second to process what was in front of her....and when it did, she absolutely could not believe her eyes.

There stood Sam, alongside her *new* family, looking at a mythical creature. They all seemed somewhat stunned, but for the most part not near as freaked as Charlie felt.

Is it still considered mythical if I saw it with my own eyes? A question she still pondered.

Too much wine...think about it tomorrow.

Charlie had done the only thing she could. She'd run...far and fast...to her car. Then she drove like Danica Patrick straight to her condo. Once inside, with all four locks secured and the curtains drawn, she'd taken her first real breath. The floodgates opened, and for the next twelve hours, she alternated between screaming, crying, and cursing.

The sun rose as she stared out her bedroom window, too drained to move. Sleep finally came.... and so did the dreams. Erotic dreams of passionate kisses and eyes as blue as the ocean, which then turned to dreams of dragons and knights fighting battles she'd only ever read about. Fortunately, her cellphone rang three hours later. Unfortunately, Sam's name came across the display. Charlie hit ignore.

And she hit ignore every hour on the hour for the next two days.

The morning of the third day she called the hospital where she and Sam were both residents. Told them she had a family emergency and needed time off. When the woman in Human Resources informed her that she had accrued six weeks of leave, all Charlie could do was sigh...it didn't seem like enough.

Mustering up her courage, she then called Sam. Curt and to the point, Charlie said, "Staying at the cottage. Do not come. I'll call when I'm ready."

It was probably a dick move since the house was Sam's, but Charlie couldn't care. Hitting the button to disconnect the call, she dropped her cell on the couch and once again fell into a mess of tears and anger.

The two weeks that followed royally sucked! After a combined eleven years of college, medical school, and residency, Charlie had never taken off more than two days in a row. Not to mention, she *always* talked to Sam.

Then there was the matter of Aaron O'Brien, the stupid jerk that made her pulse race and her temperature rise. The asshole whose kiss she couldn't forget. The moron whose lips had branded her, leaving her yearning for more. The idiot she had seen running around the lake behind the house a few times.

Even though he's the last man on earth I want to see. Yeah...I'm the biggest liar ever.

About a week after what Charlie referred to as 'the incident', she started walking to pass the time. Exercise had always been a four-letter word, but how many times could she read the same magazines or watch the same reruns? She knew whom every Bachelor had slept with and every plate Gordon Ramsay had thrown by heart.

On the morning of the third day of her new walking program, she found the large terracotta pot on Sam's redwood deck filled with daisies, one of her favorite flowers. She chalked it up to Lance trying to apologize for his wife.

Sweet gesture.

Not wanting their kindness to go to waste, she began taking care of them.

Four days later a brand new rose bush was miraculously growing on the side of the barbeque pit. It had been so expertly planted that it took Charlie an extra look to realize it hadn't been there the day before. What baffled her more than the fact that someone was bringing her beautiful flowers, were the incredibly large blooms…*out of season*. It was as though their beauty was just for her.

Laughing aloud at her own ridiculous thoughts, Charlie continued on her walk, chastising herself for thinking *anything* was *weird* after what she'd witnessed. Returning home, she decided that if anything else unexplained happened, she'd have to break down and call Sam. Enough was enough. None of it made sense. Her best friend was a sweetheart but had never been one to give flowers or anything of the sort. Charlie was still pissed, but if Samantha was willing to go so far as to anonymously leave presents, then it was time to try and mend fences.

The next morning she had coffee and a bagel, perused the newspaper, and then headed out. She looked and looked, even walked around each tree, but there were no new flowers, not a bud, not a petal…*nothing*.

The same was true for the next five days.

Convincing herself it was for the best, Charlie resumed her routine. Forgiving Sam was something she knew she had to do, but it still hurt to have been kept in the dark about something so monumentally important. Even after all the explanation filled voicemails, some that revealed more secrets, she just wasn't ready to move on. There was no denying she missed everyone, some more than others, but she wasn't at the point of rational discussion, so she ignored all of it. It was just easier.

Day fifteen was exhausting. Who knew relaxing could take so much out of a girl? Charlie hadn't been sleeping well and the days seemed to stretch on forever. There was no work and no one to talk to. Then there had been all the times her cellphone had rung. It was beginning to get harder and harder to ignore her friend. Checking her call log, she counted fifteen missed calls in all. Mostly from Sam, but some were from a number she didn't recognize.

Giving in, mostly because she couldn't take the solitude one moment longer, Charlie picked up the phone and called Sam. Whatever residual anger she felt melted away when Sam's daughter, Sydney, answered the phone. "Hey, Aunt Charlie! You still mad?"

Chuckling despite herself, Charlie answered, "No, sweetheart, I'm not mad anymore."

No sooner had the words left her mouth than squeals of delight filled the earpiece. The sounds of tennis shoes slapping against hardwood floors had Charlie picturing her adopted niece running through the house as she screamed. "Mom! Mom! It's Aunt Charlie! She's not mad anymore! She's on your cell phone!"

In less than a minute, Samantha said a tentative hello. There were exactly fifteen point two seconds of awkward silence, two more minutes of apologies, and then the friends truly started talking. They discussed, argued, and cried until both cell phones beeped at their loss of charge. Right before her phone died, Charlie told Sam to grab something alcoholic and head her way.

Four hours and two bottles of wine later, the two friends had rehashed many things, starting as far back as the first day they met. However, the ladies were still kind of dancing around the moment Charlie had unwittingly witnessed a living, breathing dragon. The reason for all the secrecy made sense, but it still stung that Sam hadn't trusted her and she couldn't keep from saying it for about the tenth time.

"You know I love you like a sister…and I forgive you…but my feelings are *still* hurt. Did you really think you couldn't trust me?" Charlie asked, working hard to focus after all the wine.

Sam shook her head. "Dammit, Charlie, you know I trust you with my life…with my *child's life*. You just have to understand…it was part of the deal. When I vowed to love Lance forever, I also vowed to keep his secrets. *And* the secrets of his people. Nothing against you, Charlie, nothing at all. It was something I *had* to do. Had it been up to me, you would've known everything *right* after I did."

Charlie could hear the honesty in Sam's voice, along with the burden of all the secrecy and all her leftover frustration simply vanished. "I forgive you," she whispered. Then added, "And I hope you forgive me for being so pigheaded."

Sam snickered as she rose from her chair, stumbled in Charlie's direction, and all but fell in her lap before hugging her tight. "Pigheaded is what I've come to expect from you. Wouldn't have you any other way."

The two laughed until tears streamed down their faces. It was Charlie that regained enough composure to speak first. "Whatever, Mrs. Dragon Lady! Let's get some of that pizza they delivered an hour ago. I'm sure it's good, cold, and greasy by now."

Heading for the kitchen, they leaned on each other to stay upright. Charlie heated up a couple slices of pizza while Sam grabbed Diet Pepsis. Eating in silence for a few minutes, Charlie felt the buzz of the alcohol wearing off. She wondered if they were ever going to address the elephant…make that *dragon* in the room.

Two bites later and unable to hold back any longer, Charlie blurted out, "All right, spill. I've seen the dragon. Know some of the secrets. Tell me what's really going on."

Sam stopped chewing and sat completely still. Charlie watched as her best friend blew out the breath she'd been holding. Several more seconds passed before Sam finally said, "Well…"

Their eyes met across the table and it was Charlie's turn to hold her breath. The staring contest lasted almost ten full seconds before Sam spoke again. "I think it would be better if you asked me questions. I honestly have no idea where to start or how much you want to know."

Charlie rolled her eyes and sighed, but saw the honesty on her friend's face and decided to play along. "All right, one of your messages said something about Anya being a dragon and that being a big deal. Was she who I saw in the clearing?"

Sam nodded. "Yes, that was the first time she had ever transformed. She's the first female dragon in *hundreds* of years. The females were all killed during their war with the hunters and wizards."

Charlie held up her index finger, signaling Sam to stop speaking, already realizing there was so much more than she could've ever imagined. Standing, she walked to the counter, grabbed a notepad and pen, and returned to her seat. After a deep, cleansing breath she said, "Go on."

Sam smiled and started again. "The dragons have two main enemies in the world that have been around almost as long as they have. They're the hunters and the wizards, and these assholes have taken damn near everything from dragon kin. First of all, the hunters are a fanatical group of killers hell bent on destroying anything supernatural. And before you ask…yes, there are more things out there than just dragon shifters, but that's for a different day."

After a sip of her soda, Sam continued, "The wizards are just bat shit crazy. That's the best description I can give you. I'm happy to say the ones that were in this area all blew up with Andrew's mansion."

Charlie wrote…*mansion?…blown up?* on her list.

"Andrew is Aidan and Aaron's younger brother and also belongs in the 'bat shit crazy' column in your notes. He turned traitor about eight years ago when he was captured and tortured by a group of wizards. He blames Aidan for what happened and Aaron too to some extent…at least, I think. Everyone thought he was dead, but then he reappeared when Kyndel met Rayne. Since then, he's tried everything possible to kill all the guys. He was in the mansion when it blew up, but Rian, Royce's brother, found a tunnel under the rubble and scented Andrew, so they're sure he's still alive somewhere."

Just the mention of Aaron's name made Charlie's pulse race. She pushed all thoughts of the irritating man to the back of her mind and focused on everything she had learned in just a few minutes. Making a few more notes, she looked up to find her friend studying her as if she was one of their patients. "I'm okay." She chuckled, hoping Sam believed her lie. The truth was she was freaking the hell out and wondered where it would all end, or if it ever would. No matter, she had to know the truth.

"Are you sure?" Sam questioned, reaching across the table and squeezing Charlie's hand.

"I'm sure I want to know. I'm not promising that I won't have a million questions when you are done. Or that I won't need to lose my shit every once in a while, but I want to hear it all."

"Okay, if you're sure. What's your next question?"

"You called Lance your mate. Isn't he your husband? And is this whole dragon thing the reason I couldn't be your maid of honor?"

Sam laughed out loud and Charlie couldn't help but smile. Replaying her question in her mind, she realized she sounded like a petulant child. Thankfully, they'd been friends for so long Sam just laughed it off and kept going.

"Yeah, that's why and you *know* I'm still sorry about that. The dragons have a special ceremony for *everything*. The mating ceremony is very private. Only Lance's brethren, the guys he calls brother, the Elders of their Clan, and I could be there."

"He's my husband," she laughed. "But in their culture we're *mates*. Actually, we're *soul mates*, destined by the Universe to be together. They have a Holy Book that better describes mates and what they mean to each other better than I ever could, and I'm sure some time or another you'll see or hear more about it. The best I can do is tell you that from the moment I saw him, I just *knew*. I felt it in my *soul*. We're supposed to be together *forever*."

Sam had a dreamy look on her face, and Charlie could actually feel the love her best friend felt for her hus…*mate* as she spoke. Charlie knew there would come a day when she would feel that way about someone…*anyone*. At that thought, Aaron's face, complete with a shit-eating grin, appeared in her mind's eye and her lips warmed just as they had when he'd kissed her.

Not wanting to think about him anymore than she had to, Charlie teased her friend. "You always were a hopeless romantic, Dr. Malone."

Sam feigned annoyance, complete with a furrowed brow, and pouted before grumping. "If I remember correctly, *you* were the one with the Backstreet Boys poster that had to be kissed every night before bed." Sam barely had the words out of her mouth before she was laughing out loud, causing Charlie to laugh right along.

"Yeah, yeah, yeah…whatever. I'm not the one waxing poetic about the man of her dreams."

"I think the lady doth protest too much, but I'll let you live with your denial for a bit longer. I know you have a million more questions, so ask away."

"Are they born dragons or is it magical or what?"

"They're born as dragon shifters *now,* but when it all started back in Arthurian times, there were still *real dragons*. The poor beasts were hunted and on the brink of extinction when some powerful magical guy found a way to combine the soul of the dragon with the soul of the man. All the men the dragons picked were Knights of the Round Table, very respectable and honorable, men they had fought alongside for years.

"Lance said there were twelve in total when they started out, one from each of the clans. The clans, just so you know, used to be divided up by their colors, but now they all coexist since their numbers never truly rebounded. There are more than there were in total, but some of the clans were wiped out altogether. Lance is a golden dragon. He's the last of his kind. I hope someday we have a boy to carry on the beautiful color and history of his father's clan. But for now, we have Syd, and Heaven knows she's one special little girl."

Sam stopped, once again looking right at Charlie, letting her know what she was about to say was very important. "And when I say special…I mean *special*. Devon's mom, Siobhan, is trying to figure out exactly what makes my girl the wonder that she is. Siobhan is an Elder Healer in the Clan and a super intelligent woman. I've learned so much from her already. More on that later."

Charlie made a little note to remind her to find out more about her niece another day and almost missed what Samantha had gone on to say.

"Anyway, like I said, the guys are born as shifters but can't 'call their dragon forth', that's what they call it when they transform, until they're like seventeen or eighteen. Until then, they just have the marking of their beast somewhere on their torso."

"So those aren't tattoos? I just figured since they all rode Harleys and looked like models they were inked." Charlie chuckled.

"You would think, right?' Sam laughed. "But no, they have them from birth. It darkens as they get older, then really pops when they transform for the first time. At least that's what they all tell me. Their dragon glyphs kinda remind me of the marks on your back. Speaking of that, have yours ever moved?"

"Not that I can remember. They itch or tingle sometimes, but nothing much more than that. My mom always said they were birthmarks. I've often wondered if my birth mom had them, too. If they were a family thing…ya know? But, hey, I never really think that much about them." She hurried on, not wanting to open the whole adopted kid discussion that Sam always wanted to have with her. There would come a day when she would look for her birth parents again with hopefully better results, but it wasn't in that moment and she didn't want to think about it.

Charlie pondered why Sam had asked and thankfully, her friend didn't make her wait long. Samantha leaned closer and whispered conspiratorially, even though they were alone. "Lance's marking *moves* when I touch it." Then she did something Charlie only remembered her doing a few times in all the years she'd known her…she winked and giggled like a schoolgirl.

Giggling? Oh, I'm saving this for just the right moment.

Charlie chuckled along, not sure if she was more embarrassed or more jealous that her friend had someone so special in her life. Thoughts of Aaron threatened to invade her thoughts for about the hundredth time. Shoving them away, she worked hard to focus. Sam cleared her throat but couldn't quite control the blush in her cheeks. Charlie decided to let the moment pass without giving her friend a hard time, something that rarely happened.

Sam spoke, "The twins, Aaron and Aidan, and their crazy ass brother are the last of the silver clan. Devon is the last of the white dragon clan. Rayne's dragon is red, and I think he's the last, too, or one of the last. Well *hell*, only Royce has any family left that I'm aware of, but we always get surprises. You met Rian and Rory at his wedding right? They're his brothers."

"Yeah, I did. They all look so much alike except for the hair. There's *no way* I could miss that they are related. I have to ask though…is Kyra something 'special'?" Charlie made air quotes to make sure Sam understood. "I just get the feeling she's more than she seems."

Nodding as she finished her soda, Sam answered while she stood and made her way to the fridge for a refill. "You're catching on fast," she answered over her shoulder. "Kyra's a white witch. One of the best from what I've seen and what little I know. She saved Anya from some nasty spell Andrew had the poor girl under."

"Was that why we could never figure out what was wrong with Anya?" Charlie butted in. "Well *damn*! Now it all makes sense. I kept wondering how the hell y'all got her to wake up after less than two days at home when we had worked for weeks. I guess we never would've been able to help her, huh?"

Sam shook her head as she made her way back to her seat. "No way. And we have nothing to feel bad about. There's so much crap out there that us 'normal' people have no clue about. Just wait, some of it will completely blow your mind…even more than it is now.

"Oh! And before I forget, there are five other Guardsmen that are part of Rory's Force and a bunch of others in his clan across the pond. The Blue Dragons have been the most successful at keeping their kin alive, from what I've been told."

"What about the green dragon, Anya, I saw the night of their wedding or mating or whatever?"

"Like I said, she's the first female dragon in hundreds of years and the first green dragon in almost as long. She's like a miracle on top of a miracle and no one knew she existed until she transformed. Devon screamed through mindspeak that she was dying and we all came running. That's when you saw us."

"Mindspeak?" Charlie asked, almost afraid of what else she would find out.

"Yeah. I should've told you about that when I was explaining mating, but I kinda got off track." Sam paused, winked…*again*… and dived right back in. "There are certain perks to being the mate of a dragon shifter. First of all, we can talk mind to mind with our other half. Later, as the bond strengthens, we can do it with all his brethren, too."

"Secondly, we get to live as long as they do and that can be a thousand years, maybe longer. We age really slowly. We get some of their strength and ability to hear. And our sense of smell becomes more acute. Overall, it's a pretty sweet deal. The bummer of it all is keeping everything a secret from those you're the closest to. But you changed all that!"

Sam seemed genuinely happy that she could finally really talk to Charlie about her life. The truth was Charlie was glad there were no more secrets between them. She just wondered how she was going to keep it all straight without going crazy.

The rest of the night went pretty much the same way until they were both yawning. They made it as far as the living room before Charlie remembered to ask one thing that had been driving her crazy. "What was up with the flowers? I mean I like them and everything, but they're really not your style."

Sam looked at her like she was crazy, and after all they had discussed, that was seriously saying something. "What flowers?"

"The daisies and the rose bush…out back. That you had Lance plant for me…?"

Shaking her head with eyebrows raised, Sam answered. "I didn't have Lance plant any flowers." She scoffed. "He's really not the green-thumb type."

"Well, if you didn't do it, then who?"

"I have no idea. Guess you have a secret admirer." Sam wiggled her eyebrows before collapsing on the couch. "I call dibs on the sofa."

"Yeah, that's cool," Charlie absentmindedly answered, trying to think of who might have left the flowers.

Maybe they weren't even for me. Maybe they were for Sam. But who would've dared leave them for her. Anyone that knows her, knows Lance, and knows he will kill them just for looking at his wife. Dammit, this is gonna drive me crazy.

Snuggling into the oversized recliner while Sam curled up on the couch, she let all thoughts of flowers and annoying dragons slip away. For the first time since 'the incident', Charlie slipped into slumber with a smile on her face. Her last thought was of haunting blue eyes and the kiss that changed her life.

CHAPTER TWO

He knew Sam was aware of his presence, or at least thought she was. She'd been mated to Lance long enough that her senses were almost as sharp as those of a full-blooded dragon shifter. He would never be able to thank her for not telling Charlie that he sat outside her window like a lovesick teenager.

Aaron used his enhanced hearing to listen to their conversation, but more than that, he focused on his mate, the one destined for him by the Universe. He could hear her heart beat faster when Samantha mentioned his name and *knew* every time she'd thought of him. Their kiss just a few weeks ago had triggered the mating call and it was taking no prisoners. He'd thought of nothing but Charlie every waking minute of every day.

Since the night she'd fled from him–from them all– he had been keeping watch over her. Not only was he worried the traitor would find her, that Andrew might be able to sense that she was a mate…*his* mate, he was worried that any wizards who hadn't died in the blast might find her, or that hunters might be in the area. Basically, he couldn't stay away and was using any excuse he could come up with to be near her. Charlie was *his*, whether either of them wanted it to be true or not.

He shook his head. *Who the hell am I kidding? I want her more than I want my next breath. Heaven knows my dragon is going to turn me inside out if I don't get this shit handled.*

"You got that right, and I might just kick your ass if you don't learn to keep your thoughts to yourself," Aidan chuckled through their unique mental link.

"Sorry, Bro. I thought I was shielded."

"I'm sure you are from everyone else or Lance and Royce would be giving you shit. You're just broadcasting loud and clear to me."

After a pause where Aaron heard Aidan talking to Grace, his twin's mate, his brother continued, "Anything I can do to help?"

"Thanks, but no. You've got enough on your hands. How are Grace and the babies doing?" He smiled, thinking about how soon he would be an uncle. Aaron had never been a kid kinda guy, but Sydney, Lance's adopted daughter, had changed that for all of them.

"Siobhan says they're great and Sam did a sonogram yesterday. She said they're big and healthy. We still don't know if they're girls or boys, just that they're identical. Heavens help me if they're girls. I may have to kill every male within a thousand miles."

Aaron laughed under his breath as he imagined teenage daughters making his twin crazy. He immediately frowned, readily agreeing. "I've got your back. I remember what we were like as teenagers. There's no way in hell a hormone ridden teenage boy is getting anywhere near my nieces."

The sound of female laughter drifted through their link before Grace spoke. "You two are a mess. Whether our children are boys or girls, they will have their father's good looks and strength, along with my brains. We'll have nothing at all to worry about."

"I agree about your brains, but I'm damn sure hoping they have your looks, not his." Aaron laughed aloud, but Aidan's words stopped him short.

"We look just alike, asshole."

"Yeah, yeah, yeah. Whatever you say. You know I'm the good looking one."

"You two are incorrigible." Grace snickered. "Take care of yourself, Aaron, and man up. Just tell the girl how you feel. The rest is written in the stars."

He knew she was right but couldn't help smiling at her words. "Whatever you say, Counselor."

"Speaking of work, I'm due in court in the morning and I have briefs to read. Take care."

"You too, Grace...and thanks."

"I gotta run, too, Bro. Grace is right, stop the lovesick shit and get the girl."

"I will."

"Later," Aidan said.

"Later."

Aaron felt Aidan break their connection and concentrated on restoring the block between he and his brother. It was a true testament to how much the mating call was messing with him that he'd let his thoughts bleed through. Nothing like that had happened since they were young and still learning. Aaron was going to have to keep his shields locked and loaded. Aidan was right about the hell he would catch from the other Guardsmen of his Force if they caught a stray thought about Charlie. Of course, then he would have to kill them.

He moved to the front window when the girls talked about going to bed, listened as Charlie asked about the plants, and smiled when he heard the joy his presents had given her. She may not have known they were from him, but she now knew for sure they were *not* from Sam. It was only a matter of time before she figured it out. Dr. Charlene Gallagher was smart, as well as beautiful, strong, quick-witted, and a force to be reckoned with. All the things, he had to admit, that made her perfect for him.

When he'd realized she was his mate, Aaron had done everything in his considerable power to stay away from her. Had gone so far as to ask Rayne to take him off Sam's guard detail so that he didn't have to be at the hospital at all. Anything to avoid seeing the woman who made him think of all the things he'd sworn didn't matter.

Thoughts of her were incredibly distracting but also a lot of fun. Charlie had curves in all the right places, was tall enough to rest her head on his shoulder, and best of all, fit perfectly in his arms. The first time she'd glanced in his direction, her piercing blue eyes had grabbed him by the soul, making him helpless to do anything but stare. He'd felt the long, warm fingers of destiny wrap around his heart, embedding themselves for all time, followed by the scent of roses and dewdrops that had filled the air, a scent forever identifying her as his mate.

He closed his eyes, imagining the bounce of her short blonde hair and the sway of her perfectly rounded ass as she walked away from him. Her laugh reminded him of tiny bells singing their song, and her clear, melodious voice was smooth as the finest whisky. Aaron wanted to hear her shouting his name in passion as much as he wanted to draw his next breath.

A sigh escaped as the thought of their first kiss floated through his consciousness. Aaron had heard his brethren talk about kissing their mates. He'd scoffed and dismissed them as the musings of lovesick fools. It was now obvious he had joined the ranks of those fools, having to admit he'd never been more wrong in all of his hundred years. Her perfectly bowed lips were soft to the touch, sweet to the taste, and in that one heart-stopping kiss, he had been forever lost, helpless to do anything but claim the one miraculous woman meant for him and him alone.

I really am a lovesick idiot. The guys are never gonna let me live this one down.

He spent the night watching her sleep and wishing he were lying beside her. As the first rays of sunshine shone through the trees, Aaron touched Charlie's mind one last time. He had to be sure she was still sleeping soundly before he left. Rising from his crouch, he made his way down the dirt round to his Harley. After climbing on, he sped away, vowing to *man up* and talk to the Charlie later that day.

As he turned onto the road leading to the lair, a familiar voice sounded in his head. *"Where are ya, loser?"* Royce, the oldest of their Force and most levelheaded, laughed.

"Two minutes from home. Where are you?"

"Standing on your front porch with a bottle of scotch and an extra-large everything pizza. Hurry the hell up."

"Pizza and booze before noon?"

"Pizza at least, it's the breakfast of champions."

"I'm hurrying." Aaron chuckled.

True to his word, Royce was standing on his porch, a pizza in one hand and a bottle in the other. Parking his bike in the driveway, Aaron made quick work of opening the door and getting glasses and plates, not wanting the pizza to get cold. He also grabbed the iced tea and set the scotch aside for later while catching up with his longtime friend. "Not that I'm not glad to see you, but I thought you and Kyra weren't coming back until you found Calysta."

"Yeah, that was the plan, but Kyra found new clues and needed to talk to her Aunt Della. Plus, I think she wanted to see Grace. I have a feeling the baby bug has bitten my lovely mate."

"Oh *damn*, lucky you. You ready for the family gig?"

"Actually, I think I am. I know Kyra will be an awesome mom and having a little guy to teach to use a sword, hunt, and fish…be a mini-me, sounds cool."

"What if it's a girl?"

"Then I move us to the farthest regions of the earth and build a hundred foot wall surrounded by a moat filled with gators around our well-guarded home and have fifteen locks on every door of our castle."

Aaron choked and spit his tea across the table. "Seriously, old man? No way Kyra would let you get away with that."

"Get away with what?" Kyra asked as she made her way through the front door with another pizza and what smelled like muffins in a basket hanging from her arm.

"Your boy here says when you have a little girl…and I quote…'I'll move us to the farthest regions of the earth and build a hundred foot wall surrounded by a moat filled with gators around our well-guarded castle.' "

Kyra shook her head and chuckled. "Whatever, big guy. Just keep dreaming. If our children are anything like you and your brothers, we'll need our clan and theirs, plus the coven just to keep tabs on them."

"You know that's right," Royce agreed before pulling Kyra into his lap and kissing her like he hadn't seen her in days.

Aaron was immediately uncomfortable as thoughts of Charlie and feelings of jealousy that she was not in his arms threatened to overwhelm him. Never one for sharing his feelings, he quickly covered with his best defense…*sarcasm*. "All right you two, stop that shit or get a room."

The couple broke apart, the old man laughed, and Kyra stuck out her tongue as she crawled off Royce's lap. "Do you have anything to drink besides beer, scotch, or iced tea, nasty ass?"

"Nasty ass?" Aaron asked in mock anger.

She smacked him on the back of the head on her way past. "You heard me."

Chuckling and rubbing his head, he answered. "There's Diet Pepsi. Kyndel threatened to beat me senseless if I didn't have her favorite when she came over, so I relented." Then, as an afterthought he added, "There's also caffeine free something for Grace in the cabinet."

While Kyra was rattling around the kitchen, Royce asked, "So you gonna fill me in on what the hell's going on with Charlie?"

"You know most of the story. We danced. We kissed. She saw Anya in dragon form and ran away. End of story."

"Okay…" Royce's eyebrows rose so high they almost disappeared under the hair laying across his brow. When he spoke, his tone said he wasn't buying Aaron's story. "Why haven't you gone over there…made things right? Come on, man, you've battled hordes, wizards, and hunters, you gonna let one woman bring you down?"

Aaron chose to ignore the snort that came from the kitchen, deciding he didn't want the white witch in on the conversation any more than she already was. He stood as he spoke, "Yeah, sure, okay."

He threw his hands in the air as he paced from one end of the room to the other. "I'll just show up, knock on her door, say 'hey', then tell her all about dragons and knights and old mages that combined the two. If she hasn't fainted by then, or better yet, kicked me in the nuts, I'll also tell her she's my mate. And that the Universe said so. Wonder if I'll get the 'we're meant to be together for at least a thousand years or so' part out before she slams the door in my face?"

Turning on his heel and heading back the direction he'd come, he mumbled more to himself than his brethren, "Should go over like a fart in church."

Royce's chuckle stopped Aaron mid-pace and the words his brethren spoke grated on his nerves, especially because of their truth. "That's about the size of it. If I've learned anything, it's that straightforward and honest works the best. Oh! And then there's groveling…that seems to be a winner for me."

Kyra nodded behind him just as another voice entered the fray. "You know you really don't have to grovel. All you need to do is take your ass over there and talk to her," Sam instructed, shocking both men.

Aaron and Royce spun around at the sound of their brethren's laugh and found both with ear-to-ear grins.

Afraid to hope, Aaron asked, "You really think that's all it'll take?" Then added, pointing at Sam, "Weren't you sleeping soundly at the cottage just a few hours ago?"

"I was, but this whole dragon's mate thing means I don't need much sleep. Now, for your original question…I *know* that's all it'll take." Sam nodded and Lance shrugged behind her. Leave it to the pain in the ass of their group to lend no moral support whatsoever.

"We spent the night talking…"

"And drinking." Her husband laughed, quickly followed by a grunt as her elbow connected with his gut.

"As I was saying, we spent the night talking. She asked tons of questions. I answered them all the best I could, and when we went to sleep, she was her old self. I'm sure you could tell a difference in her."

The young doctor paused and winked with a coy smile plastered on her face. "I probably shouldn't tell you, and if any of you ever breathe a word of this, I will deny it and then kick your butts…" She looked around the room with narrowed eyes in an attempt to intimidate them all before continuing. "She's attracted to you but is resisting it, as only my stubborn bestie can do. Every time I mentioned your name, her pupils dilated and there was a catch in her breath. She's got it bad, but has no clue what's really going on. I explained mates and their connection, hoping it might lead her to a logical conclusion, but as I said, she's in denial. She's a sharp cookie, though. If she hasn't figured it out yet, it won't be long. Now it's all up to you, bud."

"See, like I said, straightforward and grovel." Royce snickered, heading to the kitchen.

Aaron slowly nodded, completely lost in thought as he tried to figure out exactly what to say to Charlie. Sam's next question caught his attention.

"Did you plant flowers for her?"

For the first time that he ever remembered, Aaron O'Brien felt his cheeks heat with embarrassment. He thought about denying what he'd done, but decided his brethren would hear the lie as quickly as it left his lips, so he did the only thing he could. He closed his eyes, took a deep breath, and answered, "Yeah, I did."

Lance and Royce roared with laughter before yelling, "*Holy Shit!*" in unison.

When Aaron opened his eyes, both Kyra and Sam were smiling at him with dreamy looks on their faces, and if that wasn't bad enough, the front door opened and in walked Aidan and Grace, just as Royce bellowed, "Lookie there, lover boy's been planting posies for his lady."

Lance slapped him on the back, laughing so hard he shook. "What's this I hear about flowers? Say it ain't so. The confirmed bachelor has been bitten by the love bug?"

The thought of punching his brethren in the mouth sounded good for a split second, but he knew there was no use. The cat was out of the bag. He had no choice but to deal with their crap.

"It was all I could think to do to make up for my monumental screw up. She'd been out walking while I was running for several mornings in a row. I saw her stop and look at flowers, and she seemed to like them. Saw daisies at the hardware store and I thought it might soften her up to find something waiting for her. I had plans to leave other presents and one day 'accidently' get caught, forcing her to talk to me." He stopped and looked around the room, surprised they were all listening and not giving him a hard time.

"But then Rian had a lead on the asshole. We were gone for over a week and I figured…" He let his words trail off, not sure what to say, and then finished barely above a whisper, "I convinced myself it wasn't working and that she probably thought it was all corny any way." He shrugged. "I just didn't go back."

Aaron knew he sounded like a whipped pup, and for the most part, that analogy was spot on. Head bowed, mortified that he had actually let his brethren *and their mates* see his soft underbelly, he almost fell out his chair when the voice of his Commander sounded from somewhere behind him. He didn't know Rayne had come into the house, proof he was in way over his head. They were all trained to be constantly vigilant, something that failed him when all he could think about was Charlie.

"Women *never* think flowers are corny, you dumbass. Now, stop making us all look like spineless wimps. Get your head out of your ass and claim your mate. Destiny waits for no man."

"And now for the voice of reason," Rayne's mate, Kyndel, laughed as she made her way around her husband and handed their son to his Auntie Kyra. "You just need to talk to her. Be honest. You're gonna have to drop all the macho shit. The little bit I've seen of Dr. Gallagher, and Sam can correct me if I'm wrong," she gestured towards the other woman as she spoke, "tells me she's not going to stand for any bullshit. She's an intelligent woman who's used to calling the shots. It's up to you to compromise."

Kyndel held up her hand, successfully halting his rebuttal and added, "Which I know is completely against your nature. You gotta suck it up, buttercup, if you want the girl."

With that, she headed to the kitchen to join the other women who had silently exited while she spoke.

Royce was the first to recover, looking at their Commander as he spoke. "That mate of yours damn sure has a way with words."

"That she does," Rayne confirmed, grabbing a glass and pouring some iced tea before sitting.

Aaron had just thanked the Universe that Devon wasn't in attendance since he'd given the most Zen of all his brethren a rash of shit like no other when Devon had found Anya. However, his prayers of thanks had come too soon. The front door burst open and in ran Sydney, Sam and Lance's daughter. A four-foot five inch bundle of curly blonde hair with boundless energy, she was chattering a mile a minute, pulling Devon and Anya along beside her.

"Hey Aaron! I brought Dev and Anya. Is Aunt Charlie here?"

Now even the kid is kicking my ass. Doesn't anybody sleep in around here?

Thankfully, Sam came in and saved the day. "No, Sweetheart, Aunt Charlie's not here. She's at the cottage, but we can go see her tomorrow if you like."

"Yay!" Sydney squealed as her mother ushered her into the kitchen with Anya close behind.

Devon grabbed a bottle of water from the small refrigerator tucked in the bottom of the antique china cabinet that had been his mother's, and took a seat next to Royce. Aaron could tell from the looks he was getting that Royce was bringing the other Guardsmen up to speed through their private link. His worst fears were confirmed when Devon took a long draw off his water, leaned back in his chair, and looked Aaron right in the eye. Devon's obnoxious grin only added to Aaron's trepidation. When he finally spoke, Devon's words caused the entire house to erupt in laughter. "I hate to throw your words back atcha, Bro, but…" the calmest of their Force paused, never breaking eye contact, "it seems as though your girl's gotcha all tied up in your underwear."

Unable to keep a straight face, Aaron laughed along, knowing he was only getting what he deserved. He'd given every single one of his brethren as much shit as he could shovel when they'd found their mates. It was only fair they return the favor. All he had to do was get it together and claim her as his own.

The razzing went on and on, but soon his brethren moved on. They ordered Chinese food for lunch since somehow several hours were wasted discussing his love life…or lack thereof. The whole crowd hung out watching soccer games he had DVRd until Royce came into the room with a determined look and his hands fisted at his sides. "Rian's found another trail."

The Guardsmen headed for the door as the older Guardsman went on, "It stops right before the mountain outside of town where we battled the wizards almost two years ago. Rian called Rory and the others to meet us there." Looking less than pleased, he went on, "I didn't know he was on patrol tonight."

"He wasn't supposed to be," Rayne answered as they loaded into the black SUVs parked outside. His tone said there would be words between the Commander of the Golden Fire Clan and the Elder of the Blue Thunder Clan in the very near future. Aaron was glad he had no dog in that fight.

The tension continued to raise the entire trip. Aaron could feel how much every Guardsman wanted this to be the time they finally caught the traitor. The vehicles stopped and they exited without a word. Rian motioned from behind a row of oak trees far off the beaten path.

Ever the Commander, Rayne was the first to speak, using their common link to avoid detection. *"What did you find?"*

"His scent ends behind the mountain on the far side of the lake. The trail is no more than a month old. Best guess is the traitor used the water to hide his tracks. Kellan found a blood trail as well. It's Andrew's. He's hurt....or was. If his dragon senses are only intermittent, he may still be healing."

As a unit they all turned, looking at the terrain. Aaron could hear several different conversations as each man tried to determine the best way to tackle the search without alerting the traitor to their presence. Rory and the rest of his Force arrived just as Royce said, *"We need to split up into four groups. Each group takes a side and we'll work our way up from the bottom. The little son of a bitch could be anywhere. There are at least a hundred caves and alcoves all over that monstrosity where he could be hiding. We don't want to spook him."*

"Roy's right," Rory agreed. "I also think we need to have a better game plan. I know Ri was excited, but a bunch of men with knives and swords running around in broad daylight are bound to freak out even the most sane human. Let's head back to the lair, make a plan, and come back after midnight when the rest of the world is asleep."

Aaron watched as the vein in Rayne's head began to bulge, a sure sign the Commander was about to lose his cool. Devon was the first to speak. "Someone needs to stay and keep watch. If Andrew is here, we need to make sure he doesn't wander off." Then volunteered. *"I'll take the far side."*

"I'll take the east side," Lennox, one of Rory's Force, said before turning and disappearing through the trees.

"I'm going west," Aidan responded. Then to Aaron alone, he said, *"You better go check on your lady."*

Aaron caught only the slightest glimpse of his twin's back as he used his enhanced speed to take his post, but his chuckle was loud and clear in his mind.

"Asshole," was Aaron's only response.

"South is mine," Kellan, another of the Blue Thunder clan, chimed in before evaporating into thin air. Aaron had heard he was what the military called a 'ghost'. Story was the man had been on more black ops missions than any other marine. He was the one they sent to places no one else could or *would* go. Whenever anyone asked about the scar on his cheek, his answer was always the same, "I could tell you, but then I'd have to kill you." Aaron knew Kellan meant what he said. He was a very scary dragon.

Rayne's voice brought him back to reality. *"All right, we'll reconvene at the Great Hall at eleven."*

Aaron glanced at his watch as he made his way back to their vehicles. *Ten hours until we're supposed to be at the Great Hall. Is that enough time?*

"I know you're not talking to me but since you asked." Aidan's laugh in his head let Aaron know he had dropped his guard again. *"Hell yes, it's enough time. Get your butt over there as soon as you can. Time's wasting."*

"I hear ya," was all he could say. He cut their connection and shored up his mental shields for the second time in less than twenty-four hours.

The return trip was quiet, but just as tension filled as the beginning of their excursion. They pulled up in front of his house, exited the vehicles, and headed inside. Aaron was almost to the house when he noticed Rayne and Rian had stayed back by the vehicles. Luckily, it looked like they were just talking, not throwing punches.

After making sure everyone was settled in, he took a quick shower, pulled on a T-shirt and jeans, and headed out the backdoor. As he pulled away, he called out to Royce, "I'm heading over to Charlie's. Be back in time for the meeting."

"Do what you gotta do. I'll cover if need be."

"Thanks."

"No worries."

He spent the ride trying to come up with something witty to say. It wasn't until he pulled in her driveway that he realized how nervous he truly was.

It's now or never and never is not an option, he heard his mother's voice repeating her favorite saying as he made his way up the walk.

What he saw made his blood run cold.

A broken clay pot, the front door was ajar, and Charlie nowhere in sight…

CHAPTER THREE

Restless and unable to stop thinking about all she and Sam had discussed the night before, Charlie decided she needed fresh air. Heading out for her walk, she glimpsed the daisies that had been anonymously planted. In the next three steps, the rose bush came into view and she became irritated.

Totally irrational, but I can't help it.

One about face later, she found herself in the kitchen making tea and looking through Sam's old cookbooks. Turning pages without even seeing them, Charlie slammed the book closed, growled under her breath, and stared out the window.

Her mind was so cluttered, a mass of pictures and thoughts…all that defied reason. She couldn't focus on any one thing for longer than a few seconds. Dragons and witches. Fate and Destiny. The Universe actually making *one* woman for *one* man. No, change that…one woman for one dragon. Hunters and wizards. It was all so confusing. There was so much more to the world then she had ever imagined. So many things that just didn't make sense.

She picked up the notes she'd made while talking to Sam, scanned the list, and tossed it across the table. Nothing on the paper was going to turn back time and make her forget all she'd learned. It was time to stop moping….time to get a grip and accept things as they were.

Come on, girlie. Up and at 'em. Do something constructive.

Making her way to the front porch, she took a deep breath of the fresh, crisp air, which amazingly cleared her mind. Charlie looked around and it was obvious no one had been paying attention to Sam's potted garden. The herbs needed weeding, vines needed trimming, and *everything* needed watered and fertilized.

Entirely focused on what she was doing, along with trying *not* to think of Aaron for the hundredth time, the sound of footsteps pulled her from her task. Gasping, Charlie spun, bobbling the pot she was working with before dropping it anyway. Of course, then she felt like a total idiot when she realized it was only Sam's neighbor walking his abnormally large dog.

Shaking her head at her lack of grace, Charlie shelved her ideas of a photo shoot for Better Homes and Garden and went in search of the broom and dustpan. Stopping in the kitchen for a quick drink of water, she once again heard footsteps, but chalked it up to her imagination and chuckled instead of freaking out.

With a glass in hand, she had just turned towards the faucet when the little hairs on the back of her neck stood on end. Worse than that, the marks on her back tingled, something that hadn't happened in years. Her heart raced. Her pulse pounded. She turned so quickly the glass she was holding slipped from her fingers. In the blink of an eye, the man she'd worked so hard to ignore was standing mere inches from her, saving the cup from certain death.

As Aaron stood to his full height of at least six feet four inches, his cerulean eyes held her captive. Tiny wrinkles at the corners of his eyes assured her she would find him grinning if she looked down at his very kissable mouth.

Staring deep into his eyes, Charlie sighed. She'd forgotten how ruggedly handsome he really was.

No one would *ever* accuse Aaron O'Brien of being pretty. His skin seemed to hold a permanent tan, showing just a few signs of years being outside in the sun and wind. No matter what time of day she saw him, he always had a five 'o'clock shadow, stubble she knew first hand that tickled when it touched her cheek.

His shoulders were broad, his waist trim, and her fingers tingled with the need to touch his chest as she'd done the night of their kiss. The longer they stood staring at one another the stronger the tingles in her back became, almost like cold chills running up and down her spine.

Somehow, his wonderful scent had slipped her mind. Standing this close, his scent filled her senses. It was as crisp as a winter morning after a fresh snowfall and made her think all sorts of thoughts that were better left tucked away.

Aaron was lethal. He was the epitome of 'sex on a stick'. The one man that could tie her in knots.

The tickle in her back reached an all-time high at the same time she realized he had no business in Sam's home, and more importantly, no business mere inches from her. Taking a step back, Charlie narrowed her eyes, pursed her lips, and slammed her fists onto her hips.

The best defense is a good offense.

"What are you doing here? You scared the hell outta me!"

His grin faltered for a split second before he cocked his hip against the counter and resumed his usual devil may care appearance. But she had seen a crack in his veneer. One she would use someday. Then he spoke, derailing her thoughts.

"I stopped by to…" He cleared his throat, the mesmerizing effect of his deep raspy voice lingering.

When he began again, his tone had softened and Charlie felt herself sway. Holding fast, she focused on his words instead of his voice. "I came to apologize… and explain. But then I saw the broken pot and the opened door and thought something had happened."

"Sam took care of that," was her retort, but it lacked the force she intended.

He was worried about me? Steady girl. Don't let him get the best of you…again.

"I know she did, but *I* owe you an apology."

"Okay. You could've done that over the phone."

"I tried several times, but you ignored my calls."

Knows that trick, does he?

"Yeah, well, there *is* such a thing as voicemail. Besides, I needed some time. It's not every day you see a real live dragon."

Aaron snorted and she immediately got the joke. Her attempt at hiding her smile was poor at best, so she gave up.

"Well, I guess it does happen every day for *you*. Does it? I mean, I can ask that, right?"

His snort turned into loud laughter. It was the first time she'd seen him really let go, except for their kiss. If possible, he was even sexier.

Asshole is gonna be the death of me.

The glance he gave her through his impossibly thick eyelashes made her think he had heard her thoughts.

Now, I've really lost it.

Before she could think further, he answered. "Yes, you can ask me anything. And no, it doesn't happen every day…but it can."

She nodded, trying to decide if she should hear what he had to say or throw him out on his butt.

Curiosity won.

"Anything, huh?"

"Yeah."

"What does it feel like to fly?" Charlie blurted out. Her cheeks heated and she thanked the Lord that Aaron chose to ignore her embarrassment.

He moved towards the table, holding out a chair and motioning for her to have a seat. When she sat, he took the chair adjacent to her before answering. "It's one of the best things about being a dragon. Most think it's being big and regal, or breathing fire, but flying is like no other feeling on earth. It is freedom, power, and it is life affirming. When I'm soaring across the skies, it gives me perspective, helps me think….makes me see my place in the world."

"Breathing fire?" she whispered, interrupting what he was about to say.

"Yeah, probably should've saved that for later," he ran his hand down his face and blew out a long breath. "But it's a fact…we *can* breathe fire. Most of the things you've read in fairy tales are true." He paused then quickly added, "Except about us being the bad guys. That's bullshit! The hunters and wizards made that up so people would rat them out. No dragon ever held a princess hostage in a tower or attacked a city they weren't battling. Truth be told, when dragons were just dragons, not shifters, they fought alongside knights to keep the King's peace. They were the good guys."

This has to be the weirdest conversation I've ever had.

No matter her internal conversation, Charlie could feel the pride in his words. Being a dragon was important to him. It was *who* he was and he loved it. Not many people could say that about themselves. Her respect for the most annoying man on the planet grew exponentially.

"What else would you like to know?" he interrupted her thoughts.

She thought for a moment and decided to ask what she really wanted to know. "Sam said each of you has a marking of their dragon, kinda like a tattoo…" Nodding his head and standing before she finished, he fisted the hem of his T-shirt and was suddenly shirtless.

Charlie sat in stunned silence. Not only was the dragon that covered most of his torso awe-inspiring, the man standing before her was absolutely breathtaking. The beast's head rested on the top of his right shoulder, the body and wings spread across his chest and abdomen, leaving the tail to wrap around his left hip. Of their own accord, her fingertips touched the tip of the dragon's wing sitting right above the waistband of his jeans. An electric current shot up her arm, through her body, and landed squarely in her womb.

She jerked her hand away and squeezed her thighs together. Their eyes met. She knew by the way his pupils dilated, he felt it, too.

Tentatively, never breaking eye contact, she let her fingers touch his dragon. Once again, she felt the spark, but this time was prepared. Her fingers traced the underside of the beast's wings, moving upward until she had to stand to continue her exploration. The dragon seemed to come alive as her fingers traced the intricate design of a beast she thought only lived in children's fantasies.

Charlie knew from her discussion with Sam that Aaron's dragon was silver, but she'd never imagined the tattoo on his skin would be so literal in its depiction. The afternoon sun danced over the glittering scales as it shone through the kitchen window.

Reaching the beast's massive body, she laid her hand flat against Aaron's chest, gently sweeping the length of its back and onto his neck. She felt the intricate design ripple against her palm. The electricity she felt at first contact grew between them the longer her hands caressed his body. Normally, Charlie resorted to her clinical expertise and logic to deal with situations that defied explanation, but standing face to face with a fairy tale come true, her imagination took over.

She saw the majestic warrior soaring across a deep blue sky, wings unfurled, head held high, basking in the glory of being alive. There would be sheer power resonating through his body. This beast knew he was at the top of the food chain, but had the dignity not to lord it over others. He was the epitome of nobility, a true master among the others.

The definition of the corded muscles in the dragon's neck was another testament of his tremendous strength. She chuckled that the position of Aaron's marking had her touching the back of the dragon's neck while lightly grazing the man's neck. His quick intake of air drew her eyes to his mouth. She watched longingly as just the tip of his tongue wet his bottom lip.

Acting on instinct alone, Charlie rose to her toes, leaned in, and laid butterfly kisses along his lip, following the path his tongue had taken. With her palms flat against his chest for support, she felt the thundering of his heart that mirrored her own. Unable to resist the man that filled her every thought, she sealed her lips to his, reveling in the feeling of completion that filled her.

Aaron groaned deep in his throat, the vibration teasing her hardened nipples as they pressed against his chest. She felt the warmth of his hands on her waist only a second before she was lifted in the air, spun around, and gently placed on the counter with him standing between her thighs.

Charlie tried to pull back and gather her wits, but Aaron would have none of it. He growled and pulled her tightly to his chest. Slammed his mouth to hers and demanded entry. Unable to do anything but follow where he led, she opened completely.

Her fingers dug into his shoulders. Her legs wrapped around his waist. His erection bumped against her excited clit, making her curse the denim that separated their bodies. Their hips moved in tandem, driving them higher. Aaron's fingers slid under her ass, lifted her against his body, and began walking towards the living room.

The sound of his cowboy boots striking hardwood told her they had reached the hallway and the little voice in the back of her head screamed, *Take me to bed or lose me forever*. Goose was nowhere around, but Aaron could fly and that was all that mattered.

His mouth left hers, nibbling along her jaw and kissing the little spot behind her ear that he somehow knew would drive her wild. She gulped air, trying to clear her mind, but all she could do was feel. Goose bumps rose all over her body at his whisper at her ear, "Which door is your room?"

"I'm upstairs, but the guestroom is the door on the right," she breathed, finding even that a difficult question to answer with her mind lost in the sensual haze the man she was presently wrapped around created.

Their forward motion stopped and Aaron's hands moved across her ass and under her shirt. His hands on her bare skin unleashed a flood of sensations and emotions so strong, Charlie was sure she would spontaneously combust. He skimmed her ribs, massaging as he went, until his thumbs rubbed the sides of her breasts, and then moved to gently tease the tips of her peaked nipples.

Charlie arched her back, threw back her head, and moaned. The markings on her back continued to tingle. Nothing had ever felt as good as his hands on her body did in that moment.

"You are absolutely gorgeous," he breathed, his low, baritone voice rumbling through her body. "Which makes what I am about to say one of the hardest things I've ever done in all my years. I…"

Aaron's hands left her breasts. Charlie was unable to stifle her disappointed groan. Just as her lips were about to touch his again, she realized she'd missed the rest of his statement. Her eyes popped open and she said, "What did you say?"

"Well…I…"

Before he could continue, Charlie slammed her hands against his chest, unlatched her ankles from behind his back, and struggled to get loose. "Put me down, you as…"

His hands tightened on her ass and he pulled her back until their bodies were flush, touching in every possible way. With an air of authority and between gritted teeth, Aaron rumbled, "Charlene. Stop. Hold still."

The strength of his grip and the force of his voice stopped Charlie cold. She looked him square in the eye and said the first thing that popped into her mind, "Did you just call me Charlene?"

"That's your name isn't it?" Any other time she would have laughed at his smartass response, but on the heels of being stopped when she was more turned on than she'd ever been in her life, Charlie snarled, "It's Dr. Gallagher to you. Now put me down."

She saw the twinkle return to his eye but couldn't be bothered with why. She wanted as far away from the biggest asshole she'd ever met in her life and she wanted that to happen *immediately*. His next remark shocked her into silence. "I will not. And you *will* listen to me."

The grin she loved to hate came to his lips. She thought about slapping it away. He slowly turned, sat on the edge of the bed, and positioned her across his lap without ever breaking eye contact. She could feel his erection against the outside of her thigh, could see his pulse pounding in the vein in his neck, and heard how he struggled to regulate his breathing, so she had no clue why they were sitting and talking instead of getting naked. They sat for the count of five, just looking into one another's eyes before he spoke.

"Let me make one thing perfectly clear. I want nothing more than to make love to you. I want it more than I want my next breath. More than I want to feel the sunshine on my skin. More than I want to wake to another day…" She started to interrupt, but his fingers magically appeared against her lips, effectively silencing her words. The grin left his face.

"I have wanted you from the moment I met you, but I promised myself when we were finally together, I would savor every moment. That it would last for *days upon days*." He paused and she could feel the importance of what he was saying, but had no idea what he was talking about.

Something big is happening and I'm clueless…perfect.

She saw a slew of emotions cross his handsome face before he finally began again. "Sam told you about my younger brother and his…*issues*?"

She nodded.

"Rian has a lead on where he may be hiding. We're going to find him tonight."

He leaned forward until their foreheads almost touched and she could feel his breath on her cheek.

"Our first time will *not* be a quickie and I will *not* leave you when it's over. I'm sorrier than you'll ever know that I let it get as far as it did. I truly only came over to apologize and talk."

His grin returned and he added, "I will admit, I like this…" he motioned between them, "better than arguing, but it will have to wait until tomorrow."

Aaron kissed the tip of her nose, set her feet on the floor, and stood beside her. Her eyes landed on his naked chest and she sighed. "All right, Mr. O'Brien, I'll let you off the hook this time, but if we're just gonna talk, then we have to get the hell out of the bedroom and you have to put your shirt back on."

She patted his chest before turning and heading out of the room. As she crossed the threshold into the hall, she chuckled over her shoulder, "I could use some iced tea. How about you?"

"And a cold shower," he grumbled.

Charlie knew she should be sorry since she was the one that started whatever it was that had just happened between them, but she wasn't and knew she wouldn't be. For once in her life, she'd let her heart run the show. Had given her head a rest. And it felt good…*really good*.

Tea poured and Aaron's shirt back on, the two retired to the deck behind the house. Several seconds of companionable silence passed before Charlie asked her first question. "How old *are* you?"

As soon as the words were out of her mouth, she wished them back in. Thankfully, he chuckled, lessening her embarrassment.

Dad always said my mouth was gonna be the death of me.

"I'll be a hundred and one in about six weeks."

"*Holy*…seriously?" Charlie spun in her seat to face him.

"Seriously." He leaned towards her and laid his hand on hers. "I will *always* be honest with you. I'm *truly* sorry we had to keep secrets from you, but that's all in the past. You ask, I'll answer."

"Cool, but back to your age… Sam said you guys live really long lives and age slowly, but I guess I had no clue you were that much older… I mean you were…Well, hell, there's no way to say this delicately. I had no clue you were that much older than me." She stopped and then immediately continued, "Are you the oldest?"

He smiled and shook his head, obviously enjoying her questions. "No, I'm actually one of the youngest you've met. As you know, Aidan and I are twins. I was born first, so technically Aidan's the youngest of our Force."

Charlie slid back into her seat, deep in thought. One of her favorite quotes from freshman English came to mind, *there are more things in heaven and earth, Horatio, than are dreamt of in your philosophy*. Nobody said it better than Shakespeare. It was one thing to have Sam tell her how old they were, it was another thing completely to get the information straight from the horse's…*oops*…dragon's mouth.

Apparently she was lost in thought, because the next thing she knew Aaron was kneeling next to her chair and asking, "Are you okay? Did I freak you out?"

"No, not at all. Just thinking," she quickly answered. "You're gonna have to excuse me. I'm the daughter of a cop *and* a doctor, so it may take a beat for me to absorb everything."

"I understand." He stood and held out his hand. "Will you take a walk with me?"

Taking his hand, Charlie stood. "Sure."

As they approached the steps leading to the yard, Charlie stopped and pointed at the daisies in the large terra cotta pot. "Did you do that?"

"Guilty." She enjoyed the shy look of a little boy busted that crossed his face.

When her feet hit the grass, she pointed to the rose bush. "That, too?"

"Yep. That, too."

"Thank you," she chuckled.

He shrugged. "I was trying to think of anything that would make you forgive me and at least speak to me. Did they work?" he asked as they started towards the trail behind Sam's cottage.

"They *are* beautiful, but I have to admit that I thought Sam had sent Lance over to plant them as an apology."

"You were half right," he responded.

"How did you know I liked daisies?"

"I saw…It was a guess." He quickly corrected.

"Nope, you don't get off that easy, dragon man. What were you going to say?"

He sighed and glanced ahead before looking back at her and finally answering. "One of the days when I was at the hospital with Devon while Anya was in a coma, I passed by the nurse's station. You were there. One of the volunteers was passing out flowers. Her cart was piled high with a variety of blooms, but out of all of them, you leaned down and smelled the daisies. Figured that was important, so I tucked it way."

Charlie was amazed to think that he'd noticed one insignificant event and even more that he'd *remembered* it. Something deep inside her heart that had been stirring since they kissed at Devon and Anya's wedding clicked into place. She wasn't sure what it meant, but knew it was something she'd have to think about when she had some time alone.

They walked on, talking about anything and everything. She was shocked at how many things they had in common. When they reached the lake, Aaron steered them towards a huge rock, sat down, and pulled her into his lap.

"But…" She started and Aaron interrupted.

"Charlie, I will take every chance I get to have you in my arms. Now, sit here and watch the sunset with me." He kissed the top of her head and together they watched the sun go down.

On the walk back, Charlie asked, "Wanna stay for supper? There's not much, but I'm sure I can whip up something."

He smiled and nodded. "I'd love to."

As soon as they reached the cottage, Charlie scoured the refrigerator and the cabinets. "I have two chicken breasts, a jar of Alfredo sauce, some noodles, and the stuff to make a salad. Sound good?"

"Sounds great. Garlic bread?"

"I don't know, check the freezer," she answered, grabbing a skillet to sauté the chicken.

Aaron slid in behind her and reached round to lay the garlic bread on the counter, placing a kiss on her cheek before backing away. Charlie took a bowl from the cabinet, handed it to him, and pointed. "The knives are in that drawer. You've got salad duty."

He chuckled as he washed his hands and proceeded to do as she instructed. Almost three hours later, they'd talked, laughed, and eaten. Aaron had even washed the dishes. He'd answered all her questions without hesitation and had even asked a few of his own. So when he got a faraway look in his eye for just a moment and missed what she said, Charlie felt comfortable enough to ask, "Something wrong?"

"No, not at all." He laid his index finger to his temple and said, "Royce was telling me our meeting was in thirty minutes and I'd better not piss Rayne off." He snickered, letting Charlie know he regularly pissed off his friends.

Nothing surprising there.

Standing, he once again held out his hand. She laid hers in his without hesitation. They walked to the front door where he proceeded to kiss her to within an inch of her life before pulling back and looking deep into her eyes. "I'll be back, *Dr. Gallagher*, and you better be ready."

It wasn't until she watched him straddle his Harley and ride off into the darkness that her brain reengaged.

That man is gonna be the death of me…but what a way to go!

She grinned and locked the door.

CHAPTER FOUR

Aaron flew back to the lair, not literally, but definitely figuratively. His Harley roared over hills, took curves like it was on rails, and damn near broke the sound barrier.... and he owed it all to one special woman. It was as if the weight of the world had been lifted from his shoulders. There'd never been a question that Charlie was attracted to him, especially after their first kiss, but the few stray thoughts he'd been able to pick up from her confirmed she was falling just as hard and fast as he was. Their mating link was growing, and as much as he'd thought he didn't want that to happen, he couldn't be happier.

A few times during the amazing hours they spent together, Aaron pondered telling Charlie she was his mate, but he was just enjoying their time together too much to start an intense conversation. Not to mention, he'd almost lost his head, as well as other important body parts, when he had to throw cold water on their passion. He knew he would have to tell her soon or she would see it as another betrayal...one he didn't think she would get over. It was a risk he wasn't willing to take.

He smiled thinking about how pissed she'd gotten. Not something most men did when the woman they wanted to spend forever with was trying to murder them, but then Aaron was no ordinary man, and his mate was no ordinary woman. She had an inner fire and a strength that matched his in every way. Whatever doubts he had in the past were wiped away after just a few hours with Dr. Charlene Gallagher. She was his...that's all there was to it.

Lance's voice sounded in his head just as he turned into the lair. *"Where you at, Bro?"*

"Just turning in." He glanced at his watch. *"What's up? I'm not late, yet."*

"Just making sure you didn't get...caught up." He heard the smile in his brethren's voice and thought about giving him shit, but decided he was in just too good of a mood.

"Oh, I wanted to, but tonight is too important."

"So everything's cool with Charlie?"

"Everything's cool." Aaron chuckled. *"And tell Sam thanks."*

Lance laughed. *"Guess you knew she was listening in?"*

"I figured as much. It's all good. I'm pulling in now. See you at the meeting."

"See ya there, and Aar?"

"Yeah?"

"'Bout time you manned up." His laughter rang through their link.

Aaron chuckled. *"Yeah, yeah, yeah, bite me."*

Almost three hours later, eight dragons, six werepanthers, and one white witch headed to the park just behind the clearing that led to the mountain, where Rian was sure the traitor was hiding out. They had been in constant communication with the four Guardsmen that stayed behind. Surges of dragon magic with an undertone of black magic let them know the traitor was close by but being careful not to disclose his exact location.

Kyra was along to provide magical cover and to scry for the little prick. Aaron had laughed when Royce had pulled her to the side, trying to convince her to stay behind. He watched the little witch twist her mate around her little finger and get exactly what she wanted. Aaron knew beyond any doubt that Charlie would do the same thing to him. A few weeks ago that knowledge would've pissed him off, but after spending time with her, it only reassured him that the Universe knew what She was doing.

Parking the SUVs on the far side of the park, the Guardsmen and their allies made their way to the picnic tables where the others waited. Rayne spread out a map and began giving instructions.

"Devon, Aidan, Kellan, and Lennox have narrowed it down to the far side of the mountain. Max and his werepanthers will take the trails closest to the lake in animal form. Devon and Kellan both have cuffs and chains that Kyra magically reinforced to keep the little shit bound. Royce, Rory, and Lennox will be in dragon form on the three largest ledges. Because of their dark color, coupled with our shielding, they should remain unseen. Everyone else take a trail. Find the little asshole."

Aaron had to laugh, it was one of the shortest speeches his Commander had given in the last eighty years. Rayne was a highly respected leader among *all* dragon kin, but brevity was not one of his strong suits. There'd been times over the years when Aaron had prayed for the man to shut the hell up, but had always listened and learned from Rayne's vast expertise. His short speech meant something was up...something he'd have to look into later.

Jogging ahead, he caught up to Aidan, Rian, and Kyra. The twins had the blood connection to the traitor. Rian's dragon magic was incredibly powerful and allowed the leader of the Blue Thunder Clan to track damn near anything, anywhere, any time. But Kyra was their ace in the hole. One of the most powerful white witches in the world, the daughter to the Grand Priestess, and fully mated to the oldest on the Force. There wasn't a spell she couldn't work. The four of them, combined with the power of the lake would enable them to scry for Andrew, as well as track even the smallest amount of magic he may use.

When they reached the lake, Kyra began to sprinkle salt in a circle from a large burlap bag while directing the others. "Aaron, will you get a fire started in the middle? Rian, fill the brass urn with water from the lake, and Aidan, I need the bags in my backpack set at the four corners, if you please?"

She winked and began chanting. From her grin, Aaron knew she was having fun, no matter the severity of the situation. He wished he could say the same. The longer it took to get the hunt started, the more tension filled his body. Charlie had been a beautiful distraction but reality was staring him in the face, and it was time for justice.

A few weeks ago, he would have savored the hunt for the traitor. He dreamed of the day they would finally remove the black mark from his family's heritage. Dreamed of watching his younger brother in chains, imprisoned for his crimes, pleading for mercy when there would be none. It would be the one time the blood of a dragon staining the ground would not make Aaron sick. The little shit had whined about torture, now he would know death.

Aaron could only imagine the shame his parents felt, looking down on their youngest from the Heavens, seeing the abomination he'd become. Andrew would be caught, stand trial before the Tribunal, and die a traitor's death. It was the only way to remove the dishonor from their family name.

Aaron dug deep, trying to find at least an ounce of sympathy for his brother turned traitor, but there was none. He'd done it to himself. Andrew was responsible for his own fate. The Heavens knew Aidan had done everything in his power to convince Andrew to turn himself in, even when the asshole had kidnapped and tortured Grace. Sure, 'A' had fought their little brother, had threatened to tear him limb from limb, but after all was said and done, Aidan still wanted to see the shithead returned to the clan.

Like that shit's ever gonna happen. Asshole needs to die. There's no redemption after what he's done.

The fire he'd built reached a good blaze. The flames licked at the night as Aaron stood staring...reliving a time when the three brothers had been thick as thieves and twice as bad.

Before their little brother had been born, the twins had been inseparable. Nothing could come between them. Their mindspeak had been immediate. They finished each other's sentences and shared each other's thoughts. Their days had been filled with fun and training, always dreaming of a future filled with honor.

Along came Andrew with his mismatched eyes and chubby little face. Things should've been awkward, but the little bugger fit right into their gang, brandishing his stick turned sword like a pro, and following orders like a true soldier. Their duo became a trio and they never missed a beat.

Andrew quickly picked up their strategy as they sought to free princesses from the clutches of the evil sea captains or liberate captives from their prisons. The brothers' days were filled with fun and dreams of the day they would assume their father's role. The three would become the proud Guardsmen they were meant to be.

All had gone as planned and they had years of ridding the world of their greatest enemies. Aaron had always been the muscle, Aidan the brains, and Andrew possessed the unique ability to see the whole picture. Their parents had attributed it to him being '*the Special One*' and maybe that was true, but Aaron always figured it was just that the three of them made the perfect team. They had completed mission after mission, enjoyed countless victories over their enemies, and been as close as three brothers could be.

Sure, Andrew had been a lazy bum most of the time. Everyone, not just the twins, took up for him, kicked his ass when he screwed up, put up with his lame excuses, and treated him like one of their own. But his ability to see the big picture had always made up for all his shortcomings. That ability was one that should've come in handy the night everything went to hell, however, there's no explaining Fate.

"Yo, dreamer, whatcha say we get this show on the road?" Kyra's words, along with the swat to his arm, brought him back to the future.

"Sounds good to me." Aaron chuckled as he backed away, taking his spot in their circle.

"We're standing at the four corners–air, water, wind, and earth. These elements will give us the power needed to track the traitor and provide the cover our friends need."

She pulled a small silver box and the antique mirror she often used from her backpack. Opening the box, the fragrance of herbs drifted on the breeze, herbs Aaron knew were also in the sachets laid at their feet. He remembered some of them from previous spells–Angelica root for protection, Caraway for protection from evil, specifically black magic, Cinnamon for success, and Holly Leaf for luck, the others he couldn't distinguish, but trusted Kyra to mix up the right concoction for their needs.

Their little witch continued, "Everyone close your eyes and imagine a large bubble with you at the center." She paused for several seconds and then said, "Now expand your bubble until it touches the others."

Magic, both Earth and Dragon, danced over his skin like fireflies on a summer's night. In his mind's eyes, Aaron watched his sphere expand until it bumped the other three. The edges of the spheres wavered. He watched the colors of his aura mix and mingle with those of the others, blurring the lines and making a kind of real life mosaic.

The pressure built to an uncomfortable level. A loud 'POP' reverberated within their containment, followed by a shock wave that almost knocked him to the ground. From the looks on Rian and Aidan's faces, they experienced it also.

"No worries, guys. Everything that happens in the bubble stays in the bubble." Kyra chuckled her answer to his unasked question.

She began the spell that sounded more like a lullaby than an incantation. "We pray to the Goddess of All and the Universe for help to bring justice where there has been none. Provide us with the cover of your dark skies, keep our scent unknown by your winds and footsteps unheard by all ears. Only you can give us the power and strength we need to conquer evil and restore the balance. So it is written, so it shall be. Blessed be."

She repeated the same words over and over. Their containment grew, surrounding the entire mountain and the lake. Her chant stopped, the immediate silence almost deafening. Kyra laid down the box and picked up the antique mirror, along with a deep purple pouch. Moving forward, she dumped the herbs on the glass, speaking in Latin as she went. Aaron had seen the white witch scry before, but on this night, her focus was more intense. Her power radiated in all directions, leaving a white stream of energy in its wake.

The mirror vibrated in her hands as Kyra's chant rose, not only in volume but also in its depth of emotion. She was pouring everything she had into finding the traitor. She looked up several long minutes later, her violet eyes glowing with power.

"Join hands and repeat after me. *We seek the traitor, blood of our blood. Once brother, now enemy. Show us his location, show us his face.*"

Over and over they repeated Kyra's words until the mirror flashed blue and then red, then back to blue in an endless loop. The witch's brow furrowed as she watched the staccato pattern. Several tense seconds passed. The lights sped to a blur then stopped on a dime, as if a switch had been flipped. There one minute, gone the next.

Kyra murmured in Latin. Nothing happened. Shaking her head, she muttered, "Well, shit!"

"What is it? Is the dick here?" Aaron asked, working hard to contain his frustration. His dragon was chuffing and blowing smoke, demanding he take action.

"I don't know…" Her words trailed off as she continued to study the mirror.

Kyra spoke, barely above a whisper. "There's something…but…it's different." She took a deep breath, and then said with more confidence, "There's dragon magic and black magic, but it *feels* different than Andrew. There's nothing really evil about it. Even the black magic is just kind of *blah*…almost worn out. It's really weird."

Dropping to her knees, Kyra dug through her large duffle. She pulled out several different colored pouches, another brass bowl, and a small silver knife. "I'm going to have to do a little blood magic. It's not black, I promise, but it's the only way I know, short of running back to the lair and looking up a new spell to figure out what it is that I'm seeing…or *not* seeing. I'm sure you can hear what's going on outside our little bubble, and to say it's nothing is a huge understatement. They're just spinning their wheels. Best guess…Andrew has laid false trails. Worst guess…there are traps. Can one of you send that along to the troops? My brain's a little busy right now." She chuckled and Aaron once again had to admire her gumption.

"Kyra says to look beyond your senses. Look for magic, might be dragon or black or even earthen. Whatever it is, it's magical and she can't get a lock on it. And whatever our little witch can't see can't be good. Also, watch for traps. The little bastard loves to fuck with us." Aaron sent it through mindspeak to all the dragons and heard Devon passing it on to the panthers.

Between wanting his little brother under lock and key, his dragon pawing at his insides like they were a scratching post, and Kyra not knowing what the hell they were up against, Aaron was about to lose his mind. Any other time he would've been pacing and ranting, but they were trapped in a magic bubble that seriously limited the space he had to work through his frustrations.

Talk about having your thumb up your ass!

He listened to the Guardsmen searching the mountainside, felt their anger and irritation at once again turning up empty-handed. Every lead was a dead end. Every scent trail led nowhere. The dragons shared no mind-to-mind communication with Max and his Pride, but their anger at Andrew's games was filling the air around the mountain as well.

The fact that his dickhead little brother had spent so much time laying false trails proved to Aaron that Andrew *had* been on that mountainside and was continuing to protect it. The little bastard was doing everything possible to hide in plain sight.

I have to do something besides stand here and watch Kyra play witch.

No sooner had the thought crossed his mind than Aidan and Rian turned in his direction, nodding their heads. Rian was the first to speak. *"Kyra will be safe inside the circle. Royce agrees. Let's get the hell outta here."*

As one unit, the Guardsmen moved from the protection of their mini circle into the massive shielding spell. Their enhanced hearing told them the location of everyone systematically searching the mountainside. They chose the trails to the east.

Rian took the lead, giving military hand signals as they combed the terrain. The Guardsmen combined their enhanced senses and connection to the traitor, building the strongest tracking net Aaron had ever seen. As they moved across the mountain, there were spikes in recognition, but with their collective powers, it was easy to spot what was old, new, and fake. Unfortunately, everything new was a trick. Fortunately, it was mostly dragon mixed with earthen magic and only a touch of black magic. Apparently, the loss of his wizards had cut off Andrew's supply of the dirty shit, which should make catching the traitor a hell of a lot easier.

"Feel that?" Rian asked, his fist in the air, stopping their forward motion.

Aaron changed his focus and felt Aidan follow suit. There was a disturbance outside the magic shield. The mountain filled the air with hate, anger, and determination. It grew in intensity as the pounding of footsteps shook the earth.

Royce spoke from high above. *"Hunters. Looks like an entire pack converging from three sides. Three sets of thirty and they know we're here."*

"Wanna blow the cover and take 'em on, Commander, or stay hidden and leave. It's your call," Rian called to Rayne.

There was a moment of silence while Aaron imagined Rayne contemplating their next move, the rest of the dragons awaiting his answer.

"Max and the panthers are good with whatever you decide," Devon interjected.

"Kyra, can you feel the hunters?" Rayne questioned.

"Yep, sure can. It'll be less than half a mile until they reach the outer border of our spell."

"Hold out until they are within twenty-five feet. If possible, let them in, and then close the door behind them. We'll handle the rest."

"Aye, aye, Captain," Kyra answered.

Aaron heard several snorts from his brethren and couldn't stop his smile. The tension level within their shield lowered. Kyra was a great witch and a *huge* smart-ass.

Perfect combination.

Ignoring the laughter, Rayne continued, *"The rest of you split up and get ready. We need to take the hunters out as quickly as possible. Royce, Rory, and Lennox, be ready to bring the fire if needed. You'll also need to burn the bodies."*

"We're ready," the Guardsmen in dragon form answered in unison.

Their minute long wait seemed to last for hours. No one said a word. Aaron was sure everyone held their breath. The sound of Kyra's voice brought them all to attention. *"One…Two…Three…and it's up."*

"Ready. They'll be here in five…four…three…two…and NOW!" Rory shouted the command.

"Let me know when to close the door," Kyra yelled over the sounds of Guardsmen engaging in battle.

The clanging of swords echoed through their enclosure. The *whish* of the hunter's arrows as they missed their targets, along with the sounds of battle, joined the skirmish. Out of the corner of his eye, Aaron saw the giant cats getting into position just as a broadsword narrowly missed his head. The hunters fighting tactics were evolving. They added swords to their repertoire.

Hell yeah! Now for some fun.

Narrowing his focus to only the black hooded figure before him, Aaron steadied his stance and loosened his grip on the leather handle of his katana. Fear flashed in the eyes of his opponent. He noted the slight shiver that shook his enemy's body and had to grin.

Scared, huh? Good for you, but it won't save your ass tonight.

Desperation and fear leaked from every pore as the hunter lunged forward, swinging his blade at Aaron's neck. The Guardsman lifted his left hand, effectively blocking the strike with his forearm while slashing his opponent's neck in one swift motion. Blood spurted from the hunter's neck as he fell to the ground.

Unable to care, Aaron prepared for the next. They came one right after the other, all unprepared for a fight with the century-old Guardsmen. He hated the loss of life, but they had attacked and he had to defend. They were brainwashed fanatics and, therefore, unable to be reformed.

The black figures were running in all directions. Some fought, most sought cover. Whatever battle plans they'd come into the fight with had once again been blown to hell by the dragons.

Still the fight continued. Hunters' screams bounced off the walls of their magical containment. Bodies dropped. Blood soaked the ground as dead hunters littered the ground.

Aaron made his way up the mountain, exterminating all threats that came his way. He had no idea how long they fought, only the sound of Royce's voice in his head slowed his siege.

"Less than a dozen remain on the ground and they're pounding against the containment to be let out. I count ten on the mountain, all in Aaron and Aidan's vicinity."

Glancing to the side, Aaron saw his twin fighting two hunters at once. His style was finesse where Aaron's was brute force. They truly were mirror images of each other. His musings were cut short when the battle cry of one fearless, or stupid, hunter cut through the air. The hunter's blade made contact with Aaron's upper arm, leaving a bloody trail in its wake.

Ignoring the fire that tore through his arm, Aaron countered with an upswing, barely missing his enemy, who spun before thrusting forward. His bravado was his undoing. A slight misstep caused the hunter to lean to his left. Aaron capitalized on the other's misfortune and swung with purpose. His blade cut through his opponent's midsection like it was no more than hot butter. A barely audible groan were the hunter's only dying words as he crumpled to the ground in a heap of blood and entrails.

"Nice work," Aidan called out before turning to engage with one of the last hunters left standing.

"You, too," Aaron responded, using his enhanced speed to tackle a hunter aiming his bow at the back of Kellan's head.

Spinning as if he had eyes in the back of his head, Kellan nodded his thanks and took off after the last armed assailant. Just as the hunter fell, Rory called out the all clear. Rayne's command quickly followed, *"Kyra, keep up the shielding until all the bodies have been burned and removed. The rest of you help with the cleanup."*

An hour later all remnants of their fight with the hunters had been eliminated, and thanks to Kyra's magic, even the grass and foliage had been returned to their original luster. Aaron and Aidan approached the original circle. The panthers and dragons had returned to human form and the other Guardsmen stood in groups discussing what had just happened.

Rian was the first to address the entire group with Max at his side. "It's obvious this was an ambush. We haven't seen hunter activity in this area for quite some time. It's also obvious who set us up. I *know* the traitor was here. Some of the clues were real, but the majority was bogus. The good thing is we took out an entire pack of hunters and Kyra and I now have a good taste of his dragon magic. Tracking him will be much easier."

Rayne picked up where Rian left off. "Good job everyone. Thank you to Max and his panthers, we couldn't have done it without you. See you all this evening at seven in the Great Hall."

It was almost daybreak as the loud 'POP', followed by what sounded like air escaping a balloon, signaled Kyra's release of the shielding spell. Aaron listened as Rory and Lance gave blow-by-blow accounts of their battles. His thoughts drifted to Charlie. He reached through their growing mating bond and found his mate blissfully asleep.

She's dreaming of me… of us.

He was so lost to the beautiful dream Charlie was having of them together, Aaron ran right into Lance's back. The other Guardsman spun in his heels, took one look at Aaron, and burst out laughing. Aaron prepared for what he knew was about to come.

"This is better than soccer on Sunday with a case of beer and no commercials. Smartass is in love."

"I must say it's refreshing to see you joining the ranks of the fallen," Royce added, sliding to the right to avoid Aaron's fist.

"How the mighty have fallen. Thank the Heavens it's not me," Rory added, slapping Aaron on the back.

Aaron was just about to respond when a voice he had hoped never to hear again blasted through his mind. He spun towards Aidan, whose facial expression mirrored his own. *"Laugh it up. Enjoy your fun. It's only a matter of time, Brothers. Soon there will be nothing left of you or your pitiful excuse of a life."*

CHAPTER FIVE

Andrew sat on the highest ledge, using the little bit of earthen magic he'd been able to gather, combined with his dragon magic, to stay hidden while he sent his useless brothers a message. He knew it was impetuous, but the idiots and their *brethren* had invaded his sanctuary. Caused him to abandon the only safe place he could make it to with all his injuries. Injuries that weren't healing, no matter how much power he forced into them.

Kyra would track him if he stayed out in the open much longer. He just had to see the looks on their pathetic faces when he made contact. It was more than worth the risk to see their dumbfounded looks. He had always been the smartest of the brothers. The *wonder twins* had all their special powers, but he was the thinker of the family, the one able to see the whole picture.

His genius plan of using the hunters had worked out perfectly. Luckily, he'd kept in touch with a few of the old network. They were happy to hear from him and even happier to come after the most elite of all the Dragon Guard Forces. Andrew had known they would fail. *Hell*, he'd even counted on it. It had been the distraction he needed to make them believe he'd abandoned the mountain in search of safer accommodations.

The last few years had been hard. Andrew had suffered more than anyone had a right to, and always because of others' incompetence. John, his apprentice, had been the only one he could trust, the only one worthy– and the dragons had killed him. Living in a cave was lonely and far beneath what he deserved, but it served his purpose.

The time was at hand when he would finally be able to exact revenge on the brother that left him for dead and the pieces of shit that he'd once called brethren. His thoughts of revenge and the prophecy had been all he'd focused on during his weeks in seclusion. Using John's notes, and what he remembered of a long forgotten dragon language, he'd translated more of the ancient texts. It was more prose and flowery writing than Andrew liked. More than once, he'd wished the writers would just get to the point, but at least it had been something to keep his mind occupied and sharp.

Clutching the old, worn volume to his chest, he pulled his remaining Concealment Amulet over his head. Creeping back to the alcove deep inside the cave he'd been inhabiting, he was careful not to dislodge the makeshift splint or tear the stitches he'd painstakingly knit into his own skin. Andrew held in the groans of pain for fear of discovery. The throbbing was debilitating as he crawled on his elbows and one knee, dragging the disabled appendage behind. The only thing that kept him moving was his promise to make every one of the useless, good for nothing dragons die… slowly and painfully.

Sweat-drenched and out of breath, Andrew leaned against the cool rocks of the cave walls. His head fell to the side merely from its weight. His mind drifted into a twilight state, something between asleep and awake, protecting as much of his body as it could from the pain. He drifted into a memory of one of his first days at the lair following his parents' death.

Andrew walked towards the training pit, looking for his brothers. He knew he had big shoes to fill and couldn't wait until the day the giant with the shocking red hair gave him the go ahead to train with the real *Guardsmen. Rounding the corner, he heard the clang of swords. The air filled with the sheer determination of the trainees trying to beat their trainer.*

Cutting through the courtyard surrounding the Great Hall, the sound of crying cut through all the other noise. It was so pitiful, such anguish, such loneliness. One of the most painful things he'd ever heard. The female's sobs reached right into his chest, squeezing his heart, making it hard for him to breathe.

Unable to move forward, Andrew changed directions. Pushing through the bushes heavy with blooms, he used the girl's pain as a beacon. Just past the fountain, he caught sight of a royal blue sweater and one small white tennis shoe peeking out from under the grape arbor.

Paying more attention to the girl than his surroundings, Andrew stubbed his toe on a bench, knocking a small brass bell from the corner. The clang scared the girl, causing her to cry out and scramble even farther under the arbor until totally hidden from view.

He crept towards her, calling out as he neared. "It's okay. I've just come to check on you."

He reached the edge of the structure draped in vines, heavy with huge leaves and grapes. The muffled sounds from underneath let him know she was trying to silence her sobs and mask her pain. Any other time he would have turned around and left her to deal with her own problems, but something about the sounds of her grief, combined with her scent and the mere fact that he felt her anguish, kept Andrew glued to the spot and forced him to speak again.

"I promise I'm a good guy. I'm a Guardsman in training. Maybe you know my brothers. They're the twins, Aaron and Aidan."

Waiting to the count of ten, Andrew wondered if maybe his transformation had left him a little crazy and he'd imagined the whole thing. He'd never heard of anyone suffering lasting damage, but there was a first time for everything. Impatient with the lack of communication from the wounded creature inside, he called out for the third time.

"Okay if I come in? I'm feeling a little crazy standing out here talking to the leaves. I'm sure if anyone can see me, they're gonna report me to Mrs. Walsh and she's going to want to check my melon."

The giggle he heard was like the sound of the little bells on his mother's favorite bracelet. His spirit soared and his dragon purred just to know that he had soothed her. Bending at the waist, he lifted the leaves out of the way and entered the arbor. There, in the corner, sat a tiny slip of a girl. Even in the limited light, her silky brown tresses shined as they swept across the top of her shoulders when she bowed her head. Her large brown eyes, red rimmed from tears, were so dark he could barely see her pupils. In the single glimpse he got, they sparkled like the rarest onyx. The sweet scent of daffodils invaded his senses and for just a moment, he felt lightheaded.

The female's sobs had stopped, but there was a lingering sadness that Andrew felt compelled to soothe. Kneeling just a few feet from where she sat, he cooed, "Wanna talk about it?"

The silence stretched between them until Andrew was sure his question would go unanswered. Just as he was about to speak again, she lifted her head and looked him right in the eye. Shaking her head, she whispered in a defeated voice, "Wouldn't do any good anyway."

"Why don't you give me a try? If nothing else, I'm a good listener."

He knew he was pleading and hoped it didn't scare her, but something in the very depth of his soul told him this one girl was important to his future. No sooner had the thought crossed his mind than his dragon chuffed in agreement. The girl sat back, stretched her legs in front of her, and simply stared.

Wanting...no needing, to hear her voice again, Andrew asked, "Can I at least know your name?"

She shrugged. "What's yours?"

"Andrew."

"Nice name."

"Thanks." He waited as patiently as possible, hoping and praying that she would talk again, but all she did was sit as still as a statue, taking in his every movement.

Before he could think of anything witty to say, she spoke. Her voice was a little higher than before, but still clear as a bell. It reminded him of the violin his uncle played during their clan celebrations.

"Would you believe me if I told you I don't remember my name?"

"Darlin', I'd believe anything you want me to." He grinned.

"Really?"

"Swear to it." She smiled and he swore his heart skipped a beat. "Now, you wanna tell me why you're so sad?"

Andrew shook himself awake, unable to endure remembering one of the best days of his life. He cursed himself, sick to his stomach that he'd become sappy enough to think about a time when he believed everything was great and that he'd be a big, bad Dragon Guardsman. He'd actually entertained the thought that the sweet girl in the grape arbor might have been his mate.

He'd seen her on and off during his time with the clan, always promising himself that he would get to know her better, but it seemed that something always stopped him, something always got in the way. Then his world had gone to hell and she'd been all but forgotten until his brief trip down memory lane.

His entire life he'd listened to stories of how great dragon kin was and how all they wanted to do was make the world a better, safer place for all kinds. Of course, Fate had shown him that it was all propaganda. A complete and total load of bullshit. Bullshit that he and he alone was going to expose and burn to the ground.

Pushing back up onto his good knee, leaning forward on his elbows, he finished the slow trek to his pallet located next to the lagoon. Collapsing next to the pool, he grabbed his cup, filled it with water, and drank until his body temperature finally started to return to normal.

Sitting up and scooting until his back touched the wall, Andrew removed the ancient text from under his shirt. Opening the book, he pulled out the pages with John's translations and began to review.

A powerful white witch sworn to the Earth, of long regal lineage made whole by human love, must mate a dragon of royal descent marked by devastating loss and the heart of not one clan but two.

The vibria born of human parents and the last female bred of two dragons lost in plain sight.

Born to an extinct race, thought to be one but actually two. Both with destinies blessed by Fate, neither knowing the other exists...

A calling to heal, a hidden nature, a history long forgotten...all protected in the heart of a woman destined to complete a warrior and his beast. The revelation of all she is brought forth from the joining with her mate.

He searched the back of the book, finding his translations.

The gift of love and the hope of a future unlocks her true nature with the surrender of a mate's heart.

The page from the ancient grimoire, written in blood and containing the spell that would deliver the forever death, fell onto his lap. He looked at it like it was the Holy Grail and in all actuality...for him it was. It was his secret weapon against the race that wronged him. The race that had forgotten him. The race that had left him to die.

Andrew held the paper to his chest, closed his eyes, and chuckled.

This is gonna be good.

CHAPTER SIX

Charlie had tossed and turned all night, dreams of Aaron fighting a black hooded figure chased her every sleeping moment. There were times it looked like his opponent might take him down, but then she would glimpse his cocky grin and watch the man that was becoming so important to her cut down *everything* in his path. His raw power was awesome and fueled by the dragon she could feel within him. He not only possessed brute strength, but also an iron will and a pure determination that would not be defeated.

Reluctantly, Charlie opened her eyes, squinting at the glare. Shards of light shone through the gaps in her light blue blackout curtains, nearly blinding her as she cursed under her breath. Those curtains had been the best investment she'd made during her first year as an intern. Working all kinds of crazy hours, never sure when she'd be able to get back to her bed, she'd learned quickly that even in the bright light of day, an hour or two of sleep was a blessing, and her curtains tricked her brain into believing it was always nighttime.

Not when you don't shut them all the way, doofus.

Throwing the blankets over her head, she groaned while rolling away from the offending light. She tossed and turned until her legs were encased in the sheets and she felt like a mummy. Laughing at her own silliness, Charlie threw off the covers, careful not to look towards the window, and stared at the far wall, once again thinking about the man that would not leave her alone, whether awake or sleeping.

He's an addiction they don't have a twelve-step program for.

After several long minutes, she sat up and threw her legs over the edge of the bed, talking to the room around her. "Might as well get this day started. Wonder how much trouble I can get into?"

Making her way to the bathroom, she brushed her teeth, took a shower, and threw on a pair of shorts and a T-shirt. She followed the smell of freshly brewed coffee to the kitchen, thanking the Lord above for coffeemakers with timers. Steaming mug in hand, she padded to the deck and plopped into the redwood Adirondack chair, propping her feet on the large terra cotta pot in front of her.

The daisies, looming big and beautiful, reached for the sun and made her smile. She knew it was silly, but knowing Aaron had planted them for her made them all the more special. Glancing to the side, she gazed at the huge red flowers of the rose bush and made a mental note to ask him where he'd gotten such a beautiful plant, and why it always seemed to be in bloom. The backyard needed some sprucing up.

That would be a great 'thank you' present to Sam for letting me use the cottage. I'll get right on it...as soon as I find the gumption.

Letting her head fall back, her eyes slid closed, and she soaked in the warmth of the sun, letting her mind wander. Thoughts of how much her world had changed and how happy she was that she and Sam were back on speaking terms floated around her brain. That made her think of her parents, which made her remember that it had been days since she'd spoken to them.

Her mom usually called at *least* every other day, especially now that her dad had retired from the police force. It was funny to hear them bicker. Marian Gallagher was a smart, sassy, retired nurse that always took care of everyone with a firm hand and a whole lot of love. Charles, aka Chuck Gallagher, was a hard-nosed retired city detective with a heart of gold and was Charlie's very own version of a superhero. After all, she was named after him.

The day Chuck Gallagher had responded to the 911 call about an abandoned newborn on the church steps was the best day of Charlie's, then, very short life. She'd heard the story so many times, she could recite it while almost perfectly imitating her dad.

You were the prettiest little thing I'd ever seen. Snow white hair and bright blue eyes, rosy cheeks and sweet, rosebud lips that spread into a smile just like sunshine. I'd never seen anything as beautiful as you, except your mom. You were all wrapped in a fluffy pink blanket, cooing like you didn't have a care in the world. The reverend said he found you safe and secure in an old-fashioned wicker basket. You know the kind with high sides and handles.

It was filled with bottles, blankets, little pink outfits of every description, and the tiniest diapers I'd ever seen. There were even two white teddy bears and a package of pacifiers. We never did figure out the meaning of the pretty copper pendant on the brown leather cord attached to the basket handle. Just knew that it exactly matched the birthmark on your hip. Your mom saved it until you were old enough to wear it, and I don't think I've ever seen you without it.

I took you straight to the hospital. Never left your side. The doctors and nurses knew me from your mother and all the times I'd brought victims in. When I said I wasn't leaving you, they just backed away and did their jobs. At first, the doc was worried about the markings on your back, but they soon said they were only a birthmark.

I was getting really impatient. Kept asking when they'd finally be done. Of course, you just smiled and even giggled a time or two. The nurses said they'd never seen a baby so young be so responsive and happy. Always so happy. I was just about to lose my mind when your mom showed up. She'd been covering a shift in surgery and recovery. Thankfully, she was just in time to hear the doctor say you were perfectly healthy.

The folks from Child Protective Services came. Marian said there was no way in hell you would spend one minute in one of those scary group homes or a crowded foster home. It took a few calls and some big time favors, but a few hours later we were taking you home and you've been ours ever since.

A flood of memories washed over Charlie: pictures of birthdays, holidays, family vacations, even simple days at the park, all the things that made her childhood so perfect. She felt like someone with a big announcer's voice should be declaring, "Charlene Gallagher…This is Your Life."

Chuckling aloud, she lifted her head just in time to see twinkling blue eyes and a handsome face blocking the rays of the sun. Lips she recognized as Aaron's slammed onto hers. A scent that was all man, specifically *him*, flooded her system, making her feel tipsy. Opening for him like it was something she was born to do, Charlie reveled in the feelings this one man brought out in her. They groaned in unison at the sheer pleasure of being together as his tongue tangled with hers.

Warm, strong hands slid around her waist, cupping her ass, and sending electric tingles throughout her entire body, making her instantly wet and needy. In the next instant she was lifted into his arms, helpless to do anything but what he commanded. The feel of his body against hers, his arms around her, his mouth on hers nearly short-circuited her brain. Her entire world narrowed to that moment, that man, and what they were together.

They moved. She felt the air at her back, recognized the sound of the sliding glass door opening and slamming shut, then the smell of her heather and dewdrop candles. The sounds of his boots on her tile floor changed as they hit the carpeting in her living room and then the hardwood floors of the hall. Upward motion told her they were on the stairs, but she really couldn't care, all that mattered was that he kept kissing her…kept touching her.

A kick to a door sounded far away, and then Aaron abruptly stopped, turned, and sat. Charlie found herself straddling his lap, the muscles in his thighs warming the inside of hers as she fought to get as close to him as possible. Sliding forward, their lips never leaving one another, his erection made contact with her engorged clit. She gasped as flashes of light burst behind her closed lids. Aaron took advantage, nipping and tasting her jawline, raising goose bumps all over her body. He worried her earlobe with his teeth and tongue. His breath on her ear and the words he whispered sent shivers up and down her spine. "Good God woman, you make me crazy. I can think of nothing else but loving you until the end of time."

She grabbed his head with both hands on the side of his head and pulled his face until she could see his eyes. Her voice was low and breathless when she spoke, "Ditto, dragon man, ditto," was all she got out before his mouth was on hers again. The fire they had started erupted into an inferno, burning her from the inside out.

Aaron's hands slipped under her shirt. Sparks flew between them at every touch of his hands on her bare skin. He moved upward, taking the flimsy fabric with him. Faster than she could track, he pulled the top over her head. Next to go were her shorts, leaving her sitting in only a bra and panties, holding her breath to see what he would say.

Good thing I wore the good stuff today.

He stood and spun in one fluid motion. The cool softness of her favorite comforter touched the markings on her back as they tingled where he'd carefully laid her down. Her legs hung over the side of the bed on either side of Aaron's incredibly muscular legs.

Charlie watched his face as his eyes surveyed every inch of her curvy form. She knew she should've been nervous or embarrassed at his intense scrutiny, but her old feelings of insecurity never rose. Instead, she watched his pupils dilate and his nostrils flare. Aaron obviously liked what he saw. Her heart soared when he spoke.

"You are absolutely stunning, *Dr. Gallagher*…absolutely stunning."

"You're not so bad yourself, Mr. O'Brien, but I think you're a little overdressed."

Aaron ripped his T-shirt over his head while kicking off his boots and stripping out of his jeans. Charlie watched in amazement as muscles she knew had to be from good genetics and hard work rippled and rolled while a mass of gorgeous tanned skin became visible. She'd seen many naked bodies in a clinical setting and a few in not-so clinical ones, but none of them compared to the near perfection that stood before her.

Holding her hostage with his eyes, Aaron slowly leaned down, capturing her between his palms as they touched down on either side of her head. The coarse hair on his legs brushed against hers as he moved to the side. The bed shifted and one of his hands lifted as he lay down beside her.

The back of his fingers skimmed her cheek and then her chin. His index finger outlined her slightly separated lips, moving across her chin and down her neck, leaving chills in its wake. He stroked across her collarbone with just his fingertips, making his way to the tops of her breasts. His fingers slipped inside the lace cup of her bra, teasing first one nipple and then the other to a painful point. She let out the breath she hadn't realized she'd been holding in a loud rush.

Aaron chuckled and she saw the passion burning in his eyes. Before another thought crossed her mind, he was lifting her shoulders from the bed and unfastening her bra. The dark burgundy material flew over her head, closely followed by her matching panties.

"How the hell?" she gasped.

"Oh, Darlin', you have only begun to know the wonders of lovin' a dragon."

He rolled to the side, taking her with him, moving until she sat atop him. Charlie was forced to let her legs fall on either side of his hips. She bent forward, kissing and tasting first his shoulder, then his neck, and finally his jaw. The fire burning at her center made it impossible for her not to move. The roll of her hips against his rock hard abs created a delicious friction, sending shivers through her excited core. She felt the moisture coat the insides of her thighs. She was sure he felt the heat on his stomach.

Aaron gently grabbed her hips, lifting her while scooting just a fraction of an inch backward. She jumped as his erection rubbed across her excited clit. He lifted his hips, slowly entering her as he lowered her inch by inch onto his cock. Her heart soared. He was a gentle and considerate lover, frequently pausing so that she might adjust to his enormous girth.

Unable to stand one more moment of separation from the man that was quickly capturing her heart, her body, and her soul, Charlie placed her hands over his, pushing her hips down until they touched his. The speed of her action forced the tip of his cock to bump the opening of her cervix. Her muscles tightened around him, making it hard for her to feel where she ended and he began. Belonging unlike anything she'd ever imagined pushed all rational thought from her mind. Charlie could only feel.

The look in Aaron's eyes told her he liked the effect he had on her, liked tearing away all her inhibitions. Winking, he slowly started to rock, barely moving in and out of her, but sending shockwaves through her body, nonetheless. It was obvious he was in no hurry. His only focus was driving their excitement higher with every stroke.

They were slow dancing to the music of their heartbeats, their bodies moving in unison. She'd never thought it possible to be simultaneously excited and so at peace. The walls of her pussy contracted harder around him the longer he continued their erotic tango. She was completely captured in the web of desire they wove together.

On the edge of what she knew would be the best orgasm of her life, Charlie threw back her head, closed her eyes, and enjoyed the ride. Words tumbled from her mouth. "Mmm, oh, oh…this feels…you are…it's…*amazing*."

Aaron swiveled his hips, moving in and out, touching all her sensitive spots and some she didn't know she had. Her clit was on fire, while the sensitive bundle of nerves at the top of her channel pulsed faster with every touch of his cock. She writhed in pleasure. Moaning so loud it was almost a scream.

"Oh, oh, oh…Aaron…"

So close to completion she felt out of control, Charlie began rotating her hips on every down stroke. Their intricate lap dance wiped all thoughts from her mind. She increased the tempo, applying more pressure as she rode Aaron, searching for the stars. She needed something more…*anything*, just could *not* think past her need, could only feel and move…her sex-addled brain unable to form one intelligent thought. Shifting forward just a bit, a squeal leapt from her lips as Aaron gave her what she needed.

"Oh. My. God! Yes! Yes! Yes!"

"You are simply spectacular. Just stunning. Come, *mo ghra'*, come for me. Come *with* me. Take whatever you need. *Ta' mo chroi istigh*." The smooth, low baritone of his voice was breathless from their lovemaking. It skittered up her spine, sending another, more potent shock of arousal through her body.

Aaron moved faster and deeper, angling himself so that every thrust in and out of her overly aroused pussy pushed the head of his penis to her very depths. Together, they panted. Sweat pooled between their bodies. The moans of pleasure that bounced off the walls were only rivaled by the sounds of their bodies as they met in passion she never knew was possible.

She heard his voice in her head. *"Open your eyes, Charlie. Look at me."*

Their eyes locked. Every muscle in her body flexed tighter than a bowstring. Aaron thrust stronger and harder, seating himself not only in her body but also in her soul. In the next second, they bellowed their release to the Heavens. Their combined orgasm went on and on until Charlie collapsed into a boneless dead weight upon his chest. She fought hard to catch her breath, praying her sanity would return. Aaron's chest rose and fell under her limp body. She worked up a weak grin as she realized he wasn't having an easy time of it either. His arms came up around her, locking her securely in place. It was then she felt their hearts beat in unison…*as one*.

The markings on her back tingled. She felt them move everywhere his skin touched them. The tingle quickly became an itch, making her squirm and wiggle against his arm.

"Got an itch, *mo ghra'*?"

"Just a bit," she answered, wanting nothing more than to fall into blissful sleep in Aaron's arms, but unable to get comfortable.

"Let me take care of that for you."

His large, calloused hand moved over her back, soothing her itch, taking away her pain…lulling her to sleep. Charlie thought she'd have to remember to thank him for the use of his magical hands. She let go of the breath she'd been holding and floated away. The last thing she heard before her world faded to black seemed like it sounded in her head and made no sense at all.

I gcónaí agus go deo. Mine grá.

CHAPTER SEVEN

Always and forever. Mine to love. He smiled, thinking of the words he'd sent directly into Charlie's mind. Speaking the old language was not something Aaron did very often, but with his mate, it just seemed natural. Aidan and the others were going to give him seven kinds of hell when they saw what a marshmallow he'd become.

Like I give a shit. She's worth all that and more.

Charlie squirmed in her sleep, her discomfort evident in her tiny moans. Every wiggle, every roll of her shoulders was like a knife to his heart. It was as if it was happening to him. His dragon growled, puffing smoke, and pushing the man to ease their mate's discomfort. Aaron's frustration grew. Helplessness, especially in this case, was *not* something he took lightly. It was his job to see to her every need, keep her from harm…make sure she was cared for in *every* way.

There had been times, specifically over the last few years, where he had scoffed when the other Guardsmen had gotten all warm and fuzzy. It was a shock to his system that he was experiencing the same thing. He'd been so sure there was no way he could ever feel what they felt, ever have a mate to call his own. The funny thing was he'd thought he was okay with it. *Hell*, he'd run as far and fast as he could, but it was to no avail. All the stories were true. Fate definitely had a way of getting what She wanted. And if Aaron had to be honest…Charlie was the best thing that had ever happened to him.

Absently moving his hands across her back, he listened to his dragon purr, noticing that every so often, the beast would chuff. It was as if the big guy was trying to tell him something, something only the beast recognized. He listened intently but heard nothing unusual. Dismissing it as excitement from finally finding the light of their soul, his thoughts drifted back to his miracle…*his mate…his Charlie.*

She was unlike any woman he'd ever known. The glimpses of her thoughts he'd gotten while they made love had blown his mind. She was not only strong, independent, and incredibly intelligent, but her compassion and empathy showed him the true beauty of her soul. The depth of commitment to her profession was a true testament to her spirit. It was not only what she wanted to do, being a physician was what she was *meant* to do.

His dragon chuffed again, this time at the precise moment her marking wiggled under his hand. Sure he'd imagined it, Aaron gently moved Charlie off his chest, carefully placing her on the bed. Using movements so slow only his enhanced vision tracked them, he traced the outermost lines of her brand with just the tips of his fingers. With his extra abilities, he could see them move, as well as feel them. What he'd originally thought to be scars, he now recognized as some type of glyph.

Connecting with Charlie through their ever-growing bond, Aaron searched for their origin, or at least everything she knew about them. He knew he'd catch hell when she found out he'd been picking through her brain, but figured it was worth it.

Besides, she's sexy when she's pissed and making up is gonna be so much fun.

Through her memories, he saw all the doctors' opinions. The professionals stated they were nothing more than birthmarks. Something they believed would disappear over time, or at least be so small they would be inconsequential. Obviously, modern medicine had been mistaken in this case.

One specific memory surfaced more than any other. Aaron saw Charlie and her mom talking about her back. His mate was adamant that her mother not look at it while her mother was just as determined to see it. It was obvious from whom she'd inherited her iron will. They reminded him of two warriors standing off on the field of battle.

Finally, Charlie had given in. It was then Mrs. Gallagher realized the marks were growing right along with her daughter. He saw their visit with another specialist who, like the others, had no answers. His pride soared as his mate told her mother not to worry, that it didn't matter. She'd even gone so far as to say that she liked her 'wings'. Those words spurred the Guardsman into action.

Moving as carefully as possible while making sure to keep one hand moving across her back at all times, he rose to his knees so he could see *all* of Charlie's back. She'd been right. The markings *did* resemble wings. They were breathtaking in their intricacy and detail. So realistic, Aaron imagined them lifting off her skin and fluttering in the breeze.

Caressing her porcelain skin, he continued to delve into Charlie's mind and spirit. There, hidden deep inside, was a spark of magic, very small but vibrant in its bid to thrive. Its origin was undeterminable, at least with his limited knowledge of anything but dragon magic, and his mate had no knowledge of its existence. She'd been adopted at such a young age, the only thing she remembered of her birth mother was the softness of her skin and the melody she sang as she rocked her babe.

He closed his eyes, imaging a young woman with white-blonde tresses and expressive blue eyes holding a child that looked so much like her, the woman thought she would burst with joy. The melody was beautiful. The woman's voice so high and clear it sounded like magic itself. And she sang in a language he recognized from his youth.

Hush-a-bye, baby, my darling, my child
My flawless jewel, my piece of the world
Hush-a-bye, baby, isn't it a great joy
My little one in bed without any sorrows.

Child of my heart, sleep calmly
And well all night and be happy
I'm by your side praying for blessings on you,
Hush-a-bye, baby, and sleep for now.

On top of the house there are white fairies
Playing and frolicking under the gentle moonlight
Here they come calling my baby
To draw her into their great fairy mound.

The recollection was buried so deep, he imagined Charlie thought of it as a dream, if she thought of it at all. Sighing in her sleep, he felt her finally relax. The lullaby gave her comfort, if only subconsciously, and for that he was grateful. Aaron knew the day would come when he would tell his mate about it and help her to remember such a beautiful memory.

His investigation of Charlie's mind and back continued until the wee hours of the morning, but he uncovered nothing new. Lots of dead ends and memories of a wonderful childhood with great parents that adored their adopted daughter. She thought of her birth mother often, but only in a dream that never quite made it to her reality. Charles and Marian Gallagher were the people her heart recognized as her mother and father.

He'd taken a few extra minutes to 'listen' to what Charlie thought of her father. After all, Aaron would be asking for her hand in what the humans called 'marriage' very soon. Charles Gallagher was a retired cop, a hard ass, but incredibly fair and rational–except where his daughter was concerned. Aaron tried to imagine what a conversation with the man would be like, but came up empty-handed and at a loss for words for one of the only times in his life. He'd faced every imaginable enemy without a second thought, but just the idea of the man his mate held in such high esteem made him nervous and jittery. Deciding it wasn't something he could control, but most definitely something that had to happen, he moved on.

Taking one more look at the magic buried deep in Charlie's soul, he just knew it was inherent, either her birth mother or father, or maybe even both, had been magical. He wondered if it had been intentionally buried, but knew that was a question for the experts. The spark was definitely a part of her, but completely unrealized by its host, and because of that he couldn't tell if it was dragon or not.

Aaron shuddered while thinking about what Devon had gone through with Anya and decided to tell Charlie what had happened first thing in the morning. He would admit he poked around in her brain and convince her to let Siobhan, their clan's Elder Healer, and Kyra take a look. There wasn't anything Siobhan didn't know about healing, and magic was the little white witch's specialty. Besides, Royce had mentioned she needed something else to think about while she waited for word from her aunt about the hunt for Calysta.

Keeping his hand on her back, he settled back into bed, carefully placing Charlie across his chest once again. His possessiveness made him chuckle. She grumbled at the motion but immediately settled when he kissed the top of her head. Her actions, even in sleep, showed that she felt the mating call just as much as he did.

Cuddling against him, a sigh slipped from her lips while her legs entwined with his, securing her place with her mate. The skin-to-skin contact calmed man and beast, as well as their mate. The scent of fresh roses and their lovemaking filled his senses while Charlie's presence in his heart and soul made him feel more complete than he ever had. He closed his eyes, took a deep breath, and just enjoyed the beginning of a very long and happy life. It was the most peaceful he could ever remember being in his entire existence.

Charlie's presence filled his mind while memories of his transformation accompanied a fear that his mate would go through what Anya did. The uncertainty of Charlie's origins was a conundrum that had to be solved as soon as possible. Her magic was good and pure…nothing but white light and a sense of peace, but there was no way she would shift without warning if he had anything to say about it.

The fear he'd heard in Devon's voice, accompanied by the pain on the older Guardsman's face when he believed Anya to be dying, had been damn near paralyzing. At the time, Aaron's thoughts had been divided between helping the couple and keeping Charlie from a total meltdown after she'd ignored his orders to return to the reception. While the details were blurry, the one thing for certain was that Anya had been in excruciating pain and Devon had been ready to follow her to the Heavens.

Neither had talked much about that night. All Devon said was that Anya was adapting to her new state of being and he was thrilled that calling her dragon forth had become a painless event. Apparently, she'd even taken to flying like a natural. He'd heard that Siobhan and Zachary, the oldest Elder in dragon kin, were searching every available archive to find Anya's heritage. Being the first female dragon in hundreds of years had to be one of the coolest and freakiest things the poor woman had ever been through.

Well, besides turning into a dragon.

Once again, Aaron thought about his and Aidan's transformation. The twins had felt the stirring of the beast at exactly the same moment. Barely making it to the valley between the two mountains that bordered the Silver Clan's lair before the crippling pain of their first shift began, the brothers drew on the knowledge buried deep in their souls and that of their dragons to survive. Aaron's last coherent thought had been to call to his father.

His extremities still tingled remembering the magic filling every molecule of his body just as his entire being began to tear and reconfigure into that of his dragon. Even his bones, that in human form were dense and heavy, became hollow and light to enable flight. Thankfully, only the first transformation was painful. Now, what had originally taken hours was instantaneous.

Of course, he and Aidan had gotten to experience it in stereo. Being identical twins, as close as two people can genetically be, they completely shared one another's transformation. They had teased each other mercilessly for years, one always accusing the other of being the bigger baby. Their father had declared it a draw and their mother had fussed over them for days after they returned home.

Some of the best times of my life.

As sleep claimed him, all he could think was that even better times were to come. It was as if his life was beginning anew.

Aaron woke to the sun in his eyes, a crick in his neck, and a cramp in his leg, but he'd never been happier or more rested. He knew he would endure absolutely anything to awaken with the woman that owned his heart and soul in his arms every morning for the rest of his life.

Sometime during the wee hours of the morning, Charlie's back had mercifully stopped bothering her. She'd wound herself around him and clung so tightly, he had to imagine they looked like a human pretzel. Aaron had never liked sharing a bed with anyone, let alone have them touching him, but now that Charlie was in his life, he couldn't imagine sleeping without her touch.

Wanting to do something special for his mate, Aaron carefully untangled their limbs, and moved her to the bed where he lovingly positioned her to make sure she got as much rest as possible, and then stood. He watched her fall back into a deep sleep. His dragon chuffed, urging him to crawl back into bed, but the man wanted to provide for their mate.

Grabbing his clothes, he quickly dressed and headed down to fix breakfast. Charlie's refrigerator was basically bare, so it was on to plan B. Two minutes later, he was roaring down the road, headed to his favorite diner to grab one of everything on the menu.

Maude, the diner owner, and her daughter, Jill, laughed at the amount of food he ordered, teasing that only a man in love ate that much. He knew they were right, but he wasn't ready to share. He grinned and said, "Wouldn't you like to know?"

"Honey, I'm old enough to be your momma," Maude cackled as she poured hotcake batter on the griddle. "There's nothing you can tell me I haven't heard once and tried twice."

He had to laugh. If Maude knew how old he really was, she'd probably flip her lid.

It wasn't long before Jill had a box packed with Styrofoam to-go containers, napkins, plastic forks and knives, and all the condiments they could ever need. Leaving them a huge tip, he secured the box to the back of his Harley and headed back to the cottage.

Sitting at a stop sign waiting to turn left, a butterfly landed on his cheek. The sensation of its wings on his skin triggered a sense of deja vu. He remembered something that felt like silk, only lighter somehow, caressing his cheek and arms. His mind filled with the scent of fresh cut roses and a warm purple glow that simply exuded happiness. A horn blasted behind him, jarring him from his memory, but the thought and feeling remained.

Following his link to Charlie, he felt her stir and knew she would be awake very soon. Hurrying into the house, he raced to the kitchen in an effort to have everything ready before she came downstairs. He slid the box on the counter, grabbed the coffee from the canister, and found plates in the cabinet.

The first drip of java hit the bottom of the pot as he heard Charlie's footsteps above his head. Figuring it would take her a few minutes to get downstairs, he ran to the patio and picked a few daisies to fill the empty vase on the table.

Timing it perfectly, he placed the plates on the table just as she rounded the corner. Her look of shock, which quickly turned to a smile, was worth all his hurried preparations. Holding out her chair, he asked, "Breakfast, milady?"

Bypassing the chair, she stood on her toes and placed a tender kiss to his cheek. Aaron wanted more. Leaning down for better contact, he held her head at the perfect angle as his lips met hers, showing her the way he wanted to start every morning. Several passion-filled moments later, they broke apart, breathless and weak-kneed.

Holding her to his chest for just a moment longer, Aaron grinned. "You're better than ham and eggs, that's for damn sure."

"You're not so bad yourself," she teased, in what had to be her best Mae West impression.

Aaron barked out a laugh as he turned Charlie around and waited until she sat. Pouring coffee and juice for both of them before taking his own seat, Aaron watched her watching him and had to grin.

"You better eat before it gets cold."

"I'm not sure where to begin. I'd ask if you made all this, but I know my cupboards were bare. Where'd you go?" she asked, adding cream and sugar to her coffee.

"Maude's on Plantation. I think we keep her in business, or did before everyone found their mates."

He watched for any sign that she knew they were fated to be together, but saw none. The thought of looking through their bond entered his mind, but he knew he already had a lot of explaining to do where that was concerned and didn't want any more to tackle.

Charlie drowned her pancakes in syrup, took a bite, and moaned, "These are amazing," with her mouth full.

Aaron loved that she was already comfortable enough around him to be herself. His mouth watered as she licked a drop of syrup from her lips. It took all of his considerable control to keep from leaning across the table and following her example. A sense of accomplishment filled not only the man, but also his beast, as he sat watching Charlie eat her fill.

I truly have turned into a big puddle of goo.

Setting her fork on her plate with an uneaten bite still on the tines, she looked up, spearing him with her brilliant gaze. "Thank you so very much. I can't remember a time I have enjoyed a breakfast as much as I have this one." She practically purred.

Always feed her breakfast, especially pancakes. Have LOTS of syrup on hand.

She paused and he watched a flurry of emotions cross her face. Clearing her throat, she spoke again, and this time it was with conviction. "I have a couple of questions for you and I have to know that you'll answer them with total honesty. Can you do that for me?"

"I told you there would be no more secrets between us and I *meant* what I said," he answered, trying to keep the hurt and frustration at her continued mistrust out of his voice.

The look on her face said she knew she'd wounded his pride and that made him even madder. She spoke before he could further respond. "Don't get upset. It's not that I don't trust you. It's that I don't know what you can and can't tell me. What are the rules? Sam said I could know everything, but what is *everything*? I guess I should've said that if there's something you can't answer, some detail you can't share, just tell me. I can handle that. I just can't handle being kept in the dark. I don't operate that way. Make sense?"

He nodded, once again in awe of her intuitive nature.

"Okay, now? I don't want you upset, but I have to know I can be straight with you and you'll be straight with me, ya know? 'Cause here's the thing…what we did last night, what we shared, I don't take lightly. And if I'm to be as honest with you as I want you to be with me, I have to admit that it has *never* been like that with anyone else…*ever*."

He restrained himself from fist pumping the air while his dragon roared his own pleasure at her comment in his head. All he could do was nod and agree as he watched just the touch of a blush highlight her cheeks.

"So we're good right?" she asked.

"Yes, *mo chroí*. We're good."

She pointed at him and rushed to ask, "That's one of the things I wanted to ask. That language…what you just called me. You used it last night, too. What is it?"

He chuckled, not surprised she had noticed it, and explained. "It is a form of Gaelic. It's the language our ancestors, the dragons used. Out of respect for their faith in us, the first shifters chose to continue its use. My parents were fluent and made sure my brothers and I knew how to read, write, and speak it. I'm ashamed to say that over time, we became used to speaking the native language of wherever we happened to live at the time to maintain our cover, and our Gaelic, at least mine, became rusty. With you, it just seems natural to use it."

"And what did you just call me?"

"My heart."

Charlie sat across the table staring at him like he'd grown an extra head while he worked hard not to laugh. She'd asked that he hold nothing back and he'd been as straight as he could be. He watched as she composed herself and had to give her credit for never breaking eye contact. When she spoke again, he heard a little waiver, but for the most part, she kept it together. His mate was truly outstanding.

"Okay, we'll get back to that."

She asked a lot of question he knew for a fact Samantha had answered and some that seemed trivial. He wondered if she was comparing their answers, but from the thoughts she was letting fly around, it seemed she was only interested in what *he* had to say. There were a few long pauses in their conversation where he was sure she was trying to get up her nerve for something. Charlie chewed on her lip when she was deep in thought or less than confident about something. It was the one tell he'd been able to pick up on while they talked.

Aaron watched one such bout of lip chewing, then saw resolve enter her eyes. When she spoke, it was a little more rushed than it had previously been, but still straight to the point. "Last night, was there a time when I could hear your thoughts or you could hear mine? I…"

"Yes, there most definitely was," he immediately answered, cutting off her next comment.

Finally, we're getting somewhere.

"How is that even possible? Are you psychic or something? Can dragons read minds?" she questioned, speaking more rapidly, tapping her nails against the table, and furrowing her brows. "Does that happen *every* time you make love?"

"No, it does not and it has never happened before. And no, dragons cannot read minds, per say. We can share thoughts with people we're connected to. Those bonds are forged through fealty, or blood, or those that mates share. In our world, we call it mindspeak. It's a really useful tool for us in battle or to pick on each other without anyone else knowing." He chuckled, adding the latter in hopes of lessening the stress he could feel in her.

She snickered, making him feel a little better, and then he said, "And I'm not psychic, although sometimes I truly wish I was. It would make things so much easier to know what was coming."

"So based on what you just said, we share a connection? Am I getting this right?"

"Yes, you are."

He could see the wheels of her mind turning, all the pieces clicking into place. He gave her the time she needed to reason through it. This was one discovery he was sure she had to make on her own.

"Not one of blood…I know that. And I haven't pledged my fealty to you or anyone for that matter. *Hell*, I don't even know how to do that."

He grinned but said nothing. Just watching her was fascinating, something he could do for days on end and never get bored.

"More than just based on the fact that I'm Sam's friend and you are a dragon like Lance, right?"

"Right."

She stood and paced. He could hear her mumbling to herself, recanting everything he'd told her, checking off one item after another. It was after her fifth pass across the kitchen that she spun on her heel, planted her hands on her hips, and glared at him.

"Well, *hell*, I'm your mate aren't I?"

Not exactly the sentiment I'd hoped for…

CHAPTER EIGHT

"I mean *you* think I'm your mate, right?"

"I *know* you're my mate," he said with all the confidence of a king and the calmness of a scholar.

I'm not gonna freak out. I'm not gonna freak out.

"How do you know? Did a bell go off? You got a sign from above? What tells you that we are meant to be together…*forever*? I mean Sam says that your guys' forever is really like…*forever*. A thousand years alive and then in the Heavens after that, right?"

"Yep, that's right. To answer your questions, no a bell didn't go off and there was no literal sign from above. I just know. In here." He pounded his fist to his chest hard enough that she thought about checking for broken bones.

"Before I go any further, I have to ask you a question. I want you to give the first answer that pops into your mind. No thinking about what is politically correct or any of that BS, just say the first thing that you think, okay?"

"Yeah. Okay. I can do that," she answered, taking a deep breath and clearing her mind.

He studied her for a moment. She stared him straight in the eye to reassure him that she would do just as he asked. Nodding once, he said, "What did you feel the first time you saw me?"

"Like I already knew you," she blurted out, surprised, even though it came out of her own mouth.

"I have another. You ready?"

"Hit me, tough guy."

"Ever been able to hear anyone else in your mind before? During sex, walking down the street holding hands, anytime?"

"Nope, never."

"Ever felt what you feel when we're together with anyone else?"

"Nope."

"How do you know we're not mates?"

"I don't," was out of her mouth before she could stop it, closely followed by a mumbled, "Oh shit!"

Aaron grinned that damn cocky grin and she felt the need to pace again. As she recounted everything she'd felt, thought, even imagined and dreamt since meeting him, Charlie had to agree that their connection defied explanation and logic. Her heart said, *go for it* while her brain said, *what about your free will?* And of course, her body said, *grab that man and never let him go.*

While she continued to pace and think, Aaron chimed in. "I think I can help you understand. Will you take a walk with me…outside? Watching you pace is making me dizzy."

She had to laugh. Pacing had always been her coping mechanism, it helped her think, got her blood pumping, and worked off the nerves, but she could see where sitting and watching might get a bit annoying after a while.

"Sure," she answered, unconsciously reaching for his hand and then shaking her head when he chuckled as he threaded his fingers through hers. He tugged her hand until she leaned into him. Placing a kiss on the top of her head, he started out the door.

Jerk! Just couldn't let it go, could he?

Taking a path she'd never been on, Aaron began to explain. "You see, all our lives we're told that there's one woman in the entire world destined to be our mate. That the Universe has fashioned one woman who will be our perfect complement and that we, in turn, will complete her. She brings the light to our souls and that of our beast. It is the job of the man and dragon to keep her safe, provide for her, and to make sure that she wants for nothing."

She started to speak, but he held up his index finger and continued. "I know these are old-fashioned ideas, but remember, we're part of a very old race. In my experience, each couple makes it work in their own way. God knows the women mated to my brethren are some of the strongest, most outspoken, independent women I've ever had the honor of knowing." He paused, kissed the back of her hand, and added, "And you, Dr. Charlene Gallagher, are no different."

A stray ray of sunshine touched his face just as he laughed. Charlie had to look away to keep from telling him just how handsome he was. She shook her head, wondering when she'd lost her mind and focused on what Aaron was saying.

"There are stories told around the campfires, older drakes, male dragons, sharing their life experiences, lessons taught to ensure we know the signs, even our Holy Book talks about it. There's a passage that all dragon shifters learn at a young age…

'When the two halves of the same whole meet, there will be instant recognition. Their souls will merge, and only then will the man and dragon know complete peace, they will have found their true home. It will be as if the time before they met their mate does not exist. All that will matter will be that they become one in body, mind, and soul with the One the Universe made for them.'

"Of course this was written when female dragons still existed. You see, later on, when the dragons entrusted their souls to the knights, almost all the female dragons had been destroyed by the wizards and their cohorts, the hunters. The ones that remained either followed their mates to the Heavens or succumbed to a sickness that swept through the clans. The Kings of all the Clans had been searching for answers. I mean without a way to reproduce, extinction was knocking at their door."

"The story goes…Their Elders met in one of the most ancient and holy places of our kin. They prayed day and night for years and years, asking the Universe to give them a solution. The night before the Joining Ceremony in which the all-powerful mage was going to combine the souls of the Dragon Kings with the Knight of their choice, the Elders' prayers were answered. Two lovebirds entered the cave where they were holed up. Now, this cave was deep in the earth, surrounded by miles and miles of rock, not some place birds would just happen into. It was a true sign from the Universe.

"The birds landed on the altar in the center of their Prayer Circle and started to sing. If that wasn't enough, words appeared in the air above them, as if handwritten with a quill or whatever people used back then, while the birds continued to sing. It was the words that gave the Elders and all dragon kin by extension, hope. It said…

"*'From the human race, women with great power will be born. Not the power to maim or destroy, but the power to love, to heal, to uplift, and to rebuild. The beautiful ones will be created as the perfect complement for the men who take up our spirits. One woman destined for one man, to live on Earth and in the Heavens, joined for all times. When the time is right, they shall discover one another. Fate will not be denied in this matter. The two will become one. The woman will provide the man and the beast with love, light, and hope. Man and beast will be protector and provider. Their partnership will be real and mutual. Together they shall provide heirs that will allow our great race to continue for all eternity.'*"

Charlie let all Aaron had said sink in. Could it be true that Fate and the Universe had designed her for him and him for her? Could everything that had happened in her life bring her to this moment with this man? Did she even have a choice in the matter?

That last question pissed her off. Charlie Gallagher was not a pushover, *no one*, not even Fate or the Universe or whoever, was going to tell her whom she was supposed to love. Letting her anger take over, she stopped on the path and asked, "I get no choice? *We* get no choice? Our free will has been taken from us? We're just supposed to skip off into the sunset because it's written in some old book somewhere?"

The minute the words were out of her mouth and she saw the look on Aaron's face, she wished them back. Replaying them in her mind, she knew she'd let her mouth get ahead of her brain. Sure, it was what she meant to say, but even she had to admit, there were about a thousand better ways to say it.

She had to give Aaron credit for a quick recovery and the amazing control of his temper. Fire flashed in his eyes and his brow furrowed, but never once did she think he might turn it on her. There was just a faith inside her that said he would never do anything to hurt her or even upset her if he could help it. That made her think about what he'd said and she went to speak, but he cut her off.

"Let me start by saying…*you* always have a choice. There is no way *anyone,* including me, will *ever* force you to do anything you don't want to do as long as I draw breath."

She heard a slight accent that hadn't been there before. It made her think of rolling, green hills and foggy moors. It all fit with what he'd told her. Even though he'd paused, he still was able to stop her when she began to speak…*again.*

"Secondly, let me ask you something…when Sam explained mates to you, what did she say?"

Thinking back to her conversation with her friend and remembering the immediate jealousy she'd felt at the way Samantha had talked about Lance, Charlie was almost embarrassed to answer, but she did it anyway. Throwing back her shoulders and faking a confidence she didn't feel, she answered, "Sam talked about the Dragon Holy Book and said that she just knew from the moment she laid eyes on the big goofball that they were meant to be together. She said she felt it in her soul. But it wasn't really what she said, it was how she said it. I could *feel* how much she loved him."

She stopped and watched, thinking Aaron would react or gloat, but he didn't. He just stood there, looking at her for several long seconds. When he spoke, she could hear more of his brogue and could see the rising conflict within him, only she didn't really know what it was all about.

"How did listening to Sam talk about her mate like that make you feel, Charlie? In here?" He reached across and laid his fingers over her heart for just a moment before stepping back and waiting.

Contemplating not answering, or at the very least just giving him some flippant answer, Charlie opened her mouth and quickly shut it again. She knew there was no way she could lie to him, even it was by omission. Something within her heart simply would not let it happen. Looking at her feet and kicking the dirt, she sighed and said, "I was jealous."

When she looked up, Aaron was still just standing there, but this time a tiny bit of the twinkle had returned to his eyes. It was nothing like usual, but it was so much better than what she'd seen just a moment ago.

"Did you think of me?"

Boy this guy just doesn't give up!

Throwing her hands in the air and starting to pace, she all but screamed, "Yes, *dammit!* Is that what you wanted to hear? I thought of you!"

Stopping in front of him, her fist on her hip and finger pointing at his face, she went on, "And before you ask…Yes! I think about you all the time! And yes, you make me crazy! And no, I've never felt this way about anyone else! But most of all, I'm scared shitless, okay?"

She gulped in a breath to continue, but never got the chance. Aaron had her in his arms and was kissing her until her toes curled and she couldn't think straight. Then, just as quickly as it had begun, it was over. Her feet touched the ground. Cool air touched her body where his had just been warming it, and her lips ached at the loss of his.

Slowly opening her eyes, she found him standing in the same spot he'd been before, looking as if nothing had happened. The thought of punching him in the gut crossed her mind, but she knew from experience, 'rock hard abs' didn't come close to describing his amazing body.

I'd probably just break my hand.

It was then she noticed the slight bulge in the crotch of his Levis. She didn't even try to hold back her evil little grin. If her brains had to be scrambled, it was good to know she had some effect on him. Still, there was no way she could let him off the hook. "What was that about?"

"I wanted to kiss you, so I did."

"But why?"

"Because I could and because you admitted to thinking about me. You could've lied or deflected or even walked away and refused to answer, but you didn't. You told me."

"Oh, well, if I expect you to be honest with me, then I have to be honest with you."

"Just another of the hundreds of reason I'm *sure* you are my mate. You have honor. Something that is rare in this day and age."

"You sound like an old geezer there, dragon guy. Be careful, I might mistake you for a dirty old man." She snickered and wiggled her eyebrows before running off down the path.

It was time for a tension breaker and she could think of nothing better than running, although 'exercise' was usually a four-letter word in her book. She could hear his footsteps pounding the ground behind her and knew he was just messing with her. He could move faster than she could track, she'd seen it with her own eyes. If he really wanted to catch her, he could.

Hearing the sounds of water crashing against rock, Charlie realized she was deeper in the woods than she'd ever been before and slowed to a stop. Aaron came up beside her, not even having the decency to pretend to be out of breath while she thought she might need a tank of oxygen.

"Everything okay there, Flo Jo?"

"HA HA HA!" She wheezed. "You could at least *act* like you're winded."

"Why would I do that? You're the one that took off running."

"Pfft…Whatever." She rolled her eyes and walked towards the water, just knowing he would follow.

The water roared, the air felt heavier, and the foliage appeared denser, a darker green, the farther they walked. Aaron grabbed her hand and electricity flew between. She shivered at the contact. He smirked. "Just another sign we're meant to be together."

She started to argue, but knew it would be an effort in futility. He was determined to convince her they were mates. And deep down inside, she knew what he was saying was the truth. She had thought of *nothing* but him since that first day in the hospital. When he'd kissed her the night of Devon and Anya's wedding, it had been a dream come true. She'd never felt anything so right. It wasn't that she didn't *want* to be with him, it was that she wanted it to be her choice. Thinking that some crazy, centuries-old lady with long, grey hair and wrinkly skin was sitting on her cloud with her crystal ball deciding who loved who pissed off the hotheaded, raised by an Irishman, Charlene Gallagher.

Stopping dead in her tracks, she looked straight ahead, and shouting over the noise of the water, asked, "Is what we feel real? I mean the whole Destiny, Fate, Universe thing is new to me. Doesn't make sense." She tapped her temple and spun to look at Aaron. "How do you know it won't change? You won't just get over it one day? Wake up and say…next!"

He laughed. The big oaf actually laughed right out loud. Turning on her heels, Charlie stomped towards the waterfall, grumbling about pigheaded dragons. She made it four whole steps before she was snatched up, thrown over Aaron's shoulder, and traveling so fast the trees were just a blur. Huffing her disgust, she just hung on, waiting for him to stop. It wasn't long before she was once again on her feet, but now by a spectacular waterfall that looked like it was straight off the pages of a Sierra Club calendar.

Aaron moved in behind her, wrapped his arms around her waist, and kissed the spot right behind her ear. Leaning against him, she shivered. "Are you cold, *mo ghra*?" he whispered at her ear.

"No, not at all. You're like a heater."

"We do run a little hotter than humans," he chuckled, teasing her earlobe for just a second. When he spoke again, his voice was lower, more serious. "Just so you know, there will never come a day that I'll wake up and shout *NEXT*. The moment you entered my life, all other women ceased to exist. You are all I see, all I think about, all I could ever want or need. I know none of this makes sense to you, but please believe me when I tell you that is the most real thing I have ever experienced in all of my hundred years."

Turning in his arms, she saw his belief and total commitment to every word he'd just spoken. That same 'something' that had clicked into place earlier, vibrated with what she could only describe as pure joy. Everything she'd been feeling, more precisely everything she'd been trying *not* to feel, was only growing stronger. Her feelings were real. She knew it was time to stop denying them. Fate, Destiny, the Universe…God, *whoever* it was that decided she and Aaron were supposed to be together, had been right. Everything she knew about him said he was her perfect match. The man somehow knew how to deal with her crap and actually had the balls to laugh in her face. Something no other man, save her father, had ever dreamt of doing.

It was then that she remembered her mom telling her about the first time she'd met Charlie's dad. "Ya know, what you're saying sounds an awful lot like the story my mom told me about meeting my dad."

"Yeah?"

"Yeah, mom's a nurse. She'd only been out of school a few months and had drawn the nightshift in the Emergency room. It was like four am and she was dog-tired when they brought in a cop that had been shot. It was only a flesh wound, but still pretty deep. He was covered in blood, looking like he might pass out, but acted all tough and macho when she came to clean the wound.

"The doctor came in and announced he needed stitches. Mom said dad almost tossed his cookies, and when she brought out the needle, he lost consciousness. She assisted, bandaged him up, and went on to her next patient. It wasn't until a couple of days later when she was heading to her car that she saw him again.

"He was sitting on a bench, holding a bunch of grocery store flowers…*daisies*. When he saw her, his whole face lit up. He asked her out for coffee and the rest, as they say, is history. Of course, she gave him a run for his money. Didn't make it easy on him. Even told him, 'no', the first time he asked her to marry him, but he never gave up. Said he knew she was the one the first time he laid eyes on her."

She stopped and thought for just a moment, then added. "I don't know that I'm in love with you… but I'm damned close, and I *have* to know what this is between us. I'm not sure if this will make sense to you, but it feels important…like as in *once in a lifetime important*. Something I was meant to do. I *have* to see where it all goes."

Aaron smiled, not his usual smirk, but a real smile. She could see in that one look how much he truly cared for her. Her heart beat just a bit harder as he kissed the tip of her nose and whispered, "Thank you, *mo ghra'*."

He lowered his lips to her. The kiss was different than any other they'd shared so far. It was deep and complete, all encompassing. There were no demands, no expectations…just two souls sharing a perfect moment in time. It seemed to go on forever but also to happen in the blink of an eye. When they broke apart, Charlie knew the look of awe on his face mirrored her own. It just felt right. They spent several hours lounging by the waterfall before Aaron announced that he was hungry.

"How about tuna salad sandwiches and chips?"

"Sounds good to me," he answered before picking her up and speeding through the woods.

Several minutes later, he sat her on the patio, turned her towards the door, and swatted her behind. Mock glaring over her shoulder, she winked. "Thanks for the ride." Aaron barked with laughter behind her and had tears in his eyes when he appeared at her side in the kitchen.

Clearing his throat he asked, "What can I do to help?"

"Nothing at all. You 'cooked' breakfast. I got lunch." She used air quotes just to give him a hard time and snorted when he stuck out his tongue.

They ate lunch, told each other embarrassing stories about growing up, and laughed until Charlie's cheeks hurt from smiling so much. While they were doing the dishes, she noticed Aaron had gotten fidgety and thought about asking him what was wrong, but somehow knew he would tell her when he was ready…which came sooner rather than later.

As soon as he'd dried the last glass and placed it in the cupboard, he said, "Can we sit and talk for a minute?"

"Isn't that what we've been doing?" she joked.

"Yes, but this is important, something I need to tell you."

"Okay," she answered, following him into the living room.

He sat on the couch, patting the spot next to him. Charlie sat, but turned so she could see his face. His arm on the back of the couch touched her shoulder and his fingers drew circles at the nape of her neck.

"You heard my voice in your head last night, right?"

"Yes," she answered, totally thrown off by his question, but curious to see where he was going.

"And you can hear me now, right?"

She jumped at the sound of his voice in her head, but nodded.

"Think your answer to me. Let's see if it's working both ways."

Not sure how it all worked, she did exactly what he said and *thought* at him, *"Can you hear me?"*

His smile was the only answer she needed, but his voice in her head still sounded good, *"Yes, I can*, mo chroi." He switched back to speaking aloud. "Now, I want you to look inside yourself and look for the link between us, the one we just used to communicate."

Charlie felt somewhat weird, but did as he asked and was surprised to find it almost immediately. "Okay I see it," she said aloud.

"Now, I want you to follow it into my mind."

She opened her eyes to make sure she'd understood him correctly. When he nodded, she again closed her eyes, located the link, and followed it to him. At first, it was like she was floating, but almost immediately she was grounded and could *feel* Aaron *everywhere*. It was absolutely extraordinary, so different from being in her own head. It sounded trite, but inside his head was *really* masculine.

The first thing she saw was a vision of herself, the way he saw her. She had to admit, he made her look like a million bucks. Attached to that mental picture were thoughts and feelings all centered on what she meant to him. Every emotion reinforced what he'd already said to her. Aaron completely believed they were meant to be together. There was not a doubt to be found. Most shockingly, he'd already begun to fall in love with her.

She also felt his dragon and thought of the huge tattoo that covered most of his torso. When she looked closer, she could actually see the beast, but in this case, he sat quietly, studying her just as she studied him. For a moment, she felt the dragon's presence in her head, along with Aaron's. He was powerful and regal, truly befitting every story she'd been told. She could feel the affection he had for her mixed with a healthy dose of admiration and more than a little possessiveness. The dragon had already claimed her as his own and was making sure she understood he took his responsibility seriously. Smiling in her mind, she laughed when he chuffed at her. Now, more than ever, she wanted to see him in person.

Charlie was humbled and more than a little freaked out, but knew it was something they would be dealing with soon. Following the link out of his head, she opened her eyes and found him observing her every move.

"That was the craziest thing I've ever done."

"I would imagine so, but it's one of the many things mates can do. I will admit, mindspeak and looking inside one another doesn't usually happen until after the official mating, but you seem to be somewhat of a quick study. That's what I wanted to talk to you about."

She nodded for him to continue.

"Last night after we made love, your back started bothering you. You moaned and wiggled like it itched, so I gave you a little massage until it settled."

She figured he'd seen her marks and was just about to explain when he started again. "When I stopped, you got really agitated, and since touching you has become my favorite pastime, I kept doing it." He winked and she rolled her eyes.

Have to keep this one on his toes.

"It wasn't long until I felt them move…and my dragon felt them, too. You were finally resting comfortably and I didn't want to wake you, so I took a look at them. They really are quite beautiful."

She went to thank him and tell him her story, but he shook his head and kept talking. "Your mind was already open to mine, so I looked to make sure you were okay. I'm sorry I was in your mind without asking. It happened because I was worried. I promise it's not something I'm in the habit of doing. We work really hard to stay *out* of each other's mind, but I just had to know that you were all right."

As he hurried on, she could see he had her best interests at heart. There was nothing malicious about his actions and the anger that had been building melted away as she continued to listen. The weirdest thing was that the longer he talked about them, the more her birthmark tingled.

"I saw that you'd had them since birth and all your visits to all the different doctors. I also saw how you came to live with your parents. They seem like really cool people. Can't wait to meet them. Anyway, while I was in there making sure everything was okay, I stumbled across…well, I found…oh *hell*, I'm just gonna say it. Charlie, you have magic inside you… pure, white, very positive magic. It's just a spark, but it's there and it's strong. I believe, and mind you this is not my area of expertise, but from what I've learned, I believe it's still small because you haven't used it. It's simply living within you."

He stopped speaking, watching her very closely. Charlie felt his hand holding hers while his other still rubbed her neck. All she could do was let everything he'd just told her sink in. It was as if she was standing outside herself watching it all take place. Her voice even sounded foreign when she spoke.

"So let me get this straight. Just a few hours ago, you told me that we were destined to spend our lives together. Then you spoke directly into my mind. You taught me how to look inside your mind and now you're telling me that I have magic inside me? Oh! And my marks moved against your fingers while I was sleeping? Is that about right? Did I leave anything out?"

Unable to sit still any longer, Charlie jumped up and paced.

Hang out with this dude any longer and I'm gonna wear out my favorite Converse.

He hadn't answered by her second pass and had a faraway look in his eye. Thinking she might've taken it too far, she plopped down in front of him, made eye contact, and waited. Aaron held up his index finger and mouthed, "One second."

Nodding in agreement but still needing to move, Charlie headed to the kitchen. It wasn't long before Aaron joined her.

"Sorry about that. Aidan was telling me that Rian has a lead on the little asshole." He tapped his temple.

"Guess you gotta go?"

"In a bit, I told him we were in the middle of something and he said he'd let me know when they needed me. It's more important that I stay with you right now, don't ya think?"

Charlie shrugged, trying to appear nonchalant when she was anything but.

Aaron shook his head and snorted. "I wanna play poker with you. You can't bluff to save your hide."

Laughing because she knew it was true, Charlie swatted him on the arm. She tried to stay mad at him, tried to be upset that he'd invaded her privacy on an unbelievable level, but she just couldn't. She knew in her heart of hearts that Aaron had only done what he thought was best...*for her.*

Waving the proverbial olive branch, she said, "Sorry I lost my cool. It's just so much to take in. There's a whole other world I knew nothing about, filled with all the things I read about as a kid, going on all around me. If that wasn't enough, I'm connected to it through you and some magic inside me. Talk about crazy...if my name was Alice, I would be looking for a white rabbit about now."

Aaron chuckled, which for some reason made her feel better, and she laughed, too.

If you can't beat 'em, join 'em.

"You want something to drink?" she asked, grabbing glasses out of the cabinet.

"Sure. Whatever you're having is fine," he answered, waiting until she returned with the iced tea to hold out her chair for her before taking a seat next to her.

"There's something else I want to talk to you about. No more surprises, scout's honor." He held up the boy scouts' hand signal and grinned.

"Hit me. Might as well get it all out of the way up front."

"I want you to come to the lair with me. Siobhan and Kyra know much more than I do about magic. They'll be able to tell you the origin of the magic inside you, as well as the meaning of the symbol on your necklace and your birthmark. You've met them both, right? Siobhan is Devon's mom and our Healer, and Kyra...well, I know you've met her. Who could miss her?"

He paused for a second and she braced herself for what was to come. Charlie was quickly learning nothing was out of bounds for her dragon man.

"I know this is hard for you. I remember what it was like for Sam. You ladies come from a world of science and logic. Everything has cause and effect. Things are rational, problems to be solved. I have to say you are simply amazing! No matter what I've thrown at you today, you've dealt with it and not looked at me like I was a total loon."

He leaned over and gave her a quick kiss before continuing. "But here's the part that might make you throw me out on my ass. I believe your magic and that symbol," he pointed to her necklace, "are part of your birthright. I just *know* they will tell us who the woman that gave birth to you is and if she was magical."

I'll be damned! Of all the things I thought he was gonna say, that *never entered my mind.*

CHAPTER NINE

Charlie hadn't thrown him out on his ass, she hadn't even raised her voice or had to pace. As a matter of fact, she was on the back of his Harley, comfortably wrapped around him, riding towards the lair to see Siobhan and Kyra.

Aaron had called the healer to make sure she had time to see them. As soon as he explained, she'd told him to come on over and said she would call Kyra. He'd then spoken to Aidan through their unique link to let him know what was going on. His twin told him he and Grace would meet them there and that he would call Sam and Lance.

"I'm sure your mate will feel more comfortable with her best friend there and I know that Sydney is dying to see her Aunt Charlie."

"Yeah, that'll be good. She's handling everything really well. I just don't want her to get overwhelmed."

"So you told her everything?" Aidan asked and Aaron could hear his skepticism.

"Yes. I told her everything." He tried to keep the exasperation out of his voice, but knew he'd failed when his brother snickered.

"Good. Dude, I know it sucks, but it's for the best in the long run, especially since she tends to run off to think."

"Yeah, yeah, yeah...the wise, old, married man. I get it, but I'm the older twin."

"Older doesn't make you wiser."

"No shit." They both busted out laughing.

"See ya when you get here."

"Yep."

Charlie put her lips next his ear and whispered, "Where you just talking to your brother in your head?"

He sent his answer directly into her mind. *"Yes, why?"*

Picking up his hint, she answered in kind. *"I kinda heard you guys. It sounded like a radio station that wasn't quite tuned in, all fuzzy, lots of static. I only picked up a word here or there, but recognized it was Aidan."*

"That's weird. I was talking to him on our private connection, the one we've had since birth, kind of a twin thing. No one, not even our parents or brother, has ever been able to hear us."

"Is that a bad thing? Promise I wasn't eavesdropping."

Patting her clasped hands that were resting at his waist, he snickered, *"I know you weren't. I don't care if you do. It's definitely not a bad thing. It means our bond is already really strong. We're sharing* everything *and in my book, that's very cool."*

Her conflicted feelings flowed through their mating bond. He really couldn't blame her and meant what he said to Aidan. Charlie was handling all of their craziness way better than he could've ever hoped.

"If you say so. By the way, I've been looking at that little glowing ball of magic on and off since you showed me, and I think you were right. The more I poke at it, for lack of a better word, it seems to be getting bigger. I really wish I had an x-ray machine or ultrasound so I could study it."

He laughed aloud. *"You're one of a kind, mo chroí'. I knew your physician's instincts would kick in soon. I'm not sure that any of those devices will show your magic, but I'm sure Siobhan and Kyra will be able to see it."*

"I've heard Sam talk about them. If both of you believe in them, then I'm on board."

Both man and dragon filled with pride. She trusted their opinion, more proof that she was meant to be theirs, that their bond was growing. Grinning to himself, he added, *"I'll be with you every step of the way."*

"That's what I'm counting on." She snuggled closer and held on tight.

Something deep inside Aaron's soul snapped into place. A little piece of happiness he hadn't known was missing, but once there, made him feel happier, more alive…more *everything*. It was the weirdest and *best* sensation he'd ever felt. Her complete belief that he would keep her safe, the undeniable trust she'd laid at his feet, was fantastic. His dragon chuffed and rolled with contentment. Yep, the stories were all true.

Turning into the lair, he headed straight to Siobhan's. He wasn't surprised to see more cars than just Aidan and Lance's. They hadn't even made it to the porch when Sydney came running out.

"Aunt Charlie! Aunt Charlie! I have missed you so much!" The girl squealed as Aaron scooped her up before she crashed into his mate's legs.

Hugging his neck with one arm while reaching for her adopted auntie, Sydney added, "Hey Aaron."

"Hey, short stuff. Happy to see you, too." He snickered.

"Ya know I love you, but I haven't seen Aunt Charlie in forever!" She wailed the last word, causing both adults to laugh so hard they had to stop walking.

Aaron handed Sydney to Charlie before she jumped, watching as the child peppered kisses all over her aunt's face.

"I missed you so much! Mom said you're all happy now and you know all the stuff. That is *awesome!*"

"Yep, I know it all, but you know what I didn't know?"

"What?"

"That you had grown almost a foot," Charlie teased.

"I know! Dad says I'm gonna be bigger than him if I keep it up."

"I think he might be right," Aaron joked, taking Sydney from Charlie's arms and gently setting her feet on the ground. "Let's head on in and see what's going on. Whatcha say, kiddo?"

Sydney jumped between them, grabbed both their hands, and held on tight as they walked into Siobhan's. No sooner had they crossed the threshold than she announced, "They're here! Hey you guys, Aaron and Charlie are here!"

Sam was the first to appear, drying her hands and laughing. "I see them, Syd. Did you give Aunt Charlie kisses?"

"I sure did. I kissed her whole face *and* I hugged Aaron's neck," she answered, running to her mom. Aaron wondered if the child ever walked anywhere.

Lance came up behind Sam, grinning like a man with a joke to tell. "I hear congratulations are in order."

"Yep, sure are," Aaron answered, wrapping his hand around Charlie's, preparing for what the jokester of their Force had to say. Little did he know it wasn't Lance he had to worry about.

A roar of laughter sounded from the kitchen, followed by a flood of his brethren and their mates all talking at once, giving him hell in one form or another.

"Look at that, will ya? Big-mouth-know-it-all with a goofy grin on his face," Royce teased.

"Must be love, huh, big brother?" Rory chimed in, patting Royce on the shoulder.

"Look how the mighty have fallen," Devon again used his own words against him.

"Good luck, Charlie, that one's got a hard head," Kyndel laughed.

Aidan and Grace brought up the rear, arm in arm, grinning ear to ear. Aaron was shocked when it was his brother's mate that spoke instead of his twin. "I think I remember hearing something about my husband being a 'big ole' marshmallow and that he was, let me see if I can get this right… 'I had him all tied up in his underwear'. She barely got the words out before a good case of the giggles took over.

How many times did I say that? I need new material.

Rayne walked in holding his son and wearing a smile that could only mean trouble. "I seem to remember you saying something about being a confirmed bachelor. That you'd be able to dodge Fate. Guess you zigged when you should've zagged, huh?"

Aaron took his medicine like a good warrior. The Heavens knew he'd given each and every one of them as much grief as he could, especially his twin and Devon. Charlie leaned into his side and looked up, winking before she teased, *"Confirmed bachelor? And here I thought you had it all figured out."*

Turning to look at the crowd that had gathered, Charlie said, "I am so glad y'all let me know the *real* story." He saw her shoulders bouncing with her contained laughter. "This one," she pointed with her thumb and cocked her head in his direction, making everyone laugh again, "wanted me to believe he had it all figured out."

Looking back up at him, she crinkled her nose and added, "You must've really slung the crap around there, big guy. I would imagine they aren't nearly done paying you back."

Loving the fact that she was already comfortable enough with his 'family' to joke around, Aaron gave Charlie a quick kiss on the forehead before looking back up at the other Guardsmen and their mates. Thinking he might be able to head off the rest of it, he looked at Lance and asked, "You gonna let everybody else have all the fun?"

"Oh Brother, I've yet to get started, but I'm thinking I'll wait…spread it out a little. If I remember correctly, you gave me hell for at least a week. The fun is just beginning. Buckle up, it's gonna be a bumpy ride."

"All right you ruffians," Siobhan called as she entered the room, "leave those poor kids alone. We have work to do and you all have dinner to cook. Let the girls rest. You boys get that meat on the grill while Charlie, Kyra, and I go have a look see."

Everyone regarded Siobhan as their surrogate mother, and as the one female Elder, she was the matriarch of their clan. She'd nursed them all back to health more times than they could count, kicked them in the butt when they needed it, and was always there, no matter what, to help them answer any and all questions. Because of that, and even more because of their love for her, when she said jump, they all asked how high. This time was no different.

Aaron watched everyone hop to it as he and Charlie followed the Healer down the hall to her study. He smelled the scent of candles and herbs before a flash of white blonde hair came flying at him and his mate. Because of the witch's height of only five feet two, both he and Charlie had to bend at the waist as Kyra hugged them tight before letting go and taking a step back.

Looking at Charlie, she smiled a knowing smile before saying, "Welcome to the family. These big lugs are a handful," she pretended to punch Aaron in the stomach, pulling it just in time. "But they're worth it."

"You better say that. I'd hate to have to come in there," Royce hollered from outside the open window.

"Oh, just make sure my steak is well done and let me take care of this, okay, big guy?" Kyra yelled back, trying to keep from laughing.

"You better listen to your mate, grandpa," Aaron threw in, making Charlie laugh beside him.

"That's enough outta you, *lover boy*," Royce hollered before grumbling something Aaron couldn't quite make out about people who don't know how to start a fire.

"I hear you have a little magic in there, right?" Kyra asked Charlie while motioning for them to follow.

"Yep, had no clue before today. He saw it," she nodded in Aaron's direction, "and then showed me how to find it."

"He also said that you have a really cool birthmark on your back. Can I see it?" Kyra asked.

Charlie readily agreed while Aaron shut the door. He was doing a pretty good job at controlling the crazy protectiveness he felt towards her since they'd gotten around his brethren, but just the thought of one of them seeing her without her shirt on made both him and his dragon growl. Looking up, he caught the grin on Siobhan's face as she and Kyra looked at Charlie's back and had to smile back.

Busted!

"That is just about the neatest thing I've ever seen. Did you know it looks like a set of wings? Of course you did." Kyra excitedly rattled on.

"Yeah, that's what I've called them since I was about twelve."

"Aaron also mentioned the birthmark on your hip and your necklace. Can I have a look at the charm?" Siobhan asked.

Charlie slipped the leather cord over her head and handed the necklace to the Healer. Siobhan immediately started flipping through a large book that reminded Aaron of his college textbooks, forcing him to hold back a shudder. He'd always been more brawn than brain. Aidan was the intellectual of the two.

He studied the pendant as it sparkled in the sun shining in the open window. At first glance, it looked like a flower contained in a circle, but the longer he looked, the clearer it became. It was actually four sets of wings joined at the center by a Celtic cross. Using his enhanced vision, he saw that each set of wings was just a bit different and the one at the top was an exact replica of the wings on Charlie's back.

"Siobhan, do you have a magnifying glass, there's something on the charm you need to see. Actually, all of you need to see this."

"In the top desk drawer," the Healer answered without looking up from the book on her lap.

Retrieving the glass, he sat beside Siobhan while Charlie and Kyra moved to her other side. Placing the pendant on the table, Aaron held the magnifying glass above it and waited while all three women took a look. It was Kyra that saw it first.

"Oh my goddess! Look at that!" she gasped.

"What? I guess I don't know what I'm looking for," Charlie muttered, still looking intently through the glass.

"I'm with you, Charlie. I don't see it either," Siobhan murmured, looking back and forth between the pendant and her book.

"Look right here," Aaron instructed, pointing at a set of the wings. "At first, I thought those were petals of a flower, but then I saw they're actually wings, four sets of wings to be exact." He outlined each set while the ladies watched, understanding dawning on both their faces.

"The details of the one at the top looks just like the markings on your back." Charlie's eyes were wide with surprise.

"Then there is this." He pointed to the center. "It's a Celtic cross and the words engraved are *chosaint agus a sha'bha'il,* which is Gaelic for protect and save."

Siobhan was nodding her head as Kyra said, "It was left with you for protection. Whoever your mom is or was, she knew magic. She protected you. I know it's kind of personal, but can I have a look at your hip. I'm wondering if it's really a birthmark. It might be something else left by your mom."

"Sure, no problem," Charlie answered, lifting the leg of her shorts while Kyra bent down to look at the birthmark on her hip.

"Just as I thought," the little witch beamed. "It's a birthmark all right, but one magically given, not naturally. The origin is feminine, so definitely from your birth mom. Now, let's check out that little spark in there," Kyra said, hopping up and pointing to the chair next to Aaron while taking the one across the table.

Pointing to the steaming copper bowl sitting on a grate over a large candle, the witch explained, "That's just some ash from the White Ash tree for protection and focus, Dragon's Blood herb for protection, Eyebright to identify the magic, Lilac and Orris for memory and focus, and Thyme for positivity. The green candle is for success, white for protection, royal blue for wisdom, and silver for the Mother Goddess. I'm gonna say a little incantation and then I should be able to see your magic. Okay?"

"I'm ready, if you are," Charlie quipped.

Aaron could feel that she was a little nervous, and from the random thoughts he picked up, it only came because of the new experiences. He could only imagine how mind boggling it had to be for someone that hadn't grown up with dragons and magic and all the other things that he just took for granted. Sending reassurance and love through their mating bond, he hoped to make things easier for her.

"Mother Goddess, provide your light. Help us focus, protect our rite. Your child is pure, her soul is bright. Her magic is beauty. Her magic is white. We seek the origin. We seek her kin. Universe of All show us the way. Give us your wisdom by end of day. Blessed be. Blessed be." Kyra chanted in English while Siobhan did the same in the language of their ancestors.

After the third time through, the little witch bowed her head and prayed, "We offer you our love, devotion, and service, Mother Goddess, God above, and the Universe that sustains us. Thank you for your gifts. Thank you for this day. Thank you for it all. Amen and amen."

"*O'n and bean naithe*," Siobhan murmured in response. Words Aaron remembered from his childhood. His mother had always said amen and blessings at the end of every prayer.

"Now, I'm going to scry," Kyra picked up the mirror that never seemed far from her side and sprinkled it with herbs, reciting the same words she'd said before.

Aaron watched the mixture on the glass shimmy and shake for almost a full minute before settling. Kyra looked at Charlie and then at him with absolute astonishment on her face.

"I have never seen anything like this before." The little witch sounded shocked, and when she set the mirror on the table for all of them to see, Aaron knew why.

The magic Kyra had called upon had arranged the herbs in the exact image of Charlie's birthmark and charm. Aaron had no idea what that meant, but from the looks on Siobhan and the little witch's face, it meant a lot more looking before they had their answers.

The Healers words confirmed his thoughts. "Well, I guess that means I'll be doing some extra reading."

"I'll help," Charlie offered.

"Me, too," Kyra chimed in.

"Well, I'll be around for moral support, ladies," Aaron joked.

"Time to eat!" Royce shouted into the window.

Saved by the food!

By the time they got to the kitchen, the table was covered with dinner and the line was long. Aaron watched Charlie watching all his brethren and their families with what could only be described as affection. He tried to imagine how his extended family looked to her, but came up short. Only a mate could deal with six huge guys that acted like a bunch of teenagers on a good day, not to mention could turn into dragons at will. Beautiful women that were smart, outspoken, and had special talents all their own *and* two children that had blessed their clan in ways no one could have predicted with their own unique qualities.

Has to be overwhelming...

Looking at Jay and Sydney made him think of Grace's pregnancy. He saw her filling her plate and laughing at something his twin had said. As she turned to head to the dining room, the proof of her pregnancy pushed against her blouse.

Heavens help them if those kids are anything like Aidan and I when we were little.

Shaking his head, he looked at Charlie. Visions of a sweet little girl with vibrant blue eyes and long blonde curls squealing with delight as he swung her in the air filled his mind. Then he thought of a tough little boy, almost identical to the little girl, but with spiky hair and the determination to accomplish anything. The little guy was swinging a stick like a sword, hurling threats at his imaginary opponent.

Royce bumped his shoulder, pulling him out of his daydream. "What's the matter, smartass?"

"Nothing, why?"

"You're standing there all starry eyed. Must be love. Look at that shit. This is gonna be fun." Royce laughed so hard, Aaron thought the old man might drop his plate.

"Yeah, yeah, yeah."

"You better get up there and get your food before the young ones get here. They can put away food faster than a swarm of locust. And your girl's already up there talking with mine and Sam. I'm sure you're in some kinda trouble."

Charlie glanced back and winked just as he looked up. Grinning, Aaron winked back.

I am the luckiest man alive.

Royce laughed all the louder, practically shouting to the other Guardsmen already eating in the dining room, "Oh man, Aar's got it bad! Y'all missed the sappy look on his face." Walking through the kitchen, the old man kept talking, "Boy oh boy, I mean he's really got it *bad*."

The dining room erupted in laughter, but Aaron just couldn't care. They were all right, he *was* in love. All was right with the world.

Plate filled, he headed into the dining room, happy to see that Charlie had saved the seat next to her. There were ten different conversations going on about ten different topics, but he zeroed in on his mate and Sam's. They were barely speaking above a whisper, but with his enhanced abilities, he heard her ask her best friend about the mating ceremony.

"You said that it's a really private thing, right?"

"Yep. Sure is. It starts with you and Aaron, the Elders, which you'll meet, and these meatheads." Sam motioned around the table. "The Elders say a passage from the Holy Book, Rayne says something on behalf of their Force, and then you and Aaron will be left alone for the Marking Ceremony."

"You mean I'll get a little tattoo like the one on your neck?"

"It's more of a brand and it happens kind of magically when you two kiss, but yeah. If you check out everyone else's, they're all similar but also different. They say the Universe decides based on what you two are together. It's pretty cool. I can't wait to see yours."

"Well, we're a long way from that."

"Whatever you say, Charlie. Whatever you say."

His mate was about to respond, but didn't when she saw him by her side.

"What are y'all talking about?" he asked as if he hadn't heard the whole thing.

"Oh nothing," they answered in unison, like two little girls caught with their hands in the cookie jar.

Smirking, Aaron sat down, deciding to let Charlie think he hadn't heard. He knew Sam would remind her about the enhanced hearing soon enough. He'd just gotten the first bite of steak in his mouth when Rian and Rory came through the door.

"What the hell, you guys? Nobody thought to holler that the steaks were ready?" Rory complained.

"We knew you'd smell them and come running," Kyndel laughed. "Heaven knows you never miss a meal."

"Hey now. I work hard to look this good." He opened his arms wide and then flexed both his biceps just as Rian elbowed him in the stomach.

Everyone howled with laughter while Rory grunted and rubbed his stomach. He turned and went into the kitchen and Aaron could hear him filling his plate. Rian looked at Rayne and Aaron immediately knew they were having a private conversation, and from the look on their faces, it was *not* about the weather.

"What's going on there?" Charlie nodded towards Rayne, whispering close to his ear.

"What do you mean?"

"I can hear the static again and it's clear from their expressions they're talking about something important. Can you hear?"

"No, we have what we call 'unique links' between each other. It's immediate with family. Then once we're bonded, either as brethren or as mates, that link is established as well. It's kinda like having a private line where we can talk and no one else can hear. You're the first one I've ever heard that can tell when others are talking. Well, others you're not somehow connected to. I mean, I know Kyra can tell when Royce and his brothers are talking, and Grace can tell when Aidan and I are talking, but I've never known anyone that could tell when *Rayne* was mindspeaking. His mind is like a steel trap."

"Wonder if it has something to do with the magic you found?"

"Might be. We'll have to tell Kyra and Siobhan."

"Yeah, I will."

He knew she would. She was going about this the same way she did diagnosing a patient. He'd heard her thinking about it. Making a chart in her head. Mentally documenting everything she learned. It may not all make sense to her, but she was open-minded and serious about learning about her origins.

Rory walked in with a plate in each hand, signaling for Rian to follow him to the only two empty chairs left at the huge oak dining table. Once they were seated, Rayne stood and looked around the table.

Oh damn, this can't be good.

"It seems we were in the right place. Andrew *is* on that mountain, just doing a good job at hiding from us. Rian and Lennox were able to catch a few of his thoughts today. His dragon is trying hard to be heard, but the little bas... I mean *traitor*..." he quickly corrected, smiling at his son and Sydney, "is working even harder to keep him at bay. That is good news. It means the black magic has burned off and he's also low on earth magic. He won't be able to hide forever, and I want him caught sooner rather than later."

"Here! Here!" was heard from everyone around the table, even the kids.

Looking at each Guardsman individually, then at Siobhan, the Commander began again. "If it's okay with you, I'd like us to discuss a strategy for catching that little piece of sh...*crap* once and for all, as soon as we're finished eating."

"Whatever you need. You know that, son," Siobhan answered while everyone else was agreeing as well.

Rayne went on, "Rian and I believe Andrew has found a way to hone in on our dragons, and maybe even our thoughts, without us knowing. He *is* the *Special One,* and because of his dalliance with black magic, we have no idea what that has done to the extra abilities he has."

"I'm certain he's almost on overload at this point," Rian took up where Rayne had stopped. "Kellan also found more fresh blood, so we know he's either injured again, not healing, or both. Kyra is sure that's because of all the conflicting types of magic he's subjected himself to. We have to use this to our advantage. We're *only* gonna get one more chance."

"Is there something more we can do?" Aidan asked Rian, pointing at Aaron.

Kyra answered, "Aunt Della found a spell to create a focus for the power of twins. She and some of the stronger ladies at the coven are crafting it now. That's gonna give you Wonder Twins the extra juice you need to hear *and* see the traitor before he knows you're anywhere around."

Aidan gave Aaron another quick look before switching his attention back to Rian, who was already talking. "All right, y'all eat up. Lennox, Kellan, and Brannoc are on their way over. Brannoc has been looking at every map he could get his hands on and has found a way for us to approach the mountain without being seen by *anyone*."

The leader of the Blue Thunder Clan sat back down just as the others of his Force came through the front door.

"Damn, it smells good in here," Lennox called out, making a beeline for the kitchen.

Brannoc dropped an armload of maps on the couch as he yelled into the dining room, "Hey in there. Pardon my manners, but I'm starving." Aaron could hear his footsteps on the tile of the kitchen floor.

Kellan, the silent, scary one of the group, dropped a duffle just inside the door, nodded his hello, and followed his comrades into the kitchen. Kyndel and Sam were up getting the kids cleaned up and making room for the Guardsmen that had just come in to sit down. Others followed suit until all the ladies were in the kitchen and the men around the table.

Any other time, Aaron would've made a smartass comment, but figured those days were long past. Charlie would kick his ass in front of everyone and smile while she did it. He grinned to himself, standing and taking his plate to the kitchen.

"Lookie there, you've already domesticated him, Charlie," Grace teased.

"Good job!" Kyndel added, squeezing his arm as he passed by.

"Y'all just keep it up. I still have a few tricks up my sleeve," Aaron joked in return.

"But he'll keep them to himself," Charlie said in mock authority, right before busting out laughing.

All the women followed suit, still laughing when he left the room.

"I see the girls are giving you the hell you deserve," Rory commented.

"Just wait loud mouth, your turns comin'," Aaron responded while everyone at the table chuckled along.

The men talked amongst themselves while the late arrivals ate, but Aaron couldn't help listening to Charlie's conversation in the kitchen. The ladies were all telling her about how they'd met their mates, at least the stories she hadn't already heard. Kyndel told the story of her and Rayne's mating ceremony. Aaron was happy to hear the excitement in Charlie's voice and had to laugh at her surprise that he was the one that planned everything…not her.

There was a lull in their conversation and then he heard Anya speak. Her voice was low and filled with trepidation, but she was a real trooper and said what she obviously thought was important. "Charlie, I want to apologize for what you saw the night of my mating ceremony. I promise I had *no idea* that was going to happen and I would do anything to take back the fear I'm sure you felt. I can't even imagine what it was like for you." Anya's nervous chuckle was hard to hear, but reinforced how strong she really was. "Heaven knows I wish I'd had a little advance warning. I just wanted you to know how happy I am that you accepted us and especially the butthead who I'm sure is out there listening in. Surprises are pretty much the rule around here, but you get used to it, I promise, and these people are so worth the angst."

"No worries, really. I admit to being completely freaked out and contemplating my own sanity for a few days, but it's all good now. I totally agree with you about the surprises. I guess I have a few of my own I knew nothing about…no dragons, but maybe a little magic. I want to thank y'all for not giving up on *me*. As for the butthead…I think I'll keep him."

The ladies all laughed, promising to share the most embarrassing story they knew about him with her. The sneaks even went so far as to tell her they were sure she would need the ammunition.

Oh, I just can't wait.

He continued to eavesdrop, hoping to catch one of the stories when a dinner roll hit him in the face.

"Snap out of it, Romeo. She's fine and you don't need to be eavesdropping. That shit will get you sleeping in the doghouse faster than anything else," Aidan said.

"Damn sure will," Lance agreed, and Aaron could tell he was speaking from experience.

No surprise there.

Kellan took his, Brannoc's, and Lennox's plate to the kitchen, surprising Aaron but apparently no one else. That man was a true enigma, one Aaron hoped he never had to figure out. Royce, Rian, and Rory trusted him and that was all Aaron needed to know. He was just damn glad the retired marine was on their side.

Brannoc spread the maps out on the freshly cleaned table, explaining as he went about the trail he'd located. It looked like if they came from the industrial park that backed up to a patch of woods behind the mountain, there was no way *anyone* would be able to see them. It appeared as if no one knew the land existed. It had taken Brannoc hacking into a government database to find the map they were looking at.

"Why couldn't we see it on a fly over?" Lance asked.

"No clue," Brannoc answered. "I'm guessing heavy cloaking magic, which makes me wonder what the hell they're hiding in there. The maps don't show any land mines or any other protection devices that we need to worry about. Royce said Kyra can null out whatever's being used magically. We'll be good to get in, get the bastard, and get out."

Rayne and Lance both popped their heads up, looked into the kitchen where Jay and Sydney were playing, and sat back down when they saw the kids were out of earshot.

"It's about time," Aidan mumbled, examining the path Brannoc had highlighted.

Their strategy session went on for several hours during which Charlie spoke directly into his mind several times. He was glad she was using their special form of communication, especially when she told him she was going to Siobhan's study with Kyra and the Healer to start looking for info on her birthmark and pendant.

Aaron showed her how to leave their connection open so he could listen in on their findings while also being a part of the hunt for his younger brother. It was shocking when it actually worked. Their connection was almost complete, and they hadn't been officially mated or even *together* for very long.

"Tell the ladies that we are able to have an open connection," he sent directly into her mind.

"I'm guessing that's important..."

"Yeah. Sorry, should've said that first, Dr. Gallagher. It appears your magic, although tiny in size, packs a wallop. That's the only reason I know of that would make our bond so strong in such a short period of time. Not that I'm complaining in the slightest. I like having you in my head. It's cozy in here."

"You are absolutely incorrigible. Now pay attention to your stuff and I'll pay attention to mine," she snickered.

He heard her talking to Kyra and Siobhan and went back to paying attention to the Guardsmen's plans to capture the dickhead. Kellan and Brannoc even impressed Rayne with their complete assessment of the situation and their suggestions for a plan of action. After just a few more adjustments, they had their strategy well laid out.

Rian told them all to get some rest and meet at the Great Hall at nightfall the following evening. Rayne had already walked away and Aaron could hear him on the phone with Max, the King of the Big Cats. The werepanthers would definitely be a huge asset on this job. Not to mention, the cats wanted the traitor caught almost as bad as the dragons did. He had wreaked enough havoc for several lifetimes and was indiscriminate in the way he spread around his special brand of pain.

Tired of being away from his mate, Aaron went directly to the study to find Charlie and Kyra sitting Indian style on the floor with books stacked all around them. The girls chatted away, not noticing him until he was right beside them.

"Y'all find anything good?"

Both shook their heads, but Kyra spoke first. "Nothing yet, but I know we will. Your girl there is made up of some strong stuff. Her magic is powerful and her momma really wanted it protected. It might take us a bit, but we'll get it figured out."

The little witch stood, stacking the books in an order Aaron guessed made sense to her, but to him looked like a game of Jenga. She looked at Charlie and smiled. "I have had a blast with you today. Want to meet back here tomorrow after lunch? I gotta go. Big guy's calling." She tapped her temple.

"Sure, I'll meet you here?" Charlie asked.

"Absolutely." Then to Siobhan, Kyra added, "I'll bring lunch. You hungry for anything specific?"

"Whatever you make will be fine, dear. Sleep well and give Royce a hug for me," the older lady answered, nose stuck in her book.

"Sure will. See y'all tomorrow." And with that, she disappeared out the door.

Squatting beside his mate, Aaron asked, "You ready to go? Or did you want to stay a while longer?"

"No, my eyes are ready for a rest. I'm ready if you are."

Standing and helping Charlie up at the same time, Aaron said, "Thanks for everything, Siobhan."

The Healer stood and approached, motioning for Aaron to lean down. When he did, she hugged his neck and whispered, "You got a good one there, son."

"Yes, ma'am, I do," he answered, returning to his normal height and pulling Charlie to his side.

She moved to Charlie and hugged her, too, but spoke only when she pulled away. "You've got your work cut out for you with this one, but I'm sure you can handle it."

Charlie laughed, snuggling closer. "My dad's a retired cop, so I'm sure I can deal with whatever he dishes out."

Siobhan's laugh was louder and fuller than Aaron had heard in a long time. She was such a vital part of their clan and so important to so many people. He loved the times she actually let loose and had fun.

Steering his mate out the door, they quickly said goodbye to everyone. Sydney made Charlie promise to come and play with her very soon. It took longer than he wanted, but when they finally stood on the porch and closed the door behind them, Aaron sighed in relief.

"What was that for? I thought it was a great evening," Charlie asked, looking up at him in surprise.

"It was. I just want you all to myself. We dragons are a possessive lot. Having all those men around you, even though I know most are mated and the unmated ones would never do anything, makes my dragon go nuts and I'm not far behind." He threaded his fingers through hers and began to walk towards his Harley. "Our bond is strong, but it's still new. *Hell*, Aidan and Grace have been together for over a year and are expecting twins and I still catch stray thoughts from him about the same thing. What can I say," he shrugged. "We're Alphas. I'll do my best not to be overbearing and I know you'll kick me if I show my ass…I'm just saying it might take a while, so be patient with me."

Charlie laughed aloud before answering. "You got it. It will be my *pleasure* to kick your ass if you get outta line."

Unable to resist her a second longer, Aaron grabbed her up and set her sidesaddle on the seat of his motorcycle. His hands on her waist held her still while his eyes took in the beauty that was his mate. He saw the question in her eyes, but loved the fact that she sat in silence, waiting for him to speak or act first.

Leaning forward, he kissed her forehead, then the tip of her nose before finally touching his lips to hers. As lightly as he could, Aaron kissed first one corner of her beautiful mouth, then the middle, then the opposite corner. Charlie let him lead the way, and when he stopped and placed his forehead to hers, they sighed in unison.

"Let's go to my house," he asked without really asking.

Charlie's nod was all the affirmation he needed. She straddled the seat while he climbed on in front of her. It took less than two minutes for him to get from Siobhan's driveway to his front door.

Not leaving anything to chance, Aaron picked her up, carried her across his front yard, and jumped onto the porch. While he was fiddling with the door, she chuckled. "You really can move fast, can't ya?"

She laid her head against his shoulder as he threw open the door, carried her across the threshold, and immediately kicked it closed with the heel of his boot. He headed straight for the stairs, whispering all the things he wanted to do to her, and was exhilarated when the scent of her arousal filled his senses.

In his bedroom, Aaron released her legs, reveling in the feel of her body sliding down his. His pulse beat faster, his heart pounded in his chest, and his cock pushed against the zipper of his jeans. He watched her eyes adjusting to only the light from his digital clock while he held her hands.

She is just the most beautiful thing in the world.

He pushed her jacket off her shoulders and let it fall to the floor before lifting her shirt over her head. She smiled a lazy smile that said she wanted him just as much as he wanted her, but would let him set the tempo. Aaron was determined to go slow, to give her the best experience of her life.

"Just being with you makes this the best," she sent directly into his mind.

"Guess I let my thoughts get away from me, huh?"

"It's all good. I kinda like knowing what's going on up there."

Bending at the waist, he kissed his way across her décolletage, sliding down one and then the other of her bra straps, pushing the pink silk cups down, and baring her full breasts to his hungry eyes. Resisting temptation, he reached behind her, completely removing the garment and also letting it fall to the floor. He then removed her shorts, leaving her standing in a tiny pair of baby pink panties.

Running the back of his hands across her hardened nipples, he smiled as she shivered at the contact.

"So receptive…so beautiful…" he whispered into her mind.

"You're teasing me, dragon man," she breathed, her arousal stealing her breath.

Charlie took a deep breath while he ran his hands across her stomach, along her ribs, and under her breasts. Her eyes closed as he watched her trying to regain some of her control. Grinning like the cat that ate the canary, she reached forward and grabbed the hem of his T-shirt.

Looking up through her lashes, she winked. *"It's only fair I get to return the favor."*

He let his hands fall to his sides, loving her playful side. He laughed when she threw his shirt over her shoulder, but could barely breathe when she ran her hands across his chest before laying a chaste kiss on both of his nipples. Aaron was sure he would lose his mind. It was the sweetest sensation. He worked hard to keep from throwing her on the bed and sinking deep inside her.

Her tiny hands rubbed along each ridge of his six-pack abs, heading downward. The glint in her eyes told him she had a plan and it was one he was going to like. Her fingertips brushed through the thin line of hair that led into the waistband of his pants. Charlie undid the button and then the zipper of his pants. When her finger touched the skin inside the waistband of his boxers, Aaron summoned all his strength not to move. He felt his pants slide down his legs just as she murmured, *"Hold on, the best is yet to come."*

It took him a second to realize what she'd said. Opening his eyes, Aaron was shocked to see Charlie on her knees in front of him. All air fled his lungs as her tongue left a glistening trail on her luscious lips. He could feel the small bead of liquid balanced on the very tip of his cock and yelped when she captured it with the end of her tongue. The sigh that flowed through their mating bond, accompanied by her excitement at being able to please him, made Aaron *and* his beast purr.

He watched as she placed her palms on his thighs, rubbing her cheek from the tip to the base of his extremely hard cock. Goose bumps danced along his spine as she nipped and tasted along the vein that ran the length of his dick, working her way back to the tip. When she licked along the ridge under the mushroom head with just the tip of her tongue, his fists clenched so hard his nails dug into his palm.

Her tongue slipped into the slit at his tip and she hummed her satisfaction at his taste. The muscles in his thighs shook. He was holding on by a thread. Aaron moved his hands to her shoulders and massaged, hoping to distract himself from exploding into her mouth.

She sucked as much of his length into her mouth as she could and hollowed her cheeks. Through gritted teeth, he spoke aloud, "*Mo ghra'*, I'm not going to last long if you keep doing that."

Charlie worked him in and out of her mouth for a few more strokes, chuckling at his words. The sensations made him weak in the knees. He shuddered as she sucked first one and then the other of his balls into her mouth. His mate licked and massaged until he thought his head might blow off his shoulders.

Releasing his sac, she kissed the top of one thigh and then the other before placing both of her hands around the base of his cock and taking him deep into her mouth. Charlie worked him in and out, across her lips, sucking and humming until he shouted and gave up the fight. Aaron released into her waiting mouth, all but blacking out at the mind-blowing experience his mate had just given him. Finally regaining some of his senses, he realized she was still massaging his sensitive cock with her precious hands and felt himself begin to harden again.

Sliding his hands under her arms, he picked her up and had her on her back in the middle of his very large bed in the blink of an eye. Kneeling on the floor, he threw her legs over his shoulders, his mouth was just a few inches from her center. He rubbed his nose against the warm wet silk covering what only his mate could give him. The scent of her arousal drove him mad. Slipping two fingers under the lace at her hip, Aaron tore the material and threw them from the bed. He breathed deep, letting his beast bathe in the scent of their wet and needy mate. Unable to wait another moment, he leaned forward, letting just the tip of his tongue lick the glistening seam of her pussy, teasing her as she had teased him.

He groaned deep in his throat. Charlie tasted like sunshine and perfection. Placing his hands under her ass, he lifted her closer to his face and began to feast. He drove his tongue deep into her warm, wet channel, licking every inch of her he could reach, curling the end to tease the bundle of nerves at her center, loving the fact that she screamed in pleasure.

Charlie's hands grabbed his hair, pulling, begging him to continue. She was wound so tightly he could hear her struggling to breathe. Aaron placed the flat of his tongue at the bottom of her outer lips and slowly licked all the way to her clit. Her excited nub pulsed as he sucked it between his lips. Flicking up and down and in circles with his tongue gave his mate just what she needed. He smiled against her throbbing pussy as she came over and over again.

He licked and swallowed the honey that flowed from his mate, nuzzling her back to earth until she released his hair and her breathing returned to normal. He let her legs slide off his shoulders and massaged the muscles in her thighs. There had never been a lovelier sight than his Charlie completely satiated, spread like a decadent courtesan across his bed.

He kissed her hip, making his way to her stomach where he paid extra attention to her belly button with his tongue and teeth. Charlie giggled as he licked his way up her stomach and then sighed when he found the sweet spot between her breasts. Palming both her breasts, he squeezed and massaged, feeling the already raised peaks grow harder against his hands. He kissed her neck, worrying the spot behind her ear until she moved her head, allowing him more access. He spent a few extra minutes nipping and kissing until her nails dug into his biceps.

Charlie grabbed him by the hair and slammed her mouth into his. He loved that she took control and opened immediately for her. They ate at each other until both were breathless. His mate was as sassy in bed as she was out and *damn* if he didn't love it. Her hands in his hair and her tongue working his mouth had him ready to explode. He shifted his hips slightly and pushed into her until he could go no farther. Her scream in his head almost had him coming again. *"Aaron! Oh My God, yes!"*

He had sworn to go slow, but the feel of her muscles contracting around him made it impossible for him to hold still. He slid out of her, leaving only the very tip of his blissfully hard cock resting inside her. *"Look at me, Charlie,"* he commanded.

Her bright blue eyes snapped to his and he thrust back inside her. Immediately pulling back out, Aaron started a rhythm that his mate met stroke for stroke. He stared into her eyes, watching as her passion reached heights that he could tell surprised even her. Grabbing her calves, he pushed her knees forward, lifting her bottom from the bed. His dick slid deeper into her. Rolling his hips, he felt the head of his cock tease the very sensitive bundle of nerves, making the walls of her vagina close so tightly around him, it felt as if they were truly one. Charlie's eyes rolled back in her head before sliding shut. Aaron slammed into her as far as he could reach, bumping her clit with his pelvis, and loving her moans of pleasure.

Reaching between their bodies, Aaron tapped her clit with the pad of his thumb and simply watched as she went into orbit. Her mouth opened in a silent scream as her eyes flew open, catching his. Those beautiful azure depths held the promise of their future. One final thrust and he was helpless but to follow her over the edge. They shared every moment, not only physically but also mentally and spiritually. Aaron knew he would never be the same, and it was the best news he'd heard in a long time.

Reluctantly pulling his still semi-erect cock out of her still quaking pussy some time later, Aaron gently lifted his drowsy mate and lay back against the pillows with her draped across his chest. It was the same position they'd been in the night before and the one he decided they would be in every night for all time.

Charlie looked up with a sleepy smile and kissed his chin. Her head landed clumsily back on his chest and in a matter of minutes, her breathing was low and deep. Aaron rubbed her back, enjoying just holding her and glad her markings weren't bothersome like the night before. All thoughts of anything but his wonderful mate fled his mind as he pulled the sheet over them and let his eyes close.

Sleep well, mo ghra'.

CHAPTER TEN

She heard Aaron's sweet words in her mind and tried to answer, but even her brain cells were tired. He had truly loved every single part of her to exhaustion. Any remaining doubts that they were meant to be together simply evaporated. It defied all explanation, as pretty much everything with her dragon did.

Charlie drifted in and out of sleep. The markings on her back tingled, but Aaron's touch kept the irritation at bay. What everyone kept referring to as her 'magic' was glowing more brightly, and in her euphoric state, she was better able to examine it. It was like the logical side of her brain was asleep, leaving the rest of her to look at the spark with a fresh set of eyes.

What Aaron had told her and Kyra had agreed with, she was now seeing for herself. What had been difficult at first to detect was now glowing in a vibrant lavender color. The longer she watched, the brighter it glowed, the more defined it became, and if she wasn't simply dreaming, there was an accompanying hum. It kind of reminded her of a note searching for the perfect pitch…high and clear, pure in origin, sweet to the ear.

Finally succumbing to sleep, her dreams came almost immediately. The vision was grainy, as if she was watching an old home movie. It took a moment for everything to come into focus, but when it did, it was as pretty as any painting she'd ever seen.

She could smell what she first thought was honeysuckle, but on closer inspection, the woody, mossy undertone told her it was heather. Turning in circles, Charlie saw rolling hills covered in the tiny lavender flowers, their fresh scent inescapable.

She heard the giggle of a little girl, followed by the sound of a woman's voice. Not able to make out what she was saying but drawn to the sound, she walked over a small bridge and up a hill. Just over the crest, she saw the woman pushing the child on a wooden swing hanging from a huge oak tree. There was no denying they were mother and daughter. Even if Charlie hadn't had umpteen genetics classes, it still would have been obvious. Their long blonde hair was identical in color, with the top layers clipped at their crowns, and even their curls twisted in the same direction.

The closer she got the more of the woman's words she could make out. She was telling her daughter a story. One that made Charlie smile. Sitting on a stump beside a clear creek, she listened as the woman wove a tale of dragons, knights, and a fairy princess.

"So you see, Ailsa, dragons are the guardians of all the Universe's secrets and treasures. She trusts them and loves them most of all. It was She that watched from above for so very many years to find human men great enough to fight beside her beloved beasts. When the Universe found the knights battling with all that they were to protect Her earth and its inhabitants, She sent the great Dragon Kings to meet with King Arthur."

"The collaboration was a success and for years knights and dragons together kept order, but as all things go, the evil of the world sought to destroy the good. The dragons were forced to join their souls, the part of them that was the most special, with that of earth's great men."

"It took boundless magic to perform such a feat, a mage that had lived almost as long as the Universe herself was the only one strong enough. He worked his magic. Man and dragon became one. All that was left was to teach the men to become a dragon and then to fly. For that he called upon the Fairy Princess, Ailsa."

The girl squealed with delight, "Her name is just like mine."

"Yes, sweetling, it is," her mother answered as she continued. "The Princess Ailsa was happy to help. Along with her came the mighty Fey Army. For who better than winged warriors to teach the knights how to soar the skies?"

"It took several days, but the warrior fairies were successful and the men who became dragons learned to fly. Princess Ailsa was so pleased that she promised the day would come when a fairy princess from her own line would wed a dragon made man. The Universe blessed the Princess' proclamation, assuring that when the time was right, it would come to pass."

"Did it happen, momma? Did the fairy and the dragon man get married?"

"Not yet, little one, and do you know why?"

The little girl jumped from the swing, dancing in a circle and clapping her hands. She sang her answer as only a child could do. "Because I am the fairy princess! Right, momma? It's me?"

The mother laughed, picking up the child and hugging her close. "Yes, my beautiful Ailsa, it is you. You are the fairy princess that will wed the dragon man."

Charlie stood to go, feeling as if she was intruding when the mother's voice rang out. "Charlene! Charlene Gallagher!"

Charlie turned, not believing her ears, to find both mother and daughter motioning her to them. The closer she got, the fainter the image of the child became. Taking the final step that brought her to within touching distance of the woman, the little girl completely disappeared.

"What happened? Where did she go?" Charlie asked.

"She had to go. You and she are one and the same," the woman answered.

"I think I'm confused. What exactly does that mean?"

"It means, here in your dream, you were able to see yourself as a child. Not the way you actually were, but the way I see you. And when you came close, your younger image had to go back where she came from." The woman patted her chest above her heart. "You two cannot occupy the same place at the same time."

"Well, I shouldn't be surprised after all I've seen, but..."

"I know, it has to be terribly disconcerting, and for that I am so very sorry, my sweetling."

"Wait a minute. If that was me, then you are..." Charlie stopped, unable to utter the word.

Smiling a sweet smile, the woman nodded and finished Charlie's question. "Your mother."

Not believing her ears, Charlie just stood, waiting for whatever was to come.

"I know it's hard to believe and I wish there had been another way. I can't come to you in person, so I had to wait until you touched your magic and then began to dream."

"Where are you? Why can't you come to me?" She had almost thirty years of questions stored up for the woman that gave her life, but those were the first two that popped out.

"I am in Fairy and for now must stay. The day will come when I can walk the mortal plane again and then I will find you. I promise with all my heart that I want nothing more than to meet you and the wonderful people that raised you. I watched the Gallaghers from the moment I knew you were growing inside me. They were the best humans I'd ever seen. Your father had gone to the Heavens and because of that, I was being called home. Fairy is no place for a hybrid, even one of Royal blood. Princess Ailsa agreed. All she asked was that you be named in her honor. I was allowed the time to make sure you were cared for. You, my sweet Ailsa, are so very important to so many people."

"Okay I have to ask...is this for real, or a byproduct of falling in love?"

The woman laughed and it sounded like the tinkling of bells, just like Charlie's dad used to describe hers.

"I assure you it is very real. I am Brynna of Princess Ailsa's blood, Keeper of the Hill. It is for that reason that I cannot come see you in person. Not until a new Keeper is born. I was given the freedom to find love by the Princess. Coming to the mortal plane, I found your father. His name was Matthew, a good man with a good heart...a fireman. One night while fighting a blaze, the building collapsed and he was caught inside. Thankfully, he did not suffer."

The sadness she saw in Brynna's eyes was palpable. Charlie felt the pain like it was her own, which she guessed it rather was.

"The following months were lonely, but I had you and the hope of your future that sustained me. The night of your birth, after I knew you were healthy, I took you to the church, made sure the priest came right to the door and persuaded him, as we fairy can do, to call Det. Gallagher. I followed you and the good detective to the hospital, waited and then watched as they took you home."

"Over the years, as Princess Ailsa allowed others of our clan to visit the mortal plane, they would check on you and send home reports of your wellbeing. Your first day of kindergarten, your high school and college graduations, and the day you became a doctor...all the milestones were recorded in this crystal."

Brynna showed Charlie a beautiful light green crystal with copper mountings on both ends. Each mounting was etched with the same symbol as Charlie's pendant and birthmark.

"Those symbols?" Charlie pointed at the fairy's necklace.

"Yes, I'm coming to that. This crystal is Apophyllite. It's very rare and very precious. It can hold the memories of someone the owner loves. The etchings are of our clan and for protection. The four wings of the four elementals to protect us no matter what direction our foes may come. The knotted ring represents the love, faith, loyalty, and friendship we share with all fey, our allies, and the Universe. And the cross to signify the Holy Creator. I prayed for you to be marked with our sigil and also gave you one made of copper and blessed by the Princess, the Holy Ones of Fairy, a man of faith from Earth, and of course, the Universe. I am happier than you will ever know that you wear it to this day."

"Wow. I have to admit it means a lot to know that you didn't just abandon me. I guess I kinda knew that all along. It was just something I felt in my heart, but to hear you say the words really means something. Thank you." Charlie spoke past the lump in her throat, trying hard not to cry.

"I am glad I can give you some solace. It warms my heart to know that even though separated, you felt my love for you. I am also overjoyed you found your magic...or should I say your mate found your magic." Brynna smiled knowingly.

"Yeah, about that."

The fairy laughed, "Do not worry. It is as it was meant to be. You heard the story I told your younger self?"

"Yes."

"That is not just a tale, but a history lesson for her and for you. Your Aaron shares blood with one of the original Dragon Kings and you, my lovely daughter, are of Ailsa's line. You are the lovers in the story."

"Yeah, right," Charlie snorted. "I would know if I was a fairy princess."

"Would you?"

Charlie thought for a moment and then looked back at Brynna. Answering with a certainty she didn't feel, the young doctor answered, "I would," then added, "wouldn't I?"

"Let me ask you a question. Did you know you had magic inside you?"

"No," Charlie answered.

"And did you know that dragons existed before a few weeks ago?"

"Well, no. But..."

Brynna held up her index finger and grinned. "One more question. Was anyone ever able to explain the markings on your back?"

No sooner had the words left her mother's mouth than Charlie's markings began to tingle. Shrugging her shoulders, she quickly answered, "No, but now that you mention it..."

"What did you call them when you were younger?"

"My wings."

"Because that is what they are, sweetling. They are your wings." Brynna nodded as she answered.

Charlie felt as if the world had somehow tilted on its axis. This woman had come to her in a dream, told her she was her birth mother, told her she'd been monitoring her, and to top it off, she was now telling her that she, Charlene Gallagher, was a fairy.

Brynna laid her hand on Charlie's arm. An immediate sense of calm washed over the younger woman, and the air around them was suddenly filled with the scent of heather. "Don't worry, Charlie. I'm not just going to drop *this on you and run away. Yes, my time is almost up for now, but I cannot leave you with so many doubts, and Princess Ailsa has said she will allow me to visit you whenever I can in your dreams. Therefore, I'll tell you what you need to know right now. First, let me ask...what is your middle name?"*

It was as if a light bulb went off in her head, and when she answered, Charlie couldn't help but sound surprised. "Well, hell, it's Ailsa, but I guess you knew that. Here you've been saying it over and over and I never put two and two together." Shaking her head, she patted her mother's hand where it still laid on her arm. "My dad used to say it was an old family name that no one had used for years, but when he saw me he thought of it and since it fit, they made it my middle name. I guess you had something to do with that?"

Winking, Brynna only nodded. *"Secondly, the Dragon Healer and the little white witch will be of great help to you. Please thank the daughter of the Grand Priestess for using her powerful earthen magic to help me find you. Tell the Healer I am in her debt for using her great intellect and wisdom to aide you and that she will find the answers to her questions. She will understand."*

"Enjoy the love the Universe has given you, daughter mine. You and your dragon mate will live long, happy lives. Fate deemed it so from the moment of your conception. And lastly, please give my undying gratitude to the Gallaghers for being exactly what you needed, for loving you like their own, and for being wonderful parents to you when I couldn't be there."

"Now I must return to Fairy and you must wake up. It is time for you to share your heritage with your mate. Never fear, he loves you and will accept you for exactly who you are. You are the light of his soul. He is dragon. He is one of the Universe's chosen. Together there is nothing you two cannot accomplish. Never forget who you are. Never forget that I love you. Wake, sweet Charlie, and wear your wings."

Brynna began to fade from view, but Charlie wasn't sad, something in her heart told her she would see her birth mother again. No sooner had the thought crossed her mind than a brilliant lavender light swept across the valley.

Turning, she walked back the way she'd come, crossed over the bridge, and headed towards what she recognized to be Aaron's house. Just before stepping onto the front porch, Charlie looked over her shoulder. Everywhere she looked the lavender light still glowed, except for the tree she'd stood under with her mother....it stood tall and proud, like a beacon for her to remember.

Charlie opened her eyes, surprised that it was dark. Still draped over Aaron's chest, she started to turn over, but was stopped when the blanket she was wrapped in pulled at the marking on her back. Trying to turn the other way and unravel from the mess they'd made out of their bedding, she once again was stopped.

Huffing her annoyance, she planted her hand on the bed at Aaron's side and pushed up, maneuvering to her knees. Trying not to disturb the snoring man, she backward crawled off the bed until she could slide off the foot and onto the floor. Standing, she turned, took two steps and stopped, dead in her tracks.

I'm not gonna freak. I'm not gonna freak.

Closing her eyes, she took a deep breath and counted to ten.

Spinning around, she looked at the bed then muttered, "Oh hell no..."

Whirling back the other way, she ran to the bathroom, flipped the light on, slammed the door shut, and stood in front of the full-length mirror. Her dream came back to her in vivid color at the same time that her vision cleared.

Once again, Charlie closed her eyes and took a deep breath, but this time she counted to twenty. When she opened her eyes, the image hadn't changed.

Doing the only thing she could think of, Charlie screamed as loud as she could, "Aaron, get your dragon ass in here! I'm a freakin' fairy!"

CHAPTER ELEVEN

One minute he was blissfully sleeping with his mate in his arms and the next he was wide awake, running for the bathroom like a man on fire. He tracked her to the bathroom, moving with blind determination. Throwing open the door, he was bathed in a soft lavender light before catching sight of Charlie standing like a raging Amazonian warrior. There was, however, one HUGE difference...she had wings...beautiful, shimmering, awe-inspiring wings. From what he could see, they were every imaginable shade of purple and lavender with silver throughout and had the same intricate detail as the markings on her back.

One question answered.

She had her hands on her hips and a less than pleased look on her face, and she had obviously forgotten she was very naked. He was still trying to process what was happening when she scoffed and said, "Can you believe this crap? My magic is *fairy* magic. I'm the descendant of a fairy princess and my birth mom came to me in a dream."

Shaking his head and trying to catch up, Aaron asked, "What did you just say?"

"I said, I had a dream and my mom was in it," she repeated as if he was two years old or hard of hearing, or both.

He could tell he was adding to her frustration but had to make sure he was hearing her correctly, so he motioned for her to go on.

Without as much as a breath, his mate railed, "Not my mom, Marian… my mom, Brynna. The one that gave birth to me. She said I'm a fairy, which must be true." She stopped and threw her arms open wide. He knew she was talking about her *new* appendages, but he couldn't focus while looking at the naked perfection that was his mate.

"And my mom, Brynna, she's a fairy, too, but that's not important. Anyway, she told me that *I'm* related to *the* Fairy Princess. There was a whole lot of other stuff, too, but the moral of the story is I woke up and I have wings…*fairy wings*! Like Tinkerbell! Did you have any idea this would happen?"

"No way! Not even a chance!" He put his hands up in the universal sign of surrender. "If I'd even had inkling, you would've been the first person I told, and I know Siobhan and Kyra had no idea either. They were stumped, and that's just not something that happens around here."

Needing to know she wasn't in any pain and also get her covered up so he could concentrate, Aaron grabbed a towel. As carefully as he could, he wrapped the cloth around her, securing it in the front and avoiding her wings until he knew she was all right.

Keeping his hands on her shoulders, he leaned back and answered the question he could see in her eyes. "Sue me. You're gorgeous…*and* standing here naked. The wings only make you more beautiful, if *that's* even possible. I needed you covered up so I could think." He winked in the hopes of easing some of her tension. Her little snort said it was working, if only a tad.

"I also *needed* to touch you, to make sure you were okay. My dragon is tearing at my brain. He does *not* do well with you in danger. Well, neither of us does. It's just a fact of who we are. Not to mention, I know how tough you are, and I wasn't sure if you'd tell me if you were in pain."

"I would've told you, but thanks for checking. I'm not in any pain…*at all*. Hell, I didn't even know it happened. I thought we were all wrapped up in the sheet when I couldn't roll over. Then I stood and realized there was *no* sheet. It was these!" She moved just enough that her wings passed over his fingers. They were softer than feathers and lighter than air. His skin tingled with magic everywhere they touched. It reminded him of something…something he'd have to think about later.

Charlie shifted from one foot to the other, drawing his attention. He looked down just in time to see her roll her eyes, which caused him to chuckle. She shook her head and huffed out a groan of frustration, which for Aaron was a relief. If she were well enough to be irritated, then she was better than most would be. He could only *imagine* how confusing yet another revelation had to be, but damn if she wasn't handling it like a pro.

Aaron needed to know exactly what had happened in her dream. It was the only clue he had to what had caused her magic to manifest. There were hundreds of cases where people were given valuable information in dreams and this had most definitely been one of those times. As he pieced together the little bit of what Charlie had blurted out, he figured her mom might be on another plane, which definitely explained the extraordinary form of communication.

"Let's go sit down and you can tell me about your dream. I'm sure we'll need Kyra and Siobhan's help, but since it's the middle of the night, let's figure out as much as we can until a decent hour. Cool?"

"Yeah, that's fine," she sighed.

They'd almost made it to the bed when she stopped and blurted out, "How on God's green earth do I get these back where they came from?" She flicked both her thumbs back towards her wings like a hitchhiker. "They are driving me *crazy*. Can you hear that humming sound? It's coming from them. It's really pretty and all, but enough is enough. Oh, and they vibrate. Not like a lawn mower or anything like that, just tiny vibrations, but I need a break."

Her pleading look told him he *had* to do something. He'd known a few fairies in his hundred years but never well enough to ask…"Hey! How do you collapse your wings?" Using his enhanced abilities, he heard the hum and saw the vibrations. He could also see the magic surrounding her. Charlie was bathed in the same iridescent purple light that had flashed at him in the bathroom, but now it had what he could only describe as tiny silver stars twinkling about.

"I'm gonna guess that it works the same as our transformation. I mean magic is magic, right?" She looked less than confident, but thankfully was still listening.

"Here's what I do…imagine what you look like without wings. Make that the only image in your mind. Focus on your magic, and then combine the two. Concentrate on collapsing your wings. When you feel the change begin, follow through, and your wings should be back where they started."

"Can I leave our link thing open so you can make sure I'm doing it right?"

He was once again overwhelmed by her complete faith in him. "Absolutely! I'll be with you every step of the way."

Nodding, she closed her eyes. He let their minds connect through their mating bond and watched as she imagined herself without wings, found her magic, and combined the two. She was a natural. Aaron felt magic fill the room as they became bathed in that same warm lavender light he already associated with Charlie.

He watched as the wings, which started just even with the top of her head and ran the length of her body, stopping behind the back of her knees, got smaller and smaller. They folded in on themselves until they were once again the glyphs on her back. Grinning from ear to ear, he pulled her to him before her eyes were even open all the way and hugged her tight.

"You did it, *mo ghra'*. You did it!" He cheered.

Looking up, she smiled. "Thank the Lord! I mean they're pretty and all but…*whew!* …I needed a break."

Snickering at her candor, he steered her to the bed, making sure she was comfortable before dashing to the closet to grab shorts for himself and a T-shirt for her. When he got back, he watched as she pulled the shirt over her head and let the towel fall to the ground. He and his dragon both highly approved of having her in his clothes. It was an overly possessive move and he knew it, but was happier than he could express that she was letting him care for her.

"How about we go down and make some coffee and you can tell me all about your dream. I'm somehow sure we're up for the day," he suggested, holding out his hand to her.

"Sounds good. There's no way I'm going back to sleep until I at least halfway understand what happened here." Charlie threaded her fingers through his and followed as he led them down the stairs, straight to the kitchen.

He was pleasantly surprised when she went to the counter, grabbed the correct canister on the first try, found the filters in the cabinet, and began making coffee. Turning, she leaned against the counter and stared straight ahead. He could feel her thinking so he simply sat down, giving her whatever time she needed to collect her thoughts.

It didn't take long before she spoke. "Can you just do that mind linky thing, again? I know it seems like we've been doing it a lot lately, but honestly, I'm not sure I can even remember everything Brynna said. Every time I think about it, something new pops up."

He started to respond just as she speared him with a determined look and asked, "It's okay to keep 'dragon mind melding' right? It doesn't hurt you or me or anything like that, right?"

Aaron wanted to laugh out loud at her Star Trek reference, but thought better of it and instead answered her questions. "Nope. Not at all. It's perfectly natural. We're mates. Looking into each other's minds is something we're *supposed* to do. I'm sure my mom and dad never left one another. I know Aidan and Grace do it more and more. It took them a bit to get the hang of it, but you have serious mojo and I've always been above average…" He winked and she snorted.

Definite progress.

"Together we are overachievers, my love."

Not waiting for her reply, he followed their mating bond and found the memory of her dream right in front. Aaron was shocked at how much the two woman looked alike. The only real difference was that Brynna's hair was long and curly.

Seeing Charlie as a child, even though it was from her mom's memory was a gift he'd never expected to receive. He let the memory play out, enjoying every second. It was amazing to him that Brynna's story was almost verbatim to what he'd been told as a child. His mate was already royalty in his eyes, so that was no surprise, and completely explained how the one little spark of magic he'd found had grown so quickly and completely.

Aaron could feel Charlie's relief that her mother was still alive and that she'd not abandoned her, but instead had made special efforts to ensure her child was cared for. He knew that Zachary, their clan's oldest Elder, had intimate knowledge of the fairies. As the story went, when Zachary was a young man he was injured in battle. Alone and unable to do more than crawl to a cave to recover, he was found by a warrior fairy and his mate. They nursed the injured Dragon Guardsman back to health and made sure he found his Force. His tale was told along with the legend of how the fairies helped the first Guardsmen to show the longstanding friendship between dragons and fairies.

When Brynna disappeared, Aaron stayed in Charlie's mind to watch the actual transformation. It was just as she'd described…no pain, nothing traumatic, just one minute no wings, next minute wings. For that, he would be eternally grateful.

He'd been watching Charlie's expressions while her dream replayed and marveled at her inner strength and complete belief that he would help her get the answers she needed. He and his dragon both puffed up with pride.

Not sure where to begin, Aaron just started rambling as he got up to get their coffee. "It's uncanny how much you look like your mom. And she is the Keeper of the Hill, which is a very important position. It's like being one of our Elders. She's a leader of her clan…your clan."

He handed her a mug of coffee and set his on the table before getting the cream from the refrigerator. Charlie hadn't responded, but was sitting still, once again deep in thought. Sitting next to her, he waited as long as he could before speaking again.

"And your dad was human, but a hero." When she still didn't respond, he asked the question he *needed* to know the answer to more than any other, but had held off asking.

"How are you? I mean *really*. All of this has to be overwhelming, to say the least. You seem to be handling it really well…like *perfectly*. I don't want to eavesdrop in your brain, but I'm kinda dying over here."

She laughed aloud. "Eavesdrop away. I'm somehow sure we'll never have secrets from one another, no matter what we do. We both speak our minds and are nosy to a fault." Charlie stopped and looked at him. He was relieved to see most of the worry and frustration gone.

Chuckling, she went on. "I'm just thinking about how strange life really is. I thought I knew all there was to know, at least about myself. I mean I'd made peace with the fact that there was no record of my birth, so I would never know who gave me life. I accepted that mom and dad were my parents. That the marks on my back were just that…marks. I've always known I was supposed to help people, so being a doctor was a logical choice. *Hell*, I even accepted dragons and witches and was prepared for almost anything. But I will tell you that I never thought about fairies and *damn* sure never in my wildest dreams imagined I could be one of them.

"When you said you found magic and Kyra and Siobhan confirmed it, I figured my birth mother was a witch or something like that…but a *fairy*. I mean that's crazy even for you, right?"

"Well, no. It's not really crazy for me. I mean you heard the story you're mom told the little version of you. Dragon shifters and fairies have been intertwined since we came to be. But did I think my mate would be one? Not even in my wildest dreams."

He stood up from his chair, turned hers to the side and knelt, taking her hands in his. "I will tell you one thing that you never, ever have to doubt, something that I will spend *every* minute of *every* day of our *very long* lives together showing you. You, Dr. Charlene Ailsa Gallagher, are absolutely perfect to me in every way."

She scoffed and tried to look away, so he gently took her chin between his thumb and forefinger, holding her in place. "I mean it, Charlie. I could not have wished for a better match. You are my equal in every way–actually better than me in most. I love you from the top of your amazing brain to the tip of your cute little toes, and everything in between."

He kissed her for just a moment, keeping her from commenting, using all of his restraint to not let things get out of control, no matter how much he wanted to grab her and run back to bed. There were things they needed to accomplish. Things that unfortunately were more important than making love.

Only just a little though.

Pulling back, he saw her grin right before saying, "I love you, too, dragon man. As crazy as it seems, I really do love you."

Kissing her again, this time more thoroughly, he spoke directly into her mind. *"Thank the Heavens."*

They broke apart, breathless and smiling. It was Aaron that recovered first. Looking out the window at the rising sun, he said, "You want to call Siobhan? Her number's in my cell phone. And I'll call Royce." He tapped his temple. "That way we can get both ladies over here, tell them what you found out, and see if there's anything else we need to know."

"Okay. I think your cell is upstairs. I'll call and then take a shower. Be back in a few."

Before he could answer, she was padding up the stairs. Aaron watched until she was out of sight, loving how comfortable she was in his house. They hadn't talked about where they would live after their mating was official, but he really hoped it would be in his home in their lair. Shaking his head, deciding to think about all that later, he called out to his brethren, *"Hey gramps, you up?"*

"Of course, I'm up. Some of us don't sleep in all day," Royce joked. *"What're you doing up already? I thought you didn't open your eyes until at least ten o'clock."*

"That's kind of a long story and why I'm calling. Let me start off with everything and everyone is okay. I just wanted to see if you and your lovely mate had time to come over. We found out what kind of magic Charlie has and I think you need to see it to believe it."

"Oh damn! I guess it's not dragon since you didn't put out the all call."

"Nope, not dragon, but still pretty cool. I'll make my famous chocolate chip pancakes."

"Deal!" The old man readily agreed. "Kyra's been listening in. She's already running around packing a bag. You called Siobhan?"

"Charlie did. See ya in a few."

"See ya."

Aaron thought about Sam and was sure his mate would want her best friend with them, but he called directly into her mind just to be sure. *"You want me to call Sam and Lance, too?"*

"Oh, please. Thank you. Siobhan is calling Devon and Anya. I figured that would be okay with you. My mind is still kinda boggled. Sam will kick my ass if we don't let her know what's going on."

"You got it. There are clothes in the closet and drawers. Wear whatever you want. You probably have about fifteen minutes before everybody's here. I'm gonna go ahead and call Rayne and Aidan. Might as well tell everybody at once."

"Whatever you think is best. I'm following your lead."

His dragon chuffed while Aaron knew he was grinning like a goof. *"All right, mo chroi. Finish your shower. Is brea' liom tu'."*

"Love you, too," she answered, surprising him that she understood the old language.

This just gets better and better.

Heading to the kitchen to start breakfast, he called Lance, Rayne, and Aidan. He'd just finished telling his twin what was going on when Charlie entered the kitchen. Hair still wet and curling around her face, she had on one of his favorite T-shirts and a pair of his sweats. He could tell she had rolled them several times around her waist, not to mention the three times he counted at her ankles.

"These were the smallest things I could find. You are huge, dude."

"Why thank you, ma'am! I'll take that as a compliment," he teased. For which, she stuck out her tongue.

Looking around at the kitchen counters, her eyes grew big and round. "Are you feeding an army?"

"Pretty much. You saw those heathens eat last night." He laughed, returning to his pancake batter.

"What can I do to help?" She'd barely gotten the question out when the front door opened and in ran a blonde-headed ball of energy. "Aunt Charlie! Aunt Charlie! Aunt Charlie! Is it true? Are you a fairy?" Sydney hugged her legs before scooting a chair over and climbing up to help Aaron with the chocolate chips.

"Well…"

"Sorry. She can hear everything, even our mindspeak unless we wear the amulets Kyra made us." Sam apologized, walking in behind her daughter with cloth grocery bags on each arm.

"No worries," Charlie answered, helping her friend with the bags. "You know me. We're family."

"That we are." Sam hugged Charlie's neck before turning to help Lance with yet more groceries. "We brought bread, fruit, juice, and two more gallons of milk," she called to Aaron.

"Sounds good," he answered over his shoulder.

It wasn't long before everyone had arrived and breakfast was ready. Aaron didn't have as large a dining room table as Siobhan, but between the one he did have, his kitchen table, and the coffee table in front of the couch, everyone had a place to sit. Thankfully, his home had an open floorplan, so the conversation wasn't hampered in the slightest.

He could tell that Kyra was busting at the seams. She and Charlie kept whispering and nodding until Aaron leaned over and said, "Y'all can go to the office or upstairs if you want some privacy, because everyone here is just pretending not to listen."

The tables erupted in laughter and several of the Guardsmen yelled, "Busted!"

"It's no big deal," Kyra said when she'd stopped laughing. "We can wait until Siobhan is finished eating. She needs to be with us. I'm just excited. It's been years since I saw a fairy."

"I have eaten all that I can and I must say, Aaron, your chocolate chip pancakes were just as good as I remembered," Siobhan said.

"I agree," Sydney chimed in with her mouth full, making everyone laugh once again.

"All right, ladies, let's get to it," Kyra jumped up and was heading towards Aaron's office before anyone else had moved.

Charlie caught his eyes and nodded before speaking through their bond, *"You're coming, too, right? Kyra wants to see my wings…"*

"Absolutely. I'll be right behind you." He picked up where she left off, returning her smile.

"All right you meatheads, Rian, Rory, and the others are on their way. They just got back from scouting. You know where everything is. I think the soccer game from the other night is on the DVR. We'll be back," he called while following Charlie down the hall.

They had hardly entered the room when Kyra began talking so fast Aaron could barely keep up.

"Oh my goddess. Siobhan found you in what we're calling 'The Prophecy'. Listen to this shit. You're not gonna believe it. You guys are in there."

"What was that?" Aaron asked.

Charlie calmly repeated exactly what the little witch had said, once again surprising Aaron.

"See, she gets me," Kyra smirked.

Siobhan opened the large ancient volume he'd seen her carry in and began reading, "A calling to heal, a hidden nature, a history long forgotten…all protected in the heart of a woman destined to complete a warrior and his beast. The revelation of all she is brought forth from the joining with her mate. There is more that I have not translated, but I recognize the words 'fairy' and 'dragon made man'."

"Oh my…" Aaron and Charlie both gasped in unison.

"What?" Siobhan and Kyra both asked.

"In my dream or vision or whatever it was, Brynna told the story about how the dragon and the knights became one, and how the fairy warriors helped them learn to fly. Princess Ailsa was happy about the collaboration and made a proclamation about someone from her line and a dragon shifter one day getting married…or mated, whatever you call it."

"No freakin' way," Kyra squealed. "That is just cool!"

"That *is* extraordinary. If it's not too much trouble, may I see the vision…just that part? I do not want to intrude. I would simply like to write down exactly what she said so I can see how closely our historians' accounts and what your mother told you coincide."

"Not a problem, but I don't know how to do that." She looked up at Aaron and asked, "Can you help with that?"

Kissing the tip of her nose, he answered, "I sure can, *evgren*. Your memory is now my memory and I share a bond with Siobhan, so I can show her while Kyra looks at your magic."

"Works for me," she responded, quickly returning his kiss before sitting down next to Kyra on the sofa.

Aaron knelt next to Siobhan and opened his mind. Thinking of the part in the story where Brynna had spoken of her proclamation, he showed the Healer, who began to write as quickly as she could. It took three times through, but she finally had it recorded word for word.

"Thank you. Now, get over there with your mate. I believe she is waiting for you," the Healer ordered with a wink and a grin.

Standing and striding toward Charlie, he leaned over the couch and kissed her cheek before asking, "You needed me?"

"Yeah I guess," she joked before both she and Kyra burst out laughing.

"See? Told you they were just big ole' babies," the little witch teased.

"Hey, you better be careful there, Broom Hilda. I might just call grandpa in here," Aaron provoked.

"And I might just turn you into a toad," Kyra retorted, trying hard to keep from cracking up.

"All right you two, take care of Charlie. Then you can tease each other all you want," Siobhan scolded from her seat behind the desk.

Kyra was the first to speak. "Okay, I already looked at your magic. Looks like it's growing, just like it should be now that it's been accessed and in direct contact with its source, your birth mom. So now, I wanna see those wings. I'm so jealous."

"All right, but this is all so new for me. Like I told you, Aaron has to help me." Charlie stood, taking off his T-shirt and pulling up the back of her sports bra.

"Whatever you need, Sweetie. Your man is always gonna give you whatever you need. I know mine does." Kyra giggled.

Holding out his hands, palms up, Charlie placed hers in his. *"You okay?"* he asked, watching her face to be sure she wasn't pushing too hard, too fast.

"I'm good. Stop worrying."

"It's my job to worry."

"Yeah, yeah, yeah…that's my line," she chuckled inside his head.

"You ready?" he inquired.

"Let's do this."

"You know the drill. Think about what you looked like with wings. Pour your magic into that image..."

"Concentrate on them coming out of my back and unfolding to their full size," she interjected, speaking over him.

Aaron was so proud of her, he couldn't hold back. *"You are just amazing. That was great!"*

Kyra squealed. Charlie's eyes flew open and Aaron and Siobhan laughed aloud.

"Those are gorgeous, Charlie!" Kyra exclaimed.

"They truly are spectacular, Charlene." Siobhan smiled.

"Thanks you guys. I guess somewhere down the line I have to learn how to use them, but for now, just getting them in and out is good with me."

"I am *so* proud of you, *mo ghra'*." Aaron hugged her close, careful of her wings but needing to feel her in his arms.

"Syd's gonna wanna see these, but I'd like to save that for another day. This magic stuff is exhausting."

"Then let's get them put away and you can rest while I talk to the guys. I heard Rian and the others come in a few minutes ago. I want to see what they found when they were out last night." Aaron was worried about the dark circles he saw under her eyes and wanted to make sure she got all the rest she needed.

Charlie held his hands but did everything else herself. He heard her reciting his instructions in her mind and watched as her wings once again folded into her back. Then he helped her straighten her bra and pull his T-shirt back over her head.

"Aaron, if you don't mind, I'm going to stay in here and translate some more of this text," Siobhan called out as he took Charlie's hand, steering her towards the door.

"Not at all, stay as long as you like. I heard Kyndel and Grace talking about sandwiches for lunch." He laughed over his shoulder.

"I'm hanging out, too. There's something familiar about Charlie's magic and I'm gonna see if I can figure it out," Kyra added.

"You got it, kiddo," Aaron responded, closing the door as he and Charlie stepped into the hall.

"Sounds like a party out there," Charlie laughed.

"Haven't you figured out it's always a party when the dragons are around?"

"I think I've heard that somewhere before."

Turning the corner, he yelled, "Well, I'm damn glad y'all have made yourselves at home."

"Oh, shut up and get the hell over here. These idiots are betting on England to beat Ireland," Aidan yelled. "And I've already threatened death to anyone that looks at the score before it's over."

Before he could tell them that he was going to rest with Charlie, she tugged on his shirt and crooked her finger for him to lean down. "Let's hang out down here," she whispered.

"Are you sure?"

"Yep, sure am. Looks like too much fun to leave."

Squeezing in beside Aidan and Grace, Aaron pulled Charlie onto his lap. Whistles and calls sounded around the room and he laughed aloud as his mate yelled, "Shut it up! We can't hear the game over here."

Everyone laughed and soon they were all cheering for one team or the other. The game ended and Ireland was victorious. Aidan jumped up and started singing the Irish National Anthem at the top of his lungs and horribly out of key. Pillows flew as most booed and hissed. As soon as he finished singing, Aidan yelled for everyone to pay up.

Aaron was laughing so hard he almost missed Rayne calling them all to the dining room. The table was covered with maps and aerial pictures of the mountain where they were sure the traitor was hiding. Brannoc started talking as soon all the Guardsmen were gathered round.

"We went back out and scouted the area between the industrial park and the mountain." He pointed to the map. "Using the amulets Kyra gave us and our dragon magic, we were able to confirm that it's protected by a white magic shielding spell. Nothing to worry about. Looks like young Earth witches are using the woods as a place to practice."

"Good news," Rayne commented, studying the maps.

"Definitely. We also found that the businesses housed there get all their deliveries tonight and tomorrow night. Based on that, I think we need to hold off. There's no use expending more energy than necessary using cloaking spells if we don't have to. Kellan was able to talk to the security guard, who's also ex-military, and get the scoop. No one, not even security, works the other nights. It's all on a system, so we'll be good to go."

"As bad as I want to get him, I think waiting is a good plan," Rayne agreed.

"The traitor's not going anywhere," Kellan spoke, a rarity when there were more than two people around. "I found more fresh blood about an hour before we pulled out. He's there, still hurt, and from the looks of the footprints, moving slowly and dragging a leg. With the cooler nights and the rain that's coming, he'll be stuck in his hidey-hole until we get there. His scent will be strong and he'll be ours for the taking."

Aaron was shocked. He'd never heard the reclusive Guardsman talk that much in all the years he'd known him. Aidan kicked him under the table before saying, *"Stop staring. The man's trying to come out of his shell."*

"No shit! Sorry. I was just shocked."

"I could tell. You looked like you were catching flies," his twin laughed.

"Brannoc and Lennox are going to prepare our strategy. Rian, Aaron, and Aidan do the mental tracking. The rest of you know what to do," the Commander looked around the room. "Let's have a good time. Get lots of rest. In two days we end this mess."

All the Guardsmen cheered, but Aaron had other plans. Looking at his twin, he motioned for him to follow. As they walked out the front door, he called out to Charlie, *"Aidan and I are gonna run some errands. You need anything?"*

"Nope. I'm good. Hurry back."

"Sure will. Love you."

"Love you, too."

Now to plan the biggest day of our lives…so far.

CHAPTER TWELVE

Charlie had no idea where Aaron and Aidan were. They had missed lunch and now Kyndel and Sam were talking about what to make for dinner and the twins were still not back. To top it off, the jerk had somehow blocked her so she couldn't listen in. Oh, she could talk to him through their bond, but she couldn't eavesdrop, and her curiosity was about to get the best of her.

She'd asked Grace if she knew what was going on, but the attorney had said she had no idea and Charlie believed her. It seemed that the brothers were out on a secret mission and she was just going to have to wait. Something Dr. Gallagher did even worse than taking orders.

Making her way to the kitchen, she saw the ladies had decided on spaghetti, garlic bread, and salad for dinner. Using that as a ploy to talk to Aaron again and try to find out what he was doing, she called to him through their link. *"The girls are making spaghetti for dinner. Are you close to the Town Square? Sam said there's a great bakery there and I would love some chocolate cake."* She used the best 'pleading tone' she could muster, hoping to find out where he was…but he wouldn't give anything away.

"Nope, not close to the bakery, but we can run by there on our way back. We shouldn't be much longer. Anything else you need?"

Trying to sound nonchalant, she said, *"That should do it. Unless you want to tell me where you are and what you're doing?"*

Laughing, Aaron's only answer was, *"It wouldn't be a surprise if I told you. Love you, gotta go."*

She paced the kitchen floor until Sam told her to help or get out of the way.

"I'm sorry. *Dammit*, I can't stand that he's keeping secrets. I know it's nothing bad, but it's making me nuts."

"Get used to it," Kyndel laughed.

"For sure," Grace added.

"Don't worry, Aunt Charlie. Aaron and Aidan are with the Elders," Sydney said, not even looking up from her coloring.

Charlie looked at the little girl with amazement. "How do you know that?"

Shrugging, she answered, "I don't know. I can just tell you where they are. Aaron's got his wall up so I can't hear them and so does Aidan, but I know where they are."

Figuring it was the best she was going to get, Charlie started making the salad, the only thing not being done. She'd chopped the last tomato when Aaron and Aidan came through the door, closely followed by four stately looking gentlemen she knew right away were dragons. Three of them looked maybe ten years older than her mate, but the last looked old enough to be her great grandfather.

The power that emanated from the men made the marking on her back tingle. Aaron started to speak, but was cut off by the tall man with gray at his temples. "I am Carrick, the Leader of the Golden Fire Clan of the Dragon Shifters. This is Riordan, Malachi, and Zachary. Also Elders of the clan, and we wanted to welcome you as our kin."

She took his outstretched hands, amazed at the strength and power radiating from him. She then shook the hands of the other three, ending with Zachary, the oldest.

He hugged her and kissed her cheek. "I hope you're ready for a lifetime with that kid." Zachary pointed at Aaron and laughed aloud. The sound seemed to fill the whole house, making everyone in it laugh along.

Aaron made his way to her side, knelt on one knee, and held out small, silver, velvet box. Before she could catch her breath, he began speaking, "I love you, Dr. Charlene Ailsa Gallagher, with all that I am. Would you please make me the happiest dragon shifter that has ever lived or will *ever* live and become my mate, my wife, my partner for all of this life and also in the Heavens?"

She opened her mouth to answer, but nothing came out. The questioning look in his eyes had her swallowing and trying to speak again. Only a squeak passed her lips, so she nodded like a bobble head doll in the back of an old Cadillac.

Aaron opened the box, revealing a huge princess cut Alexandrite, at least five carats in size. The overhead light bounced off the facets, highlighting an amazing spectrum of colors. He slid the ring on her finger, explaining as he went. "I spoke to Brynna this morning. Took some doing, but I called in a favor. Anyway, she said that Alexandrite would amplify your powers and make it possible for you to communicate with her or anyone else in Fairy you may want to talk with. It will also help you find the control and balance you asked for. I also think it looks beautiful on your finger and wanted you to have a ring as a human symbol of my love for you."

Finally finding her voice, all she could say was, "Thank you!"

Aaron stood and kissed her like they weren't in front of a room full of people. It only took a second before she didn't care and kissed him back the same way. The room erupted in clapping and cheers. Several long moments later, the couple broke apart and accepted congratulations from everyone.

During dinner, Aaron sprung another surprise on her that almost had her falling out of her chair.

"What do you think about having our official mating ceremony tomorrow?"

He continued to eat like he hadn't just asked her to plan a wedding in less than twelve hours. Aaron must have heard her thoughts, because he spoke directly into her mind. *"You don't have anything to plan. I've already taken care of everything."*

Turning her head so fast she feared whiplash, she answered aloud, "You what?"

"That's where I was all day. It's all planned. Aidan was a big help. All I need is your okay. That's one of the reasons the Elders are here."

She looked at the older men she'd met just a bit ago. They smiled in response and continued eating spaghetti like everything that was happening was completely commonplace.

Maybe it is. What the hell do I know?

Charlie continued to look around the table. Each face she landed on was smiling and filled with so much love and acceptance, she was overwhelmed with more warm fuzzies than she could ever remember having.

Aaron spoke again, drawing her attention. "I also spoke to your parents. They were a little freaked out and not too trusting, but after a long conversation and a quick call to Sam to confirm I was who I said I was, they gave their permission that we be 'married'." He made air quotes before she looked to her best friend, who at least had the decency to blush.

"The only thing your dad made me promise, beside to love you and protect you with my very life, was that we make a trip to their house and have a reception with all their friends. Sound good?"

She had no idea what she'd ever done so right to deserve a man as awesome as the one she had, but she thanked the God above for Aaron right before giving him the biggest kiss she could muster. When they broke apart, he grinned and asked, "Was that a yes?"

Nodding she said, "Sure was, dragon man. *Damn* sure was."

It was the longest night of her life. Aaron had left her and all the girls to have a 'sleepover/bachelorette party' while he went with Lance and the guys to have what she could only imagine was their version of a bachelor party. Charlie hadn't slept a wink, alternating between pacing the floor and trying to read some magazines Sam and Grace had given her. When the sun finally began to rise, she'd gone downstairs and started the coffee. Sydney joined her for a cup of hot chocolate and that's where they were when the doorbell rang.

"It's Jace," Syd squealed as she ran to answer the door.

By the time Charlie made it to the door, the child had it open and was talking to a younger version of the men she was quickly becoming to think of as family. Looking up, he bowed at the waist before handing her a huge silver box tied with a lavender satin ribbon.

"For you, Dr. Gallagher," he said.

"That's Jace, Aunt Charlie. He's gonna be a Guardsman when daddy and Royce decide he's ready."

Pink tinted the apples of the young man's cheeks. "Congratulations, Dr. Gallagher. Have a nice day," he said before once again bowing and then leaving.

"Thank you," she called after him, closing the door.

"I bet I know what's in the box," Sydney sang as she skipped alongside her.

"You think so, huh?"

"Yep. I'm gonna wait though. You need to be surprised, but hurry. I'm dying here."

Charlie laughed, sat the box on the kitchen table, and began untying the ribbon. Lifting off the lid, she unwrapped the tissue paper, and stood speechless. Reaching into the box, she pulled out an absolutely gorgeous silver chiffon gown that glistened and shimmered as she held it up. The beautifully stitched lavender flames sewn all over the skirt perfectly matched the wide satin ribbon folded in the bottom of the box, and highlighted the shimmer of the fabric.

Holding it against her chest and using the stainless steel of the refrigerator as a mirror, she marveled at the wonderful craftsmanship and wondered how they'd gotten it ready in such a short amount of time. It had a corset-like bodice with tiny pearls going down the center and ending just where the skirt began. The same pearls decorated all the way around the very top of the bodice.

Next to the ribbon in the box was a silver pair of ballet slippers and a note. She smiled as she read…*For you my beautiful mate. Today we begin our lives together. Together forever. All of my love for eternity and beyond.*

One by one the other ladies entered the kitchen, filling the room with happy chatter. Everyone was excited to get the mating ceremony over with so they could have the reception. From what she could tell, it was going to be an even bigger party than Devon and Anya's. She had to laugh when Sam made sure Charlie knew the werepanthers would be there.

"Just no transforming under the influence, right?" Charlie joked while filling the plates Grace had placed on the counter with her famous veggie omelets.

Kyndel pulled the biscuits from the oven while Sam filled the glasses with orange juice and everyone sat down to eat. All conversations centered on the list of things that had to be done for the party. Charlie tried to focus, but her mind was on one thing and one thing only…the mating ceremony.

Sitting still as long as she could, she made her excuses and headed upstairs. She filled the tub with hot, steamy water and the bath oil that Kyndel had made just for her. The fragrance of lavender and heather filled the room as she sank down into the hot, bubbly water. Relaxing as much as she could, Charlie thought about how much her life had changed in just a matter of days. If someone had told her she'd find the love of her life and marry…or mate…him in less than a month, she would've called them a liar.

She shaved her legs, washed her hair, and soaked until the water turned tepid. Drying off, she wrapped up in Aaron's huge robe, and sat in the chair by the window. Sam had told her two younger Guardsmen would come to get her at exactly four. Glancing at the clock, Charlie saw she still had two hours and decided to see what she could do with her hair and makeup.

Sam knocked on the door just as she was putting in the last curl. Sydney came running in before she had a chance to answer. "Oh, Aunt Charlie, you look beautiful."

"Why, thank you, my dear. All I have left to do is put on my dress and shoes."

"That's good, because the boys will be here to get you soon," Sam commented. "Need any help?"

"Nope. I think I got it."

"Okay, we are all heading out to get ready. See you at the reception." Both Sydney and Sam hugged her before heading out.

Charlie had just slipped her feet into her slippers when she heard a knock at the door. Holding up the skirt of her dress, she hurried down the stairs and threw open the door. There stood two young Guardsmen, dressed in what she imagined were their formal uniforms. She recognized Jace from earlier and smiled when he spoke.

"Hi again, Dr. Gallagher. This is Liam and I'm Jace, in case you forgot."

She chuckled as he continued, "We're here to escort you to the ceremony."

"Great!" Closing the door behind her, Charlie looked closer at the young men's uniforms.

They wore surcoats reminiscent of Arthurian times, made from luxurious, silvery-gray wool, trimmed in black braid with silver thread glittering throughout. From the pictures in Aaron's mind, she knew they matched the scales of his dragon almost exactly. On the front, there was an intricately embroidered picture depicting a dragon in flight, just like Aaron's marking. They each also wore a black, long-sleeved undershirt and pants, as well as knee high, polished black boots that shined in the afternoon sun.

The young men gently took her hands and placed them on their bent elbows, leading her to an ornate carriage that made her remember the story of Cinderella. *Bibbity, Bobbity, Boo* danced around in her head.

The closer they got to the carriage, the more details she was able to pick out. It was made of deep mahogany with elegant carvings bordering the door and decorating the moldings. She recognized them as fairy wings and heather blossoms and smiled at the attention to detail.

A set of steps rolled out as Jace opened the door. Liam helped her into the carriage and asked if she was comfortable before securing the door. The seats were covered in plush cream velvet, softer than any silk Charlie had ever felt. A hand painted mural depicting dragons in flight covered all four walls. She counted twelve dragons in all and remembered the story Siobhan had told her of the Dragon Kings that became the original dragon shifters.

Looking around, she saw a bouquet of silver and lavender roses tied with a single white ribbon lying on the seat opposite her. While reaching across to pick them up and inhale their succulent aroma, she saw the small card attached. The message was simple but caused her eyes to fill with tears. *All my love for eternity and beyond. Aaron.*

The carriage slowed and then came to a complete stop. Looking out the window, she saw the meadow where she'd first discovered the existence of dragons. Butterflies danced in her stomach from the excitement of the day and the prospect of a lifetime with the man who held her heart. Lost in thought, she jumped when the carriage door opened and both she and Jace laughed.

"Sorry about that. Got my head in the clouds," Charlie joked.

Her escorts helped her step down and it was then that she saw exactly what Aaron and Aidan had been up to the day before. The meadow was filled with every purple, white, and silver flower imaginable, including hundreds and hundreds of daisies. A raised circle sat in the middle, surrounded by four archways pointing to the North, South, East, and West, also decorated with flowers and hundreds of ribbons.

Four chairs resembling thrones sat at the head of the circular platform. Liam and Jace once again placed her hands on their bent elbows and led her to an ornate white chair on the side of the circle. The young men let go of her hands and took two very large steps behind, standing at attention.

From behind a line of white wooden panels that had been painted to match the décor, came the four Elders she'd met the day before. They walked in single file, stepped onto the raised platform, and took their places on the thrones.

Charlie then watched as the five men she knew were part of Aaron's Force appeared. They were all dressed in the same dress uniforms as her escorts, but with surcoats depicting what Sam had told her were the colors of their dragons. Rayne stood at the head of the line in flaming red. Royce was next, and his beautiful royal blue surcoat with green accents truly fit the gentle giant that gave her mate as much trouble as he could. Next was Aidan, her mate's twin, dressed in the same silvery gray as Jace and Liam. He winked at her as she looked from man to man.

The next in line was Lance, who attempted to look regal and noble in his dress uniform of gold and black, but had given Charlie so much crap since they met, she grinned the cheesiest grin she could, making him chuckle. Last in line was Devon, in his opalescent white surcoat with the serene smile she'd come to expect from him.

A movement to the right of the Elders caught her eye. There stood Aaron in all his magnificence, making her heart skip a beat. His short brown hair was messy as usual, but it was his brilliant blue eyes that captivated her. His shimmering dress uniform accentuated the muscular body she knew lay beneath it. His tight black pants highlighted his muscular legs and made her think of all the ways she wanted to love him.

Carrick cleared his throat before his voice rang out across the meadow. "Long ago, when knights and dragons fought side by side for King and Country, it became apparent that dragon kin was no longer safe from those that would expose and destroy them. They sought to join with the knights that had fought so valiantly by their sides. Thus, through magic and the will of both dragon and knight, the Golden Fire Clan of the Dragon Shifters became a reality. It was through the joining of many different clans that we have become the strong and powerful Force we are today.

"We are here, in the place of importance to the couple, long blessed by our ancestors that have gone before us, to honor what the Universe put into place all those many years ago. To acknowledge and bless the mating of Aaron Michael O'Brien to the one the Universe made for him, Charlene Ailsa Gallagher. Will those seeking to witness this union please step forward."

The Guardsman stepped forward, then knelt in front of the Elders and bowed their heads. Rayne stood, addressing the Elders, "We, the five of the MacLendon Force, wish to witness and offer our blessing to the union of these two souls, two halves of the same whole. May they live long, fight hard, love harder, and produce many young to flourish when their souls have gone to the Heavens." He returned to his brethren, knelt, and again bowed his head.

Carrick began again, "Your witness and blessing have been acknowledged and accepted, MacLendon Force. Aaron O'Brien, you may go to your mate and escort her to the center of the Blessed Circle." No sooner had the words been spoken than Aaron was standing in front of Charlie.

He took her in his arms, and then gently picked her up and carried her.

"You do remember that I can walk, right?"

"Yeah, but this is so much more fun," he winked.

When they reached their destination, he carefully placed her on her bare feet, never taking his hands from her waist.

"The silver dragons were forged from the very fiber of the Universe, and because of this, are often referred to as the 'Shield Dragons'," Carrick spoke with authority.

"They are protective to a fault and will fight to the death to defend those they hold dear. They have quick and ambitious attitudes and use a combination of their minds and hearts to make all decisions. They love hard, strong, and endlessly. They never lose faith in whom or what they believe in. To mate a silver dragon means to accept all that they are and honor the power shared between mates.

"Now is the time of the marking. May the Universe continue to bless you and yours all the days of your lives together."

Charlie watched as the Elders left the meadow. The guard then positioned the wooden panels around them, giving them privacy before making their exit as well.

Staring at the man that held her heart, she felt his presence not only in her heart but also in her soul. He winked, letting her know he'd heard her thoughts and that he felt it, too. The longer they stared at one another, the bluer his eyes became until she realized they were glowing.

A heat caused by more than passion, combined with wisdom even greater than his hundred years, shone out at her. Aaron lowered his mouth to hers, stopping just as their lips touched, and whispered, *"Ta' mo chroi istigh ionat,"* before capturing her lips with his.

It was as if Aaron was *everywhere*. Charlie was consumed with a heat that set her ablaze from the inside out. She was laid open...body, heart, and soul to her mate.

There was a sting on the left side of her neck that made her try to pull back. Aaron left her lips, trailing kisses across her jaw and down her neck, reaching the tender spot that had stung only a moment before. He licked and sucked the offending spot until all thoughts of anything but their naked bodies loving one another were banished from her mind.

Her fingers wound through his hair as he continued to lavish her neck and shoulders. She pulled his mouth to hers, kissing him until they were both breathless. Aaron pulled back and it was then that she saw the glint of a little boy with a secret in his eyes. She cocked one eyebrow in mock anger and asked, "What *exactly* are you up to, Mr. O'Brien?"

"Oh, nothing," he joked before picking her up and carrying her back to her chair. "There are two really quick things we need to take care of before they come looking for us. One, I want you to meet my dragon…face to face. If that's all right with you?"

"Of course it is."

He smiled like a kid at Christmas and jogged across the meadow. Stopping well out of range of her and everything else, Aaron stripped to just his pants, looked her right in the eye, and said, "Watch this."

Charlie's skin tingled as if hundreds of butterflies were landing on her right before her mate turned into a huge silver dragon with a black underbelly. Aaron lay down and chuffed in her direction as she heard his voice in her head, *"Come over. I don't bite."*

"Now, I know that's a lie." She laughed aloud, making her way toward the dragon.

The front of his snout and nostrils were black and led to numerous peaks and valleys running from his nostrils to his eyes. Charlie had never imagined there could be so many variations of the color silver, not to mention all the different patterns his scales made, and she'd only made it as far as his face. It was mesmerizing.

The scales around his eyes were much lighter, almost translucent, and smaller than any other she could see. They were layered together in a protective manner that also accentuated the large blue crystalline orb looking down at her.

A row of imposing spikes started in the middle of his head, growing in length and width as they ran down the entire the length of his spine and ending just before his tail. Glancing back to his head, she saw he also had two very lethal looking horns growing from his brow ridge and curling back over his cranium for at least six feet.

She walked closer, placing her hand on the side of his muzzle, rubbing as she moved towards his wings. His were *nothing* like hers. For one thing, they were gigantic, even folded into his sides, with thin cartilage resembling veins running throughout. The skin felt like a heavy raw silk to the touch.

Making her way back to the front of the beast, she likened his scales to hand blown glass, but the longer she touched them, the more she could feel their incredible strength. Placing one hand next to the other, she massaged under his jaw, feeling how much softer and thinner the scales were there.

Charlie walked all the way around his head, making her way to his hindquarter and back paw. She laughed aloud when faced with the huge appendage before teasing, *"I could fit between your toes."*

"Just be careful of the nails, mo ghra'.*"*

As she rounded his rear end and came to his tail, she was reminded that these creatures had been created to defend. At the end of his really long tail was a huge triangular shaped spade with what she could only think to call *tail-spikes* covering the entire surface. One swipe and Charlie was sure anything and everything in its path would be completely destroyed.

She walked back to his head, kissed what she guessed was his cheek, and stepped back. Magic filled the air and once again, Aaron stood before her. She noticed a brand, the shape of a flame with fairy wings on either side, at the exact spot where his neck touched his shoulder. Reaching out, she touched the mark and then looked up. Grinning, he said, "Yours matches."

Her fingers flew to her neck as she remembered the stinging sensation during their kiss. "Well, at least we're a pair."

"That we are," he agreed, grabbing first his clothes and then her hand before moving her under a large oak tree where a small blanket was expertly placed with an oblong silver box laying in the center. "Now, for number two."

Throwing his clothes on the blanket, he pointed to the box and said, "For you, *mo chroi.*"

"*Dammit*, Aaron, I didn't get you anything," she scolded with her hands on her hips.

"Oh, yes, you did. You gave me…*you.*"

Faster than she could track, Aaron moved to the blanket, picked up the box, and returned to standing before her with her present in hand. Charlie opened the box to find a gorgeous charm bracelet. As she picked it up, she heard the tinkle of little bells and realized that each glittering silver charm *was* a bell and in between the bells were teardrops of Alexandrite that exactly matched her ring.

"The bells are made from my dragon's scales that I have shed since meeting you."

His smile grew as he fastened the bracelet around her wrist. She couldn't help but give it a little shake, just to hear the tiny bells ring. Before she was able to utter a word, his lips were on hers. Aaron kissed her long and deep, making sure there were no doubts about to whom she belonged.

Pulling back to catch her breath, Charlie asked, "Not that I'm complaining, but what was that for?"

Taking her left hand in his, he raised it to his lips, slowly turning it over until she could feel his breath on her pulse. He held her gaze with his own and laid his lips against her wrist. After several long seconds, she heard his voice in her mind. *"Every time a dragon kisses his mate, a bell rings. And I plan to make these little guys sing."*

Hugging him as tight as she could and willing herself not to cry and mess up her makeup, Charlie spoke through their bond, *"Thank you so very much for everything. I love you to the moon and back."*

"To the moon and back, huh? I might just take you up on that."

EPILOGUE

He could hear them coming. Smell the musk of wet cat. Hear their footsteps sloshing through the puddles he knew were from last night's thunderstorms. There was no way the misdirects and traps he'd worked so hard to set could've withstood the torrential downpour. He would have no choice…he would have to fight.

His leg was infected, there was no doubt about it. He was suffering with the first fever of his life, complete with hallucinations. At first, he'd been sure he was dead and by some miracle, in the Heavens with his mother. He could hear her sweet voice and feel her hands upon his face. It had been a dream come true.

Andrew had tried to apologize. Tried to explain how he'd only played the hand Fate had dealt him, but she would hear none of it. As fair and unbiased as she'd always been, Margarite O'Brien had told him he would need to beg forgiveness from his brothers and their brethren. She'd told him that they owed him a debt as well, but that he'd gone too far and only his brother's forgiveness, combined with favor from the great Universe and Fate, could absolve him of the atrocities he'd committed against his own kin.

He'd known she was right, but had still sought to plead his case. Somewhere in the middle of his defense, the mother whose death he still grieved morphed into a beautiful young woman with deep brown eyes and hair the color of melted chocolate. Her voice had called to not only him, but also his dragon. For the first time since reemergence, the beast was behaving as Andrew remembered. Gone was the inner turmoil and fighting to return to the clan. It was as if just the vision of the girl was enough to bring his dragon to heel.

The buzz of mindspeak woke the traitor from his delusion. The Dragon Guard was approaching. They'd been searching the mountain for nearly an hour. He knew he was truly trapped, but he would not cower in the corner like a mouse. No, he was Andrew O'Brien of the mighty Silver Dragons, son of Michael O'Brien II, and most of all, the *Special One*. His last day on earth would not be spent sniveling and begging for his life. He would fight.

Andrew positioned himself in the longest and most desolate of all the caverns in the cave he presently called home. Its odd shape had afforded him the opportunity to set two traps. There was no doubt in his mind that the werepanthers would sense at least one of them and alert the others, but the time it would take them to dismantle it would give him time to stand and prepare.

His leg throbbed from just the thought of moving it. The stench of infection filled the small space he'd wedged himself into to await their attack. Andrew figured it was better to die in battle than to wither away from a slow agonizing descent into insanity.

He mourned that he'd not completed his mission. The dragons would live on. The Dragon Guard would live on. He had never gotten to use the one spell he was sure would exterminate them all. His *brothers*, the rotten cowards, would live on. He knew they had made *excuses*, especially Aidan, for his capture and torture. *Hell*, the bastard had even tried to apologize to him. Wanted *forgiveness* for the hell Andrew had been forced to endure because of his cowardice. Even his pretty little mate had tried to plead the bastard's case.

Pain shot through his entire body. He shook with chills. Cold sweat soaked his filthy clothes. He prayed to the Heavens and to Hell that someone…*anyone* but his brothers, would end his pain. There'd been another time he'd prayed the same words and just like today, he'd been ignored.

Footsteps echoed through the cavern. He could sense his brothers. His dragon chuffed with the need to reunite with its clan mates. Andrew ignored the beast, knowing it was only a matter of minutes before he would die and the dragon's soul would be released into the Heavens to find another worthy Guardsman waiting to be born. It was he, the *man*, which would die the forever death. His brothers would strike true. He had no doubt they each carried silver blades to ensure his death. It would be a welcome reprieve from all his years of suffering.

A rock skittered past the opening of his hidey-hole. Knowing they would be able to pinpoint his location, but wanting the end to come, Andrew reached out with his enhanced senses. The panthers were leading the charge with Aidan, Aaron, and Rian right behind them. They'd taken no chances. Max Prentisse and his Pride, The Blue Thunder Clan, and if he wasn't mistaken, even Kyra, were all in attendance.

He chuckled to himself, thinking how infamous he'd become. The Golden Fire Force lead by Rayne MacLendon was known worldwide as the best and most fierce Force of all dragon kin. That the *great* Commander had called in reinforcements spoke highly of Andrew's threat to them all. It was a shame he hadn't been able to make them pay for what they'd done to him, but Fate would not be denied. Those spineless bastards would get what they had coming to them. He knew somehow they would pay, not by his hand, but they would pay.

When he heard the rattle of the trap he'd set, Andrew pulled himself from his hiding place, picked up his katana, and stood at the ready. Pushing back the pain and delirium, he remembered the lessons his father and brothers had taught him. He would give his attackers a fight worthy of the O'Brien name, even if he were sure he'd been disowned.

Shadows shown long around the corner. The Guardsmen had taken over the lead from the panthers. He could still sense the panthers, but knew they would stay behind to catch him if by some chance he eluded the dragons. There was no doubt he would die today, all that was left to be seen was how many of them he would take with him.

The sounds of boots striking rock reached his ears just as Aaron came into view. He could sense the others stationed throughout the cave…all but Aidan. Somehow, his older brother, the one he truly wanted to face, had disappeared from detection. He shook his head. With his waning strength, he was only able to focus on the threat before him.

Standing at the ready, he taunted, "They only sent you? Am I so underestimated?"

"Drop the act, asshole. I know you can tell there are others."

"You always were able to call my bluff," Andrew chuckled.

"Just drop the sword. It's over. You lost. You…"

Aaron's next words were cut off as a blast rang through the cavern, reverberating over and over off the stone walls. Apparently, the werepanthers weren't as good at scouting ahead as he'd heard. The one booby trap he'd had enough magic left to create had gone undetected, and from the sounds of it, had injured at least a few of the hunting party.

Using the distraction to his advantage, Andrew grabbed the ancient volume he'd been translating, the only possession he still had, and ran for the tunnel he'd found the night before. Even drawing on his enhanced speed, dragging his wounded leg proved slower than he had counted on. Aaron's boots pounded in the dirt floor. Andrew could all but feel his brother's breath on his neck. There was nowhere to run, nowhere to hide. The fight had come to him.

Tossing the book to the side, Andrew whirled around and lifted his katana just in time to block the thrust of Aaron's broadsword. Pulling the silver knife from his belt, Andrew swiped back and forth, hoping to push back his brother's attack.

During their years of separation, Andrew had forgotten how well his brother could handle a sword. Aaron's blade was but a blur that Andrew had to work hard to avoid. The sting of a hit ran down his left arm, causing the silver blade to slip in his hand.

Stepping back, Andrew got one decent advance with a powerful thrust, but Aaron was simply too quick. Their blades clashed, filling the cavern with the sounds of their battle. Andrew could feel the others closing in, but fought to keep his attention on his brother. The man he knew would deal the fatal blow.

Andrew backed off again, this time bumping against the wall…the end of the tunnel. There was nowhere left to go. He poured all his remaining strength into the fight, blocking one blow after another. Aaron was brutal and relentless. The look in his eyes was one of sheer determination.

Aaron thrust with his right hand, immediately following with a jab of a silver dagger Andrew hadn't known his brother had. The blade struck true. Andrew groaned in pain. Warm blood wet his shirt and flowed onto his pants from what he felt was a gash about a foot long, but Andrew still refused to go down.

Swinging his katana like a wild man, Andrew advanced, but Aaron merely smirked and with extreme ease, met him blow for blow. Every clash of their blades sent crippling pain through every cell of Andrew's body. It was then he realized Aaron was toying with him, prolonging the fight.

Andrew tried to reach out with his dragon senses, but his pain and growing weakness left him unable to sense anything but the man before him. Again, Aaron advanced. This time slicing across the thigh of Andrew's good leg, striking muscles, tendons, and vessels. He toppled to the floor. His vision blurred. But even on his knees, Andrew swung both his blades, praying to draw blood before his death.

His vision darkened at the edges. He saw a shadow at his right that hadn't been there before, but chalked it up to another of his feverish delusions and continued to fight. Aaron's boot on his chest forced him to the ground. Andrew let go of his blades. Heard the clang of metal against the cavern floor.

The darkness was closing in. His vision narrowed to a pinpoint. He was now seeing double. Andrew laughed, and even to his ears, it sounded maniacal. Aaron's foot on his chest made every breath unbearable. He waited for his brother to say something…anything, but he only looked at him in disgust. A voice that sounded familiar, but so very far away, echoed through the chamber and Aaron nodded.

Andrew was only seeing shadows now. Unable to distinguish anything but shapes. More voices. More shadows.

It must be the Fates coming to take me to hell.

The rattle of chains bounced off the walls right before fire enveloped his wrists and ankles. Two sets of eyes–one cobalt, one amber–looked at him with disgust before his world faded to black.

The reaper is here and the son of a bitch brought silver.

~~*~*~*~*~*

She had no idea how many days it had been. Her captors rarely let her sleep anymore. Rarely left her alone. It was one torture after another, each more inventive than the last. Mara had come in alone several times, but Calysta had been too weak to speak. The young witch had shoved parchment after parchment in front of her blurry eyes screaming, "Is this the spell?" Over and over until the Grand Priestess thought she might lose her mind.

Only the knowledge that they would never get their hands on the incantation kept her alive. Their coven was well protected. She knew the protocols that dictated the lockdown and the addition of guards from other covens *and* the Council since her disappearance. Another layer of protection would have been added to all the artifacts. The bastards could kill her, but there was no way they would ever get ahold of Thanatos.

She heard the sound of footsteps. The huge iron door to her cell scratched against the stone floor, the smell of Old Spice and nasty magic assaulted her senses. She truly wished the man would at least use cologne that masked his pungent odor instead of adding to it.

He neared and she prepared for his questioning, or worse yet, another round of the iron knives. They seemed to be his favorite torture devices. Instead, the wizard walked around the stone slab that she felt she was growing to and began setting up an altar.

Calysta watched as a burlap bag containing the bones that she could only assume had been a child from their size and shape was dumped on the floor. He then set a cage with four huge rats beside them. Five black candles were placed at the points of a pentagram he had drawn with chalk made from Mandrake Root and Black Tang. They were smells she hated…evil and disgusting.

He built a fire and set up a large metal tripod. Sliding on gloves, he hooked a cast iron pot over the fire. The sizzle and smell of oil infused with Belladonna filled the room. He began to chant in Latin and he added Lobelia, Dandelion, and Mugwort to the pot.

And the fires shall burn
And the wheel of life shall turn
And the dead come back home on Samhain
And in the night sky
On the lunar light they fly
And the dead come back home on Samhain
Balor I come to you on bended knee
I search for your servant Thanatos
I beseech you access into your realm
Balor, Demon King, please show favor on my request.

The idiot was summoning Balor to find Thanatos. Calysta could only imagine that the wizard or warlock or whatever he was thought that the legend was true. He actually believed that Thanatos would be able to recite the spell. She wanted to laugh but couldn't work up the energy. Instead, she watched while he placed copper pots beside the five candles and filled them with water. At least the man knew his demons. Balor's followers were the Fomori, the demons who live in the dark depths of the lakes and seas. Water is the only conduit to reach them, and they are the only way to reach their boss.

The wizard continued to chant. Slimy black magic filled the room, making the air heavy. Calysta could feel it like snakes writhing all over her battered body. Placing a black stone basin on the floor, the wizard knelt beside it and opened the cage containing the rats. One by one, he slit their throats, letting the blood drain from their bodies into the container between his knees.

The blood bubbled and a grey mist rose from the pentagram. Calysta worked hard to draw her next breath. The wizard smiled and cackled like a loon. "The King is on the way, Priestess. Maybe you'll tell *him* your secrets."
~~*~*~*~*~*~*

It had been two days since the prisoner had been brought to the lair…two days of horrible nightmares. The mark on her wrist that appeared after Anya had transformed burned until she thought she might cry. She'd tried to work up the courage to tell Siobhan what was happening, but the Healer had been so busy trying to keep the traitor alive so that he might stand before the Tribunal, she had decided to wait.

She knew it was Andrew, the one that had betrayed them all, that was screaming in her dreams. His pain was alive within her every time she closed her eyes. He had seen her, too. Called out to her. At first, he'd called her by what she now knew was his mother's name, but then he'd realized that she was not Margarite O'Brien. In the few seconds that he was actually lucid before the fever took him again, he had asked her for help. Then told her she was beautiful.

Last night, after hours and hours of his constant murmuring and crying in her head, she gave up and started walking toward the cave where she knew he was sequestered. But just as she'd suspected, they had Guardsmen posted everywhere. No one but the few the Elders had approved was allowed in.

She'd taken the long way home. Ran into Sam and finally got to meet Charlie, Aaron's mate. The beautiful lavender glow that shone around the pretty blonde doctor confirmed that she was a fairy.

As they walked away and resumed talking, she heard the ladies discussing Sydney. It seemed the sweet child's abilities had strengthened and new ones had manifested since the traitor had entered the lair. She'd also heard that Kyra's magic was much stronger and Anya's dragon senses had magnified.

Finally making it home, she walked up the steps to her apartment, unlocked the door, and barely made it in before Andrew's screams almost brought her to her knees. He was calling out to her.

"Teacht anseo, maite. Teacht, mo chroi"

"Come here, mate. Come, my heart."

Fighting for Her Dragon
Dragon Guard Series #7

There Are No Coincidences.
The Universe Does Not Make Mistakes.
Fate Will Not Be Denied.

CHAPTER ONE

"Emma! Emma! Open this damn door!" Devon bellowed.

This was the third time in two days he'd pounded on her door. The only difference was this time he seemed *really* upset, almost desperate. She tried to get up, had tried every time. Wanted to answer the door or at least call out to him. Needed to tell him she had the flu or whatever this horrible feeling was and she would talk to him when she felt better. The problem was no matter how hard she tried, not even a finger would move. Her throat was so dry from crying and lack of drink she could only whisper. Emma couldn't remember how long it had been since she'd actually left her bed.

All of this had started forty-eight hours earlier, with the voice of the traitor sounding in her head, and reached its first climax when she'd collapsed on her living room floor. He'd spoken directly into her mind, had been doing so since the moment he touched the land of the Red Fire Clan lair. As shocking as it was to hear him like he was a part of her, the fact that he called her his mate and had triggered her fainting freaked her out. On the heels of his mind-boggling revelation, the traitor had begged her to come to him. He had reached for her. Not like you reach across the table, but through some invisible link she felt in the very depths of her soul and could've sworn had not been there before he reached out to her.

Pain accompanied his pleas, a crippling pain that permeated every cell of her being. It had finally become too much for her to bear. Emma landed face first in front of the couch, barely missing the corner of the coffee table with her head, and let blessed unconsciousness take her away.

She woke to wave after wave of pain racking her body. When the sun began to shine through the slats of her blinds hanging on the picture window, the pain had begun to recede. It had been almost twenty minutes since the last barrage of agony–the longest it had stayed at just a dull throb since she'd passed out. Working up her courage, Emma rose to her knees.

Cold sweat peppered her upper lip, wet her spine, and ran down her arms. Taking a long, deep breath in an attempt to end her panting and hopefully not hyperventilate, she steadied herself and began crawling towards her bedroom. Halfway to her destination, the pain returned with a vengeance. Her muscles knotted, feeling as if they were pulling away from her bones. Cramps like nothing she'd ever experienced set her insides on fire, a blaze that tore through her abdomen and chest, forcing the air from her lungs. Spots danced before her eyes before she once again found herself lying on the cold, hard tile.

With no windows in the hallway, Emma could only guess how long she'd been there when she was finally able to pry open her eyelids. Struggling to her knees for the second time, she was determined to make it to her feet and used the wall as a crutch. Finally standing, she put one foot in front of the other, her shaky legs threatening to buckle under her before she finally made it to her bed. Moaning, she fell face forward onto the sage green comforter, praying to the Heavens that she never had to move again.

Over the next few hours she floated in and out of consciousness, never quite sure if what she heard and saw was real. Andrew's voice was the only constant as she battled whatever force attacked her body, mind, and soul. He would plead with her to come to him, speaking beautiful words in the ancient language of dragon kin, telling her that she was the only one that could end his torment. Then he would demand, his tone sharp, his words direct, as if he would accept nothing but her complete surrender to his will. In between, he would whisper her name over and over, all the while pushing his need into her.

His eyes peered into her soul. She had no idea how, but his mismatched stare followed her from consciousness to restless sleep and back again, ever present, keeping watch over her. When one especially horrific wave of torment came upon her, their gazes locked. The agony she saw reflected in those hauntingly imperfect eyes confirmed her worst fears. It was not *her* pain but his attacking her.

"Why are you doing this to me?" she whispered, barely able to make out her own words.

Horror overrode the ache in his eyes and seemed to push the agony from his tone. He spoke with command and a clarity that baffled her, considering his pain. "*I'm not doing anything*, a thaisce. *It's our connection...our bond. If you come to me, I hope to free you from my influence.*"

"*But...*" Her attempt to answer through mindspeak, as he had spoken to her, was cut short by Devon's first round of knocking at her door.

The next two days were an endless loop of pain, visions, and nonsensical conversations with the traitor in her head, only interrupted by the few precious moments when she was overtaken by exhaustion. Andrew's pleas became more insistent, the power he was pushing through the invisible bond more forceful, as she continued to explain that she was trying to come to him but was physically incapable.

"*You must! It's the only way I can save you,*" was the last she heard of him. Their bond had gone silent. She called to him but to no avail, he had simply stopped communicating.

But I still hurt...

"Emma, Heavens dammit! If you don't open this door, I'm breaking it down." Devon's shouts were becoming more insistent, his pounding on the door a constant thunder that echoed through her skull at every strike.

Closing her eyes, wishing for the mindspeak the Dragon Guard all shared, Emma tried to answer her longtime friend. The harder she pushed, the more lightheaded she became. It was hard for her to breathe. The cramps were endless. Just before the darkness overtook her, she heard Devon roar and the telltale sound of splintering wood.

From the smells that assaulted her senses and the temperature that felt like they were in a meat locker, Emma could tell she was no longer in her home but in the new clinic they had just finished building.

"How long has she been unconscious?" A low, gravelly voice she didn't recognize asked.

"How the hell should I know? She hasn't responded to my calls or texts and hasn't answered her door in almost three days. Mom mentioned that Andrew had been calling her name, and in the last few hours, he had gotten frantic and then passed out. Something about it didn't feel right, so I went to check on our Emma again, and this time I didn't let the door get in the way," Devon answered.

The voice she didn't recognize barked with laughter. "I'm guessing you owe the poor girl a door."

"Damn straight, and I'll pay up as soon as you tell me she's gonna be okay. Mom's with that fucking traitor so you're all I got, Pearce."

Pearce? The dark-haired, dark-skinned, Blue Dragon from Rian's clan?

"Loving the vote of confidence there, Bro," Pearce chuckled.

"You know what I mean. I know you're damn good at what you do. It's just that she's like my little sister. We all think of her that way." Devon's voice faded off and Emma tried with all her might to wake up, to reassure him that everything would be all right.

"No worries, just tryin' to lighten the mood." The Blue Dragon cleared his throat and continued. "We'll figure this out and get her back on her feet in no time. She's very dehydrated, seems to have suffered a reoccurring fever for a number of days, and from the look of the nail marks in her palms, excruciating pain accompanied it all. There's internal bruising, which looks like it might have been from muscle cramping of some sort. It's bad enough in a few spots that I would swear she's been punched, but there's no external marks, not even a scratch on her body that I can find."

"And you're not going to find anything." She heard Siobhan's voice and wanted to cry tears of joy, but not even her tear ducts were cooperating.

"What do mean?" Both men asked in unison.

Emma felt Siobhan's hand on her arm and relaxed for the first time that she could remember. "I mean…I believe our girl is Andrew's mate…"

"WHAT!?" Devon yelled.

"You heard what I said, Son. Why do you doubt it?"

"I don't doubt it. I just don't understand it. How can that piece of crap have a mate? How could the Universe…"

"Who has a mate? How could the Universe what?" Emma immediately recognized Aidan's voice.

"Your brother," Siobhan answered.

"Well, yeah, Aaron and Charlie, we knew that."

"No, the other one," Devon growled.

The silence was deafening. Emma tried to imagine the look of disbelief on Aidan's face. She wished she could just wake up and be an active participant in her own life, but no matter what she tried, she couldn't move. Thankfully, since she'd awakened, the pain had only been a dull ache. Her head was no longer threatening to break into tiny pieces. But she still couldn't move, so it only stood to reason that her body had shut down to heal.

Couldn't be a worse time for this shit.

"You can't be serious?" Aidan's voice was low and disbelieving.

"Can't be serious about what?" Aaron was apparently entering the clinic and Emma heard another pair of boots striking the tile floor. The question of who was quickly answered when Royce spoke.

"Sorry, are we late to the party? Lance and I were working the kid here overtime when Dev sent out the call. The girls are on their way, and Rayne is coming from the Cave of the Ancients."

A hand on her shoulder and a soft, "Come on, Em, you can beat it," let her know the 'kid' they referred to was Cole, one of the Guardsman in training. A sweet kid that brought her unusable dragon scales to make her jewelry.

Emma wasn't surprised to hear Siobhan's voice. "Well, now that most of you are here, I will start over and hopefully only have to explain once. Please hold your outbursts until I am finished. It has been a rough five days and my patience is limited." The Elder Healer sounded frustrated and tired.

"It appears as though our Emma is Andrew's mate, and somehow, the mating bond has been established, although I would stake my life on the fact that they have not seen each other, much less done anything to trigger a mating. Their link has become so strong in such a short amount of time that she is sharing his pain...*on every level*. Those of us that have been around since she came to the lair have always known she was extraordinary, but just *how* extraordinary was always the mystery. We now have a clue. She is the mate of the *Special One*. Something none of us can take lightly. When I have a few extra minutes, I will go through the Books of Legend and figure out exactly what we are up against."

They've always known I was extraordinary? What the heck is she talking about? I really need to wake up. Laying here is driving me nuts!

Again there was nothing but silence and it seemed to stretch on forever. Aidan was the first to speak. "So, the little shit has a mate. How can that be after all that he's done? How can you be sure, Siobhan?"

"Well, I hate to state the obvious," Siobhan's calm had returned, but she still sounded exhausted. "But he *is* dragon and that means the Universe fashioned someone just for him at the time of his birth. As for how I know, well Andrew tipped me off. He is in an incredible amount of pain. Silver has gotten into his bloodstream and his dragon is being little to no help in pushing it out. His wounds are not healing and he has a high fever. In his delirium, he was speaking the ancient language, referring to *mate* and begging her to come to him. I chalked it up to silver poisoning, but today he called her name and said he could sever their bond."

So that's what he was talking about.

"That's when I went over *again*. I ended up knocking down the door, found her unconscious, and brought her to Pearce since Mom was with the traitor." Emma could hear some of the Zen that was Devon's trademark returning to his tone, but it was still colored with a *lot* of anger and frustration.

"This is just too hard to believe. The stupid little bastard turned his back on dragon kin, vowed to destroy us all, and basically became a black magic wielding wizard. How can his dragon still recognize its mate? How can the bond have been created?" Aaron asked.

"Hell, how can his dragon have survived the horror it's been subjected to without turning on the little shit? There were years we couldn't even sense his existence," Royce asked, resentment punctuating every word.

"Couldn't it be that his dragon merely hibernated while his human side went about his nasty business?" Cole asked, and Emma was proud that he was learning to speak up in a group of Guardsmen.

"If I may jump into this conversation," Pearce said. "I think the young'un has a good point. More importantly, we're all about to sit on Andrew's Tribunal, so we need to do our research. I, like Siobhan, remember something about the *Special One* and his mate in the history books. As much as I want to see the little shit burn for all he's done, I want to make sure your girl here's okay and that we're not setting off a chain reaction those we love won't survive."

Agreement came from all around, warming her heart. Emma loved each and every one of the big lugs and was thrilled her feelings were reciprocated. The Guardsmen continued to talk while Siobhan and Pearce resumed her exam. She felt them using their enhanced senses and listened as Pearce made sure Siobhan saw every one of her internal injuries.

"This is way off the charts. Unlike anything I've ever seen before. What about you?" Pearce asked.

"One other time," Siobhan answered. "I was a young healer. Gareth, my mate, brought a Green Dragon home from one of their many battles with the wizards. He was so badly hurt, Zachary and I were sure he would go to the Heavens, but then his little mate, Cara, wandered into our lair.

"She was a sweet girl, long dark hair, deep brown eyes, and about three months pregnant. The poor thing had made her way nearly a hundred miles over treacherous terrain after waking up in the middle of the night when her mate received the worst of his numerous injuries. Cara collapsed as soon as she was able to tell us who she was.

"I feared she'd been beaten by any number of treacherous adversaries during her travels. However, when Zachary examined her, he found wounds just like these–internal bruising identical to her mate's. The only way we could think of to end Cara's pain was to have her block her mating bond with Shane. No matter how we pleaded she refused, and he was unconscious most of the time, so couldn't help us either. The biggest difference was that Shane's dragon was active and working as hard as we were to heal the Guardsman. The beast also did everything he could to shield their mate and child. It only took a few days before they were both on their feet and heading home."

"So if we can get her to break their bond, then we can treat her." Pearce sounded optimistic. Emma wanted to feel it, too, but couldn't. She had no idea how the bond had formed and no idea how to break it, block it, or even burn it down.

"That would be a great plan, but I'm guessing almost all of it is coming from Andrew. I need you to take care of Emma while I go try to convince our 'guest' to break their bond."

Siobhan didn't ask and didn't wait for an answer. The Elder Healer always knew the Guardsmen would do whatever they could to help her. Just one of the many reasons Emma loved her family so very much.

"And you think that piece of shit is going to do anything to help any of us?" Emma could only imagine Aaron's expression from the rage that heated his tone.

"I have to believe if the Universe and Fate have let them find one another, they have also made sure Andrew is experiencing all the protective feelings a dragon has for his newfound mate. He will do *whatever* it takes to end her pain."

"Then I'm going, too," Aaron growled.

"Me, too," Aidan rumbled.

"That's fine. It might help to have you two there."

Emma could barely hear Siobhan's voice. The sound of footsteps, followed by the banging of a door, let her know the twins and the Healer were gone. The smell of healing herbs and candles let her know Pearce had decided on a course of treatment. The Guardsman began rubbing what felt like a cream and smelled like outdoors on her skin. She remembered seeing Siobhan combine healing herbs with lemongrass oil. The Elder Healer had told her it helped with pain and inflammation.

The heat of the ointment, coupled with Pearce's huge, lightly calloused hands, lulled Emma into a dreamlike state. It seemed the poultice was working its magic. The dull thud in her head and slight pain in her muscles seemed to be slipping away. With her mind clearer than it had been in the last few days, Emma began pushing to wake up.

I mean, come on, it's time to get the hell up.

She could still feel the traitor's presence, but he remained silent. It was like he was riding the waves, fading in and out, and she was helpless to do anything but follow. The link Siobhan and the Guardsmen had been talking about explained the weird light in her soul and the ray of light that flowed from it.

When waking up seemed like too much work, the young jeweler focused on her mating bond with Andrew. She knew everything he'd done. All the people he'd hurt. The plans he'd concocted to make everyone he thought was responsible for what he'd suffered pay. And until the last few days, she'd thought the only true justice would be to watch him burn, but when she looked into the white, warm, ball of energy warming her soul, it was hard to believe it was the same person.

Emma contemplated the idea that somehow the Universe's wires had gotten crossed and Andrew wasn't *really* her mate, but then she remembered the mismatched eyes and the deep timbre of his voice that was so like Aidan and Aaron's. There was no doubt it was him.

Following the bond, the traitor's memories began to come to her, recollections from his youth depicting a happy family with three rambunctious brothers and very loving parents. The longer she watched, the more she saw. It was like a synopsis of his life up to the time he left his clan of birth to train with the MacLendon Force.

Emma could feel everything he had felt, could see how much it had meant to him to follow in his father and brothers' footsteps. What truly amazed her was how heavily the responsibility of being the *Special One* weighed on him. He lived in constant fear of letting everyone down.

One memory, heavy with importance, played out like a movie in her head…

Malachi, the Spiritual Elder of their clan and one of the four that made up their Council, was sitting in the Cave of Ancients beside the Great Altar while Andrew was praying on bended knee. When the younger version of the man they all had come to despise finally looked up, he had tears in his eyes.

"Did you see that, Elder? Did you see what the Ancients said to me?"

"Yes, I saw what they wanted me to see, but what did you see?" Malachi's soft baritone voice seemed to add reverence to the moment.

Andrew hesitated before beginning. "It was daunting. The Ancient, Shavon, said… 'Wherever the Special One *goes, there so goes dragon kin.' She explained that as the* Special One, *I will have a decision to make. I'll be faced with great tragedy, and out of that I will be forced to choose either the path of light or the path of darkness. My decision will be ABSOLUTE; either completely good or completely evil.*

"If by some chance I end up on a dark path, only the one the Universe made for me can redeem my soul and wash away the taint of my mistakes. We have to 'know of each other' but not be mated, and she has to want to save me of her own free will.

"She will also be very special and will have to have…"

The rest of the memory was obliterated as a burning pain, worse than anything she'd previously experienced, forced Emma's back to bow off the table. Her arms adhered themselves to her sides and her legs snapped together as if magnetized. Her limbs became so rigid that the popping and cracking of her joints echoed in her ears. The loss of control over her body was scary as hell. She was sure at any moment her lungs would freeze and she would die where she laid.

"Holy shit! She's seizing!" Pearce's yell filled the clinic. "Devon, grab her feet! Lance and Royce, each hold an arm. We have to keep her from hurting herself while I get this Tree of Heaven syrup into her. It's the only thing I know that is strong enough to calm her."

The Guardsmen's strength held her in place so tightly she knew there would be bruises while Pearce's thumb and fingers bit into her jaw, holding her mouth open, keeping her from choking on her own tongue. Emma floated on the edge of consciousness as cold, thick liquid slid down her throat. The chanting of female voices was far in the distance and she prayed she would live long enough to thank everyone.

Out of her despair came Andrew's voice, weak and thready, as if he were drawing his last breath. *"Tharraingt ar shiúl, mo maite'. Briseadh an banna."*

"How do I do that?" She pleaded as the pain finally receded.

"You have to...I don't want...Go gcasfar le chéile sinn i na Spéartha, mo a ru'nsearc. *Please live...*"

His voice trailed off while she tried to figure out what he meant. The ball of light she'd identified as their mating bond faded to little more than a spark just before she felt Andrew let go. Their link wasn't severed, but it was clear neither the man nor the dragon were actively participating.

Terror filled her heart. She called to him through the link but was unable to wait for an answer as consciousness came rushing back to her.

Gasping, Emma's eyes flew open. She fought to sit up. Pearce yelled for her to hold still. The Guardsmen tried to keep her down, and all the while she screamed, "They're dying. Andrew and his dragon have gone into the Fades!"

CHAPTER TWO

He'd always known he'd die young...and tragically. Even before he was left for dead by his brother, tortured by wizards, and made to cavort with hunters just to survive...it had been a foregone conclusion. Of course, it would've been nice to go out in a blaze of glory like James Dean or Bruce Lee, but that hadn't happened. He'd died on the floor of cave that served as his prison, awaiting a Tribunal to convict him of treason. An offense that, by the way, carried a death sentence.

See the pattern?

No matter, he was dead and that was one thing that had finally gone his way. Since he'd buried John, his second in command and only friend, Andrew had felt his impending doom breathing down his neck. It was weird, but he was relieved.

Over the years he'd heard others say he had no soul, no heart, no remorse for the things he'd done, and they'd been partially right. Andrew had no remorse for the devastation he'd tried to deliver to the dragons. They'd left him for dead, and for that they needed to pay. Heavens knew he'd done everything in his considerable power to deliver that retribution, but the Universe protected Her favorite warriors, and in the end, Andrew had lost. So remorse was not something he felt, but regrets...oh yeah, he had those. Not the ones people might guess, and not near as many as his sanctimonious brothers would want him to carry around for all eternity, but he had them.

I'm bound for hell; isn't that enough?

First and foremost, he regretted not getting to see the look of utter defeat on Aidan's face when the Tribunal pronounced Andrew guilty of treason and sentenced him to death. Andrew knew his bleeding-heart, do-gooder of an older brother would've argued for life imprisonment. He also knew the Elders and other Guardsmen on the Tribunal would have vehemently opposed Aidan and he would've lost.

Poor, poor, Aidan....

Nope, can't keep a straight face on that one.

Secondly, he hated that he hadn't been able to take at least a few of those fucking asshole Guardsmen with him. Time after time he'd meticulously planned their deaths; dotted every 'i', crossed every 't', and every damn time those sons of bitches had escaped Andrew's brand of justice. They even blew up his home and killed his only friend. Just another in a long line of atrocities that he'd endured at the hands of the dragons with no chance for payback.

Lastly, and most importantly, which quite frankly shocked him, was that he would never know the one the Universe made for him. He hated that he'd caused her pain and surprised himself by wishing for more time to tell her how sorry he was.

When they connected after he'd been dumped on the cold stone floor of his cell, Andrew had pulled away, scorched by the virtue she possessed. Awestruck, both man and dragon had gaped at the pure selflessness flowing from his Emma. Her goodness shone so brightly it diminished the darkness that stained his soul. Andrew actually felt hope for the first time in almost ten years. She made him *want* to be better.

Those fucking dragons...

Not only had they robbed him of his heritage and the kinship of family, they'd also taken the only beautiful thing he'd ever had. If only he had one more day to make them pay. Just one more day...

He prayed to whoever was listening that his mate knew he'd done everything possible with his waning power to shield her from his pain. When he'd called to her, begging her to come to him, it had only been to break their connection. No matter how many times he'd tried mentally to release the bond, *something* held them together. He knew a spell, used only in case of an extreme emergency, that would sever the mating bond in an unconsummated relationship, but the mates had to be touching. Emma hadn't come to him, either because she couldn't or because she feared him. Another question he would never get answered. The torment of her suffering would follow him through the depths of Hell for all of eternity.

Floating in the Ether, waiting for his dragon's soul to take its leave and for the Reaper of Hell to fetch him, he continued to think of Emma. Glimpses of her soft brown hair and expressive dark eyes haunted him. He was forced to *feel* something other than hate and vengeance, a whole new experience for him as of late. His trip to the Land of the Lost Feelings didn't stop with his almost mate, it continued down Memory Lane. The first such trip not centered on his abduction and torture that he could remember, compelling him to pay close attention.

For the most part it was sappy and a complete waste of time. Andrew was well aware of what his life had been before that fateful night. He'd had great parents whom, even through it all, he'd loved, or at the very least didn't hate. Love was one of those things he'd sluffed off after deciding on the path of vengeance, so he wasn't sure what he felt for the couple that had given him life, except to say had they been alive, he wouldn't have wished them harm. No, all those feelings were saved for his *brethren*. The word stung his brain as he thought it. They could no more be called his brethren than a gecko can be called a T-Rex. Those bastards were to blame for all he'd been through. Pity his chances for retribution had passed, but it was time for him to move on...*literally*.

The scene in his mind changed, reaching deep into his past from a time when he'd just begun his training to become a Guardsman. This specific memory contained a young girl hiding in a grape arbor. The one thing he remembered more than her fear or sadness was the way he *and* his dragon responded to her. Both man and beast reveled in her laugh that sounded like the little bells on his mother's bracelet. They wanted to bath in the scent of daffodils that was purely her. Another regret was he'd never followed up and gotten to know the sweet girl better.

Oh shit!

All the pieces of the puzzle came tumbling together in painful clarity. The girl from so long ago, the one that had been crying, that hadn't remembered her name, was Emma...*his Emma!*

Well, I'll be damned.

Already done. He chuckled to himself and then laughed. *Talking to myself....wow. That's got to be somewhere on the list of things a crazy person would do.*

Everything surrounding his mate now made sense. They *had* met before, so of course the mating bond had opened wide and irrevocably linked them together. It explained why his dragon, even in the beast's weakened state, had pushed so hard to know her and had refused to help him break their connection.

He'd thought about that young girl with the silky brown tresses and sparkling onyx eyes so many times over the years. Had known she was incredible and had wanted to explore the feelings she brought out in him, but Destiny always had another plan. The chance to get to know her had passed. His heart had grown cold and hard. Love was not something Andrew had even thought about after the night his brother betrayed him.

Heaviness settled on his chest, a tightness gripped his once beating heart. It was a good thing he didn't need to breathe, because there would've been no way he could've drawn a breath. His dragon roared, sending shards of sharp, burning agony into the base of his skull that spread throughout his lifeless body. The beast was mourning the loss of their mate and there was nothing Andrew could do but let him.

Look old boy, be patient. You'll find her again. Fate always gets what She wants.

The beast continued to grieve, leaving Andrew with the option to lament with him or hop back on the Remembrance Railway and face a whole other pile of steaming bullshit. Faced with two losing propositions, he chose the least painful and spent *days* floating on a sea of nothingness, reliving every painstaking moment of his life. Sensory deprivation might be nice for meditation or relaxation or whatever Swami Sammy was selling on late night TV, but not for the hard-ass traitor of the world renowned Dragon Guard.

Maybe this is *hell and I just missed the Reaper.*

"*Now you know better than that, Son, your dragon is still here,*" the first voice, other than his own, he'd heard in what seemed like forever said.

"*Excuse me, my brain is not a party line. How the hell did you get in here?*"

"*A little respect,* mo mhac. *You're never too old to get your ass kicked by your* athair. *It has been a few years, but I'm sure it's just like taking flight...*"

"*Dad...?*"

"*Who exactly were you expecting?*"

"*In all honesty? I wasn't expecting anyone.*" He stopped talking for a second, wondering if insanity was part of the ticket to Hell, then had another thought. "*This isn't an 'Ebenezer Scrooge' thing is it? Are you here to tell me I'm going to be visited by three ghosts and all that happy horse shit? Because that has really been played out and I'm already dead, so it would be a huge waste of resources.*"

"*You always were a smartass and too damn smart for your own good and the good of those around you.*" His father sounded tired and more than a little sad. "*This is NOT a Scrooge visit. This, my son, is a visit from a father long passed to his son who is facing eternity in the fiery pits of Hell. It is a wish granted from the Ancients of our kind to me, one of their warriors.*"

Andrew immediately felt like he was six years old again and had just been caught putting spiders in his mom's apple basket. A prank that had not only gotten his butt beaten, but also landed him mucking the horse stalls for a month, and he still didn't have a regret. He knew he should be apologizing to Michael, but figured it was useless. He'd never lived up to any of his father's expectations...why try now?

"*See, Son, that's always been your problem. You always thought that you didn't live up to your potential, so you transferred those feelings to others and used them as a reason to be a complete pain in the ass. In death, you really need to be honest with yourself and grow the hell up!*

"*Yes, Aidan left you after the wizard attack, but you know damn good and well it was only because he thought you were dead. Tell me what* you *would've done if you'd seen his head thrown into a ceremonial pyre?*"

Unable to answer, Andrew waited.

"*Thoughts? Comments? None? Okay, I'll tell you what you would've done, not because I'm your father but because I'm a man, a dragon, a Guardsman, and most importantly, I had brothers of my own. You would've done exactly what Aidan did...go get help and search for any signs that he still lived.*

"*I watched from the Heavens as he tortured himself year after year, never fully giving up hope that he would find you and bring you home.*"

"*Oh, my Heavens, here we go. I know! I KNOW! I've heard it all. Poor Aidan...you don't know how he suffered. Poor Aidan...you have to forgive him. Poor Aidan...*"

"*ENOUGH!*" Michael's bellow echoed through the blankness of time and space, causing Andrew to cringe.

"*Will you NEVER take responsibility for your own actions? You fucked up! There is no two ways about it. When you broke free from the wizards, you should have gone to your own kin and helped fight the forces that threatened our race, instead, through some convoluted sense of a need to make the world pay for what you'd suffered, YOU TOOK UP WITH THE ENEMY.*

"*Now, I've listened to your reasons why and I have to call bullshit. You were always somewhat of a brat. Sorry, there's no other way to say it, you just were. I never really understood why, but I accepted you for who you were. I figured being the youngest of three drakes born into the proud, Silver Dragon clan had to be tough.*

"*Then there was the whole* Special One *thing. I'm sure it was a pain in the ass to hear about how you were destined for greatness every day of your life. And...well, I'm not sure having the fate of the dragon kin resting firmly on his shoulders would be easy for anyone, but let's face it, you let that shit go to your head.*"

Silence filled the space. Andrew wondered if Michael was gone or just waiting. Figuring out the Fades had been hard enough, but with his father dropping in for a visit, he was *almost* looking forward to Hell.

"*If you haven't figured it out, Andrew, I can hear your thoughts, so say whatever you need to say...I'm going to hear it either way. Hell will come soon enough. I didn't come to hasten your journey. I actually came here to make things easier for you.*

"*If you face what you've done, show at least a modicum of repentance, TAKE RESPONSIBILITY for the part you played in everything that happened, then you have a chance of not spending* all *of eternity in unrelenting torment. No father wants that for his child, no matter that child's shortcomings.*"

It took a minute, but Andrew finally responded. "*So you're looking for me to forgive Aidan and those fucking Guardsmen? Is that what you're saying, Dad? That I need to forgive and forget?*" He knew he was yelling, but dammit, even in death he couldn't do anything right.

Andrew counted to almost one hundred and Michael finally spoke. The older Guardsman sounded beaten and sad. "Mo mhac, *I fought in many battles, lost many brethren, didn't always know if I was going to come out the other side alive, was wounded more times than I can remember, and none of that was a hard as what I'm about to say to you. You're on your own. I tried. May the Universe, or Fate, or even the Prince of Hell himself, have mercy on you.*"

Michael was gone. Andrew knew it for sure this time. Unlike the other times when his father had merely been silent, now the nothingness around him felt empty…desolate. He was all alone except for his dragon, a fact that still baffled him. But he had to admit, the beast's companionship was nice.

Everyone always gives up on me. Why did I think my long-dead father would be any different?

The conversation he'd had with his father was on a continuous loop, playing over and over in his head until Andrew was ready to scream. Being forced to listen, he had to admit that Michael had definitely given him food for thought, but the thing that had baffled Andrew in life and now in death was, why did no one see the part Aidan played in his abduction? Why were they so ready to forgive one but condemn the other?

Sure, I was kind of a dick after escaping the wizards, but after what I experienced...

He wondered why everyone had expected him to just show back up at the lair like nothing had happened after being left for dead *by his brother*. Was he just supposed to give them all another chance to hurt him again? Maybe even achieve their ultimate goal of killing him? No way! Andrew had done what he had to. He'd made sure they knew he was alive after planning his revenge. His goals may not have been reached, but he had kept those assholes on their toes and inflicted copious amounts of anguish to the brethren who had failed him in every way possible.

Tiring of rehashing the same old shit for the millionth time, he pushed all thoughts of anything but Emma from his mind. Not that she hadn't been ever present in his thoughts no matter what he'd been thinking about, but right now *she* was *all* he wanted. His beast was on board. Together, they used all of their combined forte to blend the image he remembered from his youth with the maturity and strength he'd felt in her just a few days ago. The result was perfection.

That one thought made him both happy and sad. She had been made for him. *HIM!* By the Universe, as a perfect complement to both him and his beast. Emma was meant to complete him in every way and he *knew* she would have. That made him happier than a dead man should've been allowed to be, but also left him sad and empty. It also made him doubt his actions and *almost* wish for another outcome.

A little late to rethink your plan there, genius.

With no way to track time, no windows to see if it was day or night…

Do they have days and nights in Hell?

Andrew had no idea how long he'd been in the Fades. It felt like a week, but that was pure speculation. He wasn't sure if he'd slept or slipped in and out of a coma, he only knew there were periods of time he simply could not remember, and those times were beginning to overtake the lucid ones.

Having just awakened from one such period of lost time, Andrew was left with a vivid memory of Emma, but one he was sure was not his own. She was sad. No, that didn't begin to cover it–she was devastated.

Andrew was immediately enraged. His dragon roared. They prepared to rip whatever or *whoever* had dared to hurt their mate limb from limb. He thought of all the ways he could make the instigator of his mate's pain pay. His beast was fully on board, ready to do whatever it took to avenge their dear Emma.

Then, like a hot air balloon without a fire, his spirit fell, plummeting towards the black abyss of helplessness. There was nothing he could do. No way he could help her. He'd given up. He was dead and farther from Emma than he'd ever been in his life. Stuck in the Ether, waiting to make the long trip south, he felt impotent, enraged, and ready to fight the denizens of Hell to get back to the best person he'd ever met.

Time stood still. Where it had once been fluid and Andrew had simply floated, he now felt the absent tick of the non-existent clock, Emma's suffering his only concern. He turned his focus inward, searching for any remnant of the mating bond he'd shared with her. What he found was a dimming spark at the bottom of his soul, fighting to keep its light but obviously failing. Not sure who listened to the souls of the damned and not caring as long as someone, anyone helped his mate, he prayed.

Checking on Emma, his heart wept at the sight. She was clutching a pillow, curled in a fetal position, laying in total darkness. And as bad as that was, it was what she was feeling that would've brought him to his knees if he still had knees. Her once bright and pure light was dim and gray. Her warmth was gone, replaced by a chill that said *she* was giving up. Of all the things he'd thought would happen without him in the world, Emma losing all hope had never entered his mind. Whatever it was about her, that exceptional ingredient that made her just a little better than most, had done what no other person, place, or threat of death had been able to do. It had made Andrew O'Brien, the traitor, want to be a better a person. And although it was too late for him, there was no way he would let it be too late for her.

Doing the only thing he could think of, Andrew sucked up all his pride and 'thought' as loud as he could.

"All right, Dad, you were right! I fucked up! Now, how do I fix it? Not for me but for Emma. I can't take it, Dad. This is my fault. I have to fix it!"

He waited and waited and…waited. Listening to silence. Praying for answers. Wishing he could pace. Just about to call for his father again, he heard the words that would haunt him for all of eternity.

"My heart can't beat without him. Please just let it end…"

CHAPTER THREE

"I'm coming, I'm coming. I'm guessing it's the only way you'll stop beating on that stupid door."

Emma uncurled from the ball she'd wound herself into almost four days ago to ward off the pain of feeling her mate die. She rolled out of bed and padded towards the door, not bothering to brush her hair or change her clothes.

I could care less what I look like. I just want whoever is at my door to go away.

Opening the bedroom door, she pulled back and slammed her eyes shut. The midday sun was more than she'd bargained for. With her hand shielding her eyes and the wall for support, Emma slowly made her way to the front door, threw it open, and stared.

"Hey, Emma. We came to see how you're doing," Sydney, Lance and Samantha's daughter, remarked as she rushed by. Emma knew they were just being kind and caring, but none of that seemed to matter at the moment.

"Sydney, get back here," Sam called over Emma's shoulder before turning to the young woman and adding, "what my over exuberant daughter meant to say was…we came to see if you need anything."

"Yes, I *need* to be alone." Emma scowled and turned away from Sam, hoping to hide the tears that were filling her eyes. No one understood how she felt. Hell, Emma wasn't sure if she understood, but the fact remained, she felt as if a part of her heart and soul had died right along with Andrew.

Patting her shoulder, Sam stepped over the threshold and waited while Emma secured the door. She could feel the young doctor close at her back and rolled her eyes, then immediately felt bad. They were there because they cared, something most people would be thankful for, but right now it just exacerbated her pain and loneliness.

Her world had been turned upside-down. Her heart was crushed. She was one raw nerve of misery and the worst part was… it was over the traitor, the one that had betrayed them all. It defied explanation. Even as her mate he'd brought her nothing but pain. She hadn't even laid eyes on him until he was already dead.

But none of that mattered when she'd touched his soul, Emma had felt the *real* Andrew. The one the man himself had been running from all those years. The one that wasn't thinking of his own pain but hers, and how to keep her safe once he realized what was happening. The one that still had goodness in him.

Sam's hand on her knee drew Emma's attention. "I know you think you need to be alone and I'm not saying you don't need to grieve, but Emma, you have to stop shutting out the world. It's not good for you."

Emma knew if she opened her mouth she would scream until she collapsed in a pile of grieving woman, so she opted for silence and refused to meet Sam's gaze. It was bad enough Emma could feel the worry pouring off her friend. There was no way she could stand to *see* the pity in her eyes.

Minutes ticked by while Sydney went from channel to channel looking for My Little Pony and Sam sat silently, patiently waiting for Emma to respond. Needing to move, to escape the scrutiny, Emma headed to the kitchen. "I'm making hot chocolate. Anyone want some?"

"Me, please," Sydney called.

"Sounds good," Sam answered.

The sound of the chair scuffing across the tile floor told Emma that Sam had followed her into the kitchen. Unable to hold back any longer, she turned, leaned against the counter, and folded her arms across her chest. "What exactly did you hope to accomplish by coming here today? I mean, I'm sure you know everyone else has been calling, texting, and dropping by. It's obvious I don't want to talk. So why? Why are you here?"

Emma knew she was yelling by the time she stopped to take a breath. She even felt a tinge of guilt when she looked and saw Sydney standing in the doorway, but she'd had enough. The bullshit needed to stop.

"We came because you need us," Sydney answered.

Emma looked back at the child, shocked it had been her that answered. "I *need* you? What makes you think I need you?"

"Because you loved him and he died and now you're sad. I can feel your sadness." The child touched the tips of her fingers to her own chest just above her heart, reminding Emma that she was no ordinary seven year old. The child's 'special powers', whatever they were, were getting stronger. Something that she'd heard was happening all over the lair since the traitor's arrival.

Sydney's words cracked the first layer of the wall Emma had been expertly constructing around her feelings. Unwilling to feel anything but anger while her uninvited guests remained, Emma spun around and grabbed three mugs from the cupboard. It was only a few minutes until she was carrying the cocoa and the tube of Oreos she'd found on the counter to the small café table in the middle of her kitchen.

"This is yummy, Emma, thanks," Sydney giggled. "I really like the mini marshmallows."

"You're welcome, Syd. Why don't you take your hot chocolate and cookies to the couch and watch your cartoons?"

"Can I, Mom?"

"Sure, sweetheart. Emma said it's okay."

Emma watched as the little sweetheart carefully made her way into the living room and was immediately engrossed in the TV. Praying Sam would just sit in silence and knowing her prayer was most definitely going to go unanswered, Emma still cringed when the young doctor spoke.

"How about a compromise? You go wash your face and brush your hair so I don't have to lie when Siobhan asks if you're taking care of yourself. Then I'll make us a light lunch and watch you take two bites so I don't have to lie to any of the guys, my pushy ass husband included, then Syd and I will get outta your hair. Deal?"

Emma shook her head and sighed before looking up to find Sam smiling with a look of hope on her face. Knowing when she was beaten, Emma stood with mug in hand, nodded, and headed to the bathroom. She had to admit she needed more than a sink bath. It had been at least five days since she showered if you counted the day she spent in the clinic arguing that she was well enough to go home.

Grabbing a towel, she took a quick shower, put on clean pajamas, and returned to the kitchen. The scent of grilled cheese sandwiches and tomato soup hit her senses, making her stomach growl. Sydney's giggle said they'd heard her coming. Sam's smile as Emma crossed the threshold told her they'd also heard her hunger pangs.

They ate in companionable silence while Emma tried to decide how to apologize for her earlier behavior. She still wanted to be alone, but she'd been a real bitch to her friends and that just wasn't cool.

"You really don't need to say sorry," Sydney mumbled while shoving a huge piece of sandwich into her mouth.

"What did you say?" Emma asked a little louder than she'd planned and almost fell off her chair while spinning to look at the little girl.

Holding up her index finger in the universal 'wait' signal, Sydney quickly chewed her food before responding. "I said you don't need to say sorry. You were thinking that you needed to 'pologize for being *grumpy*." The little girl looked at Emma and winked before continuing, confirming she'd heard *everything* Emma had been thinking. "*You know*, when we got here. but you don't have to. Your heart hurts and it's hard to be nice and smiley when your heart hurts. You liked that old Andrew. I liked him, too. Did you know he bought me ice cream once? It was before Mom was my mom and Dad was my dad. We were at the hospital. He was really nice to me. He wasn't the bad old dragon they all thought he was. He was just confused…mad. I think he needed a time out."

The pain hadn't gone away. If anything, it had just shifted a little while she'd showered and eaten. But at the mention of his name, it pushed to the forefront once again. It was compounded by Syd's story. To know that he'd been nice to someone besides her confirmed what she already knew…there had been hope. With time, Andrew would've changed, or at least been repentant for what he'd done. Maybe even tried to make amends.

If 'ifs' and 'buts' were candy and nuts we'd all have a Merry Christmas.

She had no idea where that saying came from, but it summed up how she felt. No amount of ifs and buts were going to bring him back, and therefore, she would live with a huge 'what if' hanging over her head. Holding in the tears while pretending to eat the rest of her lunch, Emma mumbled, "Thanks, Syd."

They finished in silence. Sam shoed both Emma and Sydney to the living room, instructing them to find a good movie to watch while she did the dishes. Emma told the child where to find her DVDs and sat down in her favorite chair, trying to come up with an excuse that would get the mother and daughter tag team to leave.

"This looks good. It's not Christmas right now, but it looks funny." Sydney held up National Lampoon's Christmas Vacation.

"Yeah, it's pretty funny. We can watch it if you want. Doesn't matter what time of year it is," Emma answered as Sam entered the room, making her way to her daughter and helping to get the movie started before taking a seat on the couch.

Emma was shocked when Sydney climbed up in the oversized recliner with her, dragging her favorite afghan, and cuddled up to her side. It wasn't long before the child had taken her hand and squeezed. The affection was almost Emma's undoing. She really needed them to leave so she could go back to bed and cry herself to sleep.

"Emma, can you hear me?"

"Syd? You can mindspeak...to me?"

"I think I can to everybody. I know I can hear everybody if they don't put up their shields. Mom and Dad have been teaching me how to keep mine up pretty much all the time. That way I don't hear the grown up stuff, ya know?"

"Yeah, I know. But I guess what I should've asked was how are you talking to me *this way. Andrew was the only person I'd ever heard in my mind."*

"I think it's because you are his mate. I heard Ms Siobhan call Andrew the Special One*. I don't know what that means, but Mom and Dad said Kyra's magic is stronger, Anya's doing tons better with her dragon, and I know Charlie's fairy magic is more sparkly cause I can see that for myself. Anyway, I want to tell you something I haven't told anyone else. Can you keep a secret?"*

"I can as long as keeping quiet won't get anyone hurt."

"No way, silly," Sydney giggled. *"That's the stuff I tell Daddy right away."*

"Good girl."

"What I have to tell you is just about you...and...well, Andrew." It had been the only time Emma could remember that Sydney sounded unsure. The child usually just blurted out whatever was on her mind.

Curiosity won out of Emma's need to be alone. *"What is it, Syd?"*

"Andrew's still here, or well...there. He's not dead, at least not all the way. He is talking about the 'Ether' or the 'Faces'. I can hear him. I tried to talk to him, but I guess he can't hear me cause he didn't answer."

Emma wondered how much of what the child was saying was factual and how much was Sydney's imagination, but she couldn't help but hope that at least part of it was true.

"It's all true. Here, let me show you."

More than a little embarrassed that the little girl had heard her doubt, Emma could only say, *"Whatever you say, Kiddo."*

It felt a lot like when she'd been inside Andrew's mind as Sydney opened her consciousness and showed Emma the place she'd 'heard' the traitor. There were echoes of hundreds of spirits that had passed through on the way to their final resting place. Some wailing and begging to be given one more chance, others resigned to their fate. And still others happy to ascend and live with their ancestors in the Heavens.

It was amazing that Sydney could access such a holy place. Emma could only imagine how *special* the child really was, even though no one had a clue how or why or what it all meant. At first glance, Sydney looked like any other seven year old. She even had the telltale missing tooth in the front, but after spending just a few minutes with the little girl, it was obvious she was so much more.

Growing impatient and rather creeped out by her surroundings, Emma asked, *"What are we waiting on, Syd?"*

"Shhh, I'm trying to find the spot."

Feeling properly chastised, Emma sat back and waited, absentmindedly rubbing the strange heart shaped mark that had appeared on her wrist the night of Devon and Anya's mating ceremony. At first it had only been a slight irritation, then like everything else, it went nuclear when Andrew came home. Since his death it had tingled a few times with no rhyme or reason and nothing too distracting, so she'd dismissed it in favor of nurturing the pain that burned through her body and threatened her sanity. She'd even forgotten to mention it to Siobhan. But then again, she hadn't been in the mood to say much to the Elder Healer after all that had happened.

The sound of Sam's voice calling to both her and Sydney pulled Emma out of the strange 'in-between' place.

"Sydney, what are you doing? Come back here this instant." Emma had only heard the young doctor's 'mom' voice one other time, but knew the girl was in for a world of hurt if she didn't respond quickly.

Tugging on their clasped hands, Emma whispered through mindspeak, *"Your mom's calling you. It's not polite to leave her waiting. We can do this another time."*

"Oh, all right, but I was almost there."

Emma had to laugh at the petulance in Sydney's voice. She really was something else. The two opened their eyes to find Sam standing over them, fists on her hips, mouth pursed in annoyance, shaking her head.

"I guess I don't need to ask what this was all about, do I young lady. Where were you this time?"

"I was taking Emma to where I last heard Andrew."

"YOU WERE WHAT?" Emma was sure most of the Towne Square had heard Sam's shriek. "Sydney Renee Kavanaugh, what were you thinking?"

"I was thinking that my friend was sad and I didn't want her to be sad anymore. Geez, Mom. What else was I supposed to do?"

"You were suppo…"

"You were supposed to do exactly what you did, sweetheart, and I thank you for it. You seem to be the only one that cares about my feelings." Emma cut off Samantha's words and spoke to the child while never losing eye contact with her mother.

"Emma, that's just not the case."

"Really, Sam? Really *it is*."

Uncomfortable did not begin to describe the look on Samantha's face as she lifted Sydney from Emma's lap and asked her to take her bag of toys to the other room. Emma refused to look away, even when Sam had to. The soft click of her office door was the starting bell for Emma's rage.

"You wanna know what makes me the maddest? What hurts the worst? It's the fact that no one takes my feelings into account. It's like all of you hate him so I'm supposed to hate him too…and for a while that worked. Now I know him. Not *know him, know him,* but know of him and have had a look at his heart and soul, revealing the man underneath all the bullshit. Yes! He's a dick and he's done some really bad things, but that's not all that he is."

She stood, her tone becoming louder and sharper as she went. "I know you've heard me say this at least ten times in the last four days, but I think it bears repeating. Now listen carefully." Emma paused for dramatic effect and knew she was being a huge bitch, but couldn't work up the strength to care. When she spoke again, each word was heavily enunciated and had a punch to it.

"He. Protected. Me." She paused and let her words have their desired effect, then added, "He died to end *my* pain." Emma slapped her chest with the palm of her hand. "Do you have any idea what that feels like? To have gotten a glimpse of the man that was to be my mate, only to lose him in the blink of an eye? Never to truly know him, only to know what the world that had already convicted him thought of him?" She was losing control. Her actions were becoming more animated.

"To know the Universe made me, little ole Emma the jeweler, quiet little girl that never said 'boo'…yeah, that girl. The big ole wise, wonderful, Universe made *me* especially for *him*. Our love was to be epic, one for the ages. I don't know how I know, I just do." She spun away from Sam only to turn right back around and advance until they were almost nose to nose.

"It didn't matter that he was the traitor. Nothing he'd done mattered in that time. I got to see the *real* him. The one he'd worked so hard to hide. The one he thought was vulnerable and open to being hurt. And then…then he was just gone." Her tone got so low, not even she was sure where that voice came from. "And that hurt, I mean really hurt. But do you know what was even worse? What the one thing is I don't know if I'll ever be able to get over?"

She waited and watched until Sam finally shook her head.

"Well, Samantha, what cut me to the quick, hurt me worse than I thought it was possible for a person to hurt, was the fact that all the people I love more than anything, the people I consider family, the people I would die for," Emma stopped and threw her hands over her head before continuing, "they just expected me to get over it. Had the *audacity* to say I was better off without him. Even went so far as to say just brush it off. *Brush it off?* What the hell is that? No matter that he was my mate and their brethren, Andrew was a person…a living, breathing person that deserved more, no matter what he'd done, than to be *brushed off*."

Emma spat the last two words and then glared at Sam, knowing it wasn't really the young doctor she was upset with. Anyone standing there would've received the same punishment. Samantha just happened to be the lucky winner when Emma's emotional dam broke. Now that it was flowing, she had no way to stop it.

Turning her back to Samantha, Emma continued, "Sydney is the first and *only* person that has given me anything to hold on to, anything that even let me know he really existed besides the memories and the pain."

Sam went to speak and Emma spun on her, holding up a hand to silence her. "Please don't try to use psychology on me. Don't tell me that I saw the corpse so I know he was real and that he *is* now dead. Oh, and I will throw up if you tell me that grief is hard but I'll get through it."

Squinting her eyes and leaning closer to Sam she said, "How do you know I'll get over it? Has this happened before? Is there a recorded history detailing all the times mates have met and one has died before they bonded and the remaining mate has gone on to live a long, productive life?"

She waited patiently, and when Sam didn't answer, Emma shook her head. "You can't, because no such record exists. The only stories you will find will be those where the mating bond was complete and the mates either went to the Heavens together or were only separated by a small expanse of time. But because my mate was the traitor, the most notorious of the Dragon Guard's enemies, I'm just supposed to 'get over it'."

Falling into her chair, Emma let her head fall back and her eyes slide closed. She was more tired than she could ever remember being, and the pain she'd been holding at bay was barreling towards her with the promise of vengeance. Taking a deep breath and then holding it to the count of ten, she exhaled. Opening her eyes to just small slits, she found Sam sitting on the edge of the coffee table facing her, looking like the doctor she was and not someone that was going to take much more of Emma's BS.

"Finished now?"

Emma gave the slightest of shrugs, waiting to see what great advice the physician had, sure there was nothing the woman could say that would help the way she felt. But as was becoming a habit–she was wrong.

"To be honest, I had no idea anyone told you to brush it off. That is absolutely deplorable. And when you feel up to it, I will be your backup and we will pay whoever had the nerve to say that to you a visit he or she will never forget. You have every right to feel whatever *you feel*. *No one,* and I mean *no one*, has the right to tell you how to feel and most certainly not to diminish your feelings. I am so very, very sorry you had to go through that.

"Along the same lines, there's not a one of us that knows if you would've been better off with or without Andrew. Everyone has an opinion and no one has the right to impose *theirs* upon you. My momma used to say opinions were like assholes and everybody's got one. When I was younger I thought that was the stupidest saying in the world, but as I've gotten older, I've come to realize she was so very right.

"You wanna know what I think?" Not waiting but two seconds for an answer, Sam hurried on, "I think you getting to see the goodness in Andrew was the best thing that could've happened, not only for you but for all the Guardsmen, especially his brothers. Those pig-headed, stubborn, wonderful men have spent so many years hating Andrew and vilifying him, blaming him for damn near everything that's wrong with the world; somewhere along the way they forgot he was a real person, one of them. A guy that when presented with great adversity made the wrong choice and never found his way back.

"I also believe wholeheartedly that the love between you and Andrew would've been epic. You were the one thing Andrew had done right in a very long time. He would've learned to trust again. You, Emma Sinclair, are one of the strongest people I know. I have faith you would've healed the man *and* the dragon."

The tick of the clock on the mantle filled the silence as the two women simply looked at one another. Emma felt a tear roll down her cheek, saw the look of compassion in Sam's eyes, and shook her head. The doctor leaned back as the jeweler breathed a sigh of relief. She had no doubt that had Sam spoken, touched her, or made any effort to give comfort at that moment, Emma would've broken into a million pieces that not even all the king's horses and all the king's men could have put back together again.

Several minutes passed before Sam spoke, and what she said resonated within Emma's entire being. "And just to prove that the Universe does not make mistakes, you have a decision to make, one not unlike Andrew faced. Do you forgive or do you seek revenge? Do you follow your mate to the Heavens or stay with the family that loves you, even though they acted like jerks? Only you can decide–it is your path to follow."

Sometime while Sam was talking, Sydney had come back into the room. The little girl climbed up on Emma's lap and took the woman's hand. "I found him again. He's still in that weird kind of nothing place."

Emma gave the child a weak smile then looked at Sam. "I'm sorry for losing my cool."

Laying her hand on Emma's knee, the young doctor smiled. "Not a problem. That's what friends are for."

Smiling back, Emma turned Sydney on her lap until they were face to face. "I want to thank you, Syd. I think there have been times I felt Andrew's presence but was afraid to believe. You've shown me that it's okay." See kissed the child's forehead before leaning back and sighing. Exhaustion was beginning to sink in, but now that she'd had her meltdown she actually felt better, and for the first time in over a week, she didn't want to be alone.

"There is one other thing I think you should know, but if you tell anyone I told you, I'll deny it," Samantha winked. "Aaron and Aidan are having as hard a time with Andrew's death as you are, maybe more so. The difference is, they think they are hiding their pain from everyone.

"Charlie says that Aaron refuses to talk about it and trains every waking minute. She said he has one more day before the ass-kicking begins."

The thought of Charlie kicking her mate's ass brought an almost grin to Emma's lips. She would pay to watch that match and bet her life savings on the little fairy for the knockout.

"And Grace can't get Aidan out of the house," Sam went on. "He alternates between rearranging the nursery and nagging Grace to rest. The poor dear called Lance this morning and begged him to get Aidan out from under foot for just an hour or so. The poor girl is only a few weeks from giving birth and the last thing she needs is her mate making her crazy.

"She called me before Syd and I came over here to tell me he'd had nightmares the few times he actually stopped long enough to sleep. She was worried enough that she slipped into his dreams. She saw the same thing in Aidan's dream that Sydney described. I think it is something you need to talk to Siobhan and Pearce about. Something about all of this feels off and they are the only ones I know of that might be able to get you some answers."

Emma thought about what Samantha said long after the doctor and her daughter had gone. The pain returned, but not as bad as it had been. Returning to bed, she resumed her fetal position while clutching her pillow to her chest, but this time it was not to ward off the pain but to welcome it, to feel it, to let it fill her on her terms.

Samantha had been right. She *did* have a decision to make, but not the one the doctor had talked about. No, Emma had to decide if she was going to lie down and accept that Destiny had taken her mate before she ever got to know him, or if she was gonna fight for him. Sydney had made her believe Andrew was out there. It was up to Emma to find a way to him, and she knew exactly what to do.

A verse she had no memory of spun around and around through her mind. Although she had no clue how she knew, *she just knew* it would help her find Andrew's soul.

Follow the pain. Follow your heart. Follow the love, you find the start.

CHAPTER FOUR

"Better not let Emma hear you say that."

"Let me hear what, Pearce?" she asked, walking into the basement of the clinic without knocking.

"Ahh…well…It's just that…" The look on the Guardsman's face was priceless and any other time Emma would've teased back, but today there was no time and she was in no mood.

"Since the cat got Pearce's tongue, how about you tell me what's going on, Devon?"

"Emma, dear, we were just talking about something Mom found while she and Pearce were doing some research. It's really nothing."

"Devon, honey, you really should never attempt to lie. You suck at it." Emma mimicked the tone he'd used while standing in front of him with her hands on her hips.

He looked over her head as if searching for someone…anyone to save him, and all she heard was Pearce trying to hide his laughter.

"You might as well tell her. Aaron and Aidan were already here today. I'm sure they've told their mates. It's just a matter of time before she finds out anyway," Pearce commented as he hurried out the door.

She heard Devon mumble 'Chicken shit' under his breath. Any other time in her life, Emma would've given in and let her friend off the hook, but not now, not after all that had happened, not after the night she'd had. Something wasn't right. She could feel it in her heart.

Her sleep had been plagued with visions of Andrew. He was trying to tell her something, she just knew it. Sydney said he was still, in some odd way, among the living, or at least 'partially living', making Emma adamantly believe the visions were her mate trying to contact her, and not just her overactive imagination or need to have another chance at making it work. One obstacle stood in her way. No matter how hard she tried to communicate with Andrew, all that came back was a whishing sound reminiscent of the noise Siobhan's old canister vacuum used to make.

A few minutes before dawn, she'd had enough. Decision made, she'd risen from bed and headed to the living room. After opening the blinds, she'd sat in an almost lotus position watching the sun making its first appearance of the day.

Clearing her mind, Emma used the picture of Andrew she had in her mind to focus and she meditated. It was something she hadn't done in years. Meditation was something she'd used to ease her anxiety for years after coming to the lair. The memories of her early years were foggy at best. She pushed to see them, to remember, but nothing came into focus, and after a few minutes of digging, she had a terrible headache.

Moving on, praying the pain in her brain would subside, she began searching for Andrew, or rather, his spirit. It was like following footsteps through the forest after a hard rain. She could tell he'd been there, even saw traces, but for the most part was flying blind. Every once in a while she would get a burst of another type of energy. It was stronger…bigger somehow, and connected not only in the same bright spot she and Andrew were, but also one deeper within her soul. A place she hadn't known existed until that moment. The oddest thing about it was it felt old... really old.

Two hours into her pursuit and still empty handed, Emma decided it was time to see if anyone else could help. She threw on some clothes, put her hair in a ponytail, and headed to the clinic. Since its construction it seemed to be the meeting place when anything of importance was happening, and since there was never a dull moment, the joint was always hopping.

"Yeah, you might as well tell her," Emma mocked.

"All right, but I want it noted that I'm doing this against my better judgement. I think you should wait and speak to Mom. She'll have a better explanation." Devon's tone was exasperated and something else she couldn't quite put her finger on.

"Duly noted."

Shaking his head, Devon let out a sigh before beginning. "There's no easy way to say this except to just spit it out. Andrew's body is still here."

"Okay," she said, waiting for the other shoe to drop.

"Like still here, still here."

"I figured it would be. I didn't think y'all would've had a funeral without me." She frowned.

"No…you're right. We wouldn't have…OH SHIT!" He paused and gently grabbed her upper arms, bending to look directly into her eyes. "In all the years you've been with us, no Guardsmen have died, have they?"

"No, but what does that have to do with this?" Her patience was growing thin and she knew her tone reflected that.

Dropping his hands, Devon stood to his full height and motioned for her to follow. Turning, he strode down a long, winding hall. After three turns, Emma saw they were heading towards a set of huge, wooden, double doors she hadn't known were at the back of the health center. The closer they got, the more she could see the intricate carvings across the middle of both doors, unlike anything she'd seen before. The dragons had welcomed her, made her their own, and because of that she knew their language and customs, had even studied some of the old texts with Siobhan, but she'd never seen anything like the symbols and glyphs on the doors.

Pausing at the door, Devon bowed his head. Emma followed suit and listened as he said the Prayer of Remembrance. "To the Universe, to the Ancients, to the Fates, and to the Heavens, we give honor to those that have gone before us and thanks to You who protect their souls."

When he turned she saw the reverence in his eyes, which was only amplified by the respect in his tone. "The clinic was placed on this very spot for two reasons. One, the healing power we all feel here is nothing short of miraculous. And two, it backs up to the Cavern of Souls, the place where deceased Guardsmen are taken."

He stopped talking as he opened the door to the left and motioned for her to enter before him. Darkness surrounded them for a second as Devon let the door close before lighting the sconces hanging on either side of the hallway. His hand on her elbow startled her, and they both grinned before he began to speak. "The thing about Guardsmen that is so different from other types of shifters is that we truly are two souls inhabiting one body, while other shifters are what they call two-natured…one soul, two forms. I'm sure you've heard the story of how our race came to be."

She nodded her head for him to continue as they began to walk down the hall.

"The original Dragon Kings were adamant that they still be 'alive' after joining with the knights. Not in the same way as they had been for thousands of years, but alive in the sense that their soul live on even after their human counterpart's body had died and his soul gone on to the Heavens. What this meant was that the spirit of the dragon would leave the Guardsman's body at the same time as the human's soul. The dragon would then join with a newly born male child of the correct lineage, or wait for such a child to be conceived, and then join with him.

"One of the happy accidents of using all this magic and creating a new race was that when both spirits had exited the body, the vessel simply returned to the Earth. When the Guardsmen questioned the mage, he simply stated, 'Ashes to ashes and soul to soul. Magic to magic and all remains whole.' Apparently the old guy wasn't much for explanations, but at least they understood that as long as the spirit of the dragons survived, there would always be Guardsmen to protect their kin. They would never again face extinction.

"I just assumed you knew that, and understood why we have only memorial services and not funerals per se after one of our own has passed. In the case of the Guardsman, there is no body, and our Ancients decided because of that, the same form of tribute would be paid to the women and children. Each family has a crypt where the members who are not Guardsmen are laid to rest in a private familial ceremony before the clan has the memorial service.

"Okay, all of that was to tell you that in any other circumstance, five days after death, the body of a fallen Guardsman would be gone. But, true to form, Andrew is different. His body is still here and showing no signs of deterioration, if you'll please excuse the crude terminology."

They continued on in silence for a few seconds before he began again. "Carrick, Zachary, Malachi, and Mom came here together and prayed. After long hours, they all agree that the soul of the man and the dragon are still linked. However, their opinions as to why differ. Carrick believes it is because of Andrew's dealings with black magic. Zachary believes it is because he is the Special One and has not served his purpose to dragon kin. Malachi believes that Andrew is holding on for you."

Devon stopped speaking just as they came to the mouth of a cave. "And we are here."

His hand at the small of her back guided Emma through dimly lit passageways until they came upon a small cavern that smelled of herbs and oils she recognized from her years spent with Siobhan. For the first time since she marched into the clinic, less than an hour earlier, Emma was uneasy. It had been one thing to think there was a chance Andrew was still among them, but when faced with irrefutable facts her brain was having a hard time catching up.

Turning the corner, she was unable to cross the threshold. Her feet simply would not move one step forward. Thankfully, Devon was perceptive enough to see she was having difficulty and considerate enough not to call it out, but stand patiently by her side.

Laying not fifteen feet in front of her, on a stone table not unlike the ones she knew stood in many of the caverns of the caves of their lair, was a man she'd never really met but knew more intimately than any other. The man that almost everyone she loved was happy to see dead. The man that no matter how hard she tried, she'd never been able to despise like the others. The man that had used his dying breath to end her pain. The man that was to be her mate.

Taking her third deep breath and deciding the only way to get to the truth was to move forward, she exhaled and took her first step toward Andrew's body. Every subsequent step got easier until she was standing beside his shrouded body. Emma looked to Devon, unsure what her next move should be.

Very carefully and with incredible reverence, Devon folded the top of the embroidered coverlet down over the top half of Andrew's body, leaving him exposed from the waist up. Having never seen him up close, and having heard so many horror stories about him, she was surprised to see an attractive, well-muscled man, with a trimmed beard and strong jawline lying before her. In his relaxed state, he looked nothing like the villain she'd heard about, but more like his brothers than she'd ever imagined possible. He did look much older, even though he was the younger brother.

Before she realized what she was doing, her hand touched his. She was surprised at the warmth his body held after so many days, not to mention how soft his skin was. If she hadn't known better, she would've thought he was asleep. A tiny spark of electricity jumped between them, making her fingers tingle. Her hand traveled up his tattooed arm, across his collarbone, and touched the tip of the wing of the beautiful dragon resting on his chest. The image of the beast barely vibrated against her fingertips and made her wonder if she'd imagined it.

Sometime later, Emma looked up to see that Devon had backed away and was leaning against the cave wall. She smiled and continued to look at the man the Universe deemed her mate. There was a pull between them, even in his present state. It filled her with peace and contentment, which made no sense considering she was standing next to her mate's dead body.

But is he really dead?

Moving to the other side of the table, she let her hand sweep across his chest. It was as if now that she'd touched him, she was able to break the connection. She grinned at herself, thinking that once upon a time she'd pictured him as a smaller, scrawnier version of his brothers, which she now knew couldn't be further from the truth.

Her fingers began to trace the tattoos that covered almost every millimeter of his arm. They were unique, beautiful, and appeared to have been burnt into his skin. Her head popped up as she looked at Devon's arms and then asked, "None of you have tats or markings on your arms that are not part of your dragons, do you?"

"No, we don't."

Leaning forward, she closely examined an especially dark glyph that took up most of Andrew's forearm. It looked like two infinite symbols perpendicularly intersecting one another to form a cross, with a band of interlocking Celtic knots forming a circle around the edge touching the four tips. In the center with the tip pointing north was the symbol of the warrior arrow. There was power emanating from the marking that made the hairs on her arms stand on end.

"Come look at this."

She held up Andrew's arm as Devon approached and waited while the Guardsman examined the marking. "I'm sure this symbol means the balance between two opposing forces, but we really should ask Mom to be sure."

"Ask me what?" Siobhan appeared in the room carrying several large tomes, which Devon rushed to take from her.

"Can you look at this symbol, please?" Emma asked. "I would swear I can feel it."

As Siobhan made her way to Emma's side, she slid her reading glasses from her head to the bridge of her nose while calling over her shoulder, "Son, please put those books on the table at the back of the room."

Thoroughly hugging Emma and then holding her at arm's length to look her over from head to toe, Siobhan smiled that motherly expression the younger woman had come to depend on after so many years in the lair. When she spoke, Emma could feel waves of love and comfort rolling over her. "How are you, my dear? Really?"

"I'm good…really."

"Then I have to ask…what are you doing here?" Siobhan asked with a suspicious tone.

"Well, let's see: he was my mate, I never met him in person, I shared the most intense pain of both our lives with him, I felt him die, and…Oh, yeah! Sydney says she can hear him talking and I feel like he's just this far," she held her thumb and forefinger about an inch from one another and put it right in front of the Elder Healer's face to make sure she saw it before continuing, "from me every second of every day. I came here to see you and happened upon a conversation I was obviously not supposed to hear. After bullying Devon," she winked over her shoulder, "he explained the whole 'poof into oblivion thing' that was supposed to happen with Andrew's body but didn't, and then brought me here to see for myself."

Emma took a breath and stood staring at Siobhan, daring her to say another word. She knew her actions were out of character, but her 'family' had been keeping things from her and were trying to baby her, and those were two things that she could not have if she was going to get the answers she wanted…needed…deserved.

"I see," was all Siobhan said before turning to examine the symbol.

"Devon said he thought it meant the balance between two opposing forces. What do you think?"

"Devon is correct," she answered without looking up. "I can also feel power running through it. Just another anomaly of his death." Straightening up, Siobhan looked down at Andrew then reached forward and moved a wayward strand of hair from his forehead. Emma saw the same sadness she felt reflected in the Healer's face and felt bad for the way she'd spoken to her. But that quickly evaporated.

The words, *"It is too late to worry with a man that was just not good enough for you. He is gone now. Focus on yourself and getting better,"* came to her mind. Emma's spine stiffened. Her resolve to make them listen to her renewed.

"No more coddling, no more sending me away or telling me I'm better off without him, Siobhan. I know you can feel something more than just power in that symbol. Stop trying to protect me and help me find out what's going on. One way or another, I will get my mate back or send him on to his final destination so that he can find some rest. I promise you I will…with or without your help."

Siobhan looked away, bit her bottom lip, and made a 'tsk' sound before answering. "Well, I suppose you will want to stay as close to him as possible, am I right?"

"That you are."

"Okay, then we will work in here until the others come. Let me show you what Pearce and I have been able to find so far. That symbol just may be the break we needed."

Not waiting for an answer, the Healer stepped around Emma and walked to the table that held all her books. Emma stood looking at Andrew, wondering what he'd been like before his capture and knowing he'd been a real pain in the ass, but someone she would've liked. Laying her hand over his still heart and her lips upon his cool forehead, she said the words in her mind she wasn't ready to say out loud. *"Come back to me. I know life was hard and you really screwed up, but I need you…at least for a little while. I'm pretty sure if I cannot see that you're real and know that everything you've made me feel is not a figment of my imagination, I'm gonna lose my mind."*

It was several more minutes before she could move away from her mate. Nothing that had happened since the man had set foot in the lair made sense, and this new development was no exception. Emma had tried to fight it, had stayed away from him, and had ultimately hidden what was happening from all those she trusted, but now there was no way she could deny their connection or her need to have him in her life.

Fate may not be denied, but it might just kill me, too.

CHAPTER FIVE

Nothing he'd ever endured at the hands of any of his captors had left him as gutted as listening to Emma fighting for him did. It wasn't what she said, although her words were beautiful. It wasn't the vehemence with which she said them, although that was humbling to say the least. It was her complete belief that bled from every word, persuading others to believe just as she did, that he was more than the sum of his deeds. She was the first person that accepted all of him: the good, the bad, and most definitely, the ugly.

He wanted to get back to her and that shocked him more than anything. Andrew O'Brien did not want to be with anyone. He was a loner and capable of dealing with anything and everything on his own…but…he wasn't. He not only wanted to be with Emma to be a better person because of her, he *needed* to be with her. Needed to show her that her faith in him was not unfounded. He just knew if he could get back there, he could be the man and dragon she needed.

Then came the part that didn't surprise him, not even a little bit. The part, where even in his death, those fucking dragons dismissed him like yesterday's garbage. It had been bad enough when they treated him like scum at the bottom of the pond when he was alive, but when they'd had the nerve to tell his mate…*his mate*… that he wasn't worth her time. They'd gone too damn far.

Well, from what I've seen of her, I'm really not. She is the best of the best and I'm…well…I'm me.

They'd also told her to get over him, move on, and that she was better off without him. And maybe they were right on a certain level, but they had no idea how deeply he and Emma had bonded. Couldn't know that she was the ultimate light. That she wiped away the deep, dark stains of all he'd done. She couldn't offer him the forgiveness that he would have to earn from all that he had harmed, but she could cleanse his soul and accept him just as he was. He'd seen that for himself. Figured it was the only reason he was still floating around the Fades like a balloon in the Macy's Day Parade instead of barbequing in Hell like a pig on a spit.

He was glad to see Emma was no longer lying in bed wishing for death, and he had to admit she had a strength that surprised even him. He'd felt power within her but would never have guessed she could be tough and demanding. Emma was light, sunshine, and goodness, which most people, even him, took for granted. Andrew could not have been prouder of her.

Tired of waiting, he called out again, "Dad! Please! Tell me how to do this."

No answer again, and tired of being ignored by his father, Andrew asked his question to the emptiness, hoping that someone, something, anyone… would answer. "How the hell do I get back to my body, or at least communicate with my mate on the other side?"

Long silent seconds ticked by. Andrew imagined himself pacing. It was a new activity he'd learned in those few hours after Michael had left him to stew in his own juices. All he had to do was picture his body as he'd been in life and then imagine himself pacing. Next step was to give himself over to the illusion. The first time he'd tried, the vertigo made him want to hurl, but the longer he worked at it the better he became, until it actually began to combat the fury inside him.

On his fourth trip around his imaginary library, he heard a voice from his past. A voice he was sure had been lost to him forever. "Drew, love, what do you need?"

"Mom? Is that you?"

"Yes, my sweet boy. It is me."

"What are you doing here, Mom? Where is Dad?"

"He's being stubborn, mo mahc. Like father, like son." Margarite laughed and Andrew's heart swelled. He hadn't realized how much he'd truly missed his mother until that moment.

"I just came myself, dear boy. Time is running out. Your dragon can only sustain you for so long and that sweet girl of yours is going to wear herself out."

"Thank you so much, Mom. I really want to get back to her and make things right, but I've tried everything I know. How do I do it? How do I get back to the other side…back to Emma?"

"Oh, darling, you do not get back on your own. You really have little control over the process at all. It is up to those that love you, along with Fate, Destiny, and the Universe. All of their energies have to be in sync. The best that you can do is be ready when you feel the pull and follow your mating bond to the light of your soul."

"Thanks for coming, Mom, but I'm pretty sure I'm screwed. Emma's the only one that wants me there. She's the only one that'll fight for me. The others are happy I'm gone. They told her to get over me and move on, that I wasn't worth her time." He paused, feeling defeated. "Let's face it, Mom, can you blame them?"

"Don't you dare give up hope, Andrew Myles O'Brien. Your brothers are angry. They are hurt. They feel betrayed, and rightfully so. You were horrible to them and you will have to make amends, maybe even beg, but they are still your blood and in their hearts still love you as their own. It is the same with your brethren. And before you interrupt, they are still your brethren. That will never change, no matter what you do or how angry they are. But you have to believe you are worthy of their forgiveness. You have to work to earn their trust."

His mother stopped talking and he thought she was finished. Just as he was about to respond, Margarite added, "But most of all, you have to make sure you are worthy of the love of that beautiful woman. The Universe has given you a precious gift. She is perfect and she is going to need you to be there for her…your fates depend on it. DO NOT WASTE IT!"

"What? What do you mean 'our fates depend on it'? Depend on what, Mom?"

"That's enough for you now. Your father's calling, and with any luck you'll be back where you belong soon. Know that your father and I love you very much. We love all our boys. Now, get it together and make us proud."

"But, Mom, you didn't…"

From one second to the next, the air around him went from full of love and life and his mother to utter nothingness. Margarite was gone and Andrew was once again left with his thoughts. A position he was beginning to detest. He thought about the time in the cave at the lair when he'd hallucinated his mother's presence. She'd been much more direct, almost uncaring in his delusion, and he'd wondered a few times how much truth there was in his vision. Happily, there was none, and she was the wonderful mother he'd known for all those years and would love forever.

He thought about what Margarite had said, worried that Emma was going to need him and he would be stuck in the Land of the Lost unable to get to her. Cursed himself for most of the decisions he'd made and had to laugh at the fact that his mother thought Aidan and Aaron, or any of the Guardsmen for that matter, would ever forgive him, let alone ever trust him again. Of course it was ultimately their fault that things had transpired as they had, but he was beginning to see where he'd played a part in the mess he was trying to escape.

It was absolutely maddening that he could do nothing to aid in his escape from the Fades. His mother had been very specific. There was nothing he could do…or was there? A thought crossed his mind that had him once again believing there may truly be a chance. All he had to do was somehow reach the little sweetheart, Sydney.

They'd met under harrowing circumstances, but she'd never feared him and told him how one day things would be okay.

Just another of my less than stellar decisions.

Banishing his negative thoughts, he focused on Sydney. He knew she was so much more than 'just a little girl'. Had known it the first time he'd spoken to her. He also knew she'd been poking around the expanse of nothingness where he presently resided. They had not been able to make contact, but they each were aware of the other, and now that he was a little better with the inner workings of the Fades, he was ready to try again. All he had to do was focus on her extremely unique energy signal, and with the help of his dragon, who he was thankfully on speaking terms with once again, he should be able to get a message to her.

Thinking of her bright blue eyes and open smile framed by the curliest, blondest hair he'd ever seen made her more real in his mind. He then thought of her tiny voice and the caring way she'd grabbed his hand, squeezing for reassurance when in all actuality he was the villain…the traitor.

"Don't say that about yourself, Andrew. You're getting better now. I can feel it." Her childlike voice filled the space around him.

"That you, Sydney?"

"Sure is. I'm at the clinic with all the grownups and Jay. Emma's yelling at Aaron. They're fighting 'bout you. Siobhan's looking at some yucky old book with Kyra, and it looks like they are gonna work a spell. Aidan is pacing because Grace won't sit down and her babies are almost ready to come out. Everyone else is just kinda standing around. What you doing?"

He smiled at her play-by-play but was worried about Emma yelling at Aaron. That sanctimonious prick better not yell back at her, or Andrew would have to kick his ass. No one yelled at Emma…absolutely no one.

Possessive much? Chill. You don't even know for sure if she wants you. She may have just felt bad for the dead guy.

"I need you to do me a favor. Can you see if the book Siobhan is reading is the one I brought with me to the lair…please?" The word almost got stuck in his throat and he cringed at what a Neanderthal he'd become. There had been a time not so long ago that whatever he commanded was done without question or reservation, or the offending party ceased to exist right where he stood. Those times were long gone, at least in his mind. He only prayed he could make them fade away in the hearts and minds of the dragons and his mate.

"Yep. I already know it is. That book is nasty. It stinks of death and darkness. Why would you have something so ugly, Andrew?"

"I thought I needed it, but I was wrong. What I need you to do is have Siobhan look at some of the pages from other books I hid between its pages. Those passages are not evil, not at all. They might actually help me talk to Emma. She does still want to talk to me, doesn't she?"

"Well, of course she does. She wants that real bad. That's what she and Aaron are fighting about."

Andrew growled under his breath and his dragon chuffed. The beast was right. This was what the traitor needed to prepare himself for. Everyone but his mate thought he was better off in Hell and out of their lives. They would've been right had he been the same old Andrew and hell, they were partially right now. He still held them responsible for what he'd suffered, no matter how many times he'd been told Aidan had come back for him, but none of that mattered right now. If he did, by some miracle, make it back to life, there was still gonna be hell to pay and the Tribunal would want to sentence him to death. It was all part of the gig and something he'd have to worry about later.

It seemed to take forever before Sydney spoke again, and this time she was whispering. *"Siobhan already found those pages. Pearce and Kyra are helping her translate them."* The little girl giggled. *"Ms. Siobhan just told them that you did good figuring out some of the old words, but your ancient language translation was way off in some places."*

Andrew had to chuckle with the little girl. A few weeks ago he would've ordered Siobhan Walsh's death for even suggesting he didn't know what he was talking about. Now? He wanted to kiss her on the cheek for figuring it out. *"Sydney, are Emma and Aaron still fighting?"*

"No. Shhhh. Ms. Siobhan is talking, and from the looks on everyone's faces, it is not good news."

"What do you mean, Sydney? Can you tell me what she's saying?"

"Gotta go, Andrew. Mom's on the way over. She'll be mad if she knows I'm talking to you. She said this is adult business. Pfft. What does she know?"

Andrew knew Sam was only trying to protect her daughter, and in an effort to show he was turning over a new leaf, he wanted to tell Sydney to do as her mother told her. But if he did that, the little he was able to keep up with Emma would be lost, and he knew it would be a matter of hours before he lost his ever-loving mind. He could, however, ask the child to contact him when things had quieted down.

He was about to do just that when there was a loud pop and he could suddenly hear what Siobhan was saying. "Will you please stop yelling at one another? With the help of Pearce and Kyra, I have corrected the translation of several of the pages Andrew had hidden in the old tome. These appear to have been torn from an ancient journal detailing prophecies of the future. Since all of you are here, I think you need to listen. It affects all of us in one way or another. For some of us, life will never be the same."

"Sounds like SSDD." A voice he recognized as Lance shouted.

"Yes, well, be that as it may, I am not professing to understand everything I've read, but some of it is very obvious. Whatever we don't figure out here tonight, I'll work on until we understand it all. Any questions before I start?"

A few seconds of silence and she spoke again, this time with a reverence to her voice that spoke to the sacredness of not only having a prophecy, but that they would be reading the old teaching as a group, the way they'd always meant to be read.

"A powerful white witch of long regal lineage sworn to the Earth, made whole by human love, must mate a dragon of royal descent, marked by devastating loss and the heart of not one clan but two.

"The vibria born of human parents who possesses the spirit of the last female born of two dragons, then lost in plain sight.

"Born to an extinct race, thought to be one but actually two. Both with destinies blessed by Fate, neither knowing the other exists, when reunited can nullify death to bring back the one needed to complete the circle.

"A calling to heal, a hidden nature, a history long forgotten... all protected in the heart of a woman destined to complete a warrior and his beast. The revelation of all she is brought forth from the joining with her mate.

"A complete circle of all called and confirmed, their mates and their families then increased by one, the twin of the warrior, also brother of the lost one, will become the Twelve–a whole, perfect, harmonious unit that will bring about the Great Miracle.

"When all is complete and the Miracle recognized, the Ancients will speak through the Special One and the Child. They will bless the Clan the color of the summer sky and the water when it is calm. This Clan and only this Clan, along with their mates as they become known, will battle the denizens of Hell and bring the Devil himself to his knees.

"If one of the Twelve is missing or the blessing is not completed, all hope is lost. Hell has won the war."

A collective 'son of a bitch' filled the cavern after a few seconds of complete silence, Andrew's included.

When I wanted to destroy the dragons I couldn't catch a break. Now, I want them alive and it looks like I'm gonna be responsible for their downfall after all. All the planning in the world can't beat dumb luck...

CHAPTER SIX

"Sorry I'm late to the party," Rayne called out as he entered the cavern and stopped dead in his tracks, looked around, and took a stance like he was ready to take action. "What the hell happened in here?" His voice had taken on a suspicious tone.

"Oh, nothing much," Aaron growled. "Siobhan found out that without Andrew, we've pretty much doomed dragon kin and probably the world. You know, nothing we can't handle. All in a day's work." Charlie, his mate, swatted his shoulder and gave him a look that said she would deal with him later.

"What the…?" Rayne couldn't even finish his sentence, just looked from one to the other of the Guardsmen of his Force.

"Yeah, that's pretty much the consensus, only we got a little more 'flowery' with our comments," Aidan confirmed, standing behind his mate as if to protect her and his unborn children from whatever was sure to come next.

Grumbling and whispers came from all around the room. Emma was just about to speak when Siobhan stepped forward. "All right, everyone. Now is the time to pull together and look for solutions, not blame."

Rian appeared behind Rayne with Carrick and Zachary in tow. "What did we miss?"

"I have found what I can only assume to be a prophecy. It has several components that have to do with 'the Special One and the Child' receiving a blessing from the Ancients that will be passed on to the Blue Dragons and allow them to fight, and I quote 'the denizens of Hell and the Devil himself'."

The oldest of them all, Zachary, stepped forward, heading directly to Siobhan. "Let me see what you've found, my dear."

The Elder Healer handed the older dragon the original parchment. Zachary nodded as he read. Emma held her breath and realized everyone else was doing the same thing. Carrick soon joined the two Elders, reading over his counterpart's shoulder. The tension in the room was palpable, and the longer the three Elders read, the worse it got, until Emma was finding it hard to breathe.

Finally, Zachary turned to the group, looking from one to the other of the Guardsmen and nodding when he was sure he had their attention. He smiled and began to explain. "I have heard rumor of this prophecy since I was a young man. It is daunting to know that it truly exists, but it is nothing we cannot handle. I have sent word to Malachi. It has been his life's work to study every occurrence of the Special Ones throughout our history. As for the others mentioned in the document, we can worry about that later. Just as you have been taught all of your lives…tackle what you know, the rest will fall into place. I have no doubt each of you has the heart to protect what means the most." The older gentlemen laid his fist to his chest. "And the brains to know what is important." He pointed to his temple. "I am sure Malachi will be able to guide us through what is to come."

The stunned awe on every face in the cavern would have been comical had the looks not come from cataclysmic news. No one spoke. No one moved. Emma wondered if they were breathing. In the years she'd spent with the dragons, she'd never been privy to the inner workings and wondered if Kyra had a spell to turn back time.

Being in the 'in-group' isn't all it's cracked up to be.

Carrick, someone Emma had always held in high esteem, added, "You must remember all your training. Dragons do not give up. We are the Universe's chosen and as such, She will constantly test our resolve, our strength, and our ability to join together in pursuit of a common goal. But She will never give us anything we cannot overcome."

Aidan was the first to regain his composure. "I understand what you're saying, but we're dancing around the obvious. Andrew is gone…dead. How can he be present? How can he accept the Blessing, let alone present it to the Blue Dragons if he is in Hell? Is there another Special One we don't know about?"

"But he's not." A tiny little voice came from the back of the room.

Acting as one and reminding Emma of marionettes, the entire group turned one hundred and eighty degrees and looked at the little girl that had just spoken. The beautifully bright child sat playing with her dolls as if she didn't have a care in the world.

Because she doesn't. Somehow the little beauty is hooked into the Universe more than any of us. She's got a behind the scenes look and isn't worried at all.

Sam and Lance were kneeling next to their daughter, obviously embarrassed at her outburst and asking what the child had meant. Emma caught movement out of the corner of her eye. Turning, she saw Carrick and Zachary making their way towards the family. Once there, both Elders sat down on the stone floor beside the child. Not something that happened every day.

Sydney looked up and smiled at both men before confirming her previous statement. "Andrew's not dead, least not all the way, and he's not in…" She stopped and looked at her mom, who smiled and nodded. "Hell," the little girl whispered.

Both Elders chuckled, then Zachary asked, "And how do you know that, Sydney?"

"First, I saw him but couldn't talk to him, then I got to talk to him. He's not so bad, ya' know?"

She crooked her index finger and made a 'come here' motion. When the Elders' faces were next to hers, she whispered, "He wants to come back really bad. Emma's his mate and he's worried something's gonna happen to her. I think he already kinda loves her and she's thinking about him lots." Sydney stopped and Emma wished she knew how to make herself invisible as everyone looked at her like she was crazy.

Why are they surprised? I told them we were mates. I even yelled in public.

"Where is he, Sydney? Can we talk to him?" Carrick asked, the authority of years of leadership making his words more resounding…more forceful.

"Andrew called it the Fades. Don't know what that is except for a dark, blank place. Andrew's dragon is there, too. He's not happy 'bout it at all. He chuffs a lot and blows smoke."

"I see," Zachary absentmindedly answered as he stood.

Emma heard commotion outside the cavern just a second before Malachi, the Spiritual Elder of their clan, appeared carrying three of the biggest books she'd ever seen. Without a word, he approached Siobhan and the two went directly to the Healer's workspace at the back of the room.

"Emma, can you come here?" Zachary asked, making her feel like she'd been called to the principal's office for playing hooky.

"Yes, sir," she said, hurrying to the Elder.

She'd barely stopped when he asked, "Can you feel him? Has he spoken to you?"

Nodding while she found her voice, she answered barely above a whisper, "I can feel him. Syd's right. He's stuck in the In-between."

"Looks like we better bring him back if we want to keep the status quo." He started to turn away then came back to face her. "How are you? I heard you finding out you had a mate was not easy for you."

"I'm fine, sir. It wasn't, but I'm okay. I just want him back."

Placing his hand on her shoulder, Zachary drew Emma into a hug. She was immediately swamped with feelings of warmth and comfort. When the Elder set her back, he looked into her eyes, smiled, and asked, "Do you know how truly special you are?"

Unsure what to say, she shook her head and waited, hoping Zachary would explain. Instead, he turned on his heel and headed to Siobhan and Malachi. Not sure what to do, Emma just looked around the room. Carrick was speaking with Rayne, Rian, Aaron, and Aidan, and from the looks on the twins' faces, it was not a happy conversation.

Continuing her surveillance, she found Kyra and Royce talking to Sam and Lance. It was obvious from the way the adults took turns looking at Sydney that the child was the topic of conversation. She wondered what they were talking about, and in the next heartbeat, could hear their conversation.

All right I'll ask questions later. Right now I need to know what they're talking about.

"There's absolutely nothing to worry about. I only need Sydney to sit with me and say the spell at the same time I do so I can scry for Andrew's location," Kyra explained.

"It's not you I'm worried about. Andrew already used her against us once. I'll have to kill him if he does it again." Lance paused and then added, "Well, kill him again, or still, or what the hell ever, you get what I'm saying. There's no way in this world or the next I'm letting that little piece of crap get his hands on her."

Emma was infuriated. She knew what they all thought of her mate, but to hear it with her own ears was tough and more than a little insulting. Here they all were faced with some crazy ass prophecy detailing the end of the world as they knew it and they were still bitching about Andrew.

Deciding she'd heard enough, Emma turned to go to Siobhan. Three steps towards her destination and she realized she could still hear everything everyone in the room was saying. It was completely disconcerting, not to mention that listening to all the bitching and complaining was giving her one hell of a migraine. Unable to deal with the chaos a second longer, she turned towards the door and exited as quickly as she could.

Winding through the corridors, she found an empty cavern lit by one white and one blue pillar candle surrounded by a circle of golden votive candles on a small, stone table. Pushed by the need for a few moments of blessed silence, Emma crossed the threshold and moved across the room to stand before the lights.

Staring into the flame of the white candle, she concentrated all of her energy on shutting out everything but the beating of her own heart. Thump…thump…thump. She'd always heard it was more of a whish sound, but in this case, it was most definitely a thump.

With the noise of everyone else's conversations silenced, Emma was finally able to focus, to think about all that had happened and what she feared would happen if they weren't able to stop the shit storm that was heading their way. For some reason she wasn't afraid as much as irritated that she'd spent so many years keeping her head down, living among the dragons but not truly with them. She'd always felt like an outsider looking in, someone they loved and accepted, but that was different nonetheless. But that all changed the moment she'd heard Andrew's voice in her head. It was not something she'd wanted, not something she'd ever dreamt of happening, but something she now embraced.

Something inside of her had come to life. Siobhan would call it her stronger self, and maybe the Elder Healer would be right, but it was more than that. More than knowing she, Emma Sinclair, had been created especially for another being. That she would bring light to not only a man that was meant to be her partner in every way but also to his dragon. Any other time she would've felt trapped, like she was stuck in a situation she had no control over and was being made to live someone else's life, but it was just the opposite. For the first time she was actually living, not just existing. Her soul was free and becoming stronger by the day.

The pain she'd shared with Andrew had been worth it, and she would suffer it again if it meant having him back and having the opportunity to get to know him. To see if all the talk about Fate not being denied was the truth or just something left over from a long forgotten time.

Still staring into the flame, watching it flicker, she saw her mate's mismatched eyes that seemed to be trying to tell her something, then those same eyes set about the snout of a great black dragon. Emma was sure the O'Briens were silver dragons. As a matter of fact she knew they were from the jewelry she'd made for both Grace and Charlie. How then was it possible for Andrew's piercing eyes to have been looking at her from the face of a huge black beast?

Not sure what it all meant, and not ready to go back to the chaos in the other room, Emma sat cross-legged on the stone floor and was just about to begin meditating when Aaron called her name from the corridor.

"In here," she answered, trying not to sound irritated. Standing, she turned just as he entered the room.

"We've been looking all over for you. You've been gone for almost three hours." The Guardsman stood just inside the doorway, avoiding eye contact while trying to act nonchalant.

"Three hours? Time flies…"

The old Emma would've acted like nothing out of the ordinary was wrong and left the room, letting the brooding Guardsman off the hook for his behavior. The new Emma, however, wanted to know what was going on.

"Well, here I am. What's up?"

"Malachi, Siobhan, and Zachary have found something." He turned to go, but Emma was not about to be dissuaded.

Closing the distance between them in record time, she placed her hand on his shoulder. "No, I mean what is going on with you?"

"Nothing. Well, nothing more than having to find a way to bring my little brother back from the dead. The little brother who just happens to have terrorized everyone and everything I hold dear for the last ten years. The part that I just can't wrap my head around is why him? Why is the piece of shit that tried to ruin the world the one person we have to have to save it? None of this shit makes any sense. It goes against everything I believed in, fought for, and wanted to achieve my whole life." He spun around, and for the first time in all the years she'd known Aaron, she could see uncertainty in his eyes.

"Oh! Let me not forget." It was his turn to place his hand on her shoulder. "I found out that one of the best people I've ever known, a woman I think of like a little sister, is his mate. I should be happy for you. I want to be happy for you, but instead, I'm freaked the fuck out.

"If we do succeed in bringing him back, you and he will sooner or later be officially mated. It's already started. I see the signs. With him back on the earthly plane, there will be nothing to stop it. But I am so damned afraid he will destroy you like he destroys everything he touches.

"The worst part of all of this mess is that I should want to have my brother back. I should want to have him mated and happy. I should want to believe that he can change. But the truth is I don't. I don't believe he can be anything but the selfish, evil prick he's been since the night he disappeared.

"I'm sorry for what he endured. I'm sorry we couldn't find him, but none of that justifies what he did. He should have to pay for every person he injured and for every life he took. He should…"

"Aaron, Emma, please come into the main cavern." Siobhan's tone left no room for argument, and before Emma could tell Aaron their conversation was not over, the asshole disappeared. She promised herself to find him later and finish what they'd started.

I really hate how fast they can move.

Malachi began to speak as soon as she crossed the threshold. "As Zachary explained, I've made it my life's work to study the Special Ones and their impact on our race. Early in Andrew's life I was blessed enough to have been present when the Ancient, Shavon, spoke to him. At the time I had no idea how important that visit was, not only to Andrew, but to Emma and our kin."

The Elder was now looking at her as he spoke. "I must ask you this question in front of the leadership of our clan and that of the Blue Dragons. Do you, Emma Sinclair, mate of Andrew O'Brien, want to save your mate?"

Emma was confused. She immediately began to nod her head before the words were completely formed in her mind. She opened her mouth to speak and slammed her lips together. A knowing smile brightened Malachi's face. She gasped and then rushed to get the words out. "I have to want to save him of my own free will, right? That's what the Ancient said! Yes! Yes! Yes! I want to save him! I want to save my friends! I want to save my family! I want to save the dragons! Just tell me what to do."

"We have our work cut out for us, but I believe you're just the girl that can do it, Emma." Malachi's confidence made her stand taller and filled her with hope. It must've worked for everyone else, too, because for the first time that day, everyone had a smile on their face.

Emma followed the Elders, Siobhan, and Kyra out of the clinic. They were headed to the Cave of the Ancients. Malachi and Zachary had decided it was the only place strong enough to prepare the ceremony to bring Andrew back. As they were exiting the cavern, she heard Carrick instruct Aaron and Aidan to bring their brother's body along as well. A quick look over her shoulder and Emma had to smile. They wanted to be upset, she could see how hard they were trying, but not even two of the toughest Guardsmen she'd ever known could hide the hope they felt that maybe…just maybe, their brother would do what was right.

Don't worry boys, he will. I just know he will.

CHAPTER SEVEN

Emma collapsed across her bed still clothed, too tired to even remove her tennis shoes. The last three days had been some of the hardest of her life. Every waking minute had been spent poring over musty old textbooks searching for the Ancient Dragon Rite for Soul Reclamation and checking to make sure there were no changes in Andrew's body.

Zachary and Malachi had explained over and over that the ritual they were looking for contained some of the oldest and most potent dragon magic ever recorded. Siobhan had added that it could only be used when the soul of a dragon shifter had been taken before its time and only when the body remained.

Sometime the day before, one of the young healers, Shannon, had come running into Malachi's chamber lugging a huge tome, saying he'd found the ritual. After several hours, the Elders determined it was indeed what they needed and had set to work to modify the ancient spell. Kyra and Siobhan worked tirelessly alongside the Elders. Even Kyra's Aunt Della and two of their coven elders had come to help and lend their power.

After the third time Emma had nodded off when she was supposed to be reading, Siobhan had ordered her to go home and get some rest. The young jeweler's argument had been half-hearted. No matter how much she wanted to help, Emma was exhausted and seeing double. Reluctantly, she said her goodnights and even let one of the young Guardsmen-in-training escort her home.

Sleep came quickly and, for the first night since Andrew's arrival at the lair, there were no dreams, at least not that she remembered. So when the sun shining through the gap in her curtains touched her face, Emma was ready for whatever the day held. If all went as planned, she would have Andrew back, and Malachi would be able to tell them who the others named in the Prophecy were.

Nervous and excited, she all but ran to the Cave of the Ancients. Sure everyone would be starving, she stopped at the bakery and the deli and was weighed down with enough food to feed an army. Apparently, someone else had the same idea. The small table they had been working on was covered with baked goods, coffee, and tea while the counter farther behind that had bags of unpacked food.

Kyndel, Rayne's mate, came around the corner with their son, Jay, on her hip, chatting to her best friend, the very pregnant Grace. "Great minds think alike, huh?" Grace chuckled, pointing at the bags Emma was carrying as she took a seat in the first available chair. "You don't happen to have some turkey and Swiss cheese in one of those bags do you? I'm not sure if it's me or the babies, but we really want a sandwich."

"I sure do. I bought some of everything the butcher had and grabbed all the bread that was ready, too. I figured y'all would be hungry."

"Do I smell food?" Royce asked, sniffing the air as he entered the room. "I'm starving."

"Me, too," Lance echoed, right on the huge Guardsman's heels.

"How are you two starving already? You were just in here less than twenty minutes ago eating everything in sight." Kyndel laughed, setting Jay on the floor and helping Emma unpack her bags.

"Research makes me hungry," they answered in unison then burst out laughing.

Emma couldn't help but smile. This was how she remembered her friends: happy, laughing, giving each other a hard time. The last week had been hard on everyone and was about to get a lot more difficult, so it was nice to know that at least for a little while they could have fun.

For the next few minutes people filed in, looking for food, until the room was wall to wall bodies and Emma was feeling a little claustrophobic. Deciding it was probably the last time she'd be able to visit with Andrew before all hell broke loose, she quietly made her way down the corridor and into the room where his body lay.

Making her way to his side, she zeroed in on his chest, watching it carefully, praying against all odds that she would see movement. That by some miracle of the Heavens Andrew would be alive. She knew it was silly. Knew that the only way that was going to happen was through the spell they would be working as soon as the New Moon was high in the sky.

Running her fingers through his dark hair, Emma marveled at the softness and grinned as a few stray curls tickled the palm of her hand. She straightened the sheet that covered his body then just stood looking at his handsome face. The O'Brien family resemblance was unmistakable. All three men had the same strong jawbone, same high cheekbones, and same full lips. She wondered if Andrew would have some of the same facial expressions. Would he furrow his brow and turn down one side of his mouth like Aaron? Would he raise one eyebrow and try to get her to tell a secret she'd sworn not to like Aidan? Would he get a twinkle in his eye when he was about to say something funny?

Lost in thought, Emma jumped when Aidan appeared at her side. She started to ask what he was doing there but the look on his face stilled her words. It was as if he couldn't decide whether to be happy or sad. His eyes were just slightly squinted, extenuating the laugh lines. The corners of his mouth were just barely turned up, like he wanted to smile but just couldn't let himself. His head was tilted to the side as if he was contemplating something life altering, which considering what they were all about to do made perfect sense.

His voice was so soft and low when he spoke that she almost didn't hear him. "Did I ever tell you that we called him Drew when we were growing up?" He nodded his head and grinned, not waiting for her reply before continuing.

"His favorite game when we were kids was pirates. He loved pretending that we were sailing across the sea on a massive ship like the ones we'd watch come in and out of the port. Aar was always the Captain because he was the oldest. I always ended up being the Sailing Master, the Captain's second and the one in charge of navigation. Drew was the Master Gunner and no matter what, always had us manning the cannons or grabbing our swords and storming the deck of a pirate's ship to save the damsel in distress. No matter what, we all three always lived to fight another day."

He paused for so long that she looked up to find him shaking his head. He grabbed her hand and held tight when he finally began speaking again. "As we got older, pretend turned to reality as Dad started our training. Drew was so pissed when Aar and I got real steel blades on our fourteenth birthdays and he still had to use the wooden practice ones. I felt bad, so when I was sure no one else was around, I would let him use mine. That's probably how he got to be such a fantastic swordsman.

"The day we left for training was the day before Drew's fourteenth birthday. I convinced Mom and Dad to celebrate early. That night we had a huge party, partly for his birthday and partly for our departure. No matter how long I live, I'll never forget the look on his face when he opened his present and found his very own steel blade."

Emma could see that Aidan was lost in his memory and simply held his hand while he reminisced. His voice cracked and he had to start over twice before getting the words out, but what he said made her heart hurt for all the brothers. "He walked with Aar and me to the end of the forest where we met Royce, our guide to our new home, this lair...this clan. It was so hard to say goodbye to my little brother, but Drew was tough as nails. He hugged us both, patted us on the back, and told us he would take care of our home while we were gone. It was the hardest goodbye of our lives. He tried to break our private connection, but I had always been better at the mental aspect of our natures than either of my brothers, so I stayed connected. I felt what it cost him to stay strong and knew the minute he'd thought he was far enough away to break down. I never told him I knew he cried that day. Maybe I should've, maybe things would've been different.

"Years later when Drew came here for training, it was as if the Three Amigos had been reunited. We trained hard, played hard, and fought harder, but one thing remained true: we all three always lived to fight another day. At least that was the case before I let him get captured."

Emma searched for the words that would make Aidan feel better, but only came up with empty platitudes that she knew he'd heard a thousand times. The Guardsman turned and speared her with a steely gaze full of so many emotions, she immediately felt overwhelmed. "Everything, and I mean everything, is about to change. I should tell you that I'm sorry the Universe and Fate have put you in this position, but I'd be lying. Drew's gonna need somebody on his side. Somebody with a good heart and a good head on her shoulders that will stand up to him and for him.

"I wish it could be me, but I just can't get over the things he's done. I'll always love him, but he's put us through hell. Don't be mistaken, I'm not angry anymore. I'm just not ready to hand him a sword and show him my back. Plus, I have Grace and the twins to think of. I can't take a chance he'd hurt them to get back at me.

"Aaron's still angry and probably always will be. The others are mad, but mostly out of respect for us. Which I know sounds stupid, but hey, we're testosterone laden meatheads ninety percent of the time, so what do you really expect?" He chuckled, sounding more like himself.

Emma wanted to tell him that Andrew was different now. That she could feel it in her heart and soul. That he truly wanted to make amends for what he'd done. But she somehow knew Aidan wasn't ready to hear that just yet. Knew he would think it was simply the ramblings of his brother's mate and that she didn't know Andrew well enough to make that call.

Before she could dwell any longer, Kyra called to them. "Come on y'all. We need to get this show on the road."

"Thanks for listening, Em. Remember, if you ever need anything, I'm here." He pulled her into a quick hug before leaving the room.

In the passageway they met up with Lance, who was looking less than thrilled with his new position. "I'm in charge of directing people to the large grotto at the farthest corner of the cave. Seems I'd make a good butler." He rolled his eyes and Emma couldn't hold back her laughter.

"That you would. Are you up for hire after this engagement?" she asked, putting on her best British accent.

"You better watch it, kiddo," he growled while winking and trying to hide his smile.

She chuckled as they walked in the direction they'd been instructed and soon caught up with Grace. Aidan scooped her up in his arms and kissed her soundly on the lips, effectively cutting off her surprised shriek. Their kiss was short and made Emma smile, but it was Grace's comment that made her laugh out loud.

"You better be careful, dragon daddy. You're gonna make me go into labor."

"Good, I'm ready to see my sons."

"You ready to change all those diapers?" Grace chuckled

"Okay, okay, you win. I'll be careful, but I'm still gonna carry you. Those poor little feet of yours look like they could use a break."

"Thank you, dear heart. You're the best." Grace kissed Aidan on the cheek.

"All right, love birds, get it moving. Kyra's about to have a heart attack. She said we have to be ready by the time the New Moon has risen." Royce chuckled, slapping Aidan on the back as they passed the gentle giant.

"Just wait till Kyra's pregnant. Paybacks are a bitch," Aidan teased.

"Yeah, but twins don't run in my family," Royce answered.

"But triplets do in ours," Kyra's Aunt Della added to the conversation, winking at Emma conspiratorially as they entered the massive cavern where the ritual was to take place.

Laughter echoed off every surface while all Royce could do was stand dumbfounded, looking at his mate for some type of denial. Her little grin and shrug said it all. Someday in the future there were most certainly going to be some powerful dragon, witch, or mixed children running around the lair.

Serves the grumpy old dragon right. Three at a time, Grandpa.

Looking around the grotto, Emma was amazed at the incredible transformation that had taken place in just the short time she'd been with Andrew and Aidan. Everywhere she looked, every available surface held a grouping of three candles. Kyra had explained earlier in the day that the yellow one was for concentration, the large white one in the center was for balance and represented the Heavens and the Goddess of all, and the peach one was for restoration and rejuvenation.

Each grouping of luminaries was surrounded at the base by flowers, herbs, and most importantly, chips of the White Ash tree, the most magically powerful of all trees and the root of power for white witches the world over. A circle of salt and White Ash dust encircled the pond of water and most of the area of the floor, only leaving room for the participants of the ritual to form a circle around the outside.

Earlier in the day, Kyra, Aunt Della, and Siobhan had decided upon the best order for the attendees to stand. They said it would increase the power of the Sacred Circle and give them the boost they needed to complete the rite. Quietly and quickly, everyone took their positions while Kyra, Siobhan, and Aunt Della stood at the head of the Circle in silent prayer.

The moment the last person stepped into place, Kyra lifted her head and looked around the Circle, making eye contact with each person. She began speaking the spell while Aunt Della stood on her left with a golden candle for increased communication, and Siobhan stood on her right with a purple candle for ancient wisdom.

"Dear Heavens, Goddess of All, and Ancients of Dragon Kin,

"We pray for your guidance and blessings on this ritual as we seek to return the spirit of our Special One to his physical body. He was taken from us long before his time and has paid his dues to King Minos, ruler of the Fades and the City of Woe. We ask not only for those that called him family, but for the whole of dragon kin.

"His mate, the one the Universe created for him and him alone, has come of her own free will to beg favor from You three Most Sacred to return her beloved to her. She accepts the full weight and responsibility of her request. She promises to stay by his side, provide the unconditional support as only a mate can, opening her heart and soul to him completely and without reservation.

"We ask your favor and thank you for your blessings of yesterday, today, and those we pray to receive in the future. We have only the lives you have given us to offer as proper sacrifice and offer them freely when you call us home.

"Blessed be, blessed be."

The last word had barely been spoken when wind blew from every direction, howling down the corridors, forcing its way into the grotto and extinguishing every candle, leaving the participants in total darkness. Emma closed her eyes and held her breath waiting for the wind to calm, but after several minutes, decided it might never stop.

Opening her eyes, she was shocked that total darkness remained, but she was able to see as if it were daylight. Looking around the Circle, Emma saw all the Guardsmen looking around as well, making sure everyone was all right. She was glad to see they had all listened to Kyra and kept their hands clasped. The white witch had told them that breaking the Circle would break the magic and they would have to wait until the next New Moon to try the ritual again. Time they did not have.

Worried that they were still drenched in darkness while the wind continued to whip away at them, Emma was just about to speak when the water, which until that moment had remained calm, began to bubble and froth. A light shined brightly from its depths as the water began to spin, creating a whirlpool. Water hovered several feet below the rim of the whirlpool, creating an empty platform that begged her to ask…for what or whom?

The light, which until now had stayed well below the water's surface, rose quickly towards the top, breaking the surface and bathing the entire cavern in a bright white light. Not wanting to break the Circle but needing to shield her eyes from the illumination, Emma squinted as tightly as she could without completely closing her eyes.

As the group looked on, a tall ethereal woman, with hair the color of sunshine and beautifully blue translucent skin the color of the ocean, rose from the water. The name *Shavon* whispered through Emma's mind, and somehow she knew that was the name of the woman in the water. Behind Shavon, the platform that had been empty now held the transparent figure of an unconscious man. The light emanating from the woman dimmed, making the features of the man immediately distinguishable.

Andrew!

Emma froze, unable to do anything but gape, while the woman turned, took a step back, and knelt next to what Emma could only reason was Andrew's spirit. The water that had calmed when the woman sat on the platform now bubbled with even more vigor than before. The light below the surface dimmed and appeared to have been covered by something very large and very dense.

From one heartbeat to the next, the image of a huge silver dragon appeared. So large and commanding that he filled every available inch of the massive cavern. Every Guardsman, including the Elders, dropped to one knee and bowed their heads. Emma hadn't known it was possible, but she watched the huge beast smile as he took in the show of respect he received.

His voice was low and shook the rocks as he spoke. "Hello, my children. Please rise. You honor me with your presence and your request. For those of you that do not know me, I am Alarick. I am called the First Dragon because I am the King responsible for the birth of the dragon shifters."

Holy crap! No wonder they all bowed.

"I have brought the First Elder, Shavon, with me to bring the spirit of your Special One home. Will his mate please come forward?"

On shaky legs, Emma made her way to the edge of the pool. "Thank you, Emma Sinclair, for giving of yourself to bring one of my children home. I feel your commitment and strength of will. Andrew has a true mate in you. A mate that not only shares his heart and soul but his nature. I give my blessing. Know, dear child, should you ever have need of my help, you only need come to this holy place and call my name. I will always come. Now, please accompany Shavon to your mate."

Emma could only nod and watch as Shavon lifted Andrew's spirit into her arms and walked across the water. Together they took the last few steps to the pallet Aidan and Aaron had laid their brother's body upon. The Elder knelt carefully beside Andrew's lifeless body, holding his spirit just above. Leaning forward, Shavon said a verse Emma would remember until the day she died.

Return to your body,
Return to your life.
Do not waste your gifts,
Live a life free of strife.

The Elder lowered Andrew's spirit into his body then laid her forehead to his. Her hair came alive around them, cocooning all three in a warm, bright light. Emma heard music as the power grew within their bubble. Shavon repeated the verse from before, ending with *'A bheannaigh'*, 'Be blessed' in the ancient language of the dragons. The singing stopped, the light extinguished, and the Elder's hair unwound, returning to beautiful long waves cascading down her back.

Shavon stood, smiled down at Emma, and said directly into her mind, "Be blessed, Emma Sinclair. You are the best of us. When your mate wakes, you will understand the Prophecy and be able to call those mentioned by name."

Quicker than Emma's eyes could track, Shavon returned to her place in front of King Alarick. The Dragon King once again addressed everyone in attendance. "Golden Fire Clan, Blue Thunder Clan, you hold great favor with the Heavens and the Ancients. Never forget who you are and who you are destined to be. Le creideamh an ancients agus beannú na flaithis a bheith go maith."

The Dragon King's great wings spread wide before he wrapped them around Shavon and together they descended back into the water. The light below them went out, the water stilled, and the candles all around the cavern were once again lit, showing everyone's looks of shock and awe.

Before she could ask 'What the hell', a voice she'd prayed to hear but feared she never would, sounded in her mind.

"Emma? Emma, are you there? Are you okay?"

CHAPTER EIGHT

He had no idea how long he'd been unconscious. Andrew only remembered the feel of intense heat and the sensation of falling before calling to Emma, and for the first time in what seemed like forever, getting a response. After he'd heard her voice, felt her hands on his face, smelled the beautiful scent of daffodils, and knew she was not a figment of his imagination, he'd slipped back into unconsciousness without a word.

The way his body felt, he'd been lying on a relatively hard surface for three or four days. His vision was blurry, allowing him to barely make out white walls, silver counters, and what he thought were glass faced cabinets lining one wall. There didn't appear to be any windows, but his field of vision was limited so he couldn't be sure.

Turning his head to the right, his cheek brushed the rough, scratchy cotton of the pillow, causing the reality of his situation to come rushing at him. She had done it! Emma had freed him from the Fades!

Suddenly he was completely awake, hyperaware, and wanted to see Emma in the flesh. Grabbing the rails of his bed, Andrew pulled himself to a semi-sitting position, only to be pushed back down by skull-splitting pain. Black dots danced before his eyes as he struggled to catch his breath. His stomach rolled and he was sure that if he'd had anything to eat it would have made its presence known as well.

His eyes slid closed as he took several deep breaths, trying to regain the balance he'd felt just a few seconds ago. Commotion just out of his line of sight alerted him to the fact that he was about to receive visitors. Praying it was Emma, Andrew was sorely disappointed when the scent of male dragon and frustration reached his senses, along with at least four sets of footsteps.

Carrick, Rayne, Aaron, and Aidan soon surrounded his bed, and from the looks on their faces, they were not happy to see him.

Okay, this is what you expected. You're back for Emma, not them. They're the fuckers that started all the bullshit. Try to keep your mouth shut until you see your mate.

As pep talks went, it wasn't great, but it was all he had. Andrew had never been a smooth talker. More times than not, he'd ended up with his foot in his mouth or dodging punches from some guy he'd offended. Time had not given him wisdom or tempered his explosive reactions– quite the opposite. He was worse than ever. He knew it and had it been any other time, any other situation, or another person than his Emma that had been the catalyst for his present standoff with four of the most imposing Guardsmen in history, he would've come out swinging. Instead, he was chanting her name over and over in his head.

Carrick was the first to speak, his tone that of a father disappointed in his wayward son. "As hard as it may be for you to believe, Andrew, I am happy to have you back among us."

Andrew was proud of himself for not laughing in the face of the Leader of the Red Fire Clan, but knew his face displayed his doubt at the truth of the Elder's statement. Carrick's brow furrowed. "You can believe whatever you like, but it is never easy for a leader to lose one of his clan. Yours was especially difficult." The leader cleared his throat. "It is my sincerest wish that we can come to some sort of cease fire after we have handled the task at hand."

Unable to stay silent any longer and feeling like there was more going on than he knew about, Andrew asked, "And what might that 'task at hand' be?"

His tone was sharp and filled with suspicion. Aaron immediately growled low in his throat, "Watch your tone, traitor."

Shock didn't begin to describe Andrew's reaction when Carrick turned to Aaron with a sharp reprimand. "If you cannot control your temper, then you need to remove yourself from the room."

Andrew saw how much it cost his brother to give a sharp nod and take a step back from the bed. His first reaction was to laugh and tease the oldest O'Brien, but quickly held his tongue when the scent of daffodils invaded his senses. His dragon, which had remained oddly quiet, even when the man had felt threatened, came to life. The beast chuffed and all but purred, trying to get close to the woman that had stopped just inside the door with a look of disgust on her face.

When she spoke, Andrew wanted to cheer her on, but once again held his tongue. "What is going on in here?" Her tone was low and suspicious, her brows furrowed over her deep brown eyes, and her mouth pursed tight, like she'd just eaten an especially sour lemon.

Aidan, always the mediator, was the first to speak, infusing his words with calm and patience. "Nothing nefarious. Relax, Em. We're here to talk to Andrew about his knowledge of the Prophecy and the Blessing."

Andrew knew his brother well enough, even after all the years they'd been separated, to know he was leaving something important out. Something that made Aidan uncomfortable. Andrew wanted to latch onto that knowledge and ferret the real reason they were there out of one of the bastards, but that would not do in front of his mate. This was the first time in her adult life they were meeting, and he wanted it to be as special as it could be, despite the circumstances.

The thought had no sooner crossed his mind than Emma's eyes met his. She winked an almost indiscernible wink while holding his gaze. He wondered if she'd heard his thoughts. The slightest of nods from his beautiful mate confirmed she had and he had to hold back the smile that threatened to cross his face. It would not do for the dragons to think he was having a good time.

Emma looked back at Aidan, who was still waiting for her response. "Okay, Aidan, but he's just awoken after being unconscious for three days. Oh yeah! And in case you forgot…before that he came back from the dead."

More than anything Andrew wanted to jump off the bed and take Emma into his arms. She was absolutely fabulous. Not only was she gorgeous and sexy and more than he knew he deserved, but she had sass and spunk and wasn't afraid to speak her mind. He could tell these were new facets to her personality and that she was working hard not to back down from the stance she'd taken. He poured confidence through their mating bond, hoping to help her stand her ground.

"Yes, Em, but there are things we need to discuss with Andrew. It won't take long and then we'll leave him to rest." Aidan was growing more uncomfortable with the situation, which sent up red flags for Andrew. His older brother had never been good with deception, something time had not changed.

Andrew decided to wait and see what was really going on. He let his thoughts drift to Emma and watched her shoulders relax. She really was special and so much more than he knew he deserved.

"All right, get your discussion out of the way, but I'm staying."

A quick glance between the Guardsmen confirmed Andrew's original misgivings, there was definitely something big in the works. Aidan reluctantly nodded. Not that it mattered, since Emma had already moved a chair to his bedside and was making herself comfortable.

"I'm glad that's been decided. Now, if we may proceed?" Carrick asked and continued before anyone responded.

Must be nice being the boss…

"Siobhan has studied the ancient text you were carrying when you…when we found you."

Good catch, old boy. You wouldn't want to remind me that you captured me just when you are about to ask for my help, now would you?

With only a split second to regain his composure, Carrick continued. "She has been able to decipher many of your notes and complete the translation of what Zachary has identified as the Hell Fire Prophecy. Are you familiar with its contents, and more importantly, the part you play in it?"

Andrew shook his head. "I knew I was translating something ancient, but I never had enough of it in one place at one time to ascertain what it was or what it could be used for. I certainly never saw anything that led me to believe I had anything to do with it."

Rayne handed a page from a yellow legal pad to Andrew that had handwriting covering most of one side. It didn't go without the traitor's notice that Rayne pulled back as if burnt when their hands accidently bumped.

Afraid you might catch some good sense and a backbone, Commander?

Shaking his head while reading the document, Andrew would've fallen down had he not already been in bed, when he read "…the Ancients will speak through the Special One and the Child. They will bless the Clan the color of the summer sky and the water when it is calm."

"Son of a bitch! I knew it was something crazy, but damn." He looked up from the paper and asked, "So, do you know who the others are?"

Shaking his head, Carrick quickly answered, "No, it appears only Emma knows."

Andrew's head spun to look at his mate, whose cheeks were immediately red with embarrassment. His dragon chuffed with the need to comfort their mate, and Andrew had to admit he had a lot to learn about having a mate, but that would have to wait until they were alone.

Her voice seemed far away as she began to explain. The more she talked the more shocked he was, and then she dropped the biggest bomb of all. Even bigger than the spirit of the first dragon appearing at his resurrection. "So, Shavon said that when you woke up, I would understand the Prophecy and know who the other people that it described were. But you're awake and I have no clue."

Andrew thought for just a moment. If he had learned one thing in all his magical dabbling, whether it was light, dark, and everything in between, things were never as 'mystical' as they seemed. It was better to take the words at face value. With that in mind, he asked, "What exactly did she say, mo chroi'?"

Where the hell did that come from? I've never called anyone my heart.

Unaware of his internal struggles, Emma answered right away. "She said, 'Be blessed, Emma Sinclair. You are the best of us. When your mate wakes, you will understand the Prophecy and be able to call those mentioned by name'." She unconsciously rubbed her wrist while she spoke, as if it itched, not so much that it was a bother, just something she endured.

"I see," was his only response. He replayed her words in his head, never losing eye contact with his mate. They were definitely straightforward, nothing flowery or misleading, so he, like Emma, had to wonder why she didn't know now that he was awake.

"What does it mean?" Aaron gruffly asked. "Do you even know or are you just stalling? Trying to think of a way to use what you know to barter your freedom? Give it up, little brother. That ship has sailed. Your ass is gonna do whatever you have to do to receive that Blessing and pass it on to the Blue Dragons. I will make damn sure of it with everything in me and with my dying breath. And when you have done every single thing required of you, you are going back to your cell to await the Tribunal, and I pray to the Heavens they kill you slowly." Venom spewed from every word Aaron was growling. The oldest O'Brien brother leaned down until he was nose to nose with Andrew and spat, "You will pay for every fucking thing you did, traitor."

Before Andrew could say a word, Emma shot up, her chair skittering across the floor and crashing into the far wall from the force of her action. He watched, unable to move, as she flew at his older brother, her palms making contact with his chest with such force that Aaron had to take a step back or find himself on his ass. She roared like a mother dragon protecting her nest and attempted to close the distance between she and the one that had threatened her mate. Thankfully, Aidan sped around the bed, grabbed her around the waist, sprung her away from Aaron, and attempted to calm her.

Not to be deterred, Emma kicked Aidan's legs while pummeling his arm with her fists, all the while screaming, "Over my dead body will you lock up my mate, Aaron O'Brien! You spineless bastard! Come in here after all he's been through! No fucking way! All of you get the hell out of here! I swear to the Heavens I will tear apart anyone that dares touch him! Get out! GET OUT! GET THE HELL OUT NOW!!!!"

A crowd was forming outside Andrew's room. For the first time since he'd left the lair all those years ago, the voices of all the Guardsmen came alive in his mind. Carrick was calling for Siobhan. Aaron was standing dumbfounded, not sure if he should be pissed or embarrassed that a girl had gotten the drop on him. Rayne was frantically calling Kyndel, sure she could talk Emma down, and yelling for Lance to bring Sam with the hopes of sedating her. Someone, he couldn't tell who, called out to Devon to come right away and bring Royce and Kyra.

Surprisingly, it was Aidan that was the calmest while he took one hell of a beating from a very pissed off Emma. He spoke directly to Andrew through their unique link, that until that moment, Andrew had forgotten existed. "She needs you. You are her mate and the only one that can get through to her. You have to take her from me and calm her. I'm not sure how or why, but she's acting like a fully mated dragon shifter protecting her nest. I've tried to reach her through mindspeak, but she can't or won't hear me."

Andrew nodded, pushing the side rail of his bed down while calling to Emma in the calmest voice possible. "Emma, mo chroi', you need to relax. You're gonna hurt Aidan or worse yet, yourself. Just chill. We'll work it all out. Aaron was just being a dick."

He continued to speak to his mate as his brother slowly, painstakingly, moved the ten feet to the bedside, taking extra care not to hurt or drop Emma. Andrew could feel Aidan's concentration and commitment to keeping her safe and had to admit, Aidan was not the complete and total monster he'd made him out to be for all those years. Just another bit of information Andrew would have to think about later.

"Okay, you ready? This is gonna be tricky. You're gonna take the brunt of her fists and feet. There's no way to get her to you without just laying her across you and the bed, and bro, your girl is strong."

Andrew nodded. "Just do it. She's gonna hurt herself. She can't hear me either. We have to get this…this…whatever the hell it is stopped."

Without another word, Aidan took the last step, and with incredible dexterity, pushed the flailing young woman into Andrew's arms. Both man and beast embraced their mate, not caring that she was losing her mind, just reveling in the fact that they finally had her in their arms. A feeling until that very moment, Andrew had been sure he would never feel.

Their skin touched and electricity sparked all over and throughout Andrew's body, lighting him up from the inside out. His dragon roared for the first time in nearly ten years and stood to his full height in Andrew's mind's eye. The black beast pushed with a strength Andrew had thought destroyed by black magic, trying to reach his mate.

Emma felt it, too. All motion stopped, her mouth hung open, and her eyes widened. Her instantaneous shock stopped her tirade for a just split second. It was all the time Andrew needed. Without thought he slammed his lips to hers–their union unlike anything he'd experienced in all his almost hundred years.

What had started as a way to distract Emma quickly became the joining of their souls. Her hands flew to his head, her nails scratched his scalp as she held him as close as possible. His hands gripped her ample bottom, pushing their bodies as closely together as they could be while still clothed. They ate at one another's lips. Andrew was unable to distinguish where he ended and she began, and all he could think was…more!

Somewhere in the distance he heard the click of a door shutting and a lock being thrown, but he couldn't care. As long as he had Emma, there was nothing and no one else that mattered. She began to ride his growing erection and the need to feel her naked skin against his became his single focus.

Sliding his hands under the hem of her light green T-shirt, he ripped it over her head. Grinning as she moaned at the loss before returning to his lips. The brief glance he'd gotten of her ample breasts overflowing the white lace of her bra made him lightheaded. Her hands left his hair, her tiny nails scratching the sides of his neck, across his collarbone, and down his chest. They found purchase just above his nipples and dug into his pecs, causing his hips to jerk against hers. Emma moaned low in her throat, riding his sheet covered cock with renewed vigor.

Reaching around her back he unhooked her bra, massaged up her back to her shoulders, and carefully slid the straps down her arms. Leaving her mouth, he kissed along her jawline and reveled in the fact that his Emma threw her head to the side to allow him greater access. Reaching her ear, he sucked her earlobe between his teeth and worried it with the tip of his tongue until she was mewling his name. He nipped the tender spot right behind her ear and worked his way down her neck, kissing and tasting until he thought he might drown in her scent.

At the tender spot where the soft skin of her neck met the curve of her shoulder, he lavished it with his tongue while she moaned his name low and long. Unable to stop himself or his dragon, Andrew bit down with enough force to leave a mark but not break the skin. Emma screamed her release over and over, making him smile against her silky skin. His only regret was that he hadn't been inside her for the experience.

As she began to return from the clouds, Andrew licked and kissed his mark, relieving any residual pain she felt. He knew it was not permanent, but prayed that with any luck she would one day wear his mark for all to see. Emma collapsed unto his chest, boneless and satisfied. He kissed the top of her head and was just about to roll them over to rest when she began to shake.

Thinking she was cold, he reached for the blanket but never made it. Emma sat straight up, eyes rolled back in her head, mouth opened wide, and made a shrill whining noise that reminded him of a wounded animal. Needing to comfort his mate, Andrew pulled her to his chest, wrapped his arms around her, and tried to stop her shaking.

His ministrations had the opposite effect. The instant their chests touched, Emma went into full blown convulsions, shaking so badly he thought she would break apart. Fearing for her life, he did the only thing he could think of…he yelled for help.

The next thirty minutes happened in the blink of an eye, but the continuous replay in his head was in slow motion. People came from every direction. Aidan pried his arms from around Emma, explaining that Andrew had to let go so Siobhan and Zachary could help his mate. Devon and Royce gently lifted her off his chest while he screamed for them to be careful. Charlie and Sam rushed into the room with a woman who smelled of magic that he didn't know. He later found out she was a nurse who worked at the hospital with them.

People were giving instructions, others were yelling demands, and still others were demanding answers…answers Andrew didn't have. All he could do was concentrate all his energy towards Emma. He spoke through their link, constantly reminding her that she was his reason for living and how proud he was of her while pouring every ounce of strength and healing power both he and his dragon possessed into her.

His last glimpse of her beautiful face was as they covered it with an oxygen mask right before wheeling her from the room.

She has to live! Dammit, she just has to.

CHAPTER NINE

Emma had been in and out of consciousness for almost a week. During the first night, she'd screamed until they'd finally relented and moved Andrew into her room. At the touch of his hand to hers she immediately quieted. They'd remained in constant contact for the next forty-eight hours until he'd been pronounced well enough to be discharged.

It was no surprise when Aidan, Pearce, Rian, and Kellan showed up with silver cuffs to take him back to his prison. They had made no secret of the fact that they didn't trust him and did not want him uncontained before the Blessing ceremony. He smiled thinking how lucky they were that Emma was still unconscious and even chuckled when he realized Aaron had not come along for his arrest.

My mate kicked my big brother's ass. This is better than reality TV.

Not wanting to wake Emma now that she was finally resting comfortably, Andrew quietly dressed and let the Guardsmen cuff his hands behind his back before leading him out of the room. The group made it as far as the door before Emma began to call his name. By the third utterance she was beginning to thrash her head side to side.

Siobhan ran into the room, took one look at Andrew in irons, and frowned. "What do you think you are doing?"

It was Rian that answered. "What we should to keep the clan safe. He won't be harmed, merely detained where we can keep an eye on him."

The entire time the Guardsman had been talking, Emma had been steadily calling for Andrew while getting louder and louder. Siobhan looked at her patient and then back to Rian, a look of pure disgust on her face. "Either you take those filthy chains off him, which by the way are burning his skin after I spent much of my time and talent returning him to good health, or I will have to call Carrick. You may be a Head Elder, Rian O'Rielly, but not here. This is not your call."

She turned to Aidan, who until that moment had been successful at remaining unnoticed. "And you, Aidan O'Brien, his brother. Letting them lead him off to prison when his mate needs him. What would you do if it was Grace in that bed?"

Aidan didn't answer but had the decency to bow his head. Focusing again on Rian, Siobhan asked, "So what will it be, Rian? Are you going to let Emma get to a full blown tantrum and possibly hurt herself, or are you going to let her mate comfort her?"

The Healer's words could barely be heard over Emma's shouting, but Siobhan's smile spoke volumes as Rian unlocked the cuffs and left the room without another word, the other Guardsmen not far behind. Not willing to let his mate suffer a second longer, Andrew crawled into the bed with Emma, pulled her across his chest, and held her tight while she settled.

Siobhan stood at the end of her bed making notes on Emma's chart. Returning the file to its rack, she rounded the bed and took Emma's wrist in her hand. Andrew knew she was checking his mate's pulse, but also felt her probing with her mind, checking to make sure she had no internal injuries from her latest outburst.

Apparently satisfied with what she found, Andrew felt Siobhan leave his mate's mind before speaking. "You have gotten yourself into quite the mess, Andrew. You need to consider what all of this is doing to Emma."

He looked down at her stunning face, upturned in her sleep, resting right over his heart, and suddenly his mouth was too dry to speak. Siobhan was right, but what could he do? If he got too far from Emma, she lost her mind…literally. Swallowing past the lump in his throat, Andrew looked at the healer. "I would leave her if I could. I would spare her all the heartache that being my mate is going to bring her if there was a way."

"I am sure we can find a way to sedate her then bring her out of it when you are far from the lair."

Andrew shook his head. "No, you misunderstand me. Everything changed the moment I heard her in my mind, felt her in my soul, and let her into my heart. I can't walk away from her. Don't you see? She is the reason I exist. She brought me back from the dead. And not just for some prophecy, but because she is the one, the only one that can wash the stain from my soul."

"But what will it cost her?"

"I will do whatever it takes, even give up my own life if it costs her anything…anything at all."

"I'll hold you to those words." And with that, the Elder Healer disappeared into the hall.

That had been five days ago and, for the most part, nothing had changed. Emma was still unconscious and screamed if he got more than ten feet from her, which made showers and bathroom breaks interesting to say the least. On the upside, he was getting to do nothing but hold her in his arms and tell her all the shitty things he'd done in the time before he met her. He was also sure to tell her everything he'd endured at the hands of others and made sure she knew exactly who was responsible for his trials and tribulations.

With the help of Melanie, a nurse from the hospital that volunteered at the clinic, he'd just finished giving Emma her sponge bath when a sound from the far corner of the room drew his attention. Reaching for his sword out of habit, he cursed when he came back empty-handed. Positioning himself between the growing white sphere and his mate, he took a slow step forward, trying to think of something instead of his hands to fight with, but coming up with nothing.

During his internal debate, the sphere had doubled in size. With no other options, Andrew spread his feet shoulder width apart, bent his knees just slightly, and took a fighting stance.

Nothing is getting to Emma without killing me first.

The thought had barely crossed his mind when a soft, almost angelic voice answered directly into his mind. "No need for violence, warrior. I came to help your mate, not hurt her, just as I have helped you in the past."

"Shavon?"

Before his next breath, the sphere of light turned into a tall, ethereal woman with shimmering golden hair and brilliantly blue translucent skin. "Yes, Andrew. It is me." Her voice was even more melodic when spoken out loud. Emma had told him all about his trip out of the Fades in vivid detail, but actually seeing the Ancient before him was mind boggling.

Shavon went straight to Emma's bedside. She gently touched his mate's forehead then held both of Emma's hands in her much larger, ghostly fingers. A hauntingly beautiful melody filled the room, along with the scent of healing herbs. Shavon sang in the language of the Ancients for several minutes. He was able to discern healing words and words of encouragement with his limited knowledge of the oldest of all dragon dialects.

The music faded, along with the scent of herbs, and Shavon motioned for Andrew to join her at Emma's bedside. Once they were both settled beside his mate, the Ancient Dragon began to speak. "You must make your mating official. You have awakened something within your mate that until you came into her life had remained dormant. Without the official ceremony and blessing of your Elders and Force, I fear she will remain trapped within herself for eternity."

"But these are no longer my Elders and I'm no longer a Guardsman. Hell, I'm not even sure if they will bless my mating with Emma. She's one of their own, beloved, and I'm just the traitor."

The Ancient Dragon shook her head just like his mother used to when she was about to tell him and his brothers how wrong they really were. "It is time you leave the past behind. It is a new day. You have a mate and your responsibility is to her. Once a Guardsman, always a Guardsman. Just as you have your dragon, you have your training. As for your Elders, they answer to those of us that have gone before. If we feel your union is to be blessed, than it shall be blessed."

Andrew wasn't sure what to say and damn sure didn't know what to do. Shavon's next statement made his decision for him and shocked him into speechlessness. "You have twenty-four hours until Emma will no longer wake. Choose wisely or doom one of the only female dragons in hundreds of years to cease to exist."

Rising from the bed, Shavon headed back to the corner. Turning, she looked him in the eye and said the five words that would rule the rest of his life. "Her fate lies with you."

The bright white sphere she had arrived in enveloped her completely, spun on an unseen axis, and disappeared in the blink of an eye. Several minutes later, Andrew still sat on the side of Emma's bed, digesting all he'd just learned.

Climbing into bed behind her, Andrew pulled Emma as close to his body as was possible, spooning her from behind while wrapping his arms around her middle. He kissed the side of her neck that still bore the faint outline of his teeth. Smiling, he gave her one last kiss on the cheek before snuggling in for the night.

There is no decision. If they won't bless our mating, I'll find a clan that will. She will come back to me. She will be whole again. She is mine to protect, mine to love.

CHAPTER TEN

Before the sun had made it all the way over the horizon, Andrew had the nurse call Siobhan. To say the Elder Healer was thrilled to hear from him would've been the overstatement of the century, but when she stopped grumbling at him long enough to hear what he was saying, she told him she would be there in ten minutes.

True to her word, Siobhan walked into Emma's room exactly ten minutes after hanging up on him. Grabbing the wooden visitor's chair on her way in, she sat next to the bed, using the bedside table as a desk, and commanded, "Now, start from the beginning. Leave nothing out and do not embellish."

Unable to resist, Andrew answered, "'In the beginning, God created the heavens and the earth…' at least that's what I believe the human bible says."

"Feel better?"

Andrew nodded, surprised she hadn't thrown something at him, or better yet, thrown him out of the clinic.

"Good. Now, can we get to it? You said we had twenty-four hours to get you two mated and save her from life as a vegetable, right? So, if my count is right, we have about eighteen of those left."

The reality of the situation hit Andrew square in the chest. He needed to straighten up and fly right. With Emma's life his only concern, he detailed everything the Ancient Dragon had said, ending with, "And as you know she said we have, well, I guess that is *had*, twenty-four hours."

"First of all, let me see why, after practically raising this child for all those years, I had no idea she was dragon."

"If it's any consolation, Shavon said I 'unlocked it'." He hoped that would help, but from the look on the Siobhan's face, he'd once again missed the mark.

Without another word, the Healer stood and leaned over his mate, gently laying one hand on Emma's forehead and the other over her heart. He could feel the power radiating from Siobhan into his mate as the Healer concentrated her gifts on finding the dragon inside his Emma.

Andrew knew the minute she'd found it. The tension in her shoulders relaxed as she pulled back some of the energy she had been pouring into his mate. The examination continued for almost thirty more minutes, during which Andrew alternated between wanting to scream and wanting to rip out his hair. When Siobhan finally stepped away, he had to take a breath before asking, "Is it true? Is she dragon? Is she going to be okay?"

Shaking her head, the Healer gave a half chuckle before turning to answer. "Yes, it is true. She is dragon, and from what I can tell, the soul of her beast was in a type of stasis, waiting for its mate. I can say I've never seen anything like it except…"

Without another word, Siobhan was racing from the room, throwing orders over her shoulder. "Stay with her, Andrew. I will be back as soon as I can. I'll call Carrick while I'm out."

He stood in the middle of Emma's room, not sure what, if anything, he needed to do. Almost two hours passed before the Healer returned with Devon and his mate, Anya. One look at the woman Andrew had attempted to teach black magic to all those months ago and reality came rushing in from every direction. It all suddenly made sense. Why Anya had seemed special all those months ago. Why she had repelled black magic to the point where he thought she'd actually been killed by it. But most importantly, why Emma had also seemed familiar when their souls touched. They were both dragon and related.

Feeling the weight of his past mistakes, Andrew stepped forward, and in the way of their ancestors, knelt before the couple with his head bowed. He uttered the words he'd been taught as a child, "Please forgive my transgressions against you and yours. I offer my life, as worthless as it may be, as repayment for all you have suffered at my hands."

He had no idea how long he knelt, waiting for Devon to accept his apology or punch him in the face, before the Guardsman finally answered, "Your transgression is forgiven but not forgotten. We will begin anew today to rebuild what was lost. May the Heavens guide our actions and erase our memories."

Devon's words lifted a weight from Andrew's shoulders he hadn't known he was carrying. Standing, he held out his hand and forearm and the men shook in the way of warriors.

Always the Zen Master.

"You two done? Can we do what we came here for?" Anya sounded irritated but also curious, and maybe a little scared.

Andrew turned and led them to his mate's bedside. He was just about to explain what he knew when Anya grabbed Emma's hand and gasped. "Deirfiúr?"

Looking from Devon to Siobhan then to Andrew with tears in her eyes, she asked, "How? How do I have a sister I didn't know about? How is she someone I have called friend for months?"

"Do you remember the story Carrick relayed to you on the day of your transformation?"

Anya nodded and motioned for the Healer to continue. Before Siobhan could continue, Andrew butted in, "For those of us late to the party, what story?"

Sighing, Anya retold the story…

"Carrick was called to give last rites to a very old dragon before his ascension and he told of a female dragon, one of the last and mate to the Commander of the Green Dragon Guard Force. The vibria was out of the lair when her clan was attacked and escaped being caught…or worse. She took refuge in the caves high above her homelands where humans, wizards, and/or hunters never dared to venture.

"During her time in hiding, she found herself pregnant and in due course gave birth. Unfortunately, without proper nourishment, the added strain of caring for her young, and a harsh winter, she fell ill. Using what little magic she had left, she concealed herself and her child from detection and left the caves. Her condition worsened as she traveled and she began to count her remaining days. Fearing for her child's safety, she came upon a couple overflowing with white magic and kindness. With her last bit of life, she placed the child on their doorstep and hid in the bushes until she was sure they had retrieved the baby.

"Knowing her child was safe and would be cared for, she made her way into the woods and perished, returning to the Earth as is our way. They figured out I was the baby and my adoptive parents the white witches and now, you're up to speed."

Anya turned to Siobhan. "The floor is once again yours."

The Elder Healer began again. "During Zachary's research to provide Anya with the answers they'd promised, he found mention of a second child, one a bit older than Anya, that the mother had hidden away with an unnamed clan when her kinsmen were attacked the first time. After what I've seen in Emma's soul and what you've just confirmed, I believe she is that child.

I remember the day they carried her into the lair. She was so tiny and frail, barely able to hold up her head, but with a fierce determination to survive. It took almost a year for her to remember her name, and even longer than that to trust any of us. The Sinclairs had just lost their only son in battle, and our Emma gave them the child they wanted so badly, but the little stinker would run away and hide in the grape arbors every chance she got.

"It made Sophie and Samuel crazy. They were debating what to do to keep her from wandering when she came home from one such excursion talking about a young Guardsman she'd met. He'd apparently made such a great impression on her that she decided she wanted to stay. As far as I know, Emma never ran away again."

As Siobhan relayed the story from Emma's youth, all kinds of bells and whistles went off in Andrew's brain. Not to mention his dragon chuffed and pawed the ground as if he might charge.

Could it really be? Damn if Fate is not always one step ahead.

He must've spoken his thoughts aloud, because Devon looked confused. "What did you just say?"

Startled, Andrew answered without thinking. "That Guardsman was me. I found a sweet young girl crying under the grape arbor one day on my way to training, not long after I'd gotten here. She was beautiful, inside and out. We talked. We laughed. She admitted to not remembering her name and thought I would think she was weird.

"Sooner than I would've liked, Mrs. Sinclair found her and that was the last time I ever spoke to her. I thought about her all the time, even saw her around the lair, and promised to go speak to her again, but it never happened. And then, well…"

Andrew stopped and chuckled, shaking his head at his own stupidity. "No one ever accused me of being the brightest bulb in the pack. If only…"

Devon cut off Andrew's next words. "You can't think that way. Stay out of the past. There's nothing there but would've beens, could've beens, and should've beens that will keep you from moving forward. You have her now, so let's do everything we can to keep her here with you and with us. Emma is a vital part of this clan. We all think of her as family and will fight to the death to keep her safe."

"Devon is right. I have also called…"

Siobhan's words disappeared into the noise that floated into Emma's room from the hall. Andrew was shocked to not only see Kyra and Royce, but also Lance and his mate, Samantha, along with their daughter, Sydney. Before Andrew could ask what was happening, the little girl pulled her hand from her father's grasp and ran to him.

Crashing into his legs, she locked herself to him on impact, her tiny arms wrapped around his knees. Looking down, Andrew found Sydney looking up at him, her blue eyes twinkling with mischief. She smiled and giggled. "Glad you could make it, you silly dragon. Em didn't know it, but she's been waiting for you since Anya transformed. That was the day Em got the mark on her wrist. That's the day I knew she was a dragon. Pretty cool, huh?"

Pretty cool? Ya gotta love this kid.

"What are you talking about, Sydney? Emma never said a word about a mark," Siobhan asked, hurrying to the young woman and examining her wrists.

Less than a moment later, the Healer looked up at Anya, put her hand out palm side up, and made the 'give me' motion by closing and opening her fingers. Devon's mate laid her wrist across Siobhan's hand without hesitation. The older woman compared both young women's wrists and then shook her head. "They match. It is unbelievable, but they match, exactly the same mark in exactly the same place."

The Healer looked at Kyra. "Just another reason why I need your help. We have to get her awake. The Ancient Dragon gave Andrew very specific instructions."

"Do you really believe this traitor actually spoke to the Ancient? How do we know he isn't just trying to save his own neck from the Tribunal?" Royce growled, looking at Andrew as if he was the Devil incarnate.

Andrew opened his mouth to speak when Devon said, "Yes, I do believe him. I've seen the way he looks at Em, and more importantly, I've seen the way she looks at him. Maybe you've forgotten that I was the one that found her almost dead from their connection and I heard Andrew begging her to break the connection, doing everything in his power to shield her from the pain. Shit, Royce, he died to keep her safe."

Disbelief did not begin to describe what Andrew felt. Devon was defending him. The room was still completely silent when Anya added, "And he apologized. Something y'all said would never happen."

Royce and Lance exchanged looks before Lance said, "I don't trust you. I'll never trust you. You turned your back on all that we stand for. Did unspeakable things in the name of revenge. But Fate and the Universe have given you a seriously wonderful girl for a mate. She's important to all of us. She's family, and as such, we'll do whatever it takes to keep her happy and whole, even if that means tolerating you." The Guardsman paused, staring at Andrew as if he could will him out of existence. "But know that I will incur the wrath of Heaven and Hell and the Ancients themselves if you hurt her."

Lance and Royce will not be coming to the bachelor party.

Lance had always been a judgmental prick and Royce thought he was better than everyone else, even his own brothers, so Andrew was not bothered by what they thought. He lumped them with Aaron and the rest of the Guardsmen that wanted to string him up and shoved them as far out of his mind as he could. Emma was all that mattered. Having her back and keeping her safe.

Of course, his great resolution lasted exactly two point two seconds. He hadn't even made it back to his chair at her bedside when in marched Carrick, Zachary, Malachi, and Riordan, followed closely behind by Aaron, Aidan, and Rayne.

Wonder if this clinic has a bar?

Thankfully, it was Carrick that spoke. "Siobhan relayed the information concerning Shavon's visit. Based on Zachary's morning meditation and the results of Emma's examination, I believe everything you have told us, Andrew, and therefore grant your petition to marry a member of the Golden Fire Clan, Emma Sinclair. The official mating ceremony will be performed this evening at sunset with the full support of the MacLendon Force in the Prayer Garden on the grounds of this facility."

Looking to Siobhan, he asked, "Is there anything we can do to help?"

"I think we have it all under control, or will in a moment. Kyra, Andrew, and I are going to wake up our Sleeping Beauty while the others are going to decorate the garden and plan a reception."

Andrew could tell by the looks on the Guardsmen's faces that only Carrick's presence was keeping them from giving Siobhan hundreds of reasons why they could not or would not help with his and Emma's mating ceremony. Siobhan must've seen it, too, because her next statement was right out of the Mother's Manipulation Handbook.

"I know everyone here wants to make sure everything is perfect for Emma." She nodded her head for effect as she spoke.

The grin on all the Elders' faces said they knew what she was up to and agreed wholeheartedly. Their quick exit would've been comical had it not drawn Andrew's attention to the glares he was receiving from those he used to call brethren.

Except for Devon, they can all kiss my ass, especially my asshole brothers. If I had it my way, we would do this without them, but since that's not possible, they better just stay the hell outta my way.

"I just hollered at all the girls to let them know we needed to get this show on the road," Anya added, looking a little lost. He had to admire her strength. She'd just found out that she had a sister she didn't know about, who was also a dragon. Who, by the way, was about to mate the man everyone hated and had kidnapped her. If she hadn't already accepted his apology, Andrew knew he would be begging. Not for himself, but for Emma. These were her people and as much as it scared him, he would do whatever he had to for her.

"Thank you, dear. I wanted to ask if you could stay for the Awakening Ritual. Kyra and I both agree that having you here can only help." Siobhan's tone was so much softer with Anya than it had been with the Guardsmen. Andrew would've laughed out loud if he hadn't been afraid the Healer would cause him bodily harm.

"Absolutely. Nowhere else I'd rather be."

"As for you," Siobhan looked each Guardsman in the face, "we need flowers, ribbons, all the things you arranged for your own mating ceremonies."

"Yes, ma'am," was the grumbled consensus as they filed out of Emma's room.

"And as for you," Siobhan spun on Andrew, pinning him with a look that made his blood run cold. "I can tell you have good intentions and that you are doing all this for Emma, but part of that is going to be letting go of the past. She is normally a sweet and gentle person who shies away from conflict. With you at her side, I fear those things will change. Do not look for trouble, do not cause trouble, and whatever happens, do not involve my sweet girl in any of your schemes. Try to make amends and keep your nose clean, because I know with all my heart Emma will give her life to save yours, and if that happens…I will kill you myself."

"Yes ma'am," were the only words he could squeeze past the lump in his throat. The look in Siobhan's eyes said she meant every word she'd spoken. She was not threatening, she was promising him that there would be hell to pay if anything happened to Emma. What the Healer could not have known, and Andrew was not inclined to tell her, was that he felt the same way about his miraculous mate. When all was lost, she was the one person who never gave up on him, and there was no way in Heaven or Hell he would allow her to feel anything but happiness and joy.

The traitor is now the sap...whoopee!

"Now that we have that cleared up, I think we better get Em awake. I don't want to be around if she doesn't have time to do her hair," Kyra chuckled while unpacking the large duffle bag containing her magical supplies.

A sudden pang of regret hit Andrew right in the gut. He thought of how he'd misused the white witch's magic and almost caused her to be sanctioned by the Council. Unable to stop himself, he crossed the room to help her while making sure to stay close enough to Emma to keep her calm. The look Kyra shot him said she remembered, too.

Swallowing his pride because it was the right thing to do and something he was going to have to get used to doing to keep his mate happy, Andrew stood right in front of the white witch. "Kyra, I wanted to tell you that I'm sorry for being such an asshole. I never should've messed with your magic. I hope somewhere down the line you can find a way to at least tolerate me, for Emma's sake."

The little witch looked at him for a long minute, tilting her head to the side as if she wasn't sure what to say but was thinking over her options. Nodding, she finally answered. "Ya know Andrew, I should hate you. I know some of the others do, or at least think they do, but I'm not that kinda girl. Instead, I have a proposition for you. We'll be fine as long as you take care of Emma. You treat her like the treasure she is and make sure she never so much as frowns because of something you've done, and we'll be good. Deal?"

He replayed Kyra's words in his head, making sure he wasn't missing anything. It sure sounded straightforward and something he knew would make Emma happy. "It's a deal. Thank you."

Not sure if he should shake her hand or if they should hug, he followed her lead and started placing groups of yellow, white, and pink candles around the room with cachets of herbs and White Ash chips at the base. He noticed Anya and Siobhan were studying an ancient book that he recognized as the Tome of Dragon Magic. The magic of a blood relative would be so much stronger than his, the blood of a mate, but it didn't stop his jealousy from rearing its ugly head.

Shaking his head, he had to remind himself that although he wanted to be everything Emma would ever need, that was not only improbable but just plain crazy. It was going to be an everyday battle not to grab her up and take her as far from the people he still held responsible for his misfortune, but it was something he was going to fight…for her…his mate…his Emma.

"Time to wake up the bride," Kyra called from her place behind the head of Emma's bed. "There are four of us, so we will take up the positions of power. Anya, you will face the East and say, *hail to the Guardians of the Watchtowers of the East, powers of air, hear me,* before lighting the white candle. Siobhan, you will face the South and say, *hail to the Guardians of the Watchtowers of the South, powers of fire, hear me,* before lighting the red candle. Andrew, you will face the West and say, *hail to the Guardians of the Watchtowers of the West, powers of water, hear me,* before lighting the blue candle. Finally, I will face the North and say, *hail to the Guardians of the Watchtowers of the North, powers of mother and earth, hear me,* before lighting the green candle."

Each person did as the little witch had instructed. When they were all holding their lit candle, Kyra began the spell. "We pray to the Heavens. We pray to the Goddess of All. We pray to the Universe who protects us one and all. We, your humble servants, ask that you bring our Emma back to us. She is lost in the sleep of the transforming. Please calm the dragon, reassure the woman, and guide them back to their mate and family. Your will in all things. Blessed be, blessed be."

There were a few moments of silence before Kyra said, "Blow out your candles, but do not leave her bedside."

Waiting for Emma to wake, Andrew found himself praying, something he hadn't done much of over the last nine or ten years. He wasn't even sure who he was praying to, just that he was asking anyone out in the vast universe to bring his mate back to him. When no one and nothing answered while Emma continued to sleep, his thoughts took a darker turn.

This is all my fault. Had I not have come here, or been brought here, then we would never have bonded. Her dragon would've stayed dormant and she would've had a normal life. Way to go, Drew!

"But then the Prophecy could not have been fulfilled. The Blessing couldn't have been given, and those that want to bring Hell to Earth would have free reign. Would you want your Emma to suffer that fate?"

Wondering who was hijacking his thoughts, Andrew could only come up with one entity strong enough. "Shavon?"

"Yes, you are correct."

"Do you often make a habit of running through people's thoughts?"

"Only when those people require my attention. Speaking of attention, your beloved is waking. She will need you. Be strong for her, dragon. Be strong for them all."

Emma's hand moved against his. The spark of electricity he was beginning to associate with his mate shot up his arm, making his pulse race. Watching her face for any signs of lucidity, Andrew almost jumped out of his skin when her eyes opened, locked with his, and she whispered, "Damn, I've missed you."

CHAPTER ELEVEN

Emma had never seen a more stunning sight than the smile on Andrew's face when she was finally awake. Add the love she saw shining from his mismatched eyes and she was over the moon. Looking around the room, she was shocked to see Anya and Kyra.

"What's up? Y'all having a party without me?"

"No, mo chroí'. We were trying to wake you up. You've been basically comatose for five days."

For a moment she couldn't speak. Her grip on Andrew's hand tightened, it was the only thing that felt real. "Five days? What happened?"

"Before we answer that, what is the last thing you remember?" Siobhan asked.

"Well," she thought for a minute. "We were in Andrew's room and…" Emma paused as memories of her fight with Aaron came rushing back, then what she and Andrew had done, and then…nothing.

She looked up to see her mate nodding. "Why did that happen? Why did I act like a raving lunatic?"

Andrew looked at Siobhan, who nodded, then back to her. "Okay, here it is, but I want you to promise me if you start to feel weird or think you might lose control, you'll let me know, and we'll take a break."

"Afraid I'm gonna kick your ass like I did your brother's?" She laughed, trying to lighten the mood.

Andrew was obviously not up for jokes. Using the hand he held as leverage, he pulled her into his arms and lifted until they were looking into each other's eyes. "No, I don't care if you kick my ass every day for the rest of our lives and twice on Saturday, but if you ever leave me for five days again, I just might kick yours. This whole loving someone thing is way out of my wheelhouse, and the thought that you might never come back to me was…well… more than I could handle. I know how to be an asshole. I know how to cause trouble. I'm even pretty handy with a sword, but sitting and watching you day after day, not knowing when or if you're coming back to me, is just too much. Got it?" He slammed his lips to hers, kissing her with the same vehemence his words had held. Far too soon Andrew pulled back, looked into her eyes for a just a few seconds, and nodded once before gently setting her back in the bed and sitting down beside her.

"Feel better now?' Emma asked, biting the inside of her cheeks to keep from laughing.

"As a matter of fact, I do."

She could tell he was pleased with himself and just couldn't let him sit there and gloat, so she added, "You love me?"

Almost immediately a deep red blush began to work its way from under the collar of his T-shirt. Clearing his throat, Andrew simply said, "Yes, I do, and that brings us to everything that happened while you were out. Before I get started, are you hungry? Do you need anything?"

Nice change of subject there, bub.

"No, thank you. I'm good right now."

"Okay, mo ghrá', buckle up, this is gonna be one helluva ride."

Thirty minutes later, Andrew had caught her up on just about everything that had happened while she'd been out, including another visit from the Ancient Dragon, Shavon. Emma could tell there was something he needed to tell her but was stalling. She'd tried to look through their mating bond, but he had it locked up tight. Growing impatient, she blurted out, "Come on, Drew, I can tell there's more to it. Out with it. The suspense is killing me."

"You're right. There's no way to do this but just come right out and say it."

He paused and she noticed him looking from Siobhan to Kyra to Anya, as if asking them for help. Her impatience was quickly becoming irritation. She'd always seen herself as laid back, all her friends teased that nothing got under her skin, but something had changed, something elemental inside her. Whatever it was had a temper and an incredibly short fuse, and if she wasn't mistaken, had just chuffed inside her mind.

Andrew had obviously sensed it, too. His procrastination was immediately replaced with a sense of urgency that had him speaking so fast it took her ears a second to catch up. "There's no easy way to say this…you're a dragon. You've always been a dragon, but someone put your dragon to sleep, for lack of a better term. When you got angry with Aaron in defense of me, your mate, your beast started to wake up and then we…well we…you know."

At least he had the decency to look embarrassed before continuing. "Any way, all of that woke your dragon up, but it was too much for your system to handle and it shut down."

Emma wanted to call him a liar. She wanted to scream that there was no way she could be a dragon. She wanted to pull the covers over her head and pretend the last hour hadn't happened, but she could see from the looks on the four faces staring back at her that hiding was not an option.

"And there's more," Andrew added quietly.

Of course there's more. Why stop at sorta crazy–let's go for certifiable.

Unable to speak, she nodded and prepared for what was to come. True to form, it was a doozy.

"You're a green dragon."

He paused and Emma could tell that was supposed to mean something, but no bells were ringing so she said, "And?"

"And, well…"

"Good grief, why do men take so long to say everything?" Anya grumbled from the corner, making her way to Emma's bedside. "What your mate is failing so miserably at telling you is that we are sisters. The last two Green Dragons that anyone knows of and the first two female dragons in hundreds of years. It's a long story and one I can show you if you'd like?"

Emma could only nod as Anya held her hands, linked their minds, and replayed everything she knew about their heritage. It was an amazing story and one that made sense. It filled all the gaps Emma had chosen to ignore throughout her life.

When she'd seen all there was to see, Anya let go of her hands and enveloped her in a huge hug, whispering, "I couldn't have wished for a better sister."

The tears that had been threatening to fall while she'd watched Anya's memories finally did when Anya sniffled. Laughing at one another, like Emma had always imagined sisters did, warmed her heart and filled her with a sense of belonging she'd thought lost to her.

Anya slid her eyes to the right and winked. Emma followed her sister's eyes and burst out laughing at the truly pained expression on Andrew's face. Holding out her hands for him to come to her, she asked, "What's wrong?"

He held her hand and looked back and forth between the two women for a minute before asking, "Why are you two crying? Is something wrong?"

It was Kyra's turn to chime in. Coming up behind Andrew, she swatted him on the back and chuckled. "You've gotta lot to learn. But right now you need to finish getting Emma up to speed. It's gonna be sundown before you know it, and this place will be crowded."

Smiling a knowing smile that made Emma wish she knew what was going on, Siobhan added, "And on that note, we have things to check on." Looking at Andrew, she said, "Stop stalling. We'll be back in thirty minutes."

The Healer left the room with Kyra close behind while Anya stopped and whispered, "Check out the box in the closet. I might've gotten my sister something pretty to wear." Without another word, she disappeared into the hall, closing the door on the way out.

"All right, what the hell is going on?"

Andrew held both her hands in his and looked longingly into her eyes. She could feel him opening himself to her, letting her feel how much he loved her, how much he wanted her to be happy, and how inadequate he felt as her mate. On the heels of all of his feelings came pictures that soon turned into a replay of Shavon's visit.

Not that I don't appreciate it, but these memory movie things are not all they're cracked up to be.

Intent on finding out whatever it was that was making her mate so uncomfortable, Emma watched and waited. What she heard and saw made her heart race. Shavon motioned for Andrew to join her at Emma's bedside. Once they were both settled beside his mate, the Ancient Dragon began to speak. "You must make your mating official. You have awakened something within your mate that until you came into her life had remained dormant. Without the official ceremony and blessing of your Elders and Force, I fear she will remain trapped within herself for eternity."

She knew she had to resemble an owl from how wide she could feel her eyes had opened and how high her eyebrows had raised on her forehead. Afraid to look at Andrew for his reaction, but more afraid not to, Emma raised her head to find him studying her. It took less than a second for him to ask, "Are you disappointed?"

Emma burst out laughing. "No, you big goofball. Are you?"

"No," he answered, looking confused, and more than a little lost. "Why are you laughing?"

"Because you are so clueless. Did you really think I would NOT want to be your mate? To make it official?"

"Well, I didn't…I mean…Who knows… Oh dammit, Emma, do you want to be my mate? Can we have our mating ceremony at sundown? How about spending the rest of our years together in love? Any of this sound good to you?"

Tears rolled unchecked down her cheeks. It took three times but she was finally able to speak past the lump in her throat. "Yes! Yes! Yes! It all sounds good."

"Hell yeah!" Was all she heard as Andrew pulled her into his arms and spun her around the room, kissing her like she was the most precious creation in history and he was the luckiest man in the world.

"That's because you are and I am," he chuckled directly into her mind.

"Hey! No fair listening in." She pretended to be annoyed, when in all honesty, it thrilled her as little else could.

"You better get used to it." He laughed.

"And you better put me down and let me get ready or we're gonna be late to our own mating ceremony."

She could see the reluctance in his eyes, but he did as she asked and deposited her right in front of the bathroom door. Placing her hands on either side of his face, she stood on the tip of her toes and kissed the tip of his nose. She whispered, "I almost forgot…I love you, too." Then kissed his lips gently, took a step back, and closed the door while Andrew stood there shocked at her revelation.

When she exited the bathroom, body and hair wrapped in towels, Emma found all the mates of all the Guardsmen waiting patiently, even Grace, who looked like she was going to go into labor at any moment. "Bout time. Get out here and let us help you get all beautiful," Anya teased as she took Emma by the hand, bringing her into the room and pointing to the wooden chair placed before the vanity mirror on the far wall.

The next hour was filled with laughter as the ladies all took turns fixing Emma's hair and helping with her makeup until she barely recognized the woman looking back at her in the mirror. Anya appeared behind her, carrying a large white box. "Traditionally, your mate would've gotten this for you, but he was busy sitting by your bedside and worrying, so I took the liberty."

She turned around, headed for the bed, and called over her shoulder, "Hope you like it."

Never one to be able to resist a present, Emma jumped up and ran to the huge box sitting in the middle of the bed. Tearing into it like a kid on Christmas morning, she immediately stopped after pulling back the tissue paper and finding an absolutely gorgeous, silver gossamer gown with miniature black flames embroidered all over the corset-like bodice.

"It is gorgeous. Thank you so much." She turned and looked at her newly found sister and smiled.

Even in the fluorescent light, the fabric sparkled as she pulled it from the box. A full length skirt, also embellished with small black flames, had a slit that started at the hem and she guessed would end at the middle of her thigh. Holding the dress to her torso, Emma pulled a thick, black satin ribbon that would serve as a belt and a pair of silver satin ballet slippers from the box. Spinning, she couldn't help but giggle. Never in all her years had she seen such a beautiful garment.

"Hurry up. Put it on. We can't wait to see you in it and," Kyndel tapped her temple, "the guys are almost ready for us."

In no time at all, Emma was dressed and being ushered out of her room and down the hall. Her entourage stopped at the door she knew led to the Prayer Garden. Each woman kissed her on the cheek and wished her good luck before disappearing out the door. Siobhan had told her they were setting up a small reception for after the ceremony in the Butterfly Garden on the far side of the clinic, so she guessed that's where they were going.

No sooner had all the ladies gone than the door opened from the outside and she found Jace and Liam, two of the younger Guardsmen, dressed in black surcoats trimmed with thick silver braiding and embroidered with an amazing black and silver beast in the throes of battle. Their black pants tucked into the top of their polished, knee-high black boots and long-sleeved black undershirts only highlighted the silver accents, and the dragon of their surcoats transporting her back in time and creating the perfect beginning to her mating ceremony.

Both turned when they saw her, putting their arms out for her to grasp. Once she was settled between them, they escorted her down the path toward the soft glow of candlelight and the fragrance of fresh flowers. Turning the corner, she found the Prayer Garden awash in white and silver candles, black and silver ribbons, and every imaginable fresh cut flower.

A platform containing four large throne-like chairs had been placed in front of the stone carved fountain that stood in the middle of the garden. Large planters filled with the same fresh cut flowers and finished with a huge black and silver bow on the front had been placed on the dais. As she stood waiting, Jace and Liam took several steps back and stood at ease as if they were guarding her back.

The sound of boots striking wood drew her attention. Emma watched as Carrick and the other Elders took their places in the chairs on the platform. Next came the Guardsmen, each wearing a surcoat that matched the color of his dragon, and to her surprise, smiling. Well, all except Aaron.

Rayne was at the head of the line, standing tall and proud in red. He looked every bit the Commander he was. Next was Royce, whose beautiful royal blue surcoat with green accents truly fit the gentle giant that Emma loved like a brother. Then there was Aaron, dressed in a silvery gray and frowning. Standing next to him was Aidan, his twin, dressed almost identically, except he was smiling and even gave her a wink. Maybe there was hope that one day the O'Briens would be one, big, happy family.

Pushing aside all thoughts of anything but her mate and their special day, Emma continued down the line. As usual, Lance was being the joker of the group. He looked incredibly regal in his surcoat of gold and black, but his shit-eating grin made her chuckle under her breath. Last in line was Devon, the one of the Force she felt the closest to. From her earliest memory, he'd always been her friend, always looked out for her, and most of all, was her surrogate big brother.

A movement to the right of the Elders caught her eye. There stood Andrew as she'd never imagined seeing him. Dressed in head to toe in black, his surcoat identical to the ones Jace and Liam wore. He was breathtakingly handsome and he was about to be hers... forever. Her heart beat only for him and she knew it always would. While Emma was daydreaming, her mate had started striding towards her, looking better than any man had a right to look.

But damn, he does that every day.

He looked nowhere but into her eyes. The electrical current that was always present when they were together snapped to life. His pupils dilated and his nostrils flared. Her body also reacted, and she hoped to make it through the mating ceremony without dragging him back to her room and making love to him all night. He winked and said, "*I'm with you, Beautiful,*" directly into her mind.

He stopped a few feet in front of her....waiting and watching. Carrick cleared his throat and then began speaking, filling the Prayer Garden with his low, clear, baritone voice. "Long ago, when knights and dragons fought side by side for King and Country, it became apparent that dragon kin was no longer safe from those that would expose and destroy them. They sought to join with the knights that had so valiantly been their allies. Thus, through magic and the will of both dragon and knight, the Golden Fire Clan of the Dragon Shifters became a reality. It was through the joining of many different clans that we have become the strong and powerful Force we are today.

"We are here, at the Prayer Garden, to honor what the Universe put into place all those many years ago. To acknowledge and bless the mating of Andrew Myles O'Brien to the one the Universe made for him, Emma Lee Sinclair. Will those seeking to witness this union please step forward?"

From their place to the side of the dais stepped the five men Andrew had long ago called brethren. The men that she knew had trained with him, fought with him, bled with him, and had also attempted to stop him when he'd been lost to his pain and anger. They knelt as one and bowed their heads. Rayne then stood and addressed the Elders, "We, the five of the MacLendon Force, wish to witness and offer our blessing to the union of these two souls, two halves of the same whole. May they live long, fight hard, love harder, and produce many young to flourish in this world when their souls have gone to the Heavens." He stepped back and knelt next to his men, bowing his head once again.

Carrick began again, "Your witness and blessing have been acknowledged and accepted, MacLendon Force. Andrew O'Brien, you may go to your mate and escort her to the center of the Blessed Circle."

She didn't even see him move before he was standing right before her with a look in his glowing, mismatched eyes that made her feel loved–adored. He took her hands in his and she felt all the emotion and power he held within flowing through his fingertips.

Andrew walked backward, maintaining eye contact with every movement, until they reached their destination. Carrick began, "The Silver Dragons were forged from the very fiber of the Universe, and because of this, are often referred to as the 'Shield Dragons'. The Black Dragons are known for their power and authority. They encapsulate the mark of humility and respectability. They are often called the 'Power Dragons'. Not only were you born the Special One, Andrew, but you also possess the nature of two dragons.

"They are protective to a fault and will fight to the death to defend those they hold dear. They have quick and ambitious attitudes and use a combination of their minds and hearts to make all decisions. They love hard, strong, and endlessly. They never lose faith in whom or what they believe in. To mate a Silver or a Black Dragon means to accept all that they are and honor the power shared between mates.

"Now is the time of the marking. May the Universe continue to bless you and yours all the days of your lives together."

Emma watched as the Elders and the Guardsmen left the meadow. Andrew then led her over to a grouping of large White Ash trees. Once inside that grouping, it was as if the rest of the world ceased to exist.

Staring at the man she'd come to love with all her heart in just a few days, she felt his presence in the depths of her soul. They simply stood together absorbing all that they were together. The longer they stared at one another, the more brilliant his eyes became until she realized they were glowing.

Andrew lowered his mouth to hers, stopping just as their lips touched, and whispered, *"Ta' mo chroi' istigh ionat,"* before capturing her lips with his.

It was as if Andrew was everywhere. Emma was consumed with a heat that set her ablaze from the inside out. She was laid open…body, heart, and soul, to her mate.

There was a sting on the left side of her neck, little more than a pinch and nothing compared to the kiss she was sharing with her mate. Andrew left her lips, trailing kisses across her jaw and down her neck, reaching the tender spot that had stung only a moment before. He licked and sucked the offending spot until all thoughts of anything but their naked bodies loving one another were banished from her mind.

"Don't get too comfortable, Mrs. O'Brien. There's a whole party awaiting your arrival."

"My arrival? Don't you mean our arrival?"

"Let's agree to disagree."

Laughing as Andrew picked her up and carried her towards their reception, she teased, "Life with you will never be boring and I wouldn't have it any other way."

"Whatever you say, love, whatever you say…"

CHAPTER TWELVE

The reception kind of reminded her of a sixth grade dance. The Guardsmen were all standing on one side trying to act as if Andrew wasn't there while their mates mixed and mingled. Max and a few of his werepanthers had come and were also wandering around eating lots and having fun. Max had even stopped by their table, hugged her, and shook Andrew's hand.

Devon had come over, sat down, and asked if they were planning to live in Emma's apartment over her jewelry shop. The couple had to admit they hadn't even thought about it. Laughing, they decided it was all they had and discussed looking for something bigger later. Andrew made her heart flutter when he said, "As long as it's big enough for us, that's all that matters. It's gonna be a long time before I want to share you with anyone."

Right after that he'd gone and disappeared for almost an hour, and when he'd come back, he was sporting a sneaky little grin and a glint in his eyes that said he was up to no good. She'd asked twice, to which he avoided the first time and flat out told her not to ask the second. Emma became more determined but was distracted when the band started to play "The Way You Look Tonight."

"You remembered?" she squealed and kissed his cheek.

"I did," Andrew answered as he stood and held out his hand. As they walked to the dancefloor, a new singer had taken the mic. Turning to see who was singing one of her all-time favorite songs, she had to hold on to Andrew to keep from falling when she found Rory, Royce's younger brother, performing like it was something he did every day. He winked and grinned a cheeky grin Emma knew had robbed more than one girl of her panties.

She laughed out loud as Andrew spun her around and around. It took a second for her to realize that he'd maneuvered them into a secluded part of the garden. "What are you up to, Drew?"

"Drew, huh? I like hearing you say my name like that." He winked, gave her a quick kiss, and then sat her on the stone bench surrounded by candles that he carefully lit before sitting down beside her.

She could tell he was nervous but could feel through the mating bond that he was also excited, so she worked hard not to push him. They sat in silence, listening to the sounds of their reception in the distance. She saw Andrew turn in his seat and followed suit.

When they were face to face, Andrew pulled a small, black velvet bag out from under his surcoat. He held out his hand and waited for her to do the same. As soon as she did, he laid the bag on her palm and began to explain. "I understand that you make all the jewelry for the clan. I saw the beautiful pieces you made for all the ladies out of the shells of their mates. You are truly talented."

"Thank you, but what's this?" She pointed at the bag in her hand.

"Open it and find out."

Shaking her head and chuckling, Emma loosened the drawstring on the bag and carefully poured its contents into her lap. The tinkling of tiny bells accompanied the glistening of highly polished silver, closely followed by one perfect black dragon scale. It took a moment for what she was looking at to sink in, but when it did, tears began to wet her cheeks.

"How did you…it is just beautiful, Drew. Where did you get it?" she asked, taking a closer look.

"Well, the scale is mine…I mean, my dragon's, and the bracelet was my mother's. Right before she went into the Heavens to be with Dad, she gave me the bobble he'd given to her on their mating day. She made me promise to give it to my mate on our special day and here we are. I wanted you to have something that showed you how much you mean to me and it seemed really…well, tacky to ask you to make your own gift. This way I am keeping my promise to my mother and showing you that you are the best, most precious gift I have ever been given and I will spend every day of my life proving that to you. The scale is so you have a true piece of me. You may do with it what you want."

Unable to speak, Emma handed the bracelet to Andrew and held out her arm. "It is just gorgeous. I will treasure it forever, almost as much as I treasure you."

Andrew placed the bracelet on her wrist and secured the lobster claw clasp. As she pulled it back, the sweet sounds of the bells ringing as they touched one another filled the area around them. Their eyes met and in unison they said, "Every time a bell rings, a dragon kisses his mate."

Chuckling at how in tune they were, Emma leaned forward. Her only thought was to make her bracelet ring again when a shout rang out from the vicinity of their reception. It was closely followed by Aidan's bellow, "Grace is in labor! The babies are coming! The babies are coming!"

CHAPTER THIRTEEN

Ten hours and no babies. He really hoped if Emma ever decided she wanted kids that he would be more prepared than he was for the birth of his nephews. Not to mention, every time Aidan came out to give everyone an update on his mate and children, he looked a little more disheveled and a lot more worried. It had to be hell to watch his mate in pain and know there was nothing he could do about it. Andrew had suffered that fate briefly when Emma shared his pain at the beginning of their mating. It was something he never wanted to experience again.

"What are you thinking so intently about?" Emma's voice startled him.

"Nothing."

"Okay, you can tell me or I can find out for myself." She waggled her eyebrows and he couldn't help but laugh, which drew the looks of all the Guardsmen. He'd caught some of their stray thoughts and knew most were less than thrilled that he was there. He was shocked, however, to hear Aidan and Aaron were both relieved he'd shown up. They would probably think less of him if they knew it was more because of Emma and less because of his familial obligation, but no matter, maybe he was making headway with his brothers. Another thing that meant way more to his mate than to him.

His mate by the way, that was still staring at him demanding to know what he was thinking. Giving in, but not before he sighed loudly and pretended to be incredibly put out, Andrew motioned for her to come and sit beside him. "I was thinking that I will lose my ever loving mind if you are ever in labor and my brother is far stronger than I ever gave him credit for."

"Well, I think that is something you should tell your brother…when the time is right, of course. As for if I am ever in labor…I can assure you I will be in labor at least twice in our very long lives together."

Andrew groaned loudly and Emma laughed her amazing laugh that just made him feel better every time he heard it.

Note to self, keep my mate laughing…all the time.

Grinning to himself, he almost fell out of his chair when Aidan's roar of distress echoed not only throughout the entire clinic, but also within the confines of Andrew's mind. Somewhere along the way the special link he and his brother had shared most of their lives, that he was sure had been destroyed when he was left to die, had regenerated.

In that moment, Andrew was watching everything Aidan was thinking and feeling, almost like he sat on his older brother's shoulder. His eyes shot up and found Aaron staring right at him. For the first time in nearly ten years, the oldest O'Brien brother spoke directly into his mind. *"Do you see what I see? Is this shit for real?"*

One nod from Andrew and they were both up and running towards the delivery room. Emma's voiced screamed in his head. "What's happening, Drew? What's wrong?"

"One of the babies is dying," was all he could say as the fear and pain Aidan and Grace were experiencing continued to unfold in his mind. He opened the renewed link he shared with his brothers to Emma so that she too could see what was happening. Rounding the corner right on Aaron's heels, he heard Grace's cry of pure anguish, "He's not breathing! Do something! Save my baby!"

Her pain reached through their familial link, wrapped around Andrew's heart, and squeezed until he was sure he was having a heart attack. Struggling to stay on his feet, he burst into the delivery room with Aaron to find Aidan holding his sobbing mate and one of their children, while Siobhan, Zachary, and three nurses worked to revive the lifeless little body of his nephew.

Sorrow unlike anything he'd ever known stole his breath. He looked to Grace, sure the emotions were coming from her, but was met with a wall of torment and fear. Aidan's feelings were similar, but also contained a heavy dose of anger and helplessness.

Andrew looked back to the baby. He could feel a spark of life trying with all its power to hold on to the child's soul, but failing miserably. A single tear slid down his cheek as a voice he was getting used to having in his head spoke, *"You can fix this, warrior. Only you can make this right."*

"What the hell are you talking about, Shavon, I'm not a doctor."

"No, but you are the Special One. Look at your nephew's opened eyes. What do you see?"

Taking a step closer to where the Healers were still trying to save the child, Andrew used his six-foot-four inch stature to look over the tiny nurse in the corner. There, staring back at him with the dimmest spark of recognition, was one amber eye and one blue eye.

In that split second, the soul of a warrior reached out to the soul of the child in an attempt to save the baby's life. *"You must touch the child, Andrew. You must bond with him and help him join his human soul with that of his dragon."*

The Ancient Dragon must've felt Andrew's reluctance, because her next words gave him the push he needed. *"The dragon soul attempting to bond with your nephew is that of your father, Michael. You have but seconds before all is lost."*

Moving faster than even he knew he could, Andrew reached between Siobhan and Zachary, gently brought the child to his chest, and willed the dragon to bond with his human. Aaron and Aidan bellowed and dove towards him, only to be held back by Zachary with one word, "Listen," and with that he touched his temple.

Andrew felt, rather than saw, the older O'Brien twins stop mid lunge and follow the bond with him that had been reestablished. He felt their instant recognition of the Ancient in their presence and watched with apprehension as their younger brother intently followed her instructions. Grace called out to her mate, who immediately let her also see what was happening. The youngest O'Brien brother would've wished for less of an audience, but saving his nephew was all that mattered and required all of his focus.

Sweat rolled down his back, his muscles were tensed so tight he thought they might literally pull away from his bones, but still he pressed on, showing the millennia old dragon spirit to the tiny human spirit begging to have life breathed into it. The entire time he worked on the child, their eyes remained locked. Two sets of mismatched eyes, identical except for size, each willing the other to stay the course, to not give up, to be stronger than anyone had ever given them credit for being.

Hours passed while Andrew helped the dragon and human spirit build their bond and accept each other as two souls sharing one entity with a destiny greater than anyone could ever imagine. The entire time Shavon directed, uplifted, and encouraged the traitor, the dragon, and the child not to give up.

Somewhere far in the distance, Andrew heard his mother's voice. It was almost inaudible when it began, but grew stronger the longer she spoke. *"You did it, Son. You saved the little one. You've given him a chance to fulfill his destiny. I am more proud of you than I can ever express."*

"Son, you have made me a very proud father today," Michael O'Brien's voice joined his wife's and for just a moment, Andrew saw them in his mind's eye just as he had so many times while growing up, standing atop the hill behind their home watching their children at play. He felt the same love and pride flowing from them as he had all those years ago.

Unable to speak, he simply smiled at his parents. Aidan's voice startled him, reminding Andrew that he was not alone. *"I too am proud of you, Drew. What you've done here today for me and for my family proves you are a changed man. Forgiveness is still something you must earn, but as brothers, we'll find a way to make it work."*

The next voice was one Andrew never expected to hear again in his mind and the words spoken were even more shocking. *"You have your second chance. Don't blow it."* And with that, Aaron silenced his part of their link and left the delivery room.

Unable to move, Andrew stood staring into the eyes of his nephew, enjoying the abundance of life he saw in their depths. *"I must return to the Ancients. You have done well, Andrew. Now, give the child to his parents and go to your mate. You need to prepare her for tomorrow. You and Sydney will receive the Blessing and Emma must translate the Prophecy for all involved. Walk in the light, brother."*

Andrew felt the moment the Ancient had left them. Turning, he found Aidan and Grace watching him with rapt attention, their eyes filled with happiness and acceptance and their arms open wide. Never one for public displays of affection and more than a little shaken up by what had just happened, Andrew walked to the end of Grace's bed and handed the little one to his father.

Grace grabbed his arm with the hand that wasn't tending to the other twin and forced him to look into her eyes. "Thank you, Andrew. I know it's not near enough to say, but it's all I can come up with. All is forgiven where I'm concerned."

She turned to Aidan and they switched babies while she still held firmly to his arm. When she looked at him again, she was smiling so brightly he would've sworn she was glowing. "Uncle Andrew, I would like you to meet Angus Andrew O'Brien."

Pride like he'd never known filled Andrew's heart to overflowing. Words escaped him, so he nodded and smiled while backing out the door, looking for the escape he so desperately needed. As he was sure she always would be, Emma was waiting just around the first corner, his surcoat in hand, and a smile that felt like home on her face. "Wanna get out of here, lover?"

"You read my mind."

CHAPTER FOURTEEN

Emma got very little sleep and was bordering on cranky when she made her way into the kitchen in search of coffee. She and Andrew had taken the fastest route to her apartment, hoping for some time alone, only to find half the Force and their mates, along with the werepanthers and their leader, waiting outside her door with the leftovers and more champagne than was probably legal.

Deciding her tiny home would never hold everyone, they ended up in the courtyard behind her shop that connected her with the baker, the butcher, and the florist. They had just finished laying out the leftovers when the band arrived with the gorgeous black and white cake she had forgotten all about. The rest of the night became a blur of dancing and toasting, along with the few intimate moments she and Andrew could steal.

He'd told her that today would be the day he and Sydney would receive the Blessing and pass it on to the Blue Dragons and that she would be translating the Prophecy to all the pertinent people.

Woohoo! Sounds like anything but fun.

Emma knew she was being a baby but couldn't help feeling slighted that she and her mate hadn't been able to be alone at all since their mating ceremony. Andrew had assured her that as soon as the Blessing Ritual was over, they would lock the door, draw the shades, and stay locked away together and alone for at least a week. Just the thought of it warmed her to the core.

The front door opened and in walked the man of her dreams. From the huge smile on his face, she didn't have to ask where he'd been, she simply asked, "How are the babies?"

"Is it that obvious?" he chuckled. "They are great! I swear they already know who I am. Grace said they just smiled because they had gas, but I know different."

Emma laughed out loud while pouring the cream in her coffee. "I'm sure they do. You know you're gonna be the cool uncle. The one they ask about smoking, drinking, and girls."

The look of utter shock and fear on his face made her spit coffee on the counter. "Seriously?" he asked.

"Yeah, but it's not something to freak out about, and you've got a few years until that happens. For now we can just buy them the really loud toys with all the lights that have little pieces that Aiden steps on in the middle of the night."

"Now, that's a plan," he chuckled. "We're supposed be at the clearing above the Cave of the Ancients in an hour and a half…"

"I know," Emma groaned before Andrew even had a chance to finish his sentence. "I'm going."

Shuffling past her mate, she let out a squeal when his arm wrapped around her waist and she found herself straddling his lap. His lips met hers and all thoughts of prophecies, blessings, and ancient dragons slipped away. All Emma could do was enjoy the wonderful feeling of being in the arms of the man she was meant to spend forever alongside.

The tip of his tongue tasted the seam of her lips, becoming more insistent the longer they kissed, demanding entrance. Emma opened immediately and completely to him. Nothing had ever felt so right. His tongue slid alongside hers, stoking the fire building deep inside. Their kiss continued driving them both higher and higher until Emma tore her mouth from Andrew's with a gasp.

She fell deep into his lust soaked eyes, wishing they had nowhere to go but bed for weeks and weeks. Leaning forward until their foreheads touched, she sighed, "Join me in the shower?"

"Oh, that I could. If we get in there together, there is no way we're making it out of the apartment in time for the ritual. Hell, we won't make it out in time for lunch on Tuesday."

They both laughed as Andrew stood with Emma's legs wrapped around his waist, holding her securely in place. Walking towards the shower, he gave her little kisses on the tip of her nose, her eyelids, her cheeks, and her lips. When they reached the bathroom, she let her legs slide down his, happy to see he was just as affected as she was. One last kiss and Andrew backed into the hall, pulling the door shut as he went. He stopped just before it would've closed and whispered, "This will be the last shower you ever take alone."

The door clicked shut and Emma melted into a puddle of blissfully happy, irrevocably turned on, newly discovered, female dragon shifter. Stepping into the steamy spray, she thought about Andrew's words and sighed. Now, to get ready and get on with a ritual that would ultimately save the world.

The Avengers got nothing on us.

Hours later and the sun was making its descent behind the mountain they were all presently standing atop. Kyra had prepared the Sacred Circle while Jace and Liam had built the platform next to the lagoon where she, Andrew, and Sydney would stand.

Lighting the candles, Emma made her way around the Circle, giving each person in attendance a certain colored candle as Kyra and Siobhan had instructed. She'd just completed her task when a bright light shone from the bottom of the pond and Shavon and King Alarick appeared. Speaking directly into everyone's minds, the Dragon King said, *"Thank you for coming and thank you for protecting our world and our race. Tasks such as these have always fallen to the dragons. Each and every one of you has much to be proud of. We, the Ancients, will forever be in your debt."*

Shavon then spoke just to Emma. *"It is time, dragoness. Take your place in the annals of history. Prepare your people for their Blessing."*

Emma turned and looked at the people that were now and would always be her family. She unrolled the parchment Siobhan had given her and began to read, inserting the names of the actual people the Prophecy referred to as she went.

"A powerful white witch of long, regal lineage sworn to the Earth, made whole by human love, must mate a dragon of royal descent marked by devastating loss and the heart of not one clan but two. Thank you, Kyra St. Croix and Royce O'Reilly, for your service to your kin. May the white witches grow even stronger. May their light wash away the darkness.

"The vibria born of human parents who possesses the spirit of the last female born of two dragons then lost in plain sight. Thank you, Sydney Kavanaugh, for your service to your kin and to your Earthly parents whose guidance is your strength. For one so young to take on such responsibility is admirable.

"Born to an extinct race, thought to be one but actually two, both with destinies blessed by Fate, neither knowing the other exists, when reunited can nullify death to bring back the one needed to complete the circle. Thank you, Anya Walsh and Emma O'Brien, for your service to your kin. May the Green Dragons be reborn through you. Their Earth magic and power was unparalleled in the world and will be again.

"A calling to heal, a hidden nature, a history long forgotten... all protected in the heart of a woman destined to complete a warrior and his beast. The revelation of all she is brought forth from the joining with her mate. Thank you, Dr. Charlene Gallagher and Aaron O'Brien, along with your twin Aidan, for your service to your kin. May the fairies regain their magic and once again rule the Seely and Unseely courts.

"A complete circle of all called and confirmed, their mates and their families then increased by one, the twin of the warrior, also brother of the lost one, will become the Twelve – a whole, perfect, harmonious unit that will bring about the Great Miracle. Thank you again to all in attendance, along with Andrew O'Brien, who has been returned to us, for your dedication and service to dragon kin. We are those required to complete the Blessing Ritual.

"Now that all is complete and the Miracle recognized, the Ancients will speak through the Special One and the Child. They will bless the Clan the color of the summer sky and the water when it is calm. This Clan and only this Clan, along with their mates as they become known, will battle the denizens of Hell and bring the Devil himself to his knees.

"Will the Blue Thunder Clan please come to the dais?"

As soon as everyone was in place, Emma bowed to Shavon and King Alarick and left the podium, taking her place at the West point of the circle. As she stood watching her mate and waiting for what was to come next, she felt her dragon move within her. It was the first time since she'd awakened that she realized the part she was to play in the coming war against evil. It was humbling and empowering all at once, and something she could not wait to share with her mate.

A voice from the Heavens she'd never heard before spoke with such force that the flames of the candles around the Circle flickered. "Sydney Kavanaugh and Andrew O'Brien, thank you for your acceptance of your role in the Blessing. You two are examples of how truly special dragon kin is. The Mother Goddess created me, Draco, many millennia ago, and gave me the great winged warriors to help keep the earth free from evil.

"Through these many thousands of years we have been victorious more times than we have suffered defeat, and this time will be no different. Like the warriors before them, the Blue Thunder Clan will emerge victorious, slay the evil hordes and their leaders that threaten all we hold dear, and protect the humans who unknowingly depend on us to keep them safe."

Silence filled the mountaintop as Sydney and Andrew knelt before Shavon. It seemed to take forever, but in actuality only took a few minutes before the Child and the Special One rose, turned to those standing around the Sacred Circle, and then focused on the Guardsmen of the Blue Thunder Clan. They spoke in unison and with such reverence, Emma felt it to the depths of her soul.

"Great Warriors of the Clan the color of the summer sky and the water when it is calm, receive the Blessing from the Mother Goddess and Draco, the original Warrior. May you be wrapped in the Divine Protection provided by the Universe and the Heaven and stop evil with the power of the Truth and Light.

"May Divine Wisdom guide your decisions in the coming battle. Think clearly, plan tirelessly, and act decisively. Shield those that depend on you from the weapons and intentions of the enemy.

"Divine Justice will grant you the Victory!

"For the glory of the Mother Goddess, the Universe, the Heavens, the Ancients, and all who are pure of heart and spirit.

"Blessed be. Blessed be."

"To the Glory of Dragon kin," Draco's voice rang out across the clearing, right before he disappeared.

The Blue Dragons rose and returned to their places around the Circle while Emma watched her mate stride towards her like the warrior she knew him to truly be. He sat behind her, wrapped his arm around her shoulders, and placed a chaste kiss upon her upturned lips.

A sigh of relief escaped her lips. Andrew was finally back where he belonged…by her side. The entire time he'd been at the head of the Circle with Shavon and Sydney, Emma had prayed he'd come back to her. Yeah, he'd promised and everyone involved assured her he was in no danger, but she still worried. Sure, since their official mating there hadn't been a single second she didn't know what he was thinking or feeling, but she knew his past was not forgiven or forgotten by any of their kin. That was going to take time, lots and lots of time, and maybe some lithium in the water, but she really had no clue if that even worked on dragons.

Looking around, she saw people she'd known all of her life, some she'd known for only a short time, and some she knew were going to be very important to her in the years to come. All so different, but all the same. All important to one another in ways they had yet to discover.

They were family…real family.

Together they would save the world, separately they would restore their own. At least the part of her life she remembered, the part that mattered, was now her responsibility to protect. Never in her wildest dreams did she ever imagine having a sister, let alone meeting her and getting to spend hundreds of years getting to know one another.

Andrew pulled her closer and dropped a kiss on the top of her head. She snuggled into his warmth, thinking of all the ways they could sneak away and be alone. Looking up at her mate, Emma was just about to suggest their departure when a shout rang out from the other side of the clearing.

"Sydney, honey, come down from there." Sam was up on her feet, quickly making her way towards the podium with Lance right behind her.

The child let go of Shavon's hand and turned to face her parents. "It's okay, Mommy. This is what's supposed to happen. This is how it was always supposed to be."

"No, baby, you belong with me and Daddy, remember?"

Shavon, who until now had remained quiet, descended the steps with Sydney at her side. She stopped in front of Lance and Samantha while Sydney ran into her parents' outstretched arms. "Samantha, Lance, your Sydney is a special being. Just as the Prophecy states, she is the embodiment of the spirit of the last female dragon ever born of dragon parents. That vibria was lost to all of us before her birth, taken by the Goddess and protected until the time was right. She was then allowed to be reborn to human parents, parents that shared the bloodline of the original mage. They were good people and we mourn their loss at the hands of evil. You see, their car accident was no accident at all. It was engineered by our enemies to take this beautiful child from us and gain a demonic foothold in the world.

"We all owe Fate a huge debt of gratitude for getting her to you. I could not have hoped for better parents for Sydney than you, Samantha, and you, Lance. The one thing our Sydney lacked was the camaraderie of her own. She needed her dragons and you gave them to her. For that, you have great favor with the Ancients."

Sam was shaking her head as if refusing to believe what Shavon was saying would somehow make it untrue. She clung to her daughter, crying and begging Lance to do something…anything to stop what was unfolding before them.

Shavon continued, "We all grieve your loss. It was never our intention to hurt you. You will be given favor and your pain lessened by the Heavens and the Goddess. You will also have many children, none to replace our dear Sydney, but only to keep your memories and love of her alive. Your children will go on to lead the dragons to great victories against those that would oppose our kin. They will pave the way for the rebirth of dragon kin."

"No, no, no, no! I don't want new children, other children…any children but Sydney. She is mine! She is ours and you cannot take her from us," Sam wailed.

The Ancient began to speak but was immediately cut off by Sydney, who pulled herself free from her mother's grasp, placed her tiny little hands on either side of Samantha's face, and looked deeply into her eyes. "I love you, Momma, and I always will, but this is what I was made to do. Have faith, Momma, everything will be okay. We will see each other again, I promise, and in the meantime, you have to be strong. Remember what you always said, 'Us girls gotta keep Dad in line.'"

Sydney hugged her mother's neck tight and then kissed her dad on the cheek. Looking over her shoulder, she nodded to Shavon, who knelt before Samantha, held both her hands, and whispered, 'codladh go maith'. Sam immediately slumped against Lance's chest. The Guardsman, who'd spent the last few minutes trying to keep his mate from losing her mind, looked up at the Ancient with tears in his eyes. "Will she be okay?"

"Who, warrior–your mate, or your daughter?" Shavon asked, compassion coloring every word.

"Both," his voice cracked as he answered.

"Your mate will sleep until tomorrow. When she wakes there will be sadness, but also acceptance at what has transpired. Your daughter will be well. She is royalty and as such, will learn to rule over our Otherworldly court and await your family's arrival into the Heavens. Her only wish is that you give her many brothers and sisters."

Lance gave a watery chuckle while Sydney giggled and ran to him, giving him one last hug. "I love you, Daddy. You'll always be my hero."

The Guardsman could do nothing but hug her back and nod his agreement while tears ran down his face.

Sydney grabbed Shavon's hand as they walked back onto the podium. One last look over her shoulder, a wave of her chubby little hand, and Sydney followed Shavon into the bright white light that burned brightly in front of them. When they could no longer be seen, the sphere of light blinked out of existence, leaving the clearing bathed in the candles that had been lit for the Blessing.

Emma once again looked at all in attendance one by one. Each mourned the loss of Sydney, but along with that sadness she could feel the hope each person had for the continuation of their races. Bittersweet was the only word that came to mind, but seemed to pale in comparison to what she felt coming from her family.

Lance stood with Samantha in his arms and silently headed in the direction of their home. It would take time, but they would recover and be stronger than ever. Emma had faith not only in what Shavon had said, but in the couple themselves. There was nothing they couldn't accomplish together.

CHAPTER FIFTEEN

It had been three days since the Blue Dragons had received the Blessing, and three days since they'd all had to accept the loss of Sydney. Anya was keeping Emma up to date on Sam's condition while Lance had actually reached out to Andrew to help him understand, since he was as close to the Ancients as Sydney had been. Andrew was doing his best, but Emma could see the toll it was taking on him.

Thinking of him and sending wave after wave of strength and love, she went back to pacing and waiting for him to return home. Thankfully, because of the positive things he'd done since returning to the lair, the Tribunal had been cancelled. However, Andrew was to be on a type of probation, the terms of which were being given to him while Emma climbed the walls.

She was sure everything would work out. After all, they'd had black surcoats made for Andrew and the young Guardsmen and allowed them to have the official ceremony performed by the Elders and blessed by the Force. Things were going to be fine, it was just going to take time, and that was something they actually had in spades.

On her hundredth trip past the large picture window in her living room that overlooked the Town Square, she heard boots striking the iron steps leading to her apartment. Not able to wait one moment longer to see her mate, Emma threw open the door and launched herself into Andrew's waiting arms.

"Great catch," was all she said before kissing him like they'd been apart for weeks instead of just a few hours. She heard the door slam shut and felt herself being carried but could not stop kissing Andrew. In that moment, he was the very air she breathed.

One second Andrew stopped walking and the next she was sliding down his body. Her feet touched the ground and their kiss only deepened. The feel of his hands at her waist warmed her throughout, sending an electric current directly to her womb. His hands roamed her body as their kiss grew to ravenous proportions. It was all teeth, tongue, and unbridled passion that had Emma fighting to breathe. Tearing his mouth from hers, Andrew took a long, deep breath and then looked deeply into her eyes.

Slower than she thought possible, his lips touched the corner of her mouth and gently nipped and tasted from one side to other, taking special care in the middle to let the tip of his tongue just barely slide across her lips and ever so lightly touch the tip of hers, igniting her senses and causing a series of tiny contractions in her womb. Climbing back up his body, Emma locked her legs around his waist and began to move against his erection. Andrew exerted his considerable control by placing his hands on her hips, essentially trapping her right where he wanted her, and slowing their pace.

"I want to make this last, mo ghra'. I need you more than my next breath, but it has been a long time for me and it has never been with someone I love."

Emma let the abundance of beautiful emotions roll over her at Andrew's confession and sighed her resignation as he worked his way across her jaw and down the column of her neck. The rough stubble of his beard tickled and excited as he lavished special attention to the spot where her neck and shoulder met, the exact spot that held her double flamed mating mark. She felt him smile against her skin just before he bit down on the tendon lying just below her mark. The slight pinch made her jump and he took the opportunity to position his cock right against her opening. All that separated them was their clothing. He kissed and sucked the spot he had bitten until she was a mass of want and need.

As if that was not enough, he wrapped one arm under her bottom, further trapping her body against his. He then used his other to take one of her straining nipples between his thumb and forefinger and tormented the hardened peak until she was certain she would lose her mind. It may have been years since he was with a woman, but he was not at a loss for what to do.

The sound of his excited roughened voice in her ear made goose bumps rise all over her body. "I want you, Emma, more than I have ever wanted anything. I need you, mo chroi'."

Her fingers touched the buttons on her blouse, trying to get as much of her skin against as much of his skin as she could. Andrew, however, was having none of it. His hands closed over hers and he spoke with an authority she'd never heard from him, but kind of liked. "Look at me, Emma. This is about us, our beginning, and our forever. You've had my heart from the moment I saw you under that grape arbor all those years ago. You are my home. You are my reason for living. You are the reason I will never turn to the darkness again. Please don't ever shut me out. I want us to share every second of our very long lives together."

Minutes ticked by as they simply stared into one another's eyes. She watched a plethora of emotion boil in his eyes. She sighed in relief that she was not alone in the depth of her feelings. Slowly, he began working to open her buttons, kissing the spot right above each new opening.

Her hands moved of their own volition, exploring every inch she could reach of his muscular body. Sliding under the material of his shirt, the electric shock she loved set her body on fire. Andrew's lips found hers, and it was as if gasoline had been thrown on the fire, threatening to burn Emma alive.

His tongue slid alongside hers as his hands covered her breasts and his calloused palms rubbed against her raised nipples. She arched into his touch. He groaned into her mouth and her nails dug into his back. He turned their bodies, sat heavily on the side of the bed, and sat her across his lap. She saw his frustration at their lack of skin to skin contact just before he ripped the blouse from her body. A moment of embarrassment was quickly erased by the look of complete adoration and undeniable lust in his mismatched eyes. His hands slid up her sides, spread his fingers wide, and she was engulfed in his touch. Fingers from each hand made their way under her bra, igniting sensations that had her fighting to keep her eyes open.

She felt his wavy brown hair against her skin and then a cool caress of air teased her breasts. Emma shivered at the sensation. Andrew chuckled. "Are you cold, mo chroi'? Should we get under the covers and get warm?"

She knew he was joking and wanted to laugh, but speech escaped her. Emma instead shook her head and watched in amazement as he leaned forward and licked the very tip of her breast. Lost to the sensation, her head fell back, her fingers tangled in his hair, and she pulled him in as close as possible. Andrew seemed to know what she needed, even when she didn't know herself. He sucked almost all of her ample breast into his mouth and tortured her nipple with his teeth and tongue. Her hips moved against his considerable length, the friction of her clothing pushing her towards release.

Andrew moved to her other breast, showing it the same attention while his hands landed on her waist and ripped open her jeans. He slid his hand inside her panties and teased the curls seated at the top of her mound with just the tips of his fingers. Once again their eyes met and the undeniable want and need he showed her was humbling. Never had anyone looked at her with such reverence and heat. Lost in his gaze, the slight movement of his hand did not register until his finger grazed her clit. Her world exploded. He scooted back on the bed and rolled them until she was on her back and he was lying beside her, his finger tracing the outer lips of her pussy.

Emma lifted her hips in an attempt to drive his fingers back to the tiny nub of nerves that was pulsing with need, but Andrew would have none of it. The look in his eyes and the grin on his lips said he was enjoying her torture.

He leaned forward, nuzzled both of her breasts, placing kisses on the underside before moving down her stomach. His kisses became deeper. He tenderly bit the skin under her belly button as he worked her jeans down her body. Her hips lifted on instinct, and within the next breath, she was completely bare. Andrew continued working his way down her body, tasting every part of her he could reach.

Andrew even kissed her toes and the arch of her foot, which set off a whole new set of goose bumps. She felt a bite at the back of her knee and then he was very gently lifting first one leg and then the other over his shoulders. Lowering his body, he kept constant eye contact with her and ran his hands up and down her legs the entire time. When he spoke, she could hear what the effort to go slow cost him. "I have to taste you. The scent of daffodils warming in the sun is driving me mad."

The first swipe of his tongue against her aroused flesh had her clawing at the blankets and screaming to the Heavens. He pushed two fingers into her and blew a steady stream of warm air on her throbbing clit. Her pussy contracted around his fingers as his tongue licked her like she was the best thing he had ever tasted.

Her arousal built as he inserted another finger deep inside her, stretching her walls at the same time his thumb found her clit. He bent the fingers moving inside in a 'come hither' motion, touching the bundle of nerves that sent her into orbit. Her orgasm hit her like a storm, her pussy clamped tight around his fingers, her legs tightened around his head, and she rode the waves of the most powerful orgasm she'd ever felt. He continued to lick and taste until she was lying boneless beneath him, her fingers lazily running through his hair.

He removed first one leg and then the other, kneading the muscles of her thighs and setting off a whole new series of tremors in her womb. The smile that brightened his face was full of satisfaction and more than a little pride. Finally able to speak, she teased, "Proud of yourself, *Special One*?"

Andrew chuckled. The vibrations, coupled with the way his chest hair tickled her skin, made her gasp and raise her hips. He winked and his grin turned playful. "Oh yeah, dragoness, I'm downright pleased as punch." And with that he slid two fingers back into her still weeping channel. Emma pushed against his fingers and moaned low and long at her renewed arousal.

"How can I feel anything after what we just did?" she sent directly into his mind, unable to form words around the sobs of pure ecstasy he was wringing from her.

"Oh, baby, we are just getting started. You inspire me."

Emma whined as Andrew removed his fingers from her pussy, but was immediately relieved when the head of his erection pushed at her opening. He pressed forward, stopping just as the head of his extremely hard cock crossed her entrance. Her hips lifted. Her pussy contracted harder and faster, trying to pull him in, but he was so much stronger and held completely still.

"Look at me, Emma. Open those gorgeous eyes and look at the man you brought back from the dead."

Her eyes snapped to his and she tried to say with her expression what her brain could not make her mouth say.

"I need to go slow, mo ghra'. You are so tight. I don't want to hurt you."

His hands trapped her hips. His gaze darkened. "I want you more than my next breath."

He breathed deeply. Sweat dotted his upper lips and he moved a few inches further inside her. She focused on his eyes, could feel their combined strength, and in that moment knew there was nothing they could not achieve together.

She felt the head of his cock touch the mouth of her womb. He was buried so deep inside of her that she had no idea where she ended and he began, and she didn't care. All that mattered was that they were together. Together as they were meant to be, together forever.

"You are driving me absolutely crazy," he said through gritted teeth as he gently pulled out of her, only to slowly return. His cock stretched her inner walls, filling her completely. He was a big man on all accounts and every inch of him was hers. Unable to stay still any longer, she fought against his hands on her hips and pulled herself up, nipping at his neck to quicken his pace. When he refused to speed up, she drove her hands into his hair, scratching his scalp as she pulled his mouth to hers. He immediately opened to her. She kissed him with all that she was, working her tongue along his, tasting all that he was, then slid it in and out of his mouth, showing him what she wanted him to do with his cock buried deep inside her.

His pace quickened but was still nowhere near what she needed from him. She wanted him to lose control. She wanted him crazy. She needed him to show her that he was as crazy for her as she was for him. She continued her assault almost to the point of no return by wrapping her legs around him and lifting her ass completely off the bed. The change in position pushed him farther inside. Her pussy held him tight, massaging his throbbing cock. The light in his eyes turned ravenous as he thrust in and out of her with such force she was sure they would fall right off the bed, but she couldn't care. A few bumps and bruises were nothing compared to the man loving her as no other ever had.

They screamed their mutual release to the Heavens. Love flowed from the depths of her and Andrew's eyes. A love so pure, tears filled her eyes and fell unhindered as he watched with a look of complete confusion.

It took several tries, but she was finally able to calm his fears. "They are happy tears, Drew. Tears of complete and total joy."

Smiling his understanding, Andrew slowly pulled out of her, the motion causing a whole new set of convulsions to rack her body. He rolled to the right, taking her with him, and carefully placed her across his chest. She had never felt so cherished.

"I love you, Andrew O'Brien."

"Emma O'Brien, I cannot conceive of a forever where you are not the center of my world. I love you with everything I am and everything I hope to be."

EPILOGUE

A few days before, Calysta had been moved to another room farther within the compound where she was being held captive. The wizard's attempt to call Balor had failed and he had blamed her. The beating she'd received had been the worst so far. She still had pieces of iron in her wrists and ankles from the spikes he'd pounded into her flesh.

There was no doubt in her mind that she would be dead had it not been for Mara appearing and telling him their Grand Draoi was on the phone, waiting for him. Calysta had been unable to speak, but could see the disgust in Mara's eyes at what the wizard was doing to her. The priestess prayed that the young witch would grow a conscience and tell someone she was there.

The wizard returned with a smirk on his face and without a word, unlocked her chains and unceremoniously threw her over his shoulder. Every step he took jostled her wounds, sending burning shards of pain throughout her body. Somewhere along the line, Calysta thankfully lost consciousness. When she awoke, she was on her back, facing a black stained ceiling with new iron chains securing her to what felt like a metal table, and that's where she'd been ever since.

Noises outside the room alerted her to at least three people entering her prison. The smell of Old Spice told her the sadistic wizard was one of them. A sickeningly sweet, almost cloying smell that made her stomach roil, told her Mara was in attendance as well and had been practicing black magic again. The last scent was one she couldn't place, but knew she had smelled before. It was old and musty, tinged with ozone from the power the man possessed.

The wizard who'd been her captor since the beginning came into view and immediately raised his hand to slap her face. Magic flew through the air. He grabbed his arm and squealed in pain as a shout echoed throughout the chamber. "Soren! You will not!"

The sound of footsteps, combined with the click of a cane against stone, came closer. The old, musty, ozone smell assaulted her senses before a face she'd hoped to never see again came into view.

"Hello, Calysta. I understand your reticence to help our cause, but as you can see, we are quite determined. I hate that it has come to violence and want nothing more than to let you go. So, tell us where to find the Thantos spell and all of this ugliness can come to an end."

Chuckling the best she could with broken teeth, swollen lips, and bruised cheeks, Calysta gave the only answer she could. "Rot in hell, Cleland."

Of course he missed the humor in her statement. She hardly had time to brace before the thick wooden handle of his cane connected with her temple and her world faded to black.

~~*~*~*~*~*~*

Melanie tested the ropes that held her hands behind her back, trying with all her might to break free. The black bag that had been shoved over her head remained, making it unbearably hot and impossible to see. Sweat covered her face as she fought not to lose her cool while figuring a way out of the fresh hell she found herself in.

Counting to ten, she redirected her focus to her feet, happy to find they were tied together and not to the legs of the chair. She rotated her feet in opposite directions, letting the rope slide over her skin, and was happy to find it was good old fashioned jute. Mr. Addison, her high school Chemistry teacher who doubled as the P.E. teacher, would be proud she recognized its texture and even happier that she remembered with enough friction and moisture it would stretch. Ignoring the burning sensation working its way up her legs, she rubbed her ankles against one another as she continued to rotate her feet.

This is like the whole 'rub your tummy and pat your head' game only with my legs and feet. Damn, I'm talented. Now to put everything I've learned from Bruce Willis to work and get the hell outta dodge.

Her muscles ached and threatened to cramp, which only made Melanie work harder. Sweat ran down her legs, soaking the ropes as she listened for the sounds of her captors. It wouldn't do any good to work this hard only to have the rat bastards show up and redo her bindings.

Distracting herself, she thought back to the men that abducted her. It was obvious they'd used black magic. They were from the very Guard she'd taunted her grandfather about. Of course she full well planned on smacking herself in the back of the head for letting them get the jump on her and for giving the old wizard the idea. She'd like to blame her inattention on the conversation with the Grand Draoi and in all truth, it had thrown her for a loop, but it was the mind-blowing kiss from a certain tall, blue-eyed hunk that had scrambled her neurons and left her wishing for so much more. She'd been lost to her daydreaming, allowing the assholes to get the jump on her. Years and years of honing her skills of observation, always knowing everything that was going on around her, and hiding her magic from even the best mystical practitioners were skills that kept her safe for almost twenty years. Melanie had known it was the only shot she would have to live a normal life, far away from her jacked up family that put the fun in dysfunction.

Best laid plans…

Turn the page for a little note from our favorite wiz kid.

Hey y'all! Sydney here! Miss Julia let me have a few minutes to talk to you guys. I just thought I would give you a little update…

First of all, it has been a blast meeting you! I hope you stay around for more of the Dragon Guard stories. I have it on good authority I'm gonna be around for a long time. Not in the way y'all thought, but I'll never be far. And hey, it wouldn't be a story without me, right? Hahahahaha

So, by now you know I'm like some super special mystical being. How crazy it that? I'm really just a kid that knows stuff and wants her family…*all of her family*…safe. Some crazy old book says I can help make that happen, so that's what I'm gonna do, no matter what Mom and Dad say. Ms. Siobhan and Ms. Shavon say it's my Destiny, which I guess makes sense, but I would still like to know how the old dragon guys knew I was coming. It's pretty cool, but *really* creepy.

Andrew is trying really hard to win back the trust of the Guard and the Clan. With Emma by his side, I know he has a real chance. I keep telling them all he's really trying. I mean, there's still darkness within him, how could there not be? And seriously, what one of us doesn't have some little nasties running around inside our brains? They just need to remember he's trying and *that* is what matters. All I know is my people better get over it soon. The bad guys are out there and those meanies have their sights set on the Dragons. This Prophecy stuff is no joke. It's gonna take all of us working together to help Rian, Rory, and their guys keep the world in one piece. I wish I knew for sure *who* was coming. All that any of us know for sure is that they are SUPER bad and wanna destroy everything good, especially Dragon Kin. I'm more than a little scared. Thank the Universe they have Kyra and Calysta. They are *really* strong and powerful! Now, they just have to find Calysta.

Okay, enough about that. I'm sure you've figured out Miss Julia is gonna tell y'all the story of the Blue Thunder Clan and *their mates*. The guys finding their mates is my favorite part! Girl Power and all that…heeheehee. There's aren't enough of us around and I keep hoping for more babies. I *love* babies. OH! Before I forget, Mom and Dad have a BIG surprise. I'm dying to tell y'all what it is, but I made a pinkie promise to keep it a secret, so you'll have to stay tuned!

Well, Mom is calling. Kyndel taught her to make my favorite peanut butter cookies. YUM! I love these little trips home. I get to be just 'Sydney', see my family, and have all the good food that they don't have in the 'Great Beyond'. Also, there are no stuffy, ancient dragons telling me what to do…BIG BONUS!! heeheeehee

Talk to you soon.
Love you guys,
Syd ☺

CPSIA information can be obtained
at www.ICGtesting.com
Printed in the USA
LVHW060029230219
608549LV00031B/622/P